Contents

INTRODUCTION

Ernest Miller Hemingway was born in the suburban town of Oak Park, Illinois, on 21 July 1899, the year in which his father completed the purchase of a summer cottage on Walloon Lake, up in Michigan. It was here that Ernest spent the summers of his formative years, learning from his father, who was an expert shot, woodsman and fisherman, the intense love of nature and the skills in handling guns and tackle that were to dominate a major part of his life. In his seventeenth year, Ernest discovered an enthusiasm for boxing, and one of the earliest of his stories to appear in the High School's literary magazine was in the form of a tale told by an old boxing manager about 'the best frame-up we almost ever pulled off'. There had been some talk of a career in medicine, but when he left High School Hemingway managed to land a job as a reporter on the *Kansas City Star*. The paper's style-book instructed reporters to 'use short sentences. Use short first paragraphs. Use vigorous English.' It was a start.

In the next six months on the *Star*, Hemingway worked enthusiastically at his new trade and collected a certain amount of material he was later to use in his stories. But his constant concern, in these closing months of 1917, was how to get to the War. His defective left eye ruled out enlistment in the normal way, but he discovered that he could volunteer as a Red Cross Ambulance driver, and in late May 1918 he sailed from New York to Paris, en route for the Italian front. After a brief spell of driving Fiat ambulances, Hemingway was despatched to a listening post on the Piave. In mid-July he was wounded in the blast from an Austrian Minenwerfer, but he immediately picked up a seriously wounded Italian and began to carry him towards the command post. Halfway there a machine-gun bullet hit him in the right knee, but he reached the post, still carrying the soldier, before he collapsed. It was two days before Hemingway was taken to a Milan hospital, his legs were riddled with shrapnel splinters, and there were two machine-gun bullets in his right leg. He was just nineteen.

But he was alive, he was in friendly and expert hands, he had been recommended for a high military medal, and, best of all, he was falling helplessly in love with one of his nurses, the beautiful Agnes von Kurowsky. He returned to New York to find himself a celebrity, but two months later he was shattered by a letter from Agnes telling him that she had fallen in love with an Italian lieutenant. By the summer of 1919 he was sufficiently recovered to take his first fishing trip in two years, and was again experimenting with short stories. In 1920 he took a job with the *Toronto Star*, and moved to Chicago at the end of the year. It was here that he met Elizabeth Hadley Richardson; they were married in the following September.

Soon the couple were living mainly on the income from Hadley's small trust fund as Ernest tried to place freelance articles and stories and they saved money for a trip to Europe. Hemingway was all for revisiting Italy but

Sherwood Anderson persuaded them that Paris was the only place for the serious writer, and wrote a number of letters of introduction to the American galaxy then living on the Left Bank. In January 1922 they moved into a small flat in the rue du Cardinal Lemoine, and, for the first time Hemingway found himself free to work out his own standards: 'All you have to do is write one true sentence. Write the truest sentence that you know.'

It was some time before Hemingway took up Anderson's letters of introduction, but he was soon a regular in the circles that revolved around Ezra Pound, Gertrude Stein, Sylvia Beach and James Joyce. He was also rapidly enlarging his journalistic contacts; he covered the Genoa Conference, interviewed Mussolini, spent three miserable weeks reporting the war between Greece and Turkey, then went on to the Lausanne Peace Conference before taking a skiing holiday in Switzerland, a walking tour in Italy, and an extended visit to the Ruhr to write a series on Franco-German relations. He was at the same time working on short fiction, and was beginning to discover the true strengths of his own technique.

In 1923 Hemingway went on a short tour of Spain and was intoxicated by his first real contact with a *corrida*; he had written briefly on bullfighting before but had never seen the spectacle. He promptly laid plans for a further expedition to Pamplona for the July feria, an experience that was to lay the foundations for some of his finest work. But there were other developments afoot that same year; Hemingway's first book, *Three Stories and Ten Poems*, was to be published by the Contact Press in Paris, and Hadley discovered she was pregnant. The Hemingways returned to Canada for the birth of their son in October 1923, and Ernest again worked for the *Toronto Star*. However, he was determined to make his way as a full-time professional writer and by January 1924 they were back in Montparnasse.

Again he went to Pamplona, then went to Austria for the skiing. It was here that he received a telegram saying that the American publisher, Liveright, had offered to publish his first collection of stories, *In Our Time*. He accepted. When he returned to Paris it was to find an enquiry from another New York publisher, Maxwell Perkins of Scribners, who had been recommended to contact Hemingway by Scott Fitzgerald. Hemingway replied that one project he had in mind was a large illustrated study of the bullfight: the novel, he thought, was played out. Nevertheless, he was to begin on a novel that June: it petered out before 30 manuscript pages had been completed.

All that year Hemingway had been planning to follow the bulls, starting at Pamplona. A rising star, the young Cayetano Ordonez, was beginning to challenge the great matador, Belmonte, and Hemingway started work on another novel, focused on Ordonez. This time the project ran more smoothly, and in September 1925, in Paris, he completed the draft manuscript of *Fiesta*. At about the same time, his marriage was beginning to disintegrate: *Fiesta* was dedicated to his wife and son, but he and Hadley had started the machinery of divorce when he returned the proofs to America. In May 1927, Hemingway was married to Pauline Pfeiffer: again, they went to Spain for the summer bullfighting season, but in the following year Hemingway discovered new territory in Key West, Florida.

While he was travelling in America, and working on the manuscript of *A Farewell to Arms*, his reputation was growing: he was selling stories to New York magazines, and his novels were commercially successful. The book on bullfighting now became a possibility, but the structural problems of organizing and recording all that he had learned in the years of following the bullfighting circuit were formidable. He fought his way through to a solution, and in January 1931 he finished *Death in the Afternoon*. While working on the book Hemingway had first encountered the challenge of fishing for marlin off the coast of Cuba, and had formed the notion of hunting big game in Africa. In 1934 he went on safari in Tanganyika. The trip was to become the basis for *Green Hills of Africa*; conversation with the professional hunter the party had engaged planted the ideas that were to grow into two of his finest stories, *The Short Happy Life of Francis Macomber* and *The Snows of Kilimanjaro*. Hemingway had meanwhile bought himself an ocean-going boat, the *Pilar*, and had made contacts in the fisherman's paradise of Bimini.

In 1936 the shadows of war began to form and Hemingway was commissioned to go to Spain to cover the Civil War. He made, in all, four visits to Spain as a war correspondent, and some of his contacts and experiences there provided the raw material for a number of stories, and above all for his most successful novel to date, *For Whom the Bell Tolls*. Shortly after the novel was published, in 1940, Hemingway married his third wife, Martha Gellhorn, whom he had first met before the Spanish adventure.

In 1944 Hemingway accepted a commission to report on the war in Europe for *Colliers*. He arrived in time to report, at uncomfortably close quarters, on the D-Day landings. For Hemingway it was a time of huge enjoyment. He managed to use his considerable talents as an intelligence officer and (informally and probably illegally) fought his way down from Normandy through Paris to the Ardennes, and organized a hair-raising excursion for himself in the navigator's seat of a Mosquito chasing V-bombs through the flak above the south coast of England. In the spring of 1945 he returned to his home in Cuba, began work on another novel, and dealt with his third divorce: he married Mary Welsh a year later.

By now filmed versions of his stories and novels were consolidating his international reputation. Biographers and bibliographers were beginning to gather: most of them were fended off. His primary concern was still fiction, and in particular two schemes that ran in parallel. One was a novel centred on recollections of war, which, after a visit to post-war Florence, took final shape in *Across the River and into the Trees*. The book produced the most hostile press Hemingway had yet met. The second was an idea that he had been working on, intermittently, for years, based on the story of a fisherman who had hooked the biggest marlin he had seen in his life, only to have his prize eaten by sharks as he made his way back to harbour. Hemingway was fishing in the reefs off Cuba when the evening news broadcast carried the item that he had won the Pulitzer Prize for 1952 with *The Old Man and the Sea*.

Hemingway returned to Spain in 1954 to take in the festival at Pamplona on his way to revisit Africa. It was at first a triumphal progress, but the second safari rapidly slid into disaster. Hemingway's marksmanship was well below his usual expert form, and the trip was hounded by irritating misadventures. There was worse to come. On a photographic expedition over Murchison Falls, their light aircraft struck a concealed cable and crashed. The party staggered out, dazed but not seriously hurt, and made their way by a convenient steamer to an airport near Lake Albert. They boarded an elderly biplane but the aircraft crashed and burst into flames before reaching the end of the primitive runway. In this crash, their second in 48 hours, Hemingway was badly injured, but he insisted on continuing with the planned tour of Europe, and was vastly entertained by reading newspaper reports of his own death as he lay in a hospital bed in Uganda. He was 55 and had no intention of dying.

For a time he was unable to work. The news that he had been awarded the Nobel Prize for Literature threw him into confusion, but he discarded his first reactions, and accepted in a brief, graceful tape-recorded message. He continued to travel, but he was, as became increasingly evident, a sick and worried man. He went back to Europe in 1956, and in each of the three following years. His last visit to Spain was a strenuous and unnecessary trip to finish an article he was working on for a magazine. It was a dangerous journey. Disease, the effects of injury, and an indefinable malaise were catching up with him. He returned to his house in Ketchum, Idaho, in 1960, pursued by disease and paranoid delusion. In that same house, on 1 July 1961, Ernest Miller Hemingway unlocked the cellar in which his guns were stored, chose and loaded a tight-choked Boss shotgun he used for pigeon shooting, pressed the muzzles to his forehead, and fired both barrels.

Hemingway was a man of multiple contradictions. Capable of massive generosity, he repeatedly allowed imagined slights to wreck friendships of many years standing. Undeniably possessed of abundant physical courage and endurance, he frequently allowed himself to appear as a petulant bully. While he carefully cultivated the image of a hard-drinking two-fisted brawler, he was throughout his life the victim of morbid anxiety about the most trivial brushes with the law. A superb shot and fanatical sportsman, his co-ordination was poor, and he was continually dogged by a series of almost laughable but always damaging accidents. He seemed to stride free from the ruins of collapsed marriages with the same casual brutality that tore him free from the wreckage of the blazing aircraft. But the wounds were real.

The breadth of his contacts was immense, always increasing through his burning curiosity about the special expertise of, for example, Kansas crime reporters, guerrilla fighters, raddled Havana whores, the literati of Paris and New York, bomber pilots, punchdrunk boxers, professional hunters, the aristocracy and the dregs of the bullring. Always the key was professionalism, the argot and the special skills of the craftsman, and he strove to build for himself, and to live up to, the highest standards of his own chosen craft.

In the early years in Paris he developed his theory of 'omission', the principle that what was known to the author, but unstated, was as crucial as the words that appeared on the page: 'the omitted part would strengthen the story and make people feel something more than they understood.' At the peak of his career, he was writing with the same intensity. The writer, he said in his Stockholm speech, 'does his work alone and if he is a good enough writer he must face eternity, or the lack of it, each day. For a true writer each book should be a new beginning where he tries again for something that is beyond attainment. He should always try for something that has never been done or that others have tried and failed. Then sometimes, with great luck, he will succeed.'

It is possible, on one level, to interpret his work as translated autobiography, to play the game of identification that absorbed the expatriate colony of the Left Bank when *Fiesta* first appeared, to read into episode and anecdote the seeds of later novels. Certainly the parallels exist, but to treat his fiction in this way is grossly to oversimplify the achievement of a major artist. No man ever struggled harder to find the techniques that would enable him to isolate and to transmit his vision of the truth. From his earliest experiments to the masterpieces of his later years, he sought continually to develop a prose style that had to be hammered out of the raw material of life.

Taut, spare, resonant, Hemingway's prose is unique, as generations of would-be imitators have discovered to their cost. The very pungency of the style at first disguises the range of his invention. His own emphasis on writing 'one true sentence' diverts attention from his striving towards true form. Throughout his career he grappled to present his vision in the form that would best suit his purpose, and his command of structure is prodigious. He used documentary, vignette, dialogue, multiple narrative, pastiche, and soliloquy. The aim was always economy, a paring away of all redundancy, but the technique varies. *One Reader Writes* is an apparently arbitrary fragment, *For Whom the Bell Tolls* deploys a rich complexity, while the deceptive simplicity of *The Old Man and the Sea* represents perhaps his finest achievement.

For Hemingway experience was always material to be ransacked for truth: each of his fictions is a statement entire in itself. His life may be said to have been exaggerated. His art, as he intended, endures.

HEMI

GWAY

For Whom the Bell Tolls

FOR WHOM THE BELL TOLLS

This book is for Martha Gellhorn

I

He lay flat on the brown, pine-needled floor of the forest, his chin on his folded arms, and high overhead the wind blew in the tops of the pine trees. The mountainside sloped gently where he lay; but below it was steep and he could see the dark of the oiled road winding through the pass. There was a stream alongside the road and far down the pass he saw a mill beside the stream and the falling water of the dam, white in the summer sunlight.

'Is that the mill?' he asked.

'Yes.'

'I do not remember it.'

'It was built since you were here. The old mill is farther down; much below the pass.'

He spread the photostated military map out on the forest floor and looked at it carefully. The old man looked over his shoulder. He was a short and solid old man in black peasant's smock and grey iron-stiff trousers and he wore rope-soled shoes. He was breathing heavily from the climb and his hand rested on one of the two heavy packs they had been carrying.

'Then you cannot see the bridge from here?'

'No,' the old man said. 'This is the easy country of the pass where the stream flows gently. Below, where the road turns out of sight in the trees, it drops suddenly and there is a steep gorge—'

'I remember.'

'Across the gorge is the bridge.'

'And where are their posts?'

'There is a post at the mill that you see there.'

The young man, who was studying the country, took his glasses from the pocket of his faded, khaki flannel shirt, wiped the lenses with a handkerchief, screwed the eyepieces around until the boards of the mill showed suddenly clearly and he saw the wooden bench beside the door; the huge pile of sawdust that rose behind the open shed where the circular saw was, and a stretch of the flume that brought the logs down from the mountainside on the other bank of the stream. The stream showed clear and smooth-looking in the glasses and, below the curl of the falling water, the spray from the dam was blowing in the wind.

'There is no sentry.'

'There is smoke coming from the millhouse,' the old man said. 'There are also clothes hanging on a line.'

'I see them, but I do not see any sentry.'

'Perhaps he is in the shade,' the old man explained. 'It is hot there now. He would be in the shadow at the end we do not see.'

'Probably. Where is the next post?'

'Below the bridge. It is at the roadmender's hut at kilometre five from the top of the pass.'

'How many men are here?' He pointed at the mill.

'Perhaps four and a corporal.'

'And below?'

'More. I will find out.'

'And at the bridge?'

'Always two. One at each end.'

'We will need a certain number of men,' he said. 'How many men can you get?'

'I can bring as many men as you wish,' the old man said. 'There are many men now here in the hills.'

'How many?'

'There are more than a hundred. But they are in small bands. How many men will you need?'

'I will let you know when we have studied the bridge.'

'Do you wish to study it now?'

'No. Now I wish to go to where we will hide this explosive until it is time. I would like to have it hidden in utmost security at a distance no greater than half an hour from the bridge, if that is possible.'

'That is simple,' the old man said. 'From where we are going, it will all be downhill to the bridge. But now we must climb a little in seriousness to get there. Are you hungry?'

'Yes,' the young man said. 'But we will eat later. How are you called? I have forgotten.' It was a bad sign to him that he had forgotten.

'Anselmo,' the old man said. 'I am called Anselmo and I come from Barco de Avila. Let me help you with that pack.'

The young man, who was tall and thin, with sun-streaked fair hair, and a wind- and sun-burned face, who wore the sun-faded flannel shirt, a pair of peasant's trousers and rope-soled shoes, leaned over, put his arm through one of the leather pack straps and swung the heavy pack up onto his shoulders. He worked his arm through the other strap and settled the weight of the pack against his back. His shirt was still wet from where the pack had rested.

'I have it up now,' he said. 'How do we go?'

'We climb,' Anselmo said.

Bending under the weight of the packs, sweating, they climbed steadily in the pine forest that covered the mountainside. There was no trail that the young man could see, but they were working up and around the face of the mountain and now they crossed a small stream and the old man went steadily on ahead up the edge of the rocky stream bed. The climbing now was steeper and more difficult, until finally the stream seemed to drop down over the edge of a smooth granite ledge that rose above them and the old man waited at the foot of the ledge for the young man to come up to him.

'How are you making it?'

'All right,' the young man said. He was sweating heavily and his thigh muscles were twitchy from the steepness of the climb.

'Wait here now for me. I go ahead to warn them. You do not want to be shot at carrying that stuff.'

'Not even in a joke,' the young man said. 'Is it far?'

'It is very close. How do they call thee?'

'Roberto,' the young man answered. He had slipped the pack off and lowered it gently down between two boulders by the stream bed.

'Wait here, then, Roberto, and I will return for you.'

'Good,' the young man said. 'But do you plan to go down this way to the bridge?'

'No. When we go to the bridge it will be by another way. Shorter and easier.'

'I do not want this material to be stored too far from the bridge.'

'You will see. If you are not satisfied, we will take another place.'

'We will see,' the young man said.

He sat by the packs and watched the old man climb the ledge. It was not hard to climb and from the way he found hand-holds without searching for them the young man could see that he had climbed it many times before. Yet whoever was above had been very careful not to leave any trail.

The young man, whose name was Robert Jordan, was extremely hungry and he was worried. He was often hungry but he was not usually worried because he did not give any importance to what happened to himself and he knew from experience how simple it was to move behind the enemy lines in all this country. It was as simple to move behind them as it was to cross through them, if you had a good guide. It was only giving importance to what happened to you if you were caught that made it difficult; that and deciding whom to trust. You had to trust the people you worked with completely or not at all, and you had to make decisions about the trusting. He was not worried about any of that. But there were other things.

This Anselmo had been a good guide and he could travel wonderfully in the mountains. Robert Jordan could walk well enough himself and he knew from following him since before daylight that the old man could walk him to death. Robert Jordan trusted the man, Anselmo, so far, in everything except judgment. He had not yet had an opportunity to test his judgment, and, anyway, the judgment was his own responsibility. No, he did not worry about Anselmo and the problem of the bridge was no more difficult than many other problems. He knew how to blow any sort of bridge that you could name and he had blown them of all sizes and constructions. There was enough explosive and all equipment in the two packs to blow this bridge properly even if it were twice as big as Anselmo reported it, as he remembered it when he had walked over it on his way to La Granja on a walking trip in 1933, and as Golz had read him the description of it night before last in that upstairs room in the house outside of the Escorial.

'To blow the bridge is nothing,' Golz had said, the lamplight on his scarred, shaved head, pointing with a pencil on the big map. 'You understand?'

'Yes, I understand.'

'Absolutely nothing. Merely to blow the bridge is a failure.'

'Yes, Comrade General.'

'To blow the bridge at a stated hour based on the time set for the attack is how it should be done. You see that naturally. That is your right and how it should be done.'

Golz looked at the pencil, then tapped his teeth with it.

Robert Jordan had said nothing.

'You understand that is your right and how it should be done,' Golz went on, looking at him and nodding his head. He tapped on the map now with the pencil. 'That is how I should do it. That is what we cannot have.'

'Why, Comrade General?'

'Why?' Golz said, angrily. 'How many attacks have you seen and you ask me why? What is to guarantee that my orders are not changed? What is to guarantee that the attack is not annulled? What is to guarantee that the attack is not postponed? What is to guarantee that it starts within six hours of when it should start? Has *any* attack ever been as it should?'

'It will start on time if it is your attack,' Robert Jordan said.

'They are never my attacks,' Golz said. 'I make them. But they are not mine. The artillery is not mine. I must put in for it. I have never been given what I ask for even when they have it to give. That is the least of it. There are other things. You know how those people are. It is not necessary to go into all of it. Always there is something. Always some one will interfere. So now be sure you understand.'

'So when is the bridge to be blown?' Robert Jordan had asked.

'After the attack starts. As soon as the attack has started and not before. So that no reinforcements will come up over that road.' He pointed with his pencil. 'I must know that nothing will come up over that road.'

'And when is the attack?'

'I will tell you. But you are to use the date and hour only as an indication of a probability. You must be ready for that time. You will blow the bridge after the attack has started. You see?' he indicated with the pencil. 'That is the only road on which they can bring up reinforcements. That is the only road on which they can get up tanks, or artillery, or even move a truck toward the pass which I attack. I must know that bridge is gone. Not before, so it can be repaired if the attack is postponed. No. It must go when the attack starts and I must know it is gone. There are only two sentries. The man who will go with you has just come from there. He is a very reliable man, they say. You will see. He has people in the mountains. Get as many men as you need. Use as few as possible, but use enough. I do not have to tell you these things.'

'And how do I determine that the attack has started?'

'It is to be made with a full division. There will be aerial bombardment as preparation. You are not deaf, are you?'

'Then I may take it that when the planes unload, the attack has started?'

'You could not always take it like that,' Golz said and shook his head. 'But in this case, you may. It is my attack.'

'I understand it,' Robert Jordan had said. 'I do not say I like it very much.'

'Neither do I like it very much. If you do not want to undertake it, say so now. If you think you cannot do it, say so now.'

'I will do it,' Robert Jordan had said. 'I will do it all right.'

'That is all I have to know,' Golz said. 'That nothing comes up over that bridge. That is absolute.'

'I understand.'

'I do not like to ask people to do such things and in such a way,' Golz went on. 'I could not order you to do it. I understand what you may be forced to do through my putting such conditions. I explain very carefully so that you understand and that you understand all of the possible difficulties and the importance.'

'And how will you advance on La Granja if that bridge is blown?'

'We go forward prepared to repair it after we have stormed the pass. It is a very complicated and beautiful operation. As complicated and as beautiful as always. The plan has been manufactured in Madrid. It is another of Vicente Rojo, the unsuccessful professor's, masterpieces. I make the attack and I make it, as always, not in sufficient force. It is a very possible operation, in spite of that. I am much happier about it than usual. It can be successful with that bridge eliminated. We can take Segovia. Look, I show you how it goes. You see? It is not the top of the pass where we attack. We hold that. It is much beyond. Look–Here–Like this–'

'I would rather not know,' Robert Jordan said.

'Good,' said Golz. 'It is less of baggage to carry with you on the other side, yes?'

'I would always rather not know. Then, no matter what can happen, it was not me that talked.'

'It is better not to know,' Golz stroked his forehead with the pencil. 'Many times I wish I did not know myself. But you do know the one thing you must know about the bridge?'

'Yes. I know that.'

'I believe you do,' Golz said. 'I will not make you any little speech. Let us now have a drink. So much talking makes me very thirsty, Comrade Hordan. You have a funny name in Spanish, Comrade Hordown.'

'How do you say Golz in Spanish, Comrade General?'

'Hotze,' said Golz grinning, making the sound deep in his throat as though hawking with a bad cold. 'Hotze,' he croaked. 'Comrade Heneral Khotze. If I had known how they pronounced Golz in Spanish I would pick me out a better name before I come to war here. When I think I come to command a division and I can pick out any name I want and I pick out Hotze. Heneral Hotze. Now it is too late to change. How do you like *partizan* work?' It was the Russian term for guerrilla work behind the lines.

'Very much,' Robert Jordan said. He grinned. 'It is very healthy in the open air.'

'I like it very much when I was your age, too,' Golz said. 'They tell me you blow bridges very well. Very scientific. It is only hearsay. I have never seen you do anything myself. Maybe nothing ever happens really. You really blow them?' he was teasing now. 'Drink this,' he handed the glass of Spanish brandy to Robert Jordan. 'You *really* blow them?'

'Sometimes.'

'You better not have any sometimes on this bridge. No, let us not talk any more about this bridge. You understand enough now about that bridge. We are very serious, so we can make very strong jokes. Look, do you have many girls on the other side of the lines?'

'No, there is no time for girls.'

'I do not agree. The more irregular the service, the more irregular the life. You have very irregular service. Also you need a haircut.'

'I have my hair cut as it needs it,' Robert Jordan said. He would be damned if he would have his head shaved like Golz. 'I have enough to think about without girls,' he said sullenly.

'What sort of uniform am I supposed to wear?' Robert Jordan asked.

'None,' Golz said. 'Your haircut is all right. I tease you. You are very different from me,' Golz had said and filled up the glasses again.

'You never think about only girls. I never think at all. Why should I? I am *Général Sovietique*. I never think. Do not try to trap me into thinking.'

Someone on his staff, sitting on a chair working over a map on a drawing board, growled at him in the language Robert Jordan did not understand.

'Shut up,' Golz had said, in English. 'I joke if I want. I am so serious is why I can joke. Now drink this and then go. You understand, huh?'

'Yes,' Robert Jordan had said. 'I understand.'

They had shaken hands and he had saluted and gone out to the staff car where the old man was waiting asleep and in that car they had ridden over the road past Guadarrama, the old man still asleep, and up the Navacerrada road to the Alpine Club hut where he, Robert Jordan, slept for three hours before they started.

That was the last he had seen of Golz with his strange white face that never tanned, his hawk eyes, the big nose and thin lips and the shaven head crossed with wrinkles and with scars. Tomorrow night they would be outside the Escorial in the dark along the road; the long lines of trucks loading the infantry in the darkness; the men, heavy loaded, climbing up into the trucks; the machine-gun sections lifting their guns into the trucks; the tanks being run up on the skids onto the long-bodied tank trucks; pulling the Division out to move them in the night for the attack on the pass. He would not think about that. That was not his business. That was Golz's business. He had only one thing to do and that was what he should think about and he must think it out clearly and take everything as it came along, and not worry. To worry was as bad as to be afraid. It simply make things more difficult.

He sat now by the stream watching the clear water flowing between the rocks and, across the stream, he noticed there was a thick bed of watercress. He crossed the stream, picked a double handful, washed the muddy roots clean in the current and then sat down again beside his pack and ate the clean, cool green leaves and the crisp, peppery-tasting stalks. He knelt by the stream and, pushing his automatic pistol around on his belt to the small of his back so that it would not be wet, he lowered himself with a hand on each of two boulders and drank from the stream. The water was achingly cold.

Pushing himself up on his hands he turned his head and saw the old man coming down the ledge. With him was another man, also in a black peasant's smock and the dark grey trousers that were almost a uniform in that province, wearing rope-soled shoes and with a carbine slung over his back. This man was bareheaded. The two of them came scrambling down the rock like goats.

They came up to him and Robert Jordan got to his feet.

'*Salud, Camarada,*' he said to the man with the carbine and smiled.

'*Salud,*' the other said, grudgingly. Robert Jordan looked at the man's heavy, beard-stubbled face. It was almost round and his head was round and set close on his shoulders. His eyes were small and set too wide apart and his ears were small and set close to his head. He was a heavy man about five feet ten inches tall and his hands and feet were large. His nose had been broken and his mouth was cut at one corner and the line of the scar across the upper lip and lower jaw showed through the growth of beard over his face.

The old man nodded his head at this man and smiled.

'He is the boss here,' he grinned, then flexed his arms as though to make the muscles stand out and looked at the man with the carbine in a half-mocking admiration. 'A very strong man.'

'I can see it,' Robert Jordan said and smiled again. He did not like the look of this man and inside himself he was not smiling at all.

'What have you to justify your identity?' asked the man with the carbine.

Robert Jordan unpinned a safety pin that ran through his pocket flap and took a folded paper out of the left breast pocket of his flannel shirt and handed it to the man, who opened it, looked at it doubtfully and turned it in his hands.

So he cannot read, Robert Jordan noted.

'Look at the seal,' he said.

The old man pointed to the seal and the man with the carbine studied it, turning it in his fingers.

'What seal is that?'

'Have you never seen it?'

'No.'

'There are two,' said Robert Jordan. 'One is S.I.M., the service of the military intelligence. The other is the General Staff.'

'Yes, I have seen that seal before. But here no one commands but me,' the other said sullenly. 'What have you in the packs?'

'Dynamite,' the old man said proudly. 'Last night we crossed the lines in the dark and all day we have carried this dynamite over the mountain.'

'I can use dynamite,' said the man with the carbine. He handed back the paper to Robert Jordan and looked him over. 'Yes. I have use for dynamite. How much have you brought me?'

'I have brought you no dynamite,' Robert Jordan said to him evenly. 'The dynamite is for another purpose. What is your name?'

'What is that to you?'

'He is Pablo,' said the old man. The man with the carbine looked at them both sullenly.

'Good. I have heard much good of you,' said Robert Jordan.

'What have you heard of me?' asked Pablo.

'I have heard that you are an excellent guerrilla leader, that you are loyal to the republic and prove your loyalty through your acts, and that you are a man both serious and valiant. I bring you greetings from the General Staff.'

'Where did you hear all this?' asked Pablo. Robert Jordan registered that he was not taking any of the flattery.

'I heard it from Buitrago to the Escorial,' he said, naming all the stretch of country on the other side of the lines.

'I know no one in Buitrago nor in Escorial,' Pablo told him.

'There are many people on the other side of the mountains who were not there before. Where are you from?'

'Avila. What are you going to do with the dynamite?'

'Blow up a bridge.'

'What bridge?'

'That is my business.'

'If it is in this territory, it is my business. You cannot blow bridges close to where you live. You must live in one place and operate in another. I know my business. One who is alive, now, after a year, knows his business.'

'This is my business,' Robert Jordan said. 'We can discuss it together. Do you wish to help us with the sacks?'

'No,' said Pablo and shook his head.

The old man turned toward him suddenly and spoke rapidly and furiously in a dialect that Robert Jordan could just follow. It was like reading Quevedo. Anselmo was speaking old Castilian and it went something like this, 'Art thou a brute? Yes. Art thou a beast? Yes, many times. Hast thou a brain? Nay. None. Now we come for something of consummate importance and thee, with thy dwelling place to be undisturbed, puts thy fox-hole before the interests of humanity. Before the interests of thy people. I this and that in the this and that of thy father. I this and that and that in thy this. *Pick up that bag*.'

Pablo looked down.

'Every one has to do what he can do according to how it can be truly done,' he said. 'I live here and I operate beyond Segovia. If you make a disturbance here, we will be hunted out of these mountains. It is only by doing nothing here that we are able to live in these mountains. It is the principle of the fox.'

'Yes,' said Anselmo bitterly. 'It is the principle of the fox when we need the wolf.'

'I am more wolf than thee,' Pablo said and Robert Jordan knew that he would pick up the sack.

'Hi. Ho . . .' Anselmo looked at him. 'Thou art more wolf than me and I am sixty-eight years old.'

He spat on the ground and shook his head.

'You have that many years?' Robert Jordan asked, seeing that now, for the moment, it would be all right and trying to make it go easier.

'Sixty-eight in the month of July.'

'If we should ever see that month,' said Pablo. 'Let me help you with the pack,' he said to Robert Jordan. 'Leave the other to the old man.' He spoke, not sullenly, but almost sadly now. 'He is an old man of great strength.'

'I will carry the pack,' Robert Jordan said.

'Nay,' said the old man. 'Leave it to this other strong man.'

'I will take it,' Pablo told him, and in his sullenness there was a sadness that was disturbing to Robert Jordan. He knew that sadness and to see it here worried him.

'Give me the carbine, then,' he said and when Pablo handed it to him, he slung it over his back and, with the two men climbing ahead of him, they went heavily, pulling and climbing up the granite shelf and over its upper edge to where there was a green clearing in the forest.

They skirted the edge of the little meadow and Robert Jordan, striding easily now without the pack, the carbine pleasantly rigid over his shoulder after the heavy, sweating pack weight, noticed that the grass was cropped down in several places and signs that picket pins had been driven into the earth. He could see a trail through the grass where horses had been led to the stream to drink and there was the fresh manure of several horses. They picket them here to feed at night and keep them out of sight in the timber in the daytime, he thought. I wonder how many horses this Pablo has?

He remembered now noticing, without realizing it, that Pablo's trousers were worn soapy shiny in the knees and thighs. I wonder if he has a pair of boots or if he rides in those *alpargatas*, he thought. He must have quite an outfit. But I don't like that sadness, he thought. That sadness is bad. That's the sadness they get before they quit or before they betray. That is the sadness that comes before the sell-out.

Ahead of them a horse whinnied in the timber and then, through the brown trunks of the pine trees, only a little sunlight coming down through their thick, almost-touching tops, he saw the corral made by roping around the tree trunks. The horses had their heads pointed toward the men as they approached, and at the foot of a tree, outside the corral, the saddles were piled together and covered with a tarpaulin.

As they came up, the two men with the packs stopped, and Robert Jordan knew it was for him to admire the horses.

'Yes,' he said. 'They are beautiful.' He turned to Pablo. 'You have your cavalry and all.'

There were five horses in the rope corral, three bays, a sorrel, and a buckskin. Sorting them out carefully with his eyes after he had seen them first together, Robert Jordan looked them over individually. Pablo and Anselmo knew how good they were and while Pablo stood now proud and less sad-looking, watching them lovingly, the old man acted as though they were some great surprise that he had produced, suddenly, himself.

'How do they look to you?' he asked.

'All these I have taken,' Pablo said and Robert Jordan was pleased to hear him speak proudly.

'That,' said Robert Jordan, pointing to one of the bays, a big stallion with a white blaze on his forehead and a single white foot, the near front, 'is much horse.'

He was a beautiful horse that looked as though he had come out of a painting by Velasquez.

'They are all good,' said Pablo. 'You know horses?'

'Yes.'

'Less bad,' said Pablo. 'Do you see a defect in one of these?'

Robert Jordan knew that now his papers were being examined by the man who could not read.

The horses all still had their heads up looking at the man. Robert Jordan slipped through between the double rope of the corral and slapped the buckskin on the haunch. He leaned back against the ropes of the enclosure and watched the horses circle the corral, stood watching them a minute more, as they stood still, then leaned down and came out through the ropes.

'The sorrel is lame in the off hind foot,' he said to Pablo, not looking at him. 'The hoof is split and although it might not get worse soon if shod properly, she could break down if she travels over much hard ground.'

'The hoof was like that when we took her,' Pablo said.

'The best horse that you have, the white-faced bay stallion, has a swelling on the upper part of the cannon bone that I do not like.'

'It is nothing,' said Pablo. 'He knocked it three days ago. If it were to be anything it would have become so already.'

He pulled back the tarpaulin and showed the saddles. There were two ordinary vaquero's or herdsman's saddles, like American stock saddles, one very ornate vaquero's saddle, with hand-tooled leather and heavy, hooded stirrups, and two military saddles in black leather.

'We killed a pair of *guardia civil*,' he said, explaining the military saddles.

'That is big game.'

'They had dismounted on the road between Segovia and Santa Maria del Real. They had dismounted to ask papers of the driver of a cart. We were able to kill them without injuring the horses.'

'Have you killed many civil guards?' Robert Jordan asked.

'Several,' Pablo said. 'But only these two without injury to the horses.'

'It was Pablo who blew up the train at Arevalo,' Anselmo said. 'That was Pablo.'

'There was a foreigner with us who made the explosion,' Pablo said. 'Do you know him?'

'What is he called?'

'I do not remember. It was a very rare name.'

'What did he look like?'

'He was fair, as you are, but not as tall and with large hands and a broken nose.'

'Kashkin,' Robert Jordan said. 'That would be Kashkin.'

'Yes,' said Pablo. 'It was a very rare name. Something like that. What has become of him?'

'He is dead since April.'

'That is what happens to everybody,' Pablo said, gloomily. 'That is the way we will all finish.'

'That is the way all men end,' Anselmo said. 'That is the way men have always ended. What is the matter with you, man? What has thou in the stomach?'

'*They* are very strong,' Pablo said. It was as though he were talking to himself. He looked at the horses gloomily. 'You do not realize how strong they are. I see them always stronger, always better armed. Always with more material. Here am I with horses like these. And what can I look forward to? To be hunted and to die. Nothing more.'

'You hunt as much as you are hunted,' Anselmo said.

'No,' said Pablo. 'Not any more. And if we leave these mountains now, where can we go? Answer me that. Where now?'

'In Spain there are many mountains. There are the Sierra de Gredos if one leaves here.'

'Not for me,' Pablo said. 'I am tired of being hunted. Here we are all right. Now if you blow a bridge here, we will be hunted. If they know we are here and hunt for us with planes, they will find us. If they send Moors to hunt us out, they will find us and we must go. I am tired of all this. You hear?' He turned to Robert Jordan. 'What right have you, a foreigner, to come to me and tell me what I must do?'

'I have not told you anything you must do,' Robert Jordan said to him.

'You will though,' Pablo said. 'There. There is the badness.'

He pointed at the two heavy packs that they had lowered to the ground while they had watched the horses. Seeing the horses had seemed to bring this all to a head in him and seeing that Robert Jordan knew horses had seemed to loosen his tongue. The three of them stood now by the rope corral and the patchy sunlight shone on the coat of the bay stallion. Pablo looked at him and then pushed with his foot against the heavy pack. 'There is the badness.'

'I come only for my duty,' Robert Jordan told him. 'I come under orders from those who are conducting the war. If I ask you to help me, you can refuse and I will find others who will help me. I have not even asked you for help yet. I have to do what I am ordered to do and I can promise you of its importance. That I am a foreigner is not my fault. I would rather have been born here.'

'To me, now, the most important is that we be not disturbed here,' Pablo said. 'To me, now, my duty is to those who are with me and to myself.'

'Thyself. Yes,' Anselmo said. 'Thyself now since a long time. Thyself and thy horses. Until thou hadst horses thou wert with us. Now thou art another capitalist more.'

'That is unjust,' said Pablo. 'I expose the horses all the time for the cause.'

'Very little,' said Anselmo scornfully. 'Very little in my judgment. To steal, yes. To eat well, yes. To murder, yes. To fight, no.'

'You are an old man who will make himself trouble with his mouth.'

'I am an old man who is afraid of no one,' Anselmo told him. 'Also I am an old man without horses.'

'You are an old man who may not live long.'

'I am an old man who will live until I die,' Anselmo said. 'And I am not afraid of foxes.'

Pablo said nothing but picked up the pack.

'Nor of wolves either,' Anselmo said, picking up the other pack. 'If thou art a wolf.'

'Shut thy mouth,' Pablo said to him. 'Thou art an old man who always talks too much.'

'And would do whatever he said he would do,' Anselmo said, bent under the pack. 'And who now is hungry. And thirsty. Go on, guerrilla leader with the sad face. Lead us to something to eat.'

It is starting badly enough, Robert Jordan thought. But Anselmo's a man. They are wonderful when they are good, he thought. There is no people like them when they are good and when they go bad there is no people that is worse. Anselmo must have known what he was doing when he brought us here. But I don't like it. I don't like any of it.

The only good sign was that Pablo was carrying the pack and that he had given him the carbine. Perhaps he is always like that, Robert Jordan thought. Maybe he is just one of the gloomy ones.

No, he said to himself, don't fool yourself. You do not know how he was before; but you do know that he is going bad fast and without hiding it. When he starts to hide it he will have made a decision. Remember that, he told himself. The first friendly thing he does, he will have made a decision. They are awfully good horses, though, he thought, beautiful horses. I wonder what could make me feel the way those horses make Pablo feel. The old man was right. The horses made him rich and as soon as he was rich he wanted to enjoy life. Pretty soon he'll feel bad because he can't join the Jockey Club, I guess, he thought. Pauvre Pablo. Il a manqué son Jockey.

That idea made him feel better. He grinned, looking at the two bent backs and the big packs ahead of him moving through the trees. He had not made any jokes with himself all day and now that he had made one he felt much better. You're getting to be as all the rest of them, he told himself. You're getting gloomy, too. He'd certainly been solemn and gloomy with Golz. The job had overwhelmed him a little. Slightly overwhelmed, he thought. Plenty overwhelmed. Golz was gay and he had wanted him to be gay too before he left, but he hadn't been.

All the best ones, when you thought it over, were gay. It was much better to be gay and it was a sign of something too. It was like having immortality while you were still alive. That was a complicated one. There were not many of them left though. No, there were not many of the gay ones left. There were very damned few of them left. And if you keep on thinking like that, my boy, you won't be left either. Turn off the thinking now, old timer, old comrade. You're a bridge-blower now. Not a thinker. Man, I'm hungry, he thought. I hope Pablo eats well.

2

They had come through the heavy timber to the cup-shaped upper end of the little valley and he saw where the camp must be under the rim-rock that rose ahead of them through the trees.

That was the camp all right and it was a good camp. You did not see it at all until you were up to it and Robert Jordan knew it could not be spotted from the air. Nothing would show from above. It was as well hidden as a bear's den. But it seemed to be little better guarded. He looked at it carefully as they came up.

There was a large cave in the rim-rock formation, and beside the opening a man sat with his back against the rock, his legs stretched out on the ground and his carbine leaning against the rock. He was cutting away on a stick with a knife and he stared at them as they came up, then went on whittling.

'*Hola*,' said the seated man. 'What is this that comes?'

'The old man and a dynamiter,' Pablo told him and lowered the pack inside the entrance to the cave. Anselmo lowered his pack, too, and Robert Jordan unslung the rifle and leaned it against the rock.

'Don't leave it so close to the cave,' the whittling man, who had blue eyes in a dark, good-looking lazy gipsy face, the colour of smoked leather, said. 'There's a fire in there.'

'Get up and put it away thyself,' Pablo said. 'Put it by that tree.'

The gipsy did not move but said something unprintable, then, 'Leave it there. Blow thyself up,' he said lazily. ''Twill cure thy diseases.'

'What do you make?' Robert Jordan sat down by the gipsy. The gipsy showed him. It was a figure four trap and he was whittling the crossbar for it.

'For foxes,' he said. 'With a log for a dead-fall. It breaks their backs.' He grinned at Jordan. 'Like this, see?' He made a motion of the framework of the trap collapsing, the log falling, then shook his head, drew in his hand, and spread his arms to show the fox with a broken back. 'Very practical,' he explained.

'He catches rabbits,' Anselmo said. 'He is a gipsy. So if he catches rabbits he says it is foxes. If he catches a fox he would say it was an elephant.'

'And if I catch an elephant?' the gipsy asked and showed his white teeth again and winked at Robert Jordan.

'You'd say it was a tank,' Anselmo told him.

'I'll get a tank,' the gipsy told him. 'I will get a tank. And you can say it is what you please.'

'Gipsies talk much and kill little,' Anselmo told him.

The gipsy winked at Robert Jordan and went on whittling.

Pablo had gone in out of sight in the cave. Robert Jordan hoped he had gone for food. He sat on the ground by the gipsy and the afternoon sunlight came down through the tree tops and was warm on his outstretched legs. He could smell food now in the cave, the smell of oil and of onions and of meat frying and his stomach moved with hunger inside of him.

'We can get a tank,' he said to the gipsy. 'It is not too difficult.'

'With this?' the gipsy pointed toward the two sacks.

'Yes,' Robert Jordan told him. 'I will teach you. You make a trap. It is not too difficult.'

'You and me?'

'Sure,' said Robert Jordan. 'Why not?'

'Hey,' the gipsy said to Anselmo. 'Move those two sacks to where they will be safe, will you? They're valuable.'

Anselmo grunted. 'I am going for wine,' he told Robert Jordan. Robert Jordan got up and lifted the sacks away from the cave entrance and leaned them, one on each side of a tree trunk. He knew what was in them and he never liked to see them close together.

'Bring a cup for me,' the gipsy told him.

'Is there wine?' Robert Jordan asked, sitting down again by the gipsy.

'Wine? Why not? A whole skinful. Half a skinful, anyway.'

'And what to eat?'

'Everything, man,' the gipsy said. 'We eat like generals.'

'And what do gipsies do in the war?' Robert Jordan asked him.

'They keep on being gipsies.'

'That's a good job.'

'The best,' the gipsy said. 'How do they call thee?'

'Roberto. And thee?'

'Rafael. And this of the tank is serious?'

'Surely. Why not?'

Anselmo came out of the mouth of the cave with a deep stone basin full of red wine and with his fingers through the handles of three cups. 'Look,' he said. 'They have cups and all.' Pablo came out behind them.

'There is food soon,' he said. 'Do you have tobacco?'

Robert Jordan went over to the packs and opening one, felt inside an inner pocket and brought out one of the flat boxes of Russian cigarettes he had gotten at Golz's headquarters. He ran his thumbnail around the edge of the box and, opening the lid, handed them to Pablo who took half a dozen. Pablo, holding them in one of his huge hands, picked one up and looked at it against the light. They were long narrow cigarettes with pasteboard cylinders for mouthpieces.

'Much air and little tobacco,' he said. 'I know these. The other with the rare name had them.'

'Kashkin,' Robert Jordan said and offered the cigarettes to the gipsy and Anselmo, who each took one.

'Take more,' he said and they each took another. He gave them each four more, they making a double nod with the hand holding the cigarettes so that the cigarette dipped its end as a man salutes with a sword, to thank him.

'Yes,' Pablo said. 'It was a rare name.'

'Here is the wine.' Anselmo dipped a cup out of the bowl and handed it to Robert Jordan, then dipped for himself and the gipsy.

'Is there no wine for me?' Pablo asked. They were all sitting together by the cave entrance.

Anselmo handed him his cup and went into the cave for another. Coming out he leaned over the bowl and dipped the cup full and they all touched cup edges.

The wine was good, tasting faintly resinous from the wineskin, but excellent, light and clean on his tongue. Robert Jordan drank it slowly, feeling it spread warmly through his tiredness.

'The food comes shortly,' Pablo said. 'And this foreigner with the rare name, how did he die?'

'He was captured and he killed himself.'

'How did that happen?'

'He was wounded and he did not wish to be a prisoner.'

'What were the details?'

'I don't know,' he lied. He knew the details very well and he knew they would not make good talking now.

'He made us promise to shoot him in case he were wounded at the business of the train and should be unable to get away,' Pablo said. 'He spoke in a very rare manner.'

He must have been jumpy even then, Robert Jordan thought. Poor old Kashkin.

'He had a prejudice against killing himself,' Pablo said. 'He told me that. Also he had a great fear of being tortured.'

'Did he tell you that, too?' Robert Jordan asked him.

'Yes,' the gipsy said. 'He spoke like that to all of us.'

'Were you at the train, too?'

'Yes. All of us were at the train.'

'He spoke in a very rare manner,' Pablo said. 'But he was very brave.'

Poor old Kashkin, Robert Jordan thought. He must have been doing more harm than good here. I wish I would have known he was that jumpy as far back as then. They should have pulled him out. You can't have people around doing this sort of work and talking like that. That is no way to talk. Even if they accomplish their mission they are doing more harm than good, talking that sort of stuff.

'He was a little strange,' Robert Jordan said. 'I think he was a little crazy.'

'But very dexterous at producing explosions,' the gipsy said. 'And very brave.'

'But crazy,' Robert Jordan said. 'In this you have to have very much head and be very cold in the head. That was no way to talk.'

'And you,' Pablo said. 'If you are wounded in such a thing as this bridge, you would be willing to be left behind?'

'Listen,' Robert Jordan said and, leaning forward, he dipped himself another cup of the wine. 'Listen to me clearly. If ever I should have any little favours to ask of any man, I will ask him at the time.'

'Good,' said the gipsy approvingly. 'In this way speak the good ones. Ah! Here it comes.'

'You have eaten,' said Pablo.

'And I can eat twice more,' the gipsy told him. 'Look now who brings it.'

The girl stooped as she came out of the cave mouth carrying the big iron cooking platter and Robert Jordan saw her face turned at an angle and at the same time saw the strange thing about her. She smiled and said, '*Hola*, Comrade,' and Robert Jordan said, '*Salud*,' and was careful not to stare and not to look away. She set down the flat iron platter in front of him and he noticed her handsome brown hands. Now she looked him full in the face and smiled. Her teeth were white in her brown face and her skin and her eyes were the same golden tawny brown. She had high cheekbones, merry eyes and a straight mouth with full lips. Her hair was the golden brown of a grain field that has been burned dark in the sun but it was cut short all over her head so that it was but little longer than the fur on a beaver pelt. She smiled in Robert Jordan's face and put her brown hand up and ran it over her head, flattening the hair which rose again as her hand passed. She has a beautiful face, Robert Jordan thought. She'd be beautiful if they hadn't cropped her hair.

'That is the way I comb it,' she said to Robert Jordan and laughed. 'Go ahead and eat. Don't stare at me. They gave me this haircut in Valladolid. It's almost grown out now.'

She sat down opposite him and looked at him. He looked back at her and she smiled and folded her hands together over her knees. Her legs slanted long and clean from the open cuffs of the trousers as she sat with her hands across her knees and he could see the shape of her small, up-tilted breasts under the grey shirt. Every time Robert Jordan looked at her he could feel a thickness in his throat.

'There are no plates,' Anselmo said. 'Use your own knife.' The girl had leaned four forks, tines down, against the sides of the iron dish.

They were all eating out of the platter, not speaking, as is the Spanish custom. It was rabbit cooked with onions and green peppers and there were chick peas in the red wine sauce. It was well cooked, the rabbit meat flaked off the bones, and the sauce was delicious. Robert Jordan drank another cup of wine while he ate. The girl watched him all through the meal. Every one else was watching his food and eating. Robert Jordan wiped up the last of the sauce in front of him with a piece of bread, piled the rabbit bones to one side, wiped the spot where they had been for sauce, then wiped his fork clean with the bread, wiped his knife and put it away and ate the bread. He leaned over and dipped his cup full of wine and the girl still watched him.

Robert Jordan drank half the cup of wine but the thickness still came in his throat when he spoke to the girl.

'How art thou called?' he asked. Pablo looked at him quickly when he heard the tone of his voice. Then he got up and walked away.

'Maria. And thee?'

'Roberto. Have you been long in the mountains?'

'Three months.'

'Three months?' he looked at her hair, that was as thick and short and rippling when she passed her hand over it, now in embarrassment, as a grain field in the wind on a hillside. 'It was shaved,' she said. 'They shaved it regularly in the prison at Valladolid. It has taken three months to grow to this. I was on the train. They were taking me to the south. Many of the prisoners were caught after the train was blown up but I was not. I came with these.'

'I found her hidden in the rocks,' the gipsy said. 'It was when we were leaving. Man, but this one was ugly. We took her along but many times I thought we would have to leave her.'

'And the other who was with them at the train?' asked Maria. 'The other blond one. The foreigner. Where is he?'

'Dead,' Robert Jordan said. 'In April.'

'In April? The train was in April.'

'Yes,' Robert Jordan said. 'He died ten days after the train.'

'Poor man,' she said. 'He was very brave. And you do that same business?'

'Yes.'

'You have done trains, too?'

'Yes. Three trains.'

'Here?'

'In Estremadura,' he said. 'I was in Estremadura before I came here. We do very much in Estremadura. There are many of us working in Estremadura.'

'And why do you come to these mountains now?'

'I take the place of the other blond one. Also I know this country from before the movement.'

'You know it well?'

'No, not really well. But I learn fast. I have a good map and I have a good guide.'

'The old man,' she nodded. 'The old man is very good.'

'Thank you,' Anselmo said to her and Robert Jordan realized suddenly that he and the girl were not alone and he realized too that it was hard for him to look at her because it made his voice change so. He was violating the second rule of the two rules for getting on well with people that speak Spanish: give the men tobacco and leave the women alone; and he realized, very suddenly, that he did not care. There were so many things that he had not to care about, why should he care about that?

'You have a very beautiful face,' he said to Maria. 'I wish I would have had the luck to see you before your hair was cut.'

'It will grow out,' she said. 'In six months it will be long enough.'

'You should have seen her when we brought her from the train. She was so ugly it would make you sick.'

'Whose woman are you?' Robert Jordan asked, trying now to pull out of it. 'Are you Pablo's?'

She looked at him and laughed, then slapped him on the knee.

'Of Pablo? You have seen Pablo?'

'Well, then, of Rafael. I have seen Rafael.'

'Of Rafael neither.'

'Of no one,' the gipsy said. 'This is a very strange woman. Is of no one. But she cooks well.'

'Really of no one?' Robert Jordan asked her.

'Of no one. No one. Neither in joke nor in seriousness. Nor of thee either.'

'No?' Robert Jordan said and he could feel the thickness coming in his throat again. 'Good. I have no time for any woman. That is true.'

'Not fifteen minutes?' the gipsy asked teasingly. 'Not a quarter of an hour?' Robert Jordan did not answer. He looked at the girl, Maria, and his throat felt too thick for him to trust himself to speak.

Maria looked at him and laughed, then blushed suddenly but kept on looking at him.

'You are blushing,' Robert Jordan said to her. 'Do you blush much?'

'Never.'

'You are blushing now.'

'Then I will go into the cave.'

'Stay here, Maria.'

'No,' she said and did not smile at him. 'I will go into the cave now.' She picked up the iron plate they had eaten from and the four forks. She moved awkwardly as a colt moves, but with that same grace as of a young animal.

'Do you want the cups?' she asked.

Robert Jordan was still looking at her and she blushed again.

'Don't make me do that,' she said. 'I do not like to do that.'

'Leave them,' the gipsy said to her. 'Here,' he dipped into the stone bowl and handed the full cup to Robert Jordan who watched the girl duck her head and go into the cave carrying the heavy iron dish.

'Thank you,' Robert Jordan said. His voice was all right again, now that she was gone. 'This is the last one. We've had enough of this.'

'We will finish the bowl,' the gipsy said. 'There is over half a skin. We packed it in on one of the horses.'

'That was the last raid of Pablo,' Anselmo said. 'Since then he has done nothing.'

'How many are you?' Robert Jordan asked.

'We are seven and there are two women.'

'Two?'

'Yes, The *mujer* of Pablo.'

'And she?'

'In the cave. The girl can cook a little. I said she cooks well to please her. But mostly she helps the *mujer* of Pablo.'

'And how is she, the *mujer* of Pablo?'

'Something barbarous,' the gipsy grinned. 'Something *very* barbarous. If you think Pablo is ugly you should see his woman. But brave. A hundred times braver than Pablo. But something barbarous.'

'Pablo was brave in the beginning,' Anselmo said. 'Pablo was something serious in the beginning.'

'He killed more people than the cholera,' the gipsy said. 'At the start of the movement, Pablo killed more people than the typhoid fever.'

'But since a long time he is *muy flojo*,' Anselmo said. 'He is very flaccid. He is very much afraid to die.'

'It is possible that it is because he has killed so many at the beginning,' the gipsy said philosophically. 'Pablo killed more than the bubonic plague.'

'That and the riches,' Anselmo said. 'Also he drinks very much. Now he would like to retire like a *matador de toros*. Like a bull-fighter. But he cannot retire.'

'If he crosses to the other side of the lines they will take his horses and make him go in the army,' the gipsy said. 'In me there is no love for being in the army either.'

'Nor is there in any other gipsy,' Anselmo said.

'Why should there be?' the gipsy asked. 'Who wants to be in any army? Do we make the revolution to be in an army? I am willing to fight but not to be in an army.'

'Where are the others?' asked Robert Jordan. He felt comfortable and sleepy now from the wine and lying back on the floor of the forest he saw through the tree tops the small afternoon clouds of the mountains moving slowly in the high Spanish sky.

'There are two asleep in the cave,' the gipsy said. 'Two are on guard above where we have the gun. One is on guard below. They are probably all asleep.'

Robert Jordan rolled over on his side.

'What kind of a gun is it?'

'A very rare name,' the gipsy said. 'It has gone away from me for the moment. It is a machine gun.'

It must be an automatic rifle, Robert Jordan thought.

'How much does it weigh?' he asked.

'One man can carry it but it is heavy. It has three legs that fold. We got it in the last serious raid. The one before the wine.'

'How many rounds have you for it?'

'An infinity,' the gipsy said. 'One whole case of an unbelievable heaviness.'

Sounds like about five hundred rounds, Robert Jordan thought.

'Does it feed from a pan or a belt?'

'From round iron cans on the top of the gun.'

Hell, it's a Lewis gun, Robert Jordan thought.

'Do you know anything about a machine gun?' he asked the old man.

'*Nada*,' said Anselmo. 'Nothing.'

'And thou?' to the gipsy.

'That they fire with much rapidity, and become so hot the barrel burns the hand that touches it,' the gipsy said proudly.

'Every one knows that,' Anselmo said with contempt.

'Perhaps,' the gipsy said. 'But he asked me to tell what I know about a *máquina* and I told him.' Then he added, 'Also, unlike an ordinary rifle, they continue to fire as long as you exert pressure on the trigger.'

'Unless they jam, run out of ammunition or get so hot they melt,' Robert Jordan said in English.

'What do you say?' Anselmo asked him.

'Nothing,' Robert Jordan said. 'I was only looking into the future in English.'

'That is something truly rare,' the gipsy said. 'Looking into the future in *Ingles*. Can you read in the palm of the hand?'

'No,' Robert Jordan said and he dipped another cup of wine. 'But if thou canst I wish thee would read in the palm of my hand and tell me what is going to pass in the next three days.'

'The *mujer* of Pablo reads in the hands,' the gipsy said. 'But she is so irritable and of such a barbarousness that I do not know if she will do it.'

Robert Jordan sat up now and took a swallow of the wine.

'Let us see the *mujer* of Pablo now,' he said. 'If it is that bad let us get it over with.'

'I would not disturb her,' Rafael said. 'She has a strong hatred for me.'

'Why?'

'She treats me as a time waster.'

'What injustice,' Anselmo taunted.

'She is against gipsies.'

'What an error,' Anselmo said.

'She has gipsy blood,' Rafael said. 'She knows of what she speaks.' He grinned. 'But she has a tongue that scalds and that bites like a bull whip. With this tongue she takes the hide from anyone. In strips. She is of an unbelievable barbarousness.'

'How does she get along with the girl, Maria?' Robert Jordan asked.

'Good. She likes the girl. But let anyone come near her seriously—' He shook his head and clucked with his tongue.

'She is very good with the girl,' Anselmo said. 'She takes good care of her.'

'When we picked the girl up at the time of the train she was very strange,' Rafael said. 'She would not speak and she cried all the time and if anyone touched her she would shiver like a wet dog. Only lately has she been better. Lately she has been much better. To-day she was fine. Just now, talking to you, she was very good. We would have left her after the train. Certainly it was not worth being delayed by something so sad and ugly and apparently worthless. But the old woman tied a rope to her and when the girl thought she could not go farther, the old woman beat her with the end of the rope to make her go. Then when she could not really go farther, the old woman carried her over her shoulder. When the old woman could not carry her, I carried her. We were going up that hill breast high in the gorse and heather. And when I could no longer carry her, Pablo carried her. But what the old woman had to say to us to make us do it!' He shook his head at the memory. 'It is true that the girl is long in the legs but is not heavy. The bones are light and she weighs little. But she weighs enough when we had to carry her and stop to fire and then carry her again with the old woman lashing at Pablo with the rope and carrying his rifle, putting it in his hand when he would drop the girl, making him pick her up again and loading the gun for him while she cursed him; taking the shells from his pouches and shoving them down into the magazine and cursing him. The dusk was coming well on then and when the night came it was all right. But it was lucky that they had no cavalry.'

'It must have been very hard at the train,' Anselmo said. 'I was not there,' he explained to Robert Jordan. 'There was the band of Pablo, of El Sordo, whom we will see to-night, and two other bands of these mountains. I had gone to the other side of the lines.'

'In addition to the blond one with the rare name—' the gipsy said.

'Kashkin.'

'Yes. It is a name I can never dominate. We had two with a machine gun. They were sent also by the army. They could not get the gun away and lost it. Certainly it weighed no more than that girl and if the old woman had been over them they would have gotten it away.' He shook his head remembering, then went on. 'Never in my life have I seen such a thing as when the explosion was produced. The train was coming steadily. We saw it far away. And I had an excitement so great that I cannot tell it. We saw steam from it and then later came the noise of the whistle. Then it came chu-chu-chu-chu-chu-chu steadily larger and larger and then, at the moment of the explosion, the front wheels of the engine rose up and all of the earth seemed to rise in a great cloud of blackness and a roar and the engine rose high in the cloud of dirt and of the wooden ties rising in the air as in a dream and then it fell onto its side like a great wounded animal and there was an explosion of white steam before the clods of the other explosion had ceased to fall on us and the *máquina* commenced to speak ta-tat-tat-ta!' went the gipsy shaking his two clenched fists up and down in front of him, thumbs up, on an imaginary machine gun. 'Ta! Ta! Tat! Tat! Ta! Ta!' he exulted. 'Never in my life have I seen such a thing, with the troops running from the train and the *máquina* speaking into them and the men falling. It was then that I put my hand on the *máquina* in my excitement and discovered that the barrel burned and at that moment the old woman slapped me on the side of the face and said, "Shoot, you fool! Shoot or I will kick your brains in!" Then I commenced to shoot but it was very hard to hold my gun steady and the troops were running up the far hill. Later, after we had been down at the train to see what there was to take, an officer forced some troops back toward us at the point of a pistol. He kept waving the pistol and shouting at them and we were all shooting at him but no one hit him. Then some troops lay down and commenced firing and the officer walked up and down behind them with his pistol and still we could not hit him and the *máquina* could not fire on him because of the position of the train. This officer shot two men as they lay and still they would not get up and he was cursing them and finally they got up, one two and three at a time and came running toward us and the train. Then they lay flat again and fired. Then we left, with the *máquina* still speaking over us as we left. It was then I found the girl where she had run from the train to the rocks and she ran with us. It was those troops who hunted us until that night.'

'It must have been something very hard.' Anselmo said. 'Of much emotion.'

'It was the only good thing we have done,' said a deep voice. 'What are you doing now, you lazy drunken obscene unsayable son of an unnameable unmarried gipsy obscenity? What are you doing?'

Robert Jordan saw a woman of about fifty almost as big as Pablo, almost as wide as she was tall, in black peasant skirt and blouse, with heavy wool socks on heavy legs, black rope-soled shoes and a brown face like a model for a granite monument. She had big but nice looking hands and her thick curly black hair was twisted into a knot on her neck.

'Answer me,' she said to the gipsy, ignoring the others.

'I was talking to these comrades. This one comes as a dynamiter.'

'I know all that,' the *mujer* of Pablo said. 'Get out of here now and relieve Andrés who is on guard at the top.'

'*Me voy*,' the gipsy said. 'I go.' He turned to Robert Jordan. 'I will see thee at the hour of eating.'

'Not even in a joke,' said the woman to him. 'Three times you have eaten to-day according to my count. Go now and send me Andrés.'

'*Hola*,' she said to Robert Jordan and put out her hand and smiled. 'How are you and how is everything in the Republic?'

'Good,' he said and returned her strong hand grip. 'Both with me and with the Republic.'

'I am happy,' she told him. She was looking into his face and smiling and he noticed she had fine grey eyes. 'Do you come for us to do another train?'

'No,' said Robert Jordan, trusting her instantly. 'For a bridge.'

'*No es nada*,' she said. 'A bridge is nothing. When do we do another train now that we have horses?'

'Later. This bridge is of great importance.'

'The girl told me your comrade who was with us at the train is dead.'

'Yes.'

'What a pity. Never have I seen such an explosion. He was a man of talent.

He pleased me very much. Is it not possible to do another train now? There are many men here now in the hills. Too many. It is already hard to get food. It would be better to get out. And we have horses.'

'We have to do this bridge.'

'Where is it?'

'Quite close.'

'All the better,' the *mujer* of Pablo said. 'Let us blow all the bridges there are here and get out. I am sick of this place. Here is too much concentration of people. No good can come of it. Here is a stagnation that is repugnant.'

She sighted Pablo through the trees.

'*Borracho!*' she called to him. 'Drunkard. Rotten drunkard!' She turned back to Robert Jordan cheerfully. 'He's taken a leather wine bottle to drink alone in the woods,' she said. 'He's drinking all the time. This life is ruining him. Young man, I am very content that you have come.' She clapped him on the back. 'Ah,' she said. 'You're bigger than you look,' and ran her hand over his shoulder, feeling the muscle under the flannel shirt. 'Good. I am very content that you have come.'

'And I equally.'

'We will understand each other,' she said. 'Have a cup of wine.'

'We have already had some,' Robert Jordan said. 'But, will you?'

'Not until dinner,' she said. 'It gives me heartburn.' Then she sighted Pablo again. '*Borracho!*' she shouted. 'Drunkard!' She turned to Robert Jordan and shook her head. 'He was a very good man,' she told him. 'But now he is terminated. And listen to me about another thing. Be very good and careful about the girl. The Maria. She has had a bad time. Understandest thou?'

'Yes. Why do you say this?'

'I saw how she was from seeing thee when she came into the cave. I saw her watching thee before she came out.'

'I joked with her a little.'

'She was in a very bad state,' the woman of Pablo said. 'Now she is better, she ought to get out of here.'

'Clearly, she can be sent through the lines with Anselmo.'

'You and the Anselmo can take her when this terminates.'

Robert Jordan felt the ache in his throat and his voice thickening. 'That might be done,' he said.

The *mujer* of Pablo looked at him, and shook her head. 'Ayee. Ayee,' she said. 'Are all men like that?'

'I said nothing. She is beautiful, you know that.'

'No, she is not beautiful. But she begins to be beautiful, you mean,' the woman of Pablo said. 'Men. It is a shame to us women that we make them. No. In seriousness. Are there not homes to care for such as her under the Republic?'

'Yes,' said Robert Jordan. 'Good places. On the coast near Valencia. In other places too. There they will treat her well and she can work with children. There are the children from evacuated villages. They will teach her the work.'

'That is what I want,' the *mujer* of Pablo said. 'Pablo has a sickness for her already. It is another thing which destroys him. It lies on him like a sickness when he sees her. It is best that she goes now.'

'We can take her after this is over.'

'And you will be careful of her now if I trust you? I speak to you as though I knew you for a long time.'

'It is like that,' Robert Jordan said, 'when people understand one another.'

'Sit down,' the woman of Pablo said. 'I do not ask any promise because what will happen, will happen. Only if you will *not* take her out, then I ask a promise.'

'Why if I would not take her?'

'Because I do not want her crazy here after you will go. I have had her crazy before and I have enough without that.'

'We will take her after the bridge,' Robert Jordan said. 'If we are alive after the bridge, we will take her.'

'I do not like to hear you speak in that manner. That manner of speaking never brings luck.'

'I spoke in that manner only to make a promise,' Robert Jordan said. 'I am not of those who speak gloomily.'

'Let me see thy hand,' the woman said. Robert Jordan put his hand out and the woman opened it, held it in her own big hand, rubbed her thumb over it and looked at it, carefully, then dropped it. She stood up. He got up too and she looked at him without smiling.

'What did you see in it?' Robert Jordan asked her. 'I don't believe in it. You won't scare me.'

'Nothing,' she told him. 'I saw nothing in it.'

'Yes you did. I am only curious. I do not believe in such things.'

'In what do you believe?'

'In many things but not in that.'

'In what?'

'In my work.'

'Yes, I saw that.'

'Tell me what else you saw.'

'I saw nothing else,' she said bitterly. 'The bridge is very difficult, you said?'

'No. I said it is very important.'

'But it can be difficult?'

'Yes. And now I go down to look at it. How many men have you here?'

'Five that are any good. The gipsy is worthless although his intentions are good. He has a good heart. Pablo I no longer trust.'

'How many men has El Sordo that are good?'

'Perhaps eight. We will see to-night. He is coming here. He is a very practical man. He also has some dynamite. Not very much, though. You will speak with him.'

'Have you sent for him?'

'He comes every night. He is a neighbour. Also a friend as well as a comrade.'

'What do you think of him?'

'He is a very good man. Also very practical. In the business of the train he was enormous.'

'And in the other bands?'

'Advising them in time, it should be possible to unite fifty rifles of a certain dependability.'

'How dependable?'

'Dependable within the gravity of the situation.'

'And now many cartridges per rifle?'

'Perhaps twenty. Depending how many they would bring for this business. If they would come for this business. Remember thee that in this of a bridge there is no money and no loot and in thy reservations of talking, much danger, and that afterwards there must be a moving from these mountains. Many will oppose this of the bridge.'

'Clearly.'

'In this way it is better not to speak of it unnecessarily.'

'I am in accord.'

'Then after thou hast studied thy bridge we will talk to-night with El Sordo.'

'I go down now with Anselmo.'

'Wake him then,' she said. 'Do you want a carbine?'

'Thank you,' he told her. 'It is good to have but I will not use it. I go to look, not to make disturbances. Thank you for what you have told me. I like very much your way of speaking.'

'I try to speak frankly.'

'Then tell me what you saw in the hand.'

'No,' she said and shook her head. 'I saw nothing. Go now to thy bridge. I will look after thy equipment.'

'Cover it and that no one should touch it. It is better there than in the cave.'

'It shall be covered and no one shall touch it,' the woman of Pablo said. 'Go now to thy bridge.'

'Anselmo,' Robert Jordan said, putting his hand on the shoulder of the old man who lay sleeping, his head on his arms.

The old man looked up. 'Yes,' he said. 'Of course. Let us go.'

3

They came down the last two hundred yards, moving carefully from tree to tree in the shadows and now, through the last pines of the steep hillside, the bridge was only fifty yards away. The late afternoon sun that still came over the brown shoulder of the mountain showed the bridge dark against the steep emptiness of the gorge. It was a steel bridge of a single span and there was a sentry box at each end. It was wide enough for two motor cars to pass and it spanned, in solid-flung metal grace, a deep gorge at the bottom of which, far below, a brook leaped in white water through rocks and boulders down to the main stream of the pass.

The sun was in Robert Jordan's eyes and the bridge showed only in outline. Then the sun lessened and was gone and looking up through the trees at the brown, rounded height that it had gone behind, he saw, now that he no longer looked into the glare, that the mountain slope was a delicate new green and that there were patches of old snow under the crest.

Then he was watching the bridge again in the sudden short trueness of the little light that would be left, and studying its construction. The problem of its demolition was not difficult. As he watched he took out a notebook from his breast pocket and made several quick line sketches. As he made the drawings he did not figure the charges. He would do that later. Now he was noting the points where the explosive should be placed in order to cut the support of the span and drop a section of it into the gorge. It could be done unhurriedly, scientifically and correctly with a half-dozen charges laid and braced to explode simultaneously; or it could be done roughly with two big ones. They would need to be very big ones, on opposite sides and should go at the same time. He sketched quickly and happily; glad at last to have the problem under his hand; glad at last actually to be engaged upon it. Then he shut his notebook, pushed the pencil into its leather holder in the edge of the flap, put the notebook in his pocket and buttoned the pocket.

While he had sketched, Anselmo had been watching the road, the bridge and the sentry boxes. He thought they had come too close to the bridge for safety and when the sketching was finished, he was relieved.

As Robert Jordan buttoned the flap of his pocket and then lay flat behind the pine trunk, looking out from behind it, Anselmo put his hand on his elbow and pointed with one finger.

In the sentry box that faced toward them up the road, the sentry was sitting holding his rifle, the bayonet fixed, between his knees. He was smoking a cigarette and he wore a knitted cap and blanket style cape. At fifty yards, you could not see anything about his face. Robert Jordan put up his field glasses, shading the lenses carefully with his cupped hands even though there was now no sun to make a glint, and there was the rail of the bridge as clear as though you could reach out and touch it and there was the face of the sentry so clear he could see the sunken cheeks, the ash on the cigarette and the greasy shine of the bayonet. It was a peasant's face, the cheeks hollow under the high cheekbones, the beard stubbled, the eyes shaded by the heavy brows, big hands holding the rifle, heavy boots showing beneath the folds of the blanket cape. There was a worn, blackened leather wine bottle on the wall of the sentry box, there were some newspapers and there was no telephone. There could, of course, be a telephone on the side he could not see; but there were no wires running from the box that were visible. A telephone line ran along the road and its wires were carried over the bridge. There was a charcoal brazier outside the sentry box, made from an old petrol tin with the top cut off and holes punched in it, which rested on two stones; but it held no fire. There were some fire-blackened empty tins in the ashes under it.

Robert Jordan handed the glasses to Anselmo who lay flat beside him. The old man grinned and shook his head. He tapped his skull beside his eye with one finger.

'*Ya lo veo*,' he said in Spanish. 'I have seen him,' speaking from the front of his mouth with almost no movement of his lips in the way that is quieter than any whisper. He looked at the sentry as Robert Jordan smiled at him and, pointing with one finger, drew the other across his throat. Robert Jordan nodded but he did not smile.

The sentry box at the far end of the bridge faced away from them and down the road and they could not see into it. The road, which was broad and oiled and well constructed, made a turn to the left at the far end of the bridge and then swung out of sight around a curve to the right. At this point it was enlarged from the old road to its present width by cutting into the solid bastion of the rock on the far side of the gorge; and its left or western edge, looking down from the pass and the bridge, was marked and protected by a line of upright cut blocks of stone where its edge fell sheer away to the gorge. The gorge was almost a canyon here, where the brook, that the bridge was flung over, merged with the main stream of the pass.

'And the other post?' Robert Jordan asked Anselmo.

'Five hundred metres below that turn. In the roadmender's hut that is built into the side of the rock.'

'How many men?' Robert Jordan asked.

He was watching the sentry again with his glasses. The sentry rubbed his cigarette out on the plank wall of the box, then took a leather tobacco pouch from his pocket, opened the paper of the dead cigarette and emptied the remnant of used tobacco into the pouch. The sentry stood up, leaned his rifle against the wall of the box and stretched, then picked up his rifle, slung it over his shoulder and walked out onto the bridge. Anselmo flattened on the ground and Robert Jordan slipped his glasses into his shirt pocket and put his head well behind the pine tree.

'There are seven men and a corporal,' Anselmo said close to his ear. 'I informed myself from the gipsy.'

'We will go now as soon as he is quiet,' Robert Jordan said. 'We are too close.'

'Hast thou seen what thou needest?'

'Yes. All that I need.'

It was getting cold quickly now with the sun down and the light was failing as the afterglow from the last sunlight on the mountains behind them faded.

'How does it look to thee?' Anselmo said softly as they watched the sentry walk across the bridge toward the other box, his bayonet bright in the last of the afterglow, his figure unshapely in the blanket coat.

'Very good,' Robert Jordan said. 'Very, very good.'

'I am glad,' Anselmo said. 'Should we go? Now there is no chance that he sees us.'

The sentry was standing, his back toward them, at the far end of the bridge. From the gorge came the noise of the stream in the boulders. Then through this noise came another noise, a steady, racketing drone and they saw the sentry looking up, his knitted cap slanted back, and turning their heads and looking up they saw, high in the evening sky, three monoplanes in V formation, showing minute and silvery at that height where there still was sun, passing unbelievably quickly across the sky, their motors now throbbing steadily.

'Ours?' Anselmo asked.

'They seem so,' Robert Jordan said but knew that at that height you never could be sure. They could be an evening patrol of either side. But you always said pursuit planes were ours because it made people feel better. Bombers were another matter.

Anselmo evidently felt the same. 'They are ours,' he said. 'I recognize them. They are *Moscas*.'

'Good,' said Robert Jordan. 'They seem to me to be *Moscas*, too.'

'They are *Moscas*,' Anselmo said.

Robert Jordan could have put the glasses on them and been sure instantly but he preferred not to. It made no difference to him who they were to-night and if it pleased the old man to have them be ours, he did not want to take them away. Now, as they moved out of sight toward Segovia, they did not look to be the green, red wing-tipped, low wing Russian conversion of the Boeing P32 that the Spaniards called *Moscas*. You could not see the colours but the cut was wrong. No. It was a Fascist patrol coming home.

The sentry was still standing at the far box with his back turned.

'Let us go,' Robert Jordan said. He started up the hill, moving carefully and taking advantage of the cover until they were out of sight. Anselmo followed him at a hundred yards distance. When they were well out of sight of the bridge, he stopped and the old man came up and went into the lead and climbed steadily through the pass, up the steep slope in the dark.

'We have a formidable aviation,' the old man said happily.

'Yes.'

'And we will win.'

'We have to win.'

'Yes. And after we have won you must come to hunt.'

'To hunt what?'

'The boar, the bear, the wolf, the ibex—'

'You like to hunt?'

'Yes, man. More than anything. We all hunt in my village. You do not like to hunt?'

'No,' said Robert Jordan. 'I do not like to kill animals.'

'With me it is the opposite,' the old man said. 'I do not like to kill men.'

'Nobody does except those who are disturbed in the head,' Robert Jordan said. 'But I feel nothing against it when it is necessary. When it is for the cause.'

'It is a different thing, though,' Anselmo said. 'In my house, when I had a house, and now I have no house, there were the tusks of boar I had shot in the lower forest. There were the hides of wolves I had shot. In the winter, hunting them in the snow. One very big one, I killed at dusk in the outskirts of the village on my way home one night in November. There were four wolf hides on the floor of my house. They were worn by stepping on them but they were wolf hides. There were the horns of ibex that I had killed in the high Sierra, and there was an eagle stuffed by an embalmer of birds of Avila, with his wings spread, and eyes as yellow and real as the eyes of an eagle alive. It was a very beautiful thing and all of those things gave me great pleasure to contemplate.'

'Yes,' said Robert Jordan.

'On the door of the church of my village was nailed the paw of a bear that I killed in the spring, finding him on a hillside in the snow, overturning a log with this same paw.'

'When was this?'

'Six years ago. And every time I saw that paw, like the hand of a man, but with those long claws, dried and nailed through the palm to the door of the church, I received a pleasure.'

'Of pride?'

'Of pride of remembrance of the encounter with the bear on that hillside in the early spring. But of the killing of a man, who is a man as we are, there is nothing good that remains.'

'You can't nail his paw to the church,' Robert Jordan said.

'No. Such a barbarity is unthinkable. Yet the hand of a man is like the paw of a bear.'

'So is the chest of a man like the chest of a bear,' Robert Jordan said. 'With the hide removed from the bear, there are many similarities in the muscles.'

'Yes,' Anselmo said. 'The gipsies believe the bear to be a brother of man.'

'So do the Indians in America,' Robert Jordan said. 'And when they kill a bear they apologize to him and ask his pardon. They put his skull in a tree and they ask him to forgive them before they leave it.'

'The gipsies believe the bear to be a brother to man because he has the same body beneath his hide, because he drinks beer, because he enjoys music and because he likes to dance.'

'So also believe the Indians.'

'Are the Indians then gipsies?'

'No. But they believe alike about the bear.'

'Clearly. The gipsies also believe he is a brother because he steals for pleasure.'

'Have you gipsy blood?'

'No. But I have seen much of them and clearly, since the movement, more. There are many in the hills. To them it is not a sin to kill outside the tribe. They deny this, but it is true.'

'Like the Moors.'

'Yes. But the gipsies have many laws they do not admit to having. In the war many gipsies have become bad again as they were in the olden times.'

'They do not understand why the war is made. They do not know for what we fight.'

'No,' Anselmo said. 'They only know now there is a war and people may kill again as in the olden times without a surety of punishment.'

'You have killed?' Robert Jordan asked in the intimacy of the dark and of their day together.

'Yes. Several times. But not with pleasure. To me it is a sin to kill a man. Even Fascists whom we must kill. To me there is a great difference between the bear and the man and I do not believe the wizardry of the gipsies about the brotherhood with animals. No. I am against all killing of men.'

'Yet you have killed.'

'Yes. And will again. But if I live later, I will try to live in such a way, doing no harm to any one, that it will be forgiven.'

'By whom?'

'Who knows? Since we do not have God here any more, neither His Son nor the Holy Ghost, who forgives? I do not know.'

'You have not God any more?'

'No. Man. Certainly not. If there were God, never would He have permitted what I have seen with my eyes. Let *them* have God.'

'They claim Him.'

'Clearly I miss Him been brought up in religion. But now a man must be responsible to himself.'

'Then it is thyself who will forgive thee for killing.'

'I believe so,' Anselmo said. 'Since you put it clearly in that way I believe that must be it. But with or without God, I think it is a sin to kill. To take the life of another is to me very grave. I will do it whenever necessary but I am not of the race of Pablo.'

'To win a war we must kill our enemies. That has always been true.'

'Clearly. In war we must kill. But I have very rare ideas,' Anselmo said.

They were walking now close together in the dark and he spoke softly, sometimes turning his head as he climbed. 'I would not kill even a Bishop. I would not kill a proprietor of any kind. I would make them work each day as we have worked in the fields and as we work in the mountains with the timber, all of the rest of their lives. So they would see what man is born to. That they should sleep where we sleep. That they should eat as we eat. But above all that they should work. Thus they would learn.'

'And they would survive to enslave thee again.'

'To kill them teaches nothing,' Anselmo said. 'You cannot exterminate them because from their seed comes more with greater hatred. Prison is nothing. Prison only makes hatred. That all our enemies should learn.'

'But still thou hast killed.'

'Yes,' Anselmo said. 'Many times and will again. But not with pleasure and regarding it as a sin.'

'And the sentry. You joked of killing the sentry.'

'That was in joke. I would kill the sentry. Yes. Certainly and with a clear heart considering our task. But not with pleasure.'

'We will leave them to those who enjoy it,' Robert Jordan said. 'There are eight and five. That is thirteen for those who enjoy it.'

'There are many of those who enjoy it,' Anselmo said in the dark. 'We have many of those. More of those than of men who would serve for a battle.'

'Hast thou ever been in a battle?'

'Nay,' the old man said. 'We fought in Segovia at the start of the movement but we were beaten and we ran. I ran with the others. We did not truly understand what we were doing, nor how it should be done. Also I had only a shotgun with cartridges of large buckshot and the *guardia civil* had Mausers. I could not hit them with buckshot at a hundred yards, and at three hundred yards they shot us as they wished as though we were rabbits. They shot much and well and we were like sheep before them.' He was silent. Then asked, 'Thinkest thou there will be a battle at the bridge?'

'There is a chance.'

'I have never seen a battle without running,' Anselmo said. 'I do not know how I would comport myself. I am an old man and I have wondered.'

'I will respond for thee,' Robert Jordan told him.

'And hast thou been in many battles?'

'Several.'

'And what thinkest thou of this of the bridge?'

'First I think of the bridge. That is my business. It is not difficult to destroy the bridge. Then we will make the dispositions for the rest. For the preliminaries. It will all be written.'

'Very few of these people read,' Anselmo said.

'It will be written for every one's knowledge so that all know, but also it will be clearly explained.'

'I will do that to which I am assigned,' Anselmo said. 'But remembering the shooting in Segovia, if there is to be a battle or even much exchanging of shots, I would wish to have it very clear what I must do under all circumstances to avoid running. I remember that I had a great tendency to run at Segovia.'

'We will be together,' Robert Jordan told him. 'I will tell you what there is to do at all times.'

'Then there is no problem,' Anselmo said. 'I can do anything that I am ordered.'

'For us will be the bridge and the battle, should there be one,' Robert Jordan said and saying it in the dark, he felt a little theatrical but it sounded well in Spanish.

'It should be of the highest interest,' Anselmo said and hearing him say it honestly and clearly and with no pose, neither the English pose of understatement nor any Latin bravado, Robert Jordan thought he was very lucky to have this old man and having seen the bridge and worked out and simplified the problem it would have been to surprise the posts and blow it in a normal way, he resented Golz's orders, and the necessity for them. He resented them for what they could do to him and for what they could do to this old man. They were bad orders all right for those who would have to carry them out.

And that is not the way to think, he told himself, and there is not you, and there are no people that things must not happen to. Neither you nor this old man is anything. You are instruments to do your duty. There are necessary orders that are no fault of yours and there is a bridge and that bridge can be the point on which the future of the human race can turn. As it can turn on everything that happens in this war. You have only one thing to do and you must do it. Only one thing, hell, he thought. If it were one thing it was easy. Stop worrying, you windy bastard, he said to himself. Think about something else.

So he thought about the girl Maria, with her skin, the hair and the eyes all the same golden tawny brown, the hair a little darker than the rest but it would be lighter as her skin tanned deeper, the smooth skin, pale gold on the surface with a darkness underneath. Smooth it would be, all of her body smooth, and she moved awkwardly as though there were something of her and about her that embarrassed her as though it were visible, though it was not, but only in her mind. And she blushed when he looked at her, and she sitting, her hands clasped around her knees and the shirt open at the throat, the cup of her breasts uptilted against the shirt, and as he thought of her, his throat was choky and there was a difficulty in walking and he and Anselmo spoke no more until the old man said, 'Now we go down through these rocks and to the camp.'

As they came through the rocks in the dark, a man spoke to them, 'Halt. Who goes?' They heard a rifle bolt snick as it was drawn back and then the knock against the wood as it was pushed forward and down on the stock.

'Comrades,' Anselmo said.

'What comrades?'

'Comrades of Pablo,' the old man told him. 'Dost thou not know us?'

'Yes,' the voice said. 'But it is an order. Have you the password?'

'No. We come from below.'

'I know,' the man said in the dark. 'You come from the bridge. I know all of that. The order is not mine. You must know the second half of a password.'

'What is the first half then?' Robert Jordan said.

'I have forgotten it,' the man said in the dark and laughed. 'Go then unprintably to the campfire with thy obscene dynamite.'

'That is called guerrilla discipline,' Anselmo said. 'Uncock thy piece.'

'It is uncocked,' the man said in the dark. 'I let it down with my thumb and forefinger.'

'Thou wilt do that with a Mauser sometime which has no knurl on the bolt and it will fire.'

'This is a Mauser,' the man said. 'But I have a grip of thumb and forefinger beyond description. Always I let it down that way.'

'Where is the rifle pointed?' asked Anselmo into the dark.

'At thee,' the man said, 'all the time that I descended the bolt. And when thou comest to the camp, order that some one should relieve me because I have indescribable and unprintable hunger and I have forgotten the password.'

'How art thou called?' Robert Jordan asked.

'Agustín,' the man said. 'I am called Agustín and I am dying with boredom in this spot.'

'We will take the message,' Robert Jordan said and he thought how the word *aburmiento* which means boredom in Spanish was a word no peasant would use in any other language. Yet it is one of the most common words in the mouth of a Spaniard of any class.

'Listen to me,' Agustín said, and coming close he put his hand on Robert Jordan's shoulder. Then striking a flint and steel together he held it up and blowing on the end of the cork, looked at the young man's face in its glow.

'You look like the other one,' he said. 'But something different. Listen,' he put the lighter down and stood holding his rifle. 'Tell me this. Is it true about the bridge?'

'What about the bridge?'

'That we blow up an obscene bridge and then have to obscenely well obscenity ourselves off out of these mountains?'

'I know not.'

'*You* know not,' Agustín said. 'What a barbarity! Whose then is the dynamite?'

'Mine.'

'And knowest thou not what it is for? Don't tell me tales.'

'I know what it is for and so will you in time,' Robert Jordan said. 'But now we go to the camp.'

'Go to the unprintable,' Agustín said. 'And unprint thyself. But do you want me to tell you something of service to you?'

'Yes,' said Robert Jordan. 'If it is not unprintable,' naming the principal obscenity that had larded the conversation. The man, Agustín, spoke so obscenely, coupling an obscenity to every noun as an adjective, using the same obscenity as a verb, that Robert Jordan wondered if he could speak a straight sentence. Agustín laughed in the dark when he heard the word. 'It is a way of speaking I have. Maybe it is ugly. Who knows? Each one speaks according to his manner. Listen to me. The bridge is nothing to me. As well the bridge as another thing. Also I have a boredom in these mountains. That we should go if it is needed. These mountains say nothing to me. That we should leave them. But I would say one thing. Guard well thy explosive.'

'Thank you,' Robert Jordan said. 'From thee?'

'No,' Agustín said. 'From people less unprintably equipped than I.'

'So?' asked Robert Jordan.

'You understand Spanish,' Agustín said seriously now. 'Care well for thy unprintable explosive.'

'Thank you.'

'No. Don't thank me. Look after thy stuff.'

'Has anything happened to it?'

'No, or I would not waste thy time talking in this fashion.'

'Thank you all the same. We go now to camp.'

'Good,' said Agustín, 'and that they send some one here who knows the password.'

'Will we see you at the camp?'

'Yes, man. And shortly.'

'Come on,' Robert Jordan said to Anselmo.

They were walking down the edge of the meadow now and there was a grey mist. The grass was lush underfoot after the pine-needle floor of the forest and the dew on the grass wet through their canvas rope-soled shoes. Ahead, through the trees, Robert Jordan could see a light where he knew the mouth of the cave must be.

'Agustín is a very good man,' Anselmo said. 'He speaks very filthily and always in jokes but he is a very serious man.'

'You know him well?'

'Yes. For a long time. I have much confidence in him.'

'And what he says?'

'Yes, man. This Pablo is bad now, as you could see.'

'And the best thing to do?'

'One shall guard it at all times.'

'Who?'

'You. Me. The woman and Agustín. Since he sees the danger.'

'Did you think things were as bad as they are here?'

'No,' Anselmo said. 'They have gone bad very fast. But it was necessary to come here. This is the country of Pablo and of El Sordo. In their country we must deal with them unless it is something that can be done alone.'

'And El Sordo?'

'Good,' Anselmo said. 'As good as the other is bad.'

'You believe now that he is truly bad?'

'All afternoon I have thought of it and since we have heard what we have heard, I think now, yes. Truly.'

'It would not be better to leave, speaking of another bridge, and obtain men from other bands?'

'No,' Anselmo said. 'This is his country. You could not move that he would not know it. But one must move with much precautions.'

4

They came down to the mouth of the cave, where a light shone out from the edge of a blanket that hung over the opening. The two packs were at the foot of the tree covered with a canvas and Robert Jordan knelt down and felt the canvas wet and stiff over them. In the dark he felt under the canvas in the outside pocket of one of the packs and took out a leather-covered flask and slipped it in his pocket. Unlocking the long barred padlocks that passed through the grummet that closed the opening of the mouth of the packs, and untying the drawstring at the top of each pack, he felt inside them and verified their contents with his hands. Deep in one pack he felt the bundled blocks in the sacks, the sacks wrapped in the sleeping robe, and tying the strings of that and pushing the lock shut again, he put his hands into the other and felt the sharp wood outline of the box of the old exploder, the cigar box with the caps, each little cylinder wrapped round and round with its two wires (the lot of them packed as carefully as he had packed his collection of wild bird eggs when he was a boy), the stock of the sub-machine gun, disconnected from the barrel and wrapped in his leather jacket, the two pans and five clips in one of the inner pockets of the big pack-sack and the small coils of copper wire and the big coil of light insulated wire in the other. In the pocket with the wire he felt his pliers and the two wooden awls for making holes in the end of the blocks and then, from the last inside pocket, he took a big box of the Russian cigarettes of the lot he had from Golz's headquarters and tying the mouth of the pack shut, he pushed the lock in, buckled the flaps down and again covered both packs with the canvas. Anselmo had gone on into the cave.

Robert Jordan stood up to follow him, then reconsidered and, lifting the canvas off the two packs, picked them up, one in each hand, and started with them, just able to carry them, for the mouth of the cave. He laid one pack down and lifted the blanket aside, then with his head stooped and with a pack in each hand, carrying by the leather shoulder straps, he went into the cave.

It was warm and smoky in the cave. There was a table along one wall with a tallow candle stuck in a bottle on it and at the table were seated Pablo, three men he did not know, and the gipsy, Rafael. The candle made shadows on the wall behind the men and Anselmo stood where he had come in to the right of the table. The wife of Pablo was standing over the charcoal fire on the open fire hearth in the corner of the cave. The girl knelt by her stirring in an iron pot. She lifted the wooden spoon out and looked at Robert Jordan as he stood there in the doorway and he saw, in the glow from the fire the woman was blowing with a bellows, the girl's face, her arm and the drops running down from the spoon and dropping into the iron pot.

'What do you carry?' Pablo said.

'My things,' Robert Jordan said and set the two packs down a little way apart where the cave opened out on the side away from the table.

'Are they not well outside?' Pablo asked.

'Some one might trip over them in the dark,' Robert Jordan said and walked over to the table and laid the box of cigarettes on it.

'I do not like to have dynamite here in the cave,' Pablo said.

'It is far from the fire,' Robert Jordan said. 'Take some cigarettes.' He ran his thumbnail along the side of the paper box with the big coloured figure of a warship on the cover and pushed the box toward Pablo.

Anselmo brought him a rawhide-covered stool and he sat down at the table. Pablo looked at him as though he were going to speak again, then reached for the cigarettes.

Robert Jordan pushed them toward the others. He was not looking at them yet. But he noted one man took cigarettes and two did not. All of his concentration was on Pablo.

'How goes it, gipsy?' he said to Rafael.

'Good,' the gipsy said. Robert Jordan could tell they had been talking about him when he came in. Even the gipsy was not at ease.

'She is going to let you eat again?' Robert Jordan asked the gipsy.

'Yes. Why not?' the gipsy said. It was a long way from the friendly joking they had together in the afternoon.

The woman of Pablo said nothing and went on blowing up the coals of the fire.

'One called Agustín says he dies of boredom above,' Robert Jordan said.

'That doesn't kill,' Pablo said. 'Let him die a little.'

'Is there wine?' Robert Jordan asked the table at large, leaning forward, his hands on the table.

'There is little left,' Pablo said sullenly. Robert Jordan decided he had better look at the other three and try to see where he stood.

'In that case, let me have a cup of water. Thou,' he called to the girl.

'Bring me a cup of water.'

The girl looked at the woman, who said nothing, and gave no sign of having heard, then she went to a kettle containing water and dipped a cup full. She brought it to the table and put it down before him. Robert Jordan smiled at her. At the same time he sucked in on his stomach muscles and swung a little to the left on his stool so that his pistol slipped around on his belt closer to where he wanted it. He reached his hand down toward his hip pocket and Pablo watched him. He knew they all were watching him, too, but he watched only Pablo. His hand came up from the hip pocket with the leather-covered flask and he unscrewed the top and then, lifting the cup, drank half the water and poured very slowly from the flask into the cup.

'It is too strong for thee or I would give thee some,' he said to the girl and smiled at her again. 'There is little left or I would offer some to thee,' he said to Pablo.

'I do not like anis,' Pablo said.

The acrid smell had carried across the table and he had picked out the one familiar component.

'Good,' said Robert Jordan. 'Because there is very little left.'

'What drink is that?' the gipsy asked.

'A medicine,' Robert Jordan said. 'Do you want to taste it?'

'What is it for?'

'For everything,' Robert Jordan said. 'It cures everything. If you have anything wrong this will cure it.'

'Let me taste it,' the gipsy said.

Robert Jordan pushed the cup toward him. It was a milky yellow now with the water and he hoped the gipsy would not take more than a swallow. There was very little of it left and one cup of it took the place of the evening papers, of all the old evenings in cafés, of all chestnut trees that would be in bloom now in this month, of the great slow horses of the outer boulevards, of book shops, of kiosks, and of galleries, of the Parc Montsouris, of the Stade Buffalo, and of the Butte Chaumont, of the Guaranty Trust Company and the Ile de la Cité, of Foyot's old hotel, and of being able to read and relax in the evening; of all the things he had enjoyed and forgotten and that came back to him when he tasted that opaque, bitter, tongue-numbing, brain-warming, stomach-warming, idea-changing liquid alchemy.

The gipsy made a face and handed the cup back. 'It smells of anis but it is bitter as gall,' he said. 'It is better to be sick than have that medicine.'

'That's the wormwood,' Robert Jordan told him. 'In this, the real absinthe, there is wormwood. It's supposed to rot your brain out but I don't believe it. It only changes the ideas. You should pour water into it very slowly, a few drops at a time. But I poured it into the water.'

'What are you saying?' Pablo said angrily, feeling the mockery.

'Explaining the medicine,' Robert Jordan told him and grinned. 'I bought it in Madrid. It was the last bottle and it's lasted me three weeks.' He took a big swallow of it and felt it coasting over his tongue in delicate anaesthesia. He looked at Pablo and grinned again.

'How's business?' he asked.

Pablo did not answer and Robert Jordan looked carefully at the other three men at the table. One had a large flat face, flat and brown as a Serrano ham with a nose flattened and broken, and the long thin Russian cigarette, projecting at an angle, made the face look even flatter. This man had short grey hair and a grey stubble of beard and wore the usual black smock buttoned at the neck. He looked down at the table when Robert Jordan looked at him but his eyes were steady and they did not blink. The other two were evidently brothers. They looked much alike and were both short, heavily built, dark haired, their hair growing low on their foreheads, dark-eyed and brown. One had a scar across his forehead above his left eye and as he looked at them, they looked back at him steadily. One looked to be about twenty-six or eight, the other perhaps two years older.

'What are you looking at?' one brother, the one with the scar, asked.

'Thee,' Robert Jordan said.

'Do you see anything rare?'

'No,' said Robert Jordan. 'Have a cigarette?'

'Why not?' the brother said. He had not taken any before. 'These are like the other had. He of the train.'

'Were you at the train?'

'We were all at the train,' the brother said quietly. 'All except the old man.'

'That is what we should do now,' Pablo said. 'Another train.'

'We can do that,' Robert Jordan said. 'After the bridge.'

He could see that the wife of Pablo had turned now from the fire and was listening. When he said the word bridge every one was quiet.

'After the bridge,' he said again deliberately, and took a sip of the absinthe. I might as well bring it on, he thought. It's coming anyway.

'I do not go for the bridge,' Pablo said, looking down at the table, 'Neither me nor my people.'

Robert Jordan said nothing. He looked at Anselmo and raised the cup. 'Then we shall do it alone, old one,' he said and smiled.

'Without this coward,' Anselmo said.

'What did you say?' Pablo spoke to the old man.

'Nothing for thee. I did not speak to thee,' Anselmo told him.

Robert Jordan now looked past the table to where the wife of Pablo was standing by the fire. She had said nothing yet, nor given any sign. But now she said something he could not hear to the girl and the girl rose from the cooking fire, slipped along the wall, opened the blanket that hung over the mouth of the cave and went out. I think it is going to come now, Robert Jordan thought. I believe this is it. I did not want it to be this way but this seems to be the way it is.

'Then we will do the bridge without thy aid,' Robert Jordan said to Pablo.

'No,' Pablo said, and Robert Jordan watched his face sweat. 'Thou wilt blow no bridge here.'

'No?'

'Thou wilt blow no bridge,' Pablo said heavily.

'And thou?' Robert Jordan spoke to the wife of Pablo who was standing, still and huge, by the fire. She turned toward them and said, 'I am for the bridge.' Her face was lit by the fire and it was flushed and it shone warm and dark and handsome now in the fire-light as it was meant to be.

'What do you say?' Pablo said to her and Robert Jordan saw the betrayed look on his face and the sweat on his forehead as he turned his head.

'I am for the bridge and against thee,' the wife of Pablo said. 'Nothing more.'

'I am also for the bridge,' the man with the flat face and the broken nose said, crushing the end of the cigarette on the table.

'To me the bridge means nothing,' one of the brothers said. 'I am for the *mujer* of Pablo.'

'Equally,' said the other brother.

'Equally,' the gipsy said.

Robert Jordan watching Pablo and as he watched, letting his right hand hang lower and lower, ready if it should be necessary, half hoping it would be (feeling perhaps that were the simplest and easiest yet not wishing to spoil what had gone so well, knowing how quickly all of a family, all of a clan, all of a band, can turn against a stranger in a quarrel, yet thinking what could be done with the hand were the simplest and best and surgically the most sound now that this had happened), saw also the wife of Pablo, standing there and watched her blush proudly and soundly and healthily as the allegiances were given.

'I am for the Republic,' the woman of Pablo said happily. 'And the Republic is the bridge. Afterwards we will have time for other projects.'

'And thou,' Pablo said bitterly. 'With your head of a seed bull and your heart of a whore. Thou thinkest there will be an afterwards from this bridge? Thou hast an idea of that which will pass?'

'That which must pass,' the woman of Pablo said. 'That which must pass, will pass.'

'And it means nothing to thee to be hunted then like a beast after this thing from which we derive no profit? Nor to die in it?'

'Nothing,' the woman of Pablo said. 'And do not try to frighten me, coward.'

'Coward,' Pablo said bitterly. 'You treat a man as coward because he has a tactical sense. Because he can see the results of an idiocy in advance. It is not cowardly to know what is foolish.'

'Neither is it foolish to know what is cowardly,' said Anselmo, unable to resist making the phrase.

'Do you want to die?' Pablo said to him seriously and Robert Jordan saw how unrhetorical was the question.

'No.'

'Then watch thy mouth. You talk too much about things you do not understand. Don't you see that this is serious?' he said almost pitifully. 'Am I the only one who sees the seriousness of this?'

I believe so, Robert Jordan thought. Old Pablo, old boy, I believe so. Except me. You can see it and I see it and the woman read it in my hand but she doesn't see it, yet. Not yet she doesn't see it.

'Am I a leader for nothing?' Pablo asked. 'I know what I speak of. You others do not know. This old man talks nonsense. He is an old man who is nothing but a messenger and a guide for foreigners. This foreigner comes here to do a thing for the good of the foreigners. For his good we must be sacrificed. I am for the good and the safety of all.'

'Safety,' the wife of Pablo said. 'There is no such thing as safety. There are so many seeking safety here now that they make a great danger. In seeking safety now you lose all.'

She stood now by the table with the big spoon in her hand.

'There is safety,' Pablo said. 'Within the danger there is the safety of knowing what chances to take. It is like the bullfighter who knowing what he is doing takes no chances and is safe.'

'Until he is gored,' the woman said bitterly. 'How many times have I heard matadors talk like that before they took a goring. How often have I heard Finito say that it is all knowledge and that the bull never gored the man; rather the man gored himself on the horn of the bull. Always do they talk that way in their arrogance before a goring. Afterwards we visit them in the clinic.' Now she was mimicking a visit to a bedside. '"Hello, old timer. Hello,"' she boomed. Then, '"*Buenas, Compadre*. How goes it, Pilar?"' imitating the weak voice of the wounded bullfighter. '"How did this happen, Finito, *Chico*, how did this dirty accident occur to thee?"' booming it out in her own voice. Then talking weak and small, '"It is nothing, woman. Pilar, it is nothing. It shouldn't have happened. I killed him very well, you understand. Nobody could have killed him better. Then having killed him exactly as I should and him absolutely dead, swaying on his legs, and ready to fall of his own weight, I walked away from him with a certain amount of arrogance and much style and from the back he throws me this horn between the cheeks of my buttocks and it comes out of my liver."' She commenced to laugh, dropping the imitation of the almost effeminate bullfighter's voice and booming again now. 'You and your safety! Did I live nine years with three of the worst paid matadors in the world not to learn about fear and about safety? Speak to me of anything but safety. And thee. What illusions I put in thee and how they have turned out! From one year of war thou hast become lazy, a drunkard and a coward.'

'In that way thou hast no right to speak,' Pablo said. 'And less even before the people and a stranger.'

'In that way will I speak,' the wife of Pablo went on. 'Have you not heard? Do you still believe that you command here?'

'Yes,' Pablo said. 'Here I command.'

'Not in joke,' the woman said. 'Here I command! Haven't you heard *la gente*? Here no one commands but me. You can stay if you wish and eat of the food and drink of the wine, but not too bloody much, and share in the work if thee wishes. But here I command.'

'I should shoot thee and the foreigner both,' Pablo said sullenly.

'Try it,' the woman said. 'And see what happens.'

'A cup of water for me,' Robert Jordan said, not taking his eyes from the man with his sullen heavy head and the woman standing proudly and confidently holding the big spoon as authoritatively as though it were a baton.

'Maria,' called the woman of Pablo and when the girl came in the door she said, 'Water for this comrade.'

Robert Jordan reached for his flask and, bringing the flask out, as he brought it he loosened the pistol in the holster and swung it on top of his thigh. He poured a second absinthe into his cup and took the cup of water the girl brought him and commenced to drip it into the cup, a little at a time. The girl stood at his elbow, watching him.'

'Outside,' the woman of Pablo said to her, gesturing with the spoon.

'It is cold outside,' the girl said, her cheek close to Robert Jordan's, watching what was happening in the cup where the liquor was clouding.

'Maybe,' the woman of Pablo said. 'But in here it is too hot.' Then she said, kindly, 'It is not for long.'

The girl shook her head and went out.

I don't think he is going to take this much more, Robert Jordan thought to himself. He held the cup in one hand and his other hand rested, frankly now, on the pistol. He had slipped the safety catch and he felt the worn comfort of the checked grip chafed almost smooth and touched the round, cool companionship of the trigger guard. Pablo no longer looked at him but only at the woman. She went on, 'Listen to me, drunkard. You understand who commands here?'

'I command.'

'No. Listen. Take the wax from thy hairy ears. Listen well. I command.'

Pablo looked at her and you could tell nothing of what he was thinking by his face. He looked at her quite deliberately and then he looked across the table at Robert Jordan. He looked at him a long time contemplatively and then he looked back at the woman again.

'All right. You command,' he said. 'And if you want he can command too. And the two of you can go to hell.' He was looking the woman straight in the face and he was neither dominated by her nor seemed to be much affected by her. 'It is possible that I am lazy and that I drink too much. You may consider me a coward but there you are mistaken. But I am not stupid.' He paused. 'That you should command and that you should like it. Now if you are a woman as well as a commander, that we should have something to eat.'

'Maria,' the woman of Pablo called.

The girl put her head inside the blanket across the cave mouth. 'Enter now and serve the supper.'

The girl came in and walked across to the low table by the hearth and picked up the enamelled-ware bowls and brought them to the table.

'There is wine enough for all,' the woman of Pablo said to Robert Jordan. 'Pay no attention to what that drunkard says. When this is finished we will get more. Finish that rare thing thou art drinking and take a cup of wine.'

Robert Jordan swallowed down the last of the absinthe, feeling it, gulped that way, making a warm, small, fume-rising, wet, chemical-change-producing heat in him and passed the cup for wine. The girl dipped it full for him and smiled.

'Well, did you see the bridge?' the gipsy asked. The others, who had not opened their mouths after the change of allegiance, were all leaning forward to listen now.

'Yes,' Robert Jordan said. 'It is something easy to do. Would you like me to show you?'

'Yes, man. With much interest?'

Robert Jordan took out the notebook from his shirt pocket and showed them the sketches.

'Look how it seems,' the flat-faced man, who was named Primitivo, said. 'It is the bridge itself.'

Robert Jordan with the point of the pencil explained how the bridge should be blown and the reason for the placing of the charges.

'What simplicity,' the scarred-faced brother, who was called Andrés, said. 'And how do you explode them?'

Robert Jordan explained that too and, as he showed them, he felt the girl's arm resting on his shoulder as he looked. The woman of Pablo was watching too. Only Pablo took no interest, sitting by himself with a cup of wine that he replenished by dipping into the big bowl Maria had filled from the wine-skin that hung to the left of the entrance to the cave.

'Hast thou done much of this?' the girl asked Robert Jordan softly.

'Yes.'

'And can we see the doing of it?'

'Yes. Why not?'

'You will see it,' Pablo said from his end of the table. 'I believe that you will see it.'

'Shut up,' the woman of Pablo said to him and suddenly remembering what she had seen in the hand in the afternoon she was wildly, unreasoningly angry. 'Shut up, coward. Shut up, bad luck bird. Shut up, murderer.'

'Good,' Pablo said. 'I shut up. It is thou who commands now and you should continue to look at the pretty pictures. But remember that I am not stupid.'

The woman of Pablo could feel her rage changing to sorrow and to a feeling of the thwarting of all hope and promise. She knew this feeling from when she was a girl and she knew the things that caused it all through her life. It came now suddenly and she put it away from her and would not let it touch her, neither her nor the Republic, and she said, 'Now we will eat. Serve the bowls from the pot, Maria.'

5

Robert Jordan pushed aside the saddle blanket that hung over the mouth of the cave and, stepping out, took a deep breath of the cold night air. The mist had cleared away and the stars were out. There was no wind, and, outside now of the warm air of the cave, heavy with smoke of both tobacco and charcoal, with the odour of cooked rice and meat, saffron, pimentos, and oil, the tarry, wine-spilled smell of the big skin hung beside the door, hung by the neck and the four legs extended, wine drawn from a plug fitted in one leg, wine that spilled a little onto the earth of the floor, settling the dust smell; out now from the odours of different herbs whose names he did not know that hung in bunches from the ceiling, with long ropes of garlic, away now from the copper-penny, red wine and garlic, horse sweat and man sweat dried in the clothing (acrid and grey the man sweat, sweet and sickly the dried brushed-off lather of horse sweat), of the men at the table, Robert Jordan breathed deeply of the clear night air of the mountains that smelled of the pines and of the dew on the grass in the meadow by the stream. Dew had fallen heavily since the wind had dropped, but, as he stood there, he thought there would be frost by morning.

As he stood breathing deep and then listening to the night, he heard first, firing far away, and then he heard an owl cry in the timber below, where the horse corral was slung. Then inside the cave he could hear the gipsy starting to sing and the soft chording of a guitar.

'I had an inheritance from my father,' the artificially hardened voice rose harshly and hung there. Then went on:

'It was the moon and the sun
And though I roam all over the world
The spending of it's never done.'

The guitar thudded with chorded applause for the singer. 'Good,' Robert Jordan heard someone say. 'Give us the Catalan, gipsy.'

'No.'

'Yes. Yes. The Catalan.'

'All right,' the gipsy said and sang mournfully:

'My nose is flat,
My face is black,
But still I am a man.'

'Olé!' someone said. 'Go on, gipsy!'

The gipsy's voice rose tragically and mockingly:

'Thank God I am a Negro,
And not a Catalan!'

'There is much noise,' Pablo's voice said. 'Shut up, gipsy.'

'Yes,' he heard the woman's voice. 'There is too much noise. You could call the *guardia civil* with that voice and still it has no quality.'

'I know another verse,' the gipsy said and the guitar commenced.

'Save it,' the woman told him.

The guitar stopped.

'I am not good in voice to-night. So there is no loss,' the gipsy said and pushing the blanket aside he came out into the dark.

Robert Jordan watched him walk over to a tree and then come toward him.

'Roberto,' the gipsy said softly.

'Yes, Rafael,' he said. He knew the gipsy had been affected by the wine from his voice. He himself had drunk the two absinthes and some wine but his head was clear and cold from the strain of the difficulty with Pablo.

'Why didst thou not kill Pablo?' the gipsy said very softly.

'Why kill him?'

'You have to kill him sooner or later. Why did you not approve of the moment?'

'Do you speak seriously?'

'What do you think that all waited for? What do you think the woman sent the girl away for? Do you believe that it is possible to continue after what has been said?'

'That you all should kill him.'

'*Qué va*,' the gipsy said quietly. 'That is your business. Three or four times we waited for you to kill him. Pablo has no friends.'

'I had the idea,' Robert Jordan said. 'But I left it.'

'Surely all could see that. Every one noted your preparations. Why didn't you do it?'

'I thought it might molest you others or the woman.'

'*Qué va*. And the woman waiting as a whore waits for the flight of the big bird. Thou art younger than thou appearest.'

'It is possible.'

'Kill him now,' the gipsy urged.

'That is to assassinate.'

'Even better,' the gipsy said very softly. 'Less danger. Go on. Kill him now.'

'I cannot in that way. It is repugnant to me and it is not how one should act for the cause.'

'Provoke him then,' the gipsy said. 'But you have to kill him. There is no remedy.'

As they spoke, the owl flew between the trees with the softness of all silence, dropping past them, then rising, the wings beating quickly, but with no noise of feathers moving as the bird hunted.

'Look at him,' the gipsy said in the dark. 'Thus should men move.'

'And in the day, blind in a tree with crows around him,' Robert Jordan said.

'Rarely,' said the gipsy. 'And then by hazard. Kill him,' he went on. 'Do not let it become difficult.'

'Now the moment is passed.'

'Provoke it,' the gipsy said. 'Or take advantage of the quiet.'

The blanket that closed the cave door opened and light came out. Someone came toward where they stood.

'It is a beautiful night,' the man said in a heavy, dull voice. 'We will have good weather.'

It was Pablo.

He was smoking one of the Russian cigarettes and in the glow, as he drew on the cigarette, his round face showed. They could see his heavy, long-armed body in the starlight.

'Do not pay any attention to the woman,' he said to Robert Jordan. In the dark the cigarette glowed bright, then showed in his hand as he lowered it. 'She is difficult sometimes. She is a good woman. Very loyal to the Republic.' The light of the cigarette jerked slightly now as he spoke. He must be talking with it in the corner of his mouth, Robert Jordan thought. 'We should have no difficulties. We are of accord. I am glad you have come.' The cigarette glowed brightly. 'Pay no attention to arguments,' he said. 'You are very welcome here.'

'Excuse me now,' he said. 'I go to see how they have picketed the horses.'

He went off through the trees to the edge of the meadow and they heard a horse whinny from below.

'You see?' the gipsy said. 'Now you see? In this way has the moment escaped.'

Robert Jordan said nothing.

'I go down there,' the gipsy said angrily.

'To do what?'

'*Qué va*, to do what. At least to prevent him leaving.'

'Can he leave with a horse from below?'

'No.'

'Then go to the spot where you can prevent him.'

'Agustín is there.'

'Go then and speak with Agustín. Tell him that which has happened.'

'Agustín will kill him with pleasure.'

'Less bad,' Robert Jordan said. 'Go then above and tell him all as it happened.'

'And then?'

'I go to look below in the meadow.'

'Good. Man. Good,' he could not see Rafael's face in the dark but he could feel him smiling. 'Now you have tightened your garters,' the gipsy said approvingly.

'Go to Agustín,' Robert Jordan said to him.

'Yes, Roberto, yes,' said the gipsy.

Robert Jordan walked through the pines, feeling his way from tree to tree to the edge of the meadow. Looking across it in the darkness, lighter here in the open from the starlight, he saw the dark bulks of the picketed horses. He counted them where they were scattered between him and the stream. There were five. Robert Jordan sat down at the foot of a pine tree and looked out across the meadow.

I am tired, he thought, and perhaps my judgment is not good. But my obligation is the bridge and to fulfil that, I must take no useless risk of myself until I complete that duty. Of course it is sometimes more of a risk not to accept chances which are necessary to take but I have done this so far, trying to let the situation take its own course. If it is true, as the gipsy says, that they expected me to kill Pablo then I should have done that. But it was never clear to me that they did expect that. For a stranger to kill where he must work with the people afterwards is very bad. It may be done in action, and it may be done if backed by sufficient discipline, but in this case I think it would be very bad, although it was a temptation and seemed a short and simple way. But I do not believe anything is that short nor that simple in this country and, while I trust the woman absolutely, I could not tell how she would react to such a drastic thing. One dying in such a place can be very ugly, dirty and repugnant. You could not tell how she would react. Without the woman there is no organization nor any discipline here and with the woman it can be very good. It would be ideal if she would kill him, or if the gipsy would (but he will not), or if the sentry, Agustín, would. Anselmo will if I ask it, though he says he is against all killing. He hates him, I believe, and he already trusts me and believes in me as a representative of what he believes in. Only he and the woman really believe in the Republic as far as I can see; but it is too early to know that yet.

As his eyes became used to the starlight he could see that Pablo was standing by one of the horses. The horse lifted his head from grazing; then dropped it impatiently. Pablo was standing by the horse, leaning against him, moving with him as he swung with the length of the picket rope and patting him on the neck. The horse was impatient at the tenderness while he was feeding. Robert Jordan could not see what Pablo was doing, nor hear what he was saying to the horse, but he could see that he was neither unpicketing nor saddling. He sat watching him, trying to think his problem out clearly.

'Thou my big good little pony,' Pablo was saying to the horse in the dark; it was the big bay stallion he was speaking to. 'Thou lovely white-faced big beauty. Thou with the big neck arching like the viaduct of my pueblo,' he stopped. 'But arching more and much finer.' The horse was snatching grass, swinging his head sideways as he pulled, annoyed by the man and his talking. 'Thou art no woman nor a fool,' Pablo told the bay horse. 'Thou, oh, thou, thee, thee, my big little pony. Thou art no woman like a rock that is burning. Thou art no colt of a girl with cropped head and the movement of a foal still wet from its mother. Thou dost not insult nor lie nor not understand. Thou, oh, thee, oh my good big little pony.'

It would have been very interesting for Robert Jordan to have heard Pablo speaking to the bay horse but he did not hear him because now, convinced that Pablo was only down checking on his horses, and having decided that it was not a practical move to kill him at this time, he stood up and walked back to the cave. Pablo stayed in the meadow talking to the horse for a long time. The horse understood nothing that he said; only, from the tone of the voice, that they were endearments and he had been in the corral all day and was hungry now, grazing impatiently at the limits of his picket rope, and the man annoyed him. Pablo shifted the picket pin finally and stood by the horse, not talking now. The horse went on grazing and was relieved now that the man did not bother him.

6

Inside the cave, Robert Jordan sat on one of the rawhide stools in a corner by the fire listening to the woman. She was washing the dishes and the girl, Maria, was drying them and putting them away, kneeling to place them in the hollow dug in the wall that was used as a shelf.

'It is strange,' she said, 'that El Sordo has not come. He should have been here an hour ago.'

'Did you advise him to come?'

'No. He comes each night.'

'Perhaps he is doing something. Some work.'

'It is possible,' she said. 'If he does not come we must go to see him to-morrow.'

'Yes. Is it far from here?'

'No. It will be a good trip. I lack exercise.'

'Can I go?' Maria asked. 'May I go too, Pilar?'

'Yes, beautiful,' the woman said, then turning her big face, 'Isn't she pretty?' she asked Robert Jordan. 'How does she seem to thee? A little thin?'

'To me she seems very well,' Robert Jordan said. Maria filled his cup with wine. 'Drink that,' she said. 'It will make me seem even better. It is necessary to drink much of that for me to seem beautiful.'

'Then I had better stop,' Robert Jordan said. 'Already thou seemest beautiful and more.'

'That's the way to talk,' the woman said. 'You talk like the good ones. What more does she seem?'

'Intelligent,' Robert Jordan said lamely. Maria giggled and the woman shook her head sadly. 'How well you begin and how it ends, Don Roberto.'

'Don't call me Don Roberto.'

'It is a joke. Here we say Don Pablo for a joke. As we say the Señorita Maria for a joke.'

'I don't joke that way,' Robert Jordan said. 'Camarada to me is what all should be called with seriousness in this war. In the joking commences a rottenness.'

'Thou are very religious about thy politics,' the woman teased him. 'Thou makest no jokes?'

'Yes. I care much for jokes but not in the form of address. It is like a flag.'

'I could make jokes about a flag. Any flag,' the woman laughed. 'To me no one can joke of anything. The old flag of yellow and gold we called pus and blood. The flag of the Republic with the purple added we call blood, pus and permanganate. It is a joke.'

'He is a communist,' Maria said. 'They are very serious *gente*.'

'Are you a communist?'

'No I am an anti-fascist.'

'For a long time?'

'Since I have understood fascism.'

'How long is that?'

'For nearly ten years.'

'That is not much time,' the woman said. 'I have been a republican for twenty years.'

'My father was a republican all his life,' Maria said. 'It was for that they shot him.'

'My father was also a republican all his life. Also my grandfather,' Robert Jordan said.

'In what country?'

'The United States.'

'Did they shoot them?' the woman asked.

'*Qué va*,' Maria said. 'The United States is a country of republicans. They don't shoot you for being a republican there.'

'All the same it is a good thing to have a grandfather who was a republican,' the woman said. 'It shows a good blood.'

'My grandfather was on the Republican national committee,' Robert Jordan said. That impressed even Maria.

'And is thy father still active in the Republic?' Pilar asked.

'No. He is dead.'

'Can one ask how he died?'

'He shot himself.'

'To avoid being tortured?' the woman asked.

'Yes,' Robert Jordan said. 'To avoid being tortured.'

Maria looked at him with tears in her eyes. 'My father,' she said, 'could not obtain a weapon. Oh, I am very glad that your father had the good fortune to obtain a weapon.'

'Yes. It was pretty lucky,' Robert Jordan said. 'Should we talk about something else?'

'Then you and me we are the same,' Maria said. She put her hand on his arm and looked in his face. He looked at her brown face and at the eyes that, since he had seen them, had never been as young as the rest of her face but that now were suddenly hungry and young and wanting.

'You could be brother and sister by the look,' the woman said. 'But I believe it is fortunate that you are not.'

'Now I know why I have felt as I have,' Maria said. 'Now it is clear.'

'*Qué va*,' Robert Jordan said and reaching over, he ran his hand over the top of her head. He had been wanting to do that all day and now he did it, he could feel his throat swelling. She moved her head under his hand and smiled up at him and he felt the thick but silky roughness of the cropped head rippling between his fingers. Then his hand was on her neck and then he dropped it.

'Do it again,' she said. 'I wanted you to do that all day.'

'Later,' Robert Jordan said and his voice was thick.

'And me,' the woman of Pablo said in her booming voice, 'I am expected to watch all this? I am expected not to be moved? One cannot. For fault of anything better; that Pablo should come back.'

Maria took no notice of her now, nor of the others playing cards at the table by the candlelight.

'Do you want another cup of wine, Roberto?' she asked.

'Yes,' he said. 'Why not?'

'You're going to have a drunkard like I have,' the woman of Pablo said. 'With that rare thing he drank in the cup and all. Listen to me, *Inglés*.'

'Not *Inglés*. American.'

'Listen, then, American. Where do you plan to sleep?'

'Outside. I have a sleeping robe.'

'Good,' she said. 'The night is clear?'

'And will be cold.'

'Outside then,' she said. 'Sleep thee outside. And thy materials can sleep with me.'

'Good,' said Robert Jordan.

'Leave us for a moment,' Robert Jordan said to the girl and put his hand on her shoulder.

'Why?'

'I wish to speak to Pilar.'

'Must I go?'

'Yes.'

'What is it?' the woman of Pablo said when the girl had gone over to the mouth of the cave where she stood by the big wineskin, watching the card players.

'The gipsy said I should have—' he began.

'No,' the woman interrupted. 'He is mistaken.'

'If it is necessary that I—' Robert Jordan said quietly but with difficulty.

'Thee would have done it, I believe,' the woman said. 'Nay, it is not necessary. I was watching thee. But thy judgment was good.'

'But if it is needful—'

'No,' the woman said. 'I tell you it is not needful. The mind of the gipsy is corrupt.'

'But in weakness a man can be a great danger.'

'No. Thou dost not understand. Out of this one has passed all capacity for danger.'

'I do not understand.'

'Thou art very young still,' she said. 'You will understand.' Then, to the girl, 'Come, Maria. We are not talking more.'

The girl came over and Robert Jordan reached his hand out and patted her head. She stroked under his hand like a kitten. Then he thought that she was going to cry. But her lips drew up again and she looked at him and smiled.

'Thee would do well to go to bed now,' the woman said to Robert Jordan. 'Thou hast had a long journey.'

'Good,' said Robert Jordan. 'I will get my things.'

7

He was asleep in the robe and he had been asleep, he thought, for a long time. The robe was spread on the forest floor in the lee of the rocks beyond the cave mouth and as he slept, he turned, and turning rolled on his pistol which was fastened by a lanyard to one wrist and had been by his side under the cover when he went to sleep, shoulder and back weary, leg-tired, his muscles pulled with tiredness so that the ground was soft, and simply stretching in the robe against the flannel lining was voluptuous with fatigue. Waking, he wondered where he was, knew, and then shifted the pistol from under his side and settled happily to stretch back into sleep, his hand on the pillow of his clothing that was bundled neatly around his rope-soled shoes. He had one arm around the pillow.

Then he felt her hand on his shoulder and turned quickly, his right hand holding the pistol under the robe.

'Oh, it is thee,' he said and dropping the pistol he reached both arms up and pulled her down. With his arms around her he could feel her shivering.

'Get in,' he said softly. 'It is cold out there.'

'No. I must not.'

'Get in,' he said. 'And we can talk about it later.'

She was trembling and he held her wrist now with one hand and held her lightly with the other arm. She had turned her head away.

'Get in, little rabbit,' he said and kissed her on the back of the neck.

'I am afraid.'

'No. Do not be afraid. Get in.'

'How?'

'Just slip in. There is much room. Do you want me to help you?'

'No,' she said and then she was in the robe and he was holding her tight to him and trying to kiss her lips and she was pressing her face against the pillow of clothing but holding her arms close around his neck. Then he felt her arms relax and she was shivering again as he held her.

'No,' he said and laughed. 'Do not be afraid. That is the pistol.'

He lifted it and slipped it behind him.

'I am ashamed,' she said, her face away from him.

'No. You must not be. Here. Now.'

'No, I must not. I am ashamed and frightened.'

'No. My rabbit. Please.'

'I must not. If thou dost not love me.'

'I love thee.'

'I love thee. Oh, I love thee. Put thy hand on my head,' she said away from him, her face still in the pillow. He put his hand on her head and stroked it and then suddenly her face was away from the pillow and she was in his arms, pressed close against him, and her face was against his and she was crying.

He held her still and close, feeling the long length of the young body, and he stroked her head and kissed the wet saltiness of her eyes, and as she cried he could feel the rounded, firm-pointed breasts touching through the shirt she wore.

'I cannot kiss,' she said. 'I do not know how.'

'There is no need to kiss.'

'Yes. I must kiss. I must do everything.'

'There is no need to do anything. We are all right. But thou has many clothes.'

'What should I do?'

'I will help you.'

'Is that better?'

'Yes. Much. Is it not better to thee?'

'Yes. Much better. And I can go with thee as Pilar said?'

'Yes.'

'But not to a home. With thee.'

'No, to a home.'

'No. No. No. With thee and I will be thy woman.'

Now as they lay all that before had been shielded was unshielded. Where there had been roughness of fabric all was smooth with a smoothness and firm rounded pressing and a long warm coolness, cool outside and warm within, long and light and closely holding, closely held, lonely, hollow-making with contours, happy-making, young and loving and now all warmly smooth with a hollowing, chest-aching, tight-held loneliness that was such that Robert Jordan felt he could not stand it and he said, 'Hast thou loved others?'

'Never.'

Then suddenly, going dead in his arms, 'But things were done to me.'

'By whom?'

'By various.'

Now she lay perfectly quietly and as though her body were dead and turned her head away from him.

'Now you will not love me.'

'I love you,' he said.

But something had happened to him and she knew it.

'No,' she said and her voice had gone dead and flat. 'Thou wilt not love me. But perhaps thou wilt take me to the home. And I will go to the home and I will never be thy woman nor anything.'

'I love thee, Maria.'

'No. It is not true,' she said. Then as a last thing pitifully and hopefully: 'But I have never kissed any man.'

'Then kiss me now.'

'I wanted to,' she said. 'But I know not how. Where things were done to me I fought until I could not see. I fought until–until–until one sat upon my head–and I bit him–and then they tied my mouth and held my arms behind my head–and others did things to me.'

'I love thee, Maria,' he said. 'And no one has done anything to thee. Thee, they cannot touch. No one has touched thee, little rabbit.'

'You believe that?'

'I know it.'

'And you can love me?' warm again against him now.

'I can love thee more.'

'I will try to kiss thee very well.'

'Kiss me a little.'

'I do not know how.'

'Just kiss me.'

She kissed him on the cheek.

'No.'

'Where do the noses go? I always wondered where the noses would go.'

'Look, turn thy head,' and then their mouths were tight together and she lay close pressed against him and her mouth opened a little gradually and then, suddenly, holding her against him, he was happier than he had ever been, lightly, lovingly, exultingly, innerly happy and unthinking and untired and unworried and only feeling a great delight and he said, 'My little rabbit, My darling. My sweet. My long lovely.'

'What do you say?' she said as though from a great distance away.

'My lovely one,' he said.

They lay there and he felt her heart beating against his and with the side of his foot he stroked very lightly against the side of hers.

'Thee came barefooted,' he said.

'Yes.'

'Then thee knew thou wert coming to the bed.'

'Yes.'

'And you had no fear.'

'Yes. Much. But more fear of how it would be to take my shoes off.'

'And what time is it now? *lo sabes?*'

'No. Thou has no watch?'

'Yes. But it is behind thy back.'

'Take it from there.'

'No.'

'Then look over my shoulder.'

It was one o'clock. The dial showed bright in the darkness that the robe made.

'Thy chin scratches my shoulder.'

'Pardon it. I have no tools to shave.'

'I like it. Is thy beard blond?'

'Yes.'

'And will it be long?'

'Not before the bridge. Maria, listen. Dost thou—?'

'Do I what?'

'Dost thou wish?'

'Yes. Everything. Please. And if we do everything together, the other maybe never will have been.'

'Did you think of that?'

'No. I think it in myself but Pilar told me.'

'She is very wise.'

'And another thing,' Maria said softly. 'She said for me to tell you that I am not sick. She knows about such things and she said to tell you that.'

'She told you to tell me?'

'Yes. I spoke to her and told her that I love you. I loved you when I saw you to-day and I loved you always but I never saw you before and I told Pilar and she said if I ever told you anything about anything, to tell you that I was not sick. The other thing she told me long ago. Soon after the train.'

'What did she say?'

'She said that nothing is done to oneself that one does not accept and that if I loved someone it would take it all away. I wished to die, you see.'

'What she said is true.'

'And now I am happy that I did not die. I am so happy that I did not die. And you can love me?'

'Yes. I love you now.'

'And I can be thy woman?'

'I cannot have a woman doing what I do. But thou art my woman now.'

'If once I am, then I will keep on. Am I thy woman now?'

'Yes, Maria. Yes, my little rabbit.'

She held herself tight to him and her lips looked for his and then found them and were against them and he felt her, fresh, new and smooth and young and lovely with the warm, scalding, coolness and unbelievable to be there in the robe that was as familiar as his clothes, or his shoes, or his duty and then she said, frightenedly, 'And now let us do quickly what it is we do so that the other is all gone.'

'You want?'

'Yes,' she said almost fiercely. 'Yes. Yes. Yes.'

8

It was cold in the night and Robert Jordan slept heavily. Once he woke and, stretching, realized that the girl was there, curled far down in the robe, breathing lightly and regularly, and in the dark, bringing his head in from the cold, the sky hard and sharp with stars, the air cold in his nostrils, he put his head under the warmth of the robe and kissed her smooth shoulder. She did not wake and he rolled onto his side away from her and with his head out of the robe in the cold again, lay awake a moment feeling the long, seeping luxury of his fatigue and then the smooth tactile happiness of their two bodies touching and then, as he pushed his legs out deep as they would go in the robe, he slipped down steeply into sleep.

He woke at first daylight and the girl was gone. He knew it as he woke and, putting out his arm, he felt the robe warm where she had been. He looked at the mouth of the cave where the blanket showed frost-rimmed and saw the thin grey smoke from the crack in the rocks that meant the kitchen fire was lighted.

A man came out of the timber, a blanket worn over his head like a poncho. Robert Jordan saw it was Pablo and that he was smoking a cigarette. He's been down corralling the horses, he thought.

Pablo pulled open the blanket and went into the cave without looking toward Robert Jordan.

Robert Jordan felt with his hand the light frost that lay on the worn, spotted green balloon silk outer covering of the five-year-old down robe, then settled into it again. *Bueno*, he said to himself, feeling the familiar caress of the flannel lining as he spread his legs wide, then drew them together and then turned on his side so that his head would be away from the direction where he knew the sun would come. *Qué más da*, I might as well sleep some more.

He slept until the sound of airplane motors woke him.

Lying on his back, he saw them, a fascist patrol of three Fiats, tiny, bright, fast-moving across the mountain sky, headed in the direction from which Anselmo and he had come yesterday. The three passed and then came nine more, flying much higher in the minute, pointed formations of threes, threes and threes.

Pablo and the gipsy were standing at the cave mouth, in the shadow, watching the sky and as Robert Jordan lay still, the sky now full of the high hammering roar of motors, there was a new droning roar and three more planes came over at less than a thousand feet above the clearing. These three were Heinkel one-elevens, twin-motor bombers.

Robert Jordan, his head in the shadow of the rocks, knew they would not see him, and that it did not matter if they did. He knew they could possibly see the horses in the corral if they were looking for anything in these mountains. If they were not looking for anything they might still see them but would naturally take them for some of their own cavalry mounts. Then came a new and louder droning roar and three more Heinkel one-elevens showed coming steeply, stiffly, lower yet, crossing in rigid formation, their pounding roar approaching in crescendo to an absolute of noise and then receding as they passed the clearing.

Robert Jordan unrolled the bundle of clothing that made his pillow and pulled on his shirt. It was over his head and he was pulling it down when he heard the next planes coming and he pulled his trousers on under the robe and lay still as three more of the Heinkel bi-motor bombers came over. Before they were gone over the shoulder of the mountain, he had buckled on his pistol, rolled the robe and placed it against the rocks and sat now, close against the rocks, tying his rope-soled shoes when the approaching droning turned to a greater clattering roar than ever before and nine more Heinkel light bombers came in echelons; hammering the sky apart as they went over.

Robert Jordan slipped along the rocks to the mouth of the cave where one of the brothers, Pablo, the gipsy, Anselmo, Agustín and the woman stood in the mouth looking out.

'Have there been planes like this before?' he asked.

'Never,' said Pablo. 'Get in. They will see thee.'

The sun had not yet hit the mouth of the cave. It was just now shining on the meadow by the stream and Robert Jordan knew they could not be seen in the dark, early morning shadow of the trees and the solid shade the rocks made, but he went in the cave in order not to make them nervous.

'They are many,' the woman said.

'And there will be more,' Robert Jordan said.

'How do you know?' Pablo asked suspiciously.

'Those, just now, will have pursuit planes with them.'

Just then they heard them, the higher, whining drone, and as they passed at about five thousand feet, Robert Jordan counted fifteen Fiats in echelon of echelons like a wild-goose flight of the V-shaped threes.

In the cave entrance their faces all looked very sober and Robert Jordan said, 'You have not seen this many planes?'

'Never,' said Pablo.

'There are not many at Segovia?'

'Never has there been, we have seen three usually. Sometimes six of the chasers. Perhaps three Junkers, the big ones with the three motors, with the chasers with them. Never have we seen planes like this.'

It is bad, Robert Jordan thought. This is really bad. Here is a concentration of planes which means something very bad. I must listen for them to unload. But no, they cannot have brought up the troops yet for the attack. Certainly not before to-night or to-morrow night, certainly not yet. Certainly they will not be moving anything at this hour.

He could still hear the receding drone. He looked at his watch. By now they should be over the lines, the first ones anyway. He pushed the knob that set the second hand to clicking and watched it move around. No, perhaps not yet. By now. Yes. Well over by now. Two hundred and fifty miles an hour for those one-elevens anyway. Five minutes would carry them there. By now they're well beyond the pass with Castile all yellow and tawny beneath them now in the morning, the yellow crossed by white roads and spotted with the small villages and the shadows of the Heinkels moving over the land as the shadows of sharks pass over a sandy floor of the ocean.

There was no bump, bump, bumping thud of bombs. His watch ticked on.

They're going on to Colmenar, to Escorial, or to the flying field at Manzanares el Real, he thought, with the old castle above the lake with the ducks in the reeds and the fake airfield just behind the real field with the dummy planes, not quite hidden, their props turning in the wind. That's where they must be headed. They can't know about the attack, he told himself and something in him said, why can't they? They've known about all the others.

'Do you think they saw the horses?' Pablo asked.

'Those weren't looking for horses,' Robert Jordan said.

'But did they see them?'

'Not unless they were asked to look for them.'

'Could they see them?'

'Probably not,' Robert Jordan said. 'Unless the sun were on the trees.'

'It is on them very early,' Pablo said miserably.

'I think they have other things to think of besides thy horses,' Robert Jordan said.

It was eight minutes since he had pushed the lever on the stop watch and there was still no sound of bombing.

'What do you do with the watch?' the woman asked.

'I listen where they have gone.'

'Oh,' she said. At ten minutes he stopped looking at the watch knowing it would be too far away to hear, now, even allowing a minute for the sound to travel, and said to Anselmo, 'I would speak to thee.'

Anselmo came out of the cave mouth and they walked a little way from the entrance and stood beside a pine tree.

'*Qué tal?*' Robert Jordan asked him. 'How goes it?'

'All right.'

'Hast thou eaten?'

'No. No one has eaten.'

'Eat then and take something to eat at midday. I want you to go to watch the road. Make a note of everything that passes both up and down the road.'

'I do not write.'

'There is no need to,' Robert Jordan took out two leaves from his notebook and with his knife cut an inch from the end of his pencil. 'Take this and make a mark for tanks thus,' he drew a slanted tank, 'and then a mark for each one and when there are four, cross the four strokes for the fifth.'

'In this way we count also.'

'Good. Make another mark, two wheels and a box, for trucks. If they are empty make a circle. If they are full of troops make a straight mark. Mark for guns. Big ones, thus. Small ones, thus. Mark for cars. Mark for ambulances. Thus, two wheels and a box with a cross on it. Mark for troops on foot by companies, like this, see? A little square and then mark beside it. Mark for cavalry, like this, you see? Like a horse. A box with four legs. That is a troop of twenty horse. You understand? Each troop a mark.'

'Yes. It is ingenious.'

'Now,' he drew two large wheels with circles around them and a short line for a gun barrel. 'These are anti-tanks. They have rubber tires. Mark for them. These are anti-aircraft,' two wheels with the gun barrel slanted up. 'Mark for them also. Do you understand? Have you seen such guns?'

'Yes,' Anselmo said. 'Of course. It is clear.'

'Take the gipsy with you that he will know from what point you will be watching so you may be relieved. Pick a place that is safe, not too close and from where you can see well and comfortably. Stay until you are relieved.'

'I understand.'

'Good. And that when you come back, I should know everything that moved upon the road. One paper is for movement up. One is for movement down the road.'

They walked over toward the cave.

'Send Rafael to me,' Robert Jordan said and waited by the tree. He watched Anselmo go into the cave, the blanket falling behind him. The gipsy sauntered out, wiping his mouth with his hand.

'*Qué tal?*' the gipsy said. 'Did you divert yourself last night?'

'I slept.'

'Less bad,' the gipsy said and grinned. 'Have you a cigarette?'

'Listen,' Robert Jordan said and felt in his pocket for the cigarettes. 'I wish you to go with Anselmo to a place from which he will observe the road. There you will leave him, noting the place in order that you may guide me to it or guide whoever will relieve him later. You will then go to where you can observe the saw mill and note if there are any changes in the post there.'

'What changes?'

'How many men are there now?'

'Eight. The last I knew.'

'See how many are there now. See at what intervals the guard is relieved at that bridge.'

'Intervals?'

'How many hours the guard stays on and at what time a change is made.'

'I have no watch.'

'Take mine.' He unstrapped it.

'What a watch,' Rafael said admiringly. 'Look at what complications.

Such a watch should be able to read and write. Look at what complications of numbers. It's a watch to end watches.'

'Don't fool with it,' Robert Jordan said. 'Can you tell time?'

'Why not? Twelve o'clock midday. Hunger. Twelve o'clock midnight. Sleep. Six o'clock in the morning, hunger. Six o'clock at night, drunk. With luck. Ten o'clock at night—'

'Shut up,' Robert Jordan said. 'You don't need to be a clown. I want you to check on the guard at the big bridge and the post on the road below in the same manner as the post and the guard at the saw mill and the small bridge.'

'It is much work,' the gipsy smiled. 'You are sure there is no one you would rather send than me?'

'No, Rafael. It is very important. That you should do it very carefully and keeping out of sight with care.'

'I believe I will keep out of sight,' the gipsy said. 'Why do you tell me to keep out of sight? You think I want to be shot?'

'Take things a little seriously,' Robert Jordan said. 'This is serious.'

'Thou askest me to take things seriously? After what thou didst last night. When thou needest to kill a man and instead did what you did? You were supposed to kill one, not make one! When we have just seen the sky full of airplanes of a quantity to kill us back to our grandfathers and forward to all unborn grandsons including all cats, goats, and bedbugs. Airplanes making a noise to curdle the milk in your mother's breasts as they pass over darkening the sky and roaring like lions and you ask me to take things seriously. I take them too seriously already.'

'All right,' said Robert Jordan and laughed and put his hand on the gipsy's shoulder. '*Don't* take them too seriously then. Now finish your breakfast and go.'

'And thou?' the gipsy asked. 'What do you do?'

'I go to see El Sordo.'

'After those airplanes it is very possible that thou wilt find nobody in the whole mountains,' the gipsy said. 'There must have been many people sweating the big drop this morning when those passed.'

'Those have other work than hunting guerrillas.'

'Yes,' the gipsy said. Then shook his head. 'But when they care to undertake that work.'

'*Qué va*,' Robert Jordan said. 'Those are the best of the German light bombers. They do not send those after gipsies.'

'They give me a horror,' Rafael said. 'Of such things, yes, I am frightened.'

'They go to bomb an airfield,' Robert Jordan told him as they went into the cave. 'I am almost sure they go for that.'

'What do you say?' the woman of Pablo asked. She poured him a bowl of coffee and handed him a can of condensed milk.

'There is milk? What luxury!'

'There is everything,' she said. 'And since the planes there is much fear. Where did you say they went?'

Robert Jordan dripped some of the thick milk into his coffee from the slit cut in the can, wiped the can on the rim of the cup, and stirred the coffee until it was a light brown.

'They go to bomb an airfield, I believe. They might go to Escorial and Colmenar. Perhaps all three.'

'That they should go a long way and keep away from here,' Pablo said.

'And why are they here now?' the woman asked. 'What brings them now? Never have we seen such planes. Nor in such quantity. Do they prepare an attack?'

'What movement was there on the road last night?' Robert Jordan asked. The girl Maria was close to him but he did not look at her.

'You,' the woman said. 'Fernando. You were in La Granja last night. What movement was there?'

'Nothing,' a short, open-faced man of about thirty-five with a cast in one eye, whom Robert Jordan had not seen before, answered. 'A few camions as usual. Some cars. No movement of troops while I was there.'

'You go into La Granja every night?' Robert Jordan asked him.

'I or another,' Fernando said. 'Someone goes.'

'They go for the news. For tobacco. For small things,' the woman said.

'We have people there?'

'Yes. Why not? Those who work the power plant. Some others.'

'What was the news?'

'*Pues nada*. There was nothing. It still goes badly in the north. That is not news. In the north it has gone badly now since the beginning.'

'Did you hear anything from Segovia?'

'No, *hombre*. I did not ask.'

'Do you go into Segovia?'

'Sometimes,' Fernando said. 'But there is danger. There are controls where they ask for your papers.'

'Do you know the airfield?'

'No, *hombre*. I know where it is but I was never close to it. There, there is much asking for papers.'

'No one spoke about these planes last night?'

'In La Granja? Nobody. But they will talk about them to-night certainly. They talked about the broadcast of Quiepo de Llano. Nothing more. Oh, yes. It seems that the Republic is preparing an offensive.'

'That what?'

'That the Republic is preparing an offensive.'

'Where?'

'It is not certain. Perhaps here. Perhaps for another part of the Sierra. Hast thou heard of it?'

'They say this in La Granja?'

'Yes, *hombre*. I had forgotten it. But there is always much talk of offensives.'

'Where does this talk come from?'

'Where? Why from different people. The officers speak in the cafés in Segovia and Avila and the waiters note it. The rumours come running. Since some time they speak of an offensive by the Republic in these parts.'

'By the Republic or by the Fascists?'

'By the Republic. If it were by the Fascists all would know of it. No, this is an offensive of quite some size. Some say there are two. One here and the other over the Alto del Léon near the Escorial. Have you heard aught of this?'

'What else did you hear?'

'*Nada, hombre*. Nothing. Oh, yes. There was some talk that Republicans would try to blow up the bridges, if there was to be an offensive. But the bridges are guarded.'

'Art thou joking?' Robert Jordan said, sipping his coffee.

'No, *hombre*,' said Fernando.

'This one doesn't joke,' the woman said. 'Bad luck that he doesn't.'

'Then,' said Robert Jordan. 'Thank you for all the news. Did you hear nothing more?'

'No. They talk, as always, of troops to be sent to clear out these mountains. There is some talk that they are on the way. That they have been sent already from Valladolid. But they always talk in that way. It is not to give any importance to.'

'And thou,' the woman of Pablo said to Pablo almost viciously. 'With thy talk of safety.'

Pablo looked at her reflectively and scratched his chin. 'Thou,' he said. 'And thy bridges.'

'What bridges?' asked Fernando cheerfully.

'Stupid,' the woman said to him. 'Thick head. *Tonto*. Take another cup of coffee and try to remember more news.'

'Don't be angry, Pilar,' Fernando said calmly and cheerfully. 'Neither should one become alarmed at rumours. I have told thee and this comrade all that I remember.'

'You don't remember anything more?' Robert Jordan asked.

'No,' Fernando said with dignity. 'And I am fortunate to remember this because, since it was but rumours, I paid no attention to any of it.'

'Then there may have been more?'

'Yes. It is possible. But I paid no attention. For a year I have heard nothing but rumours.'

Robert Jordan heard a quick, control-breaking sniff of laughter from the girl Maria, who was standing behind him.

'Tell us one more rumour, Fernandito,' she said and then her shoulders shook again.

'If I could remember, I would not,' Fernando said. 'It is beneath a man's dignity to listen and give importance to rumours.'

'And with this we will save the Republic,' the woman said.

'No. *You* will save it by blowing bridges,' Pablo told her.

'Go,' said Robert Jordan to Anselmo and Rafael. 'If you have eaten.'

'We go now,' the old man said and the two of them stood up. Robert Jordan felt a hand on his shoulder. It was Maria. 'Thou shouldst eat,' she said and let her hand rest there. 'Eat well so that thy stomach can support more rumours.'

'The rumours have taken the place of the appetite.'

'No. It should not be so. Eat this now before more rumours come.' She put the bowl before him.

'Do not make a joke of me,' Fernando said to her. 'I am thy good friend, Maria.'

'I do not joke at thee, Fernando. I only joke with him and he should eat or he will be hungry.'

'We should all eat,' Fernando said. 'Pilar, what passes that we are not served?'

'Nothing, man,' the woman of Pablo said and filled his bowl with the meat stew. 'Eat. Yes, that's what you *can* do. Eat now.'

'It is very good, Pilar,' Fernando said, all dignity intact.

'Thank you,' said the woman. 'Thank you and thank you again.'

'Are you angry at me?' Fernando asked.

'No. Eat. Go ahead and eat.'

'I will,' said Fernando. 'Thank you.'

Robert Jordan looked at Maria and her shoulders started shaking again and she looked away. Fernando ate steadily, a proud and dignified expression on his face, the dignity of which could not be affected even by the huge spoon that he was using or the slight dripping of juice from the stew which ran from the corners of his mouth.

'Do you like the food?' the woman of Pablo asked him.

'Yes, Pilar,' he said with his mouth full. 'It is the same as usual.'

Robert Jordan felt Maria's hand on his arm and felt her fingers tighten with delight.

'It is for *that* that you like it?' the woman asked Fernando.

'Yes,' she said. 'I see. The stew; as usual. *Como siempre*. Things are bad in the north; as usual. An offensive here; as usual. That troops come to hunt us out; as usual. You could serve as a monument to as usual.'

'But the last two are only rumours, Pilar.'

'Spain,' the woman of Pablo said bitterly. Then turned to Robert Jordan. 'Do they have people such as this in other countries?'

'There are no other countries like Spain,' Robert Jordan said politely.

'You are right,' Fernando said. 'There is no other country in the world like Spain.'

'Hast thou ever seen any other country?' the woman asked him.

'Nay,' said Fernando. 'Nor do I wish to.'

'You see?' the woman of Pablo said to Robert Jordan.

'Fernandito,' Maria said to him. 'Tell us of the time thee went to Valencia.'

'I did not like Valencia.'

'Why?' Maria asked and pressed Robert Jordan's arm again. 'Why did thee not like it?'

'The people had no manners and I could not understand them. All they did was shout *ché* at one another.'

'Could they understand thee?' Maria asked.

'They pretended not to,' Fernando said.

'And what did thee there?'

'I left without even seeing the sea,' Fernando said. 'I did not like the people.'

'Oh, get out of here, you old maid,' the woman of Pablo said. 'Get out of here before you make me sick. In Valencia I had the best time of my life. *Vamos!* Valencia. Don't talk to me of Valencia.'

'What did thee there?' Maria asked. The woman of Pablo sat down at the table with a bowl of coffee, a piece of bread and a bowl of the stew.

'*Qué*? what did we there? I was there when Finito had a contract for three fights at the Feria. Never have I seen so many people. Never have I seen cafés so crowded. For hours it would be impossible to get a seat and it was impossible to board the tram cars. In Valencia there was movement all day and all night.'

'But what did you do?' Maria asked.

'All things,' the woman said. 'We went to the beach and lay in the water and boats with sails were hauled up out of the sea by oxen. The oxen driven to the water until they must swim; then harnessed to the boats, and, when they found their feet, staggering up the sand. Ten yokes of oxen dragging a boat with sails out of the sea in the morning with the line of the small waves breaking on the beach. That is Valencia.'

'But what did thee besides watch oxen?'

'We ate in pavilions on the sand. Pastries made of cooked and shredded fish and red and green peppers and small nuts like grains of rice. Pastries delicate and flaky and the fish of a richness that was incredible. Prawns fresh from the sea sprinkled with lime juice. They were pink and sweet and there were four bites to a prawn. Of those we ate many. Then we ate *paella* with fresh sea food, clams in their shells, mussels, crayfish, and small eels. Then we ate even smaller eels alone cooked in oil and as tiny as bean sprouts and curled in all directions and so tender they disappeared in the mouth without chewing. All the time drinking a white wine, cold, light and good at thirty centimos the bottle. And for an end; melon. That is the home of the melon.'

'The melon of Castile is better,' Fernando said.

'*Qué va*,' said the woman of Pablo. 'The melon of Castile is for self abuse. The melon of Valencia for eating. When I think of those melons long as one's arm, green like the sea and crisp and juicy to cut and sweeter than the early morning in summer. Aye, when I think of those smallest eels, tiny, delicate and in mounds on the plate. Also the beer in pitchers all through the afternoon, the beer sweating in its coldness in pitchers the size of water jugs.'

'And what did thee when not eating nor drinking?'

'We made love in the room with the strip wood blinds hanging over the balcony and a breeze through the opening of the top of the door which turned on hinges. We made love there, the room dark in the day time from the hanging blinds, and from the streets there was the scent of the flower market and the smell of burned powder from the firecrackers of the *traca* that ran through the streets exploding each noon during the Feria. It was a line of fireworks that ran through all the city, the firecrackers linked together and the explosions running along on poles and wires of the tramways, exploding with great noise and a jumping from pole to pole with a sharpness and a cracking of explosion you could not believe.

'We made love and then sent for another pitcher of beer with the drops of its coldness on the glass and when the girl brought it, I took it from the door and I placed the coldness of the pitcher against the back of Finito as he lay, now, asleep, not having wakened when the beer was brought and he said, "No, Pilar, No, woman, let me sleep." And I said, "No, wake up and drink this to see how cold," and he drank without opening his eyes and went to sleep again and I lay with my back against a pillow at the foot of the bed and watched him sleep, brown and dark-haired and young and quiet in his sleep, and drank the whole pitcher, listening now to the music of a band that was passing. "You," she said to Pablo. "Do you know aught of such things?"'

'We have done things together,' Pablo said.

'Yes,' the woman said. 'Why not? And thou wert more man than Finito in your time. But never did we go to Valencia. Never did we lie in bed together and hear a band pass in Valencia.'

'It was impossible,' Pablo told her. 'We have had no opportunity to go to Valencia. Thou knowest that if thou wilt be reasonable. But, with Finito, neither did thee blow up any train.'

'No,' said the woman. 'That is what is left to us. The train. Yes. Always the train. No one can speak against that. That remains of all the laziness, sloth and failure. That remains of the cowardice of this moment. There were many other things before too. I do not want to be unjust. But no one can speak against Valencia either. You hear me?'

'I did not like it,' Fernando said quietly. 'I did not like Valencia.'

'Yet they speak of the mule as stubborn,' the woman said. 'Clean up, Maria, that we may go.'

As she said this they heard the first sound of the planes returning.

9

They stood in the mouth of the cave and watched them. The bombers were high now in fast, ugly arrow-heads beating the sky apart with the noise of their motors. They *are* shaped like sharks, Robert Jordan thought, the wide-finned, sharp-nosed sharks of the Gulf Stream. But these, wide-finned in silver, roaring, the night mist of their propellers in the sun, these do not move like sharks. They move like nothing there has ever been. They move like mechanized doom.

You ought to write, he told himself. Maybe you will again sometime. He felt Maria holding to his arm. She was looking up and he said to her, 'What do they look like to you, *guapa*?'

'I don't know,' she said. 'Death, I think.'

'They look like planes to me,' the woman of Pablo said. 'Where are the little ones?'

'They may be crossing at another part,' Robert Jordan said. 'Those bombers are too fast to have to wait for them and have come back alone. We never follow them across the lines to fight. There aren't enough planes to risk it.'

Just then three Heinkel fighters in V formation came low over the clearing coming toward them, just over the tree tops, like clattering, wing-tilting, pinch-nosed ugly toys, to enlarge suddenly, fearfully to their actual size; pouring past in a whining roar. They were so low that from the cave mouth all of them could see the pilots, helmeted, goggled, a scarf blowing back from behind the patrol leader's head.

'*Those* can seen the horses,' Pablo said.

'Those can see thy cigarette butts,' the woman said. 'Let fall the blanket.'

No more planes came over. The others must have crossed farther up the range and when the droning was gone they went out of the cave into the open.

The sky was empty now and high and blue and clear.

'It seems as though they were a dream that you wake from,' Maria said to Robert Jordan. There was not even the last almost unheard hum that comes like a finger faintly touching and leaving and touching again after the sound is gone almost past hearing.

'They are no dream and you go in and clean up,' Pilar said to her. 'What about it,' she turned to Robert Jordan. 'Should we ride or walk?'

Pablo looked at her and grunted.

'As you will,' Robert Jordan said.

'Then let us walk,' she said. 'I would like it for the liver.'

'Riding is good for the liver.'

'Yes, but hard on the buttocks. We will walk and thou—' She turned to Pablo. 'Go down and count thy beasts and see they have not flown away with any.'

'Do you want a horse to ride?' Pablo asked Robert Jordan.

'No. Many thanks. What about the girl?'

'Better for her to walk,' Pilar said. 'She'll get stiff in too many places and serve for nothing.'

Robert Jordan felt his face reddening.

'Did you sleep well?' Pilar asked. Then said, 'It is true that there is no sickness. There could have been. I know not why there wasn't. There probably still is God after all, although we have abolished Him. Go on,' she said to Pablo. 'This does not concern thee. This is of people younger than thee. Made of other material. Get on.' Then to Robert Jordan, 'Agustín is looking after thy things. We go when he comes.'

It was a clear, bright day and warm now in the sun. Robert Jordan looked at the big, brown-faced woman with her kind, widely set eyes and her square, heavy face, lined and pleasantly ugly, the eyes merry, but the face sad until the lips moved. He looked at her and then at the man, heavy and stolid, moving off through the trees toward the corral. The woman, too, was looking after him.

'Did you make love?' the woman said.

'What did she say?'

'She would not tell me.'

'I neither.'

'Then you made love,' the woman said. 'Be as careful with her as you can.'

'What if she has a baby?'

'That will do no harm,' the woman said. 'That will do less harm.'

'This is no place for that.'

'She will not stay here. She will go with you.'

'And where will I go? I can't take a woman where I go.'

'Who knows? You may take two where you go.'

'That is no way to talk.'

'Listen,' the woman said. 'I am no coward, but I see things very clearly in the early morning and I think there are many that we know that are alive now who will never see another Sunday.'

'In what day are we?'

'Sunday.'

'*Qué va*,' said Robert Jordan. 'Another Sunday is very far. If we see Wednesday we are all right. But I do not like to hear thee talk like this.'

'Everyone needs to talk to someone,' the woman said. 'Before we had religion and other nonsense. Now for everyone there should be someone to whom one can speak frankly, for all the valour that one could have one becomes very alone.'

'We are not alone. We are all together.'

'The sight of those machines does things to one,' the woman said. 'We are nothing against such machines.'

'Yet we can beat them.'

'Look,' the woman said. 'I confess a sadness to you, but do not think I lack resolution. Nothing has happened to my resolution.'

'The sadness will dissipate as the sun rises. It is like a mist.'

'Clearly,' the woman said. 'If you want it that way. Perhaps it came from talking that foolishness about Valencia. And that failure of a man who has gone to look at his horses. I wounded him much with the story. Kill him, yes. Curse him, yes. But wound him, no.'

'How came you to be with him?'

'How is one with anyone? In the first days of the movement and before too, he was something. Something serious. But now he is finished. The plug has been drawn and the wine has all run out of the skin.'

'I do not like him.'

'Nor does he like you, and with reason. Last night I slept with him.' She smiled now and shook her head. '*Vamos a ver*,' she said. 'I said to him, "Pablo, why did you not kill the foreigner?"

'"He's a good boy, Pilar," he said. "He's a good boy."

'So I said, "You understand now that I command?"

'"Yes, Pilar. Yes," he said. Later in the night I hear him awake and he is crying. He is crying in a short and ugly manner as a man cries when it is as though there is an animal inside that is shaking him.

'"What passes with thee, Pablo?" I said to him and I took hold of him and held him.

'"Nothing, Pilar. Nothing."

'"Yes. Something passes with thee."

'"The people," he said. "The way they left me. The *gente*."

'"Yes, but they are with me," I said, "and I am thy woman."

'"Pilar," he said, "remember the train." Then he said, "May God aid thee, Pilar."

'"What are you talking of God for?" I said to him. "What way is that to speak?"

'"Yes," he said. "God and the *Virgen*."

'"*Qué va*, God and the *Virgen*," I said to him. "Is that any way to talk?"

'"I am afraid to die, Pilar," he said. "*Tengo miedo de morir*. Dost thou understand?"

'"Then get out of bed," I said to him. "There is not room in one bed for me and thee and thy fear all together."

'Then he was ashamed and was quiet and I went to sleep but, man, he's a ruin.'

Robert Jordan said nothing.

'All my life I have had this sadness at intervals,' the woman said. 'But it is not like the sadness of Pablo. It does not affect my resolution.'

'I believe that.'

'It may be it is like the times of a woman,' she said. 'It may be it is nothing,' she paused, then went on. 'I put great illusion in the Republic. I believe firmly in the Republic and I have faith. I believe in it with fervour as those who have religious faith believe in the mysteries.'

'I believe you.'

'And you have this same faith?'

'In the Republic?'

'Yes.'

'Yes,' he said, hoping it was true.

'I am happy,' the woman said. 'And you have no fear?'

'Not to die,' he said truly.

'But other fears?'

'Only of not doing my duty as I should.'

'Not of capture, as the other had?'

'No,' he said truly. 'Fearing that, one would be so preoccupied as to be useless.'

'You are a very cold boy.'

'No, he said. 'I do not think so.'

'No. In the head you are very cold.'

'It is that I am very preoccupied with my work.'

'But you do not like the things of life?'

'Yes. Very much. But not to interfere with my work.'

'You like to drink, I know. I have seen.'

'Yes. Very much. But not to interfere with my work.'

'And women?'

'I like them very much, but I have not given them much importance.'

'You do not care for them?'

'Yes. But I have not found one that moved me as they say they should move you.'

'I think you lie.'

'Maybe a little.'

'But you care for Maria.'

'Yes. Suddenly and very much.'

'I, too. I care for her very much. Yes. Much.'

'I, too,' said Robert Jordan, and could feel his voice thickening. 'I, too. Yes.' It gave him pleasure to say it and he said it quite formally in Spanish. 'I care for her very much.'

'I will leave you alone with her after we have seen El Sordo.'

Robert Jordan said nothing. Then he said, 'That is not necessary.'

'Yes, man. It is necessary. There is not much time.'

'Did you see that in the hand?' he asked.

'No. Do not remember that nonsense of the hand.'

She had put that away with all the other things that might do ill to the Republic.

Robert Jordan said nothing. He was looking at Maria putting away the dishes inside the cave. She wiped her hands and turned and smiled at him. She could not hear what Pilar was saying, but as she smiled at Robert Jordan she blushed dark under the tawny skin and then smiled at him again.

'There is the day also,' the woman said. 'You have the night, but there is the day, too. Clearly, there is no such luxury as in Valencia in my time. But you could pick a few wild strawberries or something.' She laughed.

Robert Jordan put his arm on her big shoulder. 'I care for thee, too,' he said. 'I care for thee very much.'

'Thou art a regular Don Juan Tenorio,' the woman said, embarrassed now with affection. 'There is a commencement of caring for everyone. Here comes Agustín.'

Robert Jordan went into the cave and up to where Maria was standing. She watched him come toward her, her eyes bright, the blush again on her cheeks and throat.

'Hello, little rabbit,' he said and kissed her on the mouth. She held him tight to her and looked in his face and said, 'Hello. Oh, hello. Hello.'

Fernando, still sitting at the table smoking a cigarette, stood up, shook his head and walked out, picking up his carbine from where it leaned against the wall.

'It is very informal,' he said to Pilar. 'And I do not like it. You should take care of the girl.'

'I am,' said Pilar. 'That comrade is her *novio*.'

'Oh,' said Fernando. 'In that case, since they are engaged, I encounter it to be perfectly normal.'

'I am pleased,' the woman said.

'Equally,' Fernando agreed gravely. '*Salud*, Pilar.'

'Where are you going?'

'To the upper post to relieve Primitivo.'

'Where the hell are you going,' Agustín asked the grave little man as he came up.

'To my duty,' Fernando said with dignity.

'Thy duty,' said Agustín mockingly. 'I besmirch the milk of thy duty.' Then turning to the woman, 'Where the un-nameable is this vileness that I am to guard?'

'In the cave,' Pilar said. 'In two sacks. And I am tired of thy obscenity.'

'I obscenity in the milk of thy tiredness,' Agustín said.

'Then go and befoul thyself,' Pilar said to him without heat.

'Thy mother,' Agustín replied.

'Thou never had one,' Pilar told him, the insults having reached the ultimate formalism in Spanish in which the acts are never stated but only implied.

'What are they doing in there?' Agustín now asked confidentially.

'Nothing,' Pilar told him. '*Nada*. We are, after all, in the spring, animal.'

'Animal,' said Agustín, relishing the word. 'Animal. And thou. Daughter of the great whore of whores. I befoul myself in the milk of the springtime.'

Pilar slapped him on the shoulder.

'You,' she said, and laughed that booming laugh. 'You lack variety in your cursing. But you have force. Did you see the planes?'

'I un-name in the milk of their motors,' Agustín said, nodding his head and biting his lower lip.

'That's something,' Pilar said. 'That is really something. But really difficult of execution.'

'At that altitude, yes,' Agustín grinned. '*Desde luego*. But it is better to joke.'

'Yes,' the woman of Pablo said. 'It is much better to joke, and you are a good man and you joke with force.'

'Listen, Pilar,' Agustín said seriously. 'Something is preparing. Is it not true?'

'How does it seem to you?'

'Of a foulness that cannot be worse. Those were many planes, woman. Many planes.'

'And thou has caught fear from them like all the others?'

'*Qué va*,' said Agustín. 'What do you think they are preparing?'

'Look,' Pilar said. 'From this boy coming for the bridges obviously the Republic is preparing an offensive. From these planes obviously the fascists are preparing to meet it. But why show the planes?'

'In this war are many foolish things,' Agustín said. 'In this war there is an idiocy without bounds.'

'Clearly,' said Pilar. 'Otherwise we could not be here.'

'Yes,' said Agustín. 'We swim within the idiocy for a year now. But Pablo is a man of much understanding. Pablo is very wily.'

'Why do you say this?'

'I say it.'

'But you must understand,' Pilar explained. 'It is now too late to be saved by wiliness and he has lost the other.'

'I understand,' said Agustín. 'I know we must go. And since we must win to survive ultimately, it is necessary that the bridges must be blown. But Pablo, for the coward that he now is, is very smart.'

'I, too, am smart.'

'No, Pilar,' Agustín said. 'You are not smart. You are brave. You are loyal. You have decision. You have intuition. Much decision and much heart. But you are not smart.'

'You believe that?' the woman asked thoughtfully.

'Yes, Pilar.'

'The boy is smart,' the woman said. 'Smart and cold. Very cold in the head.'

'Yes,' Agustín said. 'He must know his business or they would not have him doing this. But I do not know that he is smart. Pablo I *know* is smart.'

'But rendered useless by his fear and his disinclination to action.'

'But still smart.'

'And what do you say?'

'Nothing. I try to consider it intelligently. In this moment we need to act with intelligence. After the bridge we must leave at once. All must be prepared. We must know for where we are leaving and how.'

'Naturally.'

'For this–Pablo. It must be done smartly.'

'I have no confidence in Pablo.'

'In this, yes.'

'No. You do not know how far he is ruined.'

'*Pero es muy vivo*. He is very smart. And if we do not do this smartly we are obscenitied.'

'I will think about it,' Pilar said. 'I have the day to think about it.'

'For the bridges; the boy,' Agustín said. 'This he must know. Look at the fine manner in which the other organized the train.'

'Yes,' Pilar said. 'It was really he who planned all.'

'You for energy and resolution,' Agustín said. 'But Pablo for the moving. Pablo for the retreat. Force him now to study it.'

'You are a man of intelligence.'

'Intelligent, yes,' Agustín said. 'But *sin picardía*. Pablo for that.'

'With his fear and all?'

'With his fear and all.'

'And what do you think of the bridges?'

'It is necessary. That I know. Two things we must do. We must leave here and we must win. The bridges are necessary if we are to win.'

'If Pablo is so smart, why does he not see that?'

'He wants things as they are for his own weakness. He wants to stay in the eddy of his own weakness. But the river is rising. Forced to a change, he will be smart in the change. *Es muy vivo*.'

'It is good that the boy did not kill him.'

'*Qué va*. The gipsy wanted me to kill him last night. The gipsy is an animal.'

'You're an animal, too,' she said. 'But intelligent.'

'We are both intelligent,' Agustín said. 'But the talent is Pablo!'

'But difficult to put up with. You do not know how ruined.'

'Yes. But a talent. Look, Pilar. To make war all you need is intelligence. But to win you need talent and material.'

'I will think it over,' she said. 'We must start now. We are late.' Then, raising her voice, 'English!' she called. '*Inglés!* Come on! Let us go.'

10

'Let us rest,' Pilar said to Robert Jordan. 'Sit down here, Maria, and let us rest.'

'We should continue,' Robert Jordan said. 'Rest when we get there. I must see this man.'

'You will see him,' the woman told him. 'There is no hurry. Sit down here, Maria.'

'Come on,' Robert Jordan said. 'Rest at the top.'

'I rest now,' the woman said, and sat down by the stream. The girl sat by her in the heather, the sun shining on her hair. Only Robert Jordan stood looking across the high mountain meadow with the trout brook running through it. There was heather growing where he stood. There were grey boulders rising from the yellow bracken that replaced the heather in the lower part of the meadow and below was the dark line of the pines.

'How far is it to El Sordo's?' he asked.

'Not far,' the woman said. 'It is across this open country, down into the next valley and above the timber at the head of the stream. Sit thee down and forget thy seriousness.'

'I want to see him and get it over with.'

'I want to bathe my feet,' the woman said, and, taking off her rope-soled shoes and pulling off a heavy wool stocking, she put her right foot into the stream. 'My God, it's cold.'

'We should have taken horses,' Robert Jordan told her.

'This is good for me,' the woman said. 'This is what I have been missing. What's the matter with you?'

'Nothing, except that I am in a hurry.'

'Then calm yourself. There is much time. What a day it is and how I am contented not to be in pine trees. You cannot imagine how one can tire of pine trees. Aren't you tired of the pines, *guapa*?'

'I like them,' the girl said.

'What can you like about them?'

'I like the odour and the feel of the needles under foot. I like the wind in the high trees and the creaking they make against each other.'

'You like anything,' Pilar said. 'You are a gift to any man if you could cook a little better. But the pine tree makes a forest of boredom. Thou hast never known a forest of beech, nor of oak, nor of chestnut. Those are forests. In such forests each tree differs and there is character and beauty. A forest of pine trees is boredom. What do you say, *Inglés*?'

'I like the pines, too.'

'*Pero, venga*,' Pilar said. 'Two of you. So do I like the pines, but we have been too long in these pines. Also I am tired of the mountains. In mountains there are only two directions. Down and up and down leads only to the road and the towns of the fascists.'

'Do you ever go to Segovia?'

'*Qué va*. With this face? This is a face that is known. How would you like to be ugly, beautiful one?' she said to Maria.

'Thou art not ugly.'

'*Vamos*, I'm not ugly. I was born ugly. All my life I have been ugly. You, *Inglés*, who know nothing about women. Do you know how an ugly woman feels? Do you know what it is to be ugly all your life and inside to feel that you are beautiful? It is very rare,' she put the other foot in the stream, then removed it. 'God, it's cold. Look at the water wagtail,' she said and pointed to the grey ball of a bird that was bobbing up and down on a stone up the stream. 'Those are no good for anything. Neither to sing nor to eat. Only to jerk their tails up and down. Give me a cigarette, *Inglés*,' she said and taking it, lit it from a flint and steel lighter in the pocket of her shirt. She puffed on the cigarette and looked at Maria and Robert Jordan.

'Life is very curious,' she said, and blew smoke from her nostrils. 'I would have made a good man, but I am all woman and all ugly. Yet many men have loved me and I have loved many men. It is curious. Listen, *Inglés*, this is interesting. Look at me, as ugly as I am. Look closely, *Inglés*.'

'Thou art not ugly.'

'*Qué no?* Don't lie to me. Or,' she laughed the deep laugh. 'Has it begun to work with thee? No. That is a joke. No. Look at the ugliness. Yet one has a feeling within one that blinds a man while he loves you. You, with that feeling, blind him, and blind yourself. Then one day, for no reason, he sees you ugly as you really are and he is not blind any more and then you see yourself as ugly as he sees you and you lose your man and your feeling. Do you understand, *guapa*?' She patted the girl on the shoulder.

'No,' said Maria. 'Because thou art not ugly.'

'Try to use thy head and not thy heart, and listen,' Pilar said. 'I am telling you things of much interest. Does it not interest you, *Inglés*?'

'Yes. But we should go.'

'*Qué va*, go. I am very well here. Then,' she went on, addressing herself to Robert Jordan now as though she were speaking to a classroom; almost as though she were lecturing. 'After a while, when you are as ugly as I am, as ugly as women can be, then, as I say, after a while the feeling, the idiotic feeling that you are beautiful, grows slowly in one again. It grows like a cabbage. And then, when the feeling is grown, another man sees you and thinks you are beautiful and it is all to do over. Now I think I am past it, but it still might come. You are lucky, *guapa*, that you are not ugly.'

'But I *am* ugly,' Maria insisted.

'Ask *him*,' said Pilar. 'And don't put thy feet in the stream because it will freeze them.'

'If Roberto says we should go, I think we should go,' Maria said.

'Listen to you,' Pilar said. 'I have as much at stake in this as thy Roberto and I say that we are well off resting here by the stream and that there is much time. Furthermore, I like to talk. It is the only civilized thing we have.

How otherwise can we divert ourselves? Does what I say not hold interest for you, *Inglés*?'

'You speak very well. But there are other things that interest me more than talk of beauty or lack of beauty.'

'Then let us talk of what interests thee.'

'Where were you at the start of the movement?'

'In my town.'

'Avila?'

'*Qué va*, Avila.'

'Pablo said he was from Avila.'

'He lies. He wanted to take a big city for his town. It was this town,' and she named a town.

'And what happened?'

'Much,' the woman said. 'Much. And all of it ugly. Even that which was glorious.'

'Tell me about it,' Robert Jordan said.

'It is brutal,' the woman said. 'I do not like to tell it before the girl.'

'Tell it,' said Robert Jordan. 'And if it is not for her, that she should not listen.'

'I can hear it,' Maria said. She put her hand on Robert Jordan's. 'There is nothing that I cannot hear.'

'It isn't whether you can hear it,' Pilar said. 'It is whether I should tell it to thee and make thee bad dreams.'

'I will not get bad dreams from a story,' Maria told her. 'You think after all that has happened with us I should get bad dreams from a story?'

'Maybe it will give the *Inglés* bad dreams.'

'Try it and see.'

'No, *Inglés*, I am not joking. Didst thou see the start of the movement in any small town?'

'No,' Robert Jordan said.

'Then thou hast seen nothing. Thou hast seen the ruin that now is Pablo, but you should have seen Pablo on that day.'

'Tell it.'

'Nay, I do not want to.'

'Tell it.'

'All right, then. I will tell it truly as it was. But thee, *guapa*, if it reaches a point that it molests thee, tell me.'

'I will not listen to it if it molests me,' Maria told her. 'It cannot be worse than many things.'

'I believe it can,' the woman said. 'Give me another cigarette, *Inglés*, and *vamonos*.'

The girl leaned back against the heather on the bank of the stream and Robert Jordan stretched himself out, his shoulders against the ground and his head against a clump of the heather. He reached out and found Maria's hand and held it in his, rubbing their two hands against the heather until she opened her hand and laid it flat on top of his as they listened.

'It was early in the morning when the *civiles* surrendered at the barracks,' Pilar began.

'You had assaulted the barracks?' Robert Jordan asked.

'Pablo had surrounded it in the dark, cut the telephone wires, placed dynamite under one wall and called on the *guardia civil* to surrender. They would not. And at daylight he blew the wall open. There was fighting. Two *civiles* were killed. Four were wounded and four surrendered.

'We all lay on roofs and on the ground and at the edge of walls and of buildings in the early morning light and the dust cloud of the explosion had not yet settled, for it rose high in the air and there was no wind to carry it, and all of us were firing into the broken side of the building, loading and firing into the smoke, and from within there was still the flashing of rifles and then there was a shout from in the smoke not to fire more, and out came the four *civiles* with their hands up. A big part of the roof had fallen in and the wall was gone and they came out to surrender.

'"Are there more inside?" Pablo shouted.

'"There are wounded."

'"Guard these," Pablo said to four who had come up from where we were firing. "Stand there. Against the wall," he told the *civiles*. The four *civiles* stood against the wall, dirty, dusty, smoke-grimed, with the four who were guarding them pointing their guns at them and Pablo and the others went in to finish the wounded.

'After they had done this and there was no longer any noise of the wounded, neither groaning, nor crying out, nor the noise of shooting in the barracks, Pablo and the others came out and Pablo had his shotgun slung over his back and was carrying in his hand a Mauser pistol.

'"Look, Pilar," he said. "This was in the hand of the officer who killed himself. Never have I fired a pistol. You," he said to one of the guards, "show me how it works. No. Don't show me. Tell me."

'The four *civiles* had stood against the wall, sweating and saying nothing while the shooting had gone on inside the barracks. They were all tall men with the faces of *guardias civiles*, which is the same model of face as mine is. Except that their faces were covered with the small stubble of this their last morning of not yet being shaved and they stood there against the wall and said nothing.

'"You," said Pablo to the one who stood nearest him. "Tell me how it works."

'"Pull the small lever down," the man said in a very dry voice. "Pull the receiver back and let it snap forward."

'"What is the receiver?" asked Pablo, and he looked at the four *civiles*. "What is the receiver?"

'"The block on top of the action."

'Pablo pulled it back, but it stuck. "What now?" he said. "It is jammed. You have lied to me."

'"Pull it farther back and let it snap lightly forward," the *civil* said, and I have never heard such a tone of voice. It was greyer than a morning without sunrise.

'Pablo pulled and let go as the man had told him and the block snapped forward into place and the pistol was cocked with the hammer back. It is an ugly pistol, small in the round handle, large and flat in the barrel, and unwieldy. All this time the *civiles* had been watching him and they had said nothing.

'"What are you going to do with us?" one asked him.

'"Shoot thee," Pablo said.

'"When?" the man asked in the same grey voice.

'"Now," said Pablo.

'"Where?" asked the man.

'"Here,' said Pablo. "Here. Now. Here and now. Have you anything to say?"

'"*Nada*," said the *civil*. "Nothing. But it is an ugly thing."

'"And you are an ugly thing," Pablo said. "You murderer of peasants. You who would shoot your own mother."

'"I have never killed anyone," the *civil* said. "And do not speak of my mother."

'"Show us how to die. You, who have always done the killing."

'"There is no necessity to insult us," another *civil* said. "And we know how to die."

'"Kneel down against the wall with your head against the wall," Pablo told them. The *civiles* looked at one another.

'"Kneel, I say," Pablo said. "Get down and kneel."

'"How does it seem to you, Paco?" one *civil* said to the tallest, who had spoken with Pablo about the pistol. He wore a corporal's stripes on his sleeves and was sweating very much although the early morning was still cool.

'"It is as well to kneel," he answered. "It is of no importance."

'"It is closer to the earth," the first one who had spoken said, trying to make a joke, but they were all too grave for a joke and no one smiled.

'"Then let us kneel," the first *civil* said, and the four knelt, looking very awkward with their heads against the wall and their hands by their sides, and Pablo passed behind them and shot each in turn in the back of the head with the pistol, going from one to another and putting the barrel of the pistol against the back of their heads, each man slipping down as he fired. I can hear the pistol still, sharp and yet muffled, and see the barrel jerk and the head of the man drop forward. One held his head still when the pistol touched it. One pushed his head forward and pressed his forehead against the stone. One shivered in his whole body and his head was shaking. Only one put his hands in front of his eyes, and he was the last one, and the four bodies were slumped against the wall when Pablo turned away from them and came toward us with the pistol still in his hand.

'"Hold this for me, Pilar," he said. "I do not know how to put down the hammer," and he handed me the pistol and stood there looking at the four guards as they lay against the wall of the barracks. All those who were with us stood there too, looking at them, and no one said anything.

'We had won the town and it was still early in the morning and no one had eaten nor had any one drunk coffee and we looked at each other and we were all powdered with dust from the blowing up of the barracks, as powdered as men are at a threshing, and I stood holding the pistol and it was heavy in my hand and I felt weak in the stomach when I looked at the guards dead there against the wall; they all as grey and as dusty as we were, but each one was now moistening with his blood the dry dirt by the wall where they lay. And as we stood there the sun rose over the far hills and shone now on the road where we stood and on the white wall of the barracks and the dust in the air was golden in that first sun and the peasant who was beside me looked at the wall of the barracks and what lay there and then looked at us and then at the sun and said, "*Vaya*, a day that commences."

'"Now let us go and get coffee," I said.

'"Good, Pilar, good," he said. And we went up into the town to the Plaza, and those were the last people who were shot in the village.'

'What happened to the others?' Robert Jordan asked. 'Were there no other fascists in the village?'

'*Qué va*, were there no other fascists? There were more than twenty. But none was shot.'

'What was done?'

'Pablo had them beaten to death with flails and thrown from the top of the cliff into the river.'

'All twenty?'

'I will tell you. It is not so simple. And in my life never do I wish to see such a scene as the flailing to death in the plaza on the top of the cliff above the river.

'The town is built on the high bank above the river and there is a square there with a fountain and there are benches and there are big trees that give a shade for the benches. The balconies of the houses look out on the plaza. Six streets enter on the plaza and there is an arcade from the houses that goes around the plaza so that one can walk in the shade of the arcade when the sun is hot. On three sides of the plaza is the arcade and on the fourth side is the walk shaded by the trees beside the edge of the cliff with, far below, the river. It is three hundred feet down to the river.

'Pablo organized it all as he did the attack on the barracks. First he had the entrances to the streets blocked off with carts as though to organize the plaza for a *capea*. For an amateur bull fight. The fascists were all held in the *Ayuntamiento*, the city hall, which was the largest building on one side of the plaza. It was there the clock was set in the wall and it was in the buildings under the arcade that the club of the fascists was. And under the arcade on the sidewalk in front of their club was where they had their chairs and tables for their club. It was there, before the movement, that they were accustomed to take their apéritifs. The chairs and the tables were of wicker. It looked like a café but was more elegant.'

'But was there no fighting to take them?'

'Pablo had them seized in the night before he assaulted the barracks. But he had already surrounded the barracks. They were all seized in their homes at the same hour the attack started. That was intelligent. Pablo is an organizer. Otherwise he would have had people attacking him at his flanks and at his rear while he was assaulting the barracks of the *guardia civil*.

'Pablo is very intelligent but very brutal. He has this of the village well planned and well ordered. Listen. After the assault was successful, and the last four guards had surrendered, and he had shot them against the wall, and we had drunk coffee at the café that always opened earliest in the morning by the corner from which the early bus left, he proceeded to the organization of the plaza. Carts were piled exactly as for a *capea* except that the side toward the river was not enclosed. That were left open. Then Pablo ordered the priest to confess the fascists and give them the necessary sacraments.'

'Where was this done?'

'In the *Ayuntamiento*, as I said. There was a great crowd outside and while this was going on inside with the priest, there was some levity outside and shouting of obscenities, but most of the people were very serious and respectful. Those who made jokes were those who were already drunk from the celebration of the taking of the barracks and there were useless characters who would have been drunk at any time.

'While the priest was engaged in these duties, Pablo organized those in the plaza into two lines.

'He placed them in two lines as you would place men for a rope pulling contest, or as they stand in a city to watch the ending of a bicycle road race with just room for the cyclists to pass between, or as men stood to allow the passage of a holy image in a procession. Two metres was left between the lines and they extended from the door of the *Ayuntamiento* clear across the plaza to the edge of the cliff. So that, from the doorway of the *Ayuntamiento*, looking across the plaza, one coming out would see two solid lines of people waiting.

'They were armed with flails such as are used to beat out the grain and they were a good flail's length apart. All did not have flails, as enough flails could not be obtained. But most had flails obtained from the store of Don Guillermo Martín, who was a fascist and sold all sorts of agricultural implements. And those who did not have flails had heavy herdsman's clubs, or ox-goads, and some had wooden pitchforks; those with wooden tines that are used to fork the chaff and straw into the air after the flailing. Some had sickles and reaping hooks but these Pablo placed at the far end where the lines reached the edge of the cliff.

'These lines were quiet and it was a clear day, as to-day is clear, and there were clouds high in the sky, as there are now, and the plaza was not yet dusty for there had been a heavy dew in the night, and the trees cast a shadow over the men in the lines and you could hear the water running from the brass pipe in the mouth of the lion and falling into the bowl of the fountain where the women bring the water jars to fill them.

'Only near the *Ayuntamiento*, where the priest was complying with his duties with the fascists, was there any ribaldry, and that came from those worthless ones who, as I said, were already drunk and were crowded around the windows shouting obscenities and jokes in bad taste in through the iron bars of the windows. Most of the men in the lines were waiting quietly and I heard one say to another, "Will there be women?"

'And another said, "I hope to Christ, no."

'Then one said, "Here is the woman of Pablo. Listen, Pilar, will there be women?"

'I looked at him and he was a peasant dressed in his Sunday jacket and sweating heavily and I said, "No, Joaquín. There are no women. We are not killing the women. Why should we kill their women?"

'And he said, "Thanks be to Christ, there are no women and when does it start?"

'And I said, "As soon as the priest finishes."

'"And the priest?"

'"I don't know," I told him, and I saw his face working and the sweat coming down on his forehead. "I have never killed a man," he said.

'"Then you will learn," the peasant next to him said. "But I do not think one blow with this will kill a man," and he held his flail in both hands and looked at it with doubt.

'"That is the beauty of it," another peasant said. "There must be many blows."

'"*They* have taken Valladolid. *They* have Avila," someone said. "I heard that before we came into town."

'"*They* will never take this town. *This* town is ours. We have struck ahead of them," I said. "Pablo is not one to wait for them to strike."

'"Pablo is able," another said. "But in this finishing off of the *civiles* he was egoistic. Don't you think so, Pilar?"

'"Yes," I said. "But now all are participating in this."

'"Yes," he said. "It is well organized. But why do we not hear more news of the movement?"

'"Pablo cut the telephone wires before the assault on the barracks. They are not yet repaired."

'"Ah," he said. "It is for this we hear nothing. I had my news from the roadmender's station early this morning."

'"Why is this done thus, Pilar?" he said to me.

'"To save bullets," I said. "And that each man should have his share in the responsibility."

'"That it should start then. That it should start." And I looked at him and saw that he was crying.

'"Why are you crying, Joaquín?" I asked him. "This is not to cry about."

'"I cannot help it, Pilar," he said. "I have never killed any one."

'If you have not seen the day of revolution in a small town where all know all in the town and always have known all, you have seen nothing. And on this day most of the men in the double line across the plaza wore the clothes in which they worked in the fields, having come into town hurriedly, but some, not knowing how one should dress for the first day of a movement, wore their clothes for Sundays or holidays, and these, seeing that the others, including those who had attacked the barracks, wore their oldest clothes, were ashamed of being wrongly dressed. But they did not like to take off their jackets for fear of losing them, or that they might be stolen by the worthless ones, and so they stood, sweating in the sun and waiting for it to commence.

'Then the wind rose and the dust was now dry in the plaza for the men walking and standing and shuffling had loosened it and it commenced to blow and a man in a dark blue Sunday jacket shouted "Agua! Agua!" and the caretaker of the plaza, whose duty it was to sprinkle the plaza each morning with a hose, came and turned the hose on and commenced to lay the dust at the edge of the plaza, and then toward the centre. Then the two lines fell back and let him lay the dust over the centre of the plaza; the hose sweeping in wide arcs and the water glistening in the sun and the men leaning on their flails or the clubs or the white wood pitchforks and watching the sweep of the stream of water. And then, when the plaza was nicely moistened and the dust settled, the lines formed up again and a peasant shouted, "When do we get the first fascist? When does the first one come out of the box?"

'"Soon," Pablo shouted from the door of the *Ayuntamiento*. "Soon the first one comes out." His voice was hoarse from shouting in the assault and from the smoke of the barracks.

'"What's the delay?" someone asked.

'"They're still occupied with their sins," Pablo shouted.

'"Clearly, there are twenty of them," a man said.

'"More," said another.

'"Among twenty there are many sins to recount."

'"Yes, but I think it's a trick to gain time. Surely facing such an emergency one could not remember one's sins except for the biggest."

'"Then have patience. For with more than twenty of them there are enough of the biggest sins to take some time."

'"I have patience," said the other. "But it is better to get it over with. Both for them and for us. It is July and there is much work. We have harvested but we have not threshed. We are not yet in the time of fairs and festivals."

'"But this will be a fair and festival to-day," another said. "The Fair of Liberty and from this day, when these are extinguished, the town and the land are ours."

'"We thresh fascists to-day," said one, "and out of the chaff comes the freedom of this pueblo."

'"We must administer it well to deserve it," said another. "Pilar," he said to me, "when do we have a meeting for organization?"

'"Immediately after this is completed," I told him. "In the same building of the *Ayuntamiento*."

'I was wearing one of the three-cornered patent leather hats of the *guardia civil* as a joke and I had put the hammer down on the pistol, holding it with my thumb to lower it as I pulled on the trigger as seemed natural, and the pistol was held in a rope I had around my waist, the long barrel stuck under the rope. And when I put it on the joke seemed very good to me, although afterwards I wished I had taken the holster of the pistol instead of the hat. But one of the men in the line said to me, "Pilar, daughter. It seems to me bad taste for thee to wear that hat. Now we have finished with such things as the *guardia civil*."

'"Then," I said, "I will take it off." And I did.

'"Give it to me," he said. "It should be destroyed."

'And as we were at the far end of the line where the walk runs along the cliff by the river, he took the hat in his hand and sailed it off over the cliff with the motion a herdsman makes throwing a stone underhand at the bulls to herd them. The hat sailed far out into space and we could see it smaller and smaller, the patent leather shining in the clear air, sailing down to the river. I looked back over the square and at all the windows and all the balconies there were people crowded and there was the double line of men across the square to the doorway of the *Ayuntamiento* and the crowd swarmed outside against the windows of that building and there was the noise of many people talking, and then I heard a shout and someone said, "Here comes the first one," and it was Don Benito Garcia, the Mayor, and he came out bareheaded walking slowly from the door and down the porch and nothing happened; and he walked between the line of men with the flails and nothing happened. He passed two men, four men, eight men, ten men and nothing happened and he was walking between that line of men, his head up, his fat face grey, his eyes looking ahead and then flickering from side to side and walking steadily. And nothing happened.

'From a balcony someone cried out, "*Qué pasa, cobardes?* What is the matter, cowards?" and still Don Benito walked along between the men and nothing happened. Then I saw a man three men down from where I was standing and his face was working and he was biting his lips and his hands were white on his flail. I saw him looking toward Don Benito, watching him come on. And still nothing happened. Then, just before Don Benito came abreast of this man, the man raised his flail high so that it struck the man beside him and smashed a blow at Don Benito that hit him on the side of the head and Don Benito looked at him and the man struck again and shouted, "That for you, *Cabron*," and the blow hit Don Benito in the face and he raised his hands to his face and they beat him until he fell and the man who had struck him first called to others to help him and he pulled on the collar of Don Benito's shirt and others took hold of his arms and with his face in the dust of the plaza, they dragged him over the walk to the edge of the cliff and threw him over and into the river. And the man who hit him first was kneeling by the edge of the cliff looking over after him and saying, "The Cabron! The Cabron! Oh, the Cabron!" He was a tenant of Don Benito and they had never gotten along together. There had been a dispute about a piece of land by the river that Don Benito had taken from this man and let to another and this man had long hated him. This man did not join the line again but sat by the cliff looking down where Don Benito had fallen.

'After Don Benito no one would come out. There was no noise now in the plaza as all were waiting to see who it was that would come out. Then a drunkard shouted in a great voice, "*Qué salga el toro!* Let the bull out!"

'Then someone from by the windows of the *Ayuntamiento* yelled, "They won't move! They are all praying!"

'Another drunkard shouted, "Pull them out. Come on, pull them out. The time for praying is finished."

'But none came out and then I saw a man coming out of the door.

'It was Don Federico González, who owned the mill and feed store and was a fascist of the first order. He was tall and thin and his hair was brushed over the top of his head from one side to the other to cover a baldness and he wore a nightshirt that was tucked into his trousers. He was barefooted as when he had been taken from his home and he walked ahead of Pablo holding his hands above his head, and Pablo walked behind him with the barrels of his shotgun pressing against the back of Don Federico González until Don Federico entered the double line. But when Pablo left him and returned to the door of the *Ayuntamiento*, Don Federico could not walk forward, and stood there, his eyes turned up to heaven and his hands reaching up as though they would grasp the sky.

'"He has no legs to walk," someone said.

'"What's the matter, Don Federico? Can't you walk?" someone shouted to him. But Don Federico stood there with his hands up and only his lips were moving.

'"Get on," Pablo shouted to him from the steps. "Walk."

'Don Federico stood there and could not move. One of the drunkards poked him in the backside with a flail handle and Don Federico gave a quick jump as a balky horse might, but still stood in the same place, his hands up, and his eyes up toward the sky.

'Then the peasant who stood beside me said, "This is shameful. I have nothing against him but such a spectacle must terminate." So he walked down the line and pushed through to where Don Federico was standing and said. "With your permission," and hit him a great blow alongside of the head with a club.

'Then Don Federico dropped his hands and put them over the top of his head where the bald place was and with his head bent and covered by his hands, the thin long hairs that covered the bald place escaping through his fingers, he ran fast through the double line with flails falling on his back and shoulders until he fell and those at the end of the line picked him up and swung him over the cliff. Never did he open his mouth from the moment he came out pushed by the shotgun of Pablo. His only difficulty was to move forward. It was as though he had no command of his legs.

'After Don Federico, I saw there was a concentration of the hardest men at the end of the lines by the edge of the cliff and I left there and I went to the arcade of the *Ayuntamiento* and pushed aside two drunkards and looked in the window. In the big room of the *Ayuntamiento* they were all kneeling in a half circle praying and the priest was kneeling and praying with them. Pablo and one named Cuatro Dedos, Four Fingers, a cobbler, who was much with Pablo then, and two others were standing with shotguns and Pablo said to the priest, "Who goes now?" and the priest went on praying and did not answer him.

'"Listen, you," Pablo said to the priest in his hoarse voice, "Who goes now? Who is ready now?"

'The priest would not speak to Pablo and acted as though he were not there and I could see Pablo was becoming very angry.

'"Let us all go together," Don Ricardo Montalvo, who was a land-owner, said to Pablo, raising his head and stopping praying to speak.

'"*Qué va*,' said Pablo. "One at a time as you are ready."

'"Then I go now," Don Ricardo said. "I'll never be any more ready." The priest blessed him as he spoke and blessed him again as he stood up, without interrupting his praying, and held up a crucifix for Don Ricardo to kiss and Don Ricardo kissed it and then turned and said to Pablo, "Nor ever again as ready. You *Cabron* of the bad milk. Let us go."

'Don Ricardo was a short man with grey hair and a thick neck and he had a shirt on with no collar. He was bow-legged from much horseback riding.

"Good-bye," he said to all those who were kneeling. "Don't be sad. To die is nothing. The only bad thing is to die at the hands of this *canalla*. Don't touch me," he said to Pablo. "Don't touch me with your shotgun."

'He walked out of the front of the *Ayuntamiento* with his grey hair and his small grey eyes and his thick neck looking very short and angry. He looked at the double line of peasants and he spat on the ground. He could spit actual saliva which, in such a circumstance, as you should know, *Inglés*, is very rare and he said, "*Arriba España!* Down with the miscalled Republic and I obscenity in the milk of your fathers."

'So they clubbed him to death very quickly because of the insult, beating him as soon as he reached the first of the men, beating him as he tried to walk with his head up, beating him until he fell and chopping at him with reaping hooks and the sickles, and many men bore him to the edge of the cliff to throw him over and there was blood now on their hands and on their clothing, and now began to be the feeling that these who came out were truly enemies and should be killed.

'Until Don Ricardo came out with that fierceness and calling those insults, many in the line would have given much, I am sure, never to have been in the line. And if anyone had shouted from the line, "Come, let us pardon the rest of them. Now they have had their lesson," I am sure most would have agreed.

'But Don Ricardo with all his bravery did a great dis-service to the others. For he aroused the men in the line and where, before, they were performing a duty and with no great taste for it, now they were angry, and the difference was apparent.

'"Let the priest out and the thing will go faster," someone shouted.

'"Let out the priest."

'"We've had three thieves, let us have the priest."

'"Two thieves," a short peasant said to the man who had shouted. "It was two thieves with Our Lord."

'"Whose Lord?" the man said, his face angry and red.

'"In the manner of speaking it is said Our Lord."

'"He isn't my Lord; not in joke," said the other. "And thee hadst best watch thy mouth if thou dost not want to walk between the lines."

'"I am as good a Libertarian republican as thou," the short peasant said. "I struck Don Ricardo across the mouth. I struck Don Federico across the back. I missed Don Benito. But I say Our Lord is the formal way of speaking of the man in question and that it was two thieves."

'"I obscenity in the milk of thy Republicanism. You speak of Don this and Don that."

'"Here are they so called."

'"Not by me, the *cabrones*. And thy Lord–Hi! Here comes a new one!"

'It was then that we saw a disgraceful sight, for the man who walked out of the doorway of the *Ayuntamiento* was Don Faustino Rivero, the oldest son of his father, Don Celestino Rivero, a land-owner. He was tall and his hair was yellow and it was freshly combed back from his forehead for he always carried a comb in his pocket and he had combed his hair now before coming out. He was a great annoyer of girls, and he was a coward, and he had always wished to be an amateur bullfighter. He went much with gipsies and with bullfighters and with bull raisers and delighted to wear the Andalucian costume, but he had no courage and was considered a joke. One time he was announced to appear in an amateur benefit fight for the old people's home in Avila and to kill a bull from on horseback in the Andalucian style, which he had spent much time practising, and when he had seen the size of the bull that had been substituted for him in place of the little one, weak in the legs, he had picked out himself, he had said he was sick and, some said, put three fingers down his throat to make himself vomit.

'When the lines saw him, they commenced to shout, "*Hola*, Don Faustino. Take care not to vomit."

'"Listen to me, Don Faustino. There are beautiful girls over the cliff."

'"Don Faustino. Wait a minute and we will bring out a bull bigger than the other."

'And another shouted, "Listen to me, Don Faustino. Hast thou ever heard speak of death?"

'Don Faustino stood there, still acting brave. He was still under the impulse that had made him announce to the others that he was going out. It was the same impulse that had made him announce himself for the bullfight. That had made him believe and hope that he could be an amateur matador. Now he was inspired by the example of Don Ricardo and he stood there looking both handsome and brave and he made his face scornful. But he could not speak.

'"Come, Don Faustino," someone called from the line. "Come, Don Faustino. Here is the biggest bull of all."

'Don Faustino stood looking out and I think as he looked, that there was no pity for him on either side of the line. Still he looked both handsome and superb; but time was shortening and there was only one direction to go.

'"Don Faustino," someone called. "What are you waiting for, Don Faustino?"

'"He is preparing to vomit," someone said and the lines laughed.

'"Don Faustino," a peasant called. "Vomit if it will give thee pleasure. To me it is all the same."

'Then, as we watched, Don Faustino looked along the lines and across the square to the cliff and then when he saw the cliff and the emptiness beyond, he turned quickly and ducked back toward the entrance of the *Ayuntamiento*.

'All the lines roared and someone shouted in a high voice, "Where do you go, Don Faustino? Where do you go?"

'"He goes to throw up," shouted another and they all laughed again.

'Then we saw Don Faustino coming out again with Pablo behind him with the shotgun. All of his style was gone now. The sight of the lines had taken away his type and his style and he came out now with Pablo behind him as though Pablo were cleaning a street and Don Faustino was what he was pushing ahead of him. Don Faustino came out now and he was crossing himself and praying and then he put his hands in front of his eyes and walked down the steps toward the lines.

'"Leave him alone," someone shouted. "Don't touch him."

'The lines understood and no one made a move to touch Don Faustino and, with his hands shaking and held in front of his eyes, and, with his mouth moving, he walked along between the lines.

'No one said anything and no one touched him and, when he was halfway through the lines, he could go no farther and fell to his knees.

'No one struck him. I was walking along parallel to the line to see what happened to him and a peasant leaned down and lifted him to his feet and said, "Get up, Don Faustino, and keep walking. The bull has not yet come out."

'Don Faustino could not walk alone and the peasant in a black smock helped him on one side and another peasant in a black smock and herdsman's boots helped him on the other, supporting him by the arms and Don Faustino walking along between the lines with his hands over his eyes, his lips never quiet, and his yellow hair slicked on his head and shining in the sun, and as he passed the peasants would say, "Don Faustino, *buen provecho*. Don Faustino, that you should have a good appetite," and others said, "Don Faustino, *a sus ordenes*. Don Faustino at your orders," and one, who had failed at bullfighting himself, said, "Don Faustino, *Matador, a sus ordenes*," and another said, "Don Faustino, there are beautiful girls in heaven, Don Faustino." And they walked Don Faustino through the lines, holding him close on either side, holding him up as he walked, with him with his hands over his eyes. But he must have looked through his fingers, because when they came to the edge of the cliff with him, he knelt again, throwing himself down and clutching the ground and holding to the grass, saying, "No. No. No. Please. NO. Please. Please. No. No."

'Then the peasants who were with him and the others, the hard ones of the end of the lines, squatted quickly behind him as he knelt, and gave him a rushing push and he was over the edge without ever having been beaten and you heard him crying loud and high as he fell.

'It was then I knew that the lines had become cruel and it was first the insults of Don Ricardo and second the cowardice of Don Faustino that had made them so.

'"Let us have another," a peasant called out and another peasant slapped him on the back and said, "Don Faustino! What a thing! Don Faustino!"

'"He's seen the big bull now," another said. "Throwing up will never help him, now."

'"In my life," another peasant said, "in my life I've never seen a thing like Don Faustino."

'"There are others," another peasant said. "Have patience. Who knows what we may yet see?"

'"There may be giants and dwarfs," the first peasant said. "There may be Negroes and rare beasts from Africa. But for me never, never will there be anything like Don Faustino. But let's have another one! Come on. Let's have another one!"

'The drunkards were handing around bottles of anis and cognac that they had looted from the bar of the club of the fascists, drinking them down like wine, and many of the men in the lines were beginning to be a little drunk, too, from drinking after the strong emotion of Don Benito, Don Federico, Don Ricardo and especially Don Faustino. Those who did not drink from the bottles of liquor were drinking from leather wineskins that were passed about and one handed a wineskin to me and I took a long drink, letting the wine run cool down my throat from the leather *bota* for I was very thirsty, too.

'"To kill gives much thirst," the man with the wineskin said to me.

'"*Quó va*," I said. "Hast thou killed?"

'"We have killed four," he said proudly. "Not counting the *civiles*. Is it true that thee killed one of the *civiles*, Pilar?"

'"Not one," I said. "I shot into the smoke when the wall fell, as did the others. That is all."

'"Where got thee the pistol, Pilar?"

'"From Pablo. Pablo gave it to me after he killed the *civiles*."

'"Killed he them with this pistol?"

'"With no other," I said. "And then he armed me with it."

'"Can I see it, Pilar? Can I hold it?"

'"Why not, man?" I said, and I took it out from under the rope and handed it to him. But I was wondering why no one else had come out and just then who should come out but Don Guillermo Martín from whose store the flails, the herdsman's clubs, and the wooden pitchforks had been taken. Don Guillermo was a fascist but otherwise there was nothing against him.

'It is true he paid little to those who made the flails but he charged little for them too and if one did not wish to buy flails from Don Guillermo, it was possible to make them for nothing more than the cost of the wood and the leather. He had a rude way of speaking and he was undoubtedly a fascist and a member of their club and he sat at noon and at evening in the cane chairs of their club to read *El Debate*, to have his shoes shined, and to drink vermouth and seltzer and eat roasted almonds, dried shrimps, and anchovies. But one does not kill for that, and I am sure if it had not been for the insults of Don Ricardo Montalvo and the lamentable spectacle of Don Faustino, and the drinking consequent on the emotion of them and the others, someone would have shouted, "That Don Guillermo should go in peace. We have his flails. Let him go."

'Because the people of this town are as kind as they can be cruel and they have a natural sense of justice and a desire to do that which is right. But cruelty had entered into the lines and also drunkenness or the beginning of drunkenness and the lines were not as they were when Don Benito had come out. I do not know how it is in other countries, and no one cares more for the pleasure of drinking than I do, but in Spain drunkenness, when produced by other elements than wine, is a thing of great ugliness and the people do things that they would not have done. Is it not so in your country, *Inglés*?'

'It is so,' Robert Jordan said. 'When I was seven years old and going with my mother to attend a wedding in the state of Ohio at which I was to be the boy of a pair of boy and girl who carried flowers—'

'Did you do that?' asked Maria. 'How nice!'

'In this town a Negro was hanged to a lamp-post and later burned. It was an arc light. A light which lowered from the post to the pavement. And he was hoisted, first by the mechanism which was used to hoist the arc light but this broke—'

'A Negro,' Maria said. 'How barbarous!'

'Were the people drunk?' asked Pilar. 'Were they drunk thus to burn a Negro?'

'I do not know,' Robert Jordan said. 'Because I saw it only looking out from under the blinds of a window in the house which stood on the corner where the arc light was. The street was full of people and when they lifted the Negro up for the second time—'

'If you had only seven years and were in a house, you could not tell if they were drunk or not,' Pilar said.

'As I said, when they lifted the Negro up for the second time, my mother pulled me away from the window, so I saw no more.' Robert Jordan said. 'But since I have had experiences which demonstrate that drunkenness is the same in my country. It is ugly and brutal.'

'You were too young at seven,' Maria said. 'You were too young for such things. I have never seen a Negro except in a circus. Unless the Moors are Negroes.'

'Some are Negroes and some are not,' Pilar said. 'I can talk to you of the Moors.'

'Not as I can,' Maria said. 'Nay, not as I can.'

'Don't speak of such things,' Pilar said. 'It is unhealthy. Where were we?'

'Speaking of the drunkenness of the lines,' Robert Jordan said. 'Go on.'

'It is not fair to say drunkenness,' Pilar said. 'For, yet, they were a long way from drunkenness. But already there was a change in them, and when Don Guillermo came out, standing straight, near-sighted, grey-headed, of medium height, with a shirt with a collar button but no collar, standing there and crossing himself once and looking ahead, but seeing little without his glasses, but walking forward well and calmly, he was an appearance to excite pity. But someone shouted from the line, 'Here, Don Guillermo. Up here, Don Guillermo. In this direction. Here we all have your products."

'They had had such success joking at Don Faustino that they could not see, now, that Don Guillermo was a different thing, and if Don Guillermo was to be killed, he should be killed quickly and with dignity.

'"Don Guillermo," another shouted. "Should we send to the house for thy spectacles?"

'Don Guillermo's house was no house, since he had not much money and was only a fascist to be a snob and to console himself that he must work for little, running a wooden-implement shop. He was a fascist, too, from the religiousness of his wife which he accepted as his own due to his love for her. He lived in an apartment in the building three houses down the square and when Don Guillermo stood there, looking near-sightedly at the lines, the double lines he knew he must enter, a woman started to scream from the balcony of the apartment where he lived. She could see him from the balcony and she was his wife.

'"Guillermo," she cried. "Guillermo. Wait and I will be with thee."

'Don Guillermo turned his head toward where the shouting came from. He could not see her. He tried to say something but he could not. Then he waved his hand in the direction the woman had called from and started to walk between the lines.

'"Guillermo!" she cried. "Guillermo! Oh, Guillermo!" She was holding her hands on the rail of the balcony and shaking back and forth. "Guillermo!"

'Don Guillermo waved his hand again toward the noise and walked into the lines with his head up and you would not have known what he was feeling except for the colour of his face.

'Then some drunkard yelled, "Guillermo!" from the lines, imitating the high cracked voice of his wife and Don Guillermo rushed toward the man, blindly, with tears now running down his cheeks and the man hit him hard across the face with his flail and Don Guillermo sat down from the force of the blow and sat there crying, but not from fear, while the drunkards beat him and one drunkard jumped on top of him, astride his shoulders, and beat him with a bottle. After this many of the men left the lines and their places were taken by the drunkards who had been jeering and saying things in bad taste through the windows of the *Ayuntamiento*.

'I myself had felt much emotion at the shooting of the *guardia civil* by Pablo,' Pilar said. 'It was a thing of great ugliness, but I had thought if this is how it must be, this how it must be, and at least there was no cruelty, only the depriving of life which, as we all have learned in these years, is a thing of ugliness but also a necessity to do if we are to win, and to preserve the Republic.

'When the square had been closed off and the lines formed, I had admired and understood it as a conception of Pablo, although it seemed to me to be somewhat fantastic and that it would be necessary for all that was to be done to be done in good taste if it were not to be repugnant. Certainly if the fascists were to be executed by the people, it was better for all the people to have a part in it, and I wished to share the guilt as much as any, just as I hoped to share in the benefits when the town should be ours. But after Don Guillermo I felt a feeling of shame and distaste, and with the coming of the drunkards and the worthless ones into the lines, and the abstention of those who left the lines as a protest after Don Guillermo, I wished that I might disassociate myself altogether from the lines, and I walked away, across the square, and sat down on a bench under one of the big trees that gave shade there.

'Two peasants from the lines walked over, talking together, and one of them called to me, "What passes with thee, Pilar?"

'"Nothing, man," I told him.

'"Yes," he said. "Speak. What passes?"

'"I think that I have a belly-full," I told him.

'"Us, too," he said and they both sat down on the bench. One of them had a leather wineskin and he handed it to me.

'"Rinse out thy mouth," he said and other said, going on with the talking they had been engaged in, "The worst is that it will bring bad luck. Nobody can tell me that such things as the killing of Don Guillermo in that fashion will not bring bad luck."

'Then the other said, "If it is necessary to kill them all, and I am not convinced of that necessity, let them be killed decently and without mockery."

'"Mockery is justified in the case of Don Faustino," the other said. "Since he was always a farcer and was never a serious man. But to mock such a serious man as Don Guillermo is beyond all right."

'"I have a belly-full," I told him, and it was literally true because I felt an actual sickness in all of me inside and a sweating and a nausea as though I had swallowed bad sea food.

'"Then, nothing," the one peasant said. "We will take no further part in it. But I wonder what happens in the other towns."

'"They have not repaired the telephone wires yet,' I said. "It is a lack that should be remedied."

'"Clearly," he said. "Who knows but what we might be better employed putting the town into a state of defence than massacring people with this slowness and brutality."

'"I will go to speak with Pablo," I told them and I stood up from the bench and started toward the arcade that led to the door of the *Ayuntamiento* from where the lines spread across the square. The lines now were neither straight nor orderly and there was much and very grave drunkenness. Two men had fallen down and lay on their backs in the middle of the square and were passing a bottle back and forth between them. One would take a drink and then shout, "*Viva la Anarquia!*" lying on his back and shouting as though he were a madman. He had a red-and-black handkerchief around his neck. The other shouted, "*Viva la Libertad!*" and kicked his feet in the air and then bellowed, "*Viva la Libertad!*" again. He had a red-and-black handkerchief too and he waved it in one hand and waved the bottle with the other.

'A peasant who had left the lines and now stood in the shade of the arcade looked at them in disgust and said, "They should shout, 'Long live drunkenness.' That's all they believe in."

'"They don't believe even in that," another peasant said. "Those neither understand nor believe in anything."

'"Just then, one of the drunkards got to his feet and raised both arms with his fists clenched over his head and shouted, "Long live Anarchy and Liberty and I obscenity in the milk of the Republic!"

'The other drunkard, who was still lying on his back, took hold of the ankle of the drunkard who was shouting and rolled over, so that the shouting drunkard fell with him, and they rolled over together and then sat up and the one who had pulled the other down put his arm around the shouter's neck and then handed the shouter a bottle and kissed the red-and-black handkerchief he wore and they both drank together.

'Just then, a yelling went up from the lines and, looking up the arcade, I could not see who it was that was coming out because the man's head did not show above the heads of those crowded about the door of the *Ayuntamiento*. All I could see was that someone was being pushed out by Pablo and Cuatro Dedos with their shotguns but I could not see who it was and I moved on close toward the lines where they were packed against the door to try to see.

'There was much pushing now and the chairs and the tables of the fascists' café had been overturned except for one table on which a drunkard was lying with his head hanging down and his mouth open and I picked up a chair and set it against one of the pillars and mounted on it so that I could see over the heads of the crowd.

'The man who was being pushed out by Pablo and Cuatro Dedos was Don Anastasio Rivas, who was an undoubted fascist and the fattest man in the town. He was a grain buyer and the agent for several insurance companies and he also loaned money at high rates of interest. Standing on the chair, I saw him walk down the steps and toward the lines, his fat neck bulging over the back of the collar band of his shirt, and his bald head shining in the sun, but he never entered them because there was a shout, not as of different men shouting, but of all of them. It was an ugly noise and was the cry of the drunken lines all yelling together and the lines broke with the rush of men toward him and I saw Don Anastasio throw himself down with his hands over his head and then you could not see him for the men piled on top of him. And when the men got up from him, Don Anastasio was dead from his head being beaten against the stone flags of the paving of the arcade and there were no more lines but only a mob.

'"We're going in," they commenced to shout. "We're going in after them."

'"He's too heavy to carry," a man kicked at the body of Don Anastasio, who was lying there on his face. "Let him stay there."

'"Why should we lug that tub of tripe to the cliff? Let him lie there."

'"We are going to enter and finish with them inside," a man shouted. "We're going in."

'"Why wait all day in the sun?" another yelled. "Come on. Let us go."

'The mob was now pressing into the arcade. They were shouting and pushing and they made a noise now like an animal and they were all shouting, "Open up! Open up! Open up!" for the guards had shut the doors of the *Ayuntamiento* when the lines broke.

'Standing on the chair, I could see in through the barred window into the hall of the *Ayuntamiento* and in there it was as it had been before. The priest was standing, and those who were left were kneeling in a half circle around him and they were all praying. Pablo was sitting on the big table in front of the Mayor's chair with his shotgun slung over his back. His legs were hanging down from the table and he was rolling a cigarette. Cuatro Dedos was sitting in the Mayor's chair with his feet on the table and he was smoking a cigarette. All the guards were sitting in different chairs of the administration, holding their guns. The key to the big door was on the table beside Pablo.

'The mob was shouting, "Open up! Open up! Open up!" as though it were a chant and Pablo was sitting there as though he did not hear them. He said something to the priest but I could not hear what he said for the noise of the mob.

'The priest, as before, did not answer him but kept on praying. With many people pushing me, I moved the chair close against the wall, shoving it ahead of me as they shoved me from behind. I stood on the chair with my face close against the bars of the window and held on by the bars. A man climbed on the chair too and stood with his arms around mine, holding the wider bars.

'"The chair will break," I said to him.

'"What does it matter?" he said. "Look at them. Look at them pray."

'His breath on my neck smelled like the smell of the mob, sour, like vomit on paving stones and the smell of drunkenness, and then he put his mouth against the opening in the bars with his head over my shoulder, and shouted, "Open up! Open up!" and it was as though the mob were on my back as a devil is on your back in a dream.

'Now the mob was pressed tight against the door so that those in front were being crushed by all the others who were pressing and from the square a big drunkard in a black smock with a red-and-black handkerchief around his neck ran and threw himself against the press of the mob and fell forward on to the pressing men and then stood up and backed away and then ran forward again and threw himself against the backs of those men who were pushing, shouting, "Long live me and long live Anarchy."

'As I watched, this man turned away from the crowd and went and sat down and drank from a bottle and then, while he was sitting down, he saw Don Anastasio, who was still lying face down on the stones, but much trampled now, and the drunkard got up and went over to Don Anastasio and leaned over and poured out of the bottle on to the head of Don Anastasio and on to his clothes, and then he took a matchbox out of his pocket and lit several matches, trying to make a fire with Don Anastasio. But the wind was blowing hard now and it blew the matches out and after a little the big drunkard sat there by Don Anastasio, shaking his head and drinking out of the bottle and every once in a while, leaning over and patting Don Anastasio on the shoulders of his dead body.

'All this time the mob was shouting to open up and the man on the chair with me was holding tight to the bars of the window and shouting to open up until it deafened me with his voice roaring past my ear and his breath foul on me and I looked away from watching the drunkard who had been trying to set fire to Don Anastasio and into the hall of the *Ayuntamiento* again; and it was just as it had been. They were still praying as they had been, the men all kneeling, with their shirts open, some with their heads down, others with their heads up, looking toward the priest and toward the crucifix that he held, and the priest praying fast and hard and looking out over their heads, and behind them Pablo, with his cigarette now lighted, was sitting there on the table swinging his legs, his shotgun slung over his back, and he was playing with the key.

'I saw Pablo speak to the priest again, leaning forward from the table and I could not hear what he said for the shouting. But the priest did not answer him but went on praying. Then a man stood up from among the half circle of those who were praying and I saw he wanted to go out. It was Don José Castro, whom everyone called Don Pepe, a confirmed fascist, and a dealer in horses, and he stood up now small, neat-looking even unshaven and wearing a pyjama top tucked into a pair of grey-striped trousers. He kissed the crucifix and the priest blessed him and he stood up and looked at Pablo and jerked his head toward the door.

'Pablo shook his head and went on smoking. I could see Don Pepe say something to Pablo but could not hear it. Pablo did not answer; he simply shook his head again and nodded toward the door.

'Then I saw Don Pepe look full at the door and realized that he had not known it was locked. Pablo showed him the key and he stood looking at it an instant and then he turned and went and knelt down again. I saw the priest look around at Pablo and Pablo grinned at him and showed him the key and the priest seemed to realize for the first time that the door was locked and he seemed as though he started to shake his head, but he only inclined it and went back to praying.

'I do not know how they could not have understood the door was locked unless it was that they were so concentrated on their praying and their own thoughts; but now they certainly understood and they understood the shouting and they must have known now, that all was changed. But they remained the same as before.

'By now the shouting was so that you could hear nothing and the drunkard who stood on the chair with me shook with his hands at the bars and yelled, "Open up! Open up!" until he was hoarse.

'I watched Pablo speak to the priest again and the priest did not answer. Then I saw Pablo unsling his shotgun and he reached over and tapped the priest on the shoulder with it. The priest paid no attention to him and I saw Pablo shake his head. Then he spoke over his shoulder to Cuatro Dedos and Cuatro Dedos spoke to the other guards and they all stood up and walked back to the far end of the room and stood there with their shotguns.

'I saw Pablo say something to Cuatro Dedos and he moved over two tables and some benches and the guards stood behind them with their shotguns. It made a barricade in that corner of the room. Pablo leaned over and tapped the priest on the shoulder again with the shotgun and the priest did not pay any attention to him but I saw Don Pepe watching him while the others paid no attention but went on praying. Pablo shook his head and, seeing Don Pepe looking at him, he shook his head at Don Pepe and showed him the key, holding it up in his hand. Don Pepe understood and he dropped his head and commenced to pray very fast.

'Pablo swung his legs down from the table and walked around it to the big chair of the Mayor on the raised platform behind the long council table. He sat down in it and rolled himself a cigarette, all the time watching the fascists who were praying with the priest. You could not see any expression on his face at all. The key was on the table in front of him. It was a big key of iron, over a foot long. Then Pablo called to the guards something I could not hear and one guard went down to the door. I could see them all praying faster than ever and I knew that they all knew now.

'Pablo said something to the priest but the priest did not answer. Then Pablo leaned forward, picked up the key and tossed it underhand to the guard at the door. The guard caught it and Pablo smiled at him. Then the guard put the key in the door, turned it, and pulled the door toward him, ducking behind it as the mob rushed in.

'I saw them come in and just then the drunkard on the chair with me commenced to shout, "Ayee! Ayee! Ayee!" and pushed his head forward so I could not see and then he shouted "Kill them! Kill them! Club them! Kill them!" and he pushed me aside with his two arms and I could see nothing.

'I hit my elbow into his belly and I said, "Drunkard, whose chair is this? Let me see."

'But he just kept shaking his hands and arms against the bars and shouting, "Kill them! Club them! Club them! that's it. Club them! Kill them! *Carbrones! Cabrones! Cabrones!*"

'I hit him hard with my elbow and said, "*Cabron!* Drunkard! Let me see."

'Then he put both his hands on my head to push me down and so he might see better and leaned all his weight on my head and went on shouting, "Club them! that's it. Club them!"

'"Club yourself," I said, and I hit him hard where it would hurt him and it hurt him and he dropped his hands from my head and grabbed himself and said, "*No hay derecho, mujer.* This, woman, you have no right to do." And in that moment, looking through the bars, I saw the hall full of men flailing away with clubs and striking with flails, and poking and striking and pushing and heaving against people with the white wooden pitchforks that now were red and with their tines broken, and this was going on all over the room while Pablo sat in the big chair with his shotgun on his knees, watching, and they were shouting and clubbing and stabbing and men were screaming as horses scream in a fire. And I saw the priest with his skirts tucked up scrambling over a bench and those after him were chopping at him with the sickles and the reaping hooks and then someone had hold of his robe and there was another scream and another scream and I saw two men chopping into his back with sickles while a third man held the skirt of his robe and the priest's arms were up and he was clinging to the back of a chair and then the chair I was standing on broke and the drunkard and I were on the pavement that smelled of spilled wine and vomit and the drunkard was shaking his finger at me and saying, "*No hay derecho mujer, no hay derecho.* You could have done me an injury," and the people were trampling over us to get into the hall of the *Ayuntamiento* and all I could see was legs of people going in the doorway and the drunkard sitting there facing me and holding himself where I had hit him.

'That was the end of the killing of the fascists in our town and I was glad I did not see more of it and, but for that drunkard, I would have seen it all. So he served some good because in the *Ayuntamiento* it was a thing one is sorry to have seen.

'But the other drunkard was something rarer still. As we got up after the breaking of the chair, and the people were still crowding into the *Ayuntamiento*, I saw this drunkard of the square with his red-and-black scarf, again pouring something over Don Anastasio. He was shaking his head from side to side and it was very hard for him to sit up, but he was pouring and lighting matches and then pouring and lighting matches and I walked over to him and said, "What are you doing, shameless?"

'"*Nada, mujer, nada,*" he said, "Let me alone."

'And perhaps because I was standing there so that my legs made a shelter from the wind, the match caught and a blue flame began to run up the shoulder of the coat of Don Anastasio and to the back of his neck and the drunkard put his head up and shouted in a huge voice, "They're burning the dead! They're burning the dead!"

'"Who?" somebody said.

'"Where?" shouted someone else.

'"Here," bellowed the drunkard. "Exactly here!"

'Then someone hit the drunkard a great blow alongside the head with a flail and he fell back, and lying on the ground, he looked up at the man who had hit him and then shut his eyes and crossed his hands on his chest, and laid there beside Don Anastasio as though he were asleep. The man did not hit him again and he lay there and he was still there when they picked up Don Anastasio and put him with the others in the cart that hauled them all over to the cliff where they were thrown over that evening with the others after there had been a cleaning up in the *Ayuntamiento*. It would have been better for the town if they had thrown over twenty or thirty of the drunkards, especially those of the red-and-black scarves, and if we ever have another revolution I believe they should be destroyed at the start. But then we did not know this. But in the next days we were to learn.

'But that night we did not know what was to come. After the slaying in the *Ayuntamiento* there was no more killing but we could not have a meeting that night because there were too many drunkards. It was impossible to obtain order and so the meeting was postponed until the next day.

'That night I slept with Pablo. I should not say this to you, *guapa*, but on the other hand, it is good for you to know everything and at least what I tell you is true. Listen to this, *Inglés*. It is very curious.

'As I say, that night we ate and it was very curious. It was as after a storm or a flood or a battle and everyone was tired and no one spoke much. I, myself, felt hollow and not well and I was full of shame and a sense of wrongdoing, and I had a great feeling of oppression and of bad to come, as this morning after the planes. And certainly, bad came within three days.

'Pablo, when we ate, spoke little.

'"Did you like it, Pilar?" he asked, finally, with his mouth full of roast young goat. We were eating at the inn from where the buses leave and the room was crowded and people were singing and there was difficulty serving.

'"No," I said. "Except for Don Faustino, I did not like it."

'"I liked it," he said.

'"All of it?" I asked him.

'"All of it," he said and cut himself a big piece of bread with his knife and commenced to mop up gravy with it. "All of it, except the priest."

'"You didn't like it about the priest?" because I knew he hated priests even worse than he hated fascists.

'"He was a disillusionment to me," Pablo said sadly.

'So many people were singing that we had to almost shout to hear one another.

'"Why?"

'"He died very badly," Pablo said. "He had very little dignity."

'"How did you want him to have dignity when he was being chased by the mob," I said. "I thought he had much dignity all the time before. All the dignity that one could have."

'"Yes," Pablo said. "But in the last minute he was frightened."

'"Who wouldn't be?" I said. "Did you see what they were chasing him with?"

'"Why would I not see?" Pablo said. "But I find he died badly."

'"In such circumstances anyone dies badly," I told him. "What do you want for your money? Everything that happened in the *Ayuntamiento* was scabrous."

'"Yes," said Pablo. "There was little organization. But a priest. He has an example to set."

'"I thought you hated priests."

'"Yes," said Pablo and cut some more bread. "But a *Spanish* priest. A *Spanish* priest should die very well."

'"I think he died well enough," I said. "Being deprived of all formality."

'"No," Pablo said. "To me he was a great disillusionment. All day I had waited for the death of the priest. I had thought he would be the last to enter the lines. I awaited it with great anticipation. I expected something of a culmination. I had never seen a priest die."

'"There is time," I said sarcastically. "Only to-day did the movement start."

'"No," he said. "I am disillusioned."

'"Now," I said, "I suppose you will lose your faith."

'"You do not understand, Pilar," he said. "He was a *Spanish* priest."

'"What people the Spaniards are," I said to him. And what a people they are for pride, eh, *Inglés*? What a people.'

'We must get on,' Robert Jordan said. He looked at the sun. 'It's nearly noon.'

'Yes,' Pilar said. 'We will go now. But let me tell you about Pablo. That night he said to me, "Pilar, to-night we will do nothing."

'"Good," I told him. "That pleases me."

'"I think it would be bad taste after the killing of so many people."

'"*Qué va*," I told him. "What a saint you are. You think I lived years with bullfighters not to know how they are after the Corrida?"

'"Is it true, Pilar?" he asked me.

'"When did I lie to you?" I told him.

'"It is true, Pilar, I am a finished man this night. You do not reproach me?"

'"No, *hombre*," I said to him. "But don't kill people every day, Pablo."

'And he slept that night like a baby and I woke him in the morning at daylight but I could not sleep that night and I got up and sat in a chair and looked out of the window and I could see the square in the moonlight where the lines had been and across the square the trees shining in the moonlight, and the darkness of their shadows, and the benches bright too in the moonlight, and the scattered bottles shining, and beyond the edge of the cliff where they had all been thrown. And there was no sound but the splashing of the water in the fountain and I sat there and I thought we have begun badly.

'The window was open and up the square from the Fonda I could hear a woman crying. I went out on the balcony standing there in my bare feet on the iron and the moon shone on the faces of all the buildings of the square and the crying was coming from the balcony of the house of Don Guillermo. It was his wife and she was on the balcony kneeling and crying.

'Then I went back inside the room and I sat there and I did not wish to think, for that was the worst day of my life until one other day.'

'What was the other?' Maria asked.

'Three days later when the fascists took the town.'

'Do not tell me about it,' said Maria. 'I do not want to hear it. This is enough. This was too much.'

'I told you that you should not have listened,' Pilar said. 'See, I did not want you to hear it. Now you will have bad dreams.'

'No,' said Maria. 'But I do not want to hear more.'

'I wish you would tell me of it sometime,' Robert Jordan said.

'I will,' Pilar said. 'But it is bad for Maria.'

'I don't want to hear it,' Maria said pitifully. 'Please Pilar. And do not tell it if I am there, for I might listen in spite of myself.'

Her lips were working and Robert Jordan thought she would cry.

'Please, Pilar, do not tell it.'

'Do not worry, little cropped head,' Pilar said. 'Do not worry. But I will tell the *Inglés* sometime.'

'But I want to be there when he is there,' Maria said. 'Oh, Pilar, do not tell it at all.'

'I will tell it when thou art working.'

'No. No. Please. Let us not tell it at all,' Maria said.

'It is only fair to tell it since I have told what we did,' Pilar said. 'But you shall never hear it.'

'Are there no pleasant things to speak of?' Maria said. 'Do we have to talk always of horrors?'

'This afternoon,' Pilar said, 'thou and the *Inglés*. The two of you can speak of what you wish.'

'Then that the afternoon should come,' Maria said. 'That it should come flying.'

'It will come,' Pilar told her. 'It will come flying and go the same way and to-morrow will fly, too.'

'This afternoon,' Maria said. 'This afternoon. That this afternoon should come.'

11

As they came up, still deep in the shadow of the pines, after dropping down from the high meadow into the wooded valley and climbing up it on a trail that paralleled the stream and then left it to gain, steeply, the top of a rimrock formation, a man with a carbine stepped out from behind a tree.

'Halt,' he said. Then, '*Hola*, Pilar. Who is this with thee?'

'An *Inglés*,' Pilar said. 'But with a Christian name–Roberto. And what an obscenity of steepness it is to arrive here.'

'*Salud, Camarada*,' the guard said to Robert Jordan and put out his hand. 'Are you well?'

'Yes,' said Robert Jordan. 'And thee?'

'Equally,' the guard said. He was very young, with a light build, thin, rather hawk-nosed face, high cheekbones and grey eyes. He wore no hat, his hair was black and shaggy and his handclasp was strong and friendly. His eyes were friendly too.

'Hello, Maria,' he said to the girl. 'You did not tire yourself?'

'*Qué va*, Joaquín' the girl said. 'We have sat and talked more than we have walked.'

'Are you the dynamiter?' Joaquín asked. 'We have heard you were here.'

'We passed the night at Pablo's,' Robert Jordan said. 'Yes, I am the dynamiter.'

'We are glad to see you,' Joaquín said. 'Is it for a train?'

'Were you at the last train?' Robert Jordan asked and smiled.

'Was I not!' Joaquín said. 'That's where we got this,' he grinned at Maria. 'You are pretty now,' he said to Maria. 'Have they told thee how pretty?'

'Shut up, Joaquín, and thank you very much,' Maria said. 'You'd be pretty with a haircut.'

'I carried thee,' Joaquín told the girl. 'I carried thee over my shoulder.'

'As did many others,' Pilar said in the deep voice. 'Who didn't carry her? Where is the old man?'

'At the camp.'

'Where was he last night?'

'In Segovia.'

'Did he bring news?'

'Yes,' Joaquín said, 'there is news.'

'Good or bad?'

'I believe bad.'

'Did you see the planes?'

'Ay,' said Joaquín and shook his head. 'Don't talk to me of that. Comrade Dynamiter, what planes were those?'

'Heinkel one-eleven bombers. Heinkel and Fiat pursuit,' Robert Jordan told him.

'What were the big ones with the low wings?'

'Heinkel one-elevens.'

'By any names they are as bad,' Joaquín said. 'But I am delaying you. I will take you to the commander.'

'The commander?' Pilar asked.

Joaquín nodded seriously. 'I like it better than "chief",' he said. 'It is more military.'

'You are militarizing heavily,' Pilar said and laughed at him.

'No,' Joaquín said. 'But I like military terms because it makes orders clearer and for better discipline.'

'Here is one according to thy taste, *Inglés*,' Pilar said. 'A very serious boy.'

'Should I carry thee?' Joaquín asked the girl and put his arm on her shoulder and smiled in her face.

'Once was enough,' Maria told him. 'Thank you just the same.'

'Can you remember it?' Joaquín asked her.

'I can remember being carried,' Maria said. 'By you, no. I remember the gipsy because he dropped me so many times. But I thank thee, Joaquín, and I'll carry thee sometime.'

'I can remember it well enough,' Joaquín said. 'I can remember holding thy two legs and thy belly was on my shoulder and thy head over my back and thy arms hanging down against my back.'

'Thou hast much memory,' Maria said and smiled at him. 'I remember nothing of that. Neither thy arms nor thy shoulders nor thy back.'

'Do you want to know something?' Joaquín asked her.

'What is it?'

'I was glad thou wert hanging over my back when the shots were coming from behind us.'

'What a swine,' Maria said. 'And was it for this the gipsy too carried me so much?'

'For that and to hold on to thy legs.'

'My heroes,' Maria said. 'My saviours.'

'Listen, *guapa*,' Pilar told her. 'This boy carried thee much, and in that moment thy legs said nothing to anyone. In that moment only the bullets talked clearly. And if he would have dropped thee he could soon have been out of range of the bullets.'

'I have thanked him,' Maria said. 'And I will carry him sometime. Allow us to joke. I do not have to cry, do I, because he carried me.'

'I'd have dropped thee,' Joaquín went on teasing her. 'But I was afraid Pilar would shoot me.'

'I shoot no one,' Pilar said.

'*No hace falta*,' Joaquín told her. 'You don't need to. You scare them to death with your mouth.'

'What a way to speak,' Pilar told him. 'And you used to be such a polite little boy. What did you do before the movement, little boy?'

'Very little,' Joaquín said. 'I was sixteen.'

'But what, exactly?'

'A few pairs of shoes from time to time.'

'Make them?'

'No. Shine them.'

'*Qué va*,' said Pilar. 'There is more to it than that.' She looked at his brown face, his lithe build, his shock of hair, and the quick heel-and-toe way that he walked. 'Why did you fail at it?'

'Fail at what?'

'What? You know what. You're growing the pigtail now.'

'I guess it was fear,' the boy said.

'You've a nice figure,' Pilar told him. 'But the face isn't much. So it was fear, was it? You were all right at the train.'

'I have no fear of them now,' the boy said. 'None. And we have seen much worse things and more dangerous than the bulls. It is clear no bull is as dangerous as a machine-gun. But if I were in the ring with one now I do not know if I could dominate my legs.'

'He wanted to be bullfighter,' Pilar explained to Robert Jordan. 'But he was afraid.'

'Do you like the bulls, Comrade Dynamiter?' Joaquín grinned, showing white teeth.

'Very much,' Robert Jordan said. 'Very, very much.'

'Have you seen them in Valladolid?' asked Joaquín.

'Yes. In September at the feria.'

'That's my town,' Joaquín said. 'What a fine town but how the *buena gente*, the good people of that town, have suffered in this war.' Then, his face grave, 'There they shot my father. My mother. My brother-in-law and now my sister.'

'What barbarians,' Robert Jordan said.

How many times had he heard this? How many times had he watched people say it with difficulty? How many times had he seen their eyes fill and their throats harden with the difficulty of saying my father, or my brother, or my mother, or my sister? He could not remember how many times he had heard them mention their dead in this way. Nearly always they spoke as this boy did now; suddenly and apropos of the mention of the town and always you said, 'What barbarians.'

You only heard the statement of the loss. You did not see the father fall as Pilar made him see the fascists die in that story she had told by the stream. You knew the father died in some courtyard, or against some wall, or in some field or orchard, or at night, in the lights of a truck, beside some road. You had seen the lights of the car from the hills and heard the shooting and afterwards you had come down to the road and found the bodies. You did not see the mother shot, nor the sister, nor the brother. You heard about it; you heard the shots; and you saw the bodies.

Pilar had made him see it in that town.

If that woman could only write. He would try to write it and if he had luck and could remember it perhaps he could get it down as she told it. God, how she could tell a story. She's better than Quevedo, he thought. He never wrote the death of any Don Faustino as well as she told it. I wish I could write well enough to write that story, he thought. What we did. Not what the others did to us. He knew enough about that. He knew plenty about that behind the lines. But you had to have known the people before. You had to know what they had been in the village.

Because of our mobility and because we did not have to stay afterwards to take the punishment we never knew how anything really ended, he thought. You stayed with a peasant and his family. You came at night and ate with them. In the day you were hidden and the next night you were gone. You did your job and cleared out. The next time you came that way you heard that they had been shot. It was as simple as that.

But you were always gone when it happened. The *partizans* did their damage and pulled out. The peasants stayed and took the punishment. I've always known about the other, he thought. What we did to them at the start. I've always known it and hated it and I have heard it mentioned shamelessly and shamefully, bragged of, boasted of, defended, explained and denied. But that damned woman made me see it as though I had been there.

Well, he thought, it is part of one's education. It will be quite an education when it's finished. You learn in this war if you listen. You most certainly did. He was lucky that he had lived parts of ten years in Spain before the war. They trusted you on the language, principally. They trusted you on understanding the language completely and speaking it idiomatically and having a knowledge of the different places. A Spaniard was only really loyal to his village in the end. First Spain of course, then his own tribe, then his province, then his village, his family and finally his trade. If you knew Spanish he was prejudiced in your favour, if you knew his province it was that much better, but if you knew his village and his trade you were in as far as any foreigner ever could be. He never felt like a foreigner in Spanish and they did not really treat him like a foreigner most of the time; only when they turned on you.

Of course they turned on you. They turned on you often but they always turned on everyone. They turned on themselves, too. If you had three together, two would unite against you, and then the two would start to betray each other. Not always, but often enough for you to take enough cases and start to draw it as a conclusion.

This was no way to think; but who censored his thinking; Nobody but himself. He would not think himself into any defeatism. The first thing was to win the war. If we did not win the war everything was lost. But he noticed, and listened to, and remembered everything. He was serving in a war and he gave absolute loyalty and as complete performance as he could give while he was serving. But nobody owned his mind, nor his faculties for seeing and hearing, and if he were going to form judgments he would form them afterwards. And there would be plenty of material to draw them from. There was plenty already. There was a little too much sometimes.

Look at the Pilar woman, he thought. No matter what comes, if there is time, I must make her tell me the rest of that story. Look at her walking along with those two kids. You could not get three better-looking products of Spain than those. She is like a mountain and the boy and the girl are like young trees. The old trees are all cut down and the young trees are growing clean like that. In spite of what has happened to the two of them they look as fresh and clean and new and untouched as though they had never heard of misfortune. But according to Pilar, Maria has just gotten sound again. She must have been in an awful shape.

He remembered a Belgian boy in the Eleventh Brigade who had enlisted with five other boys from his village. It was a village of about two hundred people and the boy had never been away from the village before. When he first saw the boy out, at Hans' Brigade Staff, the other five from the village had all been killed and the boy was in very bad shape and they were using him as an orderly to wait on table at the staff. He had a big, blond, ruddy Flemish face and huge awkward peasant hands and he moved, with the dishes, as powerfully and awkwardly as a draught horse. But he cried all the time. All during the meal he cried with no noise at all.

You looked up and there he was, crying. If you asked for the wine, he cried and if you passed your plate for stew, he cried; turning away his head. Then he would stop; but if you looked up at him, tears would start coming again. Between courses he cried in the kitchen. Everyone was very gentle with him. But it did no good. He would have to find out what became of him and whether he ever cleared up and was fit for soldiering again.

Maria was sound enough now. She seemed so anyway. But he was no psychiatrist. Pilar was the psychiatrist. It probably had been good for them to have been together last night. Yes, unless it stopped. It certainly had been good for him. He felt fine to-day; sound and good and unworried and happy. The show looked bad enough but he was awfully lucky, too. He had been in others that announced themselves badly. Announced themselves; that was thinking in Spanish. Maria was lovely.

Look at her, he said to himself. Look at her.

He looked at her striding happily in the sun; her khaki shirt open at the neck. She walks like a colt moves, he thought. You do not run on to something like that. Such things don't happen. Maybe it never did happen, he thought. Maybe you dreamed it or made it up and it never did happen. Maybe it is like the dreams you have when someone you have seen in the cinema comes to your bed at night and is so kind and lovely. He'd slept with them all that way when he was asleep in bed. He could remember Garbo still, and Harlow. Yes, Harlow many times. Maybe it was like those dreams.

But he could still remember the time Garbo came to his bed the night before the attack at Pozoblanco and she was wearing a soft silky wool sweater when he put his arm around her and when she leaned forward her hair swept forward and over his face and she said why had he never told her that he loved her when she had loved him all this time? She was not shy, nor cold, nor distant. She was just lovely to hold and kind and lovely and like the old days with Jack Gilbert and it was as true as though it happened and he loved her much more than Harlow though Garbo was only there once while Harlow–maybe this was like those dreams.

Maybe it isn't too, he said to himself. Maybe I could reach over and touch that Maria now, he said to himself. Maybe you are afraid to he said to himself. Maybe you would find out that it never happened and it was not true and it was something you made up like those dreams about the people of the cinema or how all your old girls come back and sleep in that robe at night on all the bare floors, in the straw of the haybarns, the stables, the *corrales* and *cortijos*, the woods, the garages, the trucks and all the hills of Spain. They all came to that robe when he was asleep and they were all much nicer than they ever had been in life. Maybe it was like that. Maybe you would be afraid to touch her to see if it was true. Maybe you would, and probably it is something that you made up or that you dreamed.

He took a step across the trail and put his hand on the girl's arm. Under his fingers he felt the smoothness of her arm in the worn khaki. She looked at him and smiled.

'Hello, Maria,' he said.

'Hello, *Inglés*,' she answered and he saw her tawny brown face and the yellow-grey eyes and the full lips smiling and the cropped sunburned hair and she lifted her face at him and smiled in his eyes. It was true all right.

Now they were in sight of El Sordo's camp in the last of the pines, where there was a rounded gulch-head shaped like an upturned basin. All these limestone upper basins must be full of caves, he thought. There are two caves there ahead. The scrub pines growing in the rock hide them well. This is as good or a better place than Pablo's.

'How was this shooting of thy family?' Pilar was saying to Joaquín.

'Nothing, woman,' Joaquín said. 'They were of the left as many others in Valladolid. When the fascists purified the town they shot first the father. He had voted Socialist. Then they shot the mother. She had voted the same. It was the first time she had ever voted. After that they shot the husband of one of the sisters. He was a member of the syndicate of tramway drivers. Clearly he could not drive a tram without belonging to the syndicate. But he was without politics. I knew him well. He was even a little bit shameless. I do not think he was even a good comrade. Then the husband of the other girl, the other sister, who was also in the trams, had gone to the hills as I had. They thought she knew where he was. But she did not. So they shot her because she would not tell them where he was.'

'What barbarians,' said Pilar. 'Where is El Sordo? I do not see him.'

'He is here. He is probably inside,' answered Joaquín and stopping now, and resting the rifle butt on the ground, said, 'Pilar, listen to me. And thou, Maria. Forgive me if I have molested you speaking of things of the family. I know that all have the same troubles and it is more valuable not to speak of them.'

'That you should speak,' Pilar said. 'For what are we born if not to aid one another? And to listen and say nothing is a cold enough aid.'

'But it can molest the Maria. She has too many things of her own.'

'*Qué va*,' Maria said. 'Mine are such a big bucket that yours falling in will never fill it. I am sorry, Joaquín, and I hope thy sister is well.'

'So far she's all right,' Joaquín said. 'They have her in prison and it seems they do not mistreat her much.'

'Are there others in the family?' Robert Jordan asked.

'No,' the boy said. 'Me. Nothing more. Except the brother-in-law who went to the hills and I think he is dead.'

'Maybe he is all right,' Maria said. 'Maybe he is with a band in other mountains.'

'For me he is dead,' Joaquín said. 'He was never too good at getting about and he was conductor of a tram and that is not the best preparation for the hills. I doubt if he could last a year. He was somewhat weak in the chest too.'

'But he may be all right,' Maria put her arm on his shoulder.

'Certainly, girl. Why not?' said Joaquín.

As the boy stood there, Maria reached up, put her arms around his neck and kissed him. Joaquín turned his head away because he was crying.

'That is as a brother,' Maria said to him. 'I kiss thee as a brother.'

The boy shook his head, crying without making any noise.

'I am thy sister,' Maria said. 'And I love thee and thou hast a family. We are all thy family.'

'Including the *Inglés*,' boomed Pilar. 'Isn't it true, *Inglés*?'

'Yes,' Robert Jordan said to the boy. 'We are all thy family, Joaquín.'

'He's your brother,' Pilar said. 'Hey, *Inglés*?'

Robert Jordan put his arm around the boy's shoulder. 'We are all brothers,' he said. The boy shook his head.

'I am ashamed to have spoken,' he said. 'To speak of such things makes it more difficult for all. I am ashamed of molesting you.'

'I obscenity in the milk of thy shame,' Pilar said in her deep lovely voice.

'And if the Maria kisses thee again I will commence kissing thee myself. It's years since I've kissed a bullfighter, even an unsuccessful one like thee. I would like to kiss an unsuccessful bullfighter turned Communist. Hold him, *Inglés*, till I get a good kiss at him.'

'*Deja*,' the boy said and turned away sharply. 'Leave me alone. I am all right and I am ashamed.'

He stood there, getting his face under control. Maria put her hand in Robert Jordan's. Pilar stood with her hands on her hips looking at the boy mockingly now.

'When I kiss thee,' she said to him, 'it will not be as any sister. This trick of kissing as a sister.'

'It is not necessary to joke,' the boy said. 'I told you I am all right, I am sorry that I spoke.'

'Well then, let us go and see the old man,' Pilar said. 'I tire myself with such emotion.'

The boy looked at her. From his eyes you could see he was suddenly very hurt.

'Not thy emotion,' Pilar said to him. 'Mine. What a tender thing thou art for a bullfighter.'

'I was a failure,' Joaquín said. 'You don't have to keep insisting on it.'

'But you are growing the pigtail another time.'

'Yes, and why not? Fighting stock serves best for that purpose economically. It gives employment to many and the State will control it. And perhaps now I would not be afraid.'

'Perhaps not,' Pilar said. 'Perhaps not.'

'Why do you speak in such a brutal manner, Pilar?' Maria said to her. 'I love thee very much but thou art acting very barbarous.'

'It is possible that I am barbarous,' Pilar said. 'Listen, *Inglés*. Do you know what you are going to say to El Sordo?'

'Yes.'

'Because he is a man of few words unlike me and thee and this sentimental menagerie.'

'Why do you talk thus?' Maria asked again, angrily.

'I don't know,' said Pilar as she strode along. 'Why do you think?'

'I do not know.'

'At times many things tire me,' Pilar said angrily. 'You understand? And one of them is to have forty-eight years. You hear me? Forty-eight years and an ugly face. And another is to see panic in the face of a failed bullfighter of Communist tendencies when I say, as a joke, I might kiss him.'

'It's not true, Pilar,' the boy said. 'You did not see that.'

'*Qué va*, it's not true. And I obscenity in the milk of all of you. Ah, there he is. *Hola*, Santiago! *Qué tal*?'

The man to whom Pilar spoke was short and heavy, brown-faced, with broad cheekbones; grey haired, with wide-set yellow-brown eyes, a thin-bridged, hooked nose like an Indian's, a long upper lip and a wide, thin mouth. He was clean shaven and he walked toward them from the mouth of the cave, moving with the bow-legged walk that went with his cattle herdsman's breeches and boots. The day was warm but he had on a sheep's wool-lined short leather jacket buttoned up to the neck. He put out a big brown hand to Pilar. '*Hola*, woman,' he said. '*Hola*,' he said to Robert Jordan and shook his hand and looked him keenly in the face. Robert Jordan saw his eyes were yellow as a cat's and flat as a reptile's eyes are. '*Guapa*,' he said to Maria and patted her shoulder.

'Eaten?' he asked Pilar. She shook her head.

'Eat,' he said and looked at Robert Jordan. 'Drink?' he asked, making a motion with his hand decanting his thumb downward.

'Yes, thanks.'

'Good,' El Sordo said. 'Whisky?'

'You have whisky?'

El Sordo nodded. '*Inglés*?' he asked. 'Not *Ruso*?'

'*Americano*.'

'Few Americans here,' he said.

'Now more.'

'Less bad. North or South?'

'North.'

'Same as *Inglés*. When blow bridge?'

'You know about the bridge?'

El Sordo nodded.

'Day after to-morrow morning.'

'Good,' said El Sordo.

'Pablo?' he asked Pilar.

She shook her head. El Sordo grinned.

'Go away,' he said to Maria and grinned again. 'Come back,' he looked at a large watch he pulled out on a leather thong from inside his coat. 'Half an hour.'

He motioned to them to sit down on a flattened log that served as a bench and looking at Joaquín, jerked his thumb down the trail in the direction they had come from.

'I'll walk down with Joaquín and come back,' Maria said.

El Sordo went into the cave and came out with a pinch bottle of Scotch whisky and three glasses. The bottle was under one arm, the three glasses were in the hand of that arm, a finger in each glass, and his other hand was around the neck of an earthenware jar of water. He put the glasses and the bottle down on the log and set the jug on the ground.

'No ice,' he said to Robert Jordan and handed him the bottle.

'I don't want any,' Pilar said and covered her glass with her hand.

'Ice last night on ground,' El Sordo said and grinned. 'All melt. Ice up there,' El Sordo said and pointed to the snow that showed on the bare crest of the mountains. 'Too far.'

Robert Jordan started to pour into El Sordo's glass but the deaf man shook his head and made a motion for the other to pour for himself.

Robert Jordan poured a big drink of whisky into the glass and El Sordo watched him eagerly and when he had finished, handed him the water jug and Robert Jordan filled the glass with the cold water that ran in a stream from the earthenware spout as he tipped up the jug.

El Sordo poured himself half a glassful and filled the glass with water.

'Wine?' he asked Pilar.

'No. Water.'

'Take it,' he said. 'No good,' he said to Robert Jordan and grinned. 'Knew many English. Always much whisky.'

'Where?'

'Ranch,' El Sordo said. 'Friends of boss.'

'Where do you get the whisky?'

'What?' he could not hear.

'You have to shout,' Pilar said. 'Into the other ear.'

El Sordo pointed to his better ear and grinned.

'Where do you get the whisky?' Robert Jordan shouted.

'Make it,' El Sordo said and watched Robert Jordan's hand check on its way to his mouth with the glass.

'No,' El Sordo said and patted his shoulder. 'Joke. Comes from La Granja. Heard last night comes English dynamiter. Good. Very happy. Get whisky. For you. You like?'

'Very much,' said Robert Jordan. 'It's very good whisky.'

'Am contented,' Sordo grinned. 'Was bringing to-night with information.'

'What information?'

'Much troop movement.'

'Where?'

'Segovia. Planes you saw?'

'Yes.'

'Bad, eh?'

'Bad.'

'Troop movement?'

'Much between Villacastín and Segovia. On Valladolid road. Much between Villacastín and San Rafael. Much. Much.'

'What do you think?'

'We prepare something?'

'Possibly.'

'They know. Prepare too.'

'It is possible.'

'Why not blow bridge to-night?'

'Orders.'

'Whose orders?'

'General Staff.'

'So.'

'Is the time of the blowing important?' Pilar asked.

'Of all importance.'

'But if they are moving up troops?'

'I will send Anselmo with a report of all movement and concentrations. He is watching the road.'

'You have someone at road?' Sordo asked.

Robert Jordan did not know how much he had heard. You never know with a deaf man.

'Yes,' he said.

'Me, too. Why not blow bridge now?'

'I have my orders.'

'I don't like it,' El Sordo said. 'This I do not like.'

'Nor I,' said Robert Jordan.

El Sordo shook his head and took a sip of the whisky. 'You want of me?'

'How many men have you?'

'Eight.'

'To cut the telephone, attack the post at the house of the roadmenders, take it, and fall back on the bridge.'

'It is easy.'

'It will all be written out.'

'Don't trouble. And Pablo?'

'Will cut the telephone below, attack the post at the sawmill, take it and fall back on the bridge.'

'And afterwards for the retreat?' Pilar asked. 'We are seven men, two women and five horses. You are?' she shouted into Sordo's ear.

'Eight men and four horses. *Faltan caballos*,' he said. 'Lacks horses.'

'Seventeen people and nine horses,' Pilar said. 'Without accounting for transport.'

Sordo said nothing.

'There is no way of getting horses?' Robert Jordan said into Sordo's best ear.

'In war a year,' Sordo said. 'Have four.' He showed four fingers. 'Now you want eight for to-morrow.'

'Yes,' said Robert Jordan. 'Knowing you are leaving. Having no need to be careful as you have been in this neighbourhood. Not having to be cautious here now. You could not cut out and steal eight head of horses?'

'Maybe,' Sordo said. 'Maybe none. Maybe more.'

'You have an automatic rifle?' Robert Jordan asked.

Sordo nodded.

'Where?'

'Up the hill.'

'What kind?'

'Don't know name. With pans.'

'How many rounds?'

'Five pans.'

'Does anyone know how to use it?'

'Me. A little. Not shoot too much. Not want make noise here. Not want use cartridges.'

'I will look at it afterwards,' Robert Jordan said. 'Have you hand grenades?'

'Plenty.'

'How many rounds per rifle?'

'Plenty.'

'How many?'

'One hundred fifty. More maybe.'

'What about other people?'

'For what?'

'To have sufficient force to take the posts and cover the bridge while I am blowing it. We should have double what we have.'

'Take posts don't worry. What time day?'

'Daylight.'

'Don't worry.'

'I could use twenty more men, to be sure,' Robert Jordan said.

'Good ones do not exist. You want undependables?'

'No. How many good ones?'

'Maybe four.'

'Why so few?'

'No trust.'

'For horseholders?'

'Must trust much to be horseholders.'

'I'd like ten more good men if I could get them.'

'Four.'

'Anselmo told me there were over a hundred here in these hills.'

'No good.'

'You said thirty,' Robert Jordan said to Pilar. 'Thirty of a certain degree of dependability.'

'What about the people of Elias?' Pilar shouted to Sordo. He shook his head.

'No good.'

'You can't get ten?' Robert Jordan asked. Sordo looked at him with his flat, yellow eyes and shook his head.

'Four,' he said and held up four fingers.

'Yours are good?' Robert Jordan asked, regretting it as he said it.

Sordo nodded.

'*Dentro de la gravedad*,' he said in Spanish. 'Within the limits of the danger.' He grinned. 'Will be bad, eh?'

'Possibly.'

'It is the same to me,' Sordo said simply and not boasting. 'Better four good than much bad. In this war always much bad, very little good. Every day fewer good. And Pablo?' he looked at Pilar.

'As you know,' Pilar said. 'Worse every day.'

Sordo shrugged his shoulders.

'Take drink,' Sordo said to Robert Jordan. 'I bring mine and four more. Makes twelve. To-night we discuss all. I have sixty sticks dynamite. You want?'

'What per cent?'

'Don't know. Common dynamite. I bring.'

'We'll blow the small bridge above with that,' Robert Jordan said. 'That is fine. You'll come down to-night? Bring that, will you? I've no orders for that but it should be blown.'

'I come to-night. Then hunt horses.'

'What chance for horses?'

'Maybe. Now eat.'

Does he talk that way to everyone? Robert Jordan thought. Or is that his idea of how to make foreigners understand?

'And where are we going to go when this is done?' Pilar shouted into Sordo's ear.

He shrugged his shoulders.

'All that must be arranged,' the woman said.

'Of course,' said Sordo. 'Why not?'

'It is bad enough,' Pilar said. 'It must be planned very well.'

'Yes, woman,' Sordo said. 'What has thee worried?'

'Everything,' Pilar shouted.

Sordo grinned at her.

'You've been going about with Pablo,' he said.

So he does only speak that pidgin Spanish for foreigners, Robert Jordan thought. Good. I'm glad to hear him talking straight.

'Where do you think we should go?' Pilar asked.

'Where?'

'Yes, where.'

'There are many places,' Sordo said. 'Many places. You know Gredos?'

'There are many people there. All these places will be cleaned up as soon as they have time.'

'Yes. But it is a big country and very wild.'

'It would be very difficult to get there,' Pilar said.

'Everything is difficult,' El Sordo said. 'We can get to Gredos as well as to anywhere else. Travelling at night. Here it is very dangerous now. It is a miracle we have been here this long. Gredos is safer country than this.'

'Do you know where I want to go?' Pilar asked him.

'Where? The Paramera? That's no good.'

'No,' Pilar said. 'Not the Sierra de Paramera. I want to go to the Republic.'

'That is possible.'

'Would your people go?'

'Yes. If I say to.'

'Of mine, I do not know,' Pilar said. 'Pablo would not want to although, truly, he might feel safer there. He is too old to have to go for a soldier unless they call more classes. The gipsy will not wish to go. I do not know about the others.'

'Because nothing passes here for so long they do not realize the danger,' El Sordo said.

'Since the planes to-day they will see it more,' Robert Jordan said. 'But I should think you could operate very well from the Gredos.'

'What?' El Sordo said and looked at him with his eyes very flat. There was no friendliness in the way he asked the question.

'You could raid more effectively from there,' Robert Jordan said.

'So,' El Sordo said. 'You know Gredos?'

'Yes. You could operate against the main line of the railway from there. You could keep cutting it as we are doing farther south in Estremadura. To operate from there would be better than returning to the Republic,' Robert Jordan said. 'You are more useful there.'

They had both gotten sullen as he talked.

Sordo looked at Pilar and she looked back at him.

'You know Gredos?' Sordo asked. 'Truly?'

'Sure,' said Robert Jordan.

'Where would you go?'

'Above Barco de Avila. Better places than here. Raid against the main road and the railroad between Béjar and Plasencia.'

'Very difficult,' Sordo said.

'We have worked against that same railroad in much more dangerous country in Estremadura,' Robert Jordan said.

'Who is we?'

'The *guerrilleros* group of Estremadura.'

'You are many?'

'About forty.'

'Was the one with the bad nerves and the strange name from there?' asked Pilar.

'Yes.'

'Where is he now?'

'Dead, as I told you.'

'You are from there, too?'

'Yes.'

'You see what I mean?' Pilar said to him.

And I have made a mistake, Robert Jordan thought to himself. I have told Spaniards we can do something better than they can when the rule is never to speak of your own exploits or abilities. When I should have flattered them I have told them what I think they should do and now they are furious. Well, they will either get over it or they will not. They are certainly much more useful in the Gredos than here. The proof is that here they have done nothing since that train that Kashkin organized. It was not much of a show. It costs the fascists one engine and killed a few troops but they all talk as though it were the high point of the war. Maybe they will shame into going to the Gredos. Yes and maybe I will get thrown out of here too. Well, it is not a very rosy-looking dish any way that you look into it.

'Listen, *Inglés*,' Pilar said to him. 'How are your nerves?'

'All right,' said Robert Jordan. 'O.K.'

'Because the last dynamiter they sent to work with us, although a formidable technician, was very nervous.'

'We have nervous ones,' Robert Jordan said.

'I do not say that he was a coward, because he comported himself very well,' Pilar went on. 'But he spoke in a very rare and windy way.' She raised her voice. 'Isn't it true, Santiago, that the last dynamiter, he of the train, was a little rare?'

'*Algo raro*,' the deaf man nodded and his eyes went over Robert Jordan's face in a way that reminded him of the round opening at the end of the wand of a vacuum cleaner. '*Si, algo raro, pero bueno*.'

'*Murió*,' Robert Jordan said into the deaf man's ear. 'He is dead.'

'How was that?' the deaf man asked, dropping his eyes down from Robert Jordan's eyes to his lips.

'I shot him,' Robert Jordan said. 'He was too badly wounded to travel and I shot him.'

'He was always talking of such a necessity,' Pilar said. 'It was his obsession.'

'Yes,' said Robert Jordan. 'He was always talking of such a necessity and it was his obsession.'

'*Como fué?*' the deaf man asked. 'Was it a train?'

'It was returning from a train,' Robert Jordan said. 'The train was successful. Returning in the dark we encountered a fascist patrol and as we ran he was shot high in the back but without hitting any bone except the shoulder blade. He travelled quite a long way, but with the wound was unable to travel more. He was unwilling to be left behind and I shot him.'

'*Menos mal*,' said El Sordo. 'Less bad.'

'Are you sure your nerves are all right?' Pilar said to Robert Jordan.

'Yes,' he told her. 'I am sure that my nerves are all right and I think that when we terminate this of the bridge you would do well to go to the Gredos.'

As he said that, the woman started to curse in a flood of obscene invective that rolled over and around him like the hot white water splashing down from the sudden eruption of a geyser.

The deaf man shook his head at Robert Jordan, and grinned in delight. He continued to shake his head happily as Pilar went on vilifying and Robert Jordan knew that it was all right again now. Finally she stopped cursing, reached for the water jug, tipped it up and took a drink and said, calmly, 'Then just shut up about what we are to do afterwards, will you, *Inglés*? You go back to the Republic and you take your piece with you and leave us others alone here to decide what part of these hills we'll die in.'

'Live in,' El Sordo said. 'Calm thyself, Pilar.'

'Live in and die in,' Pilar said. 'I can see the end of it well enough. I like thee, *Inglés*, but keep thy mouth off of what we must do when thy business is finished.'

'It is thy business,' Robert Jordan said. 'I do not put my hand in it.'

'But you did,' Pilar said. 'Take thy little cropped-headed whore and go back to the Republic but do not shut the door on others who are not foreigners and who loved the Republic when thou wert wiping thy mother's milk off thy chin.'

Maria had come up the trail while they were talking and she heard this last sentence which Pilar, raising her voice again, shouted at Robert Jordan. Maria shook her head at Robert Jordan violently and shook her finger warningly. Pilar saw Robert Jordan looking at the girl and saw him smile and she turned and said, 'Yes. I said whore and I mean it. And I suppose that you'll go to Valencia together and we can eat goat crut in Gredos.'

'I'm a whore if thee wishes, Pilar,' Maria said. 'I suppose I am in all case if you say so. But calm thyself. What passes with thee?'

'Nothing,' Pilar said and sat down on the bench, her voice calm now and all the metallic rage gone out of it. 'I do not call thee that. But I have such a desire to go to the Republic.'

'We can all go,' Maria said.

'Why not?' Robert Jordan said. 'Since thou seemest not to love the Gredos.'

Sordo grinned at him.

'We'll see,' Pilar said, her rage gone now. 'Give me a glass of that rare drink. I have worn my throat out with anger. We'll see. We'll see what happens.'

'You see, comrade,' El Sordo explained. 'It is the morning that is difficult.' He was not talking the pidgin Spanish now and he was looking into Robert Jordan's eyes calmly and explainingly; not searchingly nor suspiciously, nor with the flat superiority of the old campaigner that had been in them before. 'I understand your needs and I know the posts must be exterminated and the bridge covered while you do your work. This I understand perfectly. This is easy to do before daylight or at daylight.'

'Yes,' Robert Jordan said. 'Run along a minute, will you?' he said to Maria without looking at her.

The girl walked away out of hearing and sat down, her hands clasped over her ankles.

'You see,' Sordo said. 'In that there is no problem. But to leave afterward and get out of this country in daylight presents a grave problem.'

'Clearly,' said Robert Jordan. 'I have thought of it. It is daylight for me also.'

'But you are one,' El Sordo said. 'We are various.'

'There is the possibility of returning to the camps and leaving from there at dark,' Pilar said, putting the glass to her lips and then lowering it.

'That is very dangerous, too,' El Sordo explained. 'That is perhaps even more dangerous.'

'I can see how it would be,' Robert Jordan said.

'To do the bridge in the night would be easy,' El Sordo said. 'Since you make the condition that it must be done at daylight, it brings grave consequences.'

'I know it.'

'You could not do it at night?'

'I would be shot for it.'

'It is very possible we will all be shot for it if you do it in the day-time.'

'For me myself that is less important once the bridge is blown,' Robert Jordan said. 'But I see your viewpoint. You cannot work out a retreat for daylight?'

'Certainly,' El Sordo said. 'We will work out such a retreat. But I explain to you why one is preoccupied and why one is irritated. You speak of going to Gredos as though it were a military manœuvre to be accomplished. To arrive at Gredos would be a miracle.'

Robert Jordan said nothing.

'Listen to me,' the deaf man said. 'I am speaking much. But it is so we may understand one another. We exist here by a miracle. By a miracle of laziness and stupidity of the fascists which they will remedy in time. Of course we are very careful and we make no disturbance in these hills.'

'I know.'

'But now, with this, we must go. We must think much about the manner of our going.'

'Clearly.'

'Then,' said El Sordo. 'Let us eat now, I have talked much.'

'Never have I heard thee talk so much,' Pilar said. 'Is it this?' she held up the glass.

'No,' El Sordo shook his head. 'It isn't whisky. It is that never have I had so much to talk of.'

'I appreciate your aid and you loyalty,' Robert Jordan said. 'I appreciate the difficulty caused by the timing of the blowing of the bridge.'

'Don't talk of that,' El Sordo said. 'We are here to do what we can do. But this is complicated.'

'And on paper very simple,' Robert Jordan grinned. 'On paper the bridge is blown at the moment the attack starts in order that nothing shall come up the road. It is very simple.'

'That they should let us do something on paper,' El Sordo said. 'That we should conceive and execute something on paper.'

'"Paper bleeds little,"' Robert Jordan quoted the proverb.

'But it is very useful,' Pilar said. '"*Es muy util.*" What I would like to do is use thy orders for that purpose.'

'Me too,' said Robert Jordan. 'But you could never win a war like that.'

'No,' the big woman said. 'I suppose not. But do you know what I would like?'

'To go to the Republic,' El Sordo said. He had put his good ear close to her as she spoke. '*Ya irás, mujer*. Let us win this and it will all be Republic.'

'All right,' Pilar said. 'And now, for God's sake let us eat.'

12

They left El Sordo's after eating and started down the trail. El Sordo had walked with them as far as the lower post.

'*Salud*,' he said. 'Until to-night.'

'*Salud, camarada*,' Robert Jordan had said to him and the three of them had gone on down the trail, the deaf man standing looking after them. Maria had turned and waved her hand at him and El Sordo waved disparagingly with the abrupt, Spanish upward flick of the forearm as though something were being tossed away which seems the negation of all salutation which has not to do with business. Through the meal he had never unbuttoned his sheepskin coat and he had been carefully polite, careful to turn his head to hear and had returned to speaking his broken Spanish, asking Robert Jordan about conditions in the Republic politely; but it was obvious he wanted to be rid of them.

As they had left him, Pilar had said to him, 'Well, Santiago?'

'Well, nothing, woman,' the deaf man said. 'It is all right. But I am thinking.'

'Me, too,' Pilar had said and now as they walked down the trail, the walking easy and pleasant down the steep trail through the pines that they had toiled up, Pilar said nothing. Neither Robert Jordan nor Maria spoke and the three of them travelled along fast until the trail rose steeply out of the wooded valley to come up through the timber, leave it, and come out into the high meadow.

It was hot in the late May afternoon and half way up this last steep grade the woman stopped. Robert Jordan, stopping and looking back, saw the sweat beading on her forehead. He thought her brown face looked pallid and the skin sallow and that were dark areas under her eyes.

'Let us rest a minute,' he said. 'We go too fast.'

'No,' she said, 'Let us go on.'

'Rest, Pilar,' Maria said. 'You look badly.'

'Shut up,' the woman said. 'Nobody asked for thy advice.'

She started on up the trail but at the top she was breathing heavily and her face was wet with perspiration and there was no doubt about her pallor now.

'Sit down, Pilar,' Maria said. 'Please, please sit down.'

'All right,' said Pilar, and the three of them sat down under a pine tree and looked across the mountain meadow to where the tops of the peaks seemed to jut out from the roll of the high country with snow shining bright on them now in the early afternoon sun.

'What rotten stuff is the snow and how beautiful it looks,' Pilar said. 'What an illusion is the snow.' She turned to Maria. 'I am sorry I was rude to thee, *guapa*. I don't know what has held me today. I have an evil temper.'

'I never mind what you say when you are angry,' Maria told her. 'And you are angry often.'

'Nay, it is worse than anger,' Pilar said, looking across at the peaks.

'Thou art not well,' Maria said.

'Neither is it that,' the woman said. 'Come here, *guapa*, and put thy head in my lap.'

Maria moved close to her, put her arms out and folded them as one does who goes to sleep without a pillow and lay with her head on her arms. She turned her face up to Pilar and smiled at her but the big woman looked on across the meadow at the mountains. She stroked the girl's head without looking down at her and ran a blunt finger across the girl's forehead and then around the line of her ear and down the line where the hair grew on her neck.

'You can have her in a little while, *Inglés*,' she said. Robert Jordan was sitting behind her.

'Do not talk like that,' Maria said.

'Yes, he can have thee,' Pilar said and looked at neither of them. 'I have never wanted thee. But I am jealous.'

'Pilar,' Maria said. 'Do not talk thus.'

'He can have thee,' Pilar said, and ran her finger around the lobe of the girl's ear. 'But I am very jealous.'

'But Pilar,' Maria said. 'It was thee explained to me there was nothing like that between us.'

'There is always something like that,' the woman said. 'There is always something like something that there should not be. But with me there is not. Truly there is not. I want thy happiness and nothing more.'

Maria said nothing but lay there, trying to make her head rest lightly.

'Listen, *guapa*,' said Pilar and ran her finger now absently but tracingly over the contours of her cheeks. 'Listen, *guapa*, I love thee and he can have thee, I am no *tortillera* but a woman made for men. That is true. But now it gives me pleasure to say thus, in the daytime, that I care for thee.'

'I love thee, too.'

'*Qué va*. Do not talk nonsense. Thou dost not know even of what I speak.'

'I know.'

'*Qué va*, that you know. You are for the *Inglés*. That is seen and as it should be. That I would have. Anything else I would not have. I do not make perversions. I only tell you something true. Few people will ever talk to thee truly and no women. I am jealous and say it and it is there. And I say it.'

'Do not say it,' Maria said. 'Do not say it, Pilar.'

'*Porqué*, do not say it,' the woman said, still not looking at either of them. 'I will say it until it no longer pleases me to say it. And,' she looked down at the girl now, 'that time has come already. I do not say it more, you understand?'

'Pilar,' Maria said, 'Do not talk thus.'

'Thou art a very pleasant little rabbit,' Pilar said. 'And lift thy head now because this silliness is over.'

'It was not silly,' said Maria. 'And my head is well where it is.'

'Nay. Lift it,' Pilar told her and put her big hands under the girl's head and raised it. 'And thou, *Inglés*?' she said, still holding the girl's head as she looked across the mountains. 'What cat has eaten thy tongue?'

'No cat,' Robert Jordan said.

'What animal then?' She laid the girl's head down on the ground.

'No animal,' Robert Jordan told her.

'You swallowed it yourself, eh?'

'I guess so,' Robert Jordan said.

'And did you like the taste?' Pilar turned now and grinned at him.

'Not much.'

'I thought not,' Pilar said. 'I *thought* not. But I give you back your rabbit. Nor ever did I try to take your rabbit. That's a good name for her. I heard you call her that this morning.'

Robert Jordan felt his face redden.

'You are a very hard woman,' he told her.

'No,' Pilar said. 'But so simple I am very complicated. Are you very complicated, *Inglés*?'

'No. Nor not so simple,'

'You please me, *Inglés*,' Pilar said. Then she smiled and leaned forward and smiled and shook her head. 'Now if I could take the rabbit from thee and take thee from the rabbit.'

'You could not.'

'I know it,' Pilar said and smiled again. 'Nor would I wish to. But when I was young I could have.'

'I believe it.'

'You believe it?'

'Surely,' Robert Jordan said. 'But such talk is nonsense.'

'It is not like thee,' Maria said.

'I am not much like myself to-day,' Pilar said. 'Very little like myself. Thy bridge has given me a headache, *Inglés*.'

'We can call it the Headache Bridge,' Robert Jordan said. 'But I will drop it in that gorge like a broken bird cage.'

'Good,' said Pilar. 'Keep on talking like that.'

'I'll drop it as you break a banana from which you have removed the skin.'

'I could eat a banana now,' said Pilar. 'Go on, *Inglés*. Keep on talking largely.'

'There is no need,' Robert Jordan said. 'Let us get to camp.'

'Thy duty,' Pilar said. 'It will come quickly enough. I said that I would leave the two of you.'

'No. I have much to do.'

'That is much too and does not take long.'

'Shut thy mouth, Pilar,' Maria said. 'You speak grossly.'

'I am gross,' Pilar said. 'But I am also very delicate. *Soy muy delicada*. I will leave the two of you. And the talk of jealousness is nonsense. I was angry at Joaquín because I saw from his look how ugly I am. I am only jealous that you are nineteen. It is not a jealousy which lasts. You will not be nineteen always. Now I go.'

She stood up and with a hand on one hip looked at Robert Jordan, who was also standing. Maria sat on the ground under the tree, her head dropped forward.

'Let us all go to camp together,' Robert Jordan said. 'It is better and there is much to do.'

Pilar nodded with her head toward Maria, who sat there, her head turned away from them, saying nothing.

Pilar smiled and shrugged her shoulders almost imperceptibly and said, 'You know the way?'

'I know it,' Maria said, not raising her head.

'*Pues me voy*,' Pilar said. 'Then I am going. We'll have something hearty for you to eat, *Inglés*.'

She started to walk off into the heather of the meadow toward the stream that led down through it toward the camp.

'Wait,' Robert Jordan called to her. 'It is better that we should all go together.'

Maria sat there and said nothing.

Pilar did not turn.

'*Qué va*, go together,' she said. 'I will see thee at the camp.'

Robert Jordan stood there.

'Is she all right?' he asked Maria. 'She looked ill before.'

'Let her go,' Maria said, her head still down.

'I think I should go with her.'

'Let her go,' said Maria. 'Let her go!'

13

They were walking through the heather of the mountain meadow and Robert Jordan felt the brushing of the heather against his legs, felt the weight of his pistol in its holster against his thigh, felt the sun on his head, felt the breeze from the snow of the mountain peaks cool on his back and, in his hand, he felt the girl's hand firm and strong, the fingers locked in his. From it, from the palm of her hand against the palm of his, from their fingers locked together, and from her wrist across his wrist something came from her hand, her fingers and her wrist to his that was as fresh as the first light air that moving toward you over the sea barely wrinkles the glassy surface of a calm, as light as a feather moved across one's lip, or a leaf falling when there is no breeze; so light that it could be felt with the touch of their fingers alone, but that was so strengthened, so intensified, and made so urgent, so aching and so strong by the hard pressure of their fingers and the close pressed palm and wrist, that it was as though a current moved up his arm and filled his whole body with an aching hollowness of wanting. With the sun shining on her hair, tawny as wheat, and on her gold-brown smooth-lovely face and on the curve of her throat he bent her head back and held her to him and kissed her. He felt her trembling as he kissed her and he held the length of her body tight to him and felt her breasts against his chest through the two khaki shirts, he felt them small and firm and he reached and undid the buttons on her shirt and bent and kissed her and she stood shivering, holding her head back, his arm behind her. Then she dropped her chin to his head and then he felt her hands holding his head and rocking it against her. He straightened and with his two arms around her held her so tightly that she was lifted off the ground, tight against him, and he felt her trembling and then her lips were on his throat, and then he put her down and said,' Maria, oh, my Maria.'

Then he said, 'Where should we go?'

She did not say anything but slipped her hand inside of his shirt and he felt her undoing the shirt buttons and she said, 'You, too, I want to kiss, too.'

'No, little rabbit.'

'Yes. Yes. Everything as you.'

'Nay. That is an impossibility.'

'Well, then. Oh, then. Oh, then. Oh.'

Then there was the smell of heather crushed and the roughness of the bent stalks under her head and the sun bright on her closed eyes and all his life he would remember the curve of her throat with her head pushed back into the heather roots and her lips that moved smally and by themselves and the fluttering of the lashes on the eyes tight closed against the sun and against everything, and for her everything was red, orange, gold-red from the sun on the closed eyes, and it all was that colour, all of it, the filling, the possessing, the having, all of that colour, all in a blindness of that colour. For him it was a dark passage which led to nowhere, then to nowhere, then again to nowhere, once again to nowhere, always and for ever to nowhere, heavy on the elbows in the earth to nowhere, dark, never any end to nowhere, hung on all time always to unknowing nowhere, this time and again for always to nowhere, now not to be borne once again always and to nowhere, now beyond all bearing up, up, up and into nowhere, suddenly, scaldingly, holdingly all nowhere gone and time absolutely still and they were both there, time having stopped and he felt the earth move out and away from under them.

Then he was lying on his side, his head deep in the heather, smelling it and the smell of the roots and the earth and the sun came through it and it was scratchy on his bare shoulders and along his flanks and the girl was lying opposite him with her eyes still shut and then she opened them and smiled at him and he said very tiredly and from a great but friendly distance, 'Hello, rabbit.' And she smiled and from no distance said, 'Hello, my *Inglés*.'

'I'm not an *Inglés*,' he said very lazily.

'Oh yes, you are,' she said. 'You're my *Inglés*,' and reached and took hold of both his ears and kissed him on the forehead.

'There,' she said. 'How is that? Do I kiss thee better?'

Then they were walking along the stream together and he said, 'Maria, I love thee and thou art so lovely and so wonderful and so beautiful and it does such things to me to be with thee that I feel as though I wanted to die when I am loving thee.'

'Oh,' she said. 'I die each time. Do you not die?'

'No. Almost. But did thee feel the earth move?'

'Yes. As I died. Put thy arm around me, please.'

'No. I have thy hand. Thy hand is enough.'

He looked at her and across the meadow where a hawk was hunting and the big afternoon clouds were coming now over the mountains.

'And it is not thus for thee with others?' Maria asked him, they now walking hand in hand.

'No. Truly.'

'Thou hast loved many others.'

'Some. But not as thee.'

'And it was not thus? Truly?'

'It was a pleasure but it was not thus.'

'And then the earth moved. The earth never moved before?'

'Nay. Truly never.'

'Ay,' she said. 'And this we have for one day.'

He said nothing.

'But we have had it now at least,' Maria said. 'And do you like me too? Do I please thee? I will look better later.'

'Thou art very beautiful now.'

'Nay,' she said. 'But stroke thy hand across my head.'

He did that feeling her cropped hair soft and flattening and then rising between his fingers and he put both hands on her head and turned her face up to his and kissed her.

'I like to kiss very much,' she said. 'But I do not do it well.'

'Thou hast no need to kiss.'

'Yes, I have. If I am to be thy woman I should please thee in all ways.'

'You please me enough. I would not be more pleased. There is nothing I could do if I were more pleased.'

'But you will see,' she said very happily. 'My hair amuses thee now because it is odd. But every day it is growing. It will be long and then I will not look ugly and perhaps you will love me very much.'

'Thou hast a lovely body,' he said. 'The loveliest in the world.'

'It is only young and thin.'

'No. In a fine body there is magic. I do not know what makes it in one and not in another. But thou hast it.'

'For thee,' she said.

'Nay.'

'Yes. For thee and for thee always and only for thee. But it is little to bring thee. I would learn to take good care of thee. But tell me truly. Did the earth never move for thee before?'

'Never,' he said truly.

'Now am I happy,' she said. 'Now am I truly happy.'

'You are thinking of something else now?' she asked him.

'Yes. My work.'

'I wish we had horses to ride,' Maria said. 'In my happiness I would like to be on a good horse and ride fast with thee riding fast beside me and we would ride faster and faster, galloping, and never pass my happiness.'

'We could take thy happiness in a plane,' he said absently.

'And go over and over in the sky like the little pursuit planes shining in the sun,' she said. 'Rolling it in loops and in dives. *Qué bueno!*' she laughed. 'My happiness would not even notice it.'

'Thy happiness has a good stomach,' he said half hearing what she said.

Because now he was not there. He was walking beside her but his mind was thinking of the problem of the bridge now and it was all clear and hard and sharp as when a camera lens is brought into focus. He saw the two posts and Anselmo and the gipsy watching. He saw the road empty and he saw movement on it. He saw where he would place the two automatic rifles to get the most level field of fire, and who will serve them, he thought, me at the end, but who at the start? He placed the charges, wedged and lashed them, sunk his caps and crimped them, ran his wires, hooked them up and got back to where he had placed the old box of the exploder and then he started to think of all the things that could have happened and that might go wrong. Stop it, he told himself. You have made love to this girl and now your head is clear, properly clear, and you start to worry. It is one thing to think you must do and it is another thing to worry. Don't worry. You mustn't worry. You know the things that you may have to do and you know what may happen. Certainly it may happen.

You went into it knowing what you were fighting for. You were fighting against exactly what you were doing and being forced into doing to have any chance of winning. So now he was compelled to use these people whom he liked as you should use troops toward whom you have no feeling at all if you were to be successful. Pablo was evidently the smartest. He knew how bad it was instantly. The woman was all for it, and still was; but the realization of what it really consisted in had overcome her steadily and it had done plenty to her already. Sordo recognized it instantly and would do it but he did not like it any more than he, Robert Jordan, liked it.

So you say that it is not that which will happen to yourself but that which may happen to the woman and the girl and to the others that you think of. All right. What would have happened to them if you had not come? What happened to them and what passed with them before you were ever here? You must not think in that way. You have no responsibility for them except in action. The orders do not come from you. They come from Golz. And who is Golz? A good general. The best you've ever served under. But should a man carry out impossible orders knowing what they lead to? Even though they come from Golz, who is the party as well as the army? Yes. He should carry them out because it is only in the performing of them that they can prove to be impossible. How do you know they are impossible until you have tried them? If everyone said orders were impossible to carry out when they were received where would you be? Where would we all be if you just said, 'Impossible,' when orders came?

He had seen enough of commanders to whom all orders were impossible. That swine Gomez in Estremadura. He had seen enough attacks when the flanks did not advance because it was impossible. No, he would carry out the orders and it was bad luck that you liked the people you must do it with.

In all the work that they, the *partizans*, did, they brought added danger and bad luck to the people that sheltered them and worked with them. For what? So that, eventually, there should be no more danger and so that the country should be a good place to live in. That was true no matter how trite it sounded.

If the Republic lost it would be impossible for those who believed in it to live in Spain. But would it? Yes, he knew that it would be, from the things that happened in the parts the fascists had already taken.

Pablo was a swine but the others were fine people and was it not a betrayal of them all to get them to do this? Perhaps it was. But if they did not do it two squadrons of cavalry would come and hunt them out of these hills in a week.

No. There was nothing to be gained by leaving them alone. Except that all people should be left alone and you should interfere with no one. So he believed that, did he? Yes, he believed that. And what about a planned society and the rest of it? That was for the others to do. He had something else to do after this war. He fought now in this war because it had started in a country that he loved and he believed in the Republic and that if it were destroyed life would be unbearable for all those people who believed in it. He was under Communist discipline for the duration of the war. Here in Spain the Communists offered the best discipline and the soundest and sanest for the prosecution of the war. He accepted their discipline for the duration of the war because, in the conduct of the war, they were the only party whose programme and whose discipline he could respect.

What were his politics then? He had none now, he told himself. But do not tell anyone else that, he thought. Don't ever admit that. And what are you going to do afterwards? I am going back and earn my living teaching Spanish as before, and I am going to write a true book. I'll bet, he said. I'll bet that will be easy.

He would have to talk with Pablo about politics. It would certainly be interesting to see what his political development had been. The classical move from left to right, probably: like old Lerroux. Pablo was quite a lot like Lerroux. Prieto was as bad. Pablo and Prieto had about an equal faith in the ultimate victory. They all had the politics of horse thieves. He believed in the Republic as a form of government but the Republic would have to get rid of all of that bunch of horse thieves that brought it to the pass it was in when the rebellion started. Was there ever a people whose leaders were as truly their enemies as this one?

Enemies of the people. That was a phrase he might omit. That was a catch phrase he would skip. That was one thing that sleeping with Maria had done. He had gotten to be as bigoted and hide-bound about his politics as a hard-shelled Baptist and phrases like enemies of the people came into his mind without his much criticizing them in any way. Any sort of *clichés* both revolutionary and patriotic. His mind employed them without criticism. Of course they were true but it was too easy to be nimble about using them. But since last night and this afternoon his mind was much clearer and cleaner on that business. Bigotry is an odd thing. To be bigoted you have to be absolutely sure that you are right and nothing makes that surety and righteousness like continence. Continence is the foe of heresy.

How would that premise stand up if he examined it? That was probably why the Communists were always cracking down on Bohemianism. When you were drunk or when you committed either fornication or adultery you recognized your own personal fallibility of that so mutable substitute for the apostles' creed, the party line. Down with Bohemianism, the sin of Mayakovsky.

But Mayakovsky was a saint again. That was because he was safely dead. You'll be safely dead yourself, he told himself. Now stop thinking that sort of thing. Think about Maria.

Maria was very hard on his bigotry. So far she had not affected his resolution but he would much prefer not to die. He would abandon a hero's or a martyr's end gladly. He did not want to make a Thermopylae, nor be Horatius at any bridge, nor be the Dutch boy with his finger in that dyke. No. He would like to spend some time with Maria. That was the simplest expression of it. He would like to spend a long, long time with her.

He did not believe there was ever going to be any such thing as a long time any more but if there ever was such a thing he would like to spend it with her. We could go into the hotel and register as Doctor and Mrs. Livingstone I presume, he thought.

Why not marry her? Sure, he thought. I will marry her. Then we will be Mr. and Mrs. Robert Jordan of Sun Valley, Idaho. Or Corpus Christi, Texas, or Butte, Montana.

Spanish girls make wonderful wives. I've never had one so I know. And when I get my job back at the university she can be an instructor's wife and when undergraduates who take Spanish IV come in to smoke pipes in the evening and I have those so valuable informal discussions about Quevedo, Lope de Vega, Galdós and the other always admirable dead, Maria can tell them about how some of the blue-shirted crusaders for the true faith sat on her head while others twisted her arms and pulled her skirts and stuffed them in her mouth.

I wonder how they will like Maria in Missoula, Montana? That is if I can get a job back in Missoula. I suppose that I am ticketed as a Red there now for good and will be on the general blacklist. Though you never know. You never can tell. They've no proof of what you do, and as a matter of fact they would never believe it if you told them, and my passport was valid for Spain before they issued the restrictions.

The time for getting back will not be until the fall of thirty-seven. I left in the summer of thirty-six and though the leave is for a year you do not need to be back until the fall term opens in the following year. There is a lot of time between now and the fall term. There is a lot of time between now and day after to-morrow if you want to put it that way. No. I think there is no need to worry about the university. Just you turn up there in the fall and it will be all right. Just try and turn up there.

But it has been a strange life for a long time now. Damned if it hasn't. Spain was your work and your job, so being in Spain was natural and sound. You had worked summers on engineering projects and in the forest service building roads and in the park and learned to handle powder, so the demolition was a sound and normal job too. Always a little hasty, but sound.

Once you accept the idea of demolition as a problem it is only a problem. But there was plenty that was not so good that went with it although God knows you took it easily enough. There was the constant attempt to approximate the conditions of successful assassination that accompanied the demolition. Did big words make it more defensible? Did they make killing any more palatable? You took to it a little too readily if you ask me, he told himself. And what you will be like or just exactly what you will be suited for when you leave the service of the Republic is, to me, he thought, extremely doubtful. But my guess is you will get rid of all that by writing about it, he said. Once you write it down it is all gone. It will be a good book if you can write it. Much better than the other.

But in the meantime all the life you have or ever will have is to-day, to-night, to-morrow, to-day, to-night, to-morrow, over and over again (I hope), he thought, and so you had better take what time there is and be very thankful for it. If the bridge goes bad. It does not look too good just now.

But Maria has been good. Has she not? Oh, has she not, he thought. Maybe that is what I am to get now from life. Maybe that is my life and instead of it being three-score years and ten it is forty-eight hours or just three-score hours and ten or twelve rather. Twenty-four hours in a day would be three-score and twelve for the three full days.

I suppose it is possible to live as full a life in seventy hours as in seventy years; granted that your life has been full up to the time that the seventy hours start and that you have reached a certain age.

What nonsense, he thought. What rot you get to thinking by yourself. That is *really* nonsense. And maybe it isn't nonsense too. Well, we will see. The last time I slept with a girl was in Madrid. No it wasn't. It was in the Escorial and, except that I woke in the night and thought it was someone else and was excited until I realized who it really was, it was just dragging ashes; except that it was pleasant enough. And the time before that was in Madrid and except for some lying and pretending I did to myself as to identity while things were going on, it was the same or something less. So I am no romantic glorifier of the Spanish Woman nor did I ever think of a casual piece as anything much other than a casual piece in any country. But when I am with Maria I love her so that I feel, literally, as though I would die and I never believed in that nor thought that it could happen.

So if your life trades its seventy years for seventy hours I have that value now and I am lucky enough to know it. And if there is not any such thing as a long time, nor the rest of your lives, nor from now on, but there is only now, why then now is the thing to praise and I am very happy with it. Now, *ahora*, *maintenant*, *heute*. *Now*, it has a funny sound to be a whole world and your life. *Esta noche*, to-night, *ce soir*, *heute abend*. Life and wife, *Vie* and *Mari*. No it didn't work out. The French turned it into husband. There was now and *frau*; but that did not prove anything either. Take dead, *mort*, *muerto*, and *todt*. *Todt* was the deadest of them all. War, *guerre*, *guerra*, and *krieg*. *Krieg* was the most like war, or was it? Or was it only that he knew German the least well? Sweetheart, *chérie*, *prenda*, and *schatz*. He would trade them all for Maria. There was a name.

Well, they would all be doing it together and it would not be long now. It certainly looked worse all the time. It was just something that you could not bring off in the morning. In an impossible situation you hang on until night to get away. You try to last out until night to get back in. You are all right, maybe, if you can stick it out until dark and then get in. So what if you start this sticking it out at daylight? How about that? And that poor bloody Sordo abandoning his pidgin Spanish to explain it to him so carefully. As though he had not thought about that whenever he had done any particularly bad thinking ever since Golz had first mentioned it. As though he hadn't been living with that like a lump of undigested dough in the pit of his stomach ever since the night before the night before last.

What a business. You go along your whole life and they seem as though they mean something and they always end up not meaning anything. There was never any of what this is. You think that is one thing that you will never have. And then, on a lousy show like this, co-ordinating two chicken-crut guerrilla bands to help you blow a bridge under impossible conditions, to abort a counter-offensive that will probably already be started, you run into a girl like this Maria. Sure. That is what you would do. You ran into her rather late, that was all.

So a woman like that Pilar practically pushed this girl into your sleeping bag and what happens? Yes, what happens? What happens? You tell me what happens, please. Yes. That is just what happens. That is exactly what happens.

Don't lie to yourself about Pilar pushing her into your sleeping robe and try to make it nothing or to make it lousy. You were gone when you first saw her. When she first opened her mouth and spoke to you it was there already and you know it. Since you have it and you never thought you would have it, there is no sense throwing dirt at it, when you know what it is and you know it came the first time you looked at her as she came out bent over carrying that iron cooking platter.

It hit you then and you know it and so why lie about it. You went all strange inside every time you looked at her and every time she looked at you. So why don't you admit it? All right. I'll admit it. And as for Pilar, pushing her on to you, all Pilar did was be an intelligent woman. She had taken good care of the girl and she saw what was coming the minute the girl came back into the cave with the cooking dish.

So she made things easier. She made things easier so that there was last night and this afternoon. She is a damned sight more civilized than you are and she knows what time is all about. Yes, he said to himself, I think we can admit that she has certain notions about the value of time. She took a beating and all because she did not want other people losing what she'd lost and then the idea of admitting it was lost was too big a thing to swallow. So she took a beating back there on the hill and I guess we did not make it any easier for her.

Well, so that is what happens and what has happened and you might as well admit it and now you will never have two whole nights with her. Not a lifetime, not to live together, not to have what people were always supposed to have, not at all. One night that is past, once one afternoon, one night to come; may be. No, sir.

Not time, not happiness, not fun, not children, not a house, not a bathroom, not a clean pair of pyjamas, not the morning paper, not to wake up together, not to wake and know she's there and that you're not alone. No. None of that. But why, when this is all you are going to get in life of what you want; when you have found it; why not just one night in bed with sheets?

You ask for the impossible. You ask for the ruddy impossible. So if you love this girl as much as you say you do, you had better love her very hard and make up in intensity what the relation will lack in duration and in continuity. Do you hear that? In the old days people devoted a lifetime to it. And now when you have found it if you get two nights you wonder where all the luck came from. Two nights. Two nights to love, honour and cherish. For better and for worse. In sickness and in death. No that wasn't it. In sickness and in health. Till death do us part. In two nights. Much more than likely. Much more than likely and now lay off that sort of thinking. You can stop that now. That's not good for you. Do nothing that is not good for you. Sure that's it.

This was what Golz had talked about. The longer he was around, the smarter Golz seemed. So this was what he was asking about; the compensation of irregular service. Had Golz had this and was it the urgency and the lack of time and the circumstances that made it? Was this something that happened to everyone given comparable circumstances? And did he only think it was something special because it was happening to him? Had

Golz slept around in a hurry when he was commanding irregular cavalry in the Red Army and had the combination of the circumstances and the rest of it made the girls seem the way Maria was?

Probably Golz knew all about this too and wanted to make the point that you must make your whole life in the two nights that are given to you; that living as we do now you must concentrate all of that which you should always have into the short time that you can have it.

It was a good system of belief. But he did not believe that Maria had only been made by the circumstances. Unless, of course, she is a reaction from her own circumstances as well as his. Her one circumstance is not so good, he thought. No, not so good.

If this was how it was then this was how it was. But there was no law that made him say he liked it. I did not know that I could ever feel what I have felt, he thought. Nor that this could happen to me. I would like to have it for my whole life. You will, the other part of him said. You will. You have it *now* and that is all your whole life is; now. There is nothing else than now. There is neither yesterday, certainly, nor is there any to-morrow. How old must you be before you know that? There is only now, and if now is only two days, then two days is your life and everything in it will be in proportion. This is how you live a life in two days. And if you stop complaining and asking for what you never will get, you will have a good life. A good life is not measured by any biblical span.

So now do not worry, take what you have, and do your work and you will have a long life and a very merry one. Hasn't it been merry lately? What are you complaining about? That's the thing about this sort of work, he told himself, and was very pleased with the thought, it isn't so much what you learn as it is the people you meet. He was pleased then because he was joking and he came back to the girl.

'I love you, rabbit,' he said to the girl. 'What was it you were saying?'

'I was saying,' she told him, 'that you must not worry about your work because I will not bother you nor interfere. If there is anything I can do you will tell me.'

'There's nothing,' he said. 'It is really very simple.'

'I will learn from Pilar what I should do to take care of a man well and those things I will do,' Maria said. 'Then, as I learn, I will discover things for myself and other things you can tell me.'

'There is nothing to do.'

'*Qué va*, man, there is nothing! Thy sleeping robe, this morning, should have been shaken and aired and hung somewhere in the sun. Then, before the dew comes, it should be taken into shelter.'

'Go on, rabbit.'

'Thy socks should be washed and dried. I would see thee had two pair.'

'What else?'

'If thou would show me I would clean and oil thy pistol.'

'Kiss me,' Robert Jordan said.

'Nay, this is serious. Wilt thou show me about the pistol? Pilar has rags and oil. There is a cleaning rod inside the cave that should fit it.'

'Sure. I'll show you.'

'Then,' Maria said. 'If you will teach me to shoot it either one of us could shoot the other and himself, or herself, if one were wounded and it were necessary to avoid capture.'

'Very interesting,' Robert Jordan said. 'Do you have many ideas like that?'

'Not many,' Maria said. 'But it is a good one. Pilar gave me this and showed me how to use it,' she opened the breast pocket of her shirt and took out a cut-down leather holder such as pocket combs are carried in and, removing a wide rubber band that closed both ends, took out a Gem type, single-edged razor blade. 'I keep this always,' she explained. 'Pilar says you must make the cut here just below the ear and draw it toward here.' She showed him with her finger. 'She says there is big artery there and that drawing the blade from there you cannot miss it. Also, she says there is no pain and you must simply press firmly below the ear and draw it downward. She says it is nothing and that they cannot stop it if it is done.'

'That's right,' said Robert Jordan. 'That's the carotid artery.'

So she goes around with that all the time, he thought, as a definitely accepted and properly organized possibility.

'But I would rather have thee shoot me,' Maria said. 'Promise if there is ever any need that thou wilt shoot me.'

'Sure,' Robert Jordan said. 'I promise.'

'Thank thee very much,' Maria told him. 'I know it is not easy to do.'

'That's all right,' Robert Jordan said.

You forget all this, he thought. You forget about the beauties of a civil war when you keep your mind too much on your work. You have forgotten this. Well, you are supposed to. Kashkin couldn't forget it and it spoiled his work. Or do you think the old boy had a hunch? It was very strange because he had experienced absolutely no emotion about the shooting of Kashkin. He expected that at some time he might have it. But so far there had been absolutely none.

'But there are other things I can do for thee,' Maria told him, walking close beside him, now, very serious and womanly.

'Besides shoot me?'

'Yes. I can roll cigarettes for thee when thou hast no more of those with tubes. Pilar has taught me to roll them very well, tight and neat and not spilling.'

'Excellent,' said Robert Jordan. 'Do you lick them yourself?'

'Yes,' the girl said, 'and when thou art wounded I will care for thee and dress thy wound and wash thee and feed thee—'

'Maybe I won't be wounded,' Robert Jordan said.

'Then when you are sick I will care for thee and make thee soups and clean thee and do all for thee. And I will read to thee.'

'Maybe I won't get sick.'

'Then I will bring thee coffee in the morning when thou wakest—'

'Maybe I don't like coffee,' Robert Jordan told her.

'Nay, but you do,' the girl said happily. 'This morning you took two cups.'

'Suppose I get tired of coffee and there's no need to shoot me and I'm neither wounded nor sick and I give up smoking and have only one pair of socks and hang up my robe myself. What then, rabbit?' he patted her on the back. 'What then?'

'Then,' said Maria, 'I will borrow the scissors of Pilar and cut thy hair.'

'I don't like to have my hair cut.'

'Neither do I,' said Maria. 'And I like thy hair as it is. So. If there is nothing to do for thee, I will sit by thee and watch thee and in the nights we will make love.'

'Good,' Robert Jordan said. 'The last project is very sensible.'

'To me it seems the same,' Maria smiled. 'Oh, *Inglés*,' she said.

'My name is Roberto.'

'Nay. But I call thee *Inglés* as Pilar does.'

'Still it is Roberto.'

'No,' she told him. 'Now for a whole day it is *Inglés*. And *Inglés*, can I help thee with thy work?'

'No. What I do now I do alone and very coldly in my head.'

'Good,' she said. 'And when will it be finished?'

'To-night, with luck.'

'Good,' she said.

Below them were the last woods that led to the camp.

'Who is that?' Robert Jordan asked and pointed.

'Pilar,' the girl said, looking along his arm. 'Surely it is Pilar.'

At the lower edge of the meadow where the first trees grew the woman was sitting, her head on her arms. She looked like a dark bundle from where they stood; black against the brown of the tree trunk.

'Come on,' Robert Jordan said and started to run toward her through the knee-high heather. It was heavy and hard to run in and when he had run a little way, he slowed and walked. He could see the woman's head was on her folded arms and she looked broad and black against the tree trunk. He came up to her and said, 'Pilar!' sharply.

The woman raised her head and looked up at him.

'Oh,' she said. 'You have terminated already?'

'Art thou ill?' he asked and bent down by her.

'*Qué va*,' she said. 'I was asleep.'

'Pilar,' Maria, who had come up, said and kneeled down by her. 'How are you? Are you all right?'

'I'm magnificent,' Pilar said but she did not get up. She looked at the two of them. 'Well, *Inglés*,' she said. 'You have been doing manly tricks again?'

'You are all right?' Robert Jordan asked, ignoring the words.

'Why not? I slept. Did you?

'No.'

'Well,' Pilar said to the girl. 'It seems to agree with you.'

Maria blushed and said nothing.

'Leave her alone,' Robert Jordan said.

'No one spoke to thee,' Pilar told him. 'Maria,' she said and her voice was hard. The girl did not look up.

'Maria,' the woman said again. 'I said it seems to agree with thee.'

'Oh, leave her alone,' Robert Jordan said again.

'Shut up, you,' Pilar said without looking at him. 'Listen, Maria, tell me one thing.'

'No,' Maria said and shook her head.

'Maria,' Pilar said, and her voice was as hard as her face and there was nothing friendly in her face. 'Tell me one thing of thy own volition.'

The girl shook her head.

Robert Jordan was thinking, if I did not have to work with this woman and her drunken man and her chicken-crut outfit, I would slap her so hard across the face that—

'Go ahead and tell me,' Pilar said to the girl.

'No,' Maria said. 'No.'

'Leave her alone,' Robert Jordan said and his voice did not sound like his own voice. I'll slap her anyway and the hell with it, he thought.

Pilar did not even speak to him. It was not like a snake charming a bird, nor a cat with a bird. There was nothing predatory. Nor was there anything perverted about it. There was a spreading, though, as a cobra's hood spreads. He could feel this. He could feel the menace of the spreading. But the spreading was a domination, not of evil, but of searching. I wish I did not see this, Robert Jordan thought. But it is not a business for slapping.

'Maria,' Pilar said. 'I will not touch thee. Tell me now of thy own volition.'

'*De tu propia voluntad*,' the words were in Spanish.

The girl shook her head.

'Maria,' Pilar said. 'Now and of thy own volition. You hear me? Anything at all.'

'No,' the girl said softly. 'No and no.'

'Now you will tell me,' Pilar told her. 'Anything at all. You will see. Now you will tell me.'

'The earth moved,' Maria said, not looking at the woman. 'Truly. It was a thing I cannot tell thee.'

'So,' Pilar said and her voice was warm and friendly and there was no compulsion in it. But Robert Jordan noticed there were small drops of perspiration on her forehead and her lips. 'So there was that. So that was it.'

'It is true,' Maria said and bit her lip.

'Of course it is true,' Pilar said kindly. 'But do not tell it to your own people for they never will believe you. You have no *Cali* blood, *Inglés*?'

She got to her feet, Robert Jordan helping her up.

'No,' he said. 'Not that I know of.'

'Nor has the Maria that she knows of,' Pilar said. '*Pues es muy raro*. It is very strange.'

'But it happened, Pilar,' Maria said.

'*Cómo que no, hija?*' Pilar said. 'Why not, daughter? When I was young the earth moved so that you could feel it all shift in space and were afraid it would go out from under you. It happened every night.'

'You lie,' Maria said.

'Yes,' Pilar said. 'I lie. It never moves more than three times in a lifetime. Did it *really* move?'

'Yes,' the girl said. 'Truly.'

'For you, *Inglés*?' Pilar looked at Robert Jordan. 'Don't lie.'

'Yes,' he said. 'Truly.'

'Good,' said Pilar. 'Good. That is something.'

'What do you mean about the three times?' Maria asked. 'Why do you say that?'

'Three times,' said Pilar. 'Now you've had one.'

'Only three times?'

'For most people, never,' Pilar told her. 'You are sure it moved?'

'One could have fallen off,' Maria said.

'I guess it moved, then,' Pilar said. 'Come, then, and let us get to camp.'

'What's this nonsense about three times?' Robert Jordan said to the big woman as they walked through the pines together.

'Nonsense?' she looked at him wryly. 'Don't talk to me of nonsense, little English.'

'Is it a wizardry like the palms of the hands?'

'Nay, it is common and proven knowledge with *Gitanos*.'

'But we are not *Gitanos*.'

'Nay. But you have had a little luck. Non-gipsies have a little luck sometimes.'

'You mean it truly about the three times?'

She looked at him again, oddly. 'Leave me, *Inglés*,' she said. 'Don't molest me. You are too young for me to speak to.'

'But, Pilar,' Maria said.

'Shut up,' Pilar told her. 'You have had one and there are two more in the world for thee.'

'And you?' Robert Jordan asked her.

'Two,' said Pilar and put up two fingers. 'Two. And there will never be a third.'

'Why not?' Maria asked.

'Oh, shut up,' Pilar said. 'Shut up. *Busnes* of thy age bore me.'

'Why not a third?' Robert Jordan asked.

'Oh, shut up, will you?' Pilar said. 'Shut up!'

All right, Robert Jordan said to himself. Only I am not having any. I've known a lot of gipsies and they are strange enough. But so are we. The difference is we have to make an honest living. Nobody knows what tribes we came from nor what our tribal inheritance is nor what the mysteries were in the woods where the people lived that we came from. All we know is that we do not know. We know nothing about what happens to us in the nights. When it happens in the day though, it *is* something. Whatever happened, happened and now this woman not only has to make the girl say it when she did not want to; but she has to take it over and make it her own. She has to make it into a gipsy thing. I thought she took a beating up the hill but she was certainly dominating just now back there. If it had been evil she should have been shot. But it wasn't evil. It was only wanting to keep her hold on life. To keep it through Maria.

When you get through with this war you might take up the study of women, he said to himself. You could start with Pilar. She has put in a pretty complicated day, if you ask me. She never brought in the gipsy stuff before.

Except the hand, he thought. Yes, of course the hand. And I don't think she was faking about the hand. She wouldn't tell me what she saw, of course. Whatever she saw she believed in herself. But that proves nothing.

'Listen, Pilar,' he said to the woman.

Pilar looked at him and smiled.

'What is it?' she asked.

'Don't be so mysterious,' Robert Jordan said. 'These mysteries tire me very much.'

'So?' Pilar said.

'I do not believe in ogres, soothsayers, fortune tellers, or chicken-crut gipsy witchcraft.'

'Oh,' said Pilar.

'No. And you can leave the girl alone.'

'I will leave the girl alone.'

'And leave the mysteries,' Robert Jordan said. 'We have enough work and enough things that will be done without complicating it with chicken-crut. Fewer mysteries and more work.'

'I see,' said Pilar and nodded her head in agreement. 'And listen, *Inglés*,' she said and smiled at him. 'Did the earth move?'

'Yes, God-damn you. It moved.'

Pilar laughed and laughed and stood looking at Robert Jordan laughing.

'Oh, *Inglés. Inglés*,' she said laughing. 'You are very comical. You must do much work now to regain thy dignity.'

The hell with you, Robert Jordan thought. But he kept his mouth shut. While they had spoken the sun had clouded over and as he looked back up toward the mountains the sky was now heavy and grey.

'Sure,' Pilar said to him, looking at the sky. 'It will snow.'

'Now? almost in June?'

'Why not? These mountains do not know the names of the months. We are in the moon of May.'

'It can't be snow,' he said. 'It *can't* snow.'

'Just the same, *Inglés*,' she said to him, 'it will snow.'

Robert Jordan looked up at the thick grey of the sky with the sun gone faintly yellow, and now as he watched gone completely and the grey becoming uniform so that it was soft and heavy; the grey now cutting off the tops of the mountains.

'Yes,' he said. 'I guess you are right.'

14

By the time they reached the camp it was snowing and the flakes were dropping diagonally through the pines. They slanted through the trees, sparse at first and circling as they fell, and then, as the cold wind came driving down the mountain, they came whirling and thick and Robert

Jordan stood in front of the cave in a rage and watched them.

'We will have much snow,' Pablo said. His voice was thick and his eyes were red and bleary.

'Has the gipsy come in?' Robert Jordan asked him.

'No,' Pablo said. 'Neither him nor the old man.'

'Will you come with me to the upper post on the road?'

'No,' Pablo said. 'I will take no part in this.'

'I will find it myself.'

'In this storm you might miss it,' Pablo said. 'I would not go now.'

'It's just downhill to the road and then follow it up.'

'You could find it. But thy two sentries will be coming up now with the snow and you would miss them on the way.'

'The old man is waiting for me.'

'Nay. He will come in now with the snow.'

Pablo looked at the snow that was blowing fast now past the mouth of the cave and said, 'You do not like the snow, *Inglés*?'

Robert Jordan swore and Pablo looked at him through his bleary eyes and laughed.

'With this thy offensive goes, *Inglés*,' he said. 'Come into the cave and thy people will be in directly.'

Inside the cave Maria was busy at the fire and Pilar at the kitchen table. The fire was smoking but, as the girl worked with it, poking in a stick of wood and then fanning it with a folded paper, there was a puff and then a flare and the wood was burning, drawing brightly as the wind sucked a draught out of the hole in the roof.

'And this snow,' Robert Jordan said. 'You think there will be much?'

'Much,' Pablo said contentedly. Then called to Pilar, 'You don't like it, woman, either? Now that you command you do not like this snow?'

'*A mi qué?*' Pilar said, over her shoulder. 'If it snows it snows.'

'Drink some wine, *Inglés*,' Pablo said. 'I have been drinking all day waiting for the snow.'

'Give me a cup,' Robert Jordan said.

'To the snow,' Pablo said and touched cups with him. Robert Jordan looked him in the eyes and clinked his cup. You bleary-eyed murderous sod, he thought. I'd like to clink this cup against your teeth. *Take it easy*, he told himself, *take it easy*.

'It is very beautiful the snow,' Pablo said. 'You won't want to sleep outside with the snow falling.'

So *that's* on your mind too is it? Robert Jordan thought. 'You've a lot of troubles, haven't you, Pablo?'

'No?' he said, politely.

'No. Very cold,' Pablo said. 'Very wet.'

You don't know why those old eiderdowns cost sixty-five dollars, Robert Jordan thought. I'd like to have a dollar for every time I've slept in that thing in the snow.

'Then I should sleep in here?' he asked politely.

'Yes.'

'Thanks,' Robert Jordan said. 'I'll be sleeping outside.'

'In the snow?'

'Yes' (damn your bloody, red pig-eyes and your swine-bristly swines-end of a face). 'In the snow.' (In the utterly-damned, ruinous, unexpected, slutting, defeat-conniving, bastard-cessery of the snow.)

He went over to where Maria had just put another piece of pine on the fire.

'Very beautiful, the snow,' he said to the girl.

'But it is bad for the work, isn't it?' she asked him. 'Aren't you worried?'

'*Qué va*,' he said. 'Worrying is no good. When will supper be ready?'

'I thought you would have an appetite,' Pilar said. 'Do you want a cut of cheese now?'

'Thanks,' he said and she cut him a slice, reaching up to unhook the big cheese that hung in a net from the ceiling, drawing a knife across the open end and handing him the heavy slice. He stood, eating it. It was just a little too goaty to be enjoyable.

'Maria,' Pablo said from the table where he was sitting.

'What?' the girl asked.

'Wipe the table clean, Maria,' Pablo said and grinned at Robert Jordan.

'Wipe thine own spillings,' Pilar said to him. 'Wipe first thy chin and thy shirt and then the table.'

'Maria,' Pablo called.

'Pay no heed to him. He is drunk,' Pilar said.

'Maria,' Pablo called. 'It is still snowing and the snow is beautiful.'

He doesn't know about that robe, Robert Jordan thought. Good old pig-eyes doesn't know why I paid the Woods boys sixty-five dollars for that robe. I wish the gipsy would come in though. As soon as the gipsy comes I'll go after the old man. I should go now but it is very possible that I would miss them. I don't know where he is posted.

'Want to make snowballs?' he said to Pablo. 'Want to have a snowball fight?'

'What?' Pablo asked. 'What do you propose?'

'Nothing,' Robert Jordan said. 'Got your saddles covered up good?'

'Yes.'

Then in English Robert Jordan said, 'Going to grain those horses or peg them out and let them dig for it?'

'What?'

'Nothing. It's your problem, old pal. I'm going out of here on my feet.'

'Why do you speak in English?' Pablo asked.

'I don't know,' Robert Jordan said. 'When I get very tired sometimes I speak English. Or when I get very disgusted. Or baffled, say. When I get highly baffled I just talk English to hear the sound of it. It's a reassuring noise. You ought to try it sometime.'

'What do you say, *Inglés*?' Pilar said. 'It sounds very interesting but I do not understand.'

'Nothing,' Robert Jordan said. 'I said, "nothing" in English.'

'Well, then, talk Spanish,' Pilar said. 'It's shorter and simpler in Spanish.'

'Surely,' Robert Jordan said. But oh boy, he thought, oh Pablo, oh Pilar, oh Maria, oh you two brothers in the corner whose names I've forgotten and must remember, but I get tired of it sometimes. Of it and of you and of me and of the war and why in all why, did it have to snow now? That's too bloody much. No, it's not. Nothing is too bloody much. You just have to take it and fight out of it and now stop prima-donnaing and accept the fact that it is snowing as you did a moment ago and the next thing is to check with your gipsy and pick up your old man. But to snow! Now in this month. Cut it out, he said to himself. Cut it out and take it. It's that cup, you know. How did it go about that cup? He'd either have to improve his memory or else never think of quotations because when you missed one it hung in your mind like a name you had forgotten and you could not get rid of it. How did it go about that cup?

'Let me have a cup of wine, please,' he said in Spanish. Then, 'Lots of snow? Eh?' he said to Pablo. '*Mucha nieve.*'

The drunken man looked up at him and grinned. He nodded his head and grinned again.

'No offensive. No *aviones*. No bridge. Just snow,' Pablo said.

'You expect it to last a long time?' Robert Jordan sat down by him. 'You think we're going to be snowed in all summer, Pablo, old boy?'

'All summer, no,' Pablo said. 'To-night and to-morrow, yes.'

'What makes you think so?'

'There are two kinds of storms,' Pablo said, heavily and judiciously. 'One comes from the Pyrenees. With this one there is great cold. It is too late for this one.'

'Good,' Robert Jordan said. 'That's something.'

'This storms comes from the Cantabrico,' Pablo said. 'It comes from the sea. With the wind in this direction there will be a great storm and much snow.'

'Where did you learn all this, old timer?' Robert Jordan asked.

Now that his rage was gone he was excited by this storm as he was always by all storms. In a blizzard, a gale, a sudden line squall, a tropical storm, or a summer thunder shower in the mountains there was an excitement that came to him from no other thing. It was like the excitement of battle except that it was clean. There is a wind that blows through battle but that was a hot wind; hot and dry as your mouth; and it blew heavily; hot and dirtily; and it rose and died away with the fortunes of the day. He knew that wind well.

But a snowstorm was the opposite of all of that. In the snowstorm you came close to wild animals and they were not afraid. They travelled across country not knowing where they were and the deer stood sometimes in the lee of the cabin. In a snowstorm you rode up to a moose and he mistook your horse for another moose and trotted forward to meet you. In a snowstorm it always seemed, for a time, as though there were no enemies. In a snowstorm the wind could blow a gale; but it blew a white cleanness and the air was full of a driving whiteness and all things were changed and when the wind stopped there would be the stillness. This was a big storm and he might as well enjoy it. It was ruining everything, but you might as well enjoy it.

'I was an arroyero for many years,' Pablo said. 'We trucked freight across the mountains with the big carts before the camions came into use. In that business we learned the weather.'

'And how did you get into the movement?'

'I was always of the left,' Pablo said. 'We had many contacts with the people of Asturias where they are much developed politically. I have always been for the Republic.'

'But what were you doing before the movement?'

'I worked then for a horse contractor of Zaragoza. He furnished horses for the bull rings as well as remounts for the army. It was then that I met Pilar who was, as she told you, with the matador Finito de Palencia.'

He said this with considerable pride.

'He wasn't much of a matador,' one of the brothers at the table said looking at Pilar's back where she stood in front of the stove.

'No?' Pilar said, turning around and looking at the man. 'He wasn't much of a matador?'

Standing there now in the cave by the cooking fire she could see him, short and brown and sober-faced, with the sad eyes, the cheeks sunken and the black hair curled wet on his forehead where the tight-fitting matador's hat had made a red line that no one else noticed. She saw him stand, now, facing the five-year-old bull, facing the horns that had lifted the horses high, the great neck thrusting the horse up, up, as the rider poked into that neck with the spiked pole, thrusting up and up until the horse went over with a crash and the rider fell against the wooden fence and, with the bull's legs thrusting him forward, the big neck swung the horns that searched the horse for the life that was in him. She saw him, Finito, the not-so-good matador, now standing in front of the bull and turning sideways toward him. She saw him now clearly as he furled the heavy flannel cloth around the stick; the flannel hanging blood-heavy from the passes where it had swept over the bull's head and shoulders and the wet streaming shine of his withers and on down and over his back as the bull raised into the air and the banderillas clattered. She saw Finito stand five paces from the bull's head, profiled, the bull standing still and heavy, and draw the sword slowly up until it was level with his shoulder and then sight along the dipping blade at a point he could not yet see because the bull's head was higher than his eyes. He would bring that head down with the sweep his left arm would make with the wet, heavy cloth; but now he rocked back a little on his heels and sighted along the blade, profiled in front of the splintered horn; the bull's chest heaving and his eyes watching the cloth.

She saw him very clearly now and she heard his thin, clear voice as he turned his head and looked toward the people in the first row of the ring above the red fence and said, 'Let's see if we can kill him like this!'

She could hear the voice and then see the first bend of the knee as he started forward and watch his voyage in on to the horn that lowered now magically as the bull's muzzle followed the low swept cloth, the thin, brown wrist controlled, sweeping the horns down and past, as the sword entered the dusty height of the withers.

She saw its brightness going in slowly and steadily as though the bull's rush plucked it into himself and out from the man's hand and she watched it move in until the brown knuckles rested against the taut hide and the short, brown man whose eyes had never left the entry place of the sword now swung his sucked-in belly clear of the horn and rocked clear from the animal, to stand holding the cloth on the stick in his left hand, raising his right hand to watch the bull die.

She saw him standing, his eyes watching the bull trying to hold the ground, watching the bull sway like a tree before it falls, watching the bull fight to hold his feet to the earth, the short man's hand raised in a formal gesture of triumph. She saw him standing there in the sweated, hollow relief of it being over, feeling the relief that the bull was dying, feeling the relief that there had been no shock, no blow of the horn as he came clear from it and then, as he stood, the bull could hold to the earth no longer and crashed over, rolling dead with all four feet in the air, and she could see the short, brown man walking tired and unsmiling to the fence.

She knew he could not run across the ring if his life depended on it and she watched him walk slowly to the fence and wipe his mouth on a towel and look up at her and shake his head and then wipe his face on the towel and start his triumphant circling of the ring.

She saw him moving slowly, dragging around the ring, smiling, bowing, smiling, his assistants walking behind him, stooping, picking up cigars, tossing back hats; he circling the ring sad-eyed and smiling, to end the circle before her. Then she looked over and saw him sitting now on the step of the wooden fence, his mouth in a towel.

Pilar saw all this as she stood there over the fire and she said, 'So he wasn't a good matador? With what class of people is my life passed now!'

'He was a good matador,' Pablo said. 'He was handicapped by his short stature.'

'And clearly he was tubercular,' Primitivo said.

'Tubercular?' Pilar said. 'Who wouldn't be tubercular from the punishment he received? In this country where no poor man can ever hope to make money unless he is a criminal like Juan March, or a bullfighter, or a tenor in the opera? Why wouldn't he be tubercular? In a country where the bourgeoisie over-eat so that their stomachs are all ruined and they cannot live without bicarbonate of soda and the poor are hungry from their birth till the day they die, why wouldn't he be tubercular? If you travelled under the seats in third-class carriages to ride free when you were following the fairs learning to fight as a boy, down there in the dust and dirt with the fresh spit and the dry spit, wouldn't you be tubercular if your chest was beaten out by horns?'

'Clearly,' Primitivo said. 'I only said he was tubercular.'

'Of course he was tubercular,' Pilar said, standing there with the big wooden stirring spoon in her hand. 'He was short of stature and he had a thin voice and much fear of bulls. Never have I seen a man with more fear before the bullfight and never have I seen a man with less fear in the ring. You,' she said to Pablo. 'You are afraid to die now. You think that is something of importance. But Finito was afraid all the time and in the ring he was like a lion.'

'He had the fame of being very valiant,' the second brother said.

'Never have I known a man with so much fear,' Pilar said. 'He would not even have a bull's head in the house. One time at the feria of Valladolid he killed a bull of Pablo Romero very well—'

'I remember,' the first brother said. 'I was at the ring. It was a soap-coloured one with a curly forehead and with very high horns. It was a bull of over thirty arrobas. It was the last bull he killed in Valladolid.'

'Exactly,' Pilar said. 'And afterwards the club of enthusiasts who met in the Café Colon and had taken his name for their club had the head of the bull mounted and presented it to him at a small banquet at the Café Colon. During the meal they had the head on the wall, but it was covered with a cloth. I was at the table and others were there, Pastora, who is uglier than I am, and the Niña de los Pienes, and other gipsies and whores of great category. It was a banquet, small but of great intensity and almost of a violence due to a dispute between Pastora and one of the most significant whores over a question of propriety. I, myself, was feeling more than happy and I was sitting by Finito and I noticed he would not look up at the bull's head, which was shrouded in a purple cloth as the images of the saints are covered in church during the week of the passion of our former Lord.

'Finito did not eat much because he had received a *palotazo*, a blow from the flat of the horn when he had gone in to kill in his last corrida of the year at Zaragoza, and it had rendered him unconscious for some time and even now he could not hold food on his stomach and he would put his handkerchief to his mouth and deposit a quantity of blood in it at intervals throughout the banquet. What was I going to tell you?'

'The bull's head,' Primitivo said. 'The stuffed head of the bull.'

'Yes,' Pilar said. 'Yes. But I must tell certain details so that you will see it. Finito was never very merry, you know. He was essentially solemn and I had never known him when we were alone to laugh at anything. Not even at things which were very comic. He took everything with great seriousness. He was almost as serious as Fernando. But this was a banquet given him by a club of *aficionados* banded together into the *Club Finito* and it was necessary for him to give an appearance of gaiety and friendliness and merriment. So all during the meal he smiled and made friendly remarks and it was only I who noticed what he was doing with the handkerchief. He had three handkerchiefs with him and he filled the three of them and then he said to me in a very low voice, "Pilar, I can support this no further. I think I must leave."

'"Let us leave then," I said. For I saw he was suffering much. There was great hilarity by this time at the banquet and the noise was tremendous.

'"No. I cannot leave," Finito said to me. "After all it is a club named for me and I have an obligation."

'"If thou art ill let us go," I said.

'"Nay," he said. "I will stay. Give me some of that manzanilla."

'I did not think it was wise of him to drink, since he had eaten nothing, and since he had such a condition of the stomach; but he was evidently unable to support the merriment and the hilarity and the noise longer without taking something. So I watched him drink, very rapidly, almost a bottle of the manzanilla. Having exhausted his handkerchiefs he was now employing his napkin for the use he had previously made of his handkerchiefs.

'Now indeed the banquet had reached a stage of great enthusiasm and some of the least heavy of the whores were being paraded around the table on the shoulders of various of the club members. Pastora was prevailed upon to sing and El Niño Ricardo played the guitar and it was very moving and an occasion of true joy and drunken friendship of the highest order. Never have I seen a banquet at which a higher pitch of real *flamenco* enthusiasm was reached and yet we have not arrived at the unveiling of the bull's head which was, after all, the reason for the celebration of the banquet.

'I was enjoying myself to such an extent and I was so busy clapping my hands to the playing of Ricardo and aiding to make up a team to clap for the singing of the Niña de los Peines that I did not notice that Finito had filled his own napkin by now, and that he had taken mine. He was drinking more manzanilla now and his eyes were very bright and he was nodding very happily to everyone. He could not speak much because at any time, while speaking, he might have to resort to his napkin; but he was giving an appearance of great gaiety and enjoyment which, after all, was what he was there for.

'So the banquet proceeded and the man who sat next to me had been the former manager of Rafael el Gallo and he was telling me a story, and the end of it was, "So Rafael came to me and said, 'You are the best friend I have in the world and the noblest. I love you like a brother and I wish to make you a present.' So then he gave me a beautiful diamond scarf-pin and kissed me on both cheeks and we were both very moved. Then Rafael el Gallo, having given me the diamond scarf-pin, walked out of the café and I said to Retana who was sitting at the table, 'That dirty gipsy had just signed a contract with another manager.'"

'"'What do you mean?' Retana asked."

'"I've managed him for ten years and he has never given me a present before," the manager of El Gallo had said. "That's the only thing it can mean." And sure enough it was true and that was how El Gallo left him.

'But at this point, Pastora intervened in the conversation, not perhaps as much to defend the good name of Rafael, since no one had ever spoken harder against him than she had herself, but because the manager had spoken against the gipsies by employing the phrase, "Dirty gipsy". She intervened so forcibly and in such terms that the manager was reduced to silence. I intervened to quiet Pastora and another *Gitana* intervened to quiet me and the din was such that no one could distinguish any words which passed except the one great word whore which roared out above all other words until quiet was restored and the three of us who had intervened sat looking down into our glasses and then I noticed Finito was staring at the bull's head, still draped in the purple cloth, with a look of horror on his face.

'At this moment the president of the Club commenced the speech which was to precede the unveiling of the head and all through the speech which was applauded with shouts of "*Olé*!" and poundings on the table I was watching Finito who was making use of his, no, my napkin, and sinking farther back in his chair and staring with horror and fascination at the shrouded bull's head on the wall opposite him.

'Toward the end of the speech, Finito began to shake his head and he got farther back in the chair all the time.

'"How are you, little one?" I said to him but when he looked at me he did not recognize me and he only shook his head and said, "No. No. No."

'So the president of the Club reached the end of the speech and then, with everybody cheering him, he stood on a chair and reached up and untied the cord that bound the purple shroud over the head and slowly pulled it clear of the head and it stuck on one of the horns and he lifted it clear and pulled it off the sharp polished horns and there was that great yellow bull with black horns that swung way out and pointed forward, their white tips sharp as porcupine quills, and the head of the bull was as though he were alive; his forehead was curly as in life and his nostrils were open and his eyes were bright and he was there looking straight at Finito.

'Everyone shouted and applauded and Finito sank farther back in the chair and then everyone was quiet and looking at him and he said, "No, No," and looked at the bull and pulled farther back and then he said, "No!" very loudly and a big blob of blood came out and he didn't even put up the napkin and it slid down his chin and he was still looking at the bull and he said, "All season, yes. To make money, yes. To eat, yes. But I can't eat. Hear me? My stomach's bad. But now with the season finished! No! No! No!" He looked around at the table and then he looked at the bull's head and said, "No," once more and then he put his head down and he put his napkin up to his mouth and then he just sat there like that and said nothing and the banquet, which had started so well, and promised to mark an epoch in hilarity and good fellowship was not a success.'

'Then how long after that did he die?' Primitivo asked.

'That winter,' Pilar said. 'He never recovered from that last blow with the flat of the horn in Zaragoza. They are worse than a goring, for the injury is internal and it does not heal. He received one almost every time he went in to kill and it was for this reason he was not more successful. It was difficult for him to get out from over the horn because of his short stature. Nearly always the side of the horn struck him. But of course many were only glancing blows.'

'If he was so short he should not have tried to be a matador,' Primitivo said.

Pilar looked at Robert Jordan and shook her head. Then she bent over the big iron pot, still shaking her head.

What a people they are, she thought. What a people are the Spaniards, and 'if he was so short he should not have tried to be a matador.' And I hear it and say nothing. I have no rage for that and having made an explanation I am silent. How simple it is when one knows nothing. *Qué sencillo!* Knowing nothing one says, 'He was not much of a matador.' Knowing nothing another says, 'He was tubercular.' And another says, after one, knowing, has explained, 'If he was so short he should not have tried to be a matador.'

Now, bending over the fire, she saw on the bed again the naked brown body with the gnarled scars in both thighs, the deep, seared whorl below the ribs on the right side of the chest and the long white welt along the side that ended in the armpit. She saw the eyes closed and the solemn brown face and the curly black hair pushed back now from the forehead and she was sitting by him on the bed rubbing the legs, chafing the taut muscles of the calves, kneading them, loosening them, and then tapping them lightly with her folded hands, loosening the cramped muscles.

'How is it?' she said to him. 'How are the legs, little one?'

'Very well, Pilar,' he would say without opening his eyes.

'Do you want me to rub the chest?'

'Nay, Pilar. Please do not touch it.'

'And the upper legs?'

'No. They hurt too badly.'

'But if I rub them and put liniment on, it will warm them and they will be better.'

'Nay, Pilar. Thank thee. I would rather they were not touched.'

'I will wash thee with alcohol.'

'Yes. Do it very lightly.'

'You were enormous in the last bull,' she would say to him and he would say, 'Yes, I killed him very well.'

Then, having washed him and covered him with a sheet, she would lie by him in the bed and he would put a brown hand out and touch her and say, 'Thou art much woman, Pilar.' It was the nearest to a joke he ever made and then, usually, after the fight, he would go to sleep and she would lie there, holding his hand in her two hands and listening to him breathe.

He was often frightened in his sleep and she would feel his hand grip tightly and see the sweat bead on his forehead and if he woke, she said, 'It's nothing,' and he slept again. She was with him thus five years and never was unfaithful to him, that is almost never, and then after the funeral, she took up with Pablo who led picador horses in the ring and was like all the bulls that Finito had spent his life killing. But neither bull force nor bull courage lasted, she knew now, and what did last? I last, she thought. Yes, I have lasted. But for what?

'Maria,' she said. 'Pay some attention to what you are doing. That is a fire to cook with. Not to burn down a city.'

Just then the gipsy came in the door. He was covered with snow and he stood there holding his carbine and stamping the snow from his feet.

Robert Jordan stood up and went over to the door. 'Well?' he said to the gipsy.

'Six-hour watches, two men at a time on the big bridge,' the gipsy said. 'There are eight men and a corporal at the roadmenders' hut. Here is thy chronometer.'

'What about the sawmill post?'

'The old man is there. He can watch that and the road both.'

'And the road?' Robert Jordan asked.

'The same movement as always,' the gipsy said. 'Nothing out of the usual. Several motor cars.'

The gipsy looked cold, his dark face was drawn with the cold and his hands were red. Standing in the mouth of the cave he took off his jacket and shook it.

'I stayed until they changed the watch,' he said. 'It was changed at noon and at six. That is a long watch. I am glad I am not in their army.'

'Let us go for the old man,' Robert Jordan said, putting on his leather coat.

'Not me,' the gipsy said. 'I go now for the fire and the hot soup. I will tell one of these where he is and he can guide you. Hey, loafers,' he called to the men who sat at the table. 'Who wants to guide the *Inglés* to where the old man is watching the road?'

'I will go,' Fernando rose. 'Tell me where it is.'

'Listen,' the gipsy said. 'It is here—' and he told him where the old man, Anselmo, was posted.

15

Anselmo was crouched in the lee of the trunk of a big tree and the snow blew past on either side. He was pressed close against the tree and his hands were inside of the sleeves of his jacket, each hand shoved up into the opposite sleeve, and his head was pulled as far down into the jacket as it would go. If I stay here much longer I will freeze, he thought, and that will be of no value. The *Inglés* told me to stay until I was relieved but he did not know then about this storm. There has been no abnormal movement on the road and I know the dispositions and the habits of this post at the sawmill across the road. I should go now to the camp. Anybody with sense would be expecting me to return to the camp. I will stay a little longer, he thought, and then go to the camp. It is the fault of the orders, which are too rigid. There is no allowance for a change in circumstance. He rubbed his feet together and then took his hands out of the jacket sleeves and bent over and rubbed his legs with them and patted his feet together to keep the circulation going. It was less cold there, out of the wind in the shelter of the tree, but he would have to start walking shortly.

As he crouched, rubbing his feet, he heard a motor car on the road. It had on chains and one link of chain was slapping, and, as he watched, it came up the snow-covered road, green and brown painted, in broken patches of daubed colour, the windows blued over so that you could not see in, with only a half circle left clear in the blue for the occupants to look out through. It was a two-year-old Rolls-Royce town car camouflaged for the use of the General Staff but Anselmo did not know that. He could not see into the car where three officers sat wrapped in their capes. Two were on the back seat and one sat on the folding chair. The officer on the folding chair was looking out of the slit in the blue of the window as the car passed but Anselmo did not know this. Neither of them saw the other.

The car passed in the snow directly below him. Anselmo saw the chauffeur, red-faced and steel-helmeted, his face and helmet projecting out of the blanket cape he wore and he saw the forward jut of the automatic rifle the orderly who sat beside the chauffeur carried. Then the car was gone up the road and Anselmo reached into the inside of his jacket and took out from his shirt pocket the two sheets torn from Robert Jordan's notebook and made a mark after the drawing of a motor car. It was the tenth car up for the day. Six had come down. Four were still up. It was not an unusual amount of cars to move upon that road but Anselmo did not distinguish between the Fords, Fiats, Opels, Renauits, and Citroens of the staff of the Division that held the passes and the line of the mountain and the Rolls-Royces, Lancias, Mercedes, and Isottas of the General Staff. This was the sort of distinction that Robert Jordan should have made and, if he had been there instead of the old man, he would have appreciated the significance of these cars which had gone up. But he was not there and the old man simply made a mark for a motor car going up the road, on the sheet of note paper.

Anselmo was now so cold that he decided he had best go to camp before it was dark. He had no fear of missing the way, but he thought it was useless to stay longer and the wind was blowing colder all the time and there was no lessening of the snow. But when he stood up and stamped his feet and looked through the driving snow at the road he did not start off up the hillside but stayed leaning against the sheltered side of the pine tree.

The *Inglés* told me to stay, he thought. Even now he may be on the way here and, if I leave this place, he may lose himself in the snow searching for me. All through this war we have suffered from a lack of discipline and from the disobeying of orders and I will wait a while still for the *Inglés*. But if he does not come soon I must go in spite of all orders for I have a report to make now, and I have much to do in these days, and to freeze here is an exaggeration and without utility.

Across the road at the sawmill smoke was coming out of the chimney and Anselmo could smell it blown toward him through the snow. The fascists are warm, he thought, and they are comfortable, and to-morrow night we will kill them. It is a strange thing and I do not like to think of it. I have watched them all day and they are the same men that we are. I believe that I could walk up to the mill and knock on the door and I would be welcome except that they have orders to challenge all travellers and ask to see their papers. It is only orders that come between us. Those men are not fascists. I call them so, but they are not. They are poor men as we are. They should never be fighting against us and I do not like to think of the killing.

These at this post are Gallegos. I know that from hearing them talk this afternoon. They cannot desert because if they do their families will be shot. Gallegos are either very intelligent or very dumb and brutal. I have known both kinds. Lister is a Gallego from the same town as Franco. I wonder what these Gallegos think of this snow now at this time of year. They have no high mountains such as these and in their country it always rains and it is always green.

A light showed in the window of the sawmill and Anselmo shivered and thought, damn that *Inglés*! There are the Gallegos warm and in a house here in our country, and I am freezing behind a tree and we live in a hole in the rocks like beasts in the mountain. But to-morrow, he thought, the beasts will come out of their hole and these that are now so comfortable will die warm in their blankets. As those died in the night when we raided Otero, he thought. He did not like to remember Otero.

In Otero, that night, was when he first killed and he hoped he would not have to kill in this of the suppressing of these posts. It was in Otero that

Pablo knifed the sentry when Anselmo pulled the blanket over his head and the sentry caught Anselmo's foot and held it, smothered as he was in the blanket, and made a crying noise in the blanket and Anselmo had to feel in the blanket and knife him until he let go of the foot and was still. He had his knee across the man's throat to keep him silent and he was knifing into the bundle when Pablo tossed the bomb through the window into the room where the men of the post were all sleeping. And when the flash came it was as though the whole world burst red and yellow before your eyes and two more bombs were in already. Pablo had pulled the pins and tossed them quickly through the window, and those who were not killed in their beds were killed as they rose from bed when the second bomb exploded. That was in the great days of Pablo when he scourged the country like a tartar and no fascist post was safe at night.

And now, he is as finished and as ended as a boar that has been altered, Anselmo thought, and, when the altering has been accomplished and the squealing is over you cast the two stones away and the boar, that is a boar no longer, goes snouting and rooting up to them and eats them. No, he is not that bad, Anselmo grinned, one can think too badly even of Pablo. But he is ugly enough and changed enough.

It is too cold, he thought. That the *Inglés* should come and that I should not have to kill in this of the posts. These four Gallegos and their corporal are for those who like the killing. The *Inglés* said that. I will do it if it is my duty but the *Inglés* said that I would be with him at the bridge and that this would be left to others. At the bridge there will be a battle and, if I am able to endure the battle, then I will have done all that an old man may do in this war. But let the *Inglés* come now, for I am cold and to see the light in the mill where I know that the Gallegos are warm makes me colder still. I wish that I were in my own house again and that this war were over. But you have no house now, he thought. We must win this war before you can ever return to your house.

Inside the sawmill one of the soldiers was sitting on his bunk and greasing his boots. Another lay in his bunk sleeping. The third was cooking and the corporal was reading a paper. Their helmets hung on nails driven into the wall and their rifles leaned against the plank wall.

'What kind of country is this where it snows when it is almost June?' the soldier who was sitting on the bunk said.

'It is a phenomenon,' the corporal said.

'We are in the moon of May,' the soldier who was cooking said. 'The moon of May has not yet terminated.'

'What kind of a country is it where it snows in May?' the soldier on the bunk insisted.

'In May snow is no rarity in these mountains,' the corporal said. 'I have been colder in Madrid in May than in any other month.'

'And hotter, too,' the soldier who was cooking said.

'May is a month of great contrasts in temperature,' the corporal said. 'Here, in Castile, May is a month of great heat but it can have much cold.'

'Or rain,' the soldier on the bunk said. 'In this past May it rained almost every day.'

'It did not,' the soldier who was cooking said. 'And anyway this past May was the moon of April.'

'One could go crazy listening to thee and thy moons,' the corporal said. 'Leave this of the moons alone.'

'Anyone who lives either by the sea or by the land knows that it is the moon and not the month which counts,' the soldier who was cooking said. 'Now for example, we have just started the moon of May. Yet it is coming on June.'

'Why then do we not get definitely behind in the seasons?' the corporal said. 'The whole proposition gives me a headache.'

'You are from a town,' the soldier who was cooking said. 'You are from Lugo. What would you know of the sea or of the land?'

'One learns more in a town than you *analfabetos* learn in thy sea or thy land.'

'In this moon the first of the big schools of sardines come,' the soldier who was cooking said. 'In this moon the sardine boats will be outfitting and the mackerel will have gone north.'

'Why are you not in the navy if you come from Noya?' the corporal asked.

'Because I am not inscribed from Noya but from Negreira, where I was born. And from Negreira which is up the river Tambre, they take you for the army.'

'Worse luck,' said the corporal.

'Do not think the navy is without peril,' the soldier who was sitting on the bunk said. 'Even without the possibility of combat that is a dangerous coast in the winter.'

'Nothing can be worse than the army,' the corporal said.

'And you a corporal,' the soldier who was cooking said. 'What a way of speaking is that?'

'Nay,' the corporal said. 'I mean for dangers. I mean the endurance of bombardments, the necessity to attack, the life of the parapet.'

'Here we have little of that,' the soldier on the bunk said.

'By the Grace of God,' the corporal said. 'But who knows when we will be subject to it again? Certainly we will not have something as easy as this for ever!'

'How much longer do you think we will have this detail?'

'I don't know,' the corporal said. 'But I wish we could have it for all the war.'

'Six hours is too long to be on guard,' the soldier who was cooking said.

'We will have three-hour watches as long as this storm holds,' the corporal said. 'That is only normal.'

'What about all those staff cars?' the soldier on the bunk asked. 'I did not like the look of all those staff cars.'

'Nor I,' the corporal said. 'All such things are of evil omen.'

'And aviation,' the soldier who was cooking said. 'Aviation is another bad sign.'

'But we have formidable aviation,' the corporal said. 'The reds have no aviation such as we have. Those planes this morning were something to make any man happy.'

'I have seen the red planes when they were something serious,' the soldier on the bunk said. 'I have seen those two-motor bombers when they were a horror to endure.'

'Yes. But they are not as formidable as our aviation,' the corporal said. 'We have an aviation that is insuperable.'

This was how they were talking in the sawmill while Anselmo waited in the snow watching the road and the light in the sawmill window.

I hope I am not for the killing, Anselmo was thinking. I think that after the war there will have to be some great penance done for the killing. If we no longer have religion after the war then I think there must be some form of civic penance organized that all may be cleansed from the killing or else we will never have a true and human basis for living. The killing is necessary, I know, but still the doing of it is very bad for a man and I think that, after all this is over and we have won the war, there must be a penance of some kind for the cleansing of us all.

Anselmo was a very good man and whenever he was alone for long, and he was alone much of the time, this problem of the killing returned to him.

I wonder about the *Inglés*, he thought. He told me that he did not mind it. Yet he seems to be both sensitive and kind. It may be that in the younger people it does not have an importance. It may be that in foreigners, or in those who have not had our religion, there is not the same attitude. But I think anyone doing it will be brutalized in time and I think that even though necessary, it is a great sin and that afterwards we must do something very strong to atone for it.

It was dark now and he looked at the light across the road and shook his arms against his chest to warm them. Now, he thought, he would certainly leave for the camp; but something kept him there beside the tree above the road. It was snowing harder and Anselmo thought: if only we could blow the bridge to-night. On a night like this it would be nothing to take the posts and blow the bridge and it would be all over and done with. On a night like this you could do anything.

Then he stood there against the tree stamping his feet softly and he did not think any more about the bridge. The coming of the dark always made him feel lonely and to-night he felt so lonely that there was a hollowness in him as of hunger. In the old days he could help this loneliness by the saying of prayers and often coming home from hunting he would repeat a great number of the same prayer and it made him feel better. But he had not prayed once since the movement. He missed the prayers but he thought it would be unfair and hypocritical to say them and he did not wish to ask any favours or for any different treatment than all the men were receiving.

No, he thought, I am lonely. But so are all the soldiers and the wives of all the soldiers and all those who have lost families or parents. I have no wife, but I am glad that she died before the movement. She would not have understood it. I have no children and I never will have any children. I am lonely in the day when I am not working but when the dark comes it is a time of great loneliness. But one thing I have that no man nor any God can take from me and that is that I have worked well for the Republic. I have worked hard for the good that we will all share later. I have worked my best from the first of the movement and I have done nothing that I am ashamed of.

All that I am sorry for is the killing. But surely there will be an opportunity to atone for that because for a sin of that sort that so many bear, certainly some just relief will be devised. I would like to talk with the *Inglés* about it but, being young, he might not understand. He mentioned the killing before. Or was it I that mentioned it? He must have killed much, but he shows no signs of liking it. In those who like it there is always a rottenness.

It must really be a great sin, he thought. Because certainly it is the one thing we have no right to do even though, as I know, it is necessary. But in Spain it is done too lightly and often without true necessity and there is much quick injustice which, afterwards, can never be repaired. I wish I did not think about it so much, he thought. I wish there were a penance for it that one could commence now because it is the only thing that I have done in all my life that makes me feel badly when I am alone. All the other things are forgiven or one had a chance to atone for them by kindness or in some decent way. But I think this of the killing must be a very great sin and I would like to fix it up. Later on there may be certain days that one can work for the state or something that one can do that will remove it. It will probably be something that one pays as in the days of the Church, he thought, and smiled. The Church was well organized for sin. That pleased him and he was smiling in the dark when Robert Jordan came up to him. He came silently and the old man did not see him until he was there.

'*Hola, viejo*,' Robert Jordan whispered and clapped him on the back. 'How's the old one?'

'Very cold,' Anselmo said. Fernando was standing a little apart, his back turned against the driving snow.

'Come on,' Robert Jordan whispered. 'Get on up to camp and get warm. It was a crime to leave you here so long.'

'That is their light,' Anselmo pointed.

'Where's the sentry?'

'You do not see him from here. He is around the bend.'

'The hell with them,' Robert Jordan said. 'You tell me at camp. Come on, let's go.'

'Let me show you,' Anselmo said.

'I'm going to look at it in the morning,' Robert Jordan said. 'Here, take a swallow of this.'

He handed the old man his flask. Anselmo tipped it up and swallowed.

'*Ayee*,' he said and rubbed his mouth. 'It is fire.'

'Come on,' Robert Jordan said in the dark. 'Let us go.'

It was so dark now you could only see the flakes blowing past and the rigid dark of the pine trunks. Fernando was standing a little way up the hill. Look at that cigar store Indian, Robert Jordan thought. I suppose I have to offer him a drink.

'Hey, Fernando,' he said as he came up to him. 'A swallow?'

'No,' said Fernando. 'Thank you.'

Thank *you*, I mean, Robert Jordan thought. I'm glad cigar store Indians don't drink. There isn't too much of that left. Boy, I'm glad to see this old man, Robert Jordan thought. He looked at Anselmo and then clapped him on the back again as they started up the hill.

'I'm glad to see you, *viejo*,' he said to Anselmo. 'If I ever get gloomy, when I see you it cheers me up. Come on, let's get up there.'

They were going up the hill in the snow.

'Back to the palace of Pablo,' Robert Jordan said to Anselmo. It sounded wonderful in Spanish.

'*El Palacio del Miedo*,' Anselmo said. 'The Palace of Fear.'

'*La cueva de los huevos perdidos*,' Robert Jordan capped the other happily. 'The cave of the lost eggs.'

'What eggs?' Fernando asked.

'A joke,' Robert Jordan said. 'Just a joke. Not eggs, you know. The others.'

'But why are they lost?' Fernando asked.

'I don't know,' said Robert Jordan. 'Take a book to tell you. Ask Pilar,' then he put his arm around Anselmo's shoulder and held him tight as they walked and shook him. 'Listen,' he said. 'I'm glad to see you, hear? You don't know what it means to find somebody in this country in the same place they were left.'

It showed what confidence and intimacy he had that he could say anything against the country.

'I am glad to see thee,' Anselmo said. 'But I was just about to leave.'

'Like hell you would have,' Robert Jordan said happily. 'You'd have frozen first.'

'How was it up above?' Anselmo asked.

'Fine,' said Robert Jordan. 'Everything is fine.'

He was very happy with that sudden, rare happiness that can come to anyone with a command in a revolutionary army; the happiness of finding that even one of your flanks holds. If both flanks ever held I suppose it would be too much to take, he thought. I don't know who is prepared to stand that. And if you extend along a flank, any flank, it eventually becomes one man. Yes, one man. This was not the axiom he wanted. But this was a good man. One good man. You are going to be the left flank when we have the battle, he thought. I better not tell you that yet. It's going to be an awfully small battle, he thought. But it's going to be an awfully good one. Well, I always wanted to fight one on my own. I always had an opinion on what was wrong with everybody else's, from Agincourt down. I will have to make this a good one. It is going to be small but very select. If I have to do what I think I will have to do it will be very select indeed.

'Listen,' he said to Anselmo. 'I'm awfully glad to see you.'

'And me to see thee,' the old man said.

As they went up the hill in the dark, the wind at their backs, the storm blowing past them as they climbed, Anselmo did not feel lonely. He had not been lonely since the *Inglés* had clapped him on the shoulder. The *Inglés* was pleased and happy and they joked together. The *Inglés* said it all went well and he was not worried. The drink in his stomach warmed him and his feet were warming, now climbing.

'Not much on the road,' he said to the *Inglés*.

'Good,' the *Inglés* told him. 'You will show me when we get there.'

Anselmo was happy now and he was very pleased that he had stayed there at the post of observation.

If he had come into camp it would have been all right. It would have been the intelligent and correct thing to have done under the circumstances, Robert Jordan was thinking. But he stayed as he was told, Robert Jordan thought. That's the rarest thing that can happen in Spain. To stay in a storm, in a way, corresponds to a lot of things. It's not for nothing that the Germans call an attack a storm. I could certainly use a couple more who would stay. I most certainly could. I wonder if that Fernando would stay. It's just possible. After all, he is the one who suggested coming out just now. Do you suppose he would stay? Wouldn't that be good? He's just about stubborn enough. I'll have to make some inquiries. Wonder what the old cigar store Indian is thinking about now.

'What are you thinking about, Fernando?' Robert Jordan asked.

'Why do you ask?'

'Curiosity,' Robert Jordan said. 'I am a man of great curiosity.'

'I was thinking of supper,' Fernando said.

'Do you like to eat?'

'Yes. Very much.'

'How's Pilar's cooking?'

'Average,' Fernando answered.

He's a second Coolidge, Robert Jordan thought. But, you know, I have just a hunch that he would stay.

The three of them plodded up the hill in the snow.

16

'El Sordo was here,' Pilar said to Robert Jordan. They had come in out of the storm to the smoky warmth of the cave and the woman had motioned Robert Jordan over to her with a nod of her head. 'He's gone to look for horses.'

'Good. Did he leave any word for me?'

'Only that he had gone for horses.'

'And we?'

'*No sé*,' she said. 'Look at him.'

Robert Jordan had seen Pablo when he came in and Pablo had grinned at him. Now he looked over at him sitting at the board table and grinned and waved his hand.

'*Inglés*,' Pablo called. 'It's still falling, *Inglés*.'

Robert Jordan nodded at him.

'Let me take thy shoes and dry them,' Maria said. 'I will hang them here in the smoke of the fire.'

'Watch out you don't burn them,' Robert Jordan told her. 'I don't want to go around here barefoot. What's the matter?' he turned to Pilar. 'Is this a meeting? Haven't you any sentries out?'

'In this storm? *Qué va.*'

There were six men sitting at the table and leaning back against the wall. Anselmo and Fernando were still shaking the snow from their jackets, beating their trousers and rapping their feet against the wall by the entrance.

'Let me take thy jacket,' Maria said. 'Do not let the snow melt on it.'

Robert Jordan slipped out of his jacket, beat the snow from his trousers, and untied his shoes.

'You will get everything wet here,' Pilar said.

'It was thee who called me.'

'Still there is no impediment to returning to the door for thy brushing.'

'Excuse me,' Robert Jordan said, standing in his bare feet on the dirty floor. 'Hunt me a pair of socks, Maria.'

'The Lord and Master,' Pilar said and poked a piece of wood into the fire.

'*Hay que aprovechar el tiempo*,' Robert Jordan told her. 'You have to take advantage of what time there is.'

'It is locked,' Maria said.

'Here is the key,' and he tossed it over.

'It does not fit this sack.'

'It is the other sack. They're on top and at the side.'

The girl found the pair of socks, closed the sack, locked it and brought them over with the key.

'Sit down and put them on and rub thy feet well,' she said. Robert Jordan grinned at her.

'Thou canst not dry them with thy hair?' he said for Pilar to hear.

'What a swine,' she said. 'First he is the Lord of the Manor. Now he is our ex-Lord Himself. Hit him with a chunk of wood, Maria.'

'Nay,' Robert Jordan said to her. 'I am joking because I am happy.'

'You are happy?'

'Yes,' he said. 'I think everything goes very well.'

'Roberto,' Maria said. 'Go sit down and dry thy feet and let me bring thee something to drink to warm thee.'

'You would think that man had never dampened foot before,' Pilar said. 'Nor that a flake of snow had ever fallen.'

Maria brought him a sheepskin and put it on the dirt floor of the cave.

'There,' she said. 'Keep that under thee until thy shoes are dry.'

The sheepskin was fresh dried and not tanned and as Robert Jordan rested his stockinged feet on it he could feel it crackle like parchment.

The fire was smoking and Pilar called to Maria, 'Blow up the fire, worthless one. This is no smokehouse.'

'Blow it thyself,' Maria said. 'I am searching for the bottle that El Sordo left.'

'It is behind his packs,' Pilar told her. 'Must you care for him as a sucking child?'

'No,' Maria said. 'As a man who is cold and wet. And a man who has just come to his house. Here it is.' She brought the bottle to where Robert Jordan sat. 'It is the bottle of this noon. With this bottle one could make a beautiful lamp. When we have electricity again, what a lamp we can make of this bottle.' She looked at the pinch-bottle admiringly. 'How do you take this, Roberto?'

'I thought I was *Inglés*,' Robert Jordan said to her.

'I call thee Roberto before the others,' she said in a low voice and blushed. 'How do you want it, Roberto?'

'Roberto,' Pablo said thickly and nodded his head at Robert Jordan. 'How do you want it, Don Roberto?'

'Do you want some?' Robert Jordan asked him.

Pablo shook his head. 'I am making myself drunk with wine,' he said with dignity.

'Go with Bacchus,' Robert Jordan said in Spanish.

'Who is Bacchus?' Pablo asked.

'A comrade of thine,' Robert Jordan said.

'Never have I heard of him,' Pablo said heavily. 'Never in these mountains.'

'Give a cup to Anselmo,' Robert Jordan said to Maria. 'It is he who is cold.' He was putting on the dry pair of socks and the whisky and water in the cup tasted clean and thinly warming. But it does not curl around inside of you the way the absinthe does, he thought. There is nothing like absinthe.

Who would imagine they would have whisky up here, he thought. But La Granja was the most likely place in Spain to find it when you thought it over. Imagine Sordo getting a bottle for the visiting dynamiter and then remembering to bring it down and leave it. It wasn't just manners that they had. Manners would have been producing the bottle and having a formal drink. That was what the French would have done and then they would have saved what was left for another occasion. No, the true thoughtfulness of thinking the visitor would like it and then bringing it down for him to enjoy when you yourself were engaged in something where there was every reason to think of no one else but yourself and of nothing but the matter in hand–that was Spanish. One kind of Spanish, he thought. Remembering to bring the whisky was one of the reasons you loved these people. Don't go romanticizing them, he thought. There are as many sorts of Spanish as there are Americans. But still, bringing the whisky was very handsome.

'How do you like it?' he asked Anselmo.

The old man was sitting by the fire with a smile on his face, his big hands holding the cup. He shook his head.

'No?' Robert Jordan asked him.

'The child put water in it,' Anselmo said.

'Exactly as Roberto takes it,' Maria said. 'Art thou something special?'

'No,' Anselmo told her. 'Nothing special at all. But I like to feel it burn as it goes down.'

'Give me that,' Robert Jordan told the girl, 'and pour him some of that which burns.'

He tipped the contents of the cup into his own and handed it back empty to the girl, who poured carefully into it from the bottle.

'Ah,' Anselmo took the cup, put his head back and let it run down his throat. He looked at Maria standing holding the bottle and winked at her, tears coming from both his eyes. 'That,' he said. 'That.' Then he licked his lips. '*That* is what kills the worm that haunts us.'

'Roberto,' Maria said and came over to him, still holding the bottle. 'Are you ready to eat?'

'Is it ready?'

'It is ready when you wish it.'

'Have the others eaten?'

'All except you, Anselmo and Fernando.'

'Let us eat then,' he told her. 'And thou?'

'Afterwards with Pilar.'

'Eat now with us.'

'No. It would not be well.'

'Come on and eat. In my country a man does not eat before his woman.'

'That is thy country. Here it is better to eat after.'

'Eat with him,' Pablo said, looking up from the table. 'Eat with him. Drink with him. Sleep with him. Die with him. Follow the customs of his country.'

'Are you drunk?' Robert Jordan said, standing in front of Pablo. The dirty, stubble-faced man looked at him happily.

'Yes,' Pablo said. 'Where is thy country, *Inglés*, where the women eat with the men?'

'In *Estados Unidos* in the state of Montana.'

'Is it there that the men wear skirts as do the women?'

'No. That is in Scotland.'

'But listen,' Pablo said. 'When you wear skirts like that, *Inglés*—'

'I don't wear them,' Robert Jordan said.

'When you are wearing those skirts,' Pablo went on, 'what do you wear under them?'

'I don't know what the Scotch wear,' Robert Jordan said. 'I've wondered myself.'

'Not the *Escoceses*,' Pablo said. 'Who cares about the *Escoceses*? Who cares about anything with a name as rare as that? Not me. I don't care. You, I say, *Inglés*. You. What do you wear under your skirts in your country?'

'Twice I have told you that we do not wear skirts,' Robert Jordan said. 'Neither drunk nor in joke.'

'But under your skirts,' Pablo insisted. 'Since it is well known that you wear skirts. Even the soldiers. I have seen photographs and also I have seen them in the Circus of Price. What do you wear under your skirts, *Inglés*?'

'*Los cojones*,' Robert Jordan said.

Anselmo laughed and so did the others who were listening; all except Fernando. The sound of the word, of the gross word spoken before the women, was offensive to him.

'Well, that is normal,' Pablo said. 'But it seems to me that with enough *cojones* you would not wear skirts.'

'Don't let him get started again, *Inglés*,' the flat faced man with the broken nose who was called Primitivo said. 'He is drunk. Tell me, what do they raise in your country?'

'Cattle and sheep,' Robert Jordan said. 'Much grain also and beans. And also much beets for sugar.'

The three were at the table now and the others sat close by except Pablo, who sat by himself in front of a bowl of the wine. It was the same stew as the night before and Robert Jordan ate it hungrily.

'In your country there are mountains? With that name surely there are mountains,' Primitivo asked politely to make conversation. He was embarrassed at the drunkenness of Pablo.

'Many mountains and very high.'

'And are there good pastures?'

'Excellent; high pasture in the summer in forests controlled by the government. Then in the fall the cattle are brought down to the lower ranges.'

'Is the land there owned by the peasants?'

'Most land is owned by those who farm it. Originally the land was owned by the state and by living on it and declaring the intention of improving it, a man could obtain title to a hundred and fifty hectares.'

'Tell me how this is done,' Agustín asked. 'That is an agrarian reform which means something.'

Robert Jordan explained the process of homesteading. He had never thought of it before as an agrarian reform.

'That is magnificent,' Primitivo said. 'Then you have a communism in your country?'

'No. That is done under the Republic.'

'For me,' Agustín said, 'everything can be done under the Republic. I see no need for other form of government.'

'Do you have no big proprietors?' Andrés asked.

'Many.'

'Then there must be abuses.'

'Certainly. There are many abuses.'

'But you will do away with them?'

'We try to more and more. But there are many abuses still.'

'But there are not great estates that must be broken up?'

'Yes. But there are those who believe that taxes will break them up.'

'How?'

Robert Jordan, wiping out the stew bowl with bread, explained how the income tax and inheritance tax worked. 'But the big estates remain. Also there are taxes on the land,' he said.

'But surely the big proprietors and the rich will make a revolution against such taxes. Such taxes appear to me to be revolutionary. They will revolt against the government when they see that they are threatened, exactly as the fascists have done here,' Primitivo said.

'It is possible.'

'Then you will have to fight in your country as we fight here.'

'Yes, we will have to fight.'

'But are there not many fascists in your country?'

'There are many who do not know they are fascists but will find it out when the time comes.'

'But you cannot destroy them until they rebel?'

'No,' Robert Jordan said. 'We cannot destroy them. But we can educate the people so that they will fear fascism and recognize it as it appears and combat it.'

'Do you know where there are no fascists?' Andrés asked.

'Where?'

'In the town of Pablo,' Andrés said and grinned.

'You know what was done in that village?' Primitivo asked Robert Jordan.

'Yes. I have heard the story.'

'From Pilar?'

'Yes.'

'You could not hear all of it from the woman,' Pablo said heavily. 'Because she did not see the end of it because she fell from a chair outside of the window,'

'You tell him what happened then,' Pilar said. 'Since I know not the story, let you tell it.'

'Nay,' Pablo said. 'I have never told it.'

'No,' Pilar said. 'And you will not tell it. And now you wish it had not happened.'

'No,' Pablo said. 'That is not true. And if all had killed the fascists as I did we would not have this war. But I would not have had it happen as it happened.'

'Why do you say that?' Primitivo asked him. 'Are you changing your politics?'

'No. But it was barbarous,' Pablo said. 'In those days I was very barbarous.'

'And now you are drunk,' Pilar said.

'Yes,' Pablo said. 'With your permission.'

'I liked you better when you were barbarous,' the woman said. 'Of all men the drunkard is the foulest. The thief when he is not stealing is like another. The extortioner does not practise in the home. The murderer when he is at home can wash his hands. But the drunkard stinks and vomits in his own bed and dissolves his organs in alcohol.'

'You are a woman and you do not understand,' Pablo said equably. 'I am drunk on wine and I would be happy except for those people I have killed. All of them fill me with sorrow.' He shook his head lugubriously.

'Give him some of that which Sordo brought,' Pilar said. 'Give him something to animate him. He is becoming too sad to bear.'

'If I could restore them to life, I would,' Pablo said.

'Go and obscenity thyself,' Agustín said to him. 'What sort of place is this?'

'I would bring them all back to life,' Pablo said sadly. 'Every one.'

'Thy mother,' Agustín shouted at him. 'Stop talking like this or get out. Those were fascists you killed.'

'You heard me,' Pablo said. 'I would restore them all to life.'

'And then you would walk on the water,' Pilar said. 'In my life I have never seen such a man. Up until yesterday you preserved some remnants of manhood. And to-day there is not enough of you left to make a sick kitten. Yet you are happy in your soddenness.'

'We should have killed all or none,' Pablo nodded his head. 'All or none.'

'Listen, *Inglés*,' Agustín said. 'How did you happen to come to Spain? Pay no attention to Pablo. He is drunk.'

'I came first twelve years ago to study the country and the language,' Robert Jordan said. 'I teach Spanish in a university.'

'You look very like a professor,' Primitivo said.

'He has no beard,' Pablo said. 'Look at him. He has no beard.'

'Are you truly a professor?'

'An instructor.'

'But you teach?'

'Yes.'

'But why Spanish?' Andrés asked. 'Would it not be easier to teach English since you are English?'

'He speaks Spanish as we do,' Anselmo said. 'Why should he not teach Spanish?'

'Yes. But it is, in a way, presumptuous for a foreigner to teach Spanish,' Fernando said. 'I mean nothing against you, Don Roberto.'

'He's a false professor,' Pablo said, very pleased with himself. 'He hasn't got a beard.'

'Surely you know English better,' Fernando said. 'Would it not be better and easier and clearer to teach English?'

'He doesn't teach it to Spaniards—' Pilar started to intervene.

'I should hope not,' Fernando said.

'Let me finish, you mule,' Pilar said to him. 'He teaches Spanish to Americans. North Americans.'

'Can they not speak Spanish?' Fernando asked. 'South Americans can.'

'Mule,' Pilar said. 'He teaches Spanish to North Americans who can speak English.'

'Still and all I think it would be easier for him to teach English if that is what he speaks,' Fernando said.

'Can't you hear he speaks Spanish?' Pilar shook her head hopelessly at Robert Jordan.

'Yes. But with an accent.'

'Of where?' Robert Jordan asked.

'Of Estremadura,' Fernando said primly.

'Oh my mother,' Pilar said. 'What a people!'

'It is possible,' Robert Jordan said. 'I have come here from there.'

'As he well knows,' Pilar said. 'You old maid,' she turned to Fernando. 'Have you had enough to eat?'

'I could eat more if there is a sufficient quantity,' Fernando told her. 'And do not think that I wish to say anything against you, Don Roberto—'

'Milk,' Agustín said simply. 'And milk again. Do we make the revolution in order to say Don Roberto to a comrade?'

'For me the revolution is so that all will say Don to all,' Fernando said. 'Thus should it be under the Republic.'

'Milk,' Agustín said. 'Black milk.'

'And I still think it would be easier and clearer for Don Roberto to teach English.'

'Don Roberto has no beard,' Pablo said. 'He is a false professor.'

'What do you mean, I have no beard?' Robert Jordan said. 'What's this?'

He stroked his chin and his cheeks where the three-day growth made a blond stubble.

'Not a beard,' Pablo said. He shook his head. 'That's not a beard.' He was almost jovial now. 'He's a false professor.'

'I obscenity in the milk of all,' Agustín said, 'if it does not seem like a lunatic asylum here.'

'You should drink,' Pablo said to him. 'To me everything appears normal. Except the lack of beard of Don Roberto.'

Maria ran her hand over Robert Jordan's cheek.

'He has a beard,' she said to Pablo.

'You should know,' Pablo said and Robert Jordan looked at him.

I don't think he is so drunk, Robert Jordan thought. No, not so drunk. And I think I had better watch myself.

'Thou,' he said to Pablo. 'Do you think this snow will last?'

'What do you think?'

'I asked you.'

'Ask another,' Pablo told him. 'I am not thy service of information. You have a paper from thy service of information. Ask the woman. She commands.'

'I asked thee.'

'Go and obscenity thyself,' Pablo told him. 'Thee and the woman and the girl.'

'He is drunk,' Primitivo said. 'Pay him no heed, *Inglés*.'

'I do not think he is so drunk,' Robert Jordan said.

Maria was standing behind him and Robert Jordan saw Pablo watching her over his shoulder. The small eyes, like a boar's, were watching her out of the round, stubble-covered head and Robert Jordan thought: I have known many killers in this war and some before and they were all different; there is no common trait nor feature; nor any such thing as the criminal type; but Pablo is certainly not handsome.

'I don't believe you can drink,' he said to Pablo. 'Nor that you're drunk.'

'I am drunk,' Pablo said with dignity. 'To drink is nothing. It is to be drunk that is important. *Estoy muy borracho*.'

'I doubt it,' Robert Jordan told him. 'Cowardly, yes.'

It was so quiet in the cave, suddenly, that he could hear the hissing noise the wood made burning on the hearth where Pilar cooked. He heard the sheepskin crackle as he rested his weight on his feet. He thought he could almost hear the snow falling outside. He could not, but he could hear the silence where it fell.

I'd like to kill him and have it over with, Robert Jordan was thinking. I don't know what he is going to do, but it is nothing good. Day after tomorrow is the bridge and this man is bad and he constitutes a danger to the success of the whole enterprise. Come on. Let us get it over with.

Pablo grinned at him and put one finger up and wiped it across his throat. He shook his head that turned only a little each way on his thick, short neck.

'Nay, *Inglés*,' he said. 'Do not provoke me.' He looked at Pilar and said to her, 'It is not thus that you get rid of me.'

'*Sinverguenza*,' Robert Jordan said to him, committed now in his own mind to the action. '*Cobarde.*'

'It is very possible,' Pablo said. 'But I am not to be provoked. Take something to drink, *Inglés*, and signal to the woman it was not successful.'

'Shut thy mouth,' Robert Jordan said. 'I provoke thee for myself.'

'It is not worth the trouble,' Pablo told him. 'I do not provoke.'

'Thou art a *bicho raro*,' Robert Jordan said, not wanting to let it go; not wanting to have it fail for the second time; knowing as he spoke that this had all been gone through before; having that feeling that he was playing a part from memory of something that he had read or had dreamed, feeling it all moving in a circle.

'Very rare, yes,' Pablo said. 'Very rare and very drunk. To your health, *Inglés*.' He dipped a cup in the wine bowl and held it up. '*Salud y cojones*.'

He's rare, all right, Robert Jordan thought, and smart, and very complicated. He could no longer hear the fire for the sound of his own breathing.

'Here's to you,' Robert Jordan said, and dipped a cup into the wine. Betrayal wouldn't amount to anything without all these pledges, he thought. Pledge up. '*Salud*,' he said. '*Salud* and *Salud* again,' you *salud*, he thought. *Salud*, you *salud*.

'Don Roberto,' Pablo said heavily.

'Don Pablo,' Robert Jordan said.

'You're no professor,' Pablo said, 'because you haven't got a beard. And also to do away with me you have to assassinate me and, for this, you have not *cojones*.'

He was looking at Robert Jordan with his mouth closed so that his lips made a tight line, like the mouth of a fish, Robert Jordan thought. With that head it is like one of those porcupine fish that swallow air and swell up after they are caught.

'*Salud*, Pablo,' Robert Jordan said and raised the cup up and drank from it. 'I am learning much from thee.'

'I am teaching the professor,' Pablo nodded his head. 'Come on, Don Roberto, we will be friends.'

'We are friends already,' Robert Jordan said.

'But now we will be good friends.'

'We are good friends already.'

'I'm going to get out of here,' Agustín said. 'Truly, it is said that we must eat a ton of it in this life but I have twenty-five pounds of it stuck in each of my ears this minute.'

'What is the matter, *negro*?' Pablo said to him. 'Do you not like to see friendship between Don Roberto and me?'

'Watch your mouth about calling me *negro*.' Agustín went over to him and stood in front of Pablo holding his hands low.

'So you are called,' Pablo said.

'Not by thee.'

'Well, then, *blanco*—'

'Nor that, either.'

'What are you then, red?'

'Yes. Red. *Rojo*. With the red star of the army and in favour of the

Republic. And my name is Agustín.'

'What a patriotic man,' Pablo said. 'Look, *Inglés*, what an exemplary patriot.'

Agustín hit him hard across the mouth with his left hand, bringing it forward in a slapping, backhand sweep. Pablo sat there. The corners of his mouth were wine-stained and his expression did not change, but Robert Jordan watched his eyes narrow, as a cat's pupils close to vertical slits in a strong light.

'Nor this,' Pablo said. 'Do not count on this, woman.' He turned his head toward Pilar. 'I am not provoked.'

Agustín hit him again. This time he hit him on the mouth with his closed fist. Robert Jordan was holding his pistol in his hand under the table. He had shoved the safety catch off and he pushed Maria away with his left hand. She moved a little way and he pushed her hard in the ribs with his left hand again to make her get really away. She was gone now and he saw her from the corner of his eye, slipping along the side of the cave toward the fire, and now Robert Jordan watched Pablo's face.

The round-headed man sat staring at Agustín from his flat little eyes. The pupils were even smaller now. He licked his lips, then put up an arm and wiped his mouth with the back of his hand, looked down and saw the blood on his hand. He ran his tongue over his lips, then spat.

'Nor that,' he said. 'I am not a fool. I do not provoke.'

'*Cabrón*,' Agustín said.

'You should know,' Pablo said. 'You know the woman.'

Agustín hit him again hard in the mouth and Pablo laughed at him, showing the yellow, bad, broken teeth in the reddened line of his mouth.

'Leave it alone,' Pablo said and reached with a cup to scoop some wine from the bowl. 'Nobody here has *cojones* to kill me and this of the hands is silly.'

'*Cobarde*,' Agustín said.

'Nor words either,' Pablo said and made a swishing noise rinsing the wine in his mouth. He spat on the floor. 'I am far past words.'

Agustín stood there looking down at him and cursed him, speaking slowly, clearly, bitterly and contemptuously and cursing as steadily as though he were dumping manure on a field, lifting it with a dung fork out of a wagon.

'Nor of those,' Pablo said. 'Leave it, Agustín. And do not hit me more. Thou wilt injure thy hands.'

Agustín turned from him and went to the door.

'Do not go out,' Pablo said. 'It is snowing outside. Make thyself comfortable in here.'

'And thou! Thou!' Agustín turned from the door and spoke to him, putting all his contempt in the single, '*Tu*.'

'Yes, me,' said Pablo. 'I will be alive when you are dead.'

He dipped up another cup of wine and raised it to Robert Jordan. 'To the professor,' he said. Then turned to Pilar. 'To the Señora Commander.' Then toasted them all, 'To all the illusioned ones.'

Agustín walked over to him and, striking quickly with the side of his hand, knocked the cup out of his hand.

'That is a waste,' Pablo said. 'That is silly.'

Agustín said something vile to him.

'No,' Pablo said, dipping up another cup. 'I am drunk, seest thou? When I am drunk I do not talk. You have never heard me talk much. But an intelligent man is sometimes forced to be drunk to spend his time with fools.'

'Go and obscenity in the milk of thy cowardice,' Pilar said to him. 'I know too much about thee and thy cowardice.'

'How the woman talks,' Pablo said. 'I will be going out to see the horses.'

'Go and befoul them,' Agustín said. 'Is not that one of thy customs?'

'No,' Pablo said and shook his head. He was taking down his big blanket cape from the wall and he looked at Agustín. 'Thou,' he said, 'and thy violence.'

'What do you go to do with the horses?' Agustín said.

'Look to them,' Pablo said.

'Befoul them,' Agustín said. 'Horse lover.'

'I care for them very much,' Pablo said. 'Even from behind they are handsomer and have more sense than these people. Divert yourselves,' he said and grinned. 'Speak to them of the bridge, *Inglés*. Explain their duties in the attack. Tell them how to conduct the retreat. Where will you take them, *Inglés*, after the bridge? Where will you take your patriots? I have thought of it all day while I have been drinking.'

'What have you thought?' Agustín asked.

'What have I thought?' Pablo said and moved his tongue around exploringly inside his lips. '*Qué te importa*, what have I thought.'

'Say it,' Agustín said to him.

'Much,' Pablo said. He pulled the blanket coat over his head, the roundness of his head protruding now from the dirty yellow folds of the blanket. 'I have thought much.'

'What?' Agustín said. 'What?'

'I have thought you are a group of illusioned people,' Pablo said. 'Led by a woman with her brains between her thighs and a foreigner who comes to destroy you.'

'Get out,' Pilar shouted at him. 'Get out and fist yourself into the snow. Take your bad milk out of here, you horse exhausted *maricón*.'

'Thus one talks,' Agustín said admiringly, but absent-mindedly. He was worried.

'I go,' said Pablo. 'But I will be back shortly.' He lifted the blanket over the door of the cave and stepped out. Then from the door he called, 'It's still falling, *Inglés*.'

17

The only noise in the cave now was the hissing from the hearth where snow was falling through the hole in the roof on to the coals of the fire.

'Pilar,' Fernando said. 'Is there more of the stew?'

'Oh, shut up, the woman said. But Maria took Fernando's bowl over to the big pot set back from the edge of the fire and ladled into it. She brought it over to the table and set it down and then patted Fernando on the shoulder as he bent to eat. She stood for a moment beside him, her hand on his shoulder. But Fernando did not look up. He was devoting himself to the stew.

Agustín stood beside the fire. The others were seated. Pilar sat at the table opposite Robert Jordan.

'Now, *Inglés*,' she said, 'you have seen how he is.'

'What will he do?' Robert Jordan asked.

'Anything,' the woman looked down at the table. 'Anything. He is capable of doing anything.'

'Where is the automatic rifle?' Robert Jordan asked.

'There in the corner wrapped in the blanket,' Primitivo said. 'Do you want it?'

'Later,' Robert Jordan said. 'I wished to know where it is.'

'It is there,' Primitivo said. 'I brought it in and I have wrapped it in my blanket to keep the action dry. The pans are in that sack.'

'He would not do that,' Pilar said. 'He would not do anything with the *máquina*.'

'I thought you said he would do anything.'

'He might,' she said. 'But he has no practice with the *máquina*. He could toss in a bomb. That is more his style.'

'It is an idiocy and a weakness not to have killed him,' the gipsy said. He had taken no part in any of the talk all evening. 'Last night Roberto should have killed him.'

'Kill him,' Pilar said. Her big face was dark and tired looking. 'I am for it now.'

'I was against it,' Agustín said. He stood in front of the fire, his long arms hanging by his sides, his cheeks, stubble-shadowed below the cheekbones, hollow in the firelight. 'Now I am for it,' he said. 'He is poisonous now and he would like to see us all destroyed.'

'Let all speak,' Pilar said and her voice was tired. 'Thou, Andrés?'

'*Matarlo*', the brother with the dark hair growing far down in the point on his forehead said and nodded his head.

'Eladio?'

'Equally,' the other brother said. 'To me he seems to constitute a great danger. And he serves for nothing.'

'Primitivo?'

'Equally.'

'Fernando?'

'Could we not hold him as a prisoner?' Fernando asked.

'Who would look after a prisoner?' Primitivo said. 'It would take two men to look after a prisoner and what would we do with him in the end?'

'We could sell him to the fascists,' the gipsy said.

'None of that,' Agustín said. 'None of that filthiness.'

'It was only an idea,' Rafael, the gipsy, said. 'It seems to me that the *facciosos* would be happy to have him.'

'Leave it alone,' Agustín said. 'That is filthy.'

'No filthier than Pablo,' the gipsy justified himself.

'One filthiness does not justify another,' Agustín said. 'Well, that is all. Except for the old man and the *Inglés*.'

'They are not in it,' Pilar said. 'He has not been their leader.'

'One moment,' Fernando said. 'I have not finished.'

'Go ahead,' Pilar said. 'Talk until he comes back. Talk until he rolls a hand grenade under that blanket and blows this all up. Dynamite and all.'

'I think that you exaggerate, Pilar,' Fernando said. 'I do not think that he has any such conception.'

'I do not think so either,' Agustín said. 'Because that would blow the wine up too and he will be back in a little while to the wine.'

'Why not turn him over to El Sordo and let El Sordo sell him to the fascists?' Rafael suggested. 'You could blind him and he would be easy to handle.'

'Shut up,' Pilar said. 'I feel something very justified against thee too when thou talkest.'

'The fascists would pay nothing for him anyway,' Primitivo said. 'Such things have been tried by others and they pay nothing. They will shoot thee too.'

'I believe that blinded he could be sold for something,' Rafael said.

'Shut up,' Pilar said. 'Speak of blinding again and you can go with the other.'

'But he, Pablo, blinded the *guardia civil* who was wounded,' the gipsy insisted. 'You have forgotten that?'

'Close thy mouth,' Pilar said to him. She was embarrassed before Robert Jordan by this talk of blinding.

'I have not been allowed to finish,' Fernando interrupted.

'Finish,' Pilar told him. 'Go on. Finish.'

'Since it is impractical to hold Pablo as a prisoner,' Fernando commenced, 'and since it is repugnant to offer him—'

'Finish,' Pilar said. 'For the love of God, finish.'

'—in any class of negotiation,' Fernando proceeded calmly, 'I am agreed that it is perhaps best that he should be eliminated in order that the operations projected should be insured of the maximum possibility of success.'

Pilar looked at the little man, shook her head, bit her lips and said nothing.

'That is my opinion,' Fernando said. 'I believe we are justified in believing that he constitutes a danger to the Republic—'

'Mother of God,' Pilar said. 'Even here one man can make a bureaucracy with his mouth.'

'Both from his own words and his recent actions,' Fernando continued. 'And while he is deserving of gratitude for his actions in the early part of the movement and up until the most recent time—'

Pilar had walked over to the fire. Now she came up to the table.

'Fernando,' Pilar said quietly and handed a bowl to him. 'Take this stew please in all formality and fill thy mouth with it and talk no more. We are in possession of thy opinion.'

'But, how then—' Primitivo asked and paused without completing the sentence.

'*Estoy listo*,' Robert Jordan said. 'I am ready to do it. Since you are all decided that it should be done it is a service that I can do.'

What's the matter? he thought. From listening to him I am beginning to talk like Fernando. That language must be infectious. French, the language of diplomacy. Spanish, the language of bureaucracy.

'No,' Maria said. 'No.'

'This is none of thy business,' Pilar said to the girl. 'Keep thy mouth shut.'

'I will do it to-night,' Robert Jordan said.

He saw Pilar looking at him, her fingers on her lips. She was looking toward the door.

The blanket fastened across the opening of the cave was lifted and Pablo put his head in. He grinned at them all, pushed under the blanket and then turned and fastened it again. He turned around and stood there, then pulled the blanket cape over his head and shook the snow from it.

'You were speaking of me?' he addressed them all. 'I am interrupting?'

No one answered him and he hung the cape on a peg in the wall and walked over to the table.

'*Qué tal*?' he asked, and picked up his cup which had stood empty on the table and dipped it into the wine bowl. 'There is no wine,' he said to Maria. 'Go draw some from the skin.'

Maria picked up the bowl and went over to the dusty, heavily distended, black-tarred wineskin that hung neck down from the wall and unscrewed the plug from one of the legs enough so that the wine squirted from the edge of the plug into the bowl. Pablo watched her kneeling, holding the bowl up and watched the light red wine flooding into the bowl so fast that it made a whirling motion as it filled it.

'Be careful,' he said to her. 'The wine's below the chest now.'

No one said anything.

'I drank from the belly-button to the chest to-day,' Pablo said. 'It's a day's work. What's the matter with you all? Have you lost your tongues?'

No one said anything at all.

'Screw it up, Maria,' Pablo said. 'Don't let it spill.'

'There'll be plenty of wine,' Agustín said. 'You'll be able to be drunk.'

'One has encountered his tongue,' Pablo said and nodded to Agustín. 'Felicitations. I thought you'd been struck dumb.'

'By what?' Agustín asked.

'By my entry.'

'Thinkest thou that thy entry carries importance?'

He's working himself up to it, maybe, Robert Jordan thought. Maybe Agustín is going to do it. He certainly hates him enough. I don't hate him, he thought. No, I don't hate him. He is disgusting but I do not hate him. Though that blinding business puts him in a special class. Still this is their war. But he is certainly nothing to have around for the next two days. I am going to keep away out of it, he thought. I made a fool of myself with him once to-night and I am perfectly willing to liquidate him. But I am not going to fool with him beforehand. And there are not going to be any shooting matches or monkey business in here with that dynamite around either. Pablo thought of that, of course. And did you think of it, he said to himself? No, you did not and neither did Agustín. You deserve whatever happens to you, he thought.

'Agustín,' he said.

'What?' Agustín looked up sullenly and turned his head away from Pablo.

'I wish to speak to thee,' Robert Jordan said.

'Later.'

'Now,' Robert Jordan said. '*Por favor.*'

Robert Jordan had walked to the opening of the cave and Pablo followed him with his eyes. Agustín, tall and sunken cheeked, stood up and came over to him. He moved reluctantly and contemptuously.

'Thou hast forgotten what is in the sacks?' Robert Jordan said to him, speaking so low that it could not be heard.

'Milk!' Agustín said. 'One becomes accustomed and one forgets.'

'I, too, forgot.'

'Milk!' Agustín said. '*Leche!* What fools we are.' He swung back loose-jointedly to the table and sat down. 'Have a drink, Pablo, old boy,' he said. 'How were the horses?'

'Very good,' Pablo said. 'And it is snowing less.'

'Do you think it will stop?'

'Yes,' Pablo said. 'It is thinning now and there are small, hard pellets. The wind will blow but the snow is going. The wind has changed.'

'Do you think it will clear to-morrow?' Robert Jordan asked him.

'Yes,' Pablo said. 'I believe it will be cold and clear. This wind is shifting.'

Look at him, Robert Jordan thought. Now he is friendly. He has shifted like the wind. He has the face and the body of a pig and I know he is many times a murderer and yet he has the sensitivity of a good aneroid. Yes, he thought, and the pig is a very intelligent animal, too. Pablo has hatred for us, or perhaps it is only for our projects, and pushes his hatred with insults to the point where you are ready to do away with him and when he sees that this point has been reached he drops it and starts all new and clean again.

'We will have good weather for it, *Inglés*,' Pablo said to Robert Jordan.

'*We*,' Pilar said. '*We*?'

'Yes, we,' Pablo grinned at her and drank some of the wine. 'Why not? I thought it over while I was outside. Why should we not agree?'

'In what?' the woman asked. 'In what now?'

'In all,' Pablo said to her. 'In this of the bridge. I am with thee now.'

'You are with us now?' Agustín said to him. 'After what you have said?'

'Yes,' Pablo told him. 'With the change of the weather I am with thee.'

Agustín shook his head. 'The weather,' he said and shook his head again. 'And after me hitting thee in the face?'

'Yes,' Pablo grinned at him and ran his fingers over his lips. 'After that too.'

Robert Jordan was watching Pilar. She was looking at Pablo as at some strange animal. On her face there was still a shadow of the expression the mention of the blinding had put there. She shook her head as though to be rid of that, then tossed it back. 'Listen,' she said to Pablo.

'Yes, woman.'

'What passes with thee?'

'Nothing,' Pablo said. 'I have changed my opinion. Nothing more.'

'You were listening at the door,' she told him.

'Yes,' he said. 'But I could hear nothing.'

'You fear that we will kill thee.'

'No,' he told her and looked at her over the wine cup. 'I do not fear that. You know that.'

'Well, what passes with thee?' Agustín said. 'One moment you are drunk and putting your mouth on all of us and disassociating yourself from the work in hand and speaking of our death in a dirty manner and insulting the women and opposing that which should be done—'

'I was drunk,' Pablo told him.

'And now—'

'I am not drunk,' Pablo said. 'And I have changed my mind.'

'Let the others trust thee. I do not,' Agustín said.

'Trust me or not,' Pablo said. 'But there is no one who can take thee to Gredos as I can.'

'Gredos?'

'It is the only place to go after this of the bridge.'

Robert Jordan, looking at Pilar, raised his hand on the side away from Pablo and tapped his right ear questioningly.

The woman nodded. Then nodded again. She said something to Maria and the girl came over to Robert Jordan's side.

'She says, "Of course he heard,"' Maria said in Robert Jordan's ear.

'Then Pablo,' Fernando said judicially. 'Thou art with us now and in favour of this of the bridge?'

'Yes, man,' Pablo said. He looked Fernando squarely in the eye and nodded.

'In truth?' Primitivo asked.

'*De veras*,' Pablo told him.

'And you think it can be successful?' Fernando asked. 'You now have confidence?'

'Why not?' Pablo said. 'Haven't you confidence?'

'Yes,' Fernando said. 'But I always have confidence.'

'I'm going to get out of here,' Agustín said.

'It is cold outside,' Pablo told him in a friendly tone.

'Maybe,' Agustín said. 'But I can't stay any longer in this *manicomio*.'

'Do not call this cave an insane asylum,' Fernando said.

'A *manicomio* for criminal lunatics,' Agustín said. 'And I'm getting out before I'm crazy, too.'

18

It is like a merry-go-round, Robert Jordan thought. Not a merry-go-round that travels fast, and with a calliope for music, and the children ride on cows with gilded horns, and there are rings to catch with sticks, and there is the blue, gas-flare-lit early dark of the Avenue du Maine, with fried fish sold from the next stall, and a wheel of fortune turning with the leather flaps slapping against the posts of the numbered compartments, and the packages of lump sugar piled in pyramids for prizes. No, it is not that kind of a merry-go-round; although the people are waiting, like the men in caps and the women in knitted sweaters, their heads bare in the gaslight and their hair shining, who stand in front of the wheel of fortune as it spins. Yes, those are the people. But this is another wheel. This is like a wheel that goes up and around.

It has been around twice now. It is a vast wheel, set at an angle, and each time it goes around and then is back to where it starts. One side is higher than the other and the sweep it makes lifts you back and down to where you started. There are no prizes either, he thought, and no one would choose to ride this wheel. You ride it each time and make the turn with no intention ever to have mounted. There is only one turn; one large, elliptical, rising and falling turn and you are back where you have started. We are back again now, he thought, and nothing is settled.

It was warm in the cave and the wind had dropped outside. Now he was sitting at the table with his notebook in front of him figuring all the technical part of the bridge-blowing. He drew three sketches, figured his formulas, marked the method of blowing with two drawings as clearly as a kindergarten project so that Anselmo could complete it in case anything should happen to himself during the process of the demolition. He finished these sketches and studied them.

Maria sat beside him and looked over his shoulder while he worked. He was conscious of Pablo across the table and of the others talking and playing cards and he smelled the odours of the cave which had changed now from those of the meal and the cooking to the fire smoke and man smell, the tobacco, red-wine and brassy, stale body smell, and when Maria, watching him finishing a drawing, put her hand on the table he picked it up with his left hand and lifted it to his face and smelled the coarse soap and water freshness from her washing of the dishes. He laid her hand down without looking at her and went on working and he could not see her blush. She let her hand lie there, close to his, but he did not lift it again.

Now he had finished the demolition project and he took a new page of the notebook and commenced to write out the operation orders. He was thinking clearly and well on these and what he wrote pleased him. He wrote two pages in the notebook and read them over carefully.

I think that is all, he said to himself. It is perfectly clear and I do not think there are any holes in it. The two posts will be destroyed and the bridge will be blown according to Golz's order and that is all of my responsibility. All of this business of Pablo is something with which I should never have been saddled and it will be solved one way or another. There will be Pablo or there will be no Pablo. I care nothing about it either way. But I am not going to get on that wheel again. Twice I have been on that wheel and twice is has gone around and come back to where it started and I am taking no more rides on it.

He shut the notebook and looked up at Maria, '*Hola, guapa*,' he said to her. 'Did you make anything out of all that?'

'No, Roberto,' the girl said and put her hand on his hand that still held the pencil. 'Have you finished?'

'Yes. Now it is all written out and ordered.'

'What have you been doing, *Inglés*?' Pablo asked from across the table. His eyes were bleary again.

Robert Jordan looked at him closely. Stay off that wheel, he said to himself. Don't step on that wheel. I think it is going to start to swing again.

'Working on the problem of the bridge,' he said civilly.

'How is it?' asked Pablo.

'Very good,' Robert Jordan said. 'All very good.'

'I have been working on the problem of the retreat,' Pablo said, and Robert Jordan looked at his drunken pig eyes and at the wine bowl. The wine bowl was nearly empty.

Keep off the wheel, he told himself. He is drinking again. Sure. But don't you get on that wheel now. Wasn't Grant supposed to be drunk a good part of the time during the Civil War? Certainly he was. I'll bet Grant would be furious at the comparison if he could see Pablo. Grant was a cigar smoker, too. Well, he would have to see about getting Pablo a cigar. That was what that face really needed to complete it; a half chewed cigar. Where could he get Pablo a cigar?

'How does it go?' Robert Jordan asked politely.

'Very well,' Pablo said and nodded his head heavily and judiciously, '*Muy bien*.'

'You've thought up something?' Agustín asked from where they were playing cards.

'Yes,' Pablo said. 'Various things.'

'Where did you find them? In that bowl?' Agustín demanded.

'Perhaps,' Pablo said. 'Who knows? Maria, fill the bowl, will you, please?'

'In the wineskin itself there should be some fine ideas,' Agustín turned back to the card game. 'Why don't you crawl in and look for them inside the skin?'

'Nay,' said Pablo equably. 'I search for them in the bowl.'

He is not getting on the wheel either, Robert Jordan thought. It must be revolving by itself. I suppose you cannot ride that wheel too long. That is probably quite a deadly wheel. I'm glad we are off it. It was making me dizzy there a couple of times. But it is the thing that drunkards and those who are truly mean or cruel ride until they die. It goes around and up and the swing is never quite the same and then it comes around down. Let it swing, he thought. They will not get me on to it again. No sir, General Grant, I am off that wheel.

Pilar was sitting by the fire, her chair turned so that she could see over the shoulders of the two card players who had their backs to her. She was watching the game.

Here it is the shift from deadliness to normal family life that is the strangest, Robert Jordan thought. It is when the damned wheel comes down that it gets you. But I am off that wheel, he thought. And nobody is going to get me on to it again.

Two days ago I never knew that Pilar, Pablo nor the rest existed, he thought. There was no such thing as Maria in the world. It was certainly a much simpler world. I had instructions from Golz that were perfectly clear and seemed perfectly possible to carry out although they presented certain difficulties and involved certain consequences. After we blew the bridge I expected either to get back to the lines or not get back and if we got back I was going to ask for some time in Madrid. No one has any leave in this war but I am sure I could get two or three days in Madrid.

In Madrid I wanted to buy some books, to go to the Florida Hotel and get a room and to have a hot bath, he thought. I was going to send Luis the porter out for a bottle of absinthe if he could locate one at the Mantequerías Leonesas or at any of the places off the Gran Via and I was going to lie in bed and read after the bath and drink a couple of absinthes and then I was going to call up Gaylord's and see if I could come up there and eat.

He did not want to eat at the Gran Via because the food was no good really and you have to get there on time or whatever there was of it would be gone. Also there were too many newspaper men there he knew and he did not want to have to keep his mouth shut. He wanted to drink the absinthes and to feel like talking and then go up to Gaylord's and eat with Karkov, where they had good food and real beer, and find out what was going on in the war.

He had not liked Gaylord's, the hotel in Madrid the Russians had taken over, when he first went there because it seemed too luxurious and the food was too good for a besieged city and the talk too cynical for a war. But I corrupted very easily, he thought. Why should you not have as good food as could be organized when you came back from something like this? And the talk that he had thought of as cynicism when he had first heard it had turned out to be much too true. This will be something to tell at Gaylord's, he thought, when this is over. Yes, when this is over.

Could you take Maria to Gaylord's. No. You couldn't. But you could leave her in the hotel and she could take a hot bath and be there when you came back from Gaylord's. Yes, you could do that and after you had told Karkov about her, you could bring her later because they would be curious about her and want to see her.

Maybe you wouldn't go to Gaylord's at all. You could eat early at the Gran Via and hurry back to the Florida. But you knew you would go to Gaylord's because you wanted to see all that again; you wanted to eat that food again and you wanted to see all the comfort of it and the luxury of it after this. Then you would come back to the Florida and there Maria would be. Sure, she would be there after this was over. After this was over. Yes, after this was over. If he did this well he would rate a meal at Gaylord's.

Gaylord's was the place where you met famous peasant and worker Spanish commanders who had sprung to arms from the people at the start of the war without any previous military training and found that many of them spoke Russian. That had been the first big disillusion to him a few months back and he had started to be cynical to himself about it. But when he realized how it happened it was all right. They *were* peasants and workers. They had been active in the 1934 revolution and had to flee the country when it failed and in Russia they had sent them to the military academy and to the Lenin Institute the Comintern maintained so they would be ready to fight the next time and have the necessary military education to command.

The Comintern had educated them there. In a revolution you could not admit to outsiders who helped you nor that anyone knew more than he was supposed to know. He had learned that. If a thing was right fundamentally the lying was not supposed to matter. There was a lot of lying though. He did not care for the lying at first. He hated it. Then later he had come to like it. It was part of being an insider but it was a very corrupting business.

It was at Gaylord's that you learned that Valentín Gonzalez, called El Campesino or The Peasant, had never been a peasant but was an ex-sergeant in the Spanish Foreign Legion who had deserted and fought with Abd el Krim. That was all right, too. Why shouldn't he be? You had to have these peasant leaders quickly in this sort of war and a real peasant leader might be a little too much like Pablo. You couldn't wait for the real Peasant Leader to arrive and he might have too many peasant characteristics when he did. So you had to manufacture one. At that, from what he had seen of Campesino, with his black beard, his thick negroid lips, and his feverish, staring eyes, he thought he might give almost as much trouble as a real peasant leader. The last time he had seen him he seemed to have gotten to believe his own publicity and think he was a peasant. He was a brave, tough man; no braver in the world. But God, how he talked too much. And when he was excited he would say anything no matter what the consequences of his indiscretion. And those consequences had been many already. He was a wonderful Brigade Commander though in a situation where it looked as though everything was lost. He never knew when everything was lost, and if it was, he would fight out of it.

At Gaylord's, too, you met the simple stonemason, Enrique Lister from Galicia, who now commanded a division and who talked Russian, too. And you met the cabinet worker, Juan Modesto from Andalucia who had just been given an Army Corps. He never learned his Russian in Puerto de Santa Maria although he might have if they had a Berlitz School there that the cabinet makers went to. He was the most trusted of the young soldiers by the Russians because he was a true party man, 'a hundred per cent' they said, proud to use the Americanism. He was much more intelligent than Lister or El Campesino.

Sure. Gaylord's was the place you needed to complete your education. It was there you learned how it was all really done instead of how it was supposed to be done. He had only started his education, he thought. He wondered whether he would continue with it long. Gaylord's was good and sound and what he needed. At the start when he had still believed all the nonsense it had come as a shock to him. But now he knew enough to accept the necessity for all the deception and what he learned at Gaylord's only strengthened him in his belief in the things that he did hold to be true. He liked to know it really was; not how it was supposed to be. There was always lying in a war. But the truth of Lister, Modesto, and El Campesino was much better than the lies and legends. Well, some day they would tell the truth to everyone and meantime he was glad there was a Gaylord's for his own learning of it.

Yes, that was where he would go in Madrid after he had bought the books and after he had lain in the hot bath and had a couple of drinks and had read awhile. But that was before Maria had come into all this that he had that plan. All right. They would have two rooms and she could do what she liked while he went up there and he'd come back from Gaylord's to her. She had waited up in the hills all this time. She could wait a little while at the Hotel Florida. They would have three days in Madrid. Three days could be a long time. He'd take her to see the Marx Brothers at the Opera. That had been running for three months now and would certainly be good for three months more. She'd like the Marx Brothers at the Opera, he thought. She'd like that very much.

It was a long way from Gaylord's to this cave though. No, that was not the long way. The long way was going to be from this cave to Gaylord's. Kashkin had taken him there first and he had not liked it. Kashkin had said he should meet Karkov because Karkov wanted to know Americans and because he was the greatest lover of Lope de Vega in the world and thought 'Fuente Ovejuna' was the greatest play ever written. Maybe it was at that, but he, Robert Jordan, did not think so.

He had liked Karkov but not the place. Karkov was the most intelligent man he had ever met. Wearing black riding boots, grey breeches, and a grey tunic, with tiny hands and feet, puffily fragile of face and body, with a spitting way of talking through his bad teeth, he looked comic when Robert Jordan first saw him. But he had more brains and more inner dignity and outer insolence and humour than any man that he had ever known.

Gaylord's itself had seemed indecently luxurious and corrupt. But why shouldn't the representatives of a power that governed a sixth of the world have a few comforts? Well, they had them and Robert Jordan had at first been repelled by the whole business and then had accepted it and enjoyed it. Kashkin had made him out to be a hell of a fellow and Karkov had at first been insultingly polite and then, when Robert Jordan had not played at being a hero but had told a story that was really funny and obscenely discreditable to himself, Karkov had shifted from the politeness to a relieved rudeness and then to insolence and they had become friends.

Kashkin had only been tolerated there. There was something wrong with Kashkin evidently and he was working it out in Spain. They would not tell him what it was but maybe they would now that he was dead. Anyway, he and Karkov had become friends and he had become friends too with the incredibly thin, drawn, dark, loving, nervous, deprived and unbitter woman with a lean, neglected body and dark, grey-streaked hair cut short who was Karkov's wife and who served as an interpreter with the tank corps. He was a friend tooo of Karkov's mistress, who had cat-eyes, reddish gold hair (sometimes more red; sometimes more gold, depending on the coiffeurs), a lazy sensual body (made to fit well against other bodies), a mouth made to fit other mouths, and a stupid, ambitious and utterly loyal mind. This mistress loved gossip and enjoyed a periodically controlled promiscuity which seemed only to amuse Karkov. Karkov was supposed to have another wife somewhere beside the tank-corps one, maybe two more, but nobody was very sure about that. Robert Jordan liked both the wife he knew and the mistress. He thought he would probably like the other wife, too, if he knew her, if there was one. Karkov had good taste in women.

There were sentries with bayonets downstairs outside the portecochere at Gaylord's and to-night it would be the pleasantest and most comfortable place in all of besieged Madrid. He would like to be there to-night instead of here. Though it was all right here, now they had stopped that wheel. And the snow was stopping too.

He would like to show his Maria to Karkov but he could not take her there unless he asked first and he would have to see how he was received after this trip. Golz would be there after this attack was over and if he had done well they would all know it from Golz. Golz would make fun of him, too, about Maria. After what he'd said to him about no girls.

He reached over to the bowl in front of Pablo and dipped up a cup of wine. 'With your permission,' he said.

Pablo nodded. He is engaged in his military studies, I imagine Robert Jordan thought. Not seeking the bubble reputation in the cannon's mouth but seeking the solution to the problem in yonder bowl. But you know the bastard must be fairly able to have run this band successfully for as long as he did. Looking at Pablo he wondered what sort of guerilla leader he would have been in the American Civil War. There were lots of them, he thought. But we know very little about them. Not the Quantrills, nor the Mosbys, nor his own grandfather, but the little ones, the bushwhackers. And about the drinking. Do you suppose Grant really was a drunk? His grandfather always claimed he was. That he was always a little drunk by four o'clock in the afternoon and that before Vicksburg sometimes during the siege he was very drunk for a couple of days. But grandfather claimed that he functioned perfectly normally no matter how much he drank except that sometimes it was very hard to wake him. But if you *could* wake him he was normal.

There wasn't any Grant, nor any Sherman nor any Stonewall Jackson on either side so far in this war. No. Nor any Jeb Stuart either. Nor any Sheridan. It was overrun with McClellans though. The fascists had plenty of McClellans and we had at least three of them.

He had certainly not seen any military geniuses in this war. Not a one. Nor anything resembling one. Kleber, Lucasz, and Hans had done a fine job of their share in the defence of Madrid with the International Brigades and then the old bald, spectacled, conceited, stupid-as-an-owl, unintelligent-in-conversation, brave-and-as-dumb-as-a-bull, propaganda-built-up defender of Madrid, Miaja, had been so jealous of the publicity Kleber received that he had forced the Russians to relieve Kleber of his command and send him to Valencia. Kleber was a good soldier; but limited and he *did* talk too much for the job he had. Golz was a good general and a fine soldier but they always kept him in a subordinate position and never gave him a free hand. This attack was going to be his biggest show so far and Robert Jordan did not like too much what he had heard about the attack. Then there was Gall, the Hungarian, who ought to be shot if you could believe half you heard at Gaylord's. Make it if you can believe ten per cent of what you hear at Gaylord's, Robert Jordan thought.

He wished that he had seen the fighting on the plateau beyond Guadalajara when they beat the Italians. But he had been down in Estremadura then. Hans had told him about it one night in Gaylord's two weeks ago and made him see it all. There was one moment when it was really lost when the Italians had broken the line near Trijueque and the Twelfth Brigade would have been cut off if the Torija-Brihuega road had been cut. 'But knowing they were Italians,' Hans had said, 'we attempted a manœuvre which would have been unjustifiable against other troops. And it was successful.'

Hans had shown it all to him on his maps of the battle. Hans carried them around with him in his map case all the time and still seemed marvelled and happy at the miracle of it. Hans was a fine soldier and a good companion. Lister's and Modesto's and Campesino's Spanish troops had all fought well in that battle, Hans had told him, and that was to be credited to their leaders and to the discipline they enforced. But Lister and Campesino and Modesto had been told many of the moves they should make by their Russian military advisers. They were like students flying a machine with dual controls which the pilot could take over whenever they made a mistake. Well, this year would show how much and how well they learned. After a while there would not be dual controls and then we would see how well they handled divisions and army corps alone.

They were Communists and they were disciplinarians. The discipline that they would enforce would make good troops. Lister was murderous in discipline. He was a true fanatic and he had the complete Spanish lack of respect for life. In few armies since the Tartar's first invasion of the West were men executed summarily for as little reason as they were under his command. But he knew how to forge a division into a fighting unit. It is one thing to hold positions. It is another to attack positions and take them and it is something very different to manœuvre an army in the field, Robert Jordan thought as he sat there at the table. From what I have seen of him, I wonder how Lister will be at that once the dual controls are gone? But maybe they won't go, he thought. I wonder if they will go? Or whether they will strengthen? I wonder what the Russian stand is on the whole business? Gaylord's is the place, he thought. There is much that I need to know now that I can learn only at Gaylord's.

At one time he had thought Gaylord's had been bad for him. It was the opposite of the puritanical, religious communism of Velazquez 63, the Madrid palace that had been turned into the International Brigade headquarters in the capital. At Velazquez 63 it was like being a member of a religious order–and Gaylord's was a long way away from the feeling you had at the headquarters of the Fifth Regiment before it had been broken up in the brigades of the new army.

At either of those places you felt that you were taking part in a crusade. That was the only word for it although it was a word that had been so worn and abused that it no longer gave its true meaning. You felt, in spite of all bureaucracy and inefficiency and party strife something that was like the feeling you expected to have and did not have when you made your first communion. It was a feeling of consecration to a duty toward all of the oppressed of the world which would be as difficult and embarrassing to speak about as religious experience and yet it was authentic as the feeling you had when you heard Bach, or stood in Chartres Cathedral or the Cathedral at Léon and saw the light coming through the great windows; or when you saw Mantegna and Greco and Brueghel in the Prado. It gave you a part in something that you could believe in wholly and completely and in which you felt an absolute brotherhood with the others who were engaged in it. It was something that you had never known before but that you had experienced now and you gave such importance to it and the reasons for it that your own death seemed of complete unimportance; only a thing to be avoided because it would interfere with the performance of your duty. But the best thing was that there was something you could do about this feeling and this necessity too. You could fight.

So you fought, he thought. And in the fighting soon there was no purity of feeling for those who survived the fighting and were good at it. Not after the first six months.

The defence of a position or of a city is a part of war in which you can feel that first sort of feeling. The fighting in the Sierras had been that way. They had fought there with the true comradeship of the revolution. Up there when there had been the first necessity for the enforcement of discipline he had approved and understood it. Under the shelling men had been cowards and had run. He had seen them shot and left to swell beside the road, nobody bothering to do more than strip them of their cartridges and their valuables. Taking their cartridges, their boots and their leather coats was right. Taking the valuables was only realistic. It only kept the anarchists from getting them.

It had seemed just and right and necessary that the men who ran were shot. There was nothing wrong about it. Their running was a selfishness. The fascists had attacked and we had stopped them on that slope in the grey rocks, the scrub pines and the gorse of the Guadarrama hillsides. We had held along the road under the bombing from the planes and the shelling when they brought their artillery up and those who were left at the end of that day had counter-attacked and driven them back. Later, when they had tried to come down on the left, sifting down between the rocks and through the trees, we had held out in the Sanitarium firing from the windows and the roof although they had passed it on both sides, and we lived through knowing what it was to be surrounded until the counter-attack had cleared them back behind the road again.

In all that, in the fear that dries your mouth and your throat, in the smashed plaster dust and the sudden panic of a wall falling, collapsing in the flash and roar of a shellburst, clearing the gun, dragging those away who had been serving it, lying face downward and covered with rubble, your head behind the shield working on a stoppage, getting the broken case out, straightening the belt again, you now lying straight behind the shield, the gun searching the roadside again; you did the thing there was to do and knew that you were right. You learned the dry-mouthed, fear-purged, purging ecstasy of battle and you fought that summer and that autumn for all the poor in the world, against all tyranny, for all the things that you believed and for the new world you had been educated into. You learned that autumn, he thought, how to endure and how to ignore suffering in the long time of cold and wetness, of mud and of digging and fortifying. And the feeling of the summer and the autumn was buried deep under tiredness, sleepiness, and nervousness and discomfort. But it was still there and all that you went through only served to validate it. It was in those days, he thought, that you had a deep and sound and selfless pride–that would have made you a bloody bore at Gaylord's, he thought suddenly.

No, you would not have been so good at Gaylord's then, he thought. You were too naïve. You were in a sort of state of grace. But Gaylord's might not have been the way it was now at that time, either. No, as a matter of fact, it was not that way, he told himself. It was not that way at all. There was not any Gaylord's then.

Karkov had told him about those days. At that time what Russians there were had lived at the Palace Hotel. Robert Jordan had known none of them then. That was before the first *partizan* groups had been formed; before he had met Kashkin or any of the others. Kashkin had been in the north at Irun, at San Sebastian and in the abortive fighting toward Vitoria. He had not arrived in Madrid until January and while Robert Jordan had fought at Carabanchel and at Usera in those three days when they stopped the right wing of the fascist attack on Madrid and drove the Moors and the *Tercio* back from house to house to clear that battered suburb on the edge of the grey, sun-baked plateau and establish a line of defence along the heights that would protect that corner of the city, Karkov had been in Madrid.

Karkov was not cynical about those times either when he talked. Those were the days they all shared when everything looked lost and each man retained now, better than any citation or decoration, the knowledge of just how he would act when everything looked lost. The government had abandoned the city, taking all the motor cars from the ministry of war in their flight and old Miaja had to ride down to inspect his defensive positions on a bicycle. Robert Jordan did not believe that one. He could not see Miaja on a bicycle even in his most patriotic imagination, but Karkov said it was true. But then he had written it for Russian papers so be probably wanted to believe it was true after writing it.

But there was another story that Karkov had not written. He had three wounded Russians in the Palace Hotel for whom he was responsible. They were two tank drivers and a flyer who were too bad to be moved, and since, at that time, it was of the greatest importance that there should be no evidence of any Russian intervention to justify an open intervention by the fascists, it was Karkov's responsibility that these wounded should not fall into the hands of the fascists in case the city should be abandoned.

In the event the city should be abandoned, Karkov was to poison them to destroy all evidence of their identity before leaving the Palace Hotel. No one could prove from the bodies of three wounded men, one with three bullet wounds in his abdomen, one with his jaw shot away and his vocal cords exposed, one with his femur smashed to bits by a bullet and his hands and face so badly burned that his face was just an eyelashless, eyebrowless, hairless blister that they were Russians. No one could tell from the bodies of these wounded men he would leave in beds at the Palace that they were Russians. Nothing proved a naked dead man was a Russian. Your nationality and your politics did not show when you were dead.

Robert Jordan had asked Karkov how he felt about the necessity of performing this act and Karkov had said that he had not looked forward to it. 'How were you going to do it?' Robert Jordan had asked him and had added, 'You know it isn't so simple just suddenly to poison people.' And Karkov had said, 'Oh, yes, it is when you carry it always for your own use.' Then he had opened his cigarette case and showed Robert Jordan what he carried in one side of it.

'But the first thing anybody would do if they took you prisoner would be to take your cigarette case,' Robert Jordan had objected. 'They would have your hands up.'

'But I have a little more here,' Karkov had grinned and showed the lapel of his jacket. 'You simply put the lapel in your mouth like this and bite it and swallow.'

'That's much better,' Robert Jordan had said. 'Tell me, does it smell like bitter almonds the way it always does in detective stories?'

'I don't know,' Karkov said delightedly. 'I have never smelled it. Should be break a little tube and smell it?'

'Better keep it.'

'Yes,' Karkov said and put the cigarette case away. 'I am not a defeatist, you understand, but it is always possible that such serious times might come again and you cannot get this anywhere. Have you seen the communiqué from the Cordoba front? It is very beautiful. It is now my favourite among all the communiqués.'

'What did it say?' Robert Jordan had come to Madrid from the Cordoban Front and he had the sudden stiffening that comes when someone jokes about a thing which you yourself may joke about but which they may not. 'Tell me?'

'*Nuestra gloriosa tropa siga avanzando sin perder ni una sola palma de terreno*,' Karkov said in his strange Spanish.

'It didn't really say that,' Robert Jordan doubted.

'Our glorious troops continue to advance without losing a foot of ground,' Karkov repeated in English. 'It is in the communiqué. I will find it for you.'

You could remember the men you knew who died in the fighting around

Pozoblanco; but it was a joke at Gaylord's.

So that was the way it was at Gaylord's now. Still there had not always been Gaylord's and if the situation was now one which produced such a thing as Gaylord's out of the survivors of the early days, he was glad to see Gaylord's and to know about it. You are a long way from how you felt in the Sierra and at Carabanchel and at Usera, he thought. You corrupt very easily, he thought. But was it corruption or was it merely that you lost the naïvety that you started with? Would it not be the same in anything? Who else kept that first chastity of mind about their work that young doctors, young priests, and young soldiers usually started with? The priests certainly kept it, or they got out. I suppose the Nazis keep it, he thought, and the Communists who have a severe enough self-discipline. But look at Karkov.

He never tired of considering the case of Karkov. The last time he had been at Gaylord's Karkov had been wonderful about a certain British economist who had spent much time in Spain. Robert Jordan had read this man's writing for years and he had always respected him without knowing anything about him. He had not cared very much for what this man had written about Spain. It was too clear and simple and too open and shut and many of the statistics he knew were faked by wishful thinking. But he thought you rarely cared for journalism written about a country you really knew about and he respected the man for his intentions.

Then he had seen the man, finally, on the afternoon when they had attacked at Carabanchel. They were sitting in the lee of the bull ring and there was shooting down the two streets and every one was nervous waiting for the attack. A tank had been promised and it had not come up and Montero was sitting with his head in his hands saying, 'The tank has not come. The tank has not come.'

It was a cold day and the yellow dust was blowing down the street and Montero had been hit in the left arm and the arm was stiffening. 'We have to have a tank,' he said. 'We must wait for the tank, but we cannot wait.' His wound was making him sound petulant.

Robert Jordan had gone back to look for the tank which Montero said he thought might have stopped behind the apartment building on the corner of the tram line. It was there all right. But it was not a tank. Spaniards called anything a tank in those days. It was an old armoured car. The driver did not want to leave the angle of the apartment house and bring it up to the bull ring. He was standing behind it with his arms folded against the metal of the car and his head in the leather-padded helmet on his arms. He shook his head when Robert Jordan spoke to him and kept it pressed against his arms. Then he turned his head without looking at Robert Jordan.

'I have no orders to go there,' he said sullenly.

Robert Jordan had taken his pistol out of the holster and pushed the muzzle of the pistol against the leather coat of the armoured car driver.

'Here are your orders,' he had told him. The man shook his head with the big padded-leather helmet like a football player's on it and said, 'There is no ammunition for the machine-gun.'

'We have ammunition at the bull ring,' Robert Jordan had told him. 'Come on, let's go. We will fill the belts there. Come on.'

'There is no one to work the gun,' the driver said.

'Where is he? Where is your mate?'

'Dead,' the driver said. 'Inside there.'

'Get him out,' Robert Jordan had said. 'Get him out of there.'

'I do not like to touch him,' the driver had said. 'And he is bent over between the gun and the wheel and I cannot get past him.'

'Come on,' Robert Jordan had said. 'We will get him out together.'

He had banged his head as he climbed into the armoured car and it had made a small cut over his eyebrow that bled down on to his face. The dead man was heavy and so stiff you could not bend him and he had to hammer at his head to get it out from where it had wedged, face-down, between his seat and the wheel. Finally he got it up by pushing with his knee up under the dead man's head and then, pulling back on the man's waist now that the head was loose, he pulled the dead man out himself toward the door.

'Give me a hand with him,' he had said to the driver.

'I do not want to touch him,' the driver had said and Robert Jordan had seen that he was crying. The tears ran straight down on each side of his nose on the powder-grimed slope of his face and his nose was running, too.

Standing beside the door he had swung the dead man out and the dead man fell on to the sidewalk beside the tram-line still in that hunched-over, doubled-up position. He lay there, his face waxy grey against the cement sidewalk, his hands bent under him as they had been in the car.

'Get in, God damn it,' Robert Jordan had said, motioning now with his pistol to the driver. 'Get in there now.'

Just then he had seen this man who had come out from the lee of the apartment house building. He had on a long overcoat and he was bareheaded and his hair was grey, his cheekbones broad and his eyes were deep and set close together. He had a package of Chesterfields in his hand and he took one out and handed it toward Robert Jordan who was pushing the driver into the armoured car with his pistol.

'Just a minute, Comrade,' he had said to Robert Jordan in Spanish. 'Can you explain to me something about the fighting?'

Robert Jordan took the cigarette and put it in the breast pocket of his blue mechanic jumper. He had recognized this comrade from his pictures. It was the British economist.

'Go muck yourself,' he said in English and then, in Spanish, to the armoured car driver. 'Down there. The bull ring. See?' And he had pulled the heavy side door to with a slam and locked it and they had started down that long slope in the car and the bullets had commenced to hit against the car, sounding like pebbles tossed against an iron boiler. Then when the machine-gun opened on them, they were like sharp hammer tappings. They had pulled up behind the shelter of the bull ring with the last October posters still pasted up beside the ticket window and the ammunition boxes knocked open and the comrades with the rifles, the grenades on their belts and in their pockets, waiting there in the lee and Montero had said, 'Good. Here is the tank. Now we can attack.'

Later that night when they had the last houses on the hill, he lay comfortable behind a brick wall with a hole knocked in the bricks for a loophole and looked across the beautiful level field of fire they had between them and the ridge the fascists had retired to and thought, with a comfort that was almost voluptuous, of the rise of the hill with the smashed villa that protected the left flank. He had lain in a pile of straw in his sweat-soaked clothes and wound a blanket around him while he dried. Lying there he thought of the economist and laughed, and then felt sorry he had been rude. But at the moment, when the man had handed him the cigarette, pushing it out almost like offering a tip for information, the combatant's hatred for the noncombatant had been too much for him.

Now he remembered Gaylord's and Karkov speaking of this same man. 'So it was there you met him,' Karkov had said. 'I did not get farther than the Puente de Toledo myself on that day. He was very far toward the front. That was the last day of his bravery, I believe. He left Madrid the next day. Toledo was where he was the bravest, I believe. At Toledo he was enormous. He was one of the architects of our capture of the Alcazar. You should have seen him at Toledo. I believe it was largely through his efforts and his advice that our siege was successful. That was the silliest part of the war. It reached an ultimate in silliness, but tell me, what is thought of him in America?'

'In America,' Robert Jordan said, 'he is supposed to be very close to Moscow.'

'He is not,' said Karkov. 'But he has a wonderful face and his face and his manners are very successful. Now with my face I could do nothing. What little I have accomplished was all done in spite of my face which does not either inspire people nor move them to love me and to trust me. But this man Mitchell has a face he makes his fortune with. It is the face of a conspirator. All who have read of conspirators in books trust him instantly. Also he has the true manner of the conspirator. Anyone seeing him enter a room knows that he is instantly in the presence of a conspirator of the first mark. All of your rich compatriots who wish sentimentally to aid the Soviet Union as they believe or to insure themselves a little against any eventual success of the party see instantly in the face of this man, and in his manner, that he can be none other than a trusted agent of the Comintern.'

'Has he no connections in Moscow?'

'None. Listen, Comrade Jordan. Do you know about the two kinds of fools?'

'Plain and damn?'

'No. The two kinds of fools we have in Russia,' Karkov grinned and began. 'First there is the winter fool. The winter fool comes to the door of your house and he knocks loudly. You go to the door and you see him there and you have never seen him before. He is an impressive sight. He is a very big man and he has on high boots and a fur coat and a fur hat and he is all covered with snow. First he stamps his boots and snow falls from them. Then he takes off his fur coat and shakes it and more snow falls. Then he takes off his fur hat and knocks it against the door. More snow falls from his fur hat. Then he stamps his boots again and advances into the room. Then you look at him and you see he is a fool. That is the winter fool.

'Now in the summer you see a fool going down the street and he is waving his arms and jerking his head from side to side and everybody from two hundred yards away can tell he is a fool. That is a summer fool. This economist is a winter fool.'

'But why do people trust him here?' Robert Jordan asked.

'His face,' Karkov said. 'His beautiful *gueule de conspirateur*. And his invaluable trick of just having come from somewhere else where he is very trusted and important. Of course,' he smiled, 'he must travel very much to keep the trick working. You know the Spanish are very strange,' Karkov went on. 'This government has had much money. Much gold. They will give nothing to their friends. You are a friend. All right. You will do it for nothing and should not be rewarded. But to people representing an important firm or a country which is not friendly but must be influenced–to such people they give much. It is very interesting when you follow it closely.'

'I do not like it. Also that money belongs to the Spanish workers.'

'You are not supposed to like things. Only to understand,' Karkov had told him. 'I teach you a little each time I see you and eventually you will acquire an education. It would be very interesting for a professor to be educated.'

'I don't know whether I'll be able to be a professor when I get back. They will probably run me out as a red.'

'Well, perhaps you will be able to come to the Soviet Union and continue your studies there. That might be the best thing for you to do.'

'But Spanish is my field.'

'There are many countries where Spanish is spoken,' Karkov had said. 'They cannot all be as difficult to do anything with as Spain is. Then you must remember that you have not been a professor now for almost nine months. In nine months you may have learned a new trade. How much dialectics have you read?'

'I have read the Handbook of Marxism that Emil Burns edited. That is all.'

'If you have read it all that is quite a little. There are fifteen hundred pages and you could spend some time on each page. But there are some other things you should read.'

'There is no time to read now.'

'I know,' Karkov had said. 'I mean eventually. There are many things to read which will make you understand some of these things that happen. But out of this will come a book which is very necessary; which will explain many things which it is necessary to know. Perhaps I will write it. I hope that it will be me who will write it.'

'I don't know who could write it better.'

'Do not flatter,' Karkov had said. 'I am a journalist. But like all journalists I wish to write literature. Just now, I am very busy on a study of Calvo Sotelo. He was a very good fascist; a true Spanish fascist. Franco and these other people are not. I have been studying all of Sotelo's writings and speeches. He was very intelligent and it was very intelligent that he was killed.'

'I thought that you did not believe in political assassination.'

'It is practised very extensively,' Karkov said. 'Very, very extensively.'

'But—'

'We do not believe in acts of terrorism by individuals,' Karkov had smiled. 'Not of course by criminal terrorist and counter-revolutionary organizations. We detest with horror the duplicity and villainy of the murderous hyenas of Bukharinite wreckers and such dregs of humanity as Zinoviev, Kamenev, Rykov and their henchmen. We hate and loathe these veritable fiends,' he smiled again. 'But I still believe that political assassination can be said to be practised very extensively.'

'You mean—'

'I mean nothing. But certainly we execute and destroy such veritable fiends and dregs of humanity and the treacherous dogs of generals and the revolting spectacle of admirals unfaithful to their trust. These are destroyed. They are not assassinated. You see the difference?'

'I see,' Robert Jordan had said.

'And because I make jokes sometime: and you know how dangerous it is to make jokes even in joke? Good. Because I make jokes, do not think that the Spanish people will not live to regret that they have not shot certain generals that even now hold commands. I do not like the shootings, you understand.'

'I don't mind them,' Robert Jordan said. 'I do not like them but I do not mind them any more.'

'I know that,' Karkov had said. 'I have been told that.'

'Is it important?' Robert Jordan said. 'I was only trying to be truthful about it.'

'It is regretful,' Karkov had said. 'But it is one of the things that makes people be treated as reliable who would ordinarily have to spend much more time before attaining that category.'

'Am I supposed to be reliable?'

'In your work you are supposed to be very reliable. I must talk to you sometime to see how you are in your mind. It is regrettable that we never speak seriously.'

'My mind is in suspension until we win the war,' Robert Jordan had said.

'Then perhaps you will not need it for a long time. But you should be careful to exercise it a little.'

'I read *Mundo Obrero*,' Robert Jordan had told him and Karkov had said, 'All right. Good. I can take a joke too. But there are very intelligent things in *Mundo Obrero*. The only intelligent things written on this war.'

'Yes,' Robert Jordan had said. 'I agree with you. But to get a full picture of what is happening you cannot read only the party organ.'

'No,' Karkov had said. 'But you will not find any such picture if you read twenty papers and then, if you had it, I do not know what you would do with it. I have such a picture almost constantly and what I do is to try to forget it.'

'It is better now than it was. We are getting rid of some of the worst. But it is very rotten. We are building a huge army now and some of the elements, those of Modesto, of El Campesino, of Lister and of Durán, are reliable. They are more than reliable. They are magnificent. You will see that. Also we still have the Brigades although their role is changing. But an army that is made up of good and bad elements cannot win a war. All must be brought to a certain level of political development; all must know why they are fighting, and its importance. All must believe in the fight they are to make and all must accept discipline. We are making a huge conscript army without the time to implant the discipline that a conscript army must have, to behave properly under fire. We call it a people's army but it will not have the assets of a true people's army and it will not have the iron discipline that a conscript army needs. You will see. It is a very dangerous procedure.

'You are not very cheerful to-day.'

'No,' Karkov had said. 'I have just come back from Valencia where I have seen many people. No one comes back very cheerful from Valencia. In Madrid you feel good and clean and with no possibility of anything but winning. Valencia is something else. The cowards who fled from Madrid still govern there. They have settled happily into the sloth and bureaucracy of governing. They have only contempt for those of Madrid. Their obsession now is the weakening of the commissariat for war. And Barcelona. You should see Barcelona.'

'How is it?'

'It is all still comic opera. First it was the paradise of the crackpots and the romantic revolutionists. Now it is the paradise of the fake soldier. The soldiers who like to wear uniforms, who like to strut and swagger and wear red-and-black scarves. Who like everything about war except to fight. Valencia makes you sick and Barcelona makes you laugh.'

'What about the P.O.U.M. putsch?'

'The P.O.U.M. was never serious. It was a heresy of crackpots and wild men and it was really just an infantilism. There were some honest misguided people. There was one fairly good brain and there was a little fascist money. Not much. The poor P.O.U.M. They were very silly people.'

'But were many killed in the putsch?'

'Not so many as were shot afterwards or will be shot. The P.O.U.M. It is like the name. Not serious. They should have called it the M.U.M.P.S. or the M.E.A.S.L.E.S. But no. The Measles is much more dangerous. It can affect both sight and hearing. But they made one plot you know to kill me, to kill Walter, to kill Modesto and to kill Prieto. You see how badly mixed up they were? We are not at all alike. Poor P.O.U.M. They never did kill anybody. Not at the front nor anywhere else. A few in Barcelona, yes.'

'Were you there?'

'Yes. I have sent a cable describing the wickedness of that infamous organization of Trotskyite murderers and their fascist machinations all beneath contempt but, between us, it is not very serious, the P.O.U.M. Nin was their only man. We had him but he escaped from our hands.'

'Where is he now?'

'In Paris. We say he is in Paris. He was a very pleasant fellow but with bad political aberrations.'

'But they were in communication with the fascists, weren't they;

'Who is not?'

'We are not.'

'Who knows? I hope we are not. You go often behind their lines,' he grinned. 'But the brother of one of the secretaries of the Republican Embassy at Paris made a trip to St Jean de Luz last week to meet people from Burgos.'

'I like it better at the front,' Robert Jordan had said. 'The closer to the front the better the people.'

'How do you like it behind the fascist lines?'

'Very much. We have fine people there.'

'Well, you see they must have their fine people behind our lines the same way. We find them and shoot them and they find ours and shoot them. When you are in their country you must always think of how many people they must send over to us.'

'I have thought about them.'

'Well,' Karkov had said. 'You have probably enough to think about for to-day, so drink that beer that is left in the pitcher and run along now because I have to go upstairs to see people. Upstairs people. Come again to see me soon.'

Yes, Robert Jordan thought. You learned a lot at Gaylord's. Karkov had read the one and only book he had published. The book had not been a success. It was only two hundred pages long and he doubted if two thousand people had ever read it. He had put in it what he had discovered about Spain in ten years of travelling in it, on foot, in third-class carriages, by bus, on horse-and mule-back and in trucks. He knew the Basque country, Navarre, Aragon, Galicia, the two Castiles and Estremadura well. There had been such good books written by Borrow and Ford and the rest that he had been able to add very little. But Karkov said it was a good book.

'It is why I bother with you,' he had said. 'I think you write absolutely truly and that is very rare. So I would like you to know some things.'

All right. He would write a book when he got through with this. But only about the things he knew, truly, and about what he knew. But I will have to be a much better writer than I am now to handle them, he thought. The things he had come to know in this war were not so simple.

19

'What do you do sitting there?' Maria asked him. She was standing close beside him and he turned his head and smiled at her.

'Nothing,' he said. 'I have been thinking.'

'What of? The bridge?'

'No. The bridge is terminated. Of thee and of a hotel in Madrid where I know some Russians, and of a book I will write some time.'

'Are there many Russians in Madrid?'

'No. Very few.'

'But in the fascist periodicals it says there are hundreds of thousands.'

'Those are lies. There are very few.'

'Do you like the Russians? The one who was here was a Russian.'

'Did you like him?'

'Yes. I was sick then but I thought he was very beautiful and very brave.'

'What nonsense, beautiful,' Pilar said. 'His nose was flat as my hand and he had cheekbones as wide as a sheep's buttocks.'

'He was a good friend and comrade of mine,' Robert Jordan said to Maria. 'I cared for him very much.'

'Sure,' Pilar said. 'But you shot him.'

When she said this the card players looked up from the table and Pablo stared at Robert Jordan. Nobody said anything and then the gipsy, Rafael, asked, 'Is it true, Roberto?'

'Yes,' Robert Jordan said. He wished Pilar had not brought this up and he wished he had not told it at El Sordo's. 'At his request. He was badly wounded.'

'*Qué cosa mas rara*,' the gipsy said. 'All the time he was with us he talked of such a possibility. I don't know how many times I have promised him to perform such an act. What a rare thing,' he said again and shook his head.

'He was a very rare man,' Primitivo said. 'Very singular.'

'Look,' Andrés, one of the brothers, said. 'You who are professor and all. Do you believe in the possibility of a man seeing ahead what is to happen to him?'

'I believe he cannot see it,' Robert Jordan said. Pablo was staring at him curiously and Pilar was watching him with no expression on her face. 'In the case of this Russian comrade he was very nervous from being too much time at the front. He had fought at Irun which, you know, was bad. Very bad. He had fought later in the north. And since the first groups who did this work behind the lines were formed he had worked here, in Estremadura and in Andalucía. I think he was very tired and nervous and he imagined ugly things.'

'He would undoubtedly have seen many evil things,' Fernando said.

'Like all the world,' Andrés said. 'But listen to me, *Inglés*. Do you think there is such a thing as a man knowing in advance what will befall him?'

'No,' Robert Jordan said. 'That is ignorance and superstition.'

'Go on,' Pilar said. 'Let us hear the viewpoint of the professor.' She spoke as though she were talking to a precocious child.

'I believe that fear produces evil visions,' Robert Jordan said. 'Seeing bad sings—'

'Such as the airplanes to-day,' Primitivo said.

'Such as thy arrival,' Pablo said softly and Robert Jordan looked across the table at him, saw it was not a provocation but only an expressed thought, then went on. 'Seeing bad signs, one, with fear, imagines an end for himself and one thinks that imagining comes by divination,' Robert Jordan concluded. 'I believe there is nothing more to it than that. I do not believe in ogres, nor soothsayers, nor in supernatural things.'

'But this one with the rare name saw his fate clearly,' the gipsy said. 'And that was how it happened.'

'He did not see it,' Robert Jordan said. 'He had a fear of such a possibility and it became an obsession. No one can tell me that he saw anything.'

'Not I?' Pilar asked him and picked some dust up from the fire and blew it off the palm of her hand. 'I cannot tell thee either?'

'No. With all wizardry, gipsy and all, thou canst not tell me either.'

'Because thou art a miracle of deafness,' Pilar said, her big face harsh and broad in the candlelight. 'It is not that thou art stupid. Thou art simply deaf. One who is deaf cannot hear music. Neither can he hear the radio. So he might say, never having heard them, that such things do not exist. *Qué va, Inglés*. I saw the death of that one with the rare name in his face as though it were burned there with a branding iron.'

'You did not,' Robert Jordan insisted. 'You saw fear and apprehension. The fear was made by what he had been through. The apprehension was for the possibility of evil he imagined.'

'*Qué va*,' Pilar said. 'I saw death there as plainly as though it were sitting on his shoulder. And what is more he smelt of death.'

'He smelt of death,' Robert Jordan jeered. 'Of fear maybe. There is a smell to fear.'

'*De la muerte*,' Pilar said. 'Listen. When Blanquet, who was the greatest *peon de brega* who ever lived, worked under the orders of Granero he told me that on the day of Manolo Granero's death, when they stopped in the chapel on the way to the ring, the odour of death was so strong on Manolo that it almost made Blanquet sick. And he had been with Manolo when he had bathed and dressed at the hotel before setting out for the ring. The odour was not present in the motor car when they had sat packed tight together riding to the bull ring. Nor was it distinguishable to anyone else but Juan Luis de la Rosa in the chapel. Neither Marcial nor Chicuelo smelled it neither then nor when the four of them lined up for the paseo. But Juan Luis was dead white, Blanquet told me, and he, Blanquet, spoke to him saying, "Thou also?"

'"So that I cannot breathe," Juan Luis said to him. "And from thy matador."

'"*Pues nada*," Blanquet said. "There is nothing to do. Let us hope we are mistaken."

'"And the others?" Juan Luis asked Blanquet.

'"*Nada*," Blanquet said. "Nothing. But this one stinks worse than José at Talavera."

'And it was on that afternoon that the bull *Pocapena* of the ranch of Veragua destroyed Manolo Granero against the planks of the barrier in front of *tendido* two in the Plaza de Toros of Madrid. I was there with Finito and I saw it. The horn entirely destroyed the cranium, the head of Manolo being wedged under the *estribo* at the base of the *barrera* where the bull had tossed him.'

'But did you smell anything?' Fernando asked.

'Nay,' Pilar said. 'I was too far away. We were in the seventh row of *tendido* three. It was thus, being at an angle, that I could see all that happened. But that same night Blanquet who had been under the orders of Joselito when he too was killed told Finito about it at Fornos, and Finito asked Juan Luis de la Rosa and he would say nothing. But he nodded his head that it was true. I was present when this happened. So, *Inglés*, it may be that thou art deaf to some things as Chicuelo and Marcial Lalanda and all of their *banderilleros* and picadors and all of the *gente* of Juan Luis and Manolo

Granero were deaf to this thing on this day. But Juan Luis and Blanquet were not deaf. Nor am I deaf to such things.'

'Why do you say deaf when it is a thing of the nose?' Fernando asked.

'*Leche!*' Pilar said. 'Thou shouldst be the professor in place of the *Inglés*. But I could tell thee of other things, *Inglés*, and do not doubt what thou simply cannot see nor cannot hear. Thou canst not hear what a dog hears. Nor canst thou smell what a dog smells. But already thou has experienced a little of what can happen to man.'

Maria put her hand on Robert Jordan's shoulder and let it rest there and he thought suddenly, let us finish all this nonsense and take advantage of what time we have. But it is too early yet. We have to kill this part of the evening. So he said to Pablo, 'Thou, believest thou in this wizardry?'

'I do not know,' Pablo said. 'I am more of thy opinion. No supernatural thing has ever happened to me. But fear, yes certainly. Plenty. But I believe that the Pilar can divine events from the hand. If she does not lie perhaps it is true that she has smelt such a thing.'

'*Qué va* that I should lie,' Pilar said. 'This is not a thing of my invention. This man Blanquet was a man of extreme seriousness and furthermore very devout. He was no gipsy but a bourgeois from Valencia. Hast thou never seen him?'

'Yes,' Robert Jordan said. 'I have seen him many times. He was small, grey-faced and no one handled a cape better. He was quick on his feet as a rabbit.'

'Exactly,' Pilar said. 'He had a grey face from heart trouble and gipsies said that he carried death with him but that he could flick it away with a cape as you might dust a table. Yet he, who was no gipsy, smelled death on Joselito when he fought at Talavera. Although I do not see how he could smell it above the smell of manzanilla. Blanquet spoke of this afterwards with much diffidence but those to whom he spoke said that it was a fantasy and that what he had smelled was the life that José led at that time coming out in sweat from his armpits. But then, later, came this of Manolo Granero in which Juan Luis de la Rosa also participated. Clearly Juan Luis was a man of very little honour, but of much sensitiveness in his work and he was also a great layer of women. But Blanquet was serious and very quiet and completely incapable of telling an untruth. And I tell you that I smelled death on your colleague who was here.'

'I do not believe it,' Robert Jordan said. 'Also you said that Blanquet smelled this just before the paseo. Just before the bullfight started. Now this was a successful action here of you and Kashkin and the train. He was not killed in that. How could you smell it then?'

'That has nothing to do with it,' Pilar explained. 'In the last season of Ignacio Sanchez Mejias he smelled so strongly of death that many refused to sit with him in the café. All gipsies knew of this.'

'After the death such things are invented,' Robert Jordan argued. 'Everyone knew that Sanchez Mejias was on the road to a *cornada* because he had been too long out of training, because his style was heavy and dangerous, and because his strength and the agility in his legs were gone and his reflexes no longer as they had been.'

'Certainly,' Pilar told him. 'All of that is true. But all the gipsies knew also that he smelled of death and when he would come into the Villa Rosa you would see such people as Ricardo and Felipe Gonzalez leaving by the small door behind the bar.'

'They probably owed him money,' Robert Jordan said.

'It is possible,' Pilar said. 'Very possible. But they also smelled the thing and all knew of it.'

'What she says is true, *Inglés*,' the gipsy, Rafael, said. 'It is a well-known thing among us.'

'I believe nothing of it,' Robert Jordan said.

'Listen, *Inglés*,' Anselmo began. 'I am against all such wizardry. But this Pilar has the fame of being very advanced in such things.'

'But what does it smell like?' Fernando asked. 'What odour has it? If there be an odour it must be a definite odour.'

'You want to know, Fernandito?' Pilar smiled at him. 'You think that you could smell it?'

'If it actually exists why should I not smell it as well as another?'

'Why not?' Pilar was making fun of him, her big hands folded across her knees. 'Hast thou ever been aboard a ship, Fernando?'

'Nay. And I would not wish to.'

'Then thou might not recognize it. For part of it is the smell that comes when, on a ship, there is a storm and the portholes are closed up. Put your nose against the brass handle of a screwed-tight porthole on a rolling ship that is swaying under you so that you are faint and hollow in the stomach and you have a part of that smell.'

'It would be impossible for me to recognize because I will go on no ship,' Fernando said.

'I have been on ships several times,' Pilar said. 'Both to go to Mexico and to Venezuela.'

'What's the rest of it?' Robert Jordan asked. Pilar looked at him mockingly, remembering now, proudly, her voyages.

'All right, *Inglés*. Learn. That's the thing. Learn. All right. After that of the ship you must go down the hill in Madrid to the Puente de Toledo early in the morning to the *matadero* and stand there on the wet paving when there is a fog from the Manzanares and wait for the old women who go before daylight to drink the blood of the beasts that are slaughtered. When such an old woman comes out of the *matadero*, holding her shawl around her, with her face grey and her eyes hollow, and the whiskers of age on her chin, and on her cheeks, set in the waxen white of her face as the sprouts grow from the seed of a bean, not bristles, but pale sprouts in the death of her face; put your arms tight around her, *Inglés*, and hold her to you and kiss her on the mouth and you will know the second part that odour is made of.'

'That one has taken my appetite,' the gipsy said. 'That of the sprouts was too much.'

'Do you want to hear some more?' Pilar asked Robert Jordan.

'Surely,' he said. 'If it is necessary for one to learn let us learn.'

'That of the sprouts in the face of the old women sickens me,' the gipsy said. 'Why should that occur in old women, Pilar? With us it is not so.'

'Nay,' Pilar mocked at him. 'With us the old woman, who was so slender in her youth, except of course for the perpetual bulge that is the mark of her husband's favour, that every gipsy pushes always before her—'

'Do not speak thus,' Rafael said. 'It is ignoble.'

'So thou art hurt,' Pilar said. 'Hast thou ever seen a *gitana* who was not about to have, or just to have had, a child?'

'Thou.'

'Leave it,' Pilar said. 'There is no one who cannot be hurt. What I was saying is that age brings its own form of ugliness to all. There is no need to detail it. But if the *Inglés* must learn that odour that he covets to recognize he must go to the *matadero* early in the morning.'

'I will go,' Robert Jordan said. 'But I will get the odour as they pass without kissing one. I fear the sprouts, too, as Rafael does.'

'Kiss one,' Pilar said. 'Kiss one, *Inglés*, for thy knowledge's sake and then, with this in thy nostrils, walk back up into the city and when thou seest a refuse pail with dead flowers in it plunge thy nose deep into it and inhale so that scent mixes with those thou has already in thy nasal passages.'

'Now have I done it,' Robert Jordan said. 'What flowers were they?'

'Chrysanthemums.'

'Continue,' Robert Jordan said. 'I smell them.'

'Then,' Pilar went on, 'it is important that the day be in autumn with rain, or at least some fog, or early winter even and now thou shouldst continue to walk through the city and down the Calle de Salud smelling what thou wilt smell where they are sweeping out the *casas de putas* and emptying the slop jars into the drains and, with this odour of love's labour lost mixed sweetly with soapy water and cigarette butts only faintly reaching thy nostrils, thou shouldst go on to the Jardín Botánico where at night those girls who can no longer work in the houses do their work against the iron gates of the park and the iron picketed fences and upon the sidewalks. It is there in the shadow of the trees against the iron railings that they will perform all that a man wishes; from the simplest requests at a remuneration of ten centimos up to a peseta for that great act that we are born to and there, on a dead flower bed that has not yet been plucked out and replanted, and so serves to soften the earth that is so much softer than the sidewalk, thou wilt find an abandoned gunny sack with the odour of the wet earth, the dead flowers, and the doings of that night. In this sack will be contained the essence of it all, both the dead earth and the dead stalks of the flowers and their rotted blooms and the smell that is both the death and birth of man. Thou wilt wrap this sack around thy head and try to breathe through it.'

'No.'

'Yes,' Pilar said. 'Thou wilt wrap this sack around thy head and try to breathe and then, if thou has not lost any of the previous odours, when thou inhalest deeply, thou wilt smell the odour of death-to-come as we know it.'

'All right,' Robert Jordan said. 'And you say Kashkin smelt like that when he was here?'

'Yes.'

'Well,' said Robert Jordan gravely. 'If that is true it is a good thing that I shot him.'

'*Olé*,' the gipsy said. The others laughed.

'Very good,' Primitivo approved. 'That should hold her for a while.'

'But Pilar,' Fernando said. 'Surely you could not expect one of Don Roberto's education to do such vile things.'

'No,' Pilar agreed.

'All of that is of the utmost repugnance.'

'Yes,' Pilar agreed.

'You would not expect him actually to perform those degrading acts?'

'No,' Pilar, 'Go to bed, will you?'

'But, Pilar—' Fernando went on.

'Shut up, will you?' Pilar said to him suddenly and viciously. 'Do not make a fool of thyself and I will try not to make a fool of myself talking with people who cannot understand what one speaks of.'

'I confess I do not understand,' Fernando began.

'Don't confess and don't try to understand,' Pilar said. 'Is it still snowing outside?'

Robert Jordan went to the mouth of the cave, lifted the blanket and looked out. It was clear and cold in the night outside and no snow was falling. He looked through the tree trunks where the whiteness lay and up through the trees to where the sky was now clear. The air came into his lungs sharp and cold as he breathed.

'El Sordo will leave plenty of tracks if he has stolen horses to-night,' he thought.

He dropped the blanket and came back into the smoky cave. 'It is clear,' he said. 'The storm is over.'

20

Now in the night he lay and waited for the girl to come to him. There was no wind now and the pines were still in the night. The trunks of the pines projected from the snow that covered all the ground, and he lay in the robe feeling the suppleness of the bed under him that he had made, his legs stretched long against the warmth of the robe, the air sharp and cold on his head and in his nostrils as he breathed. Under his head, as he lay on his side, was the bulge of the trousers and the coat that he had wrapped around his shoes to make a pillow and against his side was the cold metal of the big automatic pistol he had taken from the holster when he undressed and fastened by its lanyard to his right wrist. He pushed the pistol away and settled deeper into the robe as he watched, across the snow, the dark break in the rocks that was the entrance to the cave. The sky was clear and there was enough light reflected from the snow to see the trunks of the trees and the bulk of the rocks where the cave was.

Earlier in the evening he had taken the axe and gone outside of the cave and walked through the new snow to the edge of the clearing and cut down a small spruce tree. In the dark he had dragged it, butt first, to the lee of the rock wall. There close to the rock, he had held the tree upright, holding the trunk firm with one hand, and, holding the axe-haft close to the head had lopped off all the boughs until he had a pile of them. Then, leaving the pile of boughs, he had laid the bare pole of the trunk down in the snow and gone into the cave to get a slab of wood he had seen against the wall. With this slab he scraped the ground clear of the snow along the rock wall and then picked up his boughs and shaking them clean of snow laid them in rows, like over-lapping plumes, until he had a bed. He put the pole across the foot of the bough bed to hold the branches in place and pegged it firm with two pointed pieces of wood he split from the edge of the slab.

Then he carried the slab and the axe back into the cave, ducking under the blanket as he came in, and leaned them both against the wall.

'What do you do outside?' Pilar had asked.

'I made a bed.'

'Don't cut pieces from my new shelf for thy bed.'

'I am sorry.'

'It has no importance,' she said. 'There are more slabs at the sawmill. What sort of bed hast thou made?'

'As in my country.'

'Then sleep well in it,' she had said and Robert Jordan had opened one of the packs and pulled the robe out and replaced those things wrapped in it back in the pack and carried the robe out, ducking under the blanket again, and spread it over the boughs so that the closed end of the robe was against the pole that was pegged cross-wise at the foot of the bed. The open head of the robe was protected by the rock wall of the cliff. Then he went back into the cave for his packs but Pilar said, 'They can sleep with me as last night.'

'Will you not have sentries?' he asked. 'The night is clear and the storm is over.'

'Fernando goes,' Pilar said.

Maria was in the back of the cave and Robert Jordan could not see her.

'Good night to everyone,' he had said. 'I am going to sleep.'

Of the others, who were laying out blankets and bedrolls on the floor in front of the cooking fire, pushing back the slab tables and the rawhide-covered stools to make sleeping space, Primitivo and Andrés looked up and said, '*Buenas noches.*'

Anselmo was already asleep in a corner, rolled in his blanket and his cape, not even his nose showing. Pablo was asleep in his chair.

'Do you want a sheep hide for thy bed?' Pilar asked Robert Jordan softly.

'Nay,' he said. 'Thank thee. I do not need it.'

'Sleep well,' she said. 'I will respond for thy material.'

Fernando had gone out with him and stood a moment where Robert Jordan had spread the sleeping robe.

'You have a curious idea to sleep in the open. Don Roberto,' he said standing there in the dark, muffled in his blanket cape, his carbine slung over his shoulder.

'I am accustomed to it. Good night.'

'Since you are accustomed to it.'

'When are you relieved?'

'At four.'

'There is much cold between now and then.'

'I am accustomed to it,' Fernando said.

'Since, then, you are accustomed to it—' Robert Jordan said politely.

'Yes,' Fernando agreed. 'Now I must get up there. Good night, Don Roberto.'

'Good night, Fernando.

Then he had made a pillow of the things he took off and gotten into the robe and then lain and waited, feeling the spring of the boughs under the flannelly, feathered lightness of the robe warmth, watching the mouth of the cave across the snow; feeling his heart beat as he waited.

The night was clear and his head felt as clear and cold as the air. He smelled the odour of the pine boughs under him, the piney smell of the crushed needles and the sharper odour of the resinous sap from the cut limbs. Pilar, he thought. Pilar and the smell of death. This is the smell I love. This and fresh-cut clover, the crushed sage as you ride after cattle, wood-smoke and the burning leaves of autumn. That must be the odour of nostalgia, the smell of the smoke from the piles of raked leaves burning in the streets in the fall in Missoula. Which would you rather smell? Sweet grass the Indians used in their baskets? Smoked leather? The odour of the ground in the spring after rain? The smell of the sea as you walk through the gorse on a headland in Galicia? Or the wind from the land as you come in toward Cuba in the dark? That was the odour of the cactus flowers, mimosa and the sea-grape shrubs. Or would you rather smell frying bacon in the morning when you are hungry? Or coffee in the morning; Or a Jonathan apple as you bit into it? Or a cider mill in the grinding, or bread fresh from the oven? You must be hungry, he thought, and he lay on his side and watched the entrance of the cave in the light that the stars reflected from the snow.

Someone came out from under the blanket and he could see whoever it was standing by the break in the rock that made the entrance. Then he heard a slithering sound in the snow and then whoever it was ducked down and went back in.

I suppose she won't come until they are all asleep, he thought. It is a waste of time. The night is half gone. Oh, Maria. Come now quickly, Maria, for there is little time. He heard the soft sound of snow falling from a branch on to the snow on the ground. A little wind was rising. He felt it on his face. Suddenly he felt a panic that she might not come. The wind rising now reminded him how soon it would be morning. More snow fell from the branches as he heard the wind now moving the pine tops.

Come now, Maria. Please come here now quickly, he thought. Oh, come here now. Do not wait. There is no importance any more to your waiting until they are asleep.

Then he saw her coming out from under the blanket that covered the cave mouth. She stood there a moment and he knew it was she but he could not see what she was doing. He whistled a low whistle and she was still at the cave mouth doing something in the darkness of the rock shadow. Then she came running, carrying something in her hands and he saw her running long-legged through the snow. Then she was kneeling by the robe, her head pushed hard against him, slapping the snow from her feet. She kissed him and handed him her bundle.

'Put it with thy pillow,' she said. 'I took these off there to save time.'

'You came barefoot through the snow?'

'Yes,' she said, 'and wearing only my wedding shirt.'

He held her close and tight in his arms and she rubbed her head against his chin.

'Avoid the feet,' she said. 'They are very cold, Roberto.'

'Put them here and warm them.'

'Nay,' she said. 'They will warm quickly. But say quickly now that you love me.'

'I love thee.'

'Good. Good. Good.'

'I love thee, little rabbit.'

'Do you love my wedding shirt?'

'It is the same one as always.'

'Yes. As last night. It is my wedding shirt.'

'Put thy feet here.'

'Nay, that would be abusive. They will warm of themselves. They are warm to me. It is only that the snow has made them cold toward thee. Say it again.'

'I love thee, my little rabbit.'

'I love thee, too, and I am thy wife.'

'Were they asleep?'

'No,' she said. 'But I could support it no longer. And what importance has it?'

'None,' he said, and felt her against him, slim and long and warmly lovely. 'No other thing has importance.'

'Put thy hand on my head,' she said, 'and then let me see if I can kiss thee.'

'Was it well?' she asked.

'Yes,' he said. 'Take off thy wedding shirt.'

'You think I should?'

'Yes, if thou wilt not be cold.'

'*Qué va*, cold. I am on fire.'

'I, too. But afterwards thou wilt not be cold?'

'No. Afterwards we will be as one animal of the forest and be so close that neither one can tell that one of us is one and not the other. Can you not feel my heart be your heart?'

'Yes. There is no difference.'

'Now, feel. I am thee and thou art me and all of one is the other. And I love thee, oh, I love thee so. Are we not truly one? Canst thou not feel it?'

'Yes,' he said. 'It is true.'

'And feel now. Thou hast no heart but mine.'

'Nor any other legs, nor feet, nor of the body.'

'But we are different,' she said. 'I would have us exactly the same.'

'You do not mean that.'

'Yes I do. I do. That is a thing I had to tell thee.'

'You do not mean that.'

'Perhaps I do not,' she said speaking softly with her lips against his shoulder. 'But I wished to say it. Since we are different I am glad that thou art Roberto and I Maria. But if thou should ever wish to change I would be glad to change. I would be thee because I love thee so.'

'I do not wish to change. It is better to be one and each one to be the one he is.'

'But we will be one now and there will never be a separate one.' Then she said, 'I will be thee when thou art not there. Oh, I love thee so and I must care well for thee.'

'Maria.'

'Yes.'

'Maria.'

'Yes.'

'Maria.'

'Oh, yes. Please.'

'Art thou not cold?'

'Oh, no. Pull the robe over thy shoulders.'

'Maria.'

'I cannot speak.'

'Oh, Maria. Maria. Maria.'

Then afterwards, close, with the night cold outside, in the long warmth of the robe, her head touching his cheek, she lay quiet and happy against him and then said softly, 'And thou?'

'*Como tu*,' he said.

'Yes,' she said. 'But it was not as this afternoon.'

'No.'

'But I loved it more. One does not need to die.'

'*Ojala no*,' he said. 'I hope not.'

'I did not mean that.'

'I know. I know what thou meanest. We mean the same.'

'Then why did you say that instead of what I meant?'

'With a man there is a difference.'

'Then I am glad that we are different.'

'And so am I,' he said. 'But I understood about the dying. I only spoke thus, as a man, from habit. I feel the same as thee.'

'However thou art and however thou speakest is how I would have thee be.'

'And I love thee and I love thy name, Maria.'

'It is a common name.'

'No,' he said. 'It is not common.'

'Now should we sleep?' she said. 'I could sleep easily.'

'Let us sleep,' he said, and he felt the long light body, warm against him, comforting against him, abolishing loneliness against him, magically, by a simple touching of flanks, of shoulders and of feet, making an alliance against death with him, and he said, 'Sleep well, little long rabbit.'

She said, 'I am asleep already.'

'I am going to sleep,' he said. 'Sleep well, beloved.' Then he was asleep and happy as he slept.

But in the night he woke and held her tight as though she were all of life and it was being taken from him. He held her feeling she was all of life there was and it was true. But she was sleeping well and soundly and she did not wake. So he rolled away on to his side and pulled the robe over her head and kissed her once on her neck under the robe and then pulled the pistol lanyard up and put the pistol by his side where he could reach it handily and then he lay there in the night thinking.

21

A warm wind came with daylight and he could hear the snow melting in the trees and the heavy sound of its falling. It was a late spring morning. He knew with the first breath he drew that the snow had been only a freak storm in the mountains and it would be gone by noon. Then he heard a horse coming, the hoofs balled with the wet snow thumping dully as the horseman trotted. He heard the noise of a carbine scabbard slapping loosely and the creak of leather.

'Maria,' he said, and shook the girl's shoulder to waken her. 'Keep thyself under the robe,' and he buttoned his shirt with one hand and held the automatic pistol in the other, loosening the safety catch with his thumb. He saw the girl's cropped head disappear with a jerk under the robe and then he saw the horseman coming through the trees. He crouched now in the robe and holding the pistol in both hands aimed it at the man as he rode towards him. He had never seen this man before.

The horseman was almost opposite him now. He was riding a big grey gelding and he wore a khaki beret, a blanket cape like a poncho, and heavy black boots. From the scabbard on the right of his saddle projected the stock and the long oblong clip of a short automatic rifle. He had a young, hard face and at this moment he saw Robert Jordan.

He reached his hand down toward the scabbard and as he swung low, turning and jerking at the scabbard, Robert Jordan saw the scarlet of the formalized device he wore on the left breast of his khaki blanket cape.

Aiming at the centre of his chest, a little lower than the device, Robert Jordan fired.

The pistol roared in the snowy woods.

The horse plunged as though he had been spurred and the young man, still tugging at the scabbard, slid over toward the ground, his right foot caught in the stirrup. The horse broke off through the trees dragging him, bumping, face downward, and Robert Jordan stood up holding the pistol now in one hand.

The big grey horse was galloping through the pines. There was a broad swath in the snow where the man dragged with a scarlet streak along one side of it. People were coming out of the mouth of the cave. Robert Jordan reached down and unrolled his trousers from the pillow and began to put them on.

'Get thee dressed,' he said to Maria.

Overhead he heard the noise of a plane flying very high. Through the trees he saw where the grey horse had stopped and was standing, his rider still hanging face down from the stirrup.

'Go catch that horse,' he called to Primitivo who had started over toward him. Then, 'Who was on guard at the top?'

'Rafael,' Pilar said from the cave. She stood there, her hair still down her back in two braids.

'There's cavalry out,' Robert Jordan said. 'Get your damned gun up there.'

He heard Pilar call, 'Agustín,' into the cave. Then she went into the cave and then two men came running out, one with the automatic rifle with its tripod swung on his shoulder; the other with a sackful of the pans.

'Get up there with them,' Robert Jordan said to Anselmo. 'You lie beside the gun and hold the legs still,' he said.

The three of them went up the trail through the woods at a run.

The sun had not yet come up over the tops of the mountains and Robert Jordan stood straight buttoning his trousers and tightening his belt, the big pistol hanging from the lanyard on his wrist. He put the pistol in his holster on his belt and slipped the knot down on the lanyard and passed the loop over his head.

Somebody will choke you with that sometime, he thought. Well, this has done it. He took the pistol out of the holster, removed the clip, inserted one of the cartridges from the row alongside of the holster and shoved the clip back into the butt of the pistol.

He looked through the trees to where Primitivo, holding the reins of the horse, was twisting the rider's foot out of the stirrup. The body lay face down in the snow and as he watched Primitivo was going through the pockets.

'Come on,' he called. 'Bring the horse.'

As he knelt to put on his rope-soled shoes, Robert Jordan could feel Maria against his knees, dressing herself under the robe. She had no place in his life now.

That cavalryman did not expect anything, he was thinking. He was not following horse tracks and he was not even properly alert, let alone alarmed. he was not even following the tracks up to the post. He must have been one of a patrol scattered out in these hills. But when the patrol misses him they will follow his tracks here. Unless the snow melts first, he thought. Unless something happens to the patrol.

'You better get down below,' he said to Pablo.

They were all out of the cave now, standing there with the carbines and with grenades on their belts. Pilar held a leather bag of grenades toward Robert Jordan and he took three and put them in his pocket. He ducked into the cave, found his two packs, opened the one with the submachine gun in it and took out the barrel and stock, slipped the stock on to the forward assembly and put one clip into the gun and three in his pockets. He locked the pack and started for the door. I've got two pockets full of hardware, he thought. I hope the seams hold. He came out of the cave and said to Pablo, 'I'm going up above. Can Agustín shoot that gun?'

'Yes,' Pablo said. He was watching Primitivo leading up the horse.

'*Mira qué caballo*,' he said. 'Look, what a horse.'

The big grey was sweating and shivering a little and Robert Jordan patted him on the withers.

'I will put him with the others,' Pablo said.

'No,' Robert Jordan said. 'He has made tracks into here. He must make them out.'

'True,' agreed Pablo. 'I will ride him out and will hide him and bring him in when the snow is melted. Thou hast much head to-day, *Inglés*.'

'Send someone below,' Robert Jordan said. 'We've got to get up there.'

'It is not necessary,' Pablo said. 'Horsemen cannot come that way. But we can get out, by there and by two other places. It is better not to make tracks if there are planes coming. Give me the *bota* with wine, Pilar.'

'To go off and get drunk,' Pilar said. 'Here, take these instead.' He reached over and put two of the grenades in his pockets.

'*Qué va*, to get drunk,' Pablo said. 'There is gravity in the situation. But give me the *bota*. I do not like to do all this on water.'

He reached his arms up, took the reins and swung up into the saddle. He grinned and patted the nervous horse. Robert Jordan saw him rub his leg along the horse's flank affectionately.

'*Qué caballo más bonito*,' he said and patted his big grey again. '*Qué caballo más hermoso*. Come on. The faster this gets out of here the better.'

He reached down and pulled the light automatic rifle with its ventilated barrel, really a sub-machine gun built to take the 9 mm. pistol cartridge, from the scabbard, and looked at it. 'Look how they are armed,' he said. 'Look at modern cavalry.'

'There's modern cavalry over there on his face,' Robert Jordan said. '*Vamonos*.'

'Do you, Andrés, saddle and hold the horses in readiness. If you hear firing bring them up to the woods behind the gap. Come with thy arms and leave the women to hold the horses. Fernando, see that my sacks are brought also. Above all, that my sacks are brought carefully. Thou to look after my sacks, too,' he said to Pilar. 'Thou to verify that they come with the horses. *Vamonos*,' he said. 'Let us go.'

'The Maria and I will prepare all for leaving,' Pilar said. Then to Robert Jordan, 'Look at him,' nodding at Pablo on the grey horse, sitting him in the heavy-thighed herdsman manner, the horse's nostrils widening as Pablo replaced the clip in the automatic rifle. 'See what a horse has done for him.'

'That I should have two horses,' Robert Jordan said fervently.

'Danger is thy horse.'

'Then give me a mule,' Robert Jordan grinned.

'Strip me that,' he said to Pilar and jerked his head toward where the man lay face down in the snow. 'And bring everything, all the letters and papers, and put them in the outside pocket of my sack. Everything, understand?'

'Yes.'

'*Vamonos*,' he said.

Pablo rode ahead and the two men followed in single file in order not to track up the snow. Robert Jordan carried the sub-machine gun muzzle down, carrying it by its forward hand grip. I wish it took the same ammunition that saddle gun takes, he thought. But it doesn't. This is a German gun. This was old Kashkin's gun.

The sun was coming over the mountains now. A warm wind was blowing and the snow was melting. It was a lovely late spring morning.

Robert Jordan looked back and saw Maria now standing with Pilar. Then she came running up the trail. He dropped behind Primitivo to speak to her.

'Thou,' she said. 'Can I go with thee?'

'No. Help Pilar.'

She was walking behind him and put her hand on his arm.

'I'm coming.'

'Nay.'

She kept on walking close behind him.

'I could hold the legs of the gun in the way thou told Anselmo.'

'Thou wilt hold no legs. Neither of guns nor of nothing.'

Walking beside him she reached forward and put her hand in his pocket.

'No,' he said. 'But take good care of thy wedding shirt.'

'Kiss me,' she said, 'if thou goest.'

'Thou art shameless,' he said.

'Yes,' she said. 'Totally.'

'Get thee back now. There is much work to do. We may fight here if they follow these horse tracks.'

'Thou,' she said. 'Didst thee see what he wore on his chest?'

'Yes. Why not?'

'It was the Sacred Heart.'

'Yes. All the people of Navarre wear it.'

'And thou shot for that?'

'No. Below it. Get thee back now.'

'Thou,' she said. 'I saw all.'

'Thou saw nothing. One man. One man from a horse. *Vete*. Get thee back.'

'Say that you love me.'

'No. Not now.'

'Not love me now?'

'*Déjamos*. Get thee back. One does not do that and love all at the same moment.'

'I want to go to hold the legs of the gun and while it speaks love thee all in the same moment.'

'Thou art crazy. Get thee back now.'

'I am not crazy,' she said. 'I love thee.'

'Then get thee back.'

'Good. I go. And if thou dost not love me, I love thee enough for both.'

He looked at her and smiled through his thinking.

'When you hear firing,' he said, 'come with the horses. Aid the Pilar with my sacks. It is possible there will be nothing. I hope so.'

'I go,' she said. 'Look what a horse Pablo rides.'

The big grey was moving ahead up the trail.

'Yes. But go.'

'I go.'

Her fist, clenched tight in his pocket, beat hard against his thigh. He looked at her and saw there were tears in her eyes. She pulled her fist out of his pocket and put both arms tight around his neck and kissed him.

'I go,' she said. '*Me voy*. I go.'

He looked back and saw her standing there, the first morning sunlight on her brown face and the cropped, tawny, burned-gold hair. She lifted her fist at him and turned and walked back down the trail, her head down.

Primitivo turned around and looked after her.

'If she did not have her hair cut so short she would be a pretty girl,' he said.

'Yes,' Robert Jordan said. He was thinking of something else.

'How is she in the bed?' Primitivo asked.

'What?'

'In the bed.'

'Watch thy mouth.'

'One should not be offended when—'

'Leave it,' Robert Jordan said. He was looking at the position.

22

'Cut me pine branches,' Robert Jordan said to Primitivo, 'and bring them quickly.'

'I do not like the gun there,' he said to Agustín.

'Why?'

'Place it over there,' Robert Jordan pointed, 'and later I will tell thee.'

'Here, thus. Let me help thee. Here,' he said, then squatted down.

He looked out across the narrow oblong, noting the height of the rocks on either side.

'It must be farther,' he said, 'farther out. Good. Here. That will do until it can be done properly. There. Put the stones there. Here is one. Put another there at the side. Leave room for the muzzle to swing. The stone must be farther to this side. Anselmo. Get thee down to the cave and bring me an axe. Quickly.'

'Have you never had a proper emplacement for the gun?' he said to Agustín.

'We always placed it here.'

'Kashkin never said to put it there?'

'No. The gun was brought after he left.'

'Did no one bring it who knew how to use it?'

'No. It was brought by porters.'

'What a way to do things,' Robert Jordan said. 'It was just given to you without instruction?'

'Yes, as a gift might be given. One for us and one for El Sordo. Four men brought them. Anselmo guided them.'

'It was a wonder they did not lose them with four men to cross the lines.'

'I thought so, too,' Agustín said. 'I thought those who sent them meant for them to be lost. But Anselmo brought them well.'

'You know how to handle it?'

'Yes. I have experimented. I know. Pablo knows. Primitivo knows. So does Fernando. We have made a study of taking it apart and putting it together on the table in the cave. Once we had it apart and could not get it together for two days. Since then we have not had it apart.'

'Does it shoot now?'

'Yes. But we do not let the gipsy nor others frig with it.'

'You see? From there it was useless,' he said. 'Look. Those rocks which should protect your flanks give cover to those who will attack you. With such a gun you must seek a flatness over which to fire. Also you must take them sideways. See? Look now. All that is dominated.'

'I see,' said Agustín. 'But we have never fought in defence except when our town was taken. At the train there were soldiers with the *máquina.*'

'Then we will all learn together,' Robert Jordan said. 'There are a few things to observe. Where is the gipsy who should be here?'

'I do not know.'

'Where is it possible for him to be?'

'I do not know.'

Pablo had ridden out through the pass and turned once and ridden in a circle across the level space at the top that was the field of fire for the automatic rifle. Now Robert Jordan watched him riding down the slope alongside the tracks the horse had left when he was ridden in. He disappeared in the trees turning off to the left.

'I hope he doesn't run right into cavalry,' Robert Jordan thought. 'I'm afraid we'd have him right here in our laps.'

Primitivo brought the pine branches and Robert Jordan stuck them through the snow into the unfrozen earth, arching them over the gun from either side.

'Bring more,' he said. 'There must be cover for the two men who serve it. This is not good but it will serve until the axe comes. Listen,' he said, 'if you hear a plane lie flat wherever thou art in the shadows of the rocks. I am here with the gun.'

Now with the sun up and the warm wind blowing it was pleasant on the side of the rocks where the sun shone. Four horses, Robert Jordan thought. The two women and me, Anselmo, Primitivo, Fernando, Agustín, what the hell is the name of the other brother? That's eight. Not counting the gipsy. Makes nine. Plus Pablo gone with one horse makes ten. Andrés is his name. The other brother. Plus the other, Eladio. Makes ten. That's not one-half a horse apiece. Three men can hold this and four can get away. Five with Pablo. That's two left over. Three with Eladio. Where the hell is he?

God knows what will happen to Sordo to-day if they picked up the trail of those horses in the snow. That was tough; the snow stopping that way. But it melting to-day will even things up. But not for Sordo. I'm afraid it's too late to even it up for Sordo.

If we can last through to-day and not have to fight we can swing the whole show to-morrow with what we have. I know we can. Not well, maybe. Not as it should be, to be foolproof, not as we would have done; but using everybody we can swing it. *If we don't have to fight to-day*. God help us if we have to fight to-day.

I don't know any place better to lay up in the meantime than this. If we move now we only leave tracks. This is as good a place as any and if the worst gets to be the worst there are three ways out of this place. There is the dark then to come and from wherever we are in these hills. I can reach and do the bridge at daylight. I don't know why I worried about it before. It seems easy enough now. I hope they get the planes up on time for once. I certainly hope that. To-morrow is going to be a day with dust on the road.

Well, to-day will be very interesting or very dull. Thank God we've got that cavalry mount out and away from here. I don't think even if they ride up here they will go in the way those tracks are now. They'll think he stopped and circled and they'll pick up Pablo's tracks. I wonder where the old swine will go. He'll probably leave tracks like an old bull elk spooking out of the country and work way up and then when the snow melts circle back below. That horse certainly did things for him. Of course he may have just mucked off with him too. Well, he should be able to take care of himself. He's been doing this a long time. I wouldn't trust him farther than you can throw Mount Everest, though.

I suppose it's smarter to use these rocks and build a good blind for this gun than to make a proper emplacement for it. You'd be digging and get caught with your pants down if they come or if the planes come. She will hold this, the way she is, as long as it is any use to hold it, and anyway I can't stay to fight. I have to get out of here with that stuff and I'm going to take Anselmo with me. Who would stay to cover us while we got away if we have to fight here?

Just then, while he was watching all of the country that was visible, he saw the gipsy coming through the rocks to the left. He was walking with a loose, high-hipped, sloppy swing, his carbine was slung on his back, his brown face was grinning and he carried two big hares, one in each hand. He carried them by the legs, heads swinging.

'*Hola*, Roberto,' he called cheerfully.

Robert Jordan put his hand to his mouth, and the gipsy looked startled. He slid over behind the rocks to where Robert Jordan was crouched beside the brush-shielded automatic rifle. He crouched down and laid the hares in the snow. Robert Jordan looked up at him.

'You *hijo de la gran puta!*' he said softly. 'Where the obscenity have you been?'

'I tracked them,' the gipsy said. 'I got them both. They had made love in the snow.'

'And thy post?'

'It was not for long,' the gipsy whispered. 'What passes? Is there an alarm?'

'There is cavalry out.'

'*Rediós!*' the gipsy said. 'Hast thou seen them?'

'There is one at the camp now,' Robert Jordan said. 'He came for breakfast.'

'I thought I heard a shot or something like one,' the gipsy said. 'I obscenity in the milk! Did he come through here?'

'Here. *Thy* post.'

'*Ay, mi madre!*' the gipsy said. 'I am a poor, unlucky man.'

'If thou were not a gipsy, I would shoot thee.'

'No, Roberto. Don't say that. I am sorry. It was the hares. Before daylight I heard the male thumping in the snow. You cannot imagine what a debauch they were engaged in. I went toward the noise but they were gone. I followed the tracks in the snow and high up I found them together and slew them both. Feel the fatness of the two for this time of year. Think what the Pilar will do with those two. I am sorry, Roberto, as sorry as thee. Was the cavalryman killed?'

'Yes.'

'By thee?'

'Yes.'

'*Qué tío!*' the gipsy said in open flattery. 'Thou art a veritable phenomenon.'

'Thy mother!' Robert Jordan said. He could not help grinning at the gipsy. 'Take thy hares to camp and bring us up some breakfast.'

He put a hand out and felt of the hares that lay limp, long, heavy, thick-furred, big-footed and long-eared in the snow, their round dark eyes open.

'They *are* fat,' he said.

'Fat!' the gipsy said. 'There's a tub of lard on the ribs of each one. In my life have I never dreamed of such hares.'

'Go then,' Robert Jordan said, 'and come quickly with the breakfast and bring to me the documentation of that *requeté*. Ask Pilar for it.'

'You are not angry with me, Roberto?'

'Not angry. Disgusted that you should leave your post. Suppose it had been a troop of cavalry?'

'*Rediós*,' the gipsy said. 'How reasonable you are.'

'Listen to me. You cannot leave a post again like that. Never. I do not speak of shooting lightly.'

'Of course not. And another thing. Never would such an opportunity as the two hares present itself again. Not in the life of one man.'

'*Anda!*' Robert Jordan said. 'And hurry back.'

The gipsy picked up the two hares and slipped back through the rocks and Robert Jordan looked out across the flat opening and the slopes of the hill below. A crow circled overhead and then lit in a pine tree below. Another crow joined it and Robert Jordan, watching them, thought: those are my sentinels. As long as those are quiet there is no one coming through the trees.

The gipsy, he thought. He is truly worthless. He has no political development, nor any discipline, and you could not rely on him for anything. But I need him for to-morrow. I have a use for him to-morrow.

It's odd to see a gipsy in a war. They should be exempted like conscientious objectors. Or as the physically and mentally unfit. They are worthless. But conscientious objectors weren't exempted in this war. No one was exempted. It came to one and all alike. Well, it had come here now to this lazy outfit. They had it now.

Agustín and Primitivo came up with the brush and Robert Jordan built a good blind for the automatic rifle, a blind that would conceal the gun from the air and that would look natural from the forest. He showed them where to place a man high in the rocks to the right where he could see all the country below and to the right, and another where he could command the only stretch where the left wall might be climbed.

'Do not fire if you see anyone from there,' Robert Jordan said. 'Roll a rock down as a warning, a small rock, and signal to us with thy rifle, thus,' he lifted the rifle and held it over his head as though guarding it. 'Thus for numbers,' he lifted the rifle up and down. 'If they are dismounted point thy rifle muzzle at the ground. Thus. Do not fire from there until thou hearest the *máquina* fire. Shoot at a man's knees when you shoot from that height. If you hear me whistle twice on this whistle get down, keeping behind cover, and come to these rocks where the *máquina* is.'

Primitivo raised the rifle.

'I understand,' he said. 'It is very simple.'

'Send first the small rock as a warning and indicate the direction and the number. See that you are not seen.'

'Yes,' Primitivo said. 'If I can throw a grenade?'

'Not until the *máquina* has spoken. It may be that cavalry will come searching for their comrade and still not try to enter. They may follow the tracks of Pablo. We do not want combat if it can be avoided. Above all that we should avoid it. Now get up there.'

'*Me voy*,' Primitivo said, and climbed up into the high rocks with his carbine.

'Thou, Agustín,' Robert Jordan said. 'What do you know of the gun?'

Agustín squatted there, tall, black, stubbly-jowled, with his sunken eyes and thin mouth and his big work-worn hands.

'*Pues*, to load it. To aim it. To shoot it. Nothing more.'

'You must not fire until they are within fifty metres and only when you are sure they will be coming into the pass which leads to the cave,' Robert Jordan said.

'Yes. How far is that?'

'That rock.'

'If there is an officer shoot him first. Then move the gun on to the others. Move very slowly. It takes little movement. I will teach Fernando to tap it. Hold it tight so that it does not jump and sight carefully and do not fire more than six shots at a time if you can help it. For the fire of the gun jumps upward. But each time fire at one man and then move from him to another. At a man on a horse, shoot at his belly.'

'Yes.'

'One man should hold the tripod still so that the gun does not jump. Thus. He will load the gun for thee.'

'And where will you be?'

'I will be here on the left. Above, where I can see all and I will cover thy left with this small *máquina*. Here. If they should come it would be possible to make a massacre. But you must not fire until they are that close.'

'I believe that we could make a massacre. *Menuda matanza!*'

'But I hope they do not come.'

'If it were not for thy bridge we could make a massacre here and get out.'

'It would avail nothing. That would serve no purpose. The bridge is a part of a plan to win the war. This would be nothing. This would be an incident. A nothing.'

'*Qué va*, nothing. Every fascist dead is a fascist less.'

'Yes. But with this of the bridge we can take Segovia. The Capital of a Province. Think of that. It will be the first one we will take.'

'Thou believest in this seriously? That we can take Segovia?'

'Yes. It is possible with the bridge blown correctly.'

'I would like to have the massacre here and the bridge, too.'

'Thou hast much appetite,' Robert Jordan told him.

All this time he had been watching the crows. Now he saw one was watching something. The bird cawed and flew up. But the other crow still stayed in the tree. Robert Jordan looked up toward Primitivo's place high in the rocks. He saw him watching out over the country below but he made no signal. Robert Jordan leaned forward and worked the lock on the automatic rifle, saw the round in the chamber and let the lock down. The crow was still there in the tree. The other circled wide over the snow and then settled again. In the sun and the warm wind the snow was falling from the laden branches of the pines.

'I have a massacre for thee for to-morrow morning.' Robert Jordan said. 'It is necessary to exterminate the post at the sawmill.'

'I am ready,' Agustín said. '*Estoy listo*.'

'Also the post at the roadmender's hut below the bridge.'

'For the one or for the other,' Agustín said. 'Or for both.'

'Not for both. They will be done at the same time,' Robert Jordan said.

'Then for either one,' Agustín said. 'Now for a long time have I wished for action in this war. Pablo has rotted us here with inaction.'

Anselmo came up with the axe.

'Do you wish more branches?' he asked. 'To me it seems well hidden.'

'Not branches,' Robert Jordan said. 'Two small trees that we can plant here and there to make it look more natural. There are not enough trees here for it to be truly natural.'

'I will bring them.'

'Cut them well back, so the stumps cannot be seen.'

Robert Jordan heard the axe sounding in the woods behind him. He looked up at Primitivo above in the rocks and he looked down at the pines below across the clearing. The one crow was still there. Then he heard the first high, throbbing murmur of a plane coming. He looked up and saw it high and tiny and silver in the sun, seeming hardly to move in the high sky.

'They cannot see us,' he said to Agustín. 'But it is well to keep down. That is the second observation plane to-day.'

'And those of yesterday?' Agustín asked.

'They are like a bad dream now,' Robert Jordan said.

'They must be at Segovia. The bad dream waits there to become a reality.'

The plane was out of sight now over the mountains but the sound of its motors still persisted.

As Robert Jordan looked, he saw the crow fly up. He flew straight away through the trees without cawing.

23

'Get thee down,' Robert Jordan whispered to Agustín, and he turned his head and flicked his hand *Down, Down*, to Anselmo who was coming through the gap with a pine tree, carrying it over his shoulder like a Christmas tree. He saw the old man drop his pine tree behind a rock and then he was out of sight in the rocks and Robert Jordan was looking ahead across the open space toward the timber. He saw nothing and heard nothing but he could feel his heart pounding and then he heard the clack of stone on stone and the leaping, dropping clicks of a small rock falling. He turned his head to the right and looking up saw Primitivo's rifle raised and lowered four times horizontally. Then there was nothing more to see but the white stretch in front of him with the circle of horse tracks and the timber beyond.

'Cavalry,' he said softly to Agustín.

Agustín looked at him and his dark, sunken cheeks widened at their base as he grinned. Robert Jordan noticed he was sweating. He reached over and put his hand on his shoulder. His hand was still there as they saw the four horsemen ride out of the timber and he felt the muscles in Agustín's back twitch under his hand.

One horseman was ahead and three rode behind. The one ahead was following the horse tracks. He looked down as he rode. The other three came behind him, fanned out through the timber. They were all watching carefully. Robert Jordan felt his heart beating against the snowy ground as he lay, his elbows spread wide and watched them over the sights of the automatic rifle.

The man who was leading rode along the trail to where Pablo had circled and stopped. The others rode up to him and they all stopped.

Robert Jordan saw them clearly over the blued steel barrel of the automatic rifle. He saw the faces of the men, the sabres hanging, the sweat-darkened flanks of the horses, and the cone-like slope of the khaki capes, and the Navarrese slant of the khaki berets. The leader turned his horse directly toward the opening in the rocks where the gun was placed and Robert Jordan saw his young, sun- and wind-darkened face, his close-set eyes, hawk nose and the over-long wedge-shaped chin.

Sitting his horse there, the horse's chest toward Robert Jordan, the horse's head high, the butt of the slight automatic rifle projecting forward from the scabbard at the right of the saddle, the leader pointed toward the opening where the gun was.

Robert Jordan sunk his elbows into the ground and looked along the barrel at the four riders stopped there in the snow. Three of them had their automatic rifles out. Two carried them across the pommels of their saddles. The other sat his horse with the rifle swung out to the right, the butt resting against his hip.

You hardly ever see them at such range, he thought. Not along the barrel of one of these do you see them like this. Usually the rear sight is raised and they seem miniatures of men and you have hell to make it carry up there; or they come running, flopping, running, and you beat a slope with fire or bar a certain street, or keep it on the windows; or far away you see them marching on a road. Only at the trains do you see them like this. Only then are they like now, and with four of these you can make them scatter. Over the gun sights, at this range, it makes them twice the size of men.

Thou, he thought, looking at the wedge of the front sight placed now firm in the slot of the rear sight, the top of the wedge against the centre of the leader's chest, a little to the right of the scarlet device that showed bright in the morning sun against the khaki cape. Thou, he thought, thinking in Spanish now and pressing his fingers forward against the trigger guard to keep it away from where it would bring the quick, shocking, hurtling rush from the automatic rifle. Thou, he thought again, thou art dead now in thy youth. And thou, he thought, and thou, and thou. But let it not happen. Do not let it happen.

He felt Agustín beside him start to cough, felt him hold it, choke and swallow. Then as he looked along the oiled blue of the barrel out through the opening between the branches, his fingers still pressed forward against the trigger guard, he saw the leader turn his horse and point into the timber where Pablo's trail led. The four of them trotted into the timber and Agustín said softly. '*Cabrones!*'

Robert Jordan looked behind him at the rocks where Anselmo had dropped the tree.

The gipsy, Rafael, was coming toward them through the rocks, carrying a pair of cloth saddlebags, his rifle slung on his back. Robert Jordan waved him down and the gipsy ducked out of sight.

'We could have killed all four,' Agustín said quietly. He was still wet with sweat.

'Yes,' Robert Jordan whispered. 'But with the firing who knows what might have come?'

Just then he heard the noise of another rock falling and he looked around quickly. But both the gipsy and Anselmo were out of sight. He looked at his wrist watch and then up to where Primitivo was raising and lowering his rifle in what seemed an infinity of short jerks. Pablo has forty-five minutes' start, Robert Jordan thought, and then he heard the noise of a body of cavalry coming.

'*No te apures*,' he whispered to Agustín. 'Do not worry. They will pass as the others.'

They came into sight trotting along the edge of the timber in column of twos, twenty mounted men, armed and uniformed as the others had been, their sabres swinging, their carbines in their holsters; and then they went down into the timber as the others had.

'*Tu ves?*' Robert Jordan said to Agustín. 'Thou seest?'

'There were many,' Agustín said.

'These would we have had to deal with if we had destroyed the others,' Robert Jordan said very softly. His heart had quieted now and his shirt felt wet on his chest from the melting snow. There was a hollow feeling in his chest.

The sun was bright on the snow and it was melting fast. He could see it hollowing away from the tree trunks and just ahead of the gun, before his eyes, the snow surface was damp and lacily fragile as the heat of the sun melted the top and the warmth of the earth breathed warmly up at the snow that lay upon it.

Robert Jordan looked up at Primitivo's post and saw him signal, 'Nothing,' crossing his two hands, palm down.

Anselmo's head showed above a rock and Robert Jordan motioned him up. The old man slipped from rock to rock until he crept up and lay down flat beside the gun.

'Many,' he said, 'Many!'

'I do not need the trees,' Robert Jordan said to him. 'There is no need for further forestal improvement.'

Both Anselmo and Agustín grinned.

'This has stood scrutiny well and it would be dangerous to plant trees now because those people will return and perhaps they are not stupid.'

He felt the need to talk that, with him, was the sign that there had just been much danger. He could always tell how bad it had been by the strength of the desire to talk that came after.

'It was a good blind, eh?' he said.

'Good,' said Agustín. 'To obscenity with all fascism good. We could have killed the four of them. Didst thou see?' he said to Anselmo.

'I saw.'

'Thou,' Robert Jordan said to Anselmo. 'Thou must go to the post of yesterday or another good post of thy selection to watch the road and report on all movement as of yesterday. Already we are late in that. Stay until dark. Then come in and we will send another.'

'But the tracks that I will make?'

'Go from below as soon as the snow is gone. The road will be muddied by the snow. Note if there has been much traffic of trucks or if there are tank tracks in the softness on the road. That is all we can tell until you are there to observe.'

'With your permission?' the old man asked.

'Surely.'

'With your permission, would it not be better for me to go into La Granja and inquire there what passed last night and arrange for one to observe today thus in the manner you have taught me? Such a one could report tonight or, better, I could go again to La Granja for the report.'

'Have you no fear of encountering cavalry?'

'Not when the snow is gone.'

'Is there someone in La Granja capable of this?'

'Yes. Of this, yes. It would be a woman. There are various women of trust in La Granja.'

'I believe it,' Agustín said. 'More, I know it, and several who serve for other purposes. You do not wish me to go?'

'Let the old man go. You understand this gun and the day is not over.'

'I will go when the snow melts,' Anselmo said. 'And the snow is melting fast.'

'What think you of their chance of catching Pablo?' Robert Jordan asked Agustín.

'Pablo is smart,' Agustín said. 'Do men catch a wise stag without hounds?'

'Sometimes,' Robert Jordan said.

'Not Pablo,' Agustín said. 'Clearly, he is only a garbage of what he once was. But it is not for nothing that he is alive and comfortable in these hills and able to drink himself to death while there are so many others that have died against a wall.'

'Is he as smart as they say?'

'He is much smarter.'

'He has not seemed of great ability here.'

'*Cómo qué no?* If he were not of great ability he would have died last night. It seems to me you do not understand politics, *Inglés*, nor guerrilla warfare. In politics and this other the first thing is to continue to exist. Look how he continued to exist last night. And the quantity of dung he ate both from me and from thee.'

Now that Pablo was back in the movements of the unit, Robert Jordan did not wish to talk against him and as soon as he had uttered it he regretted saying the thing about his ability. He knew himself how smart Pablo was. It was Pablo who had seen instantly all that was wrong with the orders for the destruction of the bridge. He had made the remark only from dislike and he knew as he made it that it was wrong. It was part of the talking too much after a strain. So now he dropped the matter and said to Anselmo, 'And to go into La Granja in daylight?'

'It is not bad,' the old man said. 'I will not go with a military band.'

'Nor with a bell around his neck,' Agustín said. 'Nor carrying a banner.'

'How will you go?'

'Above and down through the forest.'

'But if they pick you up.'

'I have papers.'

'So have we all but thou must eat the wrong ones quickly.'

Anselmo shook his head and tapped the breast pocket of his smock.

'How many times have I contemplated that,' he said. 'And never did I like to swallow paper.'

'I have thought we should carry a little mustard on them all,' Robert Jordan said. 'In my left breast pocket I carry our papers. In my right the fascist papers. Thus one does not make a mistake in an emergency.'

It must have been bad enough when the leader of the first patrol of cavalry had pointed toward the entry because they were all talking very much. Too much, Robert Jordan thought.

'But look, Roberto,' Agustín said. 'They say the government moves further to the right each day. That in the Republic they no longer say Comrade but Señor and Señora. Canst shift thy pockets?'

'When it moves far enough to the right I will carry them in my hip pocket,' Robert Jordan said, 'and sew it in the centre.'

'That they should stay in thy shirt,' Agustín said. 'Are we to win this war and lose the revolution?'

'Nay,' Robert Jordan said. 'But if we do not win this war there will be no revolution nor any Republic nor any thou nor any me nor anything but the most grand *carajo*.'

'So say I,' Anselmo said. 'That we should win the war.'

'And afterwards shoot the anarchists and the Communists and all this *canalla* except the good Republicans,' Agustín said.

'That we should win this war and shoot nobody,' Anselmo said. 'That we should govern justly and that all should participate in the benefits according as they have striven for them. And that those who have fought against us should be educated to see their error.'

'We will have to shoot many,' Agustín said. 'Many, many, many.'

He thumped his closed right fist against the palm of his left hand.

'That we should shoot none. Not even the leaders. That they should be reformed by work.'

'I know the work I'd put them at,' Agustín said, and he picked up some snow and put it in his mouth.

'What, bad one?' Robert Jordan asked.

'Two trades of the utmost brilliance.'

'They are?'

Agustín put some more snow in his mouth and looked across the clearing where the cavalry had ridden. Then he spat the melted snow out. '*Vaya*. What a breakfast,' he said. 'Where is the filthy gipsy?'

'What trades?' Robert Jordan asked him. 'Speak, bad mouth.'

'Jumping from planes without parachutes,' Agustín said, and his eyes shone. 'That for those that we care for. And being nailed to the tops of fence posts to be pushed over backwards for the others.'

'That way of speaking is ignoble,' Anselmo said. 'Thus we will never have a Republic.'

'I would like to swim ten leagues in a strong soup made from the *cojones* of all of them,' Agustín said. 'And when I saw those four there and thought that we might kill them I was like a mare in the corral waiting for the stallion.'

'You know why we did not kill them, though?' Robert Jordan said quietly.

'Yes,' Agustín said. 'Yes. But the necessity was on me as it is on a mare in heat. You cannot know what it is if you have not felt it.'

'You sweated enough,' Robert Jordan said. 'I thought it was fear.'

'Fear, yes,' Agustín said. 'Fear and the other. And in this life there is no stronger thing than the other.'

Yes, Robert Jordan thought. We do it coldly but they do not, nor ever have. It is their extra sacrament. Their old one that they had before the new religion came from the far end of the Mediterranean, the one they have never abandoned but only suppressed and hidden to bring it out again in wars and inquisitions. They are the people of the Auto de Fé; the act of faith. Killing is something one must do, but ours are different from theirs. And you, he thought, you have never been corrupted by it? You never had it in the Sierra? Nor at Usera? Not through all the time in Estremadura? Nor at any time? *Qué va*, he told himself. At every train.

Stop making dubious literature about the Berbers and the old Iberians and admit that you have liked to kill as all who are soldiers by choice have enjoyed it at some time whether they lie about it or not. Anselmo does not like to because he is a hunter, not a soldier. Don't idealize him, either. Hunters kill animals and soldiers kill men. Don't lie to yourself, he thought. Nor make up literature about it. You have been tainted with it for a long time now. And do not think against Anselmo either. He is a Christian. Something very rare in Catholic countries.

But with Agustín I had thought it was fear, he thought. That natural fear before action. So it was the other, too. Of course, he may be bragging now. There was plenty of fear. I felt the fear under my hand. Well, it was time to stop talking.

'See if the gipsy brought food,' he said to Anselmo. 'Do not let him come up. He is a fool. Bring it yourself. And however much he brought, send back for more. I am hungry.'

24

Now the morning was late May, the sky was high and clear and the wind blew warm on Robert Jordan's shoulders. The snow was going fast and they were eating breakfast. There were two big sandwiches of meat and the goaty cheese apiece, and Robert Jordan had cut thick slices of onion with his clasp knife and put them on each side of the meat and cheese between the chunks of bread.

'You will have a breath that will carry through the forest to the fascists,' Agustín said, his own mouth full.

'Give me the wineskin and I will rinse the mouth,' Robert Jordan said, his mouth full of meat, cheese, onion and chewed bread.

He had never been hungrier and he filled his mouth with wine, faintly tarry-tasting from the leather bag, and swallowed. Then he took another big mouthful of wine, lifting the bag up to let the jet of wine spurt into the back of his mouth, the wineskin touching the needles of the blind of pine branches that covered the automatic rifle as he lifted his hand, his head leaning against the pine branches as he bent it back to let the wine run down.

'Dost thou want this other sandwich?' Agustín asked him, handing it toward him across the gun.

'No. Thank you. Eat it.'

'I cannot. I am not accustomed to eat in the morning.'

'You do not want it, truly?'

'Nay. Take it.'

Robert Jordan took it and laid it on his lap while he got the onion out of his side jacket pocket where the grenades were and opened his knife to slice it. He cut off a thin sliver of the surface that had dirtied in his pocket, then cut a thick slice. An outer segment fell and he picked it up and bent the circle together and put it into the sandwich.

'Eatest thou always onions for breakfast?' Agustín asked.

'When there are any.'

'Do all in thy country do this?'

'Nay,' Robert Jordan said. 'It is looked on badly there.'

'I am glad,' Agustín said' 'I had always considered America a civilized country.'

'What hast thou against the onion?'

'The odour. Nothing more. Otherwise it is like the rose.'

Robert Jordan grinned at him with his mouth full.

'Like the rose,' he said. 'Mighty like the rose. A rose is a rose is an onion.'

'Thy onions are affecting thy brain,' Agustín said. 'Take care.'

'An onion is an onion is an onion,' Robert Jordan said cheerily and, he thought, a stone is a stein is a rock is a boulder is a pebble.

'Rinse thy mouth with wine,' Agustín said. 'Thou art very rare, *Inglés*. There is great difference between thee and the last dynamiter who worked with us.'

'There is one great difference.'

'Tell it to me.'

'I am alive and he is dead,' Robert Jordan said. Then: what's the matter with you? he thought. Is that the way to talk? Does food make you that slap happy? What are you, drunk on onions? Is that all it means to you, now? It never meant much, he told himself truly. You tried to make it mean something, but it never did. There is no need to lie in the time that is left.

'No,' he said, seriously now. 'That one was a man who had suffered greatly.'

'And thou? Hast thou not suffered?'

'No,' said Robert Jordan. 'I am of those who suffer little.'

'Me also,' Agustín told him. 'There are those who suffer and those who do not. I suffer very little.'

'Less bad,' Robert Jordan tipped up the wineskin again. 'And with this, less.'

'I suffer for others.'

'As all good men should.'

'But for myself very little.'

'Hast thou a wife?'

'No.'

'Me neither.'

'But now you have the Maria.'

'Yes.'

'There is a rare thing,' Agustín said. 'Since she came to us at the train the Pilar has kept her away from all as fiercely as though she were in a convent of

Carmelites. You cannot imagine with what fierceness she guarded her. You come, and she gives her to thee as a present. How does that seem to thee?'

'It was not thus.'

'How was it, then?'

'She has put her in my care.'

'And thy care is to *joder* with her all night?'

'With luck.'

'What a manner to care for one.'

'You do not understand that one can take good care of one thus?'

'Yes, but such care could have been furnished by any one of us.'

'Let us not talk of it any more,' Robert Jordan said. 'I care for her seriously.'

'Seriously?'

'As there can be nothing more serious in this world.'

'And afterwards? After this of the bridge?'

'She goes with me.'

'Then,' Agustín said. 'That no one speaks of it further and that the two of you go with all luck.'

He lifted the leather wine bag and took a long pull, then handed it to Robert Jordan.

'One thing more, *Inglés*', he said.

'Of course.'

'I have cared much for her, too.'

Robert Jordan put his hand on his shoulder.

'Much,' Agustín said. 'Much. More than one is able to imagine.'

'I can imagine.'

'She has made an impression on me that does not dissipate.'

'I can imagine.'

'Look. I say this to thee in all seriousness.'

'Say it.'

'I have never touched her nor had anything to do with her but I care for her greatly. *Inglés*, do not treat her lightly. Because she sleeps with thee she is no whore.'

'I will care for her.'

'I believe thee. But more. You do not understand how such a girl would be if there had been no revolution. You have much responsibility. This one, truly, has suffered much. She is not as we are.'

'I will marry her.'

'Nay. Not that. There is no need for that under the revolution. But—' he nodded his head–'it would be better.'

'I will marry her,' Robert Jordan said and could feel his throat swelling as he said it. 'I care for her greatly.'

'Later,' Agustín said. 'When it is convenient. The important thing is to have the intention.'

'I have it.'

'Listen,' Agustín said. 'I am speaking too much of a matter in which I have no right to intervene, but hast thou known many girls of this country?'

'A few.'

'Whores?'

'Some who were not.'

'How many?'

'Several.'

'And did you sleep with them?'

'No.'

'You see?'

'Yes.'

'What I mean is that this Maria does not do this lightly.'

'Nor I.'

'If I thought you did I would have shot you last night as you lay with her. For this we kill much here.'

'Listen, old one,' Robert Jordan said. 'It is because of the lack of time that there has been informality. What we do not have is time. To-morrow we must fight. To me that is nothing. But for the Maria and me it means that we must live all of our life in this time.'

'And a day and a night is little time,' Agustín said.

'Yes. But there has been yesterday and the night before and last night.'

'Look,' Agustín said. 'If I can aid thee.'

'No. We are all right.'

'If I could do anything for thee or for the cropped head—'

'No.'

'Truly, there is little one man can do for another.'

'No. There is much.'

'What?'

'No matter what passes to-day and to-morrow in respect to combat, give me thy confidence and obey even though the orders may appear wrong.'

'You have my confidence. Since this of the cavalry and the sending away of the horse.'

'That was nothing. You see that we are working for one thing. To win the war. Unless we win, all other things are futile. Tomorrow we have a thing of great importance. Of true importance. Also we will have combat. In combat there must be discipline. For many things are not as they appear. Discipline must come from trust and confidence.'

Agustín spat on the ground.

'The Maria and all such things are apart,' he said. 'That you and the Maria should make use of what time there is as two human beings. If I can aid thee I am at thy orders. But for the thing of to-morrow I will obey thee blindly. If it is necessary that one should die for the thing of to-morrow one goes gladly and with the heart light.'

'Thus do I feel,' Robert Jordan said. 'But to hear it from thee brings pleasure.'

'And more,' Agustín said. 'That one above,' he pointed toward Primitivo, 'is a dependable value. The Pilar is much, much more than thou canst imagine. The old man Anselmo, also. Andrés also. Eladio also. Very quiet, but a dependable element. And Fernando. I do not know how thou hast appreciated him. It is true he is heavier than mercury. He is fuller of boredom than a steer drawing a cart on the highroad. But to fight and to do as he is told. *Es muy hombre!* Thou wilt see.'

'We are lucky.'

'No. We have two weak elements. The gipsy and Pablo. But the band of Sordo are as much better than we are as we are better than goat manure.'

'All is well then.'

'Yes,' Agustín said. 'But I wish it was for to-day.'

'Me, too. To finish with it. But it is not.'

'Do you think it will be bad?'

'It can be.'

'But thou art very cheerful now, *Inglés*.'

'Yes.'

'Me also. In spite of this of the Maria and all.'

'Do you know why?'

'No.'

'Me neither. Perhaps it is the day. The day is good.'

'Who knows? Perhaps it is that we will have action.'

'I think it is that,' Robert Jordan said. 'But not to-day. Of all things; of all importance we must avoid it to-day.'

As he spoke he heard something. It was a noise far off that came above the sound of the warm wind in the trees. He could not be sure and he held his mouth open and listened, glancing up at Primitivo as he did so. He thought he heard it but then it was gone. The wind was blowing in the pines and now Robert Jordan strained all of himself to listen. Then he heard it faintly coming down the wind.

'It is nothing tragic with me,' he heard Agustín say. 'That I should never have the Maria is nothing. I will go with the whores as always.'

'Shut up,' he said, not listening, and lying beside him, his head having been turned away. Agustín looked over at him suddenly.

'*Qué pasa?*' he asked.

Robert Jordan put his hand over his own mouth and went on listening. There it came again. It came faint, muted, dry and far away. But there was no mistaking it now. It was the precise, crackling, curling roll of automatic rifle fire. It sounded as though pack after pack of miniature firecrackers were going off at a distance that was almost out of hearing.

Robert Jordan looked up at Primitivo who had his head up now, his face looking toward them, his hand cupped to his ear. As he looked Primitivo pointed up the mountain toward the highest country.

'They are fighting at El Sordo's,' Robert Jordan said.

'Then let us go to aid them,' Agustín said. 'Collect the people. *Vamonos*.'

'No,' Robert Jordan said. 'We stay here.'

25

Robert Jordan looked up at where Primitivo stood now in his lookout post, holding his rifle and pointing. He nodded his head but the man kept pointing, putting his hand to his ear and then pointing insistently and as though he could not possibly have been understood.

'Do you stay with this gun and unless it is sure, sure, sure that they are coming in do not fire. And then not until they reach that shrub,' Robert Jordan pointed. 'Do you understand?'

'Yes. But—'

'No but. I will explain to thee later. I go to Primitivo.'

Anselmo was by him and he said to the old man:

'*Viejo*, stay there with Agustín with the gun.' He spoke slowly and unhurriedly. 'He must not fire unless cavalry is actually entering. If they merely present themselves he must let them alone as we did before. If he must fire, hold the legs of the tripod firm for him and hand him the pans when they empty.'

'Good,' the old man said. 'And La Granja?'

'Later.'

Robert Jordan climbed up, over and around the grey boulders that were wet now under his hands as he pulled himself up. The sun was melting the snow on them fast. The tops of the boulders were drying and as he climbed he looked across the country and saw the pine woods and the long open glade and the dip of the country before the high mountains beyond. Then he stood beside Primitivo in a hollow behind two boulders and the short, brown-faced man said to him, 'They are attacking Sordo. What is it that we do?'

'Nothing,' Robert Jordan said.

He heard the firing clearly here and as he looked across the country, he saw, far off, across the distant valley where the country rose steeply again, a troop of cavalry ride out of the timber and cross the snowy slope riding uphill in the direction of the firing. He saw the oblong double line of men and horses dark against the snow as they forced at an angle up the hill. He watched the double line top the ridge and go into the farther timber.

'We have to aid them,' Primitivo said. His voice was dry and flat.

'It is impossible,' Robert Jordan told him. 'I have expected this all morning.'

'How?'

'They went to steal horses last night. The snow stopped and they tracked them up there.'

'But we have to aid them,' Primitivo said. 'We cannot leave them alone to this. Those are our comrades.'

Robert Jordan put his hand on the other man's shoulder.

'We can do nothing,' he said. 'If we could I would do it.'

'There is a way to reach there from above. We can take that way with the horses and the two guns. This one below and thine. We can aid them thus.'

'Listen—' Robert Jordan said.

'*That* is what I listen to,' Primitivo said.

The firing was rolling in overlapping waves. Then they heard the noise of hand grenades heavy and sodden in the dry rolling of the automatic rifle fire.

'They are lost,' Robert Jordan said. 'They were lost when the snow stopped. If we go there we are lost, too. It is impossible to divide what force we have.'

There was a grey stubble of beard stippled over Primitivo's jaws, his lip and his neck. The rest of his face was flat brown with a broken, flattened nose and deep-set grey eyes, and watching him Robert Jordan saw the stubble twitching at the corners of his mouth and over the cords of his throat.

'Listen to it,' he said. 'It is a massacre.'

'If they have surrounded the hollow it is that,' Robert Jordan said. 'Some may have gotten out.'

'Coming on them now we could take them from behind,' Primitivo said. 'Let four of us go with the horses.'

'And then what? What happens after you take them from behind?'

'We join with Sordo.'

'To die there? Look at the sun. The day is long.'

The sky was high and cloudless and the sun was hot on their backs. There were big bare patches now on the southern slope of the open glade below them and the snow was all dropped from the pine trees. The boulders below them that had been wet as the snow melted were steaming faintly now in the hot sun.

'You have to stand it,' Robert Jordan said. '*Hay que aguantarse.* There are things like this in a war.'

'But there is nothing we can do? Truly?' Primitivo looked at him and Robert Jordan knew he trusted him. 'Thou couldst not send me and another with the small machine gun?'

'It would be useless,' Robert Jordan said.

He thought he saw something that he was looking for but it was a hawk that slid down into the wind and then rose above the line of the farthest pine woods. 'It would be useless if we all went,' he said.

Just then the firing doubled in intensity and in it was the heavy bumping of the hand grenades.

'Oh, obscenity them,' Primitivo said with an absolute devoutness of blasphemy, tears in his eyes and his cheeks twitching. 'Oh, God and the Virgin, obscenity them in the milk of their filth.'

'Calm thyself,' Robert Jordan said. 'You will be fighting them soon enough. Here comes the woman.'

Pilar was climbing up to them, making heavy going of it in the boulders.

Primitivo kept saying, 'Obscenity them. Oh, God and the Virgin, befoul them,' each time the firing rolled down the wind, and Robert Jordan climbed down to help Pilar up.

'*Qué tal*, woman,' he said, taking hold of both her wrists and hoisting as she climbed heavily over the last boulder.

'Thy binoculars,' she said and lifted their strap over her head. 'So it has come to Sordo?'

'Yes.'

'*Pobre*,' she said in commiseration. 'Poor Sordo.'

She was breathing heavily from the climb and she took hold of Robert Jordan's hand and gripped it tight in hers as she looked out over the country.

'How does the combat seem?'

'Bad. Very bad.'

'He's *jodido*?'

'I believe so.'

'*Pobre*,' she said. 'Doubtless because of the horses?'

'Probably.'

'*Pobre*,' Pilar said. Then, 'Rafael recounted me all of an entire novel of dung about cavalry. What came?'

'A patrol and part of a squadron.'

'Up to what point?'

Robert Jordan pointed out where the patrol had stopped and showed her where the gun was hidden. From where they stood they could just see one of Agustín's boots protruding from the rear of the blind.

'The gipsy said they rode to where the gun muzzle pressed against the chest of the horse of the leader,' Pilar said. 'What a race! Thy glasses were in the cave.'

'Have you packed?'

'All that can be taken. Is there news of Pablo?'

'He was forty minutes ahead of the cavalry. They took his trail.'

Pilar grinned at him. She still held his hand. Now she dropped it. 'They'll never see him,' she said. 'Now for Sordo. Can we do anything?'

'Nothing.'

'*Pobre*,' she said. 'I was very fond of Sordo. Thou art sure, *sure* that he is *jodido*?'

'Yes. I have seen much cavalry.'

'More than were here?'

'Another full troop on their way up there.'

'Listen to it,' Pilar said. '*Pobre, pobre Sordo*.'

They listened to the firing.

'Primitivo wanted to go up there,' Robert Jordan said.

'Art thou crazy?' Pilar said to the flat-faced man. 'What kind of *locos* are we producing around here?'

'I wish to aid them.'

'*Qué va*,' Pilar said. 'Another romantic. Dost thou not believe thou wilt die quick enough here without useless voyages?'

Robert Jordan looked at her, at the heavy brown face with the high Indian cheekbones, the wide-set dark eyes and the laughing mouth with the heavy, bitter upper lip.

'Thou must act like a man,' she said to Primitivo. 'A grown man. You with your grey hairs and all.'

'Don't joke at me,' Primitivo said sullenly. 'If a man has a little heart and a little imagination—'

'He should learn to control them,' Pilar said. 'Thou wilt die soon enough with us. There is no need to seek that with strangers. As for thy imagination. The gipsy has enough for all. What a novel he told me.'

'If thou hadst seen it thou wouldst not call it a novel,' Primitivo said. 'There was a moment of great gravity.'

'*Qué va*,' Pilar said. 'Some cavalry rode here and they rode away. And you all make yourselves a heroism. It is to this we have come with so much inaction.'

'And this of Sordo is not grave?' Primitivo said contemptuously now. He suffered visibly each time the firing came down the wind and he wanted either to go to the combat or have Pilar go and leave him alone.

'*Total qué?*' Pilar said. 'It has come so it has come. Don't lose thy *cojones* for the misfortune of another.'

'Go defile thyself,' Primitivo said. 'There are women of a stupidity and brutality that is insupportable.'

'In order to support and aid those men poorly equipped for procreation,' Pilar said. 'If there is nothing to see I am going.'

Just then Robert Jordan heard the plane high overhead. He looked up and in the high sky it looked to be the same observation plane that he had seen earlier in the morning. Now it was returning from the direction of the lines and it was moving in the direction of the high country where El Sordo was being attacked.

'There is the bad luck bird,' Pilar said. 'Will it see what goes on there?'

'Surely,' Robert Jordan said. 'If they are not blind.'

They watched the plane moving high and silvery and steady in the sunlight. It was coming from the left and they could see the round disks of light the two propellers made.

'Keep down,' Robert Jordan said.

Then the plane was overhead, its shadows passing over the open glade, the throbbing reaching its maximum of portent. Then it was past and headed toward the top of the valley. They watched it go steadily on its course until it was just out of sight and then they saw it coming back in a wide dipping circle, to circle twice over the high country and then disappear in the direction of Segovia.

Robert Jordan looked at Pilar. There was perspiration on her forehead and she shook her head. She had been holding her lower lip between her teeth.

'For each one there is something,' she said. 'For me it is those.'

'Thou hast not caught my fear?' Primitivo said sarcastically.

'Nay,' she put her hand on his shoulder. 'Thou hast no fear to catch. I know that. I am sorry I joked too roughly with thee. We are all in the same cauldron.' Then she spoke to Robert Jordan. 'I will send up food and wine. Dost need anything more?'

'Not in this moment. Where are the others?'

'Thy reserve is intact below with the horses,' she grinned. 'Everything is out of sight. Everything to go is ready. Maria is with thy material.'

'If by any chance we *should* have aviation keep her in the cave.'

'Yes, my Lord *Inglés*,' Pilar said. '*Thy* gipsy (I give him to thee) I have sent to gather mushrooms to cook with the hares. There are many mushrooms now and it seemed to me we might as well eat the hares although they would be better to-morrow or the day after.'

'I think it is best to eat them,' Robert Jordan said, and Pilar put her big hand on his shoulder where the strap of the sub-machine gun crossed his chest, then reached up and mussed his hair with her fingers. 'What an *Inglés*,' Pilar said. 'I will send the Maria with the *puchero* when they are cooked.'

The firing from far away and above had almost died out and now there was only an occasional shot.

'You think it is over?' Pilar asked.

'No,' Robert Jordan said. 'From the sound that we have heard they have attacked and been beaten off. Now I would say the attackers have them surrounded. They have taken cover and they wait for the planes.'

Pilar spoke to Primitivo, 'Thou. Dost understand there was no intent to insult thee?'

'*Ya lo sé*,' said Primitivo. 'I have put up with worse than that from thee. Thou hast a vile tongue. But watch thy mouth, woman. Sordo was a good comrade of mine.'

'And not of mine?' Pilar asked him. 'Listen, flat face. In war one cannot say what one feels. We have enough of our own without taking Sordo's.'

Primitivo was still sullen.

'You should take a physic,' Pilar told him. 'Now I go to prepare the meal.'

'Did you bring the documentation of that *requeté*?' Robert Jordan asked her.

'How stupid I am,' she said. 'I forgot it. I will send the Maria.'

26

It was three o'clock in the afternoon before the planes came. The snow had all been gone by noon and the rocks were hot now in the sun. There were no clouds in the sky and Robert Jordan sat in the rocks with his shirt off browning his back in the sun and reading the letters that had been in the pockets of the dead cavalryman. From time to time he would stop reading to look across the open slope to the line of the timber, look over the high country above and then return to the letters. No more cavalry had appeared. At intervals there would be the sound of a shot from the direction of El Sordo's camp. But the firing was desultory.

From examining his military papers he knew the boy was from Tafalla in Navarra, twenty-one years old, unmarried, and the son of a blacksmith. His regiment was the Nth cavalry, which surprised Robert Jordan, for he had believed that regiment to be in the North. He was a Carlist, and he had been wounded at the fighting for Irun at the start of the war.

I've probably seen him run through the streets ahead of the bulls at the

Feria in Pamplona, Robert Jordan thought. You never kill anyone that you want to kill in a war, he said to himself. Well, hardly ever, he amended and went on reading the letters.

The first letters he read were very formal, very carefully written and dealt almost entirely with local happenings. They were from his sister and Robert Jordan learned that everything was all right in Tafalla, that father was well, that mother was the same as always but with certain complaints about her back, that she hoped he was well and not in too great danger and she was happy he was doing away with the Reds to liberate Spain from the domination of the Marxist hordes. Then there was a list of those boys from Tafalla who had been killed or badly wounded since she wrote last. She mentioned ten who were killed. That is a great many for a town the size of Tafalla, Robert Jordan thought.

There was quite a lot of religion in the letter and she prayed to Saint Anthony, to the Blessed Virgin of Pilar, and to other Virgins to protect him and she wanted him never to forget that he was also protected by the Sacred Heart of Jesus that he wore still, she trusted, at all times over his own heart where it had been proven innumerable–this was underlined–times to have the power of stopping bullets. She was as always his loving sister Concha.

This letter was a little stained around the edges and Robert Jordan put it carefully back with the military papers and opened a letter with a less severe handwriting. It was from the boy's *novia*, his fiancée, and it was quietly, formally, and completely hysterical with concern for his safety. Robert Jordan read it through and then put all the letters together with the papers into his hip pocket. He did not want to read the other letters.

I guess I've done my good deed for to-day, he said to himself. I guess you have all right, he repeated.

'What are those you were reading?' Primitivo asked him.

'The documentation and the letters of that *requeté* we shot this morning. Do you want to see it?'

'I can't read,' Primitivo said. 'Was there anything interesting?'

'No,' Robert Jordan told him. 'They are personal letters.'

'How are things going where he came from? Can you tell from the letters?'

'They seem to be going all right,' Robert Jordan said. 'There are many losses in his town.' He looked down to where the blind for the automatic rifle had been changed a little and improved after the snow melted. It looked convincing enough. He looked off across the country.

'From what town is he?' Primitivo asked.

'Tafalla,' Robert Jordan told him.

All right, he said to himself. I'm sorry, if that does any good.

It doesn't, he said to himself.

All right then, drop it, he said to himself.

All right, it's dropped.

But it would not drop that easily. How many is that you have killed? he asked himself. I don't know. Do you think you have a right to kill anyone? No. But I have to. How many of those you have killed have been real fascists? Very few. But they are all the enemy to whose force we are opposing force. But you like the people of Navarra better than those of any other part of

Spain. Yes. And you kill them. Yes. If you don't believe it go down there to the camp. Don't you know it is wrong to kill? Yes. But you do it? Yes. And you still believe absolutely that your cause is right? Yes.

It is right, he told himself, not reassuringly, but proudly. I believe in the people and their right to govern themselves as they wish. But you mustn't believe in killing, he told himself. You must do it as a necessity but you must not believe in it. If you believe in it the whole thing is wrong.

But how many do you suppose you have killed? I don't know because I won't keep track. But do you know? Yes. How many? You can't be sure how many. Blowing the trains you kill many. Very many. But you can't be sure. But of those you are sure of? More than twenty. And of those how many were real fascists? Two that I am sure of. Because I had to shoot them when we took them prisoners at Usera. And you did not mind that? No. Nor did you like it? No. I decided never to do it again. I have avoided it. I have avoided killing those who are unarmed.

Listen, he told himself. You'd better cut this out. This is very bad for you and for your work. Then himself said back to him, You listen, see? Because you are doing something very serious and I have to see you understand it all the time. I have to keep you straight in your head. Because if you are not absolutely straight in your head you have no right to do the things you do for all of them are crimes and no man has a right to take another man's life unless it is to prevent something worse happening to other people. So get it straight and do not lie to yourself.

But I won't keep a count of people I have killed as though it were a trophy record or a disgusting business like notches in a gun, he told himself. I have a right not to keep count and I have a right to forget them.

No, himself said. You have no right to forget anything. You have no right to shut your eyes to any of it nor any right to forget any of it nor to soften it nor to change it.

Shut up, he told himself. You're getting awfully pompous.

Nor ever to deceive yourself about it, himself went on.

All right, he told himself. Thanks for all the good advice and is it all right for me to love Maria?

Yes, himself said.

Even if there isn't supposed to be any such thing as love in a purely materialistic conception of society?

Since when did you ever have any such conception? himself asked. Never. And you never could have. You're not a real Marxist and you know it. You believe in Liberty, Equality and Fraternity. You believe in Life, Liberty and the Pursuit of Happiness. Don't ever kid yourself with too much dialectics. They are for some but not for you. You have to know them in order not to be a sucker. You have put many things in abeyance to win a war. If this war is lost all of those things are lost.

But afterwards you can discard what you do not believe in. There is plenty you do not believe in and plenty that you do believe in.

And another thing. Don't ever kid yourself about loving someone. It is just that most people are not lucky enough ever to have it. You never had it before and now you have it. What you have with Maria, whether it lasts just through to-day and a part of to-morrow, or whether it lasts for a long life is the most important thing that can happen to a human being. There will always be people who say it does not exist because they cannot have it. But I tell you it is true and that you have it and that you are lucky even if you die to-morrow.

Cut out the dying stuff, he said to himself. That's not the way we talk. That's the way our friends the anarchists talk. Whenever things get really bad they want to set fire to something and to die. It's a very odd kind of mind they have. Very odd. Well, we're getting through to-day, old timer, he told himself. It's nearly three o'clock now and there is going to be some food sooner or later. They are still shooting up at Sordo's, which means that they have him surrounded and are waiting to bring up more people, probably. Though they have to make it before dark.

I wonder what it is like up at Sordo's. That's what we all have to expect, given enough time. I imagine it is not too jovial up at Sordo's. We certainly got Sordo into a fine jam with that horse business. How does it go in Spanish? *Un callejón sin salida*. A passageway with no exit. I suppose I could go through with it all right. You only have to do it once and it is soon over with. But wouldn't it be luxury to fight in a war some time where, when you were surrounded, you could surrender? *Estamos copados*. We are surrounded. That was the great panic cry of this war. Then the next thing was that you were shot; with nothing bad before it you were lucky. Sordo wouldn't be lucky that way. Neither would they when the time ever came.

It was three o'clock. Then he heard the far-off, distant throbbing and, looking up, he saw the planes.

27

El Sordo was making his fight on a hilltop. He did not like this hill and when he saw it he thought it had the shape of a chancre. But he had had no choice except this hill and he had picked it as far away as he could see it and galloped for it, the automatic rifle heavy on his back, the horse labouring, barrel heaving between his thighs, the sack of grenades swinging against one side, the sack of automatic rifle pans banging against the other, and Joaquín and Ignacio halting and firing, halting and firing to give him time to get the gun in place.

There had still been snow then, the snow that had ruined them, and when his horse was hit so that he wheezed in a slow, jerking, climbing stagger up the last part of the crest, splattering the snow with a bright, pulsing jet, Sordo had hauled him along by the bridle, the reins over his shoulder as he climbed. He climbed as hard as he could with the bullets spatting on the rocks, with the two sacks heavy on his shoulders, and then, holding the horse by the mane, had shot him quickly, expertly, and tenderly just where he had needed him, so that the horse pitched, head forward, down to plug a gap between two rocks. He had gotten the gun to firing over the horse's back and he fired two pans, the gun clattering, the empty shells pitching into the snow, the smell of burnt hair from the burnt hide where the hot muzzle rested, him firing at what came up to the hill, forcing them to scatter for cover, while all the time there was a chill in his back from not knowing what was behind him. Once the last of the five men had reached the hilltop the chill went out of his back and he had saved the pans he had left until he would need them.

There were two more horses dead along the slope and three more were dead here on the hilltop. He had only succeeded in stealing three horses last night and one had bolted when they tried to mount him bareback in the corral at the camp when the first shooting had started.

Of the five men who had reached the hilltop three were wounded. Sordo was wounded in the calf of his leg and in two places in his left arm. He was very thirsty, his wounds had stiffened, and one of the wounds in his left arm was very painful. He also had a bad headache and as he lay waiting for the planes to come he thought of a joke in Spanish. It was, '*Hay que tomar la muerte como si fuera aspirina*', which means, 'You will have to take death as an aspirin.' But he did not make the joke aloud. He grinned somewhere inside the pain in his head and inside the nausea that came whenever he moved his arm and looked around at what there was left of his band.

The five men were spread out like the points of a five-pointed star. They had dug with their knees and hands and made mounds in front of their heads and shoulders with the dirt and piles of stones. Using this cover, they were linking the individual mounds up with stones and dirt. Joaquín, who was eighteen years old, had a steel helmet that he dug with and he passed dirt in it.

He had gotten this helmet at the blowing up of the train. It had a bullet hole through it and everyone had always joked at him for keeping it. But he had hammered the jagged edges of the bullet hole smooth and driven a wooden plug into it and then cut the plug off and smoothed it even with the metal inside the helmet.

When the shooting started he had clapped this helmet on his head so hard it banged his head as though he had been hit with a casserole and, in the last lung-aching, leg-dead, mouth-dry, bullet-spatting, bullet-cracking, bullet-singing run up the final slope of the hill after his horse was killed, the helmet had seemed to weigh a great amount and to ring his bursting forehead with an iron band. But he had kept it. Now he dug with it in a steady, almost machine-like desperation. He had not yet been hit.

'It serves for something finally,' Sordo said to him in his deep, throaty voice.

'*Resistir y fortificar es vencer*,' Joaquín said, his mouth stiff with the dryness of fear which surpassed the normal thirst of battle. It was one of the slogans of the Communist party and it meant, 'Hold out and fortify, and you will win'.

Sordo looked away and down the slope at where a cavalryman was sniping from behind a boulder. He was very fond of this boy and he was in no mood for slogans.

'What did you say?'

One of the men turned from the building that he was doing. This man was lying flat on his face, reaching carefully up with his hands to put a rock in place while keeping his chin flat against the ground.

Joaquín repeated the slogan in his dried-up boy's voice without checking his digging for a moment.

'What was the last word?' the man with his chin on the ground asked.

'*Vencer*,' the boy said. 'Win.'

'*Mierda*,' the man with his chin on the ground said.

'There is another that applies to here,' Joaquín said, bringing them out as though they were talismans, 'Pasionaria says it is better to die on your feet than to live on your knees.'

'*Mierda* again,' the man said and another man said, over his shoulder, 'We're on our bellies, not our knees.'

'Thou. Communist. Do you know your Pasionaria has a son thy age in Russia since the start of the movement?'

'It's a lie,' Joaquín said.

'*Qué va*, it's a lie,' the other said. 'The dynamiter with the rare name told me. He was of thy party, too. Why should he lie?'

'It's a lie,' Joaquín said. 'She would not do such a thing as keep a son hidden in Russia out of the war.'

'I wish I were in Russia,' another of Sordo's men said. 'Will not thy Pasionaria send me now from here to Russia, Communist?'

'If thou believest so much in thy Pasionaria, get her to get us off this hill,' one of the men who had a bandaged thigh said.

'The fascists will do that,' the man with his chin in the dirt said.

'Do not speak thus,' Joaquín said to him.

'Wipe the pap of your mother's breast off thy lips and give me a hatful of that dirt,' the man with his chin on the ground said. 'No one of us will see the sun go down this night.'

El Sordo was thinking: It is shaped like a chancre. Or the breast of a young girl with no nipple. Or the top cone of a volcano. You have never seen a volcano, he thought. Nor will you ever see one. And this hill is like a chancre. Let the volcanoes alone. It's late now for the volcanoes.

He looked very carefully around the withers of the dead horse and there was a quick hammering of firing from behind a boulder well down the slope and he heard the bullets from the sub-machinegun thud into the horse. He crawled along behind the horse and looked out of the angle between the horse's hindquarters and the rock. There were three bodies on the slope just below him where they had fallen when the fascists had rushed the crest under cover of the automatic rifle and sub-machinegun fire and he and the others had broken down the attack by throwing and rolling down hand grenades. There were other bodies that he could not see on the other sides of the hill crest. There was no dead ground by which attackers could approach the summit and Sordo knew that as long as his ammunition and grenades held out and he had as many as four men they could not get him out of there unless they brought up a trench mortar. He did not know whether they had sent to La Granja for a trench mortar. Perhaps they had not, because surely, soon, the planes would come. It had been four hours since the observation plane had flown over them.

This hill is truly like a chancre, Sordo thought, and we are the very pus of it. But we killed many when they made that stupidness. How could they think that they would take us thus? They have such modern armament that they lose all their sense with over-confidence. He had killed the young officer who had led the assault with a grenade that had gone bouncing and rolling down the slope as they came up it, running, bent half over. In the yellow flash and grey roar of smoke he had seen the officer dive forward to where he lay now like a heavy, broken bundle of old clothing marking the farthest point that the assault had reached. Sordo looked at this body and then, down the hill, at the others.

They are brave but stupid people, he thought. But they have sense enough now not to attack us again until the planes come. Unless, of course, they have a mortar coming. It would be easy with a mortar. The mortar was the normal thing and he knew that they would die as soon as a mortar came up, but when he thought of the planes coming up he felt as naked on that hilltop as though all of his clothing and even his skin had been removed. There is no nakeder thing than I feel, he thought. A flayed rabbit is as well covered as a bear in comparison. But why should they bring planes? They could get us out of here with a trench mortar easily. They are proud of their planes, though, and they will probably bring them. Just as they were so proud of their automatic weapons that they made that stupidness. But undoubtedly they must have sent for a mortar too.

One of the men fired. Then jerked the bolt and fired again, quickly.

'Save thy cartridges,' Sordo said.

'One of the sons of the great whore tried to reach that boulder,' the man pointed.

'Did you hit him?' Sordo asked, turning his head with difficulty.

'Nay,' the man said. 'The fornicator ducked back.'

'Who is a whore of whores is Pilar,' the man with his chin in the dirt said. 'That whore knows we are dying here.'

'She could do no good,' Sordo said. The man had spoken on the side of his good ear and he had heard him without turning his head. 'What could she do?'

'Take these sluts from the rear.'

'*Qué va*,' Sordo said. 'They are spread around a hillside. How would she come on them? There are a hundred and fifty of them. Maybe more now.'

'But if we hold out until dark,' Joaquín said.

'And if Christmas comes on Easter,' the man with his chin on the ground said.

'And if thy aunt had *cojones* she would be thy uncle,' another said to him. 'Send for thy Pasionaria. She alone can help us.'

'I do not believe that about the son,' Joaquín said. 'Or if he is there he is training to be an aviator or something of that sort.'

'He is hidden there for safety,' the man told him.

'He is studying dialectics. Thy Pasionaria has been there. So have Lister and Modesto and others. The one with the rare name told me.'

'That they should go to study and return to aid us,' Joaquín said.

'That they should aid us now,' another man said. 'That all the cruts of Russian sucking swindlers should aid us now.' He fired and said, '*Me cago en tal*; I missed him again.'

'Save thy cartridges and do not talk so much or thou wilt be very thirsty,' Sordo said. 'There is no water on this hill.'

'Take this,' the man said and rolling on his side he pulled a wineskin that he wore slung from his shoulder over his head and handed it to Sordo. 'Wash thy mouth out, old one. Thou must have much thirst with thy wounds.'

'Let all take it,' Sordo said.

'Then I will have some first,' the owner said and squirted a long stream into his mouth before he handed the leather bottle around.

'Sordo, when thinkest thou the planes will come?' the man with his chin in the dirt asked.

'Any time,' said Sordo. 'They should have come before.'

'Do you think these sons of the great whore will attack again?'

'Only if the planes do not come.'

He did not think there was any need to speak about the mortar. They would know it soon enough when the mortar came.

'God knows they've enough planes with what we saw yesterday.'

'Too many,' Sordo said.

His head hurt very much and his arm was stiffening so that the pain of moving it was almost unbearable. He looked up at the bright, high, blue early summer sky as he raised the leather wine bottle with his good arm. He was fifty-two years old and he was sure this was the last time he would see that sky.

He was not at all afraid of dying but he was angry at being trapped on this hill which was only utilizable as a place to die. If we could have gotten clear, he thought. If we could have made them come up the long valley or if we could have broken loose across the road it would have been all right. But this chancre of a hill. We must use it as well as we can and we have used it very well so far.

If he had known how many men in history have had to use a hill to die on it would not have cheered him any for, in the moment he was passing through, men are not impressed by what has happened to other men in similar circumstances any more than a widow of one day is helped by the knowledge that other loved husbands have died. Whether one has fear of it or not, one's death is difficult to accept. Sordo had accepted it but there was no sweetness in its acceptance even at fifty-two, with three wounds and him surrounded on a hill.

He joked about it to himself but he looked at the sky and at the far mountains and he swallowed the wine and he did not want it. If one must die, he thought, and clearly one must, I can die. But I hate it.

Dying was nothing and he had no picture of it nor fear of it in his mind. But living was a field of grain blowing in the wind on the side of a hill. Living was a hawk in the sky. Living was an earthen jar of water in the dust of the threshing with the grain flailed out and the chaff blowing. Living was a horse between your legs and a carbine under one leg and a hill and a valley and a stream with trees along it and the far side of the valley and the hills beyond.

Sordo passed the wine bottle back and nodded his head in thanks. He leaned forward and patted the dead horse on the shoulder where the muzzle of the automatic rifle had burned the hide. He could still smell the burnt hair. He thought how he had held the horse there, trembling, with the fire around them, whispering and cracking, over and around them like a curtain, and had carefully shot him just at the intersection of the crosslines between the two eyes and the ears. Then as the horse pitched down he had dropped down behind his warm, wet back to get the gun going as they came up the hill.

'*Eras mucho caballo*,' he said, meaning, 'Thou wert plenty of horse.'

El Sordo lay now on his good side and looked up at the sky. He was lying on a heap of empty cartridge hulls but his head was protected by the rock and his body lay in the lee of the horse. His wounds had stiffened badly and he had much pain and he felt too tired to move.

'What passes with thee, old one?' the man next to him asked.

'Nothing. I am taking a little rest.'

'Sleep,' the other said. '*They* will wake us when they come.'

Just then someone shouted from down the slope.

'Listen, bandits!' the voice came from behind the rocks where the closest automatic rifle was placed. 'Surrender now before the planes blow you to pieces.'

'What is it he says?' Sordo asked.

Joaquín told him. Sordo rolled to one side and pulled himself up so that he was crouched behind the gun again.

'Maybe the planes aren't coming,' he said. 'Don't answer them and do not fire. Maybe we can get them to attack again.'

'If we should insult them a little?' the man who had spoken to Joaquín about La Pasionaria's son in Russia asked.

'No,' Sordo said. 'Give me thy big pistol. Who has a big pistol?'

'Here.'

'Give it to me.' Crouched on his knees he took the big 9 mm. Star and fired one shot into the ground beside the dead horse, waited, then fired again four times at irregular intervals. Then he waited while he counted sixty and then fired a final shot directly into the body of the dead horse. He grinned and handed back the pistol.

'Reload it,' he whispered, 'and that everyone should keep his mouth shut and no one shoot.'

'*Bandidos!*' the voice shouted from behind the rocks.

No one spoke on the hill.

'*Bandidos!* Surrender now before we blow thee to little pieces.'

'They're biting,' Sordo whispered happily.

As he watched, a man showed his head over the top of the rocks. There was no shot from the hilltop and the head went down again. El Sordo waited, watching, but nothing more happened. He turned his head and looked at the others who were all watching down their sectors of the slope. As he looked at them the others shook their heads.

'Let no one move,' he whispered.

'Sons of the great whore,' the voice came now from behind the rocks again.

'Red swine. Mother rapers. Eaters of the milk of thy fathers.'

Sordo grinned. He could just hear the bellowed insults by turning his good ear. This is better than the aspirin, he thought. How many will we get? Can they be that foolish?

The voice had stopped again and for three minutes they heard nothing and saw no movement. Then the sniper behind the boulder a hundred yards down the slope exposed himself and fired. The bullet hit a rock and ricocheted with a sharp whine. Then Sordo saw a man, bent double, run from the shelter of the rocks where the automatic rifle was across the open ground to the big boulder behind which the sniper was hidden. He almost dove behind the boulder.

Sordo looked around. They signalled to him that there was no movement on the other slopes. El Sordo grinned happily and shook his head. This is ten times better than the aspirin, he thought, and he waited, as happy as only a hunter can be happy.

Below on the slope the man who had run from the pile of stones to the shelter of the boulder was speaking to the sniper.

'Do you believe it?'

'I don't know,' the sniper said.

'It would be logical,' the man, who was the officer in command, said, 'They are surrounded. They have nothing to expect but to die.'

The sniper said nothing.

'What do you think?' the officer asked.

'Nothing,' the sniper said.

'Have you seen any movement since the shots?'

'None at all.'

The officer looked at his wrist watch. It was ten minutes to three o'clock.

'The planes should have come an hour ago,' he said. Just then another officer flopped in behind the boulder. The sniper moved over to make room for him.

'Thou, Paco,' the first officer said. 'How does it seem to thee?'

The second officer was breathing heavily from his sprint up and across the hillside from the automatic rifle position.

'For me it is a trick,' he said.

'But if it is not? What a ridicule we make waiting here and laying siege to dead men.'

'We have done something worse than ridiculous already,' the second officer said. 'Look at that slope.'

He looked up the slope to where the dead were scattered close to the top. From where he looked the line of the hilltop showed the scattered rocks, the belly, projecting legs, shod hooves jutting out, of Sordo's horse, and the fresh dirt thrown up by the digging.

'What about the mortars?' asked the second officer.

'They should be here in an hour. If not before.'

'Then wait for them. There has been enough stupidity already.'

'*Bandidos!*' the first officer shouted suddenly, getting to his feet and putting his head well up above the boulder so that the crest of the hill looked much closer as he stood upright. 'Red swine! Cowards!'

The second officer looked at the sniper and shook his head. The sniper looked away but his lips tightened.

The first officer stood there, his head all clear of the rock and with his hand on his pistol butt. He cursed and vilified the hilltop. Nothing happened. Then he stepped clear of the boulder and stood there looking up the hill.

'Fire, cowards, if you are alive,' he shouted. 'Fire on one who has no fear of any Red that ever came out of the belly of the great whore.'

This last was quite a long sentence to shout and the officer's face was red and congested as he finished.

The second officer, who was a thin sunburned man with quiet eyes, a thin, long-lipped mouth and a stubble of beard over his hollow cheeks, shook his head again. It was this officer who was shouting who had ordered the first assault. The young lieutenant who was dead up the slope had been the best friend of this other lieutenant who was named Paco Berrendo and who was listening to the shouting of the captain, who was obviously in a state of exaltation.

'Those are the swine who shot my sister and my mother,' the captain said. He had a red face and a blond, British-looking moustache and there was something wrong about his eyes. They were a light blue and the lashes were light, too. As you looked at them they seemed to focus slowly. Then 'Reds!' he shouted. 'Cowards!' and commenced cursing again.

He stood absolutely clear now and, sighting carefully, fired his pistol at the only target that the hilltop presented: the dead horse that had belonged to Sordo. The bullet threw up a puff of dirt fifteen yards below the horse. The captain fired again. The bullet hit a rock and sung off.

The captain stood there looking at the hilltop. The Lieutenant Berrendo was looking at the body of the other lieutenant just below the summit. The sniper was looking at the ground under his eyes. Then he looked up at the captain.

'There is no one alive up there,' the captain said. 'Thou,' he said to the sniper, 'go up there and see.'

The sniper looked down. He said nothing.

'Don't you hear me?' the captain shouted at him.

'Yes, my captain,' the sniper said, not looking at him.

'Then get up and go.' The captain still had his pistol out. 'Do you hear me?'

'Yes, my captain.'

'Why don't you go, then?'

'I don't want to, my captain.'

'You don't want to?' The captain pushed the pistol against the small of the man's back. 'You don't *want* to?'

'I am afraid, my captain,' the soldier said with dignity.

Lieutenant Berrendo, watching the captain's face and his odd eyes, thought he was going to shoot the man then.

'Captain Mora,' he said.

'Lieutenant Berrendo?'

'It is possible the soldier is right.'

'That he is right to say he is afraid? That he is right to say he does not *want* to obey an order?'

'No. That he is right that it is a trick.'

'They are all dead,' the captain said. 'Don't you hear me say they are all dead?'

'You mean our comrades on the slope?' Berrendo asked him. 'I agree with you.'

'Paco,' the captain said, 'don't be a fool. Do you think you are the only one who cared for Julián? I tell you the Reds are dead. Look!'

He stood up, then put both hands on top of the boulder and pulled himself up, kneeing-up awkwardly, then getting on his feet.

'Shoot,' he shouted, standing on the grey granite boulder and waved both his arms. 'Shoot me! Kill me!'

On the hilltop El Sordo lay behind the dead horse and grinned.

What a people, he thought. He laughed, trying to hold it in because the shaking hurt his arm.

'Reds,' came the shout from below. 'Red canaille. Shoot me! Kill me!'

Sordo, his chest shaking, barely peeped past the horse's crupper and saw the captain on top of the boulder waving his arms. Another officer stood by the boulder. The sniper was standing at the other side. Sordo kept his eye where it was and shook his head happily.

'Shoot me,' he said softly to himself. 'Kill me!' Then his shoulders shook again. The laughing hurt his arm and each time he laughed his head felt as though it would burst. But the laughter shook him again like a spasm.

Captain Mora got down from the boulder.

'Now do you believe me, Paco?' he questioned Lieutenant Berrendo.

'No,' said Lieutenant Berrendo.

'*Cojones!*' the captain said. 'Here there is nothing but idiots and cowards.'

The sniper had gotten carefully behind the boulder again and Lieutenant Berrendo was squatting beside him.

The captain, standing in the open beside the boulder, commenced to shout filth at the hilltop. There is no language so filthy as Spanish. There are words for all the vile words in English and there are other words and expressions that are used only in countries where blasphemy keeps pace with the austerity of religion. Lieutenant Berrendo was a very devout Catholic. So was the sniper. They were Carlists from Navarra and while both of them cursed and blasphemed when they were angry they regarded it as a sin which they regularly confessed.

As they crouched now behind the boulder watching the captain and listening to what he was shouting, they both disassociated themselves from him and what he was saying. They did not want to have that sort of talk on their consciences on a day in which they might die. Talking thus will not bring luck, the sniper thought. Speaking thus of the *Virgen* is bad luck. This one speaks worse than the Reds.

Julián is dead, Lieutenant Berrendo was thinking. Dead there on the slope on such a day as this is. And this foul mouth stands there bringing more ill fortune with his blasphemies.

Now the captain stopped shouting and turned to Lieutenant Berrendo. His eyes looked stranger than ever.

'Paco,' he said, happily, 'you and I will go up there.'

'Not me.'

'What?' The captain had his pistol out again.

I hate these pistol brandishers, Berrendo was thinking. They cannot give an order without jerking a gun out. They probably pull out their pistols when they go to the toilet and order the move they will make.

'I will go if you order me to. But under protest,' Lieutenant Berrendo told the captain.

'Then I will go alone,' the captain said. 'The smell of cowardice is too strong here.'

Holding his pistol in his right hand, he strode steadily up the slope. Berrendo and the sniper watched him. He was making no attempt to take any cover and he was looking straight ahead of him at the rocks, the dead horse, and the fresh-dug dirt of the hilltop.

El Sordo lay behind the horse at the corner of the rock, watching the captain come striding up the hill.

Only one, he thought. We get only one. But from his manner of speaking he is *caza mayor*. Look at him walking. Look what an animal. Look at him stride forward. This one is for me. This one I take with me on the trip. This one coming now makes the same voyage I do. Come on, Comrade Voyager. Come striding. Come right along. Come along to meet it. Come on. Keep on walking. Don't slow up. Come right along. Come as thou art coming. Don't stop and look at those. That's right. Don't even look down. Keep on coming with your eyes forward. Look, he has a moustache. What do you think of that? He runs to a moustache, the Comrade Voyager. He is a captain. Look at his sleeves. I said he was *caza mayor*. He has the face of an *Inglés*. Look. With a red face and blond hair and blue eyes. With no cap on and his moustache is yellow. With blue eyes. With pale blue eyes. With pale blue eyes with something wrong with them. With pale blue eyes that don't focus. Close enough. Too close. Yes, Comrade Voyager. Take it, Comrade Voyager.

He squeezed the trigger of the automatic rifle gently and it pounded back three times against his shoulder with the slippery jolt the recoil of a tripoded automatic weapon gives.

The captain lay on his face on the hillside. His left arm was under him. His right arm that had held the pistol was stretched forward of his head. From all down the slope they were firing on the hill crest again.

Crouched behind the boulder, thinking that now he would have to sprint across that open space under fire, Lieutenant Berrendo heard the deep hoarse voice of Sordo from the hilltop.

'*Bandidos!*' the voice came. '*Bandidos!* Shoot me! Kill me!'

On the top of the hill El Sordo lay behind the automatic rifle laughing so that his chest ached, so that he thought the top of his head would burst.

'*Bandidos*,' he shouted again happily. 'Kill me, *bandidos!*' Then he shook his head happily. We have lots of company for the Voyage, he thought.

He was going to try for the other officer with the automatic rifle when he would leave the shelter of the boulder. Sooner or later he would have to leave it. Sordo knew that he could never command from there and he thought he had a very good chance to get him.

Just then the others on the hill heard the first sound of the coming of the planes.

El Sordo did not hear them. He was covering the down-slope edge of the boulder with his automatic rifle and he was thinking: when I see him he will be running already and I will miss him if I am not careful. I could shoot behind him all across that stretch. I should swing the gun with him and ahead of him. Or let him start and then get on him and ahead of him. I will try to pick him up there at the edge of the rock and swing just ahead of him. Then he felt a touch on his shoulder and he turned and saw the grey, fear-drained face of Joaquín and he looked where the boy was pointing and saw the three planes coming.

At this moment Lieutenant Berrendo broke from behind the boulder and, with his head bent and his legs plunging, ran down and across the slope to the shelter of the rocks where the automatic rifle was placed.

Watching the planes, Sordo never saw him go.

'Help me to pull this out,' he said to Joaquín and the boy dragged the automatic rifle clear from between the horse and the rock.

The planes were coming on steadily. They were in echelon and each second they grew larger and their noise was greater.

'Lie on your backs to fire at them,' Sordo said. 'Fire ahead of them as they come.'

He was watching them all the time. '*Cabrones! Hijos de puta!*' he said rapidly.

'Ignacio!' he said. 'Put the gun on the shoulder of the boy.' 'Thou!' to Joaquín, 'Sit there and do not move. Crouch over. More. No. More.'

He lay back and sighted with the automatic rifle as the planes came on steadily.

'Thou, Ignacio, hold me the three legs of that tripod.' They were dangling down the boy's back and the muzzle of the gun was shaking from the jerking of his body that Joaquín could not control as he crouched with bent head hearing the droning roar of their coming.

Lying flat on his belly and looking up into the sky watching them come, Ignacio gathered the legs of the tripod into his two hands and steadied the gun.

'Keep thy head down,' he said to Joaquín. 'Keep thy head forward.'

'Pasionaria says "Better to die on thy—"' Joaquín was saying to himself as the drone came nearer them. Then he shifted suddenly into 'Hail Mary, full of grace, the Lord is with thee; Blessed art thou among women and Blessed is the fruit of thy womb, Jesus. Holy Mary, Mother of God, pray for us sinners now and at the hour of our death. Amen. Holy Mary, Mother of God,' he started, then he remembered quickly as the roar came now unbearably and started an act of contrition racing in it, 'Oh my God, I am heartily sorry for having offended thee who art worthy of all my love—'

Then there were the hammering explosions past his ears and the gun barrel hot against his shoulder. It was hammering now again and his ears were deafened by the muzzle blast. Ignacio was pulling down hard on the tripod and the barrel was burning his back. It was hammering now in the roar and he could not remember the act of contrition.

All he could remember was at the hour of our death. Amen. At the hour of our death. Amen. At the hour. At the hour. Amen. The others all were firing. Now and at the hour of our death. Amen.

Then, through the hammering of the gun, there was the whistle of the air splitting apart and then in the red black roar the earth rolled under his knees and then waved up to hit him in the face and then dirt and bits of rock were falling all over and Ignacio was lying on him and the gun was lying on him. But he was not dead because the whistle came again and the earth rolled under him with the roar. Then it came again and the earth lurched under his belly and one side of the hilltop rose into the air and then fell slowly over them where they lay.

The planes came back three times and bombed the hilltop but no one on the hilltop knew it. Then the planes machine-gunned the hilltop and went away. As they dived on the hill for the last time with their machine guns hammering, the first plane pulled up and winged over and then each plane did the same and they moved from echelon to V-formation and went away into the sky in the direction of Segovia.

Keeping a heavy fire on the hilltop, Lieutenant Berrendo pushed a patrol up to one of the bomb craters from where they could throw grenades on to the crest. He was taking no chances of anyone being alive and waiting for them in the mess that was up there and he threw four grenades into the confusion of dead horses, broken and split rocks, and torn yellow-stained explosive-stinking earth before he climbed out of the bomb crater and walked over to have a look.

No one was alive on the hilltop except the boy Joaquín, who was unconscious under the dead body of Ignacio. Joaquín was bleeding from the nose and from the ears. He had known nothing and had no feeling since he had suddenly been in the very heart of the thunder and the breath had been wrenched from his body when the one bomb struck so close and Lieutenant Berrendo made the sign of the cross and then shot him in the back of the head, as quickly and as gently, if such an abrupt movement can be gentle, as Sordo had shot the wounded horse.

Lieutenant Berrendo stood on the hilltop and looked down the slope at his own dead and then across the country seeing where they had galloped before Sordo had turned at bay here. He noticed all the dispositions that had been made of the troops and then he ordered the dead men's horses to be brought up and the bodies tied across the saddles so that they might be packed in to La Granja.

'Take that one, too,' he said. 'The one with his hands on the automatic rifle. That should be Sordo. He is the oldest and it was he with the gun. No. Cut the head off and wrap it in a poncho.' He considered a minute. 'You might as well take all the heads. And of the others below on the slope and where we first found them. Collect the rifles and pistols and pack that gun on a horse.'

Then he walked down to where the lieutenant lay who had been killed in the first assault. He looked down at him but did not touch him.

'*Qué cosa más mala es la guerra*,' he said to himself, which meant, 'What a bad thing war is.'

Then he made the sign of the cross again and as he walked down the hill he said five Our Fathers and five Hail Marys for the repose of the soul of his dead comrade. He did not wish to stay to see his orders being carried out.

28

After the planes went away Robert Jordan and Primitivo heard the firing start and his heart seemed to start again with it. A cloud of smoke drifted over the last ridge that he could see in the high country and the planes were three steadily receding specks in the sky.

'They've probably bombed hell out of their own cavalry and never touched Sordo and Company,' Robert Jordan said to himself. 'The damned planes scare you to death but they don't kill you.'

'The combat goes on,' Primitivo said, listening to the heavy firing. He had winced at each bomb thud and now he licked his dry lips.

'Why not?' Robert Jordan said. 'Those things never kill anybody.'

Then the firing stopped absolutely and he did not hear another shot. Lieutenant Berrendo's pistol shot did not carry that far.

When the firing stopped it did not affect him. Then as the quiet kept on a hollow feeling came in his chest. Then he heard the grenades burst and for a moment his heart rose. Then everything was quiet again and the quiet kept on and he knew that it was over.

Maria came up from the camp with a tin bucket of stewed hare with mushrooms sunken in the rich gravy and a sack with bread, a leather wine bottle, four tin plates, two cups and four spoons. She stopped at the gun and ladled out two plates for Agustín and Eladio, who had replaced Anselmo at the gun, and gave them bread and unscrewed the horn tip of the wine bottle and poured two cups of wine.

Robert Jordan watched her climbing lithely up to his lookout post, the sack over her shoulder, the bucket in one hand, her cropped head bright in the sun. He climbed down and took the bucket and helped her up the last boulder.

'What did the aviation do?' she asked, her eyes frightened.

'Bombed Sordo.'

He had the bucket open and was ladling out stew on to a plate.

'Are they still fighting?'

'No. It is over.'

'Oh,' she said, and bit her lip and looked out across the country.

'I have no appetite,' Primitivo said.

'Eat anyway,' Robert Jordan told him.

'I could not swallow food.'

'Take a drink of this, man,' Robert Jordan said and handed him the wine bottle. 'Then eat.'

'This of Sordo has taken away desire,' Primitivo said. 'Eat, thou. I have no desire.'

Maria went over to him and put her arms around his neck and kissed him. 'Eat, old one,' she said. 'Each one should take care of his strength.'

Primitivo turned away from her. He took the wine bottle and tipping his head back swallowed steadily while he squirted a jet of wine into the back of his mouth. Then he filled his plate from the bucket and commenced to eat.

Robert Jordan looked at Maria and shook his head. She sat down by him and put her arm around his shoulder. Each knew how the other felt and they sat there and Robert Jordan ate the stew, taking time to appreciate the mushrooms completely, and he drank the wine and they said nothing.

'You may stay here, *guapa*, if you want,' he said after a while when the food was all eaten.

'Nay,' she said. 'I must go to Pilar.'

'It is all right to stay here. I do not think that anything will happen now.'

'Nay. I must go to Pilar. She is giving me instruction.'

'What does she give thee?'

'Instruction.' She smiled at him and then kissed him. 'Did you never hear of religious instruction?' She blushed. 'It is something like that.' She blushed again. 'But different.'

'Go to thy instruction,' he said and patted her on the head. She smiled at him again, then said to Primitivo, 'Do you want anything from below?'

'No, daughter,' he said. They both saw that he was still not yet recovered.

'*Salud*, old one,' she said to him.

'Listen,' Primitivo said. 'I have no fear to die but to leave them alone thus—' his voice broke.

'There was no choice,' Robert Jordan told him.

'I know. But all the same—'

'There was no choice,' Robert Jordan repeated. 'And now it is better not to speak of it.'

'Yes. But there alone with no aid from us—'

'Much better not to speak of it,' Robert Jordan said. 'And thou, *guapa*, get thee to thy instruction.'

He watched her climb down through the rocks. Then he sat there for a long time thinking and watching the high country.

Primitivo spoke to him but he did not answer. It was hot in the sun but he did not notice the heat while he sat watching the hill slopes and the long patches of pine trees that stretched up the highest slope. An hour passed and the sun was far to his left now when he saw them coming over the crest of the slope and he picked up his glasses.

The horses showed small and minute as the first two riders came into sight on the long green slope of the high hill. Then there were four more horsemen coming down, spread out across the wide hill and then through his glasses he saw the double column of men and horses ride into the sharp clarity of his vision. As he watched them he felt sweat come from his armpits and run down his flanks. One man rode at the head of the column. Then came more horsemen. Then came the riderless horses with their burdens tied across the saddles. Then there were two riders. Then came the wounded with men walking by them as they rode. Then came more cavalry to close the column.

Robert Jordan watched them ride down the slope and out of sight among the trees. He could not see at that distance the load one saddle bore of a long rolled poncho tied at each end and at intervals so that it bulged between each lashing as a pod bulges with peas. This was tied across the saddle and at each end it was lashed to the stirrup leathers. Alongside this on the top of the saddle the automatic rifle Sordo had served was lashed arrogantly.

Lieutenant Berrendo, who was riding at the head of the column, his flankers out, his point pushed well forward, felt no arrogance. He felt only the hollowness that comes after action. He was thinking: taking the heads is barbarous. But proof and identification is necessary. I will have trouble enough about this as it is and who knows? This of the heads may appeal to them. There are those of them who like such things. It is possible they will send them all to Burgos. It is a barbarous business. The planes were *muchos*. Much. Much. But we could have done it all, and almost without losses, with a Stokes mortar. Two mules to carry the shells and a mule with a mortar on each side of the pack saddle. What an army we would be then! With the fire power of all these automatic weapons. And another mule. No, two mules to carry ammunition. Leave it alone, he told himself. It is no longer cavalry. Leave it alone. You're building yourself an army. Next you will want a mountain gun.

Then he thought of Julián, dead on the hill, dead now, tied across a horse there in the first troop, and as he rode down into the dark pine forest, leaving the sunlight behind him on the hill, riding now in the quiet dark of the forest, he started to say a prayer for him again.

'Hail, holy queen mother of mercy,' he started. 'Our life, our sweetness and our hope. To thee do we send up our sighs, mournings and weepings in this valley of tears—'

He went on with the prayer, the horses' hooves soft on the fallen pine needles, the light coming through the tree trunks in patches as it comes through the columns of a cathedral, and as he prayed he looked ahead to see his flankers riding through the trees.

He rode out of the forest on to the yellow road that led into La Granja and the horses' hooves raised a dust that hung over them as they rode. It powdered the dead who were tied face down across the saddles and the wounded, and those who walked beside them, were in thick dust.

It was here that Anselmo saw them ride past in their dust.

He counted the dead and the wounded and he recognized Sordo's automatic rifle. He did not know what the poncho wrapped bundle was which flapped against the led horse's flanks as the stirrup leathers swung, but when, on his way home, he came in the dark on to the hill where Sordo had fought, he knew at once what the long poncho roll contained. In the dark he could not tell who had been up on the hill. But he counted those that lay there and then made off across the hills for Pablo's camp.

Walking alone in the dark, with a fear like a freezing of his heart from the feeling the holes of the bomb craters had given him, from them and from what he had found on the hill, he put all thought of the next day out of his mind. He simply walked as fast as he could to bring the news. And as he walked he prayed for the souls of Sordo and of all his band. It was the first time he had prayed since the start of the movement.

'Most kind, most sweet, most clement Virgin,' he prayed.

But he could not keep from thinking of the next day finally. So he thought: I will do exactly as the *Inglés* says and as he says to do it. But let me be close to him, O Lord, and may his instructions be exact for I do not think that I could control myself under the bombardment of the planes. Help me, O Lord, to-morrow to comport myself as a man should in his last hours. Help me, O Lord, to understand clearly the needs of the day. Help me, O Lord, to dominate the movement of my legs that I should not run when the bad moment comes. Help me, O Lord, to comport myself as a man to-morrow in the day of battle. Since I have asked this aid of thee, please grant it, knowing I would not ask it if it were not serious, and I will ask nothing more of thee again.

Walking in the dark alone he felt much better from having prayed and he was sure, now, that he would comport himself well. Walking now down from the high country, he went back to praying for the people of Sordo and in a short time he had reached the upper post where Fernando challenged him.

'It is I,' he answered, 'Anselmo.'

'Good,' Fernando said.

'You know of this of Sordo, old one?' Anselmo asked Fernando, the two of them standing at the entrance of the big rocks in the dark.

'Why not?' Fernando said. 'Pablo has told us.'

'He was up there?'

'Why not?' Fernando said stolidly. 'He visited the hill as soon as the cavalry left.'

'He told you—'

'He told us all,' Fernando said. 'What barbarians these fascists are! We must do away with all such barbarians in Spain.' He stopped, then said bitterly, 'In them is lacking all conception of dignity.'

Anselmo grinned in the dark. An hour ago he could not have imagined that he would ever smile again. What a marvel, that Fernando, he thought.

'Yes,' he said to Fernando. 'We must teach them. We must take away their planes, their automatic weapons, their tanks, their artillery, and teach them dignity.'

'Exactly,' Fernando said. 'I am glad that you agree.'

Anselmo left him standing there alone with his dignity and went on down to the cave.

29

Anselmo found Robert Jordan sitting at the plank table inside the cave with Pablo opposite him. They had a bowl poured full of wine between them and each had a cup of wine on the table. Robert Jordan had his notebook out and he was holding a pencil. Pilar and Maria were in the back of the cave out of sight. There was no way for Anselmo to know that the woman was keeping the girl back there to keep her from hearing the conversation and he thought that it was odd that Pilar was not at the table.

Robert Jordan looked up as Anselmo came in under the blanket that hung over the opening. Pablo stared straight at the table. His eyes were focused on the wine bowl but he was not seeing it.

'I come from above,' Anselmo said to Robert Jordan.

'Pablo has told us,' Robert Jordan said.

'There were six dead on the hill and they had taken the heads,' Anselmo said. 'I was there in the dark.'

Robert Jordan nodded. Pablo sat there looking at the wine bowl and saying nothing. There was no expression on his face and his small pig-eyes were looking at the wine bowl as though he had never seen one before.

'Sit down,' Robert Jordan said to Anselmo.

The old man sat down at the table on one of the hide-covered stools and Robert Jordan reached under the table and brought up the pinch-bottle of whisky that had been the gift of Sordo. It was about half-full. Robert Jordan reached down the table for a cup and poured a drink of whisky into it and shoved it along the table to Anselmo.

'Drink that, old one,' he said.

Pablo looked from the wine bowl to Anselmo's face as he drank and then he looked back at the wine bowl.

As Anselmo swallowed the whisky he felt a burning in his nose, his eyes and his mouth, and then a happy, comforting warmth in his stomach. He wiped his mouth with the back of his hand.

Then he looked at Robert Jordan and said, 'Can I have another?'

'Why not?' Robert Jordan said and poured another drink from the bottle and handed it this time instead of pushing it.

This time there was not the burning when he swallowed but the warm comfort doubled. It was as good a thing for his spirit as a saline injection is for a man who has suffered a great haemorrhage.

The old man looked toward the bottle again.

'The rest is for to-morrow,' Robert Jordan said. 'What passed on the road, old one?'

'There was much movement,' Anselmo said. 'I have it all noted down as you showed me. I have one watching for me and noting now. Later I will go for her report.'

'Did you see anti-tank guns? Those on rubber tyres with the long barrels?'

'Yes,' Anselmo said. 'There were four camions which passed on the road. In each of them there was such a gun with pine branches spread across the barrels. In the trucks rode six men with each gun.'

'Four guns, you say?' Robert Jordan asked him.

'Four,' Anselmo said. He did not look at his papers.

'Tell me what else went up the road.'

While Robert Jordan noted Anselmo told him everything he had seen move past him on the road. He told it from the beginning and in order with the wonderful memory of those who cannot read or write, and twice, while he was talking, Pablo reached out for more wine from the bowl.

'There was also the cavalry which entered La Granja from the high country where El Sordo fought,' Anselmo went on.

Then he told the number of the wounded he had seen and the number of the dead across the saddles.

'There was a bundle packed across one saddle that I did not understand,' he said. 'But now I know it was the heads.' He went on without pausing. 'It was a squadron of cavalry. They had only one officer left. He was not the one who was here in the early morning when you were by the gun. He must have been one of the dead. Two of the dead were officers by their sleeves. They were lashed face down over the saddles, their arms hanging. Also they had the *máquina* of El Sordo tied to the saddle that bore the heads. The barrel was bent. That is all,' he finished.

'It is enough,' Robert Jordan said and dipped his cup into the wine bowl. 'Who beside you has been through the lines to the side of the Republic?'

'Andrés and Eladio.'

'Which is the better of those two?'

'Andrés.'

'How long would it take him to get to Navacerrada from here?'

'Carrying no pack and taking his precautions, in three hours with luck. We came by a longer, safer route because of the material.'

'He can surely make it?'

'No *sé*, there is no such thing as surely.'

'Not for thee either?'

'Nay.'

That decides that, Robert Jordan thought to himself. If he had said that he could make it surely, surely I would have sent him.

'Andrés can get there as well as thee?'

'As well or better. He is younger.'

'But this must absolutely get there.'

'If nothing happens he will get there. If anything happens it could happen to anyone.'

'I will write a dispatch and send it by him,' Robert Jordan said. 'I will explain to him where he can find the General. He will be at the Estado Mayor of the Division.'

'He will not understand all this of divisions and all,' Anselmo said.

'Always has it confused me. He should have the name of the General and where he can be found.'

'But it is at the Estado Mayor of the Division that he will be found.'

'But is that not a place?'

'Certainly it is a place, old one,' Robert Jordan explained patiently. 'But it is a place the General will have selected. It is where he will make his headquarters for the battle.'

'Where is it then?' Anselmo was tired and the tiredness was making him stupid. Also words like Brigades, Divisions, Army Corps confused him. First there had been columns, then there were regiments, then there were brigades. Now there were brigades and divisions, both. He did not understand. A place was a place.

'Take it slowly, old one,' Robert Jordan said. He knew that if he could not make Anselmo understand he could never explain it clearly to Andrés either. 'The Estado Mayor of the Division is a place the General will have picked to set up his organization to command. He commands a division, which is two brigades. I do not know where it is because I was not there when it was picked. It will probably be a cave or dugout, a refuge, and wires will run to it. Andrés must ask for the General and for the Estado Mayor of the Division. He must give this to the General or to the Chief of his Estado Mayor or to another whose name I will write. One of them will surely be there even if the others are out inspecting the preparations for the attack. Do you understand now?'

'Yes.'

'Then get Andrés and I will write it now and seal it with this seal.' He showed him the small, round, wooden-backed rubber stamp with the seal of the S.I.M. and the round, tin-covered inking pad no bigger than a fifty-cent piece he carried in his pocket. 'That seal they will honour. Get Andrés now and I will explain to him. He must go quickly but first he must understand.'

'He will understand if I do. But you must make it very clear. This of staffs and divisions is a mystery to me. Always have I gone to such things as definite places such as a house. In Navacerrada it is in the old hotel where the place of command is. In Guadarrama it is in a house with a garden.'

'With this General,' Robert Jordan said, 'it will be some place very close to the lines. It will be underground to protect it from the planes. Andrés will find it easily by asking, if he knows what to ask for. He will only need to show what I have written. But fetch him now for this should get there quickly.'

Anselmo went out, ducking under the hanging blanket. Robert Jordan commenced writing in his notebook.

'Listen, *Inglés*,' Pablo said, still looking at the wine bowl.

'I am writing,' Robert Jordan said without looking up.

'Listen, *Inglés*,' Pablo spoke directly to the wine bowl. 'There is no need to be disheartened in this. Without Sordo we have plenty of people to take the posts and blow thy bridge.'

'Good,' Robert Jordan said without stopping writing.

'Plenty,' Pablo said. 'I have admired thy judgment much to-day, *Inglés*,' Pablo told the wine bowl. 'I think thou hast much *picardia*. That thou are smarter than I am. I have confidence in thee.'

Concentrating on his report to Golz, trying to put it in the fewest words and still make it absolutely convincing, trying to put it so the attack would be cancelled, absolutely, yet convince them he wasn't trying to have it called off because of any fears he might have about the danger of his own mission, but wished only to put them in possession of all the facts, Robert Jordan was hardly half listening.

'*Inglés*,' Pablo said.

'I am writing,' Robert Jordan told him without looking up.

I probably should send two copies, he thought. But if I do we will not have enough people to blow it if I have to blow it. What do I know about why this attack is made? Maybe it is only a holding attack. Maybe they want to draw those troops from somewhere else. Perhaps they make it to draw those planes from the North. Maybe that is what it is about. Perhaps it is not expected to succeed. What do I know about it? This is my report to Golz. I do not blow the bridge until the attack starts. My orders are clear and if the attack is called off I blow nothing. But I've got to keep enough people here for the bare minimum necessary to carry the orders out.

'What did you say?' he asked Pablo.

'That I have confidence, *Inglés*.' Pablo was still addressing the wine bowl.

Man, I wish I had, Robert Jordan thought. He went on writing.

30

So now everything had been done that there was to do that night. All orders had been given. Everyone knew exactly what he was to do in the morning. Andrés had been gone three hours. Either it would come now with the coming of the daylight or it would not come. I believe that it will come, Robert Jordan told himself, walking back down from the upper post where he had gone to speak to Primitivo.

Golz makes the attack but he has not the power to cancel it. Permission to cancel it will have to come from Madrid. The chances are they won't be able to wake anybody up there and if they do wake up they will be too sleepy to think. I should have gotten the word to Golz sooner of the preparations they have made to meet the attack, but how could I send word about something until it happened? They did not move up that stuff until just at dark. They did not want to have any movement on the road spotted by planes. But what about all their planes? What about those fascist planes?

Surely our people must have been warned by them. But perhaps the fascists were faking for another offensive down through Guadalajara with them. There were supposed to be Italian troops concentrated in Soria, and at Siguenza again besides those operating in the North. They haven't enough troops or material to run two major offensives at the same time though. That is impossible; so it must be just a bluff.

But we know how many troops the Italians have landed all last month and the month before at Cadiz. It is always possible they will try again at Guadalajara, not stupidly as before, but with three main fingers coming down to broaden it out and carry it along the railway to the west of the plateau. There was a way that they could do it all right. Hans had shown him. They made many mistakes the first time. The whole conception was unsound. They had not used any of the same troops in the Arganda offensive against the Madrid–Valencia road that they used at Guadalajara. Why had they not made those same drives simultaneously? Why? Why? When would we know why?

Yet we had stopped them both times with the very same troops. We never could have stopped them if they had pulled both drives at once. Don't worry, he told himself. Look at the miracles that have happened before this. Either you will have to blow that bridge in the morning or you will not have to. But do not start deceiving yourself into thinking you won't have to blow it. You will blow it one day or you will blow it another. Or if it is not this bridge it will be some other bridge. It is not you who decides what shall be done. You follow orders. Follow them and do not try to think beyond them.

The orders on this are very clear. Too very clear. But you must not worry nor must you be frightened. For if you allow yourself the luxury of normal fear that fear will infect those who must work with you.

But that heads business was quite a thing all the same, he told himself. And the old man running on to them on the hilltop alone. How would you have liked to run into them like that? That impressed you, didn't it? Yes, that impressed you, Jordan. You have been quite impressed more than once today. But you have behaved O.K. So far you have behaved all right.

You do very well for an instructor in Spanish at the University of Montana, he joked at himself. You do all right for that. But do not start thinking that you are anything very special. You haven't gotten very far in this business. Just remember Durán, who never had any military training and who was a composer and lad about town before the movement and is now a damned good general commanding a brigade. It was all as simple and easy to learn and understand to Durán as chess to a child chess prodigy. You had read on and studied the art of war ever since you were a boy and your grandfather had started you on the American Civil War. Except that Grandfather always called it the War of the Rebellion. But compared with Durán you were like a good sound chess player against a boy prodigy. Old Durán. It would be good to see Durán again. He would see him at Gaylord's after this was over. Yes. After this was over. See how well he was behaving?

I'll see him at Gaylord's, he said to himself again, after this is over. Don't kid yourself, he said. You do it all perfectly O.K. Cold. Without kidding yourself. You aren't going to see Durán any more and it is of no importance. Don't be that way either, he told himself. Don't go in for any of those luxuries.

Nor for heroic resignation either. We do not want any citizens full of heroic resignation in these hills. Your grandfather fought four years in our Civil War and you are just finishing your first year in this war. You have a long time to go yet and you are very well fitted for the work. And now you have Maria, too. Why, you've got everything. You shouldn't worry. What is a little brush between a guerrilla band and a squadron of cavalry? That isn't anything. What if they took the heads? Does that make any difference? None at all.

The Indians always took the scalps when Grandfather was at Fort Kearny after the war. Do you remember the cabinet in your father's office with the arrowheads spread out on a shelf, and the eagle feathers of the war bonnets that hung on the wall, their plumes slanting, the smoked buckskin smell of the leggings and the shirts and the feel of the beaded moccasins? Do you remember the great stave of the buffalo bow that leaned in a corner of the cabinet and the two quivers of hunting and war arrows, and how the bundle of shafts felt when you closed your hand around them?

Remember something like that. Remember something concrete and practical. Remember Grandfather's sabre, bright and well oiled in its dented scabbard and Grandfather showed you how the blade had been thinned from the many times it had been to the grinder's. Remember Grandfather's Smith and Wesson. It was a single action, officer's model .32 calibre and there was no trigger guard. It had the softest, sweetest trigger pull you had ever felt and it was always well oiled and the bore was clean although the finish was all worn off and the brown metal of the barrel and the cylinder was worn smooth from the leather of the holster. It was kept in the holster with a U.S. on the flap in a drawer in the cabinet with its cleaning equipment and two hundred rounds of cartridges. Their cardboard boxes were wrapped and tied neatly with waxed twine.

You could take the pistol out of the drawer and hold it. 'Handle it freely,' was Grandfather's expression. But you could not play with it because it was 'a serious weapon'.

You asked Grandfather once if he had ever killed anyone with it and he said, 'Yes.'

Then you said, 'When, Grandfather?' and he said, 'In the War of the Rebellion and afterwards.'

You said, 'Will you tell me about it, Grandfather?'

And he said, 'I do not care to speak about it, Robert.'

Then after your father had shot himself with this pistol and you had come home from school and they'd had the funeral, the coroner had returned it after the inquest saying, 'Bob, I guess you might want to keep the gun. I'm supposed to hold it, but I know your dad set a lot of store by it because his dad packed it all through the War, besides out here when he first came out with the Cavalry, and it's still a hell of a good gun. I had her out trying her this afternoon. She don't throw much of a slug but you can hit things with her.'

He had put the gun back in the drawer in the cabinet where it belonged, but the next day he took it out and he had ridden up to the top of the high country above Red Lodge, with Chub, where they had built the road to Cooke City now over the pass and across the Bear Tooth plateau, and up there where the wind was thin and there was snow all summer on the hills they had stopped by the lake which was supposed to be eight hundred feet deep and was a deep green colour, and Chub held the two horses and he climbed out on a rock and leaned over and saw his face in the still water, and saw himself holding the gun, and then he dropped it, holding it by the muzzle, and saw it go down making bubbles until it was just as big as a watch charm in that clear water, and then it was out of sight. Then he came back off the rock and when he swung up into the saddle he gave old Bess such a clout with the spurs she started to buck like an old rocking horse. He bucked her out along the shore of the lake and as soon as she was reasonable they went on back along the trail.

'I know why you did that with the old gun, Bob,' Chub said.

'Well, then we don't have to talk about it,' he had said.

They never talked about it and that was the end of Grandfather's side arms except for the sabre. He still had the sabre in his trunk with the rest of his things at Missoula.

I wonder what Grandfather would think of this situation, he thought. Grandfather was a hell of a good soldier, everybody said. They said if he had been with Custer that day he never would have let him be sucked in that way. How could he ever not have seen the smoke nor the dust of all those lodges down there in the draw along the Little Big Horn unless there must have been a heavy morning mist? But there wasn't any mist.

I wish Grandfather were here instead of me. Well, maybe we will be altogether by to-morrow night. If there should be any such damn fool business as a hereafter, and I'm sure there isn't, he thought, I would certainly like to talk to him. Because there are a lot of things I would like to know. I have a right to ask him now because I have had to do the same sort of things myself. I don't think he'd mind my asking now. I had no right to ask before. I understand him not telling me because he didn't know me. But now I think that we would get along all right. I'd like to be able to talk to him now and get his advice. Hell, if I didn't get advice I'd just like to talk to him. It's a shame there is such a jump in time between ones like us.

Then, as he thought, he realized that if there was any such thing as ever meeting, both he and his grandfather would be acutely embarrassed by the presence of his father. Anyone has a right to do it, he thought. But it isn't a good thing to do. I understand it, but I do not approve of it. *Lache* was the word. But you *do* understand it? Sure, I understand it, but. Yes, but. You have to be awfully occupied with yourself to do a thing like that.

Aw hell, I wish Grandfather was here, he thought. For about an hour anyway. Maybe he sent me what little I have through that other one that misused the gun. Maybe that is the only communication that we have. But, damn it. Truly, damn it, but I wish the time-lag wasn't so long so that I could have learned from him what the other one never had to teach me. But suppose the fear he had to go through and dominate and just get rid of finally in four years of that and then in the Indian fighting, although in that, mostly, there couldn't have been so much fear, had made a *cobarde* out of the other one the way second generation bullfighters almost always are? Suppose that? And maybe the good juice only came through straight again after passing through that one?

I'll never forget how sick it made me the first time I knew he was a *cobarde*. Go on, say it in English. Coward. It's easier when you have it said and there is never any point in referring to a son of a bitch by some foreign term. He wasn't any son of a bitch, though. He was just a coward and that was the worst luck any man could have. Because if he wasn't a coward he would have stood up to that woman and not let her bully him. I wonder what I would have been like if he had married a different woman? That's something you'll never know, he thought, and grinned. Maybe the bully in her helped to supply what was missing in the other. And you. Take it a little easy. Don't get to referring to the good juice and such other things until you are through to-morrow. Don't be snotty too soon. And then don't be snotty at all. We'll see what sort of juice you have to-morrow.

But he started thinking about Grandfather again.

'George Custer was not an intelligent leader of cavalry, Robert,' his grandfather had said. 'He was not even an intelligent man.'

He remembered that when his grandfather said that he felt resentment that anyone should speak against that figure in the buckskin shirt, the yellow curls blowing, that stood on that hill holding a service revolver as the Sioux closed in around him in the old Anheuser-Busch lithograph that hung on the poolroom wall in Red Lodge.

'He just had great ability to get himself in and out of trouble,' his grandfather went on, 'and on the Little Big Horn he got into it but he couldn't get out.

'Now Phil Sheridan was an intelligent man and so was Jeb Stuart. But John Mosby was the finest cavalry leader that ever lived.'

He had a letter in his things in the trunk at Missoula from General Phil Sheridan to old Killy-the-Horse Kilpatrick that said his grandfather was a finer leader of irregular cavalry than John Mosby.

I ought to tell Golz about my grandfather, he thought. He wouldn't ever have heard of him though. He probably never even heard of John Mosby. The British all had heard of them though because they had to study our Civil War much more than people did on the Continent. Karkov said after this was over I could go to the Lenin Institute in Moscow if I wanted to. He said I could go to the military academy of the Red Army if I wanted to do that. I wonder what Grandfather would think of that? Grandfather, who never knowingly sat at a table with a Democrat in his life.

Well, I don't want to be a soldier, he thought. I know that. So that's out. I just want us to win this war. I guess really good soldiers are really good at very little else, he thought. That's obviously untrue. Look at Napoleon and Wellington. You're very stupid this evening, he thought.

Usually his mind was very good company and to-night it has been when he thought about his grandfather. Then thinking of his father had thrown him off. He understood his father and he forgave him everything and he pitied him but he was ashamed of him.

You better not think at all, he told himself. Soon you will be with Maria and you won't have to think. That's the best way now that everything is worked out. When you have been concentrating so hard on something you can't stop and your brain gets to racing like a flywheel with the weight gone. You'd better just not think.

But just suppose, he thought. Just suppose that when the planes unload they smash those anti-tank guns and just blow hell out of the positions and the old tanks roll good up whatever hill it is for once and old Golz boots that bunch of drunks, *clochards*, bums, fanatics and heroes that make up the Quatorzième Brigade ahead of him, and I *know* how good Durán's people are in Golz's other brigade, and we are in Segovia to-morrow night.

Yes. Just suppose he said to himself. I'll settle for La Granja, he told himself. But you are going to have to blow that bridge, he suddenly knew absolutely. There won't be any calling off. Because the way you have just been supposing there for a minute is how the possibilities of that attack look to those who have ordered it. Yes, you will have to blow the bridge, he knew truly. Whatever happens to Andrés doesn't matter.

Coming down the trail there in the dark, alone with the good feeling that everything that had to be done was over for the next four hours, and with the confidence that had come from thinking back to concrete things, the knowledge that he would surely have to blow the bridge came to him almost with comfort.

The uncertainty, the enlargement of the feeling of being uncertain, as when, through a misunderstanding of possible dates, one does not know whether the guests are really coming to a party, that had been with him ever since he had dispatched Andrés with the report to Golz, had all dropped from him now. He was sure now that the festival would not be cancelled. It's much better to be sure, he thought. It's always much better to be sure.

31

So now they were in the robe again together and it was late in the last night. Maria lay close against him and he felt the long smoothness of her thighs against his and her breasts like two small hills that rise out of the long plain where there is a well, and the far country beyond the hills was the valley of her throat where his lips were. He lay very quiet and did not think and she stroked his head with her hand.

'Roberto,' Maria said very softly and kissed him. 'I am ashamed. I do not wish to disappoint thee but there is a great soreness and much pain. I do not think I would be any good to thee.'

'There is always a great soreness and much pain,' he said. 'Nay, rabbit. That is nothing. We will do nothing that makes pain.'

'It is not that. It is that I am not good to receive thee as I wish to.'

'That is of no importance. That is a passing thing. We are together when we lie together.'

'Yes, but I am ashamed. I think it was from when the things were done to me that it comes. Not from thee and me.'

'Let us not talk of that.'

'Nor do I wish to. I meant I could not bear to fail thee now on this night and so I sought to excuse myself.'

'Listen, rabbit,' he said. 'All such things pass and then there is no problem.' But he thought; it was not good luck for the last night.

Then he was ashamed and said, 'Lie close against me, rabbit. I love thee as much feeling thee against me in here in the dark as I love thee making love.'

'I am deeply ashamed because I thought it might be again to-night as it was in the high country when we came down from El Sordo's.'

'*Qué va*,' he said to her. 'That is not for every day. I like it thus as well as the other.' He lied, putting aside disappointment. 'We will be here together quietly and we will sleep. Let us talk together. I know thee very little from talking.'

'Should we speak of to-morrow and of thy work? I would like to be intelligent about thy work.'

'No,' he said and relaxed completely into the length of the robe and lay now quietly with his cheek against her shoulder, his left arm under her head. 'The most intelligent is not to talk about to-morrow nor what happened to-day. In this we do not discuss the losses and what we must do to-morrow we will do. Thou art not afraid?'

'*Qué va*,' she said. 'I am always afraid. But now I am afraid for thee so much I do not think of me.'

'Thou must not, rabbit. I have been in many things. And worse than this,' he lied.

Then suddenly surrendering to something, to the luxury of going into unreality, he said, 'Let us talk of Madrid and of us in Madrid.'

'Good,' she said. Then, 'Oh, Roberto, I am sorry I have failed thee. Is there not some other thing that I can do for thee?'

He stroked her head and kissed her and then lay close and relaxed beside her, listening to the quiet of the night.

'Thou canst talk with me of Madrid,' he said and thought: I'll keep any over-supply of that for to-morrow. I'll need all of that there is to-morrow. There are no pine needles that need that now as I will need it to-morrow. Who was it cast his seed upon the ground in the Bible? Onan. How did Onan turn out? he thought. I don't remember ever hearing any more about Onan. He smiled in the dark.

Then he surrendered again and let himself slip into it, feeling a voluptuousness of surrender into unreality that was like a sexual acceptance of something that could come in the night when there was no understanding, only the delight of acceptance.

'My beloved,' he said, and kissed her. 'Listen. The other night I was thinking about Madrid and I thought how I would get there and leave thee at the hotel while I went up to see people at the hotel of the Russians. But that was false. I would not leave thee at any hotel.'

'Why not?'

'Because I will take care of thee. I will not ever leave thee. I will go with thee to the Seguridad to get papers. Then I will go with thee to buy those clothes that are needed.'

'They are few, and I can buy them.'

'Nay, they are many and we will go together and buy good ones and thou wilt be beautiful in them.'

'I would rather we stayed in the room in the hotel and sent out for the clothes. Where is the hotel?'

'It is on the Plaza del Callao. We will be much in that room in that hotel. There is a wide bed with clean sheets and there is hot running water in the bathtub and there are two closets and I will keep my things in one and thou wilt take the other. And there are tall, wide windows that open, and outside, in the streets, there is the spring. Also I know good places to eat that are illegal but with good food, and I know shops where there is still wine and whisky. And we will keep things to eat in the room for when we are hungry and also whisky for when I wish a drink and I will buy thee manzanilla.'

'I would like to try the whisky.'

'But since it is difficult to obtain and if thou likest manzanilla.'

'Keep thy whisky, Roberto,' she said. 'Oh, I love thee very much. Thou and thy whisky that I could not have. What a pig thou art.'

'Nay, you shall try it. But it is not good for a woman.'

'And I have only had things that were good for a woman,' Maria said. 'Then there in bed I will still wear my wedding shirt?'

'Nay. I will buy thee various nightgowns and pyjamas too if you should prefer them.'

'I will buy seven wedding shirts,' she said. 'One for each day of the week. And I will buy a clean wedding shirt for thee. Dost ever wash thy shirt?'

'Sometimes.'

'I will keep everything clean and I will pour thy whisky and put the water in it as it was done at Sordo's. I will obtain olives and salted codfish and hazel nuts for thee to eat while thou drinkest and we will stay in the room for a month and never leave it. If I am fit to receive thee,' she said, suddenly unhappy.

'That is nothing,' Robert Jordan told her. 'Truly it is nothing. It is possible thou wert hurt there once and now there is a scar that makes a further hurting. Such a thing is possible. All such things pass. And also there are good doctors in Madrid if there is truly anything.'

'But all was good before,' she said pleadingly.

'That is the promise that all will be good again.'

'Then let us talk again about Madrid.' She curled her legs between his and rubbed the top of her head against his shoulder. 'But will I not be so ugly there with this cropped head that thou wilt be ashamed of me?'

'Nay. Thou art lovely. Thou hast a lovely face and a beautiful body, long and light, and thy skin is smooth and the colour of burnt gold and everyone will try to take thee from me.'

'*Qué va*, take me from thee,' she said. 'No other man will ever touch me till I die. Take me from thee! *Qué va*.'

'But many will try. Thou wilt see.'

'They will see I love thee so that they will know it would be as unsafe as putting their hands into a cauldron of melted lead to touch me. But thou? When thou seest beautiful women of the same culture as thee? Thou wilt not be ashamed of me?'

'Never. And I will marry thee.'

'If you wish,' she said. 'But since we no longer have the Church I do not think it carries importance.'

'I would like us to be married.'

'If you wish. But listen. If we were ever in another country where there still was the Church perhaps we could be married in it there.'

'In my country they still have the Church,' he told her. 'There we can be married in it if it means aught to thee. I have never been married. There is no problem.'

'I am glad thou hast never been married,' she said. 'But I am glad thou knowest about such things as you have told me for that means thou hast been with many women and the Pilar told me that it is only such men who are possible for husbands. But thou wilt not run with other women now? Because it would kill me.'

'I have never run with many woman,' he said, truly. 'Until thee I did not think that I could love one deeply.'

She stroked his cheeks and then held her hands clasped behind his head. 'Thou must have known very many.'

'Not to love them.'

'Listen. The Pilar told me something—'

'Say it.'

'No. It is better not to. Let us talk again about Madrid.'

'What was it you were going to say?'

'I do not wish to say it.'

'Perhaps it would be better to say it if it could be important.'

'You think it is important?'

'Yes.'

'But how can you know when you do not know what it is?'

'From thy manner.'

'I will not keep it from you then. The Pilar told me that we would all die to-morrow and that you know it as well as she does and that you give it no importance. She said this not in criticism but in admiration.'

'She said that?' he said. The crazy bitch, he thought, and he said, 'That is more of her gipsy manure. That is the way old market women and café cowards talk. That is manuring obscenity.' He felt the sweat that came from under his armpits and slid down between his arm and his side and he said to himself, 'So you are scared, eh?' and aloud he said, 'She is a manure-mouthed superstitious bitch. Let us talk again of Madrid.'

'Then you know no such thing?'

'Of course not. Do not talk such manure,' he said, using a stronger, ugly word.

But this time when he talked about Madrid there was no slipping into make-believe again. Now he was just lying to his girl and to himself to pass the night before battle and he knew it. He liked to do it, but all the luxury of the acceptance was gone. But he started again.

'I have thought about thy hair,' he said. 'And what we can do about it. You see it grows now all over thy head the same length like the fur of an animal and it is lovely to feel and I love it very much and it is beautiful and it flattens and rises like a wheatfield in the wind when I pass my hand over it.'

'Pass thy hand over it.'

He did and left his hand there and went on talking to her throat as he felt his own throat swell. 'But in Madrid I thought we could go together to the coiffeur's and they could cut it neatly on the sides and at the back as they cut mine and that way it would look better in the town while it is growing out.'

'I would look like thee,' she said and held him close to her. 'And then I never would want to change it.'

'Nay. It will grow all the time and that will only be to keep it neat at the start while it is growing long. How long will it take it to grow long?'

'Really long?'

'No. I mean to thy shoulders. It is thus I would have thee wear it.'

'As Garbo in the cinema?'

'Yes,' he said thickly.

Now the making believe was coming back in a great rush and he would take it all to him. It had him now, and again he surrendered and went on. 'So it will hang straight to thy shoulders and curl at the ends as a wave of the sea curls, and it will be the colour of ripe wheat and thy face the colour of burnt gold and thine eyes the only colour they could be with thy hair and thy skin, gold with the dark flecks in them, and I will push thy head back and look in thy eyes and hold thee tight against me—'

'Where?'

'Anywhere. Wherever it is that we are. How long will it take for thy hair to grow?'

'I do not know because it never had been cut before. But I think in six months it should be long enough to hang well below my ears and in a year as long as thou couldst ever wish. But do you know what will happen first?'

'Tell me.'

'We will be in the big clean bed in thy famous room in our famous hotel and we will sit in the famous bed together and look into the mirror of the *armoire* and there will be thee and there will be me in the glass and then I will turn to thee thus, and put my arms around thee thus, and then I will kiss thee thus.'

Then they lay quiet and close together in the night, hot-aching, rigid, close together and holding her. Robert Jordan held closely too all those things that he knew could never happen, and he went on with it deliberately and said, 'Rabbit, we will not always live in that hotel.'

'Why not?'

'We can get an apartment in Madrid on that street that runs along the Parque of the Buen Retiro. I know an American woman who furnished apartments and rented them before the movement and I know how to get such an apartment for only the rent that was paid before the movement. There are apartments there that face on the park and you can see all the park from the windows; the iron fence, the gardens, and the gravel walks and the green of the lawns where they touch the gravel, and the trees deep with shadows and the many fountains, and now the chestnut trees will be in bloom. In Madrid we can walk in the park and row on the lake if the water is back in it now.'

'Why would the water be out?'

'They drained it in November because it made a mark to sight from when the planes came over for bombing. But I think that the water is back in it now. I am not sure. But even if there is no water in it we can walk through all the park away from the lake and there is a part that is like a forest with trees from all parts of the world with their names on them, with placards that tell what trees they are and where they come from.'

'I would almost as soon go to the cinema,' Maria said. 'But the trees sound very interesting and I will learn them all with thee if I can remember them.'

'They are not as in a museum,' Robert Jordan said. 'They grow naturally and there are hills in the park and part of the park is like a jungle. Then below it there is the book fair where along the sidewalks there are hundreds of booths with second-hand books in them and now, since the movement, there are many books, stolen in the looting of the houses which have been bombed and from the houses of the fascists, and brought to the book fair by those who stole them. I could spend all day every day at the stalls of the book fair as I once did in the days before the movement, if I ever could have any time in Madrid.'

'While thou art visiting the book fair I will occupy myself with the apartment,' Maria said. 'Will we have enough money for a servant?'

'Surely. I can get Petra who is at the hotel if she pleases thee. She cooks well and is clean. I have eaten there with newspapermen that she cooks for. They have electric stoves in their rooms.'

'If you wish her,' Maria said. 'Or I can find someone. But wilt thou not be away much with thy work? They would not let me go with thee on such work as this.'

'Perhaps I can get work in Madrid. I have done this work now for a long time and I have fought since the start of the movement. It is possible that they would give me work now in Madrid. I have never asked for it. I have always been at the front or in such work as this.

'Do you know that until I met thee I have never asked for anything? Nor wanted anything? Nor thought of anything except the movement and the winning of this war? Truly I have been very pure in my ambitions. I have worked much and now I love thee and,' he said it now in a complete embracing of all that would not be, 'I love thee as I love all that we have fought for. I love thee as I love liberty and dignity and the rights of all men to work and not be hungry. I love thee as I love Madrid that we have defended and as I love all my comrades that have died. And many have died. Many. Many. Thou canst not think how many. But I love thee as I love what I love most in the world and I love thee more. I love thee very much, rabbit. More than I can tell thee. But I say this now to tell thee a little. I have never had a wife and now I have thee for a wife and I am happy.'

'I will make thee as good a wife as I can,' Maria said. 'Clearly I am not well trained but I will try to make up for that. If we live in Madrid; good. If we must live in any other place; good. If we live nowhere and I can go with thee; better. If we go to thy country I will learn to talk *Inglés* like the most *Inglés* that there is. I will study all their manners and as they do so will I do.'

'Thou wilt be very comic.'

'Surely. I will make mistakes but you will tell me and I will never make them twice, or maybe only twice. Then in thy country if thou art lonesome for our food I can cook for thee. And I will go to a school to learn to be a wife, if there is such a school, and study at it.'

'There are such schools but thou dost not need that schooling.'

'Pilar told me that she thought they exist in your country. She had read of them in a periodical. And she told me also that I must learn to speak *Inglés* and to speak it well so thou wouldst never be ashamed of me.'

'When did she tell you this?'

'To-day while we were packing. Constantly she talked to me about what I should do to be thy wife.'

I guess she was going to Madrid too, Robert Jordan thought, and said, 'What else did she say?'

'She said I must take care of my body and guard the line of my figure as though I were a bullfighter. She said this was of great importance.'

'It is,' Robert Jordan said. 'But thou hast not to worry about that for many years.'

'No. She said those of our race must watch that always as it can come suddenly. She told me she was once as slender as I but that in those days women did not take exercise. She told me what exercises I should take and that I must not eat too much. She told me which things not to eat. But I have forgotten and must ask her again.'

'Potatoes,' he said.

'Yes,' she went on. 'It was potatoes and things that are fried. Also when I told her about this of the soreness she said I must not tell thee but must support the pain and not let thee know. But I told thee because I do not wish to lie to thee ever and also I feared that thou might think we did not have the joy in common any longer and that other, as it was in the high country, had not truly happened.'

'It was right to tell me.'

'Truly? For I am ashamed and I will do anything for thee that thou should wish. Pilar has told me of things one can do for a husband.'

'There is no need to do anything. What we have we have together and we will keep it and guard it. I love thee thus lying beside thee and touching thee and knowing thou art truly there and when thou art ready again we will have all.'

'But hast thou not necessities that I can care for? She explained that to me.'

'Nay. We will have our necessities together. I have no necessities apart from thee.'

'That seems much better to me. But understand always that I will do what you wish. But thou must tell me for I have great ignorance and much of what she told me I did not understand clearly. For I was ashamed to ask and she is of such great and varied wisdom.'

'Rabbit,' he said. 'Thou art very wonderful.'

'*Qué va*,' she said. 'But to try to learn all of that which goes into wifehood in a day while we are breaking camp and packing for a battle with another battle passing in the country above is a rare thing and if I make serious mistakes thou must tell me for I love thee. It could be possible for me to remember things incorrectly and much that she told me was very complicated.'

'What else did she tell thee?'

'*Pues* so many things I cannot remember them. She said I could tell thee of what was done to me if I ever began to think of it again because thou art a good man and already have understood it all. But that it were better never to speak of it unless it came on me as a black thing as it had been before and then that telling it to thee might rid me of it.'

'Does it weigh on thee now?'

'No. It is as though it had never happened since we were first together. There is the sorrow for my parents always. But that there will be always. But I would have thee know that which you should know for thy own pride if I am to be thy wife. Never did I submit to any one. Always I fought and always it took two of them or more to do me the harm. One would sit on my head and hold me. I tell thee this for thy pride.'

'My pride is in thee. Do not tell it.'

'Nay, I speak of thy own pride which it is necessary to have in thy wife. And another thing. My father was the mayor of the village and an honourable man. My mother was an honourable woman and a good Catholic and they shot her with my father because of the politics of my father who was a Republican. I saw both of them shot and my father said, "*Viva la República*," when they shot him standing against the wall of the slaughterhouse of our village.

'My mother standing against the same wall said, "Viva my husband who was the Mayor of this village," and I hoped they would shoot me too and I was going to say "*Viva la República y vivan mis padres*," but instead there was no shooting but instead the doing of the things.

'Listen. I will tell thee of one thing since it affects us. After the shooting at the *matadero* they took us, those relatives who had seen it but were not shot, back from the *matadero* up the steep hill into the main square of the town. Nearly all were weeping but some were numb with what they had seen and the tears had dried in them. I myself could not cry. I did not notice anything that passed for I could only see my father and my mother at the moment of the shooting and my mother saying, "Long live my husband who is Mayor of this village," and this was in my head like a scream that would not die but kept on and on. For my mother was not a Republican and she would not say, "*Viva la República*," but only *Viva* my father who lay there, on his face, by her feet.

'But what she had said, she had said very loud, like a shriek and then they shot and she fell and I tried to leave the line to go to her but we were all tied. The shooting was done by the *guardia civiles* and they were still there waiting to shoot more when the Falangist herded us away and up the hill leaving the *guardia civiles* leaning on their rifles and leaving all the bodies there against the wall. We were tied by the wrists in a long line of girls and women and they herded us up by the hill and through the streets to the square and in the square they stopped in front of the barber-shop which was across the square from the city hall.

'Then the two men looked at us and one said, "That is the daughter of the Mayor," and the other said, "Commence with her."

'Then they cut the rope that was on each of my wrists, one saying to others of them, "Tie up the line," and these two took me by the arms and into the barber-shop and lifted me up and put me in the barber's chair and held me there.

'I saw my face in the mirror of the barber-shop and the faces of those who were holding me and the faces of three others who were leaning over me and I knew none of their faces but in the glass I saw myself and them, but they saw only me. And it was as though one were in the dentist's chair and there were many dentists and they were all insane. My own face I could hardly recognize because my grief had changed it but I looked at it and knew that it was me. But my grief was so great that I had no fear nor any feeling but my grief.

'At that time I wore my hair in two braids and as I watched in the mirror one of them lifted one of the braids and pulled on it so it hurt me suddenly through my grief and then cut it off close to my head with a razor. And I saw myself with one braid and a slash where the other had been. Then he cut off the other braid but without pulling on it and the razor made a small cut on my ear and I saw blood come from it. Canst thou feel the scar with thy finger?'

'Yes. But would it be better not to talk of this?'

'This is nothing. I will not talk of that which is bad. So he had cut both braids close to my head with a razor and the others laughed and I did not even feel the cut on my ear and then he stood in front of me and struck me across the face with the braids while the other two held me and he said, "This is how we make Red nuns. This will show thee how to unite with thy proletarian brothers. Bride of the Red Christ!"

'And he struck me again and again across the face with the braids which had been mine and then he put the two of them in my mouth and tied them tight around my neck, knotting them in the back to make a gag and the two holding me laughed.

'And all of them who saw it laughed and when I saw them laugh in the mirror I commenced to cry because until then I had been too frozen in myself from the shooting to be able to cry.

'Then the one who had gagged me ran a clippers all over my head; first from the forehead all the way to the back of the neck and then across the top and then all over my head and close behind my ears and they held me so I could see into the glass of the barber's mirror all the time that they did this and I could not believe it as I saw it done and I cried and I cried but I could not look away from the horror that my face made with the mouth open and the braids tied in it and my head coming naked under the clippers.

'And when the one with the clippers was finished he took a bottle of iodine from the shelf of the barber (they had shot the barber too for he belonged to a syndicate, and he lay in the doorway of the shop and they had lifted me over him as they brought me in) and with the glass wand that is in the iodine bottle he touched me on the ear where it had been cut and the small pain of that came through my grief and through my horror.

'Then he stood in front of me and wrote U.H.P. on my forehead with the iodine, lettering it slowly and carefully as though he were an artist and I saw all of this as it happened in the mirror and I no longer cried for my heart was frozen in me for my father and my mother and what happened to me now was nothing and I knew it.

'Then when he had finished the lettering, the Falangist stepped back and looked at me to examine his work and then he put down the iodine bottle and picked up the clippers and said, "Next," and they took me out of the barber-shop holding me tight by each arm and I stumbled over the barber lying there still in the doorway on his back with his grey face up, and we nearly collided with Concepción Gracía, my best friend, that two of them were bringing in and when she saw me she did not recognize me, and then she recognized me, and she screamed, and I could hear her screaming all the time they were shoving me across the square, and into the doorway, and up the stairs of the city hall and into the office of my father where they laid me on to the couch. And it was there that the bad things were done.'

'My rabbit,' Robert Jordan said and held her as close and as gently as he could. But he was as full of hate as any man could be. 'Do not talk more about it. Do not tell me any more for I cannot bear my hatred now.'

She was stiff and cold in his arms and she said, 'Nay. I will never talk more of it. But they are bad people and I would like to kill some of them with thee if I could. But I have told thee this only for thy pride if I am to be thy wife. So thou wouldst understand.'

'I am glad you told me,' he said. 'For to-morrow, with luck, we will kill plenty.'

'But will we kill Falangists? It was they who did it.'

'They do not fight,' he said gloomily. 'They kill at the rear. It is not them we fight in battle.'

'But can we not kill them in some way? I would like to kill some very much.'

'I have killed them,' he said. 'And we will kill them again. At the trains we have killed them.'

'I would like to go for a train with thee,' Maria said. 'The time of the train that Pilar brought me back from I was somewhat crazy. Did she tell thee how I was?'

'Yes. Do not talk of it.'

'I was dead in my head with a numbness and all I could do was cry. But there is another thing that I must tell thee. This I must. Then perhaps thou wilt not marry me. But, Roberto, if thou should not wish to marry me, can we not, then, just be always together?'

'I will marry thee.'

'Nay. I had forgotten this. Perhaps you should not. It is possible that I can never bear thee either a son or a daughter for the Pilar says that if I could it would have happened to me with the things which were done. I must tell thee that. Oh, I do not know why I had forgotten that.'

'It is of no importance, rabbit,' he said. 'First it may not be true. That is for a doctor to say. Then I would not wish to bring either a son or a daughter into this world as this world is. And also you take all the love I have to give.'

'I would like to bear thy son and thy daughter,' she told him. 'And how can the world be made better if there are no children of us who fight against the fascists?'

'Thou,' he said. 'I love thee. Hearest thou? And now we must sleep, rabbit. For I must be up long before daylight and the dawn comes early in this month.'

'Then is it all right about the last thing I said? We can still be married?'

'We are married, now. I marry thee now. Thou art my wife. But go to sleep, my rabbit, for there is little time now.'

'And we will truly be married? Not just a talking?'

'Truly.'

'Then I will sleep and think of that if I wake.'

'I, too.'

'Good night, my husband.'

'Good night,' he said. 'Good night, wife.'

He heard her breathing steadily and regularly now and he knew she was asleep and he lay awake and very still not wanting to waken her by moving. He thought of all the part she had not told him and he lay there hating and he was pleased there would be killing in the morning. But I must not take any of it personally, he thought.

Though how can I keep from it? I know that we did dreadful things to them too. But it was because we were uneducated and knew no better. But they did that on purpose and deliberately. Those who did that are the last flowering of what their education has produced. Those are the flowers of Spanish chivalry. What a people they have been. What sons of bitches from Cortez, Pizarro, Mendéndez de Avila all down through Enrique Lister to Pablo. And what wonderful people. There is no finer and no worse people in the world. No kinder people and no crueller. And who understands them? Not me, because if I did I would forgive it all. To understand is to forgive. That's not true. Forgiveness has been exaggerated. Forgiveness is a Christian idea and Spain has never been a Christian country. It has always had its own special idol worship within the Church. *Otra Virgen más*. I suppose that was why they had to destroy the virgins of their enemies. Surely it was deeper with them, with the Spanish religion fanatics, than it was with the people. The people had grown away from the Church because the Church was in the government and the government had always been rotten. This was the only country that the reformation never reached. They were paying for the Inquisition now, all right.

Well, it was something to think about. Something to keep your mind from worrying about your work. It was sounder than pretending. God, he had done a lot of pretending to-night. And Pilar had been pretending all day. Sure. What if they were killed to-morrow? What did it matter as long as they did the bridge properly? That was all they had to do to-morrow.

It didn't. You couldn't do these things indefinitely. But you weren't supposed to live for ever. Maybe I have had all my life in three days, he thought. If that's true I wish we would have spent the last night differently. But last nights are never any good. Last nothings are any good. Yes, last words were good sometimes. '*Viva* my husband who was Mayor of this town' was good.

He knew it was good because it made a tingle run all over him when he said it to himself. He leaned over and kissed Maria who did not wake. In English he whispered very quietly, 'I'd like to marry you, rabbit. I'm very proud of your family.'

32

On that same night in Madrid there were many people at the Hotel Gaylord. A car pulled up under the porte-cochere of the hotel, its headlights painted over with blue calcimine and a little man in black riding boots, grey riding breeches and a short, grey high-buttoned jacket stepped out and returned the salute of the two sentries as he opened the door, nodded to the secret policeman who sat at the concierge's desk and stepped into the elevator. There were two sentries seated on chairs inside the door, one on each side of the marble entrance hall, and these only looked up as the little man passed them at the door of the elevator. It was their business to feel everyone they did not know along the flanks, under the armpits, and over the hip pockets to see if the person entering carried a pistol and, if he did, have him leave it with the concierge. But they knew the short man in riding boots very well and they hardly looked up as he passed.

The apartment where he lived in Gaylord's was crowded as he entered. People were sitting and standing about and talking together as in any drawing-room and the men and the women were drinking vodka, whisky and soda, and beer from small glasses filled from great pitchers. Four of the men were in uniform. The others wore windbreakers or leather jackets and three of the four women were dressed in ordinary street dresses while the fourth who was haggardly thin and dark, wore a sort of severely cut militia-woman's uniform with a skirt with high boots under it.

When he came into the room, Karkov went at once to the woman in the uniform and bowed to her and shook hands. She was his wife and he said something to her in Russian that no one could hear and for a moment the insolence that had been in his eyes as he entered the room was gone. Then it lighted again as he saw the mahogany-coloured head and the love-lazy face of the well-constructed girl who was his mistress and he strode with short, precise steps over to her and bowed and shook her hand in such a way that no one could tell it was not a mimicry of his greeting to his wife. His wife had not looked after him as he walked across the room. She was standing with a tall, good-looking Spanish officer and they were talking Russian now.

'Your great love is getting a little fat,' Karkov was saying to the girl. 'All of our heroes are fattening now as we approach the second year.' He did not look at the man he was speaking of.

'You are so ugly you would be jealous of a toad,' the girl told him cheerfully. She spoke in German. 'Can I go with thee to the offensive to-morrow?'

'No. Nor is there one.'

'Everyone knows about it,' the girl said. 'Don't be so mysterious. Dolores is going. I will go with her or Carmen. Many people are going.'

'Go with whoever will take you,' Karkov said. 'I will not.'

Then he turned to the girl and asked seriously, 'Who told thee of it? Be exact.'

'Richard,' she said as seriously.

Karkov shrugged his shoulders and left her standing.

'Karkov,' a man of middle height with a grey, heavy, sagging face, puffed eye pouches and a pendulous under-lip called to him in a dyspeptic voice. 'Have you heard the good news?'

Karkov went over to him and the man said. 'I only have it now. Not ten minutes ago. It is wonderful. All day the fascists have been fighting among themselves near Segovia. They have been forced to quell the mutinies with automatic rifle and machine-gun fire. In the afternoon they were bombing their own troops with planes.'

'Yes?' asked Karkov.

'That is true,' the puffy-eyed man said. 'Dolores brought the news herself. She was here with the news and was in such a state of radiant exultation as I have never seen. The truth of the news shone from her face. That great face—' he said happily.

'That great face,' Karkov said with no tone in his voice at all.

'If you could have heard her,' the puffy-eyed man said. 'The news itself shone from her with a light that was not of this world. In her voice you could tell the truth of what she said. I am putting it in an article for *Izvestia*. It was one of the greatest moments of the war to me when I heard the report in that great voice where pity, compassion and truth are blended. Goodness and truth shine from her as from a true saint of the people. Not for nothing is she called La Pasionaria.'

'Not for nothing,' Karkov said in a dull voice. 'You'd better write it for *Izvestia* now, before you forget that last beautiful lead.'

'That is a woman that is not to joke about. Not even by a cynic like you,' the puffy-eyed man said. 'If you could have been here to hear her and to see her face.'

'That great voice,' Karkov said. 'That great face. Write it,' he said. 'Don't tell it to me. Don't waste whole paragraphs on me. Go and write it now.'

'Not just now.'

'I think you'd better,' Karkov said and looked at him, and then looked away. The puffy-eyed man stood there a couple of minutes more holding his glass of vodka, his eyes, puffy as they were, absorbed in the beauty of what he had seen and heard and then he left the room to write it.

Karkov went over to another man of about forty-eight, who was short, chunky, jovial-looking with pale blue eyes, thinning blond hair and a gay mouth under a bristly yellow moustache. This man was in uniform. He was a divisional commander and he was a Hungarian.

'Were you here when the Dolores was here?' Karkov asked the man.

'Yes.'

'What was the stuff?'

'Something about the fascists fighting among themselves. Beautiful if true.'

'You hear much talk of to-morrow.'

'Scandalous. All the journalists should be shot as well as most of the people in this room and certainly the intriguing German unmentionable of a Richard. Whoever gave that Sunday *függler* command of a brigade should be shot. Perhaps you and me should be shot too. It is possible,' the General laughed. 'Don't suggest it though.'

'That is a thing I never like to talk about,' Karkov said. 'That American who comes here sometimes is over there. You know the one, Jordan, who is with the *partizan* group. He is there where this business they spoke of is supposed to happen.'

'Well, he should have a report through on it to-night then,' the General said. 'They don't like me down there or I'd go down and find out for you. He works with Golz on this, doesn't he? You'll see Golz to-morrow.'

'Early to-morrow.'

'Keep out of his way until it's going well,' the General said. 'He hates you bastards as much as I do. Though he has a much better temper.'

'But about this—'

'It was probably the fascists having manœuvres,' the General grinned. 'Well, we'll see if Golz can manœuvre them a little. Let Golz try his hand at it. We manœuvred them at Guadalajara.'

'I hear you are travelling too,' Karkov said, showing his bad teeth as he smiled. The General was suddenly angry.

'And me too. Now is the mouth on me. And on all of us always. This filthy sewing circle of gossip. One man who could keep his mouth shut could save the country if he believed he could.'

'Your friend Prieto can keep his mouth shut.'

'But he doesn't believe he can win. How can you win without belief in the people?'

'You decide that,' Karkov said. 'I am going to get a little sleep.'

He left the smoky, gossip-filled room and went into the back bedroom and sat down on the bed and pulled his boots off. He could still hear them talking so he shut the door and opened the window. He did not bother to undress because at two o'clock he would be starting for the drive by Colmenar, Cerceda, and Navacerrada up to the front where Golz would be attacking in the morning.

33

It was two o'clock in the morning when Pilar waked him. As her hand touched him he thought, at first, it was Maria and he rolled toward her and said, 'Rabbit.' Then the woman's big hand shook his shoulder and we was suddenly, completely and absolutely awake and his hand was around the butt of the pistol that lay alongside of his bare right leg and all of him was as cocked as the pistol with its safety catch slipped off.

In the dark he saw it was Pilar and he looked at the dial of his wrist watch with the two hands shining in the short angle close to the top and seeing it was only two, he said, 'What passes with thee, woman?'

'Pablo is gone,' the big woman said to him.

Robert Jordan put on his trousers and shoes. Maria had not waked.

'When?' he asked.

'It must be an hour.'

'And?'

'He has taken something of thine,' the woman said miserably.

'So. What?'

'I do not know,' she told him. 'Come and see.'

In the dark they walked over to the entrance of the cave, ducked under the blanket and went in. Robert Jordan followed her in the dead-ashes, bad-air and sleeping-men smell of the cave, shining his electric torch so that he would not step on any of those who were sleeping on the floor. Anselmo woke and said, 'Is it time?'

'No,' Robert Jordan whispered. 'Sleep, old one.'

The two sacks were at the head of Pilar's bed which was screened off with a hanging blanket from the rest of the cave. The bed smelt stale and sweat-dried and sickly-sweet the way an Indian's bed does as Robert Jordan knelt on it and shone the torch on the two sacks. There was a long slit from top to bottom in each one. Holding the torch in his left hand, Robert Jordan felt in the first sack with his right hand. This was the one that he carried his robe in and it should not be very full. It was not very full. There was some wire in it still but the square wooden box of the exploder was gone. So was the cigar box with the carefully wrapped and packed detonators. So was the screw-top tin with the fuse and the caps.

Robert Jordan felt in the other sack. It was still full of explosive. There might be one packet missing.

He stood up and turned to the woman. There is a hollow, empty feeling that a man can have when he is waked too early in the morning that is almost like the feeling of disaster and he had this multiplied a thousand times.

'And this is what you call guarding one's materials,' he said.

'I slept with my head against them and one arm touching them,' Pilar told him.

'You slept well.'

'Listen,' the woman said. 'He got up in the night and I said, "Where do you go, Pablo?" "To urinate, woman," he told me and I slept again. When I woke again I did not know what time had passed but I thought, when he was not there, that he had gone down to look at the horses as was his custom. Then,' she finished miserably, 'when he did not come I worried and when I worried I felt of the sacks to be sure all was well and there were the slit places and I came to thee.'

'Come on,' Robert Jordan said.

They were outside now and it was still so near the middle of the night that you could not feel the morning coming.

'Can he get out with the horses other ways than by the sentry?'

'Two ways.'

'Who's at the top?'

'Eladio.'

Robert Jordan said nothing more until they reached the meadow where the horses were staked out to feed. There were three horses feeding in the meadow. The big bay and the grey were gone.

'How long ago do you think it was he left you?'

'It must have been an hour.'

'Then that is that,' Robert Jordan said. 'I go to get what is left of my sacks and go back to bed.'

'I will guard them.'

'*Qué va*, you will guard them. You've guarded them once already.'

'*Inglés*,' the woman said, 'I feel in regard to this as you do. There is nothing I would not do to bring back thy property. You have no need to hurt me. We have both been betrayed by Pablo.'

As she said this Robert Jordan realized that he could not afford the luxury of being bitter, that he could not quarrel with this woman. He had to work with this woman on that day that was already two hours and more gone.

He put his hand on her shoulder. 'It is nothing, Pilar,' he told her. 'What is gone is of small importance. We shall improvise something that will do as well.'

'But what did he take?'

'Nothing, woman. Some luxuries that one permits oneself.'

'Was is part of thy mechanism for the exploding?'

'Yes. But there are other ways to do the exploding. Tell me, did Pablo not have caps and fuse? Surely they would have equipped him with those.'

'He has taken them,' she said miserably. 'I looked at once for them' They are gone, too.'

They walked back through the woods to the entrance of the cave.

'Get some sleep,' he said. 'We are better off with Pablo gone.'

'I go to see Eladio.'

'He will have gone another way.'

'I go anyway. I have betrayed thee with my lack of smartness.'

'Nay,' he said. 'Get some sleep, woman. We must be under way at four.'

He went into the cave with her and brought out the two sacks, carrying them held together in both arms so that nothing could spill from the slits.

'Let me sew them up.'

'Before we start,' he said softly. 'I take them not against you but so that I can sleep.'

'I must have them early to sew them.'

'You shall have them early,' he told her. 'Get some sleep, woman.'

'Nay,' she said. 'I have failed thee and I have failed the Republic.'

'Get thee some sleep, woman,' he told her gently. 'Get thee some sleep.'

34

The fascists held the crests of the hills here. Then there was a valley that no one held except for a fascist post in a farmhouse with its outbuildings and its barn that they had fortified. Andrés, on his way to Golz with the message from Robert Jordan, made a wide circle around this post in the dark. He knew where there was a trip wire laid that fired a set-gun and he located it in the dark, stepped over it, and started along the small stream bordered with poplars whose leaves were moving with the night wind. A cock crowed at the farmhouse that was the fascist post and as he walked along the stream he looked back and saw, through the trunks of the poplars, a light showing at the lower edge of one of the windows of the farmhouse. The night was quiet and clear and Andrés left the stream and struck across the meadow.

There were four haycocks in the meadow that had stood there ever since the fighting in July of the year before. No one had ever carried the hay away and the four seasons that had passed had flattened the cocks and made the hay worthless.

Andrés thought what a waste it was as he stepped over a trip wire that ran between two of the haycocks. But the Republicans would have had to carry the hay up the steep Guadarrama slope that rose beyond the meadow and the fascists did not need it, I suppose, he thought.

They have all the hay they need and all the grain. They have much, he thought. But we will give them a blow to-morrow morning. To-morrow morning we will give them something for Sordo. What barbarians they are! But in the morning there will be dust on the road.

He wanted to get this message-taking over and be back for the attack on the posts in the morning. Did he really want to get back though or did he only pretend he wanted to be back? He knew the reprieved feeling he had felt when the *Inglés* had told him he was to go with the message. He had faced the prospect of the morning calmly. It was what was to be done. He had voted for it and would do it. The wiping out of Sordo had impressed him deeply. But, after all, that was Sordo. That was not them. What they had to do they would do.

But when the *Inglés* had spoken to him of the message he had felt the way he used to feel when he was a boy and he had wakened in the morning of the festival of his village and heard it raining hard so that he knew that it would be too wet and that the bull-baiting in the square would be cancelled.

He loved the bull-baiting when he was a boy and he looked forward to it and to the moment when he would be in the square in the hot sun and the dust with the carts ranged all around to close the exits and to make a closed place into which the bull would come, sliding down out of his box, braking with all four feet, when they pulled the end-gate up. He looked forward with excitement, delight and sweating fear to the moment when, in the square, he would hear the clatter of the bull's horns knocking against the wood of his travelling box, and then the sight of him as he came, sliding, braking out into the square, his head up, his nostrils wide, his ears twitching, dust in the sheen of his black hide, dried crut splashed on his flanks, watching his eyes set wide apart, unblinking eyes under the widespread horns as smooth and solid as driftwood polished by the sand, the sharp tips uptilted so that to see them did something to your heart.

He looked forward all the year to that moment when the bull would come out into the square on the day when you watched his eyes while he made his choice of whom in the square he would attack in that sudden head-lowering, horn-reaching, quick cat-gallop that stopped your heart dead when it started. He had looked forward to that moment all the year when he was a boy; but the feeling when the *Inglés* gave the order about the message was the same as when you woke to hear the reprieve of the rain falling on the slate roof, against the stone wall and into the puddles on the dirt street of the village.

He had always been very brave with the bull in those village *capeas*, as brave as any in the village or of the other near-by villages, and not for anything would he have missed it any year although he did not go to the *capeas* of other villages. He was able to wait still when the bull charged and only jumped aside at the last moment. He waved a sack under his muzzle to draw him off when the bull had someone down and many times he had held and pulled on the horns when the bull had someone on the ground and pulled sideways on the horn, had slapped and kicked him in the face until he left the man to charge someone else.

He had held the bull's tail to pull him away from a fallen man, bracing hard and pulling and twisting. Once he had pulled the tail around with one hand until he could reach a horn with the other and when the bull had lifted his head to charge him he had run backwards, circling with the bull, holding the tail in one hand and the horn in the other until the crowd had swarmed on to the bull with their knives and stabbed him. In the dust and the heat, the shouting, the bull and man and wine smell, he had been in the first of the crowd that threw themselves on to the bull and he knew the feeling when the bull rocked and bucked under him and he lay across the withers with one arm locked around the base of the horn and his hand holding the other horn tight, his fingers locked as his body tossed and wrenched and his left arm felt as though it would tear from the socket while he lay on the hot, dusty, bristly, tossing slope of muscle, the ear clenched tight in his teeth, and drove his knife again and again and again into the swelling, tossing bulge of the neck that was now spouting hot on his fist as he let his weight hang on the high slope of the withers and banged and banged into the neck.

The first time he had bit the ear like that and held on to it, his neck and jaws stiffened against the tossing, they had all made fun of him afterwards. But though they joked him about it they had great respect for him. And every year after that he had to repeat it. They called him the bulldog of Villaconejos and joked about him eating cattle raw. But everyone in the village looked forward to seeing him do it and every year he knew that first the bull would come out, then there would be the charges and the tossing, and then when they yelled for the rush for the killing he would place himself to rush through the other attackers and leap for his hold. Then, when it was over, and the bull settled and sunk dead finally under the weight of the killers, he would stand up and walk away ashamed of the ear part, but also as proud as a man could be. And he would go through the carts to wash his hands at the stone fountain and men would clap him on the back and hand him wineskins and say, 'Hurray for you, Bulldog. Long life to your mother.'

Or they would say, 'That's what it is to have a pair of *cojones*! Year after year!'

Andrés would be ashamed, empty-feeling, proud and happy, and he would shake them all off, and wash his hands and his right arm and wash his knife well and then take one of the wineskins and rinse the ear-taste out of his mouth for that year; spitting the wine on the stone flags of the plaza before he lifted the wineskin high and let the wine spurt into the back of his mouth.

Surely. He was the Bull Dog of Villaconejos and not for anything would he have missed doing it each year in his village. But he knew there was no better feeling than that one the sound of the rain gave when he knew he would not have to do it.

But I must go back, he told himself. There is no question but that I must go back for the affair of the posts and the bridge. My brother Eladio is there, who is of my own bone and flesh. Anselmo, Primitivo, Fernando, Agustín, Rafael, though clearly he is not serious, the two women, Pablo and the *Inglés*, though the *Inglés* does not count since he is a foreigner and under orders. They are all in for it. It is impossible that I should escape this proving through the accident of a message. I must deliver this message now quickly and well and then make all haste to return in time for the assault on the posts. It would be ignoble of me not to participate in this action because of the accident of this message. That could not be clearer. And besides, he told himself, as one who suddenly remembers that there will be pleasure too in an engagement only the onerous aspects of which he has been considering, and besides I will enjoy the killing of some fascists. It has been too long since we have destroyed any. To-morrow can be a day of much valid action. To-morrow can be a day of concrete acts. To-morrow can be a day which is worth something. That to-morrow should come and that I should be there.

Just then, as kneedeep in the gorse he climbed the steep slope that led to the Republican lines, a partridge flew up from under his feet, exploding in a whirr of wingbeats in the dark and he felt a sudden breath-stopping fright. It is the suddenness, he thought. How can they move their wings that fast? She must be nesting now. I probably trod close to the eggs. If there were not this war I would tie a handkerchief to the bush and come back in the daytime and search out the nest and I could take the eggs and put them under a setting hen and when they hatched we would have little partridges in the poultry yard and I would watch them grow and, when they were grown, I'd use them for callers. I wouldn't blind them because they would be tame. Or do you suppose they would fly off? Probably. Then I would have to blind them.

But I don't like to do that after I have reared them. I could clip the wings or tether them by one leg when I used them for calling. If there was no war I would go with Eladio to get crayfish from that stream back there by the fascist post. One time we got four dozen from that stream in a day. If we go to the Sierra de Gredos after this of the bridge there are fine streams there for trout and for crayfish also. I hope we go to Gredos, he thought. We could make a good life in Gredos in the summer time and in the fall but it would be terribly cold in winter. But by winter maybe we will have won the war.

If our father had not been a Republican both Eladio and I would be soldiers now with the fascists and if one were a soldier with them then there would be no problem. One would obey orders and one would live or die and in the end it would be however it would be. It was easier to live under a regime than to fight it.

But this irregular fighting was a thing of much responsibility. There was much worry if you were one to worry. Eladio thinks more than I do. Also he worries. I believe truly in the cause and I do not worry. But it is a life of much responsibility.

I think that we are born into a time of great difficulty, he thought. I think any other time was probably easier. One suffers little because all of us have been formed to resist suffering. They who suffer are unsuited to this climate. But it is a time of difficult decisions. The fascists attacked and made our decision for us. We fight to live. But I would like to have it so that I could tie a handkerchief to that bush back there and come in the daylight and take the eggs and put them under a hen and be able to see the chicks of the partridge in my own courtyard. I would like such small and regular things.

But you have no house and no courtyard to your no-house, he thought. You have no family but a brother who goes to battle to-morrow and you own nothing but the wind and the sun and an empty belly. The wind is small, he thought, and there is no sun. You have four grenades in your pocket but they are only good to throw away. You have a carbine on your back but it is only good to give away bullets. You have a message to give away. And you're full of crap that you can give to the earth, he grinned in the dark. You can anoint it also with urine. Everything you have is to give. Thou art a phenomenon of philosophy and an unfortunate man, he told himself and grinned again.

But for all his noble thinking a little while before there was in him that reprieved feeling that had always come with the sound of rain in the village on the morning of the fiesta. Ahead of him now at the top of the ridge was the government position where he knew he would be challenged.

35

Robert Jordan lay in the robe beside the girl Maria who was still sleeping. He lay on his side turned away from the girl and he felt her long body against his back and the touch of it now was just an irony. You, you, he raged at himself. Yes, you. You told yourself the first time you saw him that when he would be friendly would be when the treachery would come. You damned fool. You utter blasted damned fool. Chuck all that. That's not what you have to do now.

What are the chances that he hid them or threw them away? Not so good. Besides you'd never find them in the dark. He would have kept them. He took some dynamite, too. Oh, the dirty, vile, treacherous sod. The dirty rotten crut. Why couldn't he have just mucked off and not have taken the exploder and the detonators? Why was I such an utter goddamned fool as to leave them with that bloody woman? The smart, treacherous ugly bastard. The dirty *cabrón*.

Cut it out and take it easy, he told himself. You had to take chances and that was the best there was. You're just mucked, he told himself. You're mucked for good and higher than a kite. Keep your damned head and get the anger out and stop this cheap lamenting like a damned wailing wall. It's gone. God damn you, it's gone. Oh damn the dirty swine to hell. You can muck your way out of it. You've got to, you know you've got to blow it if you have to stand there and–cut out that stuff, too. Why don't you ask your grandfather?

Oh, muck my grandfather and muck this whole treacherous muck-faced mucking country and every mucking Spaniard in it on either side and to hell for ever. Muck them to hell together, Largo, Prieto, Asensio, Miaja, Rojo, all of them. Muck every one of them to death to hell. Muck the whole treachery-ridden country. Muck their egotism and their selfishness and their selfishness and their egotism and their conceit and their treachery. Muck them to hell and always. Muck them before we die for them. Muck them after we die for them. Muck them to death and hell. God muck Pablo. Pablo is all of them. God pity the Spanish people. Any leader they have will muck them. One good man, Pablo Iglesias, in two thousand years and everybody else mucking them. How do we know how he would have stood up in this war? I remember when I thought Largo was O.K. Durruti was good and his own people shot him there at the Puente de los Franceses. Shot him because he wanted them to attack. Shot him in the glorious discipline of indiscipline. The cowardly swine. Oh muck them all to hell and be damned. And that Pablo that just mucked off with my exploder and my box of detonators. Oh muck him to deepest hell. But no. He's mucked us instead. They always muck you instead from Cortez, and Menéndez de Avila down to Miaja. Look at what Miaja did to Kleber. The bald egotistical swine. The stupid egg-headed bastard. Muck all the insane, egotistical, treacherous swine that have always governed Spain and ruled her armies. Muck everybody but the people and then be damned careful what they turn into when they have power.

His rage began to thin as he exaggerated more and more and spread his scorn and contempt so widely and unjustly that he could no longer believe in it himself. If that were true what are you here for? It's not true and you know it. Look at all the good ones. Look at all the fine ones. He could not bear to be unjust. He hated injustice as he hated cruelty and he lay in his rage that blinded his mind until gradually the anger died down and the red, black, blinding, killing anger was all gone and his mind now as quiet, empty-calm and sharp, cold-seeing as a man is after he has had sexual intercourse with a woman that he does not love.

'And you, you poor rabbit,' he leaned over and said to Maria, who smiled in her sleep and moved close against him. 'I would have struck thee there awhile back if thou had spoken. What an animal a man is in a rage.'

He lay close to the girl now with his arms around her and his chin on her shoulder and lying there he figured out exactly what he would have to do and how he would have to do it.

And it isn't so bad, he thought. It really isn't so bad at all. I don't know whether anyone has ever done it before. But there will always be people who will do it from now on, given a similar jam. If we do it and if they hear about it. If they hear about it, yes. If they do not just wonder how it was we did it. We are too short of people but there is no sense to worry about that. I will do the bridge with what we have. God, I'm glad I got over being angry. It was like not being able to breathe in a storm. That being angry is another damned luxury you can't afford.

'It's all figured out, *guapa*,' he said softly against Maria's shoulder. 'You haven't been bothered by any of it. You have not known about it. We'll be killed but we'll blow the bridge. You have not had to worry about it. That isn't much of a wedding present. But is not a good night's sleep supposed to be priceless? You had a good night's sleep. See if you can wear that like a ring on your finger. Sleep, *guapa*. Sleep well, my beloved. I do not wake thee. That is all I can do for thee now.'

He lay there holding her very lightly, feeling her breathe and feeling her heart beat, and keeping track of the time on his wrist watch.

36

Andrés had challenged at the government position. That is, he had lain down where the ground fell sharply away below the triple belt of wire and shouted up at the rock and earth parapet. There was no continual defensive line and he could easily have passed this position in the dark and made his way farther into the government territory before running into someone who would challenge him. But it seemed safer and simpler to get it over here.

'*Salud!*' he had shouted, '*Salud, milicianos!*'

He heard a bolt snick as it was pulled back. Then, from farther down the parapet, a rifle fired. There was a crashing crack and a downward stab of yellow in the dark. Andrés had flattened at the click, the top of his head hard against the ground.

'Don't shoot, comrades,' Andrés shouted. 'Don't shoot! I want to come in.'

'How many are you?' someone called from behind the parapet.

'One. Me. Alone.'

'Who are you?'

'Andrés Lopez of Villaconejos. From the band of Pablo. With a message.'

'Have you your rifle and equipment?'

'Yes, man.'

'We can take in none without rifle and equipment,' the voice said. 'Nor in larger groups than three.'

'I am alone,' Andrés shouted. 'It is important. Let me come in.'

He could hear them talking behind the parapet but not what they were saying. Then the voice shouted again, 'How many are you?'

'One. Me. Alone. For the love of God.'

They were talking behind the parapet again. Then the voice came, 'Listen, fascist.'

'I am not a fascist,' Andrés shouted. 'I am a *guerrillero* from the band of Pablo. I come with a message for the General Staff.'

'He's crazy,' he heard someone say. 'Toss a bomb at him.'

'Listen,' Andrés said. 'I am alone. I am completely by myself. I obscenity in the midst of the holy mysteries that I am alone. Let me come in.'

'He speaks like a Christian,' he heard someone say and laugh.

Then someone else said, 'The best thing is to toss a bomb down on him.'

'No,' Andrés shouted. 'That would be a great mistake. This is important. Let me come in.'

It was for this reason that he had never enjoyed trips back and forth between the lines. Sometimes it was better than others. But it was never good.

'You are alone?' the voice called down again.

'*Me cago en la leche*,' Andrés shouted. 'How many times must I tell thee? I AM ALONE.'

'Then if you should be alone stand up and hold thy rifle over thy head.'

Andrés stood up and put the carbine above his head, holding it in both hands.

'Now come through the wire. We have thee covered with the *máquina*,' the voice called.

Andrés was in the first zigzag belt of wire. 'I need my hands to get through the wire,' he shouted.

'Keep them up,' the voice commanded.

'I am held fast by the wire,' Andrés called.

'It would have been simpler to have thrown a bomb at him,' a voice said.

'Let him sling his rifle,' another voice said. 'He cannot come through there with his hands above his head. Use a little reason.'

'All these fascists are the same,' the other voice said. 'They demand one condition after another.'

'Listen,' Andrés shouted. 'I am no fascist but a *guerrillero* from the band of Pablo. We've killed more fascists than the typhus.'

'I have never heard of the band of Pablo,' the man who was evidently in command of the post said. 'Neither of Peter nor of Paul nor of any of the other saints nor apostles. Nor of their bands. Sling thy rifle over thy shoulder and use thy hands to come through the wire.'

'Before we loose the *máquina* on thee,' another shouted.

'*Qué poco amables sois!*' Andrés said. 'You're not very amiable.'

He was working his way through the wire.

'*Amables*,' someone shouted at him. 'We are in a war, man.'

'It begins to appear so,' Andrés said.

'What's he say?'

Andrés heard a bolt click again.

'Nothing,' he shouted. 'I say nothing. Do not shoot until I get through this fornicating wire.'

'Don't speak badly of our wire,' someone shouted. 'Or we'll toss a bomb on you.'

'*Quiero decir, qué buena alambrada*,' Andrés shouted. 'What beautiful wire. God in a latrine. What lovely wire. Soon I will be with thee, brothers.'

'Throw a bomb at him,' he heard the one voice say. 'I tell you that's the soundest way to deal with the whole thing.'

'Brothers,' Andrés said. He was wet through with sweat and he knew the bomb advocate was perfectly capable of tossing a grenade at any moment. 'I have no importance.'

'I believe it,' the bomb man said.

'You are right.' Andrés said. He was working carefully through the third belt of wire and he was very close to the parapet. 'I have no importance of any kind. But the affair is serious. *Muy, muy serio*.'

'There is no more serious thing than liberty,' the bomb man shouted. 'Thou thinkest there is anything more serious than liberty?' he asked challengingly.

'No, man,' Andrés said, relieved. He knew now he was up against the crazies; the ones with the black-and-red scarves. '*Viva la Libertad!*'

'*Viva la F.A.I. Viva la C.N.T.*,' they shouted back at him from the parapet. '*Viva el anarco-sindicalismo* and liberty.'

'*Viva nosotros*,' Andrés shouted. 'Long life to us.'

'He is a co-religionary of ours,' the bomb man said. 'And I might have killed him with this.'

He looked at the grenade in his hand and was deeply moved as Andrés climbed over the parapet. Putting his arms around him, the grenade still in one hand, so that it rested against Andrés's shoulder blade as he embraced him, the bomb man kissed him on both cheeks.

'I am content that nothing happened to thee, brother,' he said. 'I am very content.'

'Where is thy officer?' Andrés asked.

'I command here,' a man said. 'Let me see thy papers.'

He took them into a dugout and looked at them with the light of a candle. There was the little square of folded silk with the colours of the Republic and the seal of the S.I.M. in the centre. There was the *Salvoconducto* or safe-conduct pass giving his name, age, height, birthplace and mission that Robert Jordan had written out on a sheet from his notebook and sealed with the S.I.M. rubber stamp, and there were the four folded sheets of the dispatch to Golz which were tied around with a cord and sealed with wax and the impression of the metal S.I.M. seal that was set in the top end of the wooden handle of the rubber stamp.

'This I have seen,' the man in command of the post said and handed back the piece of silk. 'This you all have, I know. But its possession proves nothing without this.' He lifted the *Salvoconducto* and read it through again. 'Where were you born?'

'Villaconejos,' Andrés said.

'And what do they grow there?'

'Melons,' Andrés said. 'As all the world knows.'

'Who do you know there?'

'Why? Are you from there?'

'Nay. But I have been there. I am from Aranjuez.'

'Ask me about anyone.'

'Describe José Rincon.'

'Who keeps the bodega?'

'Naturally.'

'With a shaved head and a big belly and a cast in one eye.'

'Then this is valid,' the man said and handed him back the paper. 'But what do you do on their side?'

'Our father had installed himself at Villacastín before the movement,' Andrés said. 'Down there beyond the mountains on the plain. It was there we were surprised by the movement. Since the movement I have fought with the band of Pablo. But I am in a great hurry, man, to take that dispatch.'

'How goes it in the country of the fascists?' the man commanding asked. He was in no hurry.

'To-day we had much *tomate*,' Andrés said proudly. 'To-day there was plenty of dust on the road all day. To-day they wiped out the band of Sordo.'

'And who is Sordo?' the other asked deprecatingly.

'The leader of one of the best bands in the mountains.'

'All of you should come in to the Republic and join the army,' the officer said. 'There is too much of this silly guerrilla nonsense going on. All of you should come in and submit to our Libertarian discipline. Then when we wished to send out guerrillas we would send them out as they are needed.'

Andrés was a man endowed with almost supreme patience. He had taken the coming in through the wire calmly. None of this examination had flustered him. He found it perfectly normal that this man should have no understanding of them nor of what they were doing and that he should talk idiocy was to be expected. That it should all go slowly should be expected too; but now he wished to go.

'Listen, *Compadre*,' he said. 'It is very possible that you are right. But I have orders to deliver that dispatch to the General commanding the 35th Division, which makes an attack at daylight in these hills and it is already late at night and I must go.'

'What attack? What do you know of an attack?'

'Nay. I know nothing. But I must go now to Navacerrada and go on from there. Wilt thou send me to thy commander who will give me transport to go on from there? Send one with me now to respond to him that there be no delay.'

'I distrust all of this greatly,' he said. 'It might have been better to have shot thee as thou approached the wire.'

'You have seen my papers, Comrade, and I have explained my mission,' Andrés told him patiently.

'Papers can be forged,' the officer said. 'Any fascist could invent such a mission. I will go with thee myself to the Commander.'

'Good.' Andrés said. 'That you should come. But that we should go quickly.'

'Thou, Sanchez. Thou commandest in my place, the officer said. 'Thou knowest thy duties as well as I do. I take this so-called Comrade to the Commander.'

They started down the shallow trench behind the crest of the hill and in the dark Andrés smelt the foulness the defenders of the hill crest had made all through the bracken on that slope. He did not like these people who were like dangerous children; dirty, foul, undisciplined, kind, loving, silly and ignorant but always dangerous because they were armed. He, Andrés, was without politics except that he was for the Republic. He had heard these people talk many times and he thought what they said was often beautiful and fine to hear but he did not like them. It is not liberty not to bury the mess one makes, he thought. No animal has more liberty than the cat; but it buries the mess it makes. The cat is the best anarchist. Until they learn that from the cat I cannot respect them.

Ahead of him the officer stopped suddenly.

'You have your *carabine* still,' he said.

'Yes,' Andrés said. 'Why not?'

'Give it to me,' the officer said. 'You could shoot me in the back with it.'

'Why?' Andrés asked him. 'Why would I shoot thee in the back?'

'One never knows,' the officer said. 'I trust no one. Give me the carbine.'

Andrés unslung it and handed it to him.

'If it pleases thee to carry it,' he said.

'It is better,' the officer said. 'We are safer that way.'

They went on down the hill in the dark.

37

Now Robert Jordan lay with the girl and he watched time passing on his wrist. It went slowly, almost imperceptibly, for it was a small watch and he could not see the second hand. But as he watched the minute hand he found he could almost check its motion with his concentration. The girl's head was under his chin and when he moved his head to look at the watch he felt the cropped head against his cheek, and it was as soft but as alive and silkily rolling as when a marten's fur rises under the caress of your hand when you spread the trap jaws open and lift the marten clear and, holding it, stroke the fur smooth. His throat swelled when his cheek moved against Maria's hair and there was a hollow aching from his throat all through him as he held his arms around her; his head dropped, his eyes close to the watch where the lance-pointed, luminous splinter moved slowly up the left face of the dial. He could see its movement clearly and steadily now and he held Maria close now to slow it. He did not want to wake her but he could not leave her alone now in this last time and he put his lips behind her ear and moved them up along her neck, feeling the smooth skin and the soft touch of her hair on them. He could see the hand moving on the watch and he held her tighter and ran the tip of his tongue along her cheek and on to the lobe of her ear and along the lovely convolutions to the sweet, firm rim at the top, and his tongue was trembling. He felt the trembling run through all of the hollow aching and he saw the hand of the watch now mounting in sharp angle toward the top where the hour was. Now while she still slept he turned her head and put his lips to hers. They lay there, just touching lightly against the sleep-firm mouth and he swung them softly across it, feeling them brush lightly. He turned himself toward her and he felt her shiver along the long, light lovely body and then she sighed, sleeping, and then she, still sleeping, held him too and then, unsleeping, her lips were against his firm and hard and pressing and he said, 'But the pain.'

And she said, 'Nay, there is no pain.'

'Rabbit.'

'Nay, speak not.'

'My rabbit.'

'Speak not. Speak not.'

Then they were together so that as the hand on the watch moved, unseen now, they knew that nothing could ever happen to the one that did not happen to the other, that no other thing could happen more than this; that this was all and always, this was what had been and now and whatever was to come. This, that they were not to have, they were having. They were having now and before and always and now and now and now. Oh, now, now, now, the only now, and above all now, and there is no other now but thou now and now is thy prophet. Now and for ever now. Come now, now, for there is no now but now. Yes, now. Now, please now, only now, not anything else only this now, and where are you and where am I and where is the other one, and not why, not ever why, only this now; and on and always please then always now, always now, for now always one now; one only one, there is no other one but one now, one, going now, rising now, sailing now, leaving now, wheeling now, soaring now, away now, all the way now, all of all the way now; one and one is one, is one, is one, is one, is still one, is still one, is one descendingly, is one softly, is one longingly, is one kindly, is one happily, is one in goodness, is one to cherish, is one now on earth with elbows against the cut and slept-on branches of the pine tree with the smell of the pine boughs and the night; to earth conclusively now, and with the morning of the day to come. Then he said, for the other was only in his head and he had said nothing, 'Oh, Maria, I love thee and I thank thee for this.'

Maria said, 'Do not speak. It is better if we do not speak.'

'I must tell thee for it is a great thing.'

'Nay.'

'Rabbit—'

But she held him tight and turned her head away and he asked softly, 'Is it pain, rabbit?'

'Nay,' she said. 'It is that I am thankful too to have been another time in *la gloria*.'

Then afterwards they lay quiet, side by side, all length of ankle, thigh, hip and shoulder touching, Robert Jordan now with the watch where he could see it again and Maria said, 'We have had much good fortune.'

'Yes,' he said, 'we are people of much luck.'

'There is not time to sleep?'

'No,' he said, 'it starts soon now.'

'Then if we must rise let us go to get something to eat.'

'All right.'

'Thou. Thou art not worried about anything?'

'No.'

'Truly?'

'No. Not now.'

'But thou hast worried before?'

'For a while.'

'Is it aught I can help?'

'Nay,' he said. 'You have helped enough.'

'That? That was for me.'

'That was for us both,' he said. 'No one is there alone. Come, rabbit, let us dress.'

But his mind, that was his best companion, was thinking La Gloria. She said La Gloria. It has nothing to do with glory nor La Gloire that the French write and speak about. It is the thing that is in the Cante Hondo and in the Saetas. It is in Greco and in San Juan de la Cruz, of course, and in the others. I am no mystic, but to deny it is as ignorant as though you denied the telephone or that the earth revolves around the sun or that there are other planets than this.

How little we know of what there is to know. I wish that I were going to live a long time instead of going to die to-day because I have learned much about life in these four days; more, I think, than in all the other time. I'd like to be an old man and to really know. I wonder if you keep on learning or if there is only a certain amount each man can understand. I thought I knew about so many things that I know nothing of. I wish there was more time.

'You taught me a lot, *guapa*.' he said in English.

'What did you say?'

'I have learned much from thee.'

'*Qué va*,' she said, 'it is thou who art educated.'

Educated, he thought. I have the very smallest beginnings of an education. The very small beginnings. If I die on this day it is a waste because I know a few things now. I wonder if you only learn them now because you are oversensitized because of the shortness of the time? There is no such thing as a shortness of time, though. You should have sense enough to know that too. I have been all my life in these hills since I have been here. Anselmo is my oldest friend. I know him better than I know Charles, than I know Chub, than I know Guy, than I know Mike, and I know them well. Agustín, with his vile mouth, is my brother, and I never had a brother. Maria is my true love and my wife. I never had a true love. I never had a wife. She is also my sister, and I never had a sister, and my daughter, and I never will have a daughter. I hate to leave a thing that is so good. He finished tying his rope-soled shoes.

'I find life very interesting,' he said to Maria. She was sitting beside him on the robe, her hands clasped around her ankles. Someone moved the blanket aside from the entrance to the cave and they both saw the light. It was night still and there was no promise of morning except that as he looked up through the pines he saw how low the stars had swung. The morning would be coming fast now in this month.

'Roberto,' Maria said.

'Yes, *guapa*.'

'In this of to-day we will be together, will we not?'

'After the start, yes.'

'Not at the start?'

'No. Thou wilt be with the horses.'

'I cannot be with thee?'

'No. I have work that only I can do and I would worry about thee.'

'But you will come fast when it is done?'

'Very fast,' he said and grinned in the dark. 'Come, *guapa*, let us go and eat.'

'And thy robe?'

'Roll it up, if it pleases thee.'

'It pleases me,' she said.

'I will help thee.'

'Nay. Let me do it alone.'

She knelt to spread and roll the robe, then changed her mind and stood up and shook it so it flapped. Then she knelt down again to straighten it and roll it. Robert Jordan picked up the two packs, holding them carefully so that nothing would spill from the slits in them, and walked over through the pines to the cave mouth where the smoky blanket hung. It was ten minutes to three by his watch when he pushed the blanket aside with his elbow and went into the cave.

38

They were in the cave and the men were standing before the fire Maria was fanning. Pilar had coffee ready in a pot. She had not gone back to bed at all since she had roused Robert Jordan and now she was sitting on a stool in the smoky cave sewing the rip in one of Jordan's packs. The other pack was already sewed. The firelight lit up her face.

'Take more of the stew,' she said to Fernando. 'What does it matter if thy belly should be full? There is no doctor to operate if you take a goring.'

'Don't speak that way, woman,' Agustín said. 'Thou hast the tongue of the great whore.'

He was leaning on the automatic rifle, its legs folded close against the fretted barrel, his pockets were full of grenades, a sack of pans hung from one shoulder, and a full bandolier of ammunition hung over the other shoulder. He was smoking a cigarette and he held a bowl of coffee in one hand and blew smoke on to its surface as he raised it to his lips.

'Thou art a walking hardware store,' Pilar said to him. 'Thou canst not walk a hundred yards with all that.'

'*Qué va*, woman,' Agustín said. 'It is all downhill.'

'There is the climb to the post,' Fernando said. 'Before the downward slope commences.'

'I will climb it like a goat,' Agustín said.

'And thy brother?' he asked Eladio. 'Thy famous brother has mucked off?'

Eladio was standing against the wall.

'Shut up,' he said.

He was nervous and he knew they all knew it. He was always nervous and irritable before action. He moved from the wall to the table and began filling his pockets with grenades from one of the rawhide-covered panniers that leaned, open, against the table leg.

Robert Jordan squatted by the pannier beside him. He reached into the pannier and picked out four grenades. Three were the oval Mills bomb type, serrated, heavy iron with a spring lever held down in position by a cotter pin with pulling ring attached.

'Where did these come from?' he asked Eladio.

'Those? Those are from the Republic. The old man brought them.'

'How are they?'

'*Valen más que pesan*,' Eladio said. 'They are worth a fortune apiece.'

'I brought those,' Anselmo said. 'Sixty in one pack. Ninety pounds, *Inglés*.'

'Have you used those?' Robert Jordan asked Pilar.

'*Qué va* have we used them?' the woman said. 'It was with those Pablo slew the post at Otero.'

When she mentioned Pablo, Agustín started cursing. Robert Jordan saw the look on Pilar's face in the firelight.

'Leave it,' she said to Agustín sharply. 'It does no good to talk.'

'Have they always exploded?' Robert Jordan held the grey-painted grenade in his hand, trying the bend of the cotter pin with his thumbnail.

'Always,' Eladio said. 'There was not a dud in any of that lot we used.'

'And how quickly?'

'In the distance one can throw it. Quickly. Quickly enough.'

'And these?'

He held up a soup-tin shaped bomb, with a tape wrapping around a wire loop.

'They are a garbage,' Eladio told him. 'They blow. Yes. But it is all flash and no fragments.'

'But do they always blow?'

'*Qué va*, always,' Pilar said. 'There is no always either with our munitions or theirs.'

'But you said the other always blew.'

'Not me,' Pilar told him. 'You asked another, not me. I have seen no *always* in any of that stuff.'

'They all blew,' Eladio insisted. 'Speak the truth, woman.'

'How do you know they all blew?' Pilar asked him. 'It was Pablo who threw them. You killed no one at Otero.'

'That son of the great whore,' Agustín began.

'Leave it alone,' Pilar said sharply. Then she went on, 'They are all much the same, *Inglés*. But the corrugated ones are more simple.'

I'd better use one of each on each set, Robert Jordan thought. But the serrated type will lash easier and more securely.

'Are you going to be throwing bombs, *Inglés*?' Agustín asked.

'Why not?' Robert Jordan said.

But crouched there, sorting out the grenades, what he was thinking was: it is impossible. How I could have deceived myself about it I do not know. We were as sunk when they attacked Sordo as Sordo was sunk when the snow stopped. It is that you can't accept it. You have to go on and make a plan that you know is impossible to carry out. You made it and now you know it is no good. It's no good, now, in the morning. You can take either of the posts absolutely O.K. with what you've got here. But you can't take them both. You can't be sure of it, I mean. Don't deceive yourself. Not when the daylight comes.

Trying to take them both will never work. Pablo knew that all the time. I suppose he always intended to muck off but he knew we were cooked when Sordo was attacked. You can't base an operation on the presumption that miracles are going to happen. You will kill them all off and not even get your bridge blown if you have nothing better than what you have now. You will kill off Pilar, Anselmo, Agustín, Primitivo, this jumpy Eladio, the worthless gipsy and old Fernando, and you won't get your bridge blown. Do you suppose there will be a miracle and Golz will get the message from Andrés and stop it? If there isn't, you are going to kill them all off with those orders. Maria too. You'll kill her too with those orders. Can't you even get her out of it? God damn Pablo to hell, he thought.

No. Don't get angry. Getting angry is as bad as getting scared. But instead of sleeping with your girl you should have ridden all night through these hills with the woman to try to dig up enough people to make it work. Yes, he thought. And if anything happened to me so I was not here to blow it. Yes. That. That's why you weren't out. And you couldn't send anybody out because you couldn't run a chance of losing them and being short one more. You had to keep what you had and make a plan to do it with them.

But your plan stinks. It stinks, I tell you. It was a night plan and it's morning now. Night plans aren't any good in the morning. The way you think at night is no good in the morning. So now you know it is no good.

What if John Mosby did get away with things as impossible as this? Sure he did. Much more difficult. And remember, do not undervalue the element of surprise. Remember that. Remember it isn't goofy if you can make it stick. But that is not the way you are supposed to make it. You should make it not only possible but sure. But look at how it all has gone. Well, it was wrong in the first place and such things accentuate disaster as a snowball rolls up wet snow.

He looked up from where he was squatted by the table and saw Maria and she smiled at him. He grinned back with the front of his face and selected four more grenades and put them in his pockets. I could unscrew the detonators and just use them, he thought. But I don't think the fragmentation will have any bad effect. It will come instantaneously with the explosion of the charge and it won't disperse it. At least, I don't think it will. I'm sure it won't. Have a little confidence, he told himself. And you, last night, thinking about how you and your grandfather were so terrific and your father was a coward. Show yourself a little confidence now.

He grinned at Maria again but the grin was still no deeper than the skin that felt tight over his cheekbones and his mouth.

She thinks you're wonderful, he thought. I think you stink. And the *gloria* and all that nonsense that you had. You had wonderful ideas, didn't you? You had this world all taped, didn't you? The hell with all of that.

Take it easy, he told himself. Don't get into a rage. That's just a way out too. There are always ways out. You've got to bite on the nail now. There isn't any need to deny everything there's been just because you are going to lose it. Don't be like some damned snake with a broken back biting at itself; and your back isn't broken either, you hound. Wait until you're hurt before you start to cry. Wait until the fight before you get angry. There's lots of time for it in a fight. It will be some use to you in a fight.

Pilar came over to him with the bag.

'It is strong now,' she said. 'Those grenades are very good, *Inglés*. You can have confidence in them.'

'How do you feel, woman?'

She looked at him and shook her head and smiled. He wondered how far into her face the smile went. It looked deep enough.

'Good,' she said. '*Dentro de la gravedad.*'

Then she said, squatting by him, 'How does it seem to thee now that it is really starting?'

'That we are few,' Robert Jordan said to her quickly.

'To me, too,' she said. 'Very few.'

Then she said still to him alone, 'The Maria can hold the horses by herself. I am not needed for that. We will hobble them. They are cavalry horses and the firing will not panic them. I will go to the lower post and do that which was the duty of Pablo. In this way we are one more.'

'Good,' he said. 'I thought you might wish to.'

'Nay, *Inglés*,' Pilar said, looking at him closely. 'Do not be worried. All will be well. Remember they expect no such thing to come to them.'

'Yes,' Robert Jordan said.

'One other thing, *Inglés*,' Pilar said as softly as her harsh whisper could be soft. 'In that thing of the hand—'

'What thing of the hand?' he said angrily.

'Nay, listen. Do not be angry, little boy. In regard to that thing of the hand. That is all gipsy nonsense that I make to give myself an importance. There is no such thing.'

'Leave it alone,' he said coldly.

'Nay,' she said harshly and lovingly. 'It is just a lying nonsense that I make. I would not have thee worry in the day of battle.'

'I am not worried,' Robert Jordan said.

'Yes, *Inglés*,' she said. 'Thou art very worried, for good cause. But all will be well, *Inglés*. It is for this that we are born.'

'I don't need a political commissar,' Robert Jordan told her.

She smiled at him again, smiling fairly and truly with the harsh lips and the wide mouth, and said, 'I care for thee very much, *Inglés*.'

'I don't want that now,' he said. '*Ni tu, ni Dios.*'

'Yes,' Pilar said in that husky whisper. 'I know. I only wished to tell thee. And do not worry. We will do all very well.'

'Why not?' Robert Jordan said and the very thinnest edge of the skin in front of his face smiled. 'Of course we will. All will be well.'

'When do we go?' Pilar asked.

Robert Jordan looked at his watch.

'Any time,' he said.

He handed one of the packs to Anselmo.

'How are you doing, old one?' he asked.

The old man was finishing whittling the last of a pile of wedges he had copied from a model Robert Jordan had given him. These were extra wedges in case they should be needed.

'Well,' the old man said and nodded. 'So far, very well.' He held his hand out. 'Look,' he said and smiled. His hands were perfectly steady.

'*Bueno, y qué?*' Robert Jordan said to him. 'I can always keep the whole hand steady. Point with one finger.'

Anselmo pointed. The finger was trembling. He looked at Robert Jordan and shook his head.

'Mine too,' Robert Jordan showed him. 'Always. That is normal.'

'Not for me,' Fernando said. He put his right forefinger out to show them. Then the left forefinger.

'Canst thou spit?' Agustín asked him and winked at Robert Jordan.

Fernando hawked and spat proudly on to the floor of the cave, then rubbed it in the dirt with his foot.

'You filthy mule,' Pilar said to him. 'Spit in the fire if thou must vaunt thy courage.'

'I would not have spat on the floor, Pilar, if we were not leaving this place,' Fernando said primly.

'Be careful where you spit to-day,' Pilar told him. 'It may be some place you will not be leaving.'

'That one speaks like a black cat,' Agustín said. He had the nervous necessity to joke that is another form of what they all felt.

'I joke,' said Pilar.

'Me too,' said Agustín. 'But *me cago en la leche*, but I will be content when it starts.'

'Where is the gipsy?' Robert Jordan asked Eladio.

'With the horses,' Eladio said. 'You can see him from the cave mouth.'

'How is he?'

Eladio grinned. 'With much fear,' he said. It reassured him to speak of the fear of another.

'Listen, *Inglés*—' Pilar began. Robert Jordan looked toward her and as he did he saw her mouth open and the unbelieving look come on her face and he swung toward the cave mouth reaching for his pistol. There, holding the blanket aside with one hand, the short automatic rifle muzzle with its flash-cone jutting up above his shoulder, was Pablo standing short, wide, bristly-faced, his small red-rimmed eyes looking toward no one in particular.

'Thou—' Pilar said to him unbelieving. 'Thou.'

'Me,' said Pablo evenly. He came into the cave.

'*Hola, Inglés*,' he said. 'I have five from the bands of Elias and Alejandro above with their horses.'

'And the exploder and the detonators?' Robert Jordan said. 'And the other material?'

'I threw them down the gorge into the river,' Pablo said still looking at no one. 'But I have thought of a way to detonate using a grenade.'

'So have I,' Robert Jordan said.

'Have you a drink of anything?' Pablo asked wearily.

Robert Jordan handed him the flask and he swallowed fast, then wiped his mouth on the back of his hand.

'What passes with you?' Pilar asked.

'*Nada*,' Pablo said, wiping his mouth again. 'Nothing. I have come back.'

'But what?'

'Nothing. I had a moment of weakness. I went away but I am come back.'

He turned to Robert Jordan, '*En el fondo no soy cobarde*,' he said. 'At bottom I am not a coward.'

But you are very many other things, Robert Jordan thought. Damned if you're not. But I'm glad to see you, you son of a bitch.

'Five was all I could get from Elias and Alejandro,' Pablo said. 'I have ridden since I left here. Nine of you could never have done it. Never. I knew that last night when the Inglés explained it. Never. There are seven men and a corporal at the lower post. Suppose there is an alarm or that they fight?'

He looked at Robert Jordan now. 'When I left I thought you would know that it was impossible and would give it up. Then after I had thrown away thy material I saw it in another manner.'

'I am glad to see thee,' Robert Jordan said. He walked over to him. 'We are all right with the grenades. That will work. The other does not matter now.'

'Nay,' Pablo said. 'I do nothing for thee. Thou art a thing of bad omen. All of this comes from thee. Sordo also. But after I had thrown away thy material I found myself too lonely.'

'Thy mother—' Pilar said.

'So I rode for the others to make it possible for it to be successful. I have brought the best that I could get. I have left them at the top so I could speak to you, first. They think I am the leader.'

'Thou art,' Pilar said. 'If thee wishes.' Pablo looked at her and said nothing. Then he said simply and quietly, 'I have thought much since the thing of Sordo. I believe if we must finish we must finish together. But thou, *Inglés*. I hate thee for bringing this to us.'

'But Pablo—' Fernando, his pockets full of grenades, a bandolier of cartridges over his shoulder, he still wiping in his pan of stew with a piece of bread, began. 'Do you not believe the operation can be successful? Night before last you said you were convinced it would be.'

'Give him some more stew,' Pilar said viciously to Maria. Then to Pablo, her eyes softening, 'So you have come back, eh?'

'Yes, woman,' Pablo said.

'Well, thou art welcome,' Pilar said to him. 'I did not think thou couldst be the ruin thou appeared to be.'

'Having done such a thing there is a loneliness that cannot be borne,' Pablo said to her quickly.

'That cannot be borne,' she mocked him. 'That cannot be borne by thee for fifteen minutes.'

'Do not mock me, woman. I have come back.'

'And thou art welcome,' she said. 'Didst not hear me the first time? Drink thy coffee and let us go. So much theatre tires me.'

'Is that coffee?' Pablo asked.

'Certainly,' Fernando said.

'Give me some, Maria,' Pablo said. 'How art thou?' He did not look at her.

'Well,' Maria told him and brought him a bowl of coffee. 'Do you want stew?' Pablo shook his head.

'*No me gusta estar solo*,' Pablo went on explaining to Pilar as though the others were not there. 'I do not like to be alone. *Sabes?* Yesterday all day alone working for the good of all I was not lonely. But last night. *Hombre! Qué mal lo pasé!*'

'Thy predecessor the famous Judas Iscariot hanged himself,' Pilar said.

'Don't talk to me that way, woman,' Pablo said. 'Have you not seen? I am back. Don't talk of Judas nor nothing of that. I am back.'

'How are these people thee brought?' Pilar asked him. 'Hast brought anything worth bringing?'

'*Son buenos*,' Pablo said. He took a chance and looked at Pilar squarely, then looked away.

'*Buenos y bobos*. Good ones and stupids. Ready to die and all. A *tu gusto*. According to thy taste. The way you like them.'

Pablo looked Pilar in the eyes again and this time he did not look away. He kept on looking at her squarely with his small, red-rimmed pig eyes.

'Thou,' she said and her husky voice was fond again. 'Thou. I suppose if a man has something once, always something of it remains.'

'*Listo*,' Pablo said, looking at her squarely and flatly now. 'I am ready for what the day brings.'

'I believe thou art back,' Pilar said to him. 'I believe it. But, *hombre*, thou wert a long way gone.'

'Lend me another swallow from thy bottle,' Pablo said to Robert Jordan. 'And then let us be going.'

39

In the dark they came up the hill through the timber to the narrow pass at the top. They were all loaded heavily and they climbed slowly. The horses had loads too, packed over the saddles.

'We can cut them loose if it is necessary,' Pilar had said. 'But with that, if we can keep it, we can make another camp.'

'And the rest of the ammunition?' Robert Jordan had asked as they lashed the packs.

'In those saddle bags.'

Robert Jordan felt the weight of his heavy pack, the dragging on his neck from the pull of his jacket with its pockets full of grenades, the weight of his pistol against his thigh, and the bulging of his trouser pockets where the clips for the sub-machine gun were. In his mouth was the taste of the coffee, in his right hand he carried the sub-machine gun and with his left hand he reached and pulled up the collar of his jacket to ease the pull of the pack straps.

'*Inglés*,' Pablo said to him, walking close beside him the dark.

'What, man?'

'These I have brought think this is to be successful because I have brought them,' Pablo said. 'Do not say anything to disillusion them.'

'Good,' Robert Jordan said. 'But let us make it successful.'

'They have five horses, *sabes*?' Pablo said cautiously.

'Good,' said Robert Jordan. 'We will keep all the horses together.'

'Good,' said Pablo, and nothing more.

I didn't think you had experienced any complete conversion on the road to Tarsus, old Pablo, Robert Jordan thought. No. Your coming back was miracle enough. I don't think there will ever be any problem about canonizing you.

'With those five I will deal with the lower post as well as Sordo would have,' Pablo said. 'I will cut the wire and fall back upon the bridge as we agreed.'

We went over this all ten minutes ago, Robert Jordan thought. I wonder why this now—

'There is a possibility of making it to Gredos,' Pablo said. 'Truly, I have thought much of it.'

I believe you've had another flash in the last few minutes, Robert Jordan said to himself. You have had another revelation. But you're not going to convince me that I am invited. No, Pablo. Do not ask me to believe too much.

Ever since Pablo had come into the cave and said he had five men Robert Jordan felt increasingly better. Seeing Pablo again had broken the pattern of tragedy into which the whole operation had seemed grooved ever since the snow, and since Pablo had been back he felt not that his luck had turned, since he did not believe in luck, but that the whole thing had turned for the better and that now it was possible. Instead of the surety of failure he felt confidence rising in him as a tyre begins to fill with air from a slow pump. There was little difference at first, although there was a definite beginning, as when the pump starts and the rubber of the tube crawls a little, but it came now as steadily as a tide rising or the sap rising in a tree until he began to feel the first edge of that negation of apprehension that often turned into actual happiness before action.

This was the greatest gift that he had, the talent that fitted him for war; that ability not to ignore but to despise whatever bad ending there could be. This quality was destroyed by too much responsibility for others or the necessity of undertaking something ill planned or badly conceived. For in such things the bad ending, failure, could not be ignored. It was not simply a possibility of harm to one's self, which *could* be ignored. He knew he himself was nothing, and he knew death was nothing. He knew that truly, as truly as he knew anything. In the last few days he had learned that he himself, with another person, could be everything. But inside himself he knew that this was the exception. That we have had, he thought. In that I have been most fortunate. That was given to me, perhaps, because I never asked for it. That cannot be taken away nor lost. But that is over and done with now on this morning and what there is to do now is our work.

And you, he said to himself, I am glad to see you getting a little something back that was badly missing for a time. But you were pretty bad back there. I was ashamed enough of you, there for a while. Only I was you. There wasn't any me to judge you. We were all in bad shape. You and me and both of us. Come on now. Quit thinking like a schizophrenic. One at a time, now. You're all right again now. But listen, you must not think of the girl all day ever. You can do nothing now to protect her except to keep her out of it, and that you are doing. There are evidently going to be plenty of horses if you can believe the signs. The best thing you can do for her is to do the job well and fast and get out, and thinking of her will only handicap you in this. So do not think of her ever.

Having thought this out he waited until Maria came up walking with Pilar and Rafael and the horses.

'Hi, *guapa*,' he said to her in the dark, 'how are you?'

'I am well, Roberto,' she said.

'Don't worry about anything,' he said to her and shifting the gun to his left hand he put a hand on her shoulder.

'I do not,' she said.

'It is all very well organized,' he told her. 'Rafael will be with thee with the horses.'

'I would rather be with thee.'

'Nay. The horses is where thou art most useful.'

'Good,' she said. 'There I will be.'

Just then one of the horses whinnied and from the open place below the opening through the rocks a horse answered, the neigh rising into a shrill sharply broken quaver.

Robert Jordan saw the bulk of the new horses ahead in the dark. He pressed forward and came up to them with Pablo. The men were standing by their mounts.

'*Salud*,' Robert Jordan said.

'*Salud*,' they answered in the dark. He could not see their faces.

'This is the *Inglés* who comes with us,' Pablo said. 'The dynamiter.'

No one said anything to that. Perhaps they nodded in the dark.

'Let us get going, Pablo,' one man said. 'Soon we will have the daylight on us.'

'Did you bring any more grenades?' another asked.

'Plenty,' said Pablo. 'Supply yourselves when we leave the animals.'

'Then let us go,' another said. 'We've been waiting here half the night.'

'*Hola*, Pilar,' another said as the woman came up.

'*Qué me maten*, if it is not Pepe,' Pilar said huskily. 'How are you, shepherd?'

'Good,' said the man. '*Dentro de la gravedad*.'

'What are you riding?' Pilar asked him.

'The grey of Pablo,' the man said. 'It is much horse.'

'Come on,' another man said. 'Let us go. There is no good in gossiping here.'

'How art thou, Elicio?' Pilar said to him as he mounted.

'How would I be?' he said rudely. 'Come on, woman, we have work to do.'

Pablo mounted the big bay horse.

'Keep thy mouths shut and follow me,' he said. 'I will lead you to the place where we will leave the horses.'

40

During the time that Robert Jordan had slept through, the time he had spent planning the destruction of the bridge and the time that he had been with Maria, Andrés had made slow progress. Until he had reached the Republican lines he had travelled across country and through the fascist lines as fast as a countryman in good physical condition who knew the country well could travel in the dark. But once inside the Republican lines it went very slowly.

In theory he should only have had to show the safe-conduct given him by Robert Jordan stamped with the seal of the S.I.M. and the dispatch which bore the same seal and be passed along toward his destination with the greatest speed. But first he had encountered the company commander in the front line who had regarded the whole mission with owlishly grave suspicion.

He had followed this company commander to battalion headquarters where the battalion commander, who had been a barber before the movement, was filled with enthusiasm on hearing the account of his mission. This commander, who was named Gomez, cursed the company commander for his stupidity, patted Andrés on the back, gave him a drink of bad brandy and told him that he himself, the ex-barber, had always wanted to be a *guerrillero*. He had then roused his adjutant, turned over the battalion to him, and sent his orderly to wake up and bring his motor-cyclist. Instead of sending Andrés back to brigade headquarters with the motor-cyclist, Gomez had decided to take him there himself in order to expedite things and, with Andrés holding tight on to the seat ahead of him, they roared, bumping, down the shell pocked mountain road between the double row of big trees, the headlight of the motor cycle showing their whitewashed bases and the places on the trunks where the whitewash and the bark had been chipped and torn by shell fragments and bullets during the fighting along this road in the first summer of the movement. They turned into the little smashed-roofed mountain-resort town where brigade headquarters was and Gomez had braked the motor cycle like a dirt-track racer and leaned it against the wall of the house where a sleepy sentry came to attention as Gomez pushed by him into the big room where the walls were covered with maps and a very sleepy officer with a green eyeshade sat at a desk with a reading lamp, two telephones and a copy of *Mundo Obrero*.

This officer looked up at Gomez and said, 'What doest thou here? Have you never heard of the telephone?'

'I must see the Lieutenant-Colonel,' Gomez said.

'He is asleep,' the officer said. 'I could see the lights of that bicycle of thine for a mile coming down the road. Dost wish to bring on a shelling?'

'Call the Lieutenant-Colonel,' Gomez said. 'This is a matter of the utmost gravity.'

'He is asleep, I tell thee,' the officer said. 'What sort of a bandit is that with thee?' he nodded towards Andrés.

'He is a *guerrillero* from the other side of the lines with a dispatch of the utmost importance for the General Golz who commands the attack that is to be made at dawn beyond Navacerrada,' Gomez said excitedly and earnestly. 'Rouse the *Teniente-Coronel* for the love of God.'

The officer looked at him with his droopy eyes shaded by the green celluloid.

'All of you are crazy,' he said. 'I know of no General Golz nor of no attack. Take this sportsman and get back to your battalion.'

'Rouse the *Teniente-Coronel*, I say,' Gomez said and Andrés saw his mouth tightening.

'Go obscenity yourself,' the officer said to him lazily and turned away.

Gomez took his heavy 9 mm. Star pistol out of its holster and shoved it against the officer's shoulder.

'Rouse him, you fascist bastard,' he said. 'Rouse him or I'll kill you.'

'Calm yourself,' the officer said. 'All you barbers are emotional.'

Andrés saw Gomez's face draw with hate in the light of the reading lamp. But all he said was, 'Rouse him.'

'Orderly,' the officer called in a contemptuous voice.

A soldier came to the door and saluted and went out.

'His fiancée is with him,' the officer said and went back to reading the paper. 'It is certain he will be delighted to see you.'

'It is those like thee who obstruct all effort to win this war, Gomez said to the staff officer.

The officer paid no attention to him. Then, as he read on, he remarked, as though to himself, 'What a curious periodical this is!'

'Why don't you read *El Debate* then? That is your paper,' Gomez said to him naming the leading Catholic-Conservative organ published in Madrid before the movement.

'Don't forget I am thy superior officer and that a report by me on thee carries weight,' the officer said without looking up. 'I never read *El Debate*. Do not make false accusations.'

'No. You read A.B.C.,' Gomez said. 'The army is still rotten with such as thee. With professionals such as thee. But it will not always be. We are caught between the ignorant and the cynical. But we will educate the one and eliminate the other.'

'"Purge" is the word you want,' the officer said, still not looking up. 'Here it reports the purging of more of thy famous Russians. They are purging more than the epsom salts in this epoch.'

'By any name,' Gomez said passionately. 'By any name so that such as thee are liquidated.'

'Liquidated,' the officer said insolently as though speaking to himself. 'Another new word that has little of Castilian in it.'

'Shot then,' Gomez said. 'That is Castilian. Canst understand it?'

'Yes, man, but do not talk so loudly. There are others beside the *Teniente-Coronel* asleep in this Brigade Staff and thy emotion bores me. It was for that reason that I always shaved myself. I never liked the conversation.'

Gomez looked at Andrés and shook his head. His eyes were shining with the moistness that rage and hatred can bring. But he shook his head and said nothing as he stored it all away for some time in the future. He had stored much in the year and a half in which he had risen to the command of a battalion in the Sierra and now, as the Lieutenant-Colonel came into the room in his pyjamas he drew himself stiff and saluted.

The Lieutenant-Colonel Miranda, who was a short, grey-faced man, who had been in the army all his life, who had lost the love of his wife in Madrid while he was losing his digestion in Morocco, and become a Republican when he found he could not divorce his wife (there was never any question of recovering his digestion) had entered the civil war as a Lieutenant-Colonel. He had only one ambition, to finish the war with the same rank. He had defended the Sierra well and he wanted to be left alone there to defend it whenever it was attacked. He felt much healthier in the war, probably due to the forced curtailment of the number of meat courses, he had an enormous stock of sodium-bicarbonate, he had his whisky in the evening, his twenty-three-year-old mistress was having a baby, as were nearly all the other girls who had started out as *milicianas* in the July of the year before, and now he came into the room, nodded in answer to Gomez's salute and put out his hand.

'What brings thee, Gomez?' he asked and then, to the officer at the desk who was his chief of operation, 'Give me a cigarette, please, Pepe.'

Gomez showed him Andrés's papers and the dispatch. The Lieutenant-Colonel looked at the *Salvoconducto* quickly, looked at Andrés, nodded and smiled, and then looked at the dispatch hungrily. He felt of the seal, tested it with his forefinger, then handed both the safe-conduct and dispatch back to Andrés.

'Is the life very hard there in the hills?' he asked.

'No, my Lieutenant-Colonel,' Andrés said.

'Did they tell thee where would be the closest point to find General Golz's headquarters?'

'Navacerrada, my Lieutenant-Colonel,' Andrés said. 'The *Inglés* said it would be somewhere close to Navacerrada behind the lines to the right of there.'

'What *Inglés*?' the Lieutenant-Colonel asked quietly.

'The *Inglés* who is with us as a dynamiter.'

The Lieutenant-Colonel nodded. It was just another sudden unexplained rarity of this war. 'The *Inglés* who is with us as a dynamiter.'

'You had better take him, Gomez, on the motor,' the Lieutenant-Colonel said. 'Write them a very strong *Salvoconducto* to the *Estado Mayor* of General Golz for me to sign,' he said to the officer in the green celluloid eyeshade. 'Write it on the machine, Pepe. Here are the details,' he motioned for Andrés to hand over his safe-conduct, 'and put on two seals.' He turned to Gomez. 'You will need something strong to-night. It is rightly so. People should be careful when an offensive is projected. I will give you something as strong as I can make it.' Then to Andrés, very kindly, he said, 'Dost wish anything? To eat or to drink?'

'No, my Lieutenant-Colonel,' Andrés said. 'I am not hungry. They gave me cognac at the last place of command and more would make me seasick.'

'Did you see any movement or activity opposite my front as you came through?' the Lieutenant-Colonel asked Andrés politely.

'It was as usual, my Lieutenant-Colonel. Quiet. Quiet.'

'Did I not meet thee in Cercedilla about three months back?' the Lieutenant-Colonel asked.

'Yes, my Lieutenant-Colonel.'

'I thought so,' the Lieutenant-Colonel patted him on the shoulder. 'You were with the old man Anselmo. How is he?'

'He is well, my Lieutenant-Colonel,' Andrés told him.

'Good. It makes me happy,' the Lieutenant-Colonel said. The officer showed him what he had typed and he read it over and signed it. 'You must go now quickly,' he said to Gomez and Andrés. 'Be careful with the motor,' he said to Gomez. 'Use your lights. Nothing will happen from a single motor and you must be careful. My compliments to Comrade General Golz. We met after Peguerinos.' He shook hands with them both. 'Button the papers inside thy shirt,' he said. 'There is much wind on a motor.'

After they went out he went to a cabinet, took out a glass and a bottle, and poured himself some whisky and poured plain water into it from an earthenware crock that stood on the floor against the wall. Then holding the glass and sipping the whisky very slowly he stood in front of the big map on the wall and studied the offensive possibilities in the country above Navacerrada.

'I am glad it is Golz and not me,' he said finally to the officer who sat at the table. The officer did not answer and looking away from the map and at the officer the Lieutenant-Colonel saw he was asleep with his head on his arms. The Lieutenant-Colonel went over to the desk and pushed the two phones close together so that one touched the officer's head on either side. Then he walked to the cupboard, poured himself another whisky, put water in it, and went back to the map again.

Andrés, holding tight on to the seat where Gomez was forking the motor, bent his head against the wind as the motor cycle moved, noisily exploding, into the light-split darkness of the country road that opened ahead sharp with the high black of the poplars beside it, dimmed and yellow-soft now as the road dipped into the fog along a stream bed, sharpening hard again as the road rose and, ahead of them at the crossroads, the headlight showed the grey bulk of the empty trucks coming down from the mountains.

41

Pablo stopped and dismounted in the dark. Robert Jordan heard the creaking and the heavy breathing as they all dismounted and the clinking of a bridle as a horse tossed his head. He smelled the horses and the unwashed and sour slept-in-clothing smell of the new men and the wood-smoky sleep-stale smell of the others who had been in the cave. Pablo was standing close to him and he smelled the brassy, dead-wine smell that came from him like the taste of a copper coin in your mouth. He lit a cigarette, cupping his hand to hide the light, pulled deep on it, and heard Pablo say very softly, 'Get the grenade sack, Pilar, while we hobble these.'

'Agustín,' Robert Jordan said in a whisper, 'you and Anselmo come now with me to the bridge. Have you the sack of pans for the *máquina*?'

'Yes,' Agustín said. 'Why not?'

Robert Jordan went over to where Pilar was unpacking one of the horses with the help of Primitivo.

'Listen, woman,' he said softly.

'What now?' she whispered huskily, swinging a cinch hook clear from under the horse's belly.

'Thou understandest that there is to be no attack on the post until thou hearest the falling of the bombs?'

'How many times dost thou have to tell me?' Pilar said. 'You are getting like an old woman, *Inglés*.'

'Only to check,' Robert Jordan said. 'And after the destruction of the post you fall back on to the bridge and cover the road from above and my left flank.'

'The first time thou outlined it I understood it as well as I will ever understand it,' Pilar whispered to him. 'Get thee about thy business.'

'That no one should make a move nor fire a shot nor throw a bomb until the noise of the bombardment comes,' Robert Jordan said softly.

'Do not molest me more,' Pilar whispered angrily. 'I have understood this since we were at Sordo's.'

Robert Jordan went to where Pablo was tying the horses. 'I have only hobbled those which are liable to panic,' Pablo said. 'These are tied so a pull of the rope will release them, see?'

'Good.'

'I will tell the girl and the gipsy how to handle them,' Pablo said. His new men were standing in a group by themselves leaning on their carbines.

'Dost understand all?' Robert Jordan asked.

'Why not?' Pablo said. 'Destroy the post. Cut the wire. Fall back on the bridge. Cover the bridge until thou blowest.'

'And nothing to start until the commencement of the bombardment.'

'Thus it is.'

'Well then, much luck.'

Pablo grunted. Then he said, 'Thou wilt cover us well with the *máquina* and with thy small *máquina* when we come back, eh, *Inglés*?'

'De la primera,' Robert Jordan said. 'Off the top of the basket.'

'Then,' Pablo said. 'Nothing more. But in that moment thou must be very careful, *Inglés*. It will not be simple to do that unless thou art very careful.'

'I will handle the *máquina* myself,' Robert Jordan said to him.

'Hast thou much experience? For I am of no mind to be shot by Agustín with his belly full of good intentions.'

'I have much experience. Truly. And if Agustín uses either *máquina* I will see that he keeps it way above thee. Above, above and above.'

'Then nothing more,' Pablo said. Then he said softly and confidentially, 'There is still a lack of horses.'

The son of a bitch, Robert Jordan thought. Or does he think I did not understand him the first time.

'I go on foot,' he said. 'The horses are thy affair.'

'Nay, there will be a horse for thee, *Inglés*,' Pablo said softly. 'There will be horses for all of us.'

'That is thy problem,' Robert Jordan said. 'Thou dost not have to count me. Hast enough rounds for thy new *máquina*?'

'Yes,' Pablo said. 'All that the cavalryman carried. I have fired only four to try it. I tried it yesterday in the high hills.'

'We go now,' Robert Jordan said. 'We must be there early and well hidden.'

'We all go now,' Pablo said. '*Suerte, Inglés*.'

I wonder what the bastard is planning now, Robert Jordan said. But I am pretty sure I know. Well, that is his, not mine. Thank God I do not know these new men.

He put his hand out and said, '*Suerte, Pablo*,' and their two hands gripped in the dark.

Robert Jordan, when he put his hand out, expected that it would be like grasping something reptilian or touching a leper. He did not know what Pablo's hand would feel like. But in the dark Pablo's hand gripped his hard and pressed it frankly and he returned the grip. Pablo had a good hand in the dark and feeling it gave Robert Jordan the strangest feeling he had felt that morning. We must be allies now, he thought. There was always much handshaking with allies. Not to mention decorations and kissing on both cheeks, he thought. I'm glad we do not have to do that. I suppose all allies are like this. They always hate each other *au fond*. But this Pablo is a strange man.

'*Suerte*, Pablo,' he said and gripped the strange, firm, purposeful hand hard. 'I will cover thee well. Do not worry.'

'I am sorry for having taken thy material,' Pablo said. 'It was an equivocation.'

'But thou has brought what we needed.'

'I do not hold this of the bridge against thee, *Inglés*,' Pablo said. 'I see a successful termination for it.'

'What are you two doing? Becoming *maricones*?' Pilar said suddenly beside them in the dark. 'That is all thou hast lacked,' she said to Pablo. 'Get along, *Inglés*, and cut thy good-byes short before this one steals the rest of thy explosive.'

'Thou dost not understand me, woman,' Pablo said. 'The *Inglés* and I understand one another.'

'Nobody understands thee. Neither God nor thy mother,' Pilar said. 'Nor I either. Get along, *Inglés*. Make thy good-byes with thy cropped head and go. *Me cago en tu padre*, but I begin to think thou art afraid to see the bull come out.'

'Thy mother,' Robert Jordan said.

'Thou never hadst one,' Pilar whispered cheerfully. 'Now go, because I have a great desire to start this and get it over with. Go with thy people,' she said to Pablo. 'Who knows how long their stern resolution is good for? Thou hast a couple that I would not trade thee for. Take them and go.'

Robert Jordan slung his pack on his back and walked over to the horses to find Maria.

'Good-bye, *guapa*,' he said. 'I will see thee soon.'

He had an unreal feeling about all of this now as though he had said it all before or as though it were a train that were going, especially as though it were a train and he was standing on the platform of a railway station.

'Good-bye, Roberto,' she said. 'Take much care.'

'Of course,' he said. He bent his head to kiss her and his pack rolled forward against the back of his head so that his forehead bumped hers hard. As this happened he knew this had happened before too.

'Don't cry,' he said, awkward not only from the load.

'I do not,' she said. 'But come back quickly.'

'Do not worry when you hear the firing. There is bound to be much firing.'

'Nay. Only come back quickly.'

'Good-bye, *guapa*,' he said awkwardly.

'*Salud*, Roberto.'

Robert Jordan had not felt this young since he had taken the train at Red Lodge to go down to Billings to get the train there to go away to school for the first time. He had been afraid to go and he did not want anyone to know it and, at the station, just before the conductor picked up the box he would step up on to reach the steps of the day coach, his father had kissed him good-bye and said, 'May the Lord watch between thee and me while we are absent the one from the other.' His father had been a very religious man and he had said it simply and sincerely. But his moustache had been moist and his eyes were damp with emotion and Robert Jordan had been so embarrassed by all of it, the damp religious sound of the prayer, and by his father kissing him good-bye, that he had felt suddenly so much older than his father and sorry for him that he could hardly bear it.

After the train started he had stood on the rear platform and watched the station and the water tower grow smaller and smaller and the rails crossed by the ties narrowed toward a point where the station and the water tower stood now minute and tiny in the steady clicking that was taking him away.

The brakeman said, 'Dad seemed to take your going sort of hard, Bob.'

'Yes,' he had said watching the sagebrush that ran from the edge of the road bed between the passing telegraph poles across to the streaming-by dusty stretching of the road. He was looking for sage hens.

'You don't mind going away to school?'

'No,' he had said and it was true.

It would not have been true before but it was true that minute and it was only now, at this parting, that he ever felt as young again as he had felt before that train left. He felt very young now and very awkward and he was saying good-bye as awkwardly as one can be when saying good-bye to a young girl when you are a boy in school, saying good-bye at the front porch, not knowing whether to kiss the girl or not. Then he knew it was not the good-bye he was being awkward about. It was the meeting he was going to. The good-bye was only a part of the awkwardness he felt about the meeting.

You're getting them again, he told himself. But I suppose there is no one that does not feel that he is too young to do it. He would not put a name to it. Come on, he said to himself. Come on. It is too early for your second childhood.

'Good-bye, *guapa*,' he said. 'Good-bye, rabbit.'

'Good-bye, my Roberto,' she said and he went over to where Anselmo and Agustín were standing and said, '*Vámonos.*'

Anselmo swung his heavy pack up. Agustín, fully loaded since the cave, was leaning against a tree, the automatic rifle jutting over the top of his load.

'Good,' he said. '*Vámonos.*'

The three of them started down the hill.

'*Buena suerte*, Don Roberto,' Fernando said as the three of them passed him as they moved in single file between the trees. Fernando was crouched on his haunches a little way from where they passed but he spoke with great dignity.

'*Buena suerte* thyself, Fernando,' Robert Jordan said.

'In everything thou doest,' Agustín said.

'Thank you, Don Roberto,' Fernando said, undisturbed by Agustín.

'That one is a phenomenon, *Inglés*,' Agustín whispered.

'I believe thee,' Robert Jordan said. 'Can I help thee? Thou art loaded like a horse.'

'I am all right,' Agustín said. 'Man, but I am content we are started.'

'Speak softly,' Anselmo said. 'From now on speak little and softly.'

Walking carefully, downhill, Anselmo in the lead, Agustín next, Robert Jordan placing his feet carefully so that he would not slip, feeling the dead pine needles under his rope-soled shoes, bumping a tree root with one foot and putting a hand forward and feeling the cold metal jut of the automatic rifle barrel and the folded legs of the tripod, then working sideways down the hill, his shoes sliding and grooving the forest floor, putting his left hand out again and touching the rough bark of a tree trunk, then as he braced himself his hand feeling a smooth place, the base of the palm of his hand coming away sticky from the resinous sap where a blaze had been cut, they dropped down the steep wooded hillside to the point above the bridge where Robert Jordan and Anselmo had watched the first day.

Now Anselmo was halted by a pine tree in the dark and he took Robert Jordan's wrist and whispered, so low Jordan could hardly hear him. 'Look. There is the fire in his brazier.'

It was a point of light below where Robert Jordan knew the bridge joined the road.

'Here is where we watched,' Anselmo said. He took Robert Jordan's hand and bent it down to touch a small fresh blaze low on a tree trunk. 'This I marked while thou watched. To the right is where thou wished to put the *máquina*.'

'We will place it there.'

'Good.'

They put the packs down behind the base of the pine trunks and the two of them followed Anselmo over to the level place where there was a clump of seedling pines.

'It is here,' Anselmo said. 'Just here.'

'From here, with daylight,' Robert Jordan crouched behind the small trees whispered to Agustín, 'thou wilt see a small stretch of road and the entrance to the bridge. Thou wilt see the length of the bridge and a small stretch of road at the other end before it rounds the curve of the rocks.'

Agustín said nothing.

'Here thou wilt lie while we prepare the exploding and fire on anything that comes from above or below.'

'Where is that light?' Agustín asked.

'In the sentry box at this end,' Robert Jordan whispered.

'Who deals with the sentries?'

'The old man and I, as I told thee. But if we do not deal with them, thou must fire into the sentry boxes and at them if thou seest them.'

'Yes. You told me that.'

'After the explosion when the people of Pablo come around that corner, thou must fire over their heads if others come after them. Thou must fire high above them when they appear in any event that others must not come. Understandest thou?'

'Why not? It is as thou saidst last night.'

'Hast any questions?'

'Nay. I have two sacks. I can load them from above where it will not be seen and bring them here.'

'But do no digging here. Thou must be as well hid as we were at the top.'

'Nay. I will bring the dirt in them in the dark. You will see. They will not show as I will fix them.'

'Thou art very close. *Sabes?* In the daylight this clump shows clearly from below.'

'Do not worry, *Inglés*. Where goest thou?'

'I go close below with the small *máquina* of mine. The old man will cross the gorge now to be ready for the box of the other end. It faces in that direction.'

'Then nothing more,' said Agustín. '*Salud, Inglés*. Hast thou tobacco?'

'Thou canst not smoke. It is too close.'

'Nay. Just to hold in the mouth. To smoke later.'

Robert Jordan gave him his cigarette case and Agustín took three cigarettes and put them inside the front flap of his herdsman's flat cap. He spread the legs of his tripod with the gun muzzle in the low pines and commenced unpacking his load by touch and laying the things where he wanted them.

'*Nada mas*,' he said. 'Well, nothing more.'

Anselmo and Robert Jordan left him there and went back to where the packs were.

'Where had we best leave them?' Robert Jordan whispered.

'I think here. But canst thou be sure of the sentry with thy small *máquina* from here?'

'Is this exactly where we were on that day?'

'The same tree,' Anselmo said so low Jordan could barely hear him and he knew he was speaking without moving his lips as he had spoken that first day. 'I marked it with my knife.'

Robert Jordan had the feeling again of it all having happened before, but this time it came from his own repetition of a query and Anselmo's answer. It had been the same with Agustín, who had asked a question about the sentries although he knew the answer.

'It is close enough. Even too close,' he whispered. 'But the light is behind us. We are all right here.'

'Then I will go now to cross the gorge and be in position at the other end,' Anselmo said. Then he said, 'Pardon me, *Inglés*. So that there is no mistake. In case I am stupid.'

'What?' breathed very softly.

'Only to repeat it so that I will do it exactly.'

'When I fire, thou wilt fire. When thy man is eliminated, cross the bridge to me. I will have the packs down there and thou wilt do as I tell thee in the placing of the charges. Everything I will tell thee. If aught happens to me do it thyself as I showed thee. Take thy time and do it well, wedging all securely with the wooden wedges and lashing the grenades firmly.'

'It is all clear to me,' Anselmo said. 'I remember it all. Now I go. Keep thee well covered, *Inglés*, when daylight comes.'

'When thou firest,' Robert Jordan said, 'take a rest and make very sure. Do not think of it as a man but as a target, *de acuerdo*? Do not shoot at the whole man but at a point. Shoot for the exact centre of the belly–if he faces thee. At the middle of the back, if he is looking away. Listen, old one. When I fire if the man is sitting down he will stand up before he runs or crouches. Shoot then. If he is still sitting down shoot. Do not wait. But make sure. Get to within fifty yards. Thou art a hunter. Thou hast no problem.'

'I will do as thou orderest,' Anselmo said.

'Yes. I order it thus,' Robert Jordan said.

'I'm glad I remembered to make it an order, he thought. That helps him out. That takes some of the curse off. I hope it does, anyway. Some of it. I had forgotten about what he told me that first day about the killing.

'It is thus I have ordered,' he said. 'Now go.'

'*Me voy*,' said Anselmo. 'Until soon, *Inglés*.'

'Until soon, old one,' Robert Jordan said.

He remembered his father in the railway station and the wetness of that farewell and he did not say *Salud* nor good-bye nor good luck nor anything like that.

'Hast wiped the oil from the bore of thy gun, old one?' he whispered. 'So it will not throw wild?'

'In the cave,' Anselmo said. 'I cleaned them all with the pull-through.'

'Then until soon,' Robert Jordan said and the old man went off, noiseless on his rope-soled shoes, swinging wide through the trees.

Robert Jordan lay on the pine-needle floor of the forest and listened to the first stirring in the branches of the pines of the wind that would come with daylight. He took the clip out of the sub-machine gun and worked the lock back and forth. Then he turned the gun, with the lock open and in the dark he put the muzzle to his lips and blew through the barrel, the metal tasting greasy and oily as his tongue touched the edge of the bore. He laid the gun across his forearm, the action up so that no pine needles or rubbish could get in it, and shucked all the cartridges out of the clip with his thumb and on to a handkerchief he had spread in front of him. Then, feeling each cartridge in the dark and turning it in his fingers, he pressed and slid them one at a time back into the clip. Now the clip was heavy again in his hand and he slid it back into the sub-machine gun and felt it click home. He lay on his belly behind the pine trunk, the gun across his left forearm and watched the point of light below him. Sometimes he could not see it and then he knew that the man in the sentry box had moved in front of the brazier. Robert Jordan lay there and waited for daylight.

42

During the time that Pablo had ridden back from the hills to the cave and the time the band had dropped down to where they had left the horses Andrés had made rapid progress toward Golz's headquarters. Where they came on to the main highroad to Navacerrada on which the trucks were rolling back from the mountain there was a control. But when Gomez showed the sentry at the control his safe-conduct from the Lieutenant-Colonel Miranda the sentry put the light from a flashlight on it, showed it to the other sentry with him, then handed it back and saluted.

'*Siga*,' he said. 'Continue. But without lights.'

The motor cycle roared again and Andrés was holding tight on to the forward seat and they were moving along the highway, Gomez riding carefully in the traffic. None of the trucks had lights and they were moving down the road in a long convoy. There were loaded trucks moving up the road too, and all of them raised a dust that Andrés could not see in that dark but could only feel as a cloud that blew in his face and that he could bite between his teeth.

They were close behind the tailboard of a truck now, the motor cycle chugging, then Gomez speeded up and passed it and another, and another, and another with the other trucks roaring and rolling down past them on the left. There was a motor car behind them now and it blasted into the truck noise and the dust with its klaxon again and again; then flashed on lights that showed the dust like a solid yellow cloud and surged past them in a whining rise of gears and a demanding, threatening, bludgeoning of klaxoning.

Then ahead all the trucks were stopped and riding on, working his way ahead past ambulances, staff cars, an armoured car, another, and a third, all halted, like heavy, metal, gun-jutting turtles in the not yet settled dust, they found another control where there had been a smash-up. A truck, halting, had not been seen by the truck which followed it and the following truck had run into it, smashing the rear of the first truck in and scattering cases of small-arms ammunition over the road. One case had burst open on landing and as Gomez and Andrés stopped and wheeled the motor cycle forward through the stalled vehicles to show their safe-conduct at the control Andrés walked over the brass hulls of the thousand of cartridges scattered across the road in the dust. The second truck had its radiator completely smashed in. The truck behind it was touching its tail-gate. A hundred more were piling up behind and an overbooted officer was running back along the road shouting to the drivers to back so that the smashed truck could be gotten off the road.

There were too many trucks for them to be able to back unless the officer reached the end of the ever mounting line and stopped it from increasing and Andrés saw him running, stumbling, with his flashlight, shouting and cursing and, in the dark, the trucks kept coming up.

The man at the control would not give the safe-conduct back. There were two of them, with rifles slung on their backs and flashlights in their hands and they were shouting too. The one carrying the safe-conduct in his hand crossed the road to a truck going in the downhill direction to tell it to proceed to the next control and tell them there to hold all trucks until this jam was straightened out. The truck driver listened and went on. Then, still holding the safe-conduct, the control patrol came over, shouting, to the truck driver whose load was spilled.

'Leave it and get ahead for the love of God so we can clear this!' he shouted at the driver.

'My transmission is smashed,' the driver, who was bent over by the rear of his truck, said.

'Obscene your transmission. Go ahead, I say.'

'They do not go ahead when the differential is smashed,' the driver told him and bent down again.

'Get thyself pulled then, get ahead so that we can get this other obscenity off the road.'

The driver looked at him sullenly as the control man shone the electric torch on the smashed rear of the truck.

'Get ahead. Get ahead,' the man shouted, still holding the safe-conduct pass in his hand.

'And my paper,' Gomez spoke to him. 'My safe-conduct. We are in a hurry.'

'Take thy safe-conduct to hell,' the man said and handing it to him ran across the road to halt a down-coming truck.

'Turn thyself at the crossroads and put thyself in position to pull this wreck forward,' he said to the driver.

'My orders are—'

'Obscenity thy orders. Do as I say.'

The driver let his truck into gear and rolled straight ahead down the road and was gone in the dust.

As Gomez started the motor cycle ahead on to the now clear right-hand side of the road past the wrecked truck, Andrés, holding right again, saw the control guard halting another truck and the driver leaning from the cab and listening to him.

Now they went fast, swooping along the road that mounted steadily toward the mountain. All forward traffic had been stalled at the control and there were only the descending trucks passing, passing and passing on their left as the motor cycle climbed fast and steadily now until it began to overtake the mounting traffic which had gone on ahead before the disaster at the control.

Still without lights they passed four more armoured cars, then a long line of trucks loaded with troops. The troops were silent in the dark and at first Andrés only felt their presence rising above him, bulking above the truck bodies through the dust as they passed. Then another staff car came behind them blasting with its klaxon and flicking its lights off and on, and each time the lights shone Andrés saw the troops, steel-helmeted, their rifles vertical, their machine guns pointed up against the dark sky, etched sharp against the night that they dropped into when the light flicked off. Once as he passed close to a troop truck and the lights flashed he saw their faces fixed and sad in the sudden light. In their steel helmets, riding in the trucks in the dark toward something that they only knew was an attack, their faces were drawn with each man's own problem in the dark and the light revealed them as they would not have looked in day, from shame to show it to each other, until the bombardment and the attack would commence, and no man would think about his face.

Andrés now passing them truck after truck, Gomez still keeping successfully ahead of the following staff car, did not think any of this about their faces. He only thought, 'What an army. What equipment. What a mechanization. *Vaya gente!* Look at such people. Here we have the army of the Republic. Look at them. Camion after camion. All uniformed alike. All with casques of steel on their heads. Look at the *máquinas* rising from the trucks against the coming of planes. Look at the army that has been builded!'

And as the motor cycle passed the high grey trucks full of troops, grey trucks with high square cabs and square ugly radiators, steadily mounting the road in the dust and the flicking lights of the pursuing staff car, the red star of the army showing in the light when it passed over the tail gates, showing when the light came on to the sides of the dusty truck bodies, as they passed, climbing steadily now, the air colder and the road starting to turn in bends and switchbacks now, the trucks labouring and grinding, some steaming in the light flashes, the motor cycle labouring now, too, and Andrés clinging tight to the front seat as they climbed. Andrés thought this ride on a motor cycle was *mucho*, *mucho*. He had never been on a motor cycle before and now they were climbing a mountain in the midst of all the movement that was going to an attack and, as they climbed, he knew now there was no problem of ever being back in time for the assault on the posts. In this movement and confusion he would be lucky to get back by the next night. He had never seen an offensive or any of the preparations for one before and as they rode up the road he marvelled at the size and power of this army that the Republic had built.

Now they rode on a long slanting, rising stretch of road that ran across the face of the mountain and the grade was so steep as they neared the top that Gomez told him to get down and together they pushed the motor cycle up the last steep grade of the pass. At the left, just past the top, there was a loop of road where cars could turn and there were lights winking in front of a big stone building that bulked long and dark against the night sky.

'Let us go to ask there where the headquarters is,' Gomez said to Andrés and they wheeled the motor cycle over to where two sentries stood in front of the closed door of the great stone building. Gomez leaned the motor cycle against the wall as a motor cyclist in a leather suit, showing against the light from inside the building as the door opened, came out of the door with a dispatch case hung over his shoulder, a wooden-holstered Mauser pistol swung against his hip. As the light went off, he found his motor cycle in the dark by the door, pushed it until it sputtered and caught, then roared off up the road.

At the door Gomez spoke to one of the sentries. 'Captain Gomez of the Sixty-Fifth Brigade,' he said. 'Can you tell me where to find the headquarters of General Golz commanding the Thirty-Fifth Division?'

'It isn't here,' the sentry said.

'What is here?'

'The Comandancia.'

'What comandancia?'

'Well, the Comandancia.'

'The comandancia of what?'

'What art thou to ask so many questions?' the sentry said to Gomez in the dark. Here on the top of the pass the sky was very clear with the stars out and Andrés, out of the dust now, could see quite clearly in the dark. Below them, where the road turned to the right, he could see clearly the outline of the trucks and cars that passed against the sky line.

'I am Captain Rogelio Gomez of the first battalion of the Sixty-Fifth Brigade and I ask where is the headquarters of General Golz,' Gomez said.

The sentry opened the door a little way. 'Call the corporal of the guard,' he shouted inside.

Just then a big staff car came up over the turn of the road and circled toward the big stone building where Andrés and Gomez were standing waiting for the corporal of the guard. It came toward them and stopped outside the door.

A large man, old and heavy, in an oversized khaki beret, such as *chasseurs à pied* wear in the French Army, wearing an overcoat, carrying a map case and wearing a pistol strapped around his greatcoat, got out of the back of the car with two other men in the uniform of the International Brigades.

He spoke in French, which Andrés did not understand and of which Gomez, who had been a barber, knew only a few words, to his chauffeur telling him to get the car away from the door and into shelter.

As he came into the door with the other two officers, Gomez saw his face clearly in the light and recognized him. He had seen him at political meetings and he had often read articles by him in *Mundo Obrero* translated from the French. He recognized his bushy eyebrows, his watery grey eyes, his chin and the double chin under it, and he knew him for one of France's great modern revolutionary figures who had led the mutiny of the French Navy in the Black Sea. Gomez knew this man's high political place in the International Brigades and he knew this man would know where Golz's headquarters were and be able to direct him there. He did not know what this man had become with time, disappointment, bitterness both domestic and political, and thwarted ambition and that to question him was one of the most dangerous things that any man could do. Knowing nothing of this he stepped forward into the path of this man, saluted with his clenched fist and said, 'Comrade Massart, we are the bearers of a dispatch for General Golz. Can you direct us to his headquarters? It is urgent.'

The tall, heavy old man looked at Gomez with his out-thrust head and considered him carefully with his watery eyes. Even here at the front in the light of a bare electric bulb, he having just come in from driving in an open car on a brisk night, his grey face had a look of decay. His face looked as though it were modelled from the waste material you find under the claws of a very old lion.

'You have what, Comrade?' he asked Gomez, speaking Spanish with a strong Catalan accent. His eyes glanced sideways at Andrés, slid over him, and went back to Gomez.

'A dispatch for General Golz to be delivered at his headquarters, Comrade Massart.'

'Where is it from, Comrade?'

'From behind the fascist lines,' Gomez said.

André Massart extended his hand for the dispatch and the other papers. He glanced at them and put them in his pocket.

'Arrest them both,' he said to the corporal of the guard. 'Have them searched and bring them to me when I send for them.'

With the dispatch in his pocket he strode on into the interior of the big stone house.

Outside in the guard room Gomez and Andrés were being searched by the guard.

'What passes with that man?' Gomez said to one of the guards.

'*Está loco*,' the guard said. 'He is crazy.'

'No. He is a political figure of great importance,' Gomez said. 'He is the chief commissar of the International Brigades.'

'*Apesar de eso, está loco*,' the corporal of the guard said. 'All the same he's crazy. What do you behind the fascist lines?'

'This comrade is a guerrilla from there,' Gomez told him while the man searched him. 'He brings a dispatch to General Golz. Guard well my papers. Be careful with that money and that bullet on the string. It is from my first wound at Guadarrama.'

'Don't worry,' the corporal said. 'Everything will be in this drawer. Why didn't you ask me where Golz was?'

'We tried to. I asked the sentry, and he called you.'

'But then came the crazy and you asked him. No one should ask him anything. He is crazy. Thy Golz is up the road three kilometres from here and to the right in the rocks of the forest.'

'Can you not let us go to him now?'

'Nay. It would be my head. I must take thee to the crazy. Besides, he has thy dispatch.'

'Can you not tell someone?'

'Yes,' the corporal said. 'I will tell the first responsible one I see. All know that he is crazy.'

'I had always taken him for a great figure,' Gomez said. 'For one of the glories of France.'

'He may be a glory and all,' the corporal said and put his hand on Andrés's shoulder. 'But he is as crazy as a bedbug. He has a mania for shooting people.'

'Truly shooting them?'

'*Como lo oyes*,' the corporal said. 'That old one kills more than the bubonic plague. *Mata más que la peste bubonica*. But he doesn't kill fascists like we do. *Qué va*. Not in joke. *Mata bichos raros*. He kills rare things. Trotzkyites. Divagationers. Any type of rare beasts.'

Andrés did not understand any of this.

'When we were at Escorial we shot I don't know how many for him,' the corporal said. 'We always furnish the firing party. The men of the Brigades would not shoot their own men. Especially the French. To avoid difficulties it is always us who do it. We shot French. We have shot Belgians. We have shot others of divers nationality. Of all types. *Tiene mania de fusilar gente*. Always for political things. He's crazy. *Purifica más que el Salvarsán*. He purifies more than Salvarsan.'

'But you will tell someone of this dispatch?'

'Yes, man. Surely. I know every one of these two Brigades. Everyone comes through here. I know even up to and through the Russians, although only few speak Spanish. We will keep this crazy from shooting Spaniards.'

'But the dispatch.'

'The dispatch, too. Do not worry, Comrade. We know how to deal with this crazy. He is only dangerous with his own people. We understand him now.'

'Bring in the two prisoners,' came the voice of André Massart.

'*Quereis echar un trago?*' the corporal asked. 'Do you want a drink?'

'Why not?'

The corporal took a bottle of Anis from a cupboard and both Gomez and Andrés drank. So did the corporal. He wiped his mouth on his hand.

'*Vámonos*,' he said.

They went out of the guard room with the swallowed burn of the Anis warming their mouths, their bellies and their hearts and walked down the hall and entered the room where Massart sat behind a long table, his map spread in front of him, his red-and-blue pencil, with which he played at being a general officer, in his hand. To Andrés it was only one more thing. There had been many to-night. There were always many. If your papers were in order and your heart was good you were in no danger. Eventually they turned you loose and you were on your way. But the *Inglés* had said to hurry. He knew now he could never get back for the bridge but they had a dispatch to deliver and this old man there at the table had put it in his pocket.

'Stand there,' Massart said without looking up.

'Listen, Comrade Massart,' Gomez broke out, the Anis fortifying his anger. 'Once to-night we have been impeded by the ignorance of the anarchists. Then by the sloth of a bureaucratic fascist. Now by thy oversuspicion of a Communist.'

'Close your mouth,' Massart said without looking up. 'This is not a meeting.'

'Comrade Massart, this is a matter of the utmost urgence,' Gomez said. 'Of the greatest importance.'

The corporal and the soldier with them were taking a lively interest in this as though they were at a play they had seen many times but whose excellent moments they could always savour.

'Everything is of urgence,' Massart said. 'All things are of importance.' Now he looked up at them, holding the pencil. 'How did you know Golz was here? Do you understand how serious it is to come asking for an individual general before an attack? How could you know such a general would be here?'

'Tell him, *tu*,' Gomez said to Andrés.

'Comrade General,' Andrés started–André Massart did not correct him in the mistake in rank–'I was given that packet on the other side of the lines—'

'On the other side of the lines?' Massart said. 'Yes, I heard him say you came from the fascist lines.'

'It was given to me, Comrade General, by an *Inglés* named Roberto who had come to us as a dynamiter for this of the bridge. Understandeth?'

'Continue thy story,' Massart said to Andrés; using the term story as you would say lie, falsehood, or fabrication.

'Well, Comrade General, the *Inglés* told me to bring it to the General Golz with all speed. He makes an attack in these hills now on this day and all we ask is to take it to him now promptly if it pleases the Comrade General.'

Massart shook his head again. He was looking at Andrés but he was not seeing him.

Golz, he thought in a mixture of horror and exultation as a man might feel hearing that a business enemy had been killed in a particularly nasty motor accident or that someone you hated but whose probity you had never doubted had been guilty of defalcation. That Golz should be one of them, too. That Golz should be in such obvious communication with the fascists. Golz that he had known for nearly twenty years. Golz who had captured the gold train that winter with Lucacz in Siberia. Golz who had fought against Kolchak, and in Poland. In the Caucasus. In China, and here since the first October. But he *had* been close to Tukachevsky. To Voroshilov, yes, too. But to Tukachevsky. And to who else? Here to Karkov, of course. And to Lucacz. But all the Hungarians had been intriguers. He hated Gall. Golz hated Gall. Remember that. Make a note of that. Golz has always hated Gall. But he favours Putz. Remember that. And Duval is his chief of staff. See what stems from that. You've heard him say Copic's a fool. That is definitive. That exists. And now this dispatch from the fascist lines. Only by pruning out of these rotten branches can the tree remain healthy and grow. The rot must become apparent for it is to be destroyed. But Golz of all men. That Golz should be one of the traitors. He knew that you could trust no one. No one. Ever. Not your wife. Not your brother. Not your oldest comrade. No one. Ever.

'Take them away,' he said to the guards. 'Guard them carefully.' The corporal looked at the soldier. This had been very quiet for one of Massart's performances.

'Comrade Massart,' Gomez said. 'Do not be insane. Listen to me, a loyal officer and comrade. That is a dispatch that must be delivered. This comrade has brought it through the fascist lines to give to Comrade General Golz.'

'Take them away,' Massart said, now kindly, to the guard. He was sorry for them as human beings if it should be necessary to liquidate them. But it was the tragedy of Golz that oppressed him. That it should be Golz, he thought. He would take the fascist communication at once to Varloff. No, better he would take it to Golz himself and watch him as he received it. That was what he would do. How could he be sure of Varloff if Golz was one of them? No. This was a thing to be very careful about.

Andrés turned to Gomez, 'You mean he is not going to send the dispatch?' he asked, unbelieving.

'Don't you see?' Gomez said.

'*Me cago en su puta madre!*' Andrés said. '*Está loco.*'

'Yes,' Gomez said. 'He is crazy. You are crazy! Hear! Crazy!' he shouted at Massart who was back now bending over the map with his red-and-blue pencil. 'Hear me, you crazy murderer?'

'Take them away,' Massart said to the guard. 'Their minds are unhinged by their great guilt.'

There was a phrase the corporal recognized. He had heard that before.

'You crazy murderer!' Gomez shouted.

'*Hijo de la gran puta*,' Andrés said to him. *'Loco.'*

The stupidity of this man angered him. If he was a crazy let him be removed as a crazy. Let the dispatch be taken from his pocket. God damn this crazy to hell. His heavy Spanish anger was rising out of his usual calm and good temper. In a little while it would blind him.

Massart, looking at his map, shook his head sadly as the guards took Gomez and Andrés out. The guards had enjoyed hearing him cursed but on the whole they had been disappointed in the performance. They had seen much better ones. André Massart did not mind the men cursing him. So many men had cursed him at the end. He was always genuinely sorry for them as human beings. He always told himself that and it was one of the last true ideas that was left to him that had ever been his own.

He sat there, his moustache and his eyes focused on the map, on the map that he never truly understood, on the brown tracing of the contours that were traced fine and concentric as a spider's web. He could see the heights and the valleys from the contours but he never really understood why it should be this height and why this valley was the one. But at the General Staff where, because of the system of Political Commissars, he could intervene as the political head of the Brigades, he would put his finger on such and such a numbered, brown-thin-lined encircled spot among the greens of woods cut by the lines of roads that parallel the never casual winding of a river and say, 'There. That is the point of weakness.'

Gall and Copic, who were men of politics and of ambition, would agree, and later, men who never saw the map, but heard the number of the hill before they left their starting place and had the earth of diggings on it pointed out, would climb its side to find their death along its slope or, being halted by machine-guns placed in olive groves would never get up it at all. Or on other fronts they might scale it easily and be no better off than they had been before. But when Massart put his finger on the map in Golz's staff the scar-headed, white-faced General's jaw muscles would tighten and he would think, 'I should shoot you, André Massart, before I let you put that grey rotten finger on a contour map of mine. Damn you to hell for all the men you've killed by interfering in matters you know nothing of. Damn the day they named tractor factories and villages and co-operatives for you so that you are a symbol that I cannot touch. Go and suspect and exhort and intervene and denounce and butcher in some other place and leave my staff alone.'

But instead of saying that Golz would only lean back away from the leaning bulk, the pushing finger, the watery grey eyes, the grey-white moustache and the bad breath and say, 'Yes, Comrade Massart. I see your point. It is not well taken, however, and I do not agree. You can try to go over my head if you like. Yes. You can make it a Party matter as you say. But I do not agree.'

So now André Massart sat working over his map at the bare table with the raw light on the unshaded electric light bulb over his head, the overwide beret pulled forward to shade his eyes, referring to the mimeographed copy of the orders for the attack and slowly and carefully and laboriously working them out on the maps as a young officer might work a problem at a staff college. He was engaged in war. In his mind he was commanding troops; he had the right to interfere and this he believed to constitute command. So he sat there with Robert Jordan's dispatch to Golz in his pocket and Gomez and Andrés waited in the guard room and Robert Jordan lay in the woods above the bridge.

It is doubtful if the outcome of Andrés's mission would have been any different if he and Gomez had been allowed to proceed without André

Massart's hindrance. There was no one at the front with sufficient authority to cancel the attack. The machinery had been in motion much too long for it to be stopped suddenly now. There is a great inertia about all military operations of any size. But once this inertia has been overcome and movement is under way they are almost as hard to arrest as to initiate.

But on this night the old man, his beret pulled forward, was still sitting at the table with his map when the door opened and Karkov the Russian journalist came in with two other Russians in civilian clothes, leather coats and caps. The corporal of the guard closed the door reluctantly behind them. Karkov had been the first responsible man he had been able to communicate with.

'Tovarich Massart,' said Karkov in his politely disdainful lisping voice and smiled, showing his bad teeth.

Massart stood up. He did not like Karkov, but Karkov, coming from *Pravda* and in direct communication with Stalin, was at this moment one of the three most important men in Spain.

'Tovarich Karkov,' he said.

'You are preparing the attack?' Karkov said insolently, nodding toward the map.

'I am studying it,' Massart answered.

'Are you attacking? Or is it Golz?' Karkov asked smoothly.

'I am only a commissar, as you know,' Massart told him.

'No,' Karkov said. 'You are modest. You are really a general. You have your map and your field glasses. But were you not an admiral once, Comrade Massart?'

'I was a gunner's mate,' said Massart. It was a lie. He had really been a chief yeoman at the time of the mutiny. But he thought now, always, that he had been a gunner's mate.

'Ah. I thought you were a first-class yeoman,' Karkov said. 'I always get my facts wrong. It is the mark of the journalist.'

The other Russians had taken no part in the conversation. They were both looking over Massart's shoulder at the map and occasionally making a remark to each other in their own language. Massart and Karkov spoke French after the first greeting.

'It is better not to get facts wrong in *Pravda*,' Massart said. He said it brusquely to build himself up again. Karkov always punctured him. The French word is *dégonfler* and Massart was worried and made wary by him. It was hard, when Karkov spoke, to remember with what importance he, André Massart, came from the Central Committee of the French Communist Party. It was hard to remember, too, that he was untouchable. Karkov seemed always to touch him so lightly and whenever he wished. Now Karkov said, 'I usually correct them before I send them to *Pravda*. I am quite accurate in *Pravda*. Tell me, Comrade Massart, have you heard anything of any message coming through for Golz from one of our *partizan* group operating toward Segovia? There is an American comrade there named Jordan that we should have heard from. There have been reports of fighting there behind the fascist lines. He would have sent a message through to Golz.'

'An American?' Massart asked. Andrés had said an *Inglés*. So that is what it was. So he had been mistaken. Why had those fools spoken to him anyway?

'Yes,' Karkov looked at him contemptuously, 'a young American of slight political development but a great way with the Spaniards and a fine *partizan* record. Just give me the dispatch, Comrade Massart. It has been delayed enough.'

'What dispatch?' Massart asked. It was a very stupid thing to say and he knew it. But he was not able to admit he was wrong that quickly and he said it anyway to delay the moment of humiliation.

'And the safe-conduct pass,' Karkov said through his bad teeth.

André Massart put his hand in his pocket and laid the dispatch on the table. He looked Karkov squarely in the eye. All right. He was wrong and there was nothing he could do about it now but he was not accepting any humiliation. 'And the safe-conduct pass,' Karkov said softly.

Massart laid it beside the dispatch.

'Comrade Corporal,' Karkov called in Spanish.

The corporal opened the door and came in. He looked quickly at André Massart who stared back at him like an old boar which has been brought to bay by hounds. There was no fear on Massart's face and no humiliation. He was only angry, and he was only temporarily at bay. He knew these dogs could never hold him.

'Take these to the two comrades in the guard room and direct them to General Golz's headquarters,' Karkov said. 'There has been too much delay.'

The corporal went out and Massart looked after him, then looked at Karkov.

'Tovarich Massart,' Karkov said, 'I am going to find out just how untouchable you are.'

Massart looked straight at him and said nothing.

'Don't start to have any plans about the corporal, either,' Karkov went on. 'It was not the corporal. I saw the two men in the guard room and they spoke to me' (this was a lie). 'I hope all men always will speak to me' (this was the truth although it was the corporal who had spoken). But Karkov had this belief in the good which could come from his own accessibility and the humanizing possibility of benevolent intervention. It was the one thing he was never cynical about.

'You know when I am in the U.S.S.R. people write to me in *Pravda* when there is an injustice in a town in Azerbaijan. Did you know that? They say, "Karkov will help us."'

André Massart looked at him with no expression on his face except anger and dislike. There was nothing in his mind now but that Karkov had done something against him. All right, Karkov, power and all, could watch out.

'This is something else,' Karkov went on, 'but it is the same principle. I am going to find out just how untouchable you are, Comrade Massart. I would like to know if it could not be possible to change the name of that tractor factory.'

André Massart looked away from him and back to the map.

'What did young Jordan say?' Karkov asked him.

'I did not read it,' André Massart said. '*Et maintenant fiche moi la paix*, Comrade Karkov.'

'Good,' said Karkov. 'I leave you to your military labours.'

He stepped out of the room and walked to the guard room. Andrés and Gomez were already gone and he stood there a moment looking up the road and at the mountain tops beyond that showed now in the first grey of daylight. We must get on up there, he thought. It will be soon, now.

Andrés and Gomez were on the motor cycle on the road again and it was getting light. Now Andrés, holding again to the back of the seat ahead of him as the motor cycle climbed turn after switchback turn in a faint grey mist that lay over the top of the pass, felt the motor cycle speed under him, then skid and stop and they were standing by the motor cycle on a long, down-slope of road and in the woods, on their left, were tanks covered with pine branches. There were troops here all through the woods. Andrés saw men carrying the long poles of stretchers over their shoulders. Three staff cars were off the road to the right, in under the trees, with branches laid against their sides and other pine branches over their tops.

Gomez wheeled the motor cycle up to one of them. He leaned it against a pine tree and spoke to the chauffeur who was sitting by the car, his back against a tree.

'I'll take you to him,' the chauffeur said. 'Put thy *moto* out of sight and cover it with these.' He pointed to a pile of cut branches.

With the sun just starting to come through the high branches of the pine trees, Gomez and Andrés followed the chauffeur, whose name was Vicente, through the pines across the road and up the slope to the entrance of a dugout from the roof of which signal wires ran on up over the wooded slope. They stood outside while the chauffeur went in and Andrés admired the construction of the dugout which showed only as a hole in the hillside, with no dirt scattered about, but which he could see, from the entrance, was both deep and profound with men moving around in it freely with no need to duck their heads under the heavy timbered roof.

Vicente, the chauffeur, came out.

'He is up above where they are deploying for the attack,' he said. 'I gave it to his Chief of Staff. He signed for it. Here.'

He handed Gomez the receipted envelope. Gomez gave it to Andrés, who looked at it and put it inside his shirt.

'What is the name of him who signed?' he asked.

'Duval,' Vicente said.

'Good,' said Andrés. 'He was one of three to whom I might give it.'

'Should we wait for an answer?' Gomez asked Andrés.

'It might be best. Though where I will find the *Inglés* and the others after that of the bridge neither God knows.'

'Come wait with me,' Vicente said, 'until the General returns. And I will get thee coffee. Thou must be hungry.'

'And these tanks,' Gomez said to him.

They were passing the branch-covered, mud-coloured tanks, each with two deep-ridged tracks over the pine needles showing where they had swung and backed from the road. Their 45-mm. guns jutted horizontally under the branches and the drivers and gunners in their leather coats and ridged helmets sat with their backs against the trees or lay sleeping on the ground.

'These are the reserve,' Vicente said. 'Also these troops are in reserve. Those who commence the attack are above.'

'They are many,' Andrés said.

'Yes,' Vicente said. 'It is a full division.'

Inside the dugout Duval, holding the opened dispatch from Robert Jordan in his left hand, glancing at his wrist watch on the same hand, reading the dispatch for the fourth time, each time feeling the sweat come out from under his armpit and run down his flank, said into the telephone, 'Get me position Segovia, then. He's left? Get me position Avila.'

He kept on with the phone. It wasn't any good. He had talked to both brigades. Golz had been up to inspect the dispositions for the attack and was on his way to an observation post. He called the observation post and he was not there.

'Get me planes one,' Duval said, suddenly taking all responsibility. He would take responsibility for holding it up. It was better to hold it up. You could not send them to a surprise attack against an enemy that was waiting for it. You couldn't do it. It was just murder. You couldn't. You mustn't. No matter what. They could shoot him if they wanted. He would call the airfield directly and get the bombardment cancelled. But suppose it's just a holding attack? Suppose we were supposed to draw off all that material and those forces? Suppose that is what it is for? They never tell you it is a holding attack when you make it.

'Cancel the call to planes one,' he told the signaller. 'Get me the 69th Brigade observation post.'

He was still calling there when he heard the first sound of the planes.

It was just then he got through to the observation post.

'Yes,' Golz said quietly.

He was sitting leaning back against the sandbag, his feet against a rock, a cigarette hung from his lower lip and he was looking up and over his shoulder while he was talking. He was seeing the expanding wedges of threes, silver and thundering in the sky that were coming over the far shoulder of the mountain where the first sun was striking. He watched them come shining and beautiful in the sun. He saw the twin circles of light where the sun shone on the propellers as they came.

'Yes,' he said into the telephone, speaking in French because it was Duval on the wire. '*Nous sommes foutus. Oui. Comme toujours. Oui. C'est dommage. Oui*. It's a shame it came too late.'

His eyes, watching the planes coming, were very proud. He saw the red wing markings now and he watched their steady, stately roaring advance. This was how it could be. These were our planes. They had come, crated on ships, from the Black Sea through the Straits of Marmora, through the Dardanelles, through the Mediterranean and to here, unloaded lovingly at Alicante, assembled ably, tested and found perfect and now flown in lovely hammering precision, the V's tight and pure as they came now high and silver in the morning sun to blast those ridges across there and blow them roaring high so that we can go through.

Golz knew that once they had passed overhead and on, the bombs would fall, looking like porpoises in the air as they tumbled. And then the ridge tops would spout and roar in jumping clouds and disappear in one great blowing cloud. Then the tanks would grind clanking up those two slopes and after them would go his two brigades. And if it had been a surprise they could go on and down and over and through, pausing, cleaning up, dealing with, much to do, much to be done intelligently with the tanks helping, with the tanks wheeling and returning, giving covering fire and others bringing the attackers up then slipping on and over and through and pushing down beyond. This was how it would be if there was no treason and if all did what they should.

There were the two ridges and there were the tanks ahead and there were his two good brigades ready to leave the woods and here came the planes now. Everything he had to do had been done as it should be.

But as he watched the planes, almost up to him now, he felt sick at his stomach for he knew from having heard Jordan's dispatch over the phone that there would be no one on those two ridges. They'd be withdrawn a little way below in narrow trenches to escape the fragments, or hiding in the timber and when the bombers passed they'd get back up there with their machine guns and their automatic weapons and the anti-tank guns Jordan had said went up the road, and it would be one famous balls up more. But the planes, now coming deafeningly, were how it could have been and Golz watching them, looking up, said into the telephone No. *Rien à faire. Rien. Faut pas penser. Faut accepter.*'

Golz watched the planes with his hard proud eyes that knew how things could be and how they would be instead and said, proud of how they could be, believing in how they could be, even if they never were, '*Bon. Nous ferons notre petit possible*,' and hung up.

But Duval did not hear him. Sitting at the table holding the receiver, all he heard was the roar of the planes and he thought, now, maybe this time, listen to them come, maybe the bombers will blow them all off, maybe we will get a break-through, maybe he will get the reserves he asked for, maybe this is it, maybe this is the time. Go on. Come on. Go on. The roar was such that he could not hear what he was thinking.

43

Robert Jordan lay behind the trunk of a pine tree on the slope of the hill above the road and the bridge and watched it become daylight. He loved this hour of the day always and now he watched it; feeling it grey within him, as though he were a part of the slow lightening that comes before the rising of the sun; when solid things darken and space lightens and the lights that have shone in the night go yellow and then fade as the day comes. The pine trunks below him were hard and clear now, their trunks solid and brown and the road was shiny with a wisp of mist over it. The dew had wet him and the forest floor was soft and he felt the give of the brown, dropped pine needles under his elbows. Below he saw, through the light mist that rose from the stream bed, the steel of the bridge, straight and rigid across the gap, with the wooden sentry boxes at each end. But as he looked the structure of the bridge was still spidery and fine in the mist that hung over the stream.

He saw the sentry now in his box as he stood, his back with the hanging blanket coat topped by the steel casque on his head showing as he leaned forward over the hole-punched petrol tin of the brazier, warming his hands. Robert Jordan heard the stream, far down in the rocks, and he saw a faint, thin smoke that rose from the sentry box.

He looked at his watch and thought, I wonder if Andrés got through to Golz? If we are going to blow it I would like to breathe very slowly and slow up the time again and feel it. Do you think he made it? Andrés? And if he did would they call it off? If they had time to call it off? *Qué va.* Do not worry. They will or they won't. There are no more decisions and in a little while you will know. Suppose the attack is successful. Golz said it could be. That there was a possibility. With our tanks coming down that road, the people coming through from the right and down and past La Granja and the whole left of the mountains turned. Why don't you ever think of how it is to win? You've been on the defensive for so long that you can't think of that. Sure. But that was before all that stuff went up this road. That was before all the planes came. Don't be so naïve. But remember this that as long as we can hold them here we keep the fascists tied up. They can't attack any other country until they finish with us and they can never finish with us. If the French help at all, if only they leave the frontier open and if we get planes from America they can never finish with us. Never, if we get anything at all. These people will fight for ever if they're well armed.

No you must not expect victory here, not for several years maybe. This is just a holding attack. You must not get illusions about it now. Suppose we got a break-through to-day? This is out first big attack. Keep your sense of proportion. But what if we should have it? Don't get excited, he told himself. Remember what went up the road. You've done what you could about that. We should have portable short-wave sets, though. We will, in time. But we haven't yet. You just watch now and do what you should.

To-day is only one day in all the days that will ever be. But what will happen in all the other days that ever come can depend on what you do to-day. It's been that way all this year. It's been that way so many times. All of this war is that way. You are getting very pompous in the early morning, he told himself. Look there what's coming now.

He saw the two men in blanket capes and steel helmets come around the corner of the road walking toward the bridge, their rifles slung over their shoulders. One stopped at the far end of the bridge and was out of sight in the sentry box. The other came on across the bridge, walking slowly and heavily. He stopped on the bridge and spat into the gorge, then came on slowly to the near end of the bridge where the other sentry spoke to him and then started off back over the bridge. The sentry who was relieved walked faster than the other had one (because he's going to coffee, Robert Jordan thought) but he too spat down into the gorge.

I wonder if that is superstition? Robert Jordan thought. I'll have to take me a spit in that gorge too. If I can spit by then. No. It can't be very powerful medicine. It can't work. I'll have to prove it doesn't work before I am out there.

The new sentry had gone inside the box and sat down. His rifle with the bayonet fixed was leaning against the wall. Robert Jordan took his glasses from his shirt pocket and turned the eyepieces until the end of the bridge showed sharp and grey-painted-metal clear. Then he moved them on to the sentry box.

The sentry sat leaning against the wall. His helmet hung on a peg and his face showed clearly. Robert Jordan saw he was the same man who had been there on guard two days before in the afternoon watch. He was wearing the same knitted stocking-cap. And he had not shaved. His cheeks were sunken and his cheek-bones prominent. He had bushy eyebrows that grew together in the centre. He looked sleepy and as Robert Jordan watched him he yawned. Then he took out a tobacco pouch and a packet of papers and rolled himself a cigarette. He tried to make a lighter work and finally put it in his pocket and went over to the brazier, leaned over, reached inside, brought up a piece of charcoal, juggled it in one hand while he blew on it, then lit the cigarette and tossed the lump of charcoal back into the brazier.

Robert Jordan, looking through the Zeiss 8-power glasses, watched his face as he leaned against the wall of the sentry box drawing on the cigarette. Then he took the glasses down, folded them together and put them in his pocket.

I won't look at him again, he told himself.

He lay there and watched the road and tried not to think at all. A squirrel chattered from a pine tree below him and Robert Jordan watched the squirrel come down the tree trunk, stopping on his way down to turn his head and look toward where the man was watching. He saw the squirrel's eyes, small and bright and watched his tail jerk in excitement. Then the squirrel crossed to another tree, moving on the ground in long, small-pawed, tail-exaggerated bounds. On the tree trunk he looked back at Robert Jordan, then pulled himself around the trunk and out of sight. Then Robert Jordan heard the squirrel chatter from a high branch of the pine tree and he watched him there, spread flat along the branch, his tail jerking.

Robert Jordan looked down through the pines to the sentry box again. He would like to have had the squirrel with him in his pocket. He would like to have had anything that he could touch. He rubbed his elbows against the pine needles but it was not the same. Nobody knows how lonely you can be when you do this. Me, though, I know. I hope that Rabbit will get out of this all right. Stop that now. Yes, sure. But I can hope that and I do. That I blow it well and that she gets out all right. Good. Sure. Just that. That is all I want now.

He lay there now and looked away from the road and the sentry box and across to the far mountain. Just do not think at all, he told himself. He lay there quietly and watched the morning come. It was a fine early summer morning and it came very fast now in the end of May. Once a motor cyclist in a leather coat and all-leather helmet with an automatic rifle in a holster by his left leg came across the bridge and went on up the road. Once an ambulance crossed the bridge, passed below him, and went up the road. But that was all. He smelled the pines and he heard the stream and the bridge showed clear now and beautiful in the morning light. He lay there behind the pine tree, with the sub-machine gun across his left forearm, and he never looked at the sentry box again until, long after it seemed that it was never coming, that nothing could happen on such a lovely late May morning, he heard the sudden, clustered, thudding of the bombs.

As he heard the bombs, the first thumping noise of them, before the echo of them came back in thunder from the mountain, Robert Jordan drew in a long breath and lifted the sub-machine gun from where it lay. His arm felt stiff from its weight and his fingers were heavy with reluctance.

The man in the sentry box stood up when he heard the bombs. Robert Jordan saw him reach for his rifle and step forward out of the box listening. He stood in the road with the sun shining on him. The knitted cap was on the side of his head and the sun was on his unshaved face as he looked up into the sky toward where the planes were bombing.

There was no mist on the road now and Robert Jordan saw the man, clearly and sharply, standing there on the road looking up at the sky. The sun shone bright on him through the trees.

Robert Jordan felt his own breath tight now as though a strand of wire bound his chest and, steadying his elbows, feeling the corrugations of the forward grip against his fingers, he put the oblong of the foresight, settled now in the notch of the rear, on to the centre of the man's chest and squeezed the trigger gently.

He felt the quick, liquid, spastic lurching of the gun against his shoulder and on the road the man, looking surprised and hurt, slid forward on his knees and his forehead doubled to the road. His rifle fell by him and lay there with one of the man's fingers twisted through the trigger guard, his wrist bent forward. The rifle lay, bayonet forward on the road. Robert Jordan looked away from the man lying with his head doubled under on the road to the bridge, and the sentry box at the other end. He could not see the other sentry and he looked down the slope to the right where he knew Agustín was hidden. Then he heard Anselmo shoot, the shot smashing an echo back from the gorge. Then he heard him shoot again.

With the second shot came the cracking boom of grenades from around the corner below the bridge. Then there was the noise of grenades from well up the road to the left. Then he heard rifle-firing up the road and from below came the noise of Pablo's cavalry automatic rifle spat-spat-spat-spatting into the noise of the grenades. He saw Anselmo scrambling down the steep cut to the far end of the bridge and he slung the sub-machine gun over his shoulder and picked up the two heavy packs from behind the pine trunks and with one in each hand, the packs pulling his arms so that he felt the tendons would pull out of his shoulders, he ran lurching down the steep slope to the road.

As he ran he heard Agustín shouting, '*Buena caza, Inglés. Buena cazá!*' and he thought, 'Nice hunting, like hell, nice hunting,' and just then he heard Anselmo shoot at the far end of the bridge, the noise of the shot clanging in the steel girders. He passed the sentry where he lay and ran on to the bridge, the packs swinging.

The old man came running toward him, holding his carbine in one hand, '*Sin novedad*,' he shouted. 'There's nothing wrong. *Tuve que rematarlo*. I had to finish him.'

Robert Jordan, kneeling, opening the packs in the centre of the bridge, taking out his material, saw that tears were running down Anselmo's cheeks through the grey beard stubble.

'*Ya maté uno tambien*,' he said to Anselmo. 'I killed one too,' and jerked his head toward where the sentry lay hunched over in the road at the end of the bridge.

'Yes, man, yes,' Anselmo said. 'We have to kill them and we kill them.'

Robert Jordan was climbing down into the framework of the bridge. The girders were cold and wet with dew under his hands and he climbed carefully, feeling the sun on his back, bracing himself in a bridge truss, hearing the noise of the tumbling water below him, hearing firing, too much firing, up the road at the upper post. He was sweating heavily now and it was cool under the bridge. He had a coil of wire around one arm and a pair of pliers hung by a thong from his wrist.

'Hand me that down a package at a time, *viejo*,' he called up to Anselmo. The old man leaned far over the edge handing down the oblong blocks of explosive and Robert Jordan reached up for them, shoved them in where he wanted them, packed them close, braced them, 'Wedges, *viejo*! Give me wedges!' smelling the fresh shingle smell of the new whittled wedges as he tapped them in tight to hold the charge between the girders.

Now as he worked, placing, bracing, wedging, lashing tight with wire, thinking only of demolition, working fast and skilfully as a surgeon works, he heard a rattle of firing from below on the road. Then there was the noise of a grenade. Then another, booming through the rushing noise the water made. Then it was quiet from that direction.

'Damn,' he thought. 'I wonder what hit them then?'

There was still firing up the road at the upper post. Too damned much firing, and he was lashing two grenades side by side on top of the braced blocks of explosive, winding the wire over their corrugations so they would hold tight and firm and lashing it tight; twisting it with the pliers. He felt of the whole thing and then, to make it more solid, tapped in a wedge above the grenades that blocked the whole charge firmly in against the steel.

'The other side now, *viejo*,' he shouted up to Anselmo and climbed across through the trestling, like a bloody Tarzan in a rolled steel forest, he thought, and then coming out from under the dark, the stream tumbling below him, he looked up and saw Anselmo's face as he reached the packages of explosive down to him. Goddamn good face, he thought. Not crying now. That's all to the good. And one side done. This side now and we're done. This will drop it like what all. Come on. Don't get excited. Do it. Clean and fast as the last one. Don't fumble with it. Take your time. Don't try to do it faster than you can. You can't lose now. Nobody can keep you from blowing one side now. You're doing it just the way you should. This is a cool place. Christ, it feels cool as a wine cellar and there's no crap. Usually working under a stone bridge it's full of crap. This is a dream bridge. A bloody dream bridge. It's the old man on top who's in a bad spot. Don't try to do it faster than you can. I wish that shooting would be over up above. 'Give me some wedges, *viejo*.' I don't like that shooting still. Pilar has got in trouble there. Some of the post must have been out. Out back; or behind the mill. They're still shooting. That means there's somebody in the mill. And all that damned sawdust. Those big piles of sawdust. Sawdust, when it's old and packed, is good stuff to fight behind. There must be several of them still. It's quiet below with Pablo. I wonder what that second flare-up was. It must have been a car or a motor cyclist. I hope to God they don't have any armoured cars come up or any tanks. Go on. Put it in just as fast as you can and wedge it tight and lash it fast. You're shaking, like a Goddamn woman. What the hell is the matter with you? You're trying to do it too fast. I'll bet that Goddamn woman up above isn't shaking. That Pilar. Maybe she is too. She sounds as though she were in plenty trouble. She'll shake if she gets in enough. Like everybody bloody else.

He leaned out and up and into the sunlight and as he reached his hand up to take what Anselmo handed him, his head now above the noise of the falling water, the firing increased sharply up the road and then the noise of grenades again. Then more grenades.

'They rushed the sawmill then.'

It's lucky I've got this stuff in blocks, he thought. Instead of sticks. What the hell. It's just neater. Although a lousy canvas sack full of jelly would be quicker. Two sacks. No. One of that would do. And if we just had detonators and the old exploder. That son of a bitch threw my exploder in the river. That old box and the places that it's been. In this river. That old box and the places that it's been. In this river he threw it. That bastard Pablo. He gave them hell there below just now. 'Give me some more of that, *viejo*.'

The old man's doing very well. He's in quite a place up there. He hated to shoot that sentry. So did I but I didn't think about it. Nor do I think about it now. You have to do that. But then Anselmo got a cripple. I know about cripples. I think that killing a man with an automatic weapon makes it easier. I mean on the one doing it. It is different. After the first touch it is it that does it. Not you. Save that to go into some other time. You and your head. You have a nice thinking head old Jordan. Roll Jordan. Roll! They used to yell that at football when you lugged the ball. Do you know the damned Jordan is really not much bigger than that creek down there below. At the source, you mean. So is anything else at the source. This is a place here under this bridge. A home away from home. Come on Jordan, pull yourself together. This is serious, Jordan. Don't you understand? Serious. It's less so all the time. Look at that other side. *Para qué?* I'm all right now however she goes. As Maine goes so goes the nation. As Jordan goes so go the bloody Israelites. The bridge, I mean. As Jordan goes, so goes the bloody bridge, other way round, really.

'Give me some more of that, Anselmo old boy,' he said. The old man nodded. 'Almost through,' Robert Jordan said. The old man nodded again.

Finishing wiring the grenades down, he no longer heard the firing from up the road. Suddenly he was working only with the noise of the stream. He looked down and saw it boiling up white below him through the boulders and then dropping down to a clear pebbled pool where one of the wedges he had dropped swung around in the current. As he looked a trout rose for some insect and made a circle on the surface close to where the chip was turning. As he twisted the wire tight with the pliers that held these two grenades in place, he saw, through the metal of the bridge, the sunlight on the green slope of the mountain. It was brown three days ago, he thought.

Out from the cool dark under the bridge he leaned into the bright sun and shouted to Anselmo's bending face, 'Give me the big coil of wire.'

The old mand handed it down.

For God's sake don't loosen them any yet. This will pull them. I wish you could string them through. But with the length wire you are using it's O.K. Robert Jordan thought as he felt the cotter pins that held the rings that would release the levers on the hand grenades. He checked that the grenades, lashed on their sides, had room for the levers to spring when the pins were pulled (the wire that lashed them ran through under the levers), then he attached a length of wire to one ring, wired it on to the main wire that ran to the ring of the outside grenade, paid off some slack from the coil and passed it around a steel brace and then handed the coil up to Anselmo. 'Hold it carefully,' he said.

He climbed up on to the bridge, took the coils from the old man and walked back as fast as he could pay out wire toward where the sentry was slumped in the road, leaning over the side of the bridge and paying out wire from the coil as he walked.

'Bring the sacks,' he shouted to Anselmo as he walked backwards. As he passed he stooped down and picked up the sub-machine gun and slung it over his shoulder again.

It was then, looking up from paying out wire, that he saw, well up the road, those who were coming back from the upper post.

There were four of them, he saw, and then he had to watch his wire so it would be clear and not foul against any of the outer work of the bridge. Eladio was not with them.

Robert Jordan carried the wire clear past the end of the bridge, took a loop around the last stanchion and then ran along the road until he stopped beside a stone marker. He cut the wire and handed it to Anselmo.

'Hold this, *viejo*,' he said. 'Now walk back with me to the bridge. Take up on it as you walk. No. I will.'

At the bridge he pulled the wire back out through the hitch so it now ran clear and unfouled to the grenade rings and handed it, stretching alongside the bridge but running quite clear, to Anselmo.

'Take this back to that high stone,' he said. 'Hold it easily but firmly. Do not put any force on it. When thou pullest hard, hard, the bridge will blow. *Comprendes?*'

'Yes.'

'Treat it softly but do not let it sag so it would foul. Keep it lightly firm but not pulling until thou pullest. *Comprendes?*'

'Yes.'

'When thou pullest really pull. Do not jerk.'

Robert Jordan while he spoke was looking up the road at the remainder of Pilar's band. They were close now and he saw Primitivo and Rafael were supporting Fernando. He looked to be shot through the groin for he was holding himself there with both hands while the man and the boy held him on either side. His right leg was dragging, the side of the shoe scraping on the road as they walked him. Pilar was climbing the bank into the timber carrying three rifles. Robert Jordan could not see her face but her head was up and she was climbing as fast as she could.

'How does it go?' Primitivo called.

'Good. We're almost finished,' Robert Jordan shouted back.

There was no need to ask how it went with them. As he looked away the three were on the edge of the road and Fernando was shaking his head as they tried to get him up the bank.

'Give me a rifle here,' Robert Jordan heard him say in a choky voice.

'No, *hombre*. We will get thee to the horses.'

'What would I do with a horse?' Fernando said. 'I am very well here.'

Robert Jordan did not hear the rest for he was speaking to Anselmo.

'Blow it if tanks come,' he said. 'But only if they come on to it. Blow it if armoured cars come. If they come on to it. Anything else Pablo will stop.'

'I will not blow it with thee beneath it.'

'Take no account of me. Blow it if thou needest to. I fix the other wire and come back. Then we will blow it together.'

He started running for the centre of the bridge.

Anselmo saw Robert Jordan run up the bridge, coil of wire over his arm, pliers hanging from one wrist and the sub-machine gun slung over his back. He saw him climb down under the rail of the bridge and out of sight. Anselmo held the wire in his hand, his right hand, and he crouched behind the stone marker and looked down the road and across the bridge. Halfway between him and the bridge was the sentry, who had settled now closer to the road, sinking closer on to the smooth road surface as the sun weighed on his back. His rifle, lying on the road, the bayonet fixed, pointed straight toward Anselmo. The old man looked past him along the surface of the bridge crossed by the shadows of the bridge rail to where the road swung to the left along the gorge and then turned out of sight behind the rocky wall. He looked at the far sentry box with the sun shining on it and then, conscious of the wire in his hand, he turned his head to where Fernando was speaking to Primitivo and the gipsy.

'Leave me here,' Fernando said. 'It hurts much and there is much haemorrhage inside. I feel it in the inside when I move.'

'Let us get thee up the slope,' Primitivo said. 'Put thy arms around our shoulders and we will take thy legs.'

'It is inutile,' Fernando said. 'Put me here behind a stone. I am as useful here as above.'

'But when we go,' Primitivo said.

'Leave me here,' Fernando said. 'There is no question of my travelling with this. Thus it gives one horse more. I am very well here. Certainly they will come soon.'

'We can take thee up the hill,' the gipsy said. 'Easily.'

He was, naturally, in a deadly hurry to be gone, as was Primitivo. But they had brought him thus far.

'Nay,' Fernando said. 'I am very well here. What passes with Eladio?'

The gipsy put his finger on his head to show where the wound had been.

'Here,' he said. 'After thee. When we made the rush.'

'Leave me,' Fernando said. Anselmo could see he was suffering much. He held both hands against his groin now and put his head back against the bank, his legs straight out before him. His face was grey and sweating.

'Leave me now please, for a favour,' he said. His eyes were shut with pain, the edges of the lips twitching. 'I find myself very well here.'

'Here is a rifle and cartridges,' Primitivo said.

'Is it mine?' Fernando asked, his eyes shut.

'Nay, the Pilar has thine,' Primitivo said. 'This is mine.'

'I would prefer my own,' Fernando said. 'I am more accustomed to it.'

'I will bring it to thee,' the gipsy lied to him. 'Keep this until it comes.'

'I am in a very good position here,' Fernando said. 'Both for up the road and for the bridge.' He opened his eyes, turned his head and looked across the bridge, then shut them as the pain came.

The gipsy tapped his head and motioned with his thumb to Primitivo for them to be off.

'Then we will be down for thee,' Primitivo said and started up the slope after the gipsy, who was climbing fast.

Fernando lay back against the bank. In front of him was one of the whitewashed stones that marked the edge of the road. His head was in the shadow but the sun shone on his plugged and bandaged wound and on his hands that were cupped over it. His legs and his feet also were in the sun. The rifle lay beside him and there were three clips of cartridges shining in the sun beside the rifle. A fly crawled on his hands but the small tickling did not come through the pain.

'Fernando!' Anselmo called to him from where he crouched, holding the wire. He had made a loop in the end of the wire and twisted it close so he could hold it in his fist.

'Fernando!' he called again.

Fernando opened his eyes and looked at him.

'How does it go?' Fernando asked.

'Very good,' Anselmo said. 'Now in a minute we will be blowing it.'

'I am pleased. Anything you need me for advise me,' Fernando said and shut his eyes again and the pain lurched in him.

Anselmo looked away from him and out on to the bridge.

He was watching for the first sight of the coil of wire being handed up on to the bridge and for the *Inglés's* sunburnt head and face to follow it as he would pull himself up the side. At the same time he was watching beyond the bridge for anything to come around the far corner of the road. He did not feel afraid now at all and he had not been afraid all the day. It goes so fast and it is so normal, he thought. I hated the shooting of the guard and it made me an emotion but that is passed now. How could the *Inglés* say that the shooting of a man is like the shooting of an animal? In all hunting I have had an elation and no feeling of wrong. But to shoot a man gives a feeling as though one had struck one's own brother when you are grown men. And to shoot him various times to kill him. Nay, do not think of that. That gave thee too much emotion and thee ran blubbering down the bridge like a woman.

That is over, he told himself, and thou canst try to atone for it as for the others. But now thou hast what thou asked for last night coming home across the hills. Thou art in battle and thou hast no problem. If I die on this morning now it is all right.

Then he looked at Fernando lying there against the bank with his hands cupped over the groove of his hip, his lips blue, his eyes tight shut, breathing heavily and slowly, and he thought, If I die may it be quickly. Nay I said I would ask nothing more if I were granted what I needed for to-day. So I will not ask. Understand? I ask nothing. Nothing in any way. Give me what I asked for and I leave all the rest according to discretion.

He listened to the noise that came, far away, of the battle at the pass and he said to himself, Truly this is a great day. I should realize and know what a day this is.

But there was no lift or any excitement in his heart. That was all gone and there was nothing but a calmness. And now, as he crouched behind the marker stone with the looped wire in his hand and another loop of it around his wrist and the gravel beside the road under his knees he was not lonely nor did he feel in any way alone. He was one with the wire in his hand and one with the bridge, and one with the charges the *Inglés* had placed. He was one with the *Inglés* still working under the bridge and he was one with all of the battle and with the Republic.

But there was no excitement. It was all calm now and the sun beat down on his neck and on his shoulders as he crouched and as he looked up he saw the high, cloudless sky and the slope of the mountain rising beyond the river and he was not happy but he was neither lonely nor afraid.

Up the hill slope Pilar lay behind a tree watching the road that came down from the pass. She had three loaded rifles by her and she handed one to Primitivo as he dropped down beside her.

'Get down there,' she said. 'Behind that tree. Thou, gipsy, over there,' she pointed to another tree below. 'Is he dead?'

'Nay. Not yet,' Primitivo said.

'It was bad luck,' Pilar said. 'If we had had two more it need not have happened. He should have crawled around the sawdust pile. Is he all right there where he is?'

Primitivo shook his head.

'When the *Inglés* blows the bridge will fragments come this far?' the gipsy asked from behind his tree.

'I don't know,' Pilar said. 'But Agustín with the *máquina* is closer than thee. The *Inglés* would not have placed him there if it were too close.'

'But I remember with the blowing of the train the lamp of the engine blew by over my head and pieces of steel flew by like swallows.'

'Thou hast poetic memories,' Pilar said. 'Like swallows. *Joder!* They were like wash boilers. Listen, gipsy, thou hast comported thyself well to-day. Now do not let thy fear catch up with thee.'

'Well, I only asked if it would blow this far so I might keep well behind the tree trunk,' the gipsy said.

'Keep it thus,' Pilar told him. 'How many have we killed?'

'*Pues* five for us. Two here. Canst thou not see the other at the far end? Look there toward the bridge. See the box? Look! Dost see?' He pointed. 'Then there were eight below for Pablo. I watched that post for the *Inglés*.'

Pilar grunted. Then she said violently and raging, 'What passes with that *Inglés*? What is he obscenitying off under that bridge? *Vaya mandanga!* Is he building a bridge or blowing one?'

She raised her head and looked down at Anselmo crouched behind the stone marker.

'Hey, *viejo*!' she shouted. 'What passes with thy obscenity of an *Inglés*?'

'Patience, woman,' Anselmo called up, holding the wire lightly but firmly. 'He is terminating his work.'

'But what in the name of the great whore does he take so much time about?'

'*Es muy concienzudo!*' Anselmo shouted. 'It is a scientific labour.'

'I obscenity in the milk of science,' Pilar raged to the gipsy. 'Let the filth-faced obscenity blow it and be done. Maria!' she shouted in her deep voice up the hill. 'Thy *Inglés*—' and she shouted a flood of obscenity about Jordan's imaginary actions under the bridge.

'Calm yourself, woman,' Anselmo called from the road. 'He is doing an enormous work. He is finishing it now.'

'The hell with it,' Pilar raged. 'It is speed that counts.'

Just then they all heard firing start down the road where Pablo was holding the post he had taken. Pilar stopped cursing and listened. 'Ay,' she said. 'Ayee. Ayee. That's it.'

Robert Jordan heard it as he swung the coil of wire up on to the bridge with one hand and then pulled himself up after it. As his knees rested on the edge of the iron of the bridge and his hands were on the surface he heard the machine gun firing around the bend below. It was a different sound from Pablo's automatic rifle. He got to his feet, leaned over, passed his coil of wire clear and commenced to pay out wire as he walked backwards and sideways along the bridge.

He heard the firing and as he walked he felt it in the pit of his stomach as though it echoed on his own diaphragm. It was closer now as he walked and he looked back at the bend of the road. But it was still clear of any car, or tank or men. It was still clear when he was half-way to the end of the bridge. It was still clear when he was three-quarters of the way, his wire running clear and unfouled, and it was still clear as he climbed around behind the sentry box, holding his wire out to keep it from catching on the iron work. Then he was on the road and it was still clear below on the road and then he was moving fast backwards up the little washed out gully by the lower side of the road as an outfielder goes backwards for a long fly ball, keeping the wire taut, and now he was almost opposite Anselmo's stone and it was still clear below the bridge.

Then he heard the truck coming down the road and he saw it over his shoulder just coming on to the long slope and he swung his wrist once around the wire and yelled to Anselmo. 'Blow her!' and he dug his heels in and leaned back hard on to the tension of the wire with a turn of it around his wrist and the noise of the truck was coming behind and ahead there was the road with the dead sentry and the long bridge and the stretch of road below, still clear and then there was a cracking roar and the middle of the bridge rose up in the air like a wave breaking and he felt the blast from the explosion roll back against him as he dived on to his face in the pebbly gully with his hands holding tight over his head. His face was down against the pebbles as the bridge settled where it had risen and the familiar yellow smell of it rolled over him in acrid smoke and then it commenced to rain pieces of steel.

After the steel stopped falling he was still alive and he raised his head and looked across the bridge. The centre section of it was gone. There were jagged pieces of steel on the bridge with their bright, new torn edges and ends and these were all over the road. The truck had stopped up the road about a hundred yards. The driver and the two men who had been with him were running toward a culvert.

Fernando was still lying against the bank and he was still breathing. His arms straight by his sides, his hands relaxed.

Anselmo lay face down behind the white marking stone. His left arm was doubled under his head and his right arm was stretched straight out. The loop of wire was still around his right fist. Robert Jordan got to his feet, crossed the road, knelt by him and made sure that he was dead. He did not turn him over to see what the piece of steel had done. He was dead and that was all.

He looked very small, dead, Robert Jordan thought. He looked small and grey-headed and Robert Jordan thought, I wonder how he ever carried such big loads if that is the size he really was. Then he saw the shape of the calves and the thighs in the tight, grey herdsman's breeches and the worn soles of the rope-soled shoes and he picked up Anselmo's carbine and the two sacks, practically empty now and went over and picked up the rifle that lay beside Fernando. He kicked a jagged piece of steel off the surface of the road. Then he swung the two rifles over his shoulder, holding them by the muzzles, and started up the slope into the timber. He did not look back nor did he even look across the bridge at the road. They were still firing around the bend below but he cared nothing about that now.

He was coughing from the TNT fumes and he felt numb all through himself.

He put one of the rifles down by Pilar where she lay behind the tree. She looked and saw that made three rifles that she had again.

'You are too high up here,' he said. 'There's a truck up the road where you can't see it. They thought it was planes. You better get farther down. I'm going down with Agustín to cover Pablo.'

'The old one?' she asked him, looking at his face.

'Dead.'

He coughed again, wrackingly, and spat on the ground.

'Thy bridge is blown, *Inglés*.' Pilar looked at him. 'Don't forget that.'

'I don't forget anything,' he said. 'You have a big voice,' he said to Pilar.

'I have heard thee bellow. Shout up to the Maria and tell her that I am all right.'

'We lost two at the sawmill,' Pilar said, trying to make him understand.

'So I saw,' Robert Jordan said. 'Did you do something stupid?'

'Go and obscenity thyself, *Inglés*,' Pilar said. 'Fernando and Eladio were men, too.'

'Why don't you go up with the horses?' Robert Jordan said. 'I can cover here better than thee.'

'Thou art to cover Pablo.'

'The hell with Pablo. Let him cover himself with *mierda*.'

'Nay, *Inglés*. He came back. He had fought much below there. Thou hast not listened? He is fighting now. Against something bad. Do you not hear?'

'I'll cover him. But obscenity all of you. Thou and Pablo both.'

'*Inglés*,' Pilar said. 'Calm thyself. I have been with thee in this as no one could be. Pablo did thee a wrong but he returned.'

'If I had had the exploder the old man would not have been killed. I could have blown it from here.'

'If, if, if—' Pilar said.

The anger and the emptiness and the hate that had come with the let-down after the bridge, when he had looked up from where he had lain and crouching, seen Anselmo dead, were still all through him. In him, too, was despair from the sorrow that soldiers turn to hatred in order that they may continue to be soldiers. Now it was over he was lonely, detached and unelated and he hated everyone he saw.

'If there had been no snow—' Pilar said. And then, not suddenly, as a physical release could have been (if the woman would have put her arm around him, say) but slowly and from his head be began to accept it and let the hate go out. Sure, the snow. That had done it. The snow. Done it to others. Once you saw it again as it was to others, once you got rid of your own self, the always ridding of self that you had to do in war. Where there could be no self. Where yourself is only to be lost. Then, from his losing of it, he heard Pilar say, 'Sordo—'

'What?' he said.

'Sordo—'

'Yes,' Robert Jordan said. He grinned at her, a cracked, stiff, too-tightened-facial-tendoned grin. 'Forget it. I was wrong. I am sorry, woman. Let us do this well and all together. And the bridge *is* blown, as thou sayest.'

'Yes. Thou must think of things in their place.'

'Then I go now to Agustín. Put thy gipsy much farther down so that he can see well up the road. Give those guns to Primitivo and take this *máquina*. Let me show thee.'

'Keep the *máquina*,' Pilar said. 'We will not be here any time. Pablo should come now and we will be going.'

'Rafael,' Robert Jordan said, 'come down here with me. Here. Good. See those coming out of the culvert. There, above the truck? Coming toward the truck? Hit me one of those. Sit. Take it easy.'

The gipsy aimed carefully and fired and as he jerked the bolt back and ejected the shell Robert Jordan said, 'Over. You threw against the rock above. See the rock dust? Lower, by two feet. Now, careful. They're running. Good. *Sigue tirando*.'

'I got one,' the gipsy said. The man was down in the road halfway between the culvert and the truck. The other two did not stop to drag him. They ran for the culvert and ducked in.

'Don't shoot at him,' Robert Jordan said. 'Shoot for the top part of a front tyre on the truck. So if you miss you'll hit the engine. Good.' He watched with the glasses. 'A little lower. Good. You shoot like hell. *Mucho! Mucho!* Shoot me the top of the radiator. Anywhere on the radiator. Thou art a champion. Look. Don't let anything come past that point there. See?'

'Watch me break the windshield in the truck,' the gipsy said happily.

'Nay. The truck is already sick,' Robert Jordan said. 'Hold thy fire until anything comes down the road. Start firing when it is opposite the culvert. Try to hit the driver. That you all should fire, then,' he spoke to Pilar who had come farther down the slope with Primitivo. 'You are wonderfully placed here. See how that steepness guards thy flank?'

'That you should get about thy business with Agustín,' Pilar said. 'Desist from thy lecture. I have seen terrain in my time.'

'Put Primitivo farther up there,' Robert Jordan said. 'There, see, man? This side of where the bank steepens.'

'Leave me,' said Pilar. 'Get along, *Inglés*. Thou and thy perfection. Here there is no problem.'

Just then they heard the planes.

Maria had been with the horses for a long time, but they were no comfort to her. Nor was she any to them. From where she was in the forest she could not see the road nor could she see the bridge and when the firing started she put her arm around the neck of the big white-faced bay stallion that she had gentled and brought gifts to many times when the horses had been in the corral in the trees below the camp. But her nervousness made the big stallion nervous too, and he jerked his head, his nostrils widening at the firing and the noise of the bombs. Maria could not keep still and she walked around patting and gentling the horses and making them all more nervous and agitated.

She tried to think of the firing not as just a terrible thing that was happening, but to realize that it was Pablo below with the new men, and Pilar with the others above, and that she must not worry nor get into a panic but must have confidence in Roberto. But she could not do this and all the firing above and below the bridge and the distant sound of the battle that rolled down from the pass like the noise of a far-off storm with a dried, rolling rattle in it and the irregular beat of the bombs was simply a horrible thing that almost kept her from breathing.

Then later she heard Pilar's big voice from away below on the hillside shouting up some obscenity to her that she could not understand and she thought, Oh, God, no, no. Don't talk like that with him in peril. Don't offend anyone and make useless risks. Don't give any provocation.

Then she commenced to pray for Roberto quickly and automatically as she had done at school, saying the prayers as fast as she could and counting them on the fingers of her left hand, praying by tens of each of the two prayers she was repeating. Then the bridge blew and one horse snapped his halter when he rose and jerked his head at the cracking roar and he went off through the trees. Maria caught him finally and brought him back shivering, trembling, his chest dark with sweat, the saddle down, and coming back through the trees she heard shooting below and she thought, I cannot stand this longer. I cannot live not knowing any longer. I cannot breathe and my mouth is so dry. And I am afraid and I am no good and I frighten the horses and only caught this horse by hazard because he knocked the saddle down against a tree and caught himself kicking into the stirrups and now as I get the saddle up, Oh, God, I do not know. I cannot bear it. Oh please have him be all right for all my heart and all of me is at the bridge. The Republic is one thing and we must win is another thing. But, Oh, Sweet Blessed Virgin, bring him back to me from the bridge and I will do anything thou sayest ever. Because I am not here. There isn't any me. I am only with him. Take care of him for me and that will be me and then I will do the things for thee and he will not mind. Nor will it be against the Republic. Oh, please forgive me for I am very confused. I am too confused now. But if thou takest care of him I will do whatever is right. I will do what he says and what you say. With the two of me I will do it. But this now not knowing I cannot endure.

Then, the horse tied again, she with the saddle up now, the blanket smoothed, hauling tight on the cinch she heard the big, deep voice from the timber below, 'Maria! Maria! Thy *Inglés* is all right. Hear me? All right. *Sin Novedad!*'

Maria held the saddle with both hands and pressed her cropped head hard against it and cried. She heard the deep voice shouting again and she turned from the saddle and shouted, choking, 'Yes! Thank you!' Then, choking again. 'Thank you! Thank you very much!'

When they heard the planes they all looked up and the planes were coming from Segovia very high in the sky, silvery in the high sky, their drumming rising over all the other sounds.

'Those!' Pilar said. 'There has only lacked those!'

Robert Jordan put his arm on her shoulders as he watched them. 'Nay, woman,' he said. 'Those do not come for us. Those have no time for us. Calm thyself.'

'I hate them.'

'Me too. But now I must go to Agustín.'

He circled the hillside through the pines and all the time there was the throbbing, drumming of the planes and across the shattered bridge on the road below, around the bend of the road there was the intermittent hammering fire of a heavy machine gun.

Robert Jordan dropped down to where Agustín lay in the clump of scrub pines behind the automatic rifle and more planes were coming all the time.

'What passes below?' Agustín said. 'What is Pablo doing? Doesn't he know the bridge is gone?'

'Maybe he can't leave.'

'Then let us leave. The hell with him.'

'He will come now if he is able,' Robert Jordan said. 'We should see him now.'

'I have not heard him,' Agustín said. 'Not for five minutes. No. There! Listen! There he is. That's him.'

There was a burst of the spot-spot-spotting fire of the cavalry sub-machine gun, then another, then another.

'That's the bastard,' Robert Jordan said.

He watched still more planes coming over in the high cloudless blue sky and he watched Agustín's face as he looked up at them. Then he looked down at the shattered bridge and across to the stretch of road which still was clear. He coughed and spat and listened to the heavy machine gun hammer again below the bend. It sounded to be in the same place that it was before.

'And what's that?' Agustín asked. 'What the unnameable is that?'

'It has been going since before I blew the bridge,' Robert Jordan said. He looked down at the bridge now and he could see the stream through the torn gap where the centre had fallen, hanging like a bent steel apron. He heard the first of the planes that had gone over now bombing up above at the pass and more were still coming. The noise of their motors filled all the high sky and looking up he saw their pursuit, minute and tiny, circling and wheeling high above them.

'I don't think they ever crossed the lines the other morning,' Primitivo said. 'They must have swung off to the west and then come back. They could not be making an attack if they had seen these.'

'Most of these are new,' Robert Jordan said.

He had the feeling of something that had started normally and had then brought great, outsized, giant repercussions. It was as though you had thrown a stone and the stone made a ripple and the ripple returned roaring and toppling as a tidal wave. Or as though you shouted and the echo came back in rolls and peals of thunder, and the thunder was deadly. Or as though you struck one man and he fell and as far as you could see other men rose up all armed and armoured. He was glad he was not with Golz up at the pass.

Lying there, by Agustín, watching the planes going over, listening for firing behind him, watching the road below where he knew he would see something but not what it would be, he still felt numb with the surprise that he had not been killed at the bridge. He had accepted being killed so completely that all of this now seemed unreal. Shake out of that, he said to himself. Get rid of that. There is much, much, much to be done to-day. But it would not leave him and he felt, consciously, all of this becoming like a dream.

'You swallowed too much of that smoke,' he told himself. But he knew it was not that. He could feel, solidly, how unreal it all was through the absolute reality and he looked down at the bridge and then back to the sentry lying on the road, to where Anselmo lay, to Fernando against the bank and back up the smooth, brown road to the stalled truck and still it was unreal.

'You better sell out your part of you quickly,' he told himself. 'You're like one of those cocks in the pit where nobody has seen the wound given and it doesn't show and he is already going cold with it.'

'Nuts,' he said to himself. 'You are a little groggy that is all, and you have a let-down after responsibility, that is all. Take it easy.'

Then Agustín grabbed his arm and pointed and he looked across the gorge and saw Pablo.

They saw Pablo come running around the corner of the bend in the road. At the sheer rock where the road went out of sight they saw him stop and lean against the rock and fire back up the road. Robert Jordan saw Pablo, short, heavy and stocky, his cap gone, leaning against the rock wall and firing the short cavalry automatic rifle, and he could see the bright flicker of the cascading brass hulls as the sun caught them. They saw Pablo crouch and fire another burst. Then, without looking back, he came running, short, bow-legged, fast, his head bent down straight toward the bridge.

Robert Jordan had pushed Agustín over and he had the stock of the big automatic rifle against his shoulder and was sighting on the bend of the road. His own sub-machine gun lay by his left hand. It was not accurate enough for that range.

As Pablo came toward them Robert Jordan sighted on the bend but nothing came. Pablo had reached the bridge, looked over his shoulder once, glanced at the bridge, and then turned to his left and gone down into the gorge and out of sight. Robert Jordan was still watching the bend and nothing had come in sight. Agustín got up on one knee. He could see Pablo climbing down into the gorge like a goat. There had been no noise of firing below since they had first seen Pablo.

'You see anything up above? On the rocks above? Robert Jordan asked.

'Nothing.'

Robert Jordan watched the bend of the road. He knew the wall just below that was too steep for anyone to climb but below it eased and someone might have circled up above.

If things had been unreal before, they were suddenly real enough now. It was as though a reflex lens camera had been suddenly brought into focus. It was then he saw the low-bodied, angled snout and squat green, grey and brown-splashed turret with the projecting machine gun come around the bend into the bright sun. He fired on it and he could hear the spang against the steel. The little whippet tank scuttled back behind the rock wall. Watching the corner, Robert Jordan saw the nose just reappear, then the edge of the turret showed and the turret swung so that the gun was pointing down the road.

'It seems like a mouse coming out of his hole,' Agustín said. 'Look, *Inglés*.'

'He has little confidence,' Robert Jordan said.

'This is the big insect Pablo has been fighting,' Agustín said. 'Hit him again, *Inglés*.'

'Nay. I cannot hurt him. I don't want him to see where we are.'

The tank commenced to fire down the road. The bullets hit the road surface and sung off and now they were pinging and clanging in the iron of the bridge. It was the same machine gun they had heard below.

'*Cabrón!*' Agustín said. 'Is that the famous tanks, *Inglés*?'

'That's a baby one.'

'*Cabrón*. If I had a baby bottle full of gasoline I would climb up there and set fire to him. What will he do, *Inglés*?'

'After a while he will have another look.'

'And these are what men fear,' Agustín said. 'Look, *Inglés*! He's rekilling the sentries.'

'Since he has no other target,' Robert Jordan said. 'Do not reproach him.'

But he was thinking, Sure, make fun of him. But suppose it was you, way back here in your own country and they held you up with firing on the main road. Then a bridge was blown. Wouldn't you think it was mined ahead or that there was a trap? Sure you would. He's done all right. He's waiting for something else to come up. He's engaging the enemy. It's only us. But he can't tell that. Look at the little bastard.

The little tank had nosed a little further around the corner.

Just then Agustín saw Pablo coming over the edge of the gorge, pulling himself over on hands and knees, his bristly face running with sweat.

'Here comes the son of a bitch,' he said.

'Who?'

'Pablo.'

Robert Jordan looked, saw Pablo, and then he commenced firing at the part of the camouflaged turret of the tank where he knew the slit above the machine gun would be. The little tank whirred backwards, scuttling out of sight and Robert Jordan picked up the automatic rifle, clamped the tripod against the barrel and swung the gun with its still hot muzzle over his shoulder. The muzzle was so hot it burned his shoulder and he shoved it far behind him turning the stock flat in his hand.

'Bring the sack of pans and my little *máquina*,' he shouted, 'and come running.'

Robert Jordan ran up the hill through the pines. Agustín was close behind him and behind him Pablo was coming.

'Pilar!' Jordan shouted across the hill. 'Come on, woman!'

The three of them were going as fast as they could up the steep slope. They could not run any more because the grade was too severe and Pablo, who had no load but the light cavalry sub-machine gun, had closed up with the other two.

'And thy people?' Agustín said to Pablo out of his dry mouth.

'All dead,' Pablo said. He was almost unable to breathe. Agustín turned his head and looked at him.

'We have plenty of horses now, *Inglés*,' Pablo panted.

'Good,' Robert Jordan said. The murderous bastard, he thought. 'What did you encounter?'

'Everything.' Pablo said. He was breathing in lunges. 'What passed with Pilar?'

'She lost Fernando and the brother—'

'Eladio,' Agustín said.

'And thou?' Pablo asked.

'I lost Anselmo.'

'There are lots of horses,' Pablo said. 'Even for the baggage.'

Agustín bit his lip, looked at Robert Jordan and shook his head. Below them, out of sight through the trees, they heard the tank firing on the road and bridge again.

Robert Jordan jerked his head. 'What passed with that?' he said to Pablo. He did not like to look at Pablo, nor to smell him, but he wanted to hear him.

'I could not leave with that there,' Pablo said. 'We were barricaded at the lower bend of the post. Finally it went back to look for something and I came.'

'What were you shooting at, at the bend?' Agustín asked bluntly.

Pablo looked at him, started to grin, thought better of it, and said nothing.

'Did you shoot them all?' Agustín asked. Robert Jordan was thinking, keep your mouth shut. It is none of your business now. They have done all that you could expect and more. This is an inter-tribal matter. Don't make moral judgments. What do you expect from a murderer? You're working with a murderer. Keep your mouth shut. You knew enough about him before. This is nothing new. But you dirty bastard, he thought. You dirty, rotten bastard.

His chest was aching with the climbing as though it would split after the running and ahead now through the trees he saw the horses.

'Go ahead,' Agustín was saying. 'Why do you not say you shot them?'

'Shut up,' Pablo said. 'I have fought much to-day and well. Ask the *Inglés*.'

'And now get us through to-day,' Robert Jordan said. 'For it is thee who has the plan for this.'

'I have a good plan,' Pablo said. 'With a little luck we will be all right.'

He was beginning to breathe better.

'You're not going to kill any of us, are you?' Agustín said. 'For I will kill thee now.'

'Shut up,' Pablo said. 'I have to look after thy interest and that of the band. This is war. One cannot do what one would wish.'

'*Cabrón*,' said Agustín. 'You take all the prizes.'

'Tell me what thou encountered below,' Robert Jordan said to Pablo.

'Everything,' Pablo repeated. He was still breathing as though it were tearing his chest but he could talk steadily now and his face and head were running with sweat and his shoulders and chest were soaked with it. He looked at Robert Jordan cautiously to see if he were really friendly and then he grinned. 'Everything,' he said again. 'First we took the post. Then came a motor cyclist. Then another. Then an ambulance. Then a camion. Then the tank. Just before thou didst the bridge.'

'Then—'

'The tank could not hurt us but we could not leave for it commanded the road. Then it went away and I came.'

'And thy people?' Agustín put in, still looking for trouble.

'Shut up,' Pablo looked at him squarely, and his face was the face of a man who had fought well before any other thing had happened. 'They were not of our band.'

Now they could see the horses tied to the trees, the sun coming down on them through the pine branches and them tossing their heads and kicking against the botflies and Robert Jordan saw Maria and the next thing he was holding her tight, tight, with the automatic rifle leaning against his side, the flash-cone pressing against his ribs and Maria saying, 'Thou, Roberto. Oh thou.'

'Yes, rabbit. My good rabbit. Now we go.'

'Art thou here truly?'

'Yes. Yes. Truly. Oh, thou!'

He had never thought that you could know that there was a woman if there was battle; nor that any part of you could know it, or respond to it; nor that if there was a woman that she should have breasts small, round and tight against you through a shirt; nor that they, the breasts, could know about the two of them in battle. But it was true and he thought, good. That's good. I would not have believed that and he held her to him once hard, hard, but he did not look at her, and then he slapped her where he never had slapped her and said, 'Mount. Mount. Get on that saddle, *guapa*.'

Then they were untying the halters and Robert Jordan had given the automatic rifle back to Agustín and slung his own sub-machine gun over his back, and he was putting bombs out of his pockets into the saddlebags, and he stuffed one empty pack inside the other and tied that one behind his saddle. Then Pilar came up, so breathless from the climb she could not talk, but only motioned.

Then Pablo stuffed three hobbles he had in his hand into a saddlebag, stood up and said, '*Qué tal*, woman?' and she only nodded, and then they were all mounting.

Robert Jordan was on the big grey he had first seen in the snow of the morning of the day before and he felt that it was much horse between his legs and under his hands. He was wearing rope-soled shoes and the stirrups were a little too short; his sub-machine gun was slung over his shoulder, his pockets were full of clips and he was sitting reloading the one used clip, the reins under one arm, tight, watching Pilar mount into a strange sort of seat on top of the duffle lashed on to the saddle of the buckskin.

'Cut that stuff loose for God's sake,' Primitivo said. 'Thou wilt fall and the horse cannot carry it.'

'Shut up,' said Pilar. 'We go to make a life with this.'

'Canst ride like that, woman?' Pablo asked her from the *guardia-civil* saddle on the great bay horse.

'Like any milk-peddler,' Pilar told him. 'How do you go, old one?'

'Straight down. Across the road. Up the far slope and into the wood where it narrows.'

'Across the road?' Agustín wheeled beside him, kicking his soft-heeled, canvas shoes against the stiff, unresponding belly of one of the horses Pablo had recruited in the night.

'Yes, man. It is the only way,' Pablo said. He handed him one of the lead ropes. Primitivo and the gipsy had the others.

'Thou canst come at the end if thou will, *Inglés*,' Pablo said. 'We cross high enough to be out of range of that *máquina*. But we will go separately and riding much and then be together where it narrows above.'

'Good,' said Robert Jordan.

They rode down through the trees toward the edge of the road. Robert Jordan rode just behind Maria. He could not ride beside her for the trees. He caressed the grey once with his thigh muscles, and then held him steady as they dropped down fast and sliding through the pines, telling the grey with his thighs as they dropped down what the spurs would have told him if they had been on level ground.

'Thou,' he said to Maria, 'go second as they cross the road. First is not so bad though it seems bad. Second is good. It is later that they are always watching for.'

'But thou—'

'I will go suddenly. There will be no problem. It is the places in line that are bad.'

He was watching the round, bristly head of Pablo, sunk in his shoulders as he rode, his automatic rifle slung over his shoulder. He was watching Pilar, her head bare, her shoulders broad, her knees higher than her thighs as her heels hooked into the bundles. She looked back at him once and shook her head.

'Pass the Pilar before you cross the road,' Robert Jordan said to Maria.

Then he was looking through the thinning trees and he saw the oiled dark of the road below and beyond it the green slope of the hillside. We are above the culvert, he saw, and just below the height where the road drops down straight towards the bridge in that long sweep. We are around eight hundred yards above the bridge. That is not out of range for the Fiat in that little tank if they have come up to the bridge.

'Maria,' he said. 'Pass the Pilar before we reach the road and ride wide up that slope.'

She looked back at him but did not say anything. He did not look at her except to see that she had understood.

'*Comprendes?*' he asked her.

She nodded.

'Move up,' he said.

She shook her head.

'Move up!'

'Nay,' she told him, turning around and shaking her head. 'I go in the order that I am to go.'

Just then Pablo dug both his spurs into the big bay and he plunged down the last pine-needled slope and crossed the road in a pounding, sparking of shod hooves. The others came behind him and Robert Jordan saw them crossing the road and slamming on up the green slope and heard the machine gun hammer at the bridge. Then he heard a noise come sweeeish-crack-boom! The boom was a sharp crack that widened in the cracking and on the hillside he saw a small fountain of earth rise with a plume of grey smoke. Sweeeish-crack-boom! It came again, the swishing like the noise of a rocket and there was another up-pulsing of dirt and smoke farther up the hillside.

Ahead of him the gipsy was stopped beside the road in the shelter of the last trees. He looked ahead at the slope and then he looked back toward Robert Jordan.

'Go ahead, Rafael,' Robert Jordan said. 'Gallop, man!'

The gipsy was holding the lead rope with the pack-horse pulling his head taut behind him.

'Drop the pack-horse and gallop!' Robert Jordan said.

He saw the gipsy's hand extended behind him, rising higher and higher, seeming to take for ever as his heels kicked into the horse he was riding and the rope came taut, then dropped, and he was across the road and Robert Jordan was kneeing against a frightened pack-horse that bumped back into him as the gipsy crossed the hard, dark road and he heard his horse's hooves clumping as he galloped up the slope.

Wheeeeeeish-ca-rack! The flat trajectory of the shell came and he saw the gipsy jink like a running boar as the earth spouted the little black and grey geyser ahead of him. He watched him galloping, slow and reaching now, up the long green slope and the gun threw behind him and ahead of him and he was under the fold of the hill with the others.

I can't take the damned pack-horse, Robert Jordan thought. Though I wish I could keep the son of a bitch on my off side. I'd like to have him between me and that 47 mm. they're throwing with. By God, I'll try to get him up there anyway.

He rode up to the pack-horse, caught hold of the hackamore, and then, holding the rope, the horse trotting behind him, rode fifty yards up through the trees. At the edge of the trees he looked down the road past the truck to the bridge. He could see men out on the bridge and behind it looked like a traffic jam on the road. Robert Jordan looked around, saw what he wanted finally and reached up and broke a dead limb from a pine tree. He dropped the hackamore, edged the pack-horse up to the slope that slanted down to the road and then hit him hard across the rump with the tree branch. 'Go on, you son of a bitch,' he said, and threw the dead branch after him as the pack-horse crossed the road and started across the slope. The branch hit him and the horse broke from a run into a gallop.

Robert Jordan rode thirty yards farther up the road; beyond that the bank was too steep. The gun was firing now with the rocket whish and the cracking, dirt-spouting boom. 'Come on, you big grey fascist bastard,' Robert Jordan said to the horse and put him down the slope in a sliding plunge. Then he was out in the open, over the road that was so hard under the hooves he felt the pound of it come up all the way to his shoulders, his neck and his teeth, on to the smooth of the slope, the hooves finding it, cutting it, pounding it, reaching, throwing, going, and he looked down across the slope to where the bridge showed now at a new angle he had never seen. It crossed in profile now without foreshortening and in the centre was the broken place and behind it on the road was the little tank and behind the little tank was a big tank with a gun that flashed now yellow-bright as a mirror and the screech as the air ripped apart seemed almost over the grey neck that stretched ahead of him, and he turned his head as the dirt fountained up the hillside. The pack-horse was ahead of him swinging too far to the right and slowing down and Robert Jordan, galloping, his head turned a little toward the bridge, saw the line of trucks halted behind the turn that showed now clearly as he was gaining height, and he saw the bright yellow flash that signalled the instant whish and boom, and the shell fell short, but he heard the metal sailing from where the dirt rose.

He saw them all ahead in the edge of the timber watching him and he said,

'*Arre caballo!* Go on, horse!' and felt his big horse's chest surging with the steepening of the slope and saw the grey neck stretching and the grey ears ahead and he reached and patted the wet grey neck, and he looked back at the bridge and saw the bright flash from the heavy, squat, mud-coloured tank there on the road and then he did not hear any whish but only a banging acrid smelling clang like a boiler being ripped apart and he was under the grey horse and the grey horse was kicking and he was trying to pull out from under the weight.

He could move all right. He could move toward the right. But his left leg stayed perfectly flat under the horse as he moved to the right. It was as though there was a new joint in it; not the hip joint but another one that went sideways like a hinge. Then he knew what it was all right and just then the grey horse kneed himself up and Robert Jordan's right leg, that had kicked the stirrup loose just as it should, slipped clear over the saddle and came down beside him and he felt with his two hands of his thigh bone where the left leg lay flat against the ground and his hands both felt the sharp bone where it pressed against the skin.

The grey horse was standing almost over him and he could see his ribs heaving. The grass was green where he sat and there were meadow flowers in it and he looked down the slope across to the road and the bridge and the gorge and the road and saw the tank and waited for the next flash. It came almost at once with again no whish and in the burst of it, with the smell of the high explosive, the dirt clods scattering and the steel whirring off, he saw the big grey horse sit quietly down beside him as though it were a horse in a circus. And then, looking at the horse sitting there, he heard the sound the horse was making.

Then Primitivo and Agustín had him under the arm-pits and were dragging him up the last of the slope and the new joint in his leg let it swing any way the ground swung it. Once a shell whished close over them and they dropped him and fell flat, but the dirt scattered over them and the metal sung off and they picked him up again. And then they had him up to the shelter of the long draw in the trees where the horses were, and Maria, Pilar and Pablo were standing over him.

Maria was kneeling by him and saying, 'Roberto, what hast thou?'

He said, sweating heavily, 'The left leg is broken, *guapa*.'

'We will bind it up,' Pilar said. 'Thou canst ride that.' She pointed to one of the horses that was packed. 'Cut off the load.'

Robert Jordan saw Pablo shake his head and he nodded at him.

'Get along,' he said. Then he said, 'Listen, Pablo. Come here.'

The sweat-streaked, bristly face bent down by him and Robert Jordan smelt the full smell of Pablo.

'Let us speak,' he said to Pilar and Maria. 'I have to speak to Pablo.'

'Does it hurt much?' Pablo asked. He was bending close over Robert Jordan.

'No. I think the nerve is crushed. Listen. Get along, I am mucked, see? I will talk to the girl for a moment. When I say to take her, take her. She will want to stay. I will only speak to her for a moment.'

'Clearly, there is not much time,' Pablo said.

'Clearly.'

'I think you would do better in the Republic,' Robert Jordan said.

'Nay. I am for Gredos.'

'Use thy head.'

'Talk to her now,' Pablo said. 'There is little time. I am sorry thou hast this, *Inglés*.'

'Since I have it—' Robert Jordan said. 'Let us not speak of it. But use thy head. Thou hast much head. Use it.'

'Why would I not?' said Pablo. 'Talk now fast, *Inglés*. There is no time.'

Pablo went over to the nearest tree and watched down the slope, across the slope and up the road across the gorge. Pablo was looking at the grey horse on the slope with true regret on his face and Pilar and Maria were with Robert Jordan where he sat against the tree trunk.

'Slit the trouser, will thee?' he said to Pilar. Maria crouched by him and did not speak. The sun was on her hair and her face was twisted as a child's contorts before it cries. But she was not crying.

Pilar took her knife and slit his trouser leg down below the left-hand pocket. Robert Jordan spread the cloth with his hands and looked at the stretch of his thigh. Ten inches below the hip joint there was a pointed, purple swelling like a sharp-peaked little tent and as he touched it with his fingers he could feel the snapped-off thigh bone tight against the skin. His leg was lying at an odd angle. He looked up at Pilar. Her face had the same expression as Maria's.

'*Anda*,' he said to her. 'Go.'

She went away with her head down without saying anything nor looking back and Robert Jordan could see her shoulders shaking.

'*Guapa*,' he said to Maria and took hold of her two hands. 'Listen. We will not be going to Madrid—'

Then she started to cry.

'No, *guapa*, don't,' he said. 'Listen. We will not go to Madrid now but I go always with thee wherever thou goest. Understand?'

She said nothing and pushed her head against his cheek with her arms around him.

'Listen to this well, rabbit,' he said. He knew there was a great hurry and he was sweating very much, but this had to be said and understood. 'Thou wilt go now, rabbit. But I go with thee. As long as there is one of us there is both of us. Do you understand?'

'Nay, I stay with thee.'

'Nay, rabbit. What I do now I do alone. I could not do it well with thee. If thou goest then I go, too. Do you not see how it is? Whichever one there is, is both.'

'I will stay with thee.'

'Nay, rabbit. 'Listen. That people cannot do together. Each one must do it alone. But if thou goest then I go with thee. It is in that way that I go too. Thou wilt go now, I know. For thou art good and kind. Thou wilt go now for us both.'

'But it is easier if I stay with thee,' she said. 'It is better for me.'

'Yes. Therefore go for a favour. Do it for me since it is what thou canst do.'

'But you don't understand, Roberto. What about *me*? It is worse for me to go.'

'Surely,' he said. 'It is harder for thee. But I am thee also now.'

She said nothing.

He looked at her and he was sweating heavily and he spoke now, trying harder to do something than he had ever tried in all his life.

'Now you will go for us both,' he said. 'You must not be selfish, rabbit. You must do your duty now.'

She shook her head.

'You are me now,' he said. 'Surely thou must feel it, rabbit. 'Rabbit, listen,' he said. 'Truly thus I go too. I swear it to thee.'

She said nothing.

'Now you see it,' he said. 'Now I see it is clear. Now thou wilt go. Good. Now you are going. Now you have said you will go.'

She had said nothing.

'Now I thank thee for it. Now you are going well and fast and far and we both go in thee. Now put thy hand here. Now put thy head down. Nay, put it down. That is right. Now I put my hand there. Good. Thou art so good. Now do not think more. Now art thou doing what thou should. Now thou art obeying. Not me but us both. The me in thee. Now you go for us both. Truly. We both go in thee now. This I have promised thee. Thou art very good to go and very kind.'

He jerked his head at Pablo, who was half-looking at him from the tree and Pablo started over. He motioned with his thumb to Pilar.

'We will go to Madrid another time, rabbit,' he said. 'Truly. Now stand up and go and we both go. Stand up. See?'

'No,' she said and held him tight around the neck.

He spoke now still calmly and reasonably but with great authority.

'Stand up,' he said. 'Thou art me too now. Thou art all there will be of me. Stand up.'

She stood up slowly, crying, and with her head down. Then she dropped quickly beside him and then stood up again, slowly and tiredly, as he said, 'Stand up, *guapa*.'

Pilar was holding her by the arm and she was standing there.

'*Vámonos*,' Pilar said. 'Dost lack anything, *Inglés*?' She looked at him and shook her head.

'No,' he said and went on talking to Maria.

'There is no good-bye, *guapa*, because we are not apart. That it should be good in the Gredos. Go now. Go good. Nay,' he spoke now still calmly and reasonably as Pilar walked the girl along. 'Do not turn around. Put thy foot in. Yes. Thy foot in. Help her up,' he said to Pilar. 'Get her in the saddle. Swing up now.'

He turned his head, sweating, and looked down the slope, then back toward where the girl was in the saddle with Pilar by her and Pablo just behind. 'Now go,' he said. 'Go.'

She started to look around. 'Don't look around,' Robert Jordan said. 'Go.' And Pablo hit the horse across the crupper with a hobbling strap and it looked as though Maria tried to slip from the saddle but Pilar and Pablo were riding close up against her and Pilar was holding her and the three horses were going up the draw.

'Roberto,' Maria turned and shouted. 'Let me stay! Let me stay!'

'I am with thee,' Robert Jordan shouted. 'I am with thee now. We are both there. Go!' Then they were out of sight around the corner of the draw and he was soaking wet with sweat and looking at nothing.

Agustín was standing by him.

'Do you want me to shoot thee, *Inglés*?' he asked, leaning down close. '*Quieres?* It is nothing.'

'*No hace falta*,' Robert Jordan said. 'Get along. I am very well here.'

'*Me cago en la leche que me han dado!*' Agustín said. He was crying so he could not see Robert Jordan clearly. '*Salud, Inglés.*'

'*Salud*, old one,' Robert Jordan said. He was looking down the slope now. 'Look well after the cropped head, wilt thou?'

'There is no problem,' Agustín said. 'Thou has what thou needest?'

'There are very few shells for this *máquina*, so I will keep it,' Robert Jordan said. 'Thou canst not get more. For that other and the one of Pablo, yes.'

'I cleaned out the barrel,' Agustín said. 'Where thou plugged it in the dirt with the fall.'

'What became of the pack-horse?'

'The gipsy caught it.'

Agustín was on the horse now but he did not want to go. He leaned far over toward the tree where Robert Jordan lay.

'Go on, *viejo*,' Robert Jordan said to him. 'In war there are many things like this.'

'*Qué puta es la guerra*,' Agustín said. 'War is a bitchery.'

'Yes, man, yes. But get on with thee.'

'*Salud, Inglés*,' Agustín said, clenching his right fist.

'*Salud*,' Robert Jordan said. 'But get along, man.'

Agustín wheeled his horse and brought his right fist down as though he cursed again with the motion of it and rode up the draw. All the others had been out of sight long before. He looked back where the draw turned in the trees and waved his fist. Robert Jordan waved and then Agustín, too, was out of sight . . . Robert Jordan looked down the green slope of the hillside to the road and the bridge. I'm as well this way as any, he thought. It wouldn't be worth risking getting over on my belly yet, not as close as that thing was to the surface, and I can see better this way.

He felt empty and drained and exhausted from all of it and from them going and his mouth tasted of bile. Now, finally and at last, there was no problem. However all of it had been and however all of it would ever be now, for him, no longer was there any problem.

They were all gone now and he was alone with his back against a tree. He looked down across the green slope, seeing the grey horse where Agustín had shot him, and on down the slope to the road with the timber-covered country behind it. Then he looked at the bridge and across the bridge and watched the activity on the bridge and the road. He could see the trucks now, all down the lower road. The grey of the trucks showed through the trees.

Then he looked back up the road to where it came down over the hill. They will be coming soon now, he thought.

Pilar will take care of her as well as anyone can. You know that. Pablo must have a sound plan or he would not have tried it. You do not have to worry about Pablo. It does no good to think about Maria. Try to believe what you told her. That is the best. And who says it is not true? Not you. You don't say it, any more than you would say the things did not happen that happened. Stay with what you believe now. Don't get cynical. The time is too short and you have just sent her away. Each one does what he can. You can do nothing for yourself but perhaps you can do something for another. Well, we had all our luck in four days. Not four days. It was afternoon when I first got there and it will not be noon to-day. That makes not quite three days and three nights. Keep it accurate, he said. Quite accurate.

I think you better get down now, he thought. You'd better get fixed around some way where you will be useful instead of leaning against this tree like a tramp. You have had much luck. There are many worse things than this. Everyone has to do this, one day or another. You are not afraid of it once you know you have to do it, are you? No, he said, truly. It was lucky the nerve was crushed, though. I cannot even feel that there is anything below the break. He touched the lower part of his leg and it was as though it were not part of his body.

He looked down the hill slope again and he thought. I hate to leave it, that is all. I hate to leave it very much and I hope I have done some good in it. I have tried to with what talent I had. *Have, you mean. All right, have.*

I have fought for what I believed in for a year now. If we win here we will win everywhere. The world is a fine place and worth the fighting for and I hate very much to leave it. And you had a lot of luck, he told himself, to have had such a good life. You've had just as good a life as grandfather's though not as long. You've had as good a life as anyone because of these last days. You do not want to complain when you have been so lucky. I wish there was some way to pass on what I've learned, though. Christ, I was learning fast there at the end. I'd like to talk to Karkov. That is in Madrid. Just over the hills there, and down across the plain. Down out of the grey rocks and the pines, the heather and the gorse, across the yellow high plateau you see it rising white and beautiful. That part is just as true as Pilar's old women drinking the blood down at the slaughterhouse. There's no *one* thing that's true. It's all true. The way the planes are beautiful whether they are ours or theirs. The hell they are, he thought.

You take it easy, now,' he said. Get turned over now while you still have time. Listen, one thing. Do you remember? Pilar and the hand? Do you believe that crap? No, he said. Not with everything that's happened? No, I don't believe it. She was nice about it early this morning before the show started. She was afraid maybe I believed it. I don't, though. But she does. They see something. Or they feel something. Like a sporting dog. What about extra-sensory perception? What about obscenity? he said. She wouldn't say good-bye, he thought, because she knew if she did Maria would never go. That Pilar. Get yourself turned over, Jordan. But he was reluctant to try it.

Then he remembered that he had the small flask in his hip pocket and he thought, I'll take a good spot of the giant killer and then I'll try it. But the flask was not there when he felt for it. Then he felt that much more alone because he knew there was not going to be even that. I guess I'd counted on that, he said.

Do you suppose Pablo took it? Don't be silly. You must have lost it at the bridge. 'Come on now, Jordan,' he said. 'Over you go.'

Then he took hold of his left leg with both hands and pulled on it hard, pulling toward the foot while he lay down beside the tree he had been resting his back against. Then lying flat and pulling hard on the leg, so the broken end of the bone would not come up and cut through the thigh, he turned slowly around on his rump until the back of his head was facing downhill. Then with his broken leg, held by both hands, uphill, he put the sole of his right foot against the instep of his left foot and pressed hard while he rolled, sweating, over on to his face and chest. He got on to his elbows, stretched the left leg well behind him with both hands and a far, sweating, push with the right foot and there he was. He felt with his fingers on the left thigh and it was all right. The bone end had not punctured the skin and the broken end was well into the muscle now.

The big nerve must have been truly smashed when that damned horse rolled on it, he thought. It truly doesn't hurt at all. Except now in certain changes of positions. That's when the bone pinches something else. You see? he said. You see what luck is? You didn't need the giant killer at all.

He reached over for the sub-machine gun, took the clip out that was in the magazine, felt in his pocket for clips, opened the action and looked through the barrel, put the clip back into the groove of the magazine until it clicked, and then looked down the hill slope. Maybe half an hour, he thought. Now take it easy.

Then he looked at the hillside and he looked at the pines and he tried not to think at all.

He looked at the stream and he remembered how it had been under the bridge in the cool of the shadow. I wish they would come, he thought. I do not want to get in any sort of mixed-up state before they come.

Who do you suppose has it easier? Ones with religion or just taking it straight? It comforts them very much but we know there is nothing to fear. It is only missing it that's bad. Dying is only bad when it takes a long time and hurts so much that it humiliates you. That is where you have all the luck, see? You don't have any of that.

It's wonderful they've got away. I don't mind this at all now they are away. It *is* sort of the way I said. It is really very much that way. Look how different it would be if they were all scattered out across that hill where that grey horse is. Or if we were all cooped up here waiting for it. No. They're gone. They're away. Now if the attack were only a success. What to you want? Everything. I want everything and I will take whatever I get. If this attack is no good another one will be. I never noticed when the planes came back. *God, that was lucky I could make her go.*

'I'd like to tell grandfather about this one. I'll bet he never had to go over and find his people and do a show like this. How do you know? He may have done fifty. No, he said. Be accurate. Nobody did any fifty like this one. Nobody did five. Nobody did one maybe not just like this. Sure. They must have.

I wish they would come now, he said. I wish they would come right now because the leg is starting to hurt now. It must be the swelling.

We were going awfully good when that thing hit us, he thought. But it was only luck it didn't come while I was under the bridge. When a thing is wrong something's bound to happen. You were bitched when they gave Golz those orders. That was what you knew and it was probably that which Pilar felt. But later on we will have these things much better organized. We ought to have portable short-wave transmitters. *Yes, there's a lot of things we ought to have.* I ought to carry a spare leg, too.

He grinned at that sweatily because the leg, where the big nerve had been bruised by the fall, was hurting badly now. Oh, let them come, he said. I don't want to do that business that my father did. I will do it all right but I'd much prefer not to have to. I'm against that. Don't think about that. Don't think at all. I wish the bastards would come, he said. I wish so very much they'd come.

His leg was hurting very badly now. The pain had started suddenly with the swelling after he had moved and he said, Maybe I'll just do it now. I guess I'm not awfully good at pain. Listen, if I do that now you wouldn't misunderstand, would you? *Who are you talking to?* Nobody, he said. Grandfather, I guess. No. Nobody. Oh bloody it, I wish they would come.

Listen, I may have to do that because if I pass out or anything like that I am no good at all and if they bring me to they will ask me a lot of questions and do things and all and that is no good. It's much best not to have them do those things. So why wouldn't it be all right to just do it now and then the whole thing would be over with? Because oh, listen, yes, listen, *let them come now.*

You're not so good at this, Jordan, he said. Not so good at this. And who is so good at this? I don't know and I don't really care right now. But you are not. That's right. You're not at all. Oh not at all, at all. I think it would be all right to do it now? Don't you?

No, it isn't. Because there is something you can do yet. As long as you know what it is you have to do it. As long as you remember what it is you have to wait for that. *Come on, Let them come. Let them come. Let them come!*

Think about them being away, he said. Think about them going through the wood. Think about them crossing a creek. Think about them riding through the heather. Think about them going up the slope. Think about them O.K. to-night. Think about them travelling, all night. Think about them hiding up to-morrow. Think about them. God damn it, think about them. *That's just as far as I can think about them*, he said.

Think about Montana. *I can't*. Think about Madrid. *I can't*. Think about a cool drink of water. *All right*. That's what it will be like. Like a cool drink of water. *You're a liar*. It will just be nothing. That's all it will be. Just nothing. Then do it. *Do it*. Do it now. It's all right to do it now. Go on and do it now. *No, you have to wait*. What for? You know all right. *Then wait*.

I can't wait any longer now, he said. If I wait any longer I'll pass out. I know because I've felt it starting to go three times now and I've held it. I held it all right. But I don't know about any more. What I think is you've got an internal haemorrhage there from where that thigh bone's cut around inside. Especially on that turning business. That makes the swelling and that's what weakens you and makes you start to pass. It would be all right to do it now. Really, I'm telling you that it would be all right.

And if you wait and hold them up even a little while or just get the officer that may make all the difference. One thing well done can make—

All right, he said. And he lay very quietly and tried to hold on to himself that he felt slipping away from himself as you feel snow starting to slip sometimes on a mountain slope, and he said, now quietly, then let me last until they come.

Robert Jordan's luck held very good because he saw, just then, the cavalry ride out of the timber and cross the road. He watched them coming riding up the slope. He saw the trooper who stopped by the grey horse and shouted to the officer who rode over to him. He watched them both looking down at the grey horse. They recognized him of course. He and his rider had been missing since the early morning of the day before.

Robert Jordan saw them there on the slope, close to him now, and below he saw the road and the bridge and the long lines of vehicles below it. He was completely integrated now and he took a good long look at everything. Then he looked up at the sky. There were big white clouds in it. He touched the palm of his hand against the pine needles where he lay and he touched the bark of the pine trunk that he lay behind.

Then he rested as easily as he could with his two elbows in the pine needles and the muzzle of the sub-machine gun resting against the trunk of the pine tree.

As the officer came trotting now on the trail of the horses of the band he would pass twenty yards below where Robert Jordan lay. At that distance there would be no problem. The officer was Lieutenant Berrendo. He had come up from La Granja when they had been ordered up after the first report of the attack on the lower post. They had ridden hard and then had to swing back, because the bridge had been blown, to cross the gorge high above and come around through the timber. Their horses were wet and blown and they had to be urged into the trot.

Lieutenant Berrendo, watching the trail, came riding up, his thin face serious and grave. His sub-machine gun lay across his saddle in the crook of his left arm. Robert Jordan lay behind the tree, holding on to himself very carefully and delicately to keep his hands steady. He was waiting until the officer reached the sunlit place where the first trees of the pine forest joined the green slope of the meadow. He could feel his heart beating against the pine needle floor of the forest.

HEM

GWAY

The Snows of Kilimanjaro

Kilimanjaro is a snow-covered mountain 19,710 feet high, and is said to be the highest mountain in Africa. Its western summit is called the Masai 'Ngàje Ngài', the House of God. Close to the western summit there is the dried and frozen carcass of a leopard. No one has explained what the leopard was seeking at that altitude.

'The marvellous thing is that it's painless,' he said. 'That's how you know when it starts.'

'Is it really?'

'Absolutely. I'm awfully sorry about the odour, though. That must bother you.'

'Don't! Please don't.'

'Look at them,' he said. 'Now is it sight or is it scent that brings them like that?'

The cot the man lay on was in the wide shade of a mimosa tree and as he looked out past the shade on to the glare of the plain there were three of the big birds squatted obscenely, while in the sky a dozen more sailed, making quick-moving shadows as they passed.

'They've been there since the day the truck broke down,' he said. 'Today's the first time any have lit on the ground. I watched the way they sailed very carefully at first in case I ever wanted to use them in a story. That's funny now.'

'I wish you wouldn't,' she said.

'I'm only talking,' he said. 'It's much easier if I talk. But I don't want to bother you.'

'You know it doesn't bother me,' she said. 'It's that I've gotten so very nervous not being able to do anything. I think we might make it as easy as we can until the plane comes.'

'Or until the plane doesn't come.'

'Please tell me what I can do. There must be something I can do.'

'You can take the leg off and that might stop it, though I doubt it. Or you can shoot me. You're a good shot now. I taught you to shoot, didn't I?'

'Please don't talk that way. Couldn't I read to you?'

'Read what?'

'Anything in the book bag that we haven't read.'

'I can't listen to it,' he said. 'Talking is the easiest. We quarrel and that makes the time pass.'

'I don't quarrel. I never want to quarrel. Let's not quarrel any more. No matter how nervous we get. Maybe they will be back with another truck to-day. Maybe the plane will come.'

'I don't want to move,' the man said. 'There is no sense in moving now except to make it easier for you.'

'That's cowardly.'

'Can't you let a man die as comfortably as he can without calling him names? What's the use of slanging me?'

'You're not going to die.'

'Don't be silly. I'm dying now. Ask those bastards.' He looked over to where the huge, filthy birds sat, their naked heads sunk in the hunched feathers. A fourth planed down to run quick-legged and then waddle slowly toward the others.

'They are around every camp. You never notice them. You can't die if you don't give up.'

'Where did you read that? You're such a bloody fool.'

'You might think about someone else.'

'For Christ's sake,' he said. 'That's been my trade.'

He lay then and was quiet for a while and looked across the heat shimmer of the plain to the edge of the bush. There were a few Tommies that showed minute and white against the yellow and, far off, he saw a herd of zebra, white against the green of the bush. This was a pleasant camp under big trees against a hill, with good water, and close by, a nearly dry waterhole where sand grouse flighted in the mornings.

'Wouldn't you like me to read?' she asked. She was sitting on a canvas chair beside his cot. 'There's a breeze coming up.'

'No thanks.'

'Maybe the truck will come.'

'I don't give a damn about the truck.'

'I do.'

'You give a damn about so many things that I don't.'

'Not so many, Harry.'

'What about a drink?'

'It's supposed to be bad for you. It said in Black's to avoid all alcohol. You shouldn't drink.'

'Molo!' he shouted.

'Yes, Bwana.'

'Bring whisky-soda.'

'Yes, Bwana.'

'You shouldn't,' she said. 'That's what I mean by giving up. It says it's bad for you. I know it's bad for you.'

'No,' he said. 'It's good for me.'

So now it was all over, he thought. So now he would never have a chance to finish it. So this was the way it ended in a bickering over a drink. Since the gangrene started in his right leg he had no pain and with the pain the horror had gone and all he felt now was a great tiredness and anger that this was the end of it. For this, that now was coming, he had very little curiosity. For years it had obsessed him; but now it meant nothing in itself. It was strange how easy being tired enough made it.

Now he would never write the things that he had saved to write until he knew enough to write them well. Well, he would not have to fail at trying to write them either. Maybe you could never write them, and that was why you put them off and delayed the starting. Well, he would never know, now.

'I wish we'd never come,' the woman said. She was looking at him holding the glass and biting her lip. 'You never would have gotten anything like this in Paris. You always said you loved Paris. We could have stayed in Paris or gone anywhere. I'd have gone anywhere. I said I'd go anywhere you wanted. If you wanted to shoot we could have gone shooting in Hungary and been comfortable.'

'Your bloody money,' he said.

'That's not fair,' she said. 'It was always yours as much as mine. I left everything and I went wherever you wanted to go and I've done what you wanted to do. But I wish we'd never come here.'

'You said you loved it.'

'I did when you were all right. But now I hate it. I don't see why that had to happen to your leg. What have we done to have that happen to us?'

'I suppose what I did was to forget to put iodine on it when I first scratched it. Then I didn't pay any attention to it because I never infect. Then, later, when it got bad, it was probably using that weak carbolic solution when the other antiseptics ran out that paralysed the minute blood vessels and started the gangrene.' He looked at her, 'What else?'

'I don't mean that.'

'If we could have hired a good mechanic instead of a half-baked Kikuyu driver, he would have checked the oil and never burned out that bearing in the truck.'

'I don't mean that.'

'If you hadn't left your own people, your goddamned Old Westbury, Saratoga, Palm Beach people to take me on—'.

'Why, I loved you. That's not fair. I love you now. I'll always love you. Don't you love me?'

'No,' said the man. 'I don't think so. I never have.'

'Harry, what are you saying? You're out of your head.'

'No. I haven't any head to go out of.'

'Don't drink that,' she said. 'Darling, please don't drink that. We have to do everything we can.'

'You do it,' he said. 'I'm tired.'

Now in his mind he saw a railway station at Karagatch and he was standing with his pack and that was the headlight of the Simplon-Orient cutting the dark now and he was leaving Thrace then after the retreat. That was one of the things he had saved to write, with, in the morning at breakfast, looking out the window and seeing snow on the mountains in Bulgaria and Nansen's Secretary asking the old man if it were snow and the old man looking at it and saying, No, that's not snow. It's too early for snow. And the Secretary repeating to the other girls, No, you see. It's not snow and them all saying, It's not snow, we were mistaken. But it was the snow all right and he sent them on into it when he evolved exchange of populations. And it was snow they tramped along in until they died that winter.

It was snow too that fell all Christmas week that year up in the Gauertal, that year they lived in the woodcutter's house with the big square porcelain stove that filled half the room, and they slept on mattresses filled with beech leaves, the time the deserter came with his feet bloody in the snow. He said the police were right behind him and they gave him woollen socks and held the gendarmes talking until the tracks had drifted over.

In Schrunz, on Christmas day, the snow was so bright it hurt your eyes when you looked out from the weinstube and saw everyone coming home from church. That was where they walked up the sleigh-smoothed urine-yellowed road along the river with the steep pine hills, skis heavy on the shoulder, and where they ran that great run down the glacier above the Madlener-haus, the snow as smooth to see as cake frosting and as light as powder and he remembered the noiseless rush the speed made as you dropped down like a bird.

They were snow-bound a week in the Madlener-haus that time in the blizzard playing cards in the smoke by the lantern light and the stakes were higher all the time as Herr Lent lost more. Finally he lost it all. Everything, the skischule money and all the season's profit and then his capital. He could see him with his long nose, picking up the cards and then opening, 'Sans Voir'. There was always gambling then. When there was no snow you gambled and when there was too much you gambled. He thought of all the time in his life he had spent gambling.

But he had never written a line of that, nor of that cold, bright Christmas day with the mountains showing across the plain that Johnson had flown across the lines to bomb the Austrian officers' leave train, machine-gunning them as they scattered and ran. He remembered Johnson afterwards coming into the mess and starting to tell about it. And how quiet it got and then somebody saying, 'You bloody murderous bastard!'

Those were the same Austrians they killed then that he skied with later. No, not the same. Hans, that he skied with all that year, had been in the Kaiser-Jägers and when they went hunting hares together up the little valley above the saw-mill they had talked of the fighting on Pasubio and of the attack on Pertica and Asalone and he had never written a word of that. Nor of Monte Corno, nor the Siete Commum, nor of Arsiedo.

How many winters had he lived in the Voralberg and the Arlberg? It was four and then he remembered the man who had the fox to sell when they had walked into Bludenz, that time to buy presents, and the cherry pip taste of good kirsch, the fast-slipping rush of running powder-snow on crust, singing 'Hi! Ho! said Rolly!' as you ran down the last stretch to the steep drop, taking it straight, then running the orchard in three turns and out across the ditch and on to the icy road behind the inn. Knocking your bindings loose, kicking the skis free and leaning them up against the wooden wall of the inn, the lamplight coming from the window, where inside, in the smoky, new-wine smelling warmth, they were playing the accordion.

'Where did we stay in Paris?' he asked the woman who was sitting by him in a canvas chair, now, in Africa.

'At the Crillon. You know that.'

'Why do I know that?'

'That's where we always stayed.'

'No. Not always.'

'There and at the Pavillon Henri-Quatre in St. Germain. You said you loved it there.'

'Love is a dunghill,' said Harry. 'And I'm the cock that gets on it to crow.'

'If you have to go away,' she said, 'is it absolutely necessary to kill off everything you leave behind? I mean do you have to take away everything? Do you have to kill your horse, and your wife and burn your saddle and your armour?'

'Yes,' he said. 'Your damned money was my armour. My Swift and my Armour.'

'Don't.'

'All right. I'll stop that. I don't want to hurt you.'

'It's a little bit late now.'

'All right then. I'll go on hurting you. It's more amusing. The only thing I ever really liked to do with you I can't do now.'

'No, that's not true. You liked to do many things and everything you wanted to do I did.'

'Oh, for Christ sake stop bragging, will you?'

He looked at her and saw her crying.

'Listen,' he said. 'Do you think that it is fun to do this? I don't know why I'm doing it. It's trying to kill to keep yourself alive, I imagine. I was all right when we started talking. I didn't mean to start this, and now I'm crazy as a coot and being as cruel to you as I can be. Don't pay any attention, darling, to what I say. I love you, really. You know I love you. I've never loved anyone else the way I love you.'

He slipped into the familiar lie he made his bread and butter by.

'You're sweet to me.'

'You bitch,' he said. 'You rich bitch. That's poetry. I'm full of poetry now. Rot and poetry. Rotten poetry.'

'Stop it. Harry, why do you have to turn into a devil now?'

'I don't like to leave anything,' the man said. 'I don't like to leave things behind.'

It was evening now and he had been asleep. The sun was gone behind the hill and there was a shadow all across the plain and the small animals were feeding close to camp; quick dropping heads and switching tails, he watched them keeping well out away from the bush now. The birds no longer waited on the ground. They were all perched heavily in a tree. There were many more of them. His personal boy was sitting by the bed.

'Memsahib's gone to shoot,' the boy said. 'Does Bwana want?'

'Nothing.'

She had gone to kill a piece of meat and, knowing how he liked to watch the game, she had gone well away so she would not disturb this little pocket of the plain that he could see. She was always thoughtful, he thought. On anything she knew about, or had read, or that she had ever heard.

It was not her fault that when he went to her he was already over. How could a woman know that you meant nothing that you said; that you spoke only from habit and to be comfortable? After he no longer meant what he said, his lies were more successful with women than when he had told them the truth.

It was not so much that he lied as that there was no truth to tell. He had had his life and it was over and then he went on living it again with different people and more money, with the best of the same places, and some new ones.

You kept from thinking and it was all marvellous. You were equipped with good insides so that you did not go to pieces that way, the way most of them had, and you made an attitude that you cared nothing for the work you used to do, now that you could no longer do it. But, in yourself, you said that you would write about these people; about the very rich; that you were really not of them but a spy in their country; that you would leave it and write of it and for once it would be written by some one who knew what he was writing of. But he would never do it, because each day of not writing, of comfort, of being that which he despised, dulled his ability and softened his will to work so that, finally, he did no work at all. The people he knew now were all much more comfortable when he did not work. Africa was where he had been happiest in the good time of his life, so he had come out here to start again. They had made this safari with the minimum of comfort. There was no hardship; but there was no luxury and he had thought that he could get back into training that way. That in some way he could work the fat off his soul the way a fighter went into the mountains to work and train in order to burn it out of his body.

She had liked it. She said she loved it. She loved anything that was exciting, that involved a change of scene, where there were new people and where things were pleasant. And he had felt the illusion of returning strength of will to work. Now if this was how it ended, and he knew it was, he must not turn like some snake biting itself because its back was broken. It wasn't this woman's fault. If it had not been she it would have been another. If he lived by a lie he should try to die by it. He heard a shot beyond the hill.

She shot very well, this good, this rich bitch, this kindly caretaker and destroyer of his talent. Nonsense. He had destroyed his talent himself. Why should he blame this woman because she kept him well? He had destroyed his talent by not using it, by betrayals of himself and what he believed in, by drinking so much that he blunted the edge of his perceptions, by laziness, by sloth, and by snobbery, by pride and by prejudice, by hook and by crook. What was this? A catalogue of old books? What was his talent anyway? It was a talent all right but instead of using it, he had traded on it. It was never what he had done, but always what he could do. And he had chosen to make his living with something else instead of a pen or a pencil. It was strange, too, wasn't it, that when he fell in love with another woman, that woman should always have more money than the last one? But when he no longer was in love, when he was only lying, as to this woman, now, who had the most money of all, who had all the money that was, who had had a husband and children, who had taken lovers and been dissatisfied with them, and who loved him dearly as a writer, as a man, as a companion and as a proud possession; it was strange that when he did not love her at all and was lying, that he should be able to give her more for her money than when he had really loved.

We must all be cut out for what we do, he thought. However you make your living is where your talent lies. He had sold vitality, in one form or another, all his life, and when your affections are not too involved you give much better value for the money. He had found that out but he would never write that, now, either. No, he would not write that, although it was well worth writing.

Now she came in sight, walking across the open towards the camp. She was wearing jodhpurs and carrying her rifle. The two boys had a Tommie slung and they were coming along behind her. She was still a good-looking woman, he thought, and she had a pleasant body. She had a great talent and appreciation for the bed, she was not pretty, but he liked her face, she read enormously, liked to ride and shoot and, certainly, she drank too much. Her husband had died when she was still a comparatively young woman and for a while she had devoted herself to her two just-grown children, who did not need her and were embarrassed at having her about, to her stable of horses, to books, and to bottles. She liked to read in the evening before dinner and she drank Scotch and soda while she read. By dinner she was fairly drunk and after a bottle of wine at dinner she was usually drunk enough to sleep.

That was before the lovers. After she had the lovers she did not drink so much because she did not have to be drunk to sleep. But the lovers bored her. She had been married to a man who had never bored her and these people bored her very much.

Then one of her two children was killed in a plane crash and after that was over she did not want the lovers, and drink being no anaesthetic she had to make another life. Suddenly, she had been acutely frightened of being alone. But she wanted someone that she respected with her.

It had begun very simply. She liked what he wrote and she had always envied the life he led. She thought he did exactly what he wanted to. The steps by which she had acquired him and the way in which she had finally fallen in love with him were all part of a regular progression in which she had built herself a new life and he had traded away what remained of his old life.

He had traded it for security, for comfort too, there was no denying that, and for what else? He did not know. She would have brought him anything he wanted. He knew that. She was a damned nice woman too. He would as soon be in bed with her as anyone; rather with her, because she was richer, because she was very pleasant and appreciative and because she never made scenes. And now this life that she had built again was coming to a term because he had not used iodine two weeks ago when a thorn had scratched his knee as they moved forward trying to photograph a herd of waterbuck standing, their heads up, peering while their nostrils searched the air, their ears spread wide to hear the first noise that would send them rushing into the bush. They had bolted, too, before he got the picture.

Here she came now.

He turned his head on the cot to look toward her. 'Hello,' he said.

'I shot a Tommy ram,' she told him. 'He'll make you good broth and I'll have them mash some potatoes with the Klim. How do you feel?'

'Much better.'

'Isn't that lovely? You know I thought perhaps you would. You were sleeping when I left.'

'I had a good sleep. Did you walk far?'

'No. Just around behind the hill. I made quite a good shot on the Tommy.'

'You shoot marvellously, you know.'

'I love it. I've loved Africa. Really. If *you're* all right it's the most fun that I've ever had. You don't know the fun it's been to shoot with you. I've loved the country.'

'I love it too.'

'Darling, you don't know how marvellous it is to see you feeling better. I couldn't stand it when you felt that way. You won't talk to me like that again, will you? Promise me?'

'No,' he said. 'I don't remember what I said.'

'You don't have to destroy me. Do you? I'm only a middle-aged woman who loves you and wants to do what you want to do. I've been destroyed two or three times already. You wouldn't want to destroy me again, would you?'

'I'd like to destroy you a few times in bed,' he said.

'Yes. That's the good destruction. That's the way we're made to be destroyed. The plane will be here to-morrow.'

'How do you know?'

'I'm sure. It's bound to come. The boys have the wood all ready and the grass to make the smudge. I went down and looked at it again to-day. There's plenty of room to land and we have the smudges ready at both ends.'

'What makes you think it will come to-morrow?'

'I'm sure it will. It's overdue now. Then, in town, they will fix up your leg and then we will have some good destruction. Not that dreadful talking kind.'

'Should we have a drink? The sun is down.'

'Do you think you should?'

'I'm having one.'

'We'll have one together. *Molo, letti dui whisky-soda!*' she called.

'You'd better put on your mosquito boots,' he told her.

'I'll wait till I bathe . . .'

While it grew dark they drank and just before it was dark and there was no longer enough light to shoot, a hyena crossed the open on his way around the hill.

'That bastard crosses there every night,' the man said. 'Every night for two weeks.'

'He's the one makes the noise at night. I don't mind it. They're a filthy animal though.'

Drinking together, with no pain now except the discomfort of lying in the one position, the boys lighting a fire, its shadow jumping on the tents, he could feel the return of acquiescence in this life of pleasant surrender. She *was* very good to him. He had been cruel and unjust in the afternoon. She was a fine woman, marvellous really. And just then it occurred to him that he was going to die.

It came with a rush; not as a rush of water nor of wind; but of a sudden evil-smelling emptiness and the odd thing was that the hyena slipped lightly along the edge of it.

'What is it, Harry?' she asked him.

'Nothing,' he said. 'You had better move over to the other side. To windward.'

'Did Molo change the dressing?'

'Yes. I'm just using the boric now.'

'How do you feel?'

'A little wobbly.'

'I'm going in to bathe,' she said. 'I'll be right out. I'll eat with you and then we'll put the cot in.'

So, he said to himself, we did well to stop the quarrelling. He had never quarrelled much with this woman, while with the women that he loved he had quarrelled so much they had finally, always, with the corrosion of the quarrelling, killed what they had together. He had loved too much, demanded too much, and he wore it all out.

He thought about alone in Constantinople that time, having quarrelled in Paris before he had gone out. He had whored the whole time and then, when that was over, and he had failed to kill his loneliness, but only made it worse, he had written her, the first one, the one who left him, a letter telling her how he had never been able to kill it . . . How when he thought he saw her outside the Regence *one time it made him go all faint and sick inside, and that he would follow a woman who looked like her in some way, along the Boulevard, afraid to see it was not she, afraid to lose the feeling it gave him. How everyone he had slept with had only made him miss her more. How what she had done could never matter since he knew he could not cure himself of loving her. He wrote this letter at the Club, cold sober, and mailed it to New York asking her to write him at the office in Paris. That seemed safe. And that night missing her so much it made him feel hollow sick inside, he wandered up past Taxim's, picked a girl up and took her out to supper. He had gone to a place to dance with her afterwards, she danced badly, and left her for a hot Armenian slut, that swung her belly against him so it almost scalded. He took her away from a British gunner subaltern after a row. The gunner asked him outside and they fought in the street on the cobbles in the dark. He'd hit him twice, hard, on the side of the jaw and when he didn't go down he knew he was in for a fight. The gunner hit him in the body, then beside his eye. He swung with his left again and landed and the gunner fell on him and grabbed his coat and tore the sleeve off and he clubbed him twice behind the ear and then smashed him with his right as he pushed him away. When the gunner went down his head hit first and he ran with the girl because they heard the M.P.s coming. They got into a taxi and drove out to Rimmily Hissa along the Bosphorus, and around, and back in the cool night and went to bed and she felt as over-ripe as she looked but smooth, rose-petal, syrupy, smooth-bellied, big-breasted and needed no pillow under her buttocks, and he left her before she was awake looking blousy enough in the first daylight and turned up at the Pera*

Palace with a black eye, carrying his coat because one sleeve was missing.

That same night he left for Anatolia and he remembered, later on that trip, riding all day through fields of the poppies that they raised for opium and how strange it made you feel, finally, and all the distances seemed wrong, to where they had made the attack with the newly arrived Constantine officers, that did not know a god-damned thing, and the artillery had fired into the troops and the British observer had cried like a child.

That was the day he'd first seen dead men wearing white ballet skirts and upturned shoes with pompoms on them. The Turks had come steadily and lumpily and he had seen the skirted men running and the officers shooting into them and running then themselves and he and the British observer had run too until his lungs ached and his mouth was full of the taste of pennies and they stopped behind some rocks and there were the Turks coming as lumpily as ever. Later he had seen the things that he could never think of and later still he had seen, much worse. So when he got back to Paris that time he could not talk about it or stand to have it mentioned. And there in the café as he passed was that American poet with a pile of saucers in front of him and a stupid look on his potato face talking about the Dada movement with a Roumanian who said his name was Tristan Tzara, who always wore a monocle and had a headache, and, back at the apartment with his wife that now he loved again, the quarrel all over, the madness all over, glad to be home, the office sent his mail up to the flat. So then the letter in answer to the one he'd written came in on a platter one morning and when he saw the hand-writing he went cold all over and tried to slip the letter underneath another. But his wife said, 'Who is that letter from, dear?' and that was the end of the beginning of that.

He remembered the good times with them all, and the quarrels. They always picked the finest places to have the quarrels. And why had they always quarrelled when he was feeling best? He had never written any of that because, at first, he never wanted to hurt anyone and then it seemed as though there was enough to write without it. But he had always thought that he would write it finally. There was so much to write. He had seen the world change; not just the events; although he had seen many of them and had watched the people, but he had seen the subtler change and he could remember how the people were at different times. He had been in it and he had watched it and it was his duty to write of it; but now he never would.

'How do you feel?' she said. She had come out from the tent now after her bath.

'All right.'

'Could you eat now?' He saw Molo behind her with the folding table and the other boy with the dishes.

'I want to write,' he said.

'You ought to take some broth to keep your strength up.'

'I'm going to die to-night,' he said. 'I don't need my strength up.'

'Don't be melodramatic, Harry, please,' she said.

'Why don't you use your nose? I'm rotted half-way up my thigh now. What the hell should I fool with broth for? Molo, bring whisky-soda.'

'Please take the broth,' she said gently.

'All right.'

The broth was too hot. He had to hold it in the cup until it cooled enough to take it and then he just got it down without gagging.

'You're a fine woman,' he said. 'Don't pay any attention to me.'

She looked at him with her well-known, well-loved face from *Spur* and *Town and Country*, only a little the worse for drink, only a little the worse for bed, but *Town and Country* never showed those good breasts and those useful thighs and those lightly small-of-back caressing hands, and as he looked and saw her well-known pleasant smile, he felt death come again. This time there was no rush. It was a puff, as of a wind that makes a candle flicker and the flame go tall.

'They can bring my net out later and hang it from the tree and build the fire up. I'm not going in the tent to-night. It's not worth moving. It's a clear night. There won't be any rain.'

So this was how you died, in whispers that you did not hear. Well, there would be no more quarrelling. He could promise that. The one experience that he had never had he was not going to spoil now. He probably would. You spoiled everything. But perhaps he wouldn't.

'You can't take dictation, can you?'

'I never learned,' she told him.

'That's all right.'

There wasn't time, of course, although it seemed as though it telescoped so that you might put it all into one paragraph if you could get it right.

There was a log house, chinked white with mortar, on a hill above the lake. There was a bell on a pole by the door to call the people in to meals. Behind the house were fields and behind the fields was the timber. A line of lombardy poplars ran from the house to the dock. Other poplars ran along the point. A road went up to the hills along the edge of the timber and along that road he picked blackberries. Then that log house was burned down and all the guns that had been on deer foot racks above the open fire place were burned and afterwards their barrels, with the lead melted in the magazines, and the stocks burned away, lay out on the heap of ashes that were used to make lye for the big iron soap kettles, and you asked Grandfather if you could have them to play with, and he said, no. You see they were his guns still and he never bought any others. Nor did he hunt any more. The house was rebuilt in the same place out of lumber now and painted white and from its porch you saw the poplars and the lake beyond; but there were never any more guns. The barrels of the guns that had hung on the deer feet on the wall of the log house lay out there on the heap of ashes and no one ever touched them.

In the Black Forest, after the war, we rented a trout stream and there were two ways to walk to it. One was down the valley from Triberg and around the valley road in the shade of the trees that bordered the white road, and then up a side road that went up through the hills, past many small farms, with the big Schwarzwald houses, until that road crossed the stream. That was where our fishing began.

The other way was to climb steeply up to the edge of the woods and then go across the top of the hills through the pine woods, and then out to the edge of a meadow and down across this meadow to the bridge. There were birches along the stream and it was not big, but narrow, clear and fast, with pools where it had cut under the roots of the birches. At the Hotel in Triberg the proprietor had a fine season. It was very pleasant and we were all great friends. The next year came the inflation and the money he had made the year before was not enough to buy supplies to open the hotel and he hanged himself.

You could dictate that, but you could not dictate the Place Contrescarpe where the flower sellers dyed their flowers in the street and the dye ran over the paving where the autobus started and the old men and the women, always drunk on wine and bad marc; and the children with their noses running in the cold; the smell of dirty sweat and poverty and drunkenness at the Café des Amateurs and the whores at the Bal Musette they lived above. The Concierge who entertained the trooper of the Garde Republicaine in her loge, his horse-hair-plumed helmet on a chair. The locataire across the hall whose husband was a bicycle racer and her joy that morning at the Cremerie when she had opened L'Auto *and seen where he placed third in Paris-Tours, his first big race. She had blushed and laughed and then gone upstairs crying with the yellow sporting paper in her hand. The husband of the woman who ran the Bal Musette drove a taxi and when he, Harry, had to take an early plane the husband knocked upon the door to wake him and they each drank a glass of white wine at the zinc of the bar before they started. He knew his neighbours in that quarter then because they all were poor.*

Around that Place *there were two kinds: the drunkards and the sportifs. The drunkards killed their poverty that way; the sportifs took it out in exercise. They were the descendants of the Communards and it was no struggle for them to know their politics. They knew who had shot their fathers, their relatives, their brothers, and their friends when the Versailles troops came in and took the town after the Commune and executed anyone they could catch with calloused hands, or who wore a cap, or carried any other sign he was a working man. And in that poverty, and in that quarter across the street from a Boucherie Chevaline and a wine-co-operative he had written the start of all he was to do. There never was another part of Paris that he loved like that, the sprawling trees, the old white plastered houses painted brown below, the long green of the autobus in that round square, the purple flower dye upon the paving, the sudden drop down the hill of the rue Cardinal Lemoine to the River, and the other way the narrow crowded world of the rue Mouffetard. The street that ran up toward the Pantheon and the other that he always took with the bicycle, the only asphalted street in all that quarter, smooth under the tyres, with the high narrow houses and the cheap tall hotel where Paul Verlaine had died. There were only two rooms in the apartments where they lived and he had a room on the top floor of that hotel that cost him sixty francs a month where he did his writing, and from it he could see the roofs and chimney pots and all the hills of Paris.*

From the apartment you could only see the wood and coal man's place. He sold wine, too, bad wine. The golden horse's head outside the Boucherie Chevaline where the carcasses hung yellow gold and red in the open window, and the green painted co-operative where they bought their wine; good wine and cheap. The rest was plaster walls and the windows of the neighbours. The neighbours who, at night, when someone lay drunk in the street, moaning and groaning in that typical French ivresse *that you were propaganded to believe did not exist, would open their windows and then the murmur of talk.*

'Where is the policeman? When you don't want him the bugger is always there. He's sleeping with some concierge. Get the Agent.*' Till someone threw a bucket of water from a window and the moaning stopped. 'What's that? Water. Ah, that's intelligent.' And the windows shutting. Marie, his femme de ménage, protesting against the eight-hour day saying, 'If a husband works until six he gets only a little drunk on the way home and does not waste too much. If he works only until five he is drunk every night and one has no money. It is the wife of the working man who suffers from this shortening of hours.'*

'Wouldn't you like some more broth?' the woman asked now.

'No, thank you very much. It is awfully good.'

'Try just a little.'

'I would like a whisky-soda.'

'It's not good for you.'

'No. It's bad for me. Cole Porter wrote the words and the music. This knowledge that you're going mad for me.'

'You know I like you to drink.'

'Oh yes. Only it's bad for me.'

When she goes, he thought, I'll have all I want. Not all I want but all there is. Ayee, he was tired. Too tired. He was going to sleep a little while. He lay still and death was not there. It must have gone around another street. It went in pairs, on bicycles, and moved absolutely silently on the pavements.

No, he had never written about Paris. Not the Paris that he cared about. But what about the rest that he had never written?

What about the ranch and the silvered grey of the sage brush, the quick, clear water in the irrigation ditches, and the heavy green of the alfalfa? The trail went up into the hills and the cattle in the summer were shy as deer. The bawling and the steady noise and slow-moving mass raising a dust as you brought them down in the fall. And behind the mountains, the clear sharpness of the peak in the evening light and, riding down along the train in the moonlight, bright across the valley. Now he remembered coming down through the timber in the dark holding the horse's tail when you could not see and all the stories that he meant to write.

About the half-wit chore boy who was left at the ranch that time and told not to let any one get any hay, and that old bastard from the Forks who had beaten the boy when he had worked for him stopping to get some feed. The boy refusing and the old man saying he would beat him again. The boy got the rifle from the kitchen and shot him when he tried to come into the barn and when they came back to the ranch he'd been dead a week, frozen in the corral, and the dogs had eaten part of him. But what was left you packed on a sled wrapped in a blanket and roped on and you got the boy to help you haul it, and the two of you took it out over the road on skis, and sixty miles down to town to turn the boy over. He having no idea that he would be arrested. Thinking he had done his duty and that you were his friend and he would be rewarded. He'd helped to haul the old man in so everybody could know how bad the old man had been, and how he'd tried to steal some feed that didn't belong to him, and when the sheriff put the handcuffs on the boy he couldn't believe it. Then he'd started to cry. That was one story he had saved to write. He knew at least twenty good stories from out there and he had never written one. Why?

'You tell them why,' he said.

'Why what, dear?'

'Why nothing.'

She didn't drink so much, now, since she had him. But if he lived he would never write about her, he knew that now. Nor about any of them. The rich were dull and they drank too much, or they played too much backgammon. They were dull and they were repetitious. He remembered poor Julian and his romantic awe of them and how he had started a story once that began, 'The very rich are different from you and me.' And how someone had said to Julian. Yes, they have more money. But that was not humorous to Julian. He thought they were a special glamorous race and when he found they weren't it wrecked him just as much as any other thing that wrecked him.

He had been contemptuous of those who wrecked. You did not have to like it because you understood it. He could beat anything, he thought, because nothing could hurt him if he did not care.

All right. Now he would not care for death. One thing he had always dreaded was the pain. He could stand pain as well as any man, until it went on too long, and wore him out, but here he had something that had hurt frightfully and just when he had felt it breaking him, the pain had stopped.

He remembered long ago when Williamson, the bombing officer, had been hit by a stick bomb some one in a German patrol had thrown as he was coming in through the wire that night and, screaming, had begged everyone to kill him. He was a fat man, very brave, and a good officer, although addicted to fantastic shows. But that night he was caught in the wire, with a flare lighting him up and his bowels spilled out into the wire, so when they brought him in, alive, they had to cut him loose. Shoot me, Harry. For Christ sake shoot me. They had had an argument one time about our Lord never sending you anything you could not bear and someone's theory had been that meant that a certain time the pain passed you out automatically. But he had always remembered Williamson, that night. Nothing passed out Williamson until he gave him all his morphine tablets that he had always saved to use himself and then they did not work right away.

Still this now, that he had, was very easy; and if it was no worse as it went on there was nothing to worry about. Except that he would rather be in better company.

He thought a little about the company that he would like to have.

No, he thought, when everything you do, you do too long, and do too late, you can't expect to find the people still there. The people are all gone. The party's over and you are with your hostess now.

I'm getting as bored with dying as with everything else, he thought.

'It's a bore,' he said out loud.

'What is, my dear?'

'Anything you do too bloody long.'

He looked at her face between him and the fire. She was leaning back in the chair and the firelight shone on her pleasantly lined face and he could see that she was sleepy. He heard the hyena make a noise just outside the range of the fire.

'I've been writing,' he said. 'But I got tired.'

'Do you think you will be able to sleep?'

'Pretty sure. Why don't you turn in?'

'I like to sit here with you.'

'Do you feel anything strange?' he asked her.

'No. Just a little sleepy.'

'I do,' he said.

He had just felt death come by again.

'You know the only thing I've never lost is curiosity,' he said to her.

'You've never lost anything. You're the most complete man I've ever known.'

'Christ,' he said. 'How little a woman knows. What is that? Your intuition?'

Because, just then, death had come and rested its head on the foot of the cot and he could smell its breath.

'Never believe any of that about a scythe and a skull,' he told her. 'It can be two bicycle policemen as easily or be a bird. Or it can have a wide snout like a hyena.'

It had moved up on him now, but it had no shape any more. It simply occupied space.

'Tell it to go away.'

It did not go away but moved a little closer.

'You've got a hell of a breath,' he told it. 'You stinking bastard.'

It moved up closer to him still and now he could not speak to it, and when it saw he could not speak it came a little closer, and now he tried to send it away without speaking, but it moved in on him so its weight was all upon his chest, and while it crouched there and he could not move, or speak, he heard the woman say, 'Bwana is asleep now. Take the cot up very gently and carry it into the tent.'

He could not speak to tell her to make it go away and it crouched now, heavier so he could not breathe. And then, while they lifted the cot, suddenly it was all right and the weight went from his chest.

It was morning and had been morning for some time and he heard the plane. It showed very tiny and then made a wide circle and the boys ran out and lit the fires, using kerosene, and piled on grass so there were two big smudges at each end of the level place and the morning breeze blew them toward the camp and the plane circled twice more, low this time, and then glided down and levelled off and landed smoothly and, coming walking toward him, was old Compton in slacks, a tweed jacket and a brown felt hat.

'What's the matter, old cock?' Compton said.

'Bad leg,' he told him. 'Will you have some breakfast?'

'Thanks. I'll just have some tea. It's the Puss Moth, you know. I won't be able to take the Memsahib. There's only room for one. Your lorry is on the way.'

Helen had taken Compton aside and was speaking to him. Compton came back more cheery than ever.

'We'll get you right in,' he said. 'I'll be back for the Mem. Now I'm afraid I'll have to stop at Arusha to refuel. We'd better get going.'

'What about the tea?'

'I don't really care about it, you know.'

The boys had picked up the cot and carried it around the green tents and down along the rock and out on to the plain and along past the smudges that were burning brightly now, the grass all consumed, and the wind fanning the fire, to the little plane. It was difficult getting him in, but once in he lay back in the leather seat, and the leg was stuck straight out to one side of the seat where Compton sat. Compton started the motor and got in. He waved to Helen and to the boys and, as the clatter moved into the old familiar roar, they swung around with Compie watching for wart-hog holes and roared, bumping, along the stretch between the fires and with the last bump rose and he saw them all standing below, waving, and the camp beside the hill, flattening now, and the plain spreading, clumps of trees, and the bush flattening, while the game trails ran now smoothly to the dry waterholes, and there was a new water that he had never known of. The zebra, small rounded backs now, and the wildebeeste, big-headed dots seeming to climb as they moved in long fingers across the plain, now scattering as the shadow came toward them, they were tiny now, and the movement had no gallop, and the plain as far as you could see, grey-yellow now and ahead old Compie's tweed back and the brown felt hat. Then they were over the first hills and the wildebeeste were trailing up them, and then they were over mountains with sudden depths of green-rising forest and the solid bamboo slopes, and then the heavy forest again, sculptured into peaks and hollows until they crossed, and hills sloped down and then another plain, hot now, and purple-brown, bumpy with heat and Compie looking back to see how he was riding. Then there were other mountains dark ahead.

And then instead of going on to Arusha they turned left, he evidently figured that they had the gas, and looking down he saw a pink sifting cloud, moving over the ground, and in the air, like the first snow in a blizzard, that comes from nowhere, and he knew the locusts were coming up from the South. Then they began to climb and they were going to the East it seemed, and then it darkened and they were in a storm, the rain so thick it seemed like flying through a waterfall, and then they were out and Compie turned his head and grinned and pointed and there, ahead, all he could see, as wide as all the world, great, high, and unbelievably white in the sun, was the square top of Kilimanjaro. And then he knew that there was where he was going.

Just then the hyena stopped whimpering in the night and started to make a strange, human, almost crying sound. The woman heard it and stirred uneasily. She did not wake. In her dream she was at the house on Long Island and it was the night before her daughter's debut. Somehow her father was there and he had been very rude. Then the noise the hyena made was so loud she woke and for a moment she did not know where she was and she was very afraid. Then she took the flashlight and shone it on the other cot that they had carried in after Harry had gone to sleep. She could see his bulk under the mosquito bar but somehow he had gotten his leg out and it hung down alongside the cot. The dressings had all come down and she could not look at it.

'Molo,' she called. 'Molo! Molo!'

Then she said, 'Harry, Harry!' Then her voice rising, 'Harry! Please, Oh Harry!'

There was no answer and she could not hear him breathing.

Outside the tent the hyena made the same strange noise that had awakened her. But she did not hear him for the beating of her heart.

THE LIGHT OF THE WORLD

When he saw us come in the door the bartender looked up and then reached over and put the glass covers on the two free-lunch bowls.

'Give me a beer,' I said. He drew it, cut the top off with the spatula and then held the glass in his hand. I put the nickel on the wood and he slid the beer toward me.

'What's yours?' he said to Tom.

'Beer.'

He drew that beer and cut it off and when he saw the money he pushed the beer across to Tom.

'What's the matter?' Tom asked.

The bartender didn't answer him. He just looked over our heads and said, 'What's yours?' to a man who'd come in.

'Rye,' the man said. The bartender put out the bottle and glass and a glass of water.

Tom reached over and took the glass off the free-lunch bowl. It was a bowl of pickled pigs' feet and there was a wooden thing that worked like a scissors, with two wooden forks at the end to pick them up with.

'No,' said the bartender and put the glass cover back on the bowl. Tom held the wooden scissors fork in his hand. 'Put it back,' said the bartender.

'You know where,' said Tom.

The bartender reached a hand forward under the bar, watching us both. I put fifty cents on the wood and he straightened up.

'What was yours?' he said.

'Beer,' I said, and before he drew the beer he covered both the bowls.

'Your goddam pigs' feet stink,' Tom said, and spit what he had in his mouth on the floor. The bartender didn't say anything. The man who had drunk the rye paid and went out without looking back.

'You stink yourself,' the bartender said. 'All you punks stink.'

'He says we're punks,' Tommy said to me.

'Listen,' I said. 'Let's get out.'

'You punks clear the hell out of here,' the bartender said.

'I said we were going out,' I said. 'It wasn't your idea.'

'We'll be back,' Tommy said.

'No you won't,' the bartender told him.

'Tell him how wrong he is,' Tom turned to me.

'Come on,' I said.

Outside it was good and dark.

'What the hell kind of place is this?' Tommy said.

'I don't know,' I said. 'Let's go down to the station.'

We'd come in that town at one end and we were going out the other. It smelled of hides and tan bark and the big piles of sawdust. It was getting dark as we came in, and now that it was dark it was cold and the puddles of water in the road were freezing at the edges.

Down at the station there were five whores waiting for the train to come in, and six white men and four Indians. It was crowded and hot from the stove and full of stale smoke. As we came in nobody was talking and the ticket window was down.

'Shut the door, can't you!' somebody said.

I looked to see who said it. It was one of the white men. He wore stagged trousers and lumbermen's rubbers and a mackinaw shirt like the others, but he had no cap and his face was white and his hands were white and thin.

'Aren't you going to shut it?'

'Sure,' I said, and shut it.

'Thank you,' he said. One of the other men snickered.

'Ever interfere with a cook?' he said to me.

'No.'

'You can interfere with this one,' he looked at the cook. 'He likes it.'

The cook looked away from him holding his lips tight together.

'He puts lemon juice on his hands,' the man said. 'He wouldn't get them in dishwater for anything. Look how white they are.'

One of the whores laughed out loud. She was the biggest whore I ever saw in my life and the biggest woman. And she had on one of those silk dresses that change colours. There were two other whores that were nearly as big but the big one must have weighed three hundred and fifty pounds. You couldn't believe she was real when you looked at her. All three had those changeable silk dresses. They sat side by side on the bench. They were huge. The other two were just ordinary looking whores, peroxide blondes.

'Look at his hands,' the man said and nodded his head at the cook. The whore laughed again and shook all over.

The cook turned and said to her quickly. 'You big disgusting mountain of flesh.'

She just kept on laughing and shaking.

'Oh, my Christ,' she said. She had a nice voice. 'Oh, my sweet Christ.'

The other two whores, the big ones, acted very quiet and placid as though they didn't have much sense, but they were big, nearly as big as the biggest one. They'd have both gone well over two hundred and fifty pounds. The other two were dignified.

Of the men, besides the cook and the one who talked, there were two other lumberjacks, one that listened, interested but bashful, and the other that seemed getting ready to say something, and two Swedes. Two Indians were sitting down at the end of the bench and one standing up against the wall.

The man who was getting ready to say something spoke to me very low. 'Must be like getting on top of a hay mow.'

I laughed and said it to Tommy.

'I swear to Christ I've never been anywhere like this,' he said. 'Look at the three of them.' Then the cook spoke up.

'How old are you boys?'

'I'm ninety-six and he's sixty-nine,' Tommy said.

'Ho! Ho! Ho!' the big whore shook with laughing. She had a really pretty voice. The other whores didn't smile.

'Oh, can't you be decent?' the cook said. 'I asked just to be friendly.'

'We're seventeen and nineteen,' I said.

'What's the matter with you?' Tommy turned to me.

'That's all right.'

'You can call me Alice,' the big whore said and then she began to shake again.

'Is that your name?' Tommy asked.

'Sure,' she said. 'Alice. Isn't it?' she turned to the man who sat by the cook.

'Alice. That's right.'

'That's the sort of name you'd have,' the cook said.

'It's my real name,' Alice said.

'What's the other girls' names?' Tom asked.

'Hazel and Ethel,' Alice said. Hazel and Ethel smiled. They weren't very bright.

'What's your name?' I said to one of the blondes.

'Frances,' she said.

'Frances Wilson. What's it to you?'

'What's yours?' I asked the other one.

'Oh, don't be fresh,' she said.

'He just wants us all to be friends,' the man who talked said. 'Don't you want to be friends?'

'No,' the peroxide one said. 'Not with you.'

'She's just a spitfire,' the man said. 'A regular little spitfire.'

The one blonde looked at the other and shook her head.

'Goddamned mossbacks,' she said.

Alice commenced to laugh again and to shake all over.

'There's nothing funny,' the cook said. 'You all laugh but there's nothing funny. You two young lads; where are you bound for?'

'Where are you going yourself?' Tom asked him.

'I want to go to Cadillac,' the cook said. 'Have you ever been there? My sister lives there.'

'He's a sister himself,' the man in the stagged trousers said.

'Can't you stop that sort of thing?' the cook asked. 'Can't we speak decently?'

'Cadillac is where Steve Ketchel came from and where Ad Wolgast is from,' the shy man said.

'Steve Ketchel,' one of the blondes said in a high voice as though the name had pulled a trigger in her. 'His own father shot and killed him. Yes, by Christ, his own father. There aren't any more men like Steve Ketchel.'

'Wasn't his name Stanley Ketchel?' asked the cook.

'Oh, shut up,' said the blonde. 'What do you know about Steve? Stanley. He was no Stanley. Steve Ketchel was the finest and most beautiful man that ever lived. I never saw a man as clean and as white and as beautiful as Steve Ketchel. There never was a man like that. He moved just like a tiger and he was the finest, free-est spender that ever lived.'

'Did you know him?' one of the men asked.

'Did I know him? Did I know him? Did I love him? You ask me that? I knew him like you know nobody in the world and I loved him like you love God. He was the greatest, finest, whitest, most beautiful man that ever lived, Steve Ketchel, and his own father shot him down like a dog.'

'Were you out on the coast with him?'

'No. I knew him before that. He was the only man I ever loved.'

Everyone was very respectful to the peroxide blonde, who said all this in a high stagey way, but Alice was beginning to shake again. I felt it sitting by her.

'You should have married him,' the cook said.

'I wouldn't hurt his career,' the peroxide blonde said. 'I wouldn't be a drawback to him. A wife wasn't what he needed. Oh, my God, what a man he was.'

'That was a fine way to look at it,' the cook said. 'Didn't Jack Johnson knock him out though?'

'It was a trick,' Peroxide said. 'That big dinge took him by surprise. He'd just knocked Jack Johnson down, the big black bastard. That nigger beat him by a fluke.'

The ticket window went up and the three Indians went over to it.

'Steve knocked him down,' Peroxide said. 'He turned to smile at me.'

'I thought you said you weren't on the coast,' someone said.

'I went out just for that fight. Steve turned to smile at me and that black son of a bitch from hell jumped and hit him by surprise. Steve could lick a hundred like that black bastard.'

'He was a great fighter,' the lumberjack said.

'I hope to God he was,' Peroxide said. 'I hope to God they don't have fighters like that now. He was like a god, he was. So white and clean and beautiful and smooth and fast and like a tiger or like lightning.'

'I saw him in the moving pictures of the fight,' Tom said.

We were all very moved. Alice was shaking all over and I looked and saw she was crying. The Indians had gone outside on the platform.

'He was more than any husband could ever be,' Peroxide said. 'We were married in the eyes of God and I belong to him right now and always will and all of me is his. I don't care about my body. They can take my body. My soul belongs to Steve Ketchel. By God, he was a man.'

Everybody felt terribly. It was sad and embarrassing. Then Alice, who was still shaking, spoke. 'You're a dirty liar,' she said in that low voice. 'You never layed Steve Ketchel in your life and you know it.'

'How can you say that?' Peroxide said proudly.

'I say it because it's true,' Alice said. 'I'm the only one here that ever knew Steve Ketchel and I come from Mancelona and I knew him there and it's true and you know it's true and God can strike me dead if it isn't true.'

'He can strike me too,' Peroxide said.

'That is true, true, true, and you know it. Not just made up and I know exactly what he said to me.'

'What did he say?' Peroxide asked, complacently.

Alice was crying so she could hardly speak from shaking so. 'He said, "You're a lovely piece, Alice." That's exactly what he said.'

'It's a lie,' Peroxide said.

'It's true,' Alice said. 'That's truly what he said.'

'It's a lie,' Peroxide said proudly.

'No, it's true, true, true, to Jesus and Mary true.'

'Steve couldn't have said that. It wasn't the way he talked,' Peroxide said happily.

'It's true,' said Alice in her nice voice. 'And it doesn't make any difference to me whether you believe it or not.' She wasn't crying any more and she was calm.

'It would be impossible for Steve to have said that,' Peroxide declared.

'He said it,' Alice said and smiled. 'And I remember when he said it and I *was* a lovely piece then exactly as he said, and right now I'm a better piece than you, you dried-up old hot water-bottle.'

'You can't insult me,' said Peroxide. 'You big mountain of pus. I have my memories.'

'No,' Alice said in that sweet lovely voice, 'you haven't got any real memories except having your tubes out and when you started C. and M. Everything else you just read in the papers. I'm clean and you know it, and men like me, even though I'm big, and you know it, and I never lie and you know it.'

'Leave me with my memories,' Peroxide said. 'With my true, wonderful memories.'

Alice looked at her and then at us and her face lost that hurt look and she smiled and she had the prettiest face I ever saw. She had a pretty face and a nice smooth skin and a lovely voice and she was nice all right and really friendly. But my God she was big. She was as big as three women. Tom saw me looking at her and he said, 'Come on. Let's go.'

'Good-bye,' said Alice. She certainly had a nice voice.

'Good-bye,' I said.

'Which way are you boys going?' asked the cook.

'The other way from you,' Tom told him.

THE CAPITAL OF THE WORLD

Madrid is full of boys named Paco, which is the diminutive of the name Francisco, and there is a Madrid joke about a father who came to Madrid and inserted an advertisement in the personal coloumns of *El Liberal* which said: PACO MEET ME AT HOTEL MONTANA NOON TUESDAY ALL IS FORGIVEN PAPA, and how a squadron of Guardia Civil had to be called out to disperse the eight hundred young men who answered the advertisement. But this Paco, who waited on table at the Pension Luarca, had no father to forgive him, nor anything for the father to forgive. He had two older sisters who were chambermaids at the Luarca, who had gotten their place through coming from the same village as a former Luarca chambermaid who had proven hardworking and honest and hence given her village and its products a good name; and these sisters had paid his way on the autobus to Madrid and gotten him his job as an apprentice waiter. He came from a village in a part of Extremadura where conditions were incredibly primitive, food scarce, and comforts unknown, and he had worked hard ever since he could remember.

He was a well-built boy with very black, rather curly hair, good teeth and a skin that his sisters envied, and he had a ready and unpuzzled smile. He was fast on his feet and did his work well and he loved his sisters, who seemed beautiful and unsophisticated; he loved Madrid, which was still an unbelievable place, and he loved his work which, done under bright lights, with clean linen, the wearing of evening clothes, and abundant food in the kitchen, seemed romantically beautiful.

There were from eight to a dozen other people who lived at the Luarca and ate in the dining-room, but for Paco, the youngest of the three waiters who served at table, the only ones who really existed were the bull-fighters.

Second-rate matadors lived at that pension because the address in the Calle San Jeronimo was good, the food was excellent and the room and board was cheap. It is necessary for a bull-fighter to give the appearance, if not of prosperity, at least of respectability, since decorum and dignity rank above courage as the virtues most highly prized in Spain, and bull-fighters stayed at the Luarca until their last pesetas were gone. There is no record of any bull-fighter having left the Luarca for a better or more expensive hotel;

second-rate bull-fighters never became first rate; but the descent from the Luarca was swift since anyone could stay there who was making anything at all and a bill was never presented to a guest unasked until the woman who ran the place knew that the case was hopeless.

At this time there were three full matadors living at the Luarca as well as two very good picadors, and one excellent banderillero. The Luarca was luxury for the picadors and the banderillero who, with their families in Seville, required lodging in Madrid during the spring season; but they were well paid and in the fixed employ of fighters who were heavily contracted during the coming season and the three of these subalterns would probably make much more apiece than any of the three matadors. Of the three matadors one was ill and trying to conceal it; one had passed his short vogue as a novelty; and the third was a coward.

The coward had at one time, until he had received a peculiarly atrocious horn wound in the lower abdomen at the start of his first season as a full matador, been exceptionally brave and remarkably skilful and he still had many of the hearty mannerisms of his days of success. He was jovial to excess and laughed constantly with and without provocation. He had, when successful, been very addicted to practical jokes, but he had given them up now. They took an assurance that he did not feel. This matador had an intelligent, very open face and he carried himself with much style.

The matador who was ill was careful never to show it and was meticulous about eating a little of all the dishes that were presented at the table. He had a great many handkerchiefs which he laundered himself in his room and, lately, he had been selling his fighting suits. He had sold one, cheaply, before Christmas and another in the first week of April. They had been very expensive suits, had always been well kept and he had one more. Before he had become ill he had been a very promising, even a sensational, fighter and, while he himself could not read, he had clippings which said that in his debut in Madrid he had been better than Belmonte. He ate alone at a small table and looked up very little.

The matador who had once been a novelty was very short and brown and very dignified. He also ate alone at a separate table and he smiled very rarely and never laughed. He came from Valladolid, where the people are extremely serious, and he was a capable matador; but his style had become old-fashioned before he had ever succeeded in endearing himself to the public through his virtues, which were courage and a calm capability, and his name on a poster would draw no one to a bull ring. His novelty had been that he was so short that he could barely see over the bull's withers, but there were other short fighters, and he had never succeeded in imposing himself on the public's fancy.

Of the picadors one was a thin, hawk-faced, grey-haired man, lightly built, but with legs and arms like iron, who always wore cattleman's boots under his trousers, drank too much every evening and gazed amorously at any woman in the pension. The other was huge, dark, brown-faced, good-looking, with black hair like an Indian and enormous hands. Both were great picadors although the first was reputed to have lost much of his ability through drink and dissipation, and the second was said to be too headstrong and quarrelsome to stay with any matador more than a single season.

The banderillero was middle-aged, grey, cat-quick in spite of his years and, sitting at the table, he looked a moderately prosperous business man. His legs were still good for this season, and when they should go he was intelligent and experienced enough to keep regularly employed for a long time. The difference would be that when his speed of foot would be gone he would always be frightened where now he was assured and calm in the ring and out of it.

On this evening every one had left the dining-room except the hawk-faced picador who drank too much, the birthmarked-faced auctioneer of watches at the fairs and festivals of Spain, who also drank too much, and two priests from Galicia who were sitting at a corner table and drinking if not too much certainly enough. At that time wine was included in the price of the room and board at the Luarca, and the waiters had just brought fresh bottles of Valdepeñas to the tables of the auctioneer, then to the picador and, finally, to the two priests.

The three waiters stood at the end of the room. It was the rule of the house that they should remain on duty until the diners whose tables they were responsible for should all have left, but the one who served the table of the two priests had an appointment to go to an Anarcho-Syndicalist meeting and Paco had agreed to take over his table for him.

Upstairs the matador who was ill was lying face down on his bed alone. The matador who was no longer a novelty was sitting looking out of his window preparatory to walking out to the café. The matador who was a coward had the older sister of Paco in his room with him and was trying to get her to do something which she was laughingly refusing to do. This matador was saying 'Come on, little savage.'

'No,' said the sister. 'Why should I?'

'For a favour.'

'You've eaten and now you want me for dessert.'

'Just once. What harm can it do?'

'Leave me alone. Leave me alone, I tell you.'

'It is a very little thing to do.'

'Leave me alone, I tell you.'

Down in the dining-room the tallest of the waiters, who was overdue at the meeting, said, 'Look at those black pigs drink.'

'That's no way to speak,' said the second waiter. 'They are decent clients. They do not drink too much.'

'For me it is a good way to speak,' said the tall one. 'There are the two curses of Spain, the bulls and the priests.'

'Certainly not the individual bull and the individual priest,' said the second waiter.

'Yes,' said the tall waiter. 'Only through the individual can you attack the class. It is necessary to kill the individual bull and the individual priest. All of them. Then there are no more.'

'Save it for the meeting,' said the other waiter.

'Look at the barbarity of Madrid,' said the tall waiter. 'It is now half past eleven o'clock and these are still guzzling.'

'They only started to eat at ten,' said the other waiter. 'As you know there are many dishes. That wine is cheap and these have paid for it. It is not a strong wine.'

'How can there be solidarity of workers with fools like you?' asked the tall waiter.

'Look,' said the second waiter who was a man of fifty. 'I have worked all my life. In all that remains of my life I must work. I have no complaints against work. To work is normal.'

'Yes, but the lack of work kills.'

'I have always worked,' said the older waiter. 'Go on to the meeting. There is no necessity to stay.'

'You are a good comrade,' said the tall waiter. 'But you lack all ideology.'

'*Mejor si me falta eso que el otro*,' said the older waiter (meaning it is better to lack that than work). 'Go on to the *mitin.*'

Paco had said nothing. He did not yet understand politics but it always gave him a thrill to hear the tall waiter speak of the necessity for killing the priests and the Guardia Civil. The tall waiter represented to him revolution and revolution also was romantic. He himself would like to be a good Catholic, a revolutionary, and have a steady job like this, while, at the same time, being a bull-fighter.

'Go on to the meeting, Ignacio,' he said. 'I will respond for your work.'

'The two of us,' said the older waiter.

'There isn't enough for one,' said Paco. 'Go on to the meeting.'

'*Pues, me voy*,' said the tall waiter. 'And thanks.'

In the meantime, upstairs, the sister of Paco had gotten out of the embrace of the matador as skilfully as a wrestler breaking a hold and said, now angry, 'These are the hungry people. A failed bull-fighter. With your ton-load of fear. If you have so much of that, use it in the ring.'

'That is the way a whore talks.'

'A whore is also a woman, but I am not a whore.'

'You'll be one.'

'Not through you.'

'Leave me,' said the matador, who, now, repulsed and refused, felt the nakedness of his cowardice returning.

'Leave you? What hasn't left you?' said the sister. 'Don't you want me to make up the bed? I'm paid to do that.'

'Leave me,' said the matador, his broad good-looking face wrinkled into a contortion that was like crying. 'You whore. You dirty little whore.'

'Matador,' she said, shutting the door. 'My matador.'

Inside the room the matador sat on the bed. His face still had the contortion which, in the ring, he made into a constant smile which frightened those people in the first row of seats who knew what they were watching. 'and this,' he was saying aloud. 'And this. And this.'

He could remember when he had been good and it had only been three years before. He could remember the weight of the heavy gold-brocaded fighting jacket on his shoulders on that hot afternoon in May when his voice had still been the same in the ring as in the café, and how he sighted along the point-dipping blade at the place in the top of the shoulders where it was dusty in the short-haired black hump of muscle above the wide, wood-knocking, splintered-tipped horns that lowered as he went in to kill, and how the sword pushed in as easy as into a mound of stiff butter with the palm of his hand pushing the pommel, his left arm crossed low, his left shoulder forward, his weight on his left leg, and then his weight wasn't on his leg. His weight was on his lower belly and as the bull raised his head the horn was out of sight in him and he swung over on it twice before they pulled him off it. So now when he went in to kill, and it was seldom, he could not look at the horns and what did any whore know about what he went throughbefore he fought? And what had they been through that laughed at him? They were all whores and they knew what they could do with it.

Down in the dining-room the picador sat looking at the priests. If there were women in the room he stared at them. If there were no women he would stare with enjoyment at a foreigner, *un inglés*, but lacking women or strangers, he now stared with enjoyment and insolence at the two priests. While he stared the birthmarked auctioneer rose and folding his napkin went out, leaving over half the wine in the last bottle he had ordered. If his accounts had been paid up at Luarca he would have finished the bottle.

The two priests did not stare back at the picador. One of them was saying, 'It is ten days since I have been here waiting to see him and all day I sit in the ante-chamber and he will not receive me.'

'What is there to do?'

'Nothing. What can one do? One cannot go against authority.'

'I have been here for two weeks for nothing. I wait and they will not see me.'

'We are from the abandoned country. When the money runs out we can return.'

'To the abandoned country. What does Madrid care about Galicia? We are a poor province.'

'One understands the action of our bother Basilio.'

'Still I have no real confidence in the integrity of Basilio Alvarez.'

'Madrid is where one learns to understand. Madrid kills Spain.'

'If they would simply see one and refuse.'

'No. You must be broken and worn out by waiting.'

'Well, we shall see. I can wait as well as another.'

At this moment the picador got to his feet, walked over to the priests' table and stood, grey-headed and hawk-faced, staring at them and smiling.

'A torero,' said one priest to the other.

'And a good one,' said the picador and walked out of the dining-room, grey-jacketed, trim-waisted, bow-legged, in tight breeches over his high-heeled cattleman's boots that clicked on the floor as he swaggered quite steadily, smiling to himself. He lived in a small, tight, professional world of personal efficiency, nightly alcoholic triumph, and insolence. Now he lit a cigar and tilting his hat at an angle in the hallway went out to the café.

The priests left immediately after the picador, hurriedly conscious of being the last people in the dining-room, and there was no one in the room now but Paco and the middle-aged waiter. They cleared the tables and carried the bottles into the kitchen.

In the kitchen was the boy who washed the dishes. He was three years older than Paco and was very cynical and bitter.

'Take this,' the middle-aged waiter said, and poured out a glass of the Valdepeñas and handed it to him.

'Why not?' the boy took the glass.

'Tu, Paco?' the older waiter asked.

'Thank you,' said Paco. The three of them drank.

'I will be going,' said the middle-aged waiter.

'Good night,' they told him.

He went out and they were alone. Paco took a napkin one of the priests had used and standing straight, his heels planted, lowered the napkin and with head following the movement, swung his arms in the motion of a slow sweeping veronica. He turned and advancing his right foot slightly, made the second pass, gained a little terrain on the imaginary bull and made a third pass, slow, perfectly timed and suave, then gathered the napkin to his waist and swung his hips away from the bull in a media-veronica.

The dishwasher, whose name was Enrique, watched him critically and sneeringly.

'How is the bull?' he said.

'Very brave,' said Paco. 'Look.'

Standing slim and straight he made four more perfect passes, smooth, elegant and graceful.

'And the bull?' asked Enrique standing against the sink, holding his wine glass and wearing his apron.

'Still has lots of gas,' said Paco.

'You make me sick,' said Enrique.

'Why?'

'Look.'

Enrique removed his apron and citing the imaginary bull he sculptured four perfect, languid gypsy veronicas and ended up with a rebolera that made the apron swing in a stiff arc past the bull's nose as he walked away from him.

'Look at that,' he said. 'And I wash dishes.'

'Why?'

'Fear,' said Enrique. '*Miedo*. The same fear you would have in a ring with a bull.'

'No,' said Paco. 'I wouldn't be afraid.'

'*Leche!*' said Enrique. 'Everyone is afraid. But a torero can control his fear so that he can work the bull. I went in an amateur fight and I was so afraid I couldn't keep from running. Every one thought it was very funny. So would you be afraid. If it wasn't for fear every bootblack in Spain would be a bull-fighter. You, a country boy, would be frightened worse than I was.'

'No,' said Paco.

He had done it too many times in his imagination. Too many times he had seen the horns, seen the bull's wet muzzle, the ear twitching, then the head go down and the charge, the hoofs thudding and the hot bull pass him as he swung the cape, to re-charge as he swung the cape again, then again, and again, and again, to end winding the bull around him in his great media-veronica, and walk swingingly away, with bull hairs caught in the gold ornaments of his jacket from the close passes; the bull standing hypnotized and the crowd applauding. No, he would not be afraid. Others, yes. Not he. He knew he would not be afraid. Even if he ever was afraid he knew that he could do it anyway. He had confidence. 'I wouldn't be afraid,' he said.

Enrique said, '*Leche*,' again.

Then he said, 'If we should try it?'

'How!'

'Look,' said Enrique. 'You think of the bull but you do not think of the horns. The bull has such force that the horns rip like a knife, they stab like a bayonet, and they kill like a club. Look,' he opened a table drawer and took out two meat knives. 'I will bind these to the legs of a chair. Then I will play bull for you with the chair held before my head. The knives are the horns. If you make those passes then they mean something.'

'Lend me your apron,' said Paco. 'We'll do it in the dining-room.'

'No,' said Enrique, suddenly not bitter. 'Don't do it, Paco.'

'Yes,' said Paco. 'I'm not afraid.'

'You will be when you see the knives come.'

'We'll see,' said Paco. 'Give me the apron.'

At this time, while Enrique was binding the two heavy-bladed razor-sharp meat knives fast to the legs of the chair with two soiled napkins holding the half of each knife, wrapping them tight and then knotting them, the two chambermaids, Paco's sisters, were on their way to the cinema to see Greta Garbo in 'Anna Christie'. Of the two priests, one was sitting in his underwear reading his breviary and the other was wearing a nightshirt and saying the rosary. All the bull-fighters except the one who was ill had made their evening appearance at the Café Fornos, where the big, dark-haired picador was playing billiards, the short, serious matador was sitting at a crowded table before a coffee and milk, along with the middle-aged banderillero and other serious workmen.

The drinking, grey-headed picador was sitting with a glass of cazalas brandy before him staring with pleasure at a table where the matador whose courage was gone sat with another matador who had renounced the sword to become a banderillero again, and two very houseworn-looking prostitutes.

The auctioneer stood on the street corner talking with friends. The tall waiter was at the Anarcho-Syndicalist meeting waiting for an opportunity to speak. The middle-aged waiter was seated on the terrace of the Café Alvarez drinking a small beer. The woman who owned the Luarca was already asleep in her bed, where she lay on her back with the bolster between her legs; big fat, honest, clean, easy-going, very religious and never having ceased to miss or pray daily for her husband, dead, now, twenty years. In his room, alone, the matador who was ill lay face down on his bed with his mouth against a handkerchief.

Now, in the deserted dining-room, Enrique tied the last knot in the napkins that bound the knives to the chair legs and lifted the chair. He pointed the legs with the knives on them forward and held the chair over his head with the two knives pointing straight ahead, one on each side of his head.

'It's heavy,' he said. 'Look, Paco. It is very dangerous. Don't do it.' He was sweating.

Paco stood facing him, holding the apron spread, holding a fold of it bunched in each hand, thumbs up, first finger down, spread to catch the eye of the bull.

'Charge straight,' he said. 'Turn like a bull. Charge as many times as you want.'

'How will you know when to cut the pass?' asked Enrique. 'It's better to do three and then a media.'

'All right,' said Paco. 'But come straight. Huh, torito! Come on, little bull!'

Running with head down Enrique came toward him and Paco swung the apron just ahead of the knife blade as it passed close in front of his belly and as it went by it was, to him, the real horn, white-tipped, black, smooth, and as Enrique passed him and turned to rush again it was the hot, blood-flanked mass of the bull that thudded by, then turned like a cat and came again as he swung the cape slowly. Then the bull turned and came again and, as he watched the onrushing point, he stepped his left foot two inches too far forward and the knife did not pass, but had slipped in as easily as into a wineskin and there was a hot scalding rush above and around the sudden inner rigidity of steel and Enrique shouting, 'Ay! Ay! Let me get it out! Let me get it out!' and Paco slipped forward on the chair the apron cape still held, Enrique pulling on the chair as the knife turned in him, in him, Paco.

The knife was out now and he sat on the floor in the widening warm pool.

'Put the napkin over it. Hold it!' said Enrique. 'Hold it tight. I will run for the doctor. You must hold in the haemorrhage.'

'There should be a rubber cup,' said Paco. He had seen that used in the ring.

'I came straight,' said Enrique, crying. 'All I wanted was to show the danger.'

'Don't worry,' said Paco, his voice sounding far away. 'But bring the doctor.'

In the ring they lifted you and carried you, running with you, to the operating room. If the femoral artery emptied itself before you reached there they called the priest.

'Advise one of the priests,' said Paco, holding the napkin tight against his lower abdomen. He could not believe that this had happened to him.

But Enrique was running down the Carrera San Jeronimo to the all-night first-aid station and Paco was alone, first sitting up, then huddled over, then slumped on the floor, until it was over, feeling his life go out of him as dirty water empties from a bathtub when the plug is drawn. He was frightened and he felt faint and he tried to say an act of contrition and he remembered how it started but before he had said, as fast as he could, 'Oh, my God, I am heartily sorry for having offended Thee who are worthy of all my love and I firmly resolve . . .' he felt too faint and he was lying face down on the floor and it was over very quickly. A severed femoral artery empties itself faster than you can believe.

As the doctor from the first-aid station came up the stairs accompanied by a policeman who held on to Enrique by the arm, the two sisters of Paco were still in the moving-picture palace of the Gran Via, where they were intensely disappointed in the Garbo film, which showed the great star in miserable low surroundings when they had been accustomed to see her surrounded by great luxury and brilliance. The audience disliked the film thoroughly and were protesting by whistling and stamping their feet. All the other people from the hotel were doing almost what they had been doing when the accident happened, except that the two priests had finished their devotions and were preparing for sleep, and the grey-haired picador had moved his drink over to the table with the two houseworn prostitutes. A little later he went out of the café with one of them. It was the one for whom the matador who had lost his nerve had been buying drinks.

The boy Paco had never known about any of this nor about what all these people would be doing on the next day and on other days to come. He had no idea how they really lived nor how they ended. He did not even realize they ended. He died, as the Spanish phrase has it, full of illusions. He had not had time in his life to lose any of them, nor even, at the end, to complete an act of contrition.

He had not even had time to be disappointed in the Garbo picture which disappointed all Madrid for a week.

A DAY'S WAIT

He came into the room to shut the windows while we were still in bed and I saw he looked ill. He was shivering, his face was white, and he walked slowly as though it ached to move.

'What's the matter, Schatz?'

'I've got a headache.'

'You better go back to bed.'

'No, I'm all right.'

'You go to bed. I'll see you when I'm dressed.'

But when I came downstairs he was dressed, sitting by the fire, looking a very sick and miserable boy of nine years. When I put my hand on his forehead I knew he had a fever.

'You go up to bed,' I said, 'You're sick.'

'I'm all right,' he said.

When the doctor came he took the boy's temperature.

'What is it?' I asked him.

'One hundred and two.'

Downstairs, the doctor left three different medicines in different coloured capsules with instructions for giving them. One was to bring down the fever, another a purgative, the third to overcome an acid condition, he explained. He seemed to know all about influenza and said there was nothing to worry about if the fever did not go above one hundred and four degrees. This was a light epidemic of flu and there was no danger if you avoided pneumonia.

Back in the room I wrote the boy's temperature down and made a note of the time to give the various capsules.

'Do you want me to read to you?'

'All right. If you want to,' said the boy. His face was very white and there were dark areas under his eyes. He lay still in the bed and seemed very detached from what was going on.

I read aloud from Howard Pyle's *Book of Pirates*; but I could see he was not following what I was reading.

'How do you feel, Schatz?' I asked him.

'Just the same, so far,' he said.

I sat at the foot of the bed and read to myself while I waited for it to be time to give another capsule. It would have been natural for him to go to sleep, but when I looked up he was looking at the foot of the bed, looking very strangely.

'Why don't you try to go to sleep? I'll wake you up for the medicine.'

'I'd rather stay awake.'

After a while he said to me, 'You don't have to stay in here with me, Papa, if it bothers you.'

'It doesn't bother me.'

'No, I mean you don't have to stay if it's going to bother you.'

I thought perhaps he was a little lightheaded and after giving him the prescribed capsules at eleven o'clock I went out for a while.

It was a bright, cold day, the ground covered with a sleet that had frozen so that it seemed as if all the bare trees, the bushes, the cut brush and all the grass and the bare ground had been varnished with ice. I took the young Irish setter for a little walk up the road and along a frozen creek, but it was difficult to stand or walk on the glassy surface and the red dog slipped and slithered and I fell twice, hard, once dropping my gun and having it slide away over the ice.

We flushed a covey of quail under a high bank with overhanging brush and I killed two as they went out of sight over the top of the bank. Some of the covey lit in trees, but most of them scattered into brush piles and it was necessary to jump on the ice-coated mounds of brush several times before they would flush. Coming out while you were poised unsteadily on the icy, springy bush they made difficult shooting and I killed two, missed five, and started back pleased to have found a covey close to the house and happy there were so many left to find on another day.

At the house they said the boy had refused to let anyone come into the room.

'You can't come in,' he said. 'You mustn't get what I have.'

I went up to him and found him in exactly the position I had left him, white-faced, but with the tops of his cheeks flushed by the fever, staring still, as he had stared, at the foot of the bed.

I took his temperature.

'What is it?'

'Something like a hundred,' I said. It was one hundred and two and four-tenths.

'It was a hundred and two,' he said.

'Who said so?'

'The doctor.'

'Your temperature is all right,' I said. 'It's nothing to worry about.'

'I don't worry,' he said, 'but I can't keep from thinking.'

'Don't think,' I said. 'Just take it easy.'

'I'm taking it easy,' he said, and looked straight ahead. He was evidently holding tight on to himself about something.

'Take this with water.'

'Do you think it will do any good?'

'Of course it will.'

I sat down and opened the *Pirate* book and commenced to read, but I could see he was not following, so I stopped.

'About what time do you think I'm going to die?' he asked.

'What?'

'About how long will it be before I die?'

'You aren't going to die. What's the matter with you?'

'Oh, yes, I am. I heard him say a hundred and two.'

'People don't die with a fever of one hundred and two. That's a silly way to talk.'

'I know they do. At school in France the boys told me you can't live with forty-four degrees. I've got a hundred and two.'

He had been waiting to die all day, ever since nine o'clock in the morning.

'You poor Schatz,' I said. 'Poor old Schatz. It's like miles and kilometres. You aren't going to die. That's a different thermometer. On that thermometer thirty-seven is normal. On this kind it's ninety-eight.'

'Absolutely,' I said. 'It's like miles and kilometres. You know, like how many kilometres we make when we do seventy miles in the car?'

'Oh,' he said.

But his gaze at the foot of the bed relaxed slowly. The hold over himself relaxed too, finally, and the next day it was very slack and he cried very easily at little things that were of no importance.

ONE READER WRITES

She sat at the table in her bedroom with a newspaper folded open before her and only stopping to look out of the window at the snow which was falling and melting on the roofs as it fell. She wrote this letter, writing it steadily with no necessity to cross out or rewrite anything.

Roanoke, Virginia
6 February 1933

Dear Doctor,

May I write you for some very important advice–I have a decision to make and don't know just whom to trust most, I dare not ask my parents–and so I come to you–and only because I need not see you, can I confide in you even. Now here is the situation–I married a man in U.S. service in 1929 and that same year he was sent to China, Shanghai–he stayed three years–and came home–he was discharged from the service some few months ago–and went to his mother's home, in Helena, Arkansas. He wrote for me to come home–I went, and found he is taking a course of injections and I naturally ask, and found he is being treated for I don't know how to spell the word but it sounds like this 'sifilus'–Do you know what I mean–now tell me will it ever be safe for me to live with him again–I did not come in close contact with him at any time since his return from China. He assures me he will be O.K. after the doctor finishes with him–Do you think it right–I often heard my Father say one could well wish themselves dead if once they became a victim of that malady–I believe my Father but want to believe my Husband most–Please, please tell me what to do–I have a daughter born while her Father was in China—

Thanking you and trusting wholly in your advice I am

and signed her name.

Maybe he can tell me what's right to do, she said to herself. Maybe he can tell me. In the picture in the paper he looks like he'd know. He looks smart, all right. Every day he tells somebody what to do. He ought to know. I want to do whatever is right. It's such a long time though. It's a long time. And it's been a long time. My Christ, it's been a long time. He had to go wherever they sent him, I know, but I don't know what he had to get it for. Oh, I wish to Christ he wouldn't have got it. I don't care what he did to get it. But I wish to Christ he hadn't ever got it. It does seem like he didn't have to have got it. I don't know what to do. I wish to Christ he hadn't got any kind of malady. I don't know why he had to get a malady.

A WAY YOU'LL NEVER BE

The attack had gone across the field, been held up by machine-gun fire from the sunken road and from the group of farmhouses, encountered no resistance in the town, and reached the bank of the river. Coming along the road on a bicycle, getting off to push the machine when the surface of the road became too broken, Nicholas Adams saw what had happened by the position of the dead.

They lay alone or in clumps in the high grass of the fields and along the road, their pockets out, and over them were flies and around each body or group of bodies were the scattered papers.

In the grass and the grain, beside the road, and in some places scattered over the road, there was much material: a field kitchen, it must have come over when things were going well; many of the calf-skin-covered haversacks, stick bombs, helmets, rifles, sometimes one butt-up, the bayonets stuck in the dirt, they had dug quite a little at the last; stick bombs, helmets, rifles, entrenching tools, ammunition boxes, starshell pistols, their shells scattered about, medical kits, gas masks, empty gas mask cans, a squat, tripodded machine-gun in a nest of empty shells, full belts protruding from the boxes, the water-cooling can empty and on its side, the breech block gone, the crew in odd positions, and around them, in the grass, more of the typical papers.

There were mass prayer books, group postcards showing the machine-gun unit standing in ranked and ruddy cheerfulness as in a football picture for a college annual; now they were humped and swollen in the grass; propaganda postcards showing a soldier in Austrian uniform bending a woman backward over a bed; the figures were impressionistically drawn; very attractively depicted and had nothing in common with actual rape in which the woman's skirts are pulled over her head to smother her, one comrade sometimes sitting upon her head. There were many of these inciting cards which had evidently been issued just before the offensive. Now they were scattered with the smutty postcards, photographic; the small photographs of village girls by village photographers, the occasional pictures of children, and the letters, letters, letters. There was always much paper about the dead and the debris of this attack was no exception.

These were new dead and no one bothered with anything but their pockets. Our own dead, or what we thought of, still, as our own dead, were surprisingly few, Nick noticed. Their coats had been opened too and their pockets were out, and they showed, by their positions, the manner and the skill of the attack. The hot weather had swollen them all alike regardless of nationality.

The town had evidently been defended, at the last, from the line of the sunken road and there had been few or no Austrians to fall back into it. There were only three bodies in the street and they looked to have been killed running. The houses of the town were broken by the shelling and the street had much rubble of plaster and mortar and there were broken beams, broken tiles, and many holes, some of them yellow-edged from the mustard gas. There were many pieces of shell, and shrapnel balls were scattered in the rubble. There was no one in the town at all.

Nick Adams had seen no one since he had left Fornaci, although, riding along the road through the over-foliaged country, he had seen guns hidden under screens of mulberry leaves, to the left of the road, noticing them by the heatwaves in the air above the leaves where the sun hit the metal. Now he went on through the town, surprised to find it deserted, and came out on the low road beneath the bank of the river. Leaving the town there was a bare open space where the road slanted down and he could see the placid reach of the river and the low curve of the opposite bank and the whitened, sun-baked mud where the Austrians had dug. It was all very lush and overgreen since he had seen it last and becoming historical had made no change in this, the lower river.

The battalion was along the bank to the left. There was a series of holes in the top of the bank with a few men in them. Nick noticed where the machine-guns were posted and the signal rockets in their racks. The men in the holes in the side of the bank were sleeping. No one challenged. He went on and as he came around a turn in the mud bank a young second lieutenant with a stubble of beard and red-rimmed, very bloodshot eyes pointed a pistol at him.

'Who are you?'

Nick told him.

'How do I know this?'

Nick showed him the tessera with photograph and identification and the seal of the third army. He took hold of it.

'I will keep this.'

'You will not,' Nick said. 'Give me back the card and put your gun away. There, in the holster.'

'How am I to know who you are?'

'The tessera tells you.'

'And if the tessera is false? Give me that card.'

'Don't be a fool,' Nick said cheerfully. 'Take me to your company commander.'

'I should send you to battalion headquarters.'

'All right,' said Nick. 'Listen, do you know the Captain Paravicini? The tall one with the small moustache who was an architect and speaks English?'

'You know him?'

'A little.'

'What company does he command?'

'The second.'

'He is commanding the battalion.'

'Good,' said Nick. He was relieved to know that Para was all right. 'Let us go to the battalion.'

As Nick had left the edge of the town three shrapnel had burst high and to the right over one of the wrecked houses and since then there had been no shelling. But the face of this officer looked like the face of a man during a bombardment. There was the same tightness and the voice did not sound natural. His pistol made Nick nervous.

'Put it away,' he said. 'There's the whole river between them and you.'

'If I thought you were a spy I would shoot you now,' the second lieutenant said.

'Come on,' said Nick. 'Let us go to the battalion.' This officer made him very nervous.

The Captain Paravicini, acting major, thinner and more English-looking than ever, rose when Nick saluted from behind the table in the dugout that was battalion headquarters.

'Hello,' he said. 'I didn't know you. What are you doing in that uniform?'

'They've put me in it.'

'I am very glad to see you, Nicolo.'

'Right. You look well. How was the show?'

'We made a very fine attack. Truly. A very fine attack. I will show you. Look.'

He showed on the map how the attack had gone.

'I came from Fornaci,' Nick said. 'I could see how it had been. It was very good.'

'It was extraordinary. Altogether extraordinary. Are you attached to the regiment?'

'No. I am supposed to move around and let them see the uniform.'

'How odd.'

'If they see one American uniform that is supposed to make them believe others are coming.'

'But how will they know it is an American uniform?'

'You will tell them.'

'Oh. Yes, I see. I will send a corporal with you to show you about and you will make a tour of the lines.'

'Like a bloody politician,' Nick said.

'You would be much more distinguished in civilian clothes. They are what is really distinguished.'

'With a homburg hat,' said Nick.

'Or with a very furry fedora.'

'I'm supposed to have my pockets full of cigarettes and postal cards and such things,' Nick said. 'I should have a musette full of chocolate. These I should distribute with a kind word and a pat on the back. But there weren't any cigarettes and postcards and no chocolate. So they said to circulate around anyway.'

'I'm sure your appearance will be very heartening to the troops.'

'I wish you wouldn't,' Nick said. 'I feel badly enough about it as it is. In principle, I would have brought you a bottle of brandy.'

'In principle,' Para said and smiled, for the first time, showing yellowed teeth. 'Such a beautiful expression. Would you like some Grappa?'

'No, thank you,' Nick said.

'It hasn't any ether in it.'

'I can taste that still,' Nick remembered suddenly and completely.

'You know I never knew you were drunk until you started talking coming back in the camions.'

'I was stinking in every attack,' Nick said.

'I can't do it,' Para said. 'I took it in the first show, the very first show, and it only made me very upset and then frightfully thirsty.'

'You don't need it.'

'You're much braver in an attack than I am.'

'No,' Nick said. 'I know how I am and I prefer to get stinking. I'm not ashamed of it.'

'I've never seen you drunk.'

'No?' said Nick. 'Never? Not when we rode from Mestre to Portogrande that night and I wanted to go to sleep and used the bicycle for a blanket and pulled it up under my chin?'

'That wasn't in the lines.'

'Let's not talk about how I am,' Nick said. 'It's a subject I know too much about to want to think about it any more.'

'You might as well stay here a while,' Paravicini said. 'You can take a nap if you like. They didn't do much to this in the bombardment. It's too hot to go out yet.'

'I suppose there is no hurry.'

'How are you really?'

'I'm fine. I'm perfectly all right.'

'No. I mean really.'

'I'm all right. I can't sleep without a light of some sort. That's all I have now.'

'I said it should have been trepanned. I'm no doctor but I know that.'

'Well, they thought it was better to have it absorb, and that's what I got. What's the matter? I don't seem crazy to you, do I?'

'You seem in top-hole shape.'

'It's a hell of a nuisance once they've had you certified as nutty,' Nick said. 'No one ever has any confidence in you again.'

'I would take a nap, Nicolo,' Paravicini said. 'This isn't battalion headquarters as we used to know it. We're just waiting to be pulled out. You oughtn't to go out in the heat now–it's silly. Use that bunk.'

'I might just lie down,' Nick said.

Nick lay on the bunk. He was very disappointed that he felt this way and more disappointed, even, that it was so obvious to Captain Paravicini. This was not as large a dugout as the one where that platoon of the class of 1899, just out at the front, got hysterics during the bombardment before the attack, and Para had had him walk them two at a time outside to show them nothing would happen, he wearing his own chin strap tight across his mouth to keep his lips quiet. Knowing they could not hold it when they took it. Knowing it was all a bloody bells–If he can't stop crying, break his nose to give him something else to think about. I'd shoot one but it's too late now. They'd all be worse. Break his nose. They've put it back to five-twenty. We've only got four minutes more. Break that other silly bugger's nose and kick his silly ass out of here. Do you think they'll go over? If they don't, shoot two and try to scoop the others out some way. Keep behind them, sergeant. It's no use to walk ahead and find there's nothing coming behind you. Bail them out as you go. What a bloody bells. All right. That's right. Then, looking at the watch, in that quiet tone, that valuable quiet tone, 'Sovoia'. Making it cold, no time to get it, he couldn't find his own after the cave-in, one whole end had caved in; it was that started them; making it cold up that slope the only time he hadn't done it stinking. And after they came back the teleferica house burned, it seemed, and some of the wounded got down four days later and some did not get down, but we went up and we went back and we came down–we always came down. And there was Gaby Deslys, oddly enough, with feathers on; you called me baby doll a year ago tadada you said that I was rather nice to know tadada with feathers on, with feathers off, the great Gaby, and my name's Harry Pilcer, too, we used to step out of the far side of the taxis when it got steep going up the hill and he could see that hill every night when he dreamed with Sacré Coeur, blown white, like a soap bubble. Sometimes his girl was there and sometimes she was with someone else and he could not understand that, but those were the nights the river ran so much wider and stiller than it should and outside of Fossalta there was a low house painted yellow with willows all around it and a low stable and there was a canal, and he had been there a thousand times and never seen it, but there it was every night as plain as the hill, only it frightened him. That house meant more than anything and every night he had it. That was what he needed but it frightened him especially when the boat lay there quietly in the willows on the canal, but the banks weren't like this river. It was all lower, as it was at Portogrande, where they had seen them come wallowing across the flooded ground holding the rifles high until they fell with them in the water. Who ordered that one? If it didn't get so damned mixed up he could follow it all right. That was why he noticed everything in such detail to keep it all straight so he would know just where he was, but suddenly it confused without reason as now, he lying in a bunk at battalion headquarters, with Para commanding a battalion and he in a bloody American uniform. He sat up and looked around; they all watching him. Para was gone out. He lay down again.

The Paris part came earlier and he was not frightened of it except when she had gone off with someone else and the fear that they might take the same driver twice. That was what frightened about that. Never about the front. He never dreamed about the front now any more but what frightened him so that he could not get rid of it was that long yellow house and the different width of the river. Now he was back here at the river, he had gone through that same town, and there was no house. Nor was the river that way. Then where did he go each night; and what was the peril, and why would he wake, soaking wet, more frightened than he had ever been in a bombardment, because of a house and a long table and a canal?

He sat up, swung his legs carefully down; they stiffened any time they were out straight for long; returned the stares of the adjutant, the signallers and the two runners by the door and put on his cloth-covered trench helmet.

'I regret the absence of the chocolate, the postal cards and cigarettes,' he said. 'I am, however, wearing the uniform.'

'The Major is coming back at once,' the adjutant said. In that army an adjutant is not a commissioned officer.

'The uniform is not very correct,' Nick told them. 'But it gives you the idea. There will be several millions of Americans here shortly.'

'Do you think they will send Americans down here?' asked the adjutant.

'Oh, absolutely. Americans twice as large as myself, healthy, with clean hearts, sleep at night, never been wounded, never been blown up, never had their heads caved in, never been scared, don't drink, faithful to the girls they left behind them, many of them never had crabs, wonderful chaps. You'll see.'

'Are you an Italian?' asked the adjutant.

'No, American. Look at the uniform. Spagnolini made it but it's not quite correct.'

'A North or South American?'

'North,' said Nick. He felt it coming on now. He would quiet down.

'But you speak Italian.'

'Why not? Do you mind if I speak Italian? Haven't I a right to speak Italian?'

'You have Italian medals.'

'Just the ribbons and the papers. The medals come later. Or you give them to people to keep and the people go away; or they are lost with your baggage. You can purchase others in Milan. It is the papers that are of importance. You must not feel badly about them. You will have some yourself if you stay at the front long enough.'

'I am a veteran of the Eritrea campaign,' said the adjutant stiffly. 'I fought in Tripoli.'

'It's quite something to have met you,' Nick put out his hand. 'Those must have been trying days. I noticed the ribbons. Were you, by any chance, on the Carso?'

'I have just been called up for this war. My class was too old.'

'At one time I was under the age limit,' Nick said. 'But now I am reformed out of the war.'

'But why are you here now?'

'I am demonstrating the American uniform,' Nick said. 'Don't you think it is very significant? It is a little tight in the collar but you will see untold millions wearing this uniform swarming like locusts. The grasshopper, you know, what we call the grasshopper in America, is really a locust. The true grasshopper is small and green and comparatively feeble. You must not, however, make a confusion with the seven-year locust or cicada which emits a peculiar sustained sound which at the moment I cannot recall. I try to recall it but I cannot. I can almost hear it and then it is quite gone. You will pardon me if I break off our conversation?'

'See if you can find the major,' the adjutant said to one of the two runners. 'I can see you have been wounded,' he said to Nick.

'In various places,' Nick said. 'If you are interested in scars I can show you some very interesting ones but I would rather talk about grasshoppers. What we call grasshoppers that is; and what are, really locusts. These insects at one time played a very important part in my life. It might interest you and you can look at the uniform while I am talking.'

The adjutant made a motion with his hand to the second runner who went out.

'Fix your eyes on the uniform. Spagnolini made it, you know. You might as well look, too,' Nick said to the signallers. 'I really have no rank. We're under the American consul. It's perfectly all right for you to look. You can stare, if you like. I will tell you about the American locust. We always preferred one that we called the medium-brown. They last the best in water and fish prefer them. The larger ones that fly make a noise somewhat similar to that produced by a rattlesnake rattling his rattlers, a very dry sound, have vivid coloured wings, some are bright red, others yellow barred with black, but their wings go to pieces in the water and they make a very blowsy bait, while the medium-brown is a plump, compact, succulent hopper that I can recommend as far as one may well recommend something you gentlemen will probably never encounter. But I must insist that you will never gather a sufficient supply of these insects for a day's fishing by pursuing them with your hands or trying to hit them with a bat. That is sheer nonsense and a useless waste of time. I repeat, gentlemen, that you will get nowhere at it. The correct procedure, and one which should be taught all young officers at every small-arms course if I had anything to say about it, and who knows but what I will have, is the employment of a seine or net made of common mosquito netting. Two officers holding this length of netting at alternate ends, or let us say one at each end, stoop, hold the bottom extremity of the net in one hand and the top extremity in the other and run into the wind. The hoppers, flying with the wind, fly against the length of netting and are imprisoned in its folds. It is no trick at all to catch a very great quantity indeed, and no officer, in my opinion, should be without a length of mosquito netting suitable for the improvisation of one of these grasshopper seines. I hope I have made myself clear, gentlemen. Are there any questions? If there is anything in the course you do not understand please ask questions. Speak up. None? Then I would like to close on this note. In the words of that great soldier and gentleman, Sir Henry Wilson: Gentlemen, either you must govern or you must be governed. Let me repeat it. Gentlemen, there is one thing I would like to have you remember. One thing I would like you to take with you as you leave this room. Gentlemen, either you must govern–or you must be governed. That is all, gentlemen. Good day.'

He removed his cloth-covered helmet, put it on again and, stooping, went out the low entrance of the dugout. Para, accompanied by the two runners, was coming down the line of the sunken road. It was very hot in the sun and Nick removed the helmet.

'There ought to be a system for wetting these things,' he said. 'I shall wet this one in the river.' He started up the bank.

'Nicolo,' Paravicini called. 'Nicolo. Where are you going?'

'I don't really have to go,' Nick came down the slope, holding the helmet in his hands. 'They're a damned nuisance wet or dry. Do you wear yours all the time?'

'All the time,' said Para. 'It's making me bald. Come inside.'

Inside Para told him to sit down.

'You know they're absolutely no damned good,' Nick said. 'I remember when they were a comfort when we first had them, but I've seen them full of brains too many times.'

'Nicolo,' Para said. 'I think you should go back. I think it would be better if you didn't come up to the line until you had those supplies. There's nothing here for you to do. If you move around, even with something worth giving away, the men will group and that invites shelling. I won't have it.'

'I know it's silly,' Nick said. 'It wasn't my idea. I heard the brigade was here so I thought I would see you or someone else I knew. I could have gone to Zenzon or to San Dona. I'd like to go to San Dona to see the bridge again.'

'I won't have you circulating around to no purpose,' Captain Paravicini said.

'All right,' said Nick. He felt it coming on again.

'You understand?'

'Of course,' said Nick. He was trying to hold it in.

'Anything of that sort should be done at night.'

'Naturally,' said Nick. He knew he could not stop it now.

'You see, I am commanding the battalion,' Para said.

'And why shouldn't you be?' Nick said. Here it came. 'You can read and write, can't you?'

'Yes,' said Para gently.

'The trouble is you have a damned small battalion to command. As soon as it gets to strength again they'll give you back your company. Why don't they bury the dead? I've seen them now. I don't care about seeing them again. They can bury them any time as far as I'm concerned and it would be much better for you. You'll all get bloody sick.'

'Where did you leave your bicycle?'

'Inside the last house.'

'Do you think it will be all right?'

'Don't worry,' Nick said. 'I'll go in a little while.'

'Lie down a little while, Nicolo.'

'All right.'

He shut his eyes and in place of the man with the beard who looked at him over the sights of the rifle, quite calmly before squeezing off, the white flash and clublike impact, on his knees, hot-sweet choking, coughing it on to the rock while they went past him, he saw a long, yellow house with a low stable and the river much wider that it was and stiller. 'Christ,' he said, 'I might as well go.'

He stood up.

'I'm going, Para,' he said. 'I'll ride back now in the afternoon. If any supplies have come I'll bring them down tonight. If not I'll come at night when I have something to bring.'

'It is still hot to ride,' Captain Paravicini said.

'You don't need to worry,' Nick said. 'I'm all right now for quite a while. I had one then but it was easy. They're getting much better. I can tell when I'm going to have one because I talk so much.'

'I'll send a runner with you.'

'I'd rather you didn't. I know the way.'

'You'll be back soon?'

'Absolutely.'

'Let me send——'

'No,' said Nick. 'As a mark of confidence.'

'Well, Ciaou then.'

'Ciaou,' said Nick. He started back along the sunken road toward where he had left the bicycle. In the afternoon the road would be shady once he had passed the canal. Beyond that there were trees on both sides that had not been shelled at all. It was on that stretch that, marching, they had once passed the Terza Savoia cavalry regiment riding in the snow with their lances. The horses' breath made plumes in the cold air. No, that was somewhere else. Where was that?

'I'd better get to that damned bicycle,' Nick said to himself. 'I don't want to lose the way to Fornaci.'

A NATURAL HISTORY OF THE DEAD

It has always seemed to me that the war has been omitted as a field for the observations of the naturalist. We have charming and sound accounts of the flora and fauna of Patagonia by the late W. H. Hudson, the Reverend Gilbert White has written most interestingly of the Hoopoe on its occasional and not at all common visits to Selborne, and Bishop Stanley has given us a valuable, although popular, *Familiar History of Birds*. Can we not hope to furnish the reader with a few rational and interesting facts about the dead? I hope so.

When that persevering traveller, Mungo Park, was at one period of his course fainting in the vast wilderness of an African desert, naked and alone, considering his days as numbered and nothing appearing to remain for him to do but lie down and die, a small moss-flower of extraordinary beauty caught his eye. 'Though the whole plant,' says he, 'was no larger than one of my fingers, I could not contemplate the delicate formation of its roots, leaves and capsules without admiration. Can that Being who planted, watered and brought to perfection, in this obscure part of the world, a thing which appears of so small importance, look with unconcern upon the situation and suffering of creatures formed after his own image? Surely not. Reflections like these would not allow me to despair; I started up and, disregarding both hunger and fatigue, travelled forward, assured that relief was at hand: and I was not disappointed.'

With a disposition to wonder and adore in like manner, as Bishop Stanley says, can any branch of Natural History be studied without increasing that faith, love and hope which we also, every one of us, need in our journey through the wilderness of life? Let us therefore see what inspiration we may derive from the dead.

In war the dead are usually the male of the human species, although this does not hold true with animals, and I have frequently seen dead mares among the horses. An interesting aspect of war, too, is that it is only there that the naturalist has an opportunity to observe the dead of mules. In twenty years of observation in civil life I had never seen a dead mule and had begun to entertain doubts as to whether these animals were really mortal. On rare occasions I had seen what I took to be dead mules, but on close approach these always proved to be living creatures who seemed to be dead through their quality of complete repose. But in war these animals succumb in much the same manner as the more common and less hardy horse.

Most of the mules that I saw dead were along mountain roads or lying at the foot of steep declivities whence they had been pushed to rid the road of their encumbrance. They seemed a fitting enough sight in the mountains where one was accustomed to their presence, and looked less incongruous there than they did later, at Smyrna, where the Greeks broke the legs of all their baggage animals and pushed them off the quay into the shallow water to drown. The numbers of broken-legged mules and horses drowning in the shallow water called for a Goya to depict them. Although, speaking literally, one can hardly say that they called for a Goya since there has only been one Goya, long dead, and it is extremely doubtful if these animals, were they able to call, would call for pictorial representation of their plight but, more likely, would, if they were articulate, call for someone to alleviate their condition.

Regarding the sex of the dead it is a fact that one becomes so accustomed to the sight of all the dead being men that the sight of a dead woman is quite shocking. I first saw inversion of the usual sex of the dead after the explosion of a munition factory which had been situated in the countryside near Milan, Italy. We drove to the scene of the disaster in trucks along poplar-shaded roads, bordered with ditches containing much minute animal life, which I could not clearly observe because of the great clouds of dust raised by the trucks. Arriving where the munition plant had been, some of us were put to patrolling about those large stocks of munitions which for some reason had not exploded, while others were put at extinguishing a fire which had gotten into the grass of an adjacent field; which task being concluded, we were ordered to search the immediate vicinity and surrounding fields for bodies. We found and carried to an improvised mortuary a good number of these and, I must admit, frankly, the shock it was to find that these dead were women rather than men. In those days women had not yet commenced to wear their hair cut short, as they did later for several years in Europe and America, and the most disturbing thing, perhaps because it was the most unaccustomed, was the presence, and, even more disturbing, the occasional absence of this long hair. I remember that after we had searched quite thoroughly for the complete dead we collected fragments. Many of these were detached from a heavy, barbed-wire fence which had surrounded the position of the factory and from the still existent portions of which we picked many of these detached bits which illustrated only too well the tremendous energy of high explosive. Many fragments we found a considerable distance away in the fields, they being carried farther by their own weight.

On our return to Milan I recall one or two of us discussing the occurrence and agreeing that the quality of unreality and the fact that there were no wounded did much to rob the disaster of a horror which might have been much greater. Also the fact that it had been so immediate and that the dead were in consequence still as little unpleasant as possible to carry and deal with made it quite removed from the usual battlefield experience. The pleasant, though dusty, ride through the beautiful Lombard countryside also was a compensation for the unpleasantness of the duty and on our return, while we exchanged impressions, we all agreed that it was indeed fortunate that the fire which broke out just before we arrived had been brought under control as rapidly as it had and before it had attained any of the seemingly huge stocks of unexploded munitions. We agreed too that the picking up of the fragments had been an extraordinary business; it being amazing that the human body should be blown into pieces which exploded along no anatomical lines, but rather divided as capriciously as the fragmentation in the burst of a high explosive shell.

A naturalist, to obtain accuracy of observation, may confine himself in his observations to one limited period and I will take first that following the Austrian offensive of June 1918 in Italy as one in which the dead were present in their greatest numbers, a withdrawal having been forced and an advance later made to recover the ground lost so that the positions after the battle were the same as before except for the presence of the dead. Until the dead are buried they change somewhat in appearance each day. The colour change in Caucasian races is from white to yellow, to yellow-green, to black. If left long enough in the heat the flesh comes to resemble coal-tar, especially where it has been broken or torn, and it has quite a visible tar-like iridescence. The dead grow larger each day until sometimes they become quite too big for their uniforms, filling these until they seem blown tight enough to burst. The individual members may increase in girth to an unbelievable extent and faces fill as taut and globular as balloons. The surprising thing, next to their progressive corpulence, is the amount of paper that is scattered about the dead. Their ultimate position, before there is any question of burial, depends on the location of the pockets in the uniform. In the Austrian army these pockets were in the back of the breeches and the dead, after a short time, all consequently lay on their faces, the two hip pockets pulled out and, scattered around them in the grass, all those papers their pockets contained. The heat, the flies, the indicative positions of the bodies in the grass, and the amount of paper scattered are the impressions one retains. The smell of battlefield in hot weather one cannot recall. You can remember that there was such a smell, but nothing ever happens to you to bring it back. It is unlike the smell of a regiment, which may come to you suddenly while riding in the street car and you will look across and see the man who has brought it to you. But the other thing is gone as completely as when you have been in love; you remember things that happened, but the sensation cannot be recalled.

One wonders what that persevering traveller, Mungo Park, would have seen on a battlefield in hot weather to restore his confidence. There were always poppies in the wheat in the end of June, and in July, and the mulberry trees were in full leaf and one could see the heatwaves rise from the barrels of the guns where the sun struck them through the screens of leaves; the earth was turned a bright yellow at the edge of holes where mustard gas shells had been and the average broken house is finer to see than one that has been shelled, but few travellers would take a good full breath of that early summer air and have any such thoughts as Mungo Park about those formed in His own image.

The first thing that you found about the dead was that, hit badly enough, they died like animals. Some quickly from a little wound you would not think would kill a rabbit. They died from little wounds as rabbits die sometimes from three or four small grains of shot that hardly seem to break the skin. Others would die like cats; a skull broken in and iron in the brain, they lie alive two days like cats that crawl into the coal bin with a bullet in the brain and will not die until you cut their heads off. Maybe cats do not die then, they say they have nine lives. I do not know, but most men die like animals, not men. I'd never seen a natural death, so called, and so I blamed it on the war and like the persevering traveller, Mungo Park, knew that here was something else, that always absent something else, and then I saw one.

The only natural death I've ever seen, outside of loss of blood, which isn't bad, was death from Spanish influenza. In this you drown in mucus, choking and how you know the patient's dead is: at the end he turns to be a little child again, though with his manly force, and fills the sheets as full as any diaper with one vast, final, yellow cataract that flows and dribbles on after he's gone. So now I want to see the death of any self-called Humanist* because a persevering traveller like Mungo Park or me lives on and maybe yet will live to see the actual death of members of this literary sect and watch the noble exits that they make. In my musings as a naturalist it has occurred to me that while decorum is an excellent thing some must be indecorous if the race is to be carried on since the position prescribed for procreation is indecorous, highly indecorous, and it occurred to me that perhaps that is what these people are, or were: the children of decorous cohabitation. But regardless of how they started I hope to see the finish of a few, and speculate how worms will try that long preserved sterility; with their quaint pamphlets gone to bust and into footnotes all their lust.

While it is, perhaps, legitimate to deal with these self-designated citizens in a natural history of the dead, even though the designation may mean nothing by the time this work is published, yet it is unfair to the other dead, who were not dead in their youth of choice, who owned no magazines, many of whom had doubtless never even read a review, that one has seen in the hot weather with a half-pint of maggots working where their mouths have been. It was not always hot weather for the dead, much of the time it was the rain that washed them clean when they lay in it and made the earth soft when they were buried in it and sometimes then kept on until the earth was mud and washed them out and you had to bury them again. Or in the winter in the mountains you had to put them in the snow and when the snow melted in the spring someone else had to bury them. They had beautiful burying grounds in the mountains, war in the mountains is the most beautiful of all war, and in one of them, at a place called Pocol, they buried a general who was shot through the head by a sniper. This is where those writers are mistaken who write books called *Generals Die in Bed*, because this general

* The Reader's indulgence is requested for this mention of an extinct phenomenon. The reference, like all references to fashions, dates the story, but it is retained because of its mild historical interest and because its omission would spoil the rhythm.

died in a trench dug in snow, high in the mountains, wearing an Alpini hat with an eagle feather in it and a hole in front you couldn't put your little finger in and a hole in back you could put your fist in, if it were a small fist and you wanted to put it there, and much blood in the snow. He was a damned fine general, and so was General von Behr who commanded the Bavarian Alpenkorps troops at the battle of Caporetto and was killed in his staff car by the Italian rearguard as he drove into Udine ahead of his troops, and the titles of all such books should be *Generals Usually Die in Bed*, if we are to have any sort of accuracy in such things.

In the mountains, too, sometimes, the snow fell on the dead outside the dressing station on the side that was protected by the mountain from any shelling. They carried them into a cave that had been dug into the mountainside before the earth froze. It was in this cave that a man whose head was broken as a flower-pot may be broken, although it was all held together by membranes and a skilfully applied bandage now soaked and hardened, with the structure of his brain disturbed by a piece of broken steel in it, lay a day, a night, and a day. The stretcher-bearers asked the doctor to go in and have a look at him. They saw him each time they made a trip and even when they did not look at him they heard him breathing. The doctor's eyes were red and the lids swollen, almost shut from tear gas. He looked at the man twice; once in daylight, once with a flashlight. That too would have made a good etching for Goya, the visit with the flashlight, I mean. After looking at him the second time the doctor believed the stretcher-bearers when they said the soldier was still alive.

'What do you want me to do about it?' he asked.

There was nothing they wanted done. But after a while they asked permission to carry him out and lay him with the badly wounded.

'No. No. No!' said the doctor, who was busy. 'What's the matter? Are you afraid of him?'

'We don't like to hear him in there with the dead.'

'Don't listen to him. If you take him out of there you will have to carry him right back in.'

'We wouldn't mind that, Captain Doctor.'

'No,' said the doctor. 'No. Didn't you hear me say no?'

'Why don't you give him an overdose of morphine?' asked an artillery officer who was waiting to have a wound in his arm dressed.

'Do you think that is the only use I have for morphine? Would you like me to have to operate without morphine? You have a pistol, go out and shoot him yourself.'

'He's been shot already,' said the officer. 'If some of you doctors were shot you'd be different.'

'Thank you very much,' said the doctor, waving a forceps in the air. 'Thank you a thousand times. What about these eyes?' He pointed the forceps at them. 'How would you like these?'

'Tear gas. We call it lucky if it's tear gas.'

'Because you leave the line,' said the doctor. 'Because you come running here with your tear gas to be evacuated. You rub onions in your eyes.'

'You are beside yourself. I do not notice your insults. You are crazy.'

The stretcher-bearers came in.

'Captain Doctor,' one of them said.

'Get out of here!' said the doctor.

They went out.

'I will shoot the poor fellow,' the artillery officer said. 'I am a humane man. I will not let him suffer.'

'Shoot him then,' said the doctor. 'Shoot him. Assume the responsibility. I will make a report. Wounded shot by lieutenant of artillery in first curing post. Shoot him. Go ahead, shoot him.'

'You are not a human being.'

'My business is to care for the wounded, not to kill them. That is for gentlemen of the artillery.'

'Why don't you care for him then?'

'I have done so. I have done all that can be done.'

'Why don't you send him down on the cable railway?'

'Who are you to ask me questions? Are you my superior officer? Are you in command of this dressing-post? Do me the courtesy to answer.'

The lieutenant of artillery said nothing. The others in the room were all soldiers and there were no other officers present.

'Answer me,' said the doctor, holding a needle up in his forceps. 'Give me a response.'

'F— yourself,' said the artillery officer.

'So,' said the doctor. 'So, you said that. All right. All right. We shall see.'

The lieutenant of artillery stood up and walked toward him.

'F— yourself,' he said. 'F— yourself. F— your mother. F— your sister. . . .'

The doctor tossed the saucer full of iodine in his face. As he came toward him, blinded, the lieutenant fumbled for his pistol. The doctor skipped quickly behind him, tripped him and, as he fell to the floor, kicked him several times and picked up the pistol in his rubber gloves. The lieutenant sat on the floor holding his good hand to his eyes.

'I'll kill you!' he said. 'I'll kill you as soon as I can see.'

'I am the boss,' said the doctor. 'All is forgiven since you know I am the boss. You cannot kill me because I have your pistol. Sergeant! Adjutant! Adjutant!'

'The adjutant is at the cable railway,' said the sergeant.

'Wipe out this officer's eyes with alcohol and water. He has got iodine in them. Bring me the basin to wash my hands. I will take this officer next.'

'You won't touch me.'

'Hold him tight. He is a little delirious.'

One of the stretcher-bearers came in.

'Captain Doctor.'

'What do you want?'

The man in the dead-house—'

'Get out of here.'

'Is dead, Captain Doctor. I thought you would be glad to know.'

'See, my poor lieutenant? We dispute about nothing. In time of war we dispute about nothing.'

'F— you,' said the lieutenant of artillery. He still could not see. 'You've blinded me.'

'It is nothing,' said the doctor. 'Your eyes will be all right. It is nothing. A dispute about nothing.'

'Ayee! Ayee! Ayee!' suddenly screamed the lieutenant. 'You have blinded me! You have blinded me!'

'Hold him tight,' said the doctor. 'He is in much pain. Hold him very tight.'

AFTER THE STORM

It wasn't about anything, something about making punch, and then we started fighting and I slipped and he had me down kneeling on my chest and choking me with both hands like he was trying to kill me and all the time I was trying to get the knife out of my pocket to cut him loose. Everybody was too drunk to pull him off me. He was choking me and hammering my head on the floor and I got the knife out and opened it up; and I cut the muscle right across his arm and he let go of me. He couldn't have held on if he wanted to. Then he rolled and hung on to that arm and started to cry and I said:

'What the hell you want to choke me for?'

I'd have killed him. I couldn't swallow for a week. He hurt my throat bad.

Well, I went out of there and there were plenty of them with him and some came out after me and I made a turn and was down by the docks and I met a fellow and he said somebody killed a man up the street. I said, 'Who killed him?' and he said, 'I don't know who killed him but he's dead all right,' and it was dark and there was water standing in the street and no lights and windows broke and boats all up in the town and trees blown down and everything all blown and I got a skiff and went out and found my boat where I had her inside of Mango Key and she was all right only she was full of water. So I bailed her out and pumped her out and there was a moon but plenty of clouds and still plenty rough and I took it down along; and when it was daylight I was off Eastern Harbour.

Brother, that was some storm. I was the first boat out and you never saw water like that was. It was just as white as a lye barrel and coming from Eastern Harbour to Sou'west Key you couldn't recognize the shore. There was a big channel blown right out through the middle of the beach. Trees and all blown out and a channel cut through and all the water white as chalk and everything on it; branches and whole trees and dead birds, and all floating. Inside the keys were all the pelicans in the world and all kinds of birds flying. They must have gone inside there when they knew it was coming.

I lay at Sou'west Key a day and nobody came after me. I was the first boat out and I seen a spar floating and I knew there must be a wreck and I started out to look for her. I found her. She was a three-masted schooner and I could just see the stumps of her spars out of water. She was in too deep water and I didn't get anything off of her. So I went on looking for something else. I had the start on all of them and I knew I ought to get whatever there was. I went on down over the sand-bar from where I left that three-masted schooner and I didn't find anything and I went on a long way. I was way out toward the quicksands and I didn't find anything so I went on. Then when I was in sight of the Rebecca Light I saw all kinds of birds making over something and I headed over for them to see what it was and there was a cloud of birds all right.

I could see something looked like a spar up out of the water and when I got over close the birds all went up in the air and stayed all around me. The water was clear out there and there was a spar of some kind sticking out just above the water and when I come up close to it I saw it was all dark under water like a long shadow and I came right over it and there under water was a liner; just lying there all under water as big as the whole world. I drifted over her in the boat. She lay on her side and the stern was deep down. The port holes were all shut tight and I could see the glass shine in the water and the whole of her; the biggest boat I ever saw in my life laying there and I went along the whole length of her and then I went over and anchored and I had the skiff on the deck forward and I shoved it down into the water and sculled over with the birds all around me.

I had a water glass like we use sponging and my hand shook so I could hardly hold it. All the port holes were shut that you could see along over her but way down below near the bottom something must have been open because there were pieces of things floating out all the time. You couldn't tell what they were. Just pieces. That's what the birds were after. You never saw so many birds. They were all around me; crazy yelling.

I could see everything sharp and clear. I could see her rounded over and she looked a mile long under the water. She was lying on a clear white bank of sand and the spar was a sort of foremast or some sort of tackle that slanted out of the water the way she was laying on her side. Her bow wasn't very far under. I could stand on the letters of her name on her bow and my head was just out of water. But the nearest port hole was twelve feet down. I could just reach it with the grains pole and I tried to break it with that but I couldn't. The glass was too stout. So I sculled back to the boat, and got a wrench and lashed it to the end of the grains pole and I couldn't break it. There I was looking down through the glass at that liner with everything in her and I was the first one to her and I couldn't get into her. She must have had five million dollars' worth in her.

It made me shake to think how much she must have in her. Inside the port hole that was closed I could see something but I couldn't make it out through the water glass. I couldn't do any good with the grains pole and I took off my clothes and stood and took a couple of deep breaths and dove over off the stern with the wrench in my hand and swam down. I could hold on for a second to the edge of the port hole, and I could see in and there was a woman inside with her hair floating all out. I could see her floating plain and I hit the glass twice with the wrench hard and I heard the noise clink in my ears but it wouldn't break and I had to come up.

I hung on to the dinghy and got my breath and then I climbed in and took a couple of breaths and dove again. I swam down and took hold of the edge of the port hole with my fingers and held it and hit the glass as hard as I could with the wrench. I could see the woman floated in the water through the glass. Her hair was tied once close to her head and it floated all out in the water. I could see the rings on one of her hands. She was right up close to the port hole and I hit the glass twice and I didn't even crack it. When I came up I thought I wouldn't make it to the top before I'd have to breathe.

I went down once more and I cracked the glass, only cracked it, and when I came up my nose was bleeding and I stood on the bow of the liner with my bare feet in the letters of her name and my head just out and rested there and then I swam over to the skiff and pulled up into it and sat there waiting for my head to stop aching and looking down into the water glass, but I bled so I had to wash out the water glass. Then I lay back in the skiff and held my hand under my nose to stop it and I lay there with my head back looking up and there was a million birds above and all around.

When I quit bleeding I took another look through the glass and then I sculled over to the boat to try and find something heavier than the wrench but I couldn't find a thing; not even a sponge hook. I went back and the water was clearer all the time and you could see everything that floated out over that white bank of sand. I looked for sharks but there weren't any. You could have seen a shark a long way away. The water was so clear and the sand white. There was a grapple for an anchor on the skiff and I cut it off and went overboard and down with it. It carried me right down and past the port hole and I grabbed and couldn't hold anything and went on down and down, sliding along the curved side of her. I had to let go of the grapple. I heard it bump once and it seemed like a year before I came up through to the top of the water. The skiff was floated away with the tide and I swam over to her with my nose bleeding in the water while I swam and I was plenty glad there weren't sharks; but I was tired.

My head felt cracked open and I lay in the skiff and rested and then sculled back. It was getting along in the afternoon. I went down once more with the wrench and it didn't do any good. That wrench was too light. It wasn't any good diving unless you had a big hammer or something heavy enough to do good. Then I lashed the wrench to the grains pole again and I watched through the water glass and pounded on the glass and hammered until the wrench came off and I saw it in the glass, clear and sharp, go sliding down along her and then off and down to the quicksand and go in. Then I couldn't do a thing. The wrench was gone and I'd lost the grapple so I sculled back to the boat. I was too tired to get the skiff aboard and the sun was pretty low. The birds were all pulling out and leaving her and I headed for Sou'west Key towing the skiff and the birds going on ahead of me and behind me. I was plenty tired.

That night it came on to blow and it blew for a week. You couldn't get out to her. They come out from town and told me the fellow I'd had to cut was all right except for his arm and I went back to town and they put me under five hundred dollar bond. It came out all right because some of them, friends of mine, swore he was after me with an axe, but by the time we got back out to her the Greeks had blown her open and cleaned her out. They got the safe out with dynamite. Nobody ever knows how much they got. She carried gold and they got it all. They stripped her clean. I found her and I never got a nickel out of her.

It was a hell of a thing all right. They say she was just outside of Havana harbour when the hurricane hit and she couldn't get in or the owners wouldn't let the captain chance coming in; they say he wanted to try; so she had to go with it and in the dark they were running with it trying to go through the gulf between Rebecca and Tortugas when she struck on quicksands. Maybe her rudder was carried away. Maybe they weren't even steering. But anyway they couldn't have known they were quicksands and when she struck the captain must have ordered them to open up the ballast tanks so she'd lay solid. But it was quicksand she'd hit and when they opened the tank she went in stern first and then over on her beam ends. There were four hundred and fifty passengers and the crew on board of her and they must all have been aboard of her when I found her. They must have opened the tanks as soon as she struck and the minute she settled on it the quicksands took her down. Then her boilers must have burst and that must have been what made those pieces that came out. It was funny there weren't any sharks though. There wasn't a fish. I could have seen them on that clear white sand.

Plenty of fish now though; jewfish, the biggest kind. The biggest part of her's under the sand now but they live inside of her; the biggest kind of jewfish. Some weigh three to four hundred pounds. Sometime we'll go out and get some. You can see the Rebecca light from where she is. They've got a buoy on her now. She's right at the end of the quicksand right at the edge of the gulf. She only missed going through by about a hundred yards. In the dark in the storm they just missed it; raining the way it was they couldn't have seen the Rebecca. Then they're not used to that sort of thing. The captain of a liner isn't used to scudding that way. They have a course and they tell me they set some sort of a compass and it steers itself. They probably didn't know where they were when they ran with that blow but they came close to making it. Maybe they'd lost the rudder though. Anyway there wasn't another thing for them to hit till they'd get to Mexico once they were in that gulf. Must have been something though when they struck in that rain and wind and he told them to open her tanks. Nobody could have been on deck in that blow and rain. Everybody must have been below. They couldn't have lived on deck. There must have been some scenes inside all right because you know she settled fast. I saw that wrench go into the sand. The captain couldn't have known it was quicksand when she struck unless he knew these waters. He just knew it wasn't rock. He must have seen it all up in the bridge. He must have known what it was about when she settled. I wonder how fast she made it. I wonder if the mate was there with him. Do you think they stayed inside the bridge or do you think they took it outside? They never found any bodies. Not a one. Nobody floating. They float a long way with lifebelts too. They must have took it inside. Well, the Greeks got it all. Everything. They must have come fast all right. They picked her clean. First there was the birds, then me, then the Greeks, and even the birds got more out of her than I did.

OLD MAN AT THE BRIDGE

An old man with steel-rimmed spectacles and very dusty clothes sat by the side of the road. There was a pontoon bridge across the river and carts, trucks, and men, women and children were crossing it. The mule-drawn carts staggered up the steep bank from the bridge with soldiers helping push against the spokes of the wheels. The trucks ground up and away heading out of it all the peasants plodded along in the ankle-deep dust. But the old man sat there without moving. He was too tired to go any farther.

It was my business to cross the bridge, explore the bridgehead beyond and find out to what point the enemy had advanced. I did this and returned over the bridge. There were not so many carts now and very few people on foot, but the old man was still there.

'Where do you come from?' I asked him.

'From San Carlos,' he said, and smiled.

That was his native town and so it gave him pleasure to mention it and he smiled.

'I was taking care of animals,' he explained.

'Oh,' I said, not quite understanding.

'Yes,' he said, 'I stayed, you see, taking care of animals. I was the last one to leave the town of San Carlos.'

He did not look like a shepherd nor a herdsman and I looked at his black dusty clothes and his grey dusty face and his steel-rimmed spectacles and said, 'What animals were they?'

'Various animals,' he said, and shook his head. 'I had to leave them.'

I was watching the bridge and the African looking country of the Ebro Delta and wondering how long now it would be before we would see the enemy, and listening all the while for the first noises that would signal that ever mysterious event called contact, and the old man still sat there.

'What animals were they?' I asked.

'There were three animals altogether,' he explained. 'There were two goats and a cat and then there were four pairs of pigeons.'

'And you had to leave them?' I asked.

'Yes. Because of the artillery. The captain told me to go because of the artillery.'

'And you have no family?' I asked, watching the far end of the bridge where a few last carts were hurrying down the slope of the bank.

'No,' he said, 'only the animals I stated. The cat, of course, will be all right. A cat can look out for itself, but I cannot think what will become of the others.'

'What politics have you?' I asked.

'I am without politics,' he said. 'I am seventy-six years old. I have come twelve kilometres now and I think now I can go no farther.'

'This is not a good place to stop,' I said. 'If you can make it, there are trucks up the road where it forks for Tortosa.'

'I will wait a while,' he said, 'and then I will go. Where do the trucks go?'

'Towards Barcelona,' I told him.

'I know of no one in that direction,' he said, 'but thank you very much. Thank you again very much.'

He looked at me very blankly and tiredly, then said, having to share his worry with someone, 'The cat will be all right, I am sure. There is no need to be unquiet about the cat. But the others. Now what do you think about the others?'

'Why, they'll probably come through it all right.'

'You think so?'

'Why not?' I said, watching the far bank where now there were no carts.

'But what will they do under the artillery when I was told to leave because of the artillery?'

'Did you leave the dove cage unlocked?' I asked.

'Yes.'

'Then they'll fly.'

'Yes, certainly they'll fly. But the others. It's better not to think about the others,' he said.

'If you are rested I would go,' I urged. 'Get up and try to walk now.'

'Thank you,' he said and got to his feet, swayed from side to side and then sat down backwards in the dust.

'I was only taking care of animals,' he said dully, but no longer to me. 'I was only taking care of animals.'

There was nothing to do about him. It was Easter Sunday and the Fascists were advancing toward the Ebro. It was a grey overcast day with a low ceiling so their planes were not up. That and the fact that cats know how to look after themselves was all the good luck that old man would ever have.

HEMI

IGWAY

Fiesta

FIESTA

This book is for
Hadley and John Hadley Nicanor

No character in this book is the portrait of any actual person

PART I

I

Robert Cohn was once middleweight boxing champion of Princeton. Do not think that I am very much impressed by that as a boxing title, but it meant a lot to Cohn. He cared nothing for boxing, in fact, he disliked it, but he learned it painfully and thoroughly to counteract the feeling of inferiority and shyness he had felt on being treated as a Jew at Princeton. There was a certain inner comfort in knowing he could knock down anybody who was snooty to him, although, being very shy and a thoroughly nice boy, he never fought except in the gym. He was Spider Kelly's star pupil. Spider Kelly taught all his young gentlemen to box like featherweights, no matter whether they weighed one hundred and five or two hundred and five pounds. But it seemed to fit Cohn. He was really very fast. He was so good that Spider promptly overmatched him and got his nose permanently flattened. This increased Cohn's distaste for boxing, but it gave him a certain satisfaction of some strange sort, and it certainly improved his nose. In his last year at Princeton he read too much and took to wearing spectacles. I never met anyone of his class who remembered him. They did not even remember that he was middleweight boxing champion.

I mistrust all frank and simple people, especially when their stories hold together, and I always had a suspicion that perhaps Robert Cohn had never been a middleweight boxing champion, and that perhaps a horse had stepped on his face, or that maybe his mother had been frightened or seen something, or that he had, maybe, bumped into something as a young child, but I finally had somebody to verify the story from Spider Kelly. Spider Kelly not only remembered Cohn. He had often wondered what had become of him.

Robert Cohn was a member, through his father, of one of the richest Jewish families in New York, and through his mother of one of the oldest. At the military school where he prepped for Princeton, and played a very good end on the football team, no one had made him race-conscious. No one had ever made him feel he was a Jew, and hence any different from anybody else, until he went to Princeton. He was a nice boy, a friendly boy, and very shy, and it made him bitter. He took it out in boxing, and he came out of Princeton with painful self-consciousness and the flattened nose, and was married by the first girl who was nice to him. He was married five years, had three children, lost most of the fifty thousand dollars his father had left him, the balance of the estate having gone to his mother, hardened into a rather unattractive mould under domestic unhappiness with a rich wife; and just when he had made up his mind to leave his wife she left him and went off with a miniature-painter. As he had been thinking for months about leaving his wife and had not done it because it would be too cruel to deprive her of himself, her departure was a very healthful shock.

The divorce was arranged and Robert Cohn went out to the Coast. In California he fell among literary people and, as he still had a little of the fifty thousand left, in a short time he was backing a review of the Arts. The review commenced publication in Carmel, California, and finished in Provincetown, Massachusetts. By that time Cohn, who had been regarded purely as an angel, and whose name had appeared on the editorial page merely as a member of the advisory board, had become the sole editor. It was his money and he discovered he liked the authority of editing. He was sorry when the magazine became too expensive and he had to give it up.

By that time, though, he had other things to worry about. He had been taken in hand by a lady who hoped to rise with the magazine. She was very forceful, and Cohn never had a chance of not being taken in hand. Also he was sure that he loved her. When this lady saw that the magazine was not going to rise, she became a little disgusted with Cohn and decided that she might as well get what there was to get while there was still something available, so she urged that they go to Europe, where Cohn could write. They came to Europe, where the lady had been educated, and stayed three years. During these three years, the first spent in travel, the last two in Paris, Robert Cohn had two friends, Braddocks and myself. Braddocks was his literary friend. I was his tennis friend.

The lady who had him, her name was Frances, found toward the end of the second year that her looks were going, and her attitude toward Robert changed from one of careless possession and exploitation to the absolute determination that he should marry her. During this time Robert's mother had settled an allowance on him, about three hundred dollars a month. During two years and a half I do not believe that Robert Cohn looked at another woman. He was fairly happy, except that, like many people living in Europe, he would rather have been in America, and he had discovered writing. He wrote a novel, and it was not really such a bad novel as the critics later called it, although it was a very poor novel. He read many books, played bridge, played tennis, and boxed at a local gymnasium.

I first became aware of his lady's attitude toward him one night after the three of us had dined together. We had dined at l'Avenue's and afterward went to the Café de Versailles for coffee. We had several *fines* after the coffee, and I said I must be going. Cohn had been talking about the two of us going off somewhere on a week-end trip. He wanted to get out of town and get in a good walk. I suggested we fly to Strasbourg and walk up to Saint Odile, or somewhere or other in Alsace. 'I know a girl in Strasbourg who can show us the town,' I said.

Somebody kicked me under the table. I thought it was accidental and went on: 'She's been there two years and knows everything there is to know about the town. She's a swell girl.'

I was kicked again under the table, and, looking, saw Frances, Robert's lady, her chin lifting and her face hardening.

'Hell,' I said, 'why go to Strasbourg? We could go up to Bruges, or to the Ardennes.'

Cohn looked relieved. I was not kicked again. I said good-night and went out. Cohn said he wanted to buy a paper and would walk to the corner with me. 'For God's sake,' he said, 'why did you say that about that girl in Strasbourg for? Didn't you see Frances?'

'No, why should I? If I know an American girl that lives in Strasbourg what the hell is it to Frances?'

'It doesn't make any difference. Any girl. I couldn't go, that would be all.

'Don't be silly.'

'You don't know Frances. Any girl at all. Didn't you see the way she looked?'

'Oh, well,' I said, 'let's go to Senlis.'

'Don't get sore.'

'I'm not sore. Senlis is a good place and we can stay at the Grand Cerf and take a hike in the woods and come home.'

'Good, that will be fine.'

'Well, I'll see you to-morrow at the courts,' I said.

'Good-night, Jake,' he said, and started back to the café.

'You forgot to get your paper,' I said.

'That's so.' He walked with me up to the kiosque at the corner. 'You are not sore, are you, Jake?' He turned with the paper in his hand.

'No, why should I be?'

'See you at tennis,' he said. I watched him walk back to the café holding his paper. I rather liked him and evidently she led him quite a life.

2

That winter Robert Cohn went over to America with his novel, and it was accepted by a fairly good publisher. His going made an awful row, I heard, and I think that was where Frances lost him, because several women were nice to him in New York, and when he came back he was quite changed. He was more enthusiastic about America than ever, and he was not so simple, and he was not so nice. The publishers had praised his novel pretty highly and it rather went to his head. Then several women had put themselves out to be nice to him, and his horizons had all shifted. For four years his horizon had been absolutely limited to his wife. For three years, or almost three years, he had never seen beyond Frances. I am sure he had never been in love in his life.

He had married on the rebound from the rotten time he had in college, and Frances took him on the rebound from his discovery that he had not been everything to his first wife. He was not in love yet, but he realised that he was an attractive quantity to women, and that the fact of a woman caring for him and wanting to live with him was not simply a divine miracle. This changed him so that he was not so pleasant to have around. Also, playing for higher stakes than he could afford in some rather steep bridge games with his New York connections, he had held cards and won several hundred dollars. It made him rather vain of his bridge game, and he talked several times of how a man could always make a living at bridge if he were forced to.

Then there was another thing. He had been reading W. H. Hudson. That sounds like an innocent occupation, but Cohn had read and re-read *The Purple Land*. *The Purple Land* is a very sinister book if read too late in life. It recounts splendid imaginary amorous adventures of a perfect English gentleman in an intensely romantic land, the scenery of which is very well described. For a man to take it at thirty-four as a guide-book to what life holds is about as safe as it would be for a man of the same age to enter Wall Street direct from a French convent, equipped with a complete set of the more practical Alger books. Cohn, I believe, took every word of *The Purple Land* as literally as though it had been an R. G. Dun report. You understand me, he made some reservations, but on the whole the book to him was sound. It was all that was needed to set him off. I did not realise the extent to which it had set him off until one day he came into my office.

'Hello, Robert,' I said. 'Did you come in to cheer me up?'

'Would you like to go to South America, Jake?' he asked.

'No.'

'Why not?'

'I don't know. I never wanted to go. Too expensive. You can see all the South Americans you want in Paris anyway.'

'They're not the real South Americans.'

'They look awfully real to me.'

I had a boat train to catch with a week's mail stories, and only half of them written.

'Do you know any dirt?' I asked.

'No.'

'None of your exalted connections getting divorces?'

'No; listen, Jake. If I handled both our expenses, would you go to South America with me?'

'Why me?'

'You can talk Spanish. And it would be more fun with two of us.'

'No,' I said, 'I like this town and I go to Spain in the summer-time.'

'All my life I've wanted to go on a trip like that,' Cohn said. He sat down. 'I'll be too old before I can ever do it.'

'Don't be a fool,' I said. 'You can go anywhere you want. You've got plenty of money.'

'I know. But I can't get started.'

'Cheer up,' I said. 'All countries look just like the moving pictures.'

But I felt sorry for him. He had it badly.

'I can't stand it to think my life is going so fast and I'm not really living it.'

'Nobody ever lives their life all the way up except bull-fighters.'

'I'm not interested in bull-fighters. That's an abnormal life. I want to go back in the country in South America. We could have a great trip.'

'Did you ever think about going to British East Africa to shoot?'

'No, I wouldn't like that.'

'I'd go there with you.'

'No; that doesn't interest me.'

'That's because you never read a book about it. Go on and read a book all full of love affairs with the beautiful shiny black princesses.'

'I want to go to South America.'

He had a hard, Jewish, stubborn streak.

'Come on downstairs and have a drink.'

'Aren't you working?'

'No,' I said. We went down the stairs to the café on the ground floor. I had discovered that was the best way to get rid of friends. Once you had a drink all you had to say was: 'Well, I've got to get back and get off some cables,' and it was done. It is very important to discover graceful exits like that in the newspaper business, where it is such an important part of the ethics that you should never seem to be working. Anyway, we went downstairs to the bar and had a whiskey and soda. Cohn looked at the bottles in bins around the wall. 'This is a good place,' he said.

'There's a lot of liquor,' I agreed.

'Listen, Jake,' he leaned forward on the bar. 'Don't you ever get the feeling that all your life is going by and you're not taking advantage of it? Do you realise that you've lived nearly half the time you have to live already?'

'Yes, every once in a while.'

'Do you know that in about thirty-five years more we'll be dead?'

'What the hell, Robert?' I said. 'What the hell?'

'I'm serious.'

'It's one thing I don't worry about,' I said.

'You ought to.'

'I've had plenty to worry about one time or other. I'm through worrying.'

'Well, I want to go to South America.'

'Listen, Robert, going to another country doesn't make any difference. I've tried all that. You can't get away from yourself by moving from one place to another. There's nothing to that.'

'But you've never been to South America.'

'South America hell! If you went there the way you feel now it would be exactly the same. This is a good town. Why don't you start living your life in Paris!'

'I'm sick of Paris, and I'm sick of the Quarter.'

'Stay away from the Quarter. Cruise around by yourself and see what happens to you.'

'Nothing happens to me. I walked alone all one night and nothing happened except a bicycle cop stopped me and asked to see my papers.'

'Wasn't the town nice at night?'

'I don't care for Paris.'

So there you were. I was sorry for him, but it was not a thing you could do anything about, because right away you ran up against the two stubbornnesses: South America could fix it and he did not like Paris. He got the first idea out of a book, and I suppose the second came out of a book too.

'Well,' I said, 'I've got to go upstairs and get off some cables.'

'Do you really have to go?'

'Yes, I've got to get these cables off.'

'Do you mind if I come up and sit around the office?'

'No, come on up.'

He sat in the outer room and read the papers, and the *Editor and Publisher* and I worked hard for two hours. Then I sorted out the carbons, stamped on a by-line, put the stuff in a couple of big manila envelopes and rang for a boy to take them to the Gare St Lazare. I went out into the other room and there was Robert Cohn asleep in the big chair. He was asleep with his head on his arms. I did not like to wake him up, but I wanted to lock the office and shove off. I put my hand on his shoulder. He shook his head. 'I can't do it,' he said, and put his head deeper into his arms. 'I can't do it. Nothing will make me do it.'

'Robert,' I said, and shook him by the shoulder. He looked up. He smiled and blinked.

'Did I talk out loud just then?'

'Something. But it wasn't clear.'

'God, what a rotten dream!'

'Did the typewriter put you to sleep?'

'Guess so. I didn't sleep all last night.'

'What was the matter?'

'Talking,' he said.

I could picture it. I have a rotten habit of picturing the bedroom scenes of my friends. We went out to the Café Napolitain to have an *apéritif* and watch the evening crowd on the Boulevard.

3

It was a warm spring night and I sat at a table on the terrace of the Napolitain after Robert had gone, watching it get dark and the electric signs come on, and the red and green stop-and-go traffic-signal, and the crowd going by, and the horse-cabs clippety-clopping along at the edge of the solid taxi traffic, and the *poules* going by, singly and in pairs, looking for the evening meal. I watched a good-looking girl walk past the table and watched her go up the street and lost sight of her, and watched another, and then saw the first one coming back again. She went by once more and I caught her eye, and she came over and sat down at the table. The waiter came up.

'Well, what will you drink?' I asked.

'Pernod.'

'That's not good for little girls.'

'Little girl yourself. Dites, garcon, un pernod.'

'A pernod for me, too.'

'What's the matter?' she asked. 'Going on a party?'

'Sure. Aren't you?'

'I don't know. You never know in this town.'

'Don't you like Paris?'

'No.'

'Why don't you go somewhere else?'

'Isn't anywhere else.'

'You're happy, all right.'

'Happy, hell!'

Pernod is greenish imitation absinthe. When you add water it turns milky. It tastes like licorice and it has a good uplift, but it drops you just as far. We sat and drank it, and the girl looked sullen.

'Well,' I said, 'are you going to buy me a dinner?'

She grinned and I saw why she made a point of not laughing. With her mouth closed she was a rather pretty girl. I paid for the saucers and we walked out to the street. I hailed a horse-cab and the driver pulled up at the curb. Settled back in the slow, smoothly rolling *fiacre* we moved up the Avenue de l'Opéra, passed the locked doors of the shops, their windows lighted, the Avenue broad and shiny and almost deserted. The cab passed the New York *Herald* bureau with the window full of clocks.

'What are all the clocks for?' she asked.

'They show the hour all over America.'

'Don't kid me.'

We turned off the Avenue up the Rue des Pyramides through the traffic of the Rue de Rivoli, and through a dark gate into the Tuileries. She cuddled against me and I put my arm around her. She looked up to be kissed. She touched me with one hand and I put her hand away.

'Never mind.'

'What's the matter? You sick?'

'Yes.'

'Everybody's sick. I'm sick, too.'

We came out of the Tuileries into the light and crossed the Seine and then turned up the Rue des Saints Pères.

'You oughtn't to drink pernod if you're sick.'

'You neither.'

'It doesn't make any difference with me. It doesn't make any difference with a woman.'

'What are you called?'

'Georgette. How are you called?'

'Jacob.'

'That's a Flemish name.'

'American too.'

'You're not Flamand?'

'No, American.'

'Good. I detest Flamands.'

By this time we were at the restaurant. I called to the *cocher* to stop. We got out and Georgette did not like the looks of the place. 'This is no great thing of a restaurant.'

'No,' I said. 'Maybe you would rather go to Foyot's. Why don't you keep the cab and go on?'

I had picked her up because of a vague sentimental idea that it would be nice to eat with some one. It was a long time since I had dined with a *poule*, and I had forgotten how dull it could be. We went into the restaurant, passed Madame Lavigne at the desk and into a little room. Georgette cheered up a little under the food.

'It isn't bad here,' she said. 'It isn't chic, but the food is all right.'

'Better than you eat in Liège.'

'Brussels, you mean.'

We had another bottle of wine and Georgette made a joke. She smiled and showed all her bad teeth, and we touched glasses. 'You're not a bad type,' she said. 'It's a shame you're sick. We get on well. What's the matter with you, anyway?'

'I got hurt in the war,' I said.

'Oh, that dirty war.'

We would probably have gone on and discussed the war and agreed that it was in reality a calamity for civilisation, and perhaps would have been better avoided. I was bored enough. Just then from the other room someone called: 'Barnes! I say, Barnes! Jacob Barnes!'

'It's a friend calling me,' I explained, and went out.

There was Braddocks at a big table with a party: Cohn, Frances Clyne, Mrs Braddocks, several people I did not know.

'You're coming to the dance, aren't you?' Braddocks asked.

'What dance?'

'Why, the dancings. Don't you know we've revived them?' Mrs Braddocks put in.

'You must come, Jake. We're all going,' Frances said from the end of the table. She was tall and had a smile.

'Of course, he's coming,' Braddocks said. 'Come in and have coffee with us, Barnes.'

'Right.'

'And bring your friend,' said Mrs Braddocks, laughing. She was a Canadian and had all their easy social graces.

'Thanks, we'll be in,' I said. I went back to the small room.

'Who are your friends?' Georgette asked.

'Writers and artists.'

'There are lots of those on this side of the river.'

'Too many.'

'I think so. Still, some of them make money.'

'Oh, yes.'

We finished the meal and the wine. 'Come on,' I said. 'We're going to have coffee with the others.'

Georgette opened her bag, made a few passes at her face as she looked in the little mirror, re-defined her lips with the lip-stick, and straightened her hat.

'Good,' she said.

We went into the room full of people and Braddocks and the men at his table stood up.

'I wish to present my fiancée, Mademoiselle Georgette Leblanc,' I said. Georgette smiled that wonderful smile, and we shook hands all round.

'Are you related to Georgette Leblanc, the singer?' Mrs Braddocks asked.

'Connais pas,' Georgette answered.

'But you have the same name,' Mrs Braddocks insisted cordially.

'No,' said Georgette. 'Not at all. My name is Hobin.'

'But Mr Barnes introduced you as Mademoiselle Georgette Leblanc. Surely he did,' insisted Mrs Braddocks, who in the excitement of talking French was liable to have no idea what she was saying.

'He's a fool,' Georgette said.

'Oh, it was a joke, then,' Mrs Braddocks said.

'Yes,' said Georgette. 'To laugh at.'

'Did you hear that, Henry?' Mrs Braddocks called down the table to Braddocks. 'Mr Barnes introduced his fiancée as Mademoiselle Leblanc, and her name is actually Hobin.'

'Of course, darling. Mademoiselle Hobin, I've known her for a very long time.'

'Oh, Mademoiselle Hobin,' Frances Clyne called, speaking French very rapidly and not seeming so proud and astonished as Mrs Braddocks at its coming out really French, 'have you been in Paris long? Do you like it here? You love Paris, do you not?'

'Who's she?' Georgette turned to me. 'Do I have to talk to her?'

She turned to Frances, sitting smiling, her hands folded, her head poised on her long neck, her lips pursed ready to start talking again.

'No. I don't like Paris. It's expensive and dirty.'

'Really? I find it so extraordinarily clean. One of the cleanest cities in all Europe.'

'I find it dirty.'

'How strange! But perhaps you have not been here very long.'

'I've been here long enough.'

'But it does have nice people in it. One must grant that.'

Georgette turned to me. 'You have nice friends.'

Frances was a little drunk and would have liked to have kept it up but the coffee came, and Lavigne with the liqueurs, and after that we all went out and started for Braddocks's dancing-club.

The dancing-club was a *bal musette* in the Rue de la Montagne Sainte Geneviéve. Five nights a week the working people of the Pantheon quarter danced there. One night a week it was the dancing-club. On Monday nights it was closed. When we arrived it was quite empty, except for a policeman sitting near the door, the wife of the proprietor back of the zinc bar, and the proprietor himself. The daughter of the house came downstairs as we went in. There were long benches, and tables ran across the room, and at the far end a dancing-floor.

'I wish people would come earlier,' Braddocks said. The daughter came up and wanted to know what we would drink. The proprietor got up on a high stool beside the dancing-floor and began to play the accordion. He had a string of bells around one of his ankles and beat time with his foot as he played. Every one danced. It was hot and we came off the floor perspiring.

'My God,' Georgette said. 'What a box to sweat in!'

'It's hot.'

'Hot, my God!'

'Take off your hat.'

'That's a good idea.'

Some one asked Georgette to dance, and I went over to the bar. It was really very hot and the accordion music was pleasant in the hot night. I drank a beer, standing in the doorway and getting the cool breath of wind from the street. Two taxis were coming down the steep street. They both stopped in front of the Bal. A crowd of young men, some in jerseys and some in their shirt-sleeves, got out. I could see their hands and newly washed, wavy hair in the light from the door. The policeman standing by the door looked at me and smiled. They came in. As they went in, under the light I saw white hands, wavy hair, white faces, grimacing, gesturing, talking. With them was Brett. She looked very lovely and she was very much with them.

One of them saw Georgette and said: 'I do declare. There is an actual harlot. I'm going to dance with her, Lett. You watch me.'

The tall, dark one, called Lette, said: 'Don't you be rash.'

The wavy blond one answered: 'Don't you worry, dear.' And with them was Brett.

I was very angry. Somehow they always made me angry. I know they are supposed to be amusing, and you should be tolerant, but I wanted to swing on one, any one, anything to shatter that superior, simpering composure. Instead, I walked down the street and had a beer at the bar at the next Bal. The beer was not good and I had a worse cognac to take the taste out of my mouth. When I came back to the Bal there was a crowd on the floor and Georgette was dancing with the tall blond youth, who danced big-hippily, carrying his head on one side, his eyes lifted as he danced. As soon as the music stopped another one of them asked her to dance. She had been taken up by them. I knew then that they would all dance with her. They are like that.

I sat down at a table. Cohn was sitting there. Frances was dancing. Mrs Braddocks brought up somebody and introduced him as Robert Prentiss. He was from New York by way of Chicago, and was a rising new novelist. He had some sort of an English accent. I asked him to have a drink.

'Thanks so much,' he said, 'I've just had one.'

'Have another.'

'Thanks, I will then.'

We got the daughter of the house over and each had a *Fine à l'eau*.

'You're from Kansas City, they tell me,' he said.

'Yes.'

'Do you find Paris amusing?'

'Yes.'

'Really?'

I was a little drunk. Not drunk in any positive sense but just enough to be careless.

'For God's sake,' I said, 'yes. Don't you?'

'Oh, how charmingly you get angry,' he said. 'I wish I had that faculty.'

I got up and walked over toward the dancing-floor. Mrs Braddocks followed me. 'Don't be cross with Robert,' she said. 'He's still only a child, you know.'

'I wasn't cross,' I said. 'I just thought perhaps I was going to throw up.'

'Your fiancée is having a great success.' Mrs Braddocks looked out on the floor where Georgette was dancing in the arms of the tall, dark one, called Lett.

'Isn't she?' I said.

'Rather,' said Mrs Braddocks.

Cohn came up. 'Come on, Jake,' he said, 'Have a drink.' We walked over to the bar. 'What's the matter with you? You seem all worked up over something?'

'Nothing. This whole show makes me sick is all.'

Brett came up to the bar.

'Hello, you chaps.'

'Hello, Brett,' I said. 'Why aren't you tight?'

'Never going to get tight any more. I say, give a chap a brandy and soda.'

She stood holding the glass and I saw Robert Cohn looking at her. He looked a great deal as his compatriot must have looked when he saw the promised land. Cohn, of course, was much younger. But he had that look of eager, deserving expectation.

Brett was damned good-looking. She wore a slip-over jersey sweater and a tweed skirt, and her hair was brushed back like a boy's. She started all that. She was built with curves like a hull of a racing yacht, and you missed none of it with that wool jersey.

'It's a fine crowd you're with, Brett,' I said.

'Aren't they lovely? And you, my dear. Where did you get it?'

'At the Napolitain.'

'And have you had a lovely evening?'

'Oh, priceless,' I said.

Brett laughed. 'It's wrong of you, Jake. It's an insult to all of us. Look at Frances there, and Jo.'

This for Cohn's benefit.

'It's in restraint of trade,' Brett said. She laughed again.

'You're wonderfully sober,' I said.

'Yes. Aren't I? And when one's with the crowd I'm with, one can drink in such safety, too.'

The music started and Robert Cohn said: 'Will you dance this with me, Lady Brett?'

Brett smiled at him. 'I've promised to dance this with Jacob,' she laughed. 'You've a hell of a biblical name, Jake.'

'How about the next?' asked Cohn.

'We're going,' Brett said. 'We've a date up at Montmartre.'

Dancing, I looked over Brett's shoulder and saw Cohn, standing at the bar, still watching her.

'You've made a new one there,' I said to her.

'Don't talk about it. Poor chap. I never knew it till just now.'

'Oh, well,' I said, 'I suppose you like to add them up.'

'Don't talk like a fool.'

'You do.'

'Oh, well. What if I do?'

'Nothing,' I said. We were dancing to the accordion and someone was playing the banjo. It was hot and I felt happy. We passed close to Georgette dancing with another one of them.

'What possessed you to bring her?'

'I don't know, I just brought her.'

'You're getting damned romantic.'

'No, bored.'

'Now?'

'No, not now.'

'Let's get out of here. She's well taken care of.'

'Do you want to?'

'Would I ask you if I didn't want to?'

We left the floor and I took my coat off a hanger on the wall and put it on. Brett stood by the bar. Cohn was talking to her. I stopped at the bar and asked them for an envelope. The patronne found one. I took a fifty-franc note from my pocket, put it in the envelope, sealed it, and handed it to the patronne.

'If the girl I came with asks for me, will you give her this?' I said. 'If she goes out with one of those gentlemen, will you save this for me?'

'C'est entendu, Monsieur,' the patronne said. 'You go now? So early?'

'Yes,' I said.

We started out the door. Cohn was still talking to Brett. She said good-night and took my arm. 'Good-night, Cohn,' I said. Outside in the street we looked for a taxi.

'You're going to lose your fifty francs,' Brett said.

'Oh, yes.'

'No taxis.'

'We could walk up to the Pantheon and get one.'

'Come on and we'll get a drink in the pub next door and send for one.'

'You wouldn't walk across the street.'

'Not if I could help it.'

We went into the next bar and I sent a waiter for a taxi.

'Well,' I said, 'we're out away from them.'

We stood against the tall zinc bar and did not talk and looked at each other. The waiter came and said the taxi was outside. Brett pressed my hand hard. I gave the waiter a franc and we went out. 'Where should I tell him?' I asked.

'Oh, tell him to drive around.'

I told the driver to go to the Parc Montsouris, and got in, and slammed the door. Brett was leaning back in the corner, her eyes closed. I got in and sat beside her. The cab started with a jerk.

'Oh, darling, I've been so miserable,' Brett said.

4

The taxi went up the hill, passed the lighted square, then on into the dark, still climbing, then levelled out on to a dark street behind St Etienne du Mont, went smoothly down the asphalt, passed the trees and the standing bus at the Place de la Contrescarpe, then turned on to the cobbles of the Rue Mouffetard. There were lighted bars and late open shops on each side of the street. We were sitting apart and we jolted close together going down the old street. Brett's hat was off. Her head was back. I saw her face in the lights from the open shops, then it was dark, then I saw her face clearly as we came out on the Avenue des Gobelins. The street was torn up and men were working on the car-tracks by the light of acetylene flares. Brett's face was white and the long line of her neck showed in the bright light of the flares. The street was dark again and I kissed her. Our lips were tight together and then she turned away and pressed against the corner of the seat, as far away as she could get. Her head was down.

'Don't touch me,' she said. 'Please don't touch me.'

'What's the matter?'

'I can't stand it.'

'Oh, Brett.'

'You mustn't. You must know. I can't stand it, that's all. Oh, darling, please understand!'

'Don't you love me?'

'Love you? I simply turn all to jelly when you touch me.'

'Isn't there anything we can do about it?'

She was sitting up now. My arm was around her and she was leaning back against me, and we were quite calm. She was looking into my eyes with that way she had of looking that made you wonder whether she really saw out of her own eyes. They would look on and on after everyone else's eyes in the world would have stopped looking. She looked as though there was nothing on earth she would not look at like that, and really she was afraid of so many things.'

'And there's not a damn thing we could do,' I said.

'I don't know,' she said. 'I don't want to go through that hell again.'

'We'd better keep away from each other.'

'But darling, I have to see you. It isn't all that you know.'

'No, but it always gets to be.'

'That's my fault. Don't we pay for all the things we do, though?'

She had been looking into my eyes all the time. Her eyes had different depths; sometimes they seemed perfectly flat. Now you could see all the way into them.

'When I think of the hell I've put chaps through. I'm paying for it all now.'

'Don't talk like a fool,' I said. 'Besides, what happened to me is supposed to be funny. I never think about it.'

'Oh, no. I'll lay you don't.'

'Well, let's shut up about it.'

'I laughed about it too, myself, once.' She wasn't looking at me. 'A friend of my brother's came home that way from Mons. It seemed like a hell of a joke. Chaps never know anything, do they?'

'No,' I said. 'Nobody ever knows anything.'

I was pretty well through with the subject. At one time or another I had probably considered it from most of its various angles, including the one that certain injuries or imperfections are a subject of merriment while remaining quite serious for the person possessing them.

'It's funny,' I said. 'It's very funny. And it's a lot of fun, too, to be in love.'

'Do you think so?' Her eyes looked flat again.

'I don't mean fun that way. In a way it's an enjoyable feeling.'

'No,' she said. 'I think it's hell on earth.'

'It's good to see each other.'

'No. I don't think it is.'

'Don't you want to?'

'I have to.'

We were sitting now like two strangers. On the right was the Parc Montsouris. The restaurant where they have the pool of live trout and where you can sit and look out over the park was closed and dark. The driver leaned his head around.

'Where do you want to go?' I asked. Brett turned her head away.

'Oh, go to the Select.'

'Café Select,' I told the driver. 'Boulevard Montparnasse.' We drove straight down, turning around the Lion de Belfort that guards the passing Montrouge trams. Brett looked straight ahead. On the Boulevard Raspail, with the lights of Montparnasse in sight, Brett said: 'Would you mind very much if I asked you to do something?'

'Don't be silly.'

'Kiss me just once more before we get there.'

When the taxi stopped I got out and paid. Brett came out putting on her hat. She gave me her hand as she stepped down. Her hand was shaky. 'I say, do I look too much of a mess?' She pulled her man's felt hat down and started in for the bar. Inside, against the bar and at tables, were most of the crowd who had been at the dance.

'Hello, you chaps,' Brett said. 'I'm going to have a drink.'

'Oh, Brett! Brett!' The little Greek portrait-painter, who called himself a duke, and whom everybody called Zizi, pushed up to her. 'I got something fine to tell you.'

'Hello, Zizi,' Brett said.

'I want you to meet a friend,' Zizi said. A fat man came up.

'Count Mippipopolous, meet my friend Lady Ashley.'

'How do you do?' said Brett.

'Well, does your ladyship have a good time here in Paris?' asked Count Mippipopolous, who wore an elk's tooth on his watch-chain.

'Rather,' said Brett.

'Paris is a fine town all right,' said the count. 'But I guess you have plenty big doings yourself over in London.'

'Oh, yes,' said Brett. 'Enormous.'

Braddocks called to me from a table. 'Barnes,' he said, 'have a drink. That girl of yours got in a frightful row.'

'What about?'

'Something the patronne's daughter said. A corking row. She was rather splendid, you know. Showed her yellow card and demanded the patronne's daughter's too. I say it was a row.'

'What finally happened?'

'Oh, some one took her home. Not a bad-looking girl. Wonderful command of the idiom. Do stay and have a drink.'

'No,' I said. 'I must shove off. Seen Cohn?'

'He went home with Frances,' Mrs Braddocks put in.

'Poor chap, he looks awfully down,' Braddocks said.

'I daresay he is,' said Mrs Braddocks.

'I have to shove off,' I said. 'Good night.'

I said good night to Brett at the bar. The count was buying champagne. 'Will you take a glass of wine with us, sir?' he asked.

'No. Thanks awfully. I have to go.'

'Really going?' Brett asked.

'Yes,' I said. 'I've got a rotten headache.'

'I'll see you to-morrow?'

'Come in at the office.'

'Hardly.'

'Well, where will I see you?'

'Anywhere around five o'clock.'

'Make it the other side of town then.'

'Good. I'll be at the Crillon at five.'

'Try and be there,' I said.

'Don't worry,' Brett said. 'I've never let you down, have I?'

'Heard from Mike?'

'Letter to-day.'

'Good night, sir,' said the count.

I went out on to the sidewalk and walked down toward the Boulevard St Michel, passed the tables of the Rotonde, still crowded, looked across the street at the Dome, its tables running out to the edge of the pavement. Someone waved to me from a table. I did not see who it was, and went on. I wanted to get home. The Boulevard Montparnasse was deserted. Lavigne's was closed tight, and they were stacking the tables outside the Closerie des Lilas. I passed Ney's statue standing among the new-leaved chestnut-trees in the arc-light. There was a faded purple wreath leaning against the base. I stopped and read the inscription: from the Bonapartist Groups, some date; I forget. He looked very fine, Marshal Ney in his top-boots, gesturing with his sword among the green new horse-chestnut leaves. My flat was just across the street, a little way down the Boulevard St Michel.

There was a light in the concierge's room and I knocked on the door and she gave me my mail. I wished her good night and went upstairs. There were two letters and some papers. I looked at them under the gas-light in the dining-room. The letters were from the States. One was a bank statement. It showed a balance of $2,432.60. I got out my cheque-book and deducted four cheques drawn since the first of the month, and discovered I had a balance of $1,832.60. I wrote this on the back of the statement. The other letter was a wedding announcement. Mr and Mrs Aloysius Kirby announce the marriage of their daughter Katherine–I knew neither the girl nor the man she was marrying. They must be circularising the town. It was a funny name. I felt sure I could remember anybody with a name like Aloysius. It was a good Catholic name. There was a crest on the announcement. Like Zizi the Greek duke. And that count. The count was funny. Brett had a title, too. Lady Ashley. To hell with Brett. To hell with you, Lady Ashley.

I lit the lamp beside the bed, turned off the gas, and opened the wide windows. The bed was far back from the windows, and I sat with the windows open and undressed by the bed. Outside a night train, running on the street-car tracks, went by carrying vegetables to the markets. They were noisy at night when you could not sleep. Undressing, I looked at myself in the mirror of the big armoire beside the bed. That was a typically French way to furnish a room. Practical, too, I suppose. Of all the ways to be wounded. I suppose it was funny. I put on my pyjamas and got into bed. I had the two bull-fight papers, and I took their wrappers off. One was orange. The other yellow. They would both have the same news, so whichever I read first would spoil the other. *Le Toril* was the better paper, so I started to read it. I read it all the way through, including the Petite Correspondance and the Cornigrams. I blew out the lamp. Perhaps I would be able to sleep.

My head started to work. The old grievance. Well, it was a rotten way to be wounded and flying on a joke front like the Italian. In the Italian hospital we were going to form a society. It had a funny name in Italian. I wonder what became of the others, the Italians. That was in the Ospedale Maggiore in Milano, Padiglione Ponte. The next building was the Padiglione Zonda. There was a statue of Ponte, or maybe it was Zonda. That was where the liaison colonel came to visit me. That was funny. That was about the first funny thing. I was all bandaged up. But they had told him about it. Then he made that wonderful speech: 'You, a foreigner, an Englishman (any foreigner was an Englishman), have given more than your life.' What a speech! I would like to have it illuminated to hang in the office. He never laughed. He was putting himself in my place, I guess. 'Que mala fortuna! Que mala fortuna!'

I never used to realise it, I guess. I try and play it along and just not make trouble for people. Probably I never would have had any trouble if I hadn't run into Brett when they shipped me to England. I suppose she only wanted what she couldn't have. Well, people were that way. To hell with people. The Catholic Church had an awfully good way of handling all that. Good advice, anyway. Not to think about it. Oh, it was swell advice. Try and take it sometime. Try and take it.

I lay awake thinking and my mind jumping around. Then I couldn't keep away from it, and I started to think about Brett and all the rest of it went away. I was thinking about Brett and my mind stopped jumping around and started to go in sort of smooth waves. Then all of a sudden I started to cry. Then after a while it was better and I lay in bed and listened to the heavy trams go by and way down the street, and then I went to sleep.

I woke up. There was a row going on outside. I listened and I thought I recognised a voice. I put on a dressing-gown and went to the door. The concierge was talking downstairs. She was very angry. I heard my name and called down the stairs.

'Is that you, Monsieur Barnes?' the concierge called.

'Yes. It's me.'

'There's a species of woman here who's waked the whole street up. What kind of a dirty business at this time of night! She says she must see you. I've told her you're asleep.'

Then I heard Brett's voice. Half asleep I had been sure it was Georgette. I don't know why. She could not have known my address.

'Will you send her up, please?'

Brett came up the stairs. I saw she was quite drunk. 'Silly thing to do,' she said. 'Make an awful row. I say, you weren't asleep, were you?'

'What did you think I was doing?'

'Don't know. What time is it?'

I looked at the clock. It was half-past four. 'Had no idea what hour it was,' Brett said. 'I say, can a chap sit down? Don't be cross, darling. Just left the count. He brought me here.'

'What's he like?' I was getting brandy and soda and glasses.

'Just a little,' said Brett. 'Don't try and make me drunk. The count? Oh, rather. He's quite one of us.'

'Is he a count?'

'Here's how. I rather think so, you know. Deserves to be, anyhow. Knows hell's own amount about people. Don't know where he got it all. Owns a chain of sweet-shops in the States.'

She sipped at her glass.

'Think he called it a chain. Something like that. Linked them all up. Told me a little about it. Damned interesting. He's one of us, though. Oh, quite. No doubt. One can always tell.'

She took another drink.

'How I do buck on about all this! You don't mind, do you? He's putting up for Zizi, you know.'

'Is Zizi really a duke, too?'

'I shouldn't wonder. Greek, you know. Rotten painter. I rather liked the count.'

'Where did you go with him?'

'Oh, everywhere. He just brought me here now. Offered me ten thousand dollars to go to Biarritz with him. How much is that in pounds?'

'Around two thousand.'

'Lot of money. I told him I couldn't do it. He was awfully nice about it. Told him I knew too many people in Biarritz.'

Brett laughed.

'I say, you are slow on the up-take,' she said. I had only sipped my brandy and soda. I took a long drink.

'That's better. Very funny,' Brett said. 'Then he wanted me to go to Cannes with him. Told him I knew too many people in Cannes. Monte Carlo. Told him I knew too many people in Monte Carlo. Told him I knew too many people everywhere. Quite true, too. So I asked him to bring me here.'

She looked at me, her hand on the table, her glass raised. 'Don't look like that,' she said. 'Told him I was in love with you. True, too. Don't look like that. He was damn nice about it. Wants to drive us out to dinner to-morrow night. Like to go?'

'Why not?'

'I'd better go now.'

'Why?'

'Just wanted to see you. Damned silly idea. Want to get dressed and come down? He's got the car just up the street.'

The count?'

'Himself. And a chauffeur in livery. Going to drive me around and have breakfast in the Bois. Hampers. Got it all at Zelli's. Dozen bottles of Mumms. Tempt you?'

'I have to work in the morning,' I said. 'I'm too far behind you now to catch up and be any fun.'

'Don't be an ass.'

'Can't do it.'

'Right. Send him a tender message?'

'Anything. Absolutely.'

'Good night, darling.'

'Don't be sentimental.'

'You make me ill.'

We kissed good night and Brett shivered. 'I'd better go,' she said. 'Good night, darling.'

'You don't have to go.'

'Yes.'

We kissed again on the stairs and as I called for the cordon the concierge muttered something behind her door. I went back upstairs and from the open window watched Brett walking up the street to the big limousine drawn up to the curb under the arc-light. She got in and it started off. I turned around. On the table was an empty glass and a glass half-full of brandy and soda. I took them both out to the kitchen and poured the half-full glass down the sink. I turned off the gas in the dining-room, kicked off my slippers sitting on the bed, and got into bed. This was Brett, that I had felt like crying about. Then I thought of her walking up the street and stepping into the car, as I had last seen her, and of course in a little while I felt like hell again. It is awfully easy to be hard-boiled about everything in the daytime, but at night it is another thing.

5

In the morning I walked down the Boulevard to the Rue Soufflot for coffee and brioche. It was a fine morning. The horse-chestnut trees in the Luxembourg gardens were in bloom. There was the pleasant early-morning feeling of a hot day. I read the papers with the coffee and then smoked a cigarette. The flower-women were coming up from the market and arranging their daily stock. Students went by going up to the law school, or down to the Sorbonne. The Boulevard was busy with trams and people going to work. I got on an S bus and rode down to the Madeleine, standing on the back platform. From the Madeleine I walked along the Boulevard des Capucines to the Opera, and up to my office. I passed the man with the jumping frogs and the man with the boxer toys. I stepped aside to avoid walking into the thread with which his girl assistant manipulated the boxers. She was standing looking away, the thread in her folded hands. The man was urging two tourists to buy. Three more tourists had stopped and were watching. I walked on behind a man who was pushing a roller that printed the name CINZANO on the sidewalk in damp letters. All along people were going to work. It felt pleasant to be going to work. I walked across the avenue and turned in to my office.

Upstairs in the office I read the French morning papers, smoked, and then sat at the typewriter and got off a good morning's work. At eleven o'clock I went over to the Quai d'Orsay in a taxi and went in and sat with about a dozen correspondents, while the foreign-office mouthpiece, a young *Nouvelle Revue Française* diplomat in horn-rimmed spectacles, talked and answered questions for half an hour. The President of the Council was in Lyons making a speech, or, rather, he was on his way back. Several people asked questions to hear themselves talk and there were a couple of questions asked by news service men who wanted to know the answers. There was no news. I shared a taxi back from the Quai d'Orsay with Woolsey and Krum.

'What do you do nights, Jake?' asked Krum. 'I never see you around.'

'Oh, I'm over in the Quarter.'

'I'm coming over some night. The Dingo. That's the great place, isn't it?'

'Yes. That, or this new dive, The Select.'

'I've meant to get over,' said Krum. 'You know how it is, though, with a wife and kids.'

'Playing any tennis?' Woolsey asked.

'Well, no,' said Krum. 'I can't say I've played any this year. I've tried to get away, but Sundays it's always rained, and the courts are so damned crowded.'

'The Englishmen all have Saturday off,' Woolsey said.

'Lucky beggars,' said Krum. 'Well, I'll tell you. Some day I'm not going to be working for an agency. Then I'll have plenty of time to get out in the country.'

'That's the thing to do. Live out in the country and have a little car.'

'I've been thinking some about getting a car next year.'

I banged on the glass. The chauffeur stopped. 'Here's my street,' I said. 'Come in and have a drink.'

'Thanks, old man,' Krum said. Woolsey shook his head. 'I've got to file that line he got off this morning.'

I put a two-franc piece in Krum's hand.

'You're crazy, Jake,' he said. 'This is on me.'

'It's all on the office, anyway.'

'Nope. I want to get it.'

I waved goodbye. Krum put his head out. 'See you at the lunch on Wednesday.'

'You bet.'

I went to the office in the elevator. Robert Cohn was waiting for me. 'Hello, Jake,' he said. 'Going out to lunch?'

'Yes. Let me see if there is anything new.'

'Where will we eat?'

'Anywhere.'

I was looking over my desk. 'Where do you want to eat?'

'How about Wetzel's? They've got good hors d'œuvres.'

In the restaurant we ordered hors d'œuvres and beer. The sommelier brought the beer, tall, beaded on the outside of the steins, and cold. There were a dozen different dishes of hors d'œuvres.

'Have any fun last night?' I asked.

'No. I don't think so.'

'How's the writing going?'

'Rotten. I can't get this second book going.'

'That happens to everybody.'

'Oh, I'm sure of that. It gets me worried, though.'

'Thought any more about going to South America?'

'I mean that.'

'Well, why don't you start off?'

'Frances.'

'Well,' I said, 'take her with you.'

'She wouldn't like it. That isn't the sort of thing she likes. She likes a lot of people around.'

'Tell her to go to hell.'

'I can't. I've got certain obligations to her.'

He shoved the sliced cucumbers away and took a pickled herring.

'What do you know about Lady Brett Ashley, Jake?'

'Her name's Lady Ashley. Brett's her own name. She's a nice girl,' I said. 'She's getting a divorce and she's going to marry Mike Campbell. He's over in Scotland now. Why?'

'She's a remarkably attractive woman.'

'Isn't she?'

'There's a certain quality about her, a certain fineness. She seems to be absolutely fine and straight.'

'She's very nice.'

'I don't know how to describe the quality,' Cohn said. 'I suppose it's breeding.'

'You sound as though you liked her pretty well.'

'I do. I shouldn't wonder if I were in love with her.'

'She's a drunk,' I said. 'She's in love with Mike Campbell, and she's going to marry him. He's going to be rich as hell some day.'

'I don't believe she'll ever marry him.'

'Why not?'

'I don't know. I just don't believe it. Have you known her a long time?'

'Yes,' I said. 'She was a V.A.D. in a hospital I was in during the war.'

'She must have been just a kid then.'

'She's thirty-four now.'

'When did she marry Ashley?'

'During the war. Her own true love had just kicked off with the dysentery.'

'You talk sort of bitter.'

'Sorry. I didn't mean to. I was just trying to give you the facts.'

'I don't believe she would marry anybody she didn't love.'

'Well,' I said. 'She's done it twice.'

'I don't believe it.'

'Well,' I said, 'don't ask me a lot of fool questions if you don't like the answers.'

'I didn't ask you that.'

'You asked me what I knew about Brett Ashley.'

'I didn't ask you to insult her.'

'Oh, go to hell.'

He stood up from the table, his face white, and stood there white and angry behind the little plates of hors d'oeuvres.

'Sit down,' I said. 'Don't be a fool.'

'You've got to take that back.'

'Oh, cut out the prep-school stuff.'

'Take it back.'

'Sure. Anything. I never heard of Brett Ashley. How's that?'

'No. Not that. About me going to hell.'

'Oh, don't go to hell,' I said. 'Stick around. We're just starting lunch.'

Cohn smiled again and sat down. He seemed glad to sit down. What the hell would he have done if he hadn't sat down? 'You say such damned insulting things, Jake.'

'I'm sorry. I've got a nasty tongue. I never mean it when I say nasty things.'

'I know it,' Cohn said. 'You're really about the best friend I have, Jake.'

God help you, I thought. 'Forget what I said,' I said out loud. 'I'm sorry.'

'It's all right. It's fine. I was just sore for a minute.'

'Good. Let's get something else to eat.'

After we finished the lunch we walked up to the Café de la Paix and had coffee. I could feel Cohn wanted to bring up Brett again, but I held him off it. We talked about one thing and another, and I left him to come to the office.

6

At five o'clock I was in the Hotel Crillon waiting for Brett. She was not there, so I sat down and wrote some letters. They were not very good letters but I hoped their being on Crillon stationery would help them. Brett did not turn up, so about quarter to six I went down to the bar and had a Jack Rose with George the barman. Brett had not been in the bar either, and so I looked for her upstairs on my way out, and took a taxi to the Café Select. Crossing the Seine I saw a string of barges being towed empty down the current, riding high, the bargemen at the sweeps as they came toward the bridge. The river looked nice. It was always pleasant crossing bridges in Paris.

The taxi rounded the statue of the inventor of the semaphore engaged in doing same, and turned up the Boulevard Raspail, and I sat back to let that part of the ride pass. The Boulevard Raspail always made dull riding. It was like a certain stretch on the P.L.M. between Fontainebleau and Montereau that always made me feel bored and dead and dull until it was over. I suppose it is some association of ideas that makes those dead places in a journey. There are other streets in Paris as ugly as the Boulevard Raspail. It is a street I do not mind walking down at all. But I cannot stand to ride along it. Perhaps I had read something about it once. That was the way Robert Cohn was about all of Paris. I wondered where Cohn got that incapacity to enjoy Paris. Possibly from Mencken. Mencken hates Paris, I believe. So many young men get their likes and dislikes from Mencken.

The taxi stopped in front of the Rotonde. No matter what café in Montparnasse you ask a taxi-driver to bring you to from the right bank of the river, they always take you to the Rotonde. Ten years from now it will probably be the Dome. It was near enough, anyway. I walked past the sad tables of the Rotonde to the Select. There were a few people inside at the bar, and outside alone, sat Harvey Stone. He had a pile of saucers in front of him, and he needed a shave.

'Sit down,' said Harvey, 'I've been looking for you.'

'What's the matter?'

'Nothing? Just looking for you.'

'Been out to the races?'

'No. Not since Sunday.'

'What do you hear from the States?'

'Nothing. Absolutely nothing.'

'What's the matter?'

'I don't know. I'm through with them. I'm absolutely through with them.'

He leaned forward and looked me in the eye.

'Do you want to know something, Jake?'

'Yes.'

'I haven't had anything to eat for five days.'

I figured rapidly back in my mind. It was three days ago that Harvey had won two hundred francs from me shaking poker dice in the New York Bar.

'What's the matter?'

'No money. Money hasn't come,' he paused. 'I tell you it's strange, Jake. When I'm like this I just want to be alone. I want to stay in my own room. I'm like a cat.'

I felt in my pocket.

'Would a hundred help you any, Harvey?'

'Yes.'

'Come on. Let's go and eat.'

'There's no hurry. Have a drink.'

'Better eat.'

'No. When I get like this I don't care whether I eat or not.'

We had a drink. Harvey added my saucer to his own pile.

'Do you know Mencken, Harvey?'

'Yes. Why?'

'What's he like?'

'He's all right. He says some pretty funny things. Last time I had dinner with him we talked about Hoffenheimer. "The trouble is," he said, "he's a garter snapper." That's not bad.'

'That's not bad.'

'He's through now,' Harvey went on. 'He's written about all the things he knows, and now he's on all the things he doesn't know.'

'I guess he's all right,' I said. 'I just can't read him.'

'Oh, nobody reads him now,' Harvey said, 'except the people that used to read the Alexander Hamilton Institute.'

'Well,' I said. 'That was a good thing, too.'

'Sure,' said Harvey. So we sat and thought deeply for a while.

'Have another port?'

'All right,' said Harvey.

'There comes Cohn,' I said. Robert Cohn was crossing the street.

'That moron,' said Harvey. Cohn came up to our table.

'Hello, you bums,' he said.

'Hello, Robert, Harvey said. 'I was just telling Jake here that you're a moron.'

'What do you mean?'

'Tell us right off. Don't think. What would you rather do if you could do anything you wanted?'

Cohn started to consider.

'Don't think. Bring it right out.'

'I don't know,' Cohn said. 'What's it all about, anyway?'

'I mean what would you rather do. What comes into your head first.

No matter how silly it is.'

'I don't know,' Cohn said. 'I think I'd rather play football again with what I know about handling myself, now.'

'I misjudged you,' Harvey said. 'You're not a moron. You're only a case of arrested development.'

'You're awfully funny, Harvey,' Cohn said. 'Some day somebody will push your face in.'

Harvey Stone laughed. 'You think so. They won't, though. Because it wouldn't make any difference to me. I'm not a fighter.'

'It would make a difference to you if anybody did it.'

'No, it wouldn't. That's where you make your big mistake. Because you're not intelligent.'

'Cut it out about me.'

'Sure,' said Harvey. 'It doesn't make any difference to me. You don't mean anything to me.'

'Come on, Harvey,' I said. 'Have another porto.'

'No,' he said. 'I'm going up the street and eat. See you later, Jake.'

He walked out and up the street. I watched him crossing the street through the taxis, small, heavy, slowly sure of himself in the traffic.

'He always gets me sore,' Cohn said. 'I can't stand him.'

'I like him,' I said. 'I'm fond of him. You don't want to get sore at him.'

'I know it,' Cohn said. 'He just gets on my nerves.'

'Write this afternoon?'

'No. I couldn't get it going. It's harder to do than my first book. I'm having a hard time handling it.'

The sort of healthy conceit that he had when he returned from America early in the spring was gone. Then he had been sure of his work, only with these personal longings for adventure. Now the sureness was gone. Somehow I feel I have not shown Robert Cohn clearly. The reason is that until he fell in love with Brett, I never heard him make one remark that would, in any way, detach him from other people. He was nice to watch on the tennis-court, he had a good body, and he kept it in shape; he handled his cards well at bridge, and he had a funny sort of undergraduate quality about him. If he were in a crowd nothing he said stood out. He wore what used to be called polo shirts at school, and may be called that still, but he was not professionally youthful. I do not believe he thought about his clothes much. Externally he had been formed at Princeton. Internally he had been moulded by the two women who had trained him. He had a nice, boyish sort of cheerfulness that had never been trained out of him, and I probably have not brought it out. He loved to win at tennis. He probably loved to win as much as Lenglen, for instance. On the other hand, he was not angry at being beaten. When he fell in love with Brett his tennis game went all to pieces. People beat him who had never had a chance with him. He was very nice about it.

Anyhow, we were sitting on the terrace of the Café Select, and Harvey Stone had just crossed the street.

'Come on up to the Lilas,' I said.

'I have a date.'

'What time?'

'Frances is coming here at seven-fifteen.'

'There she is.'

Frances Clyne was coming toward us from across the street. She was a very tall girl who walked with a great deal of movement. She waved and smiled. We watched her cross the street.

'Hello,' she said, 'I'm so glad you're here, Jake. I've been wanting to talk to you.'

'Hello, Frances,' said Cohn. He smiled.

'Why, hello, Robert. Are you here?' She went on, talking rapidly. 'I've had the darndest time. This one'–shaking her head at Cohn–'didn't come home for lunch.'

'I wasn't supposed to.'

'Oh, I know. But you didn't say anything about it to the cook. Then I had a date myself, and Paula wasn't at her office. I went to the Ritz and waited for her, and she never came, and of course I didn't have enough money to lunch at the Ritz—'

'What did you do?'

'Oh, went out, of course.' She spoke in a sort of imitation joyful manner. 'I always keep my appointments. No one keeps theirs, nowadays. I ought to know better. How are you, Jake, anyway?'

'Fine.'

'That was a fine girl you had at the dance, and then went off with that Brett one.'

'Don't you like her?' Cohn asked.

'I think she's perfectly charming. Don't you?'

Cohn said nothing.

'Look, Jake. I want to talk with you. Would you come over with me to the Dome? You'll stay here, won't you, Robert? Come on, Jake.'

We crossed the Boulevard Montparnasse and sat down at a table. A boy came up with the *Paris Times*, and I bought one and opened it.

'What's the matter, Frances?'

'Oh, nothing,' she said, 'except that he wants to leave me.'

'How do you mean?'

'Oh, he told everyone that we were going to be married, and I told my mother and every one, and now he doesn't want to do it.'

'What's the matter?'

'He's decided he hasn't lived enough. I knew it would happen when he went to New York.'

She looked up, very bright-eyed and trying to talk inconsequentially.

'I wouldn't marry him if he doesn't want to. Of course I wouldn't. I wouldn't marry him now for anything. But it does seem to me to be a little late now, after we've waited three years, and I've just gotten my divorce.'

I said nothing.

'We were going to celebrate so, and instead we've just had scenes. It's so childish. We have dreadful scenes, and he cries and begs me to be reasonable, but he says he just can't do it.'

'It's rotten luck.'

'I should say it is rotten luck. I've wasted two years and a half on him now. And I don't know if any man will ever want to marry me. Two years ago I could have married anybody I wanted, down at Cannes. All the old ones that wanted to marry somebody chic and settle down were crazy about me. Now I don't think I could get anybody.'

'Sure, you could marry anybody.'

'No, I don't believe it. And I'm fond of him, too. And I'd like to have children. I always thought we'd have children.'

She looked at me very brightly. 'I never liked children much, but I don't want to think I'll never have them. I always thought I'd have them and then like them.'

'He's got children.'

'Oh, yes. He's got children, and he's got money, and he's got a rich mother, and he's written a book, and nobody will publish my stuff, nobody at all. It isn't bad, either. And I haven't got any money at all. I could have had alimony, but I got the divorce the quickest way.'

She looked at me again very brightly.

'It isn't right. It's my own fault and it's not, too. I ought to have known better. And when I tell him he just cries and says he can't marry. Why can't he marry? I'd be a good wife. I'm easy to get along with. I leave him alone. It doesn't do any good.'

'It's a rotten shame.'

'Yes, it is a rotten shame. But there's no use talking about it, is there? Come on, let's go back to the café.'

'And of course there isn't anything I can do.'

'No. Just don't let him know I talked to you. I know what he wants.' Now for the first time she dropped her bright, terribly cheerful manner. 'He wants to go back to New York alone, and be there when his book comes out. That's what he wants.'

'Maybe they won't like it. I don't think he's that way. Really.'

'You don't know him like I do, Jake. That's what he wants to do. I know it. I know it. That's why he doesn't want to marry. He wants to have a big triumph this fall all by himself.'

'Want to go back to the café?'

'Yes. Come on.'

We got up from the table–they had never brought us a drink–and started across the street toward the Select, where Cohn sat smiling at us from behind the marble-topped table.

'Well, what are you smiling at?' Frances asked him. 'Feel pretty happy?'

'I was smiling at you and Jake with your secrets.'

'Oh, what I've told Jake isn't any secret. Everybody will know it soon enough. I only wanted to give Jake a decent version.'

'What was it? About your going to England?'

'Yes, about my going to England. Oh, Jake! I forgot to tell you. I'm going to England.'

'Isn't that fine!'

'Yes, that's the way it's done in the very best families. Robert's sending me. He's going to give me two hundred pounds and then I'm going to visit friends. Won't it be lovely? The friends don't know about it, yet.'

She turned to Cohn and smiled at him. He was not smiling now.

'You were only going to give me a hundred pounds, weren't you Robert? But I made him give me two hundred. He's really very generous. Aren't you, Robert?'

I do not know how people could say such terrible things to Robert Cohn. There are people to whom you could not say insulting things. They give you a feeling that the world would be destroyed, would actually be destroyed before your eyes, if you said certain things. But here was Cohn taking it all. Here it was, all going on right before me, and I did not even feel an impulse to try and stop it. And this was friendly joking to what went on later.

'How can you say such things, Frances?' Cohn interrupted.

'Listen to him. I'm going to England. I'm going to visit friends. Ever visit friends that didn't want you? Oh, they'll have to take me, all right. "How do you do, my dear? Such a long time since we've seen you. And how is your dear mother?" Yes, how is my dear mother? She put all her money into French war bonds. Yes, she did. Probably the only person in the world that did. "And what about Robert?" or else very careful talking around Robert. "You must be most careful not to mention him, my dear. Poor Frances has had a most unfortunate experience." Won't it be fun, Robert? Don't you think it will be fun, Jake?'

She turned to me with that terribly bright smile. It was very satisfactory to her to have an audience for this.

'And where are you going to be, Robert? It's my own fault, all right. Perfectly my own fault. When I made you get rid of your little secretary on the magazine I ought to have known you'd get rid of me the same way. Jake doesn't know about that. Should I tell him?'

'Shut up, Frances, for God's sake.'

'Yes, I'll tell him. Robert had a little secretary on the magazine. Just the sweetest little thing in the world, and he thought she was wonderful, and then I came along and he thought I was pretty wonderful too. So I made him get rid of her, and he had brought her to Provincetown from Carmel when he moved the magazine, and he didn't even pay her fare back to the coast. All to please me. He thought I was pretty fine, then. Didn't you, Robert?'

'You mustn't misunderstand, Jake, it was absolutely platonic with the secretary. Not even platonic. Nothing at all, really. It was just that she was so nice. And he did that just to please me. Well, I suppose that we that live by the sword shall perish by the sword. Isn't that literary, though? You want to remember that for your next book, Robert.

'You know Robert is going to get material for a new book. Aren't you, Robert? That's why he's leaving me. He's decided I don't film well. You see, he was so busy all the time that we were living together, writing on this book, that he doesn't remember anything about us. So now he's going out and get some new material. Well, I hope he gets something frightfully interesting.

'Listen, Robert, dear. Let me tell you something. You won't mind, will you? Don't have scenes with your young ladies. Try not to. Because you can't have scenes without crying, and then you pity yourself so much you can't remember what the other person's said. You'll never be able to remember any conversations that way. Just try and be calm. I know it's awfully hard. But remember, it's for literature. We all ought to make sacrifices for literature. Look at me. I'm going to England without a protest. All for literature. We must all help young writers. Don't you think so, Jake? But you're not a young writer. Are you, Robert? You're thirty-four. Still, I suppose that is young for a great writer. Look at Hardy. Look at Anatole France. He just died a little while ago. Robert doesn't think he's any good, though. Some of his French friends told him. He doesn't read French very well himself. He wasn't a good writer like you are, was he, Robert? Do you think he ever had to go and look for material? What do you suppose he said to his mistresses when he wouldn't marry them? I wonder if he cried, too? Oh, I've just thought of something.' She put her gloved hand up to her lips. 'I know the real reason why Robert won't marry me, Jake. It's just come to me. They've sent it to me in a vision in the Café Select. Isn't it mystic? Some day they'll put a tablet up. Like at Lourdes. Do you want to hear, Robert? I'll tell you. It's so simple. I wonder why I never thought about it. Why, you see, Robert's always wanted to have a mistress, and if he doesn't marry me, why, then he's had one. She was his mistress for over two years. See how it is? And if he marries me, like he's always promised he would, that would be the end of all the romance. Don't you think that's bright of me to figure that out? It's true, too. Look at him and see if it's not. Where are you going, Jake?'

'I've got to go in and see Harvey Stone a minute.'

Cohn looked up as I went in. His face was white. Why did he sit there? Why did he keep on taking it like that?

As I stood against the bar looking out I could see them through the window. Frances was talking on to him, smiling brightly, looking into his face each time she asked: 'Isn't it so, Robert?' Or maybe she did not ask that now. Perhaps she said something else. I told the barman I did not want anything to drink and went out through the side door. As I went out the door I looked back through the two thicknesses of glass and saw them sitting there. She was still talking to him. I went down a side street to the Boulevard Raspail. A taxi came along and I got in and gave the driver the address of my flat.

7

As I started up the stairs the concierge knocked on the glass of the door of her lodge, and as I stopped she came out. She had some letters and a telegram.

'Here is the post. And there was a lady here to see you.'

'Did she leave a card?'

'No. She was with a gentleman. It was the one who was here last night. In the end I find she is very nice.'

'Was she with a friend of mine?'

'I don't know. He was never here before. He was very large. Very, very large. She was very nice. Very, very nice. Last night she was, perhaps a little—' She put her head on one hand and rocked it up and down. 'I'll speak perfectly frankly, Monsieur Barnes. Last night I found her not so gentille. Last night I formed another idea of her. But listen to what I tell you. She is très, très gentille. She is of very good family. It is a thing you can see.'

'They did not leave any word?'

'Yes. They said they would be back in an hour.'

'Send them up when they come.'

'Yes, Monsieur Barnes. And that lady, that lady there is some one. An eccentric, perhaps, but quelqu'un, quelqu'un!'

The concierge, before she became a concierge, had owned a drink-selling concession at the Paris race-courses. Her life-work lay in the *pelouse*, but she kept an eye on the people of the *pesage*, and she took great pride in telling me which of my guests were well brought up, which were of good family, who were sportsmen, a French word pronounced with the accent on the men. The only trouble was that people who did not fall into any of these three categories were very liable to be told there was no one home, chez Barnes. One of my friends, an extremely underfed-looking painter, who was obviously to Madame Duzinell neither well brought up, of good family, nor a sportsman, wrote me a letter asking if I could get him a pass to get by the concierge so he would come up and see me occasionally in the evenings.

I went up to the flat wondering what Brett had done to the concierge. The wire was a cable from Bill Gorton, saying he was arriving on the *France*. I put the mail on the table, went back to the bedroom, undressed and had a shower. I was rubbing down when I heard the door-bell pull. I put on a bathrobe and slippers and went to the door. It was Brett. Back of her was the count. He was holding a great bunch of roses.

'Hello, darling,' said Brett. 'Aren't you going to let us in?'

'Come on. I was just bathing.'

'Aren't you the fortunate man. Bathing.'

'Only a shower. Sit down, Count Mippipopolous. What will you drink?'

'I don't know whether you like flowers, sir,' the count said, 'but I took the liberty of just bringing these roses.'

'Here, give them to me.' Brett took them. 'Get me some water in this, Jake.' I filled the big earthenware jug with water in the kitchen, and Brett put the roses in it, and placed them in the centre of the dining-room table.

'I say. We have had a day.'

'You don't remember anything about a date with me at the Crillon?'

'No. Did we have one? I must have been blind.'

'You were quite drunk, my dear,' said the count.

'Wasn't I, though? and the count's been a brick, absolutely.'

'You've got hell's own drag with the concierge now.'

'I ought to have. Gave her two hundred francs.'

'Don't be a damned fool.'

'His,' she said, and nodded at the count.

'I thought we ought to give her a little something for last night. It was very late.'

'He's wonderful,' Brett said. 'He remembers everything that's happened.'

'So do you, my dear.'

'Fancy,' said Brett. 'Who'd want to? I say, Jake, *do* we get a drink?'

'You get it while I go in and dress. You know where it is.'

'Rather.'

While I dressed I heard Brett put down glasses and then a syphon, and then heard them talking. I dressed slowly, sitting on the bed. I felt tired and pretty rotten. Brett came in the room, a glass in her hand, and sat on the bed.

'What's the matter, darling? Do you feel rocky?'

She kissed me coolly on the forehead.

'Oh, Brett, I love you so much.'

'Darling,' she said. Then: 'Do you want me to send him away?'

'No. He's nice.'

'I'll send him away.'

'No, don't.'

'Yes, I'll send him away.'

'You can't just like that.'

'Can't I, though? You stay here. He's mad about me, I tell you.'

She was gone out of the room. I lay face down on the bed. I was having a bad time. I heard them talking but I did not listen. Brett came in and sat on the bed.

'Poor old darling.' She stroked my head.

'What did you say to him?' I was lying with my face away from her. I did not want to see her.

'Sent him for champagne. He loves to go for champagne.'

Then later: 'Do you feel better, darling? Is the head any better?'

'It's better.'

'Lie quiet. He's gone to the other side of town.'

'Couldn't we live together, Brett? Couldn't we just live together?'

'I don't think so. I'd just *tromper* you with everybody. You couldn't stand it.'

'I stand it now.'

'That would be different. It's my fault, Jake. It's the way I'm made.'

'Couldn't we go off in the country for a while?'

'It wouldn't be any good. I'll go if you like. But I couldn't live quietly in the country. Not with my own true love.'

'I know.'

'Isn't it rotten? There isn't any use my telling you I love you.'

'You know I love you.'

'Let's not talk. Talking's all bilge. I'm going away from you, and then Michael's coming back.'

'Why are you going away?'

'Better for you. Better for me.'

'When are you going?'

'Soon as I can.'

'Where?'

'San Sebastian.'

'Can't we go together?'

'No. That would be a hell of an idea after we'd just talked it out.'

'We never agreed.'

'Oh, you know as well as I do. Don't be obstinate, darling.'

'Oh, sure,' I said. 'I know you're right. I'm just low, and when I'm low I talk like a fool.'

I sat up, leaned over, found my shoes beside the bed and put them on. I stood up.

'Don't look like that, darling.'

'How do you want me to look?'

'Oh, don't be a fool. I'm going away to-morrow.'

'To-morrow?'

'Yes. Didn't I say so? I am.'

'Let's have a drink, then. The count will be back.'

'Yes. He should be back. You know he's extraordinary about buying champagne. It means any amount to him.'

We went into the dining-room. I took up the brandy bottle and poured Brett a drink and one for myself. There was a ring at the bell-pull. I went to the door and there was the count. Behind him was the chauffeur carrying a basket of champagne.

'Where should I have him put it, sir?' asked the count.

'In the kitchen,' Brett said.

'Put it in there, Henry,' the count motioned. 'Now go down and get the ice.' He stood looking after the basket inside the kitchen door. 'I think you'll find that's very good wine,' he said. 'I know we don't get much of a chance to judge good wine in the States now, but I got this from a friend of mine that's in the business.'

'Oh, you always have someone in the trade,' Brett said.

'This fellow raises the grapes. He's got thousands of acres of them.'

'What's his name?' asked Brett. 'Veuve Cliquot?'

'No,' said the count. 'Mumms. He's a baron.'

'Isn't it wonderful,' said Brett. 'We all have titles. Why haven't you a title, Jake?'

'I assure you, sir,' the count put his hand on my arm, 'it never does a man any good. Most of the time it costs you money.'

'Oh, I don't know. It's damned useful sometimes,' Brett said.

'I've never known it to do me any good.'

'You haven't used it properly. I've had hell's own amount of credit on mine.'

'Do sit down, count,' I said. 'Let me take that stick.'

The count was looking at Brett across the table under the gas-light. She was smoking a cigarette and flicking the ashes on the rug. She saw me notice it. 'I say, Jake, I don't want to ruin your rugs. Can't you give a chap an ash-tray?'

I found some ash-trays and spread them around. The chauffeur came up with a bucket full of salted ice. 'Put two bottles in it, Henry,' the count called.

'Anything else, sir?'

'No. Wait down in the car.' He turned to Brett and to me. 'We'll want to ride out to the Bois for dinner?'

'If you like,' Brett said. 'I couldn't eat a thing.'

'I always like a good meal,' said the count.

'Should I bring the wine in, sir?' asked the chauffeur.

'Yes. Bring it in, Henry,' said the count. He took out a heavy pigskin cigar-case and offered it to me. 'Like to try a real American cigar?'

'Thanks,' I said, 'I'll finish the cigarette.'

He cut off the end of his cigar with a gold cutter he wore on one end of his watch-chain.

'I like a cigar to really draw,' said the count. 'Half the cigars you smoke don't draw.'

He lit the cigar, puffed at it, looking across the table at Brett. 'And when you're divorced, Lady Ashley, then you won't have a title.'

'No. What a pity.'

'No,' said the count. 'You don't need a title. You got class all over you.'

'Thanks. Awfully decent of you.'

'I'm not joking you,' the count blew a cloud of smoke. 'You got the most class of anybody I ever seen. You got it. That's all.'

'Nice of you,' said Brett. 'Mummy would be pleased. Couldn't you write it out, and I'll send it in a letter to her.'

'I'd tell her, too,' said the count. 'I'm not joking you. I never joke people. Joke people and you make enemies. That's what I always say.'

'You're right,' Brett said. 'You're terribly right. I always joke people and I haven't a friend in the world. Except Jake here.'

'You don't joke him?'

'That's it.'

'Do you, now?' asked the count. 'Do you joke him?'

Brett looked at me and wrinkled up the corners of her eyes.

'No,' she said. 'I wouldn't joke him.'

'See,' said the count. 'You don't joke him.'

'This is a hell of a dull talk,' Brett said. 'How about some of that champagne?'

The count reached down and twirled the bottles in the shiny bucket. 'It isn't cold, yet. You're always drinking, my dear. Why don't you just talk?'

'I've talked too ruddy much. I've talked myself all out to Jake.'

'I should like to hear you really talk, my dear. When you talk to me you never finish your sentences at all.'

'Leave 'em for you to finish. Let anyone finish them as they like.'

'It is a very interesting system,' the count reached down and gave the bottles a twirl. 'Still I would like to hear you talk some time.'

'Isn't he a fool?' Brett asked.

'Now,' the count brought up a bottle. 'I think this is cool.'

I brought a towel and he wiped the bottle dry and held it up. 'I like to drink champagne from magnums. The wine is better but it would have been too hard to cool.' He held the bottle, looking at it. I put out the glasses.

'I say. You might open it,' Brett suggested.

'Yes, my dear. Now I'll open it.'

It was amazing champagne.

'I say, that is wine,' Brett held up her glass. 'We ought to toast something. "Here's to royalty."'

'This wine is too good for toast-drinking, my dear. You don't want to mix emotions up with a wine like that. You lose the taste.'

Brett's glass was empty.

'You ought to write a book on wines, count,' I said.

'Mr Barnes,' answered the count, 'all I want out of wines is to enjoy them.'

'Let's enjoy a little more of this,' Brett pushed her glass forward. The count poured very carefully. 'There, my dear. Now you enjoy that slowly, and then you can get drunk.'

'Drunk? Drunk?'

'My dear, you are charming when you are drunk.'

'Listen to the man.'

'Mr Barnes,' the count poured my glass full, 'she is the only lady I have ever known who was as charming when she was drunk as when she was sober.'

'You haven't been around much, have you?'

'Yes, my dear. I have been around very much. I have been around a very great deal.'

'Drink your wine,' said Brett. 'We've all been around. I dare say Jake here has seen as much as you have.'

'My dear, I am sure Mr Barnes has seen a lot. Don't think I don't think so, sir. I have seen a lot, too.'

'Of course you have, my dear,' Brett said. 'I was only ragging.'

'I have been in seven wars and four revolutions,' the count said.

'Soldiering?' Brett asked.

'Sometimes, my dear. And I have got arrow wounds. Have you ever seen arrow wounds?'

'Let's have a look at them.'

The count stood up, unbuttoned his vest, and opened his shirt. He pulled up the undershirt on to his chest and stood, his chest black, and big stomach muscles bulging under the light.

'You see them?'

Below the line where his ribs stopped were two raised white welts. 'See on the back where they came out.' Above the small of the back were the same two scars, raised as thick as a finger.

'I say. Those are something.'

'Clean through.'

The count was tucking in his shirt.

'Where did you get those?' I asked.

'In Abyssinia. When I was twenty-one years old.'

'What were you doing?' asked Brett. 'Were you in the army?'

'I was on a business trip, my dear.'

'I told you he was one of us. Didn't I?' Brett turned to me. 'I love you, count. You're a darling.'

'You make me very happy, my dear. But it isn't true.'

'Don't be an ass.'

'You see, Mr Barnes, it is because I have lived very much that now I can enjoy everything so well. Don't you find it like that?'

'Yes. Absolutely.'

'I know,' said the count. 'That is the secret. You must get to know the values.'

'Doesn't anything ever happen to your values?' Brett asked.

'No. Not any more.'

'Never fall in love?'

'Always,' said the count. 'I'm always in love.'

'What does that do to your values?'

'That, too, has got a place in my values.'

'You haven't any values. You're dead, that's all.'

'No, my dear. You're not right. I'm not dead at all.'

We drank three bottles of the champagne and the count left the basket in my kitchen. We dined at a restaurant in the Bois. It was a good dinner. Food had an excellent place in the count's values. So did wine. The count was in fine form during the meal. So was Brett. It was a good party.

'Where would you like to go?' asked the count after dinner. We were the only people left in the restaurant. The two waiters were standing over against the door. They wanted to go home.

'We might go up on the hill,' Brett said. 'Haven't we had a splendid party?'

The count was beaming. He was very happy.

'You are very nice people,' he said. He was smoking a cigar again. 'Why don't you get married, you two?'

'We want to lead our own lives,' I said.

'We have our careers,' Brett said. 'Come on. Let's get out of this.'

'Have another brandy,' the count said.

'Get it on the hill.'

'No. Have it here where it is quiet.'

'You and your quiet,' said Brett. 'What is it men feel about quiet?'

'We like it,' said the count. 'Like you like noise, my dear.'

'All right,' said Brett. 'Let's have one.'

'Sommelier!' the count called.

'Yes, sir.'

'What is the oldest brandy you have?'

'Eighteen eleven, sir.'

'Bring us a bottle.'

'I say. Don't be ostentatious. Call him off, Jake.'

'Listen, my dear. I get more value for my money in old brandy than in any other antiquities.'

'Got many antiquities?'

'I got a houseful.'

Finally we went up to Montmartre. Inside Zelli's it was crowded, smoky and noisy. The music hit you as you went in. Brett and I danced. It was so crowded we could barely move, The nigger drummer waved at Brett. We were caught in the jam, dancing in one place in front of him.

'Hah're you?'

'Great.'

'That's good.'

He was all teeth and lips.

'He's a great friend of mine,' Brett said. 'Damn good drummer.'

The music stopped and we started toward the table where the count sat. Then the music started again and we danced. I looked at the count. He was sitting at the table smoking a cigar. The music stopped again.

'Let's go over.'

Brett started toward the table. The music started and again we danced, tight in the crowd.

'You are a rotten dancer, Jake. Michael's the best dancer I know.'

'He's splendid.'

'He's got his points.'

'I like him,' I said. 'I'm damned fond of him.'

'I'm going to marry him,' Brett said. 'Funny. I haven't thought about him for a week.'

'Don't you write him?'

'Not I. Never write letters.'

'I'll bet he writes to you.'

'Rather. Damned good letters, too.'

'When are you going to get married?'

'How do I know? As soon as we can get the divorce. Michael's trying to get his mother to put up for it.'

'Could I help you?'

'Don't be an ass. Michael's people have loads of money.'

The music stopped. We walked over to the table. The count stood up.

'Very nice,' he said. 'You looked very, very nice.'

'Don't you dance, count?' I asked.

'No. I'm too old.'

'Oh, come off it,' Brett said.

'My dear, I would do it if I would enjoy it. I enjoy to watch you dance.'

'Splendid,' Brett said. 'I'll dance again for you some time. I say. What about your little friend, Zizi?'

'Let me tell you. I support that boy, but I don't want to have him around.'

'He is rather hard.'

'You know I think that boy's got a future. But personally I don't want him around.'

'Jake's rather the same way.'

'He gives me the willys.'

'Well,' the count shrugged his shoulders. 'About his future you can't ever tell. Anyhow, his father was a great friend of my father.'

'Come on. Let's dance,' Brett said.

We danced. It was crowded and close.

'Oh, darling,' Brett said. 'I'm so miserable.'

I had that feeling of going through something that had all happened before. 'You were happy a minute ago.'

The drummer shouted: 'You can't two time—'

'It's all gone.'

'What's the matter?'

'I don't know. I just feel terribly.'

' . . . . ' the drummer chanted. Then turned to his sticks.

'Want to go?'

I had the feeling as in a nightmare of it all being something repeated, something I had been through and that now I must go through again.

' . . . . ' the drummer sang softly.

'Let's go,' said Brett. 'You don't mind.'

' . . . . ' the drummer shouted and grinned at Brett.

'All right,' I said. We got out from the crowd. Brett went to the dressing-room.

'Brett wants to go,' I said to the count. He nodded. 'Does she? That's fine. You take the car. I'm going to stay here for a while, Mr Barnes.'

We shook hands.

'It was a wonderful time,' I said. 'I wish you would let me get this.' I took a note out of my pocket.

'Mr Barnes, don't be ridiculous,' the count said.

Brett came over with her wrap on. She kissed the count and put her hand on his shoulder to keep him from standing up. As we went out of the door I looked back and there were three girls at his table. We got into the big car. Brett gave the chauffeur the address of her hotel.

'No, don't come up,' she said at the hotel. She had rung and the door was unlatched.

'Really?'

'No. Please.'

'Good-night, Brett,' I said. 'I'm sorry you feel rotten.'

'Good-night, Jake. Good-night, darling. I won't see you again.' We kissed standing at the door. She pushed me away. We kissed again. 'Oh, don't!' Brett said.

She turned quickly and went into the hotel. The chauffeur drove me around to my flat. I gave him twenty francs and he touched his cap and said: 'Good-night, sir,' and drove off. I rang the bell. The door opened and I went upstairs and went to bed.

PART II

8

I did not see Brett again until she came back from San Sebastian. One card came from her there. It had a picture of the Concha, and said: 'Darling. Very quiet and healthy. Love to all the chaps. BRETT.

Nor did I see Robert Cohn again. I heard Frances had left for England and I had a note from Cohn saying he was going out in the country for a couple of weeks, he did not know where, but that he wanted to hold me to the fishing-trip in Spain we had talked about last winter. I could reach him always, he wrote, through his bankers.

Brett was gone, I was not bothered by Cohn's troubles, I rather enjoyed not having to play tennis, there was plenty of work to do, I went often to the races, dined with friends, and put in some extra time at the office getting things ahead so I could leave it in charge of my secretary when Bill Gorton and I should shove off to Spain the end of June. Bill Gorton arrived, put up a couple of days at the flat and went off to Vienna. He was very cheerful and said the States were wonderful. New York was wonderful. There had been a grand theatrical season and a whole crop of great young light heavyweights. Any one of them was a good prospect to grow up, put on weight and trim Dempsey. Bill was very happy. He had made a lot of money on his last book, and was going to make a lot more. We had a good time while he was in Paris, and then he went off to Vienna. He was coming back in three weeks and we would leave for Spain to get in some fishing and go to the fiesta at Pamplona. He wrote that Vienna was wonderful. Then a card from Budapest; 'Jake, Budapest is wonderful.' Then I got a wire: 'Back on Monday.'

Monday evening he turned up at the flat. I heard his taxi stop and went to the window and called to him; he waved and started upstairs carrying his bags. I met him on the stairs and took one of the bags.

'Well,' I said, 'I hear you had a wonderful trip.'

'Wonderful,' he said. 'Budapest is absolutely wonderful.'

'How about Vienna?'

'Not so good, Jake. Not so good. It seemed better than it was.'

'How do you mean?' I was getting glasses and a syphon.

'Tight, Jake. It was tight.'

'That's strange. Better have a drink.'

Bill rubbed his forehead. 'Remarkable thing,' he said. 'Don't know how it happened. Suddenly it happened.'

'Last long?'

'Four days, Jake. Lasted just four days.'

'Where did you go?'

'Don't remember. Wrote you a post-card. Remember that perfectly.'

'Do anything else?'

'Not so sure. Possible.'

'Go on. Tell me about it.'

'Can't remember. Tell you anything I could remember.'

'Go on. Take that drink and remember.'

'Might remember a little,' Bill said. 'Remember something about a prize-fight. Enormous Vienna prize-fight. Had a nigger in it. Remember the nigger perfectly.'

'Go on.'

'Wonderful nigger. Looked like Tiger Flowers, only four times as big. All of a sudden everybody started to throw things. Not me. Nigger'd just knocked local boy down. Nigger put up his glove. Wanted to make a speech. Awful noble-looking nigger. Started to make a speech. Then local white boy hit him. Then he knocked white boy cold. Then everybody commenced to throw chairs. Nigger went home with us in our car. Couldn't get his clothes. Wore my coat. Remember the whole thing now. Big sporting evening.'

'What happened?'

'Loaned the nigger some clothes and went around with him to try and get his money. Claimed nigger owed them money on account of wrecking hall. Wonder who translated? Was it me?'

'Probably it wasn't you.'

'You're right. Wasn't me at all. Was another fellow. Think we called him the local Harvard man. Remember him now. Studying music.'

'How'd you come out?'

'Not so good, Jake. Injustice everywhere. Promoter claimed nigger promised let local boy stay. Claimed nigger violated contract. Can't knock out Vienna boy in Vienna. "My God, Mister Gorton," said nigger, "I didn't do anything in there for forty minutes but try and let him stay. That white boy musta ruptured himself swinging at me. I never did hit him."'

'Did you get any money?'

'No money, Jake. All we could get was nigger's clothes. Somebody took his watch, too. Splendid nigger. Big mistake to have come to Vienna. Not so good, Jake. Not so good.'

'What became of the nigger?'

'Went back to Cologne. Lives there. Married. Got a family. Going to write me a letter and send me the money I loaned him. Wonderful nigger. Hope I gave him the right address.'

'You probably did.'

'Well, anyway, let's eat,' said Bill. 'Unless you want me to tell you some more travel stories.'

'Go on.'

'Let's eat.'

We went downstairs and out on to the Boulevard St Michel in the warm June evening.

'Where will we go?'

'Want to eat on the island?'

'Sure.'

We walked down the Boulevard. At the juncture of the Rue Denfert-Rochereau with the Boulevard is a statue of two men in flowing robes.

'I know who they are.' Bill eyed the monument. 'Gentlemen who invented pharmacy. Don't try and fool me on Paris.'

We went on.

'Here's a taxidermist's,' Bill said. 'Want to buy anything? Nice stuffed dog?'

'Come on,' I said. 'You're pie-eyed.'

'Pretty nice stuffed dogs,' Bill said, 'Certainly brighten up your flat.'

'Come on.'

'Just one stuffed dog. I can take 'em or leave 'em alone. But listen, Jake. Just one stuffed dog.'

'Come on.'

'Mean everything in the world to you after you bought it. Simple exchange of values. You give them money. They give you a stuffed dog.'

'We'll get one on the way back.'

'All right. Have it your own way. Road to hell paved with unbought stuffed dogs. Not my fault.'

We went on.

'How'd you feel that way about dogs so sudden?'

'Always felt that way about dogs. Always been a great lover of stuffed animals.'

We stopped and had a drink.

'Certainly like to drink,' Bill said. 'You ought to try it sometimes, Jake.'

'You're about a hundred and forty-four ahead of me.'

'Ought not to daunt you. Never be daunted. Secret of my success. Never been daunted. Never been daunted in public.'

'Where were you drinking?'

'Stopped at the Crillon. George made me a couple of Jack Roses. George's a great man. Know the secret of his success? Never been daunted.'

'You'll be daunted after about three more pernods.'

'Not in public. If I begin to feel daunted I'll go off by myself. I'm like a cat that way.'

'When did you see Harvey Stone?'

'At the Crillon. Harvey was just a little daunted. Hadn't eaten for three days. Doesn't eat any more. Just goes off like a cat. Pretty sad.'

'He's all right.'

'Splendid. Wish he wouldn't keep going off like a cat, though. Makes me nervous.'

'What'll we do to-night?'

'Doesn't make any difference. Only let's not get daunted. Suppose they got any hard-boiled eggs here? If they had hard-boiled eggs here we wouldn't have to go all the way down to the island to eat.'

'Nix,' I said. 'We're going to have a regular meal.'

'Just a suggestion,' said Bill. 'Want to start now?'

'Come on.'

We started on again down the Boulevard. A horse-cab passed us. Bill looked at it.

'See that cab-horse? Going to have that horse-cab stuffed for you for Christmas. Going to give all my friends stuffed animals. I'm a nature-writer.'

A taxi passed, someone in it waved, then banged for the driver to stop. The taxi backed up to the curb. In it was Brett.

'Beautiful lady,' said Bill. 'Going to kidnap us?'

'Hullo!' Brett said. 'Hullo!'

'This is Bill Gorton. Lady Ashley.'

Brett smiled at Bill. 'I say I'm just back. Haven't bathed even. Michael comes in to-night.'

'Good. Come on and eat with us, and we'll all go to meet him.'

'Must clean myself.'

'Oh, rot! Come on.'

'Must bathe. He doesn't get in till nine.'

'Come and have a drink, then, before you bathe.'

'Might do that. Now you're not talking rot.'

We got in the taxi. The driver looked around.

'Stop at the nearest bistro,' I said.

'We might as well go to the Closerie,' Brett said. 'I can't drink these rotten brandies.'

'Closerie des Lilas.'

Brett turned to Bill.

'Have you been in this pestilential city long?'

'Just got in to-day from Budapest.'

'How was Budapest?'

'Wonderful. Budapest was wonderful.'

'Ask him about Vienna.'

'Vienna,' said Bill, 'is a strange city.'

'Very much like Paris,' Brett smiled at him, wrinkling the corner of her eyes.

'Exactly,' Bill said, 'Very much like Paris at this moment.'

'You *have* a good start.'

Sitting on the terraces of the Lilas, Brett ordered a whiskey-and-soda, I took one, too, and Bill took another pernod.

'How are you, Jake?'

'Great,' I said. 'I've had a good time.'

Brett looked at me. 'I was a fool to go away,' she said. 'One's an ass to leave Paris.'

'Did you have a good time?'

'Oh, all right. Interesting. Not frightfully amusing.'

'See anybody?'

'No, hardly anybody. I never went out.'

'Didn't you swim?'

'No. Didn't do a thing.'

'Sounds like Vienna,' Bill said.

Brett wrinkled up the corners of her eyes at him.

'So that's the way it was in Vienna.'

'It was like everything in Vienna.'

Brett smiled at him again.

'You've a nice friend, Jake.'

'He's all right,' I said. 'He's a taxidermist.'

'That was in another country,' Bill said. 'And besides all the animals were dead.'

'One more,' Brett said, 'and I must run. Do send the waiter for a taxi.'

'There's a line of them. Right out in front.'

'Good.'

We had the drink and put Brett into her taxi.

'Mind you're at the Select around ten. Make him come. Michael will be there.'

'We'll be there,' Bill said, The taxi started and Brett waved.

'Quite a girl,' Bill said. 'She's damned nice. Who's Michael?'

'The man she's going to marry.'

'Well, well,' Bill said. 'That's always just the stage I meet anybody. What'll I send them? Think they'd like a couple of stuffed race-horses?'

'We better eat.'

'Is she really Lady Something-or-other?' Bill asked in the taxi on our way to the Ile Saint Louis.

'Oh, yes. In the stud-book and everything.'

'Well, well.'

We ate dinner at Madame Lecomte's restaurant on the far side of the island. It was crowded with Americans and we had to stand up and wait for a place. Someone had put it in the American Women's Club list as a quaint restaurant on the Paris *quais* as yet untouched by Americans, so we had to wait forty-five minutes for a table. Bill had eaten at the restaurant in 1918, and right after the armistice, and Madame Lecomte made a great fuss over seeing him.

'Doesn't get us a table, though,' Bill said. 'Grand woman, though.'

We had a good meal, a roast chicken, new green beans, mashed potatoes, a salad, and some apple-pie and cheese.

'You've got the world here all right,' Bill said to Madame Lecomte. She raised her hand. 'Oh, my God!'

'You'll be rich.'

'I hope so.'

After the coffee and a *fine* we got the bill, chalked up the same as ever on a slate, that was doubtless one of the 'quaint' features, paid it, shook hands, and went out.

'You never come here any more, Monsieur Barnes,' Madame Lecomte said.

'Too many compatriots.'

'Come at lunch time. It's not crowded then.'

'Good. 'I'll be down soon.'

We walked along under the trees that grew out over the river on the Quai d'Orléans side of the island. Across the river were the broken walls of old houses that were being torn down.

'They're going to cut a street through.'

'They would,' Bill said.

We walked on and circled the island. The river was dark and a *bâteau mouche* went by, all bright with lights, going fast and quiet up and out of sight under the bridge. Down the river was Notre Dame squatting against the night sky. We crossed to the left bank of the Seine by the wooden foot-bridge from the Quai de Bethune, and stopped on the bridge and looked down the river at Notre Dame. Standing on the bridge the island looked dark, the houses were high against the sky, and the trees were shadows.

'It's pretty grand,' Bill said. 'God, I love to get back.'

We leaned on the wooden rail of the bridge and looked up the river to the lights of the big bridges. Below, the water was smooth and black. It made no sound against the piles of the bridge. A man and a girl passed us. They were walking with their arms around each other.

We crossed the bridge and walked up the Rue du Cardinal Lemoine. It was steep walking, and we went all the way up to the Place Contrescarpe. The arc-light shone through the leaves of the trees in the square, and underneath the trees was an S bus ready to start. Music came out of the door of the Negre Joyeux. Through the window of the Café aux Amateurs I saw the long zinc bar. Outside on the terrace working people were drinking. In the open kitchen of the Amateurs a girl was cooking potato-chips in oil. There was an iron pot of stew. The girl ladled some on to a plate for an old man who stood holding a bottle of red wine in one hand.

'Want to have a drink?'

'No,' said Bill. 'I don't need it.'

We turned to the right off the Place Contrescarpe, walking along smooth narrow streets with high old houses on both sides. Some of the houses jutted out toward the street. Others were cut back. We came on to the Rue du Pot de Fer and followed it along until it brought us to the rigid north and south of the Rue Saint Jacques and then walked south, past Val de Grace, set back behind the courtyard and the iron fence, to the Boulevard du Port Royal.

'What do you want to do?' I asked. 'Go up to the café and see Brett and Mike?'

'Why not?'

We walked along Port Royal until it became Montparnasse, and then on past the Lilas, Lavinge's, and all the little cafés, Damoy's, crossed the street to the Rotonde, past its lights and tables to the Select.

Michael came toward us from the tables. He was tanned and healthy-looking.

'Hel-lo, Jake,' he said, 'Hel-lo! Hel-lo! How are you, old lad?'

'You look very fit, Mike.'

'Oh, I am. I'm frightfully fit. I've done nothing but walk. Walk all day long. One drink a day with my mother at tea.'

Bill had gone into the bar. He was standing talking with Brett, who was sitting on a high stool, her legs crossed. She had no stockings on.

'It's good to see you, Jake,' Michael said. 'I'm a little tight, you know. Amazing, isn't it? Did you see my nose?'

There was a patch of dried blood on the bridge of his nose.

'An old lady's bags did that,' Mike said. 'I reached up to help her with them and they fell on me.'

Brett gestured at him from the bar with her cigarette-holder and wrinkled the corners of her eyes.

'An old lady,' said Mike. 'Her bags *fell* on me.'

'Let's go in and see Brett. I say, she is a piece. You *are* a lovely lady, Brett. Where did you get that hat?'

'Chap bought it for me. Don't you like it?'

'It's a dreadful hat. Do get a good hat.'

'Oh, we've so much money now,' Brett said. 'I say, haven't you met Bill yet? You *are* a lovely host, Jake.'

She turned to Mike. 'This is Bill Gorton. This drunkard is Mike Campbell. Mr Campbell is an undischarged bankrupt.'

'Aren't I, though? You know I met my ex-partner yesterday in London. Chap who did me in.'

'What did he say?'

'Bought me a drink. I thought I might as well take it. I say, Brett, you *are* a lovely piece. Don't you think she's beautiful?'

'Beautiful. With this nose?'

'It's a lovely nose. Go on, point it at me. Isn't she a lovely piece?'

'Couldn't we have kept the man in Scotland?'

'I say, Brett, let's turn in early.'

'Don't be indecent, Michael. Remember there are ladies at this bar.'

'Isn't she a lovely piece? Don't you think so, Jake?'

'There's a fight to-night,' Bill said. 'Like to go?'

'Fight,' said Mike. 'Who's fighting?'

'Ledoux and somebody.'

'He's very good, Ledoux,' Mike said. 'I'd like to see it rather'–he was making an effort to pull himself together–'but I can't go. I have a date with this thing here. I say, Brett, do get a new hat.'

Brett pulled the felt hat down far over one eye and smiled out from under it. 'You two run along to the fight. I'll have to be taking Mr Campbell home directly.'

'I'm not tight,' Mike said. 'Perhaps just a little. I say, Brett, you are a lovely piece.'

'Go on to the fight,' Brett said. 'Mr Campbell's getting difficult. What are these outbursts of affection, Michael?'

'I say, you are a lovely piece.'

We said good-night. 'I'm sorry I can't go,' Mike said. Brett laughed. I looked back from the door. Mike had one hand on the bar and was leaning toward Brett, talking. Brett was looking at him quite coolly, but the corners of her eyes were smiling.

Outside on the pavement I said: 'Do you want to go to the fight?'

'Sure,' said Bill. 'If we don't have to walk.'

'Mike was pretty excited about his girl friend,' I said in the taxi.

'Well,' said Bill. 'You can't blame him such a hell of a lot.'

9

The Ledoux-Kid Francis fight was the night of the 20th of June. It was a good fight. The morning after the fight I had a letter from Robert Cohn, written from Hendaye. He was having a very quiet time, he said, bathing, playing some golf and much bridge. Hendaye had a splendid beach, but he was anxious to start on the fishing-trip. When would I be down? If I would buy him a double-tapered line he would pay me when I came down.

That same morning I wrote to Cohn from the office that Bill and I would leave Paris on the 25th unless I wired him otherwise, and would meet him at Bayonne, where we could get a bus over the mountains to Pamplona. The same evening about seven o'clock I stopped in at the Select to see Michael and Brett. They were not there, and I went over to the Dingo. They were inside sitting at the bar.

'Hello, darling.' Brett put out her hand.

'Hello, Jake,' Mike said. 'I understand I was tight last night.'

'Weren't you, though,' Brett said. 'Disgraceful business.'

'Look,' said Mike, 'when do you go down to Spain? Would you mind if we came down with you?'

'It would be grand.'

'You wouldn't mind, really? I've been at Pamplona, you know. Brett's mad to go. You're sure we wouldn't just be a bloody nuisance?'

'Don't talk like a fool.'

'I'm a little tight, you know. I wouldn't ask you like this if I weren't. You're sure you don't mind?'

'Oh, shut up, Michael,' Brett said. 'How can the man say he'd mind now? I'll ask him later.'

'But you don't mind, do you?'

'Don't ask that again unless you want to make me sore. Bill and I go down on the morning of the 25th.'

'By the way, where is Bill?' Brett asked.

'He's out at Chantilly dining with some people.'

'He's a good chap.'

'Splendid chap,' said Mike. 'He is, you know.'

'You don't remember him,' Brett said.

'I do. Remember him perfectly. Look, Jake, we'll come down the night of the 25th. Brett can't get up in the morning.'

'Indeed not!'

'If our money comes and you're sure that you don't mind.'

'It will come, all right. I'll see to that.'

'Tell me what tackle to send for.'

'Get two or three rods with reels, and lines, and some flies.'

'I won't fish,' Brett put in.

'Get two rods, then, and Bill won't have to buy one.'

'Right,' said Mike. 'I'll send a wire to the keeper.'

'Won't it be splendid,' Brett said. 'Spain! We *will* have fun.'

'The 25th. When is that?'

'Saturday.'

'We *will* have to get ready.'

'I say,' said Mike, 'I'm going to the barber's.'

'I must bathe,' said Brett. 'Walk up to the hotel with me, Jake. Be a good chap.'

'We *have* got the loveliest hotel,' Mike said. 'I think it's a brothel!'

'We left our bags here at the Dingo when we got in, and they asked us at this hotel if we wanted a room for the afternoon only. Seemed frightfully pleased we were going to stay all night.'

'I believe it's a brothel,' Mike said. 'And I should know.'

'Oh, shut up and go and get your hair cut.'

Mike went out, Brett and I sat on at the bar.

'Have another?'

'Might.'

'I needed that,' Brett said.

We walked up the Rue Delambre.

'I haven't seen you since I've been back,' Brett said.

'No.'

'How *are* you, Jake?'

'Fine.'

Brett looked at me. 'I say,' she said, 'is Robert Cohn going on this trip?'

'Yes. Why?'

'Don't you think it will be a bit rough on him?'

'Why should it?'

'Who did you think I went down to San Sebastian with?'

'Congratulations,' I said.

We walked along.

'What did you say that for?'

'I don't know. What would you like me to say?'

We walked along and turned a corner.

'He behaved rather well, too. He gets a little dull.'

'Does he?'

'I rather thought it would be good for him.'

'You might take up social service.'

'Don't be nasty.'

'I won't.'

'Didn't you really know?'

'No,' I said. 'I guess I didn't think about it.'

'Do you think it will be too rough on him?'

'That's up to him,' I said. 'Tell him you're coming. He can always not come.'

'I'll write and give him a chance to pull out of it.'

I did not see Brett again until the night of the 24th of June.

'Did you hear from Cohn?'

'Rather. He's keen about it.'

'My God!'

'I thought it was rather odd myself.'

'Says he can't wait to see me.'

'Does he think you're coming alone?'

'No. I told him we were all coming down together. Michael and all.'

'He's wonderful.'

'Isn't he?'

They expected their money the next day. We arranged to meet at Pamplona. They would go directly to San Sebastian and take the train from there. We would all meet at the Montoya in Pamplona. If they did not turn up on Monday at the latest we would go on ahead up to Burguete in the mountains, to start fishing. There was a bus to Burguete. I wrote out an itinerary so they could follow us.

Bill and I took the morning train from the Gare d'Orsay. It was a lovely day, not too hot, and the country was beautiful from the start. We went back into the diner and had breakfast. Leaving the dining-car I asked the conductor for tickets for the first service.

'Nothing until the fifth.'

'What's this?'

There were never more than two servings of lunch on that train, and always plenty of plates for both of them.

'They're all reserved,' the dining-car conductor said. 'There will be a fifth service at three-thirty.'

'This is serious,' I said to Bill.

'Give him ten francs.'

'Here,' I said. 'We want to eat in the first service.'

The conductor put the ten francs in his pocket.

'Thank you,' he said. 'I would advise you gentlemen to get some sandwiches. All the places for the first four services were reserved at the office of the company.'

'You'll go a long way, brother,' Bill said to him in English. 'I suppose if I'd given you five francs you would have advised us to jump off the train.'

'*Comment?*'

'Go to hell!' said Bill. 'Get the sandwiches made and a bottle of wine. You tell him, Jake.'

'And send it up to the next car.' I described where we were.

In our compartment were a man and his wife and their young son.

'I suppose you're Americans, aren't you?' the man asked. 'Having a good trip?'

'Wonderful,' said Bill.

'That's what you want to do. Travel while you're young. Mother and I always wanted to get over, but we had to wait a while.'

'You could have come over ten years ago, if you'd wanted to,' the wife said. 'What you always said was: "See America first!" I will say we've seen a good deal, take it one way and another.'

'Say, there's plenty of Americans on this train,' the husband said. 'They've got seven cars of them from Dayton, Ohio. They've been on a pilgrimage to Rome, and now they're going down to Biarritz and Lourdes.'

'So that's what they are. Pilgrims. Goddam Puritans,' Bill said.

'What part of the States you boys from?'

'Kansas City,' I said. 'He's from Chicago.'

'You both going to Biarritz?'

'No. We're going fishing in Spain.'

'Well, I never cared for it, myself. There's plenty that do out where I come from, though. We got some of the best fishing in the State of Montana. I've been out with the boys, but I never cared for it any.'

'Mighty little fishing you did on them trips,' his wife said.

He winked at us.

'You know how the ladies are. If there's a jug goes along, or a case of beer, they think it's hell and damnation.'

'That's the way men are,' his wife said to us. She smoothed her comfortable lap. 'I voted against prohibition to please him, and because I like a little beer in the house, and then he talks that way. It's a wonder they ever find anyone to marry them.'

'Say,' said Bill, 'do you know that gang of Pilgrim Fathers have cornered the dining-car until half-past three this afternoon?'

'How do you mean? They can't do a thing like that.'

'You try and get seats.'

'Well, mother, it looks as though we better go back and get another breakfast.'

She stood up and straightened her dress.

'Will you boys keep an eye on our things? Come on, Hubert.'

They all three went up to the waggon restaurant. A little while after they were gone a steward went through announcing the first service, and pilgrims, with their priests, commenced filing down the corridor. Our friend and his family did not come back. A waiter passed in the corridor with our sandwiches and the bottle of Chablis, and we called him in.

'You're going to work to-day,' I said.

He nodded his head. 'They start now, at ten-thirty.'

'When do we eat?'

'Huh! When do I eat?'

He left two glasses for the bottle, and we paid him for the sandwiches and tipped him.

'I'll get the plates,' he said, 'or bring them with you.'

We ate the sandwiches and drank the Chablis and watched the country out of the window. The grain was just beginning to ripen and the fields were full of poppies. The pasture land was green, and there were fine trees, and sometimes big rivers and châteaux off in the trees.

At Tours we got off and bought another bottle of wine, and when we got back in the compartment the gentleman from Montana and his wife and his son, Hubert, were sitting comfortably.

'Is there good swimming in Biarritz?' asked Hubert.

'That boy's just crazy till he can get in the water,' his mother said. 'It's pretty hard on youngsters travelling.'

'There's good swimming,' I said. 'But it's dangerous when it's rough.'

'Did you get a meal?' Bill asked.

'We sure did. We set right there when they started to come in, and they must have just thought we were in the party. One of the waiters said something to us in French, and then they just sent three of them back.'

'They thought we were snappers, all right,' the man said. 'It certainly shows you the powers of the Catholic Church. It's a pity you boys ain't Catholics. You could get a meal then, all right.'

'I am,' I said. 'That's what makes me so sore.'

Finally, at a quarter past four we had lunch. Bill had been rather difficult at the last. He button-holed a priest who was coming back with one of the returning streams of pilgrims.

'When do us Protestants get a chance to eat, father?'

'I don't know anything about it. Haven't you got tickets?'

'It's enough to make a man join the Klan,' Bill said. The priest looked back at him.

Inside the dining-car the waiters served the fifth successive table d'hôte meal. The waiter who served us was soaked through. His white jacket was purple under the arms.

'He must drink a lot of wine.'

'Or wear purple undershirts.'

'Let's ask him.'

'No. He's too tired.'

The train stopped for half an hour at Bordeaux and we went out through the station for a little walk. There was not time to get in to the town. Afterward we passed through the Landes and watched the sun set. There were wide fire-gaps cut through the pines, and you could look up them like avenues and see wooded hills way off. About seven-thirty we had dinner and watched the country through the open window in the diner. It was all sandy, pine country full of heather. There were little clearings with houses in them, and once in a while we passed a sawmill. It got dark and we could feel the country hot and sandy and dark outside of the window, and about nine o'clock we got into Bayonne. The man and his wife and Hubert all shook hands with us. They were going on to La Negresse to change for Biarritz.

'Well, I hope you have lots of luck,' he said.

'Be careful about those bull-fights.'

'Maybe we'll see you at Biarritz,' Hubert said.

We got off with our bags and rod-cases and passed through the dark station and out to the lights and the line of cabs and hotel buses. There, standing with the hotel runners, was Robert Cohn. He did not see us at first. Then he started forward.

'Hello, Jake. Have a good trip?'

'Fine,' I said. 'This is Bill Gorton.'

'How are you?'

'Come on,' said Robert. 'I've got a cab.' He was a little near-sighted. I had never noticed it before. He was looking at Bill, trying to make him out. He was shy, too.

'We'll go up to my hotel. It's all right. It's quite nice.'

We got into the cab, and the cabman put the bags up on the seat beside him and climbed up and cracked his whip, and we drove over the dark bridge and into the town.

'I'm awfully glad to meet you,' Robert said to Bill. 'I've heard so much about you from Jake, and I've read your books. Did you get my line, Jake?'

The cab stopped in front of the hotel and we all got out and went in. It was a nice hotel, and the people at the desk were very cheerful, and we each had a good small room.

10

In the morning it was bright, and they were sprinkling the streets of the town, and we all had breakfast in a café. Bayonne is a nice town. It is like a very clean Spanish town and it is on a big river. Already, so early in the morning, it was very hot on the bridge across the river. We walked out on the bridge and then took a walk through the town.

I was not at all sure Mike's rods would come from Scotland in time, so we hunted a tackle store and finally bought a rod for Bill upstairs over a dry-goods store. The man who sold the tackle was out, and we had to wait for him to come back. Finally he came in, and we bought a pretty good rod cheap, and two landing-nets.

We went into the street again and took a look at the cathedral. Cohn made some remark about it being a very good example of something or other, I forget what. It seemed like a nice cathedral, nice and dim, like Spanish churches. Then we went up past the old fort and out to the local Syndicat d'Initiative office, where the bus was supposed to start from. There they told us the bus service did not start until the 1st of July. We found out at the tourist office what we ought to pay for a motor-car to Pamplona and hired one at a big garage just around the corner from the Municipal Theatre for four hundred francs. The car was to pick us up at the hotel in forty minutes, and we stopped at the café on the square where we had eaten breakfast, and had a beer. It was hot, but the town had a cool, fresh, early-morning smell and it was pleasant sitting in the café. A breeze started to blow, and you could feel that the air came from the sea. There were pigeons out in the square, and the houses were a yellow, sun-baked colour, and I did not want to leave the café. But we had to go to the hotel to get our bags packed and pay the bill. We paid for the beers, we matched, and I think Cohn paid, and went up to the hotel. It was only sixteen francs apiece for Bill and me, with ten per cent added for the service, and we had the bags sent down and waited for Robert Cohn. While we were waiting I saw a cockroach on the parquet floor that must have been at least three inches long. I pointed him out to Bill and then put my shoe on him. We agreed he must have just come in from the garden. It was really an awfully clean hotel.

Cohn came down, finally, and we all went out to the car. It was a big, closed car, with a driver in a white duster with blue collar and cuffs, and we had him put the back of the car down. He piled in the bags and we started off up the street and out of the town. We passed some lovely gardens and had a good look back at the town, and then we were out in the country, green and rolling, and the road climbing all the time. We passed lots of Basques with oxen, or cattle, hauling carts along the road, and nice farmhouses, low roofs, and all white-plastered. In the Basque country the land all looks very rich and green and the houses and villages look well-off and clean. Every village had a pelota court and on some of them kids were playing in the hot sun. There were signs on the walls of the churches saying it was forbidden to play pelota against them, and the houses in the villages had red tiled roofs, and then the road turned off and commenced to climb and we were going way up close along a hillside, with a valley below and hills stretched off back toward the sea. You couldn't see the sea. It was too far away. You could see only hills and more hills, and you knew where the sea was.

We crossed the Spanish frontier. There was a little stream and a bridge, and Spanish carabineers, with patent-leather Bonaparte hats, and short guns on their backs, on one side, and on the other fat Frenchmen in kepis and moustaches. They only opened one bag and took the passports in and looked at them. There was a general store and inn on each side of the line. The chauffeur had to go in and fill out some papers about the car and we got out and went over to the stream to see if there were any trout. Bill tried to talk some Spanish to one of the carabineers, but it did not go very well. Robert Cohn asked, pointing with his finger, if there were any trout in the stream, and the carabineer said yes, but not many.

I asked him if he ever fished, and he said no, that he didn't care for it.

Just then an old man with long sunburned hair and beard, and clothes that looked as though they were made of gunny-sacking, came striding up to the bridge. He was carrying a long staff, and he had a kid slung on his back, tied by the four legs, the head hanging down.

The carabineer waved him back with his sword. The man turned without saying anything, and started back up the white road into Spain.

'What's the matter with the old one?' I asked.

'He hasn't got any passport.'

I offered the guard a cigarette. He took it and thanked me.

'What will he do?' I asked.

The guard spat in the dust.

'Oh, he'll just wade across the stream.'

'Do you have much smuggling?'

'Oh,' he said, 'they go through.'

The chauffeur came out, folding up the papers and putting them in the inside pocket of his coat. We all got in the car and it started up the white dusty road into Spain. For a while the country was much as it had been; then, climbing all the time, we crossed the top of a col, the road winding back and forth on itself, and then it was really Spain. There were long brown mountains and a few pines and far-off forests of beech-trees on some of the mountain-sides. The road went along the summit of the col and then dropped down, and the driver had to honk, and slow up, and turn out to avoid running into two donkeys that were sleeping in the road. We came down out of the mountains and through an oak forest. Down below there were grassy plains and clear streams, and then we crossed a stream and went through a gloomy little village, and started to climb again. We climbed up and up and crossed another high col and turned along it, and the road ran down to the right, and we saw a whole new range of mountains off to the south, all brown and baked-looking and furrowed in strange shapes.

After a while we came out of the mountains, and there were trees along both sides of the road, and a stream and ripe fields of grain, and the road went on, very white and straight ahead, and then lifted to a little rise, and off on the left was a hill with an old castle, with buildings close around it and a field of grain going right up to the walls and shifting in the wind. I was up in front with the driver and I turned around. Robert Cohn was asleep, but Bill looked and nodded his head. Then we crossed a wide plain, and there was a big river off on the right shining in the sun from between the line of trees, and away off you could see the plateau of Pamplona rising out of the plain, and the walls of the city, and the great brown cathedral, and the broken skyline of the other churches. In back of the plateau were the mountains, and every way you looked there were other mountains and ahead the road stretched out white across the plain going toward Pamplona.

We came into the town on the other side of the plateau, the road slanting up steeply and dustily with shade-trees on both sides, and then levelling out through the new part of town they are building up outside the old walls. We passed the bull-ring, high and white and concrete-looking in the sun, and then came into the big square by a side street and stopped in front of the Hotel Montoya.

The driver helped us down with the bags. There was a crowd of kids watching the car, and the square was hot, and the trees were green, and the flags hung on their staffs, and it was good to get out of the sun and under the shade of the arcade that runs all the way around the square. Montoya was glad to see us, and shook hands and gave us good rooms looking out on the square, and then we washed and cleaned up and went downstairs in the dining-room for lunch. The driver stayed for lunch, too, and afterward we paid him and he started back to Bayonne.

There are two dining-rooms in the Montoya. One is upstairs on the second floor and looks out on the square. The other is down one floor below the level of the square and has a door that opens on the back street that the bulls pass along when they run through the streets early in the morning on their way to the ring. It is always cool in the downstairs dining-room, and we had a very good lunch. The first meal in Spain was always a shock with the hors d'œuvres, an egg course, two meat courses, vegetables, salad, and dessert and fruit. You have to drink plenty of wine to get it all down. Robert Cohn tried to say he did not want any of the second meat course, but we would not interpret for him, and so the waitress brought him something else as a replacement, a plate of cold meats, I think. Cohn had been rather nervous ever since we had met in Bayonne. He did not know whether we knew Brett had been with him at San Sebastian, and it made him rather awkward.

'Well,' I said, 'Brett and Mike ought to get in to-night.'

'I'm not sure they'll come,' Cohn said.

'Why not?' Bill said. 'Of course they'll come.'

'They're always late,' I said.

'I rather think they're not coming,' Robert Cohn said.

He said it with an air of superior knowledge that irritated both of us.

'I'll bet you fifty pesetas they're here to-night,' Bill said. He always bets when he is angered, and so he usually bets foolishly.

'I'll take it,' Cohn said. 'Good. You remember it, Jake. Fifty pesetas.'

'I'll remember it myself,' Bill said. I saw he was angry and wanted to smooth him down.

'It's a sure thing they'll come,' I said. 'But maybe not to-night.'

'Want to call it off?' Cohn asked.

'No. Why should I? Make it a hundred if you like.'

'All right. I'll take that.'

'That's enough,' I said. 'Or you'll have to make a book and give me some of it.'

'I'm satisfied,' Cohn said. He smiled. 'You'll probably win it back at bridge, anyway.'

'You haven't got it yet,' Bill said.

We went out to walk around under the arcade to the Café Iruna for coffee. Cohn said he was going over and get a shave.

'Say,' Bill said to me, 'have I got any chance on that bet?'

'You've got a rotten chance. They've never been on time anywhere. If their money doesn't come it's a cinch they won't get in to-night.'

'I was sorry as soon as I opened my mouth. But I had to call him. He's all right, I guess, but where does he get this inside stuff? Mike and Brett fixed it up with us about coming here.'

I saw Cohn coming over across the square.

'Here he comes.'

'Well, let him not get superior and Jewish.'

'The barber shop's closed,' Cohn said. 'It's not open till four.'

We had coffee at the Iruna, sitting in comfortable wicker chairs looking out from the cool of the arcade at the big square. After a while Bill went to write some letters and Cohn went over to the barber-shop. It was still closed, so he decided to go up to the hotel and get a bath, and I sat out in front of the café and then went for a walk in the town. It was very hot, but I kept on the shady side of the streets and went through the market and had a good time seeing the town again. I went to the Ayuntamiento and found the old gentleman who subscribes for the bull-fight tickets for me every year, and he had gotten the money I sent him from Paris and renewed my subscriptions, so that was all set. He was the archivist, and all the archives of the town were in his office. That has nothing to do with the story. Anyway, his office had a green baize door and big wooden door, and when I went out I left him sitting among the archives that covered all the walls, and I shut both the doors, and as I went out of the building into the street the porter stopped me to brush off my coat.

'You must have been in a motor-car,' he said.

The back of the collar and the upper part of the shoulders were gray with dust.

'From Bayonne.'

'Well, well,' he said. 'I knew you were in a motor-car from the way the dust was.' So I gave him two copper coins.

At the end of the street I saw the cathedral and walked up toward it. The first time I ever saw it I thought the façade was ugly but I liked it now. I went inside. It was dim and dark and the pillars went high up, and there were people praying, and it smelt of incense, and there were some wonderful big windows. I knelt and started to pray and prayed for everybody I thought of, Brett and Mike and Bill and Robert Cohn and myself, and all the bull-fighters, separately for the ones I liked, and lumping all the rest, then I prayed for myself again, and while I was praying for myself I found I was getting sleepy, so I prayed that the bull-fights would be good, and that it would be a fine fiesta, and that we would get some fishing. I wondered if there was anything else I might pray for, and I thought that I would like to have some money, so I prayed that I would make a lot of money, and then I started to think how I would make it, and thinking of making money reminded me of the count, and I started wondering about where he was, and regretting I hadn't seen him since that night in Montmartre, and about something funny Brett told me about him, and as all the time I was kneeling with my forehead on the wood in front of me, and was thinking of myself as praying, I was a little ashamed, and regretted that I was such a rotten Catholic, but realised there was nothing I could do about it, at least for a while, and maybe never, but that anyway it was a grand religion, and I only wished I felt religious and maybe I would the next time; and then I was out in the hot sun on the steps of the cathedral, and the forefingers and the thumb of my right hand were still damp, and I felt them dry in the sun. The sunlight was hot and hard, and I crossed over beside some buildings, and walked back along side-streets to the hotel.

At dinner that night we found that Robert Cohn had taken a bath, had had a shave and a haircut and a shampoo, and something put on his hair afterward to make it stay down. He was nervous, and I did not try to help him any. The train was due in at nine o'clock from San Sebastian, and, if Brett and Mike were coming, they would be on it. At twenty minutes to nine we were not half way through dinner. Robert Cohn got up from the table and said he would go to the station. I said I would go with him, just to devil him. Bill said he would be damned if he would leave his dinner. I said we would be right back.

We walked to the station. I was enjoying Cohn's nervousness. I hoped Brett would be on the train. At the station the train was late, and we sat on a baggage-truck and waited outside in the dark. I have never seen a man in civil life as nervous as Robert Cohn–nor as eager. I was enjoying it. It was lousy to enjoy it, but I felt lousy. Cohn had a wonderful quality of bringing out the worst in anybody.

After a while we heard the train-whistle way off below on the other side of the plateau, and then we saw the headlight coming up the hill. We went inside the station and stood with a crowd of people just back of the gates, and the train came in and stopped, and everybody coming started out through the gates.

They were not in the crowd. We waited till everybody had gone through and out of the station and gotten into buses, or taken cabs, or were walking with their friends or relatives through the dark into the town.

'I knew they wouldn't come,' Robert said. We were going back to the hotel.

'I thought they might,' I said.

Bill was eating fruit when we came in and finishing a bottle of wine.

'Didn't come, eh?'

'No.'

'Do you mind if I give you that hundred pesetas in the morning, Cohn?' Bill asked. 'I haven't changed any money here yet.'

'Oh, forget about it,' Robert Cohn said. 'Let's bet on something else. Can you bet on bull-fights?'

'You could,' Bill said, 'but you don't need to.'

'It would be like betting on the war,' I said. 'You don't need any economic interest.'

'I'm very curious to see them,' Robert said.

Montoya came up to our table. He had a telegram in his hand. 'It's for you.' He handed it to me.

It read: 'Stopped night San Sebastian.'

'It's from them,' I said. I put it in my pocket. Ordinarily I should have handed it over.

'They've stopped over in San Sebastian,' I said. 'Send their regards to you.'

Why I felt that impulse to devil him I do not know. Of course I do know. I was blind, unforgivingly jealous of what had happened to him. The fact that I took it as a matter of course did not alter that any. I certainly did hate him. I do not think I ever really hated him until he had that little spell of superiority at lunch–that and when he went through all that barbering. So I put the telegram in my pocket. The telegram came to me, anyway.

'Well,' I said. 'We ought to pull out on the noon bus for Burguete. They can follow us if they get in to-morrow night.'

There were only two trains up from San Sebastian, an early morning train and the one we had just met.

'That sounds like a good idea,' Cohn said.

'The sooner we get on the stream the better.'

'It's all one to me when we start,' Bill said. 'The sooner the better.'

We sat in the Iruna for a while and had coffee and then took a little walk out to the bull-ring and across the field and under the trees at the edge of the cliff and looked down at the river in the dark, and I turned in early. Bill and Cohn stayed out in the café quite late, I believe, because I was asleep when they came in.

In the morning I bought three tickets for the bus to Burguete. It was scheduled to leave at two o'clock. There was nothing earlier. I was sitting over at the Iruna reading the papers when I saw Robert Cohn coming across the square. He came up to the table and sat down in one of the wicker chairs.

'This is a comfortable café,' he said. 'Did you have a good night, Jake?'

'I slept like a log.'

'I didn't sleep very well. Bill and I were out late, too.'

'Where were you?'

'Here. And after it shut we went over to that other café. The old man there speaks German and English.'

'The Café Suizo.'

'That's it. He seems like a nice old fellow. I think it's a better café than this one.'

'It's not so good in the daytime,' I said. 'Too hot. By the way, I got the bus tickets.'

'I'm not going up to-day. You and Bill go on ahead.'

'I've got your ticket.'

'Give it to me. I'll get the money back.'

'It's five pesetas.'

Robert Cohn took out a silver five-peseta piece and gave it to me.

'I ought to stay,' he said. 'You see, I'm afraid there's some sort of misunderstanding.'

'Why,' I said. 'They may not come here for three or four days now if they start on parties at San Sebastian.'

'That's just it,' said Robert. 'I'm afraid they expected to meet me at San Sebastian, and that's why they stopped over.'

'What makes you think that?'

'Well, I wrote suggesting it to Brett.'

'Why in hell didn't you stay there and meet them, then?' I started to say, but I stopped. I thought that idea would come to him by itself, but I do not believe it ever did.

He was being confidential now and it was giving him pleasure to be able to talk with the understanding that I knew there was something between him and Brett.

'Well, Bill and I will go up right after lunch,' I said.

'I wish I could go. We've been looking forward to this fishing all winter.' He was being sentimental about it. 'But I ought to stay. I really ought. As soon as they come I'll bring them right up.'

'Let's find Bill.'

'I want to go over to the barber-shop.'

'See you at lunch.'

I found Bill up his room. He was shaving.

'Oh, yes, he told me all about it last night,' Bill said. 'He's a great little confider. He said he had a date with Brett at San Sebastian.'

'The lying bastard!'

'Oh, no,' said Bill. 'Don't get sore. Don't get sore at this stage of the trip. How did you ever happen to know this fellow anyway?'

'Don't rub it in.'

Bill looked around, half-shaved, and then went on talking into the mirror while he lathered his face.

'Didn't you send him with a letter to me in New York last winter? Thank God, I'm a travelling man. Haven't you got some more Jewish friends you could bring along?' He rubbed his chin with his thumb, looked at it, and then started scraping again.

'You've got some fine ones yourself.'

'Oh, yes. I've got some darbs. But not alongside of this Robert Cohn. The funny thing is he's nice, too. I like him. But he's just so awful.'

'He can be damn nice.'

'I know it. That's the terrible part.'

I laughed.

'Yes. Go on and laugh,' said Bill. 'You weren't out with him last night until two o'clock.'

'Was he very bad?'

'Awful. What's all this about him and Brett, anyway? Did she ever have anything to do with him?'

He raised his chin up and pulled it from side to side.

'Sure.' She went down to San Sebastian with him.'

'What a damn-fool thing to do. Why did she do that?'

'She wanted to get out of town and she can't go anywhere alone. She said she thought it would be good for him.'

'What bloody-fool things people do. Why didn't she go off with some of her own people? Or you?–he slurred that over–'or me? Why not me?' He looked at his face carefully in the glass, put a big dab of lather on each cheek-bone. 'It's an honest face. It's a face any woman would be safe with.'

'She'd never seen it.'

'She should have. All women should see it. It's a face that ought to be thrown on every screen in the country. Every woman ought to be given a copy of this face as she leaves the altar. Mothers should tell their daughters about this face. My son'–he pointed the razor at me–'go west with this face and grow up with the country.'

He ducked down in the bowl, rinsed his face with cold water, put on some alcohol, and then looked at himself carefully in the glass, pulling down his long upper lip.

'My God!' he said, 'isn't it an awful face?'

He looked in the glass.

'And as for this Robert Cohn,' Bill said, 'he makes me sick, and he can go to hell, and I'm damn glad he's staying here so we won't have him fishing with us.'

'You're damn right.'

'We're going trout-fishing. We're going trout-fishing in the Irati River, and we're going to get tight now at lunch on the wine of the country, and then take a swell bus ride.'

'Come on. Let's go over to the Iruna and start,' I said.

II

It was baking hot in the square when we came out after lunch with our bags and the rod-case to go to Burguete. People were on top of the bus, and others were climbing up a ladder. Bill went up and Robert sat beside Bill to save a place for me, and I went back in the hotel to get a couple of bottles of wine to take with us. When I came out the bus was crowded. Men and women were sitting on all the baggage and boxes on top, and the women all had their fans going in the sun. It certainly was hot. Robert climbed down and I fitted into the place he had saved on the one wooden seat that ran across the top.

Robert Cohn stood in the shade of the arcade waiting for us to start. A Basque with a big leather wine-bag in his lap lay across the top of the bus in front of our seat, leaning back against our legs. He offered the wine-skin to Bill and to me, and when I tipped it up to drink he imitated the sound of a klaxon motor-horn so well and so suddenly that I spilled some of the wine, and everybody laughed. He apologised and made me take another drink. He made the klaxon again a little later, and it fooled me the second time. He was very good at it. The Basques liked it. The man next to Bill was talking to him in Spanish and Bill was not getting it, so he offered the man one of the bottles of wine. The man waved it away. He said it was too hot and he had drunk too much at lunch. When Bill offered the bottle a second time he took a long drink, and then the bottle went all over that part of the bus. Everyone took a drink very politely, and then they made us cork it up and put it away. They all wanted us to drink from their leather wine-bottles. They were peasants going up into the hills.

Finally, after a couple more false klaxons, the bus started and Robert Cohn waved good-bye to us, and all the Basques waved good-bye to him. As soon as we started out on the road outside of town it was cool. It felt nice riding high up and close under the trees. The bus went quite fast and made a good breeze, and as we went out along the road with the dust powdering the trees and down the hill, we had a fine view, back through the trees, of the town rising up from the bluff above the river. The Basque lying against my knees pointed out the view with the neck of the wine-bottle, and winked at us. He nodded his head.

'Pretty nice, eh?'

'These Basques are swell people,' Bill said.

The Basque lying against my legs was tanned the colour of saddle-leather. He wore a black smock like all the rest. There were wrinkles in his tanned neck. He turned around and offered his wine-bag to Bill. Bill handed him one of our bottles. The Basque wagged a forefinger at him and handed the bottle back, slapping in the cork with the palm of his hand. He shoved the wine-bag up.

'Arriba! Arriba!' he said. 'Lift it up.'

Bill raised the wine-skin and let the stream of wine spurt out and into his mouth, his head tipped back. When he stopped drinking and tipped the leather bottle down a few drops ran down his chin.

'No! No!' several Basques said. 'Not like that.'

One snatched the bottle away from the owner, who was himself about to give a demonstration. He was a young fellow and he held the wine-bottle at full arms' length and raised it high up, squeezing the leather bag with his hand so the stream of wine hissed into his mouth. He held the bag out there, the wine making a flat, hard trajectory into his mouth, and he kept on swallowing smoothly and regularly.

'Hey!' the owner of the bottle shouted. 'Whose wine is that?'

The drinker waggled his little finger at him and smiled at us with his eyes. Then he bit the stream off sharp, made a quick lift with the wine-bag and lowered it down to the owner. He winked at us. The owner shook the wine-skin sadly.

We passed through a town and stopped in front of the posada, and the driver took on several packages. Then we started on again, and outside the town the road commenced to mount. We were going through farming country with rocky hills that sloped down into the fields. The grain-fields went up the hillsides. Now as we went higher there was a wind blowing the grain. The road was white and dusty, and the dust rose under the wheels and hung in the air behind us. The road climbed up into the hills and left the rich grain-fields below. Now there were only patches of grain on the bare hillsides and on each side of the water-courses. We turned sharply out to the side of the road to give room to pass to a long string of six mules, following one after the other, hauling a high-hooded waggon loaded with freight. The waggon and the mules were covered with dust. Close behind was another string of mules and another waggon. This was loaded with lumber, and the arriero driving the mules leaned back and put on the thick wooden brakes as we passed. Up here the country was quite barren and the hills were rocky and hard-baked clay furrowed by the rain.

We came around a curve into a town, and on both sides opened out a sudden green valley. A stream went through the centre of the town, and fields of grapes touched the houses.

The bus stopped in front of a posada and many of the passengers got down, and a lot of the baggage was unstrapped from the roof from under the big tarpaulins and lifted down. Bill and I got down and went into the posada. There was a low, dark room with saddles and harness and hay-forks made of white wood and clusters of canvas rope-soled shoes and hams and slabs of bacon and white garlics and long sausages hanging from the roof. It was cool and dusky, and we stood in front of a long wooden counter with two women behind it serving drinks. Behind them were shelves stacked with supplies and goods.

We each had an aguardiente and paid forty centimes for the two drinks. I gave the woman fifty centimes to make a tip, and she gave me back the copper piece, thinking I had misunderstood the price.

Two of our Basques came in and insisted on buying a drink. So they bought a drink and then we bought a drink, and then they slapped us on the back and bought another drink. Then we bought, and then we all went out into the sunlight and the heat, and climbed back on top of the bus. There was plenty of room now for everyone to sit on the seat, and the Basque who had been lying on the tin roof now sat between us. The woman who had been serving drinks came out wiping her hands on her apron and talked to somebody inside the bus. Then the driver came out swinging two flat leather mail-pouches and climbed up and, everybody waving, we started off.

The road left the green valley at once, and we were up in the hills again. Bill and the wine-bottle Basque were having a conversation. A man leaned over from the other side of the seat and asked in English: 'You're American?'

'Sure.'

'I been there,' he said. 'Forty years ago.'

He was an old man, as brown as the others, with the stubble of a white beard.

'How was it?'

'What you say?'

'How was America?'

'Oh, I was in California. It was fine.'

'Why did you leave?'

'What you say?'

'Why did you come back here?'

'Oh! I come back to get married. I was going to go back but my wife she don't like to travel. Where you from?'

'Kansas City.'

'I been there,' he said. 'I been in Chicago, St Louis, Kansas City, Denver, Los Angeles, Salt Lake City.'

He named them carefully.

'How long were you over?'

'Fifteen years. Then I come back and got married.'

'Have a drink?'

'All right,' he said. 'You can't get this in America eh?'

'There's plenty if you can pay for it.'

'What you come over here for?'

'We're going to the fiesta at Pamplona.'

'You like the bull-fights?'

'Sure Don't you?'

'Yes,' he said. 'I guess I like them.'

Then after a little:

'Where you go now?'

'Up to Burguete to fish.'

'Well,' he said, 'I hope you catch something.'

He shook hands and turned around to the back seat again. The other Basques had been impressed. He sat back comfortably and smiled at me when I turned around to look at the country. But the effort of talking American seemed to have tired him. He did not say anything after that.

The bus climbed steadily up the road. The country was barren and rocks stuck up through the clay. There was no grass beside the road. Looking back we could see the country spread out below. Far back the fields were squares of green and brown on the hillsides. Making the horizon were the brown mountains. They were strangely shaped. As we climbed higher the horizon kept changing. As the bus ground slowly up the road we could see other mountains coming up in the south. Then the road came over the crest, flattened out, and went into a forest. It was a forest of cork oaks, and the sun came through the trees in patches, and there were cattle grazing back in the trees. We went through the forest and the road came out and turned along a rise of land, and out ahead of us was a rolling green plain, with dark mountains beyond it. These were not like the brown, heat-baked mountains we had left behind. These were wooded and there were clouds coming down from them. The green plains stretched off. It was cut by fences and the white of the road showed through the trunks of a double line of trees that crossed the plain toward the south. As we came to the edge of the rise we saw the red roofs and white houses of Burguete ahead strung out on the plain, and away off on the shoulder of the first dark mountain was the grey metal-sheathed roof of the monastery of Roncevalles.

'There's Roncevaux,' I said.

'Where?'

'Way off there where the mountain starts.'

'It's cold up here,' Bill said.

'It's high,' I said. 'It must be twelve hundred metres.'

'It's awful cold,' Bill said.

The bus levelled down on to the straight line of road that ran to Burguete. We passed a crossroads and crossed a bridge over a stream. The houses of Burguete were along both sides of the road. There were no side-streets. We passed the church and the school-yard, and the bus stopped. We got down and the driver handed down our bags and the rod-case. A carabineer in his cocked hat and yellow leather cross-straps came up.

'What's in there?' He pointed to the rod-case.

I opened it and showed him. He asked to see our fishing permits and I got them out. He looked at the date and then waved us on.

'Is that all right?' I asked.

'Yes. Of course.'

We went up the street, past the whitewashed stone houses, families sitting in their doorways watching us, to the inn.

The fat woman who ran the inn came out from the kitchen and shook hands with us. She took off her spectacles, wiped them, and put them on again. It was cold in the inn and the wind was starting to blow outside. The woman sent a girl upstairs with us to show the room. There were two beds, a wash-stand, a clothes-chest, and a big, framed steel-engraving of Nuestra Señora de Roncevalles. The wind was blowing against the shutters. The room was on the north side of the inn. We washed, put on sweaters, and came downstairs into the dining-room. It had a stone floor, low ceiling, and was oak-panelled. The shutters were all up and it was so cold you could see your breath.

'My God!' said Bill, 'It can't be this cold to-morrow. I'm not going to wade a stream in this weather.'

There was an upright piano in the far corner of the room beyond the wooden tables and Bill went over and started to play.

'I got to keep warm,' he said.

I went out to find the woman and ask her how much the room and board was. She put her hands under her apron and looked away from me.

'Twelve pesatas.'

'Why, we only paid that in Pamplona.'

She did not say anything, just took off her glasses and wiped them on her apron.

'That's too much,' I said. 'We didn't pay more than that at a big hotel.'

'We've put in a bathroom.'

'Haven't you got anything cheaper?'

'Not in the summer. Now is the big season.'

We were the only people in the inn. Well, I thought, it's only a few days.

'Is the wine included?'

'Oh, yes.'

'Well,' I said. 'It's all right.'

I went back to Bill. He blew his breath at me to show how cold it was, and went on playing. I sat at one of the tables and looked at the pictures on the wall. There was one panel of rabbits, dead, one of pheasants, also dead, and one panel of dead ducks. The panels were all dark and smoky-looking. There was a cupboard full of liqueur bottles. I looked at them all. Bill was still playing. 'How about a hot rum punch?' he said. 'This isn't going to keep me warm permanently.'

I went out and told the woman what a rum punch was and how to make it. In a few minutes a girl brought a stone pitcher, steaming, into the room. Bill came over from the piano and we drank the hot punch and listened to the wind.

'There's isn't too much rum in that.'

I went over to the cupboard and brought the rum bottle and poured a half-tumblerful into the pitcher.

'Direct action,' said Bill, 'It beats legislation.'

The girl came in and laid the table for supper.

'It blows like hell up here,' Bill said.

The girl brought in a big bowl of hot vegetable soup and the wine. We had fried trout afterward and some sort of stew and a big bowl full of wild strawberries. We did not lose money on the wine, and the girl was shy but nice about bringing it. The old woman looked in once and counted the empty bottles.

After supper we went upstairs and smoked and read in bed to keep warm. Once in the night I woke and heard the wind blowing. It felt good to be warm and in bed.

12

When I woke in the morning I went to the window and looked out. It had cleared and there were no clouds on the mountains. Outside under the window were some carts and an old diligence, the wood of the roof cracked and split by the weather. It must have been left from the days before the motor-buses. A goat hopped up on one of the carts and then to the roof of the diligence. He jerked his head at the other goats below and when I waved at him he bounded down.

Bill was still sleeping, so I dressed, put on my shoes outside in the hall, and went downstairs. No one was stirring downstairs, so I unbolted the door and went out. It was cool outside in the early morning and the sun had not yet dried the dew that had come when the wind died down. I hunted around in the shed behind the inn and found a sort of mattock, and went down toward the stream to try and dig some worms for bait. The stream was clear and shallow, but it did not look trouty. On the grassy bank where it was damp I drove the mattock into the earth and loosened a chunk of sod. There were worms underneath. They slid out of sight as I lifted the sod and I dug carefully and got a good many. Digging at the edge of the damp ground I filled two empty tobacco-tins with worms and sifted dirt on to them. The goats watched me dig.

When I went back into the inn the woman was down in the kitchen, and I asked her to get coffee for us, and that we wanted a lunch. Bill was awake and sitting on the edge of the bed.

'I saw you out of the window,' he said. 'Didn't want to interrupt you. What were you doing? Burying your money?'

'You lazy bum!'

'Been working for the common good? Splendid. I want you to do that every morning.'

'Come on,' I said. 'Get up.'

'What? Get up? I never get up.'

He climbed into bed and pulled the sheet up to his chin.

'Try and argue me into getting up.'

I went on looking for the tackle and putting it all together in the tackle-bag.

'Aren't you interested?' Bill asked.

'I'm going down and eat.'

'Eat? Why didn't you say eat? I thought you just wanted me to get up for fun. Eat? Fine. Now you're reasonable. You go out and dig some more worms and I'll be right down.'

'Oh, go to hell!'

'Work for the good of all.' Bill stepped into his underclothes. 'Show irony and pity.'

I started out of the room with the tackle-bag, the nets, and the rod-case.

'Hey! Come back!'

I put my head in the door.

'Aren't you going to show a little irony and pity?'

I thumbed my nose.

'That's not irony.'

As I went downstairs I heard Bill singing. 'Irony and Pity. When you're feeling . . . Oh, Give them Irony and Give them Pity. Oh, give them Irony. When they're feeling . . . Just a little irony. Just a little pity . . .' He kept on singing until he came downstairs. The tune was: 'The Bells are Ringing for Me and my Gal.' I was reading a week-old Spanish paper.

'What's all this irony and pity?'

'What? Don't you know about Irony and Pity?'

'No. Who got it up?'

'Everybody. They're mad about it in New York. It's just like the Fratellinis used to be.'

The girl came in with the coffee and buttered toast. Or, rather, it was bread toasted and buttered.

'Ask her if she's got any jam,' Bill said. 'Be ironical with her.'

'Have you got any jam?'

'That's not ironical. I wish I could talk Spanish.'

The coffee was good and we drank it out of big bowls. The girl brought in a glass dish of raspberry jam.

'Thank you.'

'Hey! that's not the way,' Bill said. 'Say something ironical. Make some crack about Primo de Rivera.'

'I could ask her what kind of jam they think they're gotten into in the Riff.'

'Poor,' said Bill. 'Very poor. You can't do it. That's all. You don't understand irony. You have no pity. Say something pitiful.'

'Robert Cohn.'

'Not so bad. That's better. Now why is Cohn pitiful? Be ironic.'

He took a big gulp of coffee.'

'Aw, hell!' I said. 'It's too early in the morning.'

'There you go. And you claim you want to be a writer, too. You're only a newspaper man. An expatriated newspaper man. You ought to be ironical the minute you get out of bed. You ought to wake up with your mouth full of pity.'

'Go on,' I said. 'Who did you get this stuff from?'

'Everybody. Don't you read? Don't you ever see anybody? You know what you are? You're an expatriate. Why don't you live in New York? Then you'd know these things. What do you want me to do? Come over here and tell you every year?'

'Take some more coffee,' I said.

'Good. Coffee is good for you. It's the caffeine in it. Caffeine, we are here. Caffeine puts a man on her horse and woman in his grave. You know what's the trouble with you? You're an expatriate. One of the worst type. Haven't you heard that? Nobody that ever left their own country ever wrote anything worth printing. Not even in the newspapers.'

He drank the coffee.

'You're an expatriate. You've lost touch with the soil. You get precious. Fake European standards have ruined you. You drink yourself to death. You become obsessed by sex. You spend all your time talking, not working. You are an expatriate, see? You hang around cafés.'

'It sounds like a swell life,' I said. 'When do I work?'

'You don't work. One group claims women support you. Another group claims you're impotent.'

'No,' I said. 'I just had an accident.'

'Never mention that,' Bill said. 'That's the sort of thing that can't be spoken of. That's what you ought to work up into a mystery. Like Henry's bicycle.'

He had been going splendidly, but he stopped. I was afraid he thought he had hurt me with that crack about being impotent. I wanted to start him again.

'It wasn't a bicycle,' I said. 'He was riding horseback.'

'I heard it was a tricycle.'

'Well,' I said. 'A plane is sort of like a tricycle. The joystick works the same way.'

'But you don't pedal it.'

'No,' I said, 'I guess you don't pedal it.'

'Let's lay off that,' Bill said.

'All right. I was just standing up for the tricycle.'

'I think he's a good writer, too,' Bill said. 'And you're a hell of a good guy. Anybody ever tell you you were a good guy?'

'I'm not a good guy.'

'Listen. You're a hell of a good guy, and I'm fonder of you than anybody on earth. I couldn't tell you that in New York. It'd mean I was a faggot. That was what the Civil War was about. Abraham Lincoln was a faggot. He was in love with General Grant. So was Jefferson Davis. Lincoln just freed the slaves on a bet. The Dred Scott case was framed by the Anti-Saloon League. Sex explains it all. The Colonel's Lady and Judy O'Grady are Lesbians under their skin.'

He stopped.

'Want to hear some more?'

'Shoot,' I said.

'I don't know any more. Tell you some more at lunch.'

'Old Bill,' I said.

'You bum!'

We packed the lunch and two bottles of wine in the rucksack, and Bill put it on. I carried the rod-case and the landing-nets slung over my back. We started up the road and then went across a meadow and found a path that crossed the fields and went toward the woods on the slope of the first hill. We walked across the fields on the sandy path. The fields were rolling and grassy and the grass was short from the sheep-grazing. The cattle were up in the hills. We heard their bells in the woods.

The path crossed a stream on a foot-log. The log was surfaced off, and there was a sapling bent across for a rail. In the flat pool beside the stream tadpoles spotted the sand. We went up a steep bank and across the rolling fields. Looking back we saw Burguete, white houses and red roofs, and the white road with a truck going along it and the dust rising.

Beyond the fields we crossed another faster-flowing stream. A sandy road led down to the ford and beyond into the woods. The path crossed the stream on another foot-log below the ford, and joined the road, and we went into the woods.

It was a beech wood and the trees were very old. Their roots bulked above the ground, and the branches were twisted. We walked on the road between the thick trunks of the old beeches and the sunlight came through the leaves in light patches on the grass. The trees were big, and the foliage was thick but it was not gloomy. There was no undergrowth, only the smooth grass, very green and fresh, and the big grey trees, well spaced as though it were a park.

'This is country,' Bill said.

The road went up a hill and we got into thick woods, and the road kept on climbing. Sometimes it dipped down but rose again steeply. All the time we heard the cattle in the woods. Finally, the road came out on the top of the hills. We were on the top of the height of land that was the highest part of the range of wooded hills we had seen from Burguete. There were wild strawberries growing on the sunny side of the ridge in a little clearing in the trees.

Ahead the road came out of the forest and went along the shoulder of the ridge of hills. The hills ahead were not wooded, and there were great fields of yellow gorse. Way off we saw the steep bluffs, dark with trees and jutting with grey stone, that marked the course of the Irati River.

'We have to follow this road along the ridge, cross these hills, go through the woods on the far hills, and come down to the Irati valley,' I pointed out to Bill.

'That's a hell of a hike.'

'It's too far to go and fish and come back the same day, comfortably.'

'Comfortably. That's a nice word. We'll have to go like hell to get there and back and have any fishing at all.'

It was a long walk and the country was very fine, but we were tired when we came down the steep road that led out of the wooded hills into the valley of Rio de la Fabrica.

The road came out from the shadow of the woods into the hot sun. Ahead was a river-valley. Beyond the river was a steep hill. There was a field of buck-wheat on the hill. We saw a white house under some trees on the hillside. It was very hot and we stopped under some trees beside a dam that crossed the river.

Bill put the pack against one of the trees and we jointed up the rods, put on the reels, tied on leaders, and got ready to fish.

'You're sure this thing has trout in it?' Bill asked.

'It's full of them.'

'I'm going to fish a fly. You got any McGintys?'

'There's some in there.'

'You going to fish bait?'

'Yeah. I'm going to fish the dam here.'

'Well, I'll take the fly-book, then.' He tied on a fly. 'Where'd I better go? Up or down?'

'Down is the best. They're plenty up above, too.'

Bill went down the bank.

'Take a worm-can.'

'No, I don't want one. If they won't take a fly I'll just flick it around.'

Bill was down below watching the stream.

'Say,' he called up against the noise of the dam. 'How about putting the wine in that spring up the road?'

'All right,' I shouted. Bill waved his hand and started down the stream. I found the two wine-bottles in the pack, and carried them up the road to where the water of a spring flowed out of an iron pipe. There was a board over the spring and I lifted it and, knocking the corks firmly into the bottles, lowered them down into the water. It was so cold my hand and wrist felt numbed. I put back the slab of wood, and hoped nobody would find the wine.

I got my rod that was leaning against the tree, took the bait-can and landing-net, and walked out on to the dam. It was built to provide a head of water for driving logs. The gate was up, and I sat on one of the squared timbers and watched the smooth apron of water before the river tumbled into the falls. In the white water at the foot of the dam it was deep. As I baited up, a trout shot up out of the white water into the falls and was carried down. Before I could finish baiting, another trout jumped at the falls, making the same lovely arc and disappearing into the water that was thundering down. I put on a good sized sinker and dropped into the white water close to the edge of the timbers of the dam.

I did not feel the first trout strike. When I started to pull up I felt that I had one and brought him, fighting and bending the rod almost double, out of the boiling water at the foot of the falls, and swung him up and on to the dam. He was a good trout, and I banged his head againt the timber so that he quivered out straight, and then slipped him into my bag.

While I had him on, several trout had jumped at the falls. As soon as I baited up and dropped in again I hooked another and brought him in the same way. In a little while I had six. They were all about the same size. I laid them out, side by side, all their heads pointing the same way, and looked at them. They were beautifully coloured and firm and hard from the cold water. It was a hot day, so I slit them and shucked out the insides, gills and all, and tossed them over across the river. I took the trout ashore, washed them in the cold, smoothly heavy water above the dam, and then picked some ferns and packed them all in the bag, three trout on a layer of ferns, then another layer of ferns, then three more trout, and then covered them with ferns. They looked nice in the ferns, and now the bag was bulky, and I put it in the shade of the tree.

It was very hot on the dam, so I put my worm-can in the shade with the bag, and got a book out of the pack and settled down under the tree to read until Bill should come up for lunch.

It was a little past noon and there was not much shade, but I sat against the trunk of two of the trees that grew together, and read. The book was something by A. E. W. Mason, and I was reading a wonderful story about a man who had been frozen in the Alps and then fallen into a glacier and disappeared, and his bride was going to wait twenty-four years exactly for his body to come out on the moraine, while her true love waited too, and they were still waiting when Bill came up.

'Get any?' he asked. He had his rod and his bag and his net all in one hand, and he was sweating. I hadn't heard him come up, because of the noise from the dam.

'Six. What did you get?'

Bill sat down, opened up his bag, laid out a big trout on the grass. He took out three more, each one a little bigger than the last, and laid them side by side in the shade from the tree. His face was sweaty and happy.

'How are yours?'

'Smaller.'

'Let's see them.'

'They're packed.'

'How big are they really?'

'They're all about the size of your smallest.'

'You're not holding out on me?'

'I wish I were.'

'Get them all on worms?'

'Yes.'

'You lazy bum!'

Bill put the trout in the bag and started for the river, swinging the open bag. He was wet from the waist down and I knew he must have been wading the stream.

I walked up the road and got out the two bottles of wine. They were cold. Moisture beaded on the bottles as I walked back to the trees. I spread the lunch on a newspaper, and uncorked one of the bottles and leaned the other against a tree. Bill came up drying his hands, his bag plump with ferns.

'Let's see that bottle,' he said. He pulled the cork and tipped up the bottle and drank. 'Whew! That makes my eyes ache.'

'Let's try it.'

The wine was icy cold and tasted faintly rusty.

'That's not such filthy wine,' Bill said.

'The cold helps it,' I said.

We unwrapped the little parcels of lunch.

'Chicken.'

'There's hard-boiled eggs.'

'Find any salt?'

'First the egg,' said Bill. 'Then the chicken. Even Bryan could see that.'

'He's dead. I read it in the paper yesterday.'

'No, not really?'

'Yes. Bryan's dead.'

Bill laid down the egg he was peeling.

'Gentlemen,' he said, and unwrapped a drumstick from a piece of newspaper. 'I reverse the order. For Bryan's sake. As a tribute to the Great Commoner. First the chicken; then the egg.'

'Wonder what day God created the chicken?'

'Oh,' said Bill, sucking the drumstick, 'how should we know? We should not question. Our stay on earth is not for long. Let us rejoice and believe and give thanks.'

'Eat an egg.'

Bill gestured with the drumstick in one hand and the bottle of wine in the other.

'Let us rejoice in our blessings. Let us utilise the fowls of the air. Let us utilise the product of the vine. Will you utilise a little, brother?'

'After you, brother?'

Bill took a long drink.

'Utilise a little, brother,' he handed me the bottle. 'Let us not doubt, brother. Let us not pry into the holy mysteries of the hen-coop with simian fingers. Let us accept on faith and simply say–I want you to join with me in saying–What shall we say, brother?' He pointed the drumstick at me and went on. 'Let me tell you. We will say, and I for one am proud to say and I want you to say with me, on your knees, brother. Let no man be ashamed to kneel here in the great out-of-doors. Remember the woods were God's first temples. Let us kneel and say: "Don't eat that Lady–that's Mencken."'

'Here,' I said. 'Utilise a little of this.'

We uncorked the other bottle.

'What's the matter?' I said. 'Didn't you like Bryan?'

'I loved Bryan,' said Bill. 'We were like brothers.'

'Where did you know him?'

'He and Mencken and I all went to Holy Cross together.'

'And Frankie Fritsch.'

'It's a lie. Frankie Fritsch went to Fordham.'

'Well,' I said, 'I went to Loyola with Bishop Manning.'

'It's a lie,' Bill said. 'I went to Loyola with Bishop Manning myself.'

'You're cock-eyed,' I said.

'On wine?'

'Why not?'

'It's the humidity,' Bill said. 'They ought to take this damn humidity away.'

'Have another shot.'

'Is this all we've got?'

'Only the two bottles.'

'Do you know what you are?' Bill looked at the bottle affectionately.

'No,' I said.

'You're in the pay of the Anti-Saloon League.'

'I went to Notre Dame with Wayne B. Wheeler.'

'It's a lie,' said Bill. 'I went to Austin Business College with Wayne B. Wheeler. He was class president.'

'Well,' I said, 'the saloon must go.'

'You're right there, old classmate,' Bill said. 'The saloon must go, and I will take it with me.'

'You're cock-eyed.'

'On wine?'

'On wine.'

'Well, maybe I am.'

'Want to take a nap?'

'All right.'

We lay with our heads in the shade and looked up into the trees.

'You asleep?'

'No,' Bill said. 'I was thinking.'

I shut my eyes. It felt good lying on the ground.

'Say,' Bill said, 'what about this Brett business?'

'What about it?'

'Were you ever in love with her?'

'Sure.'

'For how long?'

'Off and on for a hell of a long time.'

'Oh, hell!' Bill said. 'I'm sorry, fella.'

'It's all right,' I said. 'I don't give a damn any more.'

'Really?'

'Really. Only I'd a hell of a lot rather not talk about it.'

'You weren't sore I asked you?'

'Why the hell should I be?'

'I'm going to sleep,' Bill said. He put a newspaper over his face.

'Listen, Jake,' he said, 'are you really a Catholic?'

'Technically.'

'What does that mean?'

'I don't know.'

'All right, I'll go to sleep now,' he said. 'Don't keep me awake by talking so much.'

I went to sleep too. When I woke Bill was packing the rucksack. It was late in the afternoon and the shadow from the trees was long and went out over the dam. I was stiff from sleeping on the ground.

'What did you do? Wake up?' Bill asked. 'Why didn't you spend the night?' I stretched and rubbed my eyes.

'I had a lovely dream,' Bill said. 'I don't remember what it was about, but it was a lovely dream.'

'I don't think I dreamt.'

'You ought to dream,' Bill said. 'All our biggest business men have been dreamers. Look at Ford. Look at President Coolidge. Look at Rockefeller. Look at Joe Davidson.'

I disjointed my rod and Bill's and packed them in the rod-case. I put the reels in the tackle-bag. Bill had packed the rucksack and we put one of the trout-bags in. I carried the other.

'Well,' said Bill, 'have we got everything?'

'The worms.'

'Your worms. Put them in there.'

He had the pack on his back and I put the worm-cans in one of the outside flap pockets.

'You got everything now?'

I looked around on the grass at the foot of the elm-trees.

'Yes.'

We started up the road into the woods. It was a long walk home to Burguete, and it was dark when we came down across the fields to the road, and along the road between the houses of the town, their windows lighted, to the inn.

We stayed five days at Burguete and had good fishing. The nights were cold and the days were hot, and there was always a breeze even in the heat of the day. It was hot enough so that it felt good to wade in a cold stream, and the sun dried you when you came out and sat on the bank. We found a stream with a pool deep enough to swim in. In the evenings we played three-handed bridge with an Englishman named Harris, who had walked over from Saint Jean Pied de Port and was stopping at the inn for the fishing. He was very pleasant and went twice with us to the Irati River. There was no word from Robert Cohn nor from Brett and Mike.

13

One morning I went down to breakfast and the Englishman, Harris, was already at the table. He was reading the paper through spectacles. He looked up and smiled.

'Good-morning,' he said. 'Letter for you. I stopped at the post and they gave it me with mine.'

The letter was at my place at the table, leaning against a coffee-cup. Harris was reading the paper again. I opened the letter. It had been forwarded from Pamplona. It was dated San Sebastian, Sunday:

> Dear Jake,
>
> We got here Friday, Brett passed out on the train, so brought her here for 3 days rest with old friends of ours. We go to Montoya Hotel Pamplona Tuesday, arriving at I don't know what hour. Will you send a note by the bus to tell us what to do to rejoin you all on Wednesday. All our love and sorry to be late, but Brett was really done in and will be quite all right by Tues. and is practically so now. I know her so well and try to look after her but it's not so easy. Love to all the chaps,
>
> Michael

'What day of the week is it?' I asked Harris.

'Wednesday, I think. Yes, quite, Wednesday. Wonderful how one loses track of the days up here in the mountains.'

'Yes. We've been here nearly a week.'

'I hope you're not thinking of leaving?'

'Yes. We'll go in on the afternoon bus, I'm afraid.'

'What a rotten business. I had hoped we'd all have another go at the Irati together.'

'We have to go into Pamplona. We're meeting people there.'

'What rotten luck for me. We've had a jolly time here at Burguete.'

'Come on in to Pamplona. We can play some bridge there, and there's going to be a damned fine fiesta.'

'I'd like to. Awfully nice of you to ask me. I'd best stop on here, though. I've not much more time to fish.'

'You want those big ones in the Irati.'

'I say, I do, you know. They're enormous trout there.'

'I'd like to try them once more.'

'Do. Stop over another day. Be a good chap.'

'We really have to get into town,' I said.

'What a pity.'

After breakfast Bill and I were sitting warming in the sun on a bench out in front of the inn and talking it over. I saw a girl coming up the road from the centre of the town. She stopped in front of us and took a telegram out of the leather wallet that hung against her skirt.

'Por ustedes?'

I looked at it. The address was: 'Barnes, Burguete.'

'Yes. It's for us.'

She brought out a book for me to sign, and I gave her a couple of coppers. The telegram was in Spanish: 'Veuve Jueves Cohn.'

I handed it to Bill.

'What does the word Cohn mean?' he asked.

'What a lousy telegram!' I said. 'He could send ten words for the same price. "I come Thursday." That gives you a lot of dope, doesn't it?'

'It gives you all the dope that's of interest to Cohn.'

'We're going in, anyway,' I said. 'There's no use trying to move Brett and Mike out here and back before the fiesta. Should we answer it?'

'We might as well,' said Bill. 'There's no need for us to be snooty.'

We walked up to the post-office and asked for a telegraph blank.

'What will we say?' Bill asked.

'"Arriving to-night." That's enough.'

We paid for the message and walked back to the inn. Harris was there and the three of us walked up to Roncevalles. We went through the monastery.

'It's a remarkable place,' Harris said, when we came out. 'But you know I'm not much on those sort of places.'

'Me either,' Bill said.

'It's a remarkable place, though,' Harris said. 'I wouldn't not have seen it. I'd been intending coming up each day.'

'It isn't the same as fishing, though, is it?' Bill asked. He liked Harris.

'I say not.'

We were standing in front of the old chapel of the monastery.

'Isn't that a pub across the way?' Harris asked. 'Or do my eyes deceive me?'

'It has the look of a pub,' Bill said.

'It looks to me like a pub,' I said.

'I say,' said Harris, 'let's utilise it.' He had taken up utilising from Bill.

We had a bottle of wine apiece. Harris would not let us pay. He talked Spanish quite well, and the innkeeper would not take our money.

'I say. You don't know what it's meant to me to have you chaps up here.'

'We've had a grand time, Harris.'

Harris was a little tight.

'I say. Really, you don't know how much it means. I've not had much fun since the war.'

'We'll fish together again, some time. Don't you forget it, Harris.'

'We must. We *have* had such a jolly good time.'

'How about another bottle around?'

'Jolly good idea,' said Harris.

'This is mine,' said Bill. 'Or we don't drink it.'

'I wish you'd let me pay for it. It *does* give me pleasure, you know.'

'This is going to give me pleasure,' Bill said.

The innkeeper brought in the fourth bottle. We had kept the same glasses. Harris lifted his glass.

'I say. You know this does utilise well.'

Bill slapped him on the back.

'Good old Harris.'

'I say. You know my name isn't really Harris. It's Wilson-Harris. All one name. With a hyphen, you know.'

'Good old Wilson-Harris,' Bill said. 'We call you Harris because we're so fond of you.'

'I say, Barnes. You don't know what this all means to me.'

'Come on and utilise another glass,' I said.

'Barnes. Really, Barnes, you can't know. That's all.'

'Drink up, Harris.'

We walked back down the road from Roncevalles with Harris between us. We had lunch at the inn and Harris went with us to the bus. He gave us his card, with his address in London and his club and his business address, and as we got on the bus he handed us each an envelope. I opened mine and there were a dozen flies in it. Harris had tied them himself. He tied all his own flies.

'I say, Harris—' I began.

'No, no!' he said. He was climbing down from the bus. 'They're not first-rate flies at all. I only thought if you fished them some time it might remind you of what a good time we had.'

The bus started. Harris stood in front of the post-office. He waved. As we started along the road he turned and walked back toward the inn.

'Say, wasn't that Harris nice?' Bill said.

'I think he really did have a good time.'

'Harris? You bet he did.'

'I wish he'd come to Pamplona.'

'He wanted to fish.'

'Yes. You couldn't tell how English would mix with each other, anyway.'

'I suppose not.'

We got into Pamplona late in the afternoon and the bus stopped in front of the Hotel Montoya. Out in the plaza they were stringing electric-light wires to light the plaza for the fiesta. A few kids came up when the bus stopped, and a custom officer for the town made all the people getting down from the bus open their bundles on the sidewalk. We went into the hotel and on the stairs I met Montoya. He shook hands with us, smiling in his embarrassed way.

'Your friends are here,' he said.

'Mr Campbell?'

'Yes. Mr Cohn and Mr Campbell and Lady Ashley.'

He smiled as though there were something I would hear about.

'When did they get in?'

'Yesterday. I've saved you the rooms you had.'

'That's fine. Did you give Mr Campbell the room on the plaza?'

'Yes. All the rooms we looked at.'

'Where are our friends now?'

'I think they went to the pelota.'

'And how about the bulls?'

Montoya smiled. 'To-night,' he said. 'To-night at seven o'clock they bring in the Villar bulls, and to-morrow come the Miuras. Do you all go down?'

'Oh, yes. They've never seen a desencajonada.'

Montoya put his hand on my shoulder.

'I'll see you there.'

He smiled again. He always smiled as though bull-fighting were a very special secret between the two of us; a rather shocking but really very deep secret that we knew about. He always smiled as though there were something lewd about the secret to outsiders, but that it was something that we understood. It would not do to expose it to people who would not understand.

'Your friend, is he aficionado, too?' Montoya smiled at Bill.

'Yes. He came all the way from New York to see the San Fermines.'

'Yes?' Montoya politely disbelieved. 'But he's not aficionado like you.'

He put his hand on my shoulder again embarrassedly.

'Yes,' I said. 'He's a real aficionado.'

'But he's not aficionado like you are.'

Aficion means passion. An aficionado is one who is passionate about the bull-fights. All the good bull-fighters stayed at Montoya's hotel; that is, those with aficion stayed there. The commercial bull-fighters stayed once, perhaps, and then did not come back. The good ones came each year. In Montoya's room were their photographs. The photographs were dedicated to Juanito Montoya or to his sister. The photographs of bull-fighters Montoya had really believed in were framed. Photographs of bull-fighters who had been without aficion Montoya kept in a drawer of his desk. They often had the most flattering inscriptions. But they did not mean anything. One day Montoya took them all out and dropped them in the waste-basket. He did not want them around.

We often talked about bulls and bull-fighters. I had stopped at the

Montoya for several years. We never talked for very long at a time. It was simply the pleasure of discovering what we each felt. Men would come in from distant towns and before they left Pamplona stop and talk for a few minutes with Montoya about bulls. These men were aficionados. Those who were aficionados could always get rooms even when the hotel was full. Montoya introduced me to some of them. They were always very polite at first, and it amused them very much that I should be an American. Somehow it was taken for granted that an American could not have aficion. He might simulate it or confuse it with excitement, but he could not really have it. When they saw that I had aficion, and there was no password, no set questions that could bring it out, rather it was a sort of oral spiritual examination with the questions always a little on the defensive and never apparent, there was this same embarrassed putting the hand on the shoulder, or a 'Buen hombre.' But nearly always there was the actual touching. It seemed as though they wanted to touch you to make it certain.

Montoya could forgive anything of a bull-fighter who had aficion. He could forgive attacks of nerves, panic, bad, unexplainable actions, all sorts of lapses. For one who had aficion he could forgive anything. At once he forgave me all my friends. Without his ever saying anything they were simply a little something shameful between us, like the spilling open of the horses in bull-fighting.

Bill had gone upstairs as we came in, and I found him washing and changing in his room.

'Well,' he said, 'talk a lot of Spanish?'

'He was telling me about the bulls coming in to-night.'

'Let's find the gang and go down.'

'All right. They'll probably be at the café.'

'Have you got tickets?'

'Yes. I got them for all the unloadings.'

'What's it like?' He was pulling his cheek before the glass, looking to see if there were unshaved patches under the line of the jaw.

'It's pretty good,' I said. 'They let the bulls out of the cages one at a time, and they have steers in the corral to receive them and keep them from fighting, and the bulls tear in at the steers and the steers run around like old maids trying to quiet them down.'

'Do they ever gore the steers?'

'Sure. Sometimes they go right after them and kill them.'

'Can't the steers do anything?'

'No. They're trying to make friends.'

'What do they have them in for?'

'To quiet down the bulls and keep them from breaking their horns against the stone walls, or goring each other.'

'Must be swell being a steer.'

We went down the stairs and out of the door and walked across the square toward the Café Iruna. There were two lonely-looking ticket-houses standing in the square. Their windows, marked SOL, SOL Y SOMBRA, and SOMBRA, were shut. They would not open until the day before the fiesta.

Across the square the white wicker tables and chairs of the Iruna extended out beyond the arcade to the edge of the street. I looked for Brett and Mike at the tables. There they were. Brett and Mike and Robert Cohn. Brett was wearing a Basque beret. So was Mike. Robert Cohn was bare-headed and wearing his spectacles. Brett saw us coming and waved. Her eyes crinkled up as we came up to the table.

'Hello, you chaps!' she called.

Brett was happy. Mike had a way of getting an intensity of feeling into shaking hands. Robert Cohn shook hands because we were back.

'Where the hell have you been?' I asked.

'I brought them up here,' Cohn said.

'What rot,' Brett said. 'We'd have gotten here earlier if you hadn't come.'

'You'd never have gotten here.'

'What rot! You chaps are brown. Look at Bill.'

'Did you get good fishing?' Mike asked. 'We wanted to join you.'

'It wasn't bad. We missed you.'

'I wanted to come,' Cohn said, 'but I thought I ought to bring them.'

'You bring us. What rot!'

'Was it really good?' Mike asked. 'Did you take many?'

'Some days we took a dozen apiece. There was an Englishman up there.'

'Named Harris,' Bill said. 'Ever know him, Mike? He was in the war, too.'

'Fortunate fellow,' Mike said. 'What times we had. How I wish those dear days were back.'

'Don't be an ass.'

'Were you in the war, Mike?' Cohn asked.

'Was I not?'

'He was a very distinguished soldier,' Brett said. 'Tell them about the time your horse bolted down Piccadilly.'

'I'll not. I've told that four times.'

'You never told me,' Robert Cohn said.

'I'll not tell that story. It reflects discredit on me.'

'Tell them about your medals.'

'I'll not. That story reflects great discredit on me.'

'What story's that?'

'Brett will tell you. She tells all the stories that reflect discredit on me.'

'Go on. Tell it, Brett.'

'Should I?'

'I'll tell it myself.'

'What medals have you got, Mike?'

'I haven't got any medals.'

'You must have some.'

'I suppose I've the usual medals. But I never sent in for them. One time there was this wopping big dinner and the Prince of Wales was to be there, and the cards said medals will be worn. So naturally I had no medals, and I stopped at my tailor's and he was impressed by the invitation, and I thought that's a good piece of business, and I said to him: "You've got to fix me up with some medals." He said: "What medals, sir?" and I said: "Oh, any medals. Just give me a few medals." So he said: "What medals *have* you, sir?" And I said: "How should I know?" Did he think I spent all my time reading the bloody gazette? "Just give me a good lot. Pick them out yourself." So he got me some medals, you know, miniature medals, and handed me the box, and I put it in my pocket and forgot it. Well, I went to the dinner, and it was the night they'd shot Henry Wilson, so the Prince didn't come and the King didn't come, and no one wore any medals, and all these coves were busy taking off their medals, and I had mine in my pocket.'

He stopped for us to laugh.

'Is that all?'

'That's all. Perhaps I didn't tell it right.'

'You didn't,' said Brett. 'But no matter.'

We were all laughing.

'Ah, yes,' said Mike. 'I know it now. It was a damn dull dinner, and I couldn't stick it, so I left. Later on in the evening I found the box in my pocket. "What's this?" I said. "Medals? Bloody military medals?" So I cut them all off their backing–you know, they put them on a strip–and gave them all around. Gave one to each girl. Form of souvenir. They thought I was hell's own shakes of a soldier. Give away medals in a night club. Dashing fellow.'

'Tell the rest,' Brett said.

'Don't you think that was funny?' Mike asked. We were all laughing. 'It was. I swear it was. Any rate, my tailor wrote me and wanted the medals back. Sent a man around. Kept on writing for months. Seems some chap had left them to be cleaned. Frightfully military cove. Set hell's own store by them.' Mike paused. 'Rotten luck for the tailor,' he said.

'You don't mean it,' Bill said. 'I should think it would have been grand for the tailor.'

'Frightfully good tailor. Never believe it to see me now,' Mike said. 'I used to pay him a hundred pounds a year just to keep him quiet. So he wouldn't send me any bills. Frightful blow to him when I went bankrupt. It was right after the medals. Gave his letters rather a bitter tone.'

'How did you go bankrupt?' Bill asked.

'Two ways,' Mike said. 'Gradually and then suddenly.'

'What brought it on?'

'Friends,' said Mike. 'I had a lot of friends. False friends. Then I had creditors, too. Probably had more creditors than anybody in England.'

'Tell them about in the court,' Brett said.

'I don't remember,' Mike said. 'I was just a little tight.'

'Tight!' Brett exclaimed. 'You were blind!'

'Extraordinary thing,' Mike said. 'Met my former partner the other day. Offered to buy me a drink.'

'Tell them about your learned counsel,' Brett said.

'I will not,' Mike said. 'My learned counsel was blind, too. I say, this is a gloomy subject. Are we going down and see these bulls unloaded or not?'

'Let's go down.'

We called the waiter, paid, and started to walk through the town. I started off walking with Brett, but Robert Cohn came up and joined her on the other side. The three of us walked along, past the Ayuntamiento with the banners hung from the balcony, down past the market and down past the steep street that led to the bridge across the Arga. There were many people walking to go and see the bulls, and carriages drove down the hill and across the bridge, the drivers, the horses, and the whips rising above the walking people in the street. Across the bridge we turned up a road to the corrals. We passed a wine-shop with a sign in the window: Good Wine 30 Centimes a Liter.

'That's where we'll go when funds get low,' Brett said.

The woman standing in the door of the wine-shop looked at us as we passed. She called to someone in the house and three girls came to the window and stared. They were staring at Brett.

At the gate of the corrals two men took tickets from the people that went in. We went in through the gate. There were trees inside and a low, stone house. At the far end was the stone wall of the corrals, with apertures in the stone that were like loopholes running all along the face of each corral. A ladder led up to the top of the wall, and people were climbing up the ladder and spreading down to stand on the walls that separated the two corrals. As we came up the ladder, walking across the grass under the trees, we passed the big grey painted cages with the bulls in them. There was one bull in each travelling box. They had come by train from a bull-breeding ranch in Castile, and had been unloaded off flat-cars at the station and brought up here to be let out of their cages into the corrals. Each cage was stencilled with the name and the brand of the bull-breeder.

We climbed up and found a place on the wall looking down into the corral. The stone walls were whitewashed, and there was straw on the ground and wooden feed-boxes and water-troughs set against the wall.

'Look up there,' I said.

Beyond the river rose the plateau of the town. All along the old walls and ramparts people were standing. The three lines of fortifications made three black lines of people. Above the walls there were heads in the windows of the houses. At the far end of the plateau boys climbed into the trees.

'They must think something is going to happen,' Brett said.

'They want to see the bulls.'

Mike and Bill were on the other wall across the pit of the corral. They waved to us. People who had come late were standing behind us, pressing against us when other people crowded them.

'Why don't they start?' Robert Cohn asked.

A single mule was hitched to one of the cages and dragged it up against the gate in the corral wall. The men shoved and lifted it with crowbars into position against the gate. Men were standing on the wall ready to pull up the gate of the corral and then the gate of the cage. At the other end of the corral a gate opened and two steers came in, swaying their heads and trotting, their lean flanks swinging. They stood together at the far end, their heads toward the gate where the bull would enter.

'They don't look happy,' Brett said.

The men on top of the wall leaned back and pulled up the door of the corral. Then they pulled up the door of the cage.

I leaned way over the wall and tried to see into the cage. It was dark. Someone rapped on the cage with an iron bar. Inside something seemed to explode. The bull, striking into the wood from side to side with his horns, made a great noise. Then I saw a dark muzzle and the shadow of horns, and then, with a clattering on the wood in the hollow box, the bull charged and came out into the corral, skidding with his forefeet in the straw as he stopped, his head up, the great hump of muscle on his neck swollen tight, his body muscles quivering as he looked up at the crowd on the stone walls. The two steers backed away against the wall, their heads sunken, their eyes watching the bull.

The bull saw them and charged. A man shouted from behind one of the boxes and slapped his hat against the planks, and the bull, before he reached the steer, turned, gathered himself and charged where the man had been, trying to reach him behind the planks with half-dozen quick, searching drives with the right horn.

'My God, isn't he beautiful?' Brett said. We were looking right down on him.

'Look how he knows how to use his horns,' I said. 'He's got a left and a right just like a boxer.'

'Not really?'

'You watch.'

'It goes too fast.'

'Wait. There'll be another one in a minute.'

They had backed up another cage into the entrance. In the far corner a man, from behind one of the plank shelters, attracted the bull, and while the bull was facing away the gate was pulled up and a second bull came out into the corral.

He charged straight for the steers and two men ran out from behind the planks and shouted, to turn him. He did not change his direction and the men shouted: 'Hah! Hah! Toro!' and waved their arms; the two steers turned sideways to take the shock, and the bull drove into one of the steers.

'Don't look,' I said to Brett. She was watching, fascinated.

'Fine,' I said. 'If it doesn't buck you.'

'I saw it,' she said. 'I saw him shift from his left to his right horn.'

'Damn good!'

The steer was down now, his neck stretched out, his head twisted, he lay the way he had fallen. Suddenly the bull left off and made for the other steer which had been standing at the far end, his head swinging, watching it all. The steer ran awkwardly and the bull caught him, hooked him lightly in the flank, and then turned away and looked up at the crowd on the walls, his crest of muscle rising. The steer came up to him and made as though to nose at him and the bull hooked perfunctorily. The next time he nosed at the steer and then the two of them trotted over to the other bull.

When the next bull came out, all three, the two bulls and the steer, stood together, their heads side by side, their horns against the newcomer. In a few minutes the steer picked the new bull up, quieted him down, and made him one of the herd. When the last two bulls had been unloaded the herd were all together.

The steer who had been gored had gotten to his feet and stood against the stone wall. None of the bulls came near him, and he did not attempt to join the herd.

We climbed down from the wall with the crowd, and had a last look at the bulls through the loopholes in the wall of the corral. They were all quiet now, their heads down. We got a carriage outside and rode up to the café. Mike and Bill came in half an hour later. They had stopped on the way for several drinks.

We were sitting in the café.

'That's an extraordinary business,' Brett said.

'Will those last ones fight as well as the first?' Robert Cohn asked. 'They seemed to quiet down awfully fast.'

'They all know each other,' I said. 'They're only dangerous when they're alone, or only two or three of them together.'

'What do you mean, dangerous?' Bill said, 'They all looked dangerous to me.'

'They only want to kill when they're alone. Of course, if you went in there you'd probably detach one of them from the herd, and he'd be dangerous.'

'That's too complicated,' Bill said. 'Don't you ever detach me from the herd, Mike.'

'I say,' Mike said, 'they *were* fine bulls, weren't they? Did you see their horns?'

'Did I not?' said Brett. 'I had no idea what they were like.'

'Did you see the one hit that steer?' Mike asked. 'That was extraordinary.'

'It's no life being a steer,' Robert Cohn said.

'Don't you think so?' Mike said. 'I would have thought you'd loved being a steer, Robert.'

'What do you mean, Mike?'

'They lead such a quiet life. They never say anything and they're always hanging about so.'

We were embarrassed. Bill laughed. Robert Cohn was angry. Mike went on talking.

'I should think you'd love it. You'd never have to say a word. Come on, Robert. Do say something. Don't just sit there.'

'I said something, Mike. Don't you remember? About the steers.'

'Oh, say something more. Say something funny. Can't you see we're all having a good time here?'

'Come off it, Michael. You're drunk,' Brett said.

'I'm not drunk. I'm quite serious. *Is* Robert Cohn going to follow Brett around like a steer all the time?'

'Shut up, Michael. Try and show a little breeding.'

'Breeding be damned. Who has any breeding, anyway, except bulls? Aren't the bulls lovely? Don't you like them, Bill? Why don't you say something, Robert? Don't sit there looking like a bloody funeral. What if Brett did sleep with you? She's slept with lots of better people than you.'

'Shut up,' Cohn said. He stood up. 'Shut up, Mike.'

'Oh, don't stand up and act as though you were going to hit me. That won't make any difference to me. Tell me, Robert. Why do you follow Brett around like a poor bloody steer? Don't you know you're not wanted? I know when I'm not wanted. Why don't you know when you're not wanted. You came down to San Sebastian where you weren't wanted, and followed Brett around like a bloody steer. Do you think that's right?'

'Shut up. You're drunk.'

'Perhaps I am drunk. Why aren't you drunk? Why don't you ever get drunk, Robert? You know you didn't have a good time at San Sebastian because none of our friends would invite you on any of the parties. You can't blame them hardly. Can you? I asked them to. They wouldn't do it. You can't blame them, now. Can you? Now, answer me. Can you blame them?'

'Go to hell, Mike.'

'I can't blame them. Can you blame them? Why do you follow Brett around? Haven't you any manners? How do you think it makes *me* feel?'

'You're a splendid one to talk about manners,' Brett said. 'You've such lovely manners.'

'Come on, Robert,' Bill said.

'What do you follow her around for?'

Bill stood up and took hold of Cohn.

'Don't go,' Mike said. 'Robert Cohn's going to buy a drink.'

Bill went off with Cohn. Cohn's face was sallow. Mike went on talking. I sat and listened for a while. Brett looked disgusted.

'I say, Michael, you might not be such a bloody ass,' she interrupted. 'I'm not saying he's not right, you know.' She turned to me.

The emotion left Mike's voice. We were all friends together.

'I'm not so damn drunk as I sounded,' he said.

'I know you're not,' Brett said.

'We're none of us sober,' I said.

'I didn't say anything I didn't mean.'

'But you put it so badly,' Brett laughed.

'He was an ass, though. He came down to San Sebastian where he damn well wasn't wanted. He hung around Brett and just *looked* at her. It made me damned well sick.'

'He did behave very badly,' Brett said.

'Mark you. Brett's had affairs with men before. She tells me all about everything. She gave me this chap Cohn's letters to read. I wouldn't read them.'

'Damned noble of you.'

'No, listen, Jake. Brett's gone off with men. But they weren't ever Jews, and they didn't come and hang about afterward.'

'Damned good chaps,' Brett said. 'It's all rot to talk about it. Michael and I understand each other.'

'She gave me Robert Cohn's letters. I wouldn't read them.'

'You wouldn't read any letters, darling. You wouldn't read mine.'

'I can't read letters,' Mike said. 'Funny, isn't it?'

'You can't read anything.'

'No. You're wrong there. I read quite a bit. I read when I'm at home.'

'You'll be writing next,' Brett said. 'Come on, Michael. Do buck up. You've got to go through with this thing now. He's here. Don't spoil the fiesta.'

'Well, let him behave, then.'

'He'll behave. I'll tell him.'

'You tell him, Jake. Tell him either he must behave or get out.'

'Yes,' I said. 'It would be nice for me to tell him.'

'Look, Brett. Tell Jake what Robert calls you. That *is* perfect, you know.'

'Oh, no. I can't.'

'Go on. We're all friends. Aren't we all friends, Jake?'

'I can't tell him. It's too ridiculous.'

'I'll tell him.'

'You won't, Michael. Don't be an ass.'

'He calls her Circe,' Mike said. 'He claims she turns men into swine. Damn good. I wish I were one of these literary chaps.'

'He'd be good, you know,' Brett said. 'He writes a good letter.'

'I know,' I said. 'He wrote me from San Sebastian.'

'That was nothing,' Brett said. 'He can write a damned amusing letter.'

'She made me write that. She was supposed to be ill.'

'I damned well was, too.'

'Come on,' I said, 'we must go in and eat.'

'How should I meet Cohn?' Mike said.

'Just act as though nothing had happened.'

'It's quite all right with me,' Mike said. 'I'm not embarrassed.'

'If he says anything, just say you were tight.'

'Quite. And the funny thing is I think I was tight.'

'Come on,' Brett said. 'Are these poisonous things paid for? I must bathe before dinner.'

We walked across the square. It was dark and all around the square were the lights from the cafés under the arcades. We walked across the gravel under the trees to the hotel.

They went upstairs and I stopped to speak with Montoya.

'Well, how did you like the bulls?' he asked.

'Good. They were nice bulls.'

'They're all right'–Montoya shook his head–'but they're not too good.'

'What didn't you like about them?'

'I don't know. They just didn't give me the feeling that they were so good.'

'I know what you mean.'

'They're all right.'

'Yes. They're all right.'

'How did your friends like them?'

'Fine.'

'Good,' Montoya said.

I went upstairs. Bill was in his room, standing on the balcony looking out at the square. I stood beside him.

'Where's Cohn?'

'Upstairs in his room.'

'How does he feel?'

'Like hell, naturally. Mike was awful. He's terrible when he's tight.'

'He wasn't so tight.'

'The hell he wasn't. I know what we had before we came to the café.'

'He sobered up afterward.'

'Good. He was terrible. I don't like Cohn, God knows, and I think it was a silly trick for him to go down to San Sebastian, but nobody has any business to talk like Mike.'

'How'd you like the bulls?'

'Grand. It's grand the way they bring them out.'

'To-morrow come the Miuras.'

'When does the fiesta start?'

'Day after to-morrow.'

'We've got to keep Mike from getting so tight. That kind of stuff is terrible.'

'We'd better get cleaned up for supper.'

'Yes. That will be a pleasant meal.'

'Won't it?'

As a matter of fact, supper was a pleasant meal. Brett wore a black, sleeveless evening dress. She looked quite beautiful. Mike acted as though nothing had happened. I had to go up and bring Robert Cohn down. He was reserved and formal, and his face was still taut and sallow, but he cheered up finally. He could not stop looking at Brett. It seemed to make him happy. It must have been pleasant for him to see her looking so lovely and know he had been away with her and that everyone knew it. They could not take that away from him. Bill was very funny. So was Michael. They were good together.

It was like certain dinners I remember from the war. There was much wine, an ignored tension, and a feeling of things coming that you could not prevent happening. Under the wine I lost the disgusted feeling and was happy. It seemed they were all such nice people.

14

I do not know what time I got to bed. I remember undressing, putting on a bathrobe, and standing out on the balcony. I knew I was quite drunk, and when I came in I put on the light over the head of the bed and started to read. I was reading a book by Turgenieff. Probably I read the same two pages over several times. It was one of the stories in *A Sportsman's Sketches*. I had read it before, but it seemed quite new. The country became very clear and the feeling of pressure in my head seemed to loosen, I was very drunk and I did not want to shut my eyes because the room would go round and round. If I kept on reading that feeling would pass.

I heard Brett and Robert Cohn come up the stairs. Cohn said good-night outside the room and went on up to his room. I heard Brett go into the room next door. Mike was already in bed. He had come in with me and hour before. He woke as she came in, and they talked together. I heard them laugh. I turned off the light and tried to go to sleep. It was not necessary to read any more. I could shut my eyes without getting the wheeling sensation. But I could not sleep. There is no reason why because it is dark you should look at things differently from when it is light. The hell there isn't!

I figured that all out once, and for six months I never slept with the electric light off. That was another bright idea. To hell with women, anyway. To hell with you, Brett Ashley.

Women made such swell friends. Awfully swell. In the first place, you had to be in love with a woman to have a basis of friendship. I had been having Brett for a friend. I had not been thinking about her side of it. I had been getting something for nothing. That only delayed the presentation of the bill. The bill always came. That was one of the swell things you could count on.

I thought I had paid for everything. Not like the woman pays and pays and pays. No idea of retribution or punishment. Just exchange of values. You gave up something and got something else. Or you worked for something. You paid some way for everything that was any good. I paid my way into enough things that I liked, so that I had a good time. Either you paid by learning about them, or by experience, or by taking chances, or by money. Enjoying living was learning to get your money's worth and knowing when you had it. You could get your money's worth. The world was a good place to buy in. It seemed like a fine philosophy. In five years, I thought, it will seem just as silly as all the other fine philosophies I've had.

Perhaps that wasn't true, though. Perhaps as you went along you did learn something. I did not care what it was all about. All I wanted to know was how to live in it. Maybe if you found out how to live in it you learned from that what it was all about.

I wished Mike would not behave so terribly to Cohn, though. Mike was a bad drunk. Brett was a good drunk. Bill was a good drunk. Cohn was never drunk. Mike was unpleasant after he passed a certain point. I liked to see him hurt Cohn. I wished he would not do it, though, because afterward it made me disgusted at myself. That was morality; things that made you disgusted afterward. No, that must be immorality. That was a large statement. What a lot of bilge I could think up at night. What rot–I could hear Brett say it. What rot! When you were with English you got into the habit of using English expressions in your thinking. The English spoken language–the upper classes, anyway–must have fewer words than the Eskimo. Of course I didn't know anything about the Eskimo. Maybe the Eskimo was a fine language. Say the Cherokee. I didn't know anything about the Cherokee, either. The English talked with inflected phrases. One phrase to mean everything. I liked them, though. I liked the way they talked. Take Harris. Still Harris was not the upper classes.

I turned on the light again and read. I read the Turgenieff. I knew that now, reading it in the over-sensitised state of my mind after much too much brandy, I would remember it somewhere, and afterward it would seem as though it had really happened to me. I would always have it. That was another good thing you paid for and then had. Some time along toward daylight I went to sleep.

The next two days in Pamplona were quiet, and there were no more rows. The town was getting ready for the fiesta. Workmen put up the gate-posts that were to shut off the side streets when the bulls were released from the corrals and came running through the streets in the morning on their way to the ring. The workmen dug holes and fitted in the timbers, each timber numbered for its regular place. Out on the plateau beyond the town employees of the bull-ring exercised picador horses, galloping them stiff-legged on the hard, sun-baked fields behind the bull-ring. The big gate of the bull-ring was open, and inside the amphitheatre was being swept. The ring was rolled and sprinkled, and carpenters replaced weakened or cracked planks in the barrera. Standing at the edge of the smooth rolled sand you could look up in the empty stands and see old women sweeping out the boxes.

Outside, the fence that led from the last street of the town to the entrance of the bull-ring was already in place and made a long pen; the crowd would come running down with the bulls behind them on the morning of the day of the first bull-fight. Out across the plain, where the horse and cattle fair would be, some gypsies had camped under the trees. The wine and aguardiente sellers were putting up their booths. One booth advertised ANIS DEL TORO. The cloth sign hung against the planks in the hot sun. In the big square that was the centre of the town there was no change yet. We sat in the white wicker chairs on the terrasse of the café and watched the motor-buses come in and unload peasants from the country coming in to the market, and we watched the buses fill up and start out with peasants sitting with their saddle-bags full of the things they had bought in the town. The tall grey motor-buses were the only life of the square except for the pigeons and the man with a hose who sprinkled the gravelled square and watered the streets.

In the evening was the paseo. For an hour after dinner everyone, all the good-looking girls, the officers from the garrison, all the fashionable people of the town, walked in the street on one side of the square while the café tables filled with the regular after-dinner crowd.

During the morning I usually sat in the café and read the Madrid papers and then walked in the town or out into the country. Sometimes Bill went along. Sometimes he wrote in his room. Robert Cohn spent the mornings studying Spanish or trying to get a shave at the barber shop. Brett and Mike never got up until noon. We all had a vermouth at the café. It was a quiet life and no one was drunk. I went to church a couple of times, once with Brett. She said she wanted to hear me go to confession, but I told her that not only was it impossible, but it was not as interesting as it sounded, and, besides, it would be in a language she did not know. We met Cohn as we came out of church, and although it was obvious he had followed us, yet he was very pleasant and nice, and we all three went for a walk out to the gypsy camp, and Brett had her fortune told.

It was a good morning, there were high white clouds above the mountains. It had rained a little in the night and it was fresh and cool on the plateau, and there was a wonderful view. We all felt good and we felt healthy, and I felt quite friendly to Cohn. You could not be upset about anything on a day like that.

That was the last day before the fiesta.

15

At noon on Sunday, the 6th of July, the fiesta exploded. There is no other way to describe it. People had been coming in all day from the country, but they were assimilated in the town and you did not notice them. The square was as quiet in the hot sun as on any other day. The peasants were in the outlying wine-shops. There they were drinking, getting ready for the fiesta. They had come in so recently from the plains and the hills that it was necessary that they made their shifting in values gradually. They could not start in paying café prices. They got their money's worth in the wine-shops. Money still had a definite value in hours worked and bushels of grain sold. Late in the fiesta it would not matter what they paid, nor where they bought.

Now on the day of the starting of the fiesta of San Fermin they had been in the wine-shops of the narrow streets of the town since early morning. Going down the streets in the morning on the way to mass in the cathedral, I heard them singing through the open doors of the shops. They were warming up. There were many people at the eleven o'clock mass. San Fermin is also a religious festival.

I walked down the hill from the cathedral and up the street to the café on the square. It was a little before noon. Robert Cohn and Bill were sitting at one of the tables. The marble-topped tables and the white wicker chairs were gone. They were replaced by cast-iron tables and severe folding chairs. The café was like a battleship stripped for action. To-day the waiters did not leave you alone all morning to read without asking you if you wanted to order something. A waiter came up as soon as I sat down.

'What are you drinking?' I asked Bill and Robert.

'Sherry,' Cohn said.

'Jerez,' I said to the waiter.

Before the waiter brought the sherry the rocket that announced the fiesta went up in the square. It burst and there was a grey ball of smoke high up above the Theatre Gayarre, across on the other side of the plaza. The ball of smoke hung in the sky like a shrapnel burst, and as I watched, another rocket came up to it, trickling smoke in the bright sunlight. I saw the bright flash as it burst and another little cloud of smoke appeared. By the time the second rocket had burst there were so many people in the arcade, that had been empty a minute before, that the waiter, holding the bottle high up over his head, could hardly get through the crowd to our table. People were coming into the square from all sides, and down the street we heard the pipes and the fifes and the drums coming. They were playing the *riau-riau* music, the pipes shrill and the drums pounding, and behind them came the men and boys dancing. When the fifers stopped they all crouched down in the street, and when the reed-pipes and the fifes shrilled, and the flat, dry, hollow drums tapped it out again, they all went up in the air dancing. In the crowd you saw only the heads and shoulders of the dancers going up and down.

In the square a man, bent over, was playing on a reed-pipe, and a crowd of children were following him, shouting and pulling at his clothes. He came out of the square, the children following him, and piped them past the café and down a side street. We saw his blank pock-marked face as he went by, piping, the children close behind him shouting and pulling at him.

'He must be the village idiot,' Bill said. 'My God! look at that!'

Down the street came dancers. The street was solid with dancers, all men. They were all dancing in time behind their own fifers and drummers. They were a club of some sort, and all wore workmen's blue smocks, and red handkerchiefs around their necks, and carried a great banner on two poles. The banner danced up and down with them as they came down, surrounded by the crowd.

'Hurray for Wine! Hurray for the Foreigners!' was painted on the banner.

'Where are the foreigners?' Robert Cohn asked.

'We're the foreigners,' Bill said.

All the time rockets were going up. The café tables were all full now. The square was emptying of people and the crowd was filling the cafés.

'Where's Brett and Mike?' Bill asked.

'I'll go and get them,' Cohn said.

'Bring them here.'

The fiesta was really started. It kept up day and night for seven days. The dancing kept up, the drinking kept up, the noise went on. The things that happened could only have happened during a fiesta. Everything became quite unreal finally and it seemed as though nothing could have any consequences. It seemed out of place to think of consequences during the fiesta. All during the fiesta you had the feeling, even when it was quiet, that you had to shout any remark to make it heard. It was the same feeling about any action. It was a fiesta and it went on for seven days.

That afternoon was the big religious procession. San Fermin was translated from one church to another. In the procession were all the dignitaries, civil and religious. We could not see them because the crowd was too great. Ahead of the formal procession and behind it danced the *riau-riau* dancers. There was one mass of yellow shirts dancing up and down in the crowd. All we could see of the procession through the closely pressed people that crowded all the side streets and curbs were the great giants, cigar-store Indians, thirty feet high, Moors, a King and Queen, whirling and waltzing solemnly to the *riau-riau.*

They were all standing outside the chapel where San Fermin and the dignitaries had passed in leaving a guard of soldiers, the giants, with the men who danced in them standing beside their resting frames, and the dwarfs moving with their whacking bladders through the crowd. We started inside and there was a smell of incense and people filing back into the church, but Brett was stopped just inside the door because she had no hat, so we went out again and along the street that ran back from the chapel into town. The street was lined on both sides with people keeping their place at the curb for the return of the procession. Some dancers formed a circle around Brett and started to dance. They wore big wreaths of white garlics around their necks. They took Bill and me by the arms and put us in the circle. Bill started to dance, too. They were all chanting. Brett wanted to dance, but they did not want her to. They wanted her as an image to dance around. When the song ended with the sharp *riau-riau* they rushed us into a wine-shop.

We stood at the counter. They had Brett seated on a wine-cask. It was dark in the wine-shop and full of men singing, hard-voiced singing. Back of the counter they drew the wine from casks. I put down money for the wine, but one of the men picked it up and put it back in my pocket.

'I want a leather wine-bottle,' Bill said.

'There's a place down the street,' I said. 'I'll go get a couple.'

The dancers did not want me to go out. Three of them were sitting on the high wine-cask beside Brett, teaching her to drink out of the wine-skins. They had hung a wreath of garlics around her neck. Someone insisted on giving her a glass. Somebody was teaching Bill a song. Singing it into his ear. Beating time on Bill's back.

I explained to them that I would be back. Outside in the street I went down the street looking for the shop that made leather wine-bottles. The crowd was packed on the sidewalks and many of the shops were shuttered, and I could not find it. I walked as far as the church, looking on both sides of the street. Then I asked a man and he took me by the arm and led me to it. The shutters were up but the door was open.

Inside it smelled of fresh-tanned leather and hot tar. A man was stencilling completed wine-skins. They hung from the roof in bunches. He took one down, blew it up, screwed the nozzle tight, and then jumped on it.

'See! It doesn't leak.'

'I want another one, too. A big one.'

He took down a big one that would hold a gallon or more from the roof. He blew it up, his cheeks puffing ahead of the wine-skin, and stood on the bota holding on to a chair.

'What are you going to do? Sell them in Bayonne?'

'No. Drink out of them.'

He slapped me on the back.

'Good man. Eight pesetas for the two. The lowest price.'

The man who was stencilling the new ones and tossing them into a pile stopped.

'It's true,' he said. 'Eight pesetas is cheap.'

I paid and went out and along the street back to the wine-shop. It was darker than ever inside and very crowded. I did not see Brett and Bill, and some one said they were in the back room. At the counter the girl filled the two wine-skins for me. One held two litres. The other held five litres.

Filling them both cost three pesetas sixty centimos. Someone at the counter, that I had never seen before, tried to pay for the wine, but I finally paid for it myself. The man who had wanted to pay then bought me a drink. He would not let me buy one in return, but said he would take a rinse of the mouth from the new wine-bag. He tipped the big five-litre bag up and squeezed it so the wine hissed against the back of his throat.

'All right,' he said, and handed back the bag.

In the back room Brett and Bill were sitting on barrels surrounded by the dancers. Everybody had his arms on everybody else's shoulders, and they were all singing. Mike was sitting at a table with several men in their shirt-sleeves, eating from a bowl of tuna fish, chopped onions and vinegar. They were all drinking wine and mopping up the oil and vinegar with pieces of bread.

'Hello, Jake. Hello!' Mike called. 'Come here. I want you to meet my friends. We're all having an hors-d'œuvre.'

I was introduced to the people at the table. They supplied their names to Mike and sent for a fork for me.

'Stop eating their dinner, Michael,' Brett shouted from the wine-barrels.

'I don't want to eat up your meal,' I said when someone handed me a fork.

'Eat,' he said. 'What do you think it's here for?'

I unscrewed the nozzle of the big wine-bottle and handed it around. Everyone took a drink, tipping the wine-skin at arm's length.

Outside, above the singing, we could hear the music of the procession going by.

'Isn't that the procession?' Mike asked.

'Nada,' someone said. 'It's nothing. Drink up. Lift the bottle.'

'Where did they find you?' I asked Mike.

'Someone brought me here,' Mike said. 'They said you were here.'

'Where's Cohn?'

'He's passed out,' Brett called. 'They've put him away somewhere.'

'Where is he?'

'I don't know.'

'How should we know?' Bill said. 'I think he's dead.'

'He's not dead,' Mike said. 'I know he's not dead. He's just passed out on Anis del Mono.'

As he said Anis del Mono one of the men at the table looked up, brought out a bottle from inside his smock, and handed it to me.

'No ' I said. 'No, thanks!'

'Yes. Yes. Arriba! Up with the bottle!'

I took a drink. It tasted of licorice and warmed all the way. I could feel it warming in my stomach.

'Where the hell is Cohn?'

'I don't know,' Mike said. 'I'll ask. Where is the drunken comrade?' he asked in Spanish.

'You want to see him?'

'Yes,' I said.

'Not me,' said Mike. 'This gent.'

The Anis del Mono man wiped his mouth and stood up.

'Come on.'

In a back room Robert Cohn was sleeping quietly on some wine-casks. It was almost too dark to see his face. They had covered him with a coat and another coat was folded under his head. Around his neck and on his chest was a big wreath of twisted garlics.

'Let him sleep,' the man whispered. 'He's all right.'

Two hours later Cohn appeared. He came into the front room still with the wreath of garlics around his neck. The Spaniards shouted when he came in. Cohn wiped his eyes and grinned.

'I must have been sleeping,' he said.

'Oh, not at all,' Brett said.

'You were only dead,' Bill said.

'Aren't we going to go and have some supper?' Cohn asked.

'Do you want to eat?'

'Yes. Why not? I'm hungry.'

'Eat those garlics, Robert,' Mike said. 'I say, do eat those garlics.'

Cohn stood there. His sleep had made him quite all right.

'Do let's go and eat,' Brett said. 'I must get a bath.'

'Come on,' Bill said. 'Let's translate Brett to the hotel.'

We said good-bye to many people and shook hands with many people and went out. Outside it was dark.

'What time is it, do you suppose?' Cohn asked.

'It's to-morrow,' Mike said. 'You've been asleep two days.'

'No,' said Cohn, 'what time is it?'

'It's ten o'clock.'

'What a lot we've drunk.'

'You mean what a lot *we've* drunk. You went to sleep.'

Going down the dark streets to the hotel we saw the sky-rockets going up in the square. Down the side streets that led to the square we saw the square solid with people, those in the centre all dancing.

It was a big meal at the hotel. It was the first meal of the prices being doubled for the fiesta, and there were several new courses. After the dinner we were out in the town. I remember resolving that I would stay up all night to watch the bulls go through the streets at six o'clock in the morning, and being so sleepy that I went to bed at four o'clock. The others stayed up.

My own room was locked and I could not find the key, so I went upstairs and slept on one of the beds in Cohn's room. The fiesta was going on outside in the night, but I was too sleepy for it to keep me awake. When I woke it was the sound of the rocket exploding that announced the release of the bulls from the corrals at the edge of town. They would race through the streets and out to the bull-ring. I had been sleeping heavily and I woke feeling I was too late. I put on a coat of Cohn's and went out on the balcony. Down below the narrow street was empty. All the balconies were crowded with people. Suddenly a crowd came down the street. They were all running, packed close together. They passed along and up the street toward the bull-ring and behind them came more men running faster, and then some stragglers who were really running. Behind them was a little bare space, and then the bulls, galloping, tossing their heads up and down. It all went out of sight around the corner. One man fell, rolled to the gutter, and lay quiet. But the bulls went right on, and did not notice him. They were all running together.

After they went out of sight a great roar came from the bull-ring. It kept on. Then finally the pop of the rocket that meant the bulls had gotten through the people in the ring and into the corrals. I went back in the room and got into bed. I had been standing on the stone balcony in bare feet. I knew our crowd must have all been out at the bull-ring. Back in bed, I went to sleep.

Cohn woke me when he came in. He started to undress and went over and closed the window because the people on the balcony of the house just across the street were looking in.

'Did you see the show?' I asked.

'Yes, we were all there.'

'Anybody get hurt?'

'One of the bulls got into the crowd in the ring and tossed six or eight people.'

'How did Brett like it?'

'It was all so sudden there wasn't any time for it to bother anybody.'

'I wish I had been up.'

'We didn't know where you were. We went to your room but it was locked.'

'Where did you stay up?'

'We danced at some club.'

'I got sleepy,' I said.

'My gosh! I'm sleepy now,' Cohn said. 'Doesn't this thing ever stop?'

'Not for a week.'

Bill opened the door and put his head in.

'Where were you, Jake?'

'I saw them go through from the balcony. How was it?'

'Grand.'

'Where you going?'

'To sleep.'

No one was up before noon. We ate at tables set out under the arcade. The town was full of people. We had to wait for a table. After lunch we went over to the Iruna. It had filled up, and as the time for the bull-fight came it got fuller, and the tables were crowded closer. There was a close, crowded hum that came every day before the bull-fight. The café did not make this same noise at any other time, no matter how crowded it was. This hum went on, and we were in it and a part of it.

I had taken six seats for all the fights. Three of them were barreras, the first row at the ring-side, and three were sobrepuertos, seats with wooden backs half-way up the amphitheatre. Mike thought Brett had best sit high up for her first time, and Cohn wanted to sit with them. Bill and I were going to sit in the barreras, and I gave the extra ticket to a waiter to sell. Bill said something to Cohn about what to do and how to look so he would not mind the horses. Bill had seen one season of bull-fights.

'I'm not worried about how I'll stand it. I'm only afraid I may be bored,' Cohn said.

'You think so?'

'Don't look at the horses, after the bull hits them,' I said to Brett. 'Watch the charge and see the picador try and keep the bull off, but then don't look again until the horse is dead if it's been hit.'

'I'm a little nervy about it,' Brett said. 'I'm worried whether I'll be able to go through with it all right.'

'You'll be all right. There's nothing but that horse part that will bother you, and they're only in for a few minutes with each bull. Just don't watch when it's bad.'

'She'll be all right,' Mike said. I'll look after her.'

'I don't think you'll be bored,' Bill said.

'I'm going over to the hotel to get the glasses and the wine-skin,' I said. 'See you back here. Don't get cock-eyed.'

'I'll come along,' Bill said. Brett smiled at us.

We walked around through the arcade to avoid the heat of the square.

'That Cohn gets me,' Bill said. 'He's got this Jewish superiority so strong that he thinks the only emotion he'll get out of the fight will be being bored.'

'We'll watch him with the glasses,' I said.

'Oh, to hell with him!'

'He spends a lot of time there.'

'I want him to stay there.'

In the hotel on the stairs we met Montoya.

'Come on,' said Montoya. 'Do you want to meet Pedro Romero?'

'Fine,' said Bill. 'Let's go see him.'

We followed Montoya up a flight and down the corridor.

'He's in room number eight,' Montoya explained. 'He's getting dressed for the bull-fight.'

Montoya knocked on the door and opened it. It was a gloomy room with a little light coming in from the window on the narrow street. There were two beds separated by a monastic partition. The electric light was on. The boy stood very straight and unsmiling in his bull-fighting clothes. His jacket hung over the back of a chair. They were just finishing winding his sash. His black hair shone under the electric light. He wore a white linen shirt and the sword-handler finished his sash and stood up and stepped back. Pedro Romero nodded, seeming very far away and dignified when we shook hands. Montoya said something about what great aficionados we were, and that we wanted to wish him luck. Romero listened very seriously. Then he turned to me. He was the best-looking boy I have ever seen.

'You go to the bull-fight,' he said in English.

'You know English,' I said, feeling like an idiot.

'No,' he answered, and smiled.

One of three men who had been sitting on the beds came up and asked us if we spoke French. 'Would you like me to interpret for you? Is there anything you would like to ask Pedro Romero?'

We thanked him. What was there that you would like to ask? The boy was nineteen years old, alone except for his sword-handler, and the three hangers-on, and the bull-fight was to commence in twenty minutes. We wished him 'Mucha suerte,' shook hands, and went out. He was standing, straight and handsome and altogether by himself, alone in the room with the hangers-on as we shut the door.

'He's a fine boy, don't you think so?' Montoya asked.

'He's a good-looking kid,' I said.

'He looks like a torero,' Montoya said. 'He has the type.'

'He's a fine boy.'

'We'll see how he is in the ring,' Montoya said.

We found the big leather wine-bottle leaning against the wall in my room, took it and the field-glasses, locked the door, and went downstairs.

It was a good bull-fight. Bill and I were very excited about Pedro Romero. Montoya was sitting about ten places away. After Romero had killed his first bull Montoya caught my eye and nodded his head. This was a real one. There had not been a real one for a long time. Of the other two matadors, one was very fair and the other was passable. But there was no comparison with Romero, although neither of his bulls was much.

Several times during the bull-fight I looked up at Mike and Brett and Cohn, with the glasses. They seemed to be all right. Brett did not look upset. All three were leaning forward on the concrete railing in front of them.

'Let me take the glasses,' Bill said.

'Does Cohn look bored?' I asked.

'That kike!'

Outside the ring after the bull-fight was over, you could not move in the crowd. We could not make our way through but had to be moved with the whole thing, slowly, as a glacier, back to town. We had that disturbed emotional feeling that always comes after a bull-fight, and the feeling of elation that comes after a good bull-fight. The fiesta was going on. The drums pounded and the pipe music was shrill, and everywhere the flow of the crowd was broken by patches of dancers. The dancers were in a crowd, so you did not see the intricate play of the feet. All you saw was the heads and shoulders going up and down, up and down. Finally, we got out of the crowd and made for the café. The waiter saved chairs for the others, and we each ordered an absinthe and watched the crowd in the square and the dancers.

'What do you suppose that dance is?' Bill asked.

'It's a sort of jota.'

'They're not all the same,' Bill said. 'They dance differently to all the different tunes.'

'It's swell dancing.'

In front of us on a clear part of the street a company of boys were dancing. The steps were very intricate and their faces were intent and concentrated. They all looked down while they danced. Their rope-soled shoes tapped and spatted on the pavement. The toes touched. The heels touched. The balls of the feet touched. Then the music broke wildly and the step was finished and they were all dancing on up the street.

'Here come the gentry,' Bill said.

They were crossing the street.

'Hello, men,' I said.

'Hello, gents!' said Brett. 'You saved us seats? How nice.'

'I say,' Mike said, 'that Romero what'shisname is somebody. Am I wrong?'

'Oh, isn't he lovely,' Brett said. 'And those green trousers.'

'Brett never took her eyes off them.'

'I say, I must borrow your glasses to-morrow.'

'How did it go?'

'Wonderfully! Simply perfect. I say, it is a spectacle!'

'How about the horses?'

'I couldn't help looking at them.'

'She couldn't take her eyes off them,' Mike said. 'She's an extraordinary wench.'

'They do have some rather awful things happen to them,' Brett said. 'I couldn't look away, though.'

'Did you feel all right?'

'I didn't feel badly at all.'

'Robert Cohn did,' Mike put in. 'You were quite green, Robert.'

'The first horse did bother me,' Cohn said.

'You weren't bored, were you?' asked Bill.

Cohn laughed.

'No. I wasn't bored. I wish you'd forgive me that.'

'It's all right,' Bill said, 'so long as you weren't bored.'

'He didn't look bored,' Mike said. 'I thought he was going to be sick.'

'I never felt that bad. It was just for a minute.'

'*I* thought he was going to be sick. You weren't bored, were you, Robert?'

'Let up on that, Mike. I said I was sorry I said it.'

'He was, you know. He was positively green.'

'Oh, shove it along, Michael.'

'You mustn't ever get bored at your first bull-fight, Robert,' Mike said. 'It might make such a mess.'

'Oh, shove it along, Michael,' Brett said.

'He said Brett was a sadist,' Mike said. 'Brett's not a sadist. She's just a lovely, healthy wench.'

'Are you a sadist, Brett?' I asked.

'Hope not.'

'He said Brett was a sadist just because she has a good, healthy stomach.'

'Won't be healthy long.'

Bill got Mike started on something else than Cohn. The waiter brought the absinthe glasses.

'Did you really like it?' Bill asked Cohn.

'No, I can't say I liked it. I think it's a wonderful show.'

'Gad, yes! What a spectacle!' Brett said.

'I wish they didn't have the horse part,' Cohn said.

'They're not important,' Bill said. 'After a while you never notice anything disgusting.'

'It is a bit strong just at the start,' Brett said. 'There's a dreadful moment for me just when the bull starts for the horse.'

'The bulls were fine,' Cohn said.

'They were very good,' Mike said.

'I want to sit down below, next time.' Brett drank from her glass of absinthe.

'She wants to see the bull-fighters close by,' Mike said.

'They are something,' Brett said. 'That Romero lad is just a child.'

'He's a damned good-looking boy,' I said. 'When we were up in his room I never saw a better-looking kid.'

'How old do you suppose he is?'

'Nineteen or twenty.'

'Just imagine it.'

The bull-fight on the second day was much better than on the first. Brett sat between Mike and me at the barrera, and Bill and Cohn went up above. Romero was the whole show. I do not think Brett saw any other bull-fighter. No one else did either, except the hard-shelled technicians. It was all Romero. There were two other matadors, but they did not count. I sat beside Brett and explained to Brett what it was all about. I told her about watching the bull, not the horse, when the bulls charged the picadors, and got her to watching the picador place the point of his pic so that she saw what it was all about, so that it became more something that was going on with a definite end, and less of a spectacle with unexplained horrors. I had her watch how Romero took the bull away from a fallen horse with his cape, and how he held him with the cape and turned him, smoothly and suavely, never wasting the bull. She saw how Romero avoided every brusque movement and saved his bulls for the last when he wanted them, not winded and discomposed, but smoothly worn down. She saw how close Romero always worked to the bull, and I pointed out to her the tricks the other bull-fighters used to make it look as though they were working closely. She saw why she liked Romero's cape-work and why she did not like the others.

Romero never made any contortions, always it was straight and pure and natural in line. The others twisted themselves like corkscrews, their elbows raised, and leaned against the flanks of the bull after his horns had passed, to give a faked look of danger. Afterward, all that was faked turned bad and gave an unpleasant feeling. Romero's bull-fighting gave real emotion, because he kept the absolute purity of line in his movements and always quietly and calmly let the horns pass him close each time. He did not have to emphasise their closeness. Brett saw how something that was beautiful done close to the bull was ridiculous if it were done a little way off. I told her how since the death of Joselito all the bull-fighters had been developing a technic that simulated this appearance of danger in order to give a fake emotional feeling, while the bull-fighter was really safe. Romero had the old thing, the holding of his purity of line through the maximum of exposition, while he dominated the bull by making him realise he was unattainable, while he prepared him for the killing.

'I've never seen him do an awkward thing,' Brett said.

'You won't until he gets frightened,' I said.

'He'll never be frightened,' Mike said. 'He knows too damned much.'

'He knew everything when he started. The others can't ever learn what he was born with.'

'And God, what looks,' Brett said.

'I believe, you know, that she's falling in love with this bull-fighter chap,' Mike said.

'I wouldn't be surprised.'

'Be a good chap, Jake. Don't tell her anything more about him. Tell her how they beat their old mothers.'

'Tell me what drunks they are.'

'Oh, frightful,' Mike said. 'Drunk all day and spend all their time beating their poor old mothers.'

'He looks that way,' Brett said.

'Doesn't he?' I said.

They had hitched the mules to the dead bull and then the whips cracked, the men ran, and the mules, straining forward, their legs pushing, broke into a gallop, and the bull, one horn up, his head on its side, swept a swath smoothly across the sand and out the red gate.

'This next is the last one.'

'Not really,' Brett said. She leaned forward on the barrera. Romero waved his picadors to their places, then stood, his cape against his chest, looking across the ring to where the bull would come out.

After it was over we went out and were pressed tight in the crowd.

'These bull-fights are hell on one,' Brett said. 'I'm limp as a rag.'

'Oh, you'll get a drink,' Mike said.

The next day Pedro Romero did not fight. It was Miura bulls, and a very bad bull-fight. The next day there was no bull-fight scheduled. But all day and all night the fiesta kept on.

16

In the morning it was raining. A fog had come over the mountains from the sea. You could not see the tops of the mountains. The plateau was dull and gloomy, and the shapes of the trees and the houses were changed. I walked out beyond the town to look at the weather. The bad weather was coming over the mountains from the sea.

The flags in the square hung wet from the white poles and the banners were wet and hung damp against the front of the houses, and in between the steady drizzle the rain came down and drove everyone under the arcades and made pools of water in the square, and the streets wet and dark and deserted; yet the fiesta kept up without any pause. It was only driven under cover.

The covered seats of the bull-ring had been crowded with people sitting out of the rain watching the concourse of Basque and Navarrais dancers and singers, and afterward the Val Carlos dancers in their costumes danced down the street in the rain, the drums sounding hollow and damp, and the chiefs of the bands riding ahead on their big, heavy-footed horses, their costumes wet, the horses' coats wet in the rain. The crowd was in the cafés and the dancers came in, too, and sat, their tight-wound white legs under the tables, shaking the water from their belled caps, and spreading their red and purple jackets over the chairs to dry. It was raining hard outside.

I left the crowd in the café and went over to the hotel to get shaved for dinner. I was shaving in my room when there was a knock on the door.

'Come in,' I called.

Montoya walked in.

'How are you?' he said.

'Fine,' I said.

'No bulls to-day.'

'No,' I said, 'nothing but rain.'

'Where are your friends?'

'Over at the Iruna.'

Montoya smiled his embarrassed smile.

'Look,' he said. 'Do you know the American ambassador?'

'Yes,' I said. 'Everybody knows the American ambassador.'

'He's here in town, now.'

'Yes,' I said. 'Everybody's seen them.'

'I've seen them, too,' Montoya said. He didn't say anything. I went on shaving.

'Sit down,' I said. 'Let me send for a drink.'

'No, I have to go.'

I finished shaving and put my face down into the bowl and washed it with cold water. Montoya was standing there looking more embarrassed.

'Look,' he said. 'I've just had a message from them at the Grand Hotel that they want Pedro Romero and Marcial Lalanda to come over for coffee to-night after dinner.'

'Well,' I said, 'it can't hurt Marcial any.'

'Marcial has been in San Sebastian all day. He drove over in a car this morning with Marquez. I don't think they'll be back to-night.'

Montoya stood embarrassed. He wanted me to say something.

'Don't give Romero the message,' I said.

'You think so?'

'Absolutely.'

Montoya was very pleased.

'I wanted to ask you because you were an American,' he said.

'That's what I'd do.'

'Look,' said Montoya. 'People take a boy like that. They don't know what he's worth. They don't know what he means. Any foreigner can flatter him. They start this Grand Hotel business, and in one year they're through.'

'Like Algabeno,' I said.

'Yes, like Algabeno.'

'They're a fine lot,' I said. 'There's one American woman down here now that collects bull-fighters.'

'I know. They only want the young ones.'

'Yes,' I said. 'The old ones get fat.'

'Or crazy like Gallo.'

'Well,' I said, 'it's easy. All you have to do is not give him the message.'

'He's such a fine boy,' said Montoya. 'He ought to stay with his own people. He shouldn't mix in that stuff.'

'Won't you have a drink?' I asked.

'No,' said Montoya, 'I have to go.' He went out.

I went downstairs and out the door and took a walk around through the arcades around the square. It was still raining. I looked in at the Iruna for the gang and they were not there, so I walked on around the square and back to the hotel. They were eating dinner in the downstairs dining-room.

They were well ahead of me, and it was no use trying to catch them. Bill was buying shoe-shines for Mike. Bootblacks opened the street door and each one Bill called over and started to work on Mike.

'This is the eleventh time my boots have been polished,' Mike said. 'I say, Bill is an ass.'

The bootblacks had evidently spread the report. Another came in.

'Limpia botas?' he said to Bill.

'No,' said Bill. 'For this señor.'

The bootblack knelt down beside the one at work and started on Mike's free shoe that shone already in the electric light.

'Bill's a yell of laughter,' Mike said.

I was drinking red wine, and so far behind them that I felt a little uncomfortable about all this shoe-shining. I looked around the room. At the next table was Pedro Romero. He stood up when I nodded, and asked me to come over and meet a friend. His table was beside ours, almost touching. I met the friend, a Madrid bull-fight critic, a little man with a drawn face. I told Romero how much I liked his work, and he was very pleased. We talked Spanish and the critic knew a little French. I reached to our table for my wine-bottle, but the critic took my arm. Romero laughed.

'Drink here,' he said in English.

He was very bashful about his English, but he was really very pleased with it, and as we went on talking he brought out words he was not sure of, and asked me about them. He was anxious to know the English for *Corrida de toros*, the exact translation. Bull-fight he was suspicious of. I explained that bull-fight in Spanish was the *lidia* of a *toro*. The Spanish word *corrida* means in English the running of bulls–the French translation is *Course de taureau*. The critic put that in. There is no Spanish word for bull-fight.

Pedro Romero said he had learned a little English in Gibraltar. He was born in Ronda. That is not far above Gibraltar. He started bull-fighting in Malaga in the bull-fighting school there. He had only been at it three years. The bull-fight critic joked him about the number of *Malaguena* expressions he used. He was nineteen years old, he said. His older brother was with him as a banderillero, but he did not live in this hotel. He lived in a smaller hotel with the other people who worked for Romero. He asked me how many times I had seen him in the ring. I told him only three. It was really only two, but I did not want to explain after I had made the mistake.

'Where did you see me the other time? In Madrid?'

'Yes,' I lied. I had read the accounts of his two appearances in Madrid in the bull-fight papers, so I was all right.

'The first or the second time?'

'The first.'

'I was very bad,' he said. 'The second time I was better. You remember?' He turned to the critic.

He was not at all embarrassed. He talked of his work as something altogether apart from himself. There was nothing conceited or braggardly about him.

'I like it very much that you like my work,' he said. 'But you haven't seen it yet. To-morrow, if I get a good bull, I will try and show it to you.'

When he said this he smiled, anxious that neither the bull-fight critic nor I would think he was boasting.

'I am anxious to see it,' the critic said. 'I would like to be convinced.'

'He doesn't like my work much.' Romero turned to me. He was serious.

The critic explained that he liked it very much, but that so far it had been incomplete.

'Wait till to-morrow, if a good one comes out.'

'Have you seen the bulls for to-morrow?' the critic asked me.

'Yes. I saw them unloaded.'

Pedro Romero leaned forward.

'What did you think of them?'

'Very nice,' I said. 'About twenty-six arrobas. Very short horns. Haven't you seen them?'

'Oh, yes,' said Romero.

'They won't weigh twenty-six arrobas,' said the critic.

'No,' said Romero.

'They've got bananas for horns,' the critic said.

'You call them bananas?' asked Romero. He turned to me and smiled. '*You* wouldn't call them bananas?'

'No,' I said. 'They're horns all right.'

'They're very short,' said Pedro Romero. 'Very, very short. Still, they aren't bananas.'

'I say, Jake,' Brett called from the next table, 'you *have* deserted us.'

'Just temporarily,' I said. 'We're talking bulls.'

'You *are* superior.'

'Tell him that bulls have no horns,' Mike shouted. He was drunk.

Romero looked at me inquiringly.

'Drunk,' I said. 'Borracho! Muy borracho!'

'You might introduce your friends,' Brett said. She had not stopped looking at Pedro Romero. I asked them if they would like to have coffee with us. They both stood up. Romero's face was very brown. He had very nice manners.

I introduced them all around and they started to sit down, but there was not enough room, so we all moved over to the big table by the wall to have coffee. Mike ordered a bottle of Fundador and glasses for everybody. There was a lot of drunken talking.

'Tell him I think writing is lousy,' Bill said. 'Go on, tell him. Tell him

I'm ashamed of being a writer.'

Pedro Romero was sitting beside Brett and listening to her.

'Go on. Tell him!' Bill said.

Romero looked up smiling.

'This gentleman,' I said, 'is a writer.'

Romero was impressed. 'This other one, too,' I said, pointing at Cohn.

'He looks like Villalta,' Romero said, looking at Bill. 'Rafael, doesn't he look like Villalta?'

'I can't see it,' the critic said.

'Really,' Romero said in Spanish. 'He looks a lot like Villalta. What does the drunken one do?'

'Nothing.'

'Is that why he drinks?'

'No. He's waiting to marry this lady.'

'Tell him bulls have no horns!' Mike shouted, very drunk, from the other end of the table.

'What does he say?'

'He's drunk.'

'Jake,' Mike called. 'Tell him bulls have no horns!'

'You understand?' I said.

'Yes.'

I was sure he didn't, so it was all right.

'Tell him Brett wants to see him put on those green pants.'

'Pipe down, Mike.'

'Tell him Brett is dying to know how he can get into those pants.'

'Pipe down.'

During this Romero was fingering his glass and talking with Brett. Brett was talking French and he was talking Spanish and a little English, and laughing.

Bill was filling the glasses.

'Tell him Brett wants to come into—'

'Oh, pipe down, Mike, for Christ's sake!'

Romero looked up smiling. 'Pipe down! I know that,' he said.

Just then Montoya came into the room. He started to smile at me, then he saw Pedro Romero with a big glass of cognac in his hand, sitting laughing between me and a woman with bare shoulders, at a table full of drunks. He did not even nod.

Montoya went out of the room. Mike was on his feet proposing a toast. 'Let's all drink to—' he began. 'Pedro Romero,' I said. Everybody stood up. Romero took it very seriously, and we touched glasses and drank it down, I rushing it a little because Mike was trying to make it clear that that was not at all what he was going to drink to. But it went off all right, and Pedro Romero shook hands with everyone and he and the critic went out together.

'My God! he's a lovely boy,' Brett said. 'And how I would love to see him get into those clothes. He must use a shoe-horn.'

'I started to tell him,' Mike began. 'And Jake kept interrupting me. Why do you interrupt me? Do you think you talk Spanish better than I do?'

'Oh, shut up, Mike! Nobody interrupted you.'

'No, I'd like to get this settled.' He turned away from me. 'Do you think you amount to something, Cohn? Do you think you belong here among us? People who are out to have a good time? For God's sake don't be so noisy, Cohn!'

'Oh, cut it out, Mike,' Cohn said.

'Do you think Brett wants you here? Do you think you add to the party? Why don't you say something?'

'I said all I had to say the other night, Mike.'

'I'm not one of you literary chaps,' Mike stood shakily and leaned against the table. 'I'm not clever. But I do know when I'm not wanted. Why don't you see when you're not wanted, Cohn? Go away. Go away, for God's sake. Take that sad Jewish face away. Don't you think I'm right?'

He looked at us.

'Sure,' I said. 'Let's all go over to the Iruna.'

'No. Don't you think I'm right? I love that woman.'

'Oh, don't start that again. Do shove it along, Michael,' Brett said.

'Don't you think I'm right, Jake?'

Cohn still sat at the table. His face had the sallow, yellow look it got when he was insulted, but somehow he seemed to be enjoying it. The childish, drunken heroics of it. It was his affair with a lady of title.

'Jake,' Mike said. He was almost crying. 'You know I'm right. Listen, you!' He turned to Cohn: 'Go away! Go away now!'

'But I won't go, Mike,' said Cohn.

'Then I'll make you!' Mike started toward him around the table. Cohn stood up and took off his glasses. He stood waiting, his face sallow, his hands fairly low, proudly and firmly waiting for the assault, ready to do battle for his lady love.

I grabbed Mike. 'Come on to the café,' I said. 'You can't hit him here in the hotel.'

'Good!' said Mike. 'Good idea!'

We started off. I looked back as Mike stumbled up the stairs and saw Cohn putting his glasses on again. Bill was sitting at the table pouring another glass of Fundador. Brett was sitting looking straight ahead at nothing.

Outside on the square it had stopped raining and the moon was trying to get through the clouds. There was a wind blowing. The military band was playing and the crowd was massed on the far side of the square where the fireworks specialist and his son were trying to send up fire balloons. A balloon would start up jerkily, on a great bias, and be torn by the wind or blown against the houses of the square. Some fell into the crowd. The magnesium flared and the fireworks exploded and chased about in the crowd. There was no one dancing in the square. The gravel was too wet.

Brett came out with Bill and joined us. We stood in the crowd and watched Don Manuel Orquito, the fireworks king, standing on a little platform, carefully starting the balloons with sticks, standing above the heads of the crowd to launch the balloons off into the wind. The wind brought them all down, and Don Manuel Orquito's face was sweaty in the light of his complicated fireworks that fell into the crowd and charged and chased, sputtering and cracking, between the legs of the people. The people shouted as each new luminous paper bubble careened, caught fire, and fell.

'They're razzing Don Manuel,' Bill said.

'How do you know he's Don Manuel?' Brett said.

'His name's on the programme. Don Manuel Orquito, the pirotecnico of esta ciudad.'

'Globos illuminados,' Mike said. 'A collection of globos illuminados. That's what the paper said.'

The wind blew the band music away.

'I say, I wish one would go up,' Brett said. 'That Don Manuel chap is furious.'

'He's probably worked for weeks fixing them to go off, spelling out "Hail to San Fermin,"' Bill said.

'Globos illuminados,' Mike said. 'A bunch of bloody globos illuminados.'

'Come on,' said Brett. 'We can't stand here.'

'Her ladyship wants a drink,' Mike said.

'How you know things,' Brett said.

Inside the café was crowded and very noisy. No one noticed us come in. We could not find a table. There was a great noise going on.

'Come on, let's get out of here,' Bill said.

Outside the paseo was going in under the arcade. There were some English and Americans from Biarritz in sport clothes scattered at the tables. Some of the women stared at the people going by with lorgnons. We had acquired, at some time, a friend of Bill's from Biarritz. She was staying with another girl at the Grand Hotel. The other girl had a headache and had gone to bed.

'Here's the pub,' Mike said. It was the Bar Milano, a small, tough bar where you could get food and where they danced in the back room. We all sat down at a table and ordered a bottle of Fundador. The bar was not full. There was nothing going on.

'This is a hell of a place,' Bill said.

'It's too early.'

'Let's take the bottle and come back later,' Bill said. 'I don't want to sit here on a night like this.'

'Let's go and look at the English,' Mike said. 'I love to look at the English.'

'They're awful,' Bill said. 'Where did they all come from?'

'They come from Biarritz,' Mike said. 'They come to see the last day of the quaint little Spanish festa.'

'I'll festa them,' Bill said.

'You're an extraordinarily beautiful girl.' Mike turned to Bill's friend. 'When did you come here?'

'Come off it, Michael.'

'I say, she *is* a lovely girl. Where have I been? Where have I been looking all this while? You're a lovely thing. *Have* we met? Come along with me and Bill. We're going to festa the English.'

'I'll festa them,' Bill said. 'What the hell are they doing at this fiesta?'

'Come on,' Mike said. 'Just us three. We're going to festa the bloody

English. I hope you're not English? I'm Scotch. I hate the English. I'm going to festa them. Come on, Bill.'

Through the window we saw them, all three arm in arm, going toward the café. Rockets were going up in the square.

'I'm going to sit here,' Brett said.

'I'll stay with you,' Cohn said.

'Oh, don't!' Brett said. 'For God's sake, go off somewhere. Can't you see Jake and I want to talk?'

'I didn't,' Cohn said. 'I thought I'd sit here because I felt a little tight.'

'What a hell of a reason for sitting with anyone. If you're tight, go to bed.'

'Was I rude enough to him?' Brett asked. Cohn was gone. 'My God! I'm so sick of him!'

'He doesn't add much to the gaiety.'

'He depresses me so.'

'He's behaved very badly.'

'Damned badly. He had a chance to behave so well.'

'He's probably waiting just outside the door now.'

'Yes. He would. You know I do know how he feels. He can't believe it didn't mean anything.'

'I know.'

'Nobody else would behave as badly. Oh, I'm so sick of the whole thing. And Michael. Michael's been lovely, too.'

'It's been damned hard on Mike.'

'Yes. But he didn't need to be a swine.'

'Everybody behaves badly,' I said. 'Give them the proper chance.'

'You wouldn't behave badly.' Brett looked at me.

'I'd be as big an ass as Cohn,' I said.

'Darling, don't let's talk a lot of rot.'

'All right. Talk about anything you like.'

'Don't be difficult. You're the only person I've got, and I feel rather awful to-night.'

'You've got Mike.'

'Yes, Mike. Hasn't he been pretty?'

'Well,' I said, 'it's been damned hard on Mike, having Cohn around and seeing him with you.'

'Don't I know it, darling? Please don't make me feel any worse than I do.'

Brett was nervous as I had never seen her before. She kept looking away from me and looking ahead at the wall.

'Want to go for a walk?'

'Yes. Come on.'

I corked up the Fundador bottle and gave it to the bartender.

'Let's have one more drink of that,' Brett said. 'My nerves are rotten.'

We each drank a glass of the smooth amontillado brandy.

As we came out the door I saw Cohn walk out from under the arcade.

'He *was* there,' Brett said.

'He can't be away from you.'

'Poor devil!'

'I'm not sorry for him. I hate him, myself.'

'I hate him too,' she shivered. 'I hate his damned suffering.'

We walked arm in arm down the side street away from the crowd and the lights of the square. The street was dark and wet, and we walked along it to the fortifications at the edge of town. We passed wine-shops with light coming out from their doors on to the black, wet street, and sudden bursts of music.

'Want to go in?'

'No.'

We walked out across the wet grass and on to the stone wall of the fortifications. I spread a newspaper on the stone and Brett sat down. Across the plain it was dark, and we could see the mountains. The wind was high up and took the clouds across the moon. Below us were the dark pits of the fortifications. Behind were the trees and the shadow of the cathedral, and the town silhouetted against the moon.

'Don't feel bad,' I said.

'I feel like hell,' Brett said. 'Don't let's talk.'

We looked out at the plain. The long lines of trees were dark in the moonlight. There were the lights of a car on the road climbing the mountain. Up on the top of the mountain we saw the lights of the fort. Below to the left was the river. It was high from the rain, and black and smooth. Trees were dark along the banks. We sat and looked out. Brett stared straight ahead. Suddenly she shivered.

'It's cold.'

'Want to walk back?'

'Through the park.'

We climbed down. It was clouding over again. In the park it was dark under the trees.

'Do you still love me, Jake?'

'Yes,' I said.

'Because I'm a goner,' Brett said.

'How?'

'I'm a goner. I'm mad about the Romero boy. I'm in love with him, I think.'

'I wouldn't be if I were you.'

'I can't help it. I'm a goner. It's tearing me all up inside.'

'Don't do it.'

'I can't help it. I've never been able to help anything.'

'You ought to stop it.'

'How can I stop it? I can't stop things. Feel that?'

Her hand was trembling.

'I'm like that all through.'

'You oughtn't to do it.'

'I can't help it. I'm a goner now, anyway. Don't you see the difference?'

'No.'

'I've got to do something. I've got to do something I really want to do. I've lost my self-respect.'

'You don't have to do that.'

'Oh, darling, don't be difficult. What do you think it's meant to have that damned Jew about, and Mike the way he's acted?'

'Sure.'

'I can't just stay tight all the time.'

'No.'

'Oh, darling, please stay by me. Please stay by me and see me through this.'

'Sure.'

'I don't say it's right. It is right though for me. God knows, I've never felt such a bitch.'

'What do you want me to do?'

'Come on,' Brett said. 'Let's go and find him.'

Together we walked down the gravel path in the park in the dark, under the trees and then out from under the trees and past the gate into the street that led into town.

Pedro Romero was in the café. He was at a table with other bull-fighters and bull-fight critics. They were smoking cigars. When we came in they looked up. Romero smiled and bowed. We sat down at a table half-way down the room.

'Ask him to come over and have a drink.'

'Not yet. He'll come over.'

'I can't look at him.'

'He's nice to look at,' I said.

'I've always done just what I wanted.'

'I know.'

'I do feel such a bitch.'

'Well,' I said.

'My God!' said Brett. 'The things a woman goes through.'

'Yes?'

'Oh, I do feel such a bitch.'

I looked across at the table. Pedro Romero smiled. He said something to the other people at his table, and stood up. He came over to our table. I stood up and we shook hands.

'Won't you have a drink?'

'You must have a drink with me,' he said. He seated himself, asking Brett's permission without saying anything. He had very nice manners. But he kept on smoking his cigar. It went well with his face.

'You like cigars?' I asked.

'Oh, yes. I always smoke cigars.'

It was part of his system of authority. It made him seem older. I noticed his skin. It was clear and smooth and very brown. There was a triangular scar on his cheek-bone. I saw he was watching Brett. He felt there was something between them. He must have felt it when Brett gave him her hand. He was being very careful. I think he was sure, but he did not want to make any mistake.

'You fight to-morrow?' I said.

'Yes,' he said. 'Algabeno was hurt to-day in Madrid. Did you hear?'

'No,' I said. 'Badly?'

He shook his head.

'Nothing. Here,' he showed his hand. Brett reached out and spread the fingers apart.

'Oh!' he said in English, 'you tell fortunes?'

'Sometimes. Do you mind?'

'No. I like it.' He spread his hand flat on the table. 'Tell me I live for always, and be a millionaire.'

He was still very polite, but he was surer of himself. 'Look,' he said, 'do you see any bulls in my hand?'

He laughed. His hand was very fine and the wrist was small.

'There are thousands of bulls,' Brett said. She was not at all nervous now. She looked lovely.

'Good,' Romero laughed. 'At a thousand duros apiece,' he said to me in Spanish. 'Tell me some more.'

'It's a good hand,' Brett said. 'I think he'll live a long time.'

'Say it to me. Not to your friend.'

'I said you'd live a long time.'

'I know it,' Romero said. 'I'm never going to die.'

I tapped with my finger-tips on the table. Romero saw it. He shook his head.

'No. Don't do that. The bulls are my best friends.'

I translated to Brett.

'You kill your friends?' she asked.

'Always,' he said in English, and laughed. 'So they don't kill me.' He looked at her across the table.

'You know English well.'

'Yes,' he said. 'Pretty well, sometimes. But I must not let anybody know. It would be very bad, a torero who speaks English.'

'Why?' asked Brett.

'It would be bad. The people would not like it. Not yet.'

'Why not?'

'They would not like it. Bull-fighters are not like that.'

'What are bull-fighters like?'

He laughed and tipped his hat down over his eyes and changed the angle of his cigar and the expression of his face.

'Like at the table,' he said. I glanced over. He had mimicked exactly the expression of Nacional. He smiled, his face natural again. 'No. I must forget English.'

'Don't forget it, yet,' Brett said.

'No?'

'No.'

'All right.'

He laughed again.

'I would like a hat like that,' Brett said.

'Good. I'll get you one.'

'Right. See that you do.'

'I will. I'll get you one to-night.'

I stood up. Romero rose, too.

'Sit down,' I said. 'I must go and find our friends and bring them here.'

He looked at me. It was a final look to ask if it were understood. It was understood all right.

'Sit down,' Brett said to him. 'You must teach me Spanish.'

He sat down and looked at her across the table. I went out. The hard-eyed people at the bull-fighter table watched me go. It was not pleasant. When I came back and looked in the café, twenty minutes later, Brett and Pedro Romero were gone. The coffee-glasses and our three empty cognac-glasses were on the table. A waiter came with a cloth and picked up the glasses and mopped off the table.

17

Outside the Bar Milano I found Bill and Mike and Edna. Edna was the girl's name.

'We've been thrown out,' Edna said.

'By the police,' said Mike. 'There's some people in there that don't like me.'

'I've kept them out of four fights,' Edna said. 'You've got to help me.'

Bill's face was red.

'Come back in, Edna,' he said. 'Go on in there and dance with Mike.'

'It's silly,' Edna said. 'There'll just be another row.'

'Damned Biarritz swine,' Bill said.

'Come on,' Mike said. 'After all, it's a pub. They can't occupy a whole pub.'

'Good old Mike,' Bill said. 'Damned English swine come here and insult Mike and try and spoil the fiesta.'

'They're so bloody,' Mike said. 'I hate the English.'

'They can't insult Mike,' Bill said. 'Mike is a swell fellow. They can't insult Mike. I won't stand it. Who cares if he is a damn bankrupt?' His voice broke.

'Who cares?' Mike said. 'I don't care. Jake doesn't care. Do *you* care?'

'No,' Edna said. 'Are you a bankrupt?'

'Of course I am. You don't care, do you, Bill?'

Bill put his arm around Mike's shoulder.

'I wish to hell I was a bankrupt. I'd show those bastards.'

'They're just English,' Mike said. 'It never makes any difference what the English say.'

'The dirty swine,' Bill said. 'I'm going to clean them out.'

'Bill,' Edna looked at me. 'Please don't go in again, Bill. They're so stupid.'

'That's it,' said Mike. 'They're stupid. I knew that was what it was.'

'They can't say things like that about Mike,' Bill said.

'Do you know them?' I asked Mike.

'No. I never saw them. They say they know me.'

'I won't stand it,' Bill said.

'Come on. Let's go over to the Suizo,' I said.

'They're a bunch of Edna's friends from Biarritz,' Bill said.

'They're simply stupid,' Edna said.

'One of them's Charley Blackman, from Chicago,' Bill said.

'I was never in Chicago,' Mike said.

Edna started to laugh and could not stop.

'Take me away from here,' she said, 'you bankrupts.'

'What kind of a row was it?' I asked Edna. We were walking across the square to the Suizo. Bill was gone.

'I don't know what happened, but someone had the police called to keep Mike out of the back room. There were some people that had known Mike at Cannes. What's the matter with Mike?'

'Probably he owes them money,' I said. 'That's what people usually get bitter about.'

In front of the ticket-booths out in the square there were two lines of people waiting. They were sitting on chairs or crouched on the ground with blankets and newspapers around them. They were waiting for the wickets to open in the morning to buy tickets for the bull-fight. The night was clearing and the moon was out. Some of the people in the line were sleeping.

At the Café Suizo we had just sat down and ordered Fundador when Robert Cohn came up.

'Where's Brett?' he asked.

'I don't know.'

'She was with you.'

'She must have gone to bed.'

'She's not.'

'I don't know where she is.'

His face was sallow under the light. He was standing up.

'Tell me where she is.'

'Sit down,' I said. 'I don't know where she is.'

'The hell you don't!'

'You can shut your face.'

'Tell me where Brett is.'

'I'll not tell you a damn thing.'

'You know where she is.'

'If I did I wouldn't tell you.'

'Oh, go to hell, Cohn,' Mike called from the table. 'Brett's gone off with the bull-fighter chap. They're on their honeymoon.'

'You shut up.'

'Oh, go to hell!' Mike said languidly.

'Is that where she is?' Cohn turned to me.

'Go to hell!'

'She was with you. Is that where she is?'

'Go to hell!'

'I'll make you tell me'–he stepped forward–'you damned pimp.'

I swung at him and he ducked. I saw his face duck sideways in the light. He hit me and I sat down on the pavement. As I started to get on my feet he hit me twice. I went down backward under a table. I tried to get up and felt I did not have any legs. I felt I must get on my feet and try and hit him. Mike helped me up. Someone poured a carafe of water on my head. Mike had an arm around me, and I found I was sitting on a chair. Mike was pulling at my ears.

'I say, you were cold,' Mike said.

'Where the hell were you?'

'Oh, I was around.'

'You didn't want to mix in it?'

'He knocked Mike down, too,' Edna said.

'He didn't knock me out,' Mike said. 'I just lay there.'

'Does this happen every night at your fiestas?' Edna asked. 'Wasn't that Mr Cohn?'

'I'm all right,' I said. 'My head's a little wobbly.'

There were several waiters and a crowd of people standing around.

'Vaya!' said Mike. 'Get away. Go on.'

The waiters moved the people away.

'It was quite a thing to watch,' Edna said. 'He must be a boxer.'

'He is.'

'I wish Bill had been here,' Edna said. 'I'd like to have seen Bill knocked down, too. I've always wanted to see Bill knocked down. He's so big.'

'I was hoping he would knock down a waiter,' Mike said, 'and get arrested. I'd like to see Mr Robert Cohn in jail.'

'No,' I said.

'Oh, no,' said Edna. 'You don't mean that.'

'I do, though,' Mike said. 'I'm not one of these chaps likes being knocked about. I never play games, even.'

Mike took a drink.

'I never liked to hunt, you know. There was always the danger of having a horse fall on you. How do you feel, Jake?'

'All right.'

'You're nice,' Edna said to Mike. 'Are you really a bankrupt?'

'I'm a tremendous bankrupt,' Mike said. 'I owe money to everybody. Don't you owe any money?'

'Tons.'

'I owe everybody money,' Mike said. 'I borrowed a hundred pesetas from Montoya to-night.'

'The hell you did,' I said.

'I'll pay it back,' Mike said. 'I always pay everything back.'

'That's why you're a bankrupt, isn't it?' Edna said.

I stood up. I had heard them talking from a long way away. It all seemed like some bad play.

'I'm going over to the hotel,' I said. Then I heard them talking about me.

'Is he all right?' Edna asked.

'We'd better walk with him.'

'I'm all right,' I said. 'Don't come. I'll see you all later.'

I walked away from the café. They were sitting at the table. I looked back at them and at the empty tables. There was a waiter sitting at one of the tables with his head in his hands.

Walking across the square to the hotel everything looked new and changed. I had never seen the trees before. I had never seen the flagpoles before, nor the front of the theatre. It was all different. I felt as I felt once coming home from an out-of-town football game. I was carrying a suitcase with my football things in it, and I walked up the street from the station in the town I had lived in all my life and it was all new. They were raking the lawns and burning leaves in the road, and I stopped for a long time and watched. It was all strange. Then I went on, and my feet seemed to be a long way off, and everything seemed to come from a long way off, and I could hear my feet walking a great distance away. I had been kicked in the head early in the game. It was like that crossing the square. It was like that going up the stairs in the hotel. Going up the stairs took a long time, and I had the feeling that I was carrying my suitcase. There was a light in the room. Bill came out and met me in the hall.

'Say,' he said, 'go up and see Cohn. He's been in a jam, and he's asking for you.'

'The hell with him.'

'Go on. Go on up and see him.'

I did not want to climb another flight of stairs.

'What are you looking at me that way for?'

'I'm not looking at you. Go on up and see Cohn. He's in bad shape.'

'You were drunk a little while ago,' I said.

'I'm drunk now,' Bill said. 'But you go up and see Cohn. He wants to see you.'

'All right,' I said. It was just a matter of climbing more stairs. I went on up the stairs carrying my phantom suitcase. I walked down the hall to Cohn's room. The door was shut and I knocked.

'Who is it?'

'Barnes.'

'Come in, Jake.'

I opened the door and went in, and set down my suitcase. There was no light in the room. Cohn was lying, face down, on the bed in the dark.

'Hello, Jake.'

'Don't call me Jake.'

I stood by the door. It was just like this that I had come home. Now it was a hot bath that I needed. A deep, hot bath, to lie back in.

'Where's the bath-room?' I asked.

Cohn was crying. There he was, face down on the bed, crying. He had on a white polo shirt, the kind he'd worn at Princeton.

'I'm sorry, Jake. Please forgive me.'

'Forgive you, hell.'

'Please forgive me, Jake.'

I did not say anything. I stood there by the door.

'I was crazy. You must see how it was.'

'Oh, that's all right.'

'I couldn't stand it about Brett.'

'You called me a pimp.'

I did not care. I wanted a hot bath. I wanted a hot bath in deep water.

'I know. Please don't remember it. I was crazy.'

'That's all right.'

He was crying. His voice was funny. He lay there in his white shirt on the bed in the dark. His polo shirt.

'I'm going away in the morning.'

He was crying without making any noise.

'I just couldn't stand it about Brett. I've been through hell, Jake. It's been simply hell. When I met her down here Brett treated me as though I were a perfect stranger. I just couldn't stand it. We lived together at San Sebastian. I suppose you know it. I can't stand it any more.'

He lay there on the bed.

'Well,' I said, 'I'm going to take a bath.'

'You were the only friend I had, and I loved Brett so.'

'Well,' I said, 'so long.'

'I guess it isn't any use,' he said. 'I guess it isn't any damn use.'

'What?'

'Everything. Please say you forgive me, Jake.'

'Sure,' I said. 'It's all right.'

'I felt so terribly. I've been through such hell, Jake. Now everything's gone. Everything.'

'Well,' I said, 'so long. I've got to go.'

He rolled over, sat on the edge of the bed, and then stood up.

'So long, Jake,' he said. 'You'll shake hands, won't you?'

'Sure. Why not?'

We shook hands. In the dark I could not see his face very well.

'Well,' I said, 'see you in the morning.'

'I'm going away in the morning.'

'Oh, yes,' I said.

I went out. Cohn was standing in the door of the room.

'Are you all right, Jake?' he asked.

'Oh, yes,' I said. 'I'm all right.'

I could not find the bath-room. After a while I found it. There was a deep stone tub. I turned on the taps and the water would not run. I sat down on the edge of the bath-tub. When I got up to go I found I had taken off my shoes. I hunted for them and found them and carried them downstairs. I found my room and went inside and undressed and got into bed.

I woke with a headache and the noise of the bands going by in the street. I remembered I had promised to take Bill's friend Edna to see the bulls go through the street and into the ring. I dressed and went downstairs and out into the cold early morning. People were crossing the square, hurrying toward the bull-ring. Across the square were the two lines of men in front of the ticket-booths. They were still waiting for the tickets to go on sale at seven o'clock. I hurried across the street to the café. The waiter told me that my friends had been there and gone.

'How many were they?'

'Two gentlemen and a lady.'

That was right. Bill and Mike were with Edna. She had been afraid last night they would pass out. That was why I was to be sure to take her. I drank the coffee and hurried with the other people toward the bull-ring. I was not groggy now. There was only a bad headache. Everything looked sharp and clear, and the town smelt of the early morning.

The stretch of ground from the edge of the town to the bull-ring was muddy. There was a crowd all along the fence that led to the ring, and the outside balconies and the top of the bull-ring were solid with people. I heard the rocket and I knew I could not get into the ring in time to see the bulls come in, so I shoved through the crowd to the fence. I was pushed close against the planks of the fence. Between the two fences of the runway the police were clearing the crowd along. They walked or trotted on into the bull-ring. Then people commenced to come running. A drunk slipped and fell. Two policemen grabbed him and rushed him over to the fence. The crowd were running fast now. There was a great shout from the crowd, and putting my head through between the boards I saw the bulls just coming out of the street into the long running pen. They were going fast and gaining on the crowd. Just then another drunk started out from the fence with a blouse in his hands. He wanted to do capework with the bulls. The two policemen tore out, collared him, one hit him with a club, and they dragged him against the fence and stood flattened out against the fence as the last of the crowd and the bulls went by. There were so many people running ahead of the bulls that the mass thickened and slowed up going through the gate into the ring, and as the bulls passed, galloping together, heavy, muddy-sided, horns swinging, one shot ahead, caught a man in the running crowd in the back and lifted him in the air. Both the man's arms were by his sides, his head went back as the horn went in, and the bull lifted him and then dropped him. The bull picked up another man running in front, but the man disappeared into the crowd, and the crowd was through the gate and into the ring with the bulls behind them. The red door of the ring went shut, the crowd on the outside balconies of the bull-ring were pressing through to the inside, there was a shout, then another shout.

The man who had been gored lay face down in the trampled mud. People climbed over the fence, and I could not see the man because the crowd was so thick around him. From inside the ring came the shouts. Each shout meant a charge by some bull into the crowd. You could tell by the degree of intensity in the shout how bad a thing it was that was happening. Then the rocket went up that meant the steers had gotten the bulls out of the ring and into the corrals. I left the fence and started back toward the town.

Back in the town I went to the café to have a second coffee and some buttered toast. The waiters were sweeping out the café and mopping off the tables. One came over and took my order.

'Anything happen at the encierro?'

'I didn't see it all. One man was badly cogida.'

'Where?'

'Here.' I put one hand on the small of my back and the other on my chest, where it looked as though the horn must have come through. The waiter nodded his head and swept the crumbs from the table with his cloth.

'Badly cogida,' he said. 'All for sport. All for pleasure.'

He went away and came back with the long-handled coffee and milk pots. He poured the milk and coffee. It came out of the long spouts in two streams into the big cup. The waiter nodded his head.

'Badly cogida through the back,' he said. He put the pots down on the table and sat down in the chair at the table. 'A big horn wound. All for fun. Just for fun. What do you think of that?'

'I don't know.'

'That's it. All for fun. Fun, you understand.'

'You're not an aficionado?'

'Me? What are bulls? Animals. Brute animals.' He stood up and put his hand on the small of his back. 'Right through the back. A cornada right through the back. For fun–you understand.'

He shook his head and walked away, carrying the coffee-pots. Two men were going by in the street. The waiter shouted to them. They were grave-looking. One shook his head. 'Muerto!' he called.

The waiter nodded his head. The two men went on. They were on some errand. The waiter came over to my table.

'You hear? Muerto. Dead. He's dead. With a horn through him. All for morning fun. Es muy flamenco.'

'It's bad.'

'Not for me,' the waiter said. 'No fun in that for me.'

Later in the day we learned that the man who was killed was named Vicente Girones, and came from near Tafalla. The next day in the paper we read that he was twenty-eight years old, and had a farm, a wife, and two children. He had continued to come to the fiesta each year after he was married. The next day his wife came in from Tafalla to be with the body, and the day after there was a service in the chapel of San Fermin, and the coffin was carried to the railway-station by members of the dancing and drinking society of Tafalla. The drums marched ahead, and there was music on the fifes, and behind the men who carried the coffin walked the wife and two children. . . . Behind them marched all the members of the dancing and drinking societies of Pamplona, Estella, Tafalla, and Sanguesa who could stay over for the funeral. The coffin was loaded into the baggage-car of the train, and the widow and the two children rode, sitting, all three together, in an open third-class railway-carriage. The train started with a jerk, and then ran smoothly, going down grade around the edge of the plateau and out into the fields of grain that blew in the wind on the plain on the way to Tafalla.

The bull who killed Vicente Girones was named Bocanegra, was Number 118 of the bull-breeding establishment of Sanchez Taberno, and was killed by Pedro Romero as the third bull of that same afternoon. His ear was cut by popular acclamation and given to Pedro Romero, who, in turn, gave it to Brett, who wrapped it in a handkerchief belonging to myself, and left both ear and handkerchief, along with a number of Muratti cigarette-stubs, shoved far back in the drawer of the bed-table that stood beside her bed in the Hotel Montoya, in Pamplona.

Back in the hotel, the night watchman was sitting on a bench inside the door. He had been there all night and was very sleepy. He stood up as I came in. Three of the waitresses came in at the same time. They had been to the morning show at the bull-ring. They went upstairs laughing. I followed them upstairs and went into my room. I took off my shoes and lay down on the bed. The window was open on to the balcony and the sunlight was bright in the room. I did not feel sleepy. It must have been half-past three o'clock when I had gone to bed and the bands had waked me at six. My jaw was sore on both sides. I felt it with my thumb and fingers. That damn Cohn. He should have hit somebody the first time he was insulted, and then gone away. He was so sure that Brett loved him. He was going to stay, and true love would conquer all. Some one knocked on the door.

'Come in.'

It was Bill and Mike. They sat down on the bed.

'Some encierro,' Bill said. 'Some encierro.'

'I say, weren't you there?' Mike asked. 'Ring for some beer, Bill.'

'What a morning!' Bill said. He mopped off his face. 'My God! what a morning! And here's old Jake. Old Jake, the human punching-bag.'

'What happened inside?'

'Good God!' Bill said, 'what happened, Mike?'

'There were these bulls coming in,' Mike said. 'Just ahead of them was the crowd, and some chap tripped and brought the whole lot of them down.'

'And the bulls all came in right over them,' Bill said.

'I heard them yell.'

'That was Edna,' Bill said.

'Chaps kept coming out and waving their shirts.'

'One bull went along the barrera and hooked everybody over.'

'They took twenty chaps to the infirmary,' Mike said.

'What a morning!' Bill said. 'The damn police kept arresting chaps that wanted to go and commit suicide with the bulls.'

'The steers took them in, in the end,' Mike said.

'It took about an hour.'

'It was really about a quarter of an hour,' Mike objected.

'Oh, go to hell,' Bill said. 'You've been in the war. It was two hours and a-half for me.'

'Where's that beer?' Mike asked.

'What did you do with the lovely Edna?'

'We took her home just now. She's gone to bed.'

'How did she like it?'

'Fine. We told her it was just like that every morning.'

'She was impressed,' Mike said.

'She wanted us to go down in the ring, too,' Bill said. 'She likes action.'

'I said it wouldn't be fair to my creditors,' Mike said.

'What a morning,' Bill said. 'And what a night!'

'How's your jaw, Jake?'

'Sore,' I said.

Bill laughed.

'Why didn't you hit him with a chair?'

'You can talk,' Mike said. 'He'd have knocked you out, too. I never saw him hit me. I rather think I saw him just before, and then quite suddenly I was sitting down in the street, and Jake was lying under a table.'

'Where did he go afterward?' I asked.

'Here she is,' Mike said. 'Here's the beautiful lady with the beer.'

The chambermaid put the tray with the beer-bottles and glasses down on the table.

'Now bring up three more bottles,' Mike said.

'Where did Cohn go after he hit me?' I asked Bill.

'Don't you know about that?' Mike was opening a beer-bottle. He poured the beer into one of the glasses, holding the glass close to the bottle.

'Really?' Bill asked.

'Why, he went in and found Brett and the bull-fighter chap in the bull-fighter's room, and then he massacred the poor, bloody bull-fighter.'

'No.'

'Yes.'

'What a night!' Bill said.

'He nearly killed the poor, bloody bull-fighter. Then Cohn wanted to take Brett away. Wanted to make an honest woman of her, I imagine. Damned touching scene.'

He took a long drink of the beer.

'He is an ass.'

'What happened?'

'Brett gave him what for. She told him off. I think she was rather good.'

'I'll bet she was,' Bill said.

'Then Cohn broke down and cried, and wanted to shake hands with the bull-fighter fellow. He wanted to shake hands with Brett too.'

'I know. He shook hands with me.'

'Did he? Well, they weren't having any of it. The bull-fighter fellow was rather good. He didn't say much, but he kept getting up and getting knocked down again. Cohn couldn't knock him out. It must have been damned funny.'

'Where did you hear all this?'

'Brett. I saw her this morning.'

'What happened finally?'

'It seems the bull-fighter fellow was sitting on the bed. He'd been knocked down about fifteen times, and he wanted to fight some more. Brett held him and wouldn't let him get up. He was weak, but Brett couldn't hold him, and he got up. Then Cohn said he wouldn't hit him again. Said he couldn't do it. Said it would be wicked. So the bull-fighter chap sort of rather staggered over to him. Cohn went back against the wall.

'"So you won't hit me?"

'"No," said Cohn. "I'd be ashamed to."

'So the bull-fighter fellow hit him just as hard as he could in the face, and then sat down on the floor. He couldn't get up, Brett said. Cohn wanted to pick him up and carry him to the bed. He said if Cohn helped him he'd kill him, and he'd kill him anyway this morning if Cohn wasn't out of town. Cohn was crying, and Brett had told him off, and he wanted to shake hands. I've told you that before.'

'Tell the rest,' Bill said.

'It seems the bull-fighter chap was sitting on the floor. He was waiting to get strength enough to get up and hit Cohn again. Brett wasn't having any shaking hands, and Cohn was crying and telling her how much he loved her, and she was telling him not to be a ruddy ass. Then Cohn leaned down to shake hands with the bull-fighter fellow. No hard feelings, you know. All for forgiveness. And the bull-fighter chap hit him in the face again.'

'That's quite a kid,' Bill said.

'He ruined Cohn,' Mike said. 'You know I don't think Cohn will ever want to knock people about again.'

'When did you see Brett?'

'This morning. She came in to get some things. She's looking after this Romero lad.'

He poured out another bottle of beer.

'Brett's rather cut up. But she loves looking after people. That's how we came to go off together. She was looking after me.'

'I know,' I said.

'I'm rather drunk,' Mike said. 'I think I'll *stay* rather drunk. This is all awfully amusing, but it's not too pleasant. It's not too pleasant for me.'

He drank off the beer.

'I gave Brett what for, you know. I said if she would go about with Jews and bull-fighters and such people, she must expect trouble.' He leaned forward. 'I say, Jake, do you mind if I drink that bottle of yours? She'll bring you another one.'

'Please,' I said. 'I wasn't drinking it, anyway.'

Mike started to open the bottle. 'Would you mind opening it?' I pressed up the wire fastener and poured it for him.

'You know,' Mike went on, 'Brett was rather good. She's always rather good. I gave her a fearful hiding about Jews and bull-fighters, and all those sort of people, and do you know what she said: "Yes. I've had such a hell of a happy life with the British aristocracy!"'

He took a drink.

'That was rather good. Ashley, chap she got the title from, was a sailor, you know. Ninth baronet. When he came home he wouldn't sleep in a bed. Always made Brett sleep on the floor. Finally, when he got really bad, he used to tell her he'd kill her. Always slept with a loaded service revolver. Brett used to take the shells out when he'd gone to sleep. She hasn't had an absolutely happy life, Brett. Damned shame, too. She enjoys things so.'

He stood up. His hand was shaky.

'I'm going in the room. Try and get a little sleep.'

He smiled.

'We go too long without sleep in these fiestas. I'm going to start now and get plenty of sleep. Damn bad thing not to get sleep. Makes you frightfully nervy.'

'We'll see you at noon at the Iruna,' Bill said.

Mike went out the door. We heard him in the next room.

He rang the bell and the chambermaid came and knocked at the door.

'Bring up half a dozen bottles of beer and a bottle of Fundador,' Mike told her.

'Si, Señorito.'

'I'm going to bed,' Bill said. 'Poor old Mike. I had a hell of a row about him last night.'

'Where? At that Milano place?'

'Yes. There was a fellow there that had helped pay Brett and Mike out of Cannes, once. He was damned nasty.'

'I know the story.'

'I didn't. Nobody ought to have a right to say things about Mike.'

'That's what makes it bad.'

'They oughtn't to have any right. I wish to hell they didn't have any right. I'm going to bed.'

'Was anybody killed in the ring?'

'I don't think so. Just badly hurt.'

'A man was killed outside in the runway.'

'Was there?' said Bill.

18

At noon we were all at the café. It was crowded. We were eating shrimps and drinking beer. The town was crowded. Every street was full. Big motor cars from Biarritz and San Sebastian kept driving up and parking around the square. They brought people for the bull-fight. Sight-seeing cars came up, too. There was one with twenty-five Englishwomen in it. They sat in the big white car and looked through their glasses at the fiesta. The dancers were all quite drunk. It was the last day of the fiesta.

The fiesta was solid and unbroken, but the motor-cars and tourist-cars made little islands of onlookers. When the cars emptied, the onlookers were absorbed into the crowd. You did not see them again except as sport clothes, odd-looking at a table among the closely packed peasants in black smocks. The fiesta absorbed even the Biarritz English so that you did not see them unless you passed close to a table. All the time there was music in the street. The drums kept on pounding and the pipes were going. Inside the cafés men with their hands gripping the table, or on each other's shoulders, were singing the hard-voiced singing.

'Here comes Brett,' Bill said.

I looked and saw her coming through the crowd in the square, walking, her head up, as though the fiesta were being staged in her honour, and she found it pleasant and amusing.

'Hello, you chaps!' she said. 'I say, I *have* a thirst.'

'Get another big beer,' Bill said to the waiter.

'Shrimps?'

'Is Cohn gone?' Brett asked.

'Yes,' Bill said. 'He hired a car.'

The beer came. Brett started to lift the glass mug and her hand shook. She saw it and smiled, and leaned forward and took a long sip.

'Good beer.'

'Very good,' I said. I was nervous about Mike. I did not think he had slept. He must have been drinking all the time, but he seemed to be under control.

'I heard Cohn had hurt you, Jake,' Brett said.

'No. Knocked me out. That was all.'

'I say, he did hurt Pedro Romero,' Brett said. 'He hurt him most badly.'

'How is he?'

'He'll be all right. He won't go out of the room.'

'Does he look badly?'

'Very. He was really hurt. I told him I wanted to pop out and see you chaps for a minute.'

'Is he going to fight?'

'Rather. I'm going with you, if you don't mind.'

'How's your boy friend?' Mike asked. He had not listened to anything that Brett had said.

'Brett's got a bull-fighter,' he said. 'She had a Jew named Cohn, but he turned out badly.'

Brett stood up.

'I am not going to listen to that sort of rot from you, Michael.'

'How's your boy friend?'

'Damned well,' Brett said. 'Watch him this afternoon.'

'Brett's got a bull-fighter,' Mike said. 'A beautiful, bloody bull-fighter.'

'Would you mind walking over with me? I want to talk to you, Jake.'

'Tell him all about your bull-fighter,' Mike said. 'Oh, to hell with your bull-fighter!' He tipped the table so that all the beers and the dish of shrimps went over in a crash.

'Come on,' Brett said. 'Let's get out of this.'

In the crowd crossing the square I said: 'How is it?'

'I'm not going to see him after lunch until the fight. His people come in and dress him. They're very angry about me, he says.'

Brett was radiant. She was happy. The sun was out and the day was bright.

'I feel altogether changed,' Brett said. 'You've no idea, Jake.'

'Anything you want me to do?'

'No, just go to the fight with me.'

'We'll see you at lunch?'

'No. I'm eating with him.'

We were standing under the arcade at the door of the hotel. They were carrying tables out and setting them up under the arcade.

'Want to take a turn out to the park?' Brett asked. 'I don't want to go up yet. I fancy he's sleeping.'

We walked along past the theatre and out of the square and along through the barracks of the fair, moving with the crowd between the lines of booths. We came out on a cross-street that led to the Paseo de Sarasate. We could see the crowd walking there, all the fashionably dressed people. They were making the turn at the upper end of the park.

'Don't let's go there,' Brett said. 'I don't want staring at just now.'

We stood in the sunlight. It was hot and good after the rain and the clouds from the sea.

'I hope the wind goes down,' Brett said. 'It's very bad for him.'

'So do I.'

'He says the bulls are all right.'

'They're good.'

'Is that San Fermin's?'

Brett looked at the yellow wall of the chapel.

'Yes. Where the show started on Sunday.'

'Let's go in. Do you mind? I'd rather like to pray a little for him or something.'

We went in through the heavy leather door that moved very lightly. It was dark inside. Many people were praying. You saw them as your eyes adjusted themselves to the half-light. We knelt at one of the long wooden benches. After a little I felt Brett stiffen beside me, and saw she was looking straight ahead.

'Come on,' she whispered throatily. 'Let's get out of here. Makes me damned nervous.'

Outside in the hot brightness of the street Brett looked up at the tree-tops in the wind. The praying had not been much of a success.

'Don't know why I get so nervy in church,' Brett said. 'Never does me any good.'

We walked along.

'I'm damned bad for a religious atmosphere,' Brett said. 'I've the wrong type of face.

'You know,' Brett said, 'I'm not worried about him at all. I just feel happy about him.'

'Good.'

'I wish the wind would drop, though.'

'It's liable to go down by five o'clock.'

'Let's hope.'

'You might pray,' I laughed.

'Never does me any good. I've never gotten anything I prayed for. Have you?'

'Oh, yes.'

'Oh, rot,' said Brett. 'Maybe it works for some people, though. You don't look very religious, Jake.'

'I'm pretty religious.'

'Oh, rot,' said Brett. 'Don't start proselyting to-day. To-day's going to be bad enough as it is.'

It was the first time I had seen her in the old happy, careless way since before she went off with Cohn. We were back again in front of the hotel. All the tables were set now, and already several were filled with people eating.

'Do look after Mike,' Brett said. 'Don't let him get too bad.'

'Your friends haff gone upstairs,' the German maître d'hôtel said in English. He was a continual eavesdropper. Brett turned to him:

'Thank you so much. Have you anything else to say?'

'No, *ma'am*.'

'Good,' said Brett.

'Save us a table for three,' I said to the German. He smiled his dirty little pink-and-white smile.

'Iss madam eating here?'

'No,' Brett said.

'Den I think a tabul for two will be enuff.'

'Don't talk to him,' Brett said. 'Mike must have been in bad shape,' she said on the stairs. We passed Montoya on the stairs. He bowed and did not smile.

'I'll see you at the café,' Brett said. 'Thank you, so much, Jake.'

We had stopped at the floor our rooms were on. She went straight down the hall and into Romero's room. She did not knock. She simply opened the door, went in, and closed it behind her.

I stood in front of the door of Mike's room and knocked. There was no answer. I tried the knob and it opened. Inside the room was in great disorder. All the bags were opened and clothing was strewn around. There were empty bottles beside the bed. Mike lay on the bed looking like a death mask of himself. He opened his eyes and looked at me.

'Hello, Jake,' he said very slowly. 'I'm getting a lit-tle sleep. I've want-ed a lit-tle sleep for a long time.'

'Let me cover you over.'

'No. I'm quite warm.

'Don't go. I haven't got-ten to sleep yet.'

'You'll sleep Mike. Don't worry, boy.'

'Brett's got a bull-fighter,' Mike said. 'But her Jew has gone away.'

He turned his head and looked at me.

'Damned good thing, what?'

'Yes. Now go to sleep, Mike. You ought to get some sleep.'

'I'm just start-ing. I'm go-ing to get a lit-tle sleep.'

He shut his eyes. I went out of the room and turned the door to quietly. Bill was in my room reading the paper.

'See Mike?'

'Yes.'

'Let's go and eat.'

'I won't eat downstairs with that German head waiter. He was damned snotty when I was getting Mike upstairs.'

'He was snotty to us, too.'

'Let's go out and eat in the town.'

We went down the stairs. On the stairs we passed a girl coming up with a covered tray.

'There goes Brett's lunch,' Bill said.

'And the kid's,' I said.

Outside on the terrace under the arcade the German head waiter came up. His red cheeks were shiny. He was being polite.

'I haff a tabul for two for you gentlemen,' he said.

'Go sit at it,' Bill said. We went on out across the street.

We ate at a restaurant in a side street off the square. They were all men eating in the restaurant. It was full of smoke and drinking and singing. The food was good and so was the wine. We did not talk much. Afterward we went to the café and watched the fiesta come to the boiling-point. Brett came over soon after lunch. She said she had looked in the room and that Mike was asleep.

When the fiesta boiled over and toward the bull-ring we went with the crowd. Brett sat at the ring-side between Bill and me. Directly below us was the callejon, the passageway between the stands and the red fence of the barrera. Behind us the concrete stands filled solidly. Out in front, beyond the red fence, the sand of the ring was smooth-rolled and yellow. It looked a little heavy from the rain, but it was dry in the sun and firm and smooth. The sword-handlers and bull-ring servants came down the callejon carrying on their shoulders the wicker baskets of fighting capes and muletas. They were bloodstained and compactly folded and packed in the baskets. The sword-handlers opened the heavy leather sword-cases so the red wrapped hilts of the sheaf of swords showed as the leather case leaned against the fence. They unfolded the dark-stained red flannel of the muletas and fixed batons in them to spread the stuff and give the matador something to hold. Brett watched it all She was absorbed in the professional details.

'He's his name stencilled on all the capes and muletas,' she said. 'Why do they call them muletas?'

'I don't know.'

'I wonder if they ever launder them.'

'I don't think so. It might spoil the colour.'

'The blood must stiffen them,' Bill said.

'Funny,' Brett said, 'how one doesn't mind the blood.'

Below in the narrow passage of the callejon the sword-handlers arranged everything. All the seats were full. Above, all the boxes were full. There was not an empty seat except in the President's box. When he came in the fight would start. Across the smooth sand, in the high doorway that led into the corrals, the bull-fighters were standing, their arms furled in their capes, talking, waiting for the signal to march in across the arena. Brett was watching them with the glasses.

'Here, would you like to look?'

I looked through the glasses and saw the three matadors. Romero was in the centre, Belmonte on his left, Marcial on his right. Back of them were their people, and behind the banderilleros, back in the passageway and in the open space of the corral I saw the picadors. Romero was wearing a black suit. His tricornered hat was low down over his eyes. I could not see his face clearly under the hat, but it looked badly marked. He was looking straight ahead. Marcial was smoking a cigarette guardedly, holding it in his hand. Belmonte looked ahead, his face wan and yellow, his long wolf-jaw out. He was looking at nothing. Neither he nor Romero seemed to have anything in common with the others. They were all alone. The President came in; there was hand-clapping above us in the grandstand, and I handed the glasses to Brett. There was applause. The music started. Brett looked through the glasses.

'Here, take them,' she said.

Through the glasses I saw Belmonte speak to Romero. Marcial

straightened up and dropped his cigarette, and, looking straight ahead, their heads back, their free arms swinging, the three matadors walked out. Behind them came all the procession, opening out, all striding in step, all the capes furled, everybody with free arms swinging, and behind rode the picadors, their pics rising like lances. Behind all came the two trains of mules and the bull-ring servants. The matadors bowed, holding their hats on, before the President's box, and then came over to the barrera below us. Pedro Romero took off his heavy gold-brocaded cape and handed it over the fence to his sword-handler. He said something to the sword-handler. Close below us we saw Romero's lips were puffed, both eyes were discoloured. His face was discoloured and swollen. The sword-handler took the cape, looked up at Brett, and came over to us and handed up the cape.

'Spread it out in front of you,' I said.

Brett leaned forward. The cape was heavy and smoothly stiff with gold. The sword-handler looked back, shook his head, and said something. A man beside me leaned over toward Brett.

'He doesn't want you to spread it,' he said. 'You should fold it and keep it in your lap.'

Brett folded the heavy cape.

Romero did not look up at us. He was speaking to Belmonte. Belmonte had sent his formal cape over to some friends. He looked across at them and smiled, his wolf-smile that was only with the mouth. Romero leaned over the barrera and asked for the water-jug. The sword-handler brought it and Romero poured water over the percale of his fighting-cape, and then scuffed the lower folds in the sand with his slippered foot.

'What's that for?' Brett asked.

'To give it weight in the wind.'

'His face looks bad,' Bill said.

'He feels very badly,' Brett said. 'He should be in bed.'

The first bull was Belmonte's. Belmonte was very good. But because he got thirty thousand pesetas and people had stayed in line all night to buy tickets to see him, the crowd demanded that he should be more than very good. Belmonte's great attraction is working close to the bull. In bull-fighting they speak of the terrain of the bull and the terrain of the bull-fighter. As long as a bull-fighter stays in his own terrain he is comparatively safe. Each time he enters into the terrain of the bull he is in great danger. Belmonte, in his best days, worked always in the terrain of the bull. This way he gave the sensation of coming tragedy. People went to the corrida to see Belmonte, to be given tragic sensations, and perhaps to see the death of Belmonte. Fifteen years ago they said if you wanted to see Belmonte you should go quickly, while he was still alive. Since then he has killed more than a thousand bulls. When he retired the legend grew up about how his bull-fighting had been, and when he came out of retirement the public were disappointed because no real man could work as close to the bulls as Belmonte was supposed to have done, not, of course, even Belmonte.

Also Belmonte imposed conditions and insisted that his bulls should not be too large, nor too dangerously armed with horns, and so the element that was necessary to give the sensation of tragedy was not there, and the public, who wanted three times as much from Belmonte, who was sick with a fistula, as Belmonte had ever been able to give, felt defrauded and cheated, and Belmonte's jaw came further out in contempt, and his face turned yellower, and he moved with greater difficulty as his pain increased, and finally the crowd were actively against him, and he was utterly contemptuous and indifferent. He had meant to have a great afternoon, and instead it was an afternoon of sneers, shouted insults, and finally a volley of cushions and pieces of bread and vegetables, thrown down at him in the plaza where he had had his greatest triumphs. His jaw only went further out. Sometimes he turned to smile that toothed, long-jawed, lipless smile when he was called something particularly insulting, and always the pain that any movement produced grew stronger and stronger, until finally his yellow face was parchment colour, and after his second bull was dead and the throwing of bread and cushions was over, after he had saluted the President with the same wolf-jawed smile and contemptuous eyes, and handed his sword over the barrera to be wiped, and put back in its case, he passed through into the callejon and leaned on the barrera below us, his head on his arms, not seeing, not hearing anything, only going through his pain. When he looked up, finally, he asked for a drink of water. He swallowed a little, rinsed his mouth, spat the water, took his cape, and went back into the ring.

Because they were against Belmonte the public were for Romero. From the moment he left the barrera and went toward the bull they applauded him. Belmonte watched Romero, too, watched him always without seeming to. He paid no attention to Marcial. Marcial was the sort of thing he knew all about. He had come out of retirement to compete with Marcial, knowing it was a competition gained in advance. He had expected to compete with Marcial and the other stars of the decadence of bull-fighting, and he knew that the sincerity of his own bull-fighting would be so set off by the false aesthetics of the bull-fighters of the decadent period that he would only have to be in the ring. His return from retirement had been spoiled by Romero. Romero did always, smoothly, calmly, and beautifully, what he, Belmonte, could only bring himself to do now sometimes. The crowd felt it, even the people from Biarritz, even the American ambassador saw it, finally. It was a competition that Belmonte would not enter because it would lead only to a bad horn wound or death. Belmonte was no longer well enough. He no longer had his greatest moments in the bull-ring. He was not sure that there were any great moments. Things were not the same and now life only came in flashes. He had flashes of the old greatness with his bulls, but they were not of value because he had discounted them in advance when he had picked the bulls out for their safety, getting out of a motor and leaning on a fence, looking over at the herd on the ranch of his friend the bull-breeder. So he had two small, manageable bulls without much horns, and when he felt the greatness again coming, just a little of it through the pain that was always with him, it had been discounted and sold in advance, and it did not give him a good feeling. It was the greatness, but it did not make bull-fighting wonderful to him any more.

Pedro Romero had the greatness. He loved bull-fighting, and I think he loved the bulls, and I think he loved Brett. Everything of which he could control the locality he did in front of her all that afternoon. Never once did he look up. He made it stronger that way, and did it for himself, too, as well as for her. Because he did not look up to ask if it pleased he did it all for himself inside, and it strengthened him, and yet he did it for her too. But he did not do it for her at any loss to himself. He gained by it all through the afternoon.

His first 'quite' was directly below us. The three matadors take the bull in turn after each charge he makes at a picador. Belmonte was the first. Marcial was the second. Then came Romero. The three of them were standing at the left of the horse. The picador, his hat down over his eyes, the shaft of his pic angling sharply toward the bull, kicked in the spurs and held them and with the reins in his left hand walked the horse forward toward the bull. The bull was watching. Seemingly he watched the white horse, but really he watched the triangular steel point of the pic. Romero, watching, saw the bull start to turn his head. He did not want to charge. Romero flicked his cape so the colour caught the bull's eye. The bull charged with the reflex, charged, and found not the flash of colour but a white horse, and a man leaned far over the horse, shot the steel point of the long hickory shaft into the hump of muscle on the bull's shoulder, and pulled his horse sideways as he pivoted on the pic, making a wound, enforcing the iron into the bull's shoulder, making him bleed for Belmonte.

The bull did not insist under the iron. He did not really want to get at the horse. He turned and the group broke apart and Romero was taking him out with his cape. He took him out softly and smoothly, and then stopped and, standing squarely in front of the bull, offered him the cape. The bull's tail went up and he charged, and Romero moved his arms ahead of the bull, wheeling, his feet firmed. The dampened, mud-weighted cape swung open and full as a sail fills, and Romero pivoted with it just ahead of the bull. At the end of the pass they were facing each other again. Romero smiled. The bull wanted it again, and Romero's cape filled again, this time on the other side. Each time he let the bull pass so close that the man and the bull and the cape that filled and pivoted ahead of the bull were all one sharply etched mass. It was all so slow and so controlled. It was as though he were rocking the bull to sleep. He made four veronicas like that, and finished with a half veronica that turned his back on the bull and came away toward the applause, his hand on his hip, his cape on his arm, and the bull watching his back going away.

In his own bulls he was perfect. His first bull did not see well. After the first two passes with the cape Romero knew exactly how bad the vision was impaired. He worked accordingly. It was not brilliant bull-fighting. It was only perfect bull-fighting. The crowd wanted the bull changed. They made a great row. Nothing very fine could happen with a bull that could not see the lures, but the President would not order him replaced.

'Why don't they change him?' Brett asked.

'They've paid for him. They don't want to lose their money.'

'It's hardly fair to Romero.'

'Watch how he handles a bull that can't see the colour.'

'It's the sort of thing I don't like to see.'

It was not nice to watch if you cared anything about the person who was doing it. With the bull who could not see the colours of the capes, or the scarlet flannel of the muleta, Romero had to make the bull content with his body. He had to get so close that the bull saw his body, and would start for it, and then shift the bull's charge to the flannel and finish out the pass in the classic manner. The Biarritz crowd did not like it. They thought Romero was afraid, and that was why he gave that little side-step each time as he transferred the bull's charge from his own body to the flannel. They preferred Belmonte's imitation of himself or Marcial's imitation of Belmonte. There were three of them in the row behind us.

'What's he afraid of the bull for? The bull's so dumb he only goes after the cloth.'

'He's just a young bull-fighter. He hasn't learned it yet.'

'But I thought he was fine with the cape before.'

'Probably he's nervous now.'

Out in the centre of the ring, all alone, Romero was going on with the same thing, getting so close that the bull could see him plainly, offering the body, offering it again a little closer, the bull watching dully, then so close that the bull thought he had him, offering again, and finally drawing the charge and then, just before the horns came, giving the bull the red cloth to follow with that little, almost imperceptible, jerk that so offended the critical judgment of the Biarritz bull-fight experts.

'He's going to kill now,' I said to Brett. 'The bull's still strong. He wouldn't wear himself out.'

Out in the centre of the ring Romero profiled in front of the bull, drew the sword out from the folds of the muleta, rose on his toes, and sighted along the blade. The bull charged as Romero charged. Romero's left hand dropped the muleta over the bull's muzzle to blind him, his left shoulder went forward between the horns as the sword went in, and for just an instant he and the bull were one, Romero way out over the bull, the right arm extended high up to where the hilt of the sword had gone in between the bull's shoulders. Then the figure was broken. There was a little jolt as Romero came clear, and then he was standing, one hand up, facing the bull, his shirt ripped out from under his sleeve, the white blowing in the wind, and the bull, the red sword hilt tight between his shoulders, his head going down and his legs settling.

'There he goes,' Bill said.

Romero was close enough so the bull could see him. His hand still up, he spoke to the bull. The bull gathered himself, then his head went forward and he went over slowly, then all over, suddenly, four feet in the air.

They handed the sword to Romero, and carrying it blade down, the muleta in his other hand, he walked over to in front of the President's box, bowed, straightened, and came over to the barrera, and handed over the sword and muleta.

'Bad one,' said the sword-handler.

'He made me sweat,' said Romero. He wiped off his face. The sword-handler handed him the water-jug. Romero wiped his lips. It hurt him to drink out of the jug. He did not look up at us.

Marcial had a big day. They were still applauding him when Romero's last bull came in. It was the bull that had sprinted out and killed the man in the morning running.

During Romero's first bull his hurt face had been very noticeable. Everything he did showed it. All the concentration of the awkwardly delicate working with the bull that could not see well brought it out. The fight with Cohn had not touched his spirit, but his face had been smashed and his body hurt. He was wiping all that out now. Each thing that he did with this bull wiped that out a little cleaner. It was a good bull, a big bull, and with horns, and it turned and re-charged easily and surely. He was what Romero wanted in bulls.

When he had finished his work with the muleta and was ready to kill, the crowd made him go on. They did not want the bull killed yet, they did not want it to be over. Romero went on. It was like a course in bull-fighting. All the passes he linked up, all completed, all slow, templed and smooth. There were no tricks and no mystifications. There was no brusqueness. And each pass as it reached the summit gave you a sudden ache inside. The crowd did not want it ever to be finished.

The bull was squared on all four feet to be killed, and Romero killed directly below us. He killed not as he had been forced to by the last bull, but as he wanted to. He profiled directly in front of the bull, drew the sword out of the folds of the muleta and sighted along the blade. The bull watched him. Romero spoke to the bull and tapped one of his feet. The bull charged and Romero waited for the charge, the muleta held low, sighting along the blade, his feet firm. Then without taking a step forward, he became one with the bull, the sword was in high between the shoulders, the bull had followed the low-swung flannel, that disappeared as Romero lurched clear to the left, and it was over. The bull tried to go forward, his legs commenced to settle, he swung from side to side, hesitated, then went down on his knees, and Romero's older brother leaned forward behind him and drove a short knife into the bull's neck at the base of the horns. The first time he missed. He drove the knife in again, and the bull went over, twitching and rigid. Romero's brother, holding the bull's horn in one hand, the knife in the other, looked up at the President's box. Handkerchiefs were waving all over the bull-ring. The President looked down from the box and waved his handkerchief. The brother cut the notched black ear from the dead bull and trotted over with it to Romero. The bull lay heavy and black on the sand, his tongue out. Boys were running toward him from all parts of the arena, making a little circle around him. They were starting to dance around the bull.

Romero took the ear from his brother and held it up toward the President. The President bowed and Romero, running to get ahead of the crowd, came toward us. He leaned up against the barrera and gave the ear to Brett. He nodded his head and smiled. The crowd were all about him. Brett held down the cape.

'You liked it?' Romero called.

Brett did not say anything. They looked at each other and smiled.

Brett had the ear in her hand.

'Don't get bloody,' Romero said, and grinned. The crowd wanted him. Several boys shouted at Brett. The crowd was the boys, the dancers, and the drunks. Romero turned and tried to get through the crowd. They were all around him trying to lift him and put him on their shoulders. He fought and twisted away, and started running, in the midst of them, toward the exit. He did not want to be carried on people's shoulders. But they held him and lifted him. It was uncomfortable and his legs were spraddled and his body was very sore. They were lifting him and all running toward the gate. He had his hand on somebody's shoulder. He looked around at us apologetically. The crowd, running, went out the gate with him.

We all three went back to the hotel. Brett went upstairs. Bill and I sat in the downstairs dining-room and ate some hard-boiled eggs and drank several bottles of beer. Belmonte came down in his street clothes with his manager and two other men. They sat at the next table and ate. Belmonte ate very little. They were leaving on the seven o'clock train for Barcelona. Belmonte wore a blue-striped shirt and a dark suit, and ate soft-boiled eggs. The others ate a big meal. Belmonte did not talk. He only answered questions.

Bill was tired after the bull-fight. So was I. We both took a bull-fight very hard. We sat and ate the eggs and I watched Belmonte and the people at his table. The men with him were tough-looking and businesslike.

'Come on over to the café,' Bill said. 'I want an absinthe.'

It was the last day of the fiesta. Outside it was beginning to be cloudy again. The square was full of people and the fireworks experts were making up their set pieces for the night and covering them over with beech branches. Boys were watching. We passed stands of rockets with long bamboo stems. Outside the café there was a great crowd. The music and the dancing were going on. The giants and the dwarfs were passing.

'Where's Edna?' I asked Bill.

'I don't know.'

We watched the beginning of the evening of the last night of the fiesta. The absinthe made everything seem better. I drank it without sugar in the dripping glass, and it was pleasantly bitter.

'I feel sorry about Cohn,' Bill said. 'He had an awful time.'

'Oh, to hell with Cohn,' I said.

'Where do you suppose he went?'

'Up to Paris.'

'What do you suppose he'll do?'

'Oh, to hell with him.'

'What do you suppose he'll do?'

'Pick up with his old girl, probably.'

'Who was his old girl?'

'Somebody named Frances.'

We had another absinthe.

'When do you go back?' I asked.

'To-morrow.'

After a little while Bill said: 'Well, it was a swell fiesta.'

'Yes,' I said; 'something doing all the time.'

'You wouldn't believe it. It's like a wonderful nightmare.'

'Sure,' I said. 'I'd believe anything. Including nightmares.'

'What's the matter? Feel low?'

'Low as hell.'

'Have another absinthe. Here, waiter! Another absinthe for this señor.'

'I feel like hell,' I said.

'Drink that,' said Bill. 'Drink it slow.'

It was beginning to get dark. The fiesta was going on. I began to feel drunk but I did not feel any better.

'How do you feel?'

'I feel like hell.'

'Have another?'

'It won't do any good.'

'Try it. You can't tell; maybe this is the one that gets it. Hey, waiter! Another absinthe for this señor!'

I poured the water directly into it and stirred it instead of letting it drip. Bill put in a lump of ice. I stirred the ice around with a spoon in the brownish, cloudy mixture.

'How is it?'

'Fine.'

'Don't drink it fast that way. It will make you sick.'

I set down the glass. I had not meant to drink it fast.

'I feel tight.'

'You ought to.'

'That's what you wanted, wasn't it?'

'Sure. Get tight. Get over your damn depression.'

'Well, I'm tight. Is that what you want?'

'Sit down.'

'I won't sit down,' I said. 'I'm going over to the hotel.'

I was very drunk. I was drunker than I ever remembered having been. At the hotel I went upstairs. Brett's door was open. I put my head in the room. Mike was sitting on the bed. He waved a bottle.

'Jake,' he said. 'Come in, Jake.'

I went in and sat down. The room was unstable unless I looked at some fixed point.

'Brett, you know. She's gone off with the bull-fighter chap.'

'No.'

'Yes. She looked for you to say good-bye. They went on the seven o'clock train.'

'Did they?'

'Bad thing to do,' Mike said. 'She shouldn't have done it.'

'No.'

'Have a drink? Wait while I ring for some beer.'

'I'm drunk,' I said. 'I'm going in and lie down.'

'Are you blind? I was blind myself.'

'Yes,' I said. 'I'm blind.'

'Well, bung-o,' Mike said. 'Get some sleep, old Jake.'

I went out the door and into my own room and lay on the bed. The bed went sailing off and I sat up in bed and looked at the wall to make it stop. Outside in the square the fiesta was going on. It did not mean anything. Later Bill and Mike came in to get me to go down and eat with them. I pretended to be asleep.

'He's asleep. Better let him alone.'

'He's blind as a tick,' Mike said. They went out.

I got up and went to the balcony and looked out at the dancing in the square. The world was not wheeling any more. It was just very clear and bright, and inclined to blur at the edges. I washed, brushed my hair. I looked strange to myself in the glass, and went downstairs to the dining-room.

'Here he is!' said Bill. 'Good old Jake! I knew you wouldn't pass out.'

'Hello, you old drunk,' Mike said.

'I got hungry and woke up.'

'Eat some soup,' Bill said.

The three of us sat at the table, and it seemed as though about six people were missing.

PART III

19

In the morning it was all over. The fiesta was finished. I woke about nine o'clock, had a bath, dressed, and went downstairs. The square was empty and there were no people on the streets. A few children were picking up rocket-sticks in the square. The cafés were just opening and the waiters were carrying out the comfortable white wicker chairs and arranging them around the marble-topped tables in the shade of the arcade. They were sweeping the streets and sprinkling them with a hose.

I sat in one of the wicker chairs and leaned back comfortably. The waiter was in no hurry to come. The white-paper announcements of the unloading of the bulls and the big schedules of special trains were still up on the pillars of the arcade. A waiter wearing a blue apron came out with a bucket of water and a cloth, and commenced to tear down the notices, pulling the paper off in strips and washing and rubbing away the paper that stuck to the stone. The fiesta was over.

I drank a coffee and after a while Bill came over. I watched him come walking across the square. He sat down at the table and ordered a coffee.

'Well,' he said, 'it's all over.'

'Yes,' I said. 'When do you go?'

'I don't know. We better get a car, I think. Aren't you going back to Paris?'

'No. I can stay away another week. I think I'll go to San Sebastian.'

'I want to get back.'

'What's Mike going to do?'

'He's going to Saint Jean de Luz.'

'Let's get a car and all go as far as Bayonne. You can get the train up from there to-night.'

'Good. Let's go after lunch.'

'All right. I'll get the car.'

We had lunch and paid the bill. Montoya did not come near us. One of the maids brought the bill. The car was outside. The chauffeur piled and strapped the bags on top of the car and put them in beside him in the front seat and we got in. The car went out of the square, along through the side streets, out under the trees and down the hill and away from Pamplona. It did not seem like a very long ride. Mike had a bottle of Fundador. I only took a couple of drinks. We came over the mountains and out of Spain and down the white roads and through the over-foliaged, wet, green, Basque country, and finally into Bayonne. We left Bill's baggage at the station, and he bought a ticket to Paris. His train left at seven-ten. We came out of the station. The car was standing out in front.

'What shall we do about the car?' Bill asked.

'Oh, bother the car,' Mike said. 'Let's just keep the car with us.'

'All right,' Bill said. 'Where shall we go?'

'Let's go to Biarritz and have a drink.'

'Old Mike the spender,' Bill said.

We drove in to Biarritz and left the car outside a very Ritz place. We went into the bar and sat on high stools and drank a whiskey-and-soda.

'That drink's mine,' Mike said.

'Let's roll for it.'

So we rolled poker dice out of a deep leather dice-cup. Bill was out first roll. Mike lost to me and handed the bartender a hundred-franc note. The whiskeys were twelve francs apiece. We had another round and Mike lost again. Each time he gave the bartender a good tip. In a room off the bar there was a good jazz band playing. It was a pleasant bar. We had another round. I went out on the first roll with four kings. Bill and Mike rolled. Mike won the first roll with four jacks. Bill won the second. On the final roll Mike had three kings and let them stay. He handed the dice-cup to Bill. Bill rattled them and rolled, and there were three kings, an ace, and a queen.

'It's yours, Mike,' Bill said. 'Old Mike, the gambler.'

'I'm so sorry,' Mike said. 'I can't get it.'

'What's the matter?'

'I've no money,' Mike said. 'I'm stony. I've just twenty francs. Here, take twenty francs.'

Bill's face sort of changed.

'I just had enough to pay Montoya. Damned lucky to have it too.'

'I'll cash you a cheque,' Bill said.

'That's damned nice of you, but you see I can't write cheques.'

'What are you going to do for money?'

'Oh, some will come through. I've two weeks allowance should be here. I can live on tick at this pub in Saint Jean.'

'What do you want to do about the car?' Bill asked me. 'Do you want to keep it on?'

'It doesn't make any difference. Seems sort of idiotic.'

'Come on, let's have another drink,' Mike said.

'Fine. This one is on me,' Bill said. 'Has Brett any money?' He turned to Mike.

'I shouldn't think so. She put up most of what I gave to old Montoya.'

'She hasn't any money with her?' I asked.

'I shouldn't think so. She never has any money. She gets five hundred quid a year and pays three hundred and fifty of it in interest to Jews.'

'I suppose they get it at the source,' said Bill.

'Quite. They're not really Jews. We just call them Jews. They're

Scotsmen, I believe.'

'Hasn't she any at all with her?' I asked.

'I hardly think so. She gave it all to me when she left.'

'Well,' Bill said, 'we might as well have another drink.'

'Damned good idea,' Mike said. 'One never gets anywhere by discussing finances.'

'No,' said Bill. Bill and I rolled for the next two rounds. Bill lost and paid. We went out to the car.

'Anywhere you'd like to go, Mike?' Bill asked.

'Let's take a drive. It might do my credit good. Let's drive about a little.'

'Fine. I'd like to see the coast. Let's drive down toward Hendaye.'

'I haven't any credit along the coast.'

'You can't ever tell,' said Bill.

We drove out along the coast road. There was the green of the headlands, the white, red-roofed villas, patches of forest, and the ocean very blue with the tide out and the water curling far out along the beach. We drove through Saint Jean de Luz and passed through villages farther down the coast. Back of the rolling country we were going through we saw the mountains we had come over from Pamplona. The road went on ahead. Bill looked at his watch.

It was time for us to go back. He knocked on the glass and told the driver to turn around. The driver backed the car out into the grass to turn it. In back of us were the woods, below a stretch of meadow, then the sea.

At the hotel where Mike was going to stay in Saint Jean we stopped the car and he got out. The chauffeur carried in his bags. Mike stood by the side of the car.

'Good-bye, you chaps,' Mike said. 'It was a damned fine fiesta.'

'So long, Mike,' Bill said.

'I'll see you around,' I said.

'Don't worry about money,' Mike said. 'You can pay for the car, Jake, and I'll send you my share.'

'So long, Mike.'

'So long, you chaps. You've been damned nice.'

We all shook hands. We waved from the car to Mike. He stood in the road watching. We got to Bayonne just before the train left. A porter carried Bill's bags in from the consigne. I went as far as the inner gate to the tracks.

'So long, fella,' Bill said.

'So long, kid!'

'It was swell. I've had a swell time.'

'Will you be in Paris?'

'No. I have to sail on the 17th. So long, fella!'

'So long, old kid!'

He went in through the gate to the train. The porter went ahead with the bags. I watched the train pull out. Bill was at one of the windows. The window passed, the rest of the train passed, and the tracks were empty. I went outside to the car.

'How much do we owe you?' I asked the driver. The price to Bayonne had been fixed at a hundred and fifty pesetas.

'Two hundred pesetas.'

'How much more will it be if you drive me to San Sebastian on your way back?'

'Fifty pesetas.'

'Don't kid me.'

'Thirty-five pesetas.'

'It's not worth it,' I said. 'Drive me to the Hotel Panier Fleuri.'

At the hotel I paid the driver and gave him a tip. The car was powdered with dust. I rubbed the rod-case through the dust. It seemed the last thing that connected me with Spain and the fiesta. The driver put the car in gear and went down the street. I watched it turn off to take the road to Spain. I went into the hotel and they gave me a room. It was the same room I had slept in when Bill and Cohn and I were in Bayonne. That seemed a very long time ago. I washed, changed my shirt, and went out in the town.

At a newspaper kiosk I bought a copy of the New York *Herald* and sat in a café to read it. It felt strange to be in France again. There was a safe, suburban feeling. I wished I had gone up to Paris with Bill, except that Paris would have meant more fiesta-ing. I was through with fiestas for a while. It would be quiet in San Sebastian. The season does not open there until August. I could get a good hotel room and read and swim. There was a fine beach there. There were wonderful trees along the promenade above the beach, and there were many children sent down with their nurses before the season opened. In the evening there would be band concerts under the trees across from the Café Marinas. I could sit in the Marinas and listen.

'How does one eat inside?' I asked the waiter. Inside the café was a restaurant.

'Well. Very well. One eats very well.'

'Good.'

I went in and ate dinner. It was a big meal for France, but it seemed very carefully apportioned after Spain. I drank a bottle of wine for company. It was a Château Margaux. It was pleasant to be drinking slowly and to be tasting the wine and to be drinking alone. A bottle of wine was good company. Afterward I had coffee. The waiter recommended a Basque liqueur called Izzarra. He brought in the bottle and poured a liqueur-glass full. He said Izzarra was made of the flowers of the Pyrenees. The veritable flowers of the Pyrenees. It looked like hair-oil and smelled like Italian *strega*. I told him to take the flowers of the Pyrenees away and bring me a *vieux marc*. The *marc* was good. I had a second *marc* after the coffee.

The waiter seemed a little offended about the flowers of the Pyrenees, so I overtipped him. That made him happy. It felt comfortable to be in a country where it is so simple to make people happy. You can never tell whether a Spanish waiter will thank you. Everything is on such a clear financial basis in France. It is the simplest country to live in. No one makes things complicated by becoming your friend for any obscure reason. If you want people to like you you have only to spend a little money. I spent a little money and the waiter liked me. He appreciated my valuable qualities. He would be glad to see me back. I would dine there again some time and he would be glad to see me, and would want me at his table. It would be a sincere liking because it would have a sound basis. I was back in France.

Next morning I tipped everyone a little too much at the hotel to make more friends, and left on the morning train for San Sebastian. At the station I did not tip the porter more than I should because I did not think I would ever see him again. I only wanted a few good French friends in Bayonne to make me welcome in case I should come back there again. I knew that if they remembered me their friendship would be loyal.

At Irun we had to change trains and show passports. I hated to leave France. Life was so simple in France. I felt I was a fool to be going back into Spain. In Spain you could not tell about anything. I felt like a fool to be going back into it, but I stood in line with my passport, opened my bags for the customs, bought a ticket, went through a gate, climbed on to a train, and after forty minutes and eight tunnels I was at San Sebastian.

Even on a hot day San Sebastian has a certain early-morning quality. The trees seem as though their leaves were never quite dry. The streets feel as though they had just been sprinkled. It is always cool and shady on certain streets on the hottest day. I went to a hotel in the town where I had stopped before, and they gave me a room with a balcony that opened out above the roofs of the town. There was a green mountainside beyond the roofs.

I unpacked my bags and stacked my books on the table beside the head of the bed, put out my shaving things, hung up some clothes in the big armoire, and made up a bundle for the laundry. Then I took a shower in the bath-room and went down to lunch. Spain had not changed to summer-time, so I was early. I set my watch again. I had recovered an hour by coming to San Sebastian.

As I went into the dining-room the concierge brought me a police bulletin to fill out. I signed it and asked him for two telegraph forms, and wrote a message to the Hotel Montoya, telling them to forward all mail and telegrams for me to this address. I calculated how many days I would be in San Sebastian and then wrote out a wire to the office asking them to hold mail, but forward all wires for me to San Sebastian for six days. Then I went in and had lunch.

After lunch I went up to my room, read a while, and went to sleep. When I woke it was half-past four. I found my swimming suit, wrapped it with a comb in a towel, and went downstairs and walked up the street to the concha. The tide was about half-way out. The beach was smooth and firm, and the sand yellow. I went into a bathing cabin, undressed, put on my suit, and walked across the smooth sand to the sea. The sand was warm under bare feet. There were quite a few people in the water and on the beach. Out beyond where the headlands of the concha almost met to form the harbour there was a white line of breakers and the open sea. Although the tide was going out, there were a few slow rollers. They came in like undulations in the water, gathered weight of water, and then broke smoothly on the warm sand. I waded out. The water was cold. As a roller came I dove, swam out under the water, and came to the surface with all the chill gone. I swam out to the raft, pulled myself up, and lay on the hot planks. A boy and girl were at the other end. The girl had undone the top strap of her bathing-suit and was browning her back. The boy lay face downward on the raft and talked to her. She laughed at things he said, and turned her brown back in the sun. I lay on the raft in the sun until I was dry. Then I tried several dives. I dove deep once, swimming down to the bottom. I swam with my eyes open and it was green and dark. The raft made a dark shadow. I came out of water beside the raft, pulled up, dove once more, holding it for length, and then swam ashore. I lay on the beach until I was dry, then went into the bathing-cabin, took off my suit, sloshed myself with fresh water, and rubbed dry.

I walked around the harbour under the trees to the casino, and then up one of the cool streets to the Café Marinas. There was an orchestra playing inside the café and I sat out on the terrace and enjoyed the fresh coolness in the hot day, and had a glass of lemon juice and shaved ice and then a long whiskey-and-soda. I sat in front of the Marinas for a long time and read and watched the people, and listened to the music.

Later when it began to get dark, I walked around the harbour and out along the promenade, and finally back to the hotel for supper. There was a bicycle race on, the Tour du Pays Basque, and the riders were stopping that night in San Sebastian. In the dining-room, at one side, there was a long table of bicycle-riders, eating with their trainers and managers. They were all French and Belgians, and paid close attention to their meal, but they were having a good time. At the head of the table were two good-looking French girls, with much Rue du Faubourg Montmartre chic. I could not make out whom they belonged to. They all spoke in slang at the long table and there were many private jokes and some jokes at the far end that were not repeated when the girls asked to hear them. The next morning at five o'clock the race resumed with the last lap, San Sebastian–Bilbao. The bicycle-riders drank much wine, and were burned and browned by the sun. They did not take the race seriously except among themselves. They had raced among themselves so often that it did not make much difference who won. Especially in a foreign country. The money could be arranged.

The man who had a matter of two minutes lead in the race had an attack of boils, which were very painful. He sat on the small of his back. His neck was very red and the blond hairs were sunburned. The other riders joked him about his boils. He tapped on the table with his fork.

'Listen,' he said, 'to-morrow my nose is so tight on the handle-bars that the only thing touches those boils is a lovely breeze.'

One of the girls looked at him down the table, and he grinned and turned red. The Spaniards, they said, did not know how to pedal.

I had coffee out on the terrasse with the team manager of one of the big bicycle manufacturers. He said it had been a very pleasant race, and would have been worth watching if Bottechia had not abandoned it at Pamplona. The dust had been bad, but in Spain the roads were better than in France. Bicycle road-racing was the only sport in the world, he said. Had I ever followed the Tour de France? Only in the papers. The Tour de France was the greatest sporting event in the world. Following and organising the road races had made him know France. Few people know France. All spring and all summer and all fall he spent on the road with bicycle road-racers. Look at the number of motor-cars now that followed the riders from town to town in a road race. It was a rich country and more *sportif* every year. It would be the most *sportif* country in the world. It was bicycle road-racing did it. That and football. He knew France. *La France Sportive*. He knew road-racing. We had a cognac. After all, though, it wasn't bad to get back to Paris. There is only one Paname. In all the world, that is. Paris is the town the most *sportif* in the world. Did I know the *Chope de Negre?* Did I not. I would see him there some time. I certainly would. We would drink another *fine* together. We certainly would. They started at six o'clock less a quarter in the morning. Would I be up for the depart? I would certainly try to. Would I like him to call me? It was very interesting. I would leave a call at the desk. He would not mind calling me. I could not let him take the trouble. I would leave a call at the desk. We said good-bye until the next morning.

In the morning when I awoke the bicycle-riders and their following cars had been on the road for three hours. I had coffee and the papers in bed and then dressed and took my bathing-suit down to the beach. Everything was fresh and cool and damp in the early morning. Nurses in uniform and in peasant costume walked under the trees with children. The Spanish children were beautiful. Some bootblacks sat together under a tree talking to a soldier. The soldier had only one arm. The tide was in and there was a good breeze and a surf on the beach.

I undressed in one of the bath-cabins, crossed the narrow line of beach and went into the water. I swam out, trying to swim through the rollers, but having to dive sometimes. Then in the quiet water I turned and floated. Floating I saw only the sky, and felt the drop and lift of the swells. I swam back to the surf and coasted in, face down, on a big roller, then turned and swam, trying to keep in the trough and not have a wave break over me. It made me tired, swimming in the trough, and I turned and swam out to the raft. The water was buoyant and cold. It felt as though you could never sink. I swam slowly, it seemed like a long swim with the high tide, and then pulled up on the raft and sat, dripping on the boards that were becoming hot in the sun. I looked around at the bay, the old town, the casino, the line of trees along the promenade, and the big hotels with their white porches and gold-lettered names. Off on the right, almost closing the harbour, was a green hill with a castle. The raft rocked with the motion of the water. On the other side of the narrow gap that led into the open sea was another high headland. I thought I would like to swim across the bay, but I was afraid of cramp.

I sat in the sun and watched the bathers on the beach. They looked very small. After a while I stood up, gripped with my toes on the edge of the raft as it tipped with my weight, and dove cleanly and deeply, to come up through the lightening water, blew the salt water out of my head, and swam slowly and steadily in to shore.

After I was dressed and had paid for the bath-cabin, I walked back to the hotel. The bicycle-racers had left several copies of *L'Auto* around, and I gathered them up in the reading-room and took them out and sat in an easy-chair in the sun to read about and catch up on French sporting life. While I was sitting there the concierge came out with a blue envelope in his hand.

'A telegram for you, sir.'

I poked my finger along under the fold that was fastened down, spread it open, and read it. It had been forwarded from Paris:

Could you come Hotel Montana Madrid am rather in trouble Brett.

I tipped the concierge and read the message again. A postman was coming along the sidewalk. He turned in the hotel. He had a big moustache and looked very military. He came out of the hotel again. The concierge was just behind him.

'Here's another telegram for you, sir.'

'Thank you,' I said.

I opened it. It was forwarded from Pamplona.

Could you come Hotel Montana Madrid am rather in trouble Brett.

The concierge stood there waiting for another tip, probably.

'What time is there a train for Madrid?'

'It left at nine this morning. There is a slow train at eleven, and the Sud Express at ten to-night.'

'Get me a berth on the Sud Express. Do you want the money now?'

'Just as you wish,' he said. 'I will have it put on the bill.'

'Do that.'

Well, that meant San Sebastian all shot to hell. I suppose, vaguely, I had expected something of the sort. I saw the concierge standing in the doorway.

'Bring me a telegram form, please.'

He brought it and I took out my fountain-pen and printed:

Lady Ashley Hotel Montana Madrid Arriving Sud Express to-morrow love Jake.

That seemed to handle it. That was it. Send a girl off with one man. Introduce her to another to go off with him. Now go and bring her back. And sign the wire with love. That was it all right. I went in to lunch.

I did not sleep much that night on the Sud Express. In the morning I had breakfast in the dining-car and watched the rock and pine country between Avila and Escorial. I saw the Escorial out of the window, gray and long and cold in the sun, and did not give a damn about it. I saw Madrid come up over the plain, a compact white skyline on the top of a little cliff away off across the sun-hardened country.

The Norte station in Madrid is the end of the line. All trains finish there. They don't go on anywhere. Outside were cabs and taxis and a line of hotel runners. It was like a country town. I took a taxi and we climbed up through the gardens, by the empty palace and the unfinished church on the edge of the cliff, and on up until we were in the high, hot, modern town. The taxi coasted down a smooth street to the Puerto del Sol, and then through the traffic and out into the Carrera San Jeronimo. All the shops had their awnings down against the heat. The windows on the sunny side of the street were shuttered. The taxi stopped at the curb. I saw the sign HOTEL MONTANA on the second floor. The taxi-driver carried the bags in and left them by the elevator. I could not make the elevator work, so I walked up. On the second floor up was a cut brass sign: HOTEL MONTANA. I rang and no one came to the door. I rang again and a maid with a sullen face opened the door.

'Is Lady Ashley here?' I asked.

She looked at me dully.

'Is an Englishwoman here?'

She turned and called someone inside. A very fat woman came to the door. Her hair was grey and stiffly oiled in scallops around her face. She was short and commanding.

'Muy buenos,' I said. 'Is there an Englishwoman here? I would like to see this English lady.'

'Muy buenos. Yes, there is a female English. Certainly you can see her if she wishes to see you.'

'She wishes to see me.'

'The chica will ask her.'

'It is very hot.'

'It is very hot in the summer in Madrid.'

'And how cold in winter.'

'Yes, it is very cold in winter.'

Did I want to stay myself in person in the Hotel Montana?

Of that as yet I was undecided, but it would give me pleasure if my bags were brought up from the ground floor in order that they might not be stolen. Nothing was ever stolen in the Hotel Montana. In other fondas, yes. Not here. No. The personages of this establishment were rigidly selectioned. I was happy to hear it. Nevertheless I would welcome the upbringal of my bags.

The maid came in and said that the female English wanted to see the male English now, at once.

'Good,' I said. 'You see. It is as I said.'

'Clearly.'

I followed the maid's back down a long, dark corridor. At the end she knocked on a door.

'Hello,' said Brett. 'Is it you, Jake?'

'It's me.'

'Come in. Come in.'

I opened the door. The maid closed it after me. Brett was in bed. She had just been brushing her hair and held the brush in her hand. The room was in that disorder produced only by those who have always had servants.

'Darling!' Brett said.

I went over to the bed and put my arms around her. She kissed me, and while she kissed me I could feel she was thinking of something else. She was trembling in my arms. She felt very small.

'Darling! I've had such a hell of a time.'

'Tell me about it.'

'Nothing to tell. He only left yesterday. I made him go.'

'Why didn't you keep him?'

'I don't know. It isn't the sort of thing one does. I don't think I hurt him any.'

'You were probably damn good for him.'

'He shouldn't be living with anyone. I realised that right away.'

'No.'

'Oh, hell!' she said, 'let's not talk about it. Let's never talk about it.'

'All right.'

'It was rather a knock his being ashamed of me. He was ashamed of me for a while, you know.'

'No.'

'Oh, yes. They ragged him about me at the café, I guess. He wanted me to grow my hair out. Me, with long hair. I'd look so like hell.'

'It's funny.'

'He said it would make me more womanly. I'd look a fright.'

'What happened?'

'Oh, he got over that. He wasn't ashamed of me long.'

'What was it about being in trouble?'

'I didn't know whether I could make him go, and I didn't have a sou to go away and leave him. He tried to give me a lot of money, you know. I told him I had scads of it. He knew that was a lie. I couldn't take his money, you know.'

'No.'

'Oh, let's not talk about it. There were some funny things, though. Do give me a cigarette.'

I lit the cigarette.

'He learned his English as a waiter in Gib.'

'Yes.'

'He wanted to marry me, finally.'

'Really?'

'Of course. I can't even marry Mike.'

'Maybe he thought that would make him Lord Ashley.'

'No. It wasn't that. He really wanted to marry me. So I couldn't go away from him, he said. He wanted to make it sure I could never go away from him. After I'd gotten more womanly, of course.'

'You ought to feel set up.'

'I do. I'm all right again. He's wiped out that damned Cohn.'

'Good.'

'You know I'd have lived with him if I hadn't seen it was bad for him. We got along damned well.'

'Outside of your personal appearance.'

'Oh, he'd have gotten used to that.'

She put out the cigarette.

'I'm thirty-four, you know. I'm not going to be one of these bitches that ruins children.'

'No.'

'I'm not going to be that way. I feel rather good, you know. I feel rather set up.'

'Good.'

She looked away. I thought she was looking for another cigarette. Then I saw she was crying. I could feel her crying. Shaking and crying. She wouldn't look up. I put my arms around her.

'Don't let's ever talk about it. Please don't let's ever talk about it.'

'Dear Brett.'

'I'm going back to Mike.' I could feel her crying as I held her close. 'He's so damned nice and he's so awful. He's my sort of thing.'

She would not look up. I stroked her hair. I could feel her shaking.

'I won't be one of those bitches,' she said. 'But oh, Jake, please let's never talk about it.'

We left the Hotel Montana. The woman who ran the hotel would not let me pay the bill. The bill had been paid.

'Oh, well. Let it go,' Brett said. 'It doesn't matter now.'

We rode in a taxi down to the Palace Hotel, left the bags, arranged for berths on the Sud Express for the night, and went into the bar of the hotel for a cocktail. We sat on high stools at the bar while the barman shook the Martinis in a large nickelled shaker.

'It's funny what a wonderful gentility you get in the bar of a big hotel,' I said.

'Barmen and jockeys are the only people who are polite any more.'

'No matter how vulgar a hotel is, the bar is always nice.'

'It's odd.'

'Bartenders have always been fine.'

'You know,' Brett said, 'it's quite true. He is only nineteen. Isn't it amazing?'

We touched the two glasses as they stood side by side on the bar. They were coldly beaded. Outside the curtained window was the summer heat of Madrid.

'I like an olive in a Martini,' I said to the barman.

'Right you are, sir. There you are.'

'Thanks.'

'I should have asked, you know.'

The barman went far enough up the bar so that he would not hear our conversation. Brett had sipped from the Martini as it stood, on the wood. Then she picked it up. Her hand was steady enough to lift it after that first sip.

'It's good. Isn't it a nice bar?'

'They're all nice bars.'

'You know I didn't believe it at first. He was born in 1905. I was in school in Paris, then. Think of that.'

'Anything you want me to think about it?'

'Don't be an ass. *Would* you buy a lady a drink?'

'We'll have two more Martinis.'

'As they were before, sir?'

'They were very good.' Brett smiled at him.

'Thank you, ma'am.'

'Well, bung-o,' Brett said.

'Bung-o!'

'You know,' Brett said, 'he'd only been with two women before. He never cared about anything but bull-fighting.'

'He's got plenty of time.'

'I don't know. He thinks it was me. Not the show in general.'

'Well, it was you.'

'Yes. It was me.'

'I thought you weren't going to ever talk about it.'

'How can I help it?'

'You'll lose it if you talk about it.'

'I just talk around it. You know I feel rather damned good, Jake.'

'You should.'

'You know it makes one feel rather good deciding not to be a bitch.'

'Yes.'

'It's sort of what we have instead of God.'

'Some people have God,' I said. 'Quite a lot.'

'He never worked very well with me.'

'Should we have another Martini?'

The barman shook up two more Martinis and poured them out into fresh glasses.

'Where will we have lunch?' I asked Brett. The bar was cool. You could feel the heat outside through the window.

'Here?' asked Brett.

'It's rotten here in the hotel. Do you know a place called Botin's?' I asked the barman.

'Yes, sir. Would you like to have me write out the address?'

'Thank you.'

We lunched upstairs at Botin's. It is one of the best restaurants in the world. We had roast young suckling pig and drank *rioja alta*. Brett did not eat much. I ate a very big meal and drank three bottles of *rioja alta*.

'How do you feel, Jake?' Brett asked. 'My God! what a meal you've eaten.'

'I feel fine. Do you want a dessert?'

'Lord, no.'

Brett was smoking.

'You like to eat, don't you?' she said.

'Yes,' I said. 'I like to do a lot of things.'

'What do you like to do?'

'Oh,' I said, 'I like to do a lot of things. Don't you want a dessert?'

'You asked me that once,' Brett said.

'Yes,' I said. 'So I did. Let's have another bottle of *rioja alta*.'

'It's very good.'

'You haven't drunk much of it,' I said.

'I have. You haven't seen.'

'Let's get two bottles,' I said. The bottles came. I poured a little in my glass, then a glass for Brett, then filled my glass. We touched glasses.

'Bung-o!' Brett said. I drank my glass and poured out another. Brett put her hand on my arm.

'Don't get drunk, Jake,' she said. 'You don't have to.'

'How do you know?'

'Don't,' she said. 'You'll be all right.'

'I'm not getting drunk,' I said. 'I'm just drinking a little wine. I like to drink wine.'

'Don't get drunk,' she said. 'Jake, don't get drunk.'

'Want to go for a ride?' I said. 'Want to ride through the town?'

'Right,' Brett said. 'I haven't seen Madrid. I should see Madrid.'

'I'll finish this,' I said.

Downstairs we came out through the first-floor dining-room to the street. A waiter went for a taxi. It was hot and bright. Up the street was a little square with trees and grass where there were taxis parked. A taxi came up the street, the waiter hanging out at the side. I tipped him and told the driver where to drive, and got in beside Brett. The driver started up the street. I settled back. Brett moved close to me. We sat close against each other. I put my arm round her and she rested against me comfortably. It was very hot and bright, and the houses looked sharply white. We turned out on to the Gran Via.

'Oh, Jake,' Brett said, 'we could have had such a damned good time together.'

Ahead was a mounted policeman in khaki directing traffic. He raised his baton. The car slowed suddenly, pressing Brett against me.

'Yes,' I said. 'Isn't it pretty to think so?'

HEMI

GWAY

The Short Happy Life of Francis Macomber

It was now lunch time and they were all sitting under the double green fly of the dining tent pretending that nothing had happened.

'Will you have lime juice or lemon squash?' Macomber asked.

'I'll have a gimlet,' Robert Wilson told him.

'I'll have a gimlet too. I need something,' Macomber's wife said.

'I suppose it's the thing to do,' Macomber agreed. 'Tell him to make three gimlets.'

The mess boy had started them already, lifting the bottles out of the canvas cooling bags that sweated wet in the wind that blew through the trees that shaded the tents.

'What had I ought to give them?' Macomber asked.

'A quid would be plenty,' Wilson told him. 'You don't want to spoil them.'

'Will the headman distribute it?'

'Absolutely.'

Francis Macomber had, half an hour before, been carried to his tent from the edge of the camp in triumph on the arms and shoulders of the cook, the personal boys, the skinner and the porters. The gun-bearers had taken no part in the demonstration. When the native boys put him down at the door of his tent, he had shaken all their hands, received their congratulations, and then gone into the tent and sat on the bed until his wife came in. She did not speak to him when she came in and he left the tent at once to wash his face and hands in the portable wash basin outside and go over to the dining tent to sit in a comfortable canvas chair in the breeze and the shade.

Mrs Macomber looked at Wilson quickly. She was an extremely handsome and well-kept woman of the beauty and social position which had, five years before, commanded five thousand dollars as the price of endorsing, with photographs, a beauty product which she had never used. She had been married to Francis Macomber for eleven years.

'He is a good lion, isn't he?' Macomber said. His wife looked at him now. She looked at both these men as though she had never seen them before.

One, Wilson, the white hunter, she knew she had never truly seen before. He was about middle height with sandy hair, a stubby moustache, a very red face and extremely cold blue eyes with faint white wrinkles at the corners that grooved merrily when he smiled. He smiled at her now and she looked away from his face at the way his shoulders sloped in the loose tunic he wore with the four big cartridges held in loops where the left breast pocket should have been, at his big brown hands, his old slacks, his very dirty boots, and back to his red face again. She noticed where the baked red of his face stopped in a white line that marked the circle by his Stetson hat that hung now from one of the pegs of the tent pole.

'Well, here's to the lion,' Robert Wilson said. He smiled at her again and, not smiling, she looked curiously at her husband.

Francis Macomber was very tall, very well built if you did not mind that length of bone, dark, his hair cropped like an oarsman, rather thin-lipped, and was considered handsome. He was dressed in the same sort of safari clothes that Wilson wore except that his were new, he was thirty-five years old, kept himself very fit, was good at court games, had a number of big-game fishing records, and had just shown himself, very publicly, to be a coward.

'Here's to the lion,' he said. 'I can't ever thank you for what you did.'

Margaret, his wife, looked away from him and back to Wilson.

'Let's not talk about the lion,' she said.

Wilson looked over at her without smiling and now she smiled at him.

'It's been a very strange day,' she said. 'Hadn't you ought to put your hat on even under the canvas at noon? You told me that, you know.'

'Might put it on,' said Wilson.

'You know you have a very red face, Mr Wilson,' she told him and smiled again.

'Drink,' said Wilson.

'I don't think so,' she said. 'Francis drinks a great deal, but his face is never red.'

'It's red today,' Macomber tried a joke.

'No,' said Margaret. 'It's mine that's red today. But Mr Wilson's is always red.'

'Must be racial,' said Wilson. 'I say, you wouldn't like to drop my beauty as a topic, would you?'

'I've just started on it.'

'Let's chuck it,' said Wilson.

'Conversation is going to be so difficult,' Margaret said.

'Don't be silly, Margot,' her husband said.

'No difficulty,' Wilson said. 'Got a damn fine lion.'

Margot looked at them both and they both saw that she was going to cry. Wilson had seen it coming for a long time and he dreaded it. Macomber was past dreading it.

'I wish it hadn't happened. Oh, I wish it hadn't happened,' she said and started for her tent. She made no noise of crying but they could see that her shoulders were shaking under the rose-coloured, sun-proofed shirt she wore.

'Women upset,' said Wilson to the tall man. 'Amounts to nothing. Strain on the nerves and one thing'n another.'

'No,' said Macomber. 'I suppose that I rate that for the rest of my life now.'

'Nonsense. Let's have a spot of the giant killer,' said Wilson. 'Forget the whole thing. Nothing to it anyway.'

'We might try,' said Macomber. 'I won't forget what you did for me though.'

'Nothing,' said Wilson. 'All nonsense.'

So they sat there in the shade where the camp was pitched under some wide-topped acacia trees with a boulder-strewn cliff behind them, and a stretch of grass that ran to the bank of a boulder-filled stream in front with forest beyond it, and drunk their just-cool lime drinks and avoided one another's eyes while the boys set the table for lunch. Wilson could tell that the boys all knew about it now and when he saw Macomber's personal boy looking curiously at his master while he was putting dishes on the table he snapped at him in Swahili. The boy turned away with his face blank.

'What were you telling him?' Macomber asked.

'Nothing. Told him to look alive or I'd see he got about fifteen of the best.'

'What's that? Lashes?'

'It's quite legal,' Wilson said. 'You're supposed to fine them.'

'Do you still have them whipped?'

'Oh, yes. They could raise a row if they chose to complain. But they don't. They prefer it to the fines.'

'How strange!' said Macomber.

'Not strange, really,' Wilson said. 'Which would you rather do? Take a good birching or lose your pay?'

Then he felt embarrassed at asking it and before Macomber could answer he went on, 'We all take a beating every day, you know, one way or another.'

This was no better. 'Good God,' he thought. 'I am a diplomat, aren't I?'

'Yes, we take a beating,' said Macomber, still not looking at him. 'I'm awfully sorry about that lion business. It doesn't have to go any further, does it? I mean no one will hear about it, will they?'

'You mean will I tell it at the Mathaiga Club?' Wilson looked at him now coldly. He had not expected this. So he's a bloody four-letter man as well as a bloody coward, he thought. I rather liked him too until today. But how is one to know about an American?

'No,' said Wilson. 'I'm a professional hunter. We never talk about our clients. You can be quite easy on that. It's supposed to be bad form to ask us not to talk though.'

He had decided now that to break would be much easier. He would eat, then, by himself and could read a book with his meals. They would eat by themselves. He would see them through the safari on a very formal basis–what was it the French called it? Distinguished consideration–and it would be a damn sight easier than having to go through this emotional trash. He'd insult him and make a good clean break. Then he could read a book with his meals and he'd still be drinking their whisky. That was the phrase for it when a safari went bad. You ran into another white hunter and you asked, 'How is everything going?' and he answered, 'Oh, I'm still drinking their whisky,' and you knew everything had gone to pot.

'I'm sorry,' Macomber said and looked at him with his American face that would stay adolescent until it became middle-aged, and Wilson noted his crew-cropped hair, fine eyes only faintly shifty, good nose, thin lips and handsome jaw. 'I'm sorry I didn't realize that. There are lots of things I don't know.'

So what could he do, Wilson thought. He was all ready to break it off quickly and neatly and here the beggar was apologizing after he had just insulted him. He made one more attempt. 'Don't worry about me talking,' he said. 'I have a living to make. You know in Africa no woman ever misses her lion and no white man ever bolts.'

'I bolted like a rabbit,' Macomber said.

Now what in hell were you going to do about a man who talked like that, Wilson wondered.

Wilson looked at Macomber with his flat, blue, machinegunner's eyes and the other smiled back at him. He had a pleasant smile if you did not notice how his eyes showed when he was hurt.

'Maybe I can fix it up on buffalo,' he said. 'We're after them next, aren't we?'

'In the morning if you like,' Wilson told him. Perhaps he had been wrong. This was certainly the way to take it. You most certainly could not tell a damned thing about an American. He was all for Macomber again. If you could forget the morning. But, of course, you couldn't. The morning had been about as bad as they come.

'Here comes the Memsahib,' he said. She was walking over from her tent looking refreshed and cheerful and quite lovely. She had a very perfect oval face, so perfect that you expected her to be stupid. But she wasn't stupid, Wilson thought, no, not stupid.

'How is the beautiful red-faced Mr Wilson? Are you feeling better, Francis, my pearl?'

'Oh, much,' said Macomber.

'I've dropped the whole thing,' she said, sitting down at the table. 'What importance is there to whether Francis is any good at killing lions? That's not his trade. That's Mr Wilson's trade. Mr Wilson is really very impressive killing anything. You do kill anything, don't you?'

'Oh, anything,' said Wilson. 'Simply anything.' They are, he thought, the hardest in the world; the hardest, the cruellest, the most predatory and the most attractive and their men have softened or gone to pieces nervously as they have hardened. Or is it that they pick men they can handle? They can't know that much at the age they marry, he thought. He was grateful that he had gone through his education on American women before now because this was a very attractive one.

'We're going after buff in the morning,' he told her.

'I'm coming,' she said.

'No you're not.'

'Oh, yes, I am. Mayn't I, Francis?'

'Why not stay in camp?'

'Not for anything,' she said. 'I wouldn't miss something like today for anything.'

When she left, Wilson was thinking, when she went off to cry she seemed a hell of a fine woman. She seemed to understand, to realize, to be hurt for him and for herself and to know how things really stood. She is away for twenty minutes and now she is back, simply enamelled in that American female cruelty. They are the damnedest women. Really the damnedest.

'We'll put on another show for you tomorrow,' Francis Macomber said.

'You're not coming,' Wilson said.

'You're very mistaken,' she told him. 'And I want *so* to see you perform again. You were lovely this morning. That is if blowing things' heads off is lovely.'

'Here's the lunch,' said Wilson. 'You're very merry, aren't you?'

'Why not? I didn't come out here to be dull.'

'Well, it hasn't been dull,' Wilson said. He could see the boulders in the river and the high bank beyond with the trees and he remembered the morning.

'Oh, no,' she said. 'It's been charming. And tomorrow. You don't know how I look forward to tomorrow.'

'That's eland he's offering you,' Wilson said.

'They're the big cowy things that jump like hares, aren't they?'

'I suppose that describes them,' Wilson said.

'It's very good meat,' Macomber said.

'Did you shoot it, Francis?' she asked.

'Yes.'

'They're not dangerous, are they?'

'Only if they fall on you,' Wilson told her.

'I'm so glad.'

'Why not let up on the bitchery just a little, Margot,' Macomber said, cutting the eland steak and putting some mashed potato, gravy and carrot on the down-turned fork that tined through the piece of meat.

'I suppose I could,' she said, 'since you put it so prettily.'

'Tonight we'll have champagne for the lion,' Wilson said. 'It's a bit too hot at noon.'

'Oh, the lion,' Margot said. 'I'd forgotten the lion!'

So, Robert Wilson thought to himself, she *is* giving him a ride, isn't she? Or do you suppose that's her idea of putting up a good show? How should a woman act when she discovers her husband is a bloody coward? She's damn cruel, but they're all cruel. They govern, of course, and to govern one has to be cruel sometimes. Still, I've seen enough of their damn terrorism.

'Have some more eland,' he said to her politely.

That afternoon, late, Wilson and Macomber went out in the motor car with the native driver and the two gunbearers. Mrs Macomber stayed in the camp. It was too hot to go out, she said, and she was going with them in the early morning. As they drove off Wilson saw her standing under the big tree looking pretty rather than beautiful in her faintly rosy khaki, her dark hair drawn back off her forehead and gathered in a knot low on her neck, her face as fresh, he thought, as though she were in England. She waved to them as the car went off through the swale of high grass and curved around through the trees into the small hills of orchard bush.

In the orchard bush they found a herd of impala, and leaving the car they stalked one old ram with long, widespread horns and Macomber killed it with a very creditable shot that knocked the buck down at a good two hundred yards and sent the herd off bounding wildly and leaping over one another's backs in long, leg-drawn-up leaps as unbelievable and as floating as those one makes sometimes in dreams.

'That was a good shot,' Wilson said. 'They're a small target.'

'Is it a worth-while head?' Macomber asked.

'It's excellent,' Wilson told him. 'You shoot like that and you'll have no trouble.'

'Do you think we'll find buffalo tomorrow?'

'There's a good chance of it. They feed out early in the morning and with luck we may catch them in the open.'

'I'd like to clear away that lion business,' Macomber said. 'It's not very pleasant to have your wife see you do something like that.'

I should think it would be even more unpleasant to do it, Wilson thought, wife or no wife, or to talk about it having done it. But he said, 'I wouldn't think about that any more. Anyone could be upset by his first lion. That's all over.'

But that night after dinner and a whisky and soda by the fire before going to bed, as Francis Macomber lay on his cot with the mosquito bar over him and listened to the night noises it was not all over. It was neither all over nor was it beginning. It was there exactly as it happened with some parts of it indelibly emphasized and he was miserably ashamed of it. But more than shame he felt cold, hollow fear in him. The fear was still there like a cold slimy hollow in all the emptiness where once his confidence had been and it made him feel sick. It was still there with him now.

It had started the night before when he had awakened and heard the lion roaring somewhere up along the river. It was a deep sound and at the end there were sort of coughing grunts that made him seem just outside the tent, and when Francis Macomber woke in the night to hear it he was afraid. He could hear his wife breathing quietly, asleep. There was no one to tell he was afraid, nor to be afraid with him, and, lying alone, he did not know the Somali proverb that says a brave man is always frightened three times by a lion; when he first sees his track, when he first hears him roar and when he first confronts him. Then while they were eating breakfast by lantern light out in the dining tent, before the sun was up, the lion roared again and Francis thought he was just at the edge of camp.

'Sounds like an old-timer,' Robert Wilson said, looking up from his kippers and coffee. 'Listen to him cough.'

'Is he very close?'

'A mile or so up the stream.'

'Will we see him?'

'We'll have a look.'

'Does his roaring carry that far? It sounds as though he were right in camp.'

'Carries a hell of a long way,' said Robert Wilson. 'It's strange the way it carries. Hope he's a shootable cat. The boys said there was a very big one about here.'

'If I get a shot, where should I hit him,' Macomber asked, 'to stop him?'

'In the shoulders,' Wilson said. 'In the neck if you can make it. Shoot for bone. Break him down.'

'I hope I can place it properly,' Macomber said.

'You shoot very well,' Wilson told him. 'Take your time. Make sure of him. The first one in is the one that counts.'

'What range will it be?'

'Can't tell. Lion has something to say about that. Don't shoot unless it's close enough so you can make sure.'

'At under a hundred yards?' Macomber asked.

Wilson looked at him quickly.

'Hundred's about right. Might have to take him a bit under. Shouldn't chance a shot at much over that. A hundred's a decent range. You can hit him wherever you want at that. Here comes the Memsahib.'

'Good morning,' she said. 'Are we going after that lion?'

'As soon as you deal with your breakfast,' Wilson said. 'How are you feeling?'

'Marvellous,' she said. 'I'm very excited.'

'I'll just go and see that everything is ready.' Wilson went off. As he left the lion roared again.

'Noisy beggar,' Wilson said. 'We'll put a stop to that.'

'What's the matter, Francis?' his wife asked him.

'Nothing,' Macomber said.

'Yes, there is,' she said. 'What are you upset about?'

'Nothing,' he said.

'Tell me,' she looked at him. 'Don't you feel well?'

'It's that damned roaring,' he said. 'It's been going on all night, you know.'

'Why didn't you wake me?' she said. 'I'd love to have heard it.'

'I've got to kill the damned thing,' Macomber said, miserably.

'Well, that's what you're out here for, isn't it?'

'Yes. But I'm nervous. Hearing the thing roar gets on my nerves.'

'Well, then, as Wilson said, kill him and stop him roaring.'

'Yes, darling,' said Francis Macomber. 'It sounds easy, doesn't it?'

'You're not afraid, are you?'

'Of course not. But I'm nervous from hearing him roar all night.'

'You'll kill him marvellously,' she said. 'I know you will. I'm awfully anxious to see it.'

'Finish your breakfast and we'll be starting.'

'It's not light yet,' she said. 'This is a ridiculous hour.'

Just then the lion roared in a deep-chested moaning, suddenly guttural, ascending vibration that seemed to shake the air and ended in a sigh and a heavy, deep-chested grunt.

'He sounds almost here,' Macomber's wife said.

'My God,' said Macomber. 'I hate that damned noise.'

'It's very impressive.'

'Impressive. It's frightful.'

Robert Wilson came up then carrying his short, ugly, shockingly big-bored ·505 Gibbs and grinning.

'Come on,' he said. 'Your gun-bearer has your Springfield and the big gun. Everything's in the car. Have you solids?'

'Yes.'

'I'm ready,' Mrs Macomber said.

'Must make him stop that racket,' Wilson said. 'You get in front. The Memsahib can sit back here with me.'

They climbed into the motor car and, in the grey first daylight, moved off up the river through the trees. Macomber opened the breach of his rifle and saw he had metalcased bullets, shut the bolt and put the rifle on safety. He saw his hand was trembling. He felt in his pocket for more cartridges and moved his fingers over the cartridges in the loops of his tunic front. He turned back to where Wilson sat in the rear seat of the doorless, box-bodied motor car beside his wife, them both grinning with excitement, and Wilson leaned forward and whispered.

'See the birds dropping. Means the old boy has left his kill.'

On the far bank of the stream Macomber could see, above the trees, vultures circling and plummeting down.

'Chances are he'll come to drink along here,' Wilson whispered. 'Before he goes to lay up. Keep an eye out.'

They were driving slowly along the high bank of the stream which here cut deeply to its boulder-filled bed, and they wound in and out through big trees as they drove. Macomber was watching the opposite bank when he felt Wilson take hold of his arm. The car stopped.

'There he is,' he heard the whisper. 'Ahead and to the right. Get out and take him. He's a marvellous lion.'

Macomber saw the lion now. He was standing almost broadside, his great head up and turned toward them. The early morning breeze that blew toward them was just stirring his dark mane, and the lion looked huge, silhouetted on the rise of bank in the grey morning light, his shoulders heavy, his barrel of a body bulking smoothly.

'How far is he?' asked Macomber, raising his rifle.

'About seventy-five. Get out and take him.'

'Why not shoot from where I am?'

'You don't shoot them from cars,' he heard Wilson saying in his ear. 'Get out. He's not going to stay there all day.'

Macomber stepped out of the curved opening at the side of the front seat, on to the step and down on to the ground. The lion still stood looking majestically and coolly toward this object that his eyes only showed in silhouette, bulking like some super-rhino. There was no man smell carried toward him and he watched the object, moving his great head a little from side to side. Then watching the object, not afraid, but hesitating before going down the bank to drink with such a thing opposite him, he saw a man figure detach itself from it and he turned his heavy head and swung away toward the cover of the trees as he heard a cracking crash and felt the slam of a ·30-06 220-grain solid bullet that bit his flank and ripped in sudden hot scalding nausea through his stomach. He trotted, heavy, big-footed, swinging wounded full-bellied, through the trees toward the tall grass and cover, and the crash came again to go past him ripping the air apart. Then it crashed again and he felt the blow as it hit his lower ribs and ripped on through, blood sudden hot and frothy in his mouth, and he galloped toward the high grass where he could crouch and not be seen and make them bring the crashing thing close enough so he could make a rush and get the man that held it.

Macomber had not thought how the lion felt as he got out of the car. He only knew his hands were shaking and as he walked away from the car it was almost impossible for him to make his legs move. They were stiff in the thighs, but he could feel the muscles fluttering. He raised the rifle, sighted on the junction of the lion's head and shoulders and pulled the trigger. Nothing happened though he pulled until he thought his finger would break. Then he knew he had the safety on and as he lowered the rifle to move the safety over he moved another frozen pace forward, and the lion, seeing his silhouette now clear of the silhouette of the car, turned and started off at a trot, and, as Macomber fired, he heard a whunk that meant that the bullet was home; but the lion kept on going. Macomber shot again and everyone saw the bullet throw a spout of dirt beyond the trotting lion. He shot again, remembering to lower his aim, and they all heard the bullet hit, and the lion went into a gallop and was in the tall grass before he had the bolt pushed forward.

Macomber stood there feeling sick at his stomach, his hands that held the Springfield still cocked, shaking, and his wife and Robert Wilson were standing by him. Beside him too were the two gun-bearers chattering in Wakamba.

'I hit him,' Macomber said. 'I hit him twice.'

'You gut-shot him and you hit him somewhere forward,' Wilson said without enthusiasm. The gun-bearers looked very grave. They were silent now.

'You may have killed him,' Wilson went on. 'We'll have to wait a while before we go in to find out.'

'What do you mean?'

'Let him get sick before we follow him up.'

'Oh,' said Macomber.

'He's a hell of a fine lion,' Wilson said cheerfully. 'He's gotten into a bad place though.'

'Why is it bad?'

'Can't see him until you're on him.'

'Oh,' said Macomber.

'Come on,' said Wilson. 'The Memsahib can stay here in the car. We'll go to have a look at the blood spoor.'

'Stay here, Margot,' Macomber said to his wife. His mouth was very dry and it was hard for him to talk.

'Why?' she asked.

'Wilson says to.'

'We're going to have a look,' Wilson said. 'You stay here. You can see even better from here.'

'All right.'

Wilson spoke in Swahili to the driver. He nodded and said, 'Yes, Bwana.'

Then they went down the steep bank and across the stream, climbing over and around the boulders and up the other bank, pulling up by some projecting roots, and along it until they found where the lion had been trotting when Macomber first shot. There was dark blood on the short grass that the gun-bearers pointed out with grass stems, and that ran away behind the river bank trees.

'What do we do?' asked Macomber.

'Not much choice,' said Wilson. 'We can't bring the car over. Bank's too steep. We'll let him stiffen up a bit and then you and I'll go in and have a look for him.'

'Can't we set the grass on fire?' Macomber asked.

'Too green.'

'Can't we send beaters?'

Wilson looked at him appraisingly. 'Of course we can,' he said. 'But it's just a touch murderous. You see we know the lion's wounded. You can drive an unwounded lion–he'll move on ahead of a noise–but a wounded lion's going to charge. You can't see him until you're right on him. He'll make himself perfectly flat in cover you wouldn't think would hide a hare. You can't very well send boys in there to that sort of a show. Somebody bound to get mauled.'

'What about the gun-bearers?'

'Oh, they'll go with us. It's their *shauri*. You see, they signed on for it. They don't look too happy though, do they?'

'I don't want to go in there,' said Macomber. It was out before he knew he'd said it.

'Neither do I,' said Wilson very cheerily. 'Really no choice though.' Then, as an afterthought, he glanced at Macomber and saw suddenly how he was trembling and the pitiful look on his face.

'You don't have to go in, of course,' he said. 'That's what I'm hired for, you know. That's why I'm so expensive.'

'You mean you'd go in by yourself? Why not leave him there?'

Robert Wilson, whose entire occupation had been with the lion and the problem he presented, and who had not been thinking about Macomber except to note that he was rather windy, suddenly felt as though he had opened the wrong door in an hotel and seen something shameful.

'What do you mean?'

'Why not just leave him?'

'You mean pretend to ourselves he hasn't been hit?'

'No. Just drop it.'

'It isn't done.'

'Why not?'

'For one thing, he's certain to be suffering. For another, someone else might run on to him.'

'I see.'

'But you don't have to have anything to do with it.'

'I'd like to,' Macomber said. 'I'm just scared, you know.'

'I'll go ahead when we go in,' Wilson said, 'with Kongoni tracking. You keep behind me and a little to one side. Chances are we'll hear him growl. If we see him we'll both shoot. Don't worry about anything. I'll keep you backed up. As a matter of fact, you know, perhaps you'd better not go. It might be much better. Why don't you go over and join the Memsahib while

I just get it over with?'

'No, I want to go.'

'All right,' said Wilson. 'But don't go in if you don't want to. This is my *shauri* now, you know.'

'I want to go,' said Macomber.

They sat under a tree and smoked.

'Want to go back and speak to the Memsahib while we're waiting?' Wilson asked.

'No.'

'I'll just step back and tell her to be patient.'

'Good,' said Macomber. He sat there, sweating under arms, his mouth dry, his stomach hollow feeling, wanting to find courage to tell Wilson to go on and finish off the lion without him. He could not know that Wilson was furious because he had not noticed the state he was in earlier and sent him back to his wife. While he sat there Wilson came up. 'I have your big gun,' he said. 'Take it. We've given him time, I think. Come on.'

Macomber took the big gun and Wilson said:

'Keep behind me and about five yards to the right and do exactly as I tell you.' Then he spoke in Swahili to the two gun-bearers who looked the picture of gloom.

'Let's go,' he said.

'Could I have a drink of water?' Macomber asked. Wilson spoke to the older gun-bearer, who wore a canteen on his belt and the man unbuckled it, unscrewed the top and handed it to Macomber, who took it noticing how heavy it seemed and how hairy and shoddy the felt covering was in his hand. He raised it to drink and looked ahead at the high grass with the flat-topped trees behind it. A breeze was blowing toward them and the grass rippled gently in the wind. He looked at the gun-bearer and he could see the gun-bearer was suffering too with fear.

Thirty-five yards into the grass the big lion lay flattened out along the ground. His ears were back and his only movement was a slight twitching up and down of his long, black-tufted tail. He had turned at bay as soon as he had reached this cover and he was sick with the wound through his full belly, and weakening with the wound through his lungs that brought a thin foamy red to his mouth each time he breathed. His flanks were wet and hot and flies were on the little opening the solid bullets had made in his tawny hide, and his big yellow eyes, narrowed with hate, looked straight ahead, only blinking when the pain came as he breathed, and his claws dug in the soft baked earth. All of him, pain, sickness, hatred and all of his remaining strength, was tightening into an absolute concentration for a rush. He could hear the men talking and he waited, gathering all of himself into this preparation for a charge as soon as the men would come into the grass. As he heard their voices his tail stiffened to twitch up and down, and, as they came into the edge of the grass, he made a coughing grunt and charged.

Kongoni, the old gun-bearer, in the lead watching the blood spoor, Wilson watching the grass for any movement, his big gun ready, the second gun-bearer looking ahead and listening, Macomber close to Wilson, his rifle cocked, they had just moved into the grass when Macomber heard the blood-choked coughing grunt, and saw the swishing rush in the grass. The next thing he knew he was running, running wildly, in panic in the open, running toward the stream.

He heard the *ca-ra-wong!* of Wilson's big rifle, and again in a second crashing *carawong!* and turning saw the lion, horrible-looking now, with half his head seeming to be gone, crawling toward Wilson in the edge of the tall grass while the red-faced man worked the bolt on the short ugly rifle and aimed carefully as another blasting *carawong!* came from the muzzle, and the crawling, heavy, yellow bulk of the lion stiffened and the huge, mutilated head slid forward and Macomber, standing by himself in the clearing where he had run, holding a loaded rifle, while two black men and a white man looked back at him in contempt, knew the lion was dead. He came toward Wilson, his tallness all seeming a naked reproach, and Wilson looked at him and said:

'Want to take pictures?'

'No,' he said.

That was all anyone had said until they reached the motor car. Then Wilson had said:

'Hell of a fine lion. Boys will skin him out. We might as well stay here in the shade.'

Macomber's wife had not looked at him nor he at her and he had sat by her in the back seat with Wilson sitting in the front seat. Once he had reached over and taken his wife's hand without looking at her and she had removed her hand from his. Looking across the stream to where the gun-bearers were skinning out the lion he could see that she had been able to see the whole thing. While they sat there his wife had reached forward and put her hand on Wilson's shoulder. He turned and she had leaned forward over the low seat and kissed him on the mouth.

'Oh, I say,' said Wilson, going redder than his natural baked colour.

'Mr Robert Wilson,' she said. 'The beautifully red-faced Mr Robert Wilson.'

Then she sat down beside Macomber again and looked away across the stream to where the lion lay, with uplifted, white-muscled tendon-marked naked forearms, and white bloating belly, as the black men fleshed away the skin. Finally the gun-bearers brought the skin over, wet and heavy, and climbed in behind with it, rolling it up before they got in, and the motor car started. No one had said anything more until they were back in camp.

That was the story of the lion. Macomber did not know how the lion had felt before he started his rush, nor during it when the unbelievable smash of the ·505 with a muzzle velocity of two tons had hit him in the mouth, nor what kept him coming after that, when the second ripping crash had smashed his hind quarters and he had come crawling on toward the crashing, blasting thing that had destroyed him. Wilson knew something about it and only expressed it by saying, 'Damned fine lion', but Macomber did not know how Wilson felt about things either. He did not know how his wife felt except that she was through with him.

His wife had been through with him before but it never lasted. He was very wealthy, and would be much wealthier, and he knew she would not leave him ever now. That was one of the few things he really knew. He knew about that, about motor cycles–that was earliest–about motor cars, about duck-shooting, about fishing, trout, salmon and big-sea, about sex in books, many books, too many books, about all court games, about dogs, not much about horses, about hanging on to his money, about most of the other things his world dealt in, and about his wife not leaving him. His wife had been a great beauty and she was still a great beauty in Africa, but she was not a great enough beauty any more at home to be able to leave him and better herself and she knew it and he knew it. She had missed the chance to leave him and he knew it. If he had been better with women she would probably have started to worry about him getting another new, beautiful wife; but she knew too much about him to worry about him either. Also, he had always had a great tolerance which seemed the nicest thing about him if it were not the most sinister.

All in all they were known as a comparatively happily married couple, one of those whose disruption is often rumoured but never occurs, and as the society columnist put it, they were adding more than a spice of *adventure* to their much envied and ever-enduring *Romance* by a *Safari* in what was known as *Darkest Africa* until the Martin Johnsons lighted it on so many silver screens where they were pursuing *Old Simba* the lion, the buffalo, *Tembo* the elephant and as well collecting specimens for the Museum of Natural History. This same columnist had reported them *on the verge* at least three times in the past and they had been. But they always made it up. They had a sound basis of union. Margot was too beautiful for Macomber to divorce her and Macomber had too much money for Margot ever to leave him.

It was now about three o'clock in the morning and Francis Macomber, who had been asleep a little while after he had stopped thinking about the lion, wakened and then slept again, woke suddenly, frightened in a dream of the bloody-headed lion, standing over him, and listening while his heart pounded, he realized that his wife was not in the other cot in the tent. He lay awake with that knowledge for two hours.

At the end of that time his wife came into the tent, lifted her mosquito bar and crawled cosily into bed.

'Where have you been?' Macomber asked in the darkness.

'Hello,' she said. 'Are you awake?'

'Where have you been?'

'I just went out to get a breath of air.'

'You did, like hell.'

'What do you want me to say, darling?'

'Where have you been?'

'Out to get a breath of air.'

'That's a new name for it. You *are* a bitch.'

'Well, you're a coward.'

'All right,' he said. 'What of it?'

'Nothing as far as I'm concerned. But please let's not talk, darling, because I'm very sleepy.'

'You think that I'll take anything.'

'I know you will, sweet.'

'Well, I won't.'

'Please, darling, let's not talk. I'm so very sleepy.'

'There wasn't going to be any of that. You promised there wouldn't be.'

'Well, there is now,' she said sweetly.

'You said if we made this trip that there would be none of that. You promised.'

'Yes, darling. That's the way I meant it to be. But the trip was spoiled yesterday. We don't have to talk about it, do we?'

'You don't wait long when you have an advantage, do you?'

'Please let's not talk. I'm so sleepy, darling.'

'I'm going to talk.'

'Don't mind me then, because I'm going to sleep.' And she did.

At breakfast they were all three at the table before daylight and Francis Macomber found that, of all the many men that he had hated, he hated Robert Wilson the most.

'Sleep well?' Wilson asked in his throaty voice, filling a pipe.

'Did you?'

'Topping,' the white hunter told him.

You bastard, thought Macomber, you insolent bastard.

So she woke him when she came in, Wilson thought, looking at them both with his flat, cold eyes. Well, why doesn't he keep his wife where she belongs? What does he think I am, a bloody plaster saint? Let him keep her where she belongs. It's his own fault.

'Do you think we'll find buffalo?' Margot asked, pushing away a dish of apricots.

'Chance of it,' Wilson said and smiled at her. 'Why don't you stay in camp?'

'Not for anything,' she told him.

'Why not order her to stay in camp?' Wilson said to Macomber.

'You order her,' said Macomber coldly.

'Let's not have any ordering, nor,' turning to Macomber, 'any silliness, Francis,' Margot said quite pleasantly.

'Are you ready to start?' Macomber asked.

'Any time,' Wilson told him. 'Do you want the Memsahib to go?'

'Does it make any difference whether I do or not?'

The hell with it, thought Robert Wilson. The utter complete hell with it. So this is what it's going to be like. Well, this is what it's going to be like, then.

'Makes no difference,' he said.

'You're sure you wouldn't like to stay in camp with her yourself and let me go out and hunt the buffalo?' Macomber asked.

'Can't do that,' said Wilson. 'Wouldn't talk rot if I were you.'

'I'm not talking rot. I'm disgusted.'

'Bad word, disgusted.'

'Francis, will you please try to speak sensibly?' his wife said.

'I speak too damned sensibly,' Macomber said. 'Did you ever eat such filthy food?'

'Something wrong with the food?' asked Wilson quietly.

'No more than with everything else.'

'I'd pull yourself together, laddybuck,' Wilson said very quietly. 'There's a boy waits at table that understands a little English.'

'The hell with him.'

Wilson stood up and puffing on his pipe strolled away, speaking a few words in Swahili to one of the gun-bearers who was standing waiting for him. Macomber and his wife sat on at the table. He was staring at his coffee cup.

'If you make a scene I'll leave you, darling,' Margot said quietly.

'No, you won't.'

'You can try and see.'

'You won't leave me.'

'No,' she said. 'I won't leave you and you'll behave yourself.'

'Behave myself? That's a way to talk. Behave myself.'

'Yes. Behave yourself.'

'Why don't *you* try behaving?'

'I've tried it so long. So very long.'

'I hate that red-faced swine,' Macomber said. 'I loathe the sight of him.'

'He's really *very* nice.'

'Oh, *shut up*,' Macomber almost shouted. Just then the car came up and stopped in front of the dining tent and the driver and the two gun-bearers got out. Wilson walked over and looked at the husband and wife sitting there at the table.

'Going shooting?' he asked.

'Yes,' said Macomber, standing up. 'Yes.'

'Better bring a woolly. It will be cool in the car,' Wilson said.

'I'll get my leather jacket,' Margot said.

'The boy has it,' Wilson told her. He climbed into the front with the driver and Francis Macomber and his wife sat, not speaking, in the back seat.

Hope the silly beggar doesn't take a notion to blow the back of my head off, Wilson thought to himself. Women *are* a nuisance on safari.

The car was grinding down to cross the river at a pebbly ford in the grey daylight and then climbed, angling up the steep bank, where Wilson had ordered a way shovelled out the day before so they could reach the parklike wooded rolling country on the far side.

It was a good morning, Wilson thought. There was a heavy dew and as the wheels went through the grass and low bushes he could smell the odour of the crushed fronds. It was an odour like verbena and he liked this early morning smell of the dew, the crushed bracken and the look of the tree trunks showing black through the early morning mist, as the car made its way through the untracked, parklike country. He had put the two in the back seat out of his mind now and was thinking about buffalo. The buffalo that he was after stayed in the daytime in a thick swamp where it was impossible to get a shot, but in the night they fed out into an open stretch of country and if he could come between them and their swamp with the car, Macomber would have a good chance at them in the open. He did not want to hunt buff with Macomber in thick cover. He did not want to hunt buff or anything else with Macomber at all, but he was a professional hunter and he had hunted with some rare ones in his time. If they got buff today there would only be rhino to come and the poor man would have gone through his dangerous game and things might pick up. He'd have nothing more to do with the woman and Macomber would get over that too. He must have gone through plenty of that before by the look of things. Poor beggar. He must have a way of getting over it. Well, it was the poor sod's own bloody fault.

He, Robert Wilson, carried a double size cot on safari to accommodate any windfalls he might receive. He had hunted for a certain clientele, the international, fast, sporting set, where the women did not feel they were getting their money's worth unless they had shared that cot with the white hunter. He despised them when he was away from them although he liked some of them well enough at the time, but he made his living by them; and their standards were his standards as long as they were hiring him.

They were his standards in all except the shooting. He had his own standards about the killing and they could live up to them or get someone else to hunt them. He knew too, that they all respected him for this. This Macomber was an odd one though. Damned if he wasn't. Now the wife. Well, the wife. Yes, the wife. Mm, the wife. Well, he'd dropped all that. He looked around at them. Macomber sat grim and furious. Margot smiled at him. She looked younger today, more innocent and fresher and not so professionally beautiful. What's in her heart God knows, Wilson thought. She hadn't talked much last night. At that it was a pleasure to see her.

The motor car climbed up a slight rise and went on through the trees and then out into a grassy prairie-like opening and kept in the shelter of the trees along the edge, the driver going slowly and Wilson looking carefully out across the prairie and all along its far side. He stopped the car and studied the opening with his field glasses. Then he motioned the driver to go on and the car moved slowly along, the driver avoiding wart-hog holes and driving around the mud castles ants had built. Then, looking across the opening, Wilson suddenly turned and said:

'By God, there they are!'

And looking where he pointed, while the car jumped forward and Wilson spoke in rapid Swahili to the driver, Macomber saw three huge, black animals looking almost cylindrical in their long heaviness, like big black tank cars, moving at a gallop across the far edge of the open prairie. They moved at a stiff-necked, stiff-bodied gallop and he could see the upswept wide black horns on their heads as they galloped heads out, the heads not moving.

'They're three old bulls,' Wilson said. 'We'll cut them off before they get to the swamp.'

The car was going a wild forty-five miles an hour across the open, and as Macomber watched, the buffalo got bigger and bigger until he could see the grey, hairless, scabby look of one huge bull and how his neck was a part of his shoulders and the shiny black of his horns as he galloped a little behind the others that were strung out in that steady plunging gait; and then, the car swaying as though it had just jumped a road, they drew up close and he could see the plunging hugeness of the bull, and the dust in his sparsely haired hide, the wide boss of horn and his outstretched, wide-nostrilled muzzle, and he was raising his rifle when Wilson shouted, 'Not from the car, you fool!' and he had no fear, only hatred of Wilson, while the brakes clamped on and the car skidded, ploughing sideways to an almost stop and Wilson was out on one side and he on the other, stumbling as his feet hit the still speeding-by of the earth, and then he was shooting at the bull as he moved away, hearing the bullets whunk into him, emptying his rifle at him as he moved steadily away, finally remembering to get his shots forward into the shoulder, and as he fumbled to re-load, he saw the bull was down. Down on his knees, his big head tossing, and seeing the other two still galloping he shot at the leader and hit him. He shot again and missed and he heard the *carawonging* roar as Wilson shot and saw the leading bull slide forward on to his nose.

'Get that other,' Wilson said. 'Now you're shooting!'

But the other bull was moving steadily at the same gallop and he missed, throwing a spout of dirt, and Wilson missed and the dust rose in a cloud and Wilson shouted, 'Come on. He's too far!' and grabbed his arm and they were in the car again, Macomber and Wilson hanging on to the sides and rocketing swayingly over the uneven ground, drawing up on the steady, plunging, heavy-necked, straight-moving gallop of the bull.

They were behind him and Macomber was filling his rifle, dropping shells on to the ground, jamming it, clearing the jam, then they were almost up with the bull when Wilson yelled 'Stop!' and the car skidded so that it almost swung over and Macomber fell forward on to his feet, slammed his bolt forward and fired as far forward as he could aim into the galloping, rounded black back, aimed and shot again, then again, and the bullets, all of them hitting, had no effect on the buffalo that he could see. Then Wilson shot, the roar deafening him, and he could see the bull stagger. Macomber shot again, aiming carefully, and down he came, on to his knees.

'All right,' Wilson said. 'Nice work. That's the three.'

Macomber felt a drunken elation.

'How many times did you shoot?' he asked.

'Just three,' Wilson said. 'You killed the first bull. The biggest one. I helped you finish the other two. Afraid they might have got into cover. You had them killed. I was just mopping up a little. You shot damn well.'

'Let's go to the car,' said Macomber. 'I want a drink.'

'Got to finish off that buff first,' Wilson told him. The buffalo was on his knees and he jerked his head furiously and bellowed in pig-eyed roaring rage as they came toward him.

'Watch he doesn't get up,' Wilson said. Then, 'Get a little broadside and take him in the neck just behind the ear.'

Macomber aimed carefully at the centre of the huge, jerking, rage-driven neck and shot. At the shot the head dropped forward.

'That does it,' said Wilson. 'Got the spine. They're a hell of a looking thing, aren't they?'

'Let's get the drink,' said Macomber. In his life he had never felt so good.

In the car Macomber's wife sat very white faced. 'You were marvellous, darling,' she said to Macomber. 'What a ride.'

'Was it rough?' Wilson asked.

'It was frightful. I've never been more frightened in my life.'

'Let's all have a drink,' Macomber said.

'By all means,' said Wilson. 'Give it to the Memsahib.' She drank the neat whisky from the flask and shuddered a little when she swallowed. She handed the flask to Macomber who handed it to Wilson.

'It was frightfully exciting,' she said. 'It's given me a dreadful headache. I didn't know you were allowed to shoot them from cars though.'

'No one shot from cars,' said Wilson coldly.

'I mean chase them from cars.'

'Wouldn't ordinarily,' Wilson said. 'Seemed sporting enough to me though while we were doing it. Taking more chance driving that way across the plain full of holes and one thing and another than hunting on foot. Buffalo could have charged us each time we shot if he liked. Gave him every chance. Wouldn't mention it to anyone though. It's illegal if that's what you mean.'

'It seemed very unfair to me,' Margot said, 'chasing those big helpless things in a motor car.'

'Did it?' said Wilson.

'What would happen if they heard about it in Nairobi?'

'I'd lose my licence for one thing. Other unpleasantnesses,' Wilson said, taking a drink from the flask. 'I'd be out of business.'

'Really?'

'Yes, really.'

'Well,' said Macomber, and he smiled for the first time all day. 'Now she has something on you.'

'You have such a petty way of putting things, Francis,' Margot Macomber said. Wilson looked at them both. If a four-letter man marries a five-letter woman, he was thinking, what number of letters would their children be? What he said was 'We lost a gun-bearer. Did you notice it?'

'My God, no,' Macomber said.

'Here he comes,' Wilson said. 'He's all right. He must have fallen off when we left the first bull.'

Approaching them was the middle-aged gun-bearer, limping along in his knitted cap, khaki tunic, shorts and rubber sandals, gloomy-faced and disgusted looking. As he came up he called out to Wilson in Swahili and they all saw the change in the white hunter's face.

'What does he say?' asked Margot.

'He says the first bull got up and went into the bush,' Wilson said with no expression in his voice.

'Oh,' said Macomber blankly.

'Then it's going to be just like the lion,' said Margot, full of anticipation.

'It's not going to be a damned bit like the lion,' Wilson told her. 'Did you want another drink, Macomber?'

'Thanks, yes,' Macomber said. He expected the feeling he had had about the lion to come back but it did not. For the first time in his life he really felt wholly without fear. Instead of fear he had a feeling of definite elation.

'We'll go and have a look at the second bull,' Wilson said. 'I'll tell the driver to put the car in the shade.'

'What are you doing to do?' asked Margot Macomber.

'Take a look at the buff,' Wilson said.

'I'll come.'

'Come along.'

The three of them walked over to where the second buffalo bulked blackly in the open, head forward on the grass, the massive horns swung wide.

'He's a very good head,' Wilson said. 'That's close to a fifty-inch spread.'

Macomber was looking at him with delight.

'He's hateful looking,' said Margot. 'Can't we go into the shade?'

'Of course,' Wilson said. 'Look,' he said to Macomber, and pointed. 'See that patch of bush?'

'Yes.'

'That's where the first bull went in. The gun-bearer said when he fell off the bull was down. He was watching us helling along and the other two buff galloping. When he looked up there was the bull up and looking at him. Gun-bearer ran like hell and the bull went off slowly into that bush.'

'Can we go in after him now?' asked Macomber eagerly.

Wilson looked at him appraisingly. Damned if this isn't a strange one, he thought. Yesterday he's scared sick and today he's a ruddy fire-eater.

'No, we'll give him a while.'

'Let's please go into the shade,' Margot said. Her face was white and she looked ill.

They made their way to the car where it stood under a single wide-spreading tree and all climbed in.

'Chances are he's dead in there,' Wilson remarked. 'After a little we'll have a look.'

Macomber felt a wild unreasonable happiness that he had never known before.

'By God, that was a chase,' he said. 'I've never felt any such feeling. Wasn't it marvellous, Margot?'

'I hated it.'

'Why?'

'I hated it,' she said bitterly. 'I loathed it.'

'You know, I don't think I'd ever be afraid of anything again,' Macomber said to Wilson. 'Something happened in me after we first saw the buff and started after him. Like a dam bursting. It was pure excitement.'

'Cleans out your liver,' said Wilson. 'Damn funny things happen to people.'

Macomber's face was shining. 'You know, something did happen to me,' he said, 'I feel absolutely different.'

His wife said nothing and eyed him strangely. She was sitting far back in the seat and Macomber was sitting forward talking to Wilson who turned sideways talking over the back of the front seat.

'You know, I'd like to try another lion,' Macomber said. 'I'm not really afraid of them now. After all, what can they do to you?'

'That's it,' said Wilson. 'Worst one can do is kill you. How does it go? Shakespeare. Damned good. See if I can remember. Oh, damned good. Used to quote it to myself at one time. Let's see. "By my troth, I care not; a man can die but once; we owe God a death, and let it go which way it will he that dies this year is quit for the next." Damned fine, eh?'

He was very embarrassed, having brought out this thing he had lived by, but he had seen men come of age before and it always moved him. It was not a matter of their twenty-first birthday.

It had taken a strange chance of hunting, a sudden precipitation into action without opportunity for worrying beforehand, to bring this about with Macomber, but regardless of how it had happened it had most certainly happened. Look at the beggar now, Wilson thought. Sometimes all their lives. Their figures stay boyish when they're fifty. The great American boy-men. Damned strange people. But he liked this Macomber now. Damned strange fellow. Probably meant the end of cuckoldry too. Well, that would be a damned good thing. Damned good thing. Beggar had probably been afraid all his life. Don't know what started it. But over now. Hadn't had time to be afraid with the buff. That and being angry too. Motor car too. Motor cars made it familiar. Be a damn fire-eater now. He'd seen it in the war work the same way. More of a change than any loss of virginity. Fear gone like an operation. Something else grew in its place. Main thing a man had. Made him into a man. Women knew it too. No bloody fear.

From the far corner of the seat Margaret Macomber looked at the two of them. There was no change in Wilson. She saw Wilson as she had seen him the day before when she had first realized what his great talent was. But she saw the change in Francis Macomber now.

'Do you have that feeling of happiness about what's going to happen?' Macomber asked, still exploring his new wealth.

'You're not supposed to mention it,' Wilson said, looking in the other's face. 'Much more fashionable to say you're scared. Mind you, you'll be scared too, plenty of times.'

'Yes,' said Wilson. 'There's that. Doesn't do to talk too much about all this. Talk the whole thing away. No pleasure in anything if you mouth it up too much.'

'You're both talking rot,' said Margot. 'Just because you've chased some helpless animals in a motor car you talk like heroes.'

'Sorry,' said Wilson. 'I have been gassing too much.' She's worried about it already, he thought.

'If you don't know what we're talking about, why not keep out of it?' Macomber asked his wife.

'You've gotten awfully brave, awfully suddenly,' his wife said contemptuously, but her contempt was not secure. She was very afraid of something.

Macomber laughed, a very natural laugh. 'You know I *have*,' he said. 'I really have.'

'Isn't it sort of late?' Margot said bitterly. Because she had done the best she could for many years back and the way they were together now was no one person's fault.

'Not for me,' said Macomber.

Margot said nothing but sat back in the corner of the seat.

'Do you think we've given him time enough?' Macomber asked Wilson cheerfully.

'We might have a look,' Wilson said. 'Have you any solids left?'

'The gun-bearer has some.'

Wilson called in Swahili and the older gun-bearer, who was skinning out one of the heads, straightened up, pulled a box of solids out of his pocket, and brought them over to Macomber, who filled his magazine and put the remaining shells in his pocket.

'You might as well shoot the Springfield,' Wilson said. 'You're used to it. We'll leave the Mannlicher in the car with the Memsahib. Your gun-bearer can carry your heavy gun. I've this damned cannon. Now let me tell you about them.' He had saved this until the last because he did not want to worry Macomber. 'When a buff comes he comes with his head high and thrust straight out. The boss of the horns covers any sort of brain shot. The only shot is straight into the nose. The only other shot is into his chest, or, if you're to one side, into the neck or the shoulders. After they've been hit once they take a hell of a lot of killing. Don't try anything fancy. Take the easiest shot there is. They've finished skinning out that head now. Should we get started?'

He called to the gun-bearers, who came up wiping their hands, and the older one got into the back.

'I'll only take Kongoni,' Wilson said. 'The other can watch to keep the birds away.'

As the car moved slowly across the open space toward the island of bushy trees that ran in a tongue of foliage along a dry water-course that cut the open swale, Macomber felt his heart pounding and his mouth was dry again, but it was excitement, not fear.

'Here's where he went in,' Wilson said. Then to the gun-bearer in Swahili, 'Take the blood spoor.'

The car was parallel to the patch of brush. Macomber, Wilson and the gun-bearer got down. Macomber, looking back, saw his wife, with the rifle by her side, looking at him. He waved to her and she did not wave back.

The brush was very thick ahead and the ground was dry. The middle-aged gun-bearer was sweating heavily and Wilson had his hat down over his eyes and his red neck showed just ahead of Macomber. Suddenly the gun-bearer said something in Swahili to Wilson and ran forward.

'He's dead in there,' Wilson said. 'Good work,' and he turned to grip Macomber's hand and as they shook hands, grinning at each other, the gun-bearer shouted wildly and they saw him coming out of the bush sideways, fast as a crab, and the bull coming, nose out, mouth tight closed, blood dripping, massive head straight out, coming in a charge, his little pig eyes bloodshot as he looked at them. Wilson, who was ahead, was kneeling shooting, and Macomber, as he fired, unhearing his shot in the roaring of Wilson's gun, saw fragments like slate burst from the huge boss of the horns, and the head jerked; he shot again at the wide nostrils and saw the horns jolt again and fragments fly, and he did not see Wilson now and, aiming carefully, shot again with the buffalo's huge bulk almost on him and his rifle almost level with the coming head, nose out, and he could see the little wicked eyes and the head started to lower, and he felt a sudden white-hot, blinding flash explode inside his head and that was all he ever felt.

Wilson had ducked to one side to get in a shoulder shot. Macomber had stood solid and shot for the nose, shooting a touch high each time and hitting the heavy horns, splintering and chipping them like hitting a slate roof, and Mrs Macomber in the car, had shot at the buffalo with the 6·5 Mannlicher as it seemed about to gore Macomber and had hit her husband about two inches up and a little to one side of the base of his skull.

Francis Macomber lay now, face down, not two yards from where the buffalo lay on his side and his wife knelt over him with Wilson beside her.

'I wouldn't turn him over,' Wilson said.

The woman was crying hysterically.

'I'd get back in the car,' Wilson said. 'Where's the rifle?'

She shook her head, her face contorted. The gun-bearer picked up the rifle.

'Leave it as it is,' said Wilson. Then, 'Go get Abdulla so that he may witness the manner of the accident.'

He knelt down, took a handkerchief from his pocket, and spread it over Francis Macomber's crew-cropped head where it lay. The blood sank into the dry, loose earth.

Wilson stood up and saw the buffalo on his side, his legs out, his thinly haired belly crawling with ticks. 'Hell of a good bull,' his brain registered automatically. 'A good fifty inches, or better. Better.' He called to the driver and told him to spread a blanket over the body and stay by it. Then he walked over to the motor car where the woman sat crying in the corner.

'That was a pretty thing to do,' he said in a toneless voice. 'He *would* have left you too.'

'Stop it,' she said.

'Of course it's an accident,' he said. 'I know that.'

'Stop it,' she said.

'Don't worry,' he said. 'There will be a certain amount of unpleasantness but I will have some photographs taken that will be very useful at the inquest. There's the testimony of the gun-bearers and the driver too. You're perfectly all right.'

'Stop it,' she said.

'There's a hell of a lot to be done,' he said. 'And I'll have to send a truck off to the lake to wireless for a plane to take the three of us into Nairobi. Why didn't you poison him? That's what they do in England.'

'Stop it. Stop it. Stop it,' the woman cried.

Wilson looked at her with his flat blue eyes.

'I'm through now,' he said. 'I was a little angry. I'd begun to like your husband.'

'Oh, please stop it,' she said. 'Please, please stop it.'

'That's better,' Wilson said. 'Please is much better. Now I'll stop.'

A CLEAN, WELL-LIGHTED PLACE

It was late and everyone had left the café except an old man who sat in the shadow the leaves of the tree made against the electric light. In the daytime the street was dusty, but at night the dew settled the dust and the old man liked to sit late because he was deaf and now at night it was quiet and he felt the difference. The two waiters inside the café knew that the old man was a little drunk, and while he was a good client they knew that if he became too drunk he would leave without paying, so they kept watch on him.

'Last week he tried to commit suicide,' one waiter said.

'Why?'

'He was in despair.'

'What about?'

'Nothing.'

'How do you know it was nothing?'

'He has plenty of money.'

They sat together at a table that was close against the wall near the door of the café and looked at the terrace where the tables were all empty except where the old man sat in the shadow of the leaves of the tree that moved slightly in the wind. A girl and a soldier went by in the street. The street light shone on the brass number on his collar. The girl wore no head covering and hurried beside him.

'The guard will pick him up,' one waiter said.

'What does it matter if he gets what he's after?'

'He had better get off the street now. The guard will get him. They went by five minutes ago.'

The old man sitting in the shadow rapped on his saucer with his glass. The younger waiter went over to him.

'What do you want?'

The old man looked at him. 'Another brandy,' he said.

'You'll be drunk,' the waiter said. The old man looked at him. The waiter went away.

'He'll stay all night,' he said to his colleague. 'I'm sleepy now. I never get to bed before three o'clock. He should have killed himself last week.'

The waiter took the brandy bottle and another saucer from the counter inside the café and marched out to the old man's table. He put down the saucer and poured the glass full of brandy.

'You should have killed yourself last week,' he said to the deaf man. The old man motioned with his finger. 'A little more,' he said. The waiter poured on into the glass so that the brandy slopped over and ran down the stem into the top saucer of the pile. 'Thank you,' the old man said. The waiter took the bottle back inside the café. He sat down at the table with his colleague again.

'He's drunk now,' he said.

'He's drunk every night.'

'What did he want to kill himself for?'

'How should I know?'

'How did he do it?'

'He hung himself with a rope.'

'Who cut him down?'

'His niece.'

'Why did they do it?'

'Fear for his soul.'

'How much money has he got?'

'He's got plenty.'

'He must be eighty years old.'

'Anyway I should say he was eighty.'

'I wish he would go home. I never get to bed before three o'clock. What kind of hour is that to go to bed?'

'He stays up because he likes it.'

'He's lonely. I'm not lonely. I have a wife waiting in bed for me.'

'He had a wife once too.'

'A wife would be no good to him now.'

'You can't tell. He might be better with a wife.'

'His niece looks after him.'

'I know. You said she cut him down.'

'I wouldn't want to be that old. An old man is a nasty thing.'

'Not always. This old man is clean. He drinks without spilling. Even now, drunk. Look at him.'

'I don't want to look at him. I wish he would go home. He has no regard for those who must work.'

The old man looked from his glass across the square, then over at the waiters.

'Another brandy,' he said, pointing to his glass. The waiter who was in a hurry came over.

'Finished,' he said, speaking with that omission of syntax stupid people employ when talking to drunken people or foreigners. 'No more tonight. Close now.'

'Another,' said the old man.

'No. Finished.' The waiter wiped the edge of the table with a towel and shook his head.

The old man stood up, slowly counted the saucers, took a leather coin purse from his pocket and paid for the drinks, leaving half a peseta tip.

The waiter watched him go down the street, a very old man walking unsteadily but with dignity.

'Why didn't you let him stay and drink?' the unhurried waiter asked. They were putting up the shutters. 'It is not half past two.'

'I want to go home to bed.'

'What is an hour?'

'More to me than to him.'

'An hour is the same.'

'You talk like an old man yourself. He can buy a bottle and drink at home.'

'It's not the same.'

'No, it is not,' agreed the waiter with a wife. He did not wish to be unjust. He was only in a hurry.

'And you? You have no fear of going home before your usual hour?'

'Are you trying to insult me?'

'No, hombre, only to make a joke.'

'No,' the waiter who was in a hurry said, rising from pulling down the metal shutters. 'I have confidence. I am all confidence.'

'You have youth, confidence, and a job,' the older waiter said. 'You have everything.'

'And what do you lack?'

'Everything but work.'

'You have everything I have.'

'No. I have never had confidence and I am not young.'

'Come on. Stop talking nonsense and lock up.'

'I am of those who like to stay late at the café, the older waiter said. 'With all those who do not want to go to bed. With all those who need a light for the night.'

'I want to go home and into bed.'

'We are of two different kinds,' the older waiter said. He was now dressed to go home. 'It is not only a question of youth and confidence, although those things are very beautiful. Each night I am reluctant to close up because there may be someone who needs the café.'

'Hombre, there are bodegas open all night long.'

'You do not understand. This is a clean and pleasant café. It is well lighted. The light is very good and also, now, there are shadows of the leaves.'

'Good night,' said the younger waiter.

'Good night,' the other said. Turning off the electric light he continued the conversation with himself. It is the light of course but it is necessary that the place be clean and pleasant. You do not want music. Certainly you do not want music. Nor can you stand before a bar with dignity although that is all that is provided for these hours. What did he fear? It was not fear or dread. It was a nothing that he knew too well. It was all a nothing and a man was nothing too. It was only that and light was all it needed and a certain cleanness and order. Some lived in it and never felt it but he knew it all was nada y pues nada y nada y pues nada. Our nada who art in nada, nada be thy name thy kingdom nada thy will be nada in nada as it is in nada. Give us this nada our daily nada and nada us our nada as we nada our nadas and nada us not into nada but deliver us from nada; pues nada. Hail nothing full of nothing, nothing is with thee. He smiled and stood before a bar with a shining steam pressure coffee machine.

'What's yours?' asked the barman.

'Nada.'

'Otro loco mas,' said the barman and turned away.

'A little cup,' said the waiter.

The barman poured it for him.

'The light is very bright and pleasant but the bar is unpolished,' the waiter said.

The barman looked at him but did not answer. It was too late at night for conversation.

'You want another copita?' the barman asked.

'No, thank you,' said the waiter and went out. He disliked bars and bodegas. A clean, well-lighted café was a very different thing. Now, without thinking further, he would go home to his room. He would lie in the bed and finally, with daylight, he would go to sleep. After all, he said to himself, it is probably only insomnia. Many must have it.

THE SEA CHANGE

'All right,' said the man. 'What about it?'

'No,' said the girl. 'I can't.'

'You mean you won't.'

'I can't,' said the girl. 'That's all that I mean.'

'You mean that you won't.'

'All right,' said the girl. 'You have it your own way.'

'I don't have it my own way. I wish to God I did.'

'You did for a long time,' the girl said.

It was early, and there was no one in the café except the barman and these two who sat together at a table in the corner. It was the end of the summer and they were both tanned, so that they looked out of place in Paris. The girl wore a tweed suit, her skin was a smooth golden brown, her blonde hair was cut short and grew beautifully away from her forehead. The man looked at her.

'I'll kill her,' he said.

'Please don't,' the girl said. She had very fine hands and the man looked at them. They were slim and brown and very beautiful.

'I will. I swear to God I will.'

'It won't make you happy.'

'Couldn't you have gotten into something else? Couldn't you have gotten into some other jam?'

'It seems not,' the girl said. 'What are you going to do about it?'

'I told you.'

'No; I mean really.'

'I don't know,' he said. She looked at him and put out her hand. 'Poor old Phil,' she said. He looked at her hands, but he did not touch her hand with his.

'No, thanks,' he said.

'It doesn't do any good to say I'm sorry?'

'No.'

'Nor to tell you how it is?'

'I'd rather not hear.'

'I love you very much.'

'Yes, this proves it.'

'I'm sorry,' she said, 'if you don't understand.'

'I understand. That's the trouble. I understand.'

'You do,' she said. 'That makes it worse, of course.'

'Sure,' he said, looking at her. 'I'll understand all the time. All day and all night. Especially all night. I'll understand. You don't have to worry about that.'

'I'm sorry,' she said.

'If it was a man—'

'Don't say that. It wouldn't be a man. You know that. Don't you trust me?'

'That's funny,' he said. 'Trust you. That's really funny.'

'I'm sorry,' she said. 'That's all I seem to say. But when we do understand each other there's no use to pretend we don't.'

'No,' he said. 'I suppose not.'

'I'll come back if you want me.'

'No. I don't want you.'

Then they did not say anything for a while.

'You don't believe I love you, do you?' the girl asked.

'Let's not talk rot,' the man said.

'Don't you really believe I love you?'

'Why don't you prove it?'

'You didn't used to be that way. You never asked me to prove anything. That isn't polite.'

'You're a funny girl.'

'You're not. You're a fine man and it breaks my heart to go off and leave you—'

'You have to, of course.'

'Yes,' she said. 'I have to and you know it.'

He did not say anything and she looked at him and put her hand out again. The barman was at the far end of the bar. His face was white and so was his jacket. He knew these two and thought them a handsome young couple. He had seen many handsome young couples break up and new couples form that were never so handsome long. He was not thinking about this, but about a horse. In half an hour he could send across the street to find if the horse had won.

'Couldn't you just be good to me and let me go?' the girl asked.

'What do you think I'm going to do?'

Two people came in the door and went up to the bar.

'Yes, sir,' the barman took the orders.

'You can't forgive me? When you know about it?' the girl asked.

'No.'

'You don't think things we've had and done should make any difference in understanding?'

'"Vice is a monster of such fearful mien,"' the young man said bitterly, 'that to be something or other needs but to be seen. Then we something, something, then embrace.' He could not remember the words. 'I can't quote,' he said.

'Let's not say vice,' she said. 'That's not very polite.'

'Perversion,' he said.

'James,' one of the clients addressed the barman, 'you're looking very well.'

'You're looking very well yourself,' the barman said.

'Old James,' the other client said. 'You're better, James.'

'It's terrible,' the barman said, 'the way I put it on.'

'Don't neglect to insert the brandy, James,' the first client said.

'No, sir,' said the barman. 'Trust me.'

The two at the bar looked over at the two at the table, then looked back at the barman again. Toward the barman was the comfortable direction.

'I'd like it better if you didn't use words like that,' the girl said. 'There's no necessity to use a word like that.'

'What do you want me to call it?'

'You don't have to call it. You don't have to put any name to it.'

'That's the name for it.'

'No,' she said. 'We're made up of all sorts of things. You've known that. You've used it well enough.'

'You don't have to say that again.'

'Because that explains it to you.'

'All right,' he said. 'All right.'

'You mean all wrong. I know. It's all wrong. But I'll come back. I told you I'd come back. I'll come back right away.'

'No, you won't.'

'I'll come back.'

'No, you won't. Not to me.'

'You'll see.'

'Yes,' he said. 'That's the hell of it. You probably will.'

'Of course I will.'

'Go on, then.'

'Really?' She could not believe him, but her voice was happy.

'Go on,' his voice sounded strange to him. He was looking at her, at the way her mouth went and the curve of her cheekbones, at her eyes and at the way her hair grew on her forehead and at the edge of her ear and at her neck.

'Not really. Oh, you're too sweet,' she said. 'You're too good to me.'

'And when you come back tell me all about it.' His voice sounded very strange. He did not recognize it. She looked at him quickly. He was settled into something.

'You want me to go?' she asked seriously.

'Yes,' he said seriously. 'Right away.' His voice was not the same, and his mouth was very dry. 'Now,' he said.

She stood up and went out quickly. She did not look back at him. He watched her go. He was not the same-looking man as he had been before he had told her to go. He got up from the table, picked up the two checks and went over to the bar with them.

'I'm a different man, James,' he said to the barman. 'You see in me quite a different man.'

'Yes, sir?' said James.

'Vice,' said the brown young man, 'is a very strange thing, James.' He looked out the door. He saw her going down the street. As he looked in the glass, he saw he was really quite a different-looking man. The other two at the bar moved down to make room for him.

'You're right there, sir,' James said.

The other two moved down a little more, so that he would be quite comfortable. The young man saw himself in the mirror behind the bar. 'I said I was a different man, James,' he said. Looking into the mirror he saw that this was quite true.

'You look very well, sir,' James said. 'You must have had a very good summer.'

THE MOTHER OF A QUEEN

When his father died he was only a kid and his manager buried him perpetually. That is, so he would have the plot permanently. But when his mother died his manager thought they might not always be so hot on each other. They were sweethearts; sure he's a queen, didn't you know that, of course he is. So he just buried her for five years.

Well, when he came back to Mexico from Spain he got the first notice. It said it was the first notice that the five years were up and would he make arrangements for the continuing of his mother's grave. It was only twenty dollars for perpetual. I had the cash box then and I said let me attend to it, Paco. But he said no, he would look after it. He'd look after it right away. It was his mother and he wanted to do it himself.

Then in a week he got the second notice. I read it to him and I said I thought he had looked after it.

No, he said, he hadn't.

'Let me do it,' I said. 'It's right here in the cash box.'

No, he said. Nobody could tell him what to do. He'd do it himself when he got around to it. 'What's the sense in spending money sooner than necessary?'

'All right,' I said, 'but see you look after it.' At this time he had a contract for six fights at four thousand pesos a fight besides his benefit fight. He made over fifteen thousand dollars there in the capital alone. He was just tight, that's all.

The third notice came in another week and I read it to him. It said that if he did not make the payment by the following Saturday his mother's grave would be opened and her remains dumped on the common boneheap. He said he would go attend to it that afternoon when he went to town.

'Why not have me do it?' I asked him.

'Keep out of my business,' he said. 'It's my business and I'm going to do it.'

'All right, if that's the way you feel about it,' I said. 'Do your own business.'

He got the money out of the cash box, although then he always carried a hundred or more pesos with him all the time, and he said he would look after it. He went out with the money and so of course I thought he had attended to it.

A week later the notice came that they had no response to the final warning and so his mother's body had been dumped on the boneheap; on the public boneheap.

'Jesus Christ,' I said to him, 'you said you'd pay that and you took money out of the cash box to do it and now what's happened to your mother? My God think of it! The public boneheap and your own mother. Why didn't you let me look after it? I would have sent it when the first notice came.'

'It's none of your business. It's *my* mother.'

'It's none of *my* business, yes, but it was *your* business. What kind of blood is it in a man that will let that be done to his mother? You don't deserve to have a mother.'

'It is my mother,' he said. 'Now she is so much dearer to me. Now I don't have to think of her buried in one place and be sad. Now she is all about me in the air, like the birds and the flowers. Now she will always be with me.'

'Jesus Christ,' I said, 'what kind of blood have you anyway? I don't want you even to speak to me.'

'She is all around me,' he said. 'Now I will never be sad.'

At that time he was spending all kinds of money around women trying to make himself seem a man and fool people, but it didn't have any effect on people that knew anything about him. He owed me over six hundred pesos and he wouldn't pay me. 'Why do you want it now?' he'd say. 'Don't you trust me? Aren't we friends?'

'It isn't friends or trusting you. It's that I paid the accounts out of my own money while you were away and now I need the money back and you have it to pay me.'

'I haven't got it.'

'You have it,' I said. 'It's in the cash box now and you can pay me.'

'I need that money for something,' he said. 'You don't know all the needs I have for money.'

'I stayed here all the time you were in Spain and you authorized me to pay these things as they came up, all these things of the house, and you didn't send any money while you were gone and I paid over six hundred pesos in my own money and now I need it and you can pay me.'

'I'll pay you soon,' he said. 'Right now I need the money badly.'

'For what?'

'For my own business.'

'Why don't you pay me some on account?'

'I can't,' he said. 'I need that money too badly. But I will pay you.'

He had only fought twice in Spain, they couldn't stand him there, they saw through him quick enough, and he had seven new fighting suits made and this is the kind of thing he was: he had them packed so badly that four of them were ruined by sea water on the trip back and he couldn't even wear them.

'My God,' I said to him, 'you go to Spain. You stay there the whole season and only fight two times. You spend all the money you took with you on suits and then have them spoiled by salt water so you can't wear them.

That is the kind of season you have and then you talk to me about running your own business. Why don't you pay me the money you owe me so I can leave?'

'I want you here,' he said, 'and I will pay you. But now I need the money.'

'You need it too badly to pay for your own mother's grave to keep your mother buried. Don't you?' I said.

'I am happy about what has happened to my mother,' he said. 'You cannot understand.'

'Thank Christ I can't,' I said. 'You pay me what you owe me or I will take it out of the cash box.'

'I will keep the cash box myself,' he said.

'No, you won't,' I said.

That very afternoon he came to me with a punk, some fellow from his own town who was broke, and said, 'Here is a paesano who needs money to go home because his mother is very sick.' This fellow was just a punk, you understand, a nobody he'd never seen before, but from his home town, and he wanted to be the big, generous matador with a fellow townsman.

'Give him fifty pesos from the cash box,' he told me.

'You just told me you had no money to pay me,' I said. 'And now you want to give fifty pesos to this punk.'

'He is a fellow townsman,' he said, 'and he is in distress.'

'You bitch,' I said. I gave him the key of the cash box. 'Get it yourself. I'm going to town.'

'Don't be angry,' he said. 'I'm going to pay you.'

I got the car out to go to town. It was his car but he knew I drove it better than he did. Everything he did I could do better. He knew it. He couldn't even read and write. I was going to see somebody and see what I could do about making him pay me. He came out and said, 'I'm coming with you and I'm going to pay you. We are good friends. There is no need to quarrel.'

We drove into the city and I was driving. Just before we came into the town he pulled out twenty pesos.

'Here's the money,' he said.

'You motherless bitch,' I said to him and told him what he could do with the money. 'You give fifty pesos to that punk and then offer me twenty when you owe me six hundred. I wouldn't take a nickel from you. You know what you can do with it.'

I got out of the car without a peso in my pocket and I didn't know where I was going to sleep that night. Later I went out with a friend and got my things from his place. I never spoke to him again until this year. I met him walking with three friends in the evening on the way to the Callao cinema in the Gran Via in Madrid. He put his hand out to me.

'Hello, Roger, old friend,' he said to me. 'How are you? People say you are talking against me. That you say all sorts of unjust things about me.'

'All I say is you never had a mother,' I said to him. That's the worse thing you can say to insult a man in Spanish.

'That's true,' he said. 'My poor mother died when I was so young it seems as though I never had a mother. It's very sad.'

There's a queen for you. You can't touch them. Nothing, nothing can touch them. They spend money on themselves or for vanity, but they never pay. Try to get one to pay. I told him what I thought of him right there on the Gran Via, in front of three friends, but he speaks to me now when I meet him as though we were friends. What kind of blood is it that makes a man like that?

WINE OF WYOMING

It was a hot afternoon in Wyoming; the mountains were a long way away and you could see snow on their tops, but they made no shadow, and in the valley the grain-fields were yellow, the road was dusty with cars passing, and all the small wooden houses at the edge of town were baking in the sun. There was a tree made shade over Fontan's back porch and I sat there at a table and Madame Fontan brought up cold beer from the cellar. A motor car turned off the main road and came up the side road, and stopped beside the house. Two men got out and came in through the gate. I put the bottles under the table. Madame Fontan stood up.

'Where's Sam?' one of the men asked at the screen door.

'He ain't here. He's at the mines.'

'You got some beer?'

'No. Ain't got any beer. That's a last bottle. All gone.'

'What's he drinking?'

'That's a last bottle. All gone.'

'Go on, give us some beer. You know me.'

'Ain't got any beer. That's a last bottle. All gone.'

'Come on, let's go some place where we can get some real beer,' one of them said, and they went out to the car. One of them walked unsteadily. The motor car jerked in starting, whirled on the road, and went on and away.

'Put the beer on the table,' Madame Fontan said. 'What's the matter, yes, all right. What's the matter? Don't drink off the floor.'

'I don't know who they were,' I said.

'They're drunk,' she said. 'That's what makes the trouble. Then they go somewhere else and say they got it here. Maybe they don't even remember.' She spoke French, but it was only French occasionally, and there were many English words and some English constructions.

'Where's Fontan?'

'Il fait de la vendange. Oh, my God, il est crazy pour le vin.'

'But you like the beer?'

'Oui, j'aime la bière, mais Fontan, il est crazy pour le vin.'

She was a plump old woman with a lovely ruddy complexion and white hair. She was very clean and the house was very clean and neat. She came from Lens.

'Where did you eat?'

'At the hotel.'

'Mangez ici. Il ne faut pas manger à l'hotel ou au restaurant. Mangez ici!'

'I don't want to make you trouble. And besides they eat all right at the hotel.'

'I never eat at the hotel. Maybe they eat all right there. Only once in my life I ate at a restaurant in America. You know what they gave me? They gave me pork that was raw!'

'Really?'

'I don't lie to you. It was pork that wasn't cooked! Et mon fils il est marié avec une américaine, et tout le temps il a mangé les *beans* en *can*.'

'How long has he been married?'

'Oh, my God, I don't know. His wife weighs two hundred twenty-five pounds. She don't work. She don't cook. She gives him beans en can.'

'What does she do?'

'All the time she reads. Rien que des books. Tout le temps elle stay in bed and read books. Already she can't have another baby. She's too fat. There ain't any room.'

'What's the matter with her?'

'She reads books all the time. He's a good boy. He works hard. He worked in the mines, now he works on a ranch. He never worked on a ranch before, and the man that owns the ranch said to Fontan that he never saw anybody work better on that ranch than that boy. Then he comes home and she feeds him nothing.'

'Why doesn't he get a divorce?'

'He ain't got no money to get a divorce. Besides, il est *crazy* pour elle.'

'Is she beautiful?'

'He thinks *so*. When he brought her home I thought I would die. He's such a good boy and works hard all the time and never run around or make any trouble. Then he goes away to work in the oilfields and brings home this Indienne that weighs right then one hundred eighty-five pounds.'

'Elle est Indienne?'

'She's Indian all right. My God, yes. All the time she says sonofa bitsh goddam. She don't work.'

'Where is she now?'

'Au show.'

'Where's that?'

'*Au show. Moving* pictures. All she does is read and go to the show.'

'Have you got any more beer?'

'My God, yes. Sure. You come and eat with us tonight.'

'All right. What should I bring?'

'Don't bring anything. Nothing at all. Maybe Fontan will have some of the wine.'

That night I had dinner at Fontan's. We ate in the dining-room and there was a clean tablecloth. We tried the new wine. It was very light and clear and good, and still tasted of the grapes. At the table there were Fontan and Madame and the little boy, André.

'What did you do today?' Fontan asked. He was an old man with small mine-tired body, a drooping grey moustache, and bright eyes, and was from the Centre near Saint-Étienne.

'I worked on my book.'

'Were your books all right?' asked Madame.

'He means he writes a book like a writer. Un roman,' Fontan explained.

'Pa, can I go to the show?' André asked.

'Sure,' said Fontan. André turned to me.

'How old do you think I am? Do you think I look fourteen years old?' He was a thin little boy, but his face looked sixteen.

'Yes. You look fourteen.'

'When I go to the show I crouch down like this and try to look small.' His voice was very high and breaking. 'If I give them a quarter they keep it all, but if I give them only fifteen cents they let me in all right.'

'I only give you fifteen cents, then,' said Fontan.

'No. Give me the whole quarter. I'll get it changed on the way.'

'Il faut revenir tout de suite après le show,' Madame Fontan said.

'I come right back.' André went out the door. The night was cooling outside. He left the door open and a cool breeze came in.

'Mangez!' said Madame Fontan. 'You haven't eaten anything.' I had eaten two helpings of chicken and French fried potatoes, three ears of sweet corn, some sliced cucumbers, and two helpings of salad.

'Perhaps he wants some kek,' Fontan said.

'I should have gotten some kek for him,' Madame Fontan said. 'Mangez du fromage. Mangez du crimcheez. Vous n'avez rien mangé. I ought have gotten kek. Americans always eat kek.'

'Mais j'ai rudement bien mangé.'

'Mangez! Vous n'avez rien mangé. Eat it all. We don't save anything. Eat it all up.'

'Eat some more salad,' Fontan said.

'I'll get some more beer,' Madame Fontan said. 'If you work all day in a book-factory you get hungry.'

'Elle ne comprend pas que vou etes écrivain,' Fontan said. He was a delicate old man who used the slang and knew the popular songs of his period of military service in the end of the 1890s. 'He writes the books himself,' he explained to Madame.

'You write the books yourself?' Madame asked.

'Sometimes.'

'Oh!' she said. 'Oh! You write them yourself. Oh! Well, you get hungry if you do that too. Mangez! Je vais chercher de la bière.'

We heard her walking on the stairs to the cellar. Fontan smiled at me. He was very tolerant of people who had not his experience and worldly knowledge.

When André came home from the show we were still sitting in the kitchen and were talking about hunting.

'Labour *day* we all went to Clear Creek,' Madame said. 'Oh, my God, you ought to have been there all right. We all went in the truck. Tout le monde est allé dans le truck. Nous sommes partis le dimanche. C'est le truck de Charley.'

'On a mangé, on a bu du vin, de la bière, et il y avait aussi un français qui a apporté de l'absinthe,' Fontan said. 'Un français de la Californie!'

'My God, nous avons chanté. There's a farmer comes to see what's the matter, and we give him something to drink, and he stayed with us awhile. There was some Italians come too, and they want to stay with us too. We sung a song about the Italians and they don't understand it. They didn't know we didn't want them, but we didn't have nothing to do with them, and after a while they went away.'

'How many fish did you catch?'

'Très peu. We went to fish a little while, but then we came back to sing again. Nous avons chanté, vous savez.'

'In the night,' said Madame, 'toutes les femmes dort dans le truck. Les hommes à coté du feu. In the night I hear Fontan come to get some more wine, and I tell him, Fontan, my God, leave some for tomorrow. Tomorrow they won't have anything to drink, and then they'll be sorry.'

'Mais nous avons tout bu,' Fontan said. 'Et le lendemain il ne reste rien.'

'What did you do?'

'Nous avons peché sérieusement.'

'Good trout, all right, too. My God, yes. All the same; half-pound one ounce.'

'How big?'

'Half-pound one ounce. Just right to eat. All the same size; half-pound one ounce.'

'How do you like America?' Fontan asked me.

'It's my country, you see. So I like it, because it's my country. Mais on ne mange pas très bien. D'antan, oui. Mais maintenant, no.'

'No,' said Madame. 'On ne mange pas bien.' She shook her head. 'Et aussi, il y a trop de Polack. Quand j'étais petite ma mère m'a dit, "vous mangez comme les Polacks." Je n'ai jamais compris ce que c'est qu'un Polack. Mais maintenant en Amérique je comprends. Il y a trop de Polack. Et, my God, ils sont sales, les Polacks.'

'It is fine for hunting and fishing,' I said.

'Oui. Ça, c'est le meilleur. La chasse et la peche,' Fontan said. 'Qu'est-ce que vous avez comme fusil?'

'A twelve-gauge pump.'

'Il est bon, le pump,' Fontan nodded his head.

'Je veux aller à la chasse moi-meme,' André said in his high little boy's voice.

'Tu ne peux pas,' Fontan said. He turned to me.

'Ils sont des sauvages, les boys, vous savez. Ils sont des sauvages. Ils veulent shooter les uns les autres.'

'Je veux aller tout seul,' André said, very shrill and excited.

'You can't go,' Madame Fontan said. 'You are too young.'

'Je veux aller tout seul,' André said shrilly. 'Je veux shooter les rats d'eau.'

'What are rats d'eau?' I asked.

'You don't know them? Sure you know them. What they call the muskrats.'

André had brought the twenty-two-calibre rifle out from the cupboard and was holding it in his hands under the light.

'Ils sont des sauvages,' Fontan explained. 'Ils veulent shooter les uns les autres.'

'Je veux aller tout seul,' André shrilled. He looked desperately along the barrel of the gun. 'Je vous shooter les rats d'eau. Je connais beaucoup de rats d'eau.'

'Give me the gun,' Fontan said. He explained again to me. 'They're savages. They would shoot one another.'

André held tight on to the gun.

'On peut looker. On ne fait pas de mal. On peut looker.'

'Il est crazy pour le shooting,' Madame Fontan said. 'Mais il est trop jeune.'

André put the twenty-two calibre rifle back in the cupboard.

'When I'm bigger I'll shoot the muskrats and the jack-rabbits, too,' he said in English. 'One time I went out with papa and he shot a jack-rabbit just a little bit and I shot it and hit it.'

'C'est vrai,' Fontan nodded. 'Il a tué un jack.'

'But he hit it first,' André said. 'I want to go all by myself and shoot all by myself. Next year I can do it.' He went over in a corner and sat down to read a book. I had picked it up when we came into the kitchen to sit after supper. It was a library book–*Frank on a Gunboat*.

'Il aime les books,' Madame Fontan said. 'But it's better than to run around at night with the older boys and steal things.'

'Books are all right,' Fontan said. 'Monsieur il fait les books.'

'Yes, that's so, all right. But too many books are bad,' Madame Fontan said. 'Ici, c'est une maladie, les books. C'est comme les churches. Ici il y a trop de churches. En France il y a seulement les catholiques et les protestants–et très peu de protestants. Mais ici rien que de churches. Quand j'étais venu ici je disais, oh, my God, what are all the churches?'

'C'est vrai,' Fontan said. 'Il y a trop de churches.'

'The other day,' Madame Fontan said, 'there was a little French girl here with her mother, the cousin of Fontan, and she said to me, "En Amérique il ne faut pas etre catholique. It's not good to be catholique. The Americans don't like you to be catholique. It's like the dry law." I said to her, "What you going to be? Heh? It's better to be catholique if you're catholique." But she said, "No, it isn't any good to be catholique in America." But I think it's better to be catholique if you are. Ce n'est pas bon de changer sa religion. My God, no.'

'You go to the mass here?'

'No, I don't go in America, only sometimes in a long while. Mais je reste catholique. It's no good to change the religion.'

'On dit que Schmidt est catholique,' Fontan said.

'On dit, mais on ne sait jamais,' Madame Fontan said. 'I don't think Schmidt is catholique. There's not many catholique in America.'

'We are catholique,' I said.

'Sure, but you live in France,' Madame Fontan said. 'Je ne crois pas que Schmidt est catholique. Did he ever live in France?'

'Les Polacks sont catholiques,' Fontan said.

'That's true,' Madame Fontan said. 'They go to church, then they fight with knives all the way home and kill each other all day Sunday. But they're not real catholiques. They're Polack catholiques.'

'All catholiques are the same,' Fontan said. 'One catholique is like another.'

'I don't believe Schmidt is catholique,' Madame Fontan said. 'That's awful funny if he's catholique. Moi, je ne crois pas.'

'Il est catholique,' I said.

'Schmidt is catholique,' Madame Fontan mused. 'I wouldn't have believed it. My God, il est catholique.'

'Marie va chercher de la bière,' Fontan said. 'Monsieur a soif–moi aussi.'

'Yes, all right,' Madame Fontan said from the next room. She went downstairs and we heard the stairs creaking. André sat reading in the corner. Fontan and I sat at the table, and he poured the beer from the last bottle into our two glasses, leaving a little in the bottom.

'C'est un bon pays pour la chasse,' Fontan said. 'J'aime beaucoup shooter les canards.'

'Mais il y a très bonne chasse aussi en France,' I said.

'C'est vrai,' Fontan said. 'Nous avons beaucoup de gibier là-bas.'

Madame Fontan came up the stairs with the beer bottles in her hands. 'Il est catholique,' she said. 'My God, Schmidt est catholique.'

'You think he'll be the President?' Fontan asked.

'No,' I said.

The next afternoon I drove out to Fontan's, through the shade of the town, then along the dusty road, turning up the side road and leaving the car beside the fence. It was another hot day. Madame Fontan came to the back door. She looked like Mrs Santa Claus, clean and rosy-faced and white-haired, and waddling when she walked.

'My God, hello,' she said. 'It's hot, my God.' She went back into the house to get some beer. I sat on the back porch and looked through the screen and the leaves of the tree at the heat and, away off, the mountains. There were furrowed brown mountains, and above them three peaks and a glacier with snow that you could see through the trees. The snow looked very white and pure and unreal. Madame Fontan came out and put down the bottles on the table.

'What do you see out there?'

'The snow.'

'C'est jolie, la neige.'

'Have a glass, too.'

'All right.'

She sat down on a chair beside me. 'Schmidt,' she said. 'If he's the President, you think we get the wine and beer all right?'

'Sure,' I said. 'Trust Schmidt.'

'Already we paid seven hundred fifty-five dollars in fines when they arrested Fontan. Twice the police arrested us and once the governments. All the money we made all the time Fontan worked in the mines and I did washing. We paid it all. They put Fontan in jail. Il n'a jamais fait de mal à personne.'

'He's a good man,' I said. 'It's a crime.'

'We don't charge too much money. The wine one dollar a litre. The beer ten cents a bottle. We never sell the beer before it's good. Lots of places they sell the beer right away when they make it, and then it gives everybody a headache. What's the matter with that? They put Fontan in jail and they take seven hundred fifty-five dollars.'

'It's wicked,' I said. 'Where is Fontan?'

'He stays with the wine. He has to watch it now to catch it just right,' she smiled. She did not think about the money any more. 'Vous savez, il est crazy pour le vin. Last night he brought a little bit home with him, what you drank, and a little bit of the new. The last new. It ain't ready yet, but he drank a little bit, and this morning he put a little bit in his coffee. Dans son café, vous savez? Il est crazy pour le vin! Il est comme ça. Son pays est comme ça. Where I live in the north they don't drink any wine. Everybody drinks beer. By where we lived there was a big brewery right near us. When I was a little girl I didn't like the smell of the hops in the carts. Nor in the fields. Je n'aime pas les houblons. No, my God, not a bit. The man that owns the brewery said to me and my sister to go to the brewery and drink the beer, and then we'd like the hops. That's true. Then we liked them all right. He had them give us the beer. We liked them all right then. But Fontan, il est crazy pour le vin. One time he killed a jack-rabbit and he wanted me to cook it with a sauce with wine, make a black sauce with wine and butter and mushrooms and onion and everything in it, for the jack. My God, I make the sauce all right, and he eat it all and said, "La sauce est meilleure que le jack." Dans son pays c'est comme ça. Il y a beaucoup de gibier et de vin. Moi, j'aime les pommes de terre, le saucisson, et la bière. C'est bon, la bière. C'est très bon pour la santé.'

'It's good,' I said. 'It and wine too.'

'You're like Fontan. But there was a thing here that I never saw. I don't think you've ever seen it either. There were Americans came here and they put whisky in the beer.'

'No,' I said.

'Oui. My God, yes, that's true. Et aussi une femme qui a vomis sur la table!'

'Comment?'

'C'est vrai. Elle a vomis sur la table. Et après elle a vomis dans ses shoes. And afterward they come back and say they want to come again and have another party the next Saturday, and I say no, my God, no! When they came I locked the door.'

'They're bad when they're drunk.'

'In the winter-time when the boys go to the dance they come in the cars and wait outside and say to Fontan, "Hey, Sam, sell us a bottle wine," or they buy the beer, and then they take the moonshine out of their pockets in a bottle and pour it in the beer and drink it. My God, that's the first time I ever saw that in my life. They put whisky in the beer. My God, I don't understand *that*!'

'They want to get sick, so they'll know they're drunk.'

'One time a fellow comes here came to me and said he wanted me to cook them a big supper and they drink one two bottles of wine, and their girls come too, and then they go to the dance. All right, I said. So I made a big supper, and when they come already they drank a lot. Then they put whisky in the wine. My God, yes. I said to Fontan, "On va ètre malade!" "Oui," il dit. Then these girls were sick, nice girls, too, all-right girls. They were sick right at the table. Fontan tried to take them by the arm and show them where they could be sick all right in the cabinet, but the fellows said no, they were all right right there at the table.'

Fontan had come in. 'When they come again I locked the door. "No," I said. "Not for hundred fifty dollars." My God, no.'

'There is a word for such people when they do like that, in French,' Fontan said. He stood looking very old and tired from the heat.

'What?'

'Cochon,' he said delicately, hesitating to use such a strong word. 'They were like the cochon. C'est un mot très fort,' he apologized, 'mais vomir sur la table—' he shook his head sadly.

'Cochons,' I said. 'That's what they are–cochons. Salauds.'

The grossness of the words was distasteful to Fontan. He was glad to speak of something else.

'Il y a des gens très gentils, très sensibles, qui viennent aussi,' he said. 'There are officers from the fort. Very nice men. Good fellas. Everybody that was ever in France they want to come and drink wine. They like wine all right.'

'There was one man,' Madame Fontan said, 'and his wife never lets him get out. So he tells her he's tired, and goes to bed, and when she goes to the show he comes straight down here, cometimes in his pyjamas with just a coat over them. "Maria, some beer," he says, "for God's sake." He sits in his pyjamas and drinks the beer, and then he goes up to the fort and gets back in bed before his wife comes home from the show.'

'C'est un original,' Fontan said, 'mais vraiment gentil. He's a nice fella.'

'My God, yes, nice fella all right,' Madame Fontan said. 'He's always in bed when his wife gets back from the show.'

'I have to go away tomorrow,' I said. 'To the Crow Reservation. We go there for the opening of the prairie-chicken season.'

'Yes? You come back here before you go away. You come back here all right?'

'Absolutely.'

'Then the wine will be done,' Fontan said. 'We'll drink a bottle together.'

'Three bottles,' Madame Fontan said.

'I'll be back,' I said.

'We count on you,' Fontan said.

'Good night,' I said.

We got in early in the afternoon from the shooting-trip. We had been up that morning since five o'clock. The day before we had had good shooting, but that morning we had not seen a prairie-chicken. Riding in the open car, we were very hot and we stopped to eat our lunch out of the sun, under a tree beside the road. The sun was high and the patch of shade was very small. We ate sandwiches and crackers with sandwich filling on them, and were thirsty and tired, and glad when we finally were out and on the main road to town. We came up behind a prairie-dog town and stopped the car to shoot at the prairie-dogs with the pistol. We shot two, but then stopped because the bullets that missed glanced off the rocks and the dirt, and sung off across the fields, and beyond the fields there were some trees along a watercourse, with a house, and we did not want to get in trouble from stray bullets going toward the house. So we drove on, and finally were on the road coming downhill toward the outlying houses of the town. Across the plain we could see the mountains. They were blue that day, and the snow on the high mountains shone like glass. The summer was ending, but the new snow had not yet come to stay on the high mountains; there was only the old sun-melted snow and the ice, and from a long way away it shone very brightly.

We wanted something cool and some shade. We were sunburned and our lips blistered from the sun and alkali dust. We turned up the side road to Fontan's, stopped the car outside the house, and went in. It was cool inside the dining-room. Madame Fontan was alone.

'Only two bottles beer,' she said. 'It's all gone. The new is no good yet.'

I gave her some birds. 'That's good,' she said. 'All right. Thanks. That's good.' She went out to put the birds away where it was cooler. When we finished the beer I stood up. 'We have to go,' I said.

'You come back tonight all right? Fontan he's going to have the wine.'

'We'll come back before we go away.'

'You go away?'

'Yes. We have to leave in the morning.'

'That's too bad you go away. You come tonight. Fontan will have the wine. We'll make a fete before you go.'

'We'll come before we go.'

But that afternoon there were telegrams to send, the car to be gone over–a tyre had been cut by a stone and needed vulcanizing–and, without the car, I walked into the town, doing things that had to be done before we could go. When it was supper-time I was too tired to go out. We did not want a foreign language. All we wanted was to go early to bed.

As I lay in bed before I went to sleep, with all the things of the summer piled around ready to be packed, the windows open and the air coming in cool from the mountains, I thought it was a shame not to have gone to Fontan's–but in a little while I was asleep. The next day we were busy all morning packing and ending the summer. We had lunch and were ready to start by two o'clock.

'We must go and say good-bye to the Fontans,' I said.

'Yes, we must.'

'I'm afraid they expected us last night.'

'I suppose we could have gone.'

'I wish we'd gone.'

We said good-bye to the man at the desk at the hotel, and to Larry and our other friends in the town, and then drove out to Fontan's. Both Monsieur and Madame were there. They were glad to see us. Fontan looked old and tired.

'We thought you would come last night,' Madame Fontan said. 'Fontan had three bottles of wine. When you did not come he drank it all up.'

'We can only stay a minute,' I said. 'We just came to say good-bye. We wanted to come last night. We intended to come, but we were too tired after the trip.'

'Go get some wine,' Fontan said.

'There is no wine. You drank it all up.'

Fontan looked very upset.

'I'll go get some,' he said. 'I'll just be gone a few minutes. I drank it up last night. We had it for you.'

'I knew you were tired. "My God," I said, "they're too tired all right to come",' Madame Fontan said. 'Go get some wine, Fontan.'

'I'll take you in the car,' I said.

'All right,' Fontan said. 'That way we'll go faster.'

We drove down the road in the motor car and turned up a side road about a mile away.

'You'll like that wine,' Fontan said. 'It's come out well. You can drink it for supper tonight.'

We stopped in front of a frame house. Fontan knocked on the door. There was no answer. We went around to the back. The back door was locked too. There were empty tin cans around the back door. We looked in the window. There was nobody inside. The kitchen was dirty and sloppy, but all the doors and windows were tight shut.

'That son of a bitch. Where is she gone out?' Fontan said. He was desperate.

'I know where I can get a key,' he said. 'You stay here.' I watched him go down to the next house down the road, knock on the door, talk to the woman who came out, and finally come back. He had a key. We tried it on the front door and the back, but it wouldn't work.

'That son of a bitch,' Fontan said. 'She's gone away somewhere.'

Looking through the window I could see where the wine was stored. Close to the window you could smell the inside of the house. It smelled sweet and sickish like an Indian house. Suddenly Fontan took a loose board and commenced digging at the earth beside the back door.

'I can get in,' he said. 'Son of a bitch, I can get in.'

There was a man in the back yard of the next house doing something to one of the front wheels of an old Ford.

'You better not,' I said. 'That man will see you. He's watching.'

Fontan straightened up. 'We'll try the key once more,' he said. We tried the key and it did not work. It turned halfway in either direction.

'We can't get in,' I said. 'We better go back.'

'I'll dig up the back,' Fontan offered.

'No, I wouldn't let you take the chance.'

'I'll do it.'

'No,' I said. 'That man would see. Then they would seize it.'

We went out to the car and drove back to Fontan's, stopping on the way to leave the key. Fontan did not say anything but swear in English. He was incoherent and crushed. We went in the house.

'That son of a bitch!' he said. 'We couldn't get the wine. My own wine that I made.'

All the happiness went from Madame Fontan's face. Fontan sat down in a corner with his head in his hands.

'We must go,' I said. 'It doesn't make any difference about the wine. You drink to us when we're gone.'

'Where did that crazy go?' Madame Fontan asked.

'I don't know,' Fontan said. 'I don't know where she go. Now you go away without any wine.'

'That's all right,' I said.

'That's no good,' Madame Fontan said. She shook her head.

'We have to go,' I said. 'Good-bye and good luck. Thank you for the fine times.'

Fontan shook his head. He was disgraced. Madame Fontan looked sad.

'Don't feel bad about the wine,' I said.

'He wanted you to drink his wine,' Madame Fontan said. 'You can come back next year?'

'No. Maybe the year after.'

'You see?' Fontan said to her.

'Good-bye,' I said. 'Don't think about the wine. Drink some for us when we're gone.' Fontan shook his head. He did not smile. He knew when he was ruined.

'That son of a bitch,' Fontan said to himself.

'Last night he had three bottles,' Madame Fontan said to comfort him. He shook his head.

'Good-bye,' he said.

Madame Fontan had tears in her eyes.

'Good-bye' she said. She felt badly for Fontan.

'Good-bye,' we said. We all felt very badly. They stood in the doorway and we got in, and I started the motor. We waved. They stood together sadly on the porch. Fontan looked very old, and Madame Fontan looked sad. She waved to us and Fontan went in the house. We turned up the road.

'They felt so badly. Fontan felt terribly.'

'We ought to have gone last night.'

'Yes, we ought to have.'

We were through the town and out on the smooth road beyond, with the stubble of grain-fields on each side and the mountains off to the right. It looked like Spain, but it was Wyoming.

'I hope they have a lot of good luck.'

'They won't,' I said, 'and Schmidt won't be President either.'

The cement road stopped. The road was gravelled now and we left the plain and started up between two foothills; the road in a curve and commencing to climb. The soil of the hills was red, the sage grew in grey clumps, and as the road rose we could see across the hills and away across the plain of the valley to the mountains. They were farther now and they looked more like Spain than ever. The road curved and climbed again, and ahead there were some grouse dusting in the road. They flew as we came toward them, their wings beating fast, then sailing in long slants, and lit on the hillside below.

'They are so big and lovely. They're bigger than European partridges.'

'It's a fine country for la chasse, Fontan says.'

'And when the chasse is gone?'

'They'll be dead then.'

'The boy won't.'

'There's nothing to prove he won't,' I said.

'We ought to have gone last night.'

'Oh, yes,' I said. 'We ought to have gone.'

GOD REST YOU MERRY, GENTLEMEN

In those days the distances were all very different, the dirt blew off the hills that now have been cut down, and Kansas City was very like Constantinople. You may not believe this. No one believes this; but it is true. On this afternoon it was snowing and inside an automobile dealer's show window, lighted against the early dark, there was a racing motor car finished entirely in silver with Dans Argent lettered on the hood. This I believed to mean the silver dance or the silver dancer, and, slightly puzzled which it meant but happy in the sight of the car and pleased by my knowledge of a foreign language, I went along the street in the snow. I was walking from the Woolf Brothers' saloon where, on Christmas and Thanksgiving Day, a free turkey dinner was served, toward the city hospital which was on a high hill that overlooked the smoke, the buildings and the streets of the town. In the reception room of the hospital were the two ambulance surgeons, Doc Fischer and Doctor Wilcox, sitting, the one before a desk, the other in a chair against the wall.

Doc Fischer was thin, sand-blond, with a thin mouth, amused eyes and gambler's hands. Doctor Wilcox was short, dark and carried an indexed book, *The Young Doctor's Friend and Guide*, which, being consulted on any given subject, told symptoms and treatment. It was also cross-indexed so that being consulted on symptoms it gave diagnoses. Doc Fischer had suggested that any future editions should be further cross-indexed so that if consulted as to the treatments being given, it would reveal ailments and symptoms. 'As an aid to memory,' he said.

Doctor Wilcox was sensitive about this book but could not get along without it. It was bound in limp leather and fitted his coat pocket and he had bought it at the advice of one of his professors who had said, 'Wilcox, you have no business being a physician and I have done everything in my power to prevent you from being certified as one. Since you are now a member of this learned profession I advise you, in the name of humanity, to obtain a copy of *The Young Doctor's Friend and Guide*, and use it, Doctor Wilcox. Learn to use it.'

Doctor Wilcox had said nothing but he had bought the leather-bound guide that same day.

'Well, Horace,' Doc Fischer said as I came in the receiving room which smelt of cigarettes, iodoform, carbolic and an over-heated radiator.

'Gentlemen,' I said.

'What news along the rialto?' Doc Fischer asked. He affected a certain extravagance of speech which seemed to me to be of the utmost elegance.

'The free turkey at Woolf's,' I answered.

'You partook?'

'Copiously.'

'Many of the confrères present?'

'All of them. The whole staff.'

'Much Yuletide cheer?'

'Not much.'

'Doctor Wilcox here has partaken slightly,' Doc Fischer said. Doctor Wilcox looked up at him, then at me.

'Want a drink?' he asked.

'No, thanks,' I said.

'That's all right,' Doctor Wilcox said.

'Horace,' Doc Fischer said, 'you don't mind me calling you Horace, do you?'

'No.'

'Good old Horace. We've had an extremely interesting case.'

'I'll say,' said Doctor Wilcox.

'You know the lad who was in here yesterday?'

'Which one?'

'The lad who sought eunuch-hood.'

'Yes.' I had been there when he came in. He was a boy about sixteen. He came in with no hat on and was very excited and frightened but determined. He was curly haired and well built and his lips were prominent.

'What's the matter with you, son?' Doctor Wilcox asked him.

'I want to be castrated,' the boy said.

'Why?' Doc Fischer asked.

'I've prayed and I've done everything and nothing helps.'

'Helps what?'

'That awful lust.'

'What awful lust?'

'The way I get. That way I can't stop getting. I pray all night about it.'

'Just what happens?' Doc Fischer asked.

The boy told him. 'Listen, boy,' Doc Fischer said. 'There's nothing wrong with you. That's the way you're supposed to be. There's nothing wrong with that.'

'It is wrong,' said the boy. 'It's a sin against purity. It's a sin against our Lord and Saviour.'

'No,' said Doc Fischer. 'It's a natural thing. It's the way you are supposed to be and later on you will think you are very fortunate.'

'Oh, you don't understand,' the boy said.

'Listen,' Doc Fischer said and he told the boy certain things.

'No. I won't listen. You can't make me listen.'

'Please listen,' Doc Fischer said.

'You're just a goddamned fool,' Doctor Wilcox said to the boy.

'Then you won't do it?' the boy asked.

'Do what?'

'Castrate me.'

'Listen,' Doc Fischer said. 'No one will castrate you. There is nothing wrong with your body. You have a fine body and you must not think about that. If you are religious remember that what you complain of is no sinful state but the means of consummating a sacrament.'

'I can't stop it happening,' the boy said. 'I pray all night and I pray in the daytime. It is a sin, a constant sin against purity.'

'Oh, go and—' Doctor Wilcox said.

'When you talk like that I don't hear you,' the boy said with dignity to Doctor Wilcox. 'Won't you please do it?' he asked Doc Fischer.

'No,' said Doc Fischer. 'I've told you, boy.'

'Get him out of here,' Doctor Wilcox said.

'I'll get out,' the boy said. 'Don't touch me. I'll get out.'

That was about five o'clock on the day before.

'So what happened?' I asked.

'So at one o'clock this morning,' Doc Fischer said, 'we receive the youth self-mutilated with a razor.'

'Castrated?'

'No,' said Doc Fischer. 'He didn't know what castrate meant.'

'He may die,' Doctor Wilcox said.

'Why?'

'Loss of blood.'

'The good physician here, Doctor Wilcox, my colleague, was on call and he was unable to find this emergency listed in his book.'

'The hell with you talking that way,' Doctor Wilcox said.

'I only mean it in the friendliest way, Doctor,' Doc Fischer said, looking at his hands, at his hands that had, with his willingness to oblige and his lack of respect for Federal statutes, made him his trouble. 'Horace here will bear me out that I only speak of it in the very friendliest way. It was an amputation the young man performed, Horace.'

'Well, I wish you wouldn't ride me about it,' Doctor Wilcox said. 'There isn't any need to ride me.'

'Ride you, Doctor, on the day, the very anniversary, of our Saviour's birth?'

'*Our* Saviour? Ain't you a Jew?' Doctor Wilcox said.

'So I am. So I am. It always is slipping my mind. I've never given it its proper importance. So good of you to remind me. *Your* Saviour. That's right. *Your* Saviour, undoubtedly *your* Saviour–and the ride for Palm Sunday.'

'You're too damned smart,' Doctor Wilcox said.

'An excellent diagnosis, Doctor. I was always too damned smart. Too damned smart on the coast certainly. Avoid it, Horace. You haven't much tendency but sometimes I see a gleam. But what a diagnosis–and without the book.'

'The hell with you,' Doctor Wilcox said.

'All in good time, Doctor,' Doc Fischer said. 'All in good time. If there is such a place I shall certainly visit it. I have even had a very small look into it. No more than a peek, really. I looked away almost at once. And do you know what the young man said, Horace, when the good Doctor here brought him in? He said, "Oh, I asked you to to do it. I asked you so many times to do it."'

'On Christmas Day, too,' Doctor Wilcox said.

'The significance of the particular day is not important,' Doc Fischer said.

'Maybe not to you,' said Doctor Wilcox.

'You hear him, Horace?' Doc Gischer said. 'You hear him? Having discovered my vulnerable point, my achilles tendon, so to speak, the doctor pursues his advantage.'

'You're too damned smart,' Doctor Wilcox said.

THE GAMBLER, THE NUN, AND THE RADIO

They brought them in around midnight and then, all night long, everyone along the corridor heard the Russian.

'Where is he shot?' Mr Frazer asked the night nurse.

'In the thigh, I think.'

'What about the other one?'

'Oh, he's going to die, I'm afraid.'

'Where is he shot?'

'Twice in the abdomen. They only found one of the bullets.'

They were both beet workers, a Mexican and a Russian, and they were sitting drinking coffee in an all-night restaurant when someone came in the door and started shooting at the Mexican. The Russian crawled under a table and was hit, finally, by a stray shot fired at the Mexican as he lay on the floor with two bullets in his abdomen. That was what the paper said.

The Mexican told the police he had no idea who shot him. He believed it to be an accident.

'An accident that he fired eight shots at you and hit you twice, there?'

'Si, señor,' said the Mexican, who was named Cayetano Ruiz.

'An accident that he hit me at all, the cabron,' he said to the interpreter.

'What does he say?' asked the detective sergeant, looking across the bed at the interpreter.

'He says it was an accident.'

'Tell him to tell the truth, that he is going to die,' the detective said.

'Na,' said Cayetano. 'But tell him that I feel very sick and would prefer not to talk so much.'

'He says that he is telling the truth,' the interpreter said. Then, speaking confidently, to the detective, 'He don't know who shot him. They shot him in the back.'

'Yes,' said the detective. 'I understand that, but why did the bullets all go in the front?'

'Maybe he is spinning around,' said the interpreter.

'Listen,' said the detective, shaking his finger almost at Cayetano's nose, which projected, waxen yellow, from his dead-man's face in which his eyes were alive as a hawk's, 'I don't give a damn who shot you, but I've got to clear this thing up. Don't you want the man who shot you to be punished? Tell him that,' he said to the interpreter.

'He says to tell who shot you.'

'Mandarlo al carajo,' said Cayetano, who was very tired.

'He says he never saw the fellow at all,' the interpreter said. 'I tell you straight they shot him in the back.'

'Ask him who shot the Russian.'

'Poor Russian,' said Cayetano. 'He was on the floor with his head enveloped in his arms. He started to give cries when they shoot him and he is giving cries ever since. Poor Russian.'

'He says some fellow that he doesn't know. Maybe the same fellow that shot him.'

'Listen,' the detective said. 'This isn't Chicago. You're not a gangster. You don't have to act like a moving picture. It's all right to tell who shot you. Anybody would tell who shot them. That's all right to do. Suppose you don't tell who he is and he shoots somebody else. Suppose he shoots a woman or a child. You can't let him get away with that. You tell him,' he said to Mr Frazer. 'I don't trust that damn interpreter.'

'I am very reliable,' the interpreter said. Cayetano looked at Mr Frazer.

'Listen, amigo,' said Mr Frazer. 'The policeman says that we are not in Chicago but in Hailey, Montana. You are not a bandit and this has nothing to do with the cinema.'

'I believe him,' said Cayetano softly. 'Ya lo creo.'

'One can, with honour, denounce one's assailant. Every one does it here, he says. He says what happens if after shooting you, this man shoots a woman or a child?'

'I am not married,' Cayetano said.

'He says any woman, any child.'

'The man is not crazy,' Cayetano said.

'He says you should denounce him,' Mr Frazer finished.

'Thank you,' Cayetano said. 'You are of the great translators. I speak English, but badly. I understand it all right. How did you break your leg?'

'A fall off a horse.'

'What bad luck. I am very sorry. Does it hurt much?'

'Not now. At first, yes.'

'Listen, amigo,' Cayetano began, 'I am very weak. You will pardon me. Also I have much pain; enough pain. It is very possible that I die. Please get this policeman out of here because I am very tired.' He made as though to roll to one side; then held himself still.

'I told him everything exactly as you said and he said to tell you, truly, that he doesn't know who shot him and that he is very weak and wishes you would question him later on,' Mr Frazer said.

'He'll probably be dead later on.'

'That's quite possible.'

'That's why I want to question him now.'

'Somebody shot him in the back, I tell you,' the interpreter said.

'Oh, for Chrisake,' the detective sergeant said, and put his note-book in his pocket.

Outside in the corridor the detective sergeant stood with the interpreter beside Mr Frazer's wheeled chair.

'I suppose you think somebody shot him in the back too?'

'Yes,' Frazer said. 'Somebody shot him in the back. What's it to you?'

'Don't get sore,' the sergeant said. 'I wish I could talk spick.'

'Why don't you learn?'

'You don't have to get sore. I don't get any fun out of asking that spick questions. If I could talk spick it would be different.'

'You don't need to talk Spanish,' the interpreter said. 'I'm a very reliable interpreter.'

'Oh, for Chrisake,' the sergeant said. 'Well, so long. I'll come up and see you.'

'Thanks. I'm always in.'

'I guess you are all right. That was bad luck all right. Plenty bad luck.'

'It's coming along good now since he spliced the bone.'

'Yes, but it's a long time. A long, long time.'

'Don't let anybody shoot you in the back.'

'That's right,' he said. 'That's right. Well, I'm glad you're not sore.'

'So long,' said Mr Frazer.

Mr Frazer did not see Cayetano again for a long time, but each morning Sister Cecilia brought news of him. He was so uncomplaining she said and he was very bad now. He had peritonitis and they thought he could not live. Poor Cayetano, she said. He had such beautiful hands and such a fine face and he never complains. The odour, now, was really terrific. He would point toward his nose with one finger and smile and shake his head, she said. He felt badly about the odour. It embarrassed him, Sister Cecilia said. Oh, he was such a fine patient. He always smiled. He wouldn't go to confession to Father but he promised to say his prayers, and not a Mexican had been to see him since he had been brought in. The Russian was going out at the end of the week. I could never feel anything about the Russian, Sister Cecilia said. Poor fellow, he suffered too. It was a greased bullet and dirty and the wound infected, but he made so much noise and then I always like the bad ones. That Cayetano, he's a bad one. Oh, he must really be a bad one, a thoroughly bad one, he's so fine and delicately made and he's never done any work with the hands. He's not a beet worker. I know he's not a beet worker. His hands are as smooth and not a callous on them. I know he's a bad one of some sort. I'm going down and pray for him now. Poor Cayetano, he's having a dreadful time, and he doesn't make a sound. What did they have to shoot him for? Oh, that poor Cayetano! I'm going right down and pray for him.

She went right down and prayed for him.

In that hospital a radio did not work very well until it was dusk. They said it was because there was so much ore in the ground or something about the mountains, but anyway it did not work well at all until it began to get dark outside; but all night it worked beautifully and when one station stopped you could go farther west and pick up another. The last one that you could get was Seattle, Washington, and due to the difference in time, when they signed off at four o'clock in the morning it was five o'clock in the morning in the hospital; and at six o'clock you could get the morning revellers in Minneapolis. That was on account of the difference in time, too, and Mr Frazer used to like to think of the morning revellers arriving at the studio and picture how they would look getting off a street car before daylight in the morning carrying their instruments. Maybe that was wrong and they kept their instruments at the place they revelled, but he always pictured them with their instruments. He had never been in Minneapolis and believed he probably would never go there, but he knew what it looked like that early in the morning.

Out of the window of the hospital you could see a field with tumbleweed coming out of the snow, and a bare clay butte. One morning the doctor wanted to show Mr Frazer two pheasants that were out there in the snow, and pulling the bed toward the window, the reading light fell off the iron bedstead and hit Mr Frazer on the head. This does not sound as funny now but it was very funny then. Everyone was looking out the window, and the doctor, who was a most excellent doctor, was pointing at the pheasants and pulling the bed toward the window, and then, just as in a comic section, Mr Frazer was knocked out by the leaded base of the lamp hitting the top of his head. It seemed the antithesis of healing or whatever people were in the hospital for, and everyone thought it was very funny, as a joke on Mr Frazer and on the doctor. Everything is much simpler in a hospital, including the jokes.

From the other window, if the bed was turned, you could see the town, with a little smoke above it, and the Dawson mountains looking like real mountains with the winter snow on them. Those were the two views since the wheeled chair had proved to be premature. It is really best to be in bed if you are in a hospital; since two views, with time to observe them, from a room the temperature of which you control, are much better than any number of views seen for a few minutes from hot, empty rooms that are waiting for someone else, or just abandoned, which you are wheeled in and out of. If you stay long enough in a room the view, whatever it is, acquires a great value and becomes very important and you would not change it, not even by a different angle. Just as, with the radio, there are certain things that you become fond of, and you welcome them and resent the new things. The best tunes they had that winter were 'Sing Something Simple', 'Singsong Girl' and 'Little White Lies'. No other tunes were as satisfactory, Mr Frazer felt. 'Betty Co-ed' was a good tune too, but the parody of the words which came unavoidably into Mr Frazer's mind grew so steadily and increasingly obscene that, there being no one to appreciate it, he finally abandoned it and let the song go back to football.

About nine o'clock in the morning they would start using the X-ray machine, and then the radio, which, by then was only getting Hailey, became useless. Many people in Hailey who owned radios protested about the hospital's X-ray machine which ruined their morning reception, but there was never any action taken, although many felt it was a shame the hospital could not use their machine at a time when people were not using their radios.

About the time when it became necessary to turn off the radio Sister Cecilia came in.

'How's Cayetano, Sister Cecilia?' Mr Frazer asked.

'Oh, he's very bad.'

'Is he out of his head?'

'No, but I'm afraid he's going to die.'

'How are you?'

'I'm very worried about him, and do you know that absolutely no one has come to see him? He could die just like a dog for all those Mexicans care. They're really dreadful.'

'Do you want to come up and hear the game this afternoon?'

'Oh, no,' she said. 'I'd be too excited. I'll be in the chapel praying.'

'We ought to be able to hear it pretty well,' Mr Frazer said. 'They're playing out on the coast and the difference in time will bring it late enough so we can get it all right.'

'Oh, no. I couldn't do it. The world series nearly finished me. When the Athletics were at bat I was praying right out loud: "Oh, Lord, direct their batting eyes! Oh, Lord, may he hit one! Oh, Lord, may he hit safely!" Then when they filled the bases in the third game, you remember, it was too much for me. "Oh, Lord, may he hit it out of the lot! Oh, Lord, may he drive it clean over the fence!" Then you know when the Cardinals would come to bat it was simply dreadful. "Oh, Lord, may they not see it! Oh, Lord, don't let them even catch a glimpse of it. Oh, Lord, may they fan!" And this game is even worse. It's Notre Dame. Our Lady. No, I'll be in the chapel. For Our Lady. They're playing for Our Lady. I wish you'd write something sometime for Our Lady. You could do it. You know you could do it, Mr Frazer.'

'I don't know anything about her that I could write. It's mostly been written already,' Mr Frazer said. 'You wouldn't like the way I write. She wouldn't care for it either.'

'You'll write about her sometime,' Sister said. 'I know you will. You must write about Our Lady.'

'You'd better come up and hear the game.'

'It would be too much for me. No, I'll be in the chapel doing what I can.'

That afternoon they had been playing about five minutes when a probationer came into the room and said, 'Sister Cecilia wants to know how the game is going?'

'Tell her they have a touchdown already.'

In a little while the probationer came into the room again.

'Tell her they're playing them off their feet,' Mr Frazer said.

A little later he rang the bell for the nurse who was on floor duty. 'Would you mind going down to the chapel or sending word to Sister Cecilia that Notre Dame has them fourteen to nothing at the end of the first quarter and that it's all right. She can stop praying.'

In a few minutes Sister Cecilia came into the room. She was very excited. 'What does fourteen to nothing mean? I don't know anything about this game. That's a nice safe lead in baseball. But I don't know anything about football. It may not mean a thing. I'm going right back down to the chapel and pray until it's finished.'

'They have them beaten,' Frazer said. 'I promise you. Stay and listen with me.'

'No. No. No. No. No. No. No,' she said. 'I'm going right down to the chapel to pray.'

Mr Frazer sent down word whenever Notre Dame scored, and finally, when it had been dark a long time, the final result.

'How's Sister Cecilia?'

'They're all at chapel,' she said.

The next morning Sister Cecilia came in. She was very pleased and confident.

'I knew they couldn't beat Our Lady,' she said. 'They couldn't. Cayetano's better too. He's much better. He's going to have visitors. He can't see them yet, but they are going to come and that will make him feel better and know he's not forgotten by his own people. I went down and saw that O'Brien boy at Police Headquarters and told him that he's got to send some Mexicans up to see poor Cayetano. He's going to send some this afternoon. Then that poor man will feel better. It's wicked the way no one has come to see him.'

That afternoon about five o'clock three Mexicans came into the room.

'Can one?' asked the biggest one, who had very thick lips and was quite fat.

'Why not?' Mr Frazer answered. 'Sit down, gentlemen. Will you take something?'

'Many thanks,' said the big one.

'Thanks,' said the darkest and smallest one.

'Thanks, no,' said the thin one. 'It mounts to my head.' He tapped his head.

The nurse brought some glasses. 'Please give them the bottle,' Frazer said. 'It is from Red Lodge,' he explained.

'That of Red Lodge is the best,' said the big one. 'Much better than that of Big Timber.'

'Clearly,' said the smallest one, 'and costs more too.'

'In Red Lodge it is of all prices,' said the big one.

'How many tubes has the radio?' asked the one who did not drink.

'Seven.'

'Very beautiful,' he said. 'What does it cost?'

'I don't know,' Mr Frazer said. 'It is rented.'

'You gentlemen are friends of Cayetano?'

'No,' said the big one. 'We are friends of he who wounded him.'

'We were sent here by the police,' the smallest one said.

'We have a little place,' the big one said. 'He and I,' indicating the one who did not drink. 'He has a little place too,' indicating the small, dark one. 'The police tell us we have to come–so we came.'

'I am very happy you have come.'

'Equally,' said the big one.

'Will you have another little cup?'

'Why not?' said the big one.

'With your permission,' said the smallest one.

'Not me,' said the thin one. 'It mounts to my head.'

'It is very good,' said the smallest one.

'Why not try some?' Mr Frazer asked the thin one. 'Let a little mount to your head.'

'Afterwards comes the headache,' said the thin one.

'Could you not send friends of Cayetano to see him?' Frazer asked.

'He has no friends.'

'Every man has friends.'

'This one, no.'

'What does he do?'

'He is a card-player.'

'Is he good?'

'I believe it.'

'From me,' said the smallest one, 'he won one hundred and eighty dollars. Now there is no longer one hundred and eighty dollars in the world.'

'From me,' said the thin one, 'he won two hundred and eleven dollars. Fix yourself on that figure.'

'I never played with him,' said the fat one.

'He must be very rich,' Mr Frazer suggested.

'He is poorer than we,' said the little Mexican. 'He has no more than the shirt on his back.'

'And that shirt is of little value now,' Mr Frazer said. 'Perforated as it is.'

'Clearly.'

'The one who wounded him was a card-player?'

'No, a beet worker. He has had to leave town.'

'Fix yourself on this,' said the smallest one. 'He was the best guitar player ever in this town. The finest.'

'What a shame.'

'I believe it,' said the biggest one. 'How he could touch the guitar.'

'There are no good guitar players left?'

'Not the shadow of a guitar player.'

'There is an accordion player who is worth something,' the thin man said.

'There are a few who touch various instruments,' the big one said. 'You like music?'

'How would I not?'

'We will come one night with music? You think the sister would allow it? She seems very amiable.'

'I am sure she would permit it when Cayetano is able to hear it.'

'Is she a little crazy?' asked the thin one.

'Who?'

'That sister.'

'No,' Mr Frazer said. 'She is a fine woman of great intelligence and sympathy.'

'I distrust all priests, monks and sisters,' said the thin one.

'He had bad experiences when a boy,' the smallest one said.

'I was an acolyte,' the thin one said proudly. 'Now I believe in nothing. Neither do I go to mass.'

'Why? Does it mount to your head?'

'No,' said the thin one. 'It is alcohol that mounts to my head. Religion is the opium of the poor.'

'I thought marijuana was the opium of the poor,' Frazer said.

'Did you ever smoke opium?' the big one asked.

'No.'

'Nor I,' he said. 'It seems it is very bad. One commences and cannot stop. It is a vice.'

'Like religion,' said the thin one.

'This one,' said the smallest Mexican, 'is very strong against religion.'

'It is necessary to be very strong against something,' Mr Frazer said politely.

'I respect those who have faith even though they are ignorant,' the thin one said.

'Good,' said Mr Frazer.

'What can we bring you?' asked the big Mexican. 'Do you lack for anything?'

'I would be glad to buy some beer if there is good beer.'

'We will bring beer.'

'Another copita before you go?'

'It is very good.'

'We are robbing you.'

'I can't take it. It goes to my head. Then I have a bad headache and sick at the stomach.'

'Good-bye, gentlemen.'

'Good-bye and thanks.'

They went out and there was supper and then the radio, turned to be as quiet as possible and still be heard, and the stations finally signing off in this order: Denver, Salt Lake City, Los Angeles and Seattle. Mr Frazer received no picture of Denver from the radio. He could see Denver from the *Denver Post*, and correct the picture from the *Rocky Mountain News*. Nor did he ever have any feel of Salt Lake City or Los Angeles from what he heard from those places. All he felt about Salt Lake City was that it was clean, but dull, and there were too many ballrooms mentioned in too many big hotels for him to see Los Angeles. He could not feel it for the ballrooms. But Seattle he came to know very well, the taxicab company with the big white cabs (each cab equipped with radio itself) he rode in every night out to the roadhouse on the Canadian side where he followed the course of parties by the musical selections they phoned for. He lived in Seattle from two o'clock on, each night, hearing the pieces that all the different people asked for, and it was as real as Minneapolis, where the revellers left their beds each morning to make the trip down to the studio. Mr Frazer grew very fond of Seattle, Washington.

The Mexicans came and brought beer but it was not good beer. Mr Frazer saw them but he did not feel like talking and when they went he knew they would not come again. His nerves had become tricky and he disliked seeing people while he was in this condition. His nerves went bad at the end of five weeks, and while he was pleased they lasted that long yet he resented being forced to make the same experiment when he already knew the answer. Mr Frazer had been through this all before. The only thing which was new to him was the radio. He played it all night long, turned so low he could barely hear it, and he was learning to listen to it without thinking.

Sister Cecilia came into the room about ten o'clock in the morning on that day and brought the mail. She was very handsome, and Mr Frazer liked to see her and to hear her talk, but the mail, supposedly coming from a different world, was important. However, there was nothing in the mail of any interest.

'You look *so* much better,' she said. 'You'll be leaving us soon.'

'Yes,' Mr Frazer said. 'You look very happy this morning.'

'Oh, I am. This morning I feel as though I might be a saint.'

Mr Frazer was a little taken aback at this.

'Yes,' Sister Cecilia went on. 'That's what I want to be. A saint. Ever since I was a little girl I've wanted to be a saint. When I was a girl I thought if I renounced the world and went into the convent I would be a saint. That was what I wanted to be and that was what I thought I had to do to be one. I expected I would be a saint. I was absolutely sure I would be one. For just a moment I thought I was one. I was so happy and it seemed so simple and easy. When I awoke in the morning I expected I would be a saint, but I wasn't. I've never become one. I want so to be one. All I want is to be a saint. That is all I've ever wanted. And this morning I feel as though I might be one. Oh, I hope I will get to be one.'

'You'll be one. Everybody gets what they want. That's what they always tell me.'

'I don't know now. When I was a girl it seemed so simple. I knew I would be a saint. Only I believed it took time when I found it did not happen suddenly. Now it seems almost impossible.'

'I'd say you had a good chance.'

'Do you really think so? No, I don't want just to be encouraged. Don't just encourage me. I want to be a saint. I want to be a saint.'

'Of course you'll be a saint,' Mr Frazer said.

'No, probably I won't be. But, oh, if I could only be a saint! I'd be perfectly happy.'

'You're three to one to be a saint.'

'No, don't encourage me. But, oh, if I could only be a saint! If I could only be a saint!'

'How's your friend Cayetano?'

'He's going to get well, but he's paralysed. One of the bullets hit the big nerve that goes down through his thigh and that leg is paralysed. They only found it out when he got well enough so that he could move.'

'Maybe the nerve will regenerate.'

'I'm praying that it will,' Sister Cecilia said. 'You ought to see him.'

'I don't feel like seeing anybody.'

'You know you'd like to see him. They could wheel him in here.'

'All right.'

They wheeled him in, thin, his skin transparent, his hair black and needing to be cut, his eyes very laughing, his teeth bad when he smiled.

'Hola, amigo! Que tal?'

'As you see,' said Mr Frazer. 'And thou?'

'Alive and with the leg paralysed.'

'Bad,' Mr Frazer said. 'But the nerve can regenerate and be as good as new.'

'So they tell me.'

'What about the pain?'

'Not now. For a while I was crazy with it in the belly. I thought the pain alone would kill me.'

Sister Cecilia was observing them happily.

'She tells me you never made a sound,' Mr Frazer said.

'So many people in the ward,' the Mexican said deprecatingly. 'What class of pain do you have?'

'Big enough. Clearly not as bad as yours. When the nurse goes out I cry an hour, two hours. It rests me. My nerves are bad now.'

'You have the radio. If I had a private room and a radio I would be crying and yelling all night long.'

'I doubt it.'

'Hombre, si. It's very healthy. But you cannot do it with so many people.'

'At least,' Mr Frazer said, 'the hands are still good. They tell me you make your living with the hands.'

'And the head,' he said, tapping his forehead. 'But the head isn't worth as much.'

'Three of your countrymen were here.'

'Sent by the police to see me.'

'They brought some beer.'

'It probably was bad.'

'It was bad.'

'Tonight, sent by the police, they come to serenade me.' He laughed, then tapped his stomach. 'I cannot laugh yet. As musicians they are fatal.'

'And the one who shot you?'

'Another fool. I won thirty-eight dollars from him at cards. That is not to kill about.'

'The three told me you win much money.'

'And am poorer than the birds.'

'How?'

'I am a poor idealist. I am the victim of illusions.' He laughed, then grinned and tapped his stomach. 'I am a professional gambler but I like to gamble. To really gamble. Little gambling is all crooked. For real gambling you need luck. I have no luck.'

'Never?'

'Never. I am completely without luck. Look, this cabron who shoots me just now. Can he shoot? No. The first shot he fires into nothing. The second is intercepted by a poor Russian. That would seem to be luck. What happens? He shoots me twice in the belly. He is a lucky man. I have no luck. He could not hit a horse if he were holding the stirrup. All luck.'

'I thought he shot you first and the Russian after.'

'No, the Russian first, me after. The paper was mistaken.'

'Why didn't you shoot him?'

'I never carry a gun. With my luck, if I carried a gun I would be hanged ten times a year. I am a cheap card player, only that.' He stopped, then continued. 'When I make a sum of money I gamble and when I gamble I lose. I have passed at dice for three thousand dollars and crapped out for the six. With good dice. More than once.'

'Why continue?'

'If I live long enough the luck will change. I have bad luck now for fifteen years. If I ever get any good luck I will be rich.' He grinned. 'I am a good gambler, really I would enjoy being rich.'

'Do you have bad luck with all games?'

'With everything and with women.' He smiled again, showing his bad teeth.

'Truly?'

'Truly.'

'And what is there to do?'

'Continue, slowly, and wait for luck to change.'

'But with women?'

'No gambler has luck with women. He is too concentrated. He works nights. When he should be with the woman. No man who works nights can hold a woman if the woman is worth anything.'

'You are a philosopher.'

'No, hombre. A gambler of the small towns. One small town, then another, another, then a big town, then start over again.'

'Then shot in the belly.'

'The first time,' he said. 'That has only happened once.'

'I tire you talking?' Mr Frazer suggested.

'No,' he said. 'I must tire you.'

'And the leg?'

'I have no great use for the leg. I am all right with the leg or not. I will be able to circulate.'

'I wish you luck, truly, and with all my heart,' Mr Frazer said.

'Equally,' he said. 'And that the pain stops.'

'It will not last, certainly. It is passing. It is of no importance.'

'That it passes quickly.'

'Equally.'

That night the Mexicans played the accordion and other instruments in the ward and it was cheerful and the noise of the inhalations and exhalations of the accordion, and of the bells, the traps and the drum came down the corridor. In that ward there was a rodeo rider who had come out of the chutes on Midnight on a hot dusty afternoon with the big crowd watching, and now, with a broken back, was going to learn to work in leather and to cane chairs when he got well enough to leave the hospital. There was a carpenter who had fallen with a scaffolding and broken both ankles and both wrists. He had lit like a cat but without a cat's resiliency. They could fix him up so that he could work again but it would take a long time. There was a boy from a farm, about sixteen years old, with a broken leg that had been badly set and was to be rebroken. There was Cayetano Ruiz, a small-town gambler with a paralysed leg. Down the corridor Mr Frazer could hear them all laughing and merry with the music made by the Mexicans who had been sent by the police. The Mexicans were having a good time. They came in, very excited, to see Mr Frazer and wanted to know if there was anything he wanted them to play, and they came twice more to play at night of their own accord.

The last time they played Mr Frazer lay in his room with the door open and listened to the noisy, bad music and could not keep from thinking. When they wanted to know what he wished played, he asked for the 'Cucaracha', which has the sinister lightness and deftness of so many of the tunes men have gone to die to. They played noisily and with emotion. The tune was better than most of such tunes, to Mr Frazer's mind, but the effect was all the same.

In spite of this introduction of emotion, Mr Frazer went on thinking. Usually he avoided thinking all he could, except when he was writing, but now he was thinking about those who were playing and what the little one had said.

Religion is the opium of the people. He believed that, that dyspeptic little joint-keeper. Yes, and music is the opium of the people. Old mount-to-the-head hadn't thought of that. And now economics is the opium of the people; along with patriotism the opium of the people in Italy and Germany. What about sexual intercourse, was that an opium of the people? Of some of the people. Of some of the best of the people. But drink was a sovereign opium of the people, oh, an excellent opium. Although some prefer the radio, another opium of the people, a cheap one he had just been using. Along with these went gambling, an opium of the people if there ever was one, one of the oldest. Ambition was another, an opium of the people, along with a belief in any new form of government. What you wanted was the minimum of government, always less government. Liberty, what we believed in, now the name of a MacFadden publication. We believed in that although they had not found a new name for it yet. But what was the real one? What was the real, the actual, opium of the people? He knew it very well. It was gone just a little way around the corner in that well-lighted part of his mind that was there after two or more drinks in the evening; that he knew was there (it was not really there of course). What was it? He knew very well. What was it? Of course; bread was the opium of the people. Would he remember that and would it make sense in the daylight? Bread is the opium of the people.

'Listen,' Mr Frazer said to the nurse when she came. 'Get that little thin Mexican in here, will you please?'

'How do you like it?' the Mexican said at the door.

'Very much.'

'It is a historic tune,' the Mexican said. 'It is the tune of the real revolution.'

'Listen,' said Mr Frazer. 'Why should the people be operated on without an anaesthetic?'

'I do not understand.'

'Why are not all the opiums of the people good? What do you want to do with the people?'

'They should be rescued from ignorance.'

'Don't talk nonsense. Education is an opium of the people. You ought to know that. You've had a little.'

'You do not believe in education?'

'No,' said Mr Frazer. 'In knowledge, yes.'

'I do not follow you.'

'Many times I do not follow myself with pleasure.'

'You want to hear the "Cucaracha" another time?' asked the Mexican worriedly.

'Yes,' said Mr Frazer. 'Play the "Cucaracha" another time. It's better than the radio.'

Revolution, Mr Frazer thought, is no opium. Revolution is a catharsis; an ecstasy which can only be prolonged by tyranny. The opiums are for before and for after. He was thinking well, a little too well.

They would go now in a little while, he thought, and they would take the 'Cucaracha' with them. Then he would have a little spot of the giant killer and play the radio, you could play the radio so that you could hardly hear it.

FATHERS AND SONS

There had been a sign to detour in the centre of the main street of this town, but cars had obviously gone through, so, believing it was some repair which had been completed, Nicholas Adams drove on through the town along the empty, brick-paved street, stopped by traffic lights that flashed on and off on this traffic-less Sunday, and would be gone next year when the payments on the system were not met; on under the heavy trees of the small town that are a part of your heart if it is your town and you have walked under them, but that are only too heavy, that shut out the sun and that dampen the houses for a stranger; out past the last house and on to the highway that rose and fell straight away ahead with banks of red dirt sliced cleanly away and the second-growth timber on both sides. It was not his country but it was the middle of fall and all of this country was good to drive through and to see. The cotton was picked and in the clearings there were patches of corn, some cut with streaks of red sorghum, and, driving easily, his son asleep on the seat by his side, the day's run made, knowing the town he would reach for the night, Nick noticed which cornfields had soy beans or peas in them, how the thickets and the cut-over land lay, where the cabins and houses were in relation to the fields and the thickets; hunting the country in his mind as he went by; sizing up each clearing as to feed and cover and figuring where you would find a covey and which way they would fly.

In shooting quail you must not get between them and their habitual cover, once the dogs have found them, or when they flush they will come pouring at you, some rising steep, some skimming by your ears, whirring into a size you have never seen them in the air as they pass, the only way being to turn and take them over your shoulder as they go, before they set their wings and angle down into the thicket. Hunting this country for quail as his father taught him, Nicholas Adams started thinking about his father. When he first thought about him it was always the eyes. The big frame, the quick movements, the wide shoulders, the hooked, hawk nose, the beard that covered the weak chin, you never thought about–it was always the eyes. They were protected in his head by the formation of the brows; set deep as though a special protection had been devised for some very valuable instrument. They saw much farther and much quicker than the human eye sees and they were the great gift his father had. His father saw as a big-horn ram or as an eagle sees, literally.

He would be standing with his father on one shore of the lake, his own eyes were very good then, and his father would say, 'They've run up the flag.' Nick would not see the flag at the flag pole. 'There,' his father would say, 'it's your sister Dorothy. She's got the flag up and she's walking out on to the dock.'

Nick would look across the lake and he could see the long wooded shoreline, the higher timber behind, the point that guarded the bay, the clear hills of the farm and the white of their cottage in the trees, but he could not see any flag pole, or any dock, only the white of the beach and the curve of the shore.

'Can you see the sheep on the hillside toward the point?'

'Yes.'

They were a whitish patch on the grey-green of the hill.

'I can count them,' his father said.

Like all men with a faculty that surpasses human requirements, his father was very nervous. Then, too, he was sentimental, and, like most sentimental people, he was both cruel and abused. Also, he had much bad luck, and it was not all of it his own. He had died in a trap that he had helped only a little to set, and they had all betrayed him in their various ways before he died. All sentimental people are betrayed so many times. Nick could not write about him yet, although he would, later, but the quail country made him remember him as he was when Nick was a boy and he was very grateful to him for two things: fishing and shooting. His father was as sound on those two things as he was unsound on sex, for instance, and Nick was glad that it had been that way; for someone has to give you your first gun or the opportunity to get it and use it, and you have to live where there is game or fish if you are to learn about them, and now, at thirty-eight, he loved to fish and to shoot exactly as much as when he first had gone with his father. It was a passion that had never slackened and he was very grateful to his father for bringing him to know it.

While for the other, that his father was not sound about, all the equipment you will ever have is provided and each man learns all there is for him to know about it without advice: and it makes no difference where you live. He remembered very clearly the only two pieces of information his father had given him about that. Once when they were out shooting together Nick shot a red squirrel out of a hemlock tree. The squirrel fell, wounded, and when Nick picked him up bit the boy clean through the ball of the thumb.

'The dirty little bugger,' Nick said and smacked the squirrel's head against the tree. 'Look how he bit me.'

His father looked and said, 'Suck it out clean and put some iodine on when you get home.'

'The little bugger,' Nick said.

'Do you know what a bugger is?' his father asked him.

'We call anything a bugger,' Nick said.

'A bugger is a man who has intercourse with animals.'

'Why?' Nick said.

'I don't know,' his father said. 'But it is a heinous crime.'

Nick's imagination was both stirred and horrified by this and he thought of various animals but none seemed attractive or practical and that was the sum total of direct sexual knowledge bequeathed him by his father except on one other subject. One morning he read in the paper that Enrico Caruso had been arrested for mashing.

'What is mashing?'

'It is one of the most heinous of crimes,' his father answered. Nick's imagination pictured the great tenor doing something strange, bizarre and heinous with a potato masher to a beautiful lady who looked like the pictures of Anna Held on the inside of cigar boxes. He resolved, with considerable horror, that when he was old enough he would try mashing at least once.

His father had summed up the whole matter by stating that masturbation produced blindness, insanity and death, while a man who went with prostitutes would contract hideous venereal diseases and that the thing to do was to keep your hands off of people. On the other hand his father had the finest pair of eyes he had ever seen and Nick had loved him very much and for a long time. Now, knowing how it had all been, even remembering the earliest times before things had gone badly was not good remembering. If he wrote it he could get rid of it. He had gotten rid of many things by writing them. But it was still too early for that. There were still too many people. So he decided to think of something else. There was nothing to do about his father and he had thought it all through many times. The handsome job the undertaker had done on his father's face had not blurred in his mind and all the rest of it was quite clear, including the responsibilities. He had complimented the undertaker. The undertaker had been both proud and smugly pleased. But it was not the undertaker that had given him that last face. The undertaker had only made certain dashingly executed repairs of doubtful artistic merit. The face had been making itself and being made for a long time. It had modelled fast in the last three years. It was a good story but there were still too many people alive for him to write it.

Nick's own education in those earlier matters had been acquired in the hemlock woods behind the Indian camp. This was reached by a trail which ran from the cottage through the woods to the farm and then by a road which wound through the slashings to the camp. Now if he could feel all of that trail with bare feet. First there was the pine-needle loam through the hemlock woods behind the cottage where the fallen logs crumbled into wood dust and long splintered pieces of wood hung like javelins in the trees that had been struck by lightning. You crossed the creek on a log and if you stepped off there was the black muck of the swamp. You climbed a fence out of the woods and the trail was hard in the sun across the field with cropped grass and sheep sorrel and mullen growing and to the left the quaky bog of the creek bottom where the killdeer plover fed. The spring house was in that creek. Below the barn there was fresh warm manure and the other old manure was caked dry on top. Then there was another fence and the hard, hot trail from the barn to the house and the hot sandy road that ran down to the woods, crossing the creek, on a bridge this time, where the cat-tails grew that you soaked in kerosene to make jacklights with for spearing fish at night.

Then the main road went off to the left, skirting the woods and climbing the hill, while you went into the woods on the wide clay and shale road, cool under the trees, and broadened for them to skid out the hemlock bark the Indians cut. The hemlock bark was piled in long rows of stacks, roofed over with more bark, like houses, and the peeled logs lay huge and yellow where the trees had been felled. They left the logs in the woods to rot, they did not even clear away or burn the tops. It was only the bark they wanted for the tannery at Boyne City; hauling it across the lake on the ice in winter, and each year there was less forest and more open, hot, shadeless, weed-grown slashing.

But there was still much forest then, virgin forest where the trees grew high before there were any branches and you walked on the brown, clean, springy-needled ground with no undergrowth and it was cool on the hottest days and they three lay against the truck of a hemlock wider than two beds are long, with the breeze high in the tops and the cool light that came in patches, and Billy said:

'You want Trudy again?'

'You want to?'

'Uh Huh.'

'Come on.'

'No, here.'

'But Billy—'

'I no mind Billy. He my brother.'

Then afterwards they sat, the three of them, listening for a black squirrel that was in the top branches where they could not see him. They were waiting for him to bark again because when he barked he would jerk his tail and Nick would shoot where he saw any movement. His father gave him only three cartridges a day to hunt with and he had a single-barrel twenty-gauge shotgun with a very long barrel.

'Son of a bitch never move,' Billy said.

'You shoot, Nickie. Scare him. We see him jump. Shoot him again,' Trudy said. It was a long speech for her.

'I've only got two shells,' Nick said.

'Son of a bitch,' said Billy.

They sat against the tree and were quiet. Nick was feeling hollow and happy.

'Eddie says he going to come some night sleep in bed with your sister Dorothy.'

'What?'

'He said.'

Trudy nodded.

'That's all he want do,' she said. Eddie was their older half-brother. He was seventeen.

'If Eddie Gilby ever comes at night and even speaks to Dorothy you know what I'd do to him? I'd kill him like this.' Nick cocked the gun and hardly taking aim pulled the trigger, blowing a hole as big as your hand in the head or belly of that half-breed bastard Eddie Gilby. 'Like that. I'd kill him like that.'

'He better not come then,' Trudy said. She put her hand in Nick's pocket.

'He'd better watch out plenty,' said Billy.

'He's a big bluff.' Trudy was exploring with her hand in Nick's pocket. 'But don't you kill him. You get plenty trouble.'

'I'd kill him like that,' Nick said. Eddie Gilby lay on the ground with all his chest shot away. Nick put his foot on him proudly.

'I'd scalp him,' he said happily.

'No,' said Trudy. 'That's dirty.'

'I'd scalp him and send it to his mother.'

'His mother dead,' Trudy said. 'Don't you kill him, Nickie. Don't you kill him for me.'

'After I scalped him I'd throw him to the dogs.'

Billy was very depressed. 'He better watch out,' he said gloomily.

'They'd tear him to pieces,' Nick said, pleased with the picture. Then, having scalped that half-breed renegade and standing, watching the dogs tear him, his face unchanging, he fell backward against the tree, held tight around the neck, Trudy holding him, choking him, and crying, 'No kill him! No kill him! No kill him! No. No. No. Nickie. Nickie. Nickie!'

'What's the matter with you?'

'No kill him.'

'I got to kill him.'

'He's just a big bluff.'

'All right,' Nickie said. 'I won't kill him unless he comes around the house. Let go of me.'

'That's good,' Trudy said. 'You want to do anything now? I feel good now.'

'If Billy goes away.' Nick had killed Eddie Gilby, then pardoned him his life, and he was a man now.

'You go, Billy. You hang around all the time. Go on.'

'Son a bitch,' Billy said. 'I get tired this. What we come? Hunt or what?'

'You can take the gun. There's one shell.'

'All right. I get a big black one all right.'

'I'll holler,' Nick said.

Then, later, it was a long time after and Billy was still away.

'You think we make a baby?' Trudy folded her brown legs together happily and rubbed against him. Something inside Nick had gone a long way away.

'I don't think so,' he said.

'Make plenty baby what the hell.'

They heard Billy shoot.

'I wonder if he got one.'

'Don't care,' said Trudy.

Billy came through the trees. He had the gun over his shoulder and he held a black squirrel by the front paws.

'Look,' he said, 'bigger than a cat. You all through?'

'Where'd you get him?'

'Over there. Saw him jump first.'

'Got to go home,' Nick said.

'No,' said Trudy.

'I got to get there for supper.'

'All right.'

'Want to hunt tomorrow?'

'All right.'

'You can have the squirrel.'

'All right.'

'Come out after supper?'

'No.'

'How you feel?'

'Good.'

'All right.'

'Give me kiss on the face,' said Trudy.

Now, as he rode along the highway in the car and it was getting dark, Nick was all through thinking about his father. The end of the day never made him think of him. The end of the day had always belonged to Nick alone and he never felt right unless he was alone at it. His father came back to him in the fall of the year, or in the early spring when there had been jacksnipe on the prairie, or when he saw shocks of corn, or when he saw a lake, or if he ever saw a horse and buggy, or when he saw, or heard, wild geese, or in a duck blind; remembering the time an eagle dropped through the whirling snow to strike a canvas-covered decoy, rising, his wings beating, the talons caught in the canvas. His father was with him, suddenly, in deserted orchards and in new-ploughed fields, in thickets, on small hills, or when going through dead grass, whenever splitting wood or hauling water, by grist mills, cider mills and dams and always with open fires. The towns he lived in were not towns his father knew. After he was fifteen he had shared nothing with him.

His father had frost in his beard in cold weather and in hot weather he sweated very much. He liked to work in the sun on the farm because he did not have to and he loved manual work, which Nick did not. Nick loved his father but hated the smell of him and once when he had to wear a suit of his father's underwear that had gotten too small for his father it made him feel sick and he took it off and put it under two stones in the creek and said that he had lost it. He had told his father how it was when his father had made him put it on but his father had said it was freshly washed. It had been, too. When Nick had asked him to smell of it his father sniffed at it indignantly and said that it was clean and fresh. When Nick came home from fishing without it and said he lost it he was whipped for lying.

Afterwards he had sat inside the woodshed with the door open, his shotgun loaded and cocked, looking across at his father sitting on the screen porch reading the paper, and thought, 'I can blow him to hell. I can kill him.' Finally he felt his anger go out of him and he felt a little sick about it being the gun that his father had given him. Then he had gone to the Indian camp, walking there in the dark, to get rid of the smell. There was only one person in his family that he liked the smell of; one sister. All the others he avoided all contact with. That sense blunted when he started to smoke. It was a good thing. It was good for a bird dog but it did not help a man.

'What was it like, Papa, when you were a little boy and used to hunt with the Indians?'

'I don't know,' Nick was startled. He had not even noticed the boy was awake. He looked at him sitting beside him on the seat. He had felt quite alone but this boy had been with him. He wondered for how long. 'We used to go all day to hunt black squirrels,' he said. 'My father only gave me three shells a day because he said that would teach me to hunt and it wasn't good for a boy to go banging around. I went with a boy named Billy Gilby and his sister Trudy. We used to go out nearly every day all one summer.'

'Those are funny names for Indians.'

'Yes, aren't they,' Nick said.

'But tell me what they were like.'

'They were Ojibways,' Nick said. 'And they were very nice.'

'But what were they like to be with?'

'It's hard to say,' Nick Adams said. Could you say she did first what no one has ever done better and mention plump brown legs, flat belly, hard little breasts, well holding arms, quick searching tongue, the flat eyes, the good taste of mouth, then uncomfortably, tightly, sweetly, moistly, lovely, tightly, achingly, fully, finally, unendingly, never-endingly, never-to-endingly, suddenly ended, the great bird flown like an owl in the twilight, only in daylight in the woods and hemlock needles stuck against your belly. So that when you go in a place where Indians have lived you smell them gone and all the empty pain killer bottles and the flies that buzz do not kill the sweetgrass smell, the smoke smell and that other like a fresh cased marten skin. Nor any jokes about them nor old squaws take that away. Nor the sick sweet smell they get to have. Nor what they did finally. It wasn't how they ended. They all ended the same. Long time ago good. Now no good.

And about the other. When you have shot one bird flying you have shot all birds flying. They are all different and they fly in different ways but the sensation is the same and the last one is as good as the first. He could thank his father for that.

'You might not like them,' Nick said to the boy. 'But I think you would.'

'And my grandfather lived with them too when he was a boy, didn't he?'

'Yes. When I asked him what they were like he said that he had many friends among them.'

'Will I ever live with them?'

'I don't know,' Nick said. 'That's up to you.'

'How old will I be when I get a shotgun and can hunt by myself?'

'Twelve years old if I see you are careful.'

'I wish I was twelve now.'

'You will be, soon enough.'

'What was my grandfather like? I can't remember him except that he gave me an air rifle and an American flag when I came over from France that time. What was he like?'

'He's hard to describe. He was a great hunter and fisherman and he had wonderful eyes.'

'Was he greater than you?'

'He was a much better shot and his father was a great wing shot too.'

'I'll bet he wasn't better than you.'

'Oh, yes he was. He shot very quickly and beautifully. I'd rather see him shoot than any man I ever knew. He was always very disappointed in the way I shot.'

'Why do we never go to pray at the tomb of my grandfather?'

'We live in a different part of the country. It's a long way from here.'

'In France that wouldn't make any difference. In France we'd go. I think I ought to go to pray at the tomb of my grandfather.'

'Some time we'll go.'

'I hope we won't live somewhere so that I can never go to pray at your tomb when you are dead.'

'We'll have to arrange it.'

'Don't you think we might all be buried at a convenient place? We could all be buried in France. That would be fine.'

'I don't want to be buried in France,' Nick said.

'Well, then, we'll have to get some convenient place in America. Couldn't we all be buried out at the ranch?'

'That's an idea.'

'Then I could stop and pray at the tomb of my grandfather on the way to the ranch.'

'You're awfully practical.'

'Well, I don't feel good never to have even visited the tomb of my grandfather.'

'We'll have to go,' Nick said. 'I can see we'll have to go.'

HOMAGE TO SWITZERLAND

I

PORTRAIT OF MR WHEELER IN MONTREUX

Inside the station café it was warm and light. The wood of the tables shone from wiping and there were baskets of pretzels in glazed paper sacks. The chairs were carved, but the seats were worn and comfortable. There was a carved wooden clock on the wall and a bar at the far end of the room. Outside the window it was snowing.

Two of the station porters sat drinking new wine at the table under the clock. Another porter came in and said the Simplon-Orient Express was an hour late at Saint-Maurice. He went out. The waitress came over to Mr Wheeler's table.

'The Express is an hour late, sir,' she said. 'Can I bring you some coffee?'

'If you think it won't keep me awake.'

'Please?' asked the waitress.

'Bring me some,' said Mr Wheeler.

'Thank you.'

She brought the coffee from the kitchen and Mr Wheeler looked out the window at the snow falling in the light from the station platform.

'Do you speak other languages beside English?' he asked the waitress.

'Oh, yes, sir, I speak German and French and the dialects.'

'Would you like a drink or something?'

'Oh, no, sir. It is not permitted to drink in the café with the clients.'

'You won't take a cigar?'

'Oh, no, sir. I don't smoke, sir.'

'That is all right,' said Mr Wheeler. He looked out of the window again, drank the coffee, and lit a cigarette.

'Fraulein,' he called. The waitress came over.

'What would you like, sir?'

'You,' he said.

'You must not joke me like that.'

'I'm not joking.'

'Then you must not say it.'

'I haven't time to argue,' Mr Wheeler said. 'The train comes in forty minutes. If you'll go upstairs with me I'll give you a hundred francs.'

'You should not say such things, sir. I will ask the porter to speak with you.'

'I don't want a porter,' Mr Wheeler said. 'Nor a policeman, nor one of those boys that sell cigarettes. I want you.'

'If you talk like that you must go out. You cannot stay here and talk like that.'

'Why don't you go away then? If you go away I can't talk to you.'

The waitress went away. Mr Wheeler watched to see if she spoke to the porters. She did not.

'Mademoiselle!' he called. The waitress came over. 'Bring me a bottle of Sion, please.'

'Yes, sir.'

Mr Wheeler watched her go out, then come in with the wine and bring it to his table. He looked toward the clock.

'I'll give you two hundred francs,' he said.

'Please do not say such things.'

'Two hundred francs is a great deal of money.'

'You will not say such things!' the waitress said. She was losing her English. Mr Wheeler looked at her interestedly.

'Two hundred francs.'

'You are hateful.'

'Why don't you go away then? I can't talk to you if you're not here.'

The waitress left the table and went over to the bar. Mr Wheeler drank the wine and smiled to himself for some time.

'Mademoiselle,' he called. The waitress pretended not to hear him. 'Mademoiselle,' he called again. The waitress came over.

'You wish something?'

'Very much. I'll give you three hundred francs.'

'You are hateful.'

'Three hundred francs Swiss.'

She went away and Mr Wheeler looked after her. A porter opened the door. He was the one who had Mr Wheeler's bags in his charge.

'The train is coming, sir,' he said in French. Mr Wheeler stood up.

'Mademoiselle,' he called. The waitress came toward the table. 'How much is the wine?'

'Seven francs.'

Mr Wheeler counted out eight francs and left them on the table. He put on his coat and followed the porter on to the platform where the snow was falling.

'Au revoir, Mademoiselle,' he said. The waitress watched him go. He's ugly, she thought, ugly and hateful. Three hundred francs for a thing that is nothing to do. How many times have I done that for nothing. And no place to go here. If he had sense he would know there was no place. No time and no place to go. Three hundred francs to do that. What people those Americans.

Standing on the cement platform beside his bags, looking down the rails toward the headlight of the train coming through the snow, Mr Wheeler was thinking that it was very inexpensive sport. He had only spent, actually, aside from the dinner, seven francs for a bottle of wine and a franc for the tip. Seventy-five centimes would have been better. He would have felt better now if the tip had been seventy-five centimes. One franc Swiss is five francs French. Mr Wheeler was headed for Paris. He was very careful about money and did not care for women. He had been in that station before and he knew there was no upstairs to go to. Mr Wheeler never took chances.

2

MR JOHNSON TALKS ABOUT IT AT VEVEY

Inside the station café it was warm and light; the tables were shiny from wiping and on some there were red and white striped tablecloths; and there were blue and white striped tablecloths on others and on all of them baskets with pretzels in glazed paper sacks. The chairs were carved but the wood seats were worn and comfortable. There was a clock on the wall, a zinc bar at the far end of the room, and outside the window it was snowing. Two of the station porters sat drinking new wine at the table under the clock.

Another porter came in and said the Simplon-Orient Express was an hour late at Saint-Maurice. The waitress came over to Mr Johnson's table.

'The Express is an hour late, sir,' she said. 'Can I bring you some coffee?'

'If it's not too much trouble.'

'Please?' asked the waitress.

'I'll take some.'

'Thank you.'

She brought the coffee from the kitchen and Mr Johnson looked out the window at the snow falling in the light from the station platform.

'Do you speak other languages besides English?' he asked the waitress.

'Oh, yes, I speak German and French and the dialects.'

'Would you like a drink of something?'

'Oh, no, sir, it is not permitted to drink in the café with the clients.'

'Have a cigar?'

'Oh, no, sir,' she laughed. 'I don't smoke, sir.'

'Neither do I,' said Johnson. 'It's a dirty habit.'

The waitress went away and Johnson lit a cigarette and drank the coffee. The clock on the wall marked a quarter to ten. His watch was a little fast. The train was due at ten-thirty–an hour late meant eleven-thirty. Johnson called to the waitress.

'Signorina!'

'What would you like, sir?'

'You wouldn't like to play with me?' Johnson asked. The waitress blushed.

'No, sir.'

'I don't mean anything violent. You wouldn't like to make up a party to see the night life of Vevey? Bring a girl friend if you like.'

'I must work,' the waitress said. 'I have my duty here.'

'I know,' said Johnson. 'But couldn't you get a substitute? They used to do that in the Civil War.'

'Oh, no, sir. I must be here myself in person.'

'Where did you learn your English?'

'At the Berlitz school, sir.'

'Tell me about it,' Johnson said. 'Were the Berlitz undergraduates a wild lot? What about all this necking and petting? Were there many smoothies? Did you ever run into Scott Fitzgerald?'

'Please?'

'I mean were your college days the happiest days of your life? What sort of team did Berlitz have last fall?'

'You are joking, sir?'

'Only feebly,' said Johnson. 'You're an awfully good girl. And you don't want to play with me?'

'Oh, no, sir,' said the waitress. 'Would you like me to bring you something?'

'Yes,' said Johnson. 'Would you bring me the wine list?'

'Yes, sir.'

Johnson walked over with the wine list to the table where the three porters sat. They looked up at him. They were old men.

'Wollen Sie trinken?' he asked. One of them nodded and smiled.

'Oui, monsieur.'

'You speak French?'

'Oui, monsieur.'

'What shall we drink? Connais vous des champagnes?'

'Non, monsieur.'

'Faut les connaitre,' said Johnson. 'Fraulein,' he called the waitress. 'We will drink champagne.'

'Which champagne would you prefer, sir?'

'The best,' said Johnson. 'Laquelle est le best?' he asked the porters.

'Le meilleur?' asked the porter who had spoken first.

'By all means.'

The porter took out a pair of gold-rimmed glasses from his coat pocket and looked over the list. He ran his finger down the four typewritten names and prices.

'Sportsman,' he said. 'Sportsman is the best.'

'You agree, gentlemen?' Johnson asked the other porters. The one porter nodded. The other said in French, 'I don't know them personally but I've often heard speak of Sportsman. It's good.'

'A bottle of Sportsman,' Johnson said to the waitress. He looked at the price on the wine card: eleven francs Swiss. 'Make it two Sportsmen. Do you mind if I sit here with you?' he asked the porter who had suggested Sportsman.

'Sit down. Put yourself here, please.' The porter smiled at him. He was folding his spectacles and putting them away in their case. 'Is it the gentleman's birthday?'

'No,' said Johnson. 'It's not a fete. My wife has decided to divorce me.'

'So,' said the porter. 'I hope not.' The other porter shook his head. The third porter seemed a little deaf.

'It is doubtless a common experience,' said Johnson, 'like the first visit to the dentist or the first time a girl is unwell, but I have been upset.'

'It is understandable,' said the oldest porter. 'I understand it.'

'None of you gentlemen is divorced?' Johnson asked. He had stopped clowning with the language and was speaking good French now and had been for some time.

'No,' said the porter who had ordered Sportsman. 'They don't divorce much here. There are gentlemen who are divorced but not many.'

'With us,' said Johnson, 'it's different. Practically everyone is divorced.'

'That's true,' the porter confirmed. 'I've read it in the paper.'

'I myself am somewhat in retard,' Johnson went on. 'This is the first time I have been divorced. I am thirty-five.'

'Mais vous êtes encore jeune,' said the porter. He explained to the two others. 'Monsieur n'a que trente-cinq ans.' The other porters nodded. 'He's very young,' said one.

'And it is really the first time you've been divorced?' asked the porter.

'Absolutely,' said Johnson. 'Please open the wine, mademoiselle.'

'And it is very expensive?'

'Ten thousand francs.'

'Swiss money?'

'No, French money.'

'Oh, yes. Two thousand francs Swiss. All the same it's not cheap.'

'No.'

'And why does one do it?'

'One is asked to.'

'But why do they ask that?'

'To marry someone else.'

'But it's idiotic.'

'I agree with you,' said Johnson. The waitress filled the four glasses. They all raised them.

'Prosit,' said Johnson.

'À votre santé, monsieur,' said the porter. The other two porters said 'Salut'. The champagne tasted like sweet pink cider.

'Is it a system always to respond in a different language in Switzerland?' Johnson asked.

'No,' said the porter. 'French is more cultivated. Besides, this is la Suisse Romande.'

'But you speak German?'

'Yes. Where I come from they speak German.'

'I see,' said Johnson, 'and you say you have never been divorced?'

'No. It would be too expensive. Besides, I have never married.'

'Ah,' said Johnson. 'And these other gentlemen?'

'They are married.'

'You like being married?' Johnson asked one of the porters.

'What?'

'You like the married state?'

'Oui. C'est normale.'

'Exactly,' said Johnson. 'Et vous, monsieur?'

'Ça va,' said the other porter.

'Pour moi,' said Johnson, 'ça ne va pas.'

'Monsieur is going to divorce,' the first porter explained.

'Oh,' said the second porter.

'Ah ha,' the third porter said.

'Well,' said Johnson, 'the subject seems to be exhausted. You're not interested in my troubles,' he addressed the first porter.

'But yes,' said the porter.

'Well, let's talk about something else.'

'As you wish.'

'What can we talk about?'

'You do the sport?'

'No,' said Johnson. 'My wife does, though.'

'What do you do for amusement?'

'I am a writer.'

'Does that make much money?'

'No. But later on when you get known it does.'

'It is interesting?'

'No,' said Johnson, 'it is not interesting. I am sorry, gentlemen, but I have to leave you. Will you please drink the other bottle?'

'But the train does not come for three-quarters of an hour.'

'I know,' said Johnson. The waitress came and he paid for the wine and his dinner.

'You going out, sir?' she asked.

'Yes,' said Johnson, 'just for a little walk. I'll leave my bag here.'

He put on his muffler, his coat, and his hat. Outside the snow was falling heavily. He looked back through the window at the three porters sitting at the table. The waitress was filling their glasses from the last wine of the opened bottle. She took the unopened bottle back to the bar. That makes them three francs something apiece, Johnson thought. He turned and walked down the platform. Inside the café he had thought that talking about it would blunt it; but it had not blunted it; it had only made him feel nasty.

3

THE SON OF A FELLOW MEMBER AT TERRITET

In the station café at Territet it was a little too warm; the lights were bright and the tables shiny from polishing. There were baskets with pretzels in glazed paper sacks on the tables and cardboard pads for beer glasses in order that the moist glasses would not make rings on the wood. The chairs were carved but the wooden seats were worn and quite comfortable. There was a clock on the wall, a bar at the far end of the room, and outside the window it was snowing. There was an old man drinking coffee at a table under the clock and reading the evening paper. A porter came in and said the

Simplon-Orient Express was an hour late at Saint-Maurice. The waitress came over to Mr Harris's table. Mr Harris had just finished dinner.

'The Express is an hour late, sir. Can I bring you some coffee?'

'If you like.'

'Please?' asked the waitress.

'All right,' said Mr Harris.

'Thank you, sir,' said the waitress.

She brought the coffee from the kitchen and Mr Harris put sugar in it, crunched the lumps with his spoons, and looked out of the window at the snow falling in the light from the station platform.

'Do you speak other languages besides English?' he asked the waitress.

'Oh, yes, sir. I speak German and French and the dialects.'

'Which do you like best?'

'They are all very much the same, sir. I can't say I like one better than another.'

'Would you like a drink of something or a coffee?'

'Oh, no, sir, it is not permitted to drink in the café with the clients.'

'You wouldn't take a cigar?'

'Oh, no, sir,' she laughed. 'I don't smoke, sir.'

'Neither do I,' said Harris. 'I don't agree with David Belasco.'

'Please?'

'Belasco. David Belasco. You can always tell him because he has his collar on backwards. But I don't agree with him. Then, too, he's dead now.'

'Will you excuse me, sir?' asked the waitress.

'Absolutely,' said Harris. He sat forward in the chair and looked out of the window. Across the room the old man had folded his paper. He looked at Mr Harris and then picked up his coffee cup and saucer and walked to Harris's table.

'I beg your pardon if I intrude,' he said in English, 'but it has just occurred to me that you might be a member of the National Geographic Society.'

'Please sit down,' Harris said. The gentleman sat down.

'Won't you have another coffee or a liqueur?'

'Thank you,' said the gentleman.

'Won't you have a kirsch with me?'

'Perhaps. But you must have it with me.'

'No, I insist.' Harris called the waitress. The old gentleman took out from an inside pocket of his coat a leather pocket-book. He took off a wide rubber band and drew out several papers, selected one, and handed it to Harris.

'That is my certificate of membership,' he said. 'Do you know Frederick J. Roussel in America?'

'I'm afraid I don't.'

'I believe he is very prominent.'

'Where does he come from? Do you know what part of the States?'

'From Washington, of course. Isn't that the headquarters of the Society?'

'I believe it is.'

'You believe it is. Aren't you sure?'

'I've been away a long time,' Harris said.

'You're not a member, then?'

'No. But my father is. He's been a member for a great many years.'

'Then he would know Frederick J. Roussel. He is one of the officers of the Society. You will observe that it is by Mr Roussel that I was nominated for membership.'

'I'm awfully glad.'

'I am sorry you are not a member. But you could obtain nomination through your father?'

'I think so,' said Harris. 'I must when I go back.'

'I would advise you to,' said the gentleman. 'You see the magazine, of course?'

'Absolutely.'

'Have you seen the number with the coloured plates of the North America fauna?'

'Yes. I have it in Paris.'

'And the number containing the panorama of the volcanoes of Alaska?'

'That was a wonder.'

'I enjoyed very much, too, the wild animal photographs of George Shiras three.'

'They were damned fine.'

'I beg your pardon?'

'They were excellent. That fellow Shiras—'

'You call him that fellow?'

'We're old friends,' said Harris.

'I see. You know George Shiras three. He must be very interesting.'

'He is. He's about the most interesting man I know.'

'And do you know George Shiras two? Is he interesting too?'

'Oh, he's not so interesting.'

'I should imagine he would be very interesting.'

'You know, a funny thing. He's not so interesting. I've often wondered why.'

'H'm,' said the gentleman. 'I should have thought anyone in that family would be interesting.'

'Do you remember the panorama of the Sahara Desert?' Harris asked.

'The Sahara Desert? That was nearly fifteen years ago.'

'That's right. That was one of my father's favourites.'

'He doesn't prefer the newer numbers?'

'He probably does. But he was very fond of the Sahara panorama.'

'It was excellent. But to me its artistic value far exceeded its scientific interest.'

'I don't know,' said Harris. 'The wind blowing all that sand and that Arab with his camel kneeling toward Mecca.'

'As I recall, the Arab was standing holding the camel.'

'You're quite right,' said Harris. 'I was thinking of Colonel Lawrence's book.'

'Lawrence's book deals with Arabia, I believe.'

'Absolutely,' said Harris. 'It was the Arab reminded me of it.'

'He must be a very interesting young man.'

'I believe he is.'

'Do you know what he is doing now?'

'He's in the Royal Air Force.'

'And why does he do that?'

'He likes it.'

'Do you know if he belongs to the National Geographic Society?'

'I wonder if he does.'

'He would make a very good member. He is the sort of person they want as a member. I would be very happy to nominate him if you think they would like to have him.'

'I think they would.'

'I have nominated a scientist from Vevey and a colleague of mine from Lausanne and they were both elected. I believe they would be very pleased if I nominated Colonel Lawrence.'

'It's a splendid idea,' said Harris. 'Do you come here to the café often?'

'I come here for coffee after dinner.'

'Are you in the University?'

'I am not active any longer.'

'I'm just waiting for the train,' said Harris. 'I'm going up to Paris and sail from Havre for the States.'

'I have never been to America. But I would like to go very much. Perhaps I shall attend a meeting of the society some time. I would be very happy to meet your father.'

'I'm sure he would have liked to meet you but he died last year. Shot himself, oddly enough.'

'I am very truly sorry. I am sure his loss was a blow to science as well as to his family.'

'Science took it awfully well.'

'This is my card,' Harris said. 'His initials were E.J. instead of E.D. I know he would have liked to know you.'

'It would have been a great pleasure.' The gentleman took out a card from the pocket-book and gave it to Harris. It read:

DR SIGISMUND WYER, PH.D.

Member of the National Geographic Society, Washington, D.C., U.S.A.

'I will keep it very carefully,' Harris said.

HEMI

IGWAY

Across the River and into the Trees

I

They started two hours before daylight, and at first, it was not necessary to break the ice across the canal as other boats had gone on ahead. In each boat, in the darkness, so you could not see, but only hear him, the poler stood in the stern, with his long oar. The shooter sat on a shooting stool fastened to the top of a box that contained his lunch and shells, and the shooter's two, or more, guns were propped against the load of wooden decoys. Somewhere, in each boat, there was a sack with one or two live mallard hens, or a hen and a drake, and in each boat there was a dog who shifted and shivered uneasily at the sound of the wings of the ducks that passed overhead in the darkness.

Four of the boats went on up the main canal towards the big lagoon to the north. A fifth boat had already turned off into a side canal. Now, the sixth boat turned south into a shallow lagoon, and there was no broken water.

It was all ice, new-frozen during the sudden, windless cold of the night. It was rubbery and bending against the thrust of the boatman's oar. Then it would break as sharply as a pane of glass, but the boat made little forward progress.

'Give me an oar,' the shooter in the sixth boat said. He stood up and braced himself carefully. He could hear the ducks passing in the darkness, and feel the restless lurching of the dog. To the north he heard the sound of breaking ice from the other boats.

'Be careful,' the poler in the stern said. 'Don't tip the boat over,'

'I am a boatman, too,' the shooter said.

He took the long oar the boatman handed him and reversed it so he could hold it by the blade. Holding the blade he reached forward and punched the handle through the ice. He felt the firm bottom of the shallow lagoon, put his weight on the top of the wide oar-blade, and holding with both hands and, first pulling, then shoving, until the pole-hold was well to the stern, he drove the boat ahead to break the ice. The ice broke like sheets of plate glass as the boat drove into it, and on to it, and astern the boatman shoved them ahead into the broken passage.

After a while, the shooter, who was working hard and steadily, and sweating in his heavy clothes, asked the boatman, 'Where is the shooting barrel?'

'Off there to the left. In the middle of the next bay.'

'Should I turn for it now?'

'As you wish.'

'What do you mean, as I wish? You know the water. Is there water to carry us there?'

'The tide is low. Who knows?'

'It will be daylight before we get there if we don't hurry.'

The boatman did not answer.

All right, you surly jerk, the shooter thought to himself. We are going to get there. We've made two-thirds of the way now and if you are worried about having to work to break ice to pick up birds, that is altogether too bad.

'Get your back in it, jerk,' he said in English.

'What?' the boatman asked in Italian.

'I said let's go. It's going to be light.'

It was daylight before they reached the oaken-staved hogshead sunk in the bottom of the lagoon. It was surrounded by a sloping rim of earth that had been planted with sedge and grass, and the shooter swung carefully up on to this, feeling the frozen grasses break as he stepped on them. The boatman lifted the combination shooting stool and shell box out of the boat and handed it to the shooter, who leaned over and placed it in the bottom of the big barrel.

The shooter, wearing his hip boots and an old combat jacket, with a patch on the left shoulder that no one understood, and with the slight light places on the straps, where stars had been removed, climbed down into the barrel and the boatman handed him his two guns.

He placed them against the wall of the barrel and hung his other shell bag between them, hanging it on two hooks built into the wall of the sunken barrel. Then he leaned the guns against each side of the shell bag.

'Is there water?' he asked the boatman.

'No water,' the boatman said.

'Can you drink the lagoon water?'

'No. It is unhealthy.'

The shooter was thirsty from the hard work of breaking the ice and driving the boat in and he felt his anger rise, and then held it, and said, 'Can I help you in the boat to break ice to put out the decoys?'

'No,' the boatman said and shoved the boat savagely out on to the thin sheet ice that cracked and ripped as the boat drove up on it. The boatman commenced smashing at the ice with the blade of his oar and then started tossing decoys out to the side and behind him.

He's in a beautiful mood, the shooter thought. He's a big brute, too. I worked like a horse coming out here. He just pulled his weight and that's all. What the hell is eating him? This is his trade, isn't it?

He arranged the shooting stool so he would have the maximum swing to left and right, opened a box of shells, and filled his pockets and opened another of the boxes of shells in the shell bag so he could reach into it easily. In front of him, where the lagoon lay glazed in the first light, was the black boat and the tall, heavily built boatman smashing with his oar at the ice and tossing decoys overboard as though he were ridding himself of something obscene.

It was getting lighter now and the shooter could see the low line of the near point across the lagoon. Beyond that point he knew there were two other shooting posts and far beyond it there was more marsh and then the open sea. He loaded both his guns and checked the position of the boat that was putting out decoys.

From behind him, he heard the incoming whisper of wings and he crouched, took hold of his right-hand gun with his right hand as he looked up from under the rim of the barrel, then stood to shoot at the two ducks that were dropping down, their wings set to brake, coming down dark in the grey dim sky, slanting towards the decoys.

His head low, he swung the gun on a long slant, down, well and ahead of the second duck, then without looking at the result of his shot he raised the gun smoothly, up, up ahead and to the left of the other duck that was climbing to the left and as he pulled, saw it fold in flight and drop among the decoys in the broken ice. He looked to his right and saw the first duck a black patch on the same ice. He knew he had shot carefully on the first duck, far to the right of where the boat was and on the second, high out and to the left, letting the duck climb far up and to the left to be sure the boat was out of any line of fire. It was a lovely double, shot exactly as he should have shot, with complete consideration and respect for the position of the boat and he felt very good as he reloaded.

'Listen,' the man in the boat called. 'Don't shoot towards the boat.'

I'll be a sad son of a bitch, the shooter said to himself. I will indeed.

'Get your decoys out,' he called to the man in the boat. 'But get them out fast. I won't shoot until they are all out. Except straight overhead.'

The man in the boat said nothing that could be heard.

I can't figure it, the shooter thought to himself. He knows the game. He knows I split the work, or more, coming out. I never shot a safer or more careful duck in my life than that. What's the matter with him? I offered to put the dekes out with him. The hell with him.

Out on the right now, the boatman was still chopping angrily at the ice and tossing out the wooden decoys in a hatred that showed in every move he made.

Don't let him spoil it, the shooter told himself. There won't be much shooting with this ice unless the sun should melt it later on. You probably will only have a few birds, so don't let him spoil it for you. You don't know how many more times you will shoot ducks and do not let anything spoil it for you.

He watched the sky lightening beyond the long point of marsh and turning in the sunken barrel, he looked out across the frozen lagoon and the marsh and saw the snow-covered mountains a long way off. Low as he was, no foot-hills showed and the mountains rose abruptly from the plain. As he looked towards the mountains he could feel a breeze on his face and he knew then, the wind would come from there, rising with the sun and that some birds would surely come flying in from the sea when the wind disturbed them.

The boatman had finished putting out the decoys. They were in two bunches, one straight ahead and to the left towards where the sun would rise and the other to the shooter's right. Now he dropped over the hen mallard with her string and anchor and the calling duck bobbed her head under water and raising and dipping her head, splashed water on to her back.

'Don't you think it would be good to break more ice around the edges?' the shooter called to the boatman. 'There's not much water to attract them.'

The boatman said nothing but commenced to smash at the jagged perimeter of ice with his oar. This ice breaking was unnecessary and the boatman knew it. But the shooter did not know it and he thought, I do not understand him but I must not let him ruin it. I must keep it entire and not let him do it. Every time you shoot now can be the last shoot and no stupid son of a bitch should be allowed to ruin it. Keep your temper, boy, he told himself.

2

But he was not a boy. He was fifty and a Colonel of Infantry in the Army of the United States and to pass a physical examination that he had to take the day before he came down to Venice for this shoot, he had taken enough mannitol hexanitrate to, well he did not quite know what to—to pass, he said to himself.

The surgeon had been quite sceptical. But he noted the readings after taking them twice.

'You know, Dick,' he said. 'It isn't indicated; in fact it is definitely contra-indicated in increased intra-ocular and intra-cranial pressure.'

'I don't know what you are talking about,' the shooter, who was not a shooter, then, except potentially, and was a Colonel of Infantry in the Army of the United States, reduced from being a general officer, said.

'I have known you a long time, Colonel. Or maybe it just seems a long time,' the surgeon told him.

'It's been a long time,' the Colonel said.

'We sound like song writers,' the surgeon said. 'But don't you ever run into anything, or let any sparks strike you, when you're really souped up on nitroglycerin. They ought to make you drag a chain like a high-octane truck.'

'Wasn't my cardiograph okay?' the Colonel asked.

'Your cardiograph was wonderful, Colonel. It could have been that of a man of twenty-five. It might have been that of a boy of nineteen.'

'Then what are you talking about?' the Colonel asked.

That much mannitol hexanitrate produced a certain amount of nausea, sometimes, and he was anxious for the interview to terminate. He was also anxious to lie down and take a Seconal. I ought to write the manual of minor tactics for the heavy pressure platoon, he thought. Wish I could tell him that. Why don't I just throw myself on the mercy of the court? You never do, he told himself. You always plead them non-guilty.

'How many times have you been hit in the head?' the surgeon asked him.

'You know,' the Colonel told him. 'It's in my 201.'

'How many times have you been hit *on* the head?'

'Oh Christ.' Then he said. 'You are asking for the army or as my physician?'

'As your physician. You didn't think I'd try to wind your clock did you?'

'No, Wes. I'm sorry. Just what was it you wanted to know?'

'Concussions.'

'Real ones?'

'Any time you were cold or couldn't remember afterwards.'

'Maybe ten,' the Colonel said. 'Counting polo. Give or take three.'

'You poor old son of a bitch,' the surgeon said. 'Colonel, sir,' he added.

'Can I go now?' the Colonel asked.

'Yes, sir,' the surgeon said. 'You're in good shape.'

'Thanks,' the Colonel said. 'Want to go on a duck shoot down in the marshes at the mouth of the Tagliamento? Wonderful shoot. Some nice Italian kids I met up at Cortina own it.'

'Is that where they shoot coots?'

'No. They shoot real ducks at this one. Good kids. Good shoot. Real ducks. Mallard, pin-tail, widgeon. Some geese. Just as good as at home when we were kids.'

'I was kids in 'twenty-nine and 'thirty.'

'That's the first mean thing I ever heard you say.'

'I didn't mean it like that. I just meant I didn't remember when duck shooting was good. I'm a city boy, too.'

'That's the only goddamn trouble with you, too. I never saw a city boy yet that was worth a damn.'

'You don't mean that, do you, Colonel?'

'Of course not. You know damn well I don't.'

'You're in good shape, Colonel,' the surgeon said. 'I'm sorry I can't go on the shoot. I can't even shoot.'

'Hell,' said the Colonel. 'That doesn't make any difference. Neither can anybody else in this army. I'd like to have you around.'

'I'll give you something else to back up what you're using.'

'Is there anything?'

'Not really. They're working on stuff, though.'

'Let 'em work,' the Colonel said.

'I think that's a laudable attitude, sir.'

'Go to hell,' the Colonel said. 'You sure you don't want to go?'

'I get my ducks at Longchamps on Madison Avenue,' the surgeon said. 'It's air-conditioned in the summer and it's warm in the winter and I don't have to get up before first light and wear long-horned underwear.'

'All right, City Boy. You'll never know.'

'I never wanted to know,' the surgeon said. 'You're in good shape, Colonel, sir.'

'Thanks,' said the Colonel and went out.

3

That was day before yesterday. Yesterday he had driven down from Trieste to Venice along the old road that ran from Montfalcone to Latisana and across the flat country. He had a good driver and he relaxed completely in the front seat of the car and looked out at all this country he had known when he was a boy.

It looks quite differently now, he thought. I suppose it is because the distances are all changed. Everything is much smaller when you are older. Then, too, the roads are better now and there is no dust. The only times I used to ride through it was in a *camion*. The rest of the times we walked. I suppose what I looked for then, was patches of shade when we fell out, and wells in farmyards. And ditches, too, he thought. I certainly looked for plenty of ditches.

They made a curve and crossed the Tagliamento on a temporary bridge. It was green along the banks and men were fishing along the far shore where it ran deep. The blown bridge was being repaired with a snarl of riveting hammers, and eight hundred yards away the smashed buildings and outbuildings of what was now a ruined country house once built by Longhena showed where the mediums had dropped their loads.

'Look at it,' the driver said. 'In this country you find a bridge or a railway station. Then go half a mile from it in any direction and you find it like that.'

'I guess the lesson is,' the Colonel said, 'don't ever build yourself a country house, or a church, or hire Giotto to paint you any frescoes, if you've got a church, eight hundred yards away from any bridge.'

'I knew there must be a lesson in it, sir,' the driver said.

They were past the ruined villa now and on to the straight road with the willows growing by the ditches still dark with winter, and the fields full of mulberry trees. Ahead a man was pedalling a bicycle and using both his hands to read a paper.

'If there are heavies the lesson ought to say a mile,' the driver said. 'Would that be about right, sir?'

'If it's guided missiles,' the Colonel said. 'Better make it two hundred and fifty miles. Better give that cyclist some horn.'

The driver did, and the man moved over to the side of the road without either looking up or touching his handle-bars. As they passed him, the Colonel tried to see what paper he was reading, but it was folded over.

'I guess a man would do better now not to build himself a fine house or a church, or to get who did you say it was to paint frescoes?'

'Giotto, I said. But it could be Piero della Francesca or Mantegna. Could be Michelangelo.'

'Do you know a lot about painters, sir?' the driver asked.

They were on a straight stretch of road now and were making time so that one farm blended, almost blurred, into another farm and you could only see what was far ahead and moving towards you. Lateral vision was just a condensation of flat, low country in the winter. I'm not sure I like speed, the Colonel thought. Brueghel would have been in a hell of a shape if he had to look at the country like this.

'Painters?' he answered the driver. 'I know quite a little about them, Burnham.'

'I'm Jackson, sir. Burnham's up at the rest centre at Cortina. That's a fine place, sir.'

'I'm getting stupid,' the Colonel said. 'Excuse me, Jackson. It is a fine place. Good chow. Well run. Nobody bothers you.'

'Yes, sir,' Jackson agreed. 'Now the reason I asked you about painters, is these madonnas. I thought I ought to see some painting so I went to that big place in Florence.'

'The Uffizi? The Pitti?'

'Whatever they call it. The biggest one. And I kept looking at those paintings until madonnas started to run out of my ears. I tell you, Colonel, sir, a man who hasn't been checked out on this painting can only see just about so many madonnas and it gets him. You know my theory? You know how crazy they are about bambinis and the less they got to eat the more bambinis they got and that they have coming? Well, I think these painters were probably big bambini lovers like all Italians. I don't know these ones you mentioned just now, so I don't include them in my theory and you'll put me straight anyway. But it looks to me like these madonnas, that I really saw plenty of, sir, it looks to me like these just straight ordinary madonna painters were sort of a manifest, say, of this whole bambini business, if you understand what I mean.'

'Plus the fact that they were restricted to religious subjects.'

'Yes, sir. Then you think there is something to my theory?'

'Sure. I think it is a little more complicated, though.'

'Naturally, sir. It's just my preliminary theory.'

'Do you have any other theories on art, Jackson?'

'No, sir. That bambini theory is as far as I've thought it through. What I wish is, though, they would paint some good pictures of that high country up around the rest centre at Cortina.'

'Titian came from up there,' the Colonel said. 'At least they say he did. I went down the valley and saw the house where he was supposed to be born.'

'Was it much of a place, sir?'

'Not so much.'

'Well, if he painted any pictures of that country up around there, with those sunset colour rocks and the pines and the snow and all the pointed steeples—'

'Campaniles,' the Colonel said. 'Like that one ahead at Ceggia. It means bell tower.'

'Well, if he painted any really good pictures of that country I'd sure as hell like to trade him out of some of them.'

'He painted some wonderful women,' the Colonel said.

'If I had a joint or a roadhouse or some sort of an inn, say, I could use one of those,' the driver said. 'But if I brought home a picture of some woman, my old woman would run me from Rawlins to Buffalo. I'd be lucky if I *got* to Buffalo.'

'You could give it to the local museum.'

'All they got in the local museum is arrow heads, war bonnets, scalping knives, different scalps, petrified fish, pipes of peace, photographs of Liver Eating Johnston, and the skin of some bad man that they hanged him and some doctor skinned him out. One of those women pictures would be out of place there.'

'See that next campanile down there across the plain?' the Colonel said. 'I'll show you a place down there where we used to fight when I was a kid.'

'Did you fight here, too, sir?'

'Yeah,' the Colonel said.

'Who had Trieste in that war?'

'The Krauts. The Austrians, I mean.'

'Did we ever get it?'

'Not till the end when it was over.'

'Who had Florence and Rome?'

'We did.'

'Well, I guess you weren't so damned bad off then.'

'Sir,' the Colonel said gently.

'I'm sorry, sir,' the driver said quickly. 'I was in the Thirty-Sixth Division, sir.'

'I've seen the patch.'

'I was thinking about the Rapido, sir, I didn't mean to be insolent or lacking in respect.'

'You weren't,' the Colonel said. 'You were just thinking about the Rapido. Listen, Jackson, everybody who's soldiered a long time has had their Rapidos and more than one.'

'I couldn't take more than one, sir.'

The car went through the cheerful town of San Dona di Piave. It was built up and new, but no more ugly than a middle western town, and it was as prosperous and as cheery as Fossalta, just up the river, is miserable and gloomy, the Colonel thought. Did Fossalta never get over the first war? I never saw it before it was smacked, he thought. They shelled it badly before the big fifteenth of June offensive in 'eighteen. Then we shelled it really badly before we re-took it. He remembered how the attack had taken off from Monastier, gone through Fornace, and on this winter day he remembered how it had been that summer.

A few weeks ago he had gone through Fossalta and had gone out along the sunken road to find the place where he had been hit, out on the river bank. It was easy to find because of the bend of the river, and where the heavy machine-gun post had been the crater was smoothly grassed. It had been cropped, by sheep or goats, until it looked like a designed depression in a golf course. The river was slow and a muddy blue here, with reeds along the edges, and the Colonel, no one being in sight, squatted low, and looking across the river from the bank where you could never show your head in daylight, relieved himself in the exact place where he had determined, by triangulation, that he had been badly wounded thirty years before.

'A poor effort,' he said aloud to the river and the river bank that were heavy with autumn quiet and wet from the fall rains. 'But my own.'

He stood up and looked around. There was no one in sight and he had left the car down the sunken road in front of the last and saddest rebuilt house in Fossalta.

'Now I'll complete the monument,' he said to no one but the dead, and he took an old Solingen clasp knife, such as German poachers carry, from his pocket. It locked on opening and, twirling it, he dug a neat hole in the moist earth. He cleaned the knife on his right combat boot and then inserted a brown ten thousand lira note in the hole and tamped it down and put the grass that he had cored out over it.

'That is twenty years at five hundred lira a year for the Medaglia d'Argento al Valore Militare. The V.C. carries ten guineas, I believe. The D.S.C. is non-productive. The Silver Star is free. I'll keep the change,' he said.

It's fine now, he thought. It has *merde*, money, blood; look how that grass grows; and the iron's in the earth along with Gino's leg, both of Randolfo's legs and my right knee-cap. It's a wonderful monument. It has everything. Fertility, money, blood and iron. Sounds like a nation. Where fertility, money, blood and iron is; there is the fatherland. We need coal though. We ought to get some coal.

Then he looked across the river to the rebuilt white house that had once been rubble, and he spat in the river. It was a long spit and he just made it.

'I couldn't spit that night nor afterwards for a long time,' he said. 'But I spit good now for a man who doesn't chew.'

He walked slowly back to where the car was parked. The driver was asleep.

'Wake up, son,' he had said. 'Turn her around and take that road towards Treviso. We don't need a map on this part. I'll give you the turns.'

4

Now, on his way into Venice, keeping strictly controlled and un-thinking his great need to be there, the big Buick cleared the last of San Dona and came up on to the bridge over the Piave.

They crossed the bridge and were on the Italian side of the river and he saw the old sunken road again. It was as smooth and undistinguished now, as it was all along the river. But he could see the old positions. And now, along each side of the straight, flat, canal-bordered road they were making time on were the willows of the two canals that had contained the dead. There had been a great killing at the last of the offensive and someone, to clear the river-bank positions and the road in the hot weather, had ordered the dead thrown into the canals. Unfortunately, the canal gates were still in the Austrians' hands down the river, and they were closed.

So there was little movement to the water, and the dead had stayed there a long time, floating and bloating face up and face down regardless of nationality until they had attained colossal proportions. Finally, after organization had been established, labour troops hauled them out at night and buried them close to the road. The Colonel looked for added greenness close to the road but could not note any. However, there were many ducks and geese in the canals, and men were fishing in them all along the road.

They dug them all up anyway, the Colonel thought, and buried them in that big *ossario* up by Nervesa.

'We fought along here when I was a kid,' the Colonel told the driver.

'It's a goddamn flat country to fight in,' the driver said. 'Did you hold that river?'

'Yes,' the Colonel said. 'We held it and lost it and took it back again.'

'There isn't a contour here as far as you can see.'

'That was the trouble,' the Colonel said. 'You had to use contours you couldn't see, they were so small, and ditches and houses and canal banks and hedgerows. It was like Normandy only flatter. I think it must have been something like fighting in Holland.'

'That river sure doesn't look anything like the Rapido.'

'It was a pretty good old river,' the Colonel said. 'Up above, it had plenty of water then, before all these hydro-electric projects. And it had very deep and tricky channels in the pebbles and shingle when it was shallow.'

He knew how boring any man's war is to any other man, and he stopped talking about it. They always take it personally, he thought. No one is interested in it, abstractly, except soldiers and there are not many soldiers. You make them and the good ones are killed, and above they are always bucking for something so hard they never look or listen. They are always thinking of what they have seen and while you are talking they are thinking of what they will say and what it may lead to in their advancement or their privilege. There was no sense boring this boy, who, for all his combat infantryman badge, his Purple Heart and the other things he wore, was in no sense a soldier but only a man placed, against his will, in uniform, who had elected to remain in the army for his own ends.

'What did you do in civil life, Jackson?' he asked.

'I was partners with my brother in a garage in Rawlins, Wyoming, sir.'

'Are you going back there?'

'My brother got killed in the Pacific and the guy who was running the garage was no good,' the driver said. 'We lost what we had put in it.'

'That's bad,' the Colonel said.

'You're goddamned right it's bad,' the driver said and added, 'sir'.

The Colonel looked up the road.

He knew that if they kept on this road they would come, shortly, to the turn that he was waiting for; but he was impatient.

'Keep your eyes open and take a left hand turn on the road leading off this pike,' he told the driver.

'Do you think those low roads will be good with this big car, sir?'

'We'll see,' the Colonel said. 'Hell, man, it hasn't rained in three weeks.'

'I don't trust those side roads in this low country.'

'If we get stuck, I'll haul you out with oxen.'

'I was only thinking about the car, sir.'

'Well, think about what I told you and turn off on the first left side road you see if it looks practicable.'

'That looks like one coming up, from the hedges,' the driver said.

'You're all clear behind. Pull up just ahead of it and I'll go over and have a look.'

He stepped out of the car and walked across the wide, hard-surfaced road and looked at the narrow dirt road, with the swift flowing canal beside it, and the thick hedge beyond. Beyond the hedge, he saw a low red farmhouse with a big barn. The road was dry. There were not even cart ruts sunk in it. He got back into the car.

'It's a boulevard,' he said. 'Quit worrying.'

'Yes, sir. It's your car, sir.'

'I know,' the Colonel said. 'I'm still paying for it. Say, Jackson, do you always suffer so much any time you go off a highway on to a secondary road?'

'No, sir. But there's a lot of difference between a jeep, and a car as low hung as this. Do you know the clearance you have on your differential and your body frame on this?'

'I've got a shovel in the trunk and we've got chains. Wait till you see where we're going after we leave Venice.'

'Do we go all the way in this car?'

'I don't know. I'll see.'

'Think about your fenders, sir.'

'We'll cut the fenders off like the Indians do in Oklahoma. She's over-fendered right now. She's got too much of everything except engine. Jackson, that's a real engine she's got.'

'It certainly is, sir. It's a great pleasure to drive that big engine on the good roads. That's why I don't want anything to happen to her.'

'That's very good of you, Jackson. Now just quit suffering.'

'I'm not suffering, sir.'

'Good,' said the Colonel.

He was not, either, because just then he saw, beyond the line of close-bunched brown trees ahead, a sail moving along. It was a big red sail, raked sharply down from the peak, and it moved slowly behind the trees.

Why should it always move your heart to see a sail moving along through the country, the Colonel thought. Why does it move my heart to see the great, slow, pale oxen? It must be the gait as well as the look of them and the size and the colour.

But a good fine big mule, or a string of pack mules in good condition, moves me, too. So does a coyote every time I ever see one, and a wolf, gaited like no other animal, grey and sure of himself, carrying that heavy head and with the hostile eyes.

'Ever see any wolves out around Rawlins, Jackson?'

'No, sir. Wolves were gone before my time; they poisoned them out.

Plenty coyotes, though.'

'Do you like coyotes?'

'I like to hear them nights.'

'So do I. Better than anything, except seeing a ship sailing along through the country.'

'There's a boat doing that over there, sir.'

'On the Sile canal,' the Colonel told him. 'She's a sailing barge going to Venice. This wind is off the mountains now and she makes it along pretty good. It's liable to turn really cold tonight if this wind holds and it ought to bring in plenty ducks. Turn to your left here and we'll run along the canal. There's a good road.'

'They didn't have much duck shooting where I came from. But there was plenty of it in Nebraska along the Platte.'

'Do you want to shoot where we're going?'

'I don't believe so, sir. I'm not much of a shot, and I'd rather stay in that sack. It's a Sunday morning, you know.'

'I know,' the Colonel said. 'You can stay in the sack until noon if you want.'

'I brought my repellent. I ought to sleep okay.'

'I'm not sure you'll need it,' the Colonel said. 'Did you bring any K-rations or Ten in One? They're liable to eat Italian food, you know.'

'I brought a few cans to help out and a little stuff to give away.'

'That's good,' the Colonel said.

He was looking ahead now to see where the canal road joined the main highway again. There he knew that he would see it on a clear day such as this was. Across the marshes, brown as those at the mouths of the Mississippi around Pilot Town are in winter, and with their reeds bent by the heavy north wind, he saw the squared tower of the church at Torcello and the high companile of Burano beyond it. The sea was a slate blue and he could see the sails of twelve sailing barges running with the wind for Venice.

I'll have to wait until we cross the Dese River above Noghera to see it perfectly, he thought. It is strange to remember how we fought back there along the canal that winter to defend it and we never saw it. Then one time, I was back as far as Noghera and it was clear and cold like today, and I saw it across the water. But I never got into it. It is my city, though, because I fought for it when I was a boy, and now that I am half a hundred years old, they know I fought for it and am a part owner and they treat me well.

Do you think that's why they treat you well, he asked himself.

Maybe, he thought. Maybe they treat me well because I'm a chicken colonel on the winning side. I don't believe it, though. I hope not, anyway. It is not France, he thought.

There you fight your way into a city that you love and are very careful about breaking anything and then, if you have good sense, you are careful not to go back because you will meet some military characters who will resent your having fought your way in. *Vive la France et les pommes de terre frites. Liberté, Venalité, et Stupidité.* The great *clarté* of the French military thinking. They haven't had a military thinker since du Picq. He was a poor bloody Colonel, too. Mangin, Maginot and Gamelin. Take your choice,

Gentlemen. Three schools of thought. One; I hit them on the nose. Two; I hide behind this thing which does not cover my left flank. Three; I hide my head in the sand like an ostrich, confident in the greatness of France as a military power and then take off.

Take off is putting it very cleanly and pleasantly. Sure, he thought, whenever you over-simplify you become unjust. Remember all the fine ones in the Resistance, remember Foch both fought and organized and remember how fine the people were. Remember your good friends and remember your deads. Remember plenty things and your best friends again and the finest people that you know. Don't be a bitter nor a stupid. And what has that to do with soldiering as a trade? Cut it out, he told himself. You're on a trip to have fun.

'Jackson,' he said, 'are you happy?'

'Yes, sir.'

'Good. Shortly, we are coming to a view that I want you to see. You only have to take one look at it. The entire operation will be practically painless.'

I wonder what he's riding me for now, the driver thought. Just because he was a BG once he knows everything. If he was any good as a BG why didn't he hold it? He's been beat up so much he's slug-nutty.

'There's the view, Jackson,' the Colonel said. 'Stop her by the side of the road and we'll take a look.'

The Colonel and the driver walked over to the Venice side of the road and looked across the lagoon that was whipped by the strong, cold wind from the mountains that sharpened all the outlines of buildings so that they were geometrically clear.

'That's Torcello directly opposite us,' the Colonel pointed. 'That's where the people lived that were driven off the mainland by the Visigoths. They built that church you see there with the square tower. There were thirty thousand people lived there once and they built that church to honour their Lord and to worship him. Then, after they built it, the mouth of the Sile River silted up or a big flood changed it, and all that land we came through just now got flooded and started to breed mosquitoes and malaria hit them. They all started to die, so the elders got together and decided they should pull out to a healthy place that would be defensible with boats, and where the Visigoths and the Lombards and the other bandits couldn't get at them, because these bandits had no sea-power. The Torcello boys were all great boatmen. So they took the stones of all their houses in barges, like that one we just saw, and they built Venice.'

He stopped. 'Am I boring you, Jackson?'

'No, sir. I had no idea who pioneered Venice.'

'It was the boys from Torcello. They were very tough and they had very good taste in building. They came from a little place up the coast called Caorle. But they drew on all the people from the towns and the farms behind when the Visigoths overran them. It was a Torcello boy who was running arms into Alexandria, who located the body of St Mark and smuggled it out under a load of fresh pork so the infidel customs guards wouldn't check him. This boy brought the remains of St Mark to Venice, and he's their patron saint and they have a cathedral there to him. But by that time, they were trading so far to the east that the architecture is pretty Byzantine for my taste. They never built any better than at the start there in Torcello. That's Torcello there.'

It was, indeed.

'St Mark's Square is where the pigeons are and where they have that big cathedral that looks sort of like a moving picture palace, isn't it?'

'Right, Jackson. You're on the ball. If that's the way you look at it. Now you look beyond Torcello you will see the lovely campanile on Burano that has damn near as much list on it as the leaning tower of Pisa. That Burano is a very over-populated little island where the women make wonderful lace, and the men make bambinis and work daytimes in the glass factories in that next island you see on beyond with the other campanile, which is Murano. They make wonderful glass daytimes for the rich of all the world, and then they come home on the little *vaporetto* and make bambinis. Not everyone passes every night with his wife though. They hunt ducks nights too, with big punt guns, out along the edge of the marshes on this lagoon you're looking across now. All night long on a moonlight night you hear the shots.' He paused.

'Now when you look past Murano you see Venice. That's my town. There's plenty more I could show you, but I think we probably ought to roll now. But take one good look at it. This is where you can see how it all happened. But nobody ever looks at it from here.'

'It's a beautiful view. Thank you, sir.'

'Okay,' the Colonel said. 'Let's roll.'

5

But he continued to look and it was all as wonderful to him and it moved him as it had when he was eighteen years old and had seen it first, understanding nothing of it and only knowing that it was beautiful. The winter had come very cold that year and all the mountains were white beyond the plain. It was necessary for the Austrians to try to break through at the angle where the Sile River and the old bed of the Piave were the only lines of defence.

If you had the old bed of the Piave then you had the Sile to fall back on if the first line did not hold. Beyond the Sile there was nothing but bare-assed plain and a good road network into the Veneto plain and the plains of Lombardy, and the Austrians attacked again and again and again late through the winter, to try to get on to this fine road that they were rolling on now which led straight to Venice. That winter the Colonel, who was a lieutenant then, and in a foreign army, which had always made him slightly suspect afterwards in his own army, and had done his career no good, had a sore throat all winter. This sore throat was from being in the water so much. You could not get dry and it was better to get wet quickly and stay wet.

The Austrian attacks were ill-coordinated, but they were constant and exasperated and you first had the heavy bombardment which was supposed to put you out of business, and then, when it lifted, you checked your positions and counted the people. But you had no time to care for the wounded, since you knew that the attack was coming immediately, and then you killed the men who came wading across the marshes, holding their rifles above the water and coming as slow as men wade, waist deep.

If they did not lift the shelling when it started, the Colonel, then a lieutenant, often thought, I do not know what we would be able to do. But they always lifted it and moved it back ahead of the attack.

If we had lost the old Piave and were on the Sile they would move it back to the second and third lines; although such lines were quite untenable, and they should have brought all their guns up very close and whammed it in all the time they attacked and until they breached us. But thank God, some high fool always controls it, the Colonel thought, and they did it piecemeal.

All that winter, with a bad sore throat, he had killed men who came, wearing the stick bombs hooked up on a harness under their shoulders with the heavy, calf-hide packs and the bucket helmets. They were the enemy.

But he never hated them; nor could have any feeling about them. He commanded with an old sock around his throat, which had been dipped in turpentine, and they broke down the attacks with rifle fire and with the machine guns which still existed, or were usable, after the bombardment. He taught his people to shoot, really, which is a rare ability in continental troops, and to be able to look at the enemy when they came, and, because there was always a dead moment when the shooting was free, they became very good at it.

But you always had to count and count fast after the bombardment to know how many shooters you would have. He was hit three times that winter, but they were all gift wounds; small wounds in the flesh of the body without breaking bone, and he had become quite confident of his personal immortality since he knew he should have been killed in the heavy artillery bombardment that always preceded the attacks. Finally, he did get hit properly and for good. No one of his other wounds had ever done to him what the first big one did. I suppose it is just the loss of the immortality, he thought. Well, in a way that is quite a lot to lose.

This country meant very much to him, more than he could, or would ever tell anyone and now he sat in the car happy that in another half hour they would be in Venice. He took two mannitol hexanitrate tablets; since he had always been able to spit since 1918, he could take them dry, and asked.

'How are you doing, Jackson?'

'Fine, sir.'

'Take the left outside road when we hit the fork for Mestre and we'll be able to see the boats along the canal and miss that main traffic.'

'Yes, sir,' the driver said. 'Will you check me on the fork?'

'Of course,' the Colonel said.

They were coming up on Mestre fast, and already it was like going to New York the first time you were ever there in the old days when it was shining, white and beautiful. I stole that, he thought. But that was before the smoke.

We are coming into my town, he thought. Christ, what a lovely town.

They made the left turn and came along the canal where the fishing boats tied up, and the Colonel looked at them and his heart was happy because of the brown nets and the wicker fish traps and the clean, beautiful lines of the boats. It's not that they are picturesque. The hell with picturesque. They are just damned beautiful.

They passed the long line of boats in the slow canal that carried water from the Brenta, and he thought about the long stretch of the Brenta where the great villas were, with their lawns and their gardens and the plane trees and the cypresses. I'd like to be buried out there, he thought. I know the place very well. I don't believe you could fix it, though. I don't know. I know some people that might let me be buried on their place. I'll ask Alberto. He might think it was morbid, though.

For a long time he had been thinking about all the fine places he would like to be buried and what parts of the earth he would like to be a part of. The stinking, putrefying part doesn't last very long, really, he thought, and anyway you are just a sort of mulch, and even the bones will be some use finally. I'd like to be buried way out at the edge of the grounds, but in sight of the old graceful house and the tall, great trees. I don't think it would be much of a nuisance to them. I could be a part of the ground where the children play in the evenings, and in the mornings, maybe, they would still be training jumping horses and their hoofs would made the thudding on the turf, and trout would rise in the pool when there was a hatch of fly.

They were up on the causeway from Mestre to Venice now with ugly Breda works that might have been Hammond, Indiana.

'What do they make there, sir?' Jackson asked.

'The company makes locomotives in Milan,' the Colonel said. 'Here they make a little of everything in the metallurgic line.'

It was a miserable view of Venice now and he always disliked this causeway except that you made such good time and you could see the buoys and the channels.

'This town makes a living on its own,' he said to Jackson. 'She used to be the queen of the seas and the people are very tough and they give less of a good goddamn about things than almost anybody you'll ever meet. It's a tougher town than Cheyenne when you really know it, and everybody is very polite.'

'I wouldn't say Cheyenne was a tough town, sir.'

'Well, it's a tougher town than Casper.'

'Do you think that's a tough town, sir?'

'It's an oil town. It's a nice town.'

'But I don't think it's tough, sir. Or ever was.'

'Okay, Jackson. Maybe we move in different circles. Or maybe we have a differing definition for the word. But this town of Venice, with everybody being polite and having good manners, is as tough as Cooke City, Montana, on the day they have the Old Timers' Fish Fry.'

'My idea of a tough town is Memphis.'

'Not like Chicago, Jackson. Memphis is only tough if you are a Negro. Chicago is tough North, South, there isn't any East, and West. But nobody has any manners. But in this country, if you ever want to know a *really* tough town where they eat wonderfully, too, go to Bologna.'

'I never was there.'

'Well, there's the Fiat garage where we leave the car,' the Colonel said. 'You can leave the key at the office. They don't steal. I'll go in the bar while you park upstairs. They have people that will bring the bags.'

'Is it okay to leave your gun and shooting gear in the trunk, sir?'

'Sure. They don't steal here. I told you that once.'

'I wanted to take the necessary precautions, sir, on your valuable property.'

'You're so damned noble that sometimes you stink,' the Colonel said. 'Get the wax out of your ears and hear what I say the first time.'

'I heard you, sir,' Jackson said. The Colonel looked at him contemplatively and with the old deadliness.

He sure is a mean son of a bitch, Jackson thought, and he can be so goddamn nice.

'Get my and your bag out and park her up there and check your oil, your water and your tyres,' the Colonel said, and walked across the oil and rubber stained cement of the entry of the bar.

6

In the bar, sitting at the first table as he came in, there was a post-war rich from Milan, fat and hard as only Milanese can be, sitting with his expensive looking and extremely desirable mistress. They were drinking *negronis*, a combination of two sweet vermouths and seltzer water, and the Colonel wondered how much taxes the man had escaped to buy that sleek girl in her long mink coat and the convertible he had seen the chauffeur take up the long, winding ramp to lock away. The pair stared at him with the bad manners of their kind and he saluted, lightly, and said to them in Italian, 'I am sorry that I am in uniform. But it is a uniform. Not a costume.'

Then he turned his back on them, without waiting to see the effect of his remark, and walked to the bar. From the bar you could watch your luggage, just as well as the two *pescecani* were watching theirs.

He is probably a Commendatore, he thought. She is a beautiful, hard piece of work. She is damned beautiful, actually. I wonder what it would have been like if I had ever had the money to buy me that kind and put them into the mink? I'll settle for what I have, he thought, and they can go and hang themselves.

The bar-tender shook hands with him. This bar-tender was an Anarchist but he did not mind the Colonel being a Colonel at all. He was delighted by it and proud and loving about it as though the Anarchists had a Colonel, too, and in some ways, in the several months that they had known each other, he seemed to feel that he had invented, or at least erected, the Colonel as you might be happy about participating in the erection of a campanile, or even the old church at Torcello.

The bar-tender had heard the conversation, or, rather, the flat statement at the table and he was very happy.

He had already sent down, via the dumb-waiter, for a Gordon's Gin and Campari and he said, 'It is coming up in that hand-pulled device. How does everything go at Trieste?'

'About as you would imagine.'

'I couldn't even imagine.'

'Then don't strain,' the Colonel said, 'and you will never get piles.'

'I wouldn't mind it if I was a Colonel.'

'I never mind it.'

'You'd be overrun like a dose of salts,' the waiter said.

'Don't tell the Honourable Pacciardi,' the Colonel said.

He and the bar-tender had a joke about this because the Honourable Pacciardi was Minister of Defence in the Italian Republic. He was the same age as the Colonel and had fought very well in the First World War, and had also fought in Spain as a Battalion commander, where the Colonel had known him when he, himself, was an observer. The seriousness with which the Honourable Pacciardi took the post of Minister of Defence of an indefensible country was a bond between the Colonel and the bar-tender. The two of them were quite practical men and the vision of the Honourable Pacciardi defending the Italian Republic stimulated their minds.

'It's sort of funny up there,' the Colonel said, 'and I don't mind it.'

'We must mechanize the Honourable Pacciardi,' the bar-tender said. 'And supply him with the atomic bomb.'

'I've got three of them in the back of the car,' the Colonel said. 'The new model, complete with handles. But we can't leave him unarmed. We must supply him with botulism and anthrax.'

'We cannot fail the Honourable Pacciardi,' the bar-tender said. 'Better to live one day as a lion than a hundred years as a sheep.'

'Better to die on our feet than to live on our knees,' the Colonel said. 'Though you better get on your belly damn fast if you want to stay alive in plenty places.'

'Colonel, do not say anything subversive.'

'We will strangle them with our bare hands,' the Colonel said. 'A million men will spring to arms overnight.'

'Whose arms?' the bar-tender asked.

'All that will be attended to,' the Colonel said. 'It's only a phase in the Big Picture.'

Just then the driver came in the door. The Colonel saw that while they had been joking, he had not watched the door and he was annoyed, always, with any lapse of vigilance or of security.

'What the hell's been keeping you, Jackson? Have a drink.'

'No, thank you, sir.'

You prissy jerk, the Colonel thought. But I better stop riding him; he corrected.

'We'll be going in a minute,' the Colonel said. 'I've been trying to learn

Italian from my friend here.' He turned to look at the Milan profiteers; but they were gone.

I'm getting awfully slow, he thought. Somebody will take me any day now. Maybe even the Honourable Pacciardi, he thought.

'How much do I owe you?' he asked the bar-tender shortly.

The bar-tender told him and looked at him with his wise Italian eyes, not merry now, although the lines of merriment were clearly cut where they radiated from the corners of each eye. I hope there is nothing wrong with him, the bar-tender thought. I hope to God, or anything else, there's nothing really bad.

'Good-bye, my Colonel,' he said.

'*Ciao*,' the Colonel said. 'Jackson, we are going down the long ramp and due north from the exit to where the small launches are moored. The varnished ones. There is a porter with the two bags. It is necessary to let them carry them since they have a concession.'

'Yes, sir,' said Jackson.

The two of them went out the door and no one looked back at anyone.

At the *imbarcadero*, the Colonel tipped the man who had carried their two bags and then looked around for a boatman he knew.

He did not recognize the man in the launch that was first on call, but the boatman said, 'Good day, my Colonel. I'm the first.'

'How much is it to the Gritti?'

'You know as well as I, my Colonel. We do not bargain. We have a fixed tariff.'

'What's the tariff?'

'Three thousand five hundred.'

'We could go on the *vaporetto* for sixty.'

'And nothing prevents you going,' the boatman, who was an elderly man with a red but un-choleric face, said. 'They won't take you to the Gritti but they will stop at the *imbarcadero* past Harry's, and you can telephone for someone from the Gritti to get your bags.'

And what would I buy with the goddamn three thousand five hundred lire; and this is a good old man.

'Do you want me to send that man there?' he pointed to a destroyed old man who did odd jobs and ran errands around the docks, always ready with the un-needed aid to the elbow of the ascending or descending passenger, always ready to help when no help was needed, his old felt hat held out as he bowed after the un-needed act. 'He'll take you to the *vaporetto*. There's one in twenty minutes.'

'The hell with it,' the Colonel said. 'Take us to the Gritti.'

'*Con piacere*,' the boatman said.

The Colonel and Jackson lowered themselves into the launch which looked like a speed boat. It was radiantly varnished and lovingly kept and was powered with a marine conversion of a tiny Fiat engine that had served its allotted time in the car of a provincial doctor and had been purchased out of one of the graveyards of automobiles; those mechanical elephant cemeteries that are the one certain thing you may find in our world near any populated centre; and been reconditioned and re-converted to start this new life on the canals of this city.

'How is the motor doing?' the Colonel asked. He could hear her sounding like a stricken tank or T.D., except the noises were in miniature from the lack of power.

'So-so,' the boatman said. He moved his free hand in a parallel motion.

'You ought to get the smallest model Universal puts out. That's the best and lightest small marine engine I know.'

'Yes,' the boatman said. 'There are quite a few things I should get.'

'Maybe you'll have a good year.'

'It's always possible. Lots of *pescecani* come down from Milano to gamble at the Lido. But nobody would ride twice in this thing on purpose. As a boat, it is fine, too. It is a well built, pleasant boat. Not beautiful as a gondola is, of course. But it needs an engine.'

'I might get you a jeep engine. One that was condemned and you could work it over.'

'Don't talk about such things,' the boatman said. 'Things like that don't happen. I don't want to think about it.'

'You can think about it,' the Colonel said. 'I'm talking true.'

'You mean it.'

'Sure. I don't guarantee anything. I'll see what I can do. How many children have you got?'

'Six. Two male and four female.'

'Hell, you mustn't have believed in the Régime. Only six.'

'I *didn't* believe in the Régime.'

'You don't have to give me that stuff,' the Colonel said. 'It would have been quite natural for you to *have* believed in it. Do you think I hold that against a man after we've won?'

They were through the dull part of the canal that runs from Piazzale Roma to Ca'Foscari, though none of it is dull, the Colonel thought.

It doesn't all have to be palaces nor churches. Certainly that isn't dull. He looked to the right, the starboard, he thought. I'm on the water. It was a long low pleasant building and there was a *trattoria* next to it.

I ought to live here. On retirement pay I could make it all right. No Gritti Palace. A room in a house like that and the tides and the boats going by. I could read in the mornings and walk around town before lunch and go every day to see the Tintorettos at the Accademia and to the Scuola San Rocco and eat in good cheap joints behind the market or, maybe, the woman that ran the house would cook in the evenings.

I think it would be better to have lunch out and get some exercise walking. It's a good town to walk in. I guess the best, probably. I never walked in it that it wasn't fun. I could learn it really well, he thought, and then I'd have that.

It's a strange, tricky town and to walk from any part to any other given part of it is better than working crossword puzzles. It's one of the few things to our credit that we never smacked it, and to *their* credit that they respected it.

Christ, I love it, he said, and I'm so happy I helped defend it when I was a punk kid, and with an insufficient command of the language and I never even saw her until that clear day in the winter when I went back to have that small wound dressed, and saw her rising from the sea. *Merde*, he thought, we did very well that winter up at the junction.

I wish I could fight it again, he thought. Knowing what I know now and having what we have now. But they'd have it too and the essential problem is just the same, except who holds the air.

And all this time he had been watching the bow of the beat-up beautifully varnished, delicately brass-striped boat, with the brass all beautifully polished, cut the brown water and seen the small traffic problems.

They went under the white bridge and under the unfinished wood bridge. Then they left the red bridge on the right and passed under the first high-flying white bridge. Then there was the black iron fret-work bridge on the canal leading into the Rio Nuovo and they passed the two stakes chained together but not touching: like us the Colonel thought. He watched the tide pull at them and he saw how the chains had worn the wood since he first had seen them. That's us, he thought. That's our monument. And how many monuments are there to us in the canals of this town?

Then they still went slowly until the great lantern that was on the right of the entrance to the Grand Canal where the engine commenced its metallic agony that produced a slight increase in speed.

Now they came down and under the Accademia between the pilings where they passed, at touching distance, a heavily loaded black diesel boat full of cut timber, cut in chunks, to burn for firewood in the damp houses of the Sea City.

'That's beech, isn't it?' the Colonel asked the boatman.

'Beech and another wood that is cheaper that I do not recall, at this moment, the name of.'

'Beech is, to an open fire, as anthracite coal is to a stove. Where do they cut that beech?'

'I'm not a man of the mountains. But I think it comes from up beyond Bassano on the other side of the Grappa. I went there to the Grappa to see where my brother was buried. It was an excursion that they made from Bassano, and we went to the big *ossario*. But we returned by Feltre. I could see it was a fine timber country on the other side as you came down the mountains into the valley. We came down that military road, and they were hauling lots of wood.'

'In what year was your brother killed on Grappa?'

'In nineteen eighteen. He was a patriot and inflamed by hearing d'Annunzio talk, and he volunteered before his class was called. We never knew him very well because he went so quickly.'

'How many were you in the family?'

'We were six. We lost two beyond the Isonzo, one on the Bainsizza and one on the Carso. Then we lost this brother I speak of on the Grappa and I remained.'

'I'll get you the goddamned jeep complete with handles,' the Colonel said. 'Now let's not be morbid and look for all the places where my friends live.'

They were moving up the Grand Canal now and it was easy to see where your friends lived.

'That's the house of the Contessa Dandolo,' the Colonel said.

He did not say, but thought, she is over eighty, and she is as gay as a girl and does not have any fear of dying. She dyes her hair red and it looks very well. She is a good companion and an admirable woman.

Her palazzo was pleasant looking, set well back from the Canal with a garden in front and a landing place of its own where many gondolas had come, in their various times, bringing hearty, cheerful, sad and disillusioned people. But most of them had been cheerful because they were going to see the Contessa Dandolo.

Now, beating up the Canal, against the cold wind off the mountains, and with the houses as clear and sharp as on a winter day, which, of course, it was, they saw the old magic of the city and its beauty. But it was conditioned, for the Colonel, by his knowing many of the people who lived in the palazzos; or if no one lived there now, knowing to what use the different places had been put.

There's Alvarito's mother's house, he thought, and did not say.

She never lives there much and stays out at the country house near Treviso where they have trees. She's tired of there not being trees in Venice. She lost a fine man and nothing really interests her now except efficiency.

But the family at one time lent the house to George Gordon, Lord Byron, and nobody sleeps now in Byron's bed nor in the other bed, two flights below, where he used to sleep with the gondolier's wife. They are not sacred, nor relics. They are just extra beds that were not used afterwards for various reasons, or possibly to respect Lord Byron who was well loved in this town, in spite of all the errors he committed. You have to be a tough boy in this town to be loved, the Colonel thought. They never cared anything for Robert Browning, nor Mrs Robert Browning, nor for their dog. They weren't Venetians no matter how well he wrote of it. And what is a tough boy, he asked himself. You use it so loosely you should be able to define it. I suppose it is a man who will make his play and then backs it up. Or just a man who backs his play. And I'm not thinking of the theatre, he thought. Lovely as the theatre can be.

And yet, he thought, seeing now the little villa, close up against the water, ugly as a building you would see on the boat train from Havre or Cherbourg, coming into the banlieue before Paris as you came into town. It was overrun with badly administered trees, and not a place that you would live in if you could help it. There *he* lived.

They loved him for his talent, and because he was bad, and he was brave. A Jewish boy with nothing, he stormed the country with his talent, and his rhetoric. He was a more miserable character than any that I know and as mean. But the man I think of to compare him with never put the chips on the line and went to war, the Colonel thought, and Gabriele d'Annunzio (I always wondered what his real name was, he thought, because nobody is named d'Annunzio in a practical country and perhaps he was not Jewish and what difference did it make if he was or was not) had moved through the different arms of the service as he had moved into and out of the arms of different women.

All the arms were pleasant that d'Annunzio served with and the mission was fast and easily over, except the Infantry. He remembered how d'Annunzio had lost an eye in a crash, flying as an observer, over Trieste or Pola, and how, afterwards, he had always worn a patch over it and people who did not know, for, then, no one really knew, thought it had been shot out at the Veliki or San Michele or some other bad place beyond the Carso where everyone died, or was incapacitated, that you knew. But d'Annunzio, truly, was only making heroic gestures with the other things. An Infantryman knows a strange trade, he thought; perhaps the strangest. He, Gabriele, flew, but he was not a flier. He was in the Infantry but he was not an Infantryman and it was always the same appearances.

And the Colonel remembered one time when he had stood, commanding a platoon of assault troops, while it was raining in one of the interminable winters, when the rain fell always; or at least, always when there were parades or speeches to the troops, and d'Annunzio, with his lost eye, covered by the patch, and his white face, as white as the belly of a sole, new turned over in the market, the brown side not showing, and looking thirty hours dead, was shouting, '*Morire non à basta*,' and the Colonel, then a lieutenant, had thought, 'What the muck more do they want of us?'

But he had followed the discourse and, at the end, when the Lieutenant-Colonel d'Annunzio, writer and national hero, certified and true if you must have heroes, and the Colonel did not believe in heroes, asked for a moment of silence for our glorious dead, he had stood stiffly to attention. But his platoon, who had not followed the speech, there being no loud speakers then, and they being slightly out of hearing of the orator, responded, as one man, at the pause for the moment of silence for our glorious dead, with a solid and ringing '*Evviva d'Annunzio*'.

They had been addressed before by d'Annunzio after victories, and before defeats, and they knew what they should shout if there was any pause by an orator.

The Colonel, being then a lieutenant, and loving his platoon, had joined with them and uttered, with the tone of command, '*Evviva d'Annunzio*', thus absolving all those who had not listened to the discourse, speech, or harangue and attempting, in the small way a lieutenant can attempt anything, except to hold an indefensible position; or intelligently direct his own part in an attack; to share their guilt.

But now he was passing the house where the poor beat-up old boy had lived with his great, sad and never properly loved actress and he thought of her wonderful hands and her so transformable face, that was not beautiful, but that gave you all love, glory and delight and sadness; and of the way the curve of her forearm could break your heart, and he thought, Christ they are dead and I do not know where either one is buried even. But I certainly hope they had fun in that house.

'Jackson,' he said, 'that small villa on the left belonged to Gabriele d'Annunzio, who was a great writer.'

'Yes, sir,' said Jackson, 'I'm glad to know about him. I never heard of him.'

'I'll check you out on what he wrote if you ever want to read him,' the

Colonel said. 'There are some fair English translations.'

'Thank you, sir,' said Jackson. 'I'd like to read him any time I have time. He has a nice practical looking place. What did you say the name was?'

'D'Annunzio,' the Colonel said. 'Writer.'

He added to himself, not wishing to confuse Jackson, nor be difficult, as he had been with the man several times that day, writer, poet, national hero, phraser of the dialectic of Fascism, macabre egotist, aviator, commander, or rider, in the first of the fast torpedo attack boats, Lieutenant-Colonel of Infantry without knowing how to command a company, nor a platoon properly, the great, lovely writer of *Notturno* whom we respect, and jerk.

Up ahead now there was a crossing place of gondolas at the Santa Maria del Giglio and, beyond, was the wooden dock of the Gritti.

'That's the hotel where we are stopping at, Jackson.'

The Colonel indicated the three-storey, rose-coloured small, pleasant palace abutting on the Canal. It had been a dependence of the Grand Hotel–but now it was its own hotel and a very good one. It was probably the best hotel, if you did not wish to be fawned on, or fussed over, or overflunkied, in a city of great hotels and the Colonel loved it.

'It looks okay to me, sir,' Jackson said.

'It is okay,' the Colonel said.

The motor-boat came gallantly up beside the piling of the dock. Every move she makes, the Colonel thought, is a triumph of the gallantry of the ageing machine. We do not have war horses now like old Traveller, or Marbot's Lysette who fought, personally, at Eylau. We have the gallantry of worn-through rods that refuse to break; the cylinder head that does not blow though it has every right to and the rest of it.

'We're at the dock, sir,' Jackson said.

'Where the hell else would we be, man. Jump out while I settle with this sportsman.'

He turned to the boatman and said, 'That was thirty-five hundred, wasn't it?'

'Yes, my Colonel.'

'I'll not forget about the over-age jeep engine. Take this and buy your horse some oats.'

The porter, who was taking the bags from Jackson, heard this and laughed.

'No veterinarian will ever fix his horse.'

'She still runs,' the boatman said.

'But she doesn't win any races,' the porter said. 'How are you, my Colonel?'

'I couldn't be better,' the Colonel said. 'How are all the members of the Order?'

'All members are well.'

'Good,' said the Colonel. 'I will go in and see the Grand Master.'

'He is waiting for you, my Colonel.'

'Let us not keep him waiting, Jackson,' the Colonel said. 'You may proceed to the lobby with this gentleman and tell them to sign me in. See the Sergeant gets a room,' he said to the porter. 'We're here for the night only.'

'The Baron Alvarito was here looking for you.'

'I'll find him at Harry's.'

'Good, my Colonel.'

'Where is the Grand Master?'

'I'll find him for you.'

'Tell him I'll be in the bar.'

7

The bar was just across from the lobby of the Gritti, although lobby, the Colonel thought, was not the accurate term to describe that gracious entrance. Didn't Giotto describe a circle, he thought? No, that was in maths. What he remembered and loved best as an anecdote about that painter was: 'It was easy,' said Giotto as he drew the perfect circle. Who the hell had said that and where?

'Good evening, Privy Councillor,' he said to the barman, who was not a full paid-up member of the order but whom he did not wish to offend. 'What can I do for you?'

'Drink, my Colonel.'

The Colonel looked out of the windows and the door of the bar on to the waters of the Grand Canal. He could see the big black hitching post for the gondolas and the late afternoon winter light on the wind-swept water. Across the Canal was the old Palace and a wood barge, black and broad, was coming up the Canal, her bluff bows pushing up a wave even though she had the wind behind her.

'Make it a very dry Martini,' the Colonel said. 'A double.'

Just then the Grand Master came into the room. He was wearing his formal attire as a waiter. He was truly handsome as a man should be, from the inside out, so that his smile starts from his heart, or whatever is the centre of the body, and comes frankly and beautifully to the surface, which is the face.

He had a fine face with the long, straight nose of his part of the Veneto; the kind, gay, truthful eyes and the honourable white hair of his age, which was two years older than that of the Colonel.

He advanced smiling, lovingly and yet conspiratorially, since they both shared many secrets and he extended his hand, which was a big, long, strong, spatula-fingered hand; well kept as was becoming, as well as necessary, to his position and the Colonel extended his own hand, which had been shot through twice and was slightly misshapen. Thus contact was made between two old inhabitants of the Veneto, both men and brothers in their membership in the human race, the only club that either one paid dues to and brothers, too, in their love of an old country, much fought over and always triumphant in defeat, which they had both defended in their youth.

Their handshake was only long enough to feel, firmly, the contact and the pleasure of meeting and then the *Maître d'Hôtel* said, 'My Colonel.'

The Colonel said, '*Gran Maestro*.'

Then the Colonel asked the *Gran Maestro* to accompany him in a drink, but the *Maître d'Hôtel* said that he was working. It was impossible as well as forbidden.

'–forbidden,' said the Colonel.

'Of course,' the *Gran Maestro* said. 'But everyone must comply with his duty and here the rules are reasonable and we all should comply with them; me especially, as a matter of precept.'

'Not for nothing are you the *Gran Maestro*,' the Colonel said.

'Give me a small Carpano *punto e mezzo*,' the *Gran Maestro* said to the bar-tender, who was still outside of the Order for some small, not defined, unstated reason. 'To drink to the *ordine*.'

Thus, violating orders and the principle of precept and example in command, the Colonel and the *Gran Maestro* downed a quick one. They did not hurry nor did the *Gran Maestro* worry. They simply made it fast.

'Now, let us discuss the affairs of the Order,' the Colonel said. 'Are we in the secret chamber?'

'We are,' said the *Gran Maestro*. 'Or I declare it to be such.'

'Continue,' said the Colonel.

The Order, which was a purely fictitious organization, had been founded in a series of conversations between the *Gran Maestro* and the Colonel. Its name was *El Ordine Militar, Nobile y Espirituoso de los Caballeros de Brusadelli*. The Colonel and the head waiter both spoke Spanish and since that is the best language for founding orders, they had used it in the naming of this one, which was named after a particularly notorious multi-millionaire non-tax-paying profiteer of Milan, who had, in the course of a dispute over property, accused his young wife, publicly and legally through due process of law, of having deprived him of his judgement through her extraordinary sexual demands.

'*Gran Maestro*,' the Colonel said. 'Have you heard from our Leader, *The Reverend One*?'

'Not a word. He is silent these days.'

'He must be thinking.'

'He must.'

'Perhaps he is meditating on new and more distinguished shameful acts.'

'Perhaps. He has not given me any word.'

'But we can have confidence in him.'

'Until he dies,' the *Gran Maestro* said. 'After that he can roast in hell and we will revere his memory.'

'Giorgio,' the Colonel said. 'Give the *Gran Maestro* another short Carpano.'

'If it is your order,' the *Gran Maestro* said, 'I can only obey.'

They touched glasses.

'Jackson,' the Colonel called. 'You're on the town. You can sign here for chow. I don't want to see you until eleven hundred tomorrow in the lobby, unless you get into trouble. Do you have money?'

'Yes, sir,' Jackson said and thought, the old son of a bitch really *is* as crazy as they say. But he might have called me instead of shouting.

'I don't want to see you,' the Colonel said.

Jackson had entered the room and stood before him at a semblance of attention.

'I'm tired of seeing you, because you worry and you don't have fun. For Christ sake have yourself some fun.'

'Yes, sir.'

'You understand what I said?'

'Yes, sir.'

'Repeat it.'

'Ronald Jackson, T5 Serial Number 100678, will present himself in the lobby of this Gritti Hotel at 11.00 tomorrow morning, I don't know the date, sir, and will absent himself from the Colonel's sight and will have some fun. Or,' he added, 'will make every reasonable attempt to attain that objective.'

'I'm sorry, Jackson,' the Colonel said. 'I'm a—'

'I beg to differ with the Colonel,' Jackson said.

'Thank you, Jackson,' the Colonel told him. 'Maybe I'm not. I hope you are correct. Now muck off. You've got a room here, or you should have and you can sign for chow. Now try and have some fun.'

'Yes, sir,' said Jackson.

When he was gone, the *Gran Maestro* said to the Colonel, 'What is the boy? One of those *sad* Americans?'

'Yes,' the Colonel said. 'And by Jesus Christ we've got a lot of them. Sad, self-righteous, over-fed and under-trained. It they are under-trained, it is my fault. But we've got some good ones, too.'

'Do you think they would have done Grappa, Pasubio and the Basso Piave as we did?'

'The good ones, yes. Maybe better. But you know, in our army, they don't even shoot for self-inflicted wounds.'

'Jesus,' said the *Gran Maestro*. He and the Colonel both remembered the men who decided that they did not wish to die, not thinking that he who dies on Thursday does not have to die on Friday and how one soldier would wrap another's putteed leg in a sandbag so there would be no powder burns and loose off at his friend from as far a distance as he figured he could hit the calf of the leg without hitting bone and then fire twice over the parapet to alibi the shot. They had this knowledge shared between them and it was for this reason and for a true, good hatred of all those who profited by war that they had founded the Order.

They knew, the two of them, who loved and respected each other, how *poor* boys who did not want to die, would share the contents of a match-box to produce the infection that would keep them from the next murderous frontal attack.

They knew about the other boys who put the big ten-centime pieces under their arm-pits to produce jaundice. And they knew, too, about the richer boys who, in different cities, had paraffin injected under their knee-caps so they would not have to go to the war.

They knew how garlic could be used to produce certain effects which could absent a man from an attack and they knew all, or nearly all, of the other tricks; for one had been a sergeant and the other a lieutenant of infantry and they had fought on the three key points, Pasubio, Grappa and the Piave, where it all made sense.

They had fought, too, in the earlier stupid butchery on the Isonzo and the Carso. But they were both ashamed of those who had ordered that and they never thought about it except as a shameful, stupid thing to be forgotten and the Colonel remembered it technically as something to learn from. So, now, they had founded the Order of Brusadelli; noble, military and religious, and there were only five members.

'What is the news of the Order?' the Colonel asked the *Gran Maestro*.

'We have ascended the cook at the Magnificent to the rank of Commendatore. He comported himself as a man Three times on his fiftieth birthday. I accepted his statement without corroboration. He never lied ever.'

'No. He never lied. But it is a topic on which you must be chary in your credibility.'

'I believed him. He looked ruined.'

'I can remember him when he was a tough kid and we called him the cherry buster.'

'*Auch' io*.'

'Have you any concrete plans for the Order during the winter?'

'No, Supreme Commander.'

'Do you think we should give a homage to the honourable Pacciardi?'

'As you wish.'

'Let's defer it,' the Colonel said. He thought a moment, and signalled for another dry Martini.

'Do you think we might organize a homage and manifestation in some historic place such as San Marco or the Old Church at Torcello in favour of our Great Patron, Brusadelli, the Reverend One?'

'I doubt if the religious authorities would permit it at this moment.'

'Then let us abandon all ideas of public manifestations for this winter, and work within our cadres, for the good of the Order.'

'I think that is soundest,' the *Gran Maestro* said. 'We will regroup.'

'And how are you, yourself?'

'Awful,' the *Gran Maestro* said. 'I have low blood pressure, ulcers and I owe money.'

'Are you happy?'

'All the time,' the *Gran Maestro* said. 'I like my work very much and I meet extraordinary and interesting characters, also many Belgians. They are what we have instead of the locusts this year. Formerly we had the Germans. What was it Caesar said, "And the bravest of these are the Belgians." But not the best dressed. Do you agree?'

'I've seen them quite well costumed in Brussels,' the Colonel said. 'A well-fed, gay capital. Win, lose, or draw.'

'We should have fought in Flanders in the old days.'

'We were not born in the old days,' the Colonel said. 'So we automatically could not have fought then.'

'I wish we could have fought with the Condottieri when all you had to do was out-think them and they conceded. You could think and I would convey your orders.'

'We'd have to take a few towns for them to respect our thinking.'

'We would sack them if they defended them,' the *Gran Maestro* said. 'What towns would you take?'

'Not this one,' the Colonel said. 'I'd take Vicenza, Bergamo and Verona. Not necessarily in that order.'

'You'd have to take two more.'

'I know,' the Colonel said. He was a general now again and he was happy. 'I figured that I'd by-pass Brescia. It could fall of its own weight.'

'And how are you, Supreme Commander?' the *Gran Maestro* said, for this taking of towns had pulled him out of his depth.

He was at home in his small house in Treviso, close to the fast-flowing river under the old walls. The weeds waved in the current and the fish hung in the shelter of the weeds and rose to insects that touched the water in the dusk. He was at home, too, in all operations that did not involve more than a company and understood them as clearly as he understood the proper serving of a small dining-room; or a large dining-room.

But when the Colonel became a general officer again, as he had once been and thought in terms that were as far beyond him as calculus is distant from a man who has only the knowledge of arithmetic, then he was not at home and their contact was strained and he wished the Colonel would return to things they both knew together when they were a lieutenant and a sergeant.

'What would you do about Mantova?' the Colonel asked.

'I do not know, my Colonel. I do not know whom you are fighting, nor what forces they have, nor what forces are at your disposal.'

'I thought you said we were Condottieri. Based on this town or on Padova.'

'My Colonel,' the *Gran Maestro* said, and he had diminished in no way, 'I know nothing, truly, about Condottieri. Nor really how they fought then. I only said I would like to fight under you in such times.'

'There aren't any such times any more,' the Colonel said and the spell was broken.

What the hell, maybe there never was any spell, the Colonel thought. The hell with you, he said to himself. Cut it out and be a human being when you're half a hundred years old.

'Have another Carpano,' he said to the *Gran Maestro*.

'My Colonel, you will allow me to refuse because of the ulcers?'

'Yes. Yes. Of course. Boy, what's your name, Giorgio? Another dry Martini. *Secco, molto secco e doppio*.'

Breaking spells, he thought. It is not my trade. My trade is killing armed men. A spell should be armed if I'm to break it. But we have killed many things which were not armed. All right, spell breaker, retract.

'*Gran Maestro*,' he said. 'You are still *Gran Maestro* and—the Condottieri.'

'They were—many years ago, Supreme Commander.'

'Exactly,' the Colonel said.

But the spell was broken.

'I'll see you at dinner,' the Colonel said. 'What is there?'

'We will have anything you wish and what we do not have I will send for.'

'Do you have any fresh asparagus?'

'You know we cannot have it in these months. It comes in April and from Bassano.'

'Then you think of something and I'll eat it,' the Colonel said.

'How many will you be?' the Maître d'Hôtel asked.

'We'll be two,' the Colonel said. 'What time do you close the *bistro*?'

'We will serve dinner as late as you wish to eat, my Colonel.'

'I'll try to be in at a sound hour,' the Colonel said. 'Good-bye, *Gran Maestro*,' he said and smiled and gave the *Gran Maestro* his crooked hand.

'Good-bye, Supreme Commander,' said the *Gran Maestro* and the spell was existent again and almost complete.

But it was not quite complete and the Colonel knew it and he thought: why am I always a bastard and why can I not suspend this trade of arms and be a kind and good man as I would have wished to be.

I try always to be just, but I am brusque and I am brutal and it is not that I have erected the defence against brown-nosing my superiors and brown-nosing the world. I should be a better man with less wild boar blood in the small time which remains. We will try it out tonight, he thought. With whom, he thought and where, and God help me not to be bad.

'Giorgio,' he said to the barman, who had a face as white as a leper, but with no bulges and without the silver shine.

Giorgio did not really like the Colonel very much, or perhaps he was simply from Piemonte and cared for no one truly; which was understandable in cold people from a border province. Borderers are not trusters and the Colonel knew about this and expected nothing from anyone that they did not have to give.

'Giorgio,' he said to the pale-faced barman. 'Write these down for me please.'

He went out, walking as he had always walked, with a slightly exaggerated confidence, even when it was not needed and, in his always renewed plan of being kind, decent and good, he greeted the concierge, who was a friend, the assistant manager, who spoke Swahili and had been a prisoner of war in Kenya and was a most amiable man, young, full of juice, handsome, perhaps not yet a member of the Order, and experienced.

'And the *cavaliere ufficiale* who manages this place?' he asked. 'My friend?'

'He is not here,' the assistant manager said. 'For the moment, naturally,' he added.

'Give him my compliments,' the Colonel said. 'And have somebody show me to my room.'

'It is the usual room. You still wish it?'

'Yes. Have you taken care of the Sergeant?'

'He is well taken care of.'

'Good,' said the Colonel.

The Colonel proceeded to his room accompanied by the boy who carried his bag.

'This way, my Colonel,' the boy said, when the elevator halted with slight hydraulic inaccuracy at the top floor.

'Can't you run an elevator properly?' the Colonel asked.

'No, my Colonel,' the boy said. 'The current is not stable.'

8

The Colonel said nothing and preceded the boy down the corridor. It was large, wide and high ceilinged and there was a long and distinguished interval between the doors of the rooms on the side of the Grand Canal. Naturally, since it had been a palace, there were no rooms without excellent views, except those which had been made for the servants.

The Colonel found the walk long, although it was a very short one and when the waiter, who served the room, appeared, short, dark and with his glass eye in the left eye socket, gleaming, unable to smile his full, true smile as he worked the big key in the lock, the Colonel wished that the door would open more rapidly.

'Open it up,' he said.

'I will, my Colonel,' the waiter said. 'But you know these locks.'

Yes, the Colonel thought. I know them, but I wish that he would get it open.

'How are your family?' he said to the waiter, who had swung the door wide so that the Colonel, now entered, was within the room with the high, dark but well-mirrored *armoire*, the two good beds, the great chandelier and the view, through the still closed windows, on to the wind-beaten water of the Grand Canal.

The Canal was grey as steel now in the quick, failing, winter light and the Colonel said, 'Arnaldo, open the windows.'

'There is much wind, my Colonel, and the room is badly heated due to the lack of eletric power.'

'Due to the lack of rainfall,' the Colonel said. 'Open the windows. All of them.'

'As you wish, my Colonel.'

The waiter opened the windows and the north wind came into the room.

'Please call the desk and ask them to ring this number.' The waiter made the call while the Colonel was in the bathroom.

'The Contessa is not at home, my Colonel,' he said. 'They believe you might find her at Harry's.'

'You find everything on earth at Harry's.'

'Yes, my Colonel. Except, possibly, happiness.'

'I'll damn well find happiness, too,' the Colonel assured him. 'Happiness, as you know, is a movable feast.'

'I am aware of that,' the waiter said. 'I have brought Campari bitters and a bottle of Gordon's Gin. May I make you a Campari with gin and soda?'

'You're a good boy,' the Colonel said. 'Where did you bring them from? The bar?'

'No. I bought them while you were away so that you would not have to spend money at the bar. The bar is very costly.'

'I agree,' the Colonel agreed. 'But you should not use your own money on such a project.'

'I took a chance. We have both taken many. The gin was 3200 lire and is legitimate. The Campari was 800.'

'You're a very good boy,' the Colonel told him. 'How were the ducks?'

'My wife still speaks of them. We had never had wild ducks, since they are of such expense, and outside of our way of life. But one of our neighbours told her how to prepare them and these same neighbours ate them with us. I never knew that anything could be so wonderful to eat. When your teeth close on the small slice of meat it is an almost unbelievable delight.'

'I think so, too. There is nothing lovelier to eat than those fat iron-curtain ducks. You know their fly-way is through the great grain fields of the Danube. This is a splinter flight we have here, but they always come the same way since before there were shotguns.'

'I know nothing about shooting for sport,' the waiter said. 'We were too poor.'

'But many people without money shoot in the Veneto.'

'Yes. Of course. One hears them shoot all night. But we were poorer than that. We were poorer than you can know, my Colonel.'

'I think I can know.'

'Perhaps,' the waiter said. 'My wife also saved all the feathers and she asked me to thank you.'

'If we have any luck day after tomorrow, we'll get plenty. The big ducks with the green heads. Tell your wife, with luck, there will be good eating ducks, fat as pigs with what they have eaten from the Russians and with beautiful feathers.'

'How do you feel about the Russians, if it is not indiscreet to ask, my Colonel?'

'They are our potential enemy. So, as a soldier, I am prepared to fight them. But I like them very much and I have never known finer people nor people more as we are.'

'I have never had the good fortune to know them.'

'You will, boy. You will. Unless the Honourable Pacciardi stops them on the line of the Piave, which is a river which no longer contains water. It has been siphoned off for hydro-electric projects. Perhaps the Honourable Pacciardi will fight there. But I do not think he will fight for long.'

'I do not know the Honourable Pacciardi.'

'I know him,' said the Colonel.

'Now ask them to ring Harry's and see if the Contessa is there. If not, have them ring the house again.'

The Colonel took the drink Arnaldo, the glass-eyed waiter, made him. He did not want it and he knew that it was bad for him.

But he took it with his old wild-boar truculence, as he had taken everything all of his life and he moved, still cat-like when he moved, although it was an old cat now, over to the open window and looked out on the great Canal which was now becoming as grey as though Degas had painted it on one of his greyest days.

'Thanks very much for the drink,' the Colonel said and Arnaldo, who was talking into the telephone, nodded and smiled his glass-eyed smile.

I wish he did not have to have that glass eye, the Colonel thought. He only loved people, he thought, who had fought or been mutilated.

Other people were fine and you liked them and were good friends; but you only felt true tenderness and love for those who had been there and had received the castigation that everyone receives who goes there long enough.

So I'm a sucker for crips, he thought, drinking the unwanted drink. And any son of a bitch who has been hit solidly, as every man will be if he stays, then I love him.

Yes, his other, good, side said. You love them.

I'd rather not love anyone, the Colonel thought. I'd rather have fun.

And fun, his good side said to him, you have no fun when you do not love.

All right. I love more than any son of the great bitch alive, the Colonel said, but not aloud.

Aloud, he said, 'Where are you getting on that call, Arnaldo?'

'Cipriani has not come in,' the waiter said. 'They are expecting him at any moment and I am keeping the line open in case he arrives.'

'A costly procedure,' the Colonel said. 'Get me a reading on who's there so we don't waste time. I want to know exactly who is there.'

Arnaldo spoke guardedly into the mouthpiece of the telephone.

He covered the mouth of the phone with his hand and said, 'I am talking to Ettore. He says the Barone Alvarito is not there. The Count Andrea is there and he is rather drunk, Ettore says, but not too drunk for you to have fun together. The group of ladies that comes in each afternoon are there and there is a Greek Princess, that you know and several people that you do not know. Riff-raff from the American Consulate who have stayed on since noon.'

'Tell him to call back when the riff-raff goes and I'll come over.'

Arnaldo spoke into the phone, then turned to the Colonel who was looking out of the window at the Dome of the Dogana, 'Ettore says he will try to move them, but he is afraid Cipriani will not like it.'

'Tell him not to move them. They don't have to work this afternoon and there is no reason why they should not get drunk like any other man. I just don't want to see them.'

'Ettore says he will call back. He told me to tell you he thinks the position will fall of its own weight.'

'Thank him for calling,' the Colonel said.

He watched a gondola working up the Canal against the wind and thought, not with Americans drinking. I know they are bored. In this town, too. They are bored in this town. I know the place is cold and their wages are inadequate and what fuel costs. I admire their wives, for the valiant efforts they make to transport Keokuk to Venice, and their children already speak Italian like little Venetians. But no snapshots today, Jack. Today we are giving the snapshots, the bar-room confidences, the unwanted comradely drinks and the tedious woes of the consular services a miss.

'No second, third or fourth vice-consuls today, Arnaldo.'

'There are some very pleasant people from the Consulate.'

'Yeah,' the Colonel said. 'They had a hell of a nice consul here in 1918. Everybody liked him. I'll try to remember his name.'

'You go back a long way back, my Colonel.'

'I go back so damn far back that it isn't funny.'

'Do you remember everything from the old days?'

'Everything,' the Colonel said. 'Carroll was the man's name.'

'I have heard of him.'

'You weren't born then.'

'Do you think it is necessary to have been born at the time to know about things that have happened in this town, my Colonel?'

'You're perfectly correct. Tell me, does everybody always know about everything that happens in this town?'

'Not everybody. But nearly everybody,' the waiter said. 'After all, sheets are sheets and some one has to change them and someone has to wash them. Naturally I do not refer to the sheets in a hotel such as this.'

'I've had some damn good times in my life without sheets.'

'Naturally. But the gondoliers, while they are the most co-operative and, for me, the finest people that we have, speak among themselves.'

'Naturally.'

'Then the clergy. While they would never violate the secrecy of the confessional, talk among themselves.'

'It is to be expected.'

'Their housekeepers talk among themselves.'

'It is their right.'

'Then the waiters,' Arnaldo said. 'People talk at a table as though the waiter were stone-deaf. The waiter, according to his ethics, makes no attempt to ever overhear a conversation. But sometimes he cannot escape from hearing. Naturally, we have our own conversations among ourselves. Never in this hotel of course. I could go on.'

'I believe I get the point.'

'Not to mention the coiffeurs and the hair-dressers.'

'And what's the news from the Rialto now?'

'You will get it all at Harry's except the part you figure in.'

'Do I figure?'

'Everyone knows everything.'

'Well, it's a damn pleasant story.'

'Some people don't understand the Torcello part.'

'I'm damned if I do sometimes myself.'

'How old are you, my Colonel, if it is not too indiscreet to ask?'

'Fifty plus one. Why didn't you find out from the concierge? I fill out a slip there for the Questura.'

'I wanted to hear it from yourself and to congratulate you.'

'I don't know what you are talking about.'

'Let me congratulate you anyway.'

'I can't accept it.'

'You are very well liked in this city.'

'Thank you. That is a very great compliment.'

Just then the telephone buzzed.

'I'll take it,' the Colonel said and heard Ettore's voice say, 'Who speaks?'

'Colonel Cantwell.'

'The position has fallen, my Colonel.'

'Which way did they go?'

'Towards the Piazza.'

'Good. I will be there at once.'

'Do you want a table?'

'In the corner,' said the Colonel and hung up.

'I am off to Harry's.'

'Good hunting.'

'I hunt ducks day after tomorrow before first light in a *botte* in the marshes.'

'It will be cold, too.'

'I dare say,' the Colonel said and put on his trench coat and looked at his face in the glass of the long mirror as he put on his cap.

'An ugly face,' he said to the glass. 'Did you ever see a more ugly face?'

'Yes,' said Arnaldo. 'Mine. Every morning when I shave.'

'We both ought to shave in the dark,' the Colonel told him and went out the door.

9

As Colonel Cantwell stepped out of the door of the Gritti Palace Hotel he came out into the last sunlight of that day. There was still sunlight on the opposite side of the Square but the gondoliers preferred to be sheltered from the cold wind by lounging in the lee of the Gritti, than to use the last remaining heat of the sun on the windswept side of the Square.

After noting this, the Colonel turned to the right and walked along the Square to the paved street which turned off on the right. As he turned, he stopped for a moment and looked at the church of Santa Maria del Giglio.

What a fine, compact, and yet ready to be airborne building, he thought. I never realized a small church could look like a P47. Must find out when it was built and who built it. Damn, I wish I might walk around this town all my life. All my life, he thought. What a gag that is. A gag to gag on. A throttle to throttle you with. Come on, boy, he said to himself. No horse named Morbid ever won a race.

Besides, he thought, as he looked in the windows of the various shops he passed, the *charcuterie* with the Parmesan cheeses and the hams from San Daniele and the sausages *alla cacciatora* and the bottles of good Scotch whisky and real Gordon's Gin, the cutlery store, an antique dealer's with some good pieces and some old maps and prints, a second-rate restaurant disguised expensively as one of the first class and then came to the first bridge crossing a feeder canal with steps to be climbed; I don't feel so badly. There is only the buzzing. I remember when that started and I thought perhaps it was seven-year locusts in the trees and I did not like to ask young Lowry, but I did. And he answered, 'No, General, I don't hear any crickets or seven-year locusts. The night is perfectly quiet except for the usual noises.'

Then, as he climbed, he felt the twinges and coming down the other side, he saw two lovely looking girls. They were beautiful and hatless and poorly but chicly dressed, and they were talking very fast to each other and the wind was blowing their hair as they climbed with their long, easy striding Venetian legs and the Colonel said to himself, I'd better quit window gazing along this street and make that next bridge and two squares afterwards you turn due right and keep along it till you are in Harry's.

He did just that, twinging on the bridge, but walking with his same old stride and only seeing, quickly, the people that he passed. There's a lot of oxygen in this air, he thought, as he faced into the wind and breathed deeply.

Then he was pulling open the door of Harry's bar and was inside and he had made it again and was at home.

At the bar a tall, very tall, man, with a ravaged face of great breeding, merry blue eyes and the long, loose-coupled body of a buffalo wolf said, 'My ancient and depraved Colonel.'

'My wicked Andrea.'

They embraced and the Colonel felt the rough texture of Andrea's handsome tweed coat that must have been entering, at least, its twentieth year.

'You look well, Andrea,' the Colonel said.

It was a lie and they both knew it.

'I am,' said Andrea, returning the lie. 'I must say I never felt better. You look extraordinarily well, yourself.'

'Thank you, Andrea. Us healthy bastards shall inherit the earth.'

'Very good idea. I must say I wouldn't mind inheriting something these days.'

'You have no kick. You'll inherit well over six feet four of it.'

'Six feet six,' said Andrea. 'You wicked old man. Are you still slaving away at *la vie militaire*?'

'I don't slave too hard at it,' the Colonel said. 'I'm down to shoot at San Relajo.'

'I know. But don't make jokes in Spanish at this hour. Alvarito was looking for you. He said to tell you he'd be back.'

'Good. Is your lovely wife and are the children well?'

'Absolutely, and they asked me to remember them to you if I saw you. They're down in Rome. There comes your girl. Or one of your girls.' He was so tall he could see into the now almost dark street, but this was a girl you could recognize if it was much darker than it was at this hour.

'Ask her to have a drink with us here before you carry her off to that corner table. Isn't she a lovely girl?'

'She is.'

Then she came into the room, shining in her youth and tall striding beauty and the carelessness the wind had made of her hair. She had a pale, almost olive-coloured skin, a profile that could break your, or anyone else's, heart and her dark hair, of an olive texture, hung down over her shoulders.

'Hello, my great beauty,' the Colonel said.

'Oh, oh, hello,' she said. 'I thought I would miss you. I am so sorry to be late.'

Her voice was low and delicate and she spoke English with caution.

'*Ciao*, Andrea,' she said. 'How is Emily and are the children?'

'Probably just the same as when I answered that same question for you at noon.'

'I am so sorry,' she said and blushed. 'I am so excited and I always say the wrong things. What should I say? Have you had a good time here all afternoon?'

'Yes,' said Andrea. 'With my old friend and severest critic.'

'Who is that?'

'Scotch whisky and water.'

'I suppose if he must tease me he must,' she said to the Colonel. 'But you won't tease me, will you?'

'Take him over to that corner table and talk to him. I'm tired of you both.'

'I'm not tired of you,' the Colonel told him. 'But I think it is a good idea. Should we have a drink sitting down, Renata?'

'I'd love to if Andrea isn't angry.'

'I'm never angry.'

'Would you have a drink with us, Andrea?'

'No,' said Andrea. 'Get along to your table. I'm sick of seeing it unoccupied.'

'Good-bye, Caro. Thanks for the drink we didn't have.'

'*Ciao*, Ricardo,' Andrea said and that was all.

He turned his fine, long, tall back on them and looked into the mirror that is placed behind bars so a man can tell when he is drinking too much and decided that he did not like what he saw there. 'Ettore,' he said. 'Please put this nonsense on my bill.'

He walked out after waiting carefully for his coat, swinging into it and tipping the man who brought it exactly what he should be tipped plus twenty per cent.

At the corner table, Renata said, 'Do you think we hurt his feelings?'

'No. He loves you and he likes me.'

'Andrea is so nice. And you're so nice.'

'Waiter,' the Colonel called; then asked, 'Do you want a dry Martini, too?'

'Yes,' she said. 'I'd love one.'

'Two very dry Martinis,' the Colonel said. 'Montgomerys. Fifteen to one.'

The waiter, who had been in the desert, smiled and was gone and the Colonel turned to Renata.

'You're nice,' he said. 'You're also very beautiful and lovely and I love you.'

'You always say that and I don't know what it means but I like to hear it.'

'How old are you now?'

'Nearly nineteen. Why?'

'And you don't know what it means?'

'No. Why should I? Americans always say it to you before they go away. It seems to be necessary to them. But I love you very much, too, whatever that is.'

'Let's have a fine time,' the Colonel said. 'Let's not think about anything at all.'

'I would like that. I cannot think very well this time of day at any rate.'

'Here are the drinks,' the Colonel said. 'Remember not to say, chin-chin.'

'I remember that from before. I never say chin-chin, nor here's to you, nor bottoms up.'

'We just raise the glass to each other and, if you wish, we can touch the edges.'

'I wish,' she said.

The Martinis were icy cold and true Montgomerys and, after touching the edges, they felt them glow happily all through their upper bodies.

'And what have you been doing?' the Colonel asked.

'Nothing. I still wait to go away to school.'

'Where now?'

'God knows. Wherever I go to learn English.'

'Turn your head and raise your chin once for me.'

'You're not making fun?'

'No. I'm not making fun.'

She turned her head and raised her chin, without vanity, nor coquetry and the Colonel felt his heart turn over inside him, as though some sleeping animal had rolled over in its burrow and frightened, deliciously, the other animal sleeping close beside.

'Oh you,' he said. 'Would you ever like to run for Queen of Heaven?'

'That would be sacrilegious.'

'Yes,' he said. 'I suppose it would and I withdraw the suggestion.'

'Richard,' she said. 'No I can't say it.'

'Say it.'

'No.'

The Colonel thought, I order you to say it. And she said, 'Please never look at me like that.'

'I'm sorry,' the Colonel said. 'I had just slipped into my trade unconsciously.'

'And if we were such a thing as married would you practise your trade in the home?'

'No. I swear it. I never have. Not in my heart.'

'With no one?'

'With no one of your sex.'

'I don't like that word your sex. It sounds as though you were practising your trade.'

'I throw my trade out of that goddamn window into the Grand Canal.'

'There,' she said. 'You see how quickly you practise it?'

'All right,' he said. 'I love you and my trade can gently leave.'

'Let me feel your hand,' she said. 'It's all right. You can put it on the table.'

'Thank you,' the Colonel said.

'Please don't,' she said. 'I wanted to feel it because all last week, every night, or I think nearly every night, I dreamed about it and it was a strange mixed-up dream and I dreamed it was the hand of Our Lord.'

'That's bad. You oughtn't to do that.'

'I know it. That's just what I dreamed.'

'You aren't on the junk, are you?'

'I don't know what you mean and please don't make fun when I tell you something true. I dreamed just as I say.'

'What did the hand do?'

'Nothing. Or maybe that is not true. Mostly it was just a hand.'

'Like this one?' The Colonel asked, looking at the misshapen hand with distaste and remembering the two times that had made it that way.

'Not like. It *was* that one. May I touch it carefully with my fingers if it does not hurt?'

'It does not hurt. Where it hurts is in the head, the legs and the feet. I don't believe there's any sensation in that hand.'

'You're wrong,' she said. 'Richard. There is very much sensation in that hand.'

'I don't like to look at it much. You don't think we could skip it.'

'Of course. But you don't have to dream about it.'

'No. I have other dreams.'

'Yes. I can imagine. But I dream lately about this hand. Now that I have touched it carefully, we can talk about funny things if you like. What is there funny we should talk about?'

'Let's look at the people and discuss them.'

'That's lovely,' she said. 'And we won't do it with malice. Only with our best wit. Yours and mine.'

'Good,' the Colonel said. 'Waiter, *Ancora due Martini*.'

He did not like to call for Montgomerys in a tone that could be overheard because there were two obvious Britishers at the next table.

The male might have been wounded, the Colonel thought, although from his looks, it seems unlikely. But God help me to avoid brutality. And look at Renata's eyes, he thought. They are probably the most beautiful of all the beautiful things she has with the longest honest lashes I have ever seen and she never uses them for anything except to look at you honestly and straight. What a damn wonderful girl and what am I doing here anyway? It is wicked. She is your last and true and only love, he thought, and that's not evil. It is only unfortunate. No, he thought, it is damned fortunate and you are very fortunate.

They sat at a small table in the corner of the room and on their right there were four women at a larger table. One of the women was in mourning; a mourning so theatrical that it reminded the Colonel of the Lady Diana

Manners playing the nun in Max Reinhardt's 'The Miracle'. This woman had an attractive, plump, naturally gay face and her mourning was incongruous.

At the table there was another woman who had hair three times as white as hair can be, the Colonel thought. She, also, had a pleasant face. There were two other women whose faces meant nothing to the Colonel.

'Are they lesbians?' he asked the girl.

'I do not know,' she said. 'They are all very nice people.'

'I should say they are lesbians. But maybe they are just good friends. Maybe they are both. It means nothing to me and it was not a criticism.'

'You are nice when you are gentle.'

'Do you suppose the word gentleman derives from a man who is gentle?'

'I do not know,' the girl said, and she ran her fingers very lightly over the scarred hand. 'But I love you when you are gentle.'

'I'll try very hard to be gentle,' the Colonel said. 'Who do you suppose that son of a bitch is at the table beyond them?'

'You don't stay gentle very long,' the girl said. 'Let us ask Ettore.'

They looked at the man at the third table. He had a strange face like an over-enlarged, disappointed weasel or ferret. It looked as pock-marked and as blemished as the mountains of the moon seen through a cheap telescope and, the Colonel thought, it looked like Goebbels's face, if Herr Goebbels had ever been in a plane that burned and not been able to bale out before the fire reached him.

Above this face, which was ceaselessly peering, as though the answer might be found by enough well-directed glances and by queries, there was black hair that seemed to have no connexion with the human race. The man looked as though he had been scalped and then the hair replaced. Very interesting, the Colonel thought. Can he be a compatriot? Yes, he must.

A little spit ran out of the corner of his mouth as he spoke, peeringly, with the elderly, wholesome looking woman who was with him. She looks like anybody's mother in an illustration in *The Ladies' Home Journal,* the Colonel thought. *The Ladies' Home Journal* was one of the magazines received regularly at the Officers' Club in Trieste and the Colonel looked through it when it came. It is a wonderful magazine, he thought, because it combines sexology and beautiful foods. It makes me hungry both ways.

But who do you suppose that character is? He looks like a caricature of an American who has been run one half way through a meat chopper and then been boiled, slightly, in oil. I'm not being so gentle, he thought.

Ettore, with his emaciated face and his love of joking and fundamental and abiding disrespect, came over and the Colonel said, 'Who is that spiritual character?'

Ettore shook his head.

The man was short and dark with glossy black hair that did not seem to go with his strange face. He looked, the Colonel thought, as though he had forgotten to change his wig as he grew older. Has a wonderful face though, the Colonel thought. Looks like some of the hills around Verdun. I don't suppose he could be Goebbels and he picked up that face in the last days when they were all playing at Götterdämmerung. *Komm' Süsser Tod*, he thought. Well they sure bought themselves a nice big piece of Süsser Tod at the end.

'You don't want a nice Süsser Tod sandwich do you Miss Renata?'

'I don't think so,' the girl said. 'Though I love Bach and I am sure Cipriani could make one.'

'I was not talking against Bach,' the Colonel said.

'I know it.'

'Hell,' the Colonel said. 'Bach was practically a co-belligerent. As you were,' he added.

'I don't think we have to talk against me.'

'Daughter,' the Colonel said. 'When will you learn that I might joke against you because I love you?'

'Now,' she said. 'I've learned it. But you know it's fun not to joke too rough.'

'Good. I've learned it.'

'How often do you think of me during the week?'

'All of the time.'

'No. Tell me truly.'

'All of the time. Truly.'

'Do you think it is this bad for everyone?'

'I wouldn't know,' the Colonel said. 'That's one of the things I would not know.'

'I hope it's not this bad for everyone. I had no idea it could be this bad.'

'Well you know now.'

'Yes,' the girl said. 'I know now. I know now and for keeps and for always. Is that the correct way to say it?'

'I know now is enough,' the Colonel said. 'Ettore, that character with the inspiring face and the nice looking woman with him doesn't live at the Gritti does he?'

'No,' Ettore said. 'He lives next door but he goes to the Gritti sometimes to eat.'

'Good,' the Colonel said. 'It will be wonderful to see him if I should ever be down-hearted. Who is the woman with him? His wife? His mother? His daughter?'

'There you have me,' Ettore said. 'We haven't kept track of him in Venice. He has aroused neither love, hate, dislike, fear nor suspicion. Do you really want to know anything about him? I could ask Cipriani.'

'Let us skip him,' the girl said. 'Is that how you say it?'

'Let's skip him,' the Colonel said.

'When we have so little time, Richard. He is rather a waste of time.'

'I was looking at him as at a drawing by Goya. Faces are pictures, too.'

'Look at mine and I will look at yours. Please skip the man. He didn't come here to do anyone any harm.'

'Let me look at your face and you not look at mine.'

'No,' she said. 'That's not fair. I have to remember yours all week.'

'And what do I do?' the Colonel asked her.

Ettore came over, unable to avoid conspiracy and, having gathered his intelligence rapidly and as a Venetian should, said, 'My colleague who works at his hotel, says that he drinks three or four highballs and then writes vastly and fluently far into the night.'

'I dare say that makes marvellous reading.'

'I dare say,' Ettore said. 'But it was hardly the method of Dante.'

'Dante was another *vieux con*,' the Colonel said. 'I mean as a man. Not as a writer.'

'I agree,' Ettore said. 'I think you will find no one, outside of Firenze, who has studied his life who would not agree.'

'Eff Florence,' the Colonel said.

'A difficult manœuvre,' Ettore said. 'Many have attempted it but very few have succeeded. Why do you dislike it, my Colonel?'

'Too complicated to explain. But it was the depot,' he said *deposito*, 'of my old regiment when I was a boy.'

'That I can understand. I have my own reasons for disliking it, too. You know a good town?'

'Yes,' said the Colonel. 'This one. A part of Milano; and Bologna. And Bergamo.'

'Cipriani has a large store of vodka in case the Russians should come,' Ettore said, loving to joke rough.

'They'll bring their own vodka, duty free.'

'Still I believe Cipriani is prepared for them.'

'Then he is the only man who is,' the Colonel said. 'Tell him not to take any cheques from junior officers on the Bank of Odessa and thank you for the data on my compatriot. I won't take more of your time.'

Ettore left and the girl turned towards him and looked in his old steel eyes and put both her hands on his bad one and said, 'You were quite gentle.'

'And you are most beautiful and I love you.'

'It's nice to hear it anyway.'

'What are we going to do about dinner?'

'I will have to call my home and find out if I can come out.'

'Why do you look sad now?'

'Do I?'

'Yes.'

'I am not, really. I am as happy as I ever am. Truly. Please believe me, Richard. But how would you like to be a girl nineteen years old in love with a man over fifty years old that you knew was going to die?'

'You put it a little bluntly,' the Colonel said. 'But you are very beautiful when you say it.'

'I never cry,' the girl said. 'Never. I made a rule not to. But I would cry now.'

'Don't cry,' the Colonel said. 'I'm gentle now and the hell with the rest of it.'

'Say once again that you love me.'

'I love you and I love you and I love you.'

'Will you do your best not to die?'

'Yes.'

'What did the doctor say?'

'So-so.'

'Not worse?'

'No,' he lied.

'Then let us have another Martini,' the girl said. 'You know I never drank a Martini until we met.'

'I know. But you drink them awfully well.'

'Shouldn't you take the medicine?'

'Yes,' the Colonel said. 'I should take the medicine.'

'May I give it to you?'

'Yes,' the Colonel said. 'You may give it to me.'

They continued to sit at the table in the corner and some people went out and others came in. The Colonel felt a little dizzy from the medicine and he let it ride. That's the way it always is, he thought. To hell with it.

He saw the girl watching him and he smiled at her. It was an old smile that he had been using for fifty years, ever since he first smiled and it was still as sound as your grandfather's Purdey shotgun. I guess my older brother has that, he thought. Well, he could always shoot better than I could and he deserves it.

'Listen, Daughter,' he said. 'Don't be sorry for me.'

'I'm not. Not at all. I just love you.'

'It isn't much of a trade is it?' He said *oficio* instead of trade, because they spoke Spanish together, too, when they left French and when they did not wish to speak English before other people. Spanish is a rough language, the Colonel thought, rougher than a corncob sometimes. But you can say what you mean in it and make it stick.

'*Es un oficio bastante malo*,' he repeated, 'loving me.'

'Yes. But it is the only one I have.'

'Don't you write any more poetry.'

'It was young girl poetry. Like young girl painting. Everyone is talented at a certain age.'

At what age do you become old in this country, the Colonel thought. No one is ever old in Venice, but they grow up very fast. I grew up very rapidly in the Veneto myself and I was never as old as I was at twenty-one.

'How is your mother?' he asked, lovingly.

'She is very well. She does not receive and she sees almost no one because of her sorrow.'

'Do you think she would mind if we had a baby?'

'I don't know. She is very intelligent, you know. But I would have to marry someone, I suppose. I don't really want to.'

'We could be married.'

'No,' she said. 'I thought it over and I thought we should not. It is just a decision as the one about crying.'

'Maybe you make wrong decisions. Christ knows I've made a few and too many men are dead from when I was wrong.'

'I think, perhaps, you exaggerate. I don't believe you made many wrong decisions.'

'Not many,' the Colonel said. 'But enough. Three is plenty in my trade and I made all three.'

'I'd like to know about them.'

'They'd bore you,' the Colonel told her. 'They beat the hell out of me to remember them. So what would they do to some outsider?'

'Am I an outsider?'

'No. You're my true love. My last and only and true love.'

'Did you make them early or late? The decisions.'

'I made them early. In the middle. And late.'

'Wouldn't you tell me about them? I would like to have a share in your sad trade.'

'The hell with them,' the Colonel said. 'They were made and they've all been paid for. Only you can't pay for that.'

'Can you tell me about that and why?'

'No,' the Colonel said. And that was the end of that.

'Then let's have fun.'

'Let's,' the Colonel said. 'With our one and only life.'

'Maybe there are others. Other lives.'

'I don't think so,' the Colonel said. 'Turn your head sideways, beauty.'

'Like this?'

'Like that,' the Colonel said. 'Exactly like that.'

So, the Colonel thought, here we come into the last round and I do not know even the number of the round. I have loved but three women and have lost them thrice.

You lose them the same way you lose a battalion; by errors of judgement; orders that are impossible to fulfil and through impossible conditions. Also through brutality.

I have lost three battalions in my life and three women and now I have a fourth and loveliest and where the hell does it end?

You tell me, General, and, incidentally, while we are discussing the matter and it is a frank discussion of the situation and in no sense a Council of War, as you have so often pointed out to me General: GENERAL WHERE IS YOUR CAVALRY?

I have thought so, he said to himself. The Commanding Officer does not know where his cavalry is and his cavalry are not completely accurate as to their situation, nor their mission and they will, some of them, *enough*, muck off as cavalry have always mucked off in all the wars since they, the Cavalry, had the big horses.

'Beauty,' he said, '*Ma très chère et bien aimée*. I am very dull and I am sorry.'

'You are never dull, to me, and I love you and I only wish we could be cheerful tonight.'

'We damn well will be,' said the Colonel. 'Do you know anything particular we should be cheerful about?'

'We might be cheerful about us, and about the town. You've often been very cheerful.'

'Yes,' the Colonel agreed. 'I have been.'

'Don't you think we could do it once more?'

'Sure. Of course. Why not?'

'Do you see the boy with the wave in his hair, that is natural, and he only pushes it a little, skilfully, to be more handsome?'

'I see him,' the Colonel said.

'He is a very good painter, but he has false teeth in front because he was a little bit *pédéraste* once and other *pédérastes* attacked him one night on the Lido when there was a full moon.'

'How old are you?'

'I will be nineteen.'

'How do you know this?'

'I know it from the Gondoliere. This boy is a very good painter, for now. There aren't any really good painters now. But with false teeth, now, in his twenty-fifth year, what a thing.'

'I love you very truly,' the Colonel said.

'I love you very truly, too. Whatever that means in American. I also love you in Italian, against all my judgement and all of my wishes.'

'We shouldn't wish for too goddamn much,' the Colonel said. 'Because we are always liable to get it.'

'I agree,' she said. 'But I would like to get what I wish for now.'

Neither of them said anything and then the girl said, 'That boy, he is a man now, of course, and goes with very many women to hide what he is, painted my portrait once. You can have it if you like.'

'Thank you,' the Colonel said. 'I would love it.'

'It is very romantic. My hair is twice as long as it has ever been and I look as though I were rising from the sea without the head wet. Actually, you rise from the sea with the hair very flat and coming to points at the end. It is almost the look of a very nearly dead rat. But Daddy paid him adequately for the portrait, and, while it is not truly me, it is the way you like to think of me.'

'I think of you when you come from the sea too.'

'Of course. Very ugly. But you might like to have this portrait for a souvenir.'

'Your lovely mother would not mind?'

'Mummy would not mind. She would be glad to be rid of it, I think. We have better pictures in the house.'

'I love you and your mother both very much.'

'I must tell her,' the girl said.

'Do you think that pock-marked jerk is really a writer?'

'Yes. If Ettore says so. He loves to joke but he does not lie. Richard, what is a jerk? Tell me truly.'

'It is a little rough to state. But I think it means a man who has never worked at his trade (*oficio*) truly, and is presumptuous in some annoying way.'

'I must learn to use the term properly.'

'Don't use it,' the Colonel said.

Then the Colonel asked, 'When do I get the portrait?'

'Tonight if you wish it. I'll have someone wrap it and send it from the house. Where will you hang it?'

'In my quarters.'

'And no one will come in and make remarks and speak badly of me?'

'No. They damn well will not. Also I'll tell them it is a portrait of my daughter.'

'Did you ever have a daughter?'

'No. I always wanted one.'

'I can be your daughter as well as everything else.'

'That would be incest.'

'I don't think that would be so terrible in a city as old as this and that has seen what this city has seen.'

'Listen, Daughter.'

'Good,' she said. 'That was fine. I liked it.'

'All right,' the Colonel said and his voice was thickened a little. 'I liked it, too.'

'Do you see now why I love you when I know better than to do it?'

'Look, Daughter. Where should we dine?'

'Wherever you like.'

'Would you eat at the Gritti?'

'Of course.'

'Then call the house and ask for permission.'

'No. I decided not to ask permission but to send word where I was dining. So they would not worry.'

'But do you really prefer the Gritti?'

'I do. Because it is a lovely restaurant and it is where you live and anyone can look at us that wants to.'

'When did you get like that?'

'I have always been like that. I have never cared what anyone thought, ever. Nor have I ever done anything that I was ashamed of except tell lies when I was a little girl and be unkind to people.'

'I wish we could be married and have five sons,' the Colonel said.

'So do I,' the girl said. 'And send them to the five corners of the world.'

'Are there five corners to the world?'

'I don't know,' she said. 'It sounded as though there were when I said it. And now we are having fun again, aren't we?'

'Yes, Daughter,' the Colonel said,

'Say it again. Just as you said it.'

'Yes, Daughter.'

'Oh,' she said. 'People must be very complicated. Please may I take your hand?'

'It's so damned ugly and I dislike looking at it.'

'You don't know about your hand.'

'That's a matter of opinion,' he said. 'I'd say you were wrong, Daughter.'

'Maybe I am wrong. But we're having fun again and whatever the bad thing was is gone now.'

'It's gone the way the mist is burned off the hollows in broken ground when the sun comes out,' the Colonel said. 'And you're the sun.'

'I want to be the moon, too.'

'You are,' the Colonel told her. 'Also any particular planet that you wish to be and I will give you an accurate location of the planet. Christ, Daughter, you can be a goddamn constellation if you like. Only that's an airplane.'

'I'll be the moon. She has many troubles too.'

'Yes. Her sorrows come regularly. But she always fills before she wanes.'

'She looks so sad to me sometimes across the Canal, that I cannot stand it.'

'She's been around a long time,' the Colonel said.

'Do you think we should have one more Montgomery?' the girl asked and the Colonel noticed that the British were gone.

He had been noticing nothing but her lovely face. I'll get killed some time that way, he thought. On the other hand it is a form of concentration I suppose. But it is damned careless.

'Yes,' he said. 'Why not?'

'They make me feel very good,' the girl said.

'They have a certain effect on me, too, the way Cipriani makes them.'

'Cipriani is very intelligent.'

'He's more than that. He's able.'

'Some day he'll own all Venice.'

'Not quite all,' the Colonel disagreed. 'He'll never own you.'

'No,' she said. 'Nor will anyone else unless you want me.'

'I want you, Daughter. But I don't want to own you.'

'I know it,' the girl said. 'And that's one more reason why I love you.'

'Let's get Ettore and have him call up your house. You can tell them about the portrait.'

'You are quite correct. If you want the portrait tonight, I must speak to the butler to have it wrapped and sent. I will also ask to speak to Mummy and tell her where we are dining, and, if you like, I will ask her permission.'

'No,' the Colonel said. 'Ettore, two Montgomerys, super Montgomerys, with garlic olives, not the big ones, and please call the home of this lady and let her know when you have completed the communication. And all of this as rapidly as possible.'

'Yes, my Colonel.'

'Now, Daughter, let us resume the having of the fun.'

'It was resumed when you spoke,' she said.

10

They were walking, now, along the right side of the street that led to the Gritti. The wind was at their backs and it blew the girl's hair forward. The wind parted her hair in the back and blew it forward. They were looking in the shop windows and the girl stopped in front of the lighted window of a jewellery shop.

There were many good pieces of old jewellery in the window and they stood and looked at them and pointed out the best ones to each other, unclasping their hands to do so.

'Is there anything you really want? I could get it in the morning. Cipriani would loan me the money.'

'No,' she said. 'I do not want anything but I notice that you never give me presents.'

'You are much richer than I am. I bring you small things from the PX and I buy you drinks and meals.'

'And take me in gondolas and to lovely places in the country.'

'I never thought you wanted presents of hard stones.'

'I don't. It is just the thought of giving and then one looks at them and thinks about them when they are worn.'

'I'm learning,' the Colonel said. 'But what could I buy you on Army pay that would be like your square emeralds?'

'But don't you see. I inherited them. They came from my grandmother, and she had them from her mother who had them from her mother. Do you think it is the same to wear stones that come from dead people?'

'I never thought about it.'

'You can have them if you like, if you like stones. To me they are only something to wear like a dress from Paris. You don't like to wear your dress uniform, do you?'

'No.'

'You don't like to carry a sword, do you?'

'No, repeat, no.'

'You are not that kind of a soldier and I am not that sort of girl. But some time give me something lasting that I can wear and be happy each time I wear it.'

'I see,' the Colonel said. 'And I will.'

'You learn fast about things you do not know,' the girl said. 'And you make lovely quick decisions. I would like you to have the emeralds and you could keep them in your pocket like a lucky piece, and feel them if you were lonely.'

'I don't put my hands much in my pockets when I'm working. I usually twirl a stick, or something, or point things out with a pencil.'

'But you could put your hand in your pocket only once in a long time and feel them.'

'I'm not lonely when I'm working. I have to think too hard to ever be lonely.'

'But you are not working now.'

'No. Only preparing the best way to be overrun.'

'I'm going to give them to you anyway. I'm quite sure Mummy will understand. Also I won't need to tell her for quite a long time. She keeps no check on my things. I'm sure my maid would never tell her.'

'I don't think I should take them.'

'You should, please, to give me pleasure.'

'I'm not sure it's honourable.'

'That is like not being sure whether you are a virgin. What you do to give pleasure to another whom you love is most honourable.'

'All right,' the Colonel said. 'I will take them for better or for worse.'

'Now you say thank you,' the girl said and slipped them into his pocket as quickly and ably as a jewel thief might. 'I brought them with me because I have been thinking and deciding about this all week.'

'I thought you thought about my hand.'

'Don't be surly, Richard. And *you* should never be stupid. It is your hand you touch them with. Didn't you think of that?'

'No. And I was stupid. What would you like from that window?'

'I would like that small Negro with the ebony face and the turban made of chip diamonds with the small ruby on the crown of the turban. I should wear it as a pin. Everyone wore them in the old days in this city and the faces were those of their confidential servants. I have coveted this for a long time, but I wanted you to give it to me.'

'I'll send it in the morning.'

'No. Give it to me when we have lunch before you go.'

'Right,' the Colonel said.

'Now we must walk or we will be too late for dinner.'

They started to walk, arm through arm, and as they went up the first bridge the wind lashed at them.

When the twinge came, the Colonel said to himself, the hell with that.

'Richard,' the girl said. 'Put your hand in your pocket to please me and feel them.'

The Colonel did.

'They feel wonderful,' he said.

II

They came in, out of the wind and the cold, through the main entrance of the Gritti Palace Hotel, into the light and warmth of the lobby.

'Good evening, Contessa,' the concierge said. 'Good evening, my Colonel. It must be cold outside.'

'It is,' the Colonel said, and did not add any of the rough or obscene phrases about the extent of the cold, or the force of the wind, that he could ordinarily have employed, for their mutual pleasure when speaking, alone, with the concierge.

As they entered the long hallway that led to the big stairs and to the elevator, leaving, on your right, the bar, the doorway on to the Grand Canal, and the entrance to the dining-room, the *Gran Maestro* came out of the bar.

He was wearing a formal white jacket, cut long, and he smiled at them and said, 'Good evening, my Countess. Good evening, my Colonel.'

'*Gran Maestro*,' the Colonel said.

The *Gran Maestro* smiled and, still bowing, said, 'We are dining in the bar at the far end. There is no one here now in the winter time and the dining-room is too big. I have saved your table. We have a very fine lobster if you would like him to commence with.'

'Is he really fresh?'

'I saw him this morning when he came from the market in a basket. He was alive and a dark green and completely unfriendly.'

'Would you like lobster, Daughter, to start your dinner?'

The Colonel was conscious of using the word, and so was the *Gran Maestro*, and so was the girl. But to each one it meant a different thing.

'I wanted to have him for you in case any *pescecani* came in. They are down now to gamble at the Lido. I was not trying to sell him.'

'I would love some lobster,' the girl said. 'Cold, and with mayonnaise. The mayonnaise rather stiff.' She said this in Italian.

'It isn't too expensive?' she said to the Colonel seriously.

'*Ay hija mía*,' the Colonel said.

'Feel in your right pocket,' she said.

'I'll see that he is not too expensive,' the *Gran Maestro* said. 'Or I'll buy him myself. I could get him quite easily with a week's wages.'

'Sold to TRUST,' the Colonel said, this being the code designation of the task force occupying Trieste. 'He only costs me a day's wages.'

'Put your hand in your right-hand pocket and feel very rich,' the girl said.

The *Gran Maestro* had sensed this was a private joke and had gone; silently. He was happy about the girl, whom he respected and admired, and he was happy for his Colonel.

'I am rich,' the Colonel said. 'But if you tease me about them, I will give them back, and on the linen tablecloth, and in public.'

He was teasing rough in his turn; throwing in the counter-attack without even thinking.

'No you won't,' she said. 'Because you love them already.'

'I would take anything I love and throw it off the highest cliff you ever saw and not wait to hear it bounce.'

'No, you wouldn't,' the girl said. 'You would not throw me off any high cliffs.'

'No,' the Colonel agreed. 'And forgive me for talking badly.'

'You didn't talk very badly and I didn't believe it anyway,' the girl told him. 'Now shall I go to the women's room to comb my hair and make myself presentable, or should I come up to your room?'

'Which do you wish?'

'To come to your room, of course, and see how you live and how things are there.'

'What about the hotel?'

'Everything is known in Venice anyway. But it is also known who my family are and that I am a good girl. Also they know it is you and it is I. We have some credit to exhaust.'

'Good,' the Colonel said. 'By stairs or elevator?'

'By elevator,' she said, and he heard the change in her voice. 'You can call a boy or we can run it ourselves.'

'We run it ourselves,' the Colonel said. 'I checked out on elevators long ago.'

It was a good ride with a slight bump, and a rectification at the end, and the Colonel thought: Checked out, eh? You better be checked out again.

The corridor was now not simply beautiful, but exciting, and putting the key into the lock was not a simple process, but a rite.

'Here it is,' the Colonel said when he swung the door open. 'What there is of it.'

'It is charming,' the girl said. 'But it is awfully cold with the windows open.'

'I'll close them.'

'No, please. Leave them open if you like it that way.'

The Colonel kissed her and felt her wonderful, long, young, lithe and properly built body against his own body, which was hard and good, but beat-up, and as he kissed her he thought of nothing.

They kissed for a long time, standing straight, and kissing true, in the cold of the open windows that were on to the Grand Canal.

'Oh,' she said. Then, 'Oh.'

'We owe nothing,' the Colonel said. 'Not a thing.'

'Will you marry me and will we have the five sons?'

'I will! I will!'

'The thing is that, would you?'

'Of course.'

'Kiss me once again and make the buttons of your uniform hurt me but not too much.'

They stood there and kissed each other true. 'I have a disappointment for you, Richard,' she said. 'I have a disappointment about everything.'

She said it as a flat statement and it came to the Colonel in the same way as a message came from one of the three battalions, when the battalion commander spoke the absolute truth and told you the worst.

'You are positive?'

'Yes.'

'My poor Daughter,' he said.

Now there was nothing dark about the word and she was his daughter, truly, and he pitied her and loved her.

'No matter,' he said. 'You comb yourself and make a new mouth and all that, and we will have a good dinner.'

'Say once more, first, that you love me and make the buttons very tight.'

'I love you,' the Colonel said quite formally.

Then he whispered into her ear as gently as he knew how to whisper, as his whisper was when they are fifteen feet away and you are a young lieutenant on a patrol, 'I love you only, my best and last and only and one true love.'

'Good,' she said, and kissed him hard so he could feel the sweet salt of the blood inside his lip. And I like that too, he thought.

'Now I will comb my hair and make my mouth new and you can watch me.'

'Do you want me to shut the windows?'

'No,' she said. 'We will do it all in the cold.'

'Who do you love?'

'You,' she said. 'And we don't have too much luck, do we?'

'I don't know,' the Colonel said. 'Go ahead and comb your hair.'

The Colonel went into the bathroom to wash up for dinner. The bathroom was the only disappointing part of the room. Due to the exigencies of the Gritti having been built as a palace, there had been no site for bathrooms at the time of building, and, later, when they were introduced, they had been built down the corridor and those entitled to use them gave due warning beforehand and water was heated and towels laid out.

This bathroom had been cut, arbitrarily, from a corner of the room and it was a defensive, rather than an attacking bathroom, the Colonel felt. Washing, and forced to look in the mirror to check any traces of lipstick, he regarded his face.

It looks as though it had been cut out of wood by an indifferent craftsman, he thought.

He looked at the different welts and ridges that had come before they had plastic surgery, and at the thin, only to be observed by the initiate, lines of the excellent plastic operations after head wounds.

Well, that is what I have to offer as a *gueule* or a *façade*, he thought. It is a damn poor offer. The only thing is that it is tanned, and that takes some of the curse off of it. But, Christ, what an ugly man.

He did not notice the old used steel of his eyes nor the small, long extending laugh wrinkles at the corners of his eyes, nor that his broken nose was like a gladiator's in the oldest statues. Nor did he notice his basically kind mouth which could be truly ruthless.

The hell with you, he said to the mirror. You beat-up, miserable. Should we rejoin the ladies?

He went out from the bathroom into the room, and he was as young as at his first attack. Every worthless thing had been left in the bathroom. As always, he thought. That's the place for it.

Où sont les neiges d'antan? Où sont les neiges d'autrefois? Dans le pissoir toute la chose comme ça.

The girl, whose first name was Renata, had the doors of the tall *armoire* open. They were all mirrored inside and she was combing her hair.

She was not combing it for vanity, nor to do to the Colonel what she knew it could and would do. She was combing it with difficulty and without respect, and, since it was very heavy hair and as alive as the hair of peasants, or the hair of the beauties of the great nobility, it was resistant to the comb.

'The wind made it very tangled,' she said. 'Do you love me still?'

'Yes,' the Colonel said. 'May I help you?'

'No, I've done it all my life.'

'You *could* stand sidewise.'

'No. All contours are for our five sons and for your head to rest on.'

'I was only thinking of the face,' the Colonel said. 'But thank you for calling my attention. My attention has been faulty again.'

'I am over bold.'

'No,' the Colonel said. 'In America, they make such things of wire and of sponge-rubber, such as you use in the seats of tanks. You never know there, whether there is any truth in the matter, unless you are a bad boy, as I am.'

'Here it is not that way,' she said, and, with the comb, swung her now parted hair forward so that it came below the line of her cheek, and slanting back, hung over her shoulders.

'Do you like it neat?'

'It's not too neat but it is damn lovely.'

'I could put it up and all that sort of thing if you value neatness. But I cannot manage hairpins and it seems so silly.' Her voice was so lovely and it always reminded him of Pablo Casals playing the 'cello that it made him feel as a wound does that you think you cannot bear. But you can bear anything, he thought.

'I love you very much the way you are,' the Colonel said. 'And you are the most beautiful woman I have ever known, or seen, even in paintings by good painters.'

'I wonder why the portrait has not come.'

'The portrait is lovely to have,' the Colonel said, and now he was a General again without thinking of it. 'But it is like skinning a dead horse.'

'Please don't be rough,' the girl said. 'I don't feel at all like being rough tonight.'

'I slipped into the jargon of my *sale métier*.'

'No,' she said. 'Please put your arms around me, gently and well. Please. It is not a dirty trade. It is the oldest and the best, although most people who practise it are unworthy.'

He held her as tight as he could without hurting and she said, 'I would not have you be a lawyer nor a priest. Nor sell things. Nor be a great success. I love you to be in your trade and I love you. Please whisper to me if you wish.'

The Colonel whispered; holding her tight, and with his heart broken, honestly and fairly, in his whisper that was as barely audible as a silent dog whistle heard close to the ear, 'I love you, devil. And you're my daughter, too. And I don't care about our losses because the moon is our mother and our father. And now let's go down to dinner.'

He whispered this last so low that it was inaudible to anyone who did not love you.

'Yes,' the girl said. 'Yes. But kiss me once more first.'

12

They were at their table in the far corner of the bar, where the Colonel had both his flanks covered, and he rested solidly against the corner of the room. The *Gran Maestro* knew about this, since he had been an excellent sergeant in a good company of infantry, in a first-rate regiment, and he would no more have seated his Colonel in the middle of a room than he would have taken up a stupid defensive position.

'The lobster,' the *Gran Maestro* said.

The lobster was imposing. He was double the size a lobster should be, and his unfriendliness had gone with the boiling, so that now he looked a monument to his dead self; complete with protruding eyes and his delicate, far-extended antennae that were for knowing what rather stupid eyes could not tell him.

He looks a little bit like Georgie Patton, the Colonel thought. But he probably never cried in his life when he was moved.

'Do you think that he will be tough?' he asked the girl in Italian.

'No,' the *Gran Maestro* assured them, still bowing with the lobster. 'He's truly not tough. He's only big. You know the type.'

'All right,' the Colonel said. 'Serve him.'

'And what will you drink?'

'What do want, Daughter?'

'What you want?'

'Capri Bianco,' the Colonel said. 'Secco and really cold.'

'I have it ready,' said the *Gran Maestro*.

'We are having fun,' the girl said. 'We are having it again and without sorrow. Isn't he an imposing lobster?'

'He is,' the Colonel answered. 'And he better damn well be tender.'

'He will be,' the girl told him. 'The *Gran Maestro* doesn't lie. Isn't it wonderful to have people who do not lie?'

'Very wonderful and quite rare,' the Colonel said. 'I was thinking just now of a man named Georgie Patton who possibly never told the truth in his life.'

'Do you ever lie?'

'I've lied four times. But each time I was very tired. That's not an excuse,' he added.

'I lied a lot when I was a little girl. But mostly it was making up stories. Or I hope so. But I have never lied to my own advantage.'

'I have,' said the Colonel. 'Four times.'

'Would you have been a general if you had not lied?'

'If I had lied as others lied, I would have been a three-star general.'

'Would it make you happier to be a three-star general?'

'No,' said the Colonel. 'It would not.'

'Put your right hand, your real hand, in your pocket once and tell me how you feel.'

The Colonel did so.

'Wonderful,' he said. 'But I have to give them back, you know.'

'No. Please no.'

'We won't go into it now.'

Just then the lobster was served.

It was tender, with the peculiar slippery grace of that kicking muscle which is the tail, and the claws were excellent; neither too thin, nor too fat.

'A lobster fills with the moon,' the Colonel told the girl. 'When the moon is dark he is not worth eating.'

'I didn't know that.'

'I think it may be because, with the full moon, he feeds all night. Or maybe it is that the full moon brings him feed.'

'They come from the Dalmatian coast do they not?'

'Yes,' the Colonel said. 'That's your rich coast in fish. Maybe I should say *our* rich coast.'

'Say it,' the girl said. 'You don't know how important things that are said are.'

'They are a damn sight more important when you put them on paper.'

'No,' the girl said. 'I don't agree. The paper means nothing unless you say them in your heart.'

'And what if you haven't a heart, or your heart is worthless?'

'You have a heart and it is not worthless.'

I would sure as hell like to trade it in on a new one, the Colonel thought. I do not see why that one, of all the muscles, should fail me. But he said nothing of this, and put his hand in his pocket.

'They feel wonderful,' he said. 'And you look wonderful.'

'Thank you,' she said. 'I will remember that all week.'

'You could always just look in the glass.'

'The mirror bores me,' she said. 'Putting on lipstick and moving your lips over each to get it spread properly and combing your too heavy hair is not a life for a woman, or even a girl alone, who loves someone. When you want to be the moon and various stars and live with your man and have five sons, looking at yourself in the mirror and doing the artifices of a woman is not very exciting.'

'Then let us be married at once.'

'No,' she said. 'I had to make a decision about that, as about the other different things. All week long is my time to make decisions.'

'I make them too,' the Colonel told her. 'But I am very vulnerable on this.'

'Let's not talk about it. It makes a sweet hurt, but I think we would do better to find out what the *Gran Maestro* has for meat. Please drink your wine. You haven't touched it.'

'I'll touch it now,' the Colonel said. He did and it was pale and cold like the wines of Greece, but not resinous, and its body was as full and as lovely as that of Renata.

'It's very like you.'

'Yes. I know. That's why I wanted you to taste it.'

'I'm tasting it,' the Colonel said. 'Now I will drink a full glass.'

'You're a good man.'

'Thank you,' the Colonel said. 'I'll remember that all week and try to be one.' Then he said, '*Gran Maestro*.'

When the *Gran Maestro* came, happy, conspiratorial, and ignoring his ulcers, the Colonel asked him, 'What sort of meat have you that is worth our eating?'

'I'm not quite sure I know,' the *Gran Maestro* said. 'But I will check. Your compatriot is over there in hearing distance. He would not let me seat him in the far corner.'

'Good,' the Colonel said. 'We'll give him something to write about.'

'He writes every night, you know. I've heard that from one of my colleagues at his hotel.'

'Good,' the Colonel said. 'That shows that he is industrious even if he has outlived his talents.'

'We are all industrious,' the *Gran Maestro* said.

'In different ways.'

'I will go and check out what there actually is among the meats.'

'Check carefully.'

'I am industrious.'

'You are also damn sagacious.'

The *Gran Maestro* was gone and the girl said, 'He is a lovely man and I love how fond he is of you.'

'We are good friends,' the Colonel said. 'I hope he has a good steak for you.'

'There is one very good steak,' the *Gran Maestro* said, reappearing.

'You take it, Daughter. I get them all the time at the mess. Do you want it rare?'

'Quite rare, please.'

'*Al sangue*,' the Colonel said, 'as John said when he spoke to the waiter in French. *Crudo, bleu*, or just make it very rare.'

'It's rare,' the *Gran Maestro* said. 'And you, my Colonel?'

'The scaloppine with Marsala, and the cauliflower braised with butter. Plus an artichoke *vinaigrette* if you can find one. What do you want, Daughter?'

'Mashed potatoes and a plain salad.'

'You're a growing girl.'

'Yes. But I should not grow too much nor in the wrong directions.'

'I think that handles it,' the Colonel said. 'What about a fiasco of Valpolicella?'

'We don't have fiascos. This is a good hotel, you know. It comes in bottles.'

'I forgot,' the Colonel said. 'Do you remember when it cost thirty centesimi the litre?'

'And we would throw the empty fiascos at the station guards from the troop trains?'

'And we would throw all the left over grenades away and bounce them down the hillside coming back from the Grappa?'

'And they would think there was a break-through when they would see the bursts and you never shaved, and we wore the *fiamme nere* on the grey, open jackets with the grey sweaters?'

'And I drank grappa and could not even feel the taste?'

'We must have been tough then,' the Colonel said.

'We were tough then,' the *Gran Maestro* said. 'We were bad boys then, and you were the worst of the bad boys.'

'Yes,' the Colonel said. 'I think we were rather bad boys. You forgive this will you, Daughter?'

'You haven't a picture of then, have you?'

'No. There weren't any pictures except with Mr d'Annunzio in them. Also most of the people turned out badly.'

'Except for us,' the *Gran Maestro* said. 'Now I must go and see how the steak marches.'

The Colonel, who was a sub-lieutenant again now, riding in a *camion*, his face dust, until only his metallic eyes showed, and they were red-rimmed and sore, sat thinking.

The three key points, he thought. The massif of Grappa with Assalone and Pertica and the hill I do not remember the name of on the right. That was where I grew up, he thought, and all the nights I woke sweating, dreaming I would not be able to get them out of the trucks. They should not have gotten out, ever, of course. But what a trade it is.

'In our army, you know,' he told the girl, 'practically no Generals have ever fought. It is quite strange and the top organization dislikes those who have fought.'

'Do Generals really fight?'

'Oh yes. When they are captains and lieutenants. Later, except in retreats, it is rather stupid.'

'Did you fight much? I know you did. But tell me.'

'I fought enough to be classified as a fool by the great thinkers.'

'Tell me.'

'When I was a boy, I fought against Erwin Rommel halfway from Cortina to the Grappa, where we held. He was a captain then and I was an acting captain; really a sub-lieutenant.'

'Did you know him?'

'No. Not until after the war when we could talk together. He was very nice and I liked him. We used to ski together.'

'Did you like many Germans?'

'Very many. Ernst Udet I liked the best.'

'But they were in the wrong.'

'Of course. But who has not been?'

'I never could like them or take such a tolerant attitude as you do, since they killed my father and burned our villa on the Brenta and the day I saw a German officer shooting pigeons with a shotgun in the Piazza San Marco.'

'I understand,' the Colonel said. 'But please, Daughter, you try to understand my attitude too. When we have killed so many we can afford to be kind.'

'How many have you killed?'

'One hundred and twenty-two sures. Not counting possibles.'

'You had no remorse?'

'Never.'

'Nor had dreams about it?'

'Nor bad dreams. But usually strange ones. Combat dreams, always, for a while after combat. But then strange dreams about places mostly. We live by accidents of terrain, you know. And terrain is what remains in the dreaming part of your mind.'

'Don't you ever dream about me?'

'I try to. But I can't.'

'Maybe the portrait will help.'

'I hope so,' the Colonel said. 'Please don't forget to remind me to give back the stones.'

'Please don't be cruel.'

'I have my small necessities of honour in the same proportions as we have our great and enveloping love. You cannot have the one without the other.'

'But you could give me privileges.'

'You have them,' the Colonel said. 'The stones are in my pocket.'

The *Gran Maestro* came then with the steak and the scaloppine and the vegetables. They were brought by a sleek-headed boy who believed in nothing; but was trying hard to be a good second waiter. He was a member of the Order. The *Gran Maestro* served adroitly and with respect both for the food, and those that were to eat it.

'Now eat,' he said.

'Uncork that Valpolicella,' he said to the boy who had the eyes of an unbelieving spaniel.

'What do you have on that character?' the Colonel asked him, referring to his pitted compatriot, sitting chawing at his food, while the elderly woman with him ate with suburban grace.

'You should tell me. Not me you.'

'I never saw him before today,' the Colonel said. 'He's hard to take with food.'

'He condescends to me. He speaks bad Italian assiduously. He goes everywhere in Baedeker, and he has no taste in either food or wine. The woman is nice. I believe she is his aunt. But I have no real information.'

'He looks like something we could do without.'

'I believe we could. In a pinch.'

'Does he speak of us?'

'He asked me who you were. He was familiar with the Contessa's name and had book-visited several palaces that had belonged to the family. He was impressed by your name, Madam, which I gave to impress him.'

'Do you think he will put us in a book?'

'I'm sure of it. He puts everything in a book.'

'We ought to be in a book,' the Colonel said. 'Would you mind, Daughter?'

'Of course not,' the girl said. 'But I'd rather Dante wrote it.'

'Dante isn't around,' the Colonel said.

'Can you tell me anything about the war?' the girl asked. 'Anything that I should be permitted to know?'

'Sure. Anything you like.'

'What was General Eisenhower like?'

'Strictly the Epworth League. Probably that is unjust too. Also complicated by various other influences. An excellent politician. Political General. Very able at it.'

'The other leaders?'

'Let us not name them. They've named themselves enough in their memoirs. Most extremely plausible out of something called the Rotary Club that you would never have heard of. In this club, they have enamelled buttons with their first names and you are fined if you call them by their proper names. Never fought. Ever.'

'Were there no good ones?'

'Yes, many. Bradley, the schoolmaster, and many others. Give you

Lightning Joe as a good one. Very good.'

'Who was he?'

'Commanded the Seventh Corps when I was there. Very sound. Rapid. Accurate. Now Chief of Staff.'

'But what about the great leaders we heard about like the Generals Montgomery and Patton?'

'Forget them, Daughter. Monty was a character who needed fifteen to one to move, and then moved tardily.'

'I always supposed he was a great General.'

'He was not,' the Colonel said. 'The worst part was he knew it. I have seen him come into an hotel and change from his proper uniform into a crowd-catching kit to go out in the evening to animate the populace.'

'Do you dislike him?'

'No. I simply think he is a British General. Whatever that means. And don't you use the term.'

'But he beat General Rommel.'

'Yes. And you don't think anyone else had softened him up? And who can't win with fifteen to one? When we fought here, when we were boys, the *Gran Maestro* and I, we won for one whole year with three to four against one and we won each one. Three main bad ones. That is why we can make jokes and not be solemn. We had something over one hundred and forty thousand dead that year. That is why we can speak gaily and without pomposity.'

'It is such a sad science; if it is a science,' the girl said. 'I hate the war monuments, though I respect them.'

'I do not like them either. Nor the process which led to their construction. Have you ever seen that end of the thing?'

'No. But I would like to know.'

'Better not know,' the Colonel said. 'Eat your steak before it gets cold and forgive me for talking about my trade.'

'I hate it but I love it.'

'I believe we share the same emotions,' the Colonel said. 'But what is my pitted compatriot thinking three tables down?'

'About his next book, or about what it says in Baedeker.'

'Should we go and ride in a gondola in the wind after we have dined?'

'That would be lovely.'

'Should we tell the pitted man that we are going? I think he has the same pits on his heart and in his soul and maybe in his curiosity.'

'We tell him nothing,' the girl said. 'The *Gran Maestro* can convey him any information we wish.'

Then she chewed well and solidly on her steak and said, 'Do you think it is true that men make their own faces after fifty?'

'I hope not. Because I would not sign for mine.'

'You,' she said. 'You.'

'Is the steak good?' the Colonel asked.

'It's wonderful. How are your scaloppine?'

'Very tender and the sauce is not at all sweet. Do you like the vegetables?'

'The cauliflower is almost crisp; like celery.'

'We should have some celery. But I don't think there is any or the *Gran Maestro* would have brought it.'

'Don't we have fun with food? Imagine if we could eat together always.'

'I've suggested it.'

'Let's not talk about that.'

'All right,' the Colonel said. 'I've made a decision too. I'm going to chuck the army and live in this town, very simply, on my retirement pay.'

'That's wonderful. How do you look in civilian clothes?'

'You've seen me.'

'I know it, my dear. I said it for a joke. You make rough jokes sometimes too, you know.'

'I'll look all right. That is if you have a tailor here who can cut clothes.'

'There isn't one here, but there is in Rome. Can we drive together to Rome to get the clothes?'

'Yes. And we will live outside the town at Viterbo and only go in for the fittings and for dinner in the evening. Then we'll drive back in the night.'

'Will we see cinema people and speak about them with dorucan and perhaps not have a drink with them?'

'We'll see them by the thousands.'

'Will we see them being married for the second and third time and then being blessed by the Pope?'

'If you go in for that kind of thing.'

'I don't,' the girl said. 'That's one reason that I cannot marry you.'

'I see,' the Colonel said. 'Thank you.'

'But I will love you, whatever that means, and you and I know what it means very well, as long as either of us is alive and after.'

'I don't think you can love very much after you, yourself, are dead,' the Colonel said.

He started to eat the artichoke taking a leaf at a time, and dipping them, heavy side down, into the deep saucer of *sauce vinaigrette*.

'I don't know whether you can either,' the girl said. 'But I will try. Don't you feel better to be loved?'

'Yes,' the Colonel said. 'I feel as though I were put on some bare-assed hill where it was too rocky to dig, and the rocks all solid, but without jutting, and no bulges, and all of a sudden instead of being there naked, I was armoured. Armoured and the eighty-eights not there.'

'You should tell that to our writer friend with the craters of the moon face so he could write it tonight.'

'I ought to tell it to Dante if he was around,' the Colonel, suddenly gone as rough as the sea when a line squall comes up, said. 'I'd tell him what I'd do if I were shifted, or ascended, into an armoured vehicle under such circumstances.'

Just then the Barone Alvarito came into the dining-room. He was looking for them and, being a hunter, he saw them instantly.

He came over to the table and kissed Renata's hand, saying, '*Ciao*, Renata.' He was almost tall, beautifully built in his town clothes, and he was the shyest man the Colonel had ever known. He was not shy from ignorance, nor from being ill at ease, nor from any defect. He was basically shy, as certain animals are, such as the Bongo that you will never see in the jungle, and that must be hunted with dogs.

'My Colonel,' he said. He smiled as only the truly shy can smile.

It was not the easy grin of the confident, nor the quick slashing smile of the extremely durable and the wicked. It had no relation with the poised, intently used smile of the courtesan or the politician. It was the strange, rare smile which rises from the deep, dark pit, deeper than a well, deep as a deep mine, that is within them.

'I can only stay a moment. I came to tell you that it looks quite good for the shoot. The ducks are coming in heavily from the north. There are many big ducks. The ones you like,' he smiled again.

'Sit down, Alvarito. Please.'

'No,' the Barone Alvarito said. 'We can meet at the garage at two-thirty if you like? You have your car?'

'Yes,'

'That makes it very good. Leaving at that hour, we will have time to see the ducks in the evening.'

'Splendid,' the Colonel said.

'*Ciao*, then, Renata. Good-bye, my Colonel. Until two-thirty.'

'We knew each other as children,' the girl said. 'But he was about three years older. He was born very old.'

'Yes. I know. He is a good friend of mine.'

'Do you think your compatriot has looked him up in Baedeker?'

'I wouldn't know,' the Colonel said. '*Gran Maestro*,' he asked, 'did my illustrious compatriot look up the Barone in Baedeker?'

'Truly, my Colonel. I have not seen him pull his Baedeker during the meal.'

'Give him full marks,' the Colonel said. 'Now look. I believe that the Valpolicella is better when it is newer. It is not a *grand vin* and bottling it and putting years on it only adds sediment. Do you agree?'

'I agree.'

'Then what should we do?'

'My Colonel, you know that in a Great Hotel, wine must cost money. You cannot get Pinard at the Ritz. But I suggest that we get several fiascos of the good. You can say they come from the Contessa Renata's estates and are a gift. Then I will have them decanted for you. This way, we will have better wine and make an impressive saving. I will explain it to the manager if you like. He is a very good man.'

'Explain it to him,' the Colonel said. 'He's not a man who drinks labels either.'

'Agreed.'

'In the meantime you might as well drink this. It is very good you know.'

'It is,' the Colonel said. 'But it isn't Chambertin.'

'What did we use to drink?'

'Anything,' the Colonel said. 'But now I seek perfection. Or, rather, not absolute perfection, but perfection for my money.'

'I seek it too,' the *Gran Maestro* said. 'But rather vainly.'

'What do you want for the end of the meal?'

'Cheese,' the Colonel said. 'What do you want, Daughter?'

The girl had been quiet and a little withdrawn, since she had seen Alvarito. Something was going on in her mind, and it was an excellent mind. But, momentarily, she was not with them.

'Cheese,' she said. 'Please.'

'What cheese?'

'Bring them all and we'll look at them,' the Colonel said.

The *Gran Maestro* left and the Colonel said, 'What's the matter, Daughter?'

'Nothing. Never anything. Always nothing.'

'You might as well pull out of it. We haven't time for such luxuries.'

'No. I agree. We will devote ourselves to the cheese.'

'Do I have to take it like a corn cob?'

'No,' she said, not understanding the colloquialism, but understanding exactly what was meant, since it was she who had been doing the thinking. 'Put your right hand in your pocket.'

'Good,' the Colonel said. 'I will.'

He put his right hand in his pocket and felt what was there, first with the tips of his fingers, and then with the insides of his fingers, and then with palm of his hand; his split hand.

'I'm sorry,' she said. 'And now we begin the good part of it again. We will dedicate ourselves to the cheese with happiness.'

'Excellent,' the Colonel said. 'I wonder what cheeses he has?'

'Tell me about the last war,' the girl said. 'Then we will ride in our gondola in the cold wind.'

'It was not very interesting,' the Colonel said. 'To us, of course, such things are always interesting. But there were only three, maybe four, phases that really interested me.'

'Why?'

'We were fighting a beaten enemy whose communications had been destroyed. We destroyed many divisions on paper, but they were ghost divisions. Not real ones. They had been destroyed by our tactical aviation before they ever got up. It was only really difficult in Normandy, due to the terrain, and when we made the break for Georgie Patton's armour to go through and held it open on both sides.'

'How do you make a break for armour to go through? Tell me, please.'

'First you fight to take a town that controls all the main roads. Call the town St Lo. Then you have to open up the roads by taking other towns and villages. The enemy has a main line of resistance, but he cannot bring up his divisions to counter-attack because the fighter-bombers catch them on the roads. Does this bore you? It bores the hell out of me.'

'It does not bore me. I never heard it said understandably before.'

'Thank you,' the Colonel said. 'Are you sure you want more of the sad science?'

'Please,' she said. 'I love you, you know, and I would like to share it with you.'

'Nobody shares this trade with anybody,' the Colonel told her. 'I'm just telling you how it works. I can insert anecdotes to make it interesting, or plausible.'

'Insert some, please.'

'The taking of Paris was nothing,' the Colonel said. 'It was only an emotional experience. Not a military operation. We killed a number of typists and the screen the Germans had left, as they always do, to cover their withdrawal. I suppose they figured they were not going to need a hell of a lot of office workers any more and they left them as soldiers.'

'Was it not a great thing?'

'The people of Leclerc, another jerk of the third or fourth water, whose death I celebrated with a magnum of Perrier-Jouet Brut 1942, shot a great number of rounds to make it seem important and because we had given them what they had to shoot with. But it was not important.'

'Did you take part in it?'

'Yes,' the Colonel said. 'I think I could safely say, yes.'

'Did you have no great impressions of it? After all, it was Paris and not everyone has taken it.'

'The French, themselves, had taken it four days before. But the grand plan of what we called SHAEF, Supreme, get that word, Headquarters of the Allied Expeditionary Forces, which included all the military politicians of the rear, and who wore a badge of shame in the form of a flaming something, while we wore a four-leafed clover as a designation, and for luck, had a master plan for the envelopment of the city. So we could not simply take it.

'Also we had to wait for the possible arrival of General or Field-Marshal Bernard Law Montgomery who was unable to close, even, the gap at Falaise and found the going rather sticky and could not quite get there on time.'

'You must have missed him,' the girl said.

'Oh, we did,' the Colonel said. 'No end.'

'But was there nothing noble or truly happy about it?'

'Surely,' the Colonel told her. 'We fought from Bas Meudon, and then the Porte de Saint-Cloud, through streets I knew and loved and we had no deads and did as little damage as possible. At the Etoile I took Elsa Maxwell's butler prisoner. It was a very complicated operation. He had been denounced as a Japanese sniper. A new thing. Several Parisians were alleged to have been killed by him. So we sent three men to the roof where he had taken refuge and he was an Indo-China boy.'

'I begin to understand a little. But it is disheartening.'

'It is always disheartening as hell. But you are not supposed to have a heart in this trade.'

'But do you think it was the same in the time of the Grand Captains?'

'I am quite sure it was worse.'

'But you got your hand honourably?'

'Yes. Very honourably. On a rocky, bare-assed hill.'

'Please let me feel it,' she said.

'Just be careful around the centre,' the Colonel said. 'It's split there and it still cracks open.'

'You ought to write,' the girl said. 'I mean it truly. So someone would know about such things.'

'No,' the Colonel disagreed. 'I have not the talent for it and I know too much. Almost any liar writes more convincingly than a man who was there.'

'But other soldiers wrote.'

'Yes. Maurice de Saxe. Frederick the Great. Mr T'sun Su.'

'But soldiers of our time.'

'You use the word our with facility. I like it though.'

'But didn't many modern soldiers write?'

'Many. But did you ever read them?'

'No. I have read mostly the classics and I read the illustrated papers for the scandals. Also, I read your letters.'

'Burn them,' the Colonel said. 'They are worthless.'

'Please. Don't be rough.'

'I won't. What can I tell you that won't bore you?'

'Tell me about when you were a General.'

'Oh, that,' he said and motioned to the *Gran Maestro* to bring champagne. It was Roederer Brut '42 and he loved it.

'When you are a General you live in a trailer and your Chief of Staff lives in a trailer, and you have bourbon whisky when other people do not have it. Your Gs live in the C.P. I'd tell you what Gs are, but it would bore you. I'd tell you about G1, G2, G3, G4, G5 and on the other side there is always Kraut-6. But it would bore you. On the other hand, you have a map covered with plastic material, and on this you have three regiments composed of three battalions each. It is all marked in coloured pencil.

'You have boundary lines so that when the battalions cross their boundaries they will not then fight each other. Each battalion is composed of five companies. All should be good, but some are good, and some are not so good. Also you have divisional artillery and a battalion of tanks and many spare parts. You live by coordinates.'

He paused while the *Gran Maestro* poured the Roederer Brut '42.

'From Corps,' he translated, unlovingly, *cuerpo d'Armata,* 'they tell you what you must do, and then you decide how to do it. You dictate the orders or, most often, you give them by telephone. You ream out people you respect, to make them do what you know is fairly impossible, but is ordered. Also, you have to think hard, stay awake late and get up early.'

'And you won't write about this? Not even to please me.'

'No,' said the Colonel. 'Boys who were sensitive and cracked and kept all their valid first impressions of their day of battle, or their three days, or even their four, write books. They are good books but can be dull if you have been there. Then others write to profit quickly from the war they never fought in. The ones who ran back to tell the news. The news is hardly exact. But they ran quickly with it. Professional writers who had jobs that prevented them from fighting wrote of combat that they could not understand, as though they had been there. I do not know what category of sin that comes under.

'Also a nylon-smooth captain of the Navy who could not command a cat-boat wrote the intimate side of the truly Big Picture. Everybody will write their book sooner or later. We might even draw a good one. But I don't write, Daughter.'

He motioned for the *Gran Maestro* to fill the glasses.

'*Gran Maestro*,' he said. 'Do you like to fight?'

'No.'

'But we fought?'

'Yes. Too much.'

'How is your health?'

'Wonderful except for the ulcers and a small cardiac condition.'

'No,' the Colonel said, and his heart rose and he felt it choke him. 'You only told me about the ulcers.'

'Well, you know now,' the *Gran Maestro* said and did not finish the sentence and he smiled his best and clearest smile that came as solid as the sun rises.

'How many times?'

The *Gran Maestro* held up two fingers as a man might do giving odds where he had credit, and all the betting was on the nod.

'I'm ahead of you,' the Colonel said. 'But let's not be macabre. Ask Donna Renata if she wishes more of this excellent wine.'

'You did not tell me there were more,' the girl said. 'You owe it to me to tell me.'

'There has been nothing since we were together last.'

'Do you think it breaks for me? If so, I would come and simply be with you and care for you.'

'It's just a muscle,' the Colonel said. 'Only it is the main muscle. It works as perfectly as a Rolex Oyster Perpetual. The trouble is you cannot send it to the Rolex representative when it goes wrong. When it stops, you just do not know the time. You're dead.'

'Don't please talk about it.'

'You asked me,' the Colonel said.

'And that pitted man with the caricature face? He has no such thing?'

'Of course not,' the Colonel told her. 'If he is a mediocre writer he will live for ever.'

'But you're not a writer. How do you know this?'

'No,' the Colonel said. 'By the grace of God. But I've read several books. We have a lot of time to read when we are unmarried. Not as much as a merchant marine maybe. But plenty. I can tell one writer from another and I tell you that a mediocre writer has a long span of life. They ought to all draw longevity pay.'

'Could you tell me any anecdotes, and we stop talking about this, which is my true sorrow?'

'I can tell you hundreds of them. All true.'

'Tell me just one. Then we will finish this wine and then go in the gondola.'

'Do you think you will be warm enough?'

'Oh I'm sure I will.'

'I don't know what to tell you,' the Colonel said. 'Everything about war bores those who have not made it. Except the tales of the liars.'

'I would like to know about the taking of Paris.'

'Why? Because I told you that you looked like Marie Antoinette in the tumbril?'

'No. I was complimented by that and I know we are a little alike in profile. But I have never been in any tumbril, and I would like to hear about Paris. When you love someone and he is your hero, you like to hear about the places and the things.'

'Please turn your head,' the Colonel said, 'and I will tell you. *Gran Maestro* is there any more in that wretched bottle?'

'No,' the *Gran Maestro* answered.

'Then bring another.'

'I have one already iced.'

'Good. Serve it. Now, Daughter, we parted from the column of the General Leclerc at Clamart. They went to Montrouge and the Porte d'Orléans and we went directly to Bas Meudon and secured the bridge of the Porte de Saint-Cloud. Is this too technical and does it bore you?'

'No.'

'It would be better with a map.'

'Go on.'

'We secured the bridge and established a bridgehead on the other side of the river and we threw the Germans, living and the dead, who had defended the bridge, into the Seine River,' he stopped. 'It was a token defence of course. They should have blown it. We threw all these Germans into the River Seine. They were nearly all office workers, I believe.'

'Go on.'

'The next morning, we were informed that the Germans had strong points at various places, and artillery on Mont Valérian, and that tanks were roaming the streets. A portion of this was true. We were also requested not to enter too rapidly as the General Leclerc was to take the city. I complied with this request and entered as slowly as I could.'

'How do you do that?'

'You hold up your attack two hours and you drink champagne whenever it is offered to you by patriots, collaborators or enthusiasts.'

'But was there nothing wonderful nor great, the way it is in books?'

'Of course. There was the city itself. The people were very happy. Old general officers were walking about in their mothballed uniforms. We were very happy, too, not to have to fight.'

'Did you not have to fight at all?'

'Only three times. Then not seriously.'

'But was that all you had to fight to take such a city?'

'Daughter, we fought twelve times from Rambouillet to enter the city. But only two of them were worth describing as fights. Those at Toussus le Noble and at Le Buc. The rest was the necessary garnishing of a dish. I really did not need to fight at all except at those two places.'

'Tell me some true things about fighting.'

'Tell me you love me.'

'I love you,' the girl said. 'You can publish it in the *Gazzettino* if you like. I love your hard, flat body and your strange eyes that frighten me when they become wicked. I love your hand and all your other wounded places.'

'I better try to tell you something pretty good,' the Colonel said. 'First I can tell you that I love you Period.'

'Why don't you buy some good glass?' the girl asked, suddenly. 'We could go to Murano together.'

'I don't know anything about glass.'

'I could teach you. It would be fun.'

'We lead too nomadic a life for good glass.'

'But when you retire and live here.'

'We'll get some then.'

'I wish that that was now.'

'So do I, except that I go duck shooting tomorrow and that tonight is tonight.'

'Can I come duck shooting?'

'Only if Alvarito asks you.'

'I can make him ask me.'

'I doubt that.'

'It isn't polite to doubt what your daughter says when she is old enough not to lie.'

'All right, Daughter. I withdraw the doubt.'

'Thank you. For that I will not go and be a nuisance. I will stay in Venice and go to Mass with Mother and my aunt and my great-aunt and visit my poors. I am an only child so I have many duties.'

'I always wondered what you did.'

'That's what I do. Also, I'll have my maid wash my head and give me a manicure and a pedicure.'

'You can't do that because the shoot is on Sunday.'

'Then I'll do that on Monday. On Sunday, I will read all the illustrated papers including the outrageous ones.'

'Maybe they'll have pictures of Miss Bergman. Do you still want to be like her?'

'Not any more,' the girl said. 'I want to be like me only much, much better and I want to have you love me.'

'Also,' she said suddenly and un-maskingly, 'I want to be like you. Can I be like you a little while tonight?'

'Of course,' the Colonel said. 'In what town are we anyway?'

'Venice,' she said. 'The best town, I think.'

'I quite agree. And thank you for not asking me for more war episodes.'

'Oh, you are going to have to tell them to me later.'

'*Have to*?' the Colonel said and the cruelty and resolution showed in his strange eyes as clearly as when the hooded muzzle of the gun of a tank swings towards you.

'Did you say *have to*, Daughter?'

'I said it. But I did not mean it in that way. Or, if I did wrong, I am sorry. I meant will you please tell me more true episodes later? And explain me the things I do not understand?'

'You can use *have to* if you want, Daughter. The hell with it.'

He smiled and his eyes were as kind as they ever were, which was not too kind, as he knew. But there was nothing now that he could do about it except to try to be kind to his last and true and only love.

'I don't really mind, Daughter. Please believe me. I know about command and, at your age, I used to take considerable pleasure in exercising it.'

'But I don't want to command,' the girl said. In spite of her resolution not to cry, her eyes were wet. 'I wish to serve you.'

'I know. But you wish to command, too. There's nothing wrong in that. All people such as us have it.'

'Thank you for the such as us.'

'It wasn't hard to say,' the Colonel said. 'Daughter,' he added.

Just then the concierge came to the table and said. 'Excuse me, my Colonel. There is a man outside, I believe he is a servant of yours, my lady, with quite a large package which he says is for the Colonel. Should I keep it in the storeroom or have it sent to your room?'

'To my room,' the Colonel said.

'Please,' the girl said. 'Can't we look at it here? We don't care about anyone here, do we?'

'Have it unwrapped and brought in here.'

'Very good.'

'Later, you may have it taken with great care to my room and have it wrapped, solidly, for transport at noon tomorrow.'

'Very good, my Colonel.'

'Are you excited to see it?' the girl asked.

'Very,' said the Colonel. '*Gran Maestro*, some more of that Roederer, please, and please place a chair in such a position that we may view a portrait. We are devotees of the pictorial arts.'

'There's no more Roederer cold,' the *Gran Maestro* said. 'But if you would like some Perrier-Jouet—'

'Bring it,' the Colonel said and added, 'Please.'

'I don't talk like Georgie Patton,' the Colonel told her. 'I don't have to. And besides he's dead.'

'Poor man.'

'Yes. Poor man all his life. Although quite rich in money and with a lot of armour.'

'Do you have anything against armour?'

'Yes. Most of the people inside of it. It makes men into bullies which is the first step towards cowardice; true cowardice, I mean. Perhaps it is a little complicated by claustrophobia.'

Then he looked at her and smiled and regretted taking her beyond her depth, as you might take a new swimmer on a shallow, shelving beach, into too deep water; and he sought to reassure her.

'You forgive me, Daughter. Much of what I say is unjust. But it is truer than the things that you will read in Generals' memoirs. After a man gets one star, or more, the truth becomes as difficult for him to attain as the Holy Grail was in our ancestors' time.'

'But you were a general officer.'

'Not for too damn long,' the Colonel said. 'Now captains,' the General said, 'they know the exact truth and they can mostly tell it to you. If they can't, you reclassify them.'

'Would you reclassify me if I lied?'

'It would depend on what you lied about.'

'I'm not going to lie about anything. I don't want to be reclassified. It sounds horrible.'

'It is,' the Colonel said. 'And you send them back to have it done to them with eleven different copies of why it should be done, every one of which you sign.'

'Did you reclassify many?'

'Plenty.'

The concierge came into the room with the portrait, carrying it in its big frame, much as a ship moves when she is carrying too much sail.

'Get two chairs,' the Colonel said to the second waiter, 'and put them there. See that the canvas does not touch the chairs. And hold it so it does not slip.'

Then to the girl he said, 'We'll have to change that frame.'

'I know,' she said. 'It was not my choice. Take it unframed with you and we'll choose a good frame next week. Now look at it. Not at the frame. At what it says, or does not say, of me.'

It was a beautiful portrait; neither cold, nor snobbish, nor stylized, nor modern. It was the way you would want your girl painted if Tintoretto were still around and, if he were not around, you settled for Velazquez. It was not the way either of them painted. It was simply a splendid portrait painted, as they sometimes are, in our time.

'It's wonderful,' the Colonel said. 'It is truly lovely.'

The concierge and the second waiter were holding it and looking at it around the edges. The *Gran Maestro* was admiring fully. The American, two tables down, was looking at it with his journalistic eyes, wondering who painted it. The back of the canvas was to the other diners.

'It is wonderful,' the Colonel said. 'But you can't give me that.'

'I already have,' the girl said. 'I'm sure my hair was never that long over my shoulders.'

'I think it probably was.'

'I could try to let it get that long if you want.'

'Try,' the Colonel said. 'You great beauty you. I love you very much. You and you portrayed on canvas.'

'Tell the waiters if you like. I'm sure it won't come as a great shock to them.'

'Take the canvas upstairs to my room,' the Colonel said to the concierge. 'Thank you very much for bringing it in. If the price is right, I am going to buy it.'

'The price is right,' the girl said to him. 'Should we have them take it and the chairs down and make a special showing of it for your compatriot? The *Gran Maestro* could tell him the address of the painter and he could visit the picturesque studio.'

'It is a very lovely portrait,' the *Gran Maestro* said. 'But it should be taken to the room. One should never let Roederer or Perrier-Jouet do the talking.'

'Take it to the room, please.'

'You said please without a pause before it.'

'Thank you,' the Colonel said. 'I am very deeply moved by the portrait and I am not entirely responsible for what I say.'

'Let's neither of us be responsible.'

'Agreed,' the Colonel said. 'The *Gran Maestro* is really very responsible. He always was.'

'No,' the girl said. 'I think he did not only from responsibility but from malice. We all have malice, you know, of some kind or another in this town. I think perhaps he did not want the man to have even a journalist's look into happiness.'

'Whatever that is.'

'I learned that phrase from you and now you have relearned it back from me.'

'That's the way it goes,' the Colonel said. 'What you win in Boston you lose in Chicago.'

'I don't understand that at all.'

'Too hard to explain,' the Colonel said. Then, 'No. Of course it isn't. Making things clear is my main trade. The hell with being too hard to explain. It is like professional football, *calcio*. What you win in Milano you lose in Torino.'

'I don't care about football.'

'Neither do I,' the Colonel said. 'Especially not about the Army and Navy game and when the very high brass speaks in terms of American football so they can't understand, themselves, what they are talking of.'

'I think we will have a good time tonight. Even under the circumstances, whatever they are.'

'Should we take this new bottle in the gondola?'

'Yes,' the girl said. 'But with deep glasses. I'll tell the *Gran Maestro*. Let's get our coats and go.'

'Good. I'll take some of this medicine and sign for the G.M. and we'll go.'

'I wish it was me taking the medicine instead of you.'

'I'm glad as hell it isn't,' the Colonel said. 'Should we pick our gondola or have them bring one to the landing?'

'Let's gamble and have them bring one to the landing. What do we have to lose?'

'Nothing, I guess. Probably nothing.'

13

They went out the side door of the hotel to the *imbarcadero* and the wind hit them. The light from the hotel shone on the blackness of the gondola and made the water green. She looks as lovely as a good horse or as a racing shell, the Colonel thought. Why have I never seen a gondola before? What hand or eye framed that darkèd symmetry?

'Where should we go?' the girl asked.

Her hair, in the light from the hotel door and window, as she stood on the dock by the black gondola, was blowing back in the wind, so she looked like the figure-head on a ship. The rest of it, too, the Colonel thought.

'Let's just ride through the park,' the Colonel said. 'Or through the Bois with the top down. Let him take us out to Armenonville.'

'Will we go to Paris?'

'Sure,' the Colonel said. 'Tell him to take us for an hour where the going is easiest. I don't want to drive him into that wind.'

'The tide is quite high with this wind,' the girl said. 'Some of our places he couldn't get under the bridges. May I tell him where to go?'

'Of course, Daughter.'

'Stow that ice bucket aboard,' the Colonel said to the second waiter, who had come out with them.

'The *Gran Maestro* said to tell you, as you embarked, that this bottle of wine was his present.'

'Thank him properly and tell him he can't do that.'

'He had better go into the wind a little first,' the girl said. 'Then I know how he should go.'

'The *Gran Maestro* sent this,' the second waiter said.

It was a folded, old U.S.O.D. blanket. Renata was talking to the gondoliere, her hair blowing. The gondoliere wore a heavy blue navy sweater and he was bareheaded too.

'Thank him,' the Colonel said.

He slipped a bill into the second waiter's hand. The second waiter returned it. 'You already made the notation on the check. Neither you nor I nor the *Gran Maestro* are starving.'

'What about the moglie and the bambini?'

'I don't have that. Your mediums smacked our house in Treviso.'

'I'm sorry.'

'You needn't be,' the second waiter said. 'You were a foot soldier as I was.'

'Permit me to be sorry.'

'Sure,' the second waiter said. 'And what the hell difference does it make? Be happy, my Colonel, and be happy, my Lady.'

They got down into the gondola and there was the same magic, as always, of the light hull and the sudden displacement that you made and then the trimming in the dark privacy and then the second trimming, as the gondoliere started to scull, laying her partly on her side so that he would have more control.

'Now,' the girl said. 'We are in our home and I love you. Please kiss me and put all love into it.'

The Colonel held her close, with her head thrown back and kissed her until there was nothing left of the kiss but desperation.

'I love you.'

'Whatever that means,' she interrupted.

'I love you and I know whatever that means. The picture is lovely. But there no word for what you are.'

'Wild,' she said. 'Or careless or unkempt?'

'No.'

'The last was one of the first words I learned from my governess. It means you do not comb your hair enough. Neglectful is when you do not brush one hundred strokes at night.'

'I'm going to run my hand through it and make it unkempter still.'

'Your hurt hand?'

'Yes.'

'We're sitting on the wrong side for that. Change over.'

'Good. That is a sensible order couched in simple language and easily understood.'

It was fun moving over, trying not to disturb the balance of the gondola, but having to trim again carefully.

'Now,' she said. 'But hold me tightly with the other arm.'

'You know just what you want?'

'I do indeed. Is it un-maidenly? I learned that word, too, from my governess.'

'No,' he said. 'It's lovely. Pull up the blanket good and feel the wind.'

'It's from the high mountains.'

'Yes. And beyond there it's from somewhere else.'

The Colonel heard the slap of the waves and he felt the wind come sharply and the rough familiarity of the blanket and then he felt the girl cold-warm and lovely and with upraised breasts that his left hand coasted lightly over. Then he ran his bad hand through her hair once, twice, and three times and then he kissed her and it was worse than desperation.

'Please,' she said, from almost underneath the blanket. 'Let me kiss now.'

'No,' he said. 'Me again.'

The wind was very cold and lashed their faces but under the blanket there was no wind nor nothing; only his ruined hand that searched for the island in the great river with the high steep banks.

'That's it,' she said.

He kissed her then and he searched for the island, finding it and losing it and then finding it for good. For good and for bad, he thought and for good and for all.

'My darling,' he said. 'My well beloved. Please.'

'No. Just hold me very tight and hold the high ground, too.'

The Colonel said nothing, because he was assisting, or had made an act of presence, at the only mystery that he believed in except the occasional bravery of man.

'Please don't move,' the girl said. 'Then move a great amount.'

The Colonel, lying under the blanket in the wind, knowing it is only what man does for woman that he retains; except what he does for his fatherland or his motherland, however, you get the reading, proceeded.

'Please, darling,' the girl said. 'I don't think I can stand it.'

'Don't think of anything. Don't think of anything at all.'

'I'm not.'

'Don't think.'

'Oh please let's not talk.'

'Is it right?'

'You know.'

'You're sure.'

'Oh please not talk. Please.'

Yes, he thought. Please and please again.

She said nothing and neither did he, and when the great bird had flown far out of the closed window of the gondola and was lost and gone, neither of them said anything. He held her head lightly with his good arm and the other arm held the high ground now.

'Please put it where it should be,' she said. 'Your hand.'

'Should we?'

'No. Just hold me tight and try to love me true.'

'I love you true,' he said and just then the gondonla turned to the left, quite sharply and the wind was on his right cheek and he said, with his old eyes catching the outline of the Palace where they turned and noting it, 'You're in the lee now, Daughter.'

'But it is too soon now. Don't you know how a woman feels?'

'No. Only what you tell me.'

'Thank you for the you. But don't you really know?'

'No. I never asked, I guess.'

'Guess now,' she said. 'And please wait until after we have gone under the second bridge.'

'Take a glass of this,' the Colonel said, reaching accurately and well for the champagne bucket with the ice and uncorking the bottle the *Gran Maestro* had uncorked and then placed a common wine cork in.

'This is good for you, Daughter. It is good for all the ills that all of us have and for all sadness and indecision.'

'I have none of those,' she said, speaking grammatically as her governess had taught her. 'I am just a woman, or a girl, or whatever that is, doing whatever it is she should not do. Let's do it again, please, now I am in the lee.'

'Where is the island now and in what river?'

'You are making the discovery. I am only the unknown country.'

'Not too unknown,' the Colonel said.

'Please don't be rude,' the girl said. 'And please attack gently and with the same attack as before.'

'It's no attack,' the Colonel said. 'It is something else.'

'Whatever it is, whatever it is, while I'm still in the lee.'

'Yes,' the Colonel said. 'Yes, now if you want, or will accept from kindness.'

'Please, yes.'

She talks like a gentle cat, though the poor cats cannot speak, the Colonel thought. But then he stopped thinking and he did not think for a long time.

The gondola now was in one of the secondary canals. When it had turned from the Grand Canal, the wind had swung it so the gondoliere had to shift all his weight as ballast and the Colonel and the girl had shifted too, under the blanket, with the wind getting under the edge of the blanket; wildly.

They had not spoken for a long time and the Colonel had noted that the gondola had only inches free in passing under the last bridge.

'How are you, Daughter?'

'I'm quite lovely.'

'Do you love me?'

'Please don't ask such silly things.'

'The tide is very high and we only just made that last bridge.'

'I think I know where we are going. I was born here.'

'I've made mistakes in my home town,' the Colonel said. 'Being born there isn't everything.'

'It is very much,' the girl said. 'You know that. Please hold me very tightly so we can be a part of each other for a little while.'

'We can try,' the Colonel said.

'Couldn't I be you?'

'That's awfully complicated. We could try of course.'

'I'm you now,' she said. 'And I just took the city of Paris.'

'Jesus, Daughter,' he said. 'You've got an awful lot of problems on your hands. The next thing, they will parade the twenty-eighth division through.'

'I don't care.'

'I do.'

'Were they not good?'

'Sure. They had fine commanders, too. But they were National Guard and hard luck. What you call a T.S. division. Get your T.S. slip from the chaplain.'

'I understand none of those things.'

'They aren't worth explaining,' the Colonel said.

'Will you tell me some true things about Paris? I love it so much and when I think of you taking it, then, it is as though I were riding in this gondola with Maréchal Ney.'

'A no good job,' the Colonel said. 'Anyway, not after he fought all those rearguard actions coming back from that big Russian town. He used to fight ten, twelve, fifteen times a day. Maybe more. Afterwards, he couldn't recognize people. Please don't get in any gondolas with him.'

'He was always one of my great heroes.'

'Yeah. Mine too. Until Quatre Bras. Maybe it wasn't Quatre Bras. I'm getting rusty. Give it the generic title of Waterloo.'

'Was he bad there?'

'Awful,' the Colonel told her. 'Forget it. Too many rearguard actions coming back from Moskova.'

'But they called him the bravest of the brave.'

'You can't eat on that. You have to be that, always, and then be the smartest of the smart. Then you need a lot of stuff coming up.'

'Tell me about Paris, please. We should not make more love, I know.'

'I don't know it. Who says it?'

'I say it because I love you.'

'All right. You said it and you love me. So we act on that. The hell with it.'

'Do you think we could once more if it would not hurt you?'

'Hurt me?' the Colonel said. 'When the hell was I ever hurt?'

14

'Please don't be bad,' she said, pulling the blanket over them both. 'Please drink a glass of this with me. You know you've been hurt.'

'Exactly,' the Colonel said. 'Let's forget it.'

'All right,' she said. 'I learned that word, or those two words from you. We have forgotten it.'

'Why do you like the hand?' the Colonel asked, placing it where he should.

'Please don't pretend to be stupid and please let's not think of anything, or anything, or anything.'

'I am stupid,' the Colonel said. 'But I won't think of anything or anything nor of nothing nor of his brother, tomorrow.'

'Please be good and kind.'

'I will be. And I will tell you, now, a military secret. Top Secret equals British Most Secret. I love you.'

'That's nice,' she said. 'And you put it nicely.'

'I'm nice,' the Colonel said and checked on the bridge that was coming up and saw there was clearance. 'That's the first thing people notice about me.'

'I always use the wrong words,' the girl said. 'Please just love me. I wish it was me who could love you.'

'You do.'

'Yes, I do,' she said. 'With all my heart.'

They were going with the wind now and they were both tired.

'Do you think—'

'I don't think,' the girl said.

'Well try and think.'

'I will.'

'Drink a glass of this.'

'Why not? It's very good.'

It was. There was still ice in the bucket and the wine was cold and clear.

'Can I stay at the Gritti?'

'No.'

'Why not?'

'It wouldn't be right. For them. Nor you. The hell with me.'

'Then I suppose I should go home.'

'Yes,' the Colonel said. 'That is the logical supposition.'

'That is an awful way to say a sad thing. Can't we even pretend some things?'

'No. I'll take you home and you sleep good and well and tomorrow we will meet where and when you say.'

'May I call the Gritti?'

'Of course. I'll always be awake. Will you call when you are awake?'

'Yes. But why do you always wake so early?'

'It is a business habit.'

'Oh, I wish you were not in that business and that you were not going to die.'

'So do I,' said the Colonel. 'But I'm getting out of the business.'

'Yes,' she said, sleepily and comfortably. 'Then we go to Rome and get the clothes.'

'And live happily ever after.'

'Please don't,' she said. 'Please, please, don't. You know I made the resolution not to cry.'

'You're crying now,' the Colonel said. 'What the hell have you got to lose on the resolution?'

'Take me home please.'

'That's what I was doing in the first place,' the Colonel told her.

'Be kind once first.'

'I will,' the Colonel said.

After they, or the Colonel, rather, had paid the gondoliere who was unknowing, yet knowing all; solid, sound, respectful and trustworthy; they walked into the Piazzetta and then across the great, cold, windswept square that was hard and old under their feet. They walked holding close and hard in their sorrow and their happiness.

'This is the place where the German shot the pigeons,' the girl said.

'We probably killed him,' the Colonel said. 'Or his brother. Maybe we hanged him. I wouldn't know. I'm not in C.I.D.'

'Do you love me still on these water-worn, cold and old stones?'

'Yes. I'd like to spread a bed roll here and prove it.'

'That would be more barbarous than the pigeon shooter.'

'I'm barbarous,' the Colonel said.

'Not always.'

'Thank you for the not always.'

'We turn here.'

'I think I know that. When are they going to tear that damned Cinema Palace down and put up a real cathedral? That's what T5 Jackson wants.'

'When someone brings Saint Mark back another time under a load of pork from Alexandria.'

'That was a Torcello boy.'

'You're a Torcello boy.'

'Yes. I'm a Basso Piave boy and a Grappa boy straight here from Pertica. I'm a Pasubio boy, too, if you know what that means. It was worse just to live there than to fight anywhere else. In the platoon they used to share anyone's gonococci brought from Schio and carried in a match-box. They used to share this just so they could leave because it was intolerable.'

'But you stayed.'

'Sure,' the Colonel said. 'I'm always the last man to leave the party, fiesta I mean, not as in political party. The truly unpopular guest.'

'Should we go?'

'I thought you had made up your mind.'

'I had. But when you said it about unpopular guest it was unmade.'

'Keep it made up.'

'I can hold a decision.'

'I know. You can hold any damn thing. But, Daughter, sometimes you don't just hold. That is for stupids. Sometimes you have to switch fast.'

'I'll switch if you like.'

'No. I think the decision was sound.'

'But won't it be an awfully long time until morning?'

'That all depends on whether one has luck or not.'

'I should sleep well.'

'Yes,' the Colonel said. 'At your age if you can't sleep they ought to take you out and hang you.'

'Oh, please.'

'Sorry,' he said. 'I meant shoot you.'

'We are nearly home and you could be kind now if you wanted.'

'I'm so kind I stink. Let somebody else be kind.'

They were in front of the palace now and there it was; the palace. There was nothing to do now but pull the bell cord, or enter with the key. I've been lost in this place the Colonel thought and I was never lost in my life.

'Please kiss me good night, kindly.'

The Colonel did and loved her so he could not bear it.

She opened the door with the key, which was in her bag. Then she was gone and the Colonel was alone, with the worn pavement, the wind, which still held in the north and the shadows from where a light went on. He walked home.

Only tourists and lovers take gondolas, he thought. Except to cross the canal in the places where there are no bridges. I ought to go to Harry's, probably, or some damn place. But I think I'll go home.

15

It was really home, if a hotel room can be so described. His pyjamas were laid on the bed. There was a bottle of Valpolicella by the reading light and by the bed a bottle of mineral water, in an ice bucket with a glass beside it on the silver tray. The portrait had been deframed and was placed on two chairs where he could see it from the bed.

The Paris edition of the *New York Herald Tribune* lay on the bed beside his three pillows. He used three pillows, as Arnaldo knew and his extra bottle of medicine, not the one that he carried in his pocket, was beside the reading light. The inner doors of the *armoire*, the mirrored ones, were opened in such a way that he could see the portrait from the side. His scuffed slippers were by the bed.

I'll buy it, the Colonel said, to himself, since there was no one else there except the portrait.

He opened the Valpolicella which had been uncorked, and then re-corked, carefully, precisely and lovingly and poured himself a glass into the glass which was much better than any hotel should use which was faced with breakage.

'Here's to you, Daughter,' he said. 'You beauty and lovely. Do you know, that, among other things, you smell good always? You smell wonderfully even in a high wind or under a blanket or kissing good night. You know almost no one does and you don't use scent.'

She looked at him from the portrait and said nothing.

'The hell with it,' he said. 'I'm not going to talk to a picture.'

What do you think went wrong tonight? he thought.

Me, I guess. Well I will try to be a good boy tomorrow all day; starting at first light.

'Daughter,' he said and he was talking to her and not to a picture now. 'Please know I love you and that I wish to be delicate and good. And please stay with me always now.'

The picture was the same.

The Colonel took out the emeralds from his pocket and looked at them, feeling them slide, cold and yet warm, as they take warmth and as all good stones have warmth, from his bad hand into his good hand.

I should have put these in an envelope and locked them up, he thought. But what the–security is there better than I can give them? I have to get these back to you fast, Daughter.

It was fun, though. And they're not worth more than a quarter of a million. What I would make in four hundred years. Have to check that figure.

He put the stones in the pocket of his pyjamas and put a handkerchief over them. Then he buttoned the pocket. The first sound thing you learn, he thought, is to have flaps and buttons on all your pockets. I imagine that I learned it too early.

The stones felt good. They were hard and warm against his flat, hard, old and warm chest and he noted how the wind was blowing, looked at the portrait, poured another glass of Valpolicella and then started to read the Paris edition of the *New York Herald Tribune*.

I ought to take the pills, he thought. But the hell with the pills.

Then he took them just the same and went on reading the *New York Herald*. He was reading Red Smith and he liked him very much.

16

The Colonel woke before daylight and checked that there was no one sleeping with him.

The wind was still blowing hard and he went to the open windows to check the weather. There was no light as yet in the east across the Grand Canal, but his eyes could see how rough the water was. Be a hell of a tide today, he thought. Probably flood the square. That's always fun. Except for the pigeons.

He went to the bathroom, taking the *Herald Tribune* and Red Smith with him, as well as a glass of Valpolicella. Damn I'll be glad when the *Gran Maestro* gets those big fiascos, he thought. This wine gets awfully dreggy at the end.

He sat there, with his newspaper, thinking of the things of that day.

There would be the telephone call. But it might be very late because she would be sleeping late. The young sleep late, he thought and the beautiful sleep half again as late. She certainly would not call early and the shops did not open until nine or a little later.

Hell, he thought, I have these damned stones. How could anyone do a thing like that?

You know how, he said to himself, reading the ads in the back of the paper. You've put it on the line enough times. It isn't crazy or morbid. She just wanted to put it on the line. It was a good thing it was me, he thought.

That is the only good thing about being me, he considered. Well I'm me, goddamn it. For better or for much worse. How would you like to sit on the can as you have sat almost every morning of your damned life with this in your pocket?

He was addressing no one, except, perhaps, posterity.

How many mornings have you sat in the row with all the others? That's the worst of it. That and shaving. Or you go off to be alone and think or not think and pick a good piece of cover and there are two riflemen there already, or some boy asleep.

There's no more privacy in the army than in a professional—. I've never been in a professional–but I imagine they run much the same. I could learn to run one, he thought.

Then I'd make all my leading characters Ambassadors and the unsuccessful ones could be Corps commanders or command military districts in peace time. Don't be bitter, boy, he said to himself. It's too early in the morning and your duty's not completed yet.

What would you do with their wives, he asked himself? Buy them new hats or shoot them, he said. It's all part of the same process.

He looked at himself in the mirror, set in the half-closed door. It showed him at a slight angle. It's a deflexion shot, he said to himself and they didn't lead me enough. Boy, he said, you certainly are a beat-up, old looking bastard.

Now you have to shave and look at that face while you do it. Then you must get a hair-cut. That's easy in this town. You're a Colonel of Infantry, boy. You can't go around looking like Joan of Arc or General (Breveted) George Armstrong Custer. That beautiful horse-cavalryman. I guess it is fun to be that way and have a loving wife and use sawdust for brains. But it must have seemed like the wrong career to him when they finished up on that hill above the Little Big Horn, with the ponies making the circle around them in all the dust and the sage brush crushed by the hooves of the horses of the other people and nothing left to him for the rest of his life but that old lovely black powder smell and his own people shooting each other and themselves, because they were afraid of what the squaws would do to them.

The body was unspeakably mutilated, they used to put in this same paper. And on that hill to know you'd made one real mistake, finally and for good and complete with true handles. Poor horse-cavalryman, he thought. The end of all his dreams. That's one good thing about being an Infantryman. You never have any dreams except bad dreams.

Well, he said to himself, we're finished here and pretty soon there will be good light and I can see the portrait. I'll be damned if I'll turn that in. I keep that.

Oh Christ, he said, I wonder what she looks like now sleeping. I know how she looks, he said to himself. Wonderful. She sleeps as though she had not gone to sleep. As though she were just resting. I hope she is, he thought. I hope she's resting well. Christ Jesus how I love her and I hope I never do her harm.

17

When it started to be light, the Colonel saw the portrait. He, very probably, saw it as quickly as any man who was civilized and had to read and sign the forms he did not believe in, could see an object, as soon as it was visible. Yes, he said to himself, I have eyes and they have fairly fast perception still and once they had ambition. I have led my Ruffians where they were well peppered. There are but three of the two hundred and fifty of them left alive and they are for the town's end to beg during life.

That's from Shakespeare, he told the portrait. The winner and still the undisputed champion.

Someone might take him, in a short bout. But I would rather revere him. Did you ever read *King Lear*, Daughter? Mr Gene Tunney did and he was the champion of the world. But I read it too. Soldiers care for Mr

Shakespeare too, though it may seem impossible.

You have anything to say in your defence except to put your head back? he asked the portrait. You want some more, Shakespeare?

You don't have to defend. You just rest and leave it as it is. It's no good. Your defence and my defence is no damn good. But who could tell you to go out and hang yourself the way we do?

Nobody, he said to himself and to the portrait. And certainly not me.

He put his good hand down and found that the room waiter had left a second bottle of Valpolicella alongside of where the first had been.

If you love a country, the Colonel thought, you might as well admit it. Sure, admit it, boy.

I have loved three and lost them thrice. Give a credit. We've retook two. Retaken, he corrected.

And we will retake the other one, General Fat Ass Franco on his shooting stick with the advice of his doctor and tame ducks and a screen of Moorish cavalry when he shoots.

Yes, he said softly to the girl who looked at him clearly now in the first and best light.

We will retake and they will all be hung upside down outside of filling stations. You have been warned, he added.

'Portrait,' he said, 'why the hell can't you just get into bed with me instead of being eighteen solid stone blocks away. Maybe more. I'm not as sharp now as I was; whenever.'

'Portrait,' he said to the girl and to the portrait and to the girl both; but there wasn't any girl and the portrait was as it was painted.

'Portrait, keep your goddamn chin up so you can break my heart easier.'

It certainly was a lovely present, the Colonel thought.

'Can you manœuvre?' he asked the portrait. 'Good and fast?'

Portrait said nothing and the Colonel answered. You know damn well she can. She'd out-manœuvre you the best day you were ever born and she would stay and fight where you would–, discreetly.

'Portrait,' he said. 'Boy or daughter or my one true love or whatever it is; you know what it is, Portrait.'

The Portrait, as before, did not answer. But the Colonel, who was a General now again, early in the morning at the only time he really knew, and with Valpolicella, knew as absolutely as though he had just read his third Wassermann that there was no–in Portrait and he felt shame for having talked to Portrait roughly.

'I'll be the best goddamned boy you ever witnessed today. And you can tell your principal that.'

Portrait, as was her fashion, was silent.

She probably would speak to a horse-cavalryman, the General, for now he had two stars and they grated on his shoulders and showed white in the vague, scuffed red on the plaque in front of his jeep. He never used command cars, nor semi-armoured vehicles complete with sandbags.

'The hell with you, Portrait,' he said. 'Or get your T.S. slip from the universal chaplain of us all, with combined religions. You ought to be able to eat on that.'

'The hell with you,' the Portrait said, without speaking. 'You low class soldier.'

'Yes,' the Colonel said, for now he was a Colonel again and had relinquished all his former rank.

'I love you, Portrait, very much. But don't get rough with me. I love you very much because you are beautiful. But I love the girl better, a million times better, hear it?'

There was no sign that she heard it, so he tired of it.

'You are in a fixed position, Portrait,' he said. 'Without or with any frame. And I am going to manœuvre.'

The portrait was as silent as she had been since the concierge had brought her into the room, and aided and abetted by the second waiter, had shown her to the Colonel and to the girl.

The Colonel looked at her and saw she was indefensible, now that the light was good, or almost good.

He saw, too, that she was the portrait of his own true love and so he said, 'I am sorry for all the stupidnesses I say. I do not wish ever to be brutal. Maýbe we could both sleep a little while, with luck, and then, perhaps, your Mistress would call on the telephone?'

Maybe she will even call, he thought.

18

The hall porter pushed the *Gazzettino* under the door and the Colonel had it, noiselessly, almost as soon as it had passed through the slit.

He very nearly took it from the hall porter's hand. He did not like the hall porter since he had found him, one day, going through his bag, when he, the Colonel, had re-entered the room after having left it, presumably for some time. He had to come back to the room to get his bottle of the medicine, which he had forgotten, and the hall porter was well through his bag.

'I guess you don't say stick them up in this hotel,' the Colonel had said. 'But you're no credit to your town.'

There was silence produced and re-produced, by the striped waistcoated man with the Fascist face and the Colonel said, 'Go on, boy, look through the rest of it. I don't carry any military secrets with my toilet articles.'

Since then, there was scant friendship between them and the Colonel enjoyed trying to take the morning paper from the striped waistcoated man's hand; noiselessly, and when he heard, or saw it first make a move under the door.

'Okay, you won today, jerk,' he said in the best Venetian dialect he could summon at that hour. 'Go hang yourself.'

But they don't hang themselves, he thought. They just have to go on putting papers under other people's doors that do not even hate them. It must be quite a difficult trade being an ex-Fascist. Maybe he is not an ex-

Fascist, too. How do you know.

I can't hate Fascists, he thought. Nor Krauts either, since unfortunately, I am a soldier.

'Listen, Portrait,' he said. 'Do I have to hate the Krauts because we kill them? Do I have to hate them as soldiers and as human beings? It seems too easy a solution to me.'

Well, Portrait. Forget it. Forget it. You're not old enough to know about it. You are two years younger than the girl that you portray and she is younger and older than hell; which is quite an old place.

'Listen, Portrait,' he said and saying it, knew that now as long as he lived, he would have someone to talk to at the early hours that he woke.

'As I was saying, Portrait. The hell with that too. That's too old for you too. That is one of the things you can't say no matter how true it is. There are lots of things I can never say to you and maybe that will be good for me. It is about time something was. What do you think would be good for me, Portrait?

'What's the matter, Portrait?' he asked her. 'You getting hungry? I am.'

So he rang the bell for the waiter who would bring breakfast.

He knew that now, even though the light was so good that every wave showed on the Grand Canal, lead-coloured and solid heavy with the wind and the tide now high over the landing steps of the Palace directly opposite his room, that there would be no telephone call for several hours.

The young sleep good, he thought. They deserve it.

'Why do we have to get old?' he asked the waiter who had come in with his glass-eye and the menu.

'I don't know, my Colonel. I suppose it is a natural process.'

'Yes. I guess I imagine that too. The eggs fried with their faces up. Tea and toast.'

'You don't want anything American?'

'The hell with anything American except me. Is the *Gran Maestro* astir yet?'

'He has your Valpolicella in the big wicker fiascos of two litres and I have brought this decanter with it.'

'That one,' the Colonel said. 'I wish to Christ I could give him a regiment.'

'I don't think he would want one, really.'

'No,' the Colonel said. 'I don't want one, really, myself.'

19

The Colonel breakfasted with the leisure of a fighter who has been clipped badly, hears four and knows how to relax truly for five seconds more.

'Portrait,' he said. 'You ought to relax too. That's the only thing that is going to be difficult about you. That's what they call the static element in painting. You know, Portrait, that almost no pictures, paintings rather, move at all. A few do. But not many.

'I wish that your mistress was here and we could have movement. How do girls like you and she know so much so damn young and be so beautiful?

'With us, if a girl is really beautiful, she comes from Texas and maybe, with luck, she can tell you what month it is. They can all count good though.

'They teach them how to count and keep their legs together and how to put their hair up in pin curls. Sometime, Portrait, for your sins, if you have any, you ought to have to sleep in a bed with a girl who has put her hair up in pin curls to be beautiful tomorrow. Not tonight. They'd never be beautiful tonight. For tomorrow, when we make the competition.

'The girl, Renata, that you are, is sleeping now without ever having done anything to her hair. She is sleeping with it spread out on the pillow and all it is to her is a glorious, dark, silky annoyance, that she can hardly remember to comb, except that her governess taught her.

'I see her in the street with the lovely long-legged stride and the wind doing anything it wants to her hair and her true breasts under the sweater and then I see the nights in Texas with the pin curls; tight and subjected by metallic instruments.

'Pin me no pin curls, my beloved,' he said to the portrait, 'and I will try to lay it on the line in round, heavy, hard silver dollars or with the other.'

I mustn't get rough, he thought.

Then he said to the portrait, for he did not capitalize her now in his mind, 'You are so goddamned beautiful you stink. Also you are jail-bait. Renata's two years older now. You are under seventeen.'

And why can't I have her and love her and cherish her and never be rude, nor bad and have the five sons that go to the five corners of the world; wherever that is! I don't know. I guess the cards we draw are those we get. You wouldn't like to re-deal would you dealer?

No. They only deal to you once and then you pick them up and play them. I can play them, if I draw any damn thing at all, he told portrait; who was unimpressed.

'Portrait,' he said. 'You better look the other way so that you will not be un-maidenly. I am going to take a shower now and shave, something you will never have to do, and put on my soldier-suit and go and walk around this town even though it is too early.'

So, he got out of bed, favouring his bad leg, which hurt him always. He pulled the reading light with his bad hand. There was sufficient light and he had been wasting electricity for nearly an hour.

He regretted this as he regretted all his errors. He walked past portrait, only looking casually and looked at himself in the mirror. He had dropped both parts of his pyjamas and he looked at himself critically and truly.

'You beat-up old bastard,' he said to the mirror. Portrait was a thing of the past. Mirror was actuality and of this day.

The gut is flat, he said without uttering it. The chest is all right except where it contains the defective muscle. We are hung as we are hung, for better or worse, or something, or something awful.

You are one half a hundred years old, you bastard you. Now go in and take a shower and scrub good and afterwards put on your soldier-suit. Today is another day.

20

The Colonel stopped at the reception desk in the lobby, but the concierge was not there yet. There was only the night porter.

'Can you put something in the safe for me?'

'No, my Colonel. No one may open the safe until the assistant manager, or the concierge arrives. But I will guard anything for you that you wish.'

'Thank you. It's not worth the trouble,' and he buttoned the Gritti envelope, with the stones inside, the envelope addressed to himself, into the inside left pocket of his tunic.

'There's no real crime here now,' the night porter said.

It had been a long night and he was happy to speak to someone. 'There never really was, my Colonel. There are only differences of opinion and politics.'

'What do you have for politics?' the Colonel asked; for he was lonely too.

'About what you would expect.'

'I see. And how is your thing going?'

'I think it goes quite well. Maybe not as well as last year. But still quite well. We were beaten and we have to wait a while now.'

'Do you work at it?'

'Not much. It is more the politics of my heart than of my head. I believe in it with my head too, but I have very little political development.'

'When you get it you won't have any heart.'

'Maybe not. Do you have politics in the army?'

'Plenty,' the Colonel said. 'But not what you mean.'

'Well, we better not discuss it then. I have not meant to be intrusive.'

'I asked the question; the original question rather. It was only to talk. It was not an interrogation.'

'I don't think it was. You do not have the face of an inquisitor, my Colonel, and I know about the Order, although I am not a member.'

'You may be member material. I'll take it up with the *Gran Maestro*.'

'We come from the same town; but from distinct quarters.'

'It's a good town.'

'My Colonel, I have so little political development that I believe all honourable men are honourable.'

'Oh you'll get over that,' the Colonel assured him. 'Don't worry, boy. You've got a young party. Naturally you make errors.'

'Please don't talk like that.'

'It was just rough early morning joking.'

'Tell me, my Colonel, what do you really think about Tito?'

'I think several things. But he's my next door neighbour. I've found it better not to talk about my neighbour.'

'I'd like to learn.'

'Then learn it the hard way. Don't you know people don't give answers to such questions?'

'I had hoped they did.'

'They don't,' the Colonel said. 'Not in my position. All I can tell you is that Mr Tito has plenty problems.'

'Well, I know that now truly,' the night porter who was really only a boy said.

'I hope you do,' the Colonel said. 'I wouldn't call it, as knowledge, any pearl of great price. Now, good day, for I must take a walk for the good of my liver, or something.'

'Good day, my Colonel. *Fa brutto tempo.*'

'*Bruttissimo,*' the Colonel said and, pulling the belt of his raincoat tight and settling his shoulders into it and the skirts well down, he stepped out into the wind.

21

The Colonel took the ten centisimi gondola across the Canal, paying the usual dirty note and standing with the crowd of those condemned to early rising.

He looked back at the Gritti and saw the windows of his room; still open. There was no promise, nor threat of rain; only the same strong, wild, cold wind from the mountains. Everyone in the gondola looked cold and the Colonel thought, I wish I could issue these wind-proof coats to everyone on board. God, and every officer that ever wore one, knows they are not waterproof and who made the money out of that one?

You can't get water through a Burberry. But I suppose some able jerk has his boy in Groton now, or maybe Canterbury, where the big contractors' boys go, because our coats leaked.

And what about some brother officer of mine who split with him? I wonder who the Benny Meyers of the ground forces were? There probably wasn't only one. Probably, he thought, there must be very many. You must not be awake yet, to talk that simply. They do keep the wind out though. The raincoats. Raincoats my ass.

The gondola pulled up between the stakes on the far bank of the canal and the Colonel watched the black-clad people climb up out of the black-painted vehicle. Is she a vehicle? he thought. Or must a vehicle have wheels or be tracked?

Nobody would give you a penny for your thoughts, he thought. Not this morning. But I've seen them worth a certain amount of money when the chips were down.

He penetrated into the far side of the city, the side that finally fronted on the Adriatic and that he liked the best. He was going in by a very narrow street and he was going to not keep track of the number of more or less north and south streets that he crossed, nor count the bridges and then try and orient himself so he would come out at the market without getting up any dead ends.

It was a game you play, as some people used to play double Canfield or any solitary card games. But it had the advantage of you moving while you do it and that you look at the houses, the minor vistas, the shops and the *trattorias* and at old palaces of the city of Venice while you are walking. If you loved the city of Venice it was an excellent game.

It is a sort of *solitaire ambulante* and what you win is the happiness of your eye and heart. If you made the market, on this side of town, without ever being stymied, you won the game. But you must not make it too easy and you must not count.

On the other side of the town, game was to leave from the Gritti and make the Rialto by the Fondamente Nuove without a mistake.

Then you could climb the bridge and cross it and go down into the market. He liked the market best. It was the part of any town he always went to first.

Just then he heard the two young men behind him saying the things about him. He knew they were young men by their voices and he did not look back, but listened carefully for distance and waited for the next turn to see them, as he turned.

They are on their way to work, he decided. Maybe they are former Fascists or maybe they are something else, or maybe it is just the line that they are talking. But they are making it pretty personal now. It isn't just Americans, it is also me, myself, my grey hair, the slightly crooked way I walk, the combat boots (those, of that stripe, disliked the practicability of combat boots. They liked boots that rang on the flag-stones and took a high black polish).

It is my uniform which they find to be without grace. Now it is why I am walking at this hour and now it is their absolute security that I can no longer make love.

The Colonel swung sharp to the left at the next corner, seeing what he had to deal with and the exact distance and when the two young men came around the corner which was formed by the apse of the church of Frari there was no Colonel. He was in the dead angle behind the apse of the ancient church and as they passed, he, hearing them come by their talk, stepped out with a hand in each low pocket of his raincoat and turned himself and the raincoat, with the two hands in the pockets, towards them.

They stopped and he looked at them both in the face and smiled his old and worn death smile. Then he looked down at their feet, as you always look at the feet of such people, since they wear their shoes too tight and when you take the shoes off them you see their hammer-toes. The Colonel spat on the pavement and said nothing.

The two of them, they *were* the first thing he had suspected, looked at him with hatred and with that other thing. Then they were off like marsh-birds, walking with the long strides of herons too, the Colonel thought and something of the flight of curlews and looking back with hatred, waiting to have the last word if the distance was ever safe.

It is a pity they weren't ten against one, the Colonel thought. They might have fought. I should not blame them, since they were defeated.

But their manners were not good in respect to a man of my rank and age. Also it was not intelligent to think all fifty-year-old colonels would not understand their language. Nor was it intelligent to think old Infantrymen would not fight this early in the morning against the simple odds of two to one.

I'd hate to fight in this town where I love the people. I would avoid it. But couldn't those badly educated youths realize what sort of animal they were dealing with? Don't they know how you get to walk that way? Nor any of the other signs that combat people show as surely as a fisherman's hands tell you if he is a fisherman from the creases from the cord cuts.

It is true they only saw my back and ass and legs and boots. But you'd think they might have told from the way they must move. Maybe they don't any more. But when I had a chance to look at them and think. Take the two of them out and hang them, I believe they understood. They understood quite clearly.

What's a man's life worth anyway? Ten thousand dollars if his insurance is paid up in our army. What the hell has that got to do with it. Oh yes, that was what I was thinking about before those jerks showed; how much money I had saved my government, in my time when people like Benny Meyers were in the trough.

Yes, he said and how much you lost them at the Château that time at ten GS a head. Well nobody ever really understood it except me, I guess. There's no reason to tell them now. Your commanding general sometimes puts things down as the Fortunes of War. Back at Army they know such things are bound to happen. You do it, as ordered, with a big butcher bill and you're a hero.

Christ, I am opposed to the excessive butcher bill, he thought. But you get the orders, and you have to carry them out. It is the mistakes that are no good to sleep with. But why the hell sleep with them anyway. It never did any good. But they can certainly crawl into a sack sometimes. They can crawl in and stay in there with you.

Cheer up, boy, he said. Remember you had a lot of money on you when you picked that one. And you might have been stripped if you lost. You can't fight a lick any more with your hands and you didn't have any weapon.

So don't be gloomy, boy, or man, or Colonel, or busted General. We're almost to the market now and you made it without hardly noticing.

Hardly noticing is bad, he added.

22

He loved the market. A great part of it was close-packed and crowded into several side streets and it was so concentrated that it was difficult not to jostle people, unintentionally and each time you stopped to look, to buy, or to admire, you formed an *îlot de résistance* against the flow of the morning attack of the purchasers.

The Colonel liked to study the spread and high piled cheeses and the great sausages. People at home think *mortadella* is a sausage, he thought.

Then he said to the woman in the booth, 'Let me try a little of that sausage, please. Only a sliver.'

She cut a thin, paper thin, slice for him, ferociously and lovingly and when the Colonel tasted it, there was the half smoky, black pepper-corned, true flavour of the meat from the hogs that ate acorns in the mountains.

'I will take a quarter of a kilo.'

The Barone's lunches for the shooting blinds were of a Spartan quality, which the Colonel respected, since he knew no one should eat much while shooting. He felt, though, that he might augment the lunch with this sausage and share it with the poler and picker-upper. He might give a slice to Bobby, the retriever, who would be wet through to his hide many times and enthusiastic still, but shaking with cold.

'Is this the best sausage that you have?' he asked the woman. 'Have you nothing that does not show and is reserved for better and steadier customers?'

'This is the best sausage. There are many other sausages, as you know. But this is the best.'

'Then give me one-eighth of a kilo of a sausage that is highly fortifying, but is not highly seasoned.'

'I have it,' she said. 'It is a little new but exactly as you describe.'

This sausage was for Bobby.

But you do not say that you buy sausages for a dog in Italy where the worst crime is to be considered a fool and many people go hungry. You may give expensive sausage to a dog before a man who works for his living and knows what a dog goes through in water in cold weather. But you do not buy them, stating your purpose in possessing them, unless you are a fool, or a millionaire from the war and from after.

The Colonel paid for the wrapped-up package and proceeded on through the market inhaling the smell of roasted coffee and looking at the amount of fat on each carcass in the butcher section, as though he were enjoying the Dutch painters, whose names no one remembers, who painted, in perfection of detail, all things you shot, or that were eaten.

A market is the closest thing to a good museum like the Prado or as the Accademia is now, the Colonel thought.

He took a short cut and was at the fish-market.

In the market, spread on the slippery stone floor, or in their baskets, or their rope-handled boxes, were the heavy, grey-green lobsters with their magenta overtones that presaged their death in boiling water. They have all been captured by treachery, the Colonel thought, and their claws are pegged.

There were the small soles and there were a few *albacore* and *bonito*. These last, the Colonel thought, looked like boat-tailed bullets, dignified in death and with the huge eye of the pelagic fish.

They were not made to be caught except for their voraciousness. The poor sole exists, in shallow water, to feed man. But these other roving bullets, in their great bands, live in blue water and travel through all oceans and all seas.

A nickel for your thoughts now, he thought. Let's see what else they have.

There were many eels, alive and no longer confident in their eeldom. There were fine prawns that could make a *scampi brochetto* spitted and broiled on a rapier-like instrument that could be used as a Brooklyn ice-pick. There were medium-sized shrimps, grey and opalescent, awaiting their turn, too, for the boiling water and their immortality, to have their shucked carcasses float out easily on an ebb tide on the Grand Canal.

The speedy shrimp, the Colonel thought, with tentacles longer than the moustaches of that old Japanese admiral, comes here now to die for our benefit. Oh Christian shrimp, he thought, master of retreat, and with your wonderful intelligence service in those two light whips, why did they not teach you about nets and that lights are dangerous?

Must have been some slip-up, he thought.

Now he looked at the many small crustaceans, the razor-edge clams you only should eat raw if you had your typhoid shots up to date, and all the small delectables.

He went past these, stopping to ask one seller where his clams came from. They came from a good place, without sewerage and the Colonel asked to have six opened. He drank the juice and cut the clam out, cutting close against the shell with the curved knife the man handed him. The man had handed him the knife because he knew from experience the Colonel cut closer to the shell than he had been taught to cut.

The Colonel paid him the pittance that they cost, which must have been much greater than the pittance those received who caught them, and he thought, now I must see the stream and canal fishes and get back to the hotel.

23

The Colonel arrived at the lobby of the Hotel Gritti Palace. His gondolieres were paid off and, now, inside the hotel, there was no wind.

It had taken two men to bring the gondola up the Grand Canal from the market. They had both worked hard, and he had paid them what it was worth, and some more.

'Are there any calls for me?' he asked the concierge, who was now in attendance.

The concierge was light, fast, sharp-faced, intelligent and polite, always, without subservience. He wore the crossed keys of his office on the lapels of his blue uniform without ostentation. He was the concierge. It is a rank very close to that of Captain, the Colonel thought. An officer and not a Gentleman. Make it top sergeant in the old days; except he's dealing always with the brass.

'My lady has called twice,' the concierge said in English. Or whatever that language should be called we all speak, the Colonel thought. Leave it at English. That is about what they have left. They should be allowed to keep the name of the language. Cripps will probably ration it shortly, anyway.

'Please put me through to her at once,' he told the concierge.

The concierge commenced to dial numbers.

'You may talk over there, my Colonel,' he said. 'I have made the connexion.'

'You're fast.'

'Over there,' the concierge said.

Inside the booth the Colonel lifted the receiver and said, automatically, 'Colonel Cantwell speaking.'

'I called twice, Richard,' the girl said. 'But they explained that you were out. Where were you?'

'At the market. How are you, my lovely?'

'No one listens on this phone at this hour. I am your lovely. Whoever that is.'

'You. Did you sleep well?'

'It was like ski-ing in the dark. Not really ski-ing but really dark.'

'That's the way it should be. Why did you wake so early? You've frightened my concierge.'

'If it is not un-maidenly, how soon can we meet, and where?'

'Where you wish and when you wish.'

'Do you still have the stones and did Miss Portrait help any?'

'Yes to both questions. The stones are in my upper left hand pocket buttoned down. Miss Portrait and I talked late and early and it made everything much easier.'

'Do you love her more than me?'

'I'm not abnormal yet. Perhaps that's bragging. But she's lovely.'

'Where should we meet?'

'Should we have breakfast at the Florian, on the right hand side of the square? The square should be flooded and it will be fun to watch.'

'I'll be there in twenty minutes if you want me.'

'I want you,' the Colonel said and hung up.

Coming out of the telephone booth he, suddenly, did not feel good and then he felt as though the devil had him in an iron cage, built like an iron lung or an iron maiden, and he walked, grey-faced, to the concierge's desk and said, in Italian, 'Domenico, Ico, could you get me a glass of water, please?'

The concierge was gone and he leaned on the desk resting. He rested lightly and without illusion. Then the concierge was back with the glass of water, and he took four tablets of the type that you take two, and he continued resting as lightly as a hawk rests.

'Domenico,' he said.

'Yes.'

'I have something here in an envelope that you can put in the safe. It may be called for either by myself, in person, or in writing, or by the person you have just put that call through to. Would you like that in writing?'

'No. It would be unnecessary.'

'But what about you, boy? You're not immortal, are you?'

'Fairly so,' the concierge told him. 'But I will put it in writing, and after me, comes the Manager and the Assistant Manager.'

'Both good men,' the Colonel agreed.

'Wouldn't you like to sit down, my Colonel?'

'No. Who sits down except men and women in change of life hotels? Do you sit down?'

'No.'

'I can rest on my feet, or against a goddamned tree. My countrymen sit down, or lie down, or fall down. Give them a few energy crackers to stall their whimpers.'

He was talking too much to regain confidence quickly.

'Do they really have energy crackers?'

'Sure. It has something in it that keeps you from getting excited. It's like the atomic bomb, only played backwards.'

'I can't believe it.'

'We have the most terrific military secrets that one General's wife ever told another. Energy crackers is the least of it. Next time we will give all Venice botulism from 56,000 feet. There's nothing to it,' the Colonel explained. 'They give you anthrax, and you give them botulism.'

'But it will be horrible.'

'It will be worse than that,' the Colonel assured him. 'This isn't classified. It's all been published. And while it goes on you can hear Margaret, if you tune in right, singing the Star Spangled Banner on the radio. I think that could be arranged. The voice I would not describe as a big one. Not as we know voices who have heard the good ones in our time. But everything is a trick now. The radio can almost make the voice. And the Star Spangled Banner is fool-proof until towards the last.'

'Do you think they will drop anything here?'

'No. They never have.'

The Colonel, who was four star general now, in his wrath and in his agony and in his need for confidence, but secured temporarily through the absorption of the tablets, said, '*Ciao,* Domenico,' and left the Gritti.

He figured it took twelve and one half minutes to reach the place where his true love would probably arrive a little late. He walked it carefully and at the speed he should walk it. The bridges were all the same.

24

His true love was at the table at the exact time that she said she would be. She was as beautiful as always in the hard, morning light that came across the flooded square, and she said. 'Please, Richard. Are you all right? Please?'

'Sure,' the Colonel said. 'You wonder beauty.'

'Did you go to all our places in the market?'

'Only a few of them. I did not go to where they have the wild ducks.'

'Thank you.'

'For nothing,' the Colonel said. 'I never go there when we are not together.'

'Don't you think I should go to the shoot?'

'No. I am quite sure. Alvarito would have asked you if he wanted you.'

'He might not have asked me because he wanted me.'

'That's true,' the Colonel said, and pondered that for two seconds. 'What do you want for breakfast?'

'Breakfast is worthless here, and I don't like the square when it is flooded. It is sad and the pigeons have no place to alight. It is only really fun towards the last when the children play. Should we go and have breakfast at the Gritti?'

'Do you want to?'

'Yes.'

'Good. We'll have breakfast there. I've had mine already.'

'Really?'

'I'll have some coffee and hot rolls, and only feel them with my fingers. Are you awfully hungry?'

'Awfully,' she said, truly.

'We'll give breakfast the full treatment,' the Colonel said. 'You'll wish you have never heard of breakfast.'

As they walked, with the wind at their back, and her hair blowing better than any banner, she asked him, holding close, 'Do you still love me in the cold, hard Venice light of morning? It is really cold and hard isn't it?'

'I love you and it is cold and hard.'

'I loved you all night when I was ski-ing in the dark.'

'How do you do that?'

'It is the same runs except that it is dark and the snow is dark instead of light. You ski the same; controlled and good.'

'Did you ski all night? That would be many runs.'

'No. Afterwards I slept soundly and well and I woke happy. You were with me and you were asleep like a baby.'

'I wasn't with you and I was not asleep.'

'You're with me now,' she said and held close and tight.

'And we are almost there.'

'Yes.'

'Have I told you, yet, properly, that I love you?'

'You told me. But tell me again.'

'I love you,' he said. 'Take it frontally and formally please.'

'I take it anyway you want as long as it is true.'

'That's the proper attitude,' he said. 'You good, brave, lovely girl. Turn your hair sideways once on top of this bridge and let it blow obliquely.'

He had made a concession, with obliquely, instead of saying, correctly, oblique.

'That's easy,' she said. 'Do you like it?'

He looked and saw the profile and the wonder early morning colour and her chest upstanding in the black sweater and her eyes in the wind and he said, 'Yes, I like it.'

'I'm very glad,' she said.

25

At the Gritti, the *Gran Maestro* seated them at the table which was beside the window that looked out on the Grand Canal. There was no one else in the dining-room.

The *Gran Maestro* was festive and well with the morning. He took his ulcers day by day, and his heart the same way. When they did not hurt he did not hurt either.

'Your pitted compatriot eats in bed at his hotel, my colleague tells me,' he confided to the Colonel. 'We may have a few Belgians. "The bravest of these were the Belgians,"' he quoted. 'There is a pair of *pescecani* from you know where. But they are exhausted and I believe they will eat, as pigs, in their room.'

'An excellent situation report,' the Colonel said. 'Our problem, *Gran Maestro,* is that I have already eaten in my room as pitted does and as the *pesacani* will. But this lady—'

'Young girl,' interrupted the *Gran Maestro* with his whole-face smile. He was feeling very good since it was a completely new day.

'This very young lady wants a breakfast to end breakfasts.'

'I understand,' the *Gran Maestro* said and he looked at Renata and his heart rolled over as a porpoise does in the sea. It is a beautiful movement and only a few people in this world can feel it and accomplish it.

'What do you want to eat, Daughter?' the Colonel asked, looking at her early morning, un-retouched dark beauty.

'Everything.'

'Would you give any suggestions?'

'Tea instead of coffee and whatever the *Gran Maestro* can salvage.'

'It won't be salvage, Daughter,' said the *Gran Maestro*.

'I'm the one who calls her Daughter.'

'I said it honestly,' the *Gran Maestro* said. 'We can make or *fabricar rognons* grilled with *champignons* dug by people I know. Or, raised in damp cellars. There can be an omelet with truffles dug by pigs of distinction. There can be real Canadian bacon from maybe Canada, even.'

'Wherever that is,' the girl said happily and unillusioned.

'Wherever that is,' said the Colonel seriously. 'And I know damn well where it is.'

'I think we should stop the jokes now and get to the breakfast.'

'If it is not un-maidenly I think so too.'

'Mine is a decanted flask of the Valpolicella.'

'Nothing else?'

'Bring me one ration of the alleged Canadian bacon,' the Colonel said.

He looked at the girl, since they were alone now, and he said, 'How are you, my dearest?'

'Quite hungry, I suppose. But thank you for being good for so long a time.'

'It was easy,' the Colonel told her in Italian.

26

They sat there at the table and watched the early stormy light over the Canal. The grey had turned to a yellow grey, now, with the sun, and the waves were working against the outgoing tide.

'Mummy says she can't live here too long at any time because there are no trees,' the girl said. 'That's why she goes to the country.'

'That's why everyone goes to the country,' the Colonel said. 'We could plant a few trees if we found a place with a big enough garden.'

'I like Lombardy poplars and plane trees the best, but I am still quite uneducated.'

'I like them, and cypresses and chestnut trees. The real chestnut and the horse-chestnut. But you will never see trees, Daughter, until we go to America. Wait till you see a white pine or a ponderosa pine.'

'Will we see them when we make the long trip and stop at all the filling stations or comfort stations or whatever they are called?'

'Lodges and Tourist Camps,' the Colonel said. 'Those others we stop at; but not for the night.'

'I want so much for us to roll up to a comfort station and plank down my money and tell them to fill her up and check the oil, Mac, the way it is in American books or in the films.'

'That's a filling station.'

'Then what is a comfort station?'

'Where you go, you know—'

'Oh,' the girl said and blushed. 'I'm sorry—

'I want to learn American so much. But I suppose I shall say barbarous things the way you do sometimes in Italian.'

'It is an easy language. The further West you go the straighter and the easier it becomes.'

The *Gran Maestro* brought the breakfast and the odour of it, although it did not spread through the room, due to the silver covers on the dishes, came to them steady and as broiled bacon and kidneys, with the dark lustreless smell of grilled mushrooms added.

'It looks lovely,' the girl said. 'Thank you very much, *Gran Maestro*. Should I talk American?' she asked the Colonel. She extended her hand to the *Gran Maestro* lightly, and fastly, so that it darted as a rapier does, and said, 'Put it there, Pal. This grub is tops.'

The *Gran Maestro* said, 'Thank you, my lady.'

'Should I have said chow instead of grub?' the girl asked the Colonel.

'They are really interchangeable.'

'Did they talk like that out West when you were a boy? What would you say at breakfast?'

'Breakfast was served, or offered up, by the cook. He would say, "Come and get it, you sons of bitches, or I'll throw it away."'

'I must learn that for in the country. Sometimes when we have the British Ambassador and his dull wife for dinner I will teach the footman, who will announce dinner, to say. "Come and get it, you sons of bitches, or we will throw it away."'

'He'd devaluate,' the Colonel said. 'At any rate, it would be an interesting experiment.'

'Tell me something I can say in true American to the pitted one if he comes in. I will just whisper it in his ear as though I were making a rendezvous, as they did in the old days.'

'It would depend on how he looks. If he is very dejected looking, you might whisper to him, "Listen, Mac. You hired out to be tough, didn't you?"'

'That's lovely,' she said and repeated it in a voice she had learned from Ida Lupino. 'Can I say it to the *Gran Maestro*?'

'Sure. Why not. *Gran Maestro!*'

The *Gran Maestro* came over and leaned forward attentively.

'Listen, Mac. You hired out to be tough, didn't you?' the girl hard-worded him.

'I did indeed,' the *Gran Maestro* said. 'Thank you for stating it so exactly.'

'If that one comes in and you wish to speak to him after he has eaten, just whisper in his ear, "Wipe the egg off your chin, Jack, and straighten up and fly right."'

'I'll remember it and I'll practise it at home.'

'What are we going to do after breakfast?'

'Should we go up and look at the picture and see if it is of any value; I mean any good; in daylight?'

'Yes,' the Colonel said.

27

Upstairs the room was already done and the Colonel, who had anticipated a possible messiness of locale, was pleased.

'Stand by it once,' he said. Then remembered to add, 'Please.'

She stood by it, and he looked at it from where he had looked at it last night.

'There's no comparison, of course,' he said. 'I don't mean likeness. The likeness is excellent.'

'Was there supposed to be a comparison?' the girl asked, and swung her head back and stood there with the black sweater of the portrait.

'Of course not. But last night, and at first light, I talked to the portrait as though it were you.'

'That was nice of you and shows it has served some useful purpose.'

They were lying now on the bed and the girl said to him, 'Don't you ever close windows?'

'No. Do you?'

'Only when it rains.'

'How much alike are we?'

'I don't know. We never had much of a chance to find out.'

'We've never had a fair chance. But we've had enough of a chance for me to know.'

'And when you know what the hell have you got?' the Colonel asked.

'I don't know. Something better than there is, I suppose.'

'Sure. We ought to try for that. I don't believe in limited objectives. Sometimes you're forced to, though.'

'What is your great sorrow?'

'Other people's orders,' he said. 'What's yours?'

'You.'

'I don't want to be a sorrow. I've been a sorry son of a bitch many times. But I never was anybody's sorrow.'

'Well you are mine now.'

'All right,' he said. 'We'll take it that way.'

'You're nice to take it that way. You're very kind this morning. I'm so ashamed about how things are. Please hold me very close and let's not talk, or think, about how things might have been different.'

'Daughter, that's one of the few things I know how to do.'

'You know many, many things. Don't say such a thing.'

'Sure,' the Colonel said. 'I know how to fight forwards and how to fight backwards and what else?'

'About pictures and about books and about life.'

'That's easy. You just look at the pictures without prejudice, and you read the books with as open a mind as you have, and you have life.'

'Don't take off your tunic, please.'

'All right.'

'You do anything when I say please.'

'I have done things without.'

'Not very often.'

'No,' the Colonel agreed. 'Please is a pretty word.'

'Please, please, please.'

'*Per piacere*. It means for pleasure. I wish we always talked Italian.'

'We could in the dark. Although there are things that say better in English.

'I love you my last true and only love,' she quoted. 'When lilacs last in the door-yard bloomed. And out of the cradle endlessly rocking. And come and get it, you sons of bitches, or I'll throw it away. You don't want those in other languages do you, Richard?'

'No.'

'Kiss me again, please.'

'Unnecessary please.'

'I would probably end up as an unnecessary please myself. That is the good thing about you going to die that you can't leave me.'

'That's a little rough,' the Colonel said. 'Watch your beautiful mouth a little on that.'

'I get rough when you get rough,' she said. 'You wouldn't want me to be completely otherwise?'

'I would not want you to be in any way other than you are and I love you truly, finally and for good.'

'You say nice things very clearly sometimes. What was it happened with you and your wife, if I may ask?'

'She was an ambitious woman and I was away too much.'

'You mean she went away, from ambition, when you only were away from duty?'

'Sure,' the Colonel said and remembered, as unbitterly as he could. 'She had more ambition than Napoleon and about the talent of the average High School Valedictorian.'

'Whatever that is,' the girl said. 'But let's not speak about her. I'm sorry I asked the question. She must be sad that she is not with you.'

'No. She is too conceited ever to be sad, and she married me to advance herself in Army circles, and have better contacts for what she considered her profession, or her art. She was a journalist.'

'But they are dreadful,' the girl said.

'I agree.'

'But you couldn't have married a woman journalist that kept on being that?'

'I told you I made mistakes,' the Colonel said.

'Let's talk about something nice.'

'Let's.'

'But that was terrible. How could you have done such a thing?'

'I don't know. I could tell you in detail but let's skip it.'

'Please let's skip it. But I had no idea it was something as awful as that. You wouldn't do such a thing now, would you?'

'I promise you, my sweet.'

'But you don't ever write to her?'

'Of course not.'

'You wouldn't tell her about us, so she could write about it?'

'No. I told her about things once, and she wrote about them. But that was in another country and besides the wench is dead.'

'Is she really dead?'

'Deader than Phoebus the Phoenician. But she doesn't know it yet.'

'What would you do if we were together in the Piazza and you saw her?'

'I'd look straight through her to show her how dead she was.'

'Thank you very much,' the girl said. 'You know that another woman, or a woman in memory, is a terrible thing for a young girl to deal with when she is still without experience.'

'There isn't any other woman,' the Colonel told her, and his eyes were bad and remembering. 'Nor is there any woman of memory.'

'Thank you very much,' the girl said. 'When I look at you I believe it truly. But please never look at me nor think of me like that.'

'Should we hunt her down and hang her to a high tree?' the Colonel said with anticipation.

'No. Let us forget her.'

'She is forgotten,' the Colonel said. And, strangely enough, she was. It was strange because she had been present in the room for a moment, and she had very nearly caused a panic; which is one of the strangest things there is, the Colonel thought. He knew about panics.

But she was gone now, for good and for ever; cauterized; exorcized and with the eleven copies of her re-classification papers, in which was included the formal, notarized act of divorcement, in triplicate.

'She is forgotten,' the Colonel said. It was quite true.

'I'm so pleased,' the girl said. 'I don't know why they ever let her into the hotel.'

'We're enough alike,' the Colonel said. 'We better not carry it too goddamned far.'

'You can hang her if you wish because she is why we cannot marry.'

'She's forgotten,' the Colonel told her. 'Maybe she will take a good look at herself in the mirror sometime and hang herself.'

'Now that she is out of the room we should wish her no bad luck. But, as a good Venetian, I wish that she were dead.'

'So do I,' the Colonel said. 'And now, since she is not, let us forget her for keeps.'

'For keeps and for always,' the girl said. 'I hope that is the correct diction. Or in Spanish *para sempre.*'

'*Para sempre* and his brother,' the Colonel said.

28

They lay together now and did not speak and the Colonel felt her heart beat. It is easy to feel a heart beat under a black sweater knitted by someone in the family, and her dark hair lay, long and heavy, over his good arm. It isn't heavy, he thought, it is lighter than anything there is. She lay, quiet and loving, and whatever it was that they possessed was in complete communication. He kissed her on the mouth, gently and hungrily, and then it was as though there was static, suddenly, when communications had been perfect.

'Richard,' she said. 'I'm sorry about things.'

'Never be sorry,' the Colonel said. 'Never discuss casualties, Daughter.'

'Say it again.'

'Daughter.'

'Will you tell me some happy things I can have for during the week and some more of war for my education?'

'Let's skip war.'

'No. I need it for my education.'

'I do too,' the Colonel said. 'Not manœuvres. You know, in our army once, a general officer through chicanery obtained the plan of the manœuvre. He anticipated every move of the enemy force and comported himself so brilliantly that he was promoted over many better men. And that was why we got smacked one time. That and the prevalence of week-ends.'

'We're on a week-end now.'

'I know,' the Colonel said. 'I can still count up to seven.'

'But are you bitter about everything?'

'No. It is just that I am half a hundred years old and I know things.'

'Tell me something more about Paris because I love to think of you and Paris in the week.'

'Daughter, why don't you lay off Paris?'

'But I've been in Paris, and I will go back there again, and I want to know. It is the loveliest city in the world, next to our own, and I want to know some things truly to take with me.'

'We will go together and I will tell you there.'

'Thank you. But tell me a little now for this week only.'

'Leclerc was a high-born jerk as I think that I've explained. Very brave, very arrogant and extremely ambitious. He is dead, as I said.'

'Yes, you told me.'

'They say you should never speak ill of the dead. But I think it is the best time to speak truly of them. I have never said anything of a dead that I would not say to his face,' and he added, 'in spades.'

'Let's not talk about him. I have re-classified him in my mind.'

'What do you want then; picturesque?'

'Yes please. I have bad taste from reading the illustrated papers. But I will read Dante all week while you are gone. I'll go to Mass each morning. That should be enough.'

'Go to Harry's before lunch too.'

'I will,' she said. 'Please tell me some picturesque.'

'Don't you think we might better just go to sleep?'

'How can we go to sleep now when we have so little time? Feel this,' she said and pushed her whole head up under his chin until she forced his head back.

'All right, I'll talk.'

'Give me your hand first to hold. I'll have it in my hand when I read the Dante and do the other things.'

'Dante was an execrable character. More conceited than Leclerc.'

'I know. But he did not write execrably.'

'No. Leclerc could fight too. Excellently.'

'Now tell me.'

Her head was on his chest now, and the Colonel said, 'Why did you not want me to take off the tunic?'

'I like to feel the buttons. Is it wrong?'

'I'll be a sad son of a bitch,' the Colonel said. 'How many people fought in your family?'

'Everybody,' she said. 'Always. They were traders as well and several of them were Doges of this city as you know.'

'But they all fought?'

'All,' she said. 'As far as I know.'

'Okay,' the Colonel said. 'I'll tell you any goddamn thing you want to know.'

'Just something picturesque. As bad or worse than in the illustrated papers.'

'*Domenica Del Corriere* or *Tribuna Illustrata?*'

'Worse, if possible.'

'Kiss me first.'

She kissed him kind, and hard, and desperately, and the Colonel could not think about any fights or any picturesque or strange incidents. He only thought of her and how she felt and how close life comes to death when there is ecstasy. And what the hell is ecstasy and what's ecstasy's rank and serial number? And how does her black sweater feel? And who made all her smoothness and delight and the strange pride and sacrifice and wisdom of a child? Yes, ecstasy is what you might have had and instead you draw sleep's other brother.

Death is a lot of —, he thought. It comes to you in small fragments that hardly show where it has entered. It comes, sometimes, atrociously. It can come from unboiled water; an un-pulled-up mosquito boot, or it can come with the great, white-hot, clanging roar we have lived with. It comes in small cracking whispers that precede the noise of the automatic weapon. It can come with the smoke-emitting arc of the grenade, or the sharp, cracking drop of the mortar.

I have seen it come, loosening itself from the bomb rack, and falling with that strange curve. It comes in the metallic rending crash of a vehicle, or the simple lack of traction on a slippery road.

It comes in bed to most people, I know, like love's opposite number. I have lived with it nearly all my life and the dispensing of it has been my trade. But what can I tell this girl now on this cold, windy morning in the Gritti Palace Hotel?

'What would you like to know, Daughter?' he asked her.

'Everything.'

'All right,' the Colonel said. 'Here goes.'

29

They lay on the pleasantly hard, new-made bed with their legs pressed tight against one another, and her head was on his chest, and her hair spread across his old hard neck; and he told her.

'We landed without much opposition. They had the true opposition at the other beach. Then we had to link up with the people who had been dropped, and take and secure various towns, and then we took Cherbourg. This was difficult, and had to be done very fast, and the orders were from a General called Lightning Joe that you never would have heard of. Good General.'

'Go on please. You spoke about Lightning Joe before.'

'After Cherbourg we had everything. I took nothing but an admiral's compass because I had a small boat at that time on Chesapeake Bay. But we had all the Wehrmacht stamped Martell and some people had as much as six million German-printed French francs. They were good until a year ago, and at that time they were worth fifty to the dollar, and many a man has a tractor now instead of simply one mule who knew how to send them home through his Esses, or sometimes his GS.

'I never stole anything except the compass because I thought it was bad luck to steal, unnecessarily, in war. But I drank the cognac and I used to try to figure out the different corrections on the compass when I had time. The compass was the only friend I had, and the telephone was my life. We had more wire strung than there are — in Texas.'

'Please keep telling me and be as little rough as you can. I don't know what the word means and I don't want to know.'

'Texas is a big state,' the Colonel said. 'That is why I used it and its female population as a symbol. You cannot say more — than Wyoming because there are less than thirty thousand there, perhaps, hell, make it fifty, and there was a lot of wire, and you kept stringing it and rolling it up, and stringing it again.'

'Go on.'

'We will cut to the break-through,' the Colonel said. 'Please tell me if this bores you.'

'No.'

'So we made the mucking break-through,' the Colonel said, and now his head was turned to her head, and he was not lecturing; he was confessing.

'The first day most of them came over and dropped the Christmas tree ornaments that confuse the other people's radar and it was called off. We were ready to go but they called it off. Quite properly I am sure. I love the very highest brass like I love the pig's you know.'

'Tell it to me and don't be bad.'

'Conditions were not propitious,' the Colonel said. 'So the second day we were for it, as our British cousins, who could not fight their way out of a wet tissue towel, say, and over came the people of the wide, blue yonder.

'They were still taking off from the fields where they lived on that green-grassed aircraft carrier that they called England, when we saw the first of them.

'Shining, bright and beautiful, because they had scraped the invasion paint by then, or maybe they had not. My memory is not exact about this part.

'Anyway, Daughter, you could see the line of them going back towards the east further than you could see. It was like a great train. They were high in the sky and never more beautiful. I told my S-2 that we should call them the Valhalla Express. Are you tired of it?'

'No. I can see the Valhalla Express. We never saw it in such numbers. But we saw it. Many times.'

'We were back two thousand yards from where we were to take off from. You know what two thousand yards is, Daughter, in a war when you are attacking?'

'No. How could I?'

'Then the front part of the Valhalla Express dropped coloured smoke and turned and went home. This smoke was dropped accurately, and clearly showed the target which was the Kraut positions. They were good positions and it *might* have been impossible to move him out of them without something mighty and picturesque such as we were experiencing.

'Then, Daughter, the next sections of the Valhalla Express dropped everything in the world on the Krauts and where they lived and worked to hold us up. Later it looked as though all of the earth had erupted and the prisoners that we took shook as a man shakes when his malaria hits him. They were very brave boys from the Sixth Parachute Division and they all shook and could not control it though they tried.

'So you can see it was a good bombing. Just the thing we always need in this life. Make them tremble in fear of justice and of might.

'So then, Daughter, not to bore you, the wind was from the east and the smoke began to blow back in our direction. The heavies were bombing on the smoke line and the smoke line was now over us. Therefore they bombed us the same as they had bombed the Krauts. First it was the heavies, and no one need ever worry about hell who was there that day. Then, to really make the break-through good and to leave as few people as possible on either side, the mediums came over and bombed who was left. Then we made the break-through as soon as the Valhalla Express had gone home, stretching in its beauty and its majesty from that part of France to all over England.'

If a man has a conscience, the Colonel thought, he might think about air-power some time.

'Give me a glass of that Valpolicella,' the Colonel said, and remembered to add, 'please.'

'Excuse me,' he said. 'Be comfortable, honey dog, please. You asked me to tell you.'

'I'm not your honey dog. That must be someone else.'

'Correct. You're my last and true and only love. Is that correct? But you asked me to tell you.'

'Please tell me,' the girl said. 'I'd like to be your honey dog if I knew how to do it. But I am only a girl from this town that loves you.'

'We'll operate on that,' the Colonel said. 'And I love you. I probably picked up that phrase in the Philippines.'

'Probably,' the girl said. 'But I would rather be your straight girl.'

'You are,' the Colonel said. 'Complete with handles and with the flag on top.'

'Please don't be rough,' she said. 'Please love me true and tell me as true as you can, without hurting yourself in any way.'

'I'll tell you true,' he said. 'As true as I can tell and let it hurt who it hurts. It is better that you hear it from me if you have curiosity on this subject, than that you read it in some book with stiff covers.'

'Please don't be rough. Just tell me true and hold me tight and tell me true until you are purged of it; if that can be.'

'I don't need to purge,' he said. 'Except heavies being used tactically. I have nothing against them if they use them right even if they kill you. But for ground support give me a man like Pete Quesada. There is a man who will boot them in.'

'Please.'

'If you ever want to quit a beat-up character like me that guy could give you ground support.'

'You are not beat-up, whatever that is, and I love you.'

'Please give me two tablets from that bottle and pour the glass of Valpolicella that you neglected to pour, and I will tell you some of the rest of it.'

'You don't have to. You don't have to tell me and I know now it is not good for you. Especially not the Valhalla Express day. I am not an inquisitor; or whatever the female of inquisitor is. Let us just lie quietly and look out of the window, and watch and see what happens on our Grand Canal.'

'Maybe we better. Who gives a damn about the war anyway?'

'You and me, maybe,' she said and stroked his head. 'Here are the two things from the square bottle. Here is the glass of decanted *vino*. I'll send you better from our own estates. Please let us sleep a little while. Please be a good boy and we just lie together and love each other. Please put your hand here.'

'My good or my bad?'

'Your bad,' the girl said. 'The one I love and must think about all week. I cannot keep it like you keep the stones.'

'They're in the safe,' the Colonel said. 'In your name,' he added.

'Let's just sleep and not talk about any material things nor any sorrows.'

'The hell with sorrows,' the Colonel said with his eyes closed and his head resting lightly on the black sweater that was his fatherland. You have to have some damned fatherland, he thought. Here is mine.

'Why aren't you President?' the girl asked. 'You could be an excellent President.'

'Me President? I served in the Montana National Guard when I was sixteen. But I never wore a bow tie in my life and I am not, nor ever have been, an unsuccessful haberdasher. I have none of the qualifications for the Presidency. I couldn't even head the opposition even though I don't have to sit on telephone books to have my picture taken. Nor am I a no-fight general. Hell, I never even was at SHAEF. I couldn't even be an elder statesman. I'm not old enough. Now we are governed in some way, by the dregs. We are governed by what you find in the bottom of dead beer glasses that whores have dunked their cigarettes in. The place has not even been swept out yet and they have an amateur pianist beating on the box.'

'I don't understand it because my American is so incomplete. But it sounds awful. But don't be angry about it. Let me be angry for you.'

'Do you know what an unsuccessful haberdasher is?'

'No.'

'It is not discreditable. There are many of them in our country. There is at least one in every town. No, Daughter, I am only a fighting soldier and that is the lowest thing on earth. In that you run for Arlington, if they return the body. The family has a choice.'

'Is Arlington nice?'

'I don't know,' the Colonel said. 'I was never buried there.'

'Where would you like to be buried?'

'Up in the hills,' he said, making a quick decision. 'On any part of the high ground where we beat them.'

'I suppose you should be buried on the Grappa.'

'On the dead angle of any shell-pocked slope if they would graze cattle over me in the summer time.'

'Do they have cattle there?'

'Sure. They always have cattle where there is good grass in the summer, and the girls of the highest houses, the strong built ones, the houses *and* the girls, that resist the snow in winter, trap foxes in the fall after they bring the cattle down. They feed from pole-stacked hay.'

'And you don't want Arlington or Père Lachaise or what we have here?'

'Your miserable boneyard.'

'I know it is the most unworthy thing about the town. The city rather. I learned to call cities towns from you. But I will see that you go where you wish to go and I will go with you if you like.'

'I would not like. That is the one thing we do alone. Like going to the bathroom.'

'Please do not be rough.'

'I meant that I would love to have you with me. But it is very egotistical and an ugly process.'

He stopped, and thought truly, but off-key, and said, 'No. You get married and have five sons and call them all Richard.'

'The lion-hearted,' the girl said, accepting the situation without even a glance, and playing what there was she held as you put down all the cards, having counted exactly.

'The louse-hearted,' the Colonel said. 'The unjust bitter criticizer who speaks badly of everyone.'

'Please don't be rough in talking,' the girl said. 'And remember you speak worst of all about yourself. But hold me as close as we can and let's think about nothing.'

He held her as close as he could and he tried to think about nothing.

30

The Colonel and the girl lay quietly on the bed and the Colonel tried to think of nothing; as he had thought of nothing so many times in so many places. But it was no good now. It would not work any more because it was too late.

They were not Othello and Desdemona, thank God, although it was the same town and the girl was certainly better looking than the Shakespearean character, and the Colonel had fought as many, or more times than the garrulous Moor.

They are excellent soldiers, he thought. The damned Moors. But how many of them have we killed in my time? I think we killed more than a generation if you count the final Moroccan campaign against Abdel Krim. And each one you have to kill separately. Nobody ever killed them in mass, as we killed Krauts before they discovered *Einheit*.

'Daughter,' he said. 'Do you want me to really tell you, so you will know, if I am not rough telling it?'

'I would rather have you tell me than anything. Then we can share it.'

'It cuts pretty thin for sharing,' the Colonel said. 'It's all yours, Daughter. And it's only the high-lights. You wouldn't understand the campaigns in detail, and few others would. Rommel might. But they always had him under wraps in France and, besides, we had destroyed his communications. The two tactical air-forces had; ours and the R.A.F. But I wish I could talk over certain things with him. I'd like to talk with him and with Ernst Udet.'

'Just tell me what you wish and take this glass of Valpolicella, and stop if it makes you feel badly. Or don't tell it at all.'

'I was a spare-parts Colonel at the start,' the Colonel explained carefully. 'They are hang-around Colonels, which are given to a Division Commander to replace one that he may have killed, or that is relieved. Almost none are killed; but many are relieved. All the good ones are promoted. Fairly fast when the thing starts to move sort of like a forest fire.'

'Go on, please. Should you take your medicine?'

'The hell with my medicine,' the Colonel said. 'And the hell with SHAEF.'

'You explained that to me,' the girl said.

'I wish the hell you were a soldier with your straight true brain and your beauty memory.'

'I would wish to be a soldier if I could fight under you.'

'Never fight under me,' the Colonel said. 'I'm cagey. But I'm not lucky. Napoleon wanted them lucky and he was right.'

'We've had some luck.'

'Yes,' the Colonel said. 'Good and bad.'

'But it was all luck.'

'Sure,' the Colonel said. 'But you can't fight on luck. It is just something that you need. The people who fought on luck are all gloriously dead like Napoleon's horse cavalry.'

'Why do you hate cavalry? Almost all the good boys I know were in the three good regiments of cavalry, or in the navy.'

'I don't hate anything, Daughter,' the Colonel said, and drank a little of the light, dry, red wine which was as friendly as the house of your brother, if you and your brother are good friends. 'I only have a point of view, arrived at after careful consideration, and an estimate of their capabilities.'

'Are they not really good?'

'They are worthless,' the Colonel said. Then, remembering to be kind added, 'In our time.'

'Every day is a disillusion.'

'No. Every day is a new and fine illusion. But you can cut out everything phony about the illusion as though you would cut it with a straight-edge razor.'

'Please never cut me.'

'You're not cut-able.'

'Would you kiss me and hold me tight, and we both look at the Grand Canal where the light is lovely now, and you tell me more?'

When they were looking out at the Grand Canal where the light was, indeed, lovely, the Colonel went on, 'I got a regiment because the Commanding General relieved a boy that I had known since he was eighteen years old. He was not a boy any more, of course. It was too much regiment for him and it was all the regiment I ever could have hoped for in this life until I lost it.' He added, 'Under orders, of course.'

'How do you lose a regiment?'

'When you are working around to get up on the high ground and all you would have to do is send in a flag, and they would talk it over and come out if you were right. The professionals are very intelligent and these Krauts were all professionals; not the fanatics. The phone rings and somebody calls from Corps who has his orders from Army or maybe Army Group or maybe even SHAEF, because they read the name of the town in a newspaper, possibly sent in from Spa, by a correspondent, and the order is to take it by assault. It's important because it got into the newspapers. You have to take it.

'So you leave one company dead along a draw. You lose one company complete and you destroy three others. The tanks get smacked even as fast as they could move and they could move fast both ways.

'They hit them one, two, three, four, five.

'Three men usually get out of the five (that are inside) and they run like broken-field runners that have been shaken loose in a play when you are Minnesota and the others are Beloit, Wisconsin.

'Do I bore you?'

'No. I do not understand the local allusions. But you can explain them when you care to. Please keep on telling me.'

'You get into the town, and some handsome jerk puts an air mission on you. This mission might have been ordered and never cancelled. Let's give everyone the benefit of the doubt. I'm just telling you about things in a general way. It is better not to be specific and a civilian wouldn't understand it. Not even you.

'This air mission does not help much, Daughter. Because maybe you cannot stay in the town because you have got too few people in, and by now, you are digging them out of rubble; or leaving them in rubble. There are two schools of thought on that. So they say to take it by assault. They repeat this.

'This has been rigidly confirmed by some politician in uniform who has never killed in his life, except with his mouth over the telephone, or on paper, nor ever has been hit. Figure him as our next President if you want him. Figure him any way you like. But figure him and his people, the whole great business establishment, so far back that the best way to communicate with them rapidly would be by racing carrier pigeons. Except, with the amount of security they maintained for their proper persons, they would probably have their anti-aircraft shoot the pigeons down. If they could hit them.

'So you do it again. Then I will tell you what it looks like.'

The Colonel looked up at the play of the light on the ceiling. It was reflected, in part, from the Canal. It made strange, but steady movements, changing, as the current of a trout stream changes, but remaining, still changing as the sun moved.

Then he looked at his great beauty, with her strange, dark, grown-up child's face that broke his heart, that he would be leaving before 1335 (that was sure) and he said, 'Let's not talk about the war, Daughter.'

'Please,' she said. 'Please. Then I will have it all this week.'

'That's a short sentence. I mean using the word sentence as a jail sentence.'

'You don't know how long a week can be when you are nineteen.'

'Several times I have known how long an hour can be,' the Colonel said. 'I could tell you how long two minutes and a half can be.'

'Please tell me.'

'Well I had two days' leave in Paris between the Schnee-Eifel fight and this one, and due to my friendship with one or two people I was privileged to be present at some sort of a meeting, where only the accredited and trusted were present, and General Walter Bedell Smith explained to all of us how easy the operation that later took the name of Hürtgen Forest would be. It was not really Hürtgen Forest. That was only a small sector. It was the Stadtswald and it was where the German High Command had figured, exactly, to fight after Aachen had been taken and the road into Germany breached. I hope I am not boring you.'

'You never bore me. Nothing about fighting bores me except lies.'

'You're a strange girl.'

'Yes,' she said. 'I've known that for quite a long time.'

'Would you really like to fight?'

'I don't know if I could do it. But I could try if you taught me.'

'I'll never teach you. I'll just tell you anecdotes.'

'Sad stories of the death of kings.'

'No. G.I.S somebody christened them. God how I hate that word and how it was used. Comic book readers. All from some certain place. Most of them there unwillingly. Not all. But they all read a paper called "The Stars and Stripes" and you had to get your unit into it, or you were unsuccessful as a commander. I was mostly unsuccessful. I tried to like the correspondents and there were some very good ones present at this meeting. I will not name names because I might omit some fine ones and that would be unjust. There were good ones that I don't remember. Then, there were draft dodgers, phonies who claimed they were wounded if a piece of spent metal ever touched them, people who wore the Purple Heart from jeep accidents, insiders, cowards, liars, thieves and telephone racers. There were a few deads missing from this briefing. They had deads too. A big percentage. But none of the deads were present as I said. They had women at it though in wonderful uniforms.'

'But how did you ever marry one?'

'By mistake as I explained before.'

'Go on and tell me.'

'There were more maps in the room than Our Lord could read on his best day,' the Colonel continued. 'There were the Big Picture, the Semi-Big Picture and the Super-Big-Picture. All these people pretended to understand them, as did the boys with the pointers, a sort of half-arsed billiard cue that they used for explanation.'

'Don't say rough words. I don't know, even, what half-arsed means.'

'Shortened, or abbreviated in an inefficient manner,' the Colonel explained. 'Or deficient as an instrument, or in character. It's an old word. You could probably find it in Sanscrit.'

'Please tell me.'

'What for? Why should I perpetuate ignominy just with my mouth?'

'I'll write it if you want. I can write truly what I hear or think. I would make mistakes of course.'

'You are a lucky girl if you can write truly what you hear or think. But don't you ever write one word of this.'

He resumed, 'The place is full of correspondents dressed according to their taste. Some are cynical and some are extremely eager.

'To ride herd on them, and to wield the pointers, there is a group of pistol-slappers. We call a pistol-slapper a non-fighting man, disguised in uniform, or you might even call it costume, who gets excited every time the weapon slaps against his thighs. Incidentally, Daughter, the weapon, not the old pistol, the real pistol, has missed more people in combat than probably any weapon in the world. Don't ever let anyone give you one unless you want to hit people on the head with it in Harry's Bar.'

'I never wanted to hit anyone; except perhaps Andrea.'

'If you ever hit Andrea, hit him with the barrel; not with the butt. The butt is awfully slow, and it misses and if it lands you get blood on your hands when you put the gun away. Also please do not ever hit Andrea because he is my friend. I do not think he would be easy to hit either.'

'No. I do not think so either. Please tell me some more about the meeting, or the assembly. I think I could recognize a pistol-slapper now. But I would like to be checked out more thoroughly.'

'Well, the pistol-slappers, in all the pride of their pistol-slappery, were awaiting the arrival of the great General who was to explain the operation.

'The correspondents were muttering, or twittering, and the intelligent ones were glum or passively cheerful. Everybody sat on folding chairs as for a Chautauqua lecture. I'm sorry about these local terms; but we are a local people.

'In comes the General. He is no pistol-slapper, but a big business man; an excellent politician, the executive type. The Army is the biggest business, at that moment, in the world. He takes the half-arsed pointer, and he shows us, with complete conviction, and without forebodings, exactly what the attack will be, why we are making it, and how facilely it will succeed. There is no problem.'

'Go on,' the girl said. 'Please let me fill your glass and you, please look at the light on the ceiling.'

'Fill it and I'll look at the light and I will go on.

'This high pressure salesman, and I say this with no disrespect, but with admiration for all his talents, or his talent, also told what we would have of the necessary. There would be no lack of anything. The organization called SHAEF was then based on a town named Versailles outside of Paris. We would attack to the east of Aachen a distance of some 380 kilometres from where they were based.

'An army can get to be huge; but you can close up a little bit. They finally went as far forward as Rheims which was 240 kilometres from the fighting. That was many months later.

'I understand the necessity of the big executive being removed from contact with his working people. I understand about the size of the army and the various problems. I even understand logistics which is not difficult. But no one ever commanded from that far back in history.'

'Tell me about the town.'

'I'll tell you,' the Colonel said. 'But I don't want to hurt you.'

'You never hurt me. We are an old town and we had fighting men, always. We respect them more than all others and I hope we understand them a little. We also know they are difficult. Usually, as people, they are very boring to women.'

'Do I bore you?'

'What do you think?' the girl asked.

'I bore myself, Daughter.'

'I don't think you do, Richard, you would not have done something all your life if you were bored by it. Don't lie to me please, darling, when we have so little time.'

'I won't.'

'Don't you see you need to tell me things to purge your bitterness?'

'I know I tell them to you.'

'Don't you know I want you to die with the grace of a happy death? Oh, I'm getting all mixed up. Don't let me get too mixed up.'

'I won't, Daughter.'

'Tell me some more please and be just as bitter as you want.'

31

'Listen, Daughter,' the Colonel said. 'Now we will cut out all references to glamour and to high brass, even from Kansas, where the brass grows higher than osage-orange trees along your own road. It bears a fruit you can't eat and it is purely Kansan. Nobody but Kansans ever had anything to do with it; except maybe us who fought. We ate them every day. Osage oranges,' he added. 'Only we call them K-rations. They weren't bad. C-rations were bad. Ten in Ones were good.

'So we fought. It is dull but it is informative. This is the way it goes if anyone is ever interested; which I doubt.

'It goes like this: 1300 Red S-3: White jumped off on time. Red said they were waiting to tie in behind White. 1305 (that is one o'clock and five minutes after in the afternoon, if you can remember that, Daughter) Blue S-3, you know what an S-3 is I hope, says, "Let us know when you move." Red said they were waiting to tie in behind White.

'You can see how easy it is,' the Colonel told the girl. 'Everybody ought to do it before breakfast.'

'We cannot all be combat infantrymen,' the girl told him softly. 'I respect it more than anything except good, honest fliers. Please talk, I'm taking care of you.'

'Good fliers are very good and should be respected as such,' the Colonel said.

He looked up at the light on the ceiling and he was completely desperate at the remembrance of his loss of his battalions, and of individual people. He could never hope to have such a regiment, ever. He had not built it. He had inherited it. But, for a time, it had been his great joy. Now every second man in it was dead and the others nearly all were wounded. In the belly, the head, the feet or the hands, the neck, the back, the lucky buttocks, the unfortunate chest and the other places. Tree burst wounds hit men where they would never be wounded in open country. And all the wounded were wounded for life.

'It was a good regiment,' he said. 'You might even say it was a beautiful regiment until I destroyed it under other people's orders.'

'But why do you have to obey them when you know better?'

'In our army you obey like a dog,' the Colonel explained. 'You always hope you have a good master.'

'What kind of masters do you get?'

'I've only had two good ones so far. After I reached a certain level of command, many nice people, but only two good masters.'

'Is that why you are not a General now? I would love it if you were a General.'

'I'd love it too,' the Colonel said. 'But maybe not with the same intensity.'

'Would you try to sleep, please, to please me?'

'Yes,' the Colonel said.

'You see, I thought that if you slept you might get rid of them, just being asleep.'

'Yes. Thank you very much,' he said.

There was nothing to it, gentlemen. All a man need ever do is obey.

32

'You slept quite well for a time,' the girl told him, lovingly and gently. 'Is there anything you would like me to do?'

'Nothing,' the Colonel said. 'Thank you.'

Then he turned bad and he said. 'Daughter, I could sleep good straight up and down in the electric chair with my pants slit and my hair clipped. I sleep as, and when, I need it.'

'I can never be like that,' the girl said, sleepily. 'I sleep when I am sleepy.'

'You're lovely,' the Colonel told her. 'And you sleep better than anyone ever slept.'

'I am not proud of it,' the girl said, very sleepily. 'It is just something that I do.'

'Do it, please.'

'No. Tell me very low and soft and put your bad hand in mine.'

'The hell with my bad hand,' the Colonel said. 'Since when was it so bad.'

'It's bad,' the girl said. 'Badder, or worse, than you will ever know.

Please tell me about combat without being too brutal.'

'An easy assignment,' the Colonel said. 'I'll skip the times. The weather is cloudy and the place is 986342. What's the situation? We are smoking the enemy with artillery and mortar. S-3 advises that S-6 wants Red to button up by 1700. S-6 wants you to button up and use plenty of artillery. White reports that they are in fair shape. S-6 informs that A company will swing around and tie with B.

'B Company was stopped first by enemy action and stayed there of their own accord. S-6 isn't doing so good. This is unofficial. He wants more artillery but there isn't any more artillery.

'You wanted combat for what? I don't know really why. Or really know why. Who wants true combat? But here it is, Daughter, on the telephone and later I will put in the sounds and smells and anecdotes about who was killed when and where if you want them.'

'I only want what you will tell me.'

'I'll tell you how it was,' the Colonel said, 'and General Walter Bedell Smith doesn't know how it was yet. Though, probably, I am wrong, as I have been so many times.'

'I'm glad we don't have to know him or the nylon-smooth man,' the girl said.

'We won't have to know them this side of hell,' the Colonel assured her. 'And I will have a detail guarding the gates of hell so that no such characters enter.'

'You sound like Dante,' she said sleepily.

'I am Mister Dante,' he said. 'For the moment.'

And for a while he was and he drew all the circles. They were as unjust as Dante's but he drew them.

33

'I will skip the detailed part since you are, justifiably, and should be, sleepy,' the Colonel said. He watched, again, the strange play of the light on the ceiling. Then he looked at the girl, who was more beautiful than any girl that he had ever seen, ever.

He had seen them come and go, and they go faster, when they go, than any other thing that flies. They can go faster from fair beauty to the knocker's shop than any other animal, he thought. But I believe that this one could hold the pace and stay the course. The dark ones last the best, he thought and look at the bony structure in that face. This one has a fine blood line too, and she can go for ever. Most of our own lovely beauties come from soda counters, and they do not know their grandfather's last name, unless, maybe, it was Schultz. Or Schlitz, he thought.

This is the wrong attitude to take, he said to himself; since he did not wish to express any of these sentiments to the girl, who would not like them anyway, and was soundly sleepy now the way a cat is when it sleeps within itself.

'Sleep well, my dearest lovely, and I will just tell it for nothing.'

The girl was asleep, still holding his bad hand, that he despised, and he could feel her breathe, as the young breathe when they are easily asleep.

The Colonel told her all about it; but he did not utter it.

So after I had the privilege of hearing General Walter Bedell Smith explain the facility of the attack, we made it. There was the Big Red One, who believed their own publicity. There was the Ninth, which was a better Division than we were. There was us, who had always done it when they asked for you to do it.

We had no time to read comic books, and we had no time for practically nothing, because we always moved before first light. This is difficult and you have to throw away the Big Picture and be a division.

We wore a four-leaf clover, which meant nothing except among ourselves, who all loved it. And every time I ever see it the same thing happens in my inner guts. Some people thought that it was ivy. But it was not. It was a four-leaf clover disguised as ivy.

The orders were that we would attack with the Big Red One, the First Infantry Division of the Army of the United States, and they, and their Calypso singing PRO never let you forget it. He was a nice guy. And it was his job.

But you get fed up with horse-dung unless you like the aroma or the taste. I never liked it. Although I loved to walk through cow-dung when I was a kid and feel it between my toes. But horse-dung bores you. It bores me very rapidly, and I can detect it at over one thousand yards.

So we attacked, the three of us in line, exactly where the Germans wished us to attack. We will not mention General Walter Bedell Smith any further. He is not the villain. He only made the promises and explained how it would go. There are no villains, I presume, in a Democracy. He was only just as wrong as hell. Period, he added in his mind.

The patches had all been removed even as far back as the rear echelon so that no Kraut would know that it was us, the three he knew so well, who were going to attack. We were going to attack with the three of us in line and nothing in reserve. I won't try to explain what that means, Daughter. But it isn't any good. And the place we were going to fight in, which I had taken a good look at, was going to be Passchendaele with tree bursts. I say that too much. But I think it too much.

The poor bloody Twenty-eighth which was up on our right had been bogged down for some time and so there was pretty accurate information available about what conditions in those woods were going to be like. I think we could conservatively describe them as unfavourable.

Then we were ordered to commit one regiment before the attack started. That means that the enemy will get at least one prisoner which makes all the taking off the Divisional patches silly. They would be waiting for the old four-leaf clover people who would go straight to hell like a mule and do it for one hundred and five days. Figures of course mean nothing to civilians. Nor to the characters from SHAEF we never saw ever in these woods.

Incidentally, and of course these occurrences are always incidental at the SHAEF level, the regiment was destroyed. It was no one's bloody fault, especially not the fault of the man who commanded it. He was a man I would be glad to spend half my time in hell with; and may yet.

It certainly would be odd if instead of going to hell, as we always counted on, we should go to one of those Kraut joints like Valhalla and not be able to get along with the people. But maybe we could get a corner table with Rommel and Udet and it would be just like any winter-sports hotel. It will probably be hell though and I don't even believe in hell.

Well anyway this regiment was rebuilt as American regiments always are by the replacement system. I won't describe it since you can always read about it in a book by somebody who was a replacement. It boils down, or distils, to the fact you stay in until you are hit badly or killed or go crazy and get section-eighted. But I guess it is logical and as good as any other, given the difficulties of transport. However it leaves a core of certain un-killed characters who know what the score is and no one of these characters liked the look of those woods much.

You could sum up their attitude in this phrase, 'Don't — me, Jack.'

And since I had been an un-killed character for around twenty-eight years I could understand their attitude. But they were soldiers, so most of them got killed in those woods and when we took the three towns that looked so innocent and were really fortresses. They were just built to tempt us and we had no word on them at all. To continue to use the silly parlance of my trade: this could or could not be faulty intelligence.

'I feel terribly about the regiment,' the girl said. She had wakened and spoken straight from sleep.

'Yes,' said the Colonel. 'So do I. Let's drink to it once. Then you go to sleep, Daughter, please. The war is over and forgotten.'

Please don't think that I am conceited, Daughter, he said, without speaking. His true love was sleeping again. She slept in a different way than his career girl had slept. He did not like to remember how the career girl slept, yet he did. But he wanted to forget it. She did not sleep pretty, he thought. Not like this girl who slept as though she were awake and alive; except she was asleep. Please sleep well, he thought.

Who the hell are you to criticize career girls? he thought. What miserable career did you attempt and have failed at?

I wished to be, and was, a General Officer in the Army of the United States. I have failed and I speak badly of all who have succeeded.

Then his contrition did not last, and he said to himself, 'Except the brown-nosers, the five and ten and twenty percenters and all the jerks from wherever who never fought and hold commands.'

They killed several men from the Academy at Gettysburg. That was the big kill day of all kill days, when there was a certain amount of opposition by both sides.

Don't be bitter. They killed General McNair by mistake the day the Valhalla Express came over. Quit being bitter. People from the Academy were killed and there are statistics to prove it.

How can I remember if I am not bitter?

Be as bitter as you want. And tell the girl, now silently, and that will not hurt her, ever, because she is sleeping so lovely. He said lovely to himself since his thinking was often un-grammatical.

34

Sleep softly, my true love and when you wake, this will be over and I will joke you out of trying to learn details of the *triste métier* of war and we will go to buy the little Negro, or Moor, carved in ebony with his fine features and his jewelled turban. Then you will pin him on and we will go to have a drink at Harry's and see whoever or whatever of our friends that will be afoot at that hour.

We will lunch at Harry's, or we'll come back here and I will be packed. We will say goodbye and I will get into the *motoscafo* with Jackson and make some cheerful crack to the *Gran Maestro* and wave to any other members of the Order and ten to one, the way I feel right now, or two will get you thirty, we will not ever see one another again.

Hell, he said to no one and certainly not aloud, I've felt this way before many fights and almost always at some time in the fall of the year and always when leaving Paris. Probably it doesn't mean a thing.

Who gives a damn anyway except me and the *Gran Maestro* and this girl; I mean at command level.

I give very much of a damn myself. But I certainly should be trained and adjusted by this time not to give a muck for nothing; like the definition of a whore. A woman who does not, etc.

But we won't think about that boy, lieutenant, captain, major, colonel, general, sir. We will just lay it on the line once more and the hell with it and with its ugly face that old Hieronymus Bosch really painted. But you can sheathe your scythe, old brother death, if you have got a sheath for it. Or, he added, thinking of Hürtgen now, you can take your scythe and stick it.

It was Passchendaele with tree bursts, he told nobody except the wonder light on the ceiling. Then he looked at the girl, to see that she was sleeping well enough so even his thoughts would not hurt her.

Then he looked at the portrait and he thought, I have her in two positions, lying down, turned a little on her side and looking at me straight in front. I'm a lucky son of a bitch and I should never be sad about anything.

35

The first day there, we lost the three battalion commanders. One killed in the first twenty minutes and the other two hit later. This is only a statistic to a journalist. But good battalion commanders have never yet grown on trees; not even Christmas trees which was the basic tree of that woods. I do not know how many times we lost company commanders how many times over. But I could look it up.

They aren't made, nor grown, as fast as a crop of potatoes is either. We got a certain amount of replacements but I can remember thinking that it would be simpler and more effective, to shoot them in the area where they de-trucked, than to have to try to bring them back from where they would be killed and bury them. It takes men to bring them back and gasoline and men to bury them. These men might just as well be fighting and get killed too.

There was snow, or something, rain or fog, all the time and the roads had been mined as many as fourteen mines deep in certain stretches, so when the vehicles churned down to a new string deeper, in another part of the mud, you were always losing vehicles and, of course, the people that went with them.

Besides just mortaring it all to hell and having all the fire-lanes taped for machine gun and automatic weapon fire, they had the whole thing worked out and canalized so however you out-thought them you ran right into it. They also shelled you with heavy artillery fire and with at least one railway gun.

It was a place where it was extremely difficult for a man to stay alive even if all he did was be there. And we were attacking all the time and every day.

Let's not think about it. The hell with it. Maybe two things I will think about and get rid of them. One was a bare-arsed piece of hill that you had to cross to get into Grosshau.

Just before you had to make this run, which was under observation with fires by 88s, there was a little piece of dead ground where they could only hit you with a howitzer, only interdicting fires, or, from the right, by mortar. When we cleaned it up we found they had good observation for their mortars there too.

This was a comparatively safe place, I'm really not lying, not me nor anybody else. You can't fool those that were in Hürtgen and if you lied they would know it the minute you opened your mouth, Colonel or no Colonel.

We met a truck at this place and slowed up, and he had the usual grey face and he said, 'Sir, there is a dead G.I. in the middle of the road up ahead and every time any vehicle goes through they have to run over him and I'm afraid it is making a bad impression on the troops.'

'We'll get him off the road.'

So we got him off the road.

And I can remember just how he felt, lifting him and how he had been flattened and the strangeness of his flatness.

Then there was one other thing, I remember. We had put an awful lot of white phosphorous on the town before we got in for good, or whatever you would call it. That was the first time I ever saw a German dog eating a roasted German Kraut. Later on I saw a cat working on him too. It was a hungry cat, quite nice looking, basically. You wouldn't think a good German cat would eat a good German soldier, would you, Daughter? Or a good German dog eat a good German soldier's arse which had been roasted by white phosphorous.

How many could you tell like that? Plenty and what good would they do? You could tell a thousand and they would not prevent war. People would say we are not fighting the Krauts and besides the cat did not eat me nor my brother Gordon, because he was in the Pacific. Maybe land crabs ate Gordon. Or maybe he just deliquesced.

In Hürtgen they just froze up hard; and it was so cold they froze up with ruddy faces. Very strange. They all were grey and yellow like waxworks, in the summer. But once the winter really came they had ruddy faces.

Real soldiers never tell anyone what their own dead looked like, he told the portrait. And I'm through with this whole subject. And what about that company dead up the draw? What about them, professional soldier?

They're dead, he said. And I can hang and rattle.

Now who would join me in a glass of Valpolicella? What time do you think I should wake your opposite number, you girl? We have to get to that jewellery place. And I look forward to making jokes and to talking of the most cheerful things.

What's cheerful, portrait? You ought to know. You're smarter than I am, although you haven't been around as much.

All right, canvas girl, the Colonel told her, not saying it aloud, we'll drop the whole thing and in eleven minutes I will wake the live girl up and we will go out on the town and be cheerful and leave you here to be wrapped.

I didn't mean to be rude. I was just joking roughly. I don't wish to be rude ever because I will be living with you from now on. I hope, he added, and drank a glass of the wine.

36

It was a sharp, cold bright day and they stood outside the window of the jeweller's shop and studied the two small Negro heads and torsos that were carved in ebony and adorned with studded jewels. One was as good as the other, the Colonel thought.

'Which do you like the best, Daughter?'

'I think the one on the right. Don't you think he has the nicer face?'

'They both have nice faces. But I think I would rather have him attend you if it was the old days.'

'Good. We'll take him. Let's go in and see them. I must ask the price.'

'I will go in.'

'No, let me ask the price. They will charge me less than they would charge you. After all you are a rich American.'

'*Et toi*, Rimbaud?'

'You'd make an awfully funny Verlaine,' the girl told him. 'We'll be some other famous characters.'

'Go on in, Majesty, and we'll buy the goddamn jewel.'

'You wouldn't make a very good Louis XVI either.'

'I'd get up in that tumbril with you and still be able to spit.'

'Let's forget all the tumbrils and everyone's sorrows and buy the small object and then we can walk to Cipriani's and be famous people.'

Inside the shop they looked at the two heads and she asked the price and then, there was some very rapid talk and the price was much lower. But still it was more money than the Colonel had.

'I'll go to Cipriani's and get some money.'

'No,' the girl said. Then to the clerk, 'Put it in a box and send it to Cipriani's and say the Colonel said to pay for it and hold it for him.'

'Please,' the clerk said. 'Exactly as you say.'

They went out into the street and the sunlight and the unremitting wind.

'By the way,' the Colonel said. 'Your stones are in the safe at the Gritti in your name.'

'Your stones.'

'No,' he told her, not rough, but to make her understand truly. 'There are some things that a person cannot do. You know about that. You cannot marry me and I understand that, although I do not approve it.'

'Very well,' the girl said. 'I understand. But would you take one for a lucky stone?'

'No. I couldn't. They are too valuable.'

'But the portrait has value.'

'That is different.'

'Yes,' she agreed. 'I suppose so. I think I begin to understand.'

'I would accept a horse from you, if I was poor and young and riding very well. But I could not take a motor car.'

'I understand it now very well. Where can we go now, at this minute, where you can kiss me?'

'In this side alley, if you know no one who lives in it.'

'I don't care who lives in it. I want to feel you hold me tight and kiss me.'

They turned into the side street and walked towards its blind end.

'Oh, Richard,' she said. 'Oh, my dear.'

'I love you.'

'Please love me.'

'I do.'

The wind had blown her hair up and around his neck and he kissed her once more with it beating silkily against both his cheeks.

Then she broke away, suddenly and hard and looked at him and said, 'I suppose we had better go to Harry's.'

'I suppose so. Do you want to play historical personages?'

'Yes,' she said. 'Let us play that you are you and I am me.'

'Let's play,' the Colonel said.

37

There was no one in Harry's except some early morning drinkers that the Colonel did not know and two men that were doing business at the back of the bar.

There were hours at Harry's when it filled with the people that you knew, with the same rushing regularity as the tide coming in at Mont St Michel. Except, the Colonel thought, the hours of the tides change each day with the moon and the hours at Harry's are as the Greenwich Meridian, or the standard metre in Paris, or the good opinion the French military hold of themselves.

'Do you know any of these morning drinkers?' he asked the girl.

'No. I am not a morning drinker so I have never met them.'

'They will be swept out when the tide comes in.'

'No. They will leave, just as it comes, of their own accord.'

'Do you mind being here out of season?'

'Did you think I was a snob because I come from an old family? We're the ones who are not snobs. The snobs are what you call jerks and the people with all the new money. Did you ever see so much new money?'

'Yes,' the Colonel said. 'I saw it in Kansas City when I used to come in from Fort Riley to play polo at the Country Club.'

'Was it as bad as here?'

'No, it was quite pleasant. I liked it and that part of Kansas City is very beautiful.'

'Is it really? I wish that we could go there. Do they have the camps there too? The ones that we are going to stay at?'

'Surely. But we'll stay at the Muehlebach Hotel which has the biggest beds in the world and we'll pretend that we are oil millionaires.'

'Where will we leave the Cadillac?'

'Is it a Cadillac now?'

'Yes. Unless you want to take the big Buick Roadmaster, with the Dynaflow drive. I've driven it all over Europe. It was in that last *Vogue* you sent me.'

'We'd probably better just use one at a time,' the Colonel said. 'Whichever one we decide to use we will park in the garage alongside the Muehlebach.'

'Is the Muehlebach very splendid?'

'Wonderful. You'll love it. When we leave town we'll drive north to St Joe and have a drink in the bar at the Roubidoux, maybe two drinks and then we will cross the river and go west. You can drive and we can spell each other.'

'What is that?'

'Take turns driving.'

'I'm driving now.'

'Let's skip the dull part and get to Chimney Rock and go on to Scott's Bluff and Torrington and after that you will begin to see it.'

'I have the road maps and the guides and that man who says where to eat and the A.A.A. guide to the camps and the hotels.'

'Do you work on this much?'

'I work at it in the evening, with the things you sent me. What kind of a licence will we have?'

'Missouri. We'll buy the car in Kansas City. We fly to Kansas City, don't you remember? Or we can go on a really good train.'

'I thought we flew to Albuquerque.'

'That was another time.'

'Will we stop early in the afternoons at the best Motel in the A.A.A. book and I make you any drinks you want while you read the paper and *Life* and *Time* and *Newsweek* and I will read the new fresh *Vogue* and *Harper's Bazaar*?'

'Yes. But we come back here, too.'

'Of course. With our car. On an Italian liner; whichever one is best then. We drive straight here from Genoa.'

'You don't want to stop anywhere for the night?'

'Why? We want to get home to our own house.'

'Where will our house be?'

'We can decide that any time. There are always plenty of houses in this town. Would you like to live in the country too?'

'Yes,' the Colonel said. 'Why not?'

'Then we could see the trees when we woke up. What sort of trees will we see on this journey?'

'Pine mostly and cotton-wood along the creeks and aspen. Wait till you see the aspen turn yellow in the fall.'

'I'm waiting. Where will we stay in Wyoming?'

'We'll go to Sheridan first and then decide.'

'Is Sheridan nice?'

'It's wonderful. In the car we'll drive to where they had the Wagon-Box Fight and I'll tell you about it. We will drive up, on the way to Billings, to where they killed that fool George Armstrong Custer and you can see the markers where everybody died and I'll explain the fight to you.'

'That will be wonderful. Which is Sheridan more like; Mantova or Verona or Vicenza?'

'It isn't like any of those. It is right up against the mountains, almost like Schio.'

'Is it like Cortina then?'

'Nothing like. Cortina is in a high valley in the mountains. Sheridan lays right up against them. There aren't any foothills to the Big Horns. They rise high out of the plateau. You can see Cloud's Peak.'

'Will our cars climb them properly?'

'You're damn right they will. But I would much rather not have any hydromatic drive.'

'I can do without it,' the girl said. Then she held herself straight and hard not to cry. 'As I can do without everything else.'

'What are you drinking?' the Colonel said. 'We haven't even ordered yet.'

'I don't think I will drink anything.'

'Two very dry Martinis,' the Colonel said to the bar-tender, 'and a glass of cold water.'

He reached into his pocket and unscrewed the top of the medicine bottle and shook two of the big tablets into his left hand. With them in his hand, he screwed the top back on the bottle. It was no feat for a man with a bad right hand.

'I said I didn't want to drink anything.'

'I know, Daughter. But I thought you might need one. We can leave it on the bar. Or I can drink it myself. Please,' he said. 'I did not mean to be brusque.'

'We haven't asked for the little Negro that will look after me.'

'No. Because I did not want to ask for him until Cipriani came in and I could pay for him.'

'Is everything that rigid?'

'With me, I guess,' the Colonel said. 'I'm sorry, Daughter.'

'Say daughter three times straight.'

'*Hija, figlia,* Daughter.'

'I don't know,' she said. 'I think we should just leave here. I love to have people see us, but I don't want to see anybody.'

'The box with the Negro in it is on top of the cash register.'

'I know. I've seen it for some time.'

The bar-tender came, with the two drinks, frost cold from the chilled coldness of the glasses and he brought the glass of water.

'Give me that small packet that came in my name and is on top of the cash register,' the Colonel said to him. 'Tell Cipriani I will send him a cheque for it.'

He had made another decision.

'Do you want your drink, Daughter?'

'Yes. If you don't mind me changing my mind too.'

They drank, after touching glasses very lightly, so lightly that the contact was almost imperceptible.

'You were right,' she said feeling its warmth and its momentary destruction of sorrow.

'You were right too,' he said and palmed the two tablets.

He thought taking them with the water now, was in bad taste. So, when the girl turned her head a moment to watch a morning drinker go out the door, he swallowed them with the Martini.

'Should we go, Daughter?'

'Yes. By all means.'

'Bar-tender,' the Colonel said. 'How much are these drinks? And do not forget to tell Cipriani I am sending him a cheque for this nonsense.'

38

They ate lunch at the Gritti and the girl had unwrapped the small ebony Negro's head and torso and pinned it high on her left shoulder. It was about three inches long and was quite lovely to look at if you liked that sort of thing. And if you don't you are stupid, the Colonel thought.

But do not even think rough, he told himself. You have to be good now in every way until you say good-bye. What a word, he thought, good-bye.

It sounds like a Valentine slogan.

Good-bye and *bonne chance* and *hasta la vista*. We always just said *merde* and let it go at that. Farewell, he thought, that is a nice word. It sings well, he thought. Farewell, a long farewell and take it with you where you go. With handles, he thought.

'Daughter,' he said. 'How long has it been since I told you that I loved you?'

'Not since we sat at the table.'

'I tell you now.'

She had combed her hair with patience when they came into the hotel and she had gone into the room for women. She disliked such rooms.

She had used lipstick to make the sort of mouth she knew he most desired and she had said to herself, making the mouth correctly, 'Don't think at all. Don't think. Above all don't be sad because he is going now.'

'You look beautiful.'

'Thank you. I would like to be beautiful for you if I could and if I could be beautiful.'

'Italian is a lovely language.'

'Yes. Mister Dante thought so.'

'*Gran Maestro*,' the Colonel said. 'What is there to eat in this *Wirtschaft*?'

The *Gran Maestro* had been observing, without observing, with affection and without envy.

'Do you want meat or fish?'

'It's Saturday,' the Colonel said. 'Fish is not compulsory. So I'll take it.'

'It is sole,' the *Gran Maestro* said. 'What do you want, my Lady?'

'Whatever you decide. You know more about food than I do and I like it all.'

'Make a decision, Daughter.'

'No. I would rather leave it to someone who knows more than me. I have a boarding-school appetite.'

'It will come as a surprise,' the *Gran Maestro* said with his long and loving face with the grey eyebrows over the softly hooded eyes and the ever happy face of the old soldier who is still alive and appreciates it.

'Is there any news from the Order?' the Colonel asked.

'Only that our leader, Himself, is in trouble. They have confiscated everything he owns. Or at any rate they have intervened.'

'I hope it is not serious.'

'We will have confidence in our leader. He has ridden out worse tempests than this.'

'To our leader,' the Colonel said.

He raised his glass, which had been filled with the decanted new and true Valpolicella. 'Drink to him, Daughter.'

'I can't drink to that swine,' the girl said. 'Besides I do not belong to the Order.'

'You are a member now,' the *Gran Maestro* said. '*Por merito di guerra.*'

'I'll drink to him then,' she said. 'Am I really a member of the Order?'

'Yes,' the *Gran Maestro* said. 'You have not received your parchment yet but I appoint you Super Honorary Secretary. My Colonel will reveal to you the secrets of the Order. Reveal, please, my Colonel.'

'I reveal,' the Colonel said. 'There are no pitted folk about?'

'No. He is out with his Lady. Miss Baedeker.'

'Okay then,' the Colonel said. 'I will reveal. There is only the major secret that you must know. Correct me, *Gran Maestro*, if I fall into error.'

'Proceed to reveal,' the *Gran Maestro* said.

'I proceed to reveal,' the Colonel said. 'Listen carefully, Daughter. This is the Supreme Secret. Listen. "Love is love and fun is fun. But it is always so quiet when the gold fish die."'

'It has been revealed,' the *Gran Maestro* said.

'I am very proud and happy to be a member of the Order,' the girl said. 'But it is, in a way, a rather rough Order.'

'It is indeed,' the Colonel said. 'And now, *Gran Maestro*, what do we actually eat; without mysteries?'

'Some crab *enchillada*, in the style of this town, but cold, first. Served in the shell. Then sole for you and for my lady a mixed grill. What vegetables?'

'Whatever you have,' the Colonel said.

The *Gran Maestro* was gone and the Colonel looked at the girl and then at the Grand Canal outside the window and he saw the magic spots and changes of light that were even here, in the end of the bar, which had now by skilful handling, been made into a dining-room and he said, 'Did I tell you, Daughter, that I love you?'

'You haven't told me for quite a long time. But I love you.'

'What happens to people that love each other?'

'I suppose they have whatever they have and they are more fortunate than others. Then one of them gets the emptiness for ever.'

'I won't be rough,' the Colonel said. 'I could have made a rough response. But please don't have any emptiness.'

'I'll try,' the girl said. 'I've been trying ever since I woke up. I've tried ever since we knew each other.'

'Keep on trying, Daughter,' the Colonel said.

Then to the *Gran Maestro*, who had reappeared, having given his orders, the Colonel said, 'A bottle of that *vino secco*, from Vesuvius, for the small soles. We have the Valpolicella for the other things.'

'Can't I drink the Vesuvius wine with my mixed grill?' the girl asked.

'Renata, Daughter,' the Colonel said. 'Of course. You can do anything.'

'I like to drink the same wines as you if I drink wine.'

'Good white wine is good with a mixed grill, at your age,' the Colonel told her.

'I wish there was not such a difference in ages.'

'I like it very much,' the Colonel said. 'Except,' he added. Then he did not continue and said, 'Let's be *fraîche et rose comme au jour de bataille*.'

'Who said that?'

'I haven't the slightest idea. I picked it up when I took a course at the Collège des Maréchaux. A rather pretentious title. But I graduated. What I know best I learned from the Krauts, studying them and opposing them. They are the best soldiers. But they always overreach.'

'Let's be like you said and please tell me that you love me.'

'I love you,' he said. 'That's what you can base on. I tell you truly.'

'It is Saturday,' she said. 'And when is next Saturday?'

'Next Saturday is a movable feast, Daughter. Find me a man who can tell me about next Saturday.'

'You could tell me if you would.'

'I'll ask the *Gran Maestro*, maybe he knows. *Gran Maestro*, when will next Saturday come?'

'*À Pâques ou à la Trinité*,' the *Gran Maestro* said.

'Why don't we have any smells from the kitchen to cheer us up?'

'Because the wind is from the wrong direction.'

Yes, the Colonel thought. The wind is from the wrong direction and how lucky I would have been to have had this girl instead of the woman that I pay alimony to, who could not even make a child. She hired out for that. But who should criticize whose tubes? I only criticize Goodrich or Firestone or General.

Keep it clean, he said to himself. And love your girl.

She was there beside him, wishing to be loved, if he had any love to give.

It came back, as it always had, when he saw her and he said, 'How are you with the crow wing hair and the break-heart face?'

'I'm fine.'

'*Gran Maestro*,' the Colonel said. 'Produce a few smells or something from your off-stage kitchen, even if the wind is against us.'

39

The hall porter had telephoned, under the direction of the concierge, and it was the same motor-boat that they had ridden in before.

T5 Jackson was in the boat with the luggage and the portrait, which had been well and sturdily wrapped. It was still blowing hard.

The Colonel had paid his bill and made the proper tips. The people of the hotel had put the luggage and the picture in the boat and seen that Jackson was seated properly. Then they had retired.

'Well, Daughter,' the Colonel said.

'Can't I ride with you to the garage?'

'It would be just as bad at the garage.'

'Please let me ride to the garage.'

'All right,' the Colonel said. 'It's your show, really. Get in.'

They did not talk at all and the wind was a stern wind so that, with what speed the old calamity of a motor made, there seemed almost to be no wind at all.

At the landing-place, where Jackson was handing the luggage to a porter and looking after the portrait himself, the Colonel said, 'Do you want to say good-bye here?'

'Do I have to?'

'No.'

'May I come up to the bar in the garage while they are getting the car down?'

'That will be worse.'

'I do not care.'

'Get that stuff up to the garage and have somebody look after it until you get the car down,' the Colonel said to Jackson. 'Check on my guns and pack this stuff in a way to give the maximum space in the rear seat.'

'Yes, sir,' Jackson said.

'Am I going then?' the girl asked.

'No,' the Colonel told her.

'Why can't I go?'

'You know very well. You weren't invited.'

'Please don't be bad.'

'Christ, Daughter, if you knew how hard I am trying not to be. It's easy if you're bad. Let's pay this good man off and go over and sit on the bench there under the tree.'

He paid the owner of the motor-boat and told him that he had not forgotten about the jeep engine. He also told him not to count on it, but that there was a good chance that he could get it.

'It will be a used engine. But it will be better than that coffee pot you have in there now.'

They went up the worn stone steps and walked across the gravel and sat on a bench under the trees.

The trees were black and moved in the wind and there were no leaves on them. The leaves had fallen early that year and been swept up long ago.

A man came over to offer postcards for sale and the Colonel told him, 'Run along, son. We don't need you now.'

The girl was crying, finally, although she had made the decision never to cry.

'Look, Daughter,' the Colonel said. 'There isn't anything to say. They didn't install shock-absorbers in this vehicle we ride in now.'

'I've stopped,' she said. 'I'm not an hysterical.'

'I wouldn't say you were. I'd say you were the loveliest and most beautiful girl that ever lived. Any time. Any place. Anywhere.'

'If it were true, what difference would it make?'

'You have me there,' the Colonel said. 'But it is true.'

'So now what?'

'So now we stand up and kiss each other and say good-bye.'

'What's that?'

'I don't know,' the Colonel said. 'I guess that is one of the things everybody has to figure out for themselves.'

'I'll try to figure it.'

'Just take it as easy as you can, Daughter.'

'Yes,' the girl said. 'In the vehicle without the shock-absorbers.'

'You were tumbril bait from the start.'

'Can't you do anything kindly?'

'I guess not. But I've tried.'

'Please keep on trying. That's all the hope we have.'

'I'll keep on trying.'

So they held each other close and kissed each other hard and true and the Colonel took the girl across the stretch of gravel and down the stone steps.

'You ought to take a good one. Not that old displaced engine boat.'

'I'd rather take the displaced engine boat if you don't mind.'

'Mind?' the Colonel said. 'Not me. I only give orders and obey orders. I don't mind. Good-bye, my dear, lovely, beautiful.'

'Good-bye,' she said.

40

He was in the sunken oak hogshead that they used in the Veneto for blinds. A blind is any artifice you use to hide the shooter from that which he is attempting to shoot, which, in this case, were ducks.

It had been a good trip out with the boys, once they had met in the garage, and a good evening with excellent food cooked on the old open-hearth kitchen. Three shooters rode in the rear seat, on the way to the shooting place. Those who did not lie had permitted themselves a certain amount of exaggeration and the liars had never been in fuller flower.

A liar, in full flower, the Colonel had thought, is as beautiful as cherry trees, or apple trees when they are in blossom. Who should ever discourage a liar, he thought, unless he is giving you coordinates?

The Colonel had collected liars all his life, as some men gather postage stamps. He did not classify them, except at the moment, nor treasure them truly. He just enjoyed, completely, hearing them lie at the moment, unless, of course, something concerned with duty was involved. Last night there had been a fair amount of good lying after the *grappa* had been passed around and the Colonel had enjoyed it.

There had been smoke in the room from the open charcoal fire; no, there were logs, he thought. Anyway, a liar lies best when there is a little smoke or when the sun has set.

He had come close to lying twice himself and had held it up and merely exaggerated. I hope anyway, he thought.

Now here was the frozen lagoon to ruin everything. But it was not ruined.

A pair of pin-tails came, suddenly, from nowhere, slanting down fast in a dive no aeroplane ever made and the Colonel heard their feathered trajectory and swung and killed the drake. He lay on the ice, hitting it as solid as a duck can hit ice and, before he was down, the Colonel had killed his mate, who was climbing, long-necked and fast.

She fell alongside the drake.

So it is murder, the Colonel thought. And what isn't nowadays? But, boy, you can still shoot.

Boy, hell, he thought. You beat-up old bastard. But look at them come now.

They were widgeon and they came in a wisp that coagulated and then stretched to nothing. Then they coagulated again and the treacherous duck on the ice started to talk to them.

Let them turn once more, the Colonel said to himself. Keep your head down and do not move even your eyes. They are going to come in.

They came in well, with treachery speaking to them.

Their wings were suddenly set to alight, as when you lower the flaps. Then they saw it was ice and they rose, climbing.

The shooter, who was not a Colonel now, nor anything but a gun handler, rose in the wooden barrel and got two. They hit the ice almost as solidly as the big ducks.

Two is enough from one family, the Colonel said. Or was it one tribe?

The Colonel heard a shot behind him, where he knew there was no other blind and turned his head to look across the frozen lagoon to the far, sedge-lined shore.

That does it, he thought.

A bunch of mallards, that had been coming in low, were flaring up into the sky, seeming to stand on their tails as they climbed.

He saw one fall, then heard another shot.

It was the sullen boatman shooting at the ducks that would have come to the Colonel.

How, how can he do that? the Colonel thought.

The man had a shotgun to shoot any cripples that might be escaping where the dog could not get them. For him to fire at ducks that were coming to the Colonel's blind was, in shooting, as bad a thing as one man could do to another.

The boatman was too far away to hear a shout. So the Colonel fired at him twice.

It is too far for the pellets to reach, he thought, but at least he will know that I know what he is doing. What the hell is this all about? On a beautifully run shoot like this one too? This is the best organized and best run duck shoot I have ever shot at and I have had as much fun shooting here as I ever had in my life. What is the matter with that son of a bitch?

He knew how bad his anger was for him. So he took two of the pills and washed them down with a drink of Gordon's Gin from his flask since there was no water.

He knew the gin was bad for him too and he thought, everything is bad for me except rest and very light exercise. Okay, rest and light exercise, boy. Do you suppose that is light exercise?

You, beauty, he said to himself. I wish you were here now and we were in the double blind and if we could only just feel the backs of our shoulders touch. I'd look around and see you and I would shoot the high ducks well, to show off and try to put one in the blind without having it hit you. I'd try to pull one down like this, he said, hearing the wings in the air. He rose, turned, saw the single drake, long-necked and beautiful, the wings fast moving and travelling to the sea. He saw him sharp and clear and in the sky with the mountains behind him. He met him, covered him and pulled as he swung as far back as he could swing the gun.

The drake came down on the ice, just outside the perimeter of the blind and broke the ice as he fell. It was the ice that had been broken to put out the decoys and it had re-frozen lightly. The calling hen looked at him as he lay and shifted her feet.

'You never saw him before in your life,' the Colonel said to the hen. 'I don't believe you even saw him coming. Though you may have. But you didn't say anything.'

The drake had hit with his head down and his head was under the ice. But the Colonel could see the beautiful winter plumage on his breast and wings.

I'd like to give her a vest made of the whole plumage the way the old Mexicans used to ornament their gods, he thought. But I suppose these ducks have to go to the market and no one would know how to skin and cure the skins anyway. It could be beautiful, though, with mallard drake skins for the back and sprig for the front with two longitudinal stripes of teal. One coming down over each breast. Be a hell of a vest. I'm pretty sure she'd like it.

I wish that they would fly, the Colonel thought. A few fool ducks might come in. I have to stay ready for them if they do. But none came in and he had to think.

There were no shots from the other blinds and only occasional shots from the sea.

With the good light, the birds could see the ice and they no longer came in and instead went out to the open sea to raft up. So he had no shooting and he thought without intention, trying to find what had made it at the first. He knew he did not deserve it and he accepted it and he lived by it, but he sought, always, to understand it.

One time it had been two sailors when he had been walking with the girl at night. They had whistled at her and, the Colonel thought, that was a harmless enough thing and he should have let it go.

But there was something wrong with it. He sensed it before he knew it. Then he knew it solidly, because he had stopped under a light, in order that they might see what he wore on his shoulders, so that they might take the other side of the street.

What he wore on each shoulder was a small eagle with wings outstretched. It was embroidered on to the coat he wore in silver thread. It was not conspicuous and it had been there a long time. But it was visible.

The two sailors whistled again.

'Stay over there against the wall if you want to watch it,' the Colonel had said to the girl. 'Or look away.'

'They are very big and young.'

'They won't be big for long,' the Colonel promised her.

The Colonel walked over to the whistlers.

'Where is your shore patrol?' he asked.

'How would I know?' the biggest whistler said. 'All I want is a good look at the dame.'

'Do people like you have names and serial numbers?'

'How would I know,' one said.

The other said, 'I wouldn't tell a chicken Colonel if I had.'

Old army boy, the Colonel thought, before he hit him. Sea lawyer. Knows all his rights.

But he hit him with a left from nowhere and hit him three times as he started to go.

The other one, the first whistler, had closed fast and well, for a man who had been drinking, and the Colonel gave him the elbow in the mouth and then, under the light, had a good right hand shot at him. When it was in, he glanced at the second whistler and saw that was okay.

Then he threw a left hook. Then he put the right way into the body, coming up. He threw another left hook and then turned away and walked towards the girl because he did not want to hear the head hit the pavement.

He checked on the one that had it first and noted he slept peacefully, chin down, with the blood coming out of his mouth. But it was still the right colour, the Colonel noted.

'Well, there goes my career,' he said to the girl. 'Whatever that was. But those people certainly wear funny pants.'

'How are you?' the girl asked.

'I'm fine. Did you watch it?'

'Yes.'

'I'll have bad hands in the morning,' he said absent mindedly. 'But I think we can walk away from it all right. But let's walk slowly.'

'Please walk slowly.'

'I did not mean it that way. I meant let's not be hurried in our departure.'

'We will walk as slowly as two people can walk.'

So they walked.

'Do you want to try an experiment?'

'Of course.'

'Let's walk so we make even the backs of our legs look dangerous.'

'I'll try. But I don't think I can.'

'Well, let's just walk then.'

'But didn't they hit you?'

'One pretty good right behind the ear. The second boy when he came in.'

'Is that what fighting's like?'

'When you're lucky.'

'And when you're not lucky?'

'Your knees bend too. Either forward or backward.'

'Do you still care for me after you have fought?'

'I love you much more than before if it were possible.'

'Can't it be possible? It would be nice. I love you more since I saw that thing. Am I walking slowly enough?'

'You walk like a deer in the forest and sometimes you walk as well as a wolf, or an old, big coyote when he is not hurried.'

'I'm not sure I wish to be an old big coyote.'

'Wait till you see one,' the Colonel said. 'You'll wish. You walk like all the great predators, when they walk softly. And you are not a predator.'

'That I can promise.'

'Walk a little ahead so I can see.'

She walked ahead and the Colonel said, 'You walk like a champion before he is the champion. If you were a horse I would buy you if I had to borrow the money at twenty per cent a month.'

'You don't have to buy me.'

'I know about that. That was not what we were discussing. We were discussing your gait.'

'Tell me,' she said. 'What happens to those men? That's one of the things I don't know about fighting. Shouldn't I have stayed and cared for them?'

'Never,' the Colonel told her. 'Remember that; never. I hope they split a good concussion between them. They can rot. They caused the accident. There is no question of civil responsibility. We were all insured. If I can tell you one thing, Renata, about fighting.'

'Tell me, please.'

'If you ever fight, then you must win it. That's all that counts. All the rest is cabbage, as my old friend Dr Rommel put it.'

'Did you really like Rommel?'

'Very much.'

'But he was your enemy.'

'I love my enemies, sometimes, more than my friends. And the Navy, you know, wins all their fights always. This I learned in a place called the Pentagon building when I was still permitted to enter that building by the front door. If you like we can stroll back down this street, or walk it fast and ask those two that question.'

'I tell you truly, Richard. I have seen enough fighting for one night.'

'Me too, to tell the truth,' the Colonel said. But he said it in Italian and it started, '*Anche io*. Let's go to Harry's for one, and then I will walk you home.'

'Didn't you hurt your bad hand?'

'No,' he explained. 'I only threw it once to the head. The other times I punched to the body with it.'

'May I feel it?'

'If you will feel very softly.'

'But it is terribly swollen.'

'There is nothing broken in it and that sort of swelling always goes down.'

'Do you love me?'

'Yes. I love you with two moderately swollen hands and all my heart.'

41

So that was that and maybe it was that day or maybe it was another that made the miracle. You never knew, he thought. There was the great miracle and he had never consciously implemented it. Nor, he thought, you son of a bitch, did you ever oppose it.

It was colder than ever and the broken ice re-froze and the calling duck did not even look up now. She had abandoned treachery for an attempt at security.

You bitch, the Colonel thought. Though that is unjust. It is your trade. But why is it a hen calls better than a drake. You ought to know, he thought. And even that's not true. What the hell is true? Drakes actually call better.

Now don't think of her. Don't think of Renata because it won't do you any good, boy. It might even be bad for you. Also you said good-bye. What a good-bye that was. Complete with tumbrils. And she would have climbed up in the damned tumbril with you too. Just so long as it was a real tumbril. Very rough trade, he thought. Loving and leaving. People can get hurt at it.

Who gave you a right to know a girl like that?

Nobody, he answered. But Andrea introduced me to her.

But how could she love a sad son of a bitch like you?

I do not know, he thought truly. I truly do not know.

He did not know, among other things, that the girl loved him because he had never been sad one waking morning of his life; attack or no attack. He had experienced anguish and sorrow. But he had never been sad in the morning.

They make almost none like that and the girl, although she was a young girl, knew one when she saw one.

Now she is at home and sleeping, the Colonel thought. That is where she ought to be and not in any goddamn duck blind with the decoys frozen up on us.

I wish to hell she was here though, if this were a double blind and have her looking to the west just in case one string did come in. It would be nice if she were warm enough. Maybe I can trade somebody out of one of these real down jackets that nobody ever sold that had one. The kind they issued to the Air Force once by mistake.

I could find out how they are quilted and make one with duck down from here, he thought. I'd get a good tailor to cut it and we would make it double-breasted with no pocket on the right and lay in a chamois shooting patch so the gun butt would never catch.

I'll do it, he said to himself. I'll do it, or I will get one off some joker and have it cut down for her. I'd like to get her a good Purdey 12, not too damn light, or a pair of Boss over and unders. She should have guns as good as she is. I suppose a pair of Purdey's, he thought.

Just then he heard the light swish of pinions, fast beating in the air and looked up. But they were too high. He only looked up with his eyes. But they were so high they could see the barrel and him in it and the frozen-in decoys with the dejected hen, who saw them too and quacked hard in her loyal treachery. The ducks, they were pintails, continued on their flight out towards the sea.

I never give her anything, as she pointed out. There was the small Moor's head. But it does not mean anything. She selected it and I bought it. That is no way to give a gift.

What I would like to give her is security, which does not exist any more; all my love, which is worthless; all my worldly goods, which are practically non-existent except for two good shotguns, my soldier suits, the medals and decorations with the citations and some books. Also a retired Colonel's pay.

With all my worldly goods I thee endow, he thought.

And she gave me her love, some hard stones, which I returned, and the picture. Well, I can always give her back the picture. I could give her my ring from V.M.I., he thought, but where the hell did I lose that?

She wouldn't want a D.S.C. with cluster, nor two silver stars, nor the other junk, nor the medals of her own country. Nor those of France. Nor those of Belgium. Nor the trick ones. That would be morbid.

I better just give her my love. But how the hell do you send it? And how do you keep it fresh? They can't pack it in dry ice.

Maybe they can. I must inquire. But how do I get that condemned jeep engine to that old man?

Figure it out, he thought. Figuring things out has been your trade. Figuring things out when they were shooting at you, he added.

I wish that son of a bitch that is lousing up the duck shooting had a rifle and I had a rifle. We would find out pretty soon who could figure things out. Even in a lousy barrel in a marsh where you can't manoeuvre. He'd have to come to get me.

Stop that, he said to himself, and think about your girl. You do not want to kill anyone any more; ever.

Who are you feeding that to, he told himself. You going to run as a Christian? You might give it an honest try. She would like you better that way. Or would she? I don't know, he said frankly. I honest to God don't know.

Maybe I will get Christian towards the end. Yes, he said, maybe you will. Who wants to make a bet on that?

'You want to bet on that?' he asked the calling duck. But she was looking up at the sky behind him and had commenced her small chuckling talk.

They came over too high and never circled. They only looked down and went on towards the open sea.

They must really be rafted up out there, the Colonel thought. There's probably some punt gunner trying to sneak up on them now. They will be pretty close into the lee with the wind and someone is sneaking on to them now surely. Well, when he makes his shot some may break back this way. But with it frozen-up I suppose I really ought to pull out instead of staying here like a fool.

I have killed enough and I have shot as well or better than I can shoot. Better hell, he thought. Nobody shoots better than you here except Alvarito and he's a kid and shoots faster. But you kill fewer ducks than many bad and fair shots.

Yes, I know about that. I know about that and why and we don't go by the numbers any more and we threw away the book too, remember?

He remembered how, by some miracle of chance in a war, he had been with his best friend for a moment in action in the Ardennes and they were pursuing.

It was early fall and it was on a high upland with sandy roads and trails and the trees were scrub oak and pines. The enemy tank and half-track prints showed clearly in the moist sand.

It had rained the day before, but now it was clearing and visibility was good and you could see well across all the high, rolling country and he and his friend were glassing it as carefully as though they were hunting game.

The Colonel, who was a General then and an assistant divisional commander, knew the individual print of each tracked vehicle they were pursuing. He also knew when the enemy vehicles had run out of mines and approximately the number of rounds that remained to them. He also had figured where they had to fight before they reached the Siegfried. He was sure they would not fight at either of these two places but would race for where they were going.

'We're pretty far up for people of our exalted rank, George,' he said to his best friend.

'Ahead of the point, General.'

'It's okay,' the Colonel had said. 'Now we throw away the book and chase for keeps.'

'I couldn't agree more fully, General. Because I wrote the book myself,' his best friend said. 'But suppose they had left something there?'

He pointed to the logical place to defend.

'They didn't leave anything there,' the Colonel had said. 'They haven't enough stuff even for a fire-fight.'

'Everybody's right until he's wrong,' his best friend said, adding, 'General.'

'I'm right,' the Colonel said. He was right, too, although in obtaining his exact knowledge he had not fulfilled in complete spirit of the Geneva Convention which was alleged to govern the operation of war.

'Let's really chase,' his best friend had said.

'There's nothing holding us up and I guarantee they won't stop at either of those two. I didn't get that from any Kraut either. That's from my head.'

He looked over the country once more, and heard the wind in the trees and smelled the heather under their boots and looked once more at the tracks in the wet sand and that was the end of that story.

I wonder if she'd like that? he thought. No. It builds me up too much. I'd like to get somebody else to tell it to her though and build me solid. George can't tell it to her. He's the only one that could tell it to her and he can't. He sure as hell can't.

I've been right over ninety-five per cent of the time and that's a hell of a batting average even in something as simple as war. But that five per cent when you are wrong can certainly be something.

I'll never tell you about that, Daughter. That's just a noise heard off stage in my heart. My lousy chicken heart. That bastard heart certainly couldn't hold the pace.

Maybe he will, he thought, and took two of the tablets and a swallow of gin and looked across the grey ice.

I'm going to get that sullen character in now and pick up and get the hell to the farm house or the lodge, I suppose that I should call it. The shooting's over.

42

The Colonel had signalled the boatman in by standing up, in the sunken barrel, firing two shots towards the empty sky, and then waving him towards the blind.

The boat came in slowly, breaking ice all the way, and the man picked up the wooden decoys, caught the calling hen and put her in her sack, and, with the dog slithering on the ice, picked up the ducks. The boatman's anger seemed to be gone and to be replaced by a solid satisfaction.

'You shot very few,' he said to the Colonel.

'With your help.'

That was all they said and the boatman placed the ducks carefully, breasts up, on the bow of the boat and the Colonel handed his guns and the combination cartridge box and shooting stool into the boat.

The Colonel got into the boat and the boatman checked the blind and unhooked the pocketed, apron-like device which had hung on the inside of the blind to hold shells. Then he got into the boat too and they commenced their slow and laborious progress out through the ice to the open water of the brown canal. The Colonel worked as hard with the poling oar as he had worked coming in. But now, in the bright sunlight, with the snow mountains to the north, and the line of the sedge that marked the canal ahead of them, they worked together in complete co-ordination.

Then they were into the canal, slipping breakingly in from the last ice; then, suddenly, light-borne and the Colonel handed the big oar to the boatman and sat down. He was sweating.

The dog, who had been shivering at the Colonel's feet, pawed his way over the gunwale of the boat and swam to the canal bank. Shaking the water from his white bedraggled coat, he was into the brown sedge and brush, and the Colonel watched his progress towards home by the movement of the brush. He had never received his sausage.

The Colonel, feeling himself sweating, although he knew he was protected from the wind by his field jacket, took two tablets from the bottle and a sip of gin from his flask.

The flask was flat and of silver with a leather cover. Under the leather cover, which was worn and stained, it was engraved, on one side, to Richard From Renata With Love. No one had ever seen this inscription except the girl, the Colonel and the man who had engraved it. It had not been engraved in the same place it was purchased. That was in the earliest days, the Colonel thought. Now who cared?

On the screw-on top of the flask was engraved From R. to R.C.

The Colonel offered the flask to the boatman who looked at him, at the flask, and said, 'What is it?'

'English *grappa.*'

'I'll try it.'

He took a long drink of it; the type of drink peasants take from a flask.

'Thank you.'

'Did you have good shooting?'

'I killed four ducks. The dog found three cripples shot by other people.'

'Why did you shoot?'

'I'm sorry that I shot. I shot in anger.'

I have done that myself sometimes, the Colonel thought, and did not ask him what the anger was about.

'I am sorry they did not fly better.'

'That's the way things go,' the Colonel said.

The Colonel was watching the movement the dog made in the high grass and sedge. Suddenly he saw him stop; he was quite still. Then he pounced. It was a high leap and a dive forward and down.

'He has a crippled,' he said to the boatman.

'Bobby,' the boatman called. 'Bring, Bring.'

The sedge moved and the dog came out with a mallard drake in his jaws. The grey white neck and the green head were swaying up and down as a snake's might move. It was a movement without hope.

The boatman put the boat in sharp for shore.

'I'll take him,' the Colonel said. 'Bobby!'

He took the duck from the dog's light-holding mouth and felt him intact and sound and beautiful to hold, and with his heart beating and his captured, hopeless eyes.

He looked at him carefully, gentling him as you might gentle a horse.

'He's only wing-tipped,' he said. 'We'll keep him for a caller or to turn loose in the spring. Here, take him and put him in the sack with the hen.'

The boatman took him carefully and put him in the burlap bag that was under the bow. The Colonel heard the hen speak to him. Or, maybe she is protesting, he thought. He could not understand duck-talk through a burlap bag.

'Take a shot of this,' he said to the boatman. 'It's damned cold today.'

The boatman took the flask and drank deeply again.

'Thank you,' he said. 'Your *grappa* is very, very good.'

43

At the landing, before the long low stone house by the side of the canal, there were ducks laid out on the ground in rows.

They were laid in groups that were never of the same number. There were a few platoons, no companies, and, the Colonel thought, I barely have a squad.

The head gamekeeper was standing on the bank in his high boots, his short jacket and his pushed back old felt hat, and he looked critically at the number of ducks on the bow of the boat as they came alongshore.

'It was frozen-up at our post,' the Colonel said.

'I suspected so,' the head keeper said. 'I'm sorry. It was supposed to be the best post.'

'Who was top gun?'

'The Barone killed forty-two. There was a little current there that kept it open for a while. You probably did not hear the shooting because it was against the wind.'

'Where is everyone?'

'They're all gone except the Barone who is waiting for you. Your driver is asleep in the house.'

'He would be,' the Colonel said.

'Spread those out properly,' the head-keeper told the boatman who was a gamekeeper too. 'I want to put them in the game book.'

'There is one green-head drake in the bag who is only wing-tipped.'

'Good. I will take good care of him.'

'I will go inside and see the Barone. I'll see you later.'

'You must get warm,' the head keeper said. 'It's been a bitter day, my Colonel.'

The Colonel started to walk towards the door of the house.

'I'll see you later,' he said to the boatman.

'Yes, my Colonel,' the boatman said.

Alvarito, the Barone, was standing by the open fire in the middle of the room. He smiled his shy smile and said in his low-pitched voice, 'I am sorry you did not have better shooting.'

'We froze up completely. I enjoyed what there was very much.'

'Are you very cold?'

'Not too cold.'

'We can have something to eat.'

'Thank you. I'm not hungry. Have you eaten?'

'Yes. The others went on and I let them take my car. Can you give me a lift to Latisana or just above? I can get transportation from there.'

'Of course.'

'It was a shame that it should freeze. The prospects were so good.'

'There must have been a world of ducks outside.'

'Yes. But now they won't stay with their feed frozen over. They will be on their way south tonight.'

'Will they all go?'

'All except our local ducks that breed here. They'll stay as long as there is any open water.'

'I'm sorry for the shoot.'

'I'm sorry you came so far for so few ducks.'

'I always love the shoot,' the Colonel said. 'And I love Venice.'

The Barone Alvarito looked away and spread his hands towards the fire. 'Yes,' he said. 'We all love Venice. Perhaps you do the best of all.'

The Colonel made no small talk on this but said, 'I love Venice as you know.'

'Yes. I know,' the Barone said. He looked at nothing. Then he said, 'We must wake your driver.'

'Has he eaten?'

'Eaten and slept and eaten and slept. He has also read a little in some illustrated books he brought with him.'

'Comic books,' the Colonel said.

'I should learn to read them,' the Barone said. He smiled the shy, dark smile. 'Could you get me some from Trieste?'

'Any amount,' the Colonel told him. 'From Superman on up into the improbable. Read some for me. Look, Alvarito, what was the matter with that gamekeeper who poled my boat? He seemed to have a hatred for me at the start. Pretty well through, too.'

'It was the old battle-jacket. Allied uniform affects him that way. You see he was a bit over-liberated.'

'Go on.'

'When the Moroccans came through here they raped both his wife and his daughter.'

'I think I'd better have a drink,' the Colonel said.

'There is *grappa* there on the table.'

44

They had dropped the Barone off at a villa with great gates, a gravelled drive and a house, which, since it was over six miles from any military objective, had the good fortune not to have been bombed.

The Colonel had said good-bye and Alvarito had told him to come down and shoot any, or every, week-end.

'You're sure you won't come in?'

'No. I must get back to Trieste. Will you give my love to Renata?'

'I will. Is that her portrait that you have wrapped in the back of the car?'

'It is.'

'I'll tell her that you shot very well and that the portrait was in good condition.'

'Also my love.'

'Also your love.'

'*Ciao*, Alvarito and thank you very much.'

'*Ciao*, my Colonel. If one can say *ciao* to a Colonel.'

'Consider me not a Colonel.'

'It is very difficult. Goodbye, my Colonel.'

'In case of any unforeseen contingencies would you ask her to have the portrait picked up at the Gritti?'

'Yes, my Colonel.'

'That's all, I guess.'

'Good-bye, my Colonel.'

45

They were out on the road now and the early darkness was beginning.

'Turn left,' the Colonel said.

'That's not the road for Trieste, sir,' Jackson said.

'The hell with the road to Trieste. I ordered you to turn left. Do you think there is only one way in the world to get to Trieste?'

'No, sir. I was only pointing out to the Colonel—'

'Don't you point me out a goddamn thing and until I direct you otherwise, don't speak to me until you are spoken to.'

'Yes, sir.'

'I'm sorry, Jackson. What I mean is I know where I'm going and I want to think.'

'Yes, sir.'

They were on the old road that he knew so well and the Colonel thought, well, I sent four of the ducks I promised to those I promised them to at the Gritti. There wasn't enough shooting to be enough feathers to do that boy's wife any good with feathers. But they are all big ducks and fat and they will be good eating. I forgot to give Bobby the sausage.

There was no time to write Renata a note. But what could I say, in a note, that we did not say?

He reached into his pocket and found a pad and pencil. He put on the map-reading light, and with his bad hand, printed a short message in block letters.

'Put that in your pocket, Jackson, and act on it if necessary. If the circumstances described occur, it is an order.'

'Yes, sir,' Jackson said and took the folded order blank with one hand and put it in the top left-hand pocket of his tunic.

Now take it easy, the Colonel said to himself. Any further concern you may have is about yourself and that is just a luxury.

You are no longer of any real use to the Army of the United States. That has been made quite clear.

You have said good-bye to your girl and she has said good-bye to you.

That is certainly simple.

You shot well and Alvarito understands. That is that.

So what the hell do you have to worry about, boy? I hope you're not the type of jerk who worries about what happens to him when there's nothing to be done. Let's certainly hope not.

Just then it hit him as he had known it would since they had picked up the decoys.

Three strikes is out, he thought, and they gave me four. I've always been a lucky son of a bitch.

It hit him again badly.

'Jackson,' he said. 'Do you know what General Thomas J. Jackson said on one occasion? On the occasion of his unfortunate death. I memorized it once. I can't respond for its accuracy of course. But this is how it was reported: "Order A.P.Hill to prepare for action." Then some more delirious stuff. Then he said, "No, no, let us cross over the river and rest under the shade of the trees."'

'That's very interesting, sir,' Jackson said. 'That must have been Stonewall Jackson, sir.'

The Colonel started to speak but he stopped while it hit him the third time and gripped him so he knew he could not live.

'Jackson,' the Colonel said. 'Pull up at the side of the road and cut to your parking lights. Do you know the way to Trieste from here?'

'Yes, sir, I have my map.'

'Good. I'm now going to get into the large back seat of this goddamned, over-sized luxurious automobile.'

That was the last thing the Colonel ever said. But he made the back seat all right and he shut the door. He shut it carefully and well.

After a while Jackson drove the car down the ditch and willow lined road with the car's big lights on, looking for a place to turn. He found one, finally, and turned carefully. When he was on the right-hand side of the road, facing south towards the road junction that would put him on the highway that led to Trieste, the one he was familiar with, he put his map light on and took out the order blank and read:

IN THE EVENT OF MY DEATH THE WRAPPED PAINTING AND THE TWO SHOTGUNS IN THIS CAR WILL BE RETURNED TO THE HOTEL GRITTI VENICE WHERE THEY WILL BE CLAIMED BY THEIR RIGHTFUL OWNER SIGNED RICHARD CANTWELL, COL., INFANTRY, U.S.A.

'They'll return them all right, through channels,' Jackson thought, and put the car in gear.

HEMI

GWAY

The Old Man and the Sea

THE OLD MAN AND THE SEA

To Charlie Scribner and to Max Perkins

He was an old man who fished alone in a skiff in the Gulf Stream and he had gone eighty-four days now without taking a fish. In the first forty days without a fish the boy's parents had told him that the old man was now definitely and finally *salao*, which is the worst form of unlucky, and the boy had gone at their orders in another boat which caught three good fish the first week. It made the boy sad to see the old man come in each day with his skiff empty and he always went down to help him carry either the coiled lines or the gaff and harpoon and the sail that was furled around the mast. The sail was patched with flour sacks and, furled, it looked like the flag of permanent defeat.

The old man was thin and gaunt with deep wrinkles in the back of his neck. The brown blotches of the benevolent skin cancer the sun brings from its reflection on the tropic sea were on his cheeks. The blotches ran well down the sides of his face and his hands had the deep-creased scars from handling heavy fish on the cords. But none of these scars were fresh. They were as old as erosions in a fishless desert.

Everything about him was old except his eyes and they were the same colour as the sea and were cheerful and undefeated.

'Santiago,' the boy said to him as they climbed the bank from where the skiff was hauled up. 'I could go with you again. We've made some money.'

The old man had taught the boy to fish and the boy loved him.

'No,' the old man said. 'You're with a lucky boat. Stay with them.'

'But remember how you went eighty-seven days without fish and then we caught big ones every day for three weeks.'

'I remember,' the old man said. 'I know you did not leave me because you doubted.'

'It was papa made me leave. I am a boy and I must obey him.'

'I know,' the old man said. 'It is quite normal.'

'He hasn't much faith.'

'No,' the old man said. 'But we have. Haven't we?'

'Yes,' the boy said. 'Can I offer you a beer on the Terrace and then we'll take the stuff home.'

'Why not?' the old man said. 'Between fishermen.'

They sat on the Terrace and many of the fishermen made fun of the old man and he was not angry. Others, of the older fishermen, looked at him and were sad. But they did not show it and they spoke politely about the current and the depths they had drifted their lines at and the steady good weather and of what they had seen. The successful fishermen of that day were already in and had butchered their marlin out and carried them laid full length across two planks, with two men staggering at the end of each plank, to the fish house where they waited for the ice truck to carry them to the market in Havana. Those who had caught sharks had taken them to the shark factory on the other side of the cove where they were hoisted on a block and tackle, their livers removed, their fins cut off and their hides skinned out and their flesh cut into strips for salting.

When the wind was in the east a smell came across the harbour from the shark factory; but today there was only the faint edge of the odour because the wind had backed into the north and then dropped off and it was pleasant and sunny on the Terrace.

'Santiago,' the boy said.

'Yes,' the old man said. He was holding his glass and thinking of many years ago.

'Can I go out and get sardines for you for tomorrow?'

'No. Go and play baseball. I can still row and Rogelio will throw the net.'

'I would like to go. If I cannot fish with you, I would like to serve in some way.'

'You bought me a beer,' the old man said. 'You are already a man.'

'How old was I when you first took me in a boat?'

'Five and you nearly were killed when I brought the fish in too green and he nearly tore the boat to pieces. Can you remember?'

'I can remember the tail slapping and banging and the thwart breaking and the noise of the clubbing. I can remember you throwing me into the bow where the wet coiled lines were and feeling the whole boat shiver and the noise of you clubbing him like chopping a tree down and the sweet blood smell all over me.'

'Can you really remember that or did I just tell it to you?'

'I remember everything from when we first went together.'

The old man looked at him with his sunburned, confident, loving eyes.

'If you were my boy I'd take you out and gamble,' he said. 'But you are your father's and your mother's and you are in a lucky boat.'

'May I get the sardines? I know where I can get four baits too.'

'I have mine left from today. I put them in salt in the box.'

'Let me get four fresh ones.'

'One,' the old man said. His hope and his confidence had never gone. But now they were freshening as when the breeze rises.

'Two,' the boy said.

'Two,' the old man agreed. 'You didn't steal them?'

'I would,' the boy said. 'But I bought these.'

'Thank you,' the old man said. He was too simple to wonder when he had attained humility. But he knew he had attained it and he knew it was not disgraceful and it carried no loss of true pride.

'Tomorrow is going to be a good day with this current,' he said.

'Where are you going?' the boy asked.

'Far out to come in when the wind shifts. I want to be out before it is light.'

'I'll try to get him to work far out,' the boy said. 'Then if you hook something truly big we can come to your aid.'

'He does not like to work too far out.'

'No,' the boy said. 'But I will see something that he cannot see such as a bird working and get him to come out after dolphin.'

'Are his eyes that bad?'

'He is almost blind.'

'It is strange,' the old man said. 'He never went turtle-ing. That is what kills the eyes.'

'But you went turtle-ing for years off the Mosquito Coast and your eyes are good.'

'I am a strange old man.'

'But are you strong enough now for a truly big fish?'

'I think so. And there are many tricks.'

'Let us take the stuff home,' the boy said. 'So I can get the cast net and go after the sardines.'

They picked up the gear from the boat. The old man carried the mast on his shoulder and the boy carried the wooden box with the coiled, hard-braided brown lines, the gaff and the harpoon with its shaft. The box with the baits was under the stern of the skiff along with the club that was used to subdue the big fish when they were brought alongside. No one would steal from the old man but it was better to take the sail and the heavy lines home as the dew was bad for them and, though he was quite sure no local people would steal from him, the old man thought that a gaff and a harpoon were needless temptations to leave in a boat.

They walked up the road together to the old man's shack and went in through its open door. The old man leaned the mast with its wrapped sail against the wall and the boy put the box and the other gear beside it. The mast was nearly as long as the one room of the shack. The shack was made of the tough bud-shields of the royal palm which are called *guano* and in it there was a bed, a table, one chair, and a place on the dirt floor to cook with charcoal. On the brown walls of the flattened, overlapping leaves of the sturdy-fibred *guano* there was a picture in colour of the Sacred Heart of Jesus and another of the Virgin of Cobre. These were relics of his wife. Once there had been a tinted photograph of his wife on the wall but he had taken it down because it made him too lonely to see it and it was on the shelf in the corner under his clean shirt.

'What do you have to eat?' the boy asked.

'A pot of yellow rice with fish. Do you want some?'

'No. I will eat at home. Do you want me to make the fire?'

'No. I will make it later on. Or I may eat the rice cold.'

'May I take the cast net?'

'Of course.'

There was no cast net and the boy remembered when they had sold it. But they went through this fiction every day. There was no pot of yellow rice and fish and the boy knew this too.

'Eighty-five is a lucky number,' the old man said. 'How would you like to see me bring one in that dressed out over a thousand pounds?'

'I'll get the cast net and go for sardines. Will you sit in the sun in the doorway?'

'Yes. I have yesterday's paper and I will read the baseball.'

The boy did not know whether yesterday's paper was a fiction too. But the old man brought it out from under the bed.

'Perico gave it to me at the *bodega*,' he explained.

'I'll be back when I have the sardines. I'll keep yours and mine together on ice and we can share them in the morning. When I come back you can tell me about the baseball.'

'The Yankees cannot lose.'

'But I fear the Indians of Cleveland.'

'Have faith in the Yankees my son. Think of the great DiMaggio.'

'I fear both the Tigers of Detroit and the Indians of Cleveland.'

'Be careful or you will fear even the Reds of Cincinnati and the White Sox of Chicago.'

'You study it and tell me when I come back.'

'Do you think we should buy a terminal of the lottery with an eighty-five? Tomorrow is the eighty-fifth day.'

'We can do that,' the boy said. 'But what about the eighty-seven of your great record?'

'It could not happen twice. Do you think you can find an eighty-five?'

'I can order one.'

'One sheet. That's two dollars and a half. Who can we borrow that from?'

'That's easy. I can always borrow two dollars and a half.'

'I think perhaps I can too. But I try not to borrow. First you borrow. Then you beg.'

'Keep warm old man,' the boy said. 'Remember we are in September.'

'The month when the great fish come,' the old man said. 'Anyone can be a fisherman in May.'

'I go now for the sardines,' the boy said.

When the boy came back the old man was asleep in the chair and the sun was down. The boy took the old army blanket off the bed and spread it over the back of the chair and over the old man's shoulders. They were strange shoulders, still powerful although very old, and the neck was still strong too and the creases did not show so much when the old man was asleep and his head fallen forward. His shirt had been patched so many times that it was like the sail and the patches were faded to many different shades by the sun. The old man's head was very old though and with his eyes closed there was no life in his face. The newspaper lay across his knees and the weight of his arm held it there in the evening breeze. He was barefooted.

The boy left him there and when he came back the old man was still asleep.

'Wake up old man,' the boy said and put his hand on one of the old man's knees.

The old man opened his eyes and for a moment he was coming back from a long way away. Then he smiled.

'What have you got?' he asked.

'Supper,' said the boy. 'We're going to have supper.'

'I'm not very hungry.'

'Come on and eat. You can't fish and not eat.'

'I have,' the old man said getting up and taking the newspaper and folding it. Then he started to fold the blanket.

'Keep the blanket around you,' the boy said. 'You'll not fish without eating while I'm alive.'

'Then live a long time and take care of yourself,' the old man said. 'What are we eating?'

'Black beans and rice, fried bananas, and some stew.'

The boy had brought them in a two-decker metal container from the Terrace. The two sets of knives and forks and spoons were in his pocket with a paper napkin wrapped around each set.

'Who gave this to you?'

'Martin. The owner.'

'I must thank him.'

'I thanked him already,' the boy said. 'You don't need to thank him.'

'I'll give him the belly meat of a big fish,' the old man said. 'Has he done this for us more than once?'

'I think so.'

'I must give him something more than the belly meat then. He is very thoughtful for us.'

'He sent two beers.'

'I like the beer in cans best.'

'I know. But this is in bottles, Hatuey beer, and I take back the bottles.'

'That's very kind of you,' the old man said. 'Should we eat?'

'I've been asking you to,' the boy told him gently. 'I have not wished to open the container until you were ready.'

'I'm ready now,' the old man said, 'I only needed time to wash.'

Where did you wash? the boy thought. The village water supply was two streets down the road. I must have water here for him, the boy thought, and soap and a good towel. Why am I so thoughtless? I must get him another shirt and a jacket for the winter and some sort of shoes and another blanket.

'Your stew is excellent,' the old man said.

'Tell me about the baseball,' the boy asked him.

'In the American League it is the Yankees as I said,' the old man said happily.

'They lost today,' the boy told him.

'That means nothing. The great DiMaggio is himself again.'

'They have other men on the team.'

'Naturally. But he makes the difference. In the other league, between Brooklyn and Philadelphia I must take Brooklyn. But then I think of Dick Sisler and those great drives in the old park.'

'There was nothing ever like them. He hits the longest ball I have ever seen.'

'Do you remember when he used to come to the Terrace? I wanted to take him fishing but I was too timid to ask him. Then I asked you to ask him and you were too timid.'

'I know. It was a great mistake. He might have gone with us. Then we would have that for all of our lives.'

'I would like to take the great DiMaggio fishing,' the old man said. 'They say his father was a fisherman. Maybe he was as poor as we are and would understand.'

'The great Sisler's father was never poor and he, the father, was playing in the big leagues when he was my age.'

'When I was your age I was before the mast on a square-rigged ship that ran to Africa and I have seen lions on the beaches in the evening.'

'I know. You told me.'

'Should we talk about Africa or about baseball?'

'Baseball I think,' the boy said. 'Tell me about the great John J. McGraw.' He said *Jota* for J.

'He used to come to the Terrace sometimes too in the older days. But he was rough and harsh-spoken and difficult when he was drinking. His mind was on horses as well as baseball. At least he carried lists of horses at all times in his pocket and frequently spoke the names of horses on the telephone.'

'He was a great manager,' the boy said. 'My father thinks he was the greatest.'

'Because he came here the most times,' the old man said. 'If Durocher had continued to come here each year your father would think him the greatest manager.'

'Who is the greatest manager, really, Luque or Mike Gonzalez?'

'I think they are equal.'

'And the best fisherman is you.'

'No. I know others better.'

'*Qué va*,' the boy said. 'There are many good fishermen and some great ones. But there is only one you.'

'Thank you. You make me happy. I hope no fish will come along so great that he will prove us wrong.'

'There is no such fish if you are still strong as you say.'

'I may not be as strong as I think,' the old man said. 'But I know many tricks and I have resolution.'

'You ought to go to bed now so that you will be fresh in the morning. I will take the things back to the Terrace.'

'Good night then. I will wake you in the morning.'

'You're my alarm clock,' the boy said.

'Age is my alarm clock,' the old man said. 'Why do old men wake so early? Is it to have one longer day?'

'I don't know,' the boy said. 'All I know is that young boys sleep late and hard.'

'I can remember it,' the old man said. 'I'll waken you in time.'

'I do not like for him to waken me. It is as though I were inferior.'

'I know.'

'Sleep well old man.'

The boy went out. They had eaten with no light on the table and the old man took off his trousers and went to bed in the dark. He rolled his trousers up to make a pillow, putting the newspaper inside them. He rolled himself in the blanket and slept on the other old newspapers that covered the springs of the bed.

He was alseep in a short time and he dreamed of Africa when he was a boy and the long, golden beaches and the white beaches, so white they hurt your eyes, and the high capes and the great brown mountains. He lived along that coast now every night and in his dreams he heard the surf roar and saw the native boats come riding through it. He smelled the tar and oakum of the deck as he slept and he smelled the smell of Africa that the land breeze brought at morning.

Usually when he smelled the land breeze he woke up and dressed to go and wake the boy. But tonight the smell of the land breeze came very early and he knew it was too early in his dream and went on dreaming to see the white peaks of the Islands rising from the sea and then he dreamed of the different harbours and roadsteads of the Canary Islands.

He no longer dreamed of storms, nor of women, nor of great occurrences, nor of great fish, nor fights, nor contests of strength, nor of his wife. He only dreamed of places now and of the lions on the beach. They played like young cats in the dusk and he loved them as he loved the boy. He never dreamed about the boy. He simply woke, looked out the open door at the moon and unrolled his trousers and put them on. He urinated outside the shack and then went up the road to wake the boy. He was shivering with the morning cold. But he knew he would shiver himself warm and that soon he would be rowing.

The door of the house where the boy lived was unlocked and he opened it and walked in quietly with his bare feet. The boy was asleep on a cot in the first room and the old man could see him clearly with the light that came in from the dying moon. He took hold of one foot gently and held it until the boy woke and turned and looked at him. The old man nodded and the boy took his trousers from the chair by the bed and, sitting on the bed, pulled them on.

The old man went out the door and the boy came after him. He was sleepy and the old man put his arm across his shoulders and said, 'I am sorry.'

'*Qué va*,' the boy said. 'It is what a man must do.'

They walked down the road to the old man's shack and all along the road, in the dark, barefoot men were moving, carrying the masts of their boats.

When they reached the old man's shack the boy took the rolls of line in the basket and the harpoon and gaff and the old man carried the mast with the furled sail on his shoulder.

'Do you want coffee?' the boy asked.

'We'll put the gear in the boat and then get some.'

They had coffee from condensed-milk cans at an early morning place that served fishermen.

'How did you sleep old man?' the boy asked. He was waking up now although it was still hard for him to leave his sleep.

'Very well, Manolin,' the old man said. 'I feel confident today.'

'So do I,' the boy said. 'Now I must get your sardines and mine and your fresh baits. He brings our gear himself. He never wants anyone to carry anything.'

'We're different,' the old man said. 'I let you carry things when you were five years old.'

'I know it,' the boy said. 'I'll be right back. Have another coffee. We have credit here.'

He walked off, barefooted on the coral rocks, to the ice house where the baits were stored.

The old man drank his coffee slowly. It was all he would have all day and he knew that he should take it. For a long time now eating had bored him and he never carried a lunch. He had a bottle of water in the bow of the skiff and that was all he needed for the day.

The boy was back now with the sardines and the two baits wrapped in a newspaper and they went down the trail to the skiff, feeling the pebbled sand under their feet, and lifted the skiff and slid her into the water.

'Good luck old man.'

'Good luck,' the old man said. He fitted the rope lashings of the oars onto the thole pins and, leaning forward against the thrust of the blades in the water, he began to row out of the harbour in the dark. There were other boats from the other beaches going out to sea and the old man heard the dip and push of their oars even though he could not see them now the moon was below the hills.

Sometimes someone would speak in a boat. But most of the boats were silent except for the dip of the oars. They spread apart after they were out of the mouth of the harbour and each one headed for the part of the ocean where he hoped to find fish. The old man knew he was going far out and he left the smell of the land behind and rowed out into the clean early morning smell of the ocean. He saw the phosphorescence of the Gulf weed in the water as he rowed over the part of the ocean that the fishermen called the great well because there was a sudden deep of seven hundred fathoms where all sorts of fish congregated because of the swirl the current made against the steep walls of the floor of the ocean. Here there were concentrations of shrimp and bait fish and sometimes schools of squid in the deepest holes and these rose close to the surface at night where all the wandering fish fed on them.

In the dark the old man could feel the morning coming and as he rowed he heard the trembling sound as flying fish left the water and the hissing that their stiff set wings made as they soared away in the darkness. He was very fond of flying fish as they were his principal friends on the ocean. He was sorry for the birds, especially the small delicate dark terns that were always flying and looking and almost never finding, and he thought, 'The birds have a harder life than we do except for the robber birds and the heavy strong ones. Why did they make birds so delicate and fine as those sea swallows when the ocean can be so cruel? She is kind and beautiful. But she can be so cruel and it comes so suddenly and such birds that fly, dipping and hunting, with their small sad voices are made too delicately for the sea.'

He always thought of the sea as *la mar* which is what people call her in Spanish when they love her. Sometimes those who love her say bad things of her but they are always said as though she were a woman. Some of the younger fishermen, those who used buoys as floats for their lines and had motor-boats, bought when the shark livers had brought much money, spoke of her as *el mar* which is masculine. They spoke of her as a contestant or a place or even as an enemy. But the old man always thought of her as feminine and as something that gave or withheld great favours, and if she did wild or wicked things it was because she could not help them. The moon affects her as it does a woman, he thought.

He was rowing steadily and it was no effort for him since he kept well within his speed and the surface of the ocean was flat except for the occasional swirls of the current. He was letting the current do a third of the work and as it started to be light he saw he was already further out than he had hoped to be at this hour.

I worked the deep wells for a week and did nothing, he thought. Today I'll work out where the schools of bonita and albacore are and maybe there will be a big one with them.

Before it was really light he had his baits out and was drifting with the current. One bait was down forty fathoms. The second was at seventy-five and the third and fourth were down in the blue water at one hundred and one hundred and twenty-five fathoms. Each bait hung head down with the shank of the hook inside the bait fish, tied and sewed solid, and all the projecting part of the hook, the curve and the point, was covered with fresh sardines. Each sardine was hooked through both eyes so that they made a half-garland on the projecting steel. There was no part of the hook that a great fish could feel which was not sweet-smelling and good-tasting.

The boy had given him two fresh small tunas, or albacores, which hung on the two deepest lines like plummets and, on the others, he had a big blue runner and a yellow jack that had been used before; but they were in good condition still and had the excellent sardines to give them scent and attractiveness. Each line, as thick around as a big pencil, was looped on to a green-sapped stick so that any pull or touch on the bait would make the stick dip and each line had two forty-fathom coils which could be made fast to the other spare coils so that, if it were necessary, a fish could take out over three hundred fathoms of line.

Now the man watched the dip of the three sticks over the side of the skiff and rowed gently to keep the lines straight up and down and at their proper depths. It was quite light and any moment now the sun would rise.

The sun rose thinly from the sea and the old man could see the other boats, low on the water and well in toward the shore, spread out across the current. Then the sun was brighter and the glare came on the water and then, as it rose clear, the flat sea sent it back at his eyes so that it hurt sharply and he rowed without looking into it. He looked down into the water and watched the lines that went straight down into the dark of the water. He kept them straighter than anyone did, so that at each level in the darkness of the stream there would be a bait waiting exactly where he wished it to be for any fish that swam there. Others let them drift with the current and sometimes they were at sixty fathoms when the fishermen thought they were at a hundred.

But, he thought, I keep them with precision. Only I have no luck any more. But who knows? Maybe today. Every day is a new day. It is better to be lucky. But I would rather be exact. Then when luck comes you are ready.

The sun was two hours higher now and it did not hurt his eyes so much to look into the east. There were only three boats in sight now and they showed very low and far inshore.

All my life the early sun has hurt my eyes, he thought. Yet they are still good. In the evening I can look straight into it without getting the blackness. It has more force in the evening too. But in the morning it is painful.

Just then he saw a man-of-war bird with his long black wings circling in the sky ahead of him. He made a quick drop, slanting down on his back-swept wings, and then circled again.

'He's got something,' the old man said aloud. 'He's not just looking.'

He rowed slowly and steadily toward where the bird was circling. He did not hurry and he kept his lines straight up and down. But he crowded the current a little so that he was still fishing correctly though faster than he would have fished if he was not trying to use the bird.

The bird went higher in the air and circled again, his wings motionless. Then he dove suddenly and the old man saw flying fish spurt out of the water and sail desperately over the surface.

'Dolphin,' the old man said aloud. 'Big dolphin.'

He shipped his oars and brought a small line from under the bow. It had a wire leader and a medium-sized hook and he baited it with one of the sardines. He let it go over the side and then made it fast to a ring bolt in the stern. Then he baited another line and felt it coiled in the shade of the bow. He went back to rowing and to watching the long-winged black bird who was working, now, low over the water.

As he watched the bird dipped again slanting his wings for the dive and then swing them wildly and ineffectually as he followed the flying fish. The old man could see the slight bulge in the water that the big dolphin raised as they followed the escaping fish. The dolphin were cutting through the water below the flight of the fish and would be in the water, driving at speed, when the fish dropped. It is a big school of dolphin, he thought. They are wide spread and the flying fish have little chance. The bird has no chance. The flying fish are too big for him and they go too fast.

He watched the flying fish burst out again and again and the ineffectual movements of the bird. That school has gotten away from me, he thought. They are moving out too fast and too far. But perhaps I will pick up a stray and perhaps my big fish is around them. My big fish must be somewhere.

The clouds over the land now rose like mountains and the coast was only a long green line with the grey-blue hills behind it. The water was a dark blue now, so dark that it was almost purple. As he looked down into it he saw the red sifting of the plankton in the dark water and the strange light the sun made now. He watched his lines to see them go straight down out of sight into the water and he was happy to see so much plankton because it meant fish. The strange light the sun made in the water, now that the sun was higher, meant good weather and so did the shape of the clouds over the land. But the bird was almost out of sight now and nothing showed on the surface of the water but some patches of yellow, sun-bleached Sargasso weed and the purple, formalized, iridescent, gelatinous bladder of a Portuguese man-of-war floating close beside the boat. It turned on its side and then righted itself. It floated cheerfully as a bubble with its long deadly purple filaments trailing a yard behind it in the water.

'*Agua mala*,' the man said. 'You whore.'

From where he swung lightly against his oars he looked down into the water and saw the tiny fish that were coloured like the trailing filaments and swam between them and under the small shade the bubble made as it drifted. They were immune to its poison. But men were not and when some of the filaments would catch on a line and rest there slimy and purple while the old man was working a fish, he would have welts and sores on his arms and hands of the sort that poison ivy or poison oak can give. But these poisonings from the *agua mala* came quickly and struck like a whiplash.

The iridescent bubbles were beautiful. But they were the falsest things in the sea and the old man loved to see the big sea turtles eating them. The turtles saw them, approached them from the front, then shut their eyes so they were completely carapaced and ate them filaments and all. The old man loved to see the turtles eat them and he loved to walk on them on the beach after a storm and hear them pop when he stepped on them with the horny soles of his feet.

He loved green turtles and hawks-bills with their elegance and speed and their great value and he had a friendly contempt for the huge, stupid logger-heads, yellow in their armour-plating, strange in their love-making, and happily eating the Portuguese men-of-war with their eyes shut.

He had no mysticism about turtles although he had gone in turtle boats for many years. He was sorry for them all, even the great trunk-backs that were as long as the skiff and weighed a ton. Most people are heartless about turtles because a turtle's heart will beat for hours after he has been cut up and butchered. But the old man thought, I have such a heart too and my feet and hands are like theirs. He ate the white eggs to give himself strength. He ate them all through May to be strong in September and October for the truly big fish.

He also drank a cup of shark liver oil each day from the big drum in the shack where many of the fishermen kept their gear. It was there for all fishermen who wanted it. Most fishermen hated the taste. But it was no worse than getting up at the hours that they rose and it was very good against all colds and grippes and it was good for the eyes.

Now the old man looked up and saw that the bird was circling again.

'He's found fish,' he said aloud. No flying fish broke the surface and there was no scattering of bait fish. But as the old man watched, a small tuna rose in the air, turned and dropped head first into the water. The tuna shone silver in the sun and after he had dropped back into the water another and another rose and they were jumping in all directions, churning the water and leaping in long jumps after the bait. They were circling it and driving it.

If they don't travel too fast I will get into them, the old man thought, and he watched the school working the water white and the bird now dropping and dipping into the bait fish that were forced to the surface in their panic.

'The bird is a great help,' the old man said. Just then the stern line came taut under his foot, where he had kept a loop of the line, and he dropped his oars and felt the weight of the small tuna's shivering pull as he held the line firm and commenced to haul it in. The shivering increased as he pulled in and he could see the blue back of the fish in the water and the gold of his sides before he swung him over the side and into the boat. He lay in the stern in the sun, compact and bullet-shaped, his big, unintelligent eyes staring as he thumped his life out against the planking of the boat with the quick shivering strokes of his neat, fast-moving tail. The old man hit him on the head for kindness and kicked him, his body still shuddering, under the shade of the stern.

'Albacore,' he said aloud. 'He'll make a beautiful bait. He'll weigh ten pounds.'

He did not remember when he had first started to talk aloud when he was by himself. He had sung when he was by himself in the old days and he had sung at night sometimes when he was alone steering on his watch in the smacks or in the turtle boats. He had probably started to talk aloud, when alone, when the boy had left. But he did not remember. When he and the boy fished together they usually spoke only when it was necessary. They talked at night or when they were storm-bound by bad weather. It was considered a virtue not to talk unnecessarily at sea and the old man had always considered it so and respected it. But now he said his thoughts aloud many times since there was no one that they could annoy.

'If the others heard me talking out loud they would think that I am crazy,' he said aloud. 'But since I am not crazy, I do not care. And the rich have radios to talk to them in their boats and to bring them the baseball.'

Now is no time to think of baseball, he thought. Now is the time to think of only one thing. That which I was born for. There might be a big one around that school, he thought. I picked up only a straggler from the albacore that were feeding. But they are working far out and fast. Everything that shows on the surface today travels very fast and to the north-east. Can that be the time of day? Or is it some sign of weather that I do not know?

He could not see the green of the shore now but only the tops of the blue hills that showed white as though they were snow-capped and the clouds that looked like high snow mountains above them. The sea was very dark and the light made prisms in the water. The myriad flecks of the plankton were annulled now by the high sun and it was only the great deep prisms in the blue water that the old man saw now with his lines going straight down into the water that was a mile deep.

The tuna, the fishermen called all the fish of that species tuna and only distinguished among them by their proper names when they came to sell them or to trade them for baits, were down again. The sun was hot now and the old man felt it on the back of his neck and felt the sweat trickle down his back as he rowed.

I could just drift, he thought, and sleep and put a bight of line around my toe to wake me. But today is eighty-five days and I should fish the day well.

Just then, watching his lines, he saw one of the projecting green sticks dip sharply.

'Yes,' he said. 'Yes,' and shipped his oars without bumping the boat. He reached out for the line and held it softly between the thumb and forefinger of his right hand. He felt no strain nor weight and he held the line lightly. Then it came again. This time it was a tentative pull, not solid nor heavy, and he knew exactly what it was. One hundred fathoms down a marlin was eating the sardines that covered the point and the shank of the hook where the hand-forged hook projected from the head of the small tuna.

The old man held the line delicately, and softly, with his left hand, unleased it from the stick. Now he could let it run through his fingers without the fish feeling any tension.

This far out, he must be huge in this month, he thought. Eat them, fish. Eat them. Please eat them. How fresh they are and you down there six hundred feet in that cold water in the dark. Make another turn in the dark and come back and eat them.

He felt the light delicate pulling and then a harder pull when a sardine's head must have been more difficult to break from the hook. Then there was nothing.

'Come on,' the old man said aloud. 'Make another turn. Just smell them. Aren't they lovely? Eat them good now and then there is the tuna. Hard and cold and lovely. Don't be shy, fish. Eat them.'

He waited with the line between his thumb and his finger, watching it and the other lines at the same time for the fish might have swum up or down. Then came the same delicate pulling touch again.

'He'll take it,' the old man said aloud. 'God help him to take it.'

He did not take it though. He was gone and the old man felt nothing.

'He can't have gone,' he said. 'Christ knows he can't have gone. He's making a turn. Maybe he has been hooked before and he remembers something of it.'

Then he felt the gentle touch on the line and he was happy.

'It was only his turn,' he said. 'He'll take it.'

He was happy feeling the gentle pulling and then he felt something hard and unbelievably heavy. It was the weight of the fish and he let the line slip down, down, unrolling off the first of the two reserve coils. As it went down, slipping lightly through the old man's fingers, he still could feel the great weight, though the pressure of his thumb and finger were almost imperceptible.

'What a fish,' he said. 'He has it sideways in his mouth now and he is moving off with it.'

Then he will turn and swallow it, he thought. He did not say that because he knew that if you said a good thing it might not happen. He knew what a huge fish this was and he thought of him moving away in the darkness with the tuna held crosswise in his mouth. At that moment he felt him stopping but the weight was still there. Then the weight increased and he gave more line. He tightened the pressure of his thumb and finger for a moment and the weight increased and was going straight down.

'He's taken it,' he said. 'Now I'll let him eat it well.'

He let the line slip through his fingers while he reached down with his left hand and made fast the free end of the two reserve coils to the loop of the two reserve coils of the next line. Now he was ready. He had three forty-fathom coils of line in reserve now, as well as the coil he was using.

'Eat it a little more,' he said. 'Eat it well.'

Eat it so that the point of the hook goes into your heart and kills you, he thought. Come up easy and let me put the harpoon into you. All right. Are you ready? Have you been long enough at table?

'Now!' he said aloud and struck hard with both hands, gained a yard of line and then struck again and again, swinging with each arm alternately on the cord with all the strength of his arms and the pivoted weight of his body.

Nothing happened. The fish just moved away slowly and the old man could not raise him an inch. His line was strong and made for heavy fish and he held it against his back until it was so taut that beads of water were jumping from it. Then it began to make a slow hissing sound in the water and he still held it, bracing himself against the thwart and leaning back against the pull. The boat began to move slowly off toward the north-west.

The fish moved steadily and they travelled slowly on the calm water. The other baits were still in the water but there was nothing to be done.

'I wish I had the boy,' the old man said aloud. 'I'm being towed by a fish and I'm the towing bitt. I could make the line fast. But then he could break it. I must hold him all I can and give him line when he must have it. Thank God he is travelling and not going down.'

What I will do if he decides to go down, I don't know. What I'll do if he sounds and dies I don't know. But I'll do something. There are plenty of things I can do.

He held the line against his back and watched its slant in the water and the skiff moving steadily to the north-west.

This will kill him, the old man thought. He can't do this for ever. But four hours later the fish was still swimming steadily out to sea, towing the skiff, and the old man was still braced solidly with the line across his back.

'It was noon when I hooked him,' he said. 'And I have never seen him.'

He had pushed his straw hat hard down on his head before he hooked the fish and it was cutting his forehead. He was thirsty too and he got down on his knees and, being careful not to jerk on the line, moved as far into the bow as he could get and reached the water bottle with one hand. He opened it and drank a little. Then he rested against the bow. He rested sitting on the unstepped mast and sail and tried not to think but only to endure.

Then he looked behind him and saw that no land was visible. That makes no difference, he thought. I can always come in on the glow from Havana. There are two more hours before the sun sets and maybe he will come up before that. If he doesn't maybe he will come up with the moon. If he does not do that maybe he will come up with the sunrise. I have no cramps and I feel strong. It is he that has the hook in his mouth. But what a fish to pull like that. He must have his mouth shut tight on the wire. I wish I could see him. I wish I could see him only once to know what I have against me.

The fish never changed his course nor his direction all that night as far as the man could tell from watching the stars. It was cold after the sun went down and the old man's sweat dried cold on his back and his arms and his old legs. During the day he had taken the sack that covered the bait box and spread it in the sun to dry. After the sun went down he tied it around his neck so that it hung down over his back and he cautiously worked it down under the line that was across his shoulders now. The sack cushioned the line and he had found a way of leaning forward against the bow so that he was almost comfortable. The position actually was only somewhat less intolerable; but he thought of it as almost comfortable.

I can do nothing with him and he can do nothing with me, he thought. Not as long as he keeps this up.

Once he stood up and urinated over the side of the skiff and looked at the stars and checked his course. The line showed like a phosphorescent streak in the water straight out from his shoulders. They were moving more slowly now and the glow of Havana was not so strong, so that he knew the current must be carrying them to the eastward. If I lose the glare of Havana we must be going more to the eastward, he thought. For if the fish's course held true I must see it for many more hours. I wonder how the baseball came out in the grand leagues today, he thought. It would be wonderful to do this with a radio. Then he thought, think of it always. Think of what you are doing. You must do nothing stupid.

Then he said aloud, 'I wish I had the boy. To help me and to see this.'

No one should be alone in their old age, he thought. But it is unavoidable. I must remember to eat the tuna before he spoils in order to keep strong. Remember, no matter how little you want to, that you must eat him in the morning. Remember, he said to himself.

During the night two porpoise came around the boat and he could hear them rolling and blowing. He could tell the difference between the blowing noise the male made and the sighing blow of the female.

'They are good,' he said. 'They play and make jokes and love one another. They are our brothers like the flying fish.'

Then he began to pity the great fish that he had hooked. He is wonderful and strange and who knows how old he is, he thought. Never have I had such a strong fish nor one who acted so strangely. Perhaps he is too wise to jump. He could ruin me by jumping or by a wild rush. But perhaps he has been hooked many times before and he knows that this is how he should make his fight. He cannot know that it is only one man against him, nor that it is an old man. But what a great fish he is and what he will bring in the market if the flesh is good. He took the bait like a male and he pulls like a male and his fight has no panic in it. I wonder if he has any plans or if he is just as desperate as I am?

He remembered the time he had hooked one of a pair of marlin. The male fish always let the female fish feed first and the hooked fish, the female, made a wild, panic-stricken, despairing fight that soon exhausted her, and all the time the male had stayed with her, crossing the line and circling with her on the surface. He had stayed so close that the old man was afraid he would cut the line with his tail which was sharp as a scythe and almost of that size and shape. When the old man had gaffed her and clubbed her, holding the rapier bill with its sandpaper edge and clubbing her across the top of her head until her colour turned to a colour almost like the backing of mirrors, and then, with the boy's aid, hoisted her aboard, the male fish had stayed by the side of the boat. Then, while the old man was clearing the lines and preparing the harpoon, the male fish jumped high into the air beside the boat to see where the female was and then went down deep, his lavender wings, that were his pectoral fins, spread wide and all his wide lavender stripes showing. He was beautiful, the old man remembered, and he had stayed.

That was the saddest thing I ever saw with them the old man thought. The boy was sad too and we begged her pardon and butchered her promptly.

'I wish the boy was here,' he said aloud and settled himself against the rounded planks of the bow and felt the strength of the great fish through the line he held across his shoulders moving steadily toward whatever he had chosen.

When once, through my treachery, it had been necessary to him to make a choice, the old man thought.

His choice had been to stay in the deep dark water far out beyond all snares and traps and treacheries. My choice was to go there to find him beyond all people. Beyond all people in the world. Now we are joined together and have been since noon. And no one to help one of us.

Perhaps I should not have been a fisherman, he thought. But that was the thing that I was born for. I must surely remember to eat the tuna after it gets light.

Some time before daylight something took one of the baits that were behind him. He heard the stick break and the line begin to rush out over the gunwale of the skiff. In the darkness he loosened his sheath knife and taking all the strain of the fish on his left shoulder he leaned back and cut the line against the wood of the gunwale. Then he cut the other line closest to him and in the dark made the loose ends of the reserve coils fast. There were two from each bait he had severed and the two from the bait the fish had taken and they were all connected.

After it is light, he thought, I will work back to the forty-fathom bait and cut it away too and link up the reserve coils. I will have lost two hundred fathoms of good Catalan *cordel* and the hooks and leaders. That can be replaced. But who replaces this fish if I hook some fish and it cuts him off? I don't know what that fish was that took the bait just now. It could have been a marlin or a broadbill or a shark. I never felt him. I had to get rid of him too fast.

Aloud he said, 'I wish I had the boy.'

But you haven't got the boy, he thought. You have only yourself and you had better work back to the last line now, in the dark or not in the dark, and cut it away and hook up the two reserve coils.

So he did it. It was difficult in the dark and once the fish made a surge that pulled him down on his face and made a cut below his eye. The blood ran down his cheek a little way. But it coagulated and dried before it reached his chin and he worked his way back to the bow and rested against the wood. He adjusted the sack and carefully worked the line so that it came across a new part of his shoulders and, holding it anchored with his shoulders, he carefully felt the pull of the fish and then felt with his hand the progress of the skiff through the water.

I wonder what he made that lurch for, he thought. The wire must have slipped on the great hill of his back. Certainly his back cannot feel as badly as mine does. But he cannot pull this skiff for ever, no matter how great he is. Now everything is cleared away that might make trouble and I have a big reserve of line; all that a man can ask.

'Fish,' he said softly, aloud, 'I'll stay with you until I am dead.'

He'll stay with me too, I suppose, the old man thought and he waited for it to be light. It was cold now in the time before daylight and he pushed against the wood to be warm. I can do it as long as he can, he thought. And in the first light the line extended out and down into the water. The boat moved steadily and when the first edge of the sun rose it was on the old man's right shoulder.

'He's headed north,' the old man said. The current will have set us far to the eastward, he thought. I wish he would turn with the current. That would show he was tiring.

When the sun had risen further the old man realized that the fish was not tiring. There was only one favourable sign. The slant of the line showed he was swimming at a lesser depth. That did not necessarily mean that he would jump. But he might.

'God let him jump,' the old man said. 'I have enough line to handle him.'

Maybe if I can increase the tension just a little it will hurt him and he will jump, he thought. Now that it is daylight let him jump so that he'll fill the sacs along his backbone with air and then he cannot go deep to die.

He tried to increase the tension, but the line had been taut up to the very edge of the breaking point since he had hooked the fish and he felt the harshness as he leaned back to pull and knew he could put no more strain on it. I must not jerk it ever, he thought. Each jerk widens the cut the hook makes and then when he does jump he might throw it. Anyway I feel better with the sun and for once I do not have to look into it.

There was yellow weed on the line but the old man knew that only made an added drag and he was pleased. It was the yellow Gulf weed that had made so much phosphorescence in the night.

'Fish,' he said, 'I love you and respect you very much. But I will kill you dead before this day ends.'

Let us hope so, he thought.

A small bird came toward the skiff from the north. He was a warbler and flying very low over the water. The old man could see that he was very tired.

The bird made the stern of the boat and rested there. Then he flew around the old man's head and rested on the line where he was more comfortable.

'How old are you?' the old man asked the bird. 'Is this your first trip?'

The bird looked at him when he spoke. He was too tired even to examine the line and he teetered on it as his delicate feet gripped it fast.

'It's steady,' the old man told him. 'It's too steady. You shouldn't be that tired after a windless night. What are birds coming to?'

The hawks, he thought, that come out to sea to meet them. But he said nothing of this to the bird who could not understand him anyway and who would learn about the hawks soon enough.

'Take a good rest, small bird,' he said. 'Then go in and take your chance like any man or bird or fish.'

It encouraged him to talk because his back had stiffened in the night and it hurt truly now.

'Stay at my house if you like, bird,' he said. 'I am sorry I cannot hoist the sail and take you in with the small breeze that is rising. But I am with a friend.'

Just then the fish gave a sudden lurch that pulled the old man down on to the bow and would have pulled him overboard if he had not braced himself and given some line.

The bird had flown up when the line jerked and the old man had not even seen him go. He felt the line carefully with his right hand and noticed his hand was bleeding.

'Something hurt him then,' he said aloud and pulled back on the line to see if he could turn the fish. But when he was touching the breaking point he held steady and settled back against the strain of the line.

'You're feeling it now, fish,' he said. 'And so, God knows, am I.'

He looked around for the bird now because he would have liked him for company. The bird was gone.

You did not stay long, the man thought. But it is rougher where you are going until you make the shore. How did I let the fish cut me with that one quick pull he made? I must be getting very stupid. Or perhaps I was looking at the small bird and thinking of him. Now I will pay attention to my work and then I must eat the tuna so that I will not have a failure of strength.

'I wish the boy were here and that I had some salt,' he said aloud.

Shifting the weight of the line to his left shoulder and kneeling carefully he washed his hand in the ocean and held it there, submerged, for more than a minute watching the blood trail away and the steady movement of the water against his hand as the boat moved.

'He has slowed much,' he said.

The old man would have liked to keep his hand in the salt water longer but he was afraid of another sudden lurch by the fish and he stood up and braced himself and held his hand up against the sun. It was only a line burn that had cut his flesh. But it was in the working part of his hand. He knew he would need his hands before this was over and he did not like to be cut before it started.

'Now,' he said, when his hand had dried, 'I must eat the small tuna. I can reach him with the gaff and eat him here in comfort.'

He knelt down and found the tuna under the stern with the gaff and drew it toward him keeping it clear of the coiled lines. Holding the line with his left shoulder again, and bracing on his left hand and arm, he took the tuna off the gaff hook and put the gaff back in place. He put one knee on the fish and cut strips of dark red meat longitudinally from the back of the head to the tail. They were wedge-shaped strips and he cut them from next to the back bone to the edge of the belly. When he had cut six strips he spread them out on the wood of the bow, wiped his knife on his trousers, and lifted the carcass of the bonito by the tail and dropped it overboard.

'I don't think I can eat an entire one,' he said and drew his knife across one of the strips. He could feel the steady hard pull of the line and his left hand was cramped. It drew up tight on the heavy cord and he looked at it in disgust.

'What kind of a hand is that,' he said. 'Cramp then if you want. Make yourself into a claw. It will do you no good.'

Come on, he thought and looked down into the dark water at the slant of the line. Eat it now and it will strengthen the hand. It is not the hand's fault and you have been many hours with the fish. But you can stay with him for ever. Eat the bonito now.

He picked up a piece and put it in his mouth and chewed it slowly. It was not unpleasant.

Chew it well, he thought, and get all the juices. It would not be bad to eat with a little lime or with lemon or with salt.

'How do you feel, hand?' he asked the cramped hand that was almost as stiff as rigor mortis. 'I'll eat some more for you.'

He ate the other part of the piece that he had cut in two. He chewed it carefully and then spat out the skin.

'How does it go, hand? Or is it too early to know?'

He took another full piece and chewed it.

'It is a strong full-blooded fish,' he thought. 'I was lucky to get him instead of dolphin. Dolphin is too sweet. This is hardly sweet at all and all the strength is still in it.'

There is no sense in being anything but practical though, he thought. I wish I had some salt. And I do not know whether the sun will rot or dry what is left, so I had better eat it all although I am not hungry. The fish is calm and steady. I will eat it all and then I will be ready.

'Be patient, hand,' he said. 'I do this for you.'

I wish I could feed the fish, he thought. He is my brother. But I must kill him and keep strong to do it. Slowly and conscientiously he ate all of the wedge-shaped strips of fish.

He straightened up, wiping his hand on his trousers.

'Now,' he said. 'You can let the cord go, hand, and I will handle him with the right arm alone until you stop that nonsense.' He put his left foot on the heavy line that the left hand had held and lay back against the pull against his back.

'God help me to have the cramp go,' he said. 'Because I do not know what the fish is going to do.'

But he seems calm, he thought, and following his plan. But what is his plan, he thought. And what is mine? Mine I must improvise to his because of his great size. If he will jump I can kill him. But he stays down for ever. Then I will stay down with him for ever.

He rubbed the cramped hand against his trousers and tried to gentle the fingers. But it would not open. Maybe it will open with the sun, he thought. Maybe it will open when the strong raw tuna is digested. If I have to have it, I will open it, cost whatever it costs. But I do not want to open it now by force. Let it open by itself and come back of its own accord. After all I abused it much in the night when it was necessary to free and unite the various lines.

He looked across the sea and knew how alone he was now. But he could see the prisms in the deep dark water and the line stretching ahead and the strange undulation of the calm. The clouds were building up now for the trade wind and he looked ahead and saw a flight of wild ducks etching themselves against the sky over the water, then blurring, then etching again and he knew no man was ever alone on the sea.

He thought of how some men feared being out of sight of land in a small boat and knew they were right in the months of sudden bad weather. But now they were in hurricane months and, when there are no hurricanes, the weather of hurricane months is the best of all the year.

If there is a hurricane you always see the signs of it in the sky for days ahead, if you are at sea. They do not see it ashore because they do not know what to look for, he thought. The land must make a difference too, in the shape of the clouds. But we have no hurricane coming now.

He looked at the sky and saw the white cumulus built like friendly piles of ice cream and high above were thin feathers of the cirrus against the high September sky.

'Light *brisa*,' he said. 'Better weather for me than for you, fish.'

His left hand was still cramped, but he was unknotting it slowly.

I hate a cramp, he thought. It is a treachery of one's own body. It is humiliating before others to have a diarrhoea from ptomaine poisoning or to vomit from it. But a cramp, he thought of it as a *calambre*, humiliates oneself especially when one is alone.

If the boy were here he could rub it for me and loosen it down from the forearm, he thought. But it will loosen up.

Then, with his right hand he felt the difference in the pull of the line before he saw the slant change in the water. Then, as he leaned against the line and slapped his left hand hard and fast against his thigh he saw the line slanting slowly upward.

'He's coming up,' he said. 'Come on hand. Please come on.'

The line rose slowly and steadily and then the surface of the ocean bulged ahead of the boat and the fish came out. He came out unendingly and water poured from his sides. He was bright in the sun and his head and back were dark purple and in the sun the stripes on his sides showed wide and a light lavender. His sword was as long as a base-ball bat and tapered like a rapier and he rose his full length from the water and then re-entered it, smoothly, like a diver and the old man saw the great scythe-blade of his tail go under and the line commenced to race out.

'He is two feet longer than the skiff,' the old man said. The line was going out fast but steadily and the fish was not panicked. The old man was trying with both hands to keep the line just inside of breaking strength. He knew that if he could not slow the fish with a steady pressure the fish could take out all the line and break it.

He is a great fish and I must convince him, he thought. I must never let him learn his strength nor what he could do if he made his run. If I were him I would put in everything now and go until something broke. But, thank God, they are not as intelligent as we who kill them; although they are more noble and more able.

The old man had seen many great fish. He had seen many that weighed more than a thousand pounds and he had caught two of that size in his life, but never alone. Now alone, and out of sight of land, he was fast to the biggest fish that he had ever seen and bigger than he had ever heard of, and his left hand was still as tight as the gripped claws of an eagle.

It will uncramp though, he thought. Surely it will uncramp to help my right hand. There are three things that are brothers: the fish and my two hands. It must uncramp. It is unworthy of it to be cramped. The fish had slowed again and was going at his usual pace.

I wonder why he jumped, the old man thought. He jumped almost as though to show me how big he was. I know now, anyway, he thought. I wish I could show him what sort of man I am. But then he would see the cramped hand. Let him think I am more man than I am and I will be so. I wish I was the fish, he thought, with everything he has against only my will and my intelligence.

He settled comfortably against the wood and took his suffering as it came and the fish swam steadily and the boat moved slowly through the dark water. There was a small sea rising with the wind coming up from the east and at noon the old man's left hand was uncramped.

'Bad news for you, fish,' he said and shifted the line over the sack that covered his shoulders.

He was comfortable but suffering, although he did not admit the suffering at all.

'I am not religious,' he said. 'But I will say ten Our Fathers and ten Hail Marys that I should catch this fish, and I promise to make a pilgrimage to the Virgin de Cobre if I catch him. That is a promise.'

He commenced to say his prayers mechanically. Sometimes he would be so tired that he could not remember the prayer and then he would say them fast so that they would come automatically. Hail Marys are easier to say than Our Fathers, he thought.

'Hail Mary full of Grace the Lord is with thee. Blessed art thou among women and blessed is the fruit of thy womb, Jesus. Holy Mary, Mother of God, pray for us sinners now and at the hour of our death. Amen.' Then he added, 'Blessed Virgin, pray for the death of this fish. Wonderful though he is.'

With his prayers said, and feeling much better, but suffering exactly as much, and perhaps a little more, he leaned against the wood of the bow and began, mechanically, to work the fingers of his left hand.

The sun was hot now although the breeze was rising gently.

'I had better re-bait that little line out over the stern,' he said. 'If the fish decides to stay another night I will need to eat again and the water is low in the bottle. I don't think I can get anything but a dolphin here. But if I eat him fresh enough he won't be bad. I wish a flying fish would come on board tonight. But I have no light to attract them. A flying fish is excellent to eat raw and I would not have to cut him up. I must save all my strength now. Christ, I did not know he was so big.'

'I'll kill him though,' he said. 'In all his greatness and his glory.'

Although it is unjust, he thought. But I will show him what a man can do and what a man endures.

'I told the boy I was a strange old man,' he said. 'Now is when I must prove it.'

The thousand times that he had proved it meant nothing. Now he was proving it again. Each time was a new time and he never thought about the past when he was doing it.

I wish he'd sleep and I could sleep and dream about the lions, he thought. Why are the lions the main thing that is left? Don't think, old man, he said to himself. Rest gently now against the wood and think of nothing. He is working. Work as little as you can.

It was getting into the afternoon and the boat still moved slowly and steadily. But there was an added drag now from the easterly breeze and the old man rode gently with the small sea and the hurt of the cord across the back came to him easily and smoothly.

Once in the afternoon the line started to rise again. But the fish only continued to swim at a slightly higher level. The sun was on the old man's left arm and shoulder and on his back. So he knew the fish had turned east of north.

Now that he had seen him once, he could picture the fish swimming in the water with his purple pectoral fins set wide as wings and the great erect tail slicing through the dark. I wonder how much he sees at that depth, the old man thought. His eye is huge and a horse, with much less eye, can see in the dark. Once I could see quite well in the dark. Not in the absolute dark. But almost as a cat sees.

The sun and his steady movement of his fingers had uncramped his left hand now completely and he began to shift more of the strain to it and he shrugged the muscles of his back to shift the hurt of the cord a little.

'If you're not tired, fish,' he said aloud, 'you must be very strange.'

He felt very tired now and he knew the night would come soon and he tried to think of other things. He thought of the Big Leagues, to him they were the *Gran Ligas*, and he knew that the Yankees of New York were playing the *Tigres* of Detroit.

This is the second day now that I do not know the result of the *juegos*, he thought. But I must have confidence and I must be worthy of the great DiMaggio who does all things perfectly even with the pain of the bone spur in his heel. What is a bone spur? he asked himself. *Un espuela de hueso*. We do not have them. Can it be as painful as the spur of a fighting cock in one's heel? I do not think I could endure that or the loss of the eye and of both eyes and continue to fight as the fighting cocks do. Man is not much beside the great birds and beasts. Still I would rather be the beast down there in the darkness of the sea.

'Unless sharks come,' he said aloud. 'If sharks come, God pity him and me.'

Do you believe the great DiMaggio would stay with a fish as long as I will stay with this one? he thought. I am sure he would and more since he is young and strong. Also his father was a fisherman. But would the bone spur hurt him too much?

'I do not know,' he said aloud. 'I never had a bone spur.'

As the sun set he remembered, to give himself more confidence, the time in the tavern at Casablanca when he had played the hand game with the great negro from Cienfuegos who was the strongest man on the docks. They had gone one day and one night with their elbows on a chalk line on the table and their forearms straight up and their hands gripped tight. Each one was trying to force the other's hand down onto the table. There was much betting and people went in and out of the room under the kerosene lights and he had looked at the arm and hand of the negro and at the negro's face. They changed the referees every four hours after the first eight so that the referees could sleep. Blood came out from under the fingernails of both his and the negro's hands and they looked each other in the eye and at their hands and forearms and the bettors went in and out of the room and sat on high chairs against the wall and watched. The walls were painted bright blue and were of wood and the lamps threw their shadows against them. The negro's shadow was huge and it moved on the wall as the breeze moved the lamps.

The odds would change back and forth all night and they fed the negro rum and lighted cigarettes for him. Then the negro, after the rum, would try for a tremendous effort and once he had the old man, who was not an old man then but was Santiago *El Campeón*, nearly three inches off balance. But the old man had raised his hand up to dead even again. He was sure then that he had the negro, who was a fine man and a great athlete, beaten. And at daylight when the bettors were asking that it be called a draw and the referee was shaking his head, he had unleashed his effort and forced the hand of the negro down and down until it rested on the wood. The match had started on a Sunday morning and ended on a Monday morning. Many of the bettors had asked for a draw because they had to go to work on the docks loading sacks of sugar or at the Havana Coal Company. Otherwise everyone would have wanted it to go to a finish. But he had finished it anyway and before anyone had to go to work.

For a long time after that everyone had called him The Champion and there had been a return match in the spring. But not much money was bet and he had won it quite easily since he had broken the confidence of the negro from Cienfuegos in the first match. After that he had a few matches and then no more. He decided that he could beat anyone if he wanted to badly enough and he decided that it was bad for his right hand for fishing. He had tried a few practice matches with his left hand. But his left hand had always been a traitor and would not do what he called on it to do and he did not trust it.

The sun will bake it out well now, he thought. It should not cramp on me again unless it gets too cold in the night. I wonder what this night will bring.

An aeroplane passed overhead on its course to Miami and he watched its shadow scaring up the schools of flying fish.

'With so much flying fish there should be dolphin,' he said, and leaned back on the line to see if it was possible to gain any on his fish. But he could not and it stayed at the hardness and water-drop shivering that preceded breaking. The boat moved ahead slowly and he watched the aeroplane until he could no longer see it.

It must be very strange in an aeroplane, he thought. I wonder what the sea looks like from that height. They should be able to see the fish well if they do not fly too high. I would like to fly very slowly at two hundred fathoms high and see the fish from above. In the turtle boats I was in the cross-trees of the mast-head and even at that height I saw much. The dolphin look greener from there and you can see their stripes and their purple spots and you can see all of the school as they swim. Why is it that all the fast-moving fish of the dark current have purple backs and usually purple stripes or spots? The dolphin looks green of course because he is really golden. But when he come to feed, truly hungry, purple stripes show on his sides as on a marlin. Can it be anger, or the greater speed he makes that brings them out?

Just before it was dark, as they passed a great island of Sargasso weed that heaved and swung in the light sea as though the ocean were making love with something under a yellow blanket, his small line was taken by a dolphin. He saw it first when it jumped in the air, true gold in the last of the sun and bending and flapping wildly in the air. It jumped again and again in the acrobatics of its fear and he worked his way back to the stern and crouching and holding the big line with his right hand and arm, he pulled the dolphin in with his left hand, stepping on the gained line each time with his bare left foot. When the fish was at the stern, plunging and cutting from side to side in desperation, the old man leaned over the stern and lifted the burnished gold fish with its purple spots over the stern. Its jaws were working convulsively in quick bites against the hook and it pounded the bottom of the skiff with its long flat body, its tail and its head until he clubbed it across the shining golden head until it shivered and was still.

The old man unhooked the fish, re-baited the line with another sardine and tossed it over. Then he worked his way slowly back to the bow. He washed his left hand and wiped it on his trousers. Then he shifted the heavy line from his right hand to his left and washed his right had in the sea while he watched the sun go into the ocean and the slant of the big cord.

'He hasn't changed at all,' he said. 'But watching the movement of the water against his hand he noted that it was perceptibly slower.

'I'll lash the two oars together across the stern and that will slow him in the night,' he said. 'He's good for the night and so am I.'

It would be better to gut the dolphin a little later to save the blood in the meat, he thought. I can do that a little later and lash the oars to make a drag at the same time. I had better keep the fish quiet now and not disturb him too much at sunset. The setting of the sun is a difficult time for all fish.

He let his hand dry in the air then grasped the line with it and eased himself as much as he could and allowed himself to be pulled forward against the wood so that the boat took the strain as much, or more, than he did.

I'm learning now how to do it, he thought. This part of it anyway. Then too, remember he hasn't eaten since he took the bait and he is huge and needs much food. I have eaten the whole bonito. Tomorrow I will eat the dolphin. He called it *dorado*. Perhaps I should eat some of it when I clean it. It will be harder to eat than the bonito. But, then, nothing is easy.

'How do you feel, fish?' he asked aloud. 'I feel good and my left hand is better and I have food for a night and a day. Pull the boat, fish.'

He did not truly feel good because the pain from the cord across his back had almost passed pain and gone into a dullness that he mistrusted. But I have had worse things than that, he thought. My hand is only cut a little and the cramp is gone from the other. My legs are all right. Also now I have gained on him in the question of sustenance.

It was dark now as it becomes dark quickly after the sun sets in September. He lay against the worn wood of the bow and rested all that he could. The first stars were out. He did not know the name of Rigel but he saw it and knew soon they would all be out and he would have all his distant friends.

'The fish is my friend too,' he said aloud. 'I have never seen or heard of such a fish. But I must kill him. I am glad we do not have to try to kill the stars.'

Imagine if each day a man must try to kill the moon, he thought. The moon runs away. But imagine if a man each day should have to try to kill the sun? We were born lucky, he thought.

Then he was sorry for the great fish that had nothing to eat and his determination to kill him never relaxed in his sorrow for him. How many people will he feed, he thought. But are they worthy to eat him? No, of course not. There is no one worthy of eating him from the manner of his behaviour and his great dignity.

I do not understand these things, he thought. But it is good that we do not have to try to kill the sun or the moon or the stars. It is enough to live on the sea and kill our true brothers.

Now, he thought, I must think about the drag. It has its perils and its merits. I may lose so much line that I will lose him, if he makes his effort and the drag made by the oars is in place and the boat loses all her lightness. Her lightness prolongs both our suffering but it is my safety since he has great speed that he has never yet employed. No matter what passes I must gut the dolphin so he does not spoil and eat some of him to be strong.

Now I will rest an hour more and feel that he is solid and steady before I move back to the stern to do the work and make the decision. In the meantime I can see how he acts and if he shows any changes. The oars are a good trick; but it has reached the time to play for safety! He is much fish still and I saw that the hook was in the corner of his mouth and he has kept his mouth tight shut. The punishment of the hook is nothing. The punishment of hunger, and that he is against something that he does not comprehend, is everything. Rest now, old man, and let him work until your next duty comes.

He rested for what he believed to be two hours. The moon did not rise now until late and he had no way of judging the time. Nor was he really resting except comparatively. He was still bearing the pull of the fish across his shoulders but he placed his left hand on the gunwale of the bow and confided more and more of the resistance to the fish to the skiff itself.

How simple it would be if I could make the line fast, he thought. But with one small lurch he could break it. I must cushion the pull of the line with my body and at all times be ready to give line with both hands.

'But you have not slept yet, old man,' he said aloud. 'It is half a day and a night and now another day and you have not slept. You must devise a way so that you sleep a little if he is quiet and steady. If you do not sleep you might become unclear in the head.'

I'm clear enough in the head, he thought. Too clear. I am as clear as the stars that are my brothers. Still I must sleep. They sleep and the moon and the sun sleep and even the ocean sleeps sometimes on certain days when there is no current and a flat calm.

But remember to sleep, he thought. Make yourself do it and devise some simple and sure way about the lines. Now go back and prepare the dolphin. It is too dangerous to rig the oars as a drag if you must sleep.

I could do without sleeping, he told himself. But it would be too dangerous.

He started to work his way back to the stern on his hands and knees, being careful not to jerk against the fish. He may be half asleep himself, he thought. But I do not want him to rest. He must pull until he dies.

Back in the stern he turned so that his left hand held the strain of the line across his shoulders and drew his knife from its sheath with his right hand. The stars were bright now and he saw the dolphin clearly and he pushed the blade of his knife into his head and drew him out from under the stern. He put one of his feet on the fish and slit him quickly from the vent up to the tip of his lower jaw. Then he put his knife down and gutted him with his right hand, scooping him clean and pulling the gills clear. He felt the maw heavy and slippery in his hands and he slit it open. There were two flying fish inside. They were fresh and hard and he laid them side by side and dropped the guts and the gills over the stern. They sank leaving a trail of phosphorescence in the water. The dolphin was cold and a leprous grey-white now in the starlight and the old man skinned one side of him while he held his right foot on the fish's head. Then he turned him over and skinned the other side and cut each side off from the head down to the tail.

He slid the carcass overboard and looked to see if there was any swirl in the water. But there was only the light of its slow descent. He turned then and placed the two flying fish inside the two fillets of fish and putting his knife back in its sheath, he worked his way slowly back to the bow. His back was bent with the weight of the line across it and he carried the fish in his right hand.

Back in the bow he laid the two fillets of fish out on the wood with the flying fish beside them. After that he settled the line across his shoulders in a new place and held it again with his left hand resting on the gunwale. Then he leaned over the side and washed the flying fish in the water, noting the speed of the water against his hand. His hand was phosphorescent from skinning the fish and he watched the flow of the water against it. The flow was less strong and as he rubbed the side of his hand against the planking of the skiff, particles of phosphorous floated off and drifted slowly astern.

'He is tiring or he is resting,' the old man said. 'Now let me get through the eating of this dolphin and get some rest and a little sleep.'

Under the stars and with the night colder all the time he ate half of one of the dolphin fillets and one of the flying fish, gutted and with its head cut off.

'What an excellent fish dolphin is to eat cooked,' he said. 'And what a miserable fish raw. I will never go in a boat again without salt or limes.'

If I had brains I would have splashed water on the bow all day and drying, it would have made salt, he thought. But then I did not hook the dolphin until almost sunset. Still it was a lack of preparation. But I have chewed it all well and I am not nauseated.

The sky was clouding over to the east and one after another the stars he knew were gone. It looked now as though he were moving into great canyon of clouds and the wind had dropped.

'There will be bad weather in three or four days,' he said. 'But not tonight and not tomorrow. Rig now to get some sleep, old man, while the fish is calm and steady.'

He held the line tight in his right hand and then pushed his thigh against his right hand as he leaned all his weight against the wood of the bow. Then he passed the line a little lower on his shoulders and braced his left hand on it.

My right hand can hold it as long as it is braced, he thought. If it relaxes in sleep my left hand will wake me as the line goes out. It is hard on the right hand. But he is used to punishment. Even if I sleep twenty minutes or half an hour it is good. He lay forward cramping himself against the line with all of his body, putting all his weight on to his right hand, and he was asleep.

He did not dream of the lions but instead of a vast school of porpoise that stretched for eight or ten miles and it was in the time of their mating and they would leap high into the air and return into the same hole they had made in the water when they leaped.

Then he dreamed that he was in the village on his bed and there was a norther and he was very cold and his right arm was asleep because his head had rested on it instead of a pillow.

After that he began to dream of the long yellow beach and he saw the first of the lions come down onto it in the early dark and then the other lions came and he rested his chin on the wood of the bows where the ship lay anchored with the evening off-shore breeze and he waited to see if there would be more lions and he was happy.

The moon had been up for a long time but he slept on and the fish pulled on steadily and the boat moved into the tunnel of clouds.

He woke with the jerk of his right fist coming up against his face and the line burning out through his right hand. He had no feeling of his left hand but he braked all he could with his right and the line rushed out. Finally his left hand found the line and he leaned back against the line and now it burned his back and his left hand, and his left hand was taking all the strain and cutting badly. He looked back at the coils of the line and they were feeding smoothly. Just then the fish jumped making a great bursting of the ocean and then a heavy fall. Then he jumped again and again and the boat was going fast although the line was still racing out and the old man was raising the strain to breaking point and raising it to breaking point again and again. He had been pulled down tight on to the bow and his face was in the cut slice of dolphin and he could not move.

This is what we waited for, he thought. So now let us take it.

Make him pay for the line, he thought. Make him pay for it.

He could not see the fish's jumps but only heard the breaking of the ocean and the heavy splash as he fell. The speed of the line was cutting his hands badly but he had always known this would happen and he tried to keep the cutting across the calloused parts and not let the line slip into the palm or cut the fingers.

If the boy was here he would wet the coils of line, he thought. Yes. If the boy were here. If the boy were here.

The line went out and out but it was slowing now and he was making the fish earn each inch of it. Now he got his head up from the wood and out of the slice of fish that his cheek had crushed. Then he was on his knees and then he rose slowly to his feet. He was ceding line but more slowly all the time. He worked back to where he could feel with his foot the coils of line that he could not see. There was plenty of line still and now the fish had to pull the friction of all that new line through the water.

Yes, he thought. And now he has jumped more than a dozen times and filled the sacs along his back with air and he cannot go down deep to die where I cannot bring him up. He will start circling soon and then I must work on him. I wonder what started him so suddenly? Could it have been hunger that made him desperate, or was he frightened by something in the night? Maybe he suddenly felt fear. But he was such a calm, strong fish and he seemed so fearless and so confident. It is strange.

'You better be fearless and confident yourself, old man,' he said. 'You're holding him again but you cannot get line. But soon he has to circle.'

The old man held him with his left hand and his shoulders now and stooped down and scooped up water in his right hand to get the crushed dolphin flesh off of his face. He was afraid that it might nauseate him and he would vomit and lose his strength. When his face was cleaned he washed his right hand in the water over the side and then let it stay in the salt water while he watched the first light come before the sunrise. He's headed almost east, he thought. That means he is tired and going with the current. Soon he will have to circle. Then our true work begins.

After he judged that his right hand had been in the water long enough he took it out and looked at it.

'It is not bad,' he said. 'And the pain does not matter to a man.'

He took hold of the line carefully so that it did not fit into any of the fresh line cuts and shifted his weight so that he could put his left hand into the sea on the other side of the skiff.

'You did not do so badly for something worthless,' he said to his left hand. 'But there was a moment when I could not find you.'

Why was I not born with two good hands? he thought. Perhaps it was my fault in not training that one properly. But God knows he had had enough chances to learn. He did not do so badly in the night, though, and he had only cramped once. If he cramps again let the line cut him off.

When he thought that he knew that he was not being clear-headed and he thought he should chew some more of the dolphin. But I can't, he told himself. It is better to be light-headed than to lose your strength from nausea. And I know I cannot keep it if I eat it since my face was in it. I will keep it for an emergency until it goes bad. But it is too late to try for strength now through nourishment. You're stupid, he told himself. Eat the other flying fish.

It was there, cleaned and ready, and he picked it up with his left hand and ate it chewing the bones carefully and eating all of it down to the tail.

It has more nourishment than almost any fish, he thought. At least the kind of strength that I need. Now I have done what I can, he thought. Let him begin to circle and let the fight come.

The sun was rising for the third time since he had put to sea when the fish started to circle.

He could not see by the slant of the line that the fish was circling. It was too early for that. He just felt a faint slackening of the pressure of the line and he commenced to pull on it gently with his right hand. It tightened, as always, but just when he reached the point where it would break, line began to come in. He slipped his shoulders and head from under the line and began to pull in line steadily and gently. He used both of his hands in a swinging motion and tried to do the pulling as much as he could with his body and his legs. His old legs and shoulders pivoted with the swinging of the pulling.

'It is a very big circle,' he said. 'But he is circling.'

Then the line would not come in any more and he held it until he saw the drops jumping from it in the sun. Then it started out and the old man knelt down and let it go grudgingly back into the dark water.

'He is making the far part of his circle now,' he said. I must hold all I can, he thought. The strain will shorten his circle each time. Perhaps in an hour I will see him. Now I must convince him and then I must kill him.

But the fish kept on circling slowly and the old man was wet with sweat and tired deep into his bones two hours later. But the circles were much shorter now and from the way the line slanted he could tell the fish had risen steadily while he swam.

For an hour the old man had been seeing black spots before his eyes and the sweat salted his eyes and salted the cut under his eye and on his forehead. He was not afraid of the black spots. They were normal at the tension that he was pulling on the line. Twice, though, he had felt faint and dizzy and that had worried him.

'I could not fail myself and die on a fish like this,' he said. 'Now that I have him coming so beautifully, God help me endure. I'll say a hundred Our Fathers and a hundred Hail Marys. But I cannot say them now.'

Consider them said, he thought. I'll say them later.

Just then he felt a sudden banging and jerking on the line he held with his two hands. It was sharp and hard-feeling and heavy.

He is hitting the wire leader with his spear, he thought. That was bound to come. He had to do that. It may make him jump though and I would rather he stayed circling now. The jumps were necessary for him to take air. But after that each one can widen the opening of the hook wound and he can throw the hook.

'Don't jump, fish,' he said. 'Don't jump.'

The fish hit the wire several times more and each time he shook his head the old man gave up a little line.

I must hold his pain where it is, he thought. Mine does not matter. I can control mine. But his pain could drive him mad.

After a while the fish stopped beating at the wire and started circling slowly again. The old man was gaining line steadily now. But he felt faint again. He lifted some sea water with his left hand and put it on his head. Then he put more on and rubbed the back of his neck.

'I have no cramps,' he said. 'He'll be up soon and I can last. You have to last. Don't even speak of it.'

He kneeled against the bow and, for a moment, slipped the line over his back again. I'll rest now while he goes out on the circle and then stand up and work on him when he comes in, he decided.

It was a great temptation to rest in the bow and let the fish make one circle by himself without recovering any line. But when the strain showed the fish had turned to come toward the boat, the old man rose to his feet and started the pivoting and the weaving pulling that brought in all the line he gained.

I'm tireder than I have ever been, he thought, and now the trade wind is rising. But that will be good to take him in with. I need that badly.

'I'll rest on the next turn as he goes out,' he said. 'I feel much better. Then in two or three turns more I will have him.'

His straw hat was far on the back of his head and he sank down into the bow with the pull of the line as he felt the fish turn.

You work now, fish, he thought. I'll take you at the turn.

The sea had risen considerably. But it was a fair-weather breeze and he had to have it to get home.

'I'll just steer south and west,' he said. 'A man is never lost at sea and it is a long island.'

It was on the third turn that he saw the fish first.

He saw him first as a dark shadow that took so long to pass under the boat that he could not believe its length.

'No,' he said. 'He can't be that big.'

But he was that big and at the end of this circle he came to the surface only thirty yards away and the man saw his tail out of the water. It was higher than a big scythe blade and a very pale lavender above the dark blue water. It raked back and as the fish swam just below the surface the old man could see his huge bulk and the purple stripes that banded him. His dorsal fin was down and his huge pectorals were spread wide.

On this circle the old man could see the fish's eye and the two grey sucking fish that swam around him. Sometimes they attached themselves to him. Sometimes they darted off. Sometimes they would swim easily in his shadow. They were each over three feet long and when they swam fast they lashed their whole bodies like eels.

The old man was sweating now but from something else besides the sun. On each calm placid turn the fish made he was gaining line and he was sure that in two turns he would have a chance to get the harpoon in.

But I must get him close, close, close, he thought. I mustn't try for the head. I must get the heart.

'Be calm and strong, old man,' he said.

On the next circle the fish's back was out but he was a little too far from the boat. On the next circle he was still too far away but he was higher out of the water and the old man was sure that by gaining some more line he could have him alongside.

He had rigged his harpoon long before and its coil of light rope was in a round basket and the end was made fast to the bitt in the bow.

The fish was coming in on his circle now calm and beautiful-looking and only his great tail moving. The old man pulled on him all that he could to bring him closer. For just a moment the fish turned a little on his side. Then he straightened himself and began another circle.

'I moved him,' the old man said. 'I moved him again.'

He felt faint again now but he held on the great fish all the strain that he could. I moved him, he thought. Maybe this time I can get him over. Pull, hands, he thought. Hold up, legs. Last for me, head. Last for me. You never went. This time I'll pull him over.

But when he put all of his effort on, starting it well out before the fish came alongside and pulling with all his strength, the fish pulled part way over and then righted himself and swam away.

'Fish,' the old man said. 'Fish, you are going to have to die anyway. Do you have to kill me too?'

That way nothing is accomplished, he thought. His mouth was too dry to speak but he could not reach for the water now. I must get him alongside this time, he thought. I am not good for many more turns. Yes you are, he told himself. You're good for ever.

On the next turn, he nearly had him. But again the fish righted himself and swam slowly away.

You are killing me, fish, the old man thought. But you have a right to. Never have I seen a greater, or more beautiful, or a calmer or more noble thing than you, brother. Come on and kill me. I do not care who kills who.

Now you are getting confused in the head, he thought. You must keep your head clear. Keep your head clear and know how to suffer like a man. Or a fish, he thought.

'Clear up, head,' he said in a voice he could hardly hear. 'Clear up.'

Twice more it was the same on the turns.

I do not know, the old man thought. He had been on the point of feeling himself go each time. I do not know. But I will try it once more.

He tried it once more and he felt himself going when he turned the fish. The fish righted himself and swam off again slowly with the great tail weaving in the air.

I'll try it again, the old man promised, although his hands were mushy now and he could only see well in flashes.

He tried it again and it was the same. So, he thought, and he felt himself going before he started; I will try once again.

He took all his pain and what was left of his strength and his long-gone pride and he put it against the fish's agony and the fish came over onto his side and swam gently on his side, his bill almost touching the planking of the skiff, and started to pass the boat, long, deep, wide, silver and barred with purple and interminable in the water.

The old man dropped the line and put his foot on it and lifted the harpoon as high as he could and drove it down with all his strength, and more strength he had just summoned, into the fish's side just behind the great chest fin that rose high in the air to the altitude of the man's chest. He felt the iron go in and he leaned on it and drove it further and then pushed all his weight after it.

Then the fish came alive, with his death in him, and rose high out of the water showing all his great length and width and all his power and his beauty. He seemed to hang in the air above the old man in the skiff. Then he fell into the water with a crash that sent spray over the old man and over all of the skiff.

The old man felt faint and sick and he could not see well. But he cleared the harpoon line and let it run slowly through his raw hands and, when he could see, he saw the fish was on his back with his silver belly up. The shaft of the harpoon was projecting at an angle from the fish's shoulder and the sea was discolouring with the red of the blood from his heart. First it was dark as a shoal in the blue water that was more than a mile deep. Then it spread like a cloud. The fish was silvery and still floated with the waves.

The old man looked carefully in the glimpse of vision that he had. Then he took two turns of the harpoon line around the bitt in the bow and laid his head on his hands.

'Keep my head clear,' he said against the wood of the bow. 'I am a tired old man. But I have killed this fish which is my brother and now I must do the slave work.'

Now I must prepare the nooses and the rope to lash him alongside, he thought. Even if we were two and swamped her to load him and bailed her out, this skiff would never hold him. I must prepare everything, then bring him in and lash him well and step the mast and set sail for home.

He started to pull the fish in to have him alongside so that he could pass a line through his gills and out his mouth and make his head fast alongside the bow. I want to see him, he thought, and to touch and to feel him. He is my fortune, he thought. But that is not why I wish to feel him. I think I felt his heart, he thought. When I pushed on the harpoon shaft the second time. Bring him in now and make him fast and get the noose around his tail and another around his middle to bind him to the skiff.

'Get to work, old man,' he said. He took a very small drink of the water. 'There is very much slave work to be done now that the fight is over.'

He looked up at the sky and then out to his fish. He looked at the sun carefully. And the trade wind is rising. The lines all mean nothing now. The boy and I will splice them when we are home.

'Come on, fish,' he said. But the fish did not come. Instead he lay there wallowing now in the seas and the old man pulled the skiff up to him.

When he was even with him and had the fish's head against the bow he could not believe his size. But he untied the harpoon rope from the bitt, passed it through the fish's gills and out his jaws, made a turn around his sword then passed the rope through the other gill, made another turn around the bill and knotted the double rope and made it fast to the bitt in the bow. He cut the rope then and went astern to noose the tail. The fish had turned silver from his original purple and silver, and the stripes showed the same pale violet colour as his tail. They were wider than a man's hand with his fingers spread and the fish's eye looked as detached as the mirrors in a periscope or as a saint in a procession.

'It was the only way to kill him,' the old man said. He was feeling better since the water and he knew he would not go away and his head was clear. He's over fifteen hundred pounds the way he is, he thought. Maybe much more. If he dresses out two-thirds of that at thirty cents a pound?

'I need a pencil for that,' he said. 'My head is not that clear. But I think the great DiMaggio would be proud of me today. I had no bone spurs. But the hands and the back hurt truly.' I wonder what a bone spur is, he thought. Maybe we have them without knowing it.

He made the fish fast to bow and stern and to the middle thwart. He was so big it was like lashing a much bigger skiff alongside. He cut a piece of line and tied the fish's lower jaw against his bill so his mouth would not open and they would sail as cleanly as possible. Then he stepped the mast and, with the stick that was his gaff and with his boom rigged, the patched sail drew, the boat began to move, and half lying in the stern he sailed south-west.

He did not need a compass to tell him where south-west was. He only needed the feel of the trade wind and the drawing of the sail. I better put a small line out with a spoon on it and try and get something to eat and drink for the moisture. But he could not find a spoon and his sardines were rotten. So he hooked a patched of yellow Gulf weed with the gaff as they passed and shook it so that the small shrimps that were in it fell onto the planking skiff. There were more than a dozen of them and they jumped and kicked like sand fleas. The old man pinched their heads off with his thumb and forefinger and ate them chewing up the shells and the tails. They were very tiny but he knew they were nourishing and they tasted good.

The old man still had two drinks of water in the bottle and he used half of one after he eaten the shrimps. The skiff was sailing well considering the handicaps and he steered with the tiller under his arm. He could see the fish and he had only to look at his hands to feel his back against the stern to know that this had truly happened and was not a dream. At one time when he was feeling so badly toward the end, he had thought perhaps it was a dream. Then when he had seen the fish come out of the water and hang motionless in the sky before he fell, he was sure there was some great strangeness and he could not believe it. Then he could not see well, although now he saw as well as ever.

Now he knew there was the fish and his hands and back were no dream. The hands cure quickly, he thought. I bled them clean and the salt water will heal them. The dark water of the true Gulf is the greatest healer that there is. All I must do is keep the head clear. The hands have done their work and we sail well. With his mouth shut and his tail straight up and down we sail like brothers. Then his head started to become a little unclear and he thought, is he bringing me in or am I bringing him in? If I were towing him behind there would be no question. Nor if the fish were in the skiff, with all dignity gone, there would be no question either. But they were sailing together lashed side by side and the old man thought, let him bring me in if it pleases him. I am only better than him through trickery and he meant me no harm.

They sailed well and the old man soaked his hands in the salt water and tried to keep his head clear. There were high cumulus clouds and enough cirrus above them so that the old man knew the breeze would last all night. The old man looked at the fish constantly to make sure it was true. It was an hour before the first shark hit him.

The shark was not an accident. He had come up from deep down in the water as the dark cloud of blood had settled and dispersed in the mile-deep sea. He had come up so fast and absolutely without caution that he broke the surface of the blue water and was in the sun. Then he fell back into the sea and picked up the scent and started swimming on the course the skiff and the fish had taken.

Sometimes he lost the scent. But he would pick it up again, or have just a trace of it, and he swam fast and hard on the course. He was a very big Mako shark built to swim as fast as the fastest fish in the sea and everything about him was beautiful except his jaws. His back was as blue as a swordfish's and his belly was silver and his hide was smooth and handsome. He was built as a swordfish except for his huge jaws which were tight shut now as he swam fast, just under the surface with his high dorsal fin knifing through the water without wavering. Inside the closed lip of his jaws all of his eight rows of teeth were slanted inwards. They were not the ordinary pyramid-shaped teeth of most sharks. They were shaped like a man's fingers when they are crisped like claws. They were nearly as long as the fingers of the old man and they had razor-sharp cutting edges on both sides. This was a fish built to feed on all the fishes in the sea, that were so fast and strong and well armed that they had no other enemy. Now he speeded up as he smelled the fresher scent and his blue dorsal fin cut the water.

When the old man saw him coming he knew that this was a shark that had no fear at all and would do exactly what he wished. He prepared the harpoon and made the rope fast while he watched the shark come on. The rope was short as it lacked what he had cut away to lash the fish.

The old man's head was clear and good now and he was full of resolution but he had little hope. It was too good to last, he thought. He took one look at the great fish as he watched the shark close in. It might as well have been a dream, he thought. I cannot keep him from hitting me but maybe I can get him. *Dentuso*, he thought. Bad luck to your mother.

The shark closed fast astern and when he hit the fish the old man saw his mouth open and his strange eyes and the clicking chop of the teeth as he drove forward in the meat just above the tail. The shark's head was out of the water and his back was coming out and the old man could hear the noise of skin and flesh ripping on the big fish when he rammed the harpoon down onto the shark's head at a spot where the line between his eyes intersected with the line that ran straight back from his nose. There were no such lines. There was only the heavy sharp blue head and the big jaws. But that was the location of the brain and the old man hit it. He hit it with his blood-mushed hands driving a good harpoon with all his strength. He hit it without hope but with resolution and complete malignancy.

The shark swung over and the old man saw his eye was not alive and then he swung over once again, wrapping himself in two loops of the rope. The old man knew that he was dead but the shark would not accept it. Then, on his back, with his tail lashing and his jaws clicking, the shark ploughed over the water as a speed-boat does. The water was white where his tail beat it and three-quarters of his body was clear above the water when the rope came taut, shivered, and then snapped. The shark lay quietly for a little while on the surface and the old man watched him. Then he went down very slowly.

'He took about forty pounds,' the old man said. He took my harpoon and all the rope, he thought, and now my fish bleeds again and there will be others.

He did not like to look at the fish any more since he had been mutilated. When the fish had been hit it was as though he himself were hit.

But I killed the shark that hit my fish, he thought. And he was the biggest *Dentuso* that I have ever seen. And God knows that I have seen big ones.

It was too good to last, he thought. I wish it had been a dream now and that I had never hooked the fish and was alone in bed on the newspapers.

'But man is not made for defeat,' he said. 'A man can be destroyed but not defeated.' I am sorry that I killed the fish though, he thought. Now the bad time is coming and I do not even have the harpoon. The *dentuso* is cruel and able and strong and intelligent. But I was more intelligent than he was. Perhaps not, he thought. Perhaps I was only better armed.

'Don't think, old man,' he said aloud. 'Sail on this course and take it when it comes.'

But I must think, he thought. Because it is all I have left. That and baseball. I wonder how the great DiMaggio would have liked the way I hit him in the brain. It was no great thing, he thought. Any man could do it. But do you think my hands were as great a handicap as the bone spurs? I cannot know. I never had anything wrong with my heel except the time the sting ray stung it when I stepped on him when swimming and paralysed the lower leg and made the unbearable pain.

'Think about something cheerful, old man,' he said. 'Every minute now you are closer to home. You sail lighter for the loss of forty pounds.'

He knew quite well the pattern of what could happen when he reached the inner part of the current. But there was nothing to be done now.

'Yes there is,' he said aloud. 'I can lash my knife to the butt of one of the oars.'

So he did that with the tiller under his arm and the sheet of the sail under his foot.

'Now,' he said. 'I am still an old man. But I am not unarmed.'

The breeze was fresh now and he sailed on well. He watched only the forward part of the fish and some of his hope returned.

It is silly not to hope, he thought. Besides I believe it is a sin. Do not think about sin, he thought. There are enough problems now without sin. Also I have no understanding of it.

I have no understanding of it and I am not sure that I believe in it. Perhaps it was a sin to kill the fish. I suppose it was even though I did it to keep me alive and feed many people. But then everything is a sin. Do not think about sin. It is much too late for that and there are people who are paid to do it. Let them think about it. You were born to be a fisherman as the fish was born to be a fish. San Pedro was a fisherman as was the father of the great DiMaggio.

But he liked to think about all things that he was involved in and since there was nothing to read and he did not have a radio, he thought much and he kept on thinking about sin. You did not kill the fish only to keep alive and to sell for food, he thought. You killed him for pride and because you are a fisherman. You loved him when he was alive and you loved him after. If you love him, it is not a sin to kill him. Or is it more?

'You think too much, old man,' he said aloud.

But you enjoyed killing the *dentuso*, he thought. He lives on the live fish as you do. He is not a scavenger nor just a moving appetite as some sharks are. He is beautiful and noble and knows no fear of anything.

'I killed him in self-defence,' the old man said aloud. 'And I killed him well.'

Besides, he thought, everything kills everything else in some way. Fishing kills me exactly as it keeps me alive. The boy keeps me alive, he thought. I must not deceive myself too much.

He leaned over the side and pulled loose a piece of the meat of the fish where the shark had cut him. He chewed it and noted its quality and its good taste. It was firm and juicy, like meat, but it was not red. There was no stringiness in it and he knew that it would bring the highest price in the market. But there was no way to keep its scent out of the water and the old man knew that a very bad time was coming.

The breeze was steady. It had backed a little further into the north-east and he knew that meant that it would not fall off. The old man looked ahead of him but he could see no sails nor could he see the hull nor the smoke of any ship. There was only the flying fish that went up from his bow sailing away to either side and the yellow patches of Gulf weed. He could not even see a bird.

He had sailed for two hours, resting in the stern and sometimes chewing a bit of the meat from the marlin, trying to rest and to be strong, when he saw the first of the two sharks.

'*Ay*,' he said aloud. There is no translation for this word and perhaps it is just a noise such as a man might make, involuntarily, feeling the nail go through his hands and into the wood.

'*Galanos*,' he said aloud. He had seen the second fin now coming up behind the first and had identified them as shovel-nosed sharks by the brown, triangular fin and the sweeping movements of the tail. They had the scent and were excited and in the stupidity of their great hunger they were losing and finding the scent in their excitement. But they were closing all the time.

The old man made the sheet fast and jammed the tiller. Then he took up the oar with the knife lashed to it. He lifted it as lightly as he could because his hands rebelled at the pain. Then he opened and closed them on it lightly to loosen them. He closed them firmly so they would take the pain now and would not flinch and watched the sharks come. He could see their wide, flattened, shovel-pointed heads now and their white-tipped wide pectoral fins. They were hateful sharks, bad-smelling, scavengers as well as killers, and when they were hungry they would bite at an oar or the rudder of a boat. It was these sharks that would cut the turtles' legs and flippers off when the turtles were asleep on the surface, and they would hit a man in the water, if they were hungry, even if the man had no smell of fish blood nor of fish slime on him.

'*Ay*,' the old man said. '*Galanos*. Come on, *Galanos*.'

They came. But they did not come as the Mako had come. One turned and went out of sight under the skiff and the old man could feel the skiff shake as he jerked and pulled on the fish. The other watched the old man with his slitted yellow eyes and then came in fast with his half circle of jaws wide to hit the fish where he had already been bitten. The line showed clearly on the top of his brown head and back where the brain joined the spinal cord and the old man drove the knife on the oar into the juncture, withdrew it, and drove it in again into the shark's yellow cat-like eyes. The shark let go of the fish and slid down, swallowing what he had taken as he died.

The skiff was still shaking with the destruction the other shark was doing to the fish and the old man let go the sheet so that the skiff would swing broadside and bring the shark out from under. When he saw the shark he leaned over the side and punched at him. He hit only meat and the hide was set hard and he barely got the knife in. The blow hurt not only his hands but his shoulder too. But the shark came up fast with his head out and the old man hit him squarely in the centre of his flat-topped head as his nose came out of the water and lay against the fish. The old man withdrew the blade and punched the shark exactly in the same spot again. He still hung to the fish with his jaws locked and the old man stabbed him in his left eye. The shark still hung there.

'No?' the old man said and he drove the blade between the vertebrae and the brain. It was an easy shot now and he felt the cartilage sever. The old man reversed the oar and put the blade between the shark's jaws to open them. He twisted the blade and as the shark slid loose he said, 'Go on, *galano*. Slide down a mile deep. Go and see your friend, or maybe it's your mother.'

The old man wiped the blade of his knife and laid down the oar. Then he found the sheet and the sail filled and he brought the skiff on to her course.

'They must have taken a quarter of him and of the best meat,' he said aloud. 'I wish it were a dream and that I had never hooked him. I'm sorry about it, fish. It makes everything wrong.' He stopped and he did not want to look at the fish now. Drained of blood and awash he looked the colour of the silver backing of a mirror and his stripes still showed.

'I shouldn't have gone out so far, fish,' he said. 'Neither for you nor for me. I'm sorry, fish.'

Now, he said to himself. Look to the lashing on the knife and see if it has been cut. Then get your hand in order because there still is more to come.

'I wish I had a stone for the knife,' the old man said after he had checked the lashing on the oar butt. 'I should have brought a stone.' You should have brought many things, he thought. But you did not bring them, old man. Now is no time to think of what you do not have. Think of what you can do with what there is.

'You give me much good counsel,' he said aloud. 'I'm tired of it.'

He held the tiller under his arm and soaked both his hands in the water as the skiff drove forward.

'God knows how much that last one took,' he said. 'But she's much lighter now.' He did not want to think of the mutilated under-side of the fish. He knew that each of the jerking bumps of the shark had been meat torn away and that the fish now made a trail for all sharks as wide as a highway through the sea.

He was a fish to keep a man all winter, he thought. Don't think of that. Just rest and try to get your hands in shape to defend what is left of him. The blood smell from my hands means nothing now with all that scent in the water. Besides they do not bleed much. There is nothing cut that means anything. The bleeding may keep the left from cramping.

What can I think of now? he thought. Nothing. I must think of nothing and wait for the next ones. I wish it had really been a dream, he thought. But who knows? It might have turned out well.

The next shark that came was a single shovel-nose. He came like a pig to the trough if a pig had a mouth so wide that you could put your head in it. The old man let him hit the fish and then drove the knife on the oar down into his brain. But the shark jerked backwards as he rolled and the knife blade snapped.

The old man settled himself to steer. He did not even watch the big shark sinking slowly in the water, showing first life-size, then small, then tiny. That always fascinated the old man. But he did not even watch it now.

'I have the gaff now,' he said. 'But it will do no good. I have the two oars and the tiller and the short club.'

Now they have beaten me, he thought. I am too old to club sharks to death. But I will try it as long as I have the oars and the short club and the tiller.

He put his hands in the water again to soak them. It was getting late in the afternoon and he saw nothing but the sea and the sky. There was more wind in the sky than there had been, and soon he hoped that he would see land.

'You're tired, old man,' he said. 'You're tired inside.'

The sharks did not hit him again until just before sunset.

The old man saw the brown fins coming along the wide trail the fish must make in the water. They were not even quartering on the scent. They were headed straight for the skiff swimming side by side.

He jammed the tiller, made the sheet fast and reached under the stern for the club. It was an oar handle from a broken oar sawed off to about two and a half feet in length. He could only use it effectively with one hand because of the grip of the handle and he took good hold of it with his right hand, flexing his hand on it, as he watched the sharks come. They were both *galanos*.

I must let the first one get a good hold and hit him on the point of the nose or straight across the top of the head, he thought.

The two sharks closed together and as he saw the one nearest him open his jaws and sink them into the silver side of the fish, he raised the club high and brought it down heavy and slamming on to the top of the shark's broad head. He felt the rubbery solidity as the club came down. But he felt the rigidity of bone too and he struck the shark once more hard across the point of the nose as he slid down from the fish.

The other shark had been in and out and now came in again with his jaws wide. The old man could see pieces of the meat of the fish spilling white from the corner of his jaws as he bumped the fish and closed his jaws. He swung at him and hit only the head and the shark looked at him and wrenched the meat loose. The old man swung the club down on him again as he slipped away to swallow and hit only the heavy solid rubberiness.

'Come on, *galano*,' the old man said. 'Come in again.'

The shark came in in a rush and the old man hit him as he shut his jaws. He hit him solidly and from as high up as he could raise the club. This time he felt the bone at the base of the brain and he hit him again in the same place while the shark tore the meat loose sluggishly and slid down from the fish.

The old man watched for him to come again but neither shark showed. Then he saw one on the surface swimming in circles. He did not see the fin of the other.

I could not expect to kill them, he thought. I could have in my time. But I have hurt them both badly and neither one can feel very good. If I could have used a bat with two hands I could have killed the first one surely. Even now, he thought.

He did not want to look at the fish. He knew that half of him had been destroyed. The sun had gone down while he had been in the fight with the sharks.

'It will be dark soon,' he said. 'Then I should see the glow of Havana. If I am too far to the eastward I will see the lights of one of the new beaches.'

I cannot be too far out now, he thought. I hope no one has been too worried. There is only the boy to worry, of course. But I am sure he would have confidence. Many of the older fishermen will worry. Many others too, he thought. I live in a good town.

He could not talk to the fish any more because the fish had been ruined too badly. Then something came into his head.

'Half-fish,' he said. 'Fish that you were. I am sorry that I went too far out. I ruined us both. But we have killed many sharks, you and I, and ruined many others. How many did you ever kill, old fish? You do not have that spear on your head for nothing.'

He liked to think of the fish and what he could do to a shark if he were swimming free. I should have chopped the bill off to fight them with, he thought. But there was no hatchet and then there was no knife.

But if I had, and could have lashed it to an oar butt, what a weapon. Then we might have fought them together. What will you do now if they come in the night? What can you do?

'Fight them,' he said. 'I'll fight them until I die.'

But in the dark now and no glow showing and no lights and only the wind and the steady pull of the sail he felt that perhaps he was already dead. He put his two hands together and felt the palms. They were not dead and he could bring the pain of life by simply opening and closing them. He leaned back against the stern and knew he was not dead. His shoulders told him.

I have all those prayers I promised if I caught the fish, he thought. But I am too tired to say them now. I better get the sack and put it over my shoulders.

He lay in the stern and steered and watched for the glow to come in the sky. I have half of him, he thought. Maybe I'll have the luck to bring the forward half in. I should have some luck. No, he said. You violated your luck when you went too far outside.

'Don't be silly,' he said aloud. 'And keep awake and steer. You may have much luck yet.

'I'd like to buy some if there's any place they sell it,' he said.

What could I buy it with? he asked himself. Could I buy it with a lost harpoon and a broken knife and two bad hands?

'You might,' he said. 'You tried to buy it with eighty-four days at sea. They nearly sold it to you too.'

I must not think nonsense, he thought. Luck is a thing that comes in many forms and who can recognize her? I would take some though in any form and pay what they asked. I wish I could see the glow from the lights, he thought. I wish too many things. But that is the thing I wish for now. He tried to settle more comfortably to steer and from his pain he knew he was not dead.

He saw the reflected glare of the lights of the city at what must have been around ten o'clock at night. They were only perceptible at first as the light is in the sky before the moon rises. Then they were steady to see across the ocean which was rough now with the increasing breeze. He steered inside of the glow and he thought that now, soon, he must hit the edge of the stream.

Now it is over, he thought. They will probably hit me again. But what can a man do against them in the dark without a weapon?

He was stiff and sore now and his wounds and all of the strained parts of his body hurt with the cold of the night. I hope I do not have to fight again, he thought. I hope so much I do not have to fight again.

But by midnight he fought and this time he knew the fight was useless. They came in a pack and he could only see the lines in the water that their fins made and the phosphorescence as they threw themselves on the fish. He clubbed at heads and heard the jaws chop and the shaking of the skiff as they took hold below. He clubbed desperately at what he could only feel and hear and he felt something seize the club and it was gone.

He jerked the tiller free from the rudder and beat and chopped with it, holding it in both hands and driving it down again and again. But they were up to the bow now and driving in one after the other and together, tearing off the pieces of meat that showed glowing below the sea as they turned to come once more.

One came, finally, against the head itself and he knew that it was over. He swung the tiller across the shark's head where the jaws were caught in the heaviness of the fish's head which would not tear. He swung it once and twice and again. He heard the tiller break and he lunged at the shark with the splintered butt. He felt it go in and knowing it was sharp he drove it in again. The shark let go and rolled away. That was the last shark of the pack that came. There was nothing more for them to eat.

The old man could hardly breathe now and he felt a strange taste in his mouth. It was coppery and sweet and he was afraid of it for a moment. But there was not much of it.

He spat into the ocean and said, 'Eat that, *galanos*. And make a dream you've killed a man.'

He knew he was beaten now finally and without remedy and he went back to the stern and found the jagged end of the tiller would fit in the slot of the rudder well enough for him to steer. He settled the sack around his shoulders and put the skiff on her course. He sailed lightly now and he had no thoughts nor any feelings of any kind. He was past everything now and he sailed the skiff to make his home port as well and as intelligently as he could. In the night sharks hit the carcass as someone might pick up crumbs from the table. The old man paid no attention to them and did not pay any attention to anything except steering. He only noticed how lightly and how well the skiff sailed now there was no great weight beside her.

She's good, he thought. She is sound and not harmed in any way except for the tiller. That is easily replaced.

He could feel he was inside the current now and he could see the lights of the beach colonies along the shore. He knew where he was now and it was nothing to get home.

The wind is our friend, anyway, he thought. Then he added, sometimes. And the great sea with our friends and our enemies. And bed, he thought. Bed is my friend. Just bed, he thought. Bed will be a great thing. It is easy when you are beaten, he thought. I never knew how easy it was. And what beat you, he thought.

'Nothing,' he said aloud. 'I went out too far.'

When he sailed into the little harbour the lights of the Terrace were out and he knew everyone was in bed. The breeze had risen steadily and was blowing strongly now. It was quiet in the harbour though and he sailed up onto the little patch of shingle below the rocks. There was no one to help him so he pulled the boat up as far as he could. Then he stepped out and made her fast to a rock.

He unstepped the mast and furled the sail and tied it. Then he shouldered the mast and started to climb. It was then he knew the depth of his tiredness. He stopped for a moment and looked back and saw in the reflection from the street light the great tail of the fish standing up well behind the skiff's stern. He saw the white naked line of his backbone and the dark mass of the head with the projecting bill and all the nakedness between.

He started to climb again and at the top he fell and lay for some time with the mast across his shoulder. He tried to get up. But it was too difficult and he sat there with the mast on his shoulder and looked at the road. A car passed on the far side going about its business and the old man watched it. Then he just watched the road.

Finally he put the mast down and stood up. He picked the mast up and put it on his shoulder and started up the road. He had to sit down five times before he reached his shack.

Inside the shack he leaned the mast against the wall. In the dark he found a water bottle and took a drink. Then he lay down on the bed. He pulled the blanket over his shoulders and then over his back and legs and he slept face down on the newspapers with his arms straight and the palms of his hands up.

He was asleep when the boy looked in the door in the morning. It was blowing so hard that the drifting boats would not be going out and the boy had slept late and then come to the old man's shack as he had come each morning. The boy saw that the old man was breathing and then he saw the old man's hands and he started to cry. He went out very quietly to go to bring some coffee and all the way down the road he was crying.

Many fishermen were around the skiff looking at what was lashed beside it and one was in the water, his trousers rolled up, measuring the skeleton with a length of line.

The boy did not go down. He had been there before and one of the fishermen was looking after the skiff for him.

'How is he?' one of the fishermen shouted.

'Sleeping,' the boy called. He did not care that they saw him crying. 'Let no one disturb him.'

'He was eighteen feet from nose to tail,' the fisherman who was measuring him called.

'I believe it,' the boy said.

He went into the Terrace and asked for a can of coffee.

'Hot and with plenty of milk and sugar in it.'

'Anything more?'

'No. Afterwards I will see what he can eat.'

'What a fish it was,' the proprietor said. 'There has never been such a fish. Those were two fine fish you took yesterday too.'

'Damn my fish,' the boy said and he started to cry again.

'Do you want a drink of any kind?' the proprietor asked.

'No,' the boy said. 'Tell them not to bother Santiago. I'll be back.'

'Tell him how sorry I am.'

'Thanks,' the boy said.

The boy carried the hot can of coffee up to the old man's shack and sat by him until he woke. Once it looked as though he were waking. But he had gone back into heavy sleep and the boy had gone across the road to borrow some wood to heat the coffee.

Finally the old man woke.

'Don't sit up,' the boy said. 'Drink this.' He poured some of the coffee in a glass.

The old man took it and drank it.

'They beat me, Manolin,' he said. 'They truly beat me.'

'*He* didn't beat you. Not the fish.'

'No. Truly. It was afterwards.'

'Pedrico is looking after the skiff and the gear. What do you want done with the head?'

'Let Pedrico chop it up to use in fish traps.'

'And the spear?'

'You keep it if you want it.'

'I want it,' the boy said. 'Now we must make our plans about the other things.'

'Did they search for me?'

'Of course. With coast guard and with planes.'

'The ocean is very big and a skiff is small and hard to see,' the old man said. He noticed how pleasant it was to have someone to talk to instead of speaking only to himself and to the sea. 'I missed you,' he said. 'What did you catch?'

'One the first day. One the second and two the third.'

'Very good.'

'Now we fish together again.'

'No. I am not lucky. I am not lucky any more.'

'The hell with luck,' the boy said, 'I'll bring the luck with me.'

'What will your family say?'

'I do not care. I caught two yesterday. But we will fish together now for I still have much to learn.'

'We must get a good killing lance and always have it on board. You can make the blade from a spring leaf from an old Ford. We can grind it in Guanabacoa. It should be sharp and not tempered so it will break. My knife broke.'

'I'll get another knife and have the spring ground. How many days of heavy *brisa* have we?'

'Maybe three. Maybe more.'

'I will have everything in order,' the boy said. 'You get your hands well, old man.'

'I know how to care for them. In the night I spat something strange and felt something in my chest was broken.'

'Get that well too,' the boy said. 'Lie down, old man, and I will bring you your clean shirt. And something to eat.'

'Bring any of the papers of the time that I was gone,' the old man said.

'You must get well fast for there is much that I can learn and you can teach me everything. How much did you suffer?'

'Plenty,' the old man said.

'I'll bring the food and the papers,' the boy said. 'Rest well, old man. I will bring stuff from the drug-store for your hands.'

'Don't forget to tell Pedrico the head is his.'

'No. I will remember.'

As the boy went out the door and down the worn coral rock road he was crying again.

That afternoon there was a party of tourists at the Terrace and looking down in the water among the empty beers cans and dead barracudas a woman saw a great long white spine with a huge tail at the end that lifted and swung with the tide while the east wind blew a heavy steady sea outside the entrance to the harbour.

'What's that?' she asked a waiter and pointed to the long backbone of the n that was now just garbage waiting to go out with the tide.

ıburon,' the waiter said, 'Eshark.' He was meaning to explain what had appened.

'I didn't know sharks had such handsome, beautifully formed tails.'

'I didn't either,' her male companion said.

Up the road, in his shack, the old man was sleeping again. He was still sleeping on his face and the boy was sitting by him watching him. The old man was dreaming about the lions.